A Moment
in Camelot

A Moment in Camelot

by Maggie Rennert

published by Bernard Geis Associates

distributed by Grove Press, Inc.

Library of Congress Catalog Card Number: 68-16151

FIRST PRINTING

For Robert D. Lincoln, M.D.,

a healer

"Don't let it be forgot,
that once there was a spot,
for one brief shining moment
that was known as Camelot."

Once Upon a Time

Spring in the nation's capital has the haste and drama of a shipboard romance. The Washington climate has been described as an arctic winter followed by a tropical summer; squeezed between them is the always sudden spring, brief but complete with all the requisite births and blossomings. Everything that is supposed to happen in spring happens somehow, and with a speed and profusion astounding to the visitors and intoxicating to the citizens.

On just such a lavish, busy spring afternoon between four and five years before the events of this chronicle begin, the official cherry blossoms—though they had had their day a week ago—were still pink and white and glorious for the sun-dazzled tourists at the Tidal Basin and the monuments. All over the city private-enterprise cherry trees on quarter-acre lots offered, without benefit of press coverage, their lovely fragile blossoms for inspection by meter readers, housewives hanging out the wash, and three-year-olds pumping tricycles. In the tiny front yards of the once-autonomous city of Georgetown —now surviving as an expensively quaint neighborhood in the capital that swallowed it a hundred years ago—the blossoms were beginning to be underlined with the green of new leaf.

As Gil Kimball handed a highball to his guest and another to his wife at about five-thirty that afternoon, soft flushed petals had begun to drop from the cherry tree onto the tenderly nurtured grass at the corner of his house. The low rays of the sun filtered through the natural-linen drapes drawn over the front window, giving the comfortable room in the comfortable house on Q Street a pleasant beneficence of light that could be enjoyed without noticing it. Which was lucky, for the three people sipping at the good-enough, middle-grade bourbon had other preoccupations—some of which seemed difficult and pressing, and none of which would still be of concern in a few years.

Poor, silly, lovely—the choice of adjective depended on where in that room one sat—Andrea Langwith was seated on the big tan sofa with her cold glass resting on one of the squared-off arms and her mind possessed by painful ponderings. The dual problem under consideration, and not by any means for the first time, was whether she could possibly marry one Alec Girard, who was unsuitable for several reasons, and whether she could possibly survive if he didn't ask her. The shrouded sunlight behind her found the reddish lights in her brown hair and shadowed the extraordinarily pretty face framed by it. She was a tall girl and willow-slim, and, whether she moved or was still, she did it with the special grace of the young and athletically gifted for whom no physical feat has ever been anything but easy. Her tailored white silk shirt and slim, short skirt of a rough-textured Kelly green material were like her: easy, elegant, and interesting. In short, she was well-supplied with natural resources and obviously endowed with the taste and funds to exploit them fully—and thus she was not by any means the sort of young lady one would expect to find mulling over the problems of adjustment to spinsterhood. Nevertheless, as she tested her drink and congratulated Gil on the celebration it marked, Andrea was thinking ruefully that it might be a very good thing if there were a Sadie Hawkins Day in Washington, D.C., for she was just about out of even the less subtle stratagems for indicating her interest to Alec, leaving her nothing except possibly a few bizarre moves that would daunt her and appall him.

Gil Kimball, standing in the center of the room with his sneakered feet slightly apart like an actor ready to bow, was worrying the question of whether a truly moral man would have quoted to the admiring Andrea the total number of newspapers subscribing for his fledgling syndicated column (a number just increased by two, which was what they were celebrating) without troubling to mention that the figure included a biweekly in Mellon, Indiana, and a free Shoppers' Guide here and there. Several heres and theres, Gil admitted—but silently; he smiled down into the worshipful velvet-brown eyes and left his conscience twinges for later. It had been always thus, or anyway always since a smitten fellow who worked with Gil on the *Washington Tribune* had brought Andrea calling on the Kimballs. The luckless swain, who'd never had a chance, had disappeared soon thereafter; but Andrea had since become so familiar a figure at the Kimballs' that they were used to the dazzle of her and loved her comfortably now. Still, when those enormous eyes admired, even the sturdy Gil was tempted to feel ten feet tall.

"Oh, Gil, how wonderful," she was saying. Her wide, friendly smile was all delight. "But nobody'll be surprised. No wonder the newspapers want your columns when they're so marvelous."

"Well, some don't, you know. Oscar Bainbridge is still about three hundred papers ahead of me." That was enough of grim realities: Gil waved his glass grandly. "But I'm coming on fast, I am. Today, the gas bill got paid. Tomorrow, mink coats for the wife and three."

Betty Kimball raised her eyebrows. "Well, if you think so, dear. But the boys will look funny. Especially with their Scout uniforms." She let Gil go back to aw-shucksing Andy, who was telling him how much better he was than Bainbridge, and returned to debating whether she should make Gil his favorite orange cake to celebrate. The trouble was, if the papers kept coming in the way they had been, he'd soon be not only a full-time columnist instead of still a struggling reporter but also a fat man instead of still a husky one. She had about decided there was room yet for a few more orange cakes before his girth caught up with his stature when she saw Andy lower her curly head to read the title of a magazine on the coffee table with passionate interest—which meant that Gil must be being tactless again. Betty sat upright and said "Gil!" in a voice that threatened an end to orange cakes.

"I cite the gentleman only as an example of an eligible bachelor," Gil protested. "The handsome, rich, and gifted Senator Girard is only a metaphor so far as I'm concerned."

"Pooh," said Andy. "Senators are a dime a dozen."

"Maybe so." Gil's lazy gaze was suddenly grave. "But I can't see Alec growing old and gray in the Senate. He's something rather special, you know." But of course she knew, he thought, wincing at his own lugubriousness: if there was one thing this silly girl did know, it was that. He decided against giving her a rundown on the record Girard had been compiling since he came to Washington as a congressman notable only for his youth. Anyway, reminding Andy of Alec's glittering public career might be doing the lad no favor, Gil decided: women were contrary in general, but Andy took the prize. So he favored her with his most oracular look and told her instead, "Mark my word. All the best newspapers do."

Andy turned away in a fruitless effort to hide her discomfort. "Double pooh to pundits." But she sounded frightened.

Betty frowned at her husband. "Ignore Gil," she said kindly. "He's just fractious because everything was in an uproar today."

"Well, I *was* supposed to be working on a magazine piece. But it was a little difficult, knee-deep in hysterical women."

"Our next-door neighbor got married," Betty explained. "Well, remarried, actually."

"I understand," Andy said. "Marriage is a well-known cause of hysteria." She smiled, but behind her attentive look she was struggling with the ridiculous fact that any mention of marriage—anybody's marriage—always seemed to evoke this sort of horrid quaver . . . Complete with blushes, she said to herself disgustedly, and tightened her lips and willed herself to listen to the Kimballs gossiping amiably about their neighbor. Who, if Gil's version was to be trusted, had displayed a curious logic: having divorced her first husband because she was unhappy as a foreign correspondent's wife, she had today married some fellow in the State Department.

"Well, everybody in the State Department doesn't go off to foreign parts." Betty seemed accustomed to defending the retread bride. "Anyway, who chooses a husband on the basis of his occupation? You sound like some kind of bigot, Gil."

"Who's a bigot? A man is his work, isn't he? Surely you can't marry a guy unless you're prepared to live in the way necessary for—" He broke off, remembering their guest, who might well find his remarks unseemly for their very relevance.

Andy caught the look the Kimballs exchanged. "I suppose it's one of those things people should think over very carefully." She offered them her profile, as pure and neutral as a cameo.

Gil studied her with the shamefaced affection of a brother. "Well, if you *must* meditate on love and marriage, be careful of false analogies, for God's sake. It's the way people handle the problems that counts, not the list of problems amateur marriage counselors tick off." There were many kinds of bigotry, he thought. It was hard to look at Andy without assuming the rest of the beautiful-but-dumb stereotype—hard to remember that what lighted those particular bright eyes was not belladonna but intelligence, and that while she might get silly, she couldn't really manage to be stupid. "Anybody who attempts to instruct women in logic deserves another drink," he said gruffly, and got up to award himself one.

Andy shook her head as he reached for her nearly empty glass. "I need steady nerves." She hesitated just long enough so that it was not clear whether her added "Thank you" applied to the offered drink or the advice.

Gil opened his mouth to reply, but his wife intervened. "Marriage doesn't have to unsteady your nerves, Andy."

The bright face grew thoughtful. "No. . . But I see what happens. Like your next-door neighbor. I mean, she must have thought she could adjust. In her previous marriage."

"It doesn't have to happen," Gil said. "If you make up your mind you're married for keeps, you can do anything you have to do." He waved his glass at his wife. "She thinks I'm unfair to Marian. But I like Marian. What it really is, is I'm against the experimental approach to marriage."

"If you want a man enough, you change enough," Betty said softly. "And so does he." She watched Andy's eyes accept the message. "With a few exceptions, of course," she went on easily then. "Like Gil's aversion to fixing dripping faucets, which has remained steadfast through eleven years."

"I will not descend to manual labor. I am an artist. Did Shakespeare run around messing with plumbing? Well, he may have, that one. But did—umm—Dante Gabriel Rossetti, say?"

The telephone cut off both reply to this thought-provoking question and, more likely, comment on the lack of resemblance between Kimball and the poet. Gil put his drink on the mantel beside the hunk of driftwood nobody had got around to doing anything artistic about and went through the dining room and into the kitchen to answer it. He came back with a careless "For you, Andy." But when he added that she could take it upstairs if she wanted, she stood up so quickly, looking at him so like a student awaiting an important grade, that he relented. "It's long distance. Woodburn, Vermont."

Betty was beginning, "Is that where—" as Andy fled out into the little black-and-white-tiled hallway and up the Kimballs' stairs to their bedroom. All the way up and across the gray-carpeted upstairs hall, a voice in her mind kept saying accusingly, "Set your cap, you've set your cap"; but it didn't slow her unseemly scamper. Breathless, she picked up the phone on the bedside table. The downstairs extension was hung up with a click and an operator's voice asked, "Miss Andree Long-worth?"

She said "Yes" and held the instrument away from her ear until the clanking of coins stopped and Alec's voice blasted into the quiet of the dim room. "Andy?"

"Yes, Alec, I can hear you. What are you doing in Woodburn, Vermont?"

"Oh, nothing much. I mean, I had to make a speech." Behind his words, a jukebox singer anguished in no particular key.

"What in the world is that?" Andy demanded. "Where *are* you?"

"Well, it's sort of a . . . a pub." He cleared his throat, deafeningly. "I— er—I got away. I mean—well—how are the Kimballs?"

"Fine." Andy smiled at herself wickedly in Betty's dressing-table mirror. "And your family?"

"Oh, they're fine, too." So were the Kimball twins, Bert and Joe, stern in Cub Scout uniforms and stiff postures, saluting her from a curling snapshot.

"I'll bet the weather's nice."

"Lovely." The Senate is also lovely, Andy did not say. "The weather is fine," she said patiently, and thought, Oh dear.

Alec was plodding on. "They said at your house you were over there."

"Yes. I stopped in on my way home." She studied the toe of her shoe and then the stitching on the wine-colored taffeta of the dressing-table skirt. Finally, as the pause continued to lengthen dismally, compassion—and the simple fear that he would run out of coins—overcame her. "Will you be back in Washington soon, Alec?"

"Well, that's actually what I called about." Gratitude sang in his voice. "I was thinking. . . Well, I saw in the *Tribune* that *The Bridges at Toko-Ri* is going to be playing there, and I thought maybe . . ." He trailed off hopefully, but Andy, watching herself in the mirror, tightened her lips and went on jiggling the Cub Scouts with her forefinger. This time, by golly, he was going to have to do it by himself: she refused to say one word to help him.

"Yes?" she said encouragingly.

"I thought maybe you'd like to go see it Thursday night." The words came in a sudden rush; but his confidence was short-lived. "If you haven't already seen it? I mean, if you're not busy . . ."

Laughter threatened to rise to the surface of her voice; she shook her head warningly at her reflection. "Why, thank you, Alec. That sounds delightful."

He sighed, and the soft echo melted her laughter away instantly. Without warning, she was shaken with a need to put her arms around him.

"Okay. I mean, swell." He was brisk now, his mission accomplished. "The last show, as usual? I'll be back Wednesday and I'll call you then, if I may."

"Of course." She held tightly to the phone, refusing to let this end even though another silence threatened. "Did you . . . Were you able to get over to the lake?" Her voice grew soft with longing. "It must be so beautiful now."

"No, we bypassed Kingsley entirely. You see," he added apologetically, "it's in what we call a 'safe' district."

"Oh, yes. Naturally," said the girl who was beginning to feel dismally that she, too, might be a safe district.

Alec had heard the faint note of disdain. "Well, this is strictly a political trip," he said lamely. He waited, but she didn't answer. "But by summer . . ."

He paused to gather courage, then asked her in a rush again, "Will you be at the lake this summer, Andy?"

"In August. And you?" Her question was as intense as his had been.

"As soon as Congress adjourns," he said quickly.

Something was leaping in her throat. With difficulty, she managed coolness. "You'll have speechmaking chores up there, I suppose?"

"No." He said it forcefully. "Certainly not." Then his courage wobbled again. "I plan to— I hope we can—" He abandoned the effort, and she waited, disappointment darkening her bright face as the pause lengthened. "I think we'll have a fine summer," he said suddenly, clearly and with assurance. "Don't you?"

"Yes." Andy closed her eyes and laid her free hand against her cheek. A silence was not particularly uncomfortable when what had just been indicated was that you were worth campaigning for. And Alec Girard had never lost an election, so far as Andy knew. She was thinking about this promising statistic when the operator broke in; wanting to go on thinking about it and cringing from the prospect of more clanging of coins, Andy said hastily, "It's all right, Alec. I'll talk to you Wednesday. I've got to run."

"Well. Good-bye, Andy."

"Good-bye." She hung up, wondering whether she'd only imagined the wistfulness in his voice. But she jumped up, hugging herself, and ran to the window, where she pushed aside the heavy velvet drapes and scanned the lavender-streaked twilight sky over Q Street as though she had been called to take an emergency survey. From there she went to turn on one of the pair of delicate lamps on the dressing table and, peering into the mirror, make no appreciable adjustments to her coiffure. Waiting for calm, she picked up a white porcelain powder box to inspect the flowers painted on it; it shook in her hands and she put it down hastily. She gave up then, pulled a fierce face at her reflection, and turned off the light and ran downstairs to the others.

"Gil was just saying—" Betty's tone was stagily conversational "—that the Foreign Relations Committee—"

"Nuts." Her husband, lounging on the end of his spine with his heels dug into the carpet, silenced her with a black glance. "Was it or wasn't it, Andy?"

"Gil, you're shameless," Betty said.

Andy perched on the sofa beside Gil and sipped from her neglected drink, looking at him over the top of her glass. "Not for publication, and if your rather cryptic inquiry means what I think, it was indeed the Senator from Vermont. The silver-tongued Senator from Vermont."

"Doubtless you speak loosely. If brisk, go-getting Alec Girard had conducted his campaign the way he does his courtship, he'd be unemployed."

"Oh, shut up, Gil," his wife said amiably. "What did the Senator have to say, Andy?"

"The Senator inquired about your health."

"Is *that* all?"

"Well, no. It seems he wanted to invite me to a movie on Thursday night. I accepted. I've already seen the movie, but I didn't tell him so." She stood up, smiling happily at both of them. "I add that information so you two dreadfully unprincipled matchmakers can rub your hands and chuckle. And I leave you to it. I've got to get home."

"Well, I will rub my hands," Betty said stoutly. "He never used to call a girl until the last minute, you know. And I heard he had his secretary do it for him. But this is only Friday—almost a whole week."

Struggling to his feet, Gil watched the women with open scorn. So Alec had got around to asking the girl to the movies again. A real hero, Girard. Impatiently, the hero's friend decided to lend the inchworm suitor a hand again. "If he's coming back, why don't they come to dinner? How about Wednesday?" Turning to his wife, he knocked a package of cigarettes from the end table.

"Can't make it, thanks," Andy said briskly. "I've got to get to the hair-dresser Wednesday afternoon. And maybe a few other preparations."

"To go to a movie?" Gil asked incredulously. But it was quite believable, really, he observed sourly to himself, once you understood that Andy's self-confidence was about the same size as Alec's.

"Yes, dear," Betty said. "To go to a movie."

Gil saw the compassion in her eyes and crouched to pluck the fallen cigarettes from the deep-blue field of the rug—and then stayed down there to tell himself off, because he had it coming. Andy had a right, by God, to act like every other female he'd ever known—not excluding his daughter Rosemary, who'd begun to demand new school dresses now that she was in second grade. As for Alec: the fact, the honest truth about people, was that unless they were conscienceless fools the courtship ordeal had its painful aspects. And a man confident of his ability to represent Vermont might well suffer some self-doubt about his qualifications as a husband for Andy. If he loved her very much, he might be very gingerly indeed.

Gil, neither a gingerly nor a moderate man, made a long business of his cigarette harvesting. But even by the time he was holding Andy's jacket for her while she shrugged into it, he had not entirely finished berating himself. For real people are corny about things that count, and the earnest are always easy to mock; but good writers know better, and Gil had in mind to be a good writer. He opened the door for Andy and then stopped her with a clumsy hand on her arm. "Okay, so Alec ain't intrepid. Listen, I wouldn't— take it kindly—if he were arrogant. About you. You know what I mean?" If she did, it would be no thanks to Kimball: he scowled at her fiercely because this was hardly the kind of prose likely to grow to be the nation's breakfast-table habit.

Andy nodded, smiling; she might be vulnerable to doubt, but she knew love when she saw it. She hurried down the uneven flagstone walk toward her car, blinking against the last of the dying light flashing from the blank windows of the house next door. In the Kimballs' front yard, night was closing the trusting blossoms, folding the shiny new leaves. As she set out on the long drive to her parents' home in the Virginia countryside, Andy knew with happiness and a little fear that the time for thinking was nearly over.

The phone booth in the Woodburn Bar and Grill was, if inconveniently near the jukebox, conveniently near the door. Alec Girard slid out without attracting the attention of the handful of citizens at the bar and made it to the parking lot unnoticed. He shed his coat as he crossed the gravel under the dilute rainbow shadows cast by the neon beer signs.

Bill Bruyette had the motor running, but he was studying the darkening sky with an air of leisure that absurdly irritated his old friend. Alec slung his coat onto the back seat and got in beside Bill. "Let's go, let's go."

Bill steered the car out onto the empty two-lane road and drove at an easy forty miles an hour, his left elbow angled out of the window, the fingers of his right hand tapping out an unheard tune on the steering wheel. The car hummed along in the Vermont twilight between tangles of roadside growth that, here and there, greened a little in honor of spring. The busy, anonymous denizens of the thickets paused as the intruders passed, then fell to twittering and chittering again in their wake.

"I am a member of the world's greatest deliberative body," Alec said abruptly.

Bruyette turned long enough for a mildly curious look. "I know. I voted for you. It's a little early, but I'll promise to do it again, unless you take graft. That what you want me to say?"

Alec shook his head. "It's only that I've just finished sounding like a barefoot boy selling maple syrup from door to door." He sat still, but there was nothing of repose in the handsome face or the long body. "Inferior maple syrup, at that." He ran a hand through his thick sandy hair, thus enhancing its customary look of somewhat rambunctious vitality. The sparse and flickering light emphasized the hollows under his cheekbones, adding to an appearance of dedicated gloom.

Bill slowed the car at a crossroads. On a wooden signpost, weathered arms indicated the several directions of indecipherable towns. "May one inquire what has battered the senatorial ego?" He glanced at the familiar face, its bright-blue eyes now darkened as much by discontent as by the night. The full, usually mobile mouth was tightened mutinously against any intent of reply. Resuming speed, Bill sighed. "One may assume, then, that it has nothing to do with affairs of state, which could have been transacted without scouting for public phone booths. One concludes therefore that the administrator of a beating to our golden boy could possibly have been a woman."

"A mere slip of a girl, in fact," Alec said grudgingly. But his tense pose relaxed, and a rueful humor lighted the look he turned on his friend.

"Forget it. In a few months, we'll be lords of the Inland Waterway, and neither Senate nor skirt will trouble your peace."

Alec cleared his throat. "I'm afraid you'll have to get yourself another crew. I've come to a reluctant decision. I'm— Well, I'm going to be putting on a rather special kind of campaign this summer." He studied Bruyette's shocked face a moment. "Dammit, I have to get married." He turned away to stare out at the stony fields, but a strangled exclamation from Bruyette recalled him. Alec laughed. "I should've stated it more clearly. The compulsion is self-generated. Internal. Mental."

"Ah so. More of a—project—than a melodrama."

"Well, the project is scarcely off the drawing board. I telephone the lady. After stammering for a while, I succeed in asking her for a date."

"And she accepts?"

"Usually. She responds with, I may say, unfailing courtesy and warmth."

"Well, then, why consider any drastic moves?"

"Unfortunately," Alec said dryly, "I have heard that she responds with equal courtesy and warmth to similar requests from other gents. I've considered the matter at length, and I conclude that I don't like that."

Bill nodded in silence. He turned the car to the right and drew up at the single blinking traffic light in the center of Ardennes, Vermont. Huge old maple trees bearing the scars of many tappings stood guard around the common with its bronze tablet commemorating the town's war dead. A scent of lilac hung in the damp, cool air. A bright white light on a slim post bathed the front of the rambling white clapboard inn, and a cherry-red sign blinked like a tic in the drugstore window. But the streets were almost empty; the town had turned into its lighted houses, readying for night.

Bruyette slowed the car's speed, muttering that he was nearly out of cigarettes.

The Senator shook his head. "Keep going, old son."

"Why? I think the drugstore's still open."

"Sure. It's also the same store where the guy refused to put my poster in his window when I ran for the House. The first campaign, remember?"

Bruyette sighed and drove on, muttering that no doubt Alec's constituents appreciated his long memory and attention to detail . . . Which reminded him—had the Senator any ideas about the runaround that fellow in Newport had been complaining about getting from Washington?

Alec groaned. "Yes sir, I have. It occurs to me that his plight is a result of the nonworking of a law that I voted against because it wouldn't work."

"A tribute to your acuity."

"Hurray for me. Actually, though, I wonder whether I deserve it—it's getting so that any bill that comes to the Senate with White House backing is almost predictably unworkable." Alec watched the last of the houses fall away behind them, leaving them to the sudden night of the countryside. What he would have to do for the man from Newport, he calculated, was vote for the increased budget the Senator who counted Communists in the State Department was asking for his committee; in return, the Vermonter could expect some aid in rescuing his suffering constituents. Meanwhile, he'd better have somebody write the Newport man . . . Reminded, Alec laughed and half-turned in his seat to tell Bruyette about the reply an aide in his Washington office had concocted for the numerous letter-writers who deluge Capitol Hill offices on signal with warnings against unseen Communists. "Dear Sir," Jerry Rosenberg had written, on behalf of Senator Girard, "I thank you for your warning of the Kremlin plot, but I feel you should know of an even grander conspiracy, which is based on the shrewd decision not to overthrow the government so long as President Winkler is in office. The schemers in Moscow have seen the truth, viz., if they planted a spy in every job in the State Department, they couldn't do more for their nefarious causes than the unbelievable stupidity of the Chief Executive does every day."

This forthright epistle had been torn into small pieces and flushed down the toilet by the Senator's right-hand man, Jake Ruffing, who took a dim view of rash levity, and a purged Rosenberg had gone cheerfully back to work. "Someday I'm going to unleash Rosie," Alec told Bruyette darkly now. "If we survive the Winkler Administration at all, that is."

"We might have a better chance if our bright young men didn't waste their summers in the pursuit of ladies. Who, judging by the number of quarters that have to be borrowed to ask for a date, live in Washington and therefore can't even vote."

"Let the record read 'probably fruitless pursuit,'" Alec said glumly.

Bruyette slowed down to let a small creature make it to the other side of the road in a frantic furry blur. "To undertake your campaign in a spirit of such unseemly gloom sounds unjustified, considering that since college you've had little visible difficulty in acquiring pretty young things to wear on your well-tailored arm. And Healy complains that we have to pay the cleanup people a bonus after your speeches because of all the swooned females to be swept out."

"Dan thinks campaigns still ought to cost the same as when he was chieftain of his old satrapy and I was a knock-kneed candidate for second assistant councilman."

"Agreed. But, allowing for Healy's nostalgia, and even putting down to the excesses of sheer rumor the stories that you frequently chase ardent ladies from your bed with a baseball bat—"

"What do you mean, 'rumor'?" Alec asked indignantly. "I've worn out several Louisville Sluggers."

"Please. No sordid confessions. Now, I ask myself: why does Girard, who consistently sails off with the fairest of the fair without employing such extreme tactics as marriage proposals, now embark on a campaign with such an uncharacteristic meekness? This observer's keen eye detects a remarkable pall—almost, shall we say, a miasma of doubt—"

"Pray do," Alec said graciously. " 'A miasma of doubt.' Oh, very good, that. Quite choice."

"Irony is not responsive, Senator. The question is, can it be that in Washington handsome, rich, brainy, unmarried senators with a mystic appeal for women are a glut on the market?"

Alec peered out at the silvery river that ran alongside the road at the right. "As a matter of fact, I may be a victim of prejudice. I think she has a hard time tolerating senators." The smooth wet tops of the many stones in the river's bed gleamed in the starry night as the waters that had dealt with them long ago coursed silently and inexorably over and around them. Alec thought about the intensely private person who would have to be persuaded to embrace at least a few of the aspects of the public life and wondered whether "a miasma of doubt" wasn't apt after all. And then he thought that he was a Vermont man, native to a land where rock occurs and people and rivers find a way—and it was a hell of a thing to do but he was going to do it somehow.

"Are you sure you want to plunge into this wedding?" Bill was asking. "What other little surprises come with the lady?"

Alec smiled because the number was infinite: every time she spoke, or bent her head, or laughed, and that was what it was all about. He glanced at his friend, who didn't seem to know what it was all about, and started to say that he didn't particularly want the wedding but he did particularly want the woman. Then he saw that Bruyette was fishing for information: all that discreet dining at the Kimballs' and slipping into movies for the last show had paid off, apparently, and Andy was a secret in Vermont, if not entirely in Washington. "Have no fear, Mother," he said mildly. "She's really quite good enough for me."

"Not a Cinderella you found abloom among some ashes?"

Alec shook his head in the darkness. "Hardly. She's beautiful, intelligent, traveled, and accomplished. Her grace and poise will delight my mother. Her wealth will surely impress even my father. My sisters will twitter over her chic, my Aunt Amelia will clamber in rapture among the branches of her family tree." His face expressionless, he watched with delight the receipt of this incredible, but quite accurate, report.

Bruyette was equally expressionless. "Oh, too bad, old boy. But she can't prove much of a handicap to a fellow born to be engraved on a coin. So pour the betrothal champagne and I'll think of some tactful toast."

"I hope you get the chance." The joke was over: there was the whole courtship minuet ahead of him, and he could very well trip over his feet. And, with Andy, you either danced every step with grace and skill or she'd tap you with her fan and smile regretfully.

"I'll lend you my second-best cummerbund if you're worried about your image."

"Oddly enough," Alec said soberly, "image is my trouble." He hesitated.

"I may be destiny's tot to you, but I'm afraid I come across with her as more like old sobersides."

"You? How could you manage it?"

"Well, I'm about ten years older. But I think it's mostly the way I look beside the people she runs around with sometimes. Gay, mad, impulsive—" Alec shook his head. "Oh, you know."

"The let's-all-run-down-to-Acapulco set? Oh, my."

"And there I always am, saying, 'Sorry, but I've got to go to the library.' " He spread his hands on his knees and studied them moodily. "I get to looking a bit lugubrious."

"A snag, all right. How do you plan to cope?"

Alec went on studying his hands. "By changing, somewhat," he said quietly. "As much as I reasonably can. And hoping it'll be enough."

Touched, Bill scowled at the dark road unwinding before them. "You'll make it, Senator," he said lightly. "By a landslide." You'll always make it, he did not add. He drove attentively, but his thoughts were busy. *I hope the damn woman really is good enough for him—* He caught himself, and advised charity: the role of mate to destiny's tot was not an easy one. Aloud, he said, "So that's love, is it? I've heard about it, but I'm not sure I ever saw any before."

"Mine may be the unrequited variety."

"I don't think so. I've seen *that* before. If you don't mind my mentioning it, the little go-round you had a few years ago with the pretty actress—"

"I mind," Alec interrupted.

"All right, but I was only going to say that was the unrequited variety. Hers, I mean. You couldn't unload her fast enough."

Demands, Alec thought. *She made demands, and I wasn't having any. I guess I was really never having any until now.* "Irrelevant, incompetent, and immaterial," he told Bill. He smiled, thinking about spending August coaxing the cool Miss Langwith to go ahead and make demands.

Bill turned the car into the driveway of the big old house, where light from the front windows discovered the heart-shaped leaves of the lilac bush. "Okay, old buddy." He turned to look at Alec in the darkness that rushed in on them as the headlights went off. "But don't let's run too scared. The voter may be unpredictable, but she's intelligent, isn't she? Open to persuasion?"

Alec leaned over the seat and got his coat from the back. He climbed out of the car and stood waiting for Bill, swinging his coat and thinking of the soft voice on the phone. Surely some of that warmth was more than general, was special and for him? "Hopefully," he answered Bill. A picture of Andy splashing, sleek and laughing, from the blue water of Kingsley Lake lighted a sudden gaiety that seemed to live somewhere deep in his chest. "You know," he said, "win or lose, the campaign ought to be fun."

"That's the spirit, Senator." Bill pushed open the white-painted front door and sniffed appreciatively. "I see my mother's still contributing her Campaign Stew."

"If she ever goes over to the opposition, I'm licked." The Senator wiped his feet on the doormat as he had since he was twelve years old and an addict of Mrs. Bruyette's sugar cookies, which were sternly withheld from floor-trackers. "I'm hungry." He discovered it with surprise as he announced it. Full of hope and hunger, he followed Bill into the welcoming brightness.

I

The Old Order

"And thus the land of Cameliard was waste"

One

The *Washington Tribune,* in its wisdom, refrained from troubling its art critic with the technicalities of employment, so nobody questioned Marian Farland when she left her office early. Which was fair enough, because all the time that she waited for the bus, and all the time she was being carried to the neighborhood that, after nearly five years, still didn't seem home to her as Georgetown's Q Street had, she was working at the kind of thinking that had to happen before the kind of writing she wrote could be written.

The problem she meant to write about was constant and translatable: the busy, tireless doing of what didn't matter very much anyhow. In art, it became a matter of spiraling expertise with Nothing as its center. But to discover that Nothing among the technical delights took experience with more than art. Maybe part of what it took was simply having lived with it in other respects. To this morning's interview with a local artist, for example, Marian had brought the memory of a day in a New York apartment eight years before, when, straining for technical expertise as a sort of Mrs. America, she had devoted a whole day's mind and spirit to following an elaborate, detailed recipe for a party confection so wondrous that it evoked comment even from jaded sophisticates. The resultant insight, which the *Tribune*'s art critic had been able to turn on the painting she'd viewed this morning, was thus acquired largely at the expense of one Charles Grayson, eight years ago a correspondent for Consolidated Press and Marian's husband; partly at the expense of Charlotte "Sharlie" Grayson, eight years ago somewhere between three and four years old and in need of a less busy mother; and in no measure at the expense of the stockholders of the *Washington Tribune.*

Similarly, it was perhaps because she had once been the wife of Grayson the foreign correspondent, and had listened in a faraway country to earnest brown men being interviewed on their doomed, idealistic schemes for liberating their native lands, that the *Tribune*'s Marian Farland had been able to listen to this morning's candidate for artistic immortality with pain instead of only scorn. She had recognized the problem—too much earnestness for the amount of skill on hand—but she was still seeking a way to write about it with both truth and kindness when she looked at the French porcelain clock on her bureau and found that it was time to stop being an art critic for today. Whatever the solution was, though, it would have something to do with the fact that the art critic was also now the wife of a State Department official: something that might happen as she went about the chores that came with that role might produce the answer, or something lodged in

3

her memory would come to light tomorrow. The least likely possibility was that the answer would come from the files of the *Tribune*.

Between the acts, so to speak—in the interval between one of her roles and another—there was a slit of time for being herself, a happy-hearted woman with a way of enjoying moments. Thus, a little later, the warm waters of the shower were washing away all troubling considerations of both art and diplomacy. Twisting her body around in unintended emulation of the flamingos printed on the black shower curtain, Marian watched soapy water slide off her flank, carrying off a whole day of not-much success: in addition to her still-unwritten Sunday column, two unanswered memos, some clothes forgotten at the cleaner's, and a postponed telephone call were gurgling down the drain. But then they were gone and falling water rattled steadily on her plastic cap like martial drumbeats; she began to sing "Men of Harlech" loudly and inaccurately above the thrumming.

She had reached the best part when the knocking on the door began. So she told herself she had imagined it and went on booming out "Onward, 'tis our country needs us, He i-is bravest he who leads us," sounding thrillingly resonant to herself in the echo chamber of the shower. Clear water sluiced around her feet and folded into the current curling toward the drain. Pleasure was the only remaining reason for standing there any longer, and she knew it. "Hon-or's self now proudly heads us," she sang defiantly at the soap-streaked tiles.

"Mother!" the real world called desperately, banging at the door.

Marian turned off the water, rolling her eyes. "Yes, what is it?"

"Mom, you better come see what Peter's done," her daughter said into the sudden quiet. "You'll *kill* him."

So much for innocent pleasures, Marian thought sadly, yanking her cap off: conscience and motherhood can louse up anything. She rattled the curtain aside carefully, but it still slipped off two of its plastic hooks. She stood on tiptoe on the bathmat and patiently replaced them, then reached for the black towel on the rack; above it, a gummed red-and-white label with a large "M" penciled on it was stuck to the wall to proclaim her ownership.

"Oh boy, wait till you see," Sharlie said joyously from the other side of the door.

Toweling with only limited efficiency in the steamy bathroom, Marian asked sharply, "He's all right, isn't he?"

"Well, he's not *hurt*. But his behavior is simply not to be *borne*."

"All right. Just hold the fort, will you? I'll be there as soon as I'm dry." She flapped bath powder onto her still-damp spots in the vague hope that it would help. Reaching for the clean underclothes on the toilet lid, she barked her shin on the homemade wooden step Peter used to reach the sink. "Oh, Boltaflex," she said out loud, and tugged on bra, pants, and slip and reached for her bathrobe. She was still tying the sash when she opened the door.

Peter's dark eyes, enormous in a small solemn face, seemed to dominate the shadowy hallway. His sister's grasp on his wrist was a rather unnecessary touch of drama, his mother thought, inspecting her three-year-old swiftly. He stood very still.

"Let him go, Sharlie," Marian said. Whatever the damage, it wasn't to him or his clothing. The Band-Aid on his right hand was an old one, and his striped polo shirt and overalls were dirty but relatively whole. She came out of the bathroom, herding them before her past the sagging brick-and-plank bookshelves toward the window end of the hall, where the pale light of late afternoon was caught and framed in a neat rectangle on the worn green carpet. "Where's Rosa?"

"Gone to the store," Sharlie reported. "That's another thing—he wasn't supposed to go out till Rosa came back."

"But he did, I take it." Marian turned her gaze on her son. "Well? What's this all about, Peter?"

"Tommy did it too," he said quickly.

"They both did, Mom. They wrote *dirty words* on the sidewalk. *All* the way down Warwick Street." Sharlie leaned against the wall and waited, an unlovely gleam in her eye.

"Well, Peter?"

"It was only one word." Peter's tone implied that he and his mother were the only two left sane in a demented world. He looked at Sharlie disapprovingly, his passion for accuracy offended. "We just wrote 'shit.' "

"Peter!"

"You better stop saying that word," Sharlie warned, with satisfaction. "I *told* you you'd get in trouble."

Marian fished her watch out of her bathrobe pocket and buckled it on her wrist. Fifteen minutes from now, according to her carefully worked out schedule, she should be leaving the house. She put an experimental hand to her hair, found it damp, and the last rousing echo of "Men of Harlech" faded into silence.

Wearily, she began to cope. "Sharlie, go downstairs and get some rags." Sharlie went off down the rubber-matted back stairs, her haunches looking massive in plaid Bermuda shorts, her trim ankles buried in thick white socks that came halfway up her legs. "Put a little water in the yellow bucket and bring a can of cleanser, too," Marian called after her, noting with disgust the self-righteous joy in her daughter's upturned face. "Get your sweater," she said to her son. She waited for him at the door of his room, wondering how soon the yellow ducklings she had appliquéd on the glazed gray chintz curtains would have to give way to something more sophisticated. Judging by Dick, that would probably be rocket ships, she thought gloomily.

Dick Farland had been about seven when Marian had acquired him by marrying his father, so she had four more years or so of fumbling her way along without precedent in the strange world that being the mother of a boy sometimes seemed. The discovery that it meant an involvement in depth with outer space had been the first shock of her stepmotherhood. Rocket ships were a hell of a problem: in outline and without a chance for descriptive detail, they ended up looking only bluntly phallic. The only solution was to paint them on and—

"Where're we going, Mom?"

Glowering at present and future parental problems, she led Peter down the front stairs, past the window on the landing framing the golden autumn of the big beech tree in the side yard. Reaching for her raincoat in the downstairs hall, she looked over her shoulder and belatedly saw the fear stiffening his small body. Poor kid, she thought, her irritation melting. Did he think he was going to jail?

"We're going to repair the damage you did," she said sternly anyway. "The people who live in those houses don't want unpleasant words written on their sidewalks, you know." She saw the relief in his face and decided that she had relented too soon. "Then we'll think about a suitable punishment."

Peter hung his curly head, studying his torn red sneakers while she tugged his sweater past his ears. "Tommy—" he offered, indistinctly.

"We'll let Tommy's mother take care of Tommy." Marian tied a scarf over her hair, avoiding the hall mirror.

My God, I'll never make it, she thought, going down the steps with the bucket in one hand and Peter's grimy fist in the other. The wind found her bare toes in their black kid mules. Peter, clutching the can of cleanser and skipping along merrily, seemed happy to be off on an adventure. As they hurried past the great blue spruce at the end of their front walk and turned onto the street, he lagged, looking speculatively at Tommy's silent house next door. Marian yanked him on his way, suspecting that he was listening for cries of pain. She rounded the corner onto Warwick Street, shivering as the October wind reached under her coat to her still-damp body.

But the sight of her son's handiwork was even more chilling. "SHIT" in big, straggly, but perfectly legible block capitals was clearly visible in the mellow light. The letters had not been chalked, as she'd thought, but more or less engraved in the pavement, scratched in with a sharp stone.

"Tommy asked me how to spell 'shit,'" Peter explained nervously, as his mother set the bucket down and began scrubbing experimentally at an "S."

"Stop *saying* it!" She tried the cleanser again, to no apparent effect, while Peter watched with interest. Then she stood up, holding her scarf in place against the wind, and exploded at last. "You are an *impossible* boy," she screamed, hearing all the while that she sounded like Sharlie. "*Now* what are we going to do? What in the world did you write with?"

"We found a good writing stone." Peter dug into his pocket and produced the stone for inspection. "Tommy says it's his, but it isn't. It writes on sidewalks, but not so good on houses."

Marian, already clearly a failure as a mother and becoming with every passing minute more of a failure as a wife, failed also to give a conscientious art critic's sober attention to the possibility that a new medium had been discovered. She reached frantically for a tone of authority and managed only shrillness. "This has got to disappear, and at once. Before anyone sees it. Or you're going to be one sorry little boy."

"Mom, listen." He plucked at the skirt of her raincoat.

"I won't listen. This is the limit. I'm supposed to be downtown to pick up your father this minute."

"Mom, please listen." Peter knelt by the first square of sidewalk, his writing stone in his hand. "Mom? Don't blow your top."

Brought up short like a runner stopped by the tape, Marian bit her lip and turned away to hide her face. Everybody sounds like Sharlie, she thought, strangling on the need not to laugh. Or had "blow your top" been a hand-me-down from Dick?

"Mom?" Peter looked up at her earnestly. "The people won't mind if it's not a bad word on their sidewalk, will they?"

"So?"

"So I can just make this 'ship.' See?" Eagerly, he scratched at the final "T," turning it into a creditable "P." "There, it's fixed."

I don't know what I'm going to do about him and his high IQ, Marian told herself desperately, and I'm sure this isn't the way to build his character. But I've got to get downtown and what the hell else . . .? "What about all the others?" she asked, in what she hoped was a cold and unrelenting voice.

But Peter heard the change in her tone. "Nothing to it," he pronounced, pressing his advantage. He hopped down to the next square, plied his stone, and called out triumphantly, "Shit—*Ship*." Without waiting for further comment, he moved on to the next square. "Shit—*Ship*," his healthy young voice rang out.

Holding her coat around her, Marian scanned the empty street nervously. "Stop saying that word," she commanded, but it was hopeless: she watched him hop and crouch and scratch in joyous rhythm, cheerfully crying "Shit" in front of every house on Warwick Street. Now that he could no longer see her, she began to laugh helplessly, standing like a hysterical sentry, with nothing left in her mind but a half-formed hope that nobody she knew would come along.

Courtesy of the wind, two dried oak leaves played games with gravity, describing their doomed arcs and swoops. One, finally defeated, landed on Marian's exposed toe, where it prickled. She kicked it free, watching the lights beginning to come on in the houses—the houses, she thought bitterly, where people spoke in low and gentle voices and managed beautifully every day. The big old trees, which had seen the years when the neighborhood had been a summer resort for the rich and gracious, these days watched in equally still dignity the more frantic doings of women who no longer stepped from coaches in a swirl of silken skirts but instead parked their cars with haste and tumbled out, tugging at capacious brown-paper bags of groceries. Doing the best they could—with their hair in curlers and their feet aching and their husbands never around and their children puzzling. Turning back onto Mackintosh Place, Marian Farland, artist, housewife, often-puzzled mother, tightened her grip on Peter's warm hand for the comfort it gave her and fled into her house.

She threw her raincoat on the banister in the front hall as Rosa came toward her through the dining room. "Oh, Rosa, what a mess," she said desperately.

Rosa snapped the hall lamp on and her round face rose out of the dusk like a coffee-colored moon. "Sharlie been tellin me. You get on upstairs and put your makeup on. I come zip you in a minute. You still make it, hon."

"But—"

"Never you mind," Rosa said authoritatively. "Go on now. I fix everything fine after you gone."

No successes at all, Marian told her mirrored face, smoothing makeup base on with shaking fingers. She snaked into her garter belt, hooked up her best black stockings, and squeezed her feet into her frivolous shoes, hating them automatically. She hadn't accomplished anything permanent or useful and she was in trouble all around. She stood still submissively under Rosa's ministrations, biting her lip, which looked ridiculously pallid in her made-up face. As soon as she was zipped into the black velvet sheath that was her autumn cocktail "uniform," she moved without thought and with tremendous but unconscious efficiency, collecting the items that went with it: the black locket on which a skilled Italian hand had engraved a tiny pair of white lilies with slender dark-green leaves; the modest cameo ring, shaped like a lemon, that had been her grandmother's and then her mother's and someday would be Sharlie's; the small hat of peacock blue and dark green feathers. When she tucked the hat into place, the thick dark mounds of her hair rose softly around the brief meld of gentle color; the curling edge of the feathery strand, curving down one side of her face, was exactly the same blue-green as her eyes. Rosa handed her the black velvet purse and the long gloves and helped her into her fur jacket. Dazed, she stood somehow and at last in the downstairs hallway, staring for a moment at Rosa's familiar face, wanting to cast herself on that dear bosom and weep.

"Plenty time," Rosa said soothingly. "You quiet down, Miz Marian."

"I don't know why—it never used to be like this. You remember, when we lived on Q Street? Everything was so—*peaceful.*"

"Peaceful? Maybe sometimes." Rosa looked doubtful. "But broke, too. You forgot that. And you had all them gentlemen callers, but we didn't have no man in the house. It ain't the same thing."

"But we didn't rush around doing—oh, I don't know. We did what we really wanted to do."

"I ain't so sure that so good for folks, you know?" Rosa smiled. "You just be sure you drive careful now, hear?"

Promising dutifully, Marian grabbed her bulky everyday purse from the hall table and stumbled toward the door. In the gloom behind her, the back door slammed, the dogs began barking in syncopation, and Dick's voice rose in piercing greeting. Marian hesitated and took a step toward the medley. But Rosa reached out and turned her toward the door again. "Go on now. They all safe home."

Rosa watched Marian, tripping a little in her high heels, run recklessly to the car and back it jerkily out of the driveway. Above the wide, cheerful grin she wore until it was certain that Marian would not look back, Rosa's eyes were worried. She sighed as she closed the door; but by the time she reached the kitchen, her habitual mantle of authority was safely on her plump, strong shoulders.

She surveyed the small war in the kitchen, where Sharlie and Dick had already gone beyond the niceties of debate in discussing the question of whose turn it was to feed the dogs. The dogs reacted to the tension in their characteristic fashions. Marian's dachshund dashed up and down the waxed linoleum floor in repeated peril of capsizing, righting himself by a frantic scrabble of toenails; he yelped hysterically and his brief black tail whipped the air like a metronome gone mad. The cocker spaniel who had been raised by Will Farland was rather more adept at sticking to the point: he whined piteously, his soulful eyes turning from one to the other of the potential dog-feeders, his long golden ears and the plumes of his tail drooping like a very metaphor of grief—but he never moved more than a few inches from his feeding dish.

Can't tell me dogs ain't like their people, Rosa thought as she snaked her way among the agitated bodies to consult the list of duties posted on the bulletin board and then listened to a rundown on the deals and counterdeals by which the original list had been amended. She ruled against Sharlie, standing her ground sturdily before the dramatic accusation of betrayal the girl's eyes flashed at her, and dispatched Dick to hang up his coat. She washed her hands, absently digressing to scrub briefly at Peter's face because it was around and dirty, and then scraped a carrot and cut it into strips. Dispensing them, Rosa wished vaguely that she could give one to Marian too.

While her munching children were settling down and Rosa's brown hands were moving competently, as they always had, about the important business of getting dinner, Marian was maneuvering the car among the vehicle-clogged downtown streets. Lighting a cigarette with one hand, she reproached herself again: it was all very well, but Peter mustn't get out of things by being smart. The fact was, writing on sidewalks was wrong, and it mattered—and yet it had been wedged in and hurried past as though it were something that didn't. She claimed the last available inch between her car and the car in front and lined up with the others arrayed like a congregation before the frock-coated statue in the center of the traffic circle.

Waiting, she reached for her velvet purse and began transferring makeup from her large purse, keeping the lipstick out to use at the next red light.

But at the next red light, Washington suddenly came officially into the night and Marian sat entranced as all at once, everywhere, the street lights bloomed like moonflowers. Behind her, a red Volkswagen with a diplomatic license plate beeped tentatively. Obediently, she took her foot off the brake and inched the car on, accepting her obligation not to stand in the Volkswagen's way. But her mind banged at the bitter truth that there was never, never, never time to stand still and just look: the demands of her daily life shoved impersonally, like a policeman who was only doing his job, moving her on relentlessly from the meaningful to the meaningless. I have a right, something in her kept trying to cry out—a right to just look. She blinked beginning tears away and drove on helplessly, the unspoken words a palpable aching lump in her throat.

Her lipstick was still only half on as she turned in at the semicircle of driveway that was the State Department's back door. Will, pacing among the flags, spotted the car before she had to blow the horn. She put it in neutral and slid over on the seat, dragging her two purses and her lipstick with her.

"For God's sake, Marian. When in hell are you going to develop some idea of time?" He slammed the door irritably on the edge of his overcoat and had to open and close it again before he moved the car out of the drive and poised it to enter the traffic.

"I couldn't help it," she began. But it was more important to get the rest of her lipstick on. Looking into the mirror of her compact, she saw a hairpin escaping the roll of hair on her neck and shoved it back into place.

"You had plenty of warning. And you know these guys can be touchy." Will changed lanes skillfully, securing a possible thirty-second advantage.

Stowing her everyday purse under the seat, Marian noticed again how much higher his voice was when he was irritated. Well, what do you want him to do, she asked herself reasonably—whisper in a passionate throb? "It was Peter," she said, very like Peter saying "It was Tommy." Beyond the car window, the green-painted crenellations on the railing of the Connecticut Avenue bridge looked like the teeth of an endless monster.

"It's always something, isn't it? All I know is, I've been standing in front of that goddam building for twenty minutes, and I needed those twenty minutes upstairs." He made a daring left turn, and they fled along under the dark blur of trees on Rock Creek Parkway. "Dammit, Marian," Will was beginning again, when a fortuitous red light intervened and he pulled up and turned to look at her. His swift glance took in the woebegone droop of her mouth and the glitter of tears in her eyes, and his bony face softened at once. "Forget it." He reached out with his free hand. "You look beautiful. I don't care how long it takes, and to hell with NATO."

Marian sniffed, brightening reluctantly. "Thanks for the dubious compliment, but I'm afraid it's nearly all natural. I didn't have time for me, thanks to Peter."

"What's he done now?"

Will began to laugh when she told him, and he was still laughing away her protests when he deposited their unwashed Dodge among the shining Cadillacs and Continentals a block from the embassy.

"It's not funny to fail as parents," Marian said. She found the second earring in the pocket of her coat and screwed it on.

"Who's a parent?" Will handed her out and slammed the car door. He tucked her hand under his arm and walked her rapidly down the street. "I'm just a lucky guy taking a pretty lady to a party. Well, a couple of parties, I'm afraid. We have to go on to one more."

"Oh, Will. Not another emerging nation." Before she even began to climb the shallow steps to the great carved door, her feet were hurting.

"Yup. At the Belleview. Better fill up here, though. The food's better. Oh, and by the way, I hope to get some mileage out of having married the erstwhile Miss DiGennaro. Remember, the guest of honor's Italian."

Waiting for Will by the cloakroom in the marble hall, Marian smiled, noting fondly the politician's quaint faith in ethnic stereotypes. Her grandfather could speak Italian—at least, the old man was given to quoting Dante—and had been known to read it; but her father's favorite reading was the *Wall Street Journal*. And her mother, who was of British descent anyway, had only enough Italian to follow the composer's directions on a musical score. People were less simple than politicians, Marian decided, discovering sadly that the only Italian word she could remember was *arrivederci*, which seemed an unlikely way to open a conversation. But there was no time to tell Will, who was smoothing his fair hair as he came toward her. Over his shoulder, a curly marble cupid smirking in a niche approved his effort. Will propelled Marian with a warm hand in the small of her velvet back, muttering, "We're on, baby—a-one and, a-two, *and*" into her ear at the last possible moment as they moved into the wave of babble; her smile for the welcoming Ambassadress was genuine, if not exactly relevant.

Neither was her critical study of the enormous, heavily gold-framed portrait looming on the opposite wall; she found herself staring at it sometime later, when the first tingling of the first martini was almost forgotten. Speculation on the possibility that its rich, dark-brown patina could have been achieved with shoe polish occupied her mind but not her tongue. It would have been all right to say something about it to Sven Halversen, the white-haired, wonderful Swede who headed the International Finance Administration, but not to a Mr. Sawyer of F.A.C., who had taken it on himself to join them. Sighing, Marian abandoned her meditations on art and shoe polish to thumb through her mental card index; but the best she could do with F.A.C. was that it had something to do with distributing food to foreign countries. Looking at the rat-faced Sawyer, she thought it was easier to imagine him hoarding food than distributing it.

"I hope I shall be here next autumn," Halversen was saying, "for I always find your elections a most enthralling spectacle. Now, perhaps, this young Senator may make it even more interesting." His accent bespoke an English public school, but heavy Scandinavian cadences lurked in his voice.

"Alec Girard? He's just a playboy," Sawyer scoffed. "Nobody's about to take him seriously."

"So?" Halversen's face was empty of expression. "I have met the Senator, just once. But not, alas, his beautiful wife, whose photographs I study with pleasure."

"It's certainly not hard to find them. But no amount of publicity's going to blind the American people to what he stands for. In the grass roots—"

"You're about to go back to the grass roots, aren't you, Mr. Sawyer?" Marian asked suddenly. She watched him like a high school girl in the presence of a movie star; nothing in her respectful attention indicated that she'd just placed Sawyer as one of President Winkler's early appointees. Most of the original batch of middle-aged businessmen who'd crusaded into Washington with Winkler—honest men, though misguided—had quickly discovered that public service interfered seriously with making money; Sawyer, who may have had less to go home to, had stayed on longest. "Didn't I read that you were returning to private life?"

The bright light from the glittering chandelier found pink scalp between the carefully deployed strands of Sawyer's thinning hair. "Well, I've done my bit, you know. And of course it's been a sacrifice."

"Of course. You had a business—what was it, farm equipment?—somewhere in the middle west."

"Indiana." Sawyer expanded under her wide, innocent gaze. "I don't for a minute regret having served my country, but it's been a frustrating couple of years."

"Oh, Mr. Sawyer, I'm so sorry we didn't make you happy here."

"Still, I tell myself I've made a dent in the problem of getting the taxpayer his dollar's worth out of these government employees."

"Was it your department," Marian inquired brightly, "where they instituted the practice of beginning the day with everybody praying together?" She thought of adding, *hands clasped at their little desks;* but she resisted temptation.

"I'm glad to say I was part of that. And at least we made sure they put in their eight hours."

There was no mistaking the little man's satisfaction. "How clever." Marian paused, then drove the dagger home. "As the wife of a State Department employee who's given to attending meetings that begin at five-thirty, I can only say, Mr. Sawyer, that I wish you had extended your missionary work to us." She saw him trying to speak and stopped him with a slim, confiding hand on his sleeve. "What a joy it would be," she gushed on, "if you could arrange to have my husband prayed from the building promptly at five."

Sawyer, his rodent face a bright pink, fought back. "I imagine you'd miss that ol' overtime pay, though."

Marian laughed like a road-show coloratura practicing her scales. "Dear Mr. Sawyer! Overtime pay, indeed! Wouldn't it be wonderful if we really were paid for all those overtime hours?" She looked searchingly into his small angry eyes. "May I hope that the Administration is planning to propose it?" She waited, studying his deepening color with wicked delight. "Or perhaps, since Mr. Winkler's remaining days in the White House are numbered, I may take it that Mr. Ferris—if he is your nominee—will ask for overtime pay for people like my husband?"

Attracted by the magic name of his party's white hope, Sawyer took the bait. "Ralph Ferris is a friend of every workingman," he began, and then stopped, belatedly aware that Ferris had recently blasted "the spenders in Washington" and this pretty little booby trap not only knew it but probably could quote it word for word. He took out his handkerchief and coughed into it unconvincingly.

Marian watched her fish flap at the end of the line for a moment and then, because she was not without mercy, threw him back by turning to thank Sven Halversen, who was offering a new martini. She finished the last of her lukewarm one, though, before handing over the glass. In the interim, Sawyer, still looking a little terrified, muttered an excuse and disappeared rapidly behind a middle-aged lady encased in a glorious Spanish shawl.

"Not only a dolt but a coward, too," Marian pronounced over his retreating figure. She shook her head, disgust like a shadow over her face. "They make me sick, Dr. Halversen. And frightened, too, I think. So much sheer ignorance, and yet so much belief in their own rightness. I have a feeling sometimes that they'll kill us all."

The old man's gaze was kind. "They could—it is possible. But only if they—these blind men—are in control." He hesitated, then went on in a low voice, his words slow and deliberate. "You're correct in your intuition, my dear, but not in your despair."

"But what can I *do?* What difference does it make if I rout one idiot Sawyer at a cocktail party? He'll just rise again somewhere else. It's not even a matter of which party wins elections. There are Sawyers everywhere."

Halversen said quietly, "There are, indeed. But they are not invincible."

"Maybe I take them too seriously."

"In one respect. And not seriously enough in another. One cannot combat the Sawyers by simply dismissing them, for what troubles them also troubles their betters. But you mustn't permit their blindness to drive you to despair."

I'm so lucky, Marian thought, lifting her head to smile happily at Halversen; I always run into somebody nice, even in the unlikeliest places. "Well, I'm glad to discover that Senator Girard troubles Mr. Sawyer. I haven't been paying much attention to Girard, but maybe I'll begin."

Halversen chuckled. "You know, I have heard from my daughter some sentiments about Senator Girard that didn't seem entirely kindly."

"Your daughter's married to an American, isn't she? But she's not in politics?"

"No, no, she is a housewife and mother in Minneapolis." The heavy face softened in a smile. "Of an age with young Mrs. Girard. And in fact, I think I detected, after listening for a bit, that her quarrel was less with the Senator than with his wife. Or, more strictly speaking, with his wife's beauty."

Marian nodded. "I suppose it's hard to take, for a young woman with small children." She drained the last of her drink, making a face. "There you are, with your hair in your eyes and your skirt hanging crooked, spending your days wiping runny noses. And smiling at you from all the newsstands is Andrea Girard—rich, beautiful, chic, endowed with practically everything."

"The fact that my wife seems more tolerant of Mrs. Girard than my daughter must bear you out," Halversen agreed.

Will appeared, looming at Marian's shoulder, and claimed her. Sighing and once more aware of her aching feet as she followed him, she said, "That sweet old man almost made it worth the whole business of putting on these damned shoes."

" 'That sweet old man' is one of the best brains alive." Will looked at her curiously. She fought coming to these parties, she fought staying at them, and yet she ended by enjoying herself; certainly from the point of view of propaganda for the U.S.A., her beauty and warmth made her a smashing success. If it were only a matter of advancing her husband's career—which she probably did, but at a price: a dozen people who would have given their eyeteeth for a kind word from Halversen would now be inspired to envy of Farland—he could get along without it. But if he left her at home, she complained that they never saw each other; it was true, and not to his liking either. He took her arm to lead her away and held her there instead, studying her with pleasure and perplexity. "Baby, you know you liked Halversen. And he was obviously delighted with you. So you're not really suffering so much, are you?"

"Yes I am," Marian insisted. "Can't we go now?" But she recognized the justice of Will's argument. It was no small thing to make a friend, however it happened.

"You know we can't just skip. Let's do the guest of honor."

Marian ducked her own feathered head to avoid a long feather from the hat of a nodding lady whose back was turned and let Will lead her toward the group gathered before a tall window shrouded in golden falls of cloth. Her feet reminded her of their pain with every step on the terrazzo floor, and she concentrated on promising them fiercely that the very minute she could manage it, they would be freed.

Will left Marian listening to the guest of honor—a brilliant, inscrutable man who had heretofore seemed incapable of any but the most formal expression—talking longingly of his wife and children, whom he confided he hadn't seen for more than a month. He spoke in English, as had Marian. Will was thinking that her Italian blood still might have something to do with it—except that there had been that Indonesian last week—when Peggy McGrath floated into his ken like a surfer coming in on a wave; she began to congratulate him, without prelude, on Marian's "sweetly slaying Mr. Odious Sawyer." Will grinned and guessed happily that Sawyer would be willing to stay down on the farm machinery hereafter, and they nodded in mutual pleasure and equal lack of wonder at the speed of the news report on the encounter. For Will and Jim McGrath had once been Foreign Service classmates setting off to their first post together, each accompanied by a brand-new wife; Peggy, one of the brides, had had as long as Will to get used to the wonders of the diplomatic circuit.

"The beauty part is, she doesn't even know it," she said now, nodding in Marian's direction.

"Don't tell her, will you?" Farland smiled down at the pretty redhead who had accepted, without any of the undercover warfare that might have been expected of Kitty Farland's friend and mourner, the outsider who had become the second Mrs. Farland. Marian might be unaware that Peggy's tactful reminders of upcoming wives' luncheons and timely nudges at Middle East ladies' teas were above and beyond the call of duty; but Will knew it, and was grateful.

"Not me," Peggy said cheerfully. "Jim says when you find a natural, you don't coach him much. You just let him swing at the ball."

Will remembered Peggy's baseball metaphor a little later when, still standing on the embassy's doorstep with the door just closed behind them, Marian bent to remove her shoes. It would have been so nice if she could have waited just until— But she was a natural, all right: the door opened to disgorge a departing pair of pomposities, and Marian, pacing down the steps on her husband's arm, wished them goodnight with such queenly aplomb as to render her stockinged feet quite invisible.

Her spirits rose as the Farlands turned the corner from the embassy's imposing entrance: it was not too late, and in the kindly night, all seemed reparable. "Let's go home, Will," she said. "You could still catch Peter in time to administer a dose of authority. And then we can go for a walk. It's such a lovely night." She paused to wiggle her liberated toes in the cool air.

"You haven't been listening to a thing I said."

"Yes I have." She sighed. It was nice of Peggy to have said something complimentary about her to Will, but it had not much to do with her: for all the McGraths' friendliness, they were alien. Recalled from innocent pleasure, she thought they were, if you looked at it coldly, another example of expertise at something maybe not worth doing at all. "I'd be feeling kindly too, if I were Peggy. She's not faced with watching the Independent Republic of Whatever emerge tonight." To forgo immediate pleasure in order to look at things coldly was not Marian's natural bent: the strain of effort edged her voice.

Will stopped walking. "Now wait a minute. Let's just settle something, right here and now."

"Will, please." Her quiet voice tried desperately for calm. "I'm afraid I have just about one hour's more standing-around time left. If I have to do it here, you'll have to go on to the reception by yourself." In spite of her efforts, her tone had grown hard and biting. "You can explain, in your halting French, that your wife is home suing you for cruelty."

Will's face froze. "I don't like ultimatums."

"I'm sorry," she said, ashamed. "Really I am. I don't want to seem ill-natured—" She heard his disbelieving snort and it was suddenly too much, much too much. "*I* don't like anything, Will," she went on furiously. "Not anything I do or anything that happens to me any more." Her own words, hanging in the soft air of the quiet street, frightened and sobered her. "It's been such a very long day," she said in a small, tired voice, "and more of it to come. And there's no day in sight that won't be full of hurrying—to somewhere I don't really want to be and something I don't really want to do—" She shook her head hopelessly. "If that's an ultimatum, then—I guess the war is on."

Will shrugged. "Don't be silly. Nobody wins a war like that." He watched her through narrowed eyes. "Just tell me, what in hell would you like me to do about it, Marian?"

"I don't know. If I knew, I'd do it myself."

"And dispense with me. Is that it?"

"Oh, Will. Just make things make sense."

It was, he told himself wryly, an absolutely insane order—and absolutely valid, too. Which made it Marian, all right. He put his forefinger under her chin and tilted her face up into the shadowy light. "I'm trying to do something," he said, looking at her steadily. "But you keep tagging me as the enemy. I'm in the same foxhole, baby."

Marian blinked and then, slowly, smiled at him. "I forget, darling." She took his arm. "Tonight—just tonight, Will—let's go home. I promise I won't forget again."

Farland looked away from her and rubbed at his chin with his free hand, pondering the problem that was, in effect, a translator's. For it was a matter of the right of each of two languages to be equally represented in all its traditions and connotations. He understood Marian's language, certainly in relation to Peter, for whom the difference between acceptable and unacceptable behavior had not been defined authoritatively enough today. But the black men who had fought their way, at unbelievably bloody cost, into a precarious nationhood had to be handled as thoughtfully as Peter, and with a gingerliness Marian simply couldn't comprehend. If she had the easy kindness of the rich and lucky, she also had their history of social acceptability: in a sense, she was the American character, in spades. Even if Will could explain to her how carefully these men counted everything that might even look like a slight, an aspersion on their new status, she would never make the connection with the possibility that a nineteen- or twenty-year-old Peter might be shot at in some faraway land because of a slur imagined tonight. Missed chances for communication, failures to build faith in this country instead of another, could cost heavily. For men led countries; and men remembered snubs and honors, and either trusted or distrusted.

Will looked down at his wife, seeing again the paradox that had once stopped his life in its tracks—the small, thin, strong-boned face, denying as an ascetic's, contradicted by the soft, full mouth, luscious as a purple grape ripe on a sunny vine. At that first moment, it had come to him clearly and in so many words: "I am smitten." He had been "smitten" with her many times since, rediscovering it without warning and with a small, pleasurable shock. Now, smitten again, it occurred to him—even while he was rapidly devising ways and means to keep it from happening—that he would like nothing better at this moment than to snatch her home and, as soon as possible, into their welcoming bed. The necessary "little talk" with Peter could be accomplished with dispatch, and then . . .

"You know," Will said thoughtfully, "I wouldn't be doing you any kindness to let you miss this thing at the Belleview."

"They're all the same," Marian said. But her voice wondered, *Aren't they?* It was probably too late to catch Peter before he went to bed, her eyes began to acknowledge.

"Not this one." Will reeled her in cautiously, but with a skilled hand. "You haven't seen their costumes, and I have. I couldn't begin to describe them, but they're gorgeous." He went on talking quietly, almost diffidently; it took just about as long as he had figured.

"Well," Marian said doubtfully, "if we don't have to stay very long . . ."

"Oh, we don't. Just check in, and we're off. Put your shoes on, baby." He steadied her while she obeyed. "Now come on. 'Once more into the breach.' "

The costumes were as interesting as he had promised. And so were the faces. Marian murmured, *"Enchanté,"* to the huge and resplendent man, bowing over her hand, his smooth skin so black it was almost blue. A crimson cloak embroidered in what looked like gold filigree hung from his great shoulders, far above her. Beside such strength and authority, Will was incredibly pale and wispy-looking; it was impossible to think of him actually negotiating with this towering magnificence. But against the massed black-and-white decorum of Will and his colleagues, it was the crimson and gold that become unbelievable, as bizarrely out of place as a four-color illustration in the middle of a law book.

Marian drifted mechanically in an ordered course around the hotel ballroom, which, for all its elegant space and expensive appointments, was inescapably bland. She turned once to look back at the fairy-tale chieftain, now listening expressionlessly to a pretty blonde who talked too fast. Ah, we'll bland him down too, Marian decided gloomily. His womenfolk in their brilliant mob caps and unflattering bunched cloth at the rear—was it a bustle, or did they all just have big behinds?—would, sooner or later, learn to stand in line at the supermarket. Neatly dressed, in fatigue and malaise just like hers.

Her mind turned to the painter whose work she would review next week. His violence, his disorderly color amounted, she supposed, to a protest against the very blandness she deplored. Her sympathies were with him; but she had a responsibility to history, to the work men had put in, learning to transmute anger into art. It could not be allowed to end in scrawling dirty words on a fence, however welcome the bright, pure color and the straggly, impulsive lettering; if there was a way back to the vividnesses that attended barbarism, the adoption of barbarism wasn't it. Once you've emerged, she thought grimly, smiling at and not listening to the wife of an Undersecretary of State, you're on the road to black-and-white glories and cardboard food and deodorized armpits. Maybe Sven Halversen was right, and she was too quick to despair. Well then, there must be a side road that you found if you were lucky, or blessed, and came out into real life and real art. But you couldn't just turn back.

Though she didn't make any dent in figuring out what you could do. The sea of molasses flows right on over me, she was thinking miserably as Will helped her into their car at last. She took her hat off and slid its loop up her arm like a bracelet. The hell with it, with all the outside world: what mattered was that Peter wrote "shit" on the sidewalk. That was a reality, and she hadn't dealt with it properly because she was late for unreality.

"Sorry I left you stuck with the Undersecretary's wife," Will said humbly over the sound of the motor. "I forgot she was a Sunday painter."

"Oh well, maybe I won't run into her again for a while."

"Even if you do, it can't be often. Her husband goes when Winkler goes."

Marian approved the pattern of lighted windows in the darkness of a side street. "Oh. Well, don't those people usually loiter in Washington after they've been—er—deposed? To become chairman of something?"

"They used to." Will sounded suddenly happy. "But if, just if, the next President should turn out to be Alexander Girard, a hell of a lot will be different around the State Department. Sometimes I feel about the election like a kid waiting for Christmas."

"Oh, darling." Marian laughed indulgently, as if indeed at a child. "It's only another election."

"Baby, it isn't. Believe me, it isn't. It's a last chance, maybe: everything has just about stopped dead under Winkler, especially during his second term. Once there's no possibility of his running again, a weak President gets damn near powerless." No child who felt the despair revealed in his voice could have managed the effortful control that was also there. "The election of Girard is about the only thing that gives me any hope. Even then, we'll be years paying the price of Winkler's refusal to run the government."

Marian watched a neatly raked pile of leaves being undone by a frisking wind. "What makes Senator Girard the hope of heaven all of a sudden?"

He stopped the car at a traffic light. "For one thing, we can use some brains in the White House."

They waited in the quiet crimsoned dark among the quiet houses. "But I'm not happy about the way he backed away from fighting the witch-hunters," Marian said mildly. "I'm not sure I'd vote for him if he did get the nomination."

The light changed and Will shot the car forward abruptly, taking out on it his irritation with his regrettable wife. It was too much, that after all his patience with the ritual evening, he should be denied reward: smitten but dutiful, he had watched from behind his decorous mask as other men smiled down into the sea-colored eyes you could drown in and examined with discretion the interestingly exact fit of the simple black dress. And now, now that it was his inning at last—he shook his head angrily—she had to decide, now of all times, to air her schoolgirl politics. "Oh come on," he said in what he hoped was a tone of quiet patience. "Let's be a little realistic, baby."

"Maybe Girard is too realistic."

Will turned the car into Warwick Street. He listened to the stubborn note in her voice and sighed; but he decided on a try at getting both of the things he wanted. "Darling, the point is, what's needed now is more important than anything Girard did or didn't do before."

"There are other candidates."

"Yes, but he has something the country needs desperately. New ideas. An understanding of what it takes to try them out. Most of all, he understands the uses of power and he isn't afraid to—"

"Oh for heaven's sake, who cares about power? I just want things to stop getting more and more mixed up and fancy-shoddy. I just wish *somebody* would keep it simple."

"You have my deepest sympathy," Will snapped. He pulled into the driveway and stopped the car. "It's too bad Winkler can't run again, because simple is what he is, all right. The only trouble is, the world isn't, and we've been killing time for eight years while he talked like a Mother's Day card." He plunged out, banging the car door, and slapped at a low-hanging branch of the red maple as he went around to get Marian, who deserved a Winkler. Which wasn't fair, he knew: she had never been one of those seduced by Winkler's bland charm. But it was true anyway, Will told himself angrily, because if you gave her a Winkler who didn't murder the English language —if you offered her practically anybody who talked well, though he didn't say anything more specific than Winkler ever had, she'd run to acclaim him because he didn't sound like a politician.

"Don't you understand? The country has to get *on,* for God's sake." He heard his voice rise as he reached into the car to help her out—this damned fool woman like all the other damned fools who convinced themselves that though you need a plumber for plumbing and an electrician for wiring, what you need in the highest political office is a non-politician.

"Tu-tu-tu-tu," Marian said in her petting voice. Her gaze, puzzled but concerned, traveled over his angry eyes and tightened lips.

Tu-tu-tu-hell, was what he should have said. But it was too late: the moment he touched her, it had been too late. Will hauled her out and stood her on her feet under the maple, where she was quite small enough to fit, and kissed her long enough and thoroughly enough to accommodate his combined passions. Her lips, soft and warm, opened invitingly and she snuggled in his arms, looking at ease for the first time all evening and apparently quite willing to stay there: Marian was not given to remembering her surroundings when at ease. Will, who never forgot his, remembered the neighbors. He marched her across the lawn and up the porch steps, and he held her in one arm while he unlocked the door hastily.

But it was still a pause, and it made a difference: it gave Marian time to advance from her reflex reactions to enjoyment of them. For she had not, after all, spent the evening lusting after Will—from her point of view, his intent, though clear enough, was the result of a sudden inspiration, a just-born idea; it appealed to her, but it also brought a sense of release that made her playful. She was not by nature given to dark thoughts, and certainly not to any enjoyment of them, and she was given to easy enjoyment of everyday delights; freed abruptly, and tacitly given permission to stop doing what she didn't like and begin to do what she did well, she responded with sheer high spirits. The replacement of the grim political prophet with her ardent Willie had happened before, but it was still an event to celebrate; her eyes sparkled with the gaiety of the occasion.

Look at her, Will thought, turning to see her standing in the lighted front hall and drawing off her gloves with the lingering coquetry of a strip-teaser: if she didn't care much for talk about power, she sure took pleasure in exercising it. The evidence that she had absolute power was inescapable: there stood Farland, nearly a foot taller and nearly a hundred pounds heavier, waiting humbly for what he had been clearly promised. He grinned, without resentment and appreciating the show; she had a monopoly on what he wanted, and he was prepared to pay her price.

"Yes, ma'am," he said, and went, as ordered, to stop the dogs from waking everybody with their barking. And that was absolute power, said its aficionado and victim to himself as he came back and found Marian calmly reading the telephone messages. She knew, all right—oh, that was one thing, Farland's hunger was, that she knew more about than anybody. He halted in the dining-room doorway, looking at the medallion around her neck like a black tear fallen onto the creamy flesh; the damn thing led the eye inexorably down that gentle swell until it was stopped cruelly by a barrier of black velvet.

"The Kimballs called," Marian reported. "To invite us to a party." She turned her disturbingly sudden blue gaze on him and smiled bewitchingly. "Darling, is it too late to call Betty now, do you think?"

It was time to take a firm hand. "She's busy. This is the husband's hour," Will said pointedly. "In well-run households, anyway."

"Oh." The shrouding lashes descended demurely. "Willie? I think I'd like a drink."

"I'll bring it up to you."

"Thank you, darling." She raised her hand to her hair, arching her body lazily—in case, Will thought, grinning, he hadn't been noticing. But his grin vanished as she turned toward the stairs and then stopped. "Oh, you know what? I left my everyday purse in the car. It's under the front seat."

"I'll get it later," he told her. He would get it for her if a dragon guarded it; he would bring her a drink if an army had mounted guard over the bourbon; he would do any goddam thing in the goddam world if she would only quit playing games.

"Darling, start my zipper, will you?" She backed up to him, smiling at him over her shoulder.

This was more like it: it took him a while, but he finally found the almost invisible little tab and pulled downward. And the soft black velvet parted silently, revealing a whiteness as tempting as a ripe fruit just peeled . . . Abruptly, Will grasped the significance of that uninterrupted expanse and grabbed for her, his hand ready to cup— But she had her little tricks: she moved like lightning, and in the blink of an eye she was out of his reach. She clutched her crumpled dress to her bosom demurely, at not much below the point that had been visible to all the nations of the world all evening; her eyes danced, and she looked totally innocent of any knowledge that she was damn near naked under that dress. She'd brought it off again, whatever it was she did that turned him instantly into the yokel, lately out of overalls and still all too-long arms and legs, eyeing the small, perfect jewel displayed discreetly in Tiffany's window.

"There's a form to sign for Dick, darling," Will's dutiful wife reminded him; her luscious mouth and soft voice were devoutly applied to the important task of information. "He needs it for school—"

"Marian." He waited for her to look at him. "I will sign the form for Dick's school. I will lock all the doors, turn down the thermostat, and put out anything that has to be put out. And oh, yes—I'll fetch you your reticule, and I'll fix you a drink. But after that," he added slowly, "I'm coming upstairs. And if you aren't waiting right smack in the middle of that bed, what I'll do then is take a stick to you. You hear?"

Absolute power might not always corrupt, but its possessors weren't prone to fear: she stood motionless at the bottom of the stairs, poised so that one slim leg in its elegant sheer stocking was exposed to the hungry eye of yokels. "Yes, massa," she taunted. "I hear you-all."

Will had heard, too: the southern cadences had crept into his speech somehow, with other echoes of the men who once sat whittling and exchanging wisdom through drowsy noons. *Whut Ah say, if you got you one of them hounds jest won't mind you none, there's bound to come a day you got to take a stick to him. And damn if there ain't some women—* Will blinked, closing out both the actual temptress and a fantasy involving an easy leap, a grab, and the satisfying sound of ripping cloth. Only a fool would try a frontal assault on a bastion of so much power: what he needed was a plea disguised as a threat. He found it, and with the experienced skill that turns a disadvantage to advantage, converted the image he was stuck with into an effective weapon. Lounging against the wall, with his thumbs stuck in his belt, he growled, "Git up them stairs, Lulubelle." He took a single menacing step toward her. "Scat!"

Marian giggled, and scampered obediently.

But one of them knew, anyway, who had the real power to command obedience.

Two

At ten-thirty in the morning after the ballroom of the Belleview had seen the emergence of another baby republic, Andrea Girard, emerging from her obstetrician's office on K Street, was in a similarly celebratory mood. And certainly she was minded to observe the beauties of the day—a soft, damp, warmish October morning more like Ireland than Washington. Coming up the steps from the basement of the converted brownstone, she decided there was world enough and time at this moment for anything she wanted. And what she wanted was to walk, on her suddenly wondrously strong legs, and look, with today's marvelously seeing eyes.

She swung off toward Connecticut Avenue, a tall, straight figure in her slim beige suit with a silky chocolate-brown raincoat hung carelessly over her arm. Her shoes were trim and elegant, and she wore no hat. A narrow purplish scarf of delicate sari cloth with a fine thread of gold was tucked into the neck of her jacket; the folds stirred in the warm wind as she turned into the avenue and glimpsed her slender figure, its magical secret still invisible, in a shop window.

Even if I walk all the way home, she thought, trying to be sober and responsible, I'll be there in time to check on Alec's lunch before it goes off to the Hill. For a fraction of a second she considered taking the hot lunch down there in person and telling him then, but she knew better than to spoil her news by dumping it among the swirling currents in his office. Besides, she wanted to be alone with it as much as she also wanted to tell Alec.

Thinking about being alone, she remembered the Mayflower Hotel, looming massively ahead—and oh dear, Elizabeth Arden's, too. But it was early yet, and if she stayed on this side of the street and kept her head turned away, maybe nobody would appear. I ought to have a hat with a swooping brim, she thought, and put my coat on and turn up the collar. And then slink like mad. A mink jacket stepped out of a taxi in front of the Mayflower, and Andy turned her back swiftly and studied Magruder's window, eyeing cheeses and canned pâté until it was safe to turn around.

She had just succeeded in slinking past the danger point when she looked across the little triangular park in the middle of the avenue and saw the hat shop across the street. A message, a sign. She crossed carefully with the traffic light and gained the other side. There were no slouch hats in the window.

"Yes, madam?" The saleslady was a big, bonny woman, but fearfully corseted. Between her plucked eyebrows three deep lines of strain, the central one upright and the others curving away from it, looked like the feathers in a court headdress.

"I was—er—interested in a felt," Andy said. "Something with a wide brim." She sat down obediently at the little table, wondering why on earth she had come in here. Then she caught sight of her reflection, with its dancing eyes and the smile about to burst through the carefully composed lips, and she remembered. "Black, I guess. Or . . . well, it doesn't matter what color."

She tried on the first two offerings, which were nowhere near what she wanted or ever would want, although it was perfectly clear to her that there was no hat made in which she would not look pretty this morning. "Something with more—er—*swoop* to the brim, I think," she told the saleswoman gently.

"Would you be interested in a Kelly green, madam?" the woman asked. "Brims are a little hard to find by now, but I have one . . ." Andy smiled dazzlingly at her and agreed to try the one. Left over by soberer ladies, who planned ahead, she supposed. But I am planning ahead, her own eyes in the mirror confided to her. I'm planning for June.

The word in her mind struck her down as the woman lowered the Kelly green—which had a brim, but definitely did not swoop—as reverently as if it were a crown. A brand-new baby at convention time would make her not exactly the candidate's perfect helpmate. If he was the candidate. And if he was, it wouldn't be because his wife had poured coffee for the ladies. "No," she told the saleslady, a little unhappily. "What I had in mind is something more . . . more dramatic."

A second saleslady appeared at Andy's elbow. "What she wants," she advised her colleague, "is a Greta Garbo type."

Oh, precisely, Andy told herself, trying not to giggle. Greta Garbo—they couldn't have known it, it had never been in any of the interviews—was one of Alec's enthusiasms. "Yes, I think that must be it," she contributed to the discussion, as solemnly as she could. Darling, if you find the fact that I'm pregnant a little inconvenient, will it help if I look like your favorite movie actress? "I'm most awfully anxious to have one," she was surprised to hear herself saying. The very thing for a candidate's wife. Guaranteed not to afford the—we hope—crowds even a glimpse of her face. An image of mystery and intrigue. Oh, won't the publicity men love *that?*

She woke from an imaginary scene in which Alec's henchmen were complaining, "With Mrs. Girard got up like Mata Hari, it just doesn't help that frank and open picture we're shooting for, Senator," to discover that the second saleslady was looking her over quizzically. "Well, if you don't have anything else," Andy began, gathering up her purse and gloves.

"I was saying, madam, if you would like a Greta Garbo number, we could make one up for you," the woman replied politely. But her gaze was still intent. Where have I seen you, it said. Andy knew the answer would leap to mind soon.

"Yes, perhaps that may be necessary. Why don't I try some more, and if I can't find what I want, I'll have it made up." She rose, in great haste now, accepting the proffered card quickly. But the retreat was almost not in time: as the door swung shut behind her, she heard the deep voice of the big woman saying, "Wasn't that—"

Andy leaned close against the windows of the shoe store a few doors beyond, where she would be invisible unless they opened their door and stuck their heads out, and she didn't think it was likely that they would do that. She waited, breathing a little as though she had been running, and continued the scene she'd been inventing. Jake Ruffing would certainly be the one chosen to protest to Alec. As Andy, of course, lolled on a divan in the background, her eyes half-closed from the weight of the makeup on their lids. And, oh definitely, plying a foot-long cigarette holder. "We—er—don't feel, Alec, that Andy is quite projecting the clean-cut American girl image. I'm afraid—"

Suddenly, the houri in her picture grew the swollen belly of late pregnancy, and Andy began, helplessly and at last, to laugh out loud. She stared at the shoes in the window, trying to hide her outlandish behavior, but she knew her shoulders were shaking. Behind her on the pavement a pair of matrons went by. One of them was saying something, and she heard, with horror, the voice stop as the two heads, reflected in the store window, turned in her direction. She froze there, afraid to be seen any more clearly, until they had gone by. Then, with effort, she composed her features and joined the sprinkling of leisurely pedestrians. But she kept her face toward the store windows, just in case.

Which was how she happened to spot the witch in the window of the bookstore. She stopped at once, staring in at it with delight. It was brummagem—a little figure a few inches high, colored in black and orange—but it looked, somehow, like Elizabeth, who had just tried on her Halloween witch costume. Andy dissolved into tenderness at the memory of her daughter's impish eyes and elaborately menacing snarl under the pointed cardboard cone that was being measured on her. When would they tell Elizabeth? Not for months yet, she supposed. But when was advisable? A little research was indicated, she decided. She pushed in the door of the bookstore.

She found the witch right away and held the small figure in her hand while she went through the children's books, rejecting the silliest of them at once. A book ought to look like a book, for heaven's sake, she thought indignantly: she rejected one shaped like a shoe and another like a train. Under them, though, she spied something promising—a cover that read, in big cheerful capitals, *Our New Baby*. She was about to reach for it when she noticed the little man in the fuzzy brown suit. He stood at her elbow, eyeing her curiously, waiting to gain her attention.

"I'd like this, please," she said nervously, holding out the witch figure. But the book tempted her. "Perhaps something else," she added. "I'd like to look these over, if you don't mind."

He took the witch, but he wouldn't go away. He smiled ingratiatingly, showing tobacco-blackened teeth. "Of course. Can I help you, Mrs. Girard?"

Andy nodded in hopeful silence, wishing she dared deny it, knowing she couldn't.

"Are you looking for a book for your little girl, Mrs. Girard?"

She looked over his shoulder quickly. The only other customer in the store was all the way in the back, and perhaps it was still possible to get out of here before anyone else came in. "Please," she said. "Can you suggest something?" Under cover of the raincoat she carried over her arm, she moved one of the train-shaped books so that it covered that hugely accusing *Our New Baby*.

The man was enjoying himself. "Let's see, Elizabeth is about two, that right?"

"Two and a half."

"Ah." He picked up a large picture book with a hole in the middle— Andy thought it looked like a crude Henry Moore that had been dropped in a pot of paint. "You see, I follow the news of your little family, Mrs. Girard. I'm a great admirer of the Senator's."

Dismayed, Andy saw the door open behind him and a stout woman come in, trailed by a sullen-looking teen-age girl. "Well, thank you," she answered. A pulse in her forehead began to throb thickly. She held out her hand for the book.

But he was not finished. "Yes, indeed, Senator Girard is exactly what this country needs, if you ask me." His speech was so refined that it very nearly thinned into unintelligibility; she thought, desperately, that that might be her only hope. "I hope somebody *will* ask me," he added coyly. "We're going to have a chance to make Senator Girard our next President, I trust?"

The pulse had become a piledriver. Over its unmerciful hammering, she said, "You're very kind," and all but snatched the book from his hand. "I'll take this, please."

He went slowly to the cash register, talking all the way. The stout lady was staring, a greeting card in her hand, a puzzled frown on her rather vacuous face. The fuzzy brown man looked disappointed as he rang up the small charges and took Andy's ten-dollar bill. "You'll tell Senator Girard hello for me, won't you?" With nightmare slowness, he fetched a paper bag and inserted the book and the little witch. "Tell him there's a lot of us, and we're all for him."

Andy smiled at him, thinking that she must look like a Halloween pumpkin, all teeth in a bright-orange face, and he held out her change. She crumpled the money in her hand and took the package. "I'll be sure to tell him. Thank you very much." She smiled and smiled, going past all of them, feeling gawky and naked, trembling for the touch of the door. The little man got to it first and bowed her out, and she managed one more "Thank you" and then took the full impact of their stares and buzzes on her retreating back.

She walked as close to the edge of running as possible, afraid to look back. Another statue loomed in a triangle of dust—she *had* to get off Connecticut Avenue. Suddenly, she saw a haven, slanting off the avenue a little to the right, and she scurried up the steps of the old church as though pursuers were close behind.

It was silent in the small vestibule, and she was blessedly alone. She stood still, waiting for her breath to come back, reading a plaque on the wall. Dully, she absorbed the information that the bells had been contributed to the church in the name of a bombardier killed in World War II. That seems a singularly appropriate memorial, she thought, and realized that, in the quiet, she had begun to feel like Andy again.

Through the glass of the door leading into the vestibule, she could see that the church was empty. The door said "Exit" on a chaste little metal plate, but she pulled it open anyway, glancing around her guiltily, and went in and sat down in a pew near the back. She dropped her purse and coat and package on the dull-blue velvet cushion like the color of the veining in bleu cheese. Then she put her hands on the varnished back of the pew in front and rested her head on them, closing her eyes. Over her head, gentle light filtered through patches of green and lavender in the high window. At the altar, the great white cross loomed in its severe geometry, and nothing moved.

And Andrea found her joy again, at last. Among the shames and the fears, the elation rose as it had when she began her walk. She opened her eyes and saw now the mass of blue-green rhododendron leaves arranged at the foot of the altar steps—and then she saw the flowers of the spring and summer to come. The forsythia first, and the tulips—the baby would be moving by then, swimming in his curiously safe blindness. Then roses, and peonies, and, finally, in the fresh burst of summer, when everything had at last come to bloom— "Thank you, thank you," she said again and again somewhere very far inside her mind.

She got up then, collecting her things, and walked slowly out of the building and down the steps, a tall, beautiful woman with a happy face. On the corner, the little flower stand was selling brightly colored bunches of autumn leaves and stiff bouquets of yellow and orange and purple strawflowers. But she had things to do at home, she thought, waiting for the light to change beside the green-streaked statue. She left Connecticut Avenue, making for Georgetown, as a gentle wind lifted her short dark hair and then just as gently put it back in place along the soft curve of her cheek.

At the next traffic light, she consulted her watch and then crossed the street rapidly and went on with more haste. Alec's lunch would be dispatched to his office on time even if she wasn't home, but she liked to choose the table linens that would be sent with it. His ability to thrive among the unlovelinesses of his office had amazed her when, as a bride, she had gone there briefly—because it was where Alec worked and it was important to her to see him there. Quickly she had summarized the scene, noting the needs; since then she had moved steadily and quietly to supply what she could and discreetly maneuver the remainder. Without being consciously aware that it was happening, the whirling dervish that was Alec Girard now slowed at midday; thinking of something else, he nevertheless ate lunches as appetizing as they were nourishing. His restless mind was rested, in spite of him, by the warm glow of polished silver and the soft colors of delicate linens, and a comfortable couch in his inner office coaxed him, most days, into a brief, refreshing nap.

As Andy waited on a corner for the "Walk" sign to come on so she could get home and attend to her primary business, an occasional accidental beneficiary of her private catering service saw her from the window of the taxicab in which he was approaching her corner. Martin Halloran of the *Washington Tribune,* who had left Senator Girard's office too early today for the arrival of the daily lunch basket, looked up with a smile and prepared to roll down the window and call to her. But his taxi was three cars back when it stopped for the red light that allowed Andy to cross, so he shrugged and returned to scribbling a few notes on the morning's gleanings from Capitol Hill. This occupation had been much hampered by the chatty cabbie so far, and now, as Andy walked past up ahead, it inevitably was again.

"Hey, you see that?" The driver turned a little and pointed, to make sure Halloran knew where to look. "That's Andy Girard, you know? That one— the tall broad in the tan suit."

Halloran made a small sound that was interpreted as disbelief.

"I'm telling you. I seen her picture plenty of times." The cabbie craned his neck to watch Andy reach the sidewalk. "Real class. You can't miss it, and no mistake."

"I guess you're right," his passenger said, grinning at the disappearing back of the tall broad.

The light changed, and the cab darted through the intersection, managing to make one more block before another red light halted it. "I thought maybe you worked on the Hill when I picked you up there," the driver said.

Halloran said he didn't and went on thinking about Senator Girard, who'd invited him to stay for lunch with the careless observation that "Andy's cuisine" beat anything available on Capitol Hill—a statement that Halloran, who had lunched on *boeuf Bourguignon* from the wicker basket the week before, found it not difficult to believe. Real class, all right, though he himself was a simple man who settled without pain for any casual hamburger. But it occurred to him now that "class" might be a loose explanation for the encounter he'd witnessed this morning between Alec Girard and Ralph Ferris in the Senate Office Building. Halloran's sharp eyes had detected Girard's involuntary wince as Ferris patted his arm familiarly, and the chill in the Vermonter's voice, even when he had been trading jovialities with Ferris, did not require a trained ear to hear. By the look of the two men and the way they sounded under their words, you would have thought Ferris was somebody trying to get into Girard's country club; Martin Halloran couldn't help thinking it, but he didn't write it down because that wasn't the sort of thing he wrote. After nearly a generation on the *Tribune,* he still insisted on being identified only as "Staff Reporter," and he was never guilty, if he could help it, of public interpretation.

The taxi driver turned left in front of the church just off Connecticut Avenue and observed that everybody said Girard was going to run for President. Girard hadn't come out and said so yet, Halloran said noncommittally; but he no longer felt noncommittal, even about the timing. Following Alec Girard into his office this morning, Halloran had recognized intuition and experience nudging at him, predicting an announcement soon, even though nothing looked particularly different. When they'd waded through the outer room's bustle like bathers through the froth of the waves, they had found calm swells in the inner office, where Jake Ruffing and Girard's new press aide, Lucien Messenger, were waiting.

Jake had turned his head long enough for the exchange of greetings and then gone back to staring from the window at bronze horses pulling a bronze Civil War cannon. "I keep thinking that someday they'll have made it over the hill and be out of sight," he explained.

The Senator slouched into his desk chair and hooked his knees over the corner of his desk. "They have, as a matter of fact. The Capitol police move the next regiment in during the night. Nobody ever notices the difference."

Same old Alec Girard—except that somehow it wasn't, Marty Halloran sensed. Grinning, he began to inquire into the implications of the fact that the Senator was scheduled to accept an award at a large banquet on, coincidentally, a date very close to the time for entering a certain presidential primary.

Jolted out of memory by a sudden question from the cab driver, Halloran examined it and discovered that he didn't have an answer. "I don't know whether Girard can beat Ferris," he said truthfully. "Blackwell might have a better chance. At least he's run before, so the voters know him." He had considerable scorn for the kind of reporting that came of interviewing taxi drivers. But he had no objection to being interviewed by taxi drivers.

"If it's Girard and Ferris, it'll be an even race," the driver asserted with assurance. "They're both young guys——"

"But they've both had a good deal of experience."

"Sure. The only difference is, one's a poor boy and the other's a rich boy."

Halloran laughed aloud. "If everybody votes on that basis, Ferris is a cinch. I'm a poor boy myself, and I know for a fact we outnumber the rich boys."

The cabbie promptly launched into autobiography, establishing his membership in the poor-boy majority, and Halloran suddenly remembered a brief exchange with the Senator's new press aide. Luke Messenger looked like the grown-up version of the fat boy, rich or poor, in anybody's neighborhood, and he was good-natured besides. He was also efficient, so perhaps it could safely be thought non-coincidental that it was Luke who had dropped into the idle-seeming, cracker-barrelish conversation in the inner office the reminder that the Senator had an appointment coming up with a very important constituent. The Senator recalled it immediately and with every sign of delight.

"You know, Marty, this old fellow's coming down from Vermont today—you ought to drop by and meet him if you can. He wrote us sometime ago and said he was going to be in town to visit and he'd like to meet me because he'd once cut rock with my grandfather." Girard examined the idea with the frank pleasure of a boy looking forward to a story about once upon a time. "Imagine it, with my grandfather. All those years ago."

"Quarrying isn't an easy way to make a living," Messenger said carefully. "It's rough, hard work."

Unlike imagemaking, Halloran had just as carefully not said. He hid his grin successfully—until Alec Girard, putting out his cigar, observed with open amusement, "Doubtless Marty knows that better than anyone." Which put a stop to the imagemaking and also released Halloran's suppressed laughter.

"Now you take this Alec Girard," the taxi driver said, his voice clearly summarizing something, and Halloran thought suddenly that he might, he just might, take this Alec Girard. For the boyishness, a quality Martin Halloran believed decidedly unsuitable for Presidents, had been less evident this morning than ever before. And a fellow of irreverent wit might well be a safer bet than a man nervously intent on his image, when you considered the fog that inevitably surrounded the inhabitant of the White House.

"Now, Ferris is more like you and me, maybe," the orator in the front seat was conceding.

"How's that?" asked the startled Halloran, who had never found Ralph Ferris personally attractive.

"A poor boy, like we were saying. So does that mean he's a better bet?"

"You don't think so?"

"No sir*ree*. You know how I figure a lot of people are bound to see it? Like this: you put a rich guy in the White House and one thing you can be sure of, he's not gonna be busy trying to chisel from the taxpayers. See what I mean? A man's got a few million bucks and a rich wife besides—well, you don't have to keep your eye on him."

The cab swirled to the curb, and the driver, turning to check the address Halloran had given him, saw the great sign that had not been put up yet. "Volunteers for Girard" shouted at passersby in letters nearly as big as they, and Alec Girard's handsome features loomed from a medallion-shaped portrait at hip level. The cabbie nodded at the sign. "They oughta put Andy in a bathing suit on there. He'll get the women and she'll get the men." His eyes rolled to indicate his own readiness to be got.

Halloran, climbing out, said it was an idea while he waited for his change. He handed back a sizable tip and turned away to see if he could find out exactly how volunteer this volunteer headquarters was.

At the State Department's shiny new building not far away, Will Farland was foraging for his lunch in the bright, sterile cafeteria. "Pecan pie," he said delightedly to Ann Taswell, who had already passed it by. He held the plate invitingly over her tray but she shook her head. "You don't know what's good." He tilted the plate onto his own already crowded tray, where it wobbled dangerously.

"I'm sorry not to be able to manage something grander," he went on as they distributed the makings of a substantial meal at his place and an ascetic one at hers. He held her chair as she sat down and then took his own chair, surveying with satisfaction the numerous dishes of rather pallid-looking food in front of him. "But I have a meeting right after lunch."

"You told me. This will do, really. After all, I did invite myself at the last minute."

Will buttered half a roll and stuffed it into his mouth. "Good for my image to be seen squiring pretty women around," he said indistinctly. He tackled his soup with enthusiasm. It was tomato-colored, and mysterious-looking vegetables floated in its depths. "On the other hand, this arrangement may be even better for my image."

"Why? How can you eat that stuff?"

"It's okra," Will said in surprise. "If it weren't for Rosa, I'd never get any at home. Marian can't stand it either." He returned a nod from a man passing their table. "See? It makes me look like I can afford to be indifferent. Got so many beautiful women that I just yawn and take 'em to the cafeteria. And then don't even buy them anything but a dab of green Jell-O."

"It's a salad."

"It's still green Jell-O."

"What's the matter with Jell-O?"

"Nothing, I guess. Marian gives it to the kids when they're sick. Only red. She seems to think it's some kind of medicine."

"I saw Marian this morning," Ann said. "She looked buried in work. Harried and conscience-stricken."

"Marian and her Calvinist conscience. She was a little late to work this morning, so she probably feels she ought to be publicly whipped."

Ann smiled because it was true, but she felt slightly disloyal. Will went on eating hungrily between rapid-fire observations. As she finished with her sparse lunch and stirred her coffee, she watched him with the peculiarly perverse quiet his energy had always evoked in her. The only time she'd ever seen Will not looking as though his motor was racing was on his wedding day: Ann, having acquitted herself nobly as maid of honor by getting a very nervous Marian to the church on time, had been amused and startled to see the normally loquacious Will transformed into a white-faced and mute bridegroom, best blue suit, classic jitters, and all.

She sat in silence until Will had consumed his greasy-crusted fried chicken with every sign of enjoyment. Then she asked, "Are you ready to give out with answers?"

"For the record, no. If it's about the Honorable Hemingway Garrison's prospective jaunt to visit world leaders, the releases are available upstairs, even to Taswell of the *Trib*."

"You can do better than that. After all, since you've been designated to accompany him, you must be prepared to say *something*."

Will maneuvered the pecan pie into position before him and dug into it with his fork. "I am honored to be chosen and I hope to be able to serve Ambassador Garrison in any way he may find me useful," he said rapidly. "His forthcoming mission on behalf of President Winkler is only the latest effort in Hemingway Garrison's long and distinguished record of service to his country and to the cause of peace." He chewed on his pie, reflecting. "Make that 'world peace,' " he added, in the same toneless voice.

Ann laughed. "You're marvelous, Will. I don't know how you do it."

"Sheer genius."

"And years of experience at throwing glittering dust into the public's eye," Ann suggested. "Off the record, if you insist—why you?"

"Oh, because it's worldwide. The Undersecretary screamed that he had better things for me to do—which was true—but they couldn't get away with sending anybody of lower rank because those guys are all area-oriented. And they certainly weren't about to waste anyone of higher rank than me."

Ann sighed. "I keep telling myself there must be a hidden meaning. Surely it can't be as silly an exercise as it looks."

"It is." Will lowered his voice. "You make the same mistake all the bright folk do. You forget that Winkler simply isn't very bright."

"You mean he—"

Will nodded. "He really thinks he can accomplish something by sort of getting the fellows together. He's noticed that men seem more convivial after the last round of golf. Which they are, and judicious application of relaxed fraternizing can make a big difference—if it takes place early enough, and delicately enough. Before you have two heads of state frozen into position by their history and the opposition back home. And an eager press ready to call every gambit a policy change." He sighed. "However. Winkler's come to the conclusion that president to president is the surest way to move the world." He emptied his coffee cup and leaned back in his chair, one long arm dangling over its back. "Thus the Premier of Ruritania, after a pleasant and jovial teatime visit by Garrison, will see the light and decide to be a real pal. Which is only a little more likely than if it was Winkler who'd come to visit. But not much. My role in this brilliant effort," he added, "is to keep Garrison, who was really made for something better, from saying the hell with it and coming home."

"But Winkler will be going out of office next year. Anything Garrison recommends can't really be acted on before the election."

"You still don't understand Winkler," Will said gloomily. "He wants to be remembered as the President who made the peace. That's his dream, and it quite outweighs any facts. What he'd really like is to make the grand journey himself, but the Secretary had some help from the White House staff in talking the old boy out of that one."

"Fortunately."

"Fortunately, indeed. We'll lose enough face as it is. Want some more coffee?"

"Yes, please."

Will took their coffee cups to the machine and refilled them, slopping the coffee into the saucers a little. Coming back to the table, he saw Ann in profile, her cameo face propped on one slim, pink-tipped hand. A small hat rode on her pale hair like a little ship on a smooth sea. Even without the dark and excitable Marian to provide the usual contrast, Ann looked so very fair and composed, he thought, and wondered whether all women picked their direct opposites for their best friends.

"Thank you." Ann accepted the refilled coffee cup and stirred sugar into it thoughtfully. "Marian doesn't know about this trip yet, I take it?"

"Not from me. I've been playing with a hope that she'll hear it at the office today, so I won't have to break the news."

"Oh, she probably will. One of the copyboys is sure to show her the wire story."

"Good." Will sipped at his coffee. "Or maybe good. It takes the first edge of hysteria off, but it also gives her a chance to work up some strong feelings. The children fatherless at Christmas and all that."

Ann said sympathetically, "Well, the trip *is* a feather in your cap, and surely she'll—" She broke off under Will's quizzical look. "I guess she won't, at that. She's about as short on status-consciousness as she is allergic to absent husbands."

"The absent-husband bit can be managed, I think," Will said slowly.

"I'll be glad to do anything I can to help. You know that."

"I know, Ann, and I'm grateful. But again, the problem is not one of facts but of attitudes." He sighed. "She's got Rosa, she's got you—she's got all the support she'll ever need, and more. The point is, though, that she wouldn't need any at all, if I could just think of a way to sell her on the proposition." His eyes were calculating, and he spoke more to himself than to his listener. "Marian may look frail, but she's quite capable of managing things while I'm gone—if she wants to."

"She won't want to, I imagine."

Will shook his head. "Not unless I can think of a compelling angle. If only she could see some sort of real importance in the trip, she'd do her bit loyally. But she's not stupid." He smiled wryly. "She is an idealist, though, and idealists can be manipulated."

"I wonder if you realize something, Will." There was a distinct coolness in Ann's voice. "Do you know you sound like a lawyer working up a case?"

"I am."

"But—forgive me—is this . . . should it be an adversary proceeding? Between you and Marian?"

"Oh Lord, yes." Will shoved his chair away from the table and leaned back in it, balancing it on its two back legs. "I don't know about what it should be, but it certainly is."

"Why?"

"You disappoint me," Will said. "Do you mean to tell me that you haven't noticed, in all these years, that Marian is an adversary when it comes to marriage?"

"Marian?"

"Certainly. She doesn't understand it, so she's averse to the whole idea."

"When Marian came to work on the *Tribune*," Ann said stiffly, "Charlie Grayson was sending her flowers daily in an attempt to open negotiations for a reconciliation. Shortly after that, she got her divorce. And from there on she was knee-deep in suitors, and more were piling in the windows every minute. And they *were* suitors: every one of them with honorable intentions."

"Sure. Marriage was their intention, all right. But not Marian's. Why do you think none of them connected?"

Ann looked less confident. "I don't know. Why did you connect?"

"Ah, you've stumbled on the hidden truth of my humility." His keen eyes examined her with a glint of amusement. "I know you sometimes think I'm an arrogant bastard, Ann. Oh, I put on a good campaign, but the reason I won was my secret weapon: Dick."

"I would have thought— I mean, his mother had died such a short time before—"

"Kids are like politicians—they're practical. They mourn, but they've got a job to fill." Will shook his head. "Alone, I'd have been only another suitor. But Dick gave me a head start. I don't think any of my blandishments were half so powerful as the silent presence of one mother-hungry little boy."

Ann eyed him with respect. "You really surrounded the problem, didn't you?"

Will said irritably, "Of course. I always do." He smacked the table softly with his fist, and the dishes rattled a little. "What the hell do you think I am, a Winkler? Working at a problem seems to be out of fashion these days. You're supposed to smile it away, or pray it away, or if you get really stuck, christen it a non-problem."

"You think Senator Girard would do better?"

"He couldn't do worse. But even Ferris would be an improvement."

Ann said, shocked, "You surely don't want Ferris for President?"

"No, because I want something more than efficiency. But if he got in, we'd at least get that."

"Most of the people I know seem to want Blackwell to run again."

Will nodded. "If we got Blackwell—I mean, if he got in, which is the big if in his case—we'd get intelligence, but I'm not too sure about the efficiency. What I'd like to get is both, if possible."

"With Girard, you think?"

"Maybe. He looks like a votegetter, which Blackwell isn't, I don't think. But Girard is still something of a mystery. I can see a campaign for him, building on the best of him and the best of Blackwell. But I don't know whether it's in him. I don't know enough about him yet."

"What do you mean 'building on Blackwell'?" Ann asked.

Will thought it over, his long nicotine-stained fingers tapping the table restlessly. "I guess the best way to explain it," he said finally, "is in terms of my own problem."

"You mean Marian? And this trip?"

"Right. The fact that Marian ran out on Charlie Grayson because he couldn't stay home and hold her hand—"

Ann smiled. "The adversary of marriage. You think that could have been worked out, don't you?"

"Sure. But what the hell, Grayson's loss is my gain. The point is, the fact that she behaved like a spoiled baby with him makes her more likely to behave like a wife in the same situation with me. If I don't push it too far or too often. I build on Grayson, but carefully, if you see what I mean."

"Not entirely. Blackwell's idea of not talking down to the American people flopped, didn't it?"

"Maybe. *I* don't know for sure what flopped. I don't think anybody does. But flop or not, what Blackwell did left a foundation that can be built on next year."

"Did it leave the American people ready to be talked honestly to?"

"To a degree. To a greater degree than before." Will sighed. "They're not going to change overnight, any more than Marian is. But you're a fool if you ignore their history when you deal with people." He looked at his watch and began to disentangle himself. "My meeting," he said apologetically.

Ann gathered her purse and gloves and rose hastily. "I'm sorry, Will." She looked thoughtfully at his back as she followed him down the long room, winding between the tables. In the corridor, she smiled up at him. "Thank you for lunch."

Farland took her outstretched hand and held it. It felt firm and cool. "Come again, and I'll do you better next time, friend."

"I'll do that. And good luck, friend."

Will nodded and made a hasty thumbs-up sign. Then he took off at a lope for the bank of elevators. He would need all the luck he could get, he thought, wondering just when his wife would begin the fireworks, and how long the display would go on. He drummed his fingers impatiently against the push-button panel while he waited for the elevator, but a smile ticked at his lips as he remembered the glib version of his courtship he had produced for Ann. Not that it wasn't probably true, the parlor-psychiatry bit about Dick.

The elevator doors slid open and Will entered and rode in silence, staring straight ahead at the paneling. The little something besides Dick that he had thought it best not to go into with Ann was the key to the whole thing. And as long as that little something kept happening from time to time, the lesser and less beneficent somethings could be managed. He hoped. Frowning, he darted out of the elevator and sped down the hall.

He entered the office almost running and snatched his briefcase from the small table beside his secretary's desk. She was on the phone, and he turned to leave, but she arched her eyebrows significantly and he waited, dismay in his face.

"Oh, could you excuse me just a moment, Mrs. Farland?" Will's secretary, a middle-aged woman with softly waved gray hair, pushed a button at the foot of the instrument and laid the phone across her shoulder. "It's your wife," she told him unnecessarily as they both glanced at the wall clock. "What do you want to do?" The apparently simple question was understood by both to mean, *How are you going to slither out of this one, bright boy?* She waited with the eager interest of a baseball fan watching a promising rookie. In the complex, behind-the-scenes, unofficial organization of the State Department, secretaries of her caliber chose their bosses: liking the young Farland's style from the first and approving his subsequent batting average, she had shrewdly traded a spot in an Assistant Secretary's office for this comer—a bargain that of itself increased Farland's prestige in the eyes of his superiors, most of them graduates of the secretaries' "farm" system.

Will indicated his briefcase. "Is it all in here?"

"Yes. You'll be late, Mr. Farland." Although she knew every move of his past and studied him more intently than a psychoanalyst, it would never have occurred to her to call him anything but "Mr. Farland."

"All right. Look, give me time to get into my office, then put my wife through. Then call Harry and give him this. Tell him to go up and say I'm tied up and I'll be along pretty soon." He saw her perplexed look and smiled. "I know. Harry's been working on the Garrison trip, and he doesn't know anything about the stuff in there. But they don't know that. They won't get to us before I come, and this way we won't be holding up the meeting."

The secretary shook her head approvingly, smiling a little. Then she pushed another button on the phone. "Mrs. Farland? I think Mr. Farland is just coming in, if you can hold on. I do hope you'll excuse the delay—it's been so horribly rushed all day—"

Will dove for the door of his office and slammed it shut behind him. He crossed to his desk and flopped into his swivel chair, one long leg pulled up so that it lay across his other knee. He drew his shoulders back and wet his lips, like an actor coming on from the wings, before he lifted the phone.

"Will?" she said immediately. "Oh, Will, I saw the story on the wire."

Farland slumped in his chair, the picture of dejection. "Don't, Marian," he begged. "I was afraid you'd see it, but I was hoping you wouldn't. Please don't say it, baby."

She had begun to say "Will" again, but then his words came through to her and she stopped. "Don't say what?" she asked uncertainly.

"Please at least wait until tonight." He rode over her question, doubling the pleading in his voice. "I understand how you feel, baby, and I know I have it coming. I've been thinking of it all morning." He tightened his grip on the telephone, hunching his shoulders. "All I'm trying to do is get through the day somehow."

"Darling." Her voice was full of alarm. "Darling, please don't sound so frightened."

"I can't help it. I guess there are some things I just can't face."

"Willie, you stop that at once," she commanded. "My God, what have you been doing to yourself all morning?"

"It hasn't been fun," he said softly.

"I'll bet it hasn't. Oh, Will. Did you really think I was going to—*leave* you? Over this? Darling, you're being absurd."

"Honestly, baby," he said, as urgently as though she had not spoken, "if you knew how I've been trying, pulling strings all over the place, to get out of this. I knew I couldn't expect you to—"

"Stop it, Will. Aren't you even listening to me?"

"I'm sorry," he muttered.

"Have you been brooding about it all this time? Look, I'll bet you haven't even eaten—"

"I tried." Remembering Ann, he added, "I had to put up a front."

"Sometimes you haven't any more sense than Peter."

"All I could think of was Charlie Grayson—"

"Well, stop thinking of Charlie Grayson. If I'm not, why in the world should you? If you must think about Charlie, think about all the differences. Do you think I haven't learned *anything?*"

Will said softly, "I'm sorry, Marian. I guess I've been doing you an injustice."

"Well, you certainly have!"

He sighed. "I'm so glad you're not mad."

"Now that I think of it, I'm mad." But her voice was not really angry.

"You can yell at me all you want tonight," Will promised.

"I'm going to yell plenty, I'm afraid," Marian said morosely. "Oh, Will. Christmas. Maybe even Thanksgiving, it seems."

"They're talking about fixing a definite date—in fact, I'm due at a meeting about it now."

"Oh. You'd better go, I guess."

"Maybe I can save us Thanksgiving if I hurry." Will had stood up and was buttoning his coat.

"Oh, darling. Try."

"I will," he promised. "It'll be easier now. Marian?"

"Yes?"

"Pick you up after work? You'll wait for me?"

"I'll wait. Try to get yourself a glass of milk or some Jell-O or something this afternoon. I know you must be exhausted."

"I will. See you later."

"With Thanksgiving in the bag, I hope."

Will laughed. "Don't cry, baby. I'll be home for Halloween, anyway."

He hung up, nearly knocking over the silver carafe that was the status symbol of his office. Righting it, he grinned sheepishly at his distorted reflection in its shiny curve. He glanced around his office, taking in the rug, the couch, and the other appurtenances that marked successful jockeying in the bureaucracy. "Wow," he said in a heartfelt tone to all of them, and then he made for the door in a hurry.

His secretary handed him a fresh package of cigarettes and a book of matches as he went out, then settled down to her work with satisfaction. Farland's wife was one of the reasons his secretary always kept her eye on other openings, just in case. Mrs. Farland was the equivalent of a trick elbow. But the happy fact was, Farland had never failed to hit when a hit was needed, so whatever treatment he was using worked. The weakness hadn't cost the team a run yet, and that was all that counted.

Three

Halloween was very mild in Washington that year, which meant that the annual squabble between mothers who wanted jackets worn and kids who wanted no interference with their costumes was equally mild, finally negotiable in terms of sweaters under Superman suits.

Peter Farland was an instant success as Wee Willie Winkie and won first prize at a party in a church in his Cleveland Park neighborhood; he wore a costume designed and executed by his sister. He also did some truncated trick-or-treating with his friend Tommy, who was a spaceman, and collected far more candy than he was permitted to consume. Dick Farland, denied permission to borrow his father's homburg to be a drunk in, settled for his father's only other hat, a beat-up, rain-spotted fedora, and was a convincing bum. He attended a party briefly at the home of a girl from school, but he left early—the girls were, he told Rosa, "getting silly"—and proceeded to amuse himself among his fellows, some of whom came back with him and played Ping-Pong in the Farland basement. Sharlie Grayson, who was almost above Halloween by now, did collect for UNICEF, dressed as a ghost—which wasn't really a costume and therefore was permissible—and went to a party at which, it was to be suspected, she was one of the girls who got silly.

The witch who rang Betty Kimball's doorbell in Georgetown wasn't immediately recognizable. However, she was a talkative little thing and had to be hushed by a tall masked woman in a brown silk raincoat, who finally said, "That's enough now, Elizabeth, just say 'thank you' and get on," in a voice suspiciously like Andrea Girard's—but Betty pretended not to notice. At least, she tried to pretend—until Elizabeth, skipping over into the next yard without bothering to go down the walk first, said over her shoulder, "Thank you. That's my mommy," at which the ladies at both ends of the Kimballs' leaf-strewn walk dissolved into unmatronly giggles. Elizabeth, too businesslike for giggles, by that time was chirping "Twickertwee" at one of the three Capitol Hill secretaries who now shared the house next door.

In the largest city of a state with an important number of electoral votes, Jake Ruffing talked urgently to a man who had once been mayor, wanted to be again, and knew precisely the extent to which a big votegetter at the top of the ticket would be of help to him. Senator Girard sat in one of the uncomfortable armchairs that hotels consider adequate everywhere in the United States. He listened intermittently, but he was also reading and editing the speech he would deliver at a county fair the next day.

In the bedroom of the suite Jerry Rosenberg was writing with a pencil on a ruled pad. He raised his head to ask a question, and Luke Messenger stopped roaming disconsolately, opened a folder on which someone with a hasty hand and a black Magic Marker had scrawled "Labor," and found what Rosie wanted. Then, freed, Luke patrolled the room again, carrying his highball glass before him; he looked rather like a roly-poly acolyte, but his features were not serene with the peace of faith.

Alec Girard's basic strategy gave away, for all practical purposes, certain states and groups of states to those contending with him for the nomination: where people had grown up with Dan Daniels or with Tom Cannon, Alec reasoned, the outlander from Vermont—though he might gain polite attention and even make a few converts—was not likely to be able to manage the kind of overwhelming victory in the primary that would dislodge the prejudices of the party's professionals, who were opposed to his nomination.

But clever application of the special arithmetic of the Electoral College made time and effort lavished on appearances in this state more profitable than any victory that might be wrung from some others. Also, its variety of interest groups—rural, urban, organized labor, Negro—could, if successfully won over, serve both as a pipeline and a demonstration. A machinist living here had contacts, through his union and its newspaper, for example, that crossed state lines easily. These contacts would matter a great deal in the national election, though not in the state primary, of course. But the watching politicians, worried about Girard's "rich boy" handicap, watched for more than primary victories; they would note the machinist-converts and would take a lessened skepticism to the nominating convention.

A secretary pushed open the door to the bedroom from the corridor without knocking and said tonelessly, "Luke, the Sons of Italy called again."

"All right." Messenger put his glass down on the glass-topped bureau and reached for a pencil. "I'll take care of them. Put that stuff on the bed and lemme see the papers."

The girl said something about pictures, but Messenger wasn't listening. He read rapidly through the lead editorial in the major paper, his round face showing reasonable satisfaction, and then briefly studied the editorial cartoon, which showed a knee-pants-clad Alec Girard scooping the pulp from a pumpkin labeled "Daniels." For a second, Luke wondered why a pumpkin, for God's sake—and then remembered wearily that it was Halloween.

Right after Halloween a bookshop on Connecticut Avenue received an order from a Mrs. J. Ruffing for a children's book called *Our New Baby* and mailed it out to her home in suburban Virginia. And on the same day Andrea Girard, sifting through the mail in the foyer of her Georgetown house, spotted the frail blue envelope addressed in Paul Morisot's bold hand and carried it happily upstairs to her bright little sitting room. At her kidney-shaped desk she pried off the French stamp, working with intensity and care, and put it away to save for one of the Ruffing boys.

He was coming to Washington, Paul wrote from the provincial village where he worked at his sculpture—as distinct from Paris, where he occasionally worked *for* it—but he would not avail himself of the Girards' always-ready hospitality because he'd be on "official-culture" business and would therefore be lodged in Washington by the French government. But he'd be there for a month or more, and that was long enough, Andy thought happily, for them to manage something, however trammeled by official functions. She could hardly wait to see his dark, intense face crinkle with delight when he heard about the new baby.

As she tucked the letter into a pile of mail for Alec, her eyes were bright with anticipation. The affection between Alec and the French sculptor he'd once described as "the best part of Andy's dowry" was one of those rare wonders, the broadening of a friendship to include a newcomer. Although Alec had been the first to point out that it was not surprising.

"I'm so glad you liked Paul," Andy had said to him as they drove back from Carol Pritchard's house party, a week before their wedding.

Alec was smiling. "It was inevitable. Nobody who loves you could possibly not like Paul. Don't you know how alike you are?" He glanced down at her briefly. "He's your brother."

Perhaps that was the best word, after all, for the instant intimacy that had bloomed that afternoon long ago, inexplicably but unmistakably, in the drawing room of a Paris hotel suite. Morisot was the new "in" figure in the French art world that year, but it was Carol who enthusiastically plied the letter of introduction with which the girls had been provided before leaving home; Andrea had seen some of his work and thought he had talent, but not more than some others, and she distrusted the fuss that was being made about him. Morisot, coming dutifully to tea because of professional self-interest—Judge Pritchard was a well-known collector—had few and jaundiced expectations of an afternoon with a couple of rich American girls on the traditional postgraduation European tour. Yet, in that first moment and in the face of preconceptions on both sides, Andy and Paul had seen each other for what they really were: lucky, gifted, and humble. After that they wandered the streets of Paris easily and comfortably; already permanently related, they filled in the gaps of biography.

Paul Morisot had had a hard war, a hard life, and a hard marriage; he was unimpressed by the attention he was receiving. It had come to him because a rich patron, touched by something in one of Morisot's few exhibited works—or perhaps just bored, or maybe inspired—had taken him up; the resultant publicity and the money that came with it were giving him, he told Andrea gratefully, his first chance to learn his trade. She studied the reflection of the waters moving across his face while they leaned above the Seine, and he told her how he had made his first statue, of mud, in the hopelessness of a prison camp while his country was dying. The armature was a piece of wire stolen as a potential aid to escape, and the figure was simply a ruse to keep the wire a secret from the German guards. But the act of making it revealed to Paul Morisot the central secret of his life.

"You know, I'd think you're falling in love with Morisot," Carol had said, surveying Andy as they changed for dinner that evening. "But you don't look excited enough. Just happy."

Telling Alec about it years later, Andy added, "Of course, she'd stumbled on the whole truth. *'L'amitié est l'amour sans ailes.'* 'Friendship is love without wings.' "

He nodded. "And rare enough to make anyone look happy."

"I've been lucky."

"You put too much down to luck," Alec said. His eyes traveled over Andy's bright, eager face. "You *bring* the love to the encounter, you know. It's something inside you. And probably in Paul, too. But it's not luck."

At Paul Morisot's retrospective exhibit last year, a relatively early figure called "L'Amitié" wore at its back the faintest indications of tiny wings, unformed and vestigial. Senator and Mrs. Girard, who had flown the Atlantic for a single day at the event, stood among the glories their friend had made of his love and his learning, listening to the beat of the strong wings between them; then they went, smiling and with hands clasped, toward Paul's welcome.

The precious sunlight of November slanted now into Andrea's sitting room, picking out a small white sculpture on the desk. She reached over and stroked the smooth, cool flank of the delicately carved figure. The alabaster infant curled, small and perfect and snug, like a fairy inside an acorn. Only when you looked again could you see that the pure circular form into which the child snuggled was in fact a globe, with its oceans and continents faintly traced in the still whiteness. The soft, safe baby and its carved-out but still encircling world sat on a square base on which a date and "Elizabeth Langwith Girard"—with the Continental line through the "Z"—had been rather amateurishly lettered.

Andy folded the three flimsy, closely written sheets of Paul's letter and tucked them back into the envelope to translate for Alec later. She heard metal clink dully against stone under the window and translated the sound at once: next spring's tulips were going into their bed along the brick walk in the back yard. Reaching for her leather-bound daybook to look ahead to the time when Paul would be here, she thought fleetingly of the annual garden skirmish she'd recently lost again: the gardener fancied a border of bricks set on end at the edge of the flower border and argued that the other ends, sunk several inches into the soil, would give pause to the impudent shoots of lily of the valley that appeared, uninvited and where they chose, every spring. The barrier didn't work too well, and Andy thought the row of little brick triangles looked like nothing so much as a finicky bank clerk's pocket handkerchief. But she had yet to persuade the gardener, and she recoiled from imposing authority on what she suspected was his self-expression. It was not one of her administrative triumphs, she concluded, frowning a little as she turned a page—and then she discovered that there would be a party at the Kimballs' during Paul's visit, and meditations on defeat vanished. She picked up a pencil and sketched swiftly in the margin of the appointment book a small, dancing figure in a frothy dress wildly unsuitable for mid-November.

Mid-November, Marian Farland decided crossly on the night of the Kimballs' party—which she thought of as a "real party," to distinguish it from official parties, and by which she meant that she expected to enjoy herself— was no time for such lingering softness in the weather. As Will drove past the house on Q Street for the second time on the hunt for a place to park, she noted the Kimballs had not yet replaced their screens with storm windows and calculated gloomily that Will would resist her efforts to get him to do it this Sunday unless it turned a lot colder in a hurry. But if he didn't do it then, the prospects of getting it done before he left with Garrison looked dim. While Will edged the car into an illegal parking place, she sat in silence, marshaling storm-window arguments.

"Did I tell you Senator Girard may be here tonight?" Will asked as they waited on the Kimballs' doorstep.

"Oh dear. You didn't. I hope it's not going to be all official—" She broke off as Betty Kimball opened the door to them and led them into the little foyer. She gave Betty her coat and, listening to the laughter and the voices while she waited, was reassured. The babble was real talk; it was a real party, after all. While Will helped hang up their coats, Marian looked into the mirror over the semicircular table and poked a hairpin into place among the drifts of her hair. Will and Betty finished their small talk, and she trailed them into the living room but let them go on without her when she recognized Ann Taswell's back. Marian was beginning to chart a course toward her oblivious friend when her hostess returned suddenly.

"Come on, slowpoke," Betty said. "I want to do the honors all at once." She drew Marian forward. A moment later she was saying, "Senator Girard."

Marian smiled at the tall, good-looking man and held out her hand, surveying him with frank curiosity. There was always a distance between the pictured countenance and the one you met, but Alec Girard was conspicuously different from his photographs. For one thing, the thatch of his hair was much lighter than she'd have thought—almost sandy, with coppery highlights. But most surprising was the modeling of his face: he had deep-set eyes and hollows in his cheeks that a thousand cameras had curiously flattened out. The man they had shown her and millions of other newspaper readers—handsome, well-tailored, just heavy enough not to be gangly—was accurate but incomplete. The total effect of Alexander Wardwell Girard, junior senator from Vermont, was, Marian decided, inexplicably but decidedly greater than the sum of its parts.

Or maybe not inexplicably, she thought, watching Girard in profile as he shook hands with Will. She saw the quick, bright-blue glance having its effect on Will, too—it summarized you, asked you at once what you were and what you had to offer. Standing easily, loosely against the wall near the mantel, Girard had nevertheless the air of a busy man. His greeting was guarded but not unfriendly; it was willing, even eager, to listen to you, but it expected you to have something to say.

"Is that Farland with a 'd'?" he asked Will. His voice was surprisingly boyish. His look turned inward for a moment, then his eyes brightened as he found the information he sought in his mind. "State Department, isn't it? I thought I'd read the name," he went on as Will nodded. "You're the officer who's been selected to accompany Garrison on his fact-finding tour, aren't you?"

"Oh, Will, you're famous," Marian said.

Will smiled. "Only among the few who read clear to the bottom of the story, over on page 31."

"Mrs. Farland, Jake Ruffing and Jerry Rosenberg, of the Senator's staff," Betty was saying.

Marian offered her hand first to the small craggy Ruffing. He held it for a moment before he turned to acknowledge the introduction to Will. "You're in the Bureau of International Organizations, aren't you, Mr. Farland? I heard you speak on the UN last year. Very effective."

"I thought so, too," Rosenberg put in. "Much more realistic than the general run. How do you do, Mrs. Farland?" he added, without looking at her, and went on congratulating Will for his analysis of future voting blocs in the United Nations.

Will smiled, ducking his head a little shyly. He looked as though he was about to dig his bare toe in the dirt, Marian thought, watching him through the buzz of introductions. Huck Finn in a dinner jacket.

"I don't suppose you're especially pleased by your husband's prospective round-the-world jaunt," Senator Girard said pleasantly to Marian. As soon as he spoke, all other conversation in the group stopped. "Wives seldom are." He grinned swiftly at Jake. "I suspect Bonnie Ruffing sticks pins in my image about twice a week."

"Well, I wouldn't mind so much if it could accomplish anything useful," Marian said bluntly. "But Garrison's trip is bound to be such a fruitless exercise."

Out of the corner of his eye Alec Girard saw Ann Taswell, standing behind and a little to the left of Marian, begin a small involuntary gesture of protest and then close her eyes in resignation.

Ruffing spotted the opening and moved in quickly. "Do you share your wife's estimate of the Garrison trip, Mr. Farland?"

Laughter sparked Senator Girard's glance at Marian. "Come now, Jake," he said to his aide. "Mr. Farland is an officer at State. Aren't you putting him on a rather sticky wicket?" His smile was polite sympathy, but his eyes were teasing.

Will looked directly at Girard. "I'm not as rapid in my judgments as Marian is, Senator." His bony face was expressionless. "However," he added, "I find that I frequently plod to the same conclusion she's leaped to."

"Well-played, old boy," Rosenberg said, in a stage-British accent.

The Senator nodded. "They're right about your realism, Mr. Farland." He paused, surveying Will attentively. "But in your job, realism must have its dispiriting aspects."

It's only an observation, Marian thought, surprised at the alertness she sensed in Will. But they were all like that—alert and intense—though the Senator seemed a little more conscientiously polite than his pals. He, at least, had spoken to her; neither of the other two had even looked at her.

"There was a poem—Day-Lewis, I think, or one of that crowd around Auden." Will paused to think. "I can't remember the whole thing, but the part I mean goes something like: 'It is the logic of our times/No subject for immortal verse/That we who lived by honest dreams/Defend the bad against the worse.' The last line about sums it up, sir."

"It doesn't have to be that way," Girard said quietly.

The words hung in the oddly weighty silence. "Well, Senator, we have to start from where we are," Will said finally.

The Senator's handsome face blazed with impatience. "Right. But we don't have to end there. Which is what we do every time we sit down at a conference table. We bring nothing to it, and we take nothing away."

"There are times when even the status quo has represented something of an achievement." Will had lapsed into a drawl, Marian noticed, and she looked at him with quick curiosity; he did that when he was excited but wanted to be cautious. "We start the negotiations already minus our shirts. It's a job just to hold onto our pants."

"And do you consider that a suitable posture for us among the nations of the world, Mr. Farland?" Girard's voice was quiet, the words easy, yet all the attention of everyone there hung on them.

"No, sir, I do not," Will said quickly. He took a long breath. "Or even a necessary one."

The Senator smiled slowly. "Then it's time to alter it, isn't it? To get moving off dead center." The bright-blue eyes summed up Will Farland, soberly and efficiently. "Is a game of crack-the-whip, with the Soviet Union at the head and the U.S. at the tail, really a foreign policy?"

They had, Marian saw as she moved away with Betty Kimball, an air of getting down to business. Familiar business, so that Will looked attentive but relaxed now. The little circle in the corner of the room shifted and tightened around the dialogue, the men in their dark jackets leaning toward the calm figure of Alec Girard like black iron filings drawn to a magnet.

"Fascinating man," Marian said. "I was raised on Italian opera singers, you know, and there's something about him that reminds me of them."

"Alec?" Betty raised her eyebrows. "He's not given to chewing the scenery."

Marian shook her head. "Not the emotional thing. The presence. When Cavallone began to speak, everything stopped. As if he were—I don't know —bigger than everybody else."

Betty looked back at the group. "I was particularly eager for you two to meet the Girards. Gil keeps saying that Alec and Will are soulmates."

"He may be right," Marian speculated, following her glance. "Teammates in a debating society, anyway." Will was talking, gesticulating with a bony hand from which a cigarette sprouted and trailed its smoke, ignored. Alec Girard was listening intently; as they watched, he shook his head and interrupted Will, his quick words emphasized by a brief chopping motion of his right hand. "But where is the beauteous Mrs. Girard?"

"Coming later. He came directly from the Hill. What are you drinking? Gil's bartending."

"Good. I've seen that hire-out bartender fellow three times this week. I'll have the wine of the country, I guess. But don't bother, I can see the bar from here."

"I've got to go out to the kitchen anyway."

"Need any help?" Marian asked, following Betty into the dining room, where Gil was working at an improvised bar.

"Thanks, no. I decided to give you official-party trotters a rest by keeping things informal, but I'm no heroine. My Annabelle stayed late, and Rosemary had no homework tonight, so she's lending a hand. I'm in good shape. Marian's interested in some bourbon," Betty said to her husband. Then she made for the kitchen—closed off, for the occasion of the party, by the unaccustomed unfolding of its accordion-like door.

"Bourbon for the beautiful purple lady," Gil sang out. "Soda?"

Marian nodded, smiling at him, and took the tall cold glass.

"Stick around," Gil invited. "Put your foot up on the rail and tell me your troubles. Or just hang around to pick up men. I saw Will desert you for Alec Girard, who's not half as pretty."

"Oh well. Easy come, easy go. My real *Angst* is that I can never make up my mind which Miss Rheingold to vote for."

Gil leered at her. "Let me advise you while I look down your décolletage."

"My poor darleeng, what ees the use?" Marian asked throatily. "When you are free, come to me." She held out her hand, icy from the glass, and Gil kissed it elaborately. Betty, backing out of the kitchen with a tray, caught them at it and complained.

"Don't take on, my girl," Gil said calmly. "I'll always support you and the children."

Marian bit into one of the hot anchovy puffs from the tray. "Frankly, I'd rather have your recipe than your husband," she told Betty, licking her lips. She stole a few more, juggling them in her hand to cool them, and left the Kimballs to make for the vacancy on the wide tan sofa under the living-room window. She arrived at her objective with her drink and her provisions and sat in happy silence, looking around the room. It was a nice party, she thought contentedly—a few strangers, the rest familiars, but all with a playtime air. Although it had required the importation of a few of the blond wood dining-room chairs to achieve it, everyone could sit down if he wanted to: there was no sign of the grim ordeal by metatarsal that marked the Washington cocktail party, or of the restless swirl of movement that results, possibly, from the need to relieve aching muscles. Everybody seemed to be at home: some people perched on chair arms and some sat on the floor, but conversation, not circulation, was what was going on.

Ann Taswell was across the room, in the rust-colored wing chair near the bookshelves. The white spotlight on the brass pole lamp in the corner isolated her smooth fair head. Ann always looked so—complete, somehow: cool, lovely, and competent. One slim, very white hand was propping her cheek and forehead, but the Thinker-like pose, with the elbow braced on the arm of her chair, indicated not puzzlement but attention. Marian waved a hand at Ann, then turned to study the blues of the picture over the mantel, a reproduction of an early Picasso mother and child. The colors were beautiful in the room, and the softness and innocence of the faces lifted the heart.

"Way back when, when the old boy was just a painter."

She looked up and grinned in sympathy at her opposite number, the art critic on Washington's evening newspaper. Phil Colby perched on the arm of the sofa beside her.

"I didn't see you," she said mildly. "I wouldn't malign Picasso just because he's become a monument."

"Oh, never," Colby protested. He sipped at his drink. "Don't start a fight—I'm on my way out. But I thought I'd wait around for Paul Morisot to show, if it doesn't get too late."

"Nobody tells me anything," Marian complained.

"Read your mail, for God's sake. The new art monument hit town yesterday."

"Well, I know *that*. We sent a kid to the airport to do an interview."

"So did we. You having a full-dress Sunday piece on Morisot?"

"It seems indicated, doesn't it? How come he's coming here?"

"Andrea Girard is bringing him, somebody said."

"I haven't been looking forward to meeting him," Marian confessed. "I think I was somewhat unkind in something I wrote."

"They shouldn't really let the artists in when the grown-ups are relaxing. But cheer up." Colby got to his feet. "He probably doesn't read the *Tribune* anyway."

Marian acknowledged the dig with a grin, watching Colby go off toward the bar. She turned then and put her drink down on the long rectangular coffee table and set about arranging herself more comfortably, spreading out the deep jewel-purple chiffon of her skirt with both hands.

"Can you put up with a little crowding?" Senator Kenneth Youngblood asked.

"Plenty of room," Marian welcomed, patting the sofa.

He lowered his wiry body to the offered space, admired her dress, and asked where Will was.

Marian pointed with her chin at the group near the fireplace. "From the moment we came in. Drawn fatally into Senator Girard's orbit."

The senior Senator from Rhode Island said, with a smile, "It happens."

Marian studied the once-aquiline features now softened by the loosening flesh; Youngblood's black-and-white hair, which looked like tweed in the lamplight, grew from the high forehead in a widow's peak that might once have been less decided. But he was still an attractive man, with a face tidily and economically sculptured and wearing well enough despite its wrinkles and the puffs of middle age and weariness under the lively brown eyes.

Marian asked after his health, but in no real spirit of inquiry: Youngblood would go on as long as the Senate's Foreign Relations Committee, of which he'd been a member for longer than anybody else in the room had been voting. He was ranking minority member now, in a Winkler Congress, and would be chairman if his party won a Senate majority next year—as he had been chairman of the committee before Winkler's election eight years ago. It was known, in the informal, unstated way such things are known, that Youngblood was Gil Kimball's literary property: when the day came, it was Kimball who would write the Senator's biography. But it would be a long time before Gil began, Marian told herself, listening with a smile as Youngblood talked dryly of a bizarre letter the committee had received.

Then Senator Youngblood had stopped talking suddenly and was getting to his feet—and the whole room, Marian realized, had come to a sudden, pulsing stop. The close little group by the mantel—which now, she saw, included Gil—had opened, revealing its center, Alec Girard, watching the doorway with a happy, expectant smile.

Oh, please, please, don't all stop and look, said the dark eyes of the woman who could be no one but Andrea Girard. Over Betty Kimball's head, her eyes looked for her husband—but drawn, perhaps, by the glowing color of the purple dress, accidentally met Marian Farland's first. And Marian, wrenched with sympathy for the pleading she saw, smiled tentatively, encouragingly, as she might at a shy child.

Yet this was, at the same time, a tall, extraordinarily beautiful woman with a wide, generous mouth and thick dark hair that shouted of health and vitality. Her dress, of apricot-colored silk, represented in its intricate and subtle detail a marriage of money and taste. Now in her early thirties, she must be familiar with this stirring of men, this turning of dark-coated shoulders like a movement of plants toward light. It must have been happening for years, yet she met it with both pleasure and a noticeable shrinking. She had, it was plain, a way of having things happen to her for the first time, every time—which is both a gift and a curse.

"Andy, my dear," Senator Youngblood said. He kissed her cheek, taking her hand. "Have you any idea what a delight it is to see you?"

"Senator." Her voice was low and soft.

Still holding her slim brown hand, the Senator presented Marian, and Andrea Girard turned on the other woman a smile that was as irresistible as it was shy. She had a merry look, Marian decided, and you hardly ever saw a really merry look. "I'm very glad to meet you," she said earnestly, and felt happily certain that Mrs. Girard was glad to meet her, too.

"If the gentleman from Rhode Island will yield," Alec Girard said.

Youngblood released Andrea's hand with a sigh. "I suppose seniority has *some* limits. I yield to the gentleman from Vermont."

"I'm sorry," Marian was saying guiltily to the stranger, a dark, compact man who looked a little like a bright-eyed sailor. "I'm afraid I didn't hear —I wasn't—"

"Paul Morisot." His face wore the crinkles of much past laughter. "Please do not apologize, Mrs. Farland. To enter with *Andréa* is to be overlooked. I have known this for many years."

"How do you do, Monsieur Morisot? I have been looking forward to meeting you." She paused, and then decided she might as well be hung for a sheep as a lamb. "I have seen much of your work."

His smile broadened. "And I yours, Mrs. Farland."

Ouch, Marian thought, what do I do now? But she was saved, at least temporarily, by the appearance of Phil Colby. "Have you met my colleague, Monsieur Morisot? Philip Colby of the *Washington Herald*." Taking advantage of their exchange to extricate herself, she slithered out of the close quarters near the sofa and went over to the bar with a distinct sense of narrow escape.

Gil had apparently abandoned bartending, so Marian made herself a drink and then stood for a moment sipping it and surveying the scene in the living room. Paul Morisot was in earnest conversation with Colby, Senator Youngblood's tweedy head was bent to the gesturing narrative of Jake Ruffing, and Andrea Girard was laughing at Gil. And then Marian saw Will, alone, surprisingly, in the corner chair by the bookcase. Balancing her glass precariously, she crossed the room to him. "Don't get up," she said, as she sank down on the floor at his feet.

"Darling, I hate to tell you. I wasn't going to."

Marian made a face at him. "Peasant. You haven't said a word to me since we came in."

Will grinned. "Well, you're pretty, baby, and you can cook. But you're not the next President of the United States." He examined this statement, his head tilted, and then added judiciously, "Thank God."

"Is he going to be? You weren't so sure last week."

"I know, but I hadn't met him then."

She looked across the room at Alec Girard, who was smiling down at his hostess. In the lamplight, his face was courteous, attentive, a little weary.

"He's got so much," Will was saying. "Maybe even everything he needs." His fair hair, rumpled so that it stood up stiffly, looked like a handle. "Marian, what's 'charisma'?"

"Hah. It's a word lazy art critics use when the thing comes across but they can't tell you why."

Will sighed, getting to his feet. "My passion flower with the edgèd wit. I'm going to get a drink. You all right?"

She watched him go, suppressing an impulse to stick out her tongue.

Charisma, indeed. Still, Will wasn't given to hasty conclusions. I don't have to believe everything you say, though, she told his departing figure defiantly, and I'm not going to vote the way you say either. In fact, if I hadn't been smitten with Gary Cooper at an impressionable age, I probably never would have married you. She drank deeply from her glass, putting Will in his place, and read the titles in the Kimballs' bookcase. Raymond Aron and Edward Crankshaw flanked a weathered Modern Library copy of *Look Homeward, Angel,* and the constellation dwarfed a paperback titled *Conception, Pregnancy and Birth.* Marian was considering how neatly this bespoke the life and times of Betty and Gil when Senator Youngblood sat down in the chair Will had vacated. "I'm saying my good-nights, although in somewhat leisurely fashion." He nodded at the other side of the room. "I managed to catch Will at the bar, but I see he's reabsorbed."

Marian said, "Oh Lord," without any note of supplication. Alec Girard was seated now in one of the armchairs by the fireplace, and Will was just sitting down in the other. Jake Ruffing hovered between them, his hands spread in a gesture of appeal, and the tall Rosenberg, propped up by the mantel, stared moodily at the top of Girard's head. "Will thinks Mr. Girard's going to be President," Marian blurted.

Youngblood's wise eyes narrowed, but the slender white nape of her neck disarmed him: there was certainly nothing of the businesslike news-gatherer about her. He decided she was only impulsive.

"I don't know how I feel about that," she was continuing. "I'd rather have had Mr. Blackwell try again, but I see he's announced he absolutely won't."

She was not only impulsive, Youngblood observed silently; she was incredibly naïve. He was thinking, poker-faced, that it was rather like finding a virgin in a home for delinquents, when he saw her looking up at him with sudden admiration. "In fact, I'd rather have you," she was saying thoughtfully.

Youngblood laughed with genuine pleasure. "I am not the stuff of which Presidents are made." He lowered his glance to hide his amusement at the aptness of his unconsidered reply. A long time ago, Kenneth Youngblood had confronted his vision of Kenneth Youngblood as President of the United States: there had been one night, after a meeting with the men who made nominations, when he'd wrestled with temptation. He had paced in his pajamas, studying his character like a student cramming for an exam— and it was in the making, he had decided with the dawn, that he fell short of presidential stuff. In all humility he believed that he could be a good President; in all honesty he recognized that he could not endure the getting there.

"My back is too stiff," he told Marian now. "At home they like it that way: I'm their totem of no-compromise. But you can't win a country with a stiff back."

"I guess you can't run one that way either," Marian said uncertainly.

Startled, Youngblood knew that she was both right and wrong. For what she was perhaps implying was crookedness, and it was not crookedness but honest compromise that his back was too stiff for. Yet a Chief Executive with superior ideas might never get a legislative program through the Congress unless he knew how to compromise. He himself was, he hoped history would say, a good senator—a "senator's senator." Which was only an awkward way of characterizing the plight of the thoughtful man, insisting on the leisure and scope to point out other ways that might be invisible under the harsh light of the immediate daily need for action. He could compromise, but he could also do nothing—which was the one thing a President could not do. Leaning his head against the high back of the chair, he decided that it had truly been the way of wisdom to stay a strong legislator rather than become a weak executive.

"What do you think?" Marian was asking doubtfully. "Does Senator Girard look as though he would bend easily?"

Kenneth Youngblood smiled, thinking that she had a child's discernment. What she saw was the ruthlessness in Girard that worried Youngblood: no, the young Senator from Vermont would not bend easily; if he did, he'd never make it to the White House. But he was not rigid—he would bend; he would surrender, but inches at a time, cautiously and exacting a price, to obtain his objective. "The Presidency is a relative concept," Youngblood said aloud. "You mustn't approach it in such absolute terms. No one who can't bend could win it. But no one who bends *easily* could perform in it."

"I think I'm a fanatic," Marian said unexpectedly.

So you probably are, Youngblood thought, and so am I. "Maybe it's one of the virtues of our system—pliancy at the top, fanaticism among the 'attendant lords.' " The price of his freedom, he had decided in that long-ago dawn: *I am not Prince Hamlet, nor was meant to be:/Am an attendant lord, one that will do/To swell a progress, start a scene or two,/Advise the prince . . .*

Well, it was worth it; he would not have liked being Hamlet. "Please don't get up," he told Marian as he rose to leave. But she would anyway, and he helped her and stood beside her then, holding her hand and looking at her with pleasure but thinking of something else. "What troubles me," he told her softly, rapidly, "is an absence of awe in the man. There are so many subtleties—I worry that he'll fail to learn them in time." But, he told himself, there was also Andy, who had the personal outlook her husband either lacked or suppressed. She could make a great deal of difference. "But maybe needlessly," he added, aloud. "And one must be realistic: who else is there?"

"Oh well," Marian said cheerfully as she walked with him toward the foyer. "He's bound to be an improvement over President Winkler."

Senator Youngblood, thinking of the fears for his country that he had known on so many occasions during the last eight years, hoped she was a typical voter. He suppressed an impulse to pat her on the head as he told her good-night, and he was still smiling as Gil helped him into his coat; it occurred to him that he had told Marian more than he had yet told Gil. Gil was a fine man and a thoughtful writer; but for depth interviewing, maybe you just couldn't beat guilelessness.

Four

      Settled with a new drink on the sofa between Paul Morisot and Andrea Girard, Marian was doing her best to learn guile in a hurry. She could hardly escape conversation with Morisot when she was forced into such close quarters, yet she shrank from confronting him. Without being able to remember exactly what she had said about him, she remembered bitterly that Ann had considered it too carping. You can't win them all, Marian had thought about that column, and gone on to try to do better the next week. But she hadn't planned on a tête-à-tête with its subject. She wriggled uncomfortably, half-listening to the men by the fireplace.

      ". . . the oldest debating-society question in the world," Jake Ruffing was saying contemptuously. "When do you lead the people and when do you follow them?"

      "It may be old, but it keeps on having to be answered," Senator Girard observed. His hand, curved around his glass, was muscular, with an unusually long forefinger.

      "Right." Will stubbed out his cigarette, then went on grinding it in the ash tray, studying it absentmindedly. "These abstractions leave out the realities of public pressure. How great is it, and how solidly on which side?"

      "Doesn't it matter whether it's right or wrong?" Marian asked.

      Her husband looked at her briefly. "Don't be silly."

      Marian shrugged. I guess I'm being a schoolgirl again, she thought, and, smiling emptily at Paul Morisot, went back to considering the awkwardness of meeting him here.

      "I think you are uneasy, Mrs. Farland." Morisot's keen eyes looked directly into hers. She had a not-unpleasant feeling that he was capable of peering right through them and into her mind. "Perhaps we speak of it now, no?"

      She turned to him with gratitude for release. "You know what it is. The trouble is, I can't remember exactly what I wrote, but I remember thinking afterward that it was a little unfair."

      He shrugged. "You have the right to object to carving if you feel that the subject required modeling."

      "Oh, I remember now." The color rose in her face. "I suppose I do have. But then I yacked on about it, didn't I, and it was all the same point. Once

I objected to the approach, there was no sense in objecting to all the details."

The sculptor laughed, showing strong, even teeth. "Yak? This animal is used metaphorically, perhaps?"

What in the world? Marian wondered, and then light dawned. "Oh. No, not y-a-k, like—er—yak butter." Why yak butter? Hardly an everyday household commodity, and she didn't even know whether you eat it or put it on your hair. But Morisot's dark eyes were on her, patient and persistent. "Y-a-c-k," she said with as much confidence as she could muster in the face of the fact that she'd never seen it spelled.

"Ah. *Andréa*?" He leaned across Marian. "I have learned a new English word."

"I should have thought you had all you needed, and more," Andrea Girard said pleasantly. "I can't practice my French with Paul any more," she told Marian. "He's become too frighteningly competent in English."

"But what is this 'yack'?" the Frenchman persisted.

Marian grimaced. "It's what art critics do when they've made their point but still want to go on being clever at the artist's expense. No, please," she told Morisot as he made to stand because she rose. "I'm too full of remorse already. I insist on getting my own drink. Can I bring you something?"

But they were well provided for, and she left them. As she crossed to the dining room, she looked back over her shoulder. Andrea Girard was opening and closing her hand in the "yack-yack-yack" gesture for Morisot. Marian knew suddenly why she had thought of a sailor: he looked like the dark, agile, merry tar on the cover of a travel folder advertising Toulon. She stirred her drink with her finger and took a sizable gulp and went on meditating on the misleading appearances of artists: from their looks, Morisot ought to be wearing the French navy's pompon cap and scrambling up shrouds; the great Martigny, in a white smock, ought to be studying X rays and deciding whether to operate; Alphonse Lenard should be changing a tire on a huge truck . . .

Marian decided against keeping these marvelous insights to herself; but, when she came back into the living room, she remembered that Phil Colby had gone home. The party was settling down to the hard core—which, in effect, was the "debating society." Andrea was offering a soft-voiced contribution to it, and Marian settled in the semi-isolation near the bookcase, watching Alec Girard. He was waiting politely for his wife to finish, but —thought Marian, looking at him with sharpened attention—he wasn't listening to her. Marian smiled into her glass in sympathy with Andrea and let the voices rise and fall around her like background music until Will's drawl, clear in a sudden silence, jarred her into attention.

". . . one of my wife's tricks in domestic debates," he was saying. "It infuriates the opposition, all right, but it doesn't exactly cast light." He paused, then asked bitingly, "Why don't you quit moving the problem from where it is to where you wish it were?"

"Hear, hear," said Alec. He turned to Ruffing. "How's that for realism,

Jake? I keep reminding us," he told Will, "that Winkler's not running for office."

"No, but the citizen you're talking about voted for him," Ruffing argued.

"The citizen you're talking about is the guy who *may* vote for Ferris," Will said. "The way he voted last time doesn't matter—at least, not as much as what he does with a different set of choices, next year. All he gets is Ralph Ferris' side or your side. What he does depends on who talked to him best."

"And last." Ruffing rubbed his crew-cut head. "You theorists never ask yourselves, How close is this guy to the moment in the voting booth?"

"You technicians," Ann Taswell remarked coolly, "seldom ask yourselves anything else."

The men laughed, and Gil said "Attababy" and reached over to pat her knee. But they all subsided when Girard spoke.

"Certainly, timing is important, and so is detail work—touching all the bases, all the stuff that Ruffing has no equal in. But Farland's point is well taken: it's Ferris who's sitting across the chessboard—a pro, and a smart one, who knows all about timing and homework. The real point is, then, what does our side say to this voter that Ferris's side doesn't?"

"That depends, doesn't it?" Gil looked up at their questioning faces. "On the real question: who is this guy?"

"Well, he's not Kenneth Youngblood," Ruffing said quickly. "That's what happened last time—Blackwell went around talking to a nation of Youngbloods."

Senator Girard smiled. "You tell us who the voter is, Gil. You talk to millions of him every week."

"If I knew for sure, I'd be a better writer." Gil considered the question, scowling. "I guess, for me, he's a guy I knew in the Army. Or maybe all of them, the known and unknown soldiers."

Ruffing scoffed, "That's poetry. He's the guy who never misses his weekly chapter of a situation comedy on TV, that's who he is."

Alec Girard said slowly, "I think he's some relative of the people to whom Churchill talked about blood, sweat, and tears. Which would make him partly a Youngblood, partly Gil's unknown soldier—"

"And all the rest too," Will Farland interrupted. He glared at Ruffing. "You'll never beat Ferris if you fall into the same trap he does."

"Go on," Alec Girard said. His blue eyes probed Will.

"The people in England who were led to prodigies of work and heroism by Churchill were the same ones who sat in the music halls laughing at the kind of bathroom jokes my three-year-old goes in for." Will spoke directly to the Vermont Senator, but as formally as though he were addressing a meeting. "It's a mistake to confuse a man's attitudes toward his entertainments, of which he demands little, with his attitudes toward a leader, from whom he demands much."

"Sure you're not just idealizing the common man, Will?" Ann asked.

"The hell I am. All I'm saying is, the common man is brighter than Ferris thinks. Look at what he does when he's not sitting in front of the television. Senator," he asked Alec, "have you ever figured out your own income tax?"

"Afraid not." Girard's voice was cool and guarded.

Gil grinned. "At ease, Alec. Will's not going to yell 'Rich boy' and start a fight."

"No, I'm not," Will said seriously. "But it does have its disadvantages."

"Right. I frequently wince over my gilt-edged bonds." Alec's stiffness was gone now. "Get on, Farland. I'm not fragile."

"Okay. The point is, it's hard. If you've got a little grocery store, say, you spend a good deal of time wrestling with rather complicated forms. Besides the income tax. What I'm trying to say is, the average man who conducts a business and raises a family and buys a house and operates an automobile is the head of a complex little sovereignty that's not easy to govern and is subject to all kinds of hazard and attack. It's a hard world he's got to wrestle a living from: nobody's out to give him anything, and quite often they're out to take him. This is the man who steps into the voting booth—a guy who competes every day and wins a good part of the time. A fighter and survivor, and therefore something of a shrewdie. He may laugh at Tuesday's chapter of 'Father Is a Dope,' but *he's* no dope, and he knows it." Will dropped his oratorical tone suddenly and studied Alec Girard in the ensuing silence. "Ferris thinks he is," he said quietly.

Girard nodded. "Churchill knew he wasn't."

"Sure. And Churchill offered him what he wants."

"Eloquence?" Jake Ruffing asked. "Hell, Blackwell offered that, don't forget."

"I haven't," Will said. "And I'm not so sure that it was the presence of eloquence that defeated Blackwell. I think I can make a good case that it was the absence of organization. But more important is the question of what the eloquence is about. What it's rooted in, and what it offers."

"Blackwell's eloquence is rooted in theory," Ruffing said positively.

Will nodded. "And it offers you a theoretician's view from the mountaintop. A chance to participate in a visionary triumph. But look at what Churchill's offered."

"Heroism," Alec Girard said. "Anyway, a chance to be part of a heroic effort." His eyes were thoughtful. "It's your belief, then, Farland, that this tired man sitting in front of the television set—this man who is, by your description, something of a daily hero himself—responds better to a call for heroism than a promise of comfort?"

Will said, "I'm not trying to make us out a nation of heroes, Senator."

"We may be," Girard said. He smiled. "Though—like all heroes—unwillingly."

"One thing sure, we're a nation of hero-worshipers, though." Jake Ruffing looked at Will challengingly. "I'm inclined to agree with your estimate of what defeated Blackwell, except that I ascribe a lot more to his lack of authority. We like a leader. Or even—like Winkler—something that just looks like a leader."

Marian, transferring her attention to the Diego Rivera print over the bookcase, thought they would probably go on this way for hours, plodding along in line with their ideological loads on their backs, for all the world like the people in the picture. But I'm not talking, she said to herself, getting up to wander the room. Palaver, palaver, I'm no pal of palaver. You've had too much to drink, she accused herself.

She slid her feet out of her shoes, leaving them under one of the dining-room chairs, and wiggled her stockinged toes in the carpet. It felt sturdy and prickly. She turned round and round on it a few times in the dining-room, listening to the swish of her taffeta underskirt. Then she ran across to the French doors that opened onto the terrace, pushed aside the light linen drapes, and let herself out.

The flagstones were cool and firm under her feet as she found the light switch on the back wall of the house. White garden furniture sprang into the light, chaste and waiting. On the green-painted toolshed under the house's overhang, someone had left a small portable radio. She ducked a hanging flowerpot and switched the radio on. Nothing happened at first, no sound except a small, hesitant rain, spattering almost invisibly on the garden. The music swelled from the radio then, on swift, tumbling rhythms, and Marian stood and listened to *The Merry Wives of Windsor* overture syncopated by the irregular beat of the rain over her head. It's such a little rain that I could dance between the drops, she thought delightedly, and danced out to meet it.

The French doors opened behind her, and Paul Morisot peered out. He winked at Marian, caught startled and looking over her shoulder, and then pulled Andrea Girard out with him. Marian said, a little defiantly, "I'm going to dance between the raindrops," and then she turned her back on them, forgetting them, and began to circle the slim, satin-black bird feeder as if it were a maypole. Running with small steps, her arms raised, she laughed when she failed to reach shelter in time and called, "That one hit me." She twirled away from a particular raindrop and met another, ducked two more and came out too soon and was hit again.

She shook her head rebelliously in response and a hairpin fell out and hit the slate surface of the patio. The tiny sound seemed suddenly a bugle call to freedom, and Marian became light as dandelion down, light as Mozart, light as any microscopic thing borne on the wind of a baby's breath. Feeling free of gravity and common sense and all futures, she bent her body into grace, her gestures more ancient, more natural to man than even the earnest society-making she had left behind and would never truly understand. Alone in the simplicity of motion and joy in her body, she danced under the tree of heaven in the wet garden, uncomprehending and gay.

Turning back in a wide, dipping circle, Marian fetched up under the overhang and nearly stumbled over the shoes the others had left there. Then she saw them, Andrea and Paul, demurely meeting with upraised hands, dipping and turning in a stately minuet. Laughing, she spun to meet them, twirling with reckless indifference in and out among the tables and chairs, the hanging flowerpots, to orbit the moving pair like a satellite.

The rain began to come in earnest now, turning from freckling the flagstones to darkening them evenly, and she left the others and pirouetted dangerously onto the grass, warm and yielding under her feet. Andrea's dress, like a flame, moved rhythmically in and out of her sight, and she told it, "I'm a taranteller" and, ignoring the music—whatever it was that was now barely audible under the sound of the rain—began singing a rapid, wordless tune of her own.

Paul Morisot reached for her as she twirled past him, caught her, and took her hand.

"We're going to do a rain dance," Andrea called, reaching for her other hand.

"But it's already raining, it's raining very hard," Marian argued.

"Of course," Andrea answered, and Marian looked at the laughing, open face with eyes and teeth gleaming in the shafted light and said "Oh," bending gracefully to the logic.

Paul stomped three times on the flagstone, clapping his hands at the same time, and Andy and Marian unclasped their hands and imitated him. The spines of a dead leaf crumbled under Marian's foot.

"It is an ancient tribal dance of my people," Paul said owlishly.

"How does it go?" Andy asked. She lifted on her toes and raised her arms, waiting like a ballet student.

"I shall devise it now." Paul seized their hands and commanded, "First to the left." Andy bent obediently and pattered off to her left, with Paul following and Marian yanked along at the end. "Now to the right," he shouted, and Marian reversed her direction, hooting joyously as she felt the others following. "A bow toward the center," Paul called, and Marian kicked up her right leg and ordered, "Kick, two, three."

"From the province of the Rockettes," Andy said as she kicked, two, three, her toe elegantly pointed. "Now circle thrice."

Marian, reaching in the dark, felt Andy's cool wet hand in hers and began circling obediently as a large fat raindrop fell on her upper lip. "One," they chanted, and then, "two." The charmed circle, the small rebellion, swayed in the unison of innocence and gaiety.

But they never got to "three," for the doors opened and all the light in the world streamed out on them and they stopped dancing and stood, still holding hands, staring in the rain at the faces that stared out at them.

"Not even enough sense to come in out of the rain," Betty grumbled as she reached around for the light switch and herded Marian and Andy into her bedroom. "Towels in the bathroom. Get yourselves something to wear in my closet," she said, indicating the opposite wall. "And then come down. I'm going to fix you something hot to drink."

Left alone, they looked at each other in the lamplight and began to laugh. "We'll get everything wet," Marian said, when they had quieted.

"Your dress is soaked," Andy pointed out. She came over and began to struggle with Marian's zipper. "You'd better take your hair down, too. It's awfully soggy."

Marian looked at Andy's bent head. "You ought to see your own coiffure. Elizabeth Arden's would cast you out in the forest to die."

As soon as they got their dresses off, they made for the mirror. As Marian sat down and began to take out her hairpins, they peered in at their drowned faces reflecting rue.

"I feel foolish," said Andy.

Marian took the last pin out and shook out her hair. The ends of it tumbled halfway down her back, curling wetly against her shoulders. "I don't care. Anyway, we made 'em stop talking."

Andy laughed. "Well, we did that, all right." She marched over to the closet and slid its door back. The array of clothes extended the width of the room. "Look! I'll be all night making up my mind."

"That Betty," said Marian, coming up to peer over Andy's shoulder. "She sure can wring every drop out of her budget, can't she?" The ends of her hair were dripping on the back of her slip. "Oh hell." She padded through the dressing room to the gray-tiled bathroom, selected a huge, fluffy, wine-colored towel from the rack near the shower, and came back with it over her head like a prayer shawl. Andy was climbing into a royal-blue wool dress with a wide skirt, and she turned to let Marian zip her up. The skirt was so much too short for her that it looked like a skating costume.

"Oh dear," Andy said, looking at herself in the mirror.

"You better take an evening dress." Marian pushed the clothes along the rack, feeling at the bottom for long skirts, and found a blue silk dinner dress for Andy. "But this is for me," she cried in sudden excitement. "By cracky, it must have been a windfall of some kind. You don't manage something like this by just using hamburger ingeniously in your menus." She yanked out a floor-length red velvet housecoat and pulled it over her head to avoid unbuttoning the whole length.

Andy eyed her thoughtfully and then went back to looking at herself critically in the mirror. The blue dress, though too dark a shade for her coloring, fitted her well enough in everything except its length. Its sleeveless bodice revealed her graceful arms, smoothly muscular under the tanned skin.

Marian fumbled at the velvet buttons over her bosom, which was apparently more ample than Betty's. "Listen, is this too much cleavage, if I leave this button open? I'm afraid I may split the seam."

"Well," Andy said thoughtfully, "it does look a bit—you know. Here," she added, suddenly inspired. "Use your hair." She pulled gently at Marian's long hair, coaxing the black curls forward until they fell over the front of the housecoat and hid the unbuttoned gap. "Like Lady Godiva."

"I'd like to stay up here forever," Marian said gloomily. "They're going to make fun of us."

"I expect they are," Andy agreed. "But I want a cup of coffee. So let's do our faces and go down."

They bent to their labors, sharing the dressing table—Marian sat on the bench and leaned toward the right, and Andy stood over her and used the upper left-hand corner. "Just like in school," Marian pointed out, noticing this.

"I know," Andy agreed. "I was always one of the taller ones. After school, I hardly knew how to make up without somebody else's face in the bottom half of the mirror."

"At least you could always see."

"Oh, it had its advantages," Andy said. She fluffed out her hair. Its dark brown was beginning to lighten as it dried. "Come on. Let's face the music. You're all right."

"You look dignified," Marian said. "I don't know how you manage it."

"Well, you look like Little Red Ridinghood," Andy replied, and then, eyeing the swell of bosom straining at the cloth, added, "Sort of." They were giggling again as they went down the stairs.

Crossing the black-and-white downstairs hallway, silent in their stockinged feet, they heard Rosenberg's voice, high and irate, from the living room: "*Argumentum ad hominem,* for God's sake."

Then they were in the doorway, and the debating team, effectively stopped again, rose to its collective feet in confused greeting and expostulation. The fire had been lighted, and Paul Morisot, swathed in a faded-red sweatshirt lettered "Western," greeted them from beside the hearth. Andy's and Marian's shoes were nearby; they went over to him and put them on.

"For one moment I believe I am a cowboy," Paul explained, pointing to the letters on the sweatshirt. Under its attached hood, his dark face was lighted by a faun's wicked smile. "But it is only a school."

"I was wondering what they were going to do about dressing you," Andy remarked.

"He had his choice of my sons' un-put-away clothing," Betty told her. "Courtesy of my sloppy housekeeping."

"Welcome," Ann said, moving over to make room for Marian on the arm of her chair. "The three poets, who were out there living while the politicians schemed indoors, are back among us again."

Alec Girard watched his wife come to rest in a swirl of skirts on the floor at his feet. "Maybe our schemes make it possible for them to dance," he observed. Andy flashed a glance at him and then looked down demurely, but there was unmistakable mischief in her eyes.

Betty appeared with a loaded tray and set it down on the coffee table, sliding it in among the clutter of ash trays and cigarette box. "Come on. Poet or politician, whatever your persuasion. There's enough for both sides."

"Even the third force? That's what we are, isn't it?" Gil asked Ann.

She considered it, tilting her head, her pale hair almost silver against the background of Marian's borrowed crimson. "I suppose. Neither doers nor dreamers. Chroniclers."

Will Farland lifted his coffee cup in a toast to his hostess. "To the real fourth estate: the nourishers."

"Amen," said Alec. "The quintessential function, to keep us all alive." He drank from his coffee cup and set it down. "While the poets dream and the politicians scheme—"

"And Kimball tells us what should have been," Ann finished, forcing a near-rhyme by giving the last word its British pronunciation. "You know, I have a conditioned reflex by now—I can't drink coffee on Mondays, Wednesdays, and Fridays without Gil pontificating. One Friday my *Tribune* wasn't delivered, and I was drowsy all day."

"Well, it beats working," Gil retorted. "When I think of all those dim years I spent getting everybody's name spelled right—"

Rosenberg observed lazily, "I noticed you'd put all that behind you."

"You're being unkind, Mr. Rosenfeld," Alec Girard said in an elaborately reproving voice.

When he could make himself heard, Gil pointed out grimly, "I've never mentioned Rosie's name and you know it, Alec."

"Let's be scrupulous, Senator," Rosenberg said. "He does know how to spell 'source.' "

"I've been scrupulous all week and I find it wearing." Girard did not look worn. "But I apologize. I'll have Luke get out a retraction."

"To run on the comic page in the first edition only," Jake Ruffing stipulated.

But they were all startled out of their chatter when Andrea said, "Nuts to the press. I read a poll that said they were for Mr. Blackwell."

Alec Girard's mobile lips quivered, but he contained his grin. "If you mean the newspaper editors' poll, Andy, remember that what they were asked for was their nomination prediction, not their preference."

"I wouldn't let it worry me in any case," Ann advised. "Editors' predictions are only a feeble magic. The entrails of a few reporters—"

"A dried, ground-up senator or two—"

"They throw the bones of columnists—"

Marian, snuggling into the merriment like a tired child in its blankets, finished her second apple turnover, licked her fingers, and watched the reflection of the firelight on the toe of her shoe, counting the colors. Blue, red, orange, purple—was there really green? She looked closely at the fire and caught a flash of it, just above the heart of orange ember. She saw Paul Morisot also watching it in silence, but he was seeing nothing else; only his left hand was almost imperceptibly moving on the curve of his coffee cup as if molding it. His fingers were agile as a violinist's; but above the pushed-up sleeve of the borrowed sweatshirt his forearm had the solid muscularity of workmen who habitually handle heavy objects. Blessed are the making hands, Marian thought dreamily, searching the firelight for another flash of green. She couldn't find it for a long time, but she didn't mind waiting.

Behind her in the room, the noises of departure rose and fell: Ruffing and Rosenberg would drop off first Ann and then Morisot, the Girards would walk because the rain had stopped. Marian waited, warm and without wonder, knowing she would be told what to do.

She saw Will frowning as he held her coat for her, but she lost track of it while she wrestled with the problem of pulling her hair free of the coat collar. Morisot came to her rescue, lifting the heavy curls with a scooping motion at the back of her neck and letting them fall outside her coat. Marian joined in Andy's mild objections as Betty held out scarves for them to wear on their damp hair; but when they turned to the hall mirror to knot the scarves under their chins, Marian's reflection was in the lower right and Andy's in the upper left again, and they both began to laugh.

In the car, curled into the corner of the front seat, Marian asked Will sleepily, "Did you mean it, that you really think Alec Girard is going to be President?"

"I think there's a damn good chance. You don't object, do you?"

"I don't know."

"Well, it certainly ought to be good for your side."

Marian stirred, but she didn't answer.

"Hasn't it occurred to you that having a well-known art-lover like Andrea Girard in the White House would give art quite a boost?"

It had, actually; but the thought of her own self-interest had made Marian immediately uncomfortable. "Oh, Will. Of course, but—oh, I don't know. I don't like to think like that."

"Why the hell not?" he asked furiously. "What's wrong with thinking like that?"

"Oh, Will, please don't start." She looked out at the comforting night, soft and damp, and longed to sink into sleep.

"The whole world runs on you-scratch-my-back, I'll-scratch-yours. The whole world except Marian Farland." He threw her a scornful look. "Who has to be Jesus Christ, or something."

When she spoke, it was from the thin edge of consciousness. "Why are you so angry, darling?"

He was caught off guard by the gentle words and the sleepy voice. "I don't like you running around with your hair down. With everybody looking."

His voice lay on the air in the little world of the moving car and he heard with horror the sound of his dangerously exposed self. When Marian didn't answer, he looked at her quickly, suspiciously. She was asleep with her head against the back of the seat, her small face white among the smoky clouds of her hair. The scarf had slipped down and lay knotted loosely at her throat. Will reached out and touched one of the thick, damp curls as if it needed some kind of attention, but he took his hand away without changing anything.

Like a baby, he thought grumpily: she plays, then eats, then sleeps. But he felt relieved that she hadn't, after all, heard his unguarded admission.

Andy Girard waved at the Farlands' departing car lights, then tucked her hand under Alec's arm as they walked slowly along the uneven surface of the old street. The street lights shed a diffused glow like clouded moons.

"It was fun." Andy glanced down at the skirt of Betty's long dress, drooping unevenly from under her coat. "But I hope nobody sees us."

"You weren't worrying about that when the three of you were cavorting in the rain," Alec said mildly.

"No, I wasn't, was I? It was nice not to think about it." She looked up at him with sudden concern. "You didn't mind—I didn't disgrace you?"

Alec covered her gloved fingers with his own and told her that she was quite decorous enough to suit him. Silently, he examined the possible charge that he had been grounding butterflies and acquitted himself, but with a caution. The "let's-all-run-down-to-Acapulco set," as Bruyette had called it long ago, had its shortcomings, but chain gangs definitely did, too: Alec had not plucked Andy from the gorgeous colors of the former in order to gray her down into the dreary uniform of the latter. He smiled down at her now and decided there was nothing gray about her yet. "Your evolution has been most satisfying," he told her. His eyes mocked his pompous tone. "I didn't know you'd got as far as reading political polls, though."

"You mean those editors? Well, actually, I only read it because it was just under the art review."

Alec, whose photographic memory instantly called up the placement of the story, knew quite well that it had been on page three—and knew equally well that his wife knew he knew it. "I see," he said gravely. "Then you were spared the rather grim news of the other polls."

"They didn't prefer you?"

"Not when they were asked, anyway." Something lumped under the curious term "influential intellectuals" had gone for Blackwell, as had those of the party's state governors who were not committed to favorite sons. The unusually large number of favorite sons gave the nomination even more of an up-for-grabs look than was accurate.

"As it happens," Andy said, terribly casually, "I did somehow notice a little thing in the paper—you know those men in various states who're always quoted about politics, though it's never clear why? I mean, sometimes they're Mayor of Pittsburgh or Governor of somewhere, but that doesn't seem to have an awful lot to do with it, because they're quoted with just as much respect when it's only 'Henry Swanson of Ohio,' you know?"

"I know. They're what is known in the more excitable literature as 'king-makers,' Andy." She would probably be meeting the actual equivalent of "Henry Swanson of Ohio" soon: a primary victory in Ohio, the native state of none of the party's presidential prospects and therefore equally conquerable by any of them, would not assure convention votes, because the delegates were not committed by the primary results. Thus, the only way Ohio would arrive at the nominating convention with its large and necessary bloc of votes promised to Alec Girard would be if a Henry Swanson had been convinced that Girard, if nominated, would win. "The kingmakers came out for Tom Cannon. I know."

"If Senator Cannon is their idea of a king," Andy scoffed, "I don't see how they can be called kingmakers." She went on to draw a swift, scathing verbal caricature of the presidential favorite of the party's southern forces. It was clever, Alec conceded, but the trouble with it was that its author mistook it for a true portrayal of the shrewd and hugely talented Tom Cannon.

"Maybe you'd better sheathe your rapier, darling," he told her finally. "You may be talking about the next President of the United States."

"Oh, Alec, they couldn't. Besides, the polls of Negroes and labor show some preference for Senator Daniels." She stopped to stare at him in earnest inquiry, her hands spread and her lips parted.

With difficulty, Girard managed to preserve a grave demeanor in the face of this innocent revelation of the extent of her secret researches; he reminded himself that it was all right, nobody would ever be likely to send Andy on an espionage mission anyhow. "Daniels is the party's only announced candidate," he said. "It doesn't matter—Dan Daniels can't get the nomination. As a matter of fact, we've been wondering whether he really intends to go through with a long exercise in futility. He's intelligent enough to know that's what it is." Alec looked at his wife's upraised face, still full of indignation at the regrettable behavior of those who failed to prefer Girard. "If you'd been examining the political straws in the wind, darling—" it was mean, but he couldn't resist "—you'd know that, though only New England seems to be willing to offer me for king so far, I'm not totally scorned. In fact, I seem to be the number-one choice for crown prince." He touched her cheek just above the slanting edge of her borrowed kerchief. "Don't you think we'd better get on home, Andy? I got used to staying up late on this last speaking trip, but you've had a long day and you should be being conscientious about rest now, shouldn't you?"

She nodded and they began to walk again through the narrow, silent streets. But she looked thoughtful. "Alec?"

"Yes."

"You absolutely refuse to run for Vice-President?"

"Yes. Why?"

"I just wanted to be sure. A long time ago—maybe he told you—I asked Bill Bruyette whether you were going to be President someday."

"Did you?" A mind full of unknown corners, he told himself, pleased and surprised. The exploration and mapping might take quite a few years. "And what was his judgment?"

"Oh, he said you would, but you'd have to be Vice-President first."

"Ah. Well, Bill was probably basing his guess on the fact that there's been only one direct jump from the Senate to the White House in this century."

"And everybody says because you're so young," Andy said vaguely.

Since it was unlikely that anyone had actually said this to Alec Girard's wife, he began to wonder whether she'd spent all her time reading newspapers during his latest absence. He stopped walking and waited till she looked up to see why. "It would be handy if I were ten years older," he told her seriously. "And, if I had my absolute choice, I might prefer to run in some other year. But I don't have absolute choice because the world doesn't stand still. And I am not too young. And—for these and a number of other reasons—I think the time is now."

"All right, darling." She put the subject away with some relief, like a woman folding the finished mending.

They turned the corner at 30th Street. The willow tree before the great gray house on the corner still had its leaves, though they had lost their green. The drooping tentacles of its branches moved slightly in the soft breeze, and a little leftover rain pattered onto the sidewalk. The white bark loomed in the misty light.

Andy hadn't quite returned the mended clothes to their places, though. "Alec, did the last huddling with Jake and Rosie mean you've decided when to announce?"

"Ay-uh." They grinned at the Vermont caricature. "Next month at the labor convention in Chicago. Tentatively."

"Oh. I go along, I take it?"

"I'd planned to invite you." His look was merry in the gentle light. "You're a considerable asset, you know. I had it in mind when I asked you to marry me."

"I'm sure. I remember that summer at Kingsley, and I can see that that's what was on your mind, every minute."

"Well, I tried to remember it, but you kept shaking those curls—"

Andy smiled: she hadn't had a curl to her name all summer, which had been spent largely in clambering in and out of boats, and her hair had been nearly always wet. Still, if Alec had seen curls, she was not about to interfere at this late date . . .

They moved on, but in a few moments he stopped, halting her with him, to look into the window of the drugstore. Alone in its center, a graceful urn filled with a very blue liquid glowed in a dim nightlight. "I wonder why they do that," Alec said.

"I don't know. Maybe it's a charm against thieves. Elizabeth's very fond of it, and I can't blame her. It's pretty."

"Elizabeth. . . . You know, sometimes it startles me that she should like or dislike anything. Like a—a person." He grinned, embarrassed. "Of course, nothing is really as startling as the way she just sort of appeared, somewhere in the intervening years— One day, suddenly, you're somebody's father. Just like that."

"Oh, anyone would've been surprised, Alec," Andy assured him gravely. "Anyone a teeny bit—absentminded, shall we say?"

"All right. But the truth is even more absurd, I suspect— I think I thought of the whole baby idea as a kind of whim of yours—a foible of women, that you go along with because you love them. I simply didn't envision a person, really." They turned from the windows and walked on, their footsteps portentous on paving bricks. "In a way, I was right," he teased. "Who could've guessed such an insignificant-looking creature could turn out to be so interesting?"

"She *wasn't* insignificant-looking. She was adorable right from the minute she was born. Which," Andy added pointedly, "you couldn't be expected to know."

"Don't, Andy. I'll be around for this one's debut. I've learned. I'm rehabilitated. Forgiven?"

"Forgiven." They walked in silence for a moment, and then she said happily, "I think there's nobody left awake in the whole wide world," and hugged his arm like a delighted child.

Alec smiled. "Nonsense. This is Georgetown. In each of those houses—" he waved at the yellow house with its billowy bays rounding on the corner "—is somebody in a back bedroom, tapping away at his memoirs." Even Gil Kimball might be scrawling a few notes into a diary for future use, he thought; but he decided Andy wouldn't find the idea engaging.

"Oh, Alec." There were, clearly, no words for how good she felt. "I wish it could just stay the same—for us, Paul, the Kimballs, everybody." She knew it made no sense, and she expected no answer: Alec Girard, though he was courteous to fairy tales, did not himself indulge, and his wife knew it. She abandoned fairy tales without regret, smiling as a subject more likely to lead to agreement occurred to her. "Wasn't Paul a sight in that Western High School shirt?"

"You can afford to be fond, but I was intimidated," Alec said. "He looked just like the fellow who was quarterback on my prep school football team. I was about to curry his favor."

"Why did you have to curry favor? You were on the football team. Your mother has pictures of it."

"I let my womenfolk in on things only when I pull them off successfully. She got the photo once the problem was solved."

"But why was it a problem? Weren't you good at it?"

"Not really," he said judiciously. "But I was very determined. I found a way to *look* good at it. Then, once I made the team, I substituted daring for whatever I lacked." He thought it over. "On second thought, by the time I got through, I was good at it."

Andy stumbled a little on a gnarled tree root that had had its way with the old brick sidewalk. He caught her arm and steadied her.

"That fellow Farland," he said suddenly. "Did you notice him? He interested me. He has some pretty good notions. *And* a way with words. It's not an easy combination to find in one man."

"Except Jerry Rosenberg."

"Exception noted, with gratitude. But one of the things we're in need of, Jake was saying, is another Rosie."

"I like Mrs. Farland," Andy said. "I was thinking of having her over to lunch."

"Pretty little woman. Is she bright?"

"I think so. Certainly intuitive. She said something that made me think. You know, Alec, there's a lot we don't know."

He smiled. "That's sad, but hardly news."

"I mean," she persisted, "about how people live." She fumbled for explanation, her eyes earnest. "What they have money for. How they manage on their salaries—oh, that kind of thing."

"Well, we manage on my salary."

"I know, but—we don't have to. There's a difference. And, besides, your salary is rather grander than Gil's or Mr. Farland's, isn't it?"

"At least, we're supposed to," Alec said emphatically, ignoring her question. "That new Chinese rug appeared rather mysteriously, I thought. Have you been juggling the household funds?"

"You can do a lot by using hamburger ingeniously in your menus," she said demurely. Above her curving grin, her eyes were thoughtful.

Out of the corner of his eye Alec took note of the fact that he was being maneuvered and debated whether to try one of his own: he'd been wondering whether her recent researches had led her to discover that it was against the law for a candidate for the Presidency to finance his own campaign. The law was a good one, though not very successful on the whole—it could be, and was, got around by any number of devices. But Dan Healy, who was almost always right about this sort of thing, had been maintaining that the public wouldn't believe Alec Girard had to raise campaign funds like anybody else. If Andy was not any more knowledgeable about the legalities than the rest of the public— Abruptly, Alec decided to find out.

"I don't want to be heavyhanded," he said, "but we may have to cut down on the bric-a-brac, darling. A full-scale presidential campaign is a very large budget item, I'm afraid."

"Oh. Oh, of course," she answered at once. "I'll be terribly careful, really I will. I'll begin economizing right away."

He smiled down at her as they turned in at last at their own front walk. The bark of the small cherry tree was shiny with the late rain. She ought to have the storm windows put up, Andy thought, looking at the welcoming lamplight behind her shrouded windows. The weather was bound to change, and storm windows were supposed to save fuel.

Belatedly, it occurred to Alec that he could suffer some uncomfortable consequences if his wife's energies were turned entirely to budget-cutting. He decided it might be advisable to tip his hand a little. "One of the first economies will be the cottage at Kingsley, of course," he said, poker-faced.

Andy stopped, staring at him in horror, before she noticed the teasing gleam in his eyes. "Beast. You scared me." She watched him put the key in the lock of the white-painted front door. The shadows cast by the street lamp doubled its rectangular panels. "Alec, you're horrid—you're a swindler, one of those people who sell gold bricks."

"A con man," he supplied. He held the door for her, closed it, and turned to switch off the small outdoor light. "I'm sorry. I'll try to give it up."

"You ought to do more than just apologize. You ought to—take me to the lake. I deserve at least that."

He sighed. "Darling, I don't know. It's hard to see how."

"Please, Alec? One more weekend at Kingsley before you begin all that?"

He helped her out of her white wool coat. " 'All that' rather understates it." She waited, looking at him hopefully, and he sighed again. "We'll try." He narrowed his eyes in a caricature of the Yankee bargainer. "If you're interested in a little trade—"

"What kind of trade?" she asked suspiciously.

"Like my being excused from the National Symphony opening. And from two art exhibits."

"*Two* exhibits is robbery."

Alec thrust his hands into his pockets and pursed his mouth for a whistle. "Not two, Alec."

"Guess you don't really care about going to the lake."

Reaching to turn off the lamp, she looked at him unhappily over her shoulder. He stood still, his face composed. But her dark eyes were having their effect.

"Two art exhibits," he repeated, ready to abandon the symphony stipulation as he watched her moving across the room.

Andy switched off the lamp and came back to him. "But you go to the symphony opening," she said firmly. "They need the support."

He put on an elaborate pantomime of judicious consideration, with her hopeful face upturned to his slow deliberations. Finally, he relented. "Done." He held out his hand and Andy shook it firmly.

"I don't know, though," she was saying doubtfully as she went up the stairs before him, holding up the borrowed skirts that were too short to need it. "I have a feeling I'm coming off the worse, anyway. *Two* exhibits."

Alec concluded that her researches hadn't really gone very far: the wise negotiator, she hadn't yet discovered, doesn't make concessions to get what the other fellow is already willing to give. And it would have been nice for United States foreign policy if Winkler had discovered that, he added to himself. He decided to hold his peace—why arm her for future confrontations? —and followed her up the stairs, eyeing her legs.

Five

That smooth purveyor of gold bricks, Alexander Girard of Vermont, did not, as it happened, end by escaping attendance at two art exhibits. He squired his wife to one of the three in town, and then, just as he was congratulating himself that he had knocked off his obligation, the catalog of the second appeared at his place at the breakfast table one morning. It was turned to an inner page, and an unknown hand had circled the title of one of the paintings to be shown: Alphonse Lenard's "Portrait of Morisot."

The portrait, the catalog said, had been lent for the exhibit by its owner, Mrs. Henry Donnelly of Philadelphia. Alec looked at his wife, who could have helped him combine his obligation with his natural desire to go look at a picture of Paul by simply tipping him off that this was coming—a fact to which she was very likely to have been privy, since Mrs. Henry Donnelly was the former Carol Pritchard, who had been Andrea Langwith's college roommate and girlhood chum. Nothing could have been prettier in the morning sunlight in the pleasant room than the sight of Andrea reading the *Tribune* with the tranquillity appropriate to a lady unacquainted with con men who thought they could get out of two exhibitions. The Senator sighed, inquired whether he might have the pleasure of escorting his wife to the opening, was told pleasantly that she would be delighted, and went off to Capitol Hill to trade with perhaps less effective opponents.

Will Farland did a little better on the domestic front that week by getting out of putting up his storm windows, but with honor. He got a call from the duty officer at the State Department just as he was swallowing the last of his coffee on Saturday morning. He went "down to the office for a little while" in his corduroy shirt and paint-stained Saturday slacks and didn't reappear until about seven o'clock that night. Marian, who had spent the day alone with the children, without the car and unable to schedule any activity, was icily polite to him as he flopped wearily into the black armchair in their living room. Studying her closed face, Will considered that it would serve Her Haughtiness right if he didn't tell her the news; but his desire to see her smile was greater than his spite, so he plucked Peter off the hassock, put his feet up, and began his tale of triumph.

Gil Kimball told it this way in his Monday column: "We were all agreed that we'd been called to the White House to be informed that the Honorable Hemingway Garrison's round-the-world fact-finding journey was postponed. But nobody succeeded in untangling President Winkler's additional comment well enough to be sure why."

And sometime next year, the reporters' symposium after the press conference had concluded, Garrison would apparently be sent on a trip, but only to the Middle East. "Nobody at our little seminar," Kimball observed solemnly, "was certain how the switch had come about or quite what had happened to the President's palship for the rest of the world. A hard-bitten type, on loan from the sports page because he has shown promise in interpreting Casey Stengel to the public, dared to suggest that the President preferred not to have to act on any recommendations Garrison might make and therefore felt safer leaving the trip and its resultant report for the closing days of his own administration. The fellow was, of course, sent from the bar in disgrace.

"Here and there, a cynic hazarded a guess that the President might be planning to tie Garrison's eventual findings to his own party's election-year needs, but these doubters were soon squelched by reminders from their colleagues that President Winkler is well known to be above politics. Finally, a grizzled veteran spoke up: 'I have it, chaps!' (I have paraphrased his remark to protect his identity.) Why not, he suggested, looking about at the rapt and respectful faces of the Washington press corps, abandon the search for meaning and simply serve up, without comment, the kernel of news? Well, needless to say, we gave the old fellow three rousing cheers before we wound our scarves tightly about our throats and, with rosy cheeks and merry farewells, set off into the night.

"The news is, Hemingway Garrison will be home for Thanksgiving."

Like Hemingway Garrison, Andrea Girard was, by Thanksgiving Day, relieved of responsibility: as a guest—along with her husband and daughter, Paul Morisot, and her brother Richie and his wife and baby—at the home of Andrew and Elizabeth Langwith, deep in the hilly, wooded Virginia countryside about a hundred miles from Washington, all that was required of her was punctuality at table and similar minor marks of decorum.

Thus the erstwhile "Langwith children" disported themselves at leisure on the wide lawn: Andrea, in slacks and a worn leather jacket, succeeded in winging her brother with a vicious whip of the dead tennis ball with which they were playing catch; she laughed wickedly as he glared at her and paused to rub his stinging arm. Nearby, Elizabeth Girard, in corduroy trousers and a white sweater knitted with exquisite care by her grandmother, was engaged in a rather more decorous game, employing a considerably larger ball, with her grandfather. Andrew Langwith looked up briefly when he heard his son yowl in pain and frowned a little disapprovingly at his daughter, then turned back and bent to roll the large red-and-blue ball gravely and carefully toward Elizabeth. His trim body in handsome and well-worn riding clothes moved a little stiffly but still competently; his quiet, dark eyes, watching his grandchild successfully pounce on the rolling ball, were intent and devout.

Standing at the tall French windows of his father-in-law's study, Alec Girard studied his wife's gleeful assault on her brother with less disapproval and more curiosity than Andrew Langwith had displayed. "Every time I see Richie," Alec observed without turning around, "I decide he's growing into a hopeless stuffed shirt. Then he spends ten minutes with Andy, and the dull young architect is all gone."

"Richie perhaps received less of the heredity of the French grandmother than *Andréa*," Paul Morisot suggested. "He is more Welsh."

"Chauvinism." Alec came over to the desk and helped himself to one of his father-in-law's cigars. "But it's shortsighted of you—if you claim all Andy's gossamer for the French, that leaves the Welsh responsible for all the iron in her." He drew in on the cigar and let the smoke out with satisfaction. "Besides, I've got too much French in me to let you get away with that. I'm a very solid citizen—husband and father and positively no gossamer."

"You reverse my meaning," Paul objected mildly. "I referred to French practicality and Welsh emotionalism." He lifted a small, silver-framed photograph from Andrew Langwith's desk and studied it with a rather wistful smile. "I think, though, the explanation is clearer in here. They share more than a heredity, *Andréa* and Richie. They are a part of each other's past. Whatever each has become since, when they are together, they remember how it was."

The picture, a candid snap taken at Andy's debut and preserved by her father in preference to the more formal photographs of his beautiful eighteen-year-old daughter, showed the debutante, graceful in off-the-shoulder white, brandishing her small bouquet like a truncheon as she dodged on the curving stairway to escape her brother, soberly clad for the occasion but unmistakably twelve years old. Alec took the picture and grinned at the girl in it before he put it back on the desk. "Fun and games," he said. "I'm glad Elizabeth isn't going to be an only child any more."

Paul nodded. "It is of importance." His dark eyes brooded.

Alec Girard studied his friend unhappily, wishing Andy were here. She would just reach out, he thought, or say something, the something that was needed and somehow magically wouldn't sound silly. Alec shook his head: better to sound silly than to protect his feelings at Paul's expense. "I know occasions like this make it tough to be alone." He hesitated. "But . . . well, there's us, Paul," he added lamely.

"Of course." Paul turned back from his thoughts and smiled, laying a strong hand briefly on Alec's shoulder. Then he put his hands in his pockets and walked toward the window. Outside, Richmond Langwith made a spectacular catch and brought down Andy's wild throw, which had seemed headed for the haze of leafless trees behind him. Andy applauded enthusiastically and Elizabeth promptly dropped the big ball she was about to roll to her grandfather and began to clap her hands too.

"Thanksgiving has little to do with it," Paul explained, without looking at Alec. "It is not, after all, a holiday in my country, and so I have no troubling memories. But I am reminded, nevertheless—they are all gone: my mother, my father, my brother, everyone of the time when I was a boy. Even the little Simone, the daughter of my mother's friend." He turned briefly to Alec then, his eyes bright, perhaps with tears. "I dreamed incessantly of kissing her, and sometimes I thought to try. But I feared that she would tell her

mother, who would of course tell my mother. My brother counseled caution."
Paul smiled, lost in memory even while he watched, again, Andrea and her
luckier brother at play. "When I returned from my military service, that
would be the time, we decided: the little Simone would tremble and surrender to the swaggering soldier."

Up to a point, thought Alec, who had also been a boy with an older
brother, it could have been Vermont. Up to a point . . . "When you came
home, there was nothing left."

"Only my mother, and she was perhaps more tragic than all the rest—
tubercular, starved, dependent on the charities of neighbors. It was not possible to speak with her." He tapped his forehead. "She had been so—cloudy,
unable to recall—since the day she saw my father die."

In the years they'd known each other, Paul had seldom talked of the war
days. What Alec knew of the details had been derived largely from Andy,
whose accounts tended to be more vivid than orderly. So it was with curiosity
as well as sympathy that Alec asked now, "They took him as a hostage,
didn't they? To stop the underground?"

"Yes. I did not know for many years, of course. Till after the prison camp,
after the *Résistance,* after the peace. My mother died soon after my return.
And Simone . . ." Morisot shrugged, thrusting his hands deep into his pockets
again.

"Don't, Paul."

"Perhaps she died soon after they took her. I have learned to think this."

Alec studied his cigar thoughtfully. "When my brother was killed, we told
ourselves—my parents and the rest of us—that it was *for* something, that it
helped to win the war. So perhaps it was easier for us. We had one loss, but
a lot still left." He thought of his mother, weeping at the memorial service
for her dead son. Clear in the remembered picture, though, was his father's
arm around her.

"And you were not defeated," Paul said emphatically. "My father's death
was necessary for victory, for France and in defiance of an invader. Like your
brother, my father died a hero." He scowled. "But my brother was killed
for no purpose, to gain no objective except perhaps convenience. Stragglers
from a defeated army, shot to save the Germans the trouble of feeding
them."

Alec said suddenly, "We're a world away from those who have been leading us. We who've survived, I mean. We're a separate generation, whatever
our ages."

Paul nodded. "Your Mr. Blackwell was welcomed in France, you know—
we hoped he would become your President."

"And now?"

"Now I am not so certain. I think perhaps you need a man of what you
call our generation. Mr. Blackwell is a good man with an excellent intellect,
but he is not one of us whose lives were interrupted by the war in Europe."

"Interrupted, or somehow, in some important way, changed by it. There are millions of us here who weren't hurt, you know. Who went and came back, substantially unaffected."

"But not untouched, even if they lost no brothers."

"No," Alec said. "Not untouched. They had been and they had seen. They're different, even if it's only because they've married a girl they would never have met if they hadn't been drafted." His sudden smile was wry and self-mocking. "I'm planning to put myself forward, you know. As the spokesman of this—shall we call it the 'shaken' generation?"

But Paul would not accept the note of humor. "Yes, and it is time we of this shaken generation came forward," he said seriously. "In both our countries. But in France, the National Assembly—"

"Politics," Andrea accused them from the doorway. "I'll tell Mother. You know she doesn't allow it in the house." She untied her scarf as she spoke, shaking her thick hair loose.

"I deny it. Where did you come from?" Alec demanded. "A moment ago, we were watching you cavort out there."

"Time to dress for the feast." She looked past him at Paul, still standing by the window. "Watching me play ball couldn't have been the cause of all the sobriety I found in here. What were you talking about?"

Alec laughed. He crossed the room and took her arm. "One thing about Andy's researches," he said to Paul. "They're swift and direct."

Paul smiled gravely at her. "We were speaking of the—um—unfamilied. There is this word in English?"

Andy studied him for a moment. "No, that's not a word. And you are not unfamilied, Paul." Her eyes brightened then and she added, "In fact, you have family obligations. Elizabeth tells me the mysterious decoration you two have been secretly concocting requires some finishing touches. And you haven't time for philosophy, so you'd better get moving."

"*Oui, mon général.*"

Andy turned to go out. "I've got to dress. Coming, Alec?"

Alec, who had been watching with interest his wife's skillful restoration of morale among the troops, shook himself to attention and went.

Paul watched them start upstairs and then set out to find Elizabeth and attend to his obligations. He put the finishing touches on the table decoration, a witty construction in which figures from Mother Goose and Greek mythology combined forces in distributing the fruits of the earth to a gathering of tiny spacemen. While Paul worked, Elizabeth recounted for him the story of the Pilgrims' first Thanksgiving—which he found, in fact, quite fascinating. She illustrated her account by displaying her favorite picture book, in which severe Pilgrims regarded remarkably bronze turkeys. Morisot watched her small, earnest face and did not feel unfamilied.

No one could possibly have felt unfamilied at the Farlands' Thanksgiving dinner, which was actually a cooperative enterprise with Jim and Peggy McGrath. It had been decided to hold it at the Farlands' so that Peter, the only nap-age child, could enjoy his regular routine; but the work was shared by Peggy McGrath and, in addition, the visitors brought most of the liquid embellishments to the traditional menu. The McGraths, like other Foreign Service couples, were obliged regularly to do a certain amount of official entertaining (though they received no allowance for it from the government) at which the quality of the liquor they served had to be somewhat superior to their everyday supply. Because they contributed to the Thanksgiving dinner some leftovers of their most recent putting-on-the-dog-for-the-U.S.A., the diners were able to sip Courvoisier while the food scraps dried on the unwashed dishes, and Jim McGrath, who owned a pleasant baritone, sang for them the "Ballad of the Diplomat's Wife." The melody was a familiar one, but the lyrics had been written by Marian and featured a refrain beginning, "My Willie lies over the ocean," and ending with "Oh, bring back my liar to me." Farland and McGrath progeny, minus the sleeping Peter, roared through the house at intervals, banging doors and exciting dogs.

The children of Mrs. Rosa Little's sister and brother-in-law, Gloria and Claude Jones, were dressed-up, polite, and restrained at their aunt's dinner table. Rosa's younger daughter Trixie, who had been an Indian in the school Thanksgiving play, wore her headdress to the table and would not be persuaded to remove it. Its feathers had been painted by Marian Farland, who began doing it to be obliging and then became fascinated by the project and ended by producing a work of considerable subtlety. Also among those present was Manuel, a man of much wisdom and little education, whose family name was either unknown to or had been forgotten by most of the others, and who had been enjoying Rosa's cooking and companionship—and, on occasion, her favors—for some time.

Ann Taswell had been invited to Thanksgiving dinner by a number of married friends—among them the Farlands and the Kimballs—but she spent Thanksgiving Day at work among the skeleton staff getting out Friday's *Washington Tribune*. Among her chores was coverage of the Thanksgiving at a children's convalescent home; after a couple of hours among the frail bodies and great demanding eyes, she drove back to the office and wrote a story that moved dozens of women readers, the next morning, to hug their uncomprehending children.

Ann ate a hunk of institutional turkey in the *Tribune* cafeteria, sitting at one of the formica-topped tables with two rewrite men and a proofreader. Listening silently, she learned that a "sirvent" was an old Provençal song of a satiric nature, and that a particularly fussy editorial writer's "to founder" had got through as "to flounder" and there would be hell to pay tomorrow. She went back upstairs and read her copy over, changing only one word and recognizing with humility and pleasure that she still wrote well. Then she started home. But on the way she decided she felt lonely, so she detoured over to the Farlands' for a little society. She found Will and Jim McGrath playing Ping-Pong in the basement with the boys and Marian and Peggy doing the dishes in the kitchen with the girls. Ann joined first one group and then the other, acquitting herself well in both.

After Thanksgiving, Washington's mean, snippy cold descended with a vengeance, and, as usual, half the population took to bed with the flu. But Andy and Alec Girard flew to Chicago, where Alec, in an address to a convention of labor union officers, formally announced his intention to offer himself as a nominee for the office of President of the United States. Andy, looking glowing in a ruby silk dress that was described in detail by all the leading news services, smiled until her face hurt and tried not to shrink visibly from some of the too-tactile friendliness of the conventioneers and their wives. Gil Kimball called the event a success, as did most other journalists. Alec spent the entire trip home in conference with Jake Ruffing, while Andy, who had stood in receiving lines and shaken more hands than she ever wanted to again, tried to take a nap but was prevented by a nagging pain in the small of her back.

On a day of uncompromising winter in the second week of December, Paul Morisot drove the Girard convertible to the airport in Washington to begin his journey home. Among the papers having to do with international cultural exchange in the attaché case that lay between him and Andy on the car seat was a highly colored crayon drawing of Morisot by Elizabeth Girard; the artist, clearly, had seen her subject as composed primarily of hands. And so he was, Paul thought, looking at his gloved hands on the steering wheel. And his hands had been idle too long.

"There it is," Andy said, pointing to the left, and Paul slowed the car and pulled over so they could look at the statue of a wave and some gulls that they both liked. Andy seemed pale and tired, Paul thought—but so did the city and the countryside. A French Embassy minion would be waiting at the airport to do the official seeing-off, so Andy and Paul inspected the statue for a moment in companionable silence—each deriving a small rebirth of hope from the lofting bronze birds' valiant denial of gravity—and then Paul moved the car back into the stream of midday traffic.

"Come back again soon," Andy said softly when it was time for good-bye. Paul patted her hand without looking at her, for he was guilty of warming himself at friendship while longing for solitude. But it was undeniable—his hands, like schoolboys yearning for recess, ached with the desire to move at large.

Driving herself back from the airport, Andrea became increasingly certain that the still white sky meant snow. It was cold as she put the car into the little garage behind the house, but it was the menace in the sky rather than the actual cold that caused her shiver when she came through the back yard into the kitchen.

The kitchen was warm and smelled good and it had its effect on her tension. Prudence the cook, whose ready smile and easy tolerance cast the appropriateness of her name into doubt, surveyed Andy a little anxiously and offered a cup of tea.

"I'll wait till Mrs. Kimball arrives. Thank you, Prudence." Andy deposited a square white bakery box on the counter. "I couldn't resist these at Miro's," she added diplomatically. Not much of Washington's domestic labor supply was of a caliber sufficient to the demands of Senator Girard's household: Prudence was one of the well-paid, self-respecting Negroes—risen from the ghetto by way of development of a marketable skill—who may have been uniquely numerous in Washington. She was not so insecure as to be touchy, but respects must always be paid to her sovereignty in her domain.

Andy left the kitchen, walking briskly down the small hall into the front entry. She laid her purse and gloves on the hall table and hung her beaver jacket in the closet. She patted the soft fur, enjoying the feel of it, before she closed the closet door on it and then still stood in the small foyer, thinking about Paul's restlessness to be at his work: it occurred with a cyclical regularity that Andy, at least, recognized.

The pale winter light coming through the small squares of glass near the top of the front door softened even more the already soft aqua color of her wool skirt and the blouse-like sweater that matched it. Through the arch at her right the drawing room looked elegant but sterile in its ordered emptiness: the formal fall of heavy draperies, the subdued sheen of the pair of small sofas, with their starkly simple off-white covers relieved only by the dark-green satin stripes of the pattern, awaited not so much conversation as circumlocution. The masses of dark-green leaves in their white urn offered a background for muted voices. It was the setting where Andy worked, but she was haunted by no periodic nostalgia for it. She surveyed it with a chatelaine's eye and then turned to look with more pleasure into the family living room on her left, a place that invited her to come in and sit down. Here the same dark green on off-white exploded into large splashes of printed foliage on the slipcover of the sofa, which supported a couple of fat green brocade pillows a child could plop onto the floor or a grown-up use to curl up with a book. The graceful end tables held ash trays large enough for the smoking of many politicians, and a stack of glossy photographs and a pair of current newsmagazines piled on the coffee table bespoke everyday use. Above the sofa, a French impressionist, framed in tawny applewood, reported on the lovely golden summer of the Midi, and on a table by the front window, a bowl of bronze and gold asters warmed the Washington winter.

Andy noted the photos, promised herself that she and Alec would finish looking them over tonight, and thought briefly about having a moment's rest with her feet up. But there was just time, before Betty arrived for tea, for Andy to check on the garden and make sure everything was ready for the possibility of snow. She turned and went back out the way she had come.

"You want to have these at tea, Miz Girard?" Prudence asked her as she came into the kitchen again.

"Yes, please." Andy smiled. "They don't come within a mile of yours, of course. But I thought you might be too busy to want to bother this afternoon."

"Miro's do pretty good," Prudence conceded, eyeing the pastries. Appeased, she looked up at Andy to warn, "You better put your coat on."

"I'll be right out back. Just call me when Mrs. Kimball comes, will you?"

She stepped outside into the waiting stillness of the garden, closing the back door quietly behind her. The brick walk was shaped like an inverted "T": the horizontal arm, on which she stood, ran the width of the small house; the vertical arm ran nearly the length of the back yard. At the far end, it descended two wide flat steps and ended in a small patio where, among the garden furniture, Andy set up her easel on spring mornings.

But it was pretty desolate now, she thought, examining the dead-looking brown earth at the edge of the flower bed that, nevertheless, held next spring's tulips. She stood, hugging herself although she was not cold, reminding herself of the tulips against the desolation.

Without warning, the small persistent pain in her back that she had successfully pushed below the level of thought during the past week exploded into total claim of her thoughts. Pain rayed from its center in every direction and all at once, so hard and so fast that her head rang. She looked down cloudily and saw the gardener's aesthetic triumph—only now, the barrier of embedded bricks had evolved from an affair of domestic diplomacy to a clear danger. Andy yanked her gaze away, but the resemblance to a crocodile's teeth had registered anyway, and she shuddered.

Now the queer, huge pain gathered and swelled again, and Andy tightened her lips and focused determinedly on the bare branches of the maple tree in the yard next door. Until they began to writhe in her vision like gray snakes— She fought for control, trying to separate the fact of pain, which could be dealt with, from the illogic of fear, which could make that impossible. Her head swam, and in the gathering dizziness, she saw the looming crocodile teeth waiting, waiting, while her imagination supplied with sickening readiness the sound it would make as her head hit those implacable pointing bricks. Her body, cold with fear, strained for flight; but her legs trembled and would not obey.

The safest place was the ground, she decided desperately, finding relief in simply summoning up a plan. She bent her knees and leaned like a skier making a turn, and sank kneeling to the walk; in the moment of triumph over foreseen danger, the pain eased. Then, suddenly, overwhelmingly—as though it had only been gathering force—it struck again, and she let herself fall the rest of the way. Her hands shot out to meet the cold, gritty surface of the path. She came to rest lying there, her cheek on the same cold while, deep in her body, a great destruction went to work.

Andy set her teeth against the possibility of crying out, and won—she managed not even to whimper. But a dried stalk behind the barrier of brick triangles filled her field of vision; it blurred, and she realized that she was crying. There was nothing to do about it, or about anything: the world was a swimming grayness with corners of dark green that threatened to roll in and over even the sparse and fragile light that was left.

After a very long time, voices came out of the grayness, and a sound that was, eventually, recognizable as the tap of high heels on the walk. Then Betty Kimball's face leaned above Andy—the light hair tousled, the blue eyes wide with alarm. But Betty's voice was soft and confident. "All right, Andy, it's all right. There'll be help in a minute."

Andy managed "Elizabeth—" but no more.

A blanket was being spread over her—she felt its softness on her legs— and Betty was lifting her head a little with a hand under the back of her neck. Andy recognized the square green brocaded pillow from her living room as it slid under her head. She had a wild, unreasoning yearning to unroll time like a reel, to go back to that moment—an infinity ago—when she had stood in the hall and thought of lying down for a bit. She wept again, with the speechless human ache for a second chance.

"Miss Page is taking Elizabeth over to my house for tea," Betty was telling her. "She won't know anything."

"Alec? Don't—" Andy couldn't go on with the warning.

But Betty understood. "I won't call Alec till you get to the hospital. There's an ambulance on the way."

Andy closed her eyes gratefully. She opened them again when she heard Betty say "Thank you" and saw Prudence's black skirt and the edge of her white apron. The stitches of the hem of the cook's uniform marched across Andy's vision like a dashed line on a map, bordering her ground-level, pain-filled world. "Would you look out for the ambulance please," Betty said, and Andy watched the cook walk back toward the kitchen door. One of her broad black shoes was worn at the heel, where her weight had borne down on its outer edge.

Betty lifted Andy's knees gently and slid another pillow under them. The pain was gathering again—Andy felt it coming and gasped in fear. Betty's hand slid into hers, and she grabbed it and held on tightly, as yellow sparks shot upward before her eyes and the dark-green shades began to roll in from the corners of her vision. She tried to ask about the baby, but only a moan came out.

"Just lie still, Andy, lie still, honey." Betty was smoothing her hair away from her wet forehead and then the dark-green blinds met in the middle, blotting everything out.

Andy woke again, unwillingly, to a prick of pain in her arm. She saw the needle, just emerging from her arm under her rolled-up sweater sleeve, and followed it with her eye—to the glass tube, marked off with numbers in red, and then to the hand with black hairs beyond the knuckles, and then to the white jacket sleeve. A pale shred of late-afternoon sun glinted on the man's glasses as he turned to put the needle away. It hurt Andy's eyes, and she moved her head a little to get away from it and found that Betty was wiping her face with a damp handkerchief. Betty's hand was close to her eyes, and

Andy saw an angry red groove on the inside of the little finger where the gold wedding ring on Betty's fourth finger had been pressed into the flesh. *I did that,* Andy thought. She saw clearly how much it must have hurt Betty to have her hand squeezed so painfully, and she thought, anguished, *She was kind and I hurt her,* and struggled to apologize.

A week later, Alec Girard fought his way out of the rocky cove of his office, in which papers and decisions tumbled and seethed, to the broad sea of his life. Recovering his wife from the hospital, he flew with her and their daughter to Florida, where they stayed in a handsome house owned by Alec's father; they spent Christmas in the palmy surroundings that, to the Vermonter, had always seemed irrelevant and faintly absurd. Elizabeth executed prodigies of manual labor involving the transportation of buckets of sand under the watchful eye of her nurse, Miss Page. Andy lay in the sun and, eventually, sported in the water; on one of the few days that Alec managed to get out in a boat for any length of time, she watched him land a sizable fish. Jake Ruffing, Jerry Rosenberg, Luke Messenger, and Dan Healy appeared singly and together and conferred with Alec in his study, on the beach, and nearly everywhere else except at the dinner table, where Andy drew the line. Andy learned, by a process very like osmosis, how many votes each of most of the state delegations would have at the convention.

However, a few of the eternal conferences Andy assumed were devoted to politics were in fact devoted to art: as a result of elaborate previous arrangements with a gallery in New York and after long pondering, Senator Girard had narrowed down his selection for his Christmas present to his wife to three paintings. Some of Alec's brooding abstraction proceeded from the necessity of this entirely nonpolitical choice, although Andy laid all of it —the preoccupation, the calls to the telephone, the tête-à-têtes with one or another of his henchmen—to "politics."

The day Alec and Luke Messenger took off in the white convertible without explanation and were gone for most of the afternoon was, in fact, the day of decision. It was also a red-letter day for a local telephone operator: Alec, phoning from a gas station in a flat, sandy stretch of Florida emptiness, livened her daily routine by calling his mother in Vermont, his sister Helene in Colorado, and Andy's mother in Virginia. His final call—to Paris, France —was the first of its kind in the memory of this slow, obscure, nontourist town; the operator's cheeks were pink with excitement as she struggled with the complexities, which included transferring the charges to a number in Washington, D.C., because the caller appeared to have come out without enough money. After a long wait, during which Alec paced beside the garage and kicked at bits of broken shell, a Parisian functionary comprehended Messenger's second-year high-school French, and Monsieur Morisot was plucked from a meeting at the Ministry of Arts.

After he had inquired about Andy's health and Elizabeth's welfare, Paul listened to the problem and then gave artistic advices more succinctly and effectively than he had just been doing among his gathered countrymen. *Andréa*, he said positively, would certainly want the Martigny *"Apès-midi Provençale"* and the rigorous geometry Martigny had managed with the olive trees would be good for her to study, Morisot added sternly. When the conference was over, the Florida operator drank several Cokes purchased by those gathered to listen to one who had listened in to Olympus and was still a little fluttery.

Fortunately for Alec Girard's desire to preserve secrecy, his wife was secluded enough to miss the winging tale. She did not miss, however, his air of having completed something successfully. Unexpectedly, she chose to go with him to see Jake Ruffing off on his return trip to Washington; on the walk back from the car, she seized the time and the solitude to say, and make Alec say, some of what they had been evading.

"Well, I can't help—" He broke off, waving a hand at her helplessly. "Let's not—"

"Yes, please let's. We've been lucky—there are no complications, and by now, I'm perfectly all right again. But there *will* be complications—underneath—if we don't talk about it."

"I know, but— Look, Andy—" He stopped, then plunged onward rapidly, and she was reminded of how he used to stumble asking her for a date. "I feel as though the least I could do would be—" His eyes were agonized. "You put me in an impossible position: you know I can't drop everything now." He stopped abruptly, because it was impossible to say that he didn't want to, and it was certainly impossible to lie.

"Of course not." She said it as sharply as she could manage. "The doctor said campaigning may have had nothing to do with—what happened. And anyway, the important thing is that—that—had no permanent effect."

"You're a very remarkable woman, do you know?" His blue eyes were brilliant, and suddenly there was nothing tentative in his tone any more. "We'll have them both, Andy—the Presidency *and* the baby. What happened in Washington was a setback, that's all."

Andy's wide grin lighted her suntanned face. "I'm glad to hear that. After all, your project could possibly limp along without me—" she waved aside his polite protest "—but mine absolutely requires your cooperation."

"You can count on me," Alec assured her gallantly. Characteristically, the touch of levity released him, making it possible for him to speak soberly of things hard for him to say. Like the admission that he was "a little afraid. You know? There's that feeling—I know it's unreasonable. But, in simplistic terms, I got you into it, didn't I? And then you suffered."

Andy looked at the expanse of lawn instead of at her suffering husband and thought with gratitude that it was difficult to remember pain. "I guess the really bad part of it," she said finally, "was hurting a lot and being afraid, and all for nothing." She studied his black silhouette against the sunlight. "I guess that would be the worst thing in the world," she said, almost impersonally. "A great big pain, with no result."

Alec turned away abruptly and stared out at the gaudy flower beds along the drive. Afraid to reach for his handkerchief lest she see and know he was crying, he raised his hand furtively and knuckled at his cheeks like a small boy. *Beloved, beloved, I promise you it was not for nothing . . .* The knowledge came to him, shaking him as it had not even when he had seen her white and silent in the hospital, that he had been afraid she would die. A brisk, restorative voice in his head swung him back from the edge of that chasm by commenting on the disorder of a state of affairs in which the frailer of a pair of partners took all the risks.

When he turned back to her, his eyes were dry. And so was his observation that he was in a position to sympathize—having himself contemplated, in another context, the possibility of pains that would produce no result. But he held her hand even as they neared the house; most uncharacteristically, he kept on holding her hand even when Dan Healy came out on the terrace and saw them.

In Washington, the department stores, which had been filled with the sound of Christmas carols since Halloween, now filled also with shoppers. Will Farland, predicting against all the poop a move by a hostile government, postponed his Christmas shopping while he executed a series of skillful bureaucratic moves that simultaneously prevented his government from painting itself into a corner and insured that his name would still be attached to the triumphant insight when it had finished climbing State Department rungs from his office to the Secretary's. He bragged shamelessly about this feat to his wife, describing fluently his use of the Department's intricate clerical practices to arrange things so that his memo would be read but could not be claimed by any of the high-ranking unscrupulous. He explained the difficulty of avoiding this fate without falling into an equally undesirable appearance of grandstanding, then closed his account with the sour observation that the original cause of the whole contretemps was the absence of brains in the White House, and that still remained. Marian, who seemed to be listening, was actually watching him instead.

Gil Kimball, who was better at listening, picked the story up from the unofficial information-gathering underground and told it in confidence to the ranking minority member of the Senate Foreign Relations Committee; Senator Youngblood, turning it over in his mind, came to a conclusion similar to Farland's and privately moved a notch nearer to a conviction that Alec Girard was needed in the Presidency. At about that point, Jake Ruffing came back from Florida, selected the Farland item from among the reports of his informal intelligence service, and added it to the week's collection for his boss, who consumed information of all sorts with the unfaltering capacity of an enormous machine.

As a result of these affairs of state, Rosa Little had been pressed into service to help Will Farland arrive at Christmas properly supplied. She was tired, which may have been why she fell into an argument with Bruce

Fisher, a student and friend of her daughter. She was still steaming about the boy's smart-aleck cynicism when Manuel came in. As he washed off at the kitchen sink the white, clownlike evidence of his day's labor at the plastering trade, she grumbled at him about the disrespect of the young. Manuel remarked peaceably that Bruce was a smart boy and he'd be all right when he settled down; when you were young, you always knew it all, he reminded Rosa, watching her bend to get the biscuits out of the oven. Putting the steaming bowl of greens in the center of the table, she asked him fearfully whether there'd been any more talk of layoffs. He said, "Not yet. We got work another month if the weather hold." She called Trixie and Bettina to come eat. Manuel began to eat with gusto, and without waiting.

Paul Morisot, escaped from Paris and the telephone to the silent hills of home, walked around the stone figure in his studio, surveying it from all sides with increasing gloom. He thought of an old joke:

"How do you make a statue of an elephant?"

"Carve away anything that doesn't look like an elephant."

Trying to decide whether he'd already sacrificed too much of the elephant, he washed his hands at the stone sink and studied the beaten landscape outside. The fierce, inescapable wind that was the scourge of his native province would reign for at least three days, thrashing everything that stood upright on the earth; its cruelty was enhanced by the bright sun shining throughout, a false promise of gentleness in the midst of whipping reality. He dried his hands on a stiff white cloth with ragged edges, put on the muffler his housekeeper had knitted for him, and shrugged into the heavy, hooded jacket he had bought at Sears Roebuck in Washington—a climate of winds as bitter as the *mistral,* if less predictable. He flailed his way down the rocky path to his house for lunch and, warming his hands around a bowl of redolent soup, regarded his mail, leaving most of it unopened. A postcard from Florida, featuring a picture of a fat lady wading and a printed comment of surpassing vulgarity, required neither opening nor reading: Elizabeth Girard had explained to Paul, with unassailable logic, that because she had not yet learned to write, she would be compelled to communicate by other means. Thus, the message half of the card was adorned with some energetic scribblings in red crayon that, in fact, quite communicated their affectionate intent. The address was written neatly in Andrea's hand; Paul pictured her holding the card gingerly between thumb and forefinger and probably at arm's length. Meditating on the sacrifices motherhood could inspire, he ate his soup.

On Christmas Day, Alec Girard, basking in his wife's pleasure and surprise, discovered with further surprise that she had been up to some secret negotiations, too. And Elizabeth received many and wondrous Christmas gifts, but the book titled *Our New Baby* was not among them.

II

The Clang of Armor in the Courtyard

"... Bound upon a quest
With horse and arms ..."

Six

The year turned and the people of Washington, cursing snow and comparing catarrhal complications, hardly noticed that in the midst of lowering January spring was beginning to stir. Marian Farland, surveying the wintry back yard through the bathroom window while she brushed her teeth, wondered again why the scarlet cardinal, so brilliantly visible against the snow, alone seemed to lack the advantage of protective coloration. She asked her husband why the cardinal survived, and Will, without knowledge, hazarded a guess that it simply didn't taste good to predators. He went back to his bacon and eggs and Oscar Bainbridge's column, which contained low-keyed predictions for the new session of Congress. Marian, sipping at her coffee, lighted her first cigarette of the day and wondered how the predators knew the cardinal didn't taste good— But Will had clearly done as much for her as he could. It occurred to her as she got ready to leave for work that Sharlie or Dick might know, because schools taught all kinds of interesting things nowadays. She told this cheerfully to Will, who had been dourly warming up the car's motor while he waited for her. His reply was neither precisely intelligible nor precisely cheerful.

In February, though, she learned something from her third child. An excited Peter dragged her out into the back yard one morning to listen to "his" bird: sure enough, high in the bare, smoky-gray branches of the crepe myrtle, a tiny bird was saying distinctly, "Peter-Peter-Peter." Questioned, Peter informed his mother that he'd had it from Rosa that the bird was a titmouse. Marian, shivering her way back into the house, was filled suddenly with a wondrous feeling that the world was very wide and full of discoveries. At lunch with Phil Colby, she took her place in the chain of gossip by passing on the titmouse news.

It was still only February when Bonnie Ruffing, setting down the cocktail tray against her husband's homecoming from a quick trip to New England, glanced out of the great windows of her Virginia living room, high over the still ice-chunked Potomac, and saw that the air was full of redwing blackbirds gathering to roost in the marshes. In the next morning's *Washington Tribune*, a letter from a reader reported the sighting of a robin in East Potomac Park and claimed it as the first; a week later, though, another reader, writing heatedly from suburban Maryland, challenged the claim.

Late in February Ann Taswell drove to an assignment along the George Washington Parkway, which follows the Potomac; she spied a group of grackles feeding and admired their sleek, deep-purple elegance. The photographer with her happened to be an enthusiastic birdwatcher; he told Ann the name of the bird (which she thought unsuitable) and much more than she wanted to know about its feeding and mating habits. What she remembered about the grackle later, though, was the way it looked, so dark in the sunlight, and its slow, stately walk.

Early in March, the dean of the Washington pundits—of whom Andy Girard had once said, "He makes me nervous, as if I just got to class and found I'd left my notebook home"—cleared his throat, tapped the blackboard with the pointer, and explained to America that sober and learned opinion could be found on either side of the question: "Is the Presidential Primary a Useful Adjunct to the Election Process?"

Oscar Bainbridge's prose wound silkily through the fog of the nation's early-morning brains, noting the distinction between the primary, which is a function of membership in a political party, and the election itself, a function of national citizenship. Painstakingly, he proceeded to break the subject down some more by discussing at length the variety of power derived from the primary exercise: for instance, the designation of a state celebrity with no chance to win a national election usually amounted to an instruction to the party's delegates to drive the best bargain they could with one of the major candidates for the nomination when they arrived at the national convention that summer. On the other hand, he pointed out, some states' primaries were binding on the delegates, thus assuring whoever was chosen of that state delegation's votes at the convention. He went on to distinguish between the two types of this type, but by that time most of the readers had skipped to the last paragraph of the column in an attempt to find out how Oscar Bainbridge stood on all these matters.

They lost, as usual. In addition, they also lost the information that the New Hampshire primaries of both major parties were about to take place—which intelligence appeared, surrounded by ponderous verbiage, about two-thirds of the way through the column.

No particular diligence was required of the readers of the *Tribune* two days later, however, when a brief, crisp story by Martin Halloran relayed the news that Alexander Girard of Vermont and Ralph Ferris of Idaho had been selected by voters in the New Hampshire primaries of their respective parties to be their respective parties' nominees for President. Both had been unopposed, and each, touring the state briefly before the voting, had been accompanied by his own wife, some state notables of his own political persuasion, and the wives of the latter. Halloran concluded with the brisk note that despite a fairly heavy snowfall, the vote in both primaries had been substantial; then he went his way and left the readers to go theirs. The story was accompanied by a photograph of a hatless Girard shaking hands with an earmuffed citizen while Mrs. Girard smiled above a bunch of hothouse flowers. A similar pose involving Ferris, Mrs. Ferris, and another local citizen had been rejected by the *Tribune*'s photo editor because the picture was of poor quality and would not reproduce well, and a rather dull standby portrait of Ferris was substituted. Luke Messenger, who earned more money for his services than did his opposite number in the Ferris camp, was apparently worth it.

The next day was one of Gil Kimball's three times a week in the *Tribune*, and he began by explaining that New Hampshire held its presidential primaries before any other state because some foresighted forebear had realized that the citizens were more productive if permitted to get their politicking out of the way when there was nothing more important to do. By March, everyone would have wintered for long enough to have discussed the candidates thoroughly and be quite ready to shovel a way to the polls, visit around a little, and trudge back home until thaw. Although some in Washington saw Senator Tom Cannon's failure to oppose Alec Girard in the New Hampshire primary as a refusal to assume the disadvantages of tangling with the New Englander on what was in effect the latter's home ground, he himself —Kimball said generously—was inclined to think that Tom Cannon, raised in a kindlier clime where it was warm enough to lounge around the courthouse all year round, was simply unaware that New Hampshire's interest in whom the party would run for President leaked away with the melting snows, vanishing under the freshets of sowing and courting that came with the slow spring.

But the rest of the world took note, Kimball pointed out—and some of it drew conclusions. The New Hampshire primaries, like the Connecticut district that was believed to reflect the national presidential vote in microcosm, were part of the mythology of election-watchers. Which was to say that the latter drew conclusions from New Hampshire, but only after they had opened sentences with "Now, I don't really believe in this stuff" or variations thereof, delivered in the tone of voice in which people "explain" why they avoided walking under a ladder.

"I do believe in this stuff," Kimball un-Bainbridgely concluded his column, "I even believe that the heavy vote in both parties' New Hampshire primaries means that everybody's going to come out and vote like crazy this fall. And I believe people will feel as strongly in the rest of the country as they did in New Hampshire, and it'll make for a close horse race in November.

"And if I'm wrong, please everybody at least remember that I got in there and predicted."

On that morning in March, Andrea Girard visited her obstetrician's basement office again and emerged with a prediction of her own. Sitting alone in the back of the taxi while the driver talked on and on about the income tax, she watched the files of budding elms yellowing before her down the long perspective of K Street. When she arrived at home, she stood for a long time looking at the forsythia, covered with bright-yellow blooms like poised butterflies, at the corner of her house. Then she went in and hunted through her store of table linens until she found some delicate lawn place mats with embroidered yellow flowers to send along with Alec's lunch. Before she lay down dutifully for an hour's nap, she asked to have the garden furniture inspected and made ready for possible use that evening.

It was warm enough in the evening: the Girards, leaving the dinner table, took their coffee in their garden. Andy wore her white wool coat over her shoulders, but only to please Alec. He professed himself dazzled by the news of the new pregnancy; but Andy suspected, from the way he began to order her about, that he was a little scared. He was also somewhat abstracted, but obviously intent on assigning priorities to Andy: he asked her at least twice during dinner whether she was tired; and, after their cursory talk in the garden was interrupted once by a telephone call from Jake Ruffing, he returned to her hopeful brown eyes, hesitated, and then ordered that no further messages be relayed.

"You needn't have done that," Andy said, glad that he had.

Alec looked at her briefly, thinking that she seemed so young all of a sudden, and so terribly frail. "I think you're entitled to some relief from the effects of my megalomania."

"Oh, Alec."

He stared into the darkness at the end of the brick walk. "I suppose it must be, you know. This conviction, I mean." He paused, searching for a way to say it. "After all, I cherish the notion that I'm uniquely qualified to lead a nation of millions of people. That's at least mild megalomania, I should think."

"Not if it's correct."

Alec considered this. "Part of it certainly is. We walk the edges of precipices, while the smiling gentleman who's supposed to be in charge plays with his golf clubs and refuses to listen to anything but cheerful news. And everything that's bad gets worse. Not to mention the things that needn't have been bad at all, but shape up now as first-class future headaches . . ." His voice trailed off in disgust. "I know I can do better than that."

Andy refilled his coffee cup and passed it back. "But couldn't you do something short of all this?"

He accepted the cup and set it down without drinking from it. "How? I wanted to do something, so I ran for Congress. Then I discovered that my hands were tied half the time. So I ran for the Senate. In the Senate, I could be—and was—stopped again, whenever anything really important came up. Remember Algeria? All I could do was make a speech." He rubbed his hand over his jaw. "To be able to do any one of a hundred things that need to be done, you have to be where the power is. And the power is in the White House."

"But what about us? What about our real lives?"

He sighed, moved by her distress. "Poor Andy. Was it really such hell in New Hampshire? Because that was the easy part, you know." He hesitated. "Look, I haven't decided finally yet just what primaries we'll go into. But, in any case, I want to make sure you understand this, and it goes for you all the time, pregnant or not: you don't ever have to do what you hate. Unless," he added, his solemnity suddenly vanished into a broad, open grin, "you find you want to."

Andy got up swiftly and came to kneel by his chair, though she knew the gesture made him uncomfortable. "It's just that I—I don't want to seem to be fighting guerrilla actions against a decision you've already made. And I want so much to be what you need, darling. I feel so awfully guilty—about leaving you lonely." In the dim light from the house, her graceful body in its light dress drooped like a symbol of sorrow. "I'm supposed to at least *wish* I could be with you in some of those horrid places."

Alec laughed. "You know, if I wanted the perfect political soulmate, I should've married Jake Ruffing."

But she was intent on self-abnegation and would not be diverted. "I've been terrible and I know it. Carping, complaining. Making problems. But from now on it'll be different, I promise. I do—I really vow. I'll smile and smile. I'll entertain dreary people. I'll do anything, anything you want."

"All right, Andy," he said dryly. "It's not necessary to cast yourself into the Ganges." He stood up, helped her to her feet, and led her back to her own chair. He put her coat back around her slim, square shoulders and set about sweeping out all the drama—with which she was wont, from time to time, to clutter their scene. "Let's look at the logistics," he said. Watching him as he went on to outline "the Campaign-Pregnancy White Paper," Andy thought this was the Alec that Jake Ruffing knew.

"So we adopt the generally conservative posture. Which means simply that if Dr. Williams says you shouldn't travel some week, you don't; if he says it's probably okay but maybe not a good idea, you don't; but if he says he sees nothing against it, you do. Your part of the bargain is, you agree to be with me as much as the pregnancy permits, because I can't stay home with you and win more than—naturally—your eternal devotion. Which, with its one vote, will mean neither the nomination nor the office." He put up a warning hand. "It's true, Andy. You'll simply have to resign yourself to the fact that we live in a democracy." He fixed her with a severe, businesslike look. "And that means," he went on, "that you put up with ladies wearing large flowered hats, with rotund oratory, and, if necessary, with quite inferior food—and all without so much as wrinkling your nose."

"I sound like a rather snobbish concubine. Do I just sit around propped on pillows, delighting your fond heart and trying not to look superior? What an attractive creature you make me out!"

"Why, Andy—are you trying to enlist in the Cause?" His blue eyes twinkled at her in the shafted light. "Are you suggesting, perhaps, that there's a place for the womenfolk in politics?"

"Well, I do have a few ideas. I could write—"

"You could even speak."

All her gaiety came to an abrupt end in a swift picture of a crowd of women, all measuring her waistline. Overcome with dismay, she fell silent.

Alec smiled. "I gather—mostly from the fact that you look as though you'd just been hit in the solar plexus—that you don't feel up to the suffragette bit."

Andy rose and made a stab at gathering the coffee cups before she gave up and flung her arms around him and buried her shamed face in his shoulder. "I'm a no-good . . . Oh, darling, I don't deserve you. I really don't."

Wishing she wouldn't do this sort of thing (and outdoors!), Alec stood patiently in the dark, patting her, and thinking of what Jake had said about the latest polls in Wisconsin.

Wisconsin was a subject Will Farland expatiated on, often and at length, until even Marian understood that Tom Cannon must be the only real winner of the Wisconsin primary. The state was to Senator Dan Daniels as New Hampshire was to Alec Girard—not exactly his home, but close enough: anybody challenging Daniels there was automatically wearing lead boots in a footrace. Tom Cannon, who had some need to demonstrate to the party potentates that he could garner votes in the North, apparently thought Wisconsin no better ground for that demonstration than New Hampshire would have been; so he went about his business in the Senate, held his tongue, and waited for Girard and Daniels to knock each other out of the race for the nomination.

Senator Girard had once eyed this very posture for himself, but he lacked the standing with the party regulars that Cannon enjoyed. Dan Healy, who took the temperature of these "pols" regularly, had reported once again that it was cool: the backroom boys would continue not to notice Girard's virtues until he exhibited the only one they couldn't ignore—a marked ability to draw votes that Daniels couldn't. Daniels, perennially short of funds and aware that he was in a fight for his political life, announced that if he lost in Wisconsin he would withdraw from the race. Tom Cannon smiled quietly and settled down to watch the other two battle for the votes that probably wouldn't have been for him anyway.

And Alec Girard went on slogging through the leftover snow and the ice just beginning to thaw, tramping streets of towns whose residents were no warmer than the weather, talking sometimes to no more than one voter at a time—and when the voters thought him not worth coming out for, to their children instead. A man of frailer ego would have crawled away to eat worms, and even a relative optimist might have regarded this as the hard way to the White House. But Alec, tall and windblown and lonely, turned his capacious memory on what he saw of this alien life, its strange industries, its great empty lands, its wintry despairs, and stored it all away for use later on.

Meanwhile, his organization was being tried out, too—in high gear for the first time, the knocks in the engine and the bolts that rattle when theory is set rolling on an actual road were being detected and repaired. Daniels went about the state saying to the people, "I am one of you and I understand you"; the unspoken corollary, in his mind and theirs, was "Vote for me because you like me." Because they did like the eminently likable Daniels (as even Alec did), they turned stony faces on the outlander Girard, who knocked at their doors to say matter-of-factly that he was asking for their votes because he needed them in order to run for President of the United States.

His wife flew out to join him in the districts where Jake Ruffing had established Girard headquarters staffed by Alec's friends, who contributed talents no amount of money could have paid for. But it was without Andy that Alec walked through the frozen mud and talked to farmers. When it was over, he told Dan Healy he was certain that he could march up to any farmhouse in Wisconsin without even setting the dogs barking.

And, when it was over, it was not over: Alec listened to the returns in a hotel room whose major decorative motif was any sort of cigarette-scarred surface atop aluminum-tubing legs. He drank deeply from the exaggerated highball Bill Bruyette handed him and told his henchmen, " 'When thou hast done,/Thou has not done,/For I have more.' "

"Alec, for God's sake. This is no time to play quotations," Bruyette said irritably, and then added unreasonably, "except maybe Kipling, and that isn't Kipling."

"What's more to the point, it's irreverent," Rosenberg said primly, before he added, for Bruyette's edification, "John Donne."

"All right, you get an 'A.' But what the hell does it mean? After all, we've won the damned primary and—"

"And known April in Wisconsin," Messenger finished.

"It means," Alec Girard said, "May in West Virginia. And Maryland, too, but mostly West Virginia. And Indiana and Oregon, each delightful primary in its time, until we're delivered by the convention."

He was right, of course, though it took nearly everyone else a little longer to see that Dan Daniels, having been beaten but not by enough and not by as much as was expected, would change his mind and go into the wide-open West Virginia primary. Where Alec Girard, who had won in Wisconsin but not by nearly enough to be lofty about a Daniels success in West Virginia, would of course have to follow him.

One of those who saw it promptly was Will Farland, who called Gil Kimball and invited him to lunch. They drank martinis and ate steaks in the backroom of Eddie Lane's bistro on Pennsylvania Avenue. Will announced that it was all on him, in view of the columnist's bereavement.

"I tried to keep anybody from knowing I cared," Gil mourned.

"Oh, I don't think people will know. Not unless they put together the fact that (a) while the Wisconsin primary was going on, you were writing funny pieces about tourists in Washington, and (b) you went to the University of Wisconsin, where you learned to love Dan Daniels even before the rest of the liberals did."

"I love Alec Girard, too," Gil said. "We've been friends for years."

"I know. It must've been tough. But it's even tougher now, isn't it?" Will looked at Gil's stubbornly expressionless face and added impatiently, "Oh, come off it. You know you can't go along with what Daniels is doing now."

"What's he doing besides trying to run for President?"

"Cutting Girard's throat, and you can't make me believe it's innocent. Daniels hasn't got a chance: he never had much, and now that he's been beaten on his home ground he hasn't got any. What politician in his right mind would support a nominee who can't deliver his own region? Even as a compromise, Daniels would be unacceptable. And you can't tell me he doesn't know it."

"Maybe he just wants to give his supporters a run for their money," Gil said weakly.

Farland eyed him with sympathy. "Okay, but you know how you'd have to vote if you lived in West Virginia, and I know it must hurt. Pass the steak sauce," he added briskly. "Life must go on."

It was going on not too far away, where his wife was eating a superior lunch at Andy Girard's Georgetown house. By an effort, Marian had remembered on her arrival to congratulate Andy on Alec's Wisconsin victory. That out of the way, they had settled down to enjoy each other's company and exchange nonpolitical recollections of Miss Kingman's School for young ladies-to-be, which both had attended. Although Marian, who was a couple of years older, had been gone by the time Andy came, Miss Kingman's faculty tended to endure, so the two alumnae had memories to share nevertheless. Andy's accurate, if unkind, imitation of Miss Berle of Phys Ed reminded Marian of getting excused from gym, which in turn reminded her of her own household's great event. So the major topic at today's meeting became the fact—and, more important, Marian's feelings about the fact—that Charlotte Grayson, Marian's only daughter and firstborn child, had begun to menstruate. And that Will Farland, informed of this by his wife, had somehow imagined the remark, "Well, I guess it's time to start saving up for the wedding," to be adequate for the occasion.

Andy sighed and said softly that men were just different, that's all, and led Marian, who had to get back to her office, out the back way so she could have some flowers to take with her.

"I feel so shoved aside," Marian said morosely, watching Andy snip jonquils. "I had her all psychologically prepared, you know. But I forgot to prepare myself. For being replaced, I mean." She accepted the flowers with only absent thanks and added that she'd better get going before the *Tribune* replaced her, too.

When Marian had gone, Andy lingered in her garden, in the scent and sight of growing, and did a little dreaming about her own daughter Elizabeth, who was still not yet three years old.

Seven

On any early May day in Washington, hundreds, thousands of flowering trees all over the city—in official places, in everyone's yard, in open land waiting for the bulldozer—can be in bloom at once, and the very air, even in the downtown section where nothing is visibly in bloom except store windows, is heavy with sweetness. The cherry blossoms along the Tidal Basin, sacred to out-of-town visitors, may have gone to leaf, but out in the suburbs somebody's cherry tree is still bridally festooned (though edged with green) right next to somebody else's dogwood.

In the Farlands' Cleveland Park neighborhood, which tourists sometimes stumbled into on their way to the Washington Cathedral, everything seemed to burst into bloom overnight: the planned-for jonquils and tulips, the inherited lilacs, and the Topsy-like honeysuckle—illicit, weedy, triumphant anywhere that it hasn't actually been routed, drowning the senses with its sturdy sweetness. If, like Marian Farland, you went to work at about nine o'clock in the morning—passing, on your way out, the window on the landing that looked right into the upper branches of the great beech tree's new leaves, the only positive green among the tentative yellow-greens of other new growth—you could hardly keep your feet on the ground on the way to the bus stop.

Delight waited also in her office, after she had good-morninged her way through the ordered hustle of the city room. The note on her desk was from the paper's chief photographer, a small gray man born with an artist's eye and an engineer's knowledge of a camera. "Marian—" said the scrawl in black greasy writing on the cheap, thumbprint-smudged proof paper—"They pitched this out downstairs. Want it?"

Oh yes, she thought gratefully, lifting the covering paper and catching her breath in something close to ecstasy. "It" was the proof of a color print for Sunday's paper, rejected because the colors had "bled" at the edges of and occasionally in the midst of a photograph of orangey azaleas and white and yellow jonquils on tall green stems. It was, Marian thought, respectful and sober in the face of so much wonder, a portrait of a first try at creation—as it would be if God were not God but a working mortal, a department chief, losing a little and gaining a little, needing to try to perfect. "Let's try it again," God the patient editor might have said to one of his conscientious flower-angels. The pencil would indicate the blurred edge of a petal, its orange yellowing off into the white of the margin. "Could we get these petals a little better defined, perhaps? And here—" the pencil moving to a smudge of jonquil stem "—these yellow flowers, whatever you're going to call them. Wouldn't it be better if they had straight, slim stalks to hold this cup-thing up? Something that looks as though it's designed for the purpose." Then, recalling that it was necessary to motivate one's underlings:

"It's a fine start, and I know it'll look beautiful. Now if you'd just like to have a try at clearing that green up . . . A little less fuzzy, perhaps . . ."

They had done it, Marian knew—she had passed the growing results this morning and they were quite without fuzziness, each stem clear and green and functional, each petal neatly defined. And it *was* beautiful. But so was this portrait of on-the-way, of unfinished creation. She taped it carefully to the glass wall of her office and, wrapped in a feeling of something like holiness, reached for her mail.

The small white envelope, postmarked somewhere indistinguishable in West Virginia, was addressed to Mrs. Willard Farland at the house in Cleveland Park; but Marian had added it to her office mail because it needed a daytime reply. She held the envelope down on the desk with her elbow and extracted the note with her other hand, propping it open with the edge of the phone as she dialed. Andrea Girard's handwriting, like Marian's, showed the influence of Miss Kingman's School. Waiting, she thought of their last lunch among the cheerful yellows of Andy's small upstairs sitting room.

"This is Mrs. Farland," she told the quiet voice that answered. "Is Mrs. Girard at home?"

"Mrs. Girard is resting. May I take a message for her, Mrs. Farland?"

"Oh, certainly," Marian answered, a little surprised because she'd never for a moment thought Andy *was* home. "I only called to say that I'd be delighted to come for lunch on Wednesday."

"Thank you, Mrs. Farland. Mrs. Girard will be expecting you on Wednesday, then."

Marian hung up, smiling a little: she'd wondered, a couple of weeks ago, whether Andy could be pregnant. If today, the day of the West Virginia primary, Andy was at home and resting in the middle of the morning, it certainly looked like it. Marian turned over the pages of her calendar and wrote "A. G." next to the lunchtime slot on Wednesday, thinking of it with pleasure. It had been better since Andy—as though Marian had been alone among aliens and then had found a compatriot. Curious as it might seem, the house on O Street at lunch was about the surest place in Washington to get away from politics. Nobody would believe me, she told herself, if I said I liked to lunch with the wife of a presidential possibility so I didn't have to talk politics.

The phone rang sharply under her hand, and she jumped a little and picked it up.

"I had your daughter on this line, Marian," said Pearl, the *Tribune*'s motherly chief operator. "But she seems—"

"Hello?" Sharlie's voice came in, loud and very young. "Mother?"

"There she is again," Pearl said with relief, and cut off.

Marian said, smiling, "What is it, Sharlie?"

"Oh, Mother." Her daughter sighed as though she had been climbing

Mount Everest to reach this triumph. "Just a minute. I'm talking to my *mother*," she went on, with no excuse or change in her voice.

"Sharlie. Please try to conduct only one conversation at a time. What did you want?"

"Oh. Well, I'm sorry to bother you at your office—" She waited for this nicety to be suitably acknowledged.

Marian lifted her free hand and felt her clenched jaw. Bad for your teeth, she told herself. "You know it's quite all right. Now tell me—what is it?"

"I'll get right to the point, Mom," her daughter promised. "I know you're busy." She waited for acknowledgment of this consideration, too.

Marian began to laugh helplessly. "If you don't tell me—*instantly*—what you want permission for, I warn you that the answer will be no, whatever it is."

"Don't blow your top, Mom," Sharlie advised, in some alarm. "It's just, can I go downtown straight from school this afternoon? I haven't got much homework and I can get most of it done in study hall."

"I guess so. What for, and with whom?"

"Well," the voice breathed confidentially, "Vicky has to pick up her new sweater at Herman's."

"And?" Marian asked, with a suspicion born of experience.

"And they're having a keen sale on skirts, Mom." Marian drew breath to speak and Sharlie heard the small sound and rushed on to forestall comment. "Mom, you practically *promised* me that I could have a green this spring, and here it is May already."

"I said I'd take you downtown on Saturday."

"But, Mother—by Saturday, they'll all be *gone*. The sale is *today*. By Saturday we'll have to spend *dollars* more for the very same *thing*."

It won't be the same thing, Marian thought weakly, it'll be something a good deal wiser if I'm along.

"Mom? Please, can't I go today?" Sharlie waited briefly for an answer, and then added primly, "I'm only trying to be *thrifty*."

Marian had an instant vision of her daughter's expression and repressed a giggle. "*One* skirt," Marian said, smiling. "And Happy May."

"I can go," Sharlie reported, apparently to the waiting Vicky. "What, Mom?"

"Nothing. Be careful crossing streets. It's a beautiful day."

"You know, Mom," Sharlie said impersonally, "sometimes I think you're kooky. Thanks a million. Love and hugs and kisses." A series of little popping noises exploded against Marian's ear. "Vicky says thank you, too. Vicky says you're neat. Gotta go now, Mom—the bell's already rung." The phone crashed violently.

"Happy May," Marian said to nobody in particular and turned again to her mail. Then she pushed it aside and went out to the back hall, where the editorial writers' cubicles were, to borrow a look out of a window.

"The whole day went that way," Marian told Will, as they drove to the Harringtons' party. She threw onto the back seat of the car the manila *Tribune* interoffice envelope that contained her daytime white blouse, for which she'd substituted the royal-blue and black print top that transformed her black faille skirt into a short evening dress. "Roses, roses all the way." She inspected her pretty legs, turning her feet in the new black kid shoes that hardly hurt at all, then reached over and straightened Will's tie. His collar looked a little wilted, and she patted its points out of sight under the jacket of his gray suit. "And now politics," she said disgustedly. "The end of a perfect day. Why couldn't we watch the returns from West Virginia on our *own* television set?"

The light changed, and Will didn't answer. They drove the short distance in silence, and he maneuvered their car skillfully into the one possible parking place left in the Harringtons' turnaround. Marian kissed Will's cheek as they went up to the front door. He smiled and opened the door. Nobody ever rang at the Harringtons'.

That was all I said against it, Marian thought bitterly, standing in the Harringtons' kitchen some hours later and remembering her final remark on the way here. Nobody could say she hadn't arrived in good spirits. She opened the waist-high oven, checked the little frankfurters rolled in dough on their rack inside, and decided they weren't quite brown enough yet. She leaned her elbow on the counter—just like a short-order joint's, only elegant and expensive—and, resting her chin on her palm, peered out gloomily into the smoky vastnesses of the great room. This was no kitchen, she thought contemptuously, and this was really no house; it was all a big party machine. Try as she might, she had never been able to envision the Harringtons doing anything but giving a party.

She took a big swig from the dark-brown drink waiting at her elbow on the counter and then turned to look into the oven again. They were done this time, and she turned the oven off and found a tray, filed neatly in a row of trays at the top of the cupboard. Eleanor Harrington, in black-velvet pants and a cloth-of-gold blouse and a million bracelets, appeared at the passthrough just as Marian set the loaded tray on it.

"You're a doll," her hostess said. "I would've let them burn to death."

You would have, too, Marian thought, smiling emptily at Eleanor, who was quite clearly quite drunk. She took up her glass and wiggled past Eleanor's bracelets into the semidarkness lighted only by a few bullet-shaped spotlights and the weird blue emanations of the huge television set. The latter appeared at the moment to be showing only strings of numbers, but a voice spoke around and above them, and it went on and on, no matter how much the numbers changed. The whole mess looked, Marian thought wearily, like a scene from the *Inferno,* full of darkness, noise, and writhing figures.

John Harrington, standing by the fireplace, suddenly reached up and swiveled one of the bullet lamps around so that the spot of light impaled a couple entangled at the end of the low black sofa. The woman wore a skin-tight dress of something that looked like hammered silver, and her breasts, thrusting out sharply against the man's white shirt front as she half-sat, half-lay on his lap, echoed the outline of the cone-shaped lamp that spotlighted her now. She shrieked and brushed at the man's arm. Marian saw, feeling slightly sick, that most of the white cuff of his shirt sleeve—and presumably the hand under it—was out of sight under the silver skirt. Not the *Inferno*, she thought—nothing so grand. Instead, an illustration for a magazine printed on cheap paper and read avidly, with a guiding finger under the one-syllable words and much recourse to the pictures, by drooling morons. The laughter rose around her, loud and feverish, and she took another great swallow of her drink and looked away. Not posed by professional models, though, she told herself: the real thing, the inside story. The man was the junior senator from a great state, and the woman was Helen McElroy, whose husband had a lot of career to lose if Alec Girard won the West Virginia primary.

Which looked likely, Marian noticed, watching the television screen briefly as it registered a rising figure for Girard and a much lower one for Daniels. "Oh, poor Dan, poor, poor Dan," a woman's voice said nearby, and she looked up and saw the redheaded bachelor girl Jill—a fixture at Harrington parties, certainly, and a good many others besides—weeping bitterly on John Harrington's shoulder.

Harrington patted her ineffectually. "She gets emotional," he said to Marian, who eyed him coldly and didn't reply. Jill's emotionalism, which was usually expressed in terms of plastering herself against the nearest man as soon as she'd consumed two drinks, was neither a matter of surprise nor of interest. Not even in view of the rumor that Jill was Harrington's mistress—which, since she was also apparently Eleanor Harrington's confidante and right hand, created an interesting, if slightly nauseating, picture of the Harringtons' domestic life.

"We worked so damned bloody hard," Jill announced blearily. She disentangled herself from Harrington's grasp and wandered unevenly past Marian, lurching just enough to spill a little of her drink. The carrot-red hair looked unbelievably innocent above the puffed face, smeared with tears and mascara.

"Looks like Girard's bought himself a primary," John Harrington told Marian.

"Really? How?"

John Harrington smiled knowledgeably. "Money will do it every time."

"How?" Marian asked again.

"Yes sir. Poor Danny didn't have a chance, up against all those millions. Girard can buy the state of West Virginia three times over."

"So could Boss Crump in Tennessee," Marian pointed out. "And I happen to know that Kefauver was so broke he was borrowing from friends during that campaign. But he won."

"Well, Girard can buy the nomination, but he can't buy the election,"

Harrington announced. Marian might never have spoken. He swallowed the last of his drink, patted her familiarly on her shoulder, and asked, "Get you a refill, honey?"

"No, thanks." She looked at him in disgust, but he was unconscious of it. She turned away then, scanning the room for Will, and finally saw him in silhouette near the television set. He was deep in conversation with Rob McElroy, and he was wearing—Marian noted with amusement that he seemed entirely unaware of it—the limpetlike Jill against his left arm.

"Good evening, Rob," Marian told McElroy politely when she had navigated the crowded room. "It seems to be looking bad for your team. I'm sorry."

The bulky, untidy McElroy looked like descriptions of Heywood Broun. He mopped at his face with a crumpled handkerchief, but otherwise he seemed unconcerned. "Well, you can't win 'em all," he said.

No, Marian thought sympathetically, but you don't have to have your wife making a fool of you the same evening you're taking a professional beating. She smiled at him and then turned to Jill. "Beat it," she said to the redhead, who was making sobbing noises into Will's coat sleeve. Jill didn't move, and Marian reached out and whacked her, not gently, on her green satin behind. "I said, scram!"

"You would've lost Hamden County in any case," Will said to McElroy. "Daniels never had a prayer there, did he?"

Jill wobbled away from Will's shoulder and turned her streaked face to Marian's. "You don't have to get nasty," she said, sniffling.

"I won't if I don't have to," Marian told her expressionlessly. "Get lost."

"I was only—"

"Just get lost." Marian thought about saying, *Go find somebody else's husband,* but she decided against it on the grounds that Jill didn't need instruction.

Apparently subliminally aware of a movement in his neighborhood, Will reached around with his right hand and felt of his left coat sleeve. "Well, then," he asked McElroy, "you couldn't count on any of the northwestern precincts, could you? So what were you counting on in that corner?"

"God, I guess," McElroy said gloomily. "The trouble is, Girard wasn't. Christ, do you realize the talent he brought in for this little preliminary?"

"You take it too seriously," Jill complained, backing away from Marian's threatening look.

"I take it seriously," Marian told her, and stood there, implacable, until Jill finally vanished.

"The swivel point, the pivot point." Rob McElroy was chanting it, swaying above the words like a high priest of some esoteric religion. "The point of insufficient returns."

"Looks like it," Will said. His voice was matter-of-fact, but it held sympathy. "I'm afraid Daniels has had it, all right. But if it's any consolation," he added, smiling, "I think Tom Cannon may have had it, too. He shouldn't have been afraid of the water."

"These were dark and dirty waters. My God, you don't *know* how dirty."

"West Virginia political waters have never been known for their purity," Will answered.

Marian plucked at his coat sleeve. "John Harrington says Girard bought West Virginia."

"Does he now?" McElroy winked at Will. "And I was just starting to think up some 'Let-us-join-together-to-heal-all-wounds' speeches. But maybe I'm jumping the gun. Maybe we go on beating Girard with his daddy's moneybags for a while yet." He gazed into his glass as though it were a crystal ball. "Of course, I don't know where we'd get the money from. Who the hell's going to give Daniels a dime now, even to float scurrilous charges with?"

Marian watched him with sick fascination. "Did he?" she asked McElroy. "Did Girard—"

"Oh hell," McElroy exploded. "Look. A lot of the time, Girard rode when Daniels had to walk. Sometimes Dan had to choose between alternatives when Alec could afford to try them both." He shook his head. "Or you can get even fancier. Like listing the number of glamorous, intelligent, high-powered types who came flying down to help out old prep-school chum Alec. The boys who went to Hayseed High with Dan Daniels are back home managing supermarkets."

"I don't understand him," Marian told Will. "I don't know what he's telling me."

McElroy smiled. "I'm telling you, love, that it's better to be rich than poor."

Her eyes widened. "Then—what John said. *Did* Alec Girard buy—"

Will broke in quickly. "That's not the way you answer Harrington, baby. Time to cut the crap, Robbie," he said to the other man. "The fun's over, and you know it."

"Well, how do I answer?" Marian asked.

"With a question, darling. You just go back and ask Mr. Harrington two questions, as a matter of fact. First, would Tom Cannon be likely to maintain a polite silence about it if Girard was really doing something he could be nailed for? And, second, ask Mr. Harrington how much he figures Girard paid Kenneth Youngblood for his backing."

"But that's ridiculous. Everybody knows Senator Youngblood wouldn't—"

"Exactly," said McElroy. He nodded at Will. "That's the kind of thing that did it. Of course."

"And Girard couldn't buy it." Will's bony finger waggled, pointing across the bluish shaft of light from the ignored television set.

"No." McElroy smiled sourly. "It was a present to Alec from Danny. Who I think must've been temporarily insane."

"Is Senator Youngblood popular in West Virginia?" Marian asked. "I mean, I know everybody admires him but I didn't think the people in West Virginia would vote for somebody just because he said to."

Both men laughed, but Will recovered first and explained to her briefly that Youngblood's influence, while difficult to define, was substantial. "Once the old boy tagged Daniels' campaign as a Stop-Girard movement and announced that he wouldn't have any part of it, Daniels was all by himself on a dungheap. The fact that he was short of money had very little to do with his troubles from there on." Will threw McElroy a challenging look. "Even if Daniels' old buddies hadn't been tied to their grindstones, could any of them have matched a single speech by any one of the experienced silver tongues Youngblood's announcement sent winging down there to help Girard?"

"Point, game, and set," McElroy acknowledged. "I might as well get real noble and admit that Bill Bruyette's silver tongue, which began wagging on Girard's behalf twenty years ago, did Danny plenty of harm." He gulped the last of his drink. "And, before I fall on my sword, I'll even give you this: Jerry Rosenberg writes better speeches than I do, and I don't think money would make him write them for Daniels."

Will's look was suddenly interested. "Would money make you write for Girard if—" He broke off to free his arm from whatever was dragging on it and discovered the drag to be his wife.

"Please, Will. Can't we go home? I'm tired."

Farland's face altered comically. *"Now?"*

"I guess not." Marian sighed. "Never mind. I guess it's still early."

Will looked simultaneously relieved and guilty. "We'll go soon, baby. I just want to hear some returns from the strictly rural counties, so I can get an idea—" He stopped, inspired by a burst of music from behind them. "Look, why don't you go dance? I'll be along in a few minutes."

Marian found her way to the bar and fixed herself another dark-brown drink, with fumbling help from John Harrington. She listened to the beat of the dance music and studied his heavy face. She had once asked Will what exactly John Harrington did for a living. "Harrington?" Will had said, laughing a little. "He doesn't do. He knows."

"Is he some kind of scholar?" Marian had been understandably surprised.

Will had laughed out loud at that one. "He doesn't know facts, my little innocent, he knows people." He'd thought for a moment and then added grimly, "I take that back. I bet he knows quite a few juicy little facts."

"You mean he's one of those five-percenters?"

"He gets a hell of a lot more than five percent," Will had assured her. And that was the end of her briefing on the career of John Harrington. So I still know nothing about you, she thought, watching him now, except that you're not quite kosher.

"Yes sir," Harrington assured her solemnly, "there's nothing like a few million bucks if you want to pick up delegates."

"Oh? How does that work?"

"Easiest thing in the world, my girl," Harrington said largely. He swayed; then, returning to his bartending, he managed to pour from a bottle into a glass by balancing one against the other, feeling them with his fingers as a blind man might. "You just buy yourself the election."

"How?"

"Easiest thing in the world," Harrington replied, and Marian turned away quickly because, drunk or not, he was her host and it wouldn't do to laugh in his face. She wandered over to the big window and looked out at the lovely flower-laden yard, the small fountain splashing on the patio. *Who are you? Who wants to know? I do. And who are you? Who wants to know? I do. And who are you* . . . In self-defense, she stopped. "I think it all ends with 'I'm Jack Armstrong, the All-American Boy,' " she told the white shirt front that loomed at her eye level.

Senator Warren took her drink out of her hand. "Wrong name, right description," he announced. "I have come into your life to dance with you."

"I don't think—" Marian began, and then she listened to the music. It was an old song, and a lovely one.

"If you reject me, I'll put a bullet through my brain," the handsome young Senator told her. He held the pose, looking quite like a handsome young Senator on the verge of putting a bullet through his brain, Marian thought uncritically.

" 'One magic moment and the world tum-tum-ting new,' " Marian sang into his ear as he swung her onto the polished floor. He held her tightly and she floated in his embrace, smiling. The dark-brown drinks bubbled in her light feet in the new shoes, doing at last what they were meant for. John Harrington appeared above her as she was twirled expertly; he was dancing with the silver-clad Helen McElroy, and Marian winked boldly at him while his face ballooned and vanished. The music curled to a close with much corny sawing of violins.

Senator Warren crooned, " 'When love walked in—with you,' " and bent Marian into an elaborate dip. She laughed up at him mindlessly, and then her body stiffened as she felt his hand traveling from her waist down her flank and her leg, sleek in the tight black skirt. His hand came up again, slowly, as he brought her upright and she stood still, speechless with rage at the alien touch on her thigh. I wish I wore a girdle, she thought futilely—and then, when this incantation failed to drive the demon away, she looked frantically for Will. Because she couldn't, she simply couldn't slap a United States senator, and certainly not in the middle of this damned gossip bazaar. She twisted violently in his grasp, and the exploring hand stopped; the Senator looked at her in mild surprise. Marian wrenched herself loose, paused—absurdly—to say a hasty "Excuse me," and fled.

"I want to go home," she told Will, speaking slowly and distinctly, as if she were addressing a foreigner. She ignored, rudely, the stranger to whom Will had been talking when she accosted them. "Now," she demanded.

"The memsahib commands," Will told the other man dryly.

She waited, silent, frozen, unsmiling, while Will found her coat and helped her into it. She thought of searching for the Harringtons to deliver the thanks courtesy demanded; but then she knew that if she stayed here for one more minute, she would either scream or vomit, so she plunged for the door without a word. Will darted after her and reached it just in time to open it for her, but she didn't stop running until she had slammed the car door on the world.

"Well." Will had waited until he'd worked the car out of the jumble at the Harringtons' and got it up the hill and onto the street. "Am I to be told what *that* bizarre behavior was all about?"

"Mine was the least bizarre behavior of the evening."

His lips tightened. "I'm not accustomed to being ordered around by women, especially in front of people I hardly know. I felt like a damn Caspar Milquetoast."

"I'm not 'women.' I'm your wife." She felt the tears coming and swallowed them back. "And I'd like it if you could remember it." She tried to swallow again, but there was no way to stop the tears this time. She laid her cheek against the back of the car seat and bawled.

"Are you going to tell me what this is all about?" Will asked. "Outside of the fact that you seem to be both drunk and hysterical."

"If I'm drunk," she shrieked at him, "*if* I'm drunk, I'm not drunk enough to stand for being felt up by any damn fool who wants to try it. I've got a right to be hysterical."

Will took in her flushed face and the crumpled misery of her pose, and deliberated briefly about whether to stop and try to quiet her now or make a run for home. Noting that her sobs were slowing down, he decided to try to make it home.

"Don't talk like that," he commanded. "That kind of language isn't natural to you, and it sounds ridiculous."

"Well, that kind of—stuff—is not natural to me either, and it felt more than ridiculous. It felt—filthy."

His hands tightened on the steering wheel. "Who was it?" he asked softly.

"Senator Warren." She stared ahead of her, only sniffling a little. "The worst part is," she said quietly now, "it never seemed to occur to him that I would *mind*. He was smiling. Innocently." She crumpled and began to cry again. "I've told you and told you—I can't stand those people."

"Look. I owe you an apology. You certainly had a right to be protected from that kind of insult. I should've watched out for you. I failed you and I'm sorry."

"Let's never go there any more," Marian begged him. "They're horrid people. I know they're all terribly important, but they shouldn't be—they're just pigs."

"They're not all pigs. You know Rob McElroy's not a pig."

"Please. I don't care who is or who isn't, as long as we never have to go there again."

"Dammit!" Will burst out angrily. "Can't you ever manage to do anything but run away when you don't like something?"

"But you said—"

"Yes, I said I owed you an apology, and I do. And I admit there are undesirable things about the Harringtons and their parties. But is the only answer, always, to run away? There are some things about their parties that I enjoy. There are even some things about Steve Warren that I enjoy—though if I ever see him within six feet of you again I'll break his jaw." He stopped abruptly, then consciously lowered his voice. "But I've known John Harrington for almost twenty years. And we've had some good times there, too."

"Not me," Marian said bitterly.

Will turned the car into their driveway. "Of course you have," he reminded her. "You've just forgotten because you're tired and angry." And drunk, probably, he thought, watching her critically as he helped her out into the sweet-smelling dark. "Try to remember it's not all one way or the other."

This advice, not likely to gladden Marian at any time, all but maddened her now. "You're mixed up in your wives," she snapped. "It must've been Kitty who had such a ball with your filthy old friends."

He was stung. "Well, she was a hell of a lot more sensible than you're being."

"Is that so?"

Will paused in the midst of unlocking the front door and burst out laughing.

"Something is funny?" she asked him nastily.

He pulled her into the house and dragged her with him, holding her hand, as he went back to hush the dogs. "Shut up down there!" he roared at the basement door; there was a final yelp from below, and then silence. In the darkness of the kitchen, he turned and hugged Marian apologetically. "I'm sorry I laughed. It's just that it wasn't up to your usual wit."

She jerked away and fled ahead of him through the dark dining room and into the hall. "I'm simply not witty. Like the sainted Kitty. Witty Kitty."

"Marian," he warned, wondering how she could suddenly look so ugly.

"Well, I'll tell you something, Junior, if it's wit you want." She swayed, grabbed at the banister, and flung out her arm in an operatic gesture. " 'That was in another country, and besides, the wench is dead,' " she quoted dramatically. She bowed, making a diva's exit.

Will let her go—chiefly to avoid the temptation to hit her—and leaned against the hall table while he watched her make her uncertain way upstairs. Absently, he fingered his jaw as though it had taken a punch. She doesn't fight fair, he thought.

But as he locked up and went slowly up the stairs he remembered that she never had. The woman was a fanatic: she had none of whatever people have that lets them learn the need for compromise. He cursed, but mildly, the gay blade Steve Warren—who damn well knew better than to lay a hand on Farland's wife. The Senator had apparently got himself taken drunk, enough to decide to help himself to a pretty woman. But it was a bad mistake, especially in Washington, not to pause and look at her label. In this case, Senator Warren would find it right costly . . . Will heard something small hit the floor in the bedroom and ran up the rest of the steps.

A flying button from her blouse nearly caught him as he opened the door. Her skirt lay in a crumpled heap about her feet and she was wrenching at the blouse and sobbing bitterly. He approached with caution, trying to make out what she was saying.

"Here. I'll help you," he said soothingly.

"Off, off. I want it all off." She yanked at her slip. "Dirty." She wept. "Dirty."

Will got her blouse off, pulled down her slip straps, and went to work with fumbling fingers at the catch of the brassiere, swearing softly to himself and ducking her flailing arms as she tore at the rest of her clothing. He managed it at last and worked the bra off her and slid his hands around her breasts from behind. But she raised her arms to her hair, nearly hitting him in the eye with her elbow, and, shrugging him off, began to pull out her hairpins. "I want a shower," she announced with abrupt clarity. She handed him the collection of hairpins like a tip to a doorman and stalked out in wildly incongruous dignity. Will stood there, undecided—first, about whether to laugh and then about whether to worry; finally, he concluded that she was all right. He discovered the hairpins still in his hand and went to deposit them tidily in the milk-glass dish on the mantel. He touched the fluted edge of this object that she prized so, for reasons he had never quite understood, and then he smiled and began to undress, thinking about how little understanding had to do with it anyway. Just for instance, how could a naked two-bit Fury with eyes like water on fire look so damn beautiful?

In the bathroom, Marian surveyed the shower, counseled herself against trying it, and compromised by washing her hands and face and splashing water from the sink all over her body (and the floor). She watched fuzzily in the mirror as a rivulet ran down her shoulder onto her breast, and she giggled with the good feeling. Then she made a face and opened the medicine cabinet and took out the little round box. All you have to do is tell him you don't want to, she said to herself reasonably. "But then we won't be able to get back," a voice surely too sober to be hers said aloud. She washed again when she was through, scattering more water, and dripped the rest on the way back down the hall to the bedroom.

Will was lying on his own side of the bed, with the sheet over him and the blanket crumpled at the bottom. His eyes were closed, and his face in the lamplight looked white and tired. Just above the sheet, the light caught

the curling golden hairs on his chest. Marian saw it, closed the door carefully behind her, and said "Will?" with curious formality.

"Yes, darling?" He didn't open his eyes, and his tone was tentative.

She came over to the bed and sank on her knees beside it and bent to
kiss the hollow of his throat. He opened his eyes then and smiled with the
relief of the rescued. He reached for the switch of the lamp, but Marian
said, "No," and his hand stopped in midair when she pulled the sheet away.
His body was long and lean, straight and very tense. But he waited quietly—
because it didn't matter who started or how, as long as they were going
to be healed.

Marian held the erect penis between her palms and then began to stroke
its amazingly soft skin. He reached down and took her hands away and
moved over to make room on the bed beside him. She slid in; but then she
climbed over him to the other side so that she could still see his body in
the lamplight. She began to travel it slowly, her touch like a passing breeze
moving past the "V" of curling hair to the flat belly, skirting the round darkness of the navel. Her eyes calm, she trailed her lips along the white skin
on the inside of his arm, and then she turned his arm around and examined
the darker, hairy other side; she smiled as if at a marvelous discovery, before she put it down and resumed her journey. Will groaned softly when
her touch grew perilous again, but he didn't drive her away; he closed his
eyes, and his empty hands curled at his sides. She slid down in the bed and,
holding the penis in her hands, rolled it along the side of her neck and then
folded it between her breasts. When she bent her head and kissed it, he
grabbed at her hair and tugged without strength. She looked up and studied
the combat in his thin face with the bones almost pushing through the skin;
his body was as taut as a violin string—if you plucked it, it would surely
twang.

"Darling." His voice threatened to crack. "You'd better—" But she didn't
let him finish, and she didn't obey: she didn't stop, and she didn't stop when
he tried again. Not until he gasped and brushed her away convulsively,
rolling over toward her with outthrust seeking hands, like a blind man lost.
She gathered him close and he said "Marian" into the valley between her
breasts and then suckled like a little animal. She tightened her arms, hugging him fiercely: as though some danger threatened him, she strove to
encompass his broad shoulders with her frail arms, somehow to wrap all
his long body with her little one.

He wanted so much to be safe: he raised his head and found her mouth
and his tongue probed, seeking, while his quick fingers hunted in the folded
places of her body for all the tiniest keys. And then, with his hands full of
keys, he said "Marian" in a voice hoarse with fear and pleading, and she
knew how to help him. She used her arms and her legs to enfold him; she
held him with all her strength and whispered to him to come *in,* oh please
come *in*—urging on him surely the best course, the safest safety he could find,
all, all her shelter . . . He gasped and took her completely, violently, at her

word. Her body rose almost in self-defense, and then clung as if held by a heartbeat, shaken with its rhythm, mindlessly straining. And then she fell through rainbows under rainbows and wasn't afraid to fall.

Until she lay still at last, with the nerve-jumping quieting all through her body and Will's breathing against her shoulder. She was watching colored circles like Christmas-tree ornaments floating lazily downward through the air when she felt him stirring. She clutched at him frantically, because he mustn't spoil it: they would all crash and break.

"All right, baby, all right." He kissed her breast. He kissed her throat. He kissed the tip of her ear.

"Don't go away."

"I'll never go away." He kissed her bruised lips and her eyebrow and her temple. They lay on their sides, enfolded into and wrapped around each other. "Marian."

"What," she said unwillingly, wanting only to breathe instead.

"I love you." He let the words lie, warm with his breath, against her skin before he added, "I'm—I wasn't any hero. But I love you with all my heart."

"Hush, Willie." She wriggled a little until she could be tucked into the fold of his body, to lie against his shoulder. "I love you, too."

After only a minute, she could feel that he was asleep, and she smiled into the dark. Somehow we made it, she said in her mind; we got home again. His heartbeat was a message of drums in a jungle of loneliness. She fell asleep listening to the news of comfort.

When she woke in the morning, the first thing she knew was the loss in her body. She stirred unhappily and Will's arms came around her at once. "You went away," she said.

He smoothed her hair. "I know. You cried when I did, did you know it?"

"No. You said you wouldn't."

"I won't," he said. "Not really. I never will."

"Promise?" she asked in a sleepy child's voice.

"I promise. Oh God, Marian." His arms tightened around her until the corded muscles hurt her. She pushed at them, but they were like iron hoops.

"You're hurting me," she said petulantly.

"I'm sorry." But he didn't stop. His knee parted her thighs, roughly, hurting a little more. She raised her hand and patted his rough cheek, and she went on saying "Tu-tu-tu-tu" until he was gentled enough to turn from desperation to making love.

Eight

In July, the month of broad, open leaves and tight, closed houses in Washington, Andy Girard realized that she had passed, without much time spent thinking about it, the time when she would have had the lost baby. Some of her success in this may have been because she was thinking, hard and long, about many other things, and they were important.

For Andy and little Elizabeth were house guests of Andy's parents, and they would remain until the convention decided whatever it would decide and the little Girard family was reunited, however briefly, at the cottage in Vermont. Here Elizabeth daily delighted her grandmother, and Andy, wearing old slacks open at the side and voluminous shirts not tucked into her pants, inspected, discussed, and worried about horses with her father.

Andrew and Elizabeth Langwith were probably as far removed from politics as anyone could get and still be a citizen. Their friends and acquaintances included, and always had, Supreme Court justices and American ambassadors, but never anyone who had actually run for any office; the talk at their dinner table was, and always had been, broad, general, and intelligent, but when it became specific, it dealt with local affairs. The avoidance of everyday speculations about the affairs of the nation was not accidental.

For if Elizabeth Langwith had the general aloofness of the very rich and secure, she had also what might have been seen, in less protective circumstances, to be almost a phobia about being noticed by the world. She hid among her rolling acres and her ordered days, a devout worshiper of respectable calm who could be driven into a migraine headache by the mere threat of mention in a newspaper. Once a year she was compelled by *noblesse oblige* to appear at the county fair to smile and award prizes. The resultant notice in the local newspaper was kept from her by her family and servants, who watched over her anxiously until she left her room, after a few days' illness, and was seen about the estate again, poised, sure, kindly, and gentle. Andrea's dislike of publicity, which was certainly heartfelt and extensive, was to her mother's horror of it as the second-generation revolutionary's devotion to dogma is to his father's raw and always-revivable memory of the oppressor's jail.

Parlor psychiatry is a futile thing at best, but certainly there must have been some connection between Elizabeth Langwith's fears and her parentage; she was the daughter of her mother, and, as with the least of us, it left its mark on her. Natalie Delacroix had been a famous French beauty when she was snatched from the gayest, most influential and talked-about circles of Paris by the then United States Ambassador to France, Richmond Carter. Carter, an umpteenth-generation Virginian, heir to all the wealth and unquestioning sense of privilege that slavery and the plantation economy had awarded to a few, brought his spoiled, lovely, and vital bride back to the United States and attempted to settle with her into the life of a country gentleman. His appointment as Ambassador had been a political gesture, undertaken by the President because of the Carter wealth and influence, accepted by Carter because a man must do something and France might be fun. He had been an uninspired, unknowledgeable diplomat in an undemanding time, and no harm had been done by it all—but now he was finished with nonsense and prepared to take up his real life.

As might have been expected, however, transplanting Natalie into the peaceful world of undercover injustice and surface benevolence was about as satisfactory as sticking an orchid into a bed of zinnias. Her hat was like all the other ladies' hats at the meetings of the local ladies' organizations, but under it Natalie's brilliant brown eyes blazed with the love of political combat; in no time at all, factions had sprung up where unanimity had always been the comfortable order of the day, and the beautiful young Mrs. Carter was right in the middle, manipulating away with skill and gusto. Everything about her was hopelessly lively and different: acceding politely to the advice of her husband's sisters in the choice of suitable costumes, she had a way, when they had drunk their tea and gone home with a sense of Christian satisfaction, of digging up from somewhere a bright orange silk scarf or a curling feather that effectively, and beautifully, put her clothes on the map. Her wide, friendly mouth opened to say whatever came into her head, and it was invariably sensible, pungent, and newsworthy. In a day when ladies retired into their homes during their pregnancies, appearing at church (if they were not too unwell) in something dully black with a white Peter Pan collar, Natalie Carter turned up at a tea in her eighth month, wearing a bright-red polka-dotted maternity dress ordered from a protesting little seamstress who had wrung her hands in distress with every stitch. And no hat, but a gauzy, brilliant scarf over her thick, glossy, dark, and scandalously short hair. And her white gloves—would you believe it?— left behind on her dressing table where her maid, discovering them, stood in tears over the disgrace.

The slowest, most unpromising cub reporter who ever covered a fire for the *Centerburg Gazette and Weekly* would have known Natalie Carter instantly for a wondrously fertile source of comment; and when Mrs. Carter produced, in rapid succession, a string of three little girls who could be photographed in white dresses and blue hair ribbons along with their fatally dramatic, inevitably chic, and apparently forever photogenic mother, there was no holding back the flood of publicity. "The beautiful Carter girls" became such a common term in newspaper stories that the reader tended to absorb it in one gulp; it might as well have been represented by a symbol. Richmond Carter, who had long ago given up the hopeless fight, paled into insignificance. He became a presence, the tall figure in the background, the black-and-white, almost anonymous gentleman in white tie and tails helping the breathtaking Natalie out of a limousine in the three-column cut on the first page of the society section. Nobody ever found out whether he minded: he would not have answered if asked, but nobody ever asked him.

He had one ally, though—his eldest daughter Elizabeth, who watched in love and anguish as her father disappeared before her eyes. Elizabeth's rebellion against her mother was cool, calm, and complete. Lively, outgoing little Natalie, who couldn't bear not talking about anything, ran into a wall of polite and dutiful silence from a glossy-haired stranger who had her father's height and quiet eyes. Natalie, at first amused and then despairing, finally spread her quick, expressive hands, remarked to her husband that the girl was simply a changeling, and turned her attention to one of the hundred thousand other matters that interested her. Elizabeth went her quiet way from small, unknown finishing school to small, exclusive women's college; she found, after a while, that she could avoid the press by (a) being colorless enough to be un-newsworthy and (b) not going anywhere.

She couldn't, of course, avoid her debut—to have done so would have distressed her father too much—but a photograph of Elizabeth Carter on that sentimental occasion shows her chiseled face thin-lipped and stony and her hands clasped stiffly about her bouquet as though her muscles ached to hurl it at the photographer. The way she ducked and hid, it's possible she might never have met anyone to marry despite Natalie Carter's determination and guile. Young men were produced, sent away in confusion, and succeeded by other young men who came no closer to breaching the wall. But eventually Natalie—probably aided by biology and a soft summer night— hit a home run.

Andrew Langwith was the eldest son of an impeccable New England family of Welsh and Scottish ancestry. He had a tall, athletic body, fine dark eyes, and a well-begun and secure living for the future as a stockbroker. Somewhere in his stiff carriage and his slow, cautious speech lay a history of lifelong pressure to return the gifts of wealth and privilege with measurable success. He had made it, but it had left its mark on him; under their smooth, proper behavior and careful understatements, Andrew Langwith and Elizabeth Carter had an ache in common. Their wedding was, of course, the society event of that year, and it had everything—though, naturally, what every newspaper reader remembers best about it is the haunting photograph of Natalie Carter in a huge organdy hat with a rippled brim, her lips curved in a tremulous smile and her great eyes filled with happy tears. In the background of the photograph, the dim figure of the father of the bride can be discerned. If you look very closely at the picture of the bride and groom as they depart, though, you may see that the new Mrs. Langwith is clutching her husband's hand so hard that her knuckles show round and white.

Andrew Langwith understood his new wife and required nothing of her that would give her pain. Their luxurious Fifth Avenue apartment in New York, from which he issued every morning on his way to Wall Street, remained as much a secret as skill and money could make it. The announcement of the birth of their first child, Andrea Carter Langwith, was four lines long in the *New York Herald Tribune*. The little girl was not photographed for public delectation until her first visit to the ancestral home in Virginia, where her large dark eyes and happy grin noticeably echoed those of the still beautiful Natalie, seen in exquisitely fashioned dress and diamond earrings, holding the child on her lap. "A NEW PRINCESS," the *Washington Herald* caption writer burbled. "Mrs. Richmond Carter, Washington's beloved

'Princess Nat,' with her first grandchild, Andrea Carter Langwith, daughter of the eldest of the beautiful Carter sisters . . ." Andrew made every attempt to keep the photograph from his wife, but she may have seen it anyway; she retired to her bed with "la grippe" and remained there for the rest of the Langwiths' stay in Virginia. After that, Andrea visited at her grandparents' regularly, because her father insisted on it and her mother's sense of duty was strong; but Elizabeth Langwith's poor health usually kept her in New York.

Six years went by before the eldest of the beautiful Carter sisters produced her second and final child. Richmond Carter Langwith was only a few months old when his grandfather Carter, who had seen his namesake only once, died of a heart attack one morning while going over a few arrangements with his head stableboy. The widow was invisible, for once, behind heavy veiling at the funeral, but her graceful, grief-stricken figure at the graveside made an effective picture anyway. Interviewed a few weeks later, she seemed, for the first time, surprised by publicity. "He was a dear man," she was quoted on the *Washington Tribune*'s women's page, "but he paid no attention to the world, so why does it pay attention to him?" This naïve query appeared under the photograph of the widow, looking subdued in a black frock of exquisitely artful cut and a string of priceless pearls—but with her hands, now a little plump, caught in a gesture of surprise. Natalie was, as always, Natalie.

And she remained good copy until her death, ten years later, when her granddaughter Andrea was a student at Miss Kingman's School in New York. "Princess Nat" died grandly and effectively, after a just long enough interval for her descendants to assemble. Her last words, as she lay in the great bed among embroidered sheets of a silky percale that had never been mauled by a washing machine, were, "I hope it will be fun." She said them to her companion, a Mlle. Claudel, and an attendant doctor and nurse; she spoke in French, however, and Mlle. Claudel, deeming the sentiment unworthy of the respectably dying, did not translate it for the others. Andrea and her brother Richie, who had for some years referred to the old lady in private as "the Czarina," and who adored her for just the imperious ways and incessant demand for devotion that had inspired the name, grieved deeply and painfully. So, as a matter of fact, did their mother, who would have felt free to love Princess Nat wholly if she herself had only been someone else's daughter.

The great, rich acres in Virginia made a far better hiding place than even the anonymity of New York, so the Langwiths changed their residence fairly soon after the funeral. Andrew made a trip to New York for a few days each week for a while, and then he retired permanently, except for a few directorships that required his presence in New York or Philadelphia on special occasions during the year. Andrea made her formal Washington debut from her new home, and another under the auspices of her aunt— the second beautiful Carter sister—in New York. She was, at the time, a student at Smith College, majoring in art history. The coverage of her debut was extensive, and the photographs made it instantly clear that this youngster, beautiful as any of the Carter girls and tall and slim as her grandfather Carter, had fully inherited the photogenic glamour of the late Princess Nat.

But not Princess Nat's wholehearted enjoyment of it, and certainly not that old beauty's light view of marriage. Andrea Langwith Girard brought to contemplation of her marriage a student's earnestness, lit only occasionally by a shrug inherited from her grandmother. The late Mrs. Richmond Carter wouldn't have cared if her husband had disappeared from her ken between the times that she had any particular need of him; but Mrs. Alexander Girard cared hugely and wrestled often with a fear that she cared excessively.

Some vague guilt about this licked at the edges of Andrea's thoughts on this July afternoon when, parted from her husband by choice and circumstance, she knelt on the windowseat in her father's study, waiting for Alec's evening phone call. Outside the French windows, the land and its creatures were bedding down for the night—flowers closed, the sky darkened, birds twittered busily. Once, Elizabeth ran quickly across the hilly picture, a fleeting thing of pumping legs like all the other hurrying creatures. Andrea smiled at the sight and slid to a sitting position, her legs curled up under her like a child's and her nose against the glass. She patted the little bulge at her waist without fear: though the doctor had warned that the danger period was not yet entirely past, she knew this one would be all right. Four months, she thought, and wondered whether she had imagined a tiny flutter.

Alec Girard was in Philadelphia, where his political party was in process of choosing its candidate for President of the United States. But Philadelphia was entirely irrelevant; his hotel-suite headquarters, a smoky inferno wherein scurrying figures eddied incessantly amid the endless alarms of telephones, could have been in Los Angeles, Chicago, or Peoria. There was a window that nobody had time to look out of, and there were streets between the hotel and the vast convention hall that were seen only as measures of travel time. The convention was the skinny figure of Jake Ruffing, growing steadily more wraithlike and more hoarse; it was television cameras and their snaking, trailing wires; it was the microphone thrust in Alec's face as he walked, simultaneously smiling and avoiding; it was being tired when he would like to rest, being dirty when he would like a bath, having to talk when he needed to think, daring to move when he would give a lot to be able to wait, and daring to wait when his nerves cried out for a move— any move at all. It was, first and foremost and at last exclusively, an endless arithmetic mounting always toward the magic number 761, the total of delegate votes required for nomination.

Alec Girard had come to the convention with victory in seven primaries behind him and a certain number of votes safely in his pocket—like Vermont's, whose red-faced, excited delegates were rapidly destroying the myth of the laconic, unemotional New Englander. The rest remained to be bargained for, persuaded, pressured, and—at the last and if luck was with him —bandwagoned into his column. Going for him was a large, smooth, efficient organization. Against him was what remained of the opposition that had been there at the start, minus whatever quantity had been won over by his primary victories and plus whatever alienation those victories had inspired. This last factor tended to be mutable: it would disappear, for the most part, after the convention, when it would be transferred to the other party's nominee. But, until then, it could not be unloaded early.

"Even more than the campaign for the office of President itself," Gil Kimball wrote in his Philadelphia-datelined column that week, "the campaign for the nomination is a test of the man's ability to operate under the strains and stresses of the office. For there is only one way to campaign for the Presidency: to win. But the choices in campaigning for the nomination —especially in the case of Senator Girard, who, if nominated and elected, would be the youngest President in American history—are multiple and, I suspect, painful. There are tempting offers to accept the second spot, and others involving guarantees for next time around. There is the question of whether to go for broke on the first ballot or seek a bargaining position on succeeding ballots. These once-in-a-lifetime decisions, rich with the possibilities of later regret, must be made in haste, often without adequate data, and in the fierce light of publicity; at the same time, uneasy alliances must be bolstered, volunteer egos sustained, and an immense machinery kept oiled. Yet all this must be achieved without sewing oneself up or boxing oneself in, so as to leave room for whatever tactical maneuvers may prove necessary—even up to and including 180-degree reversals of stated positions. The whole operation is rather like dancing on a tightrope, directing an amateur performance of *Macbeth*, and playing three-dimensional chess— all at the same time. Which is a little more than will be asked of the man who finally gets to live in the White House."

Alec Girard, gulping the opening of this column in his characteristic lightning glance, smiled and remarked to Jake Ruffing over his morning coffee that Gil was a sharp observer. Then he went on to the passage Jake had marked: "On the basis of their performance in Philadelphia this week, I conclude that both Alec Girard, the leading contender, and his closest rival, Tom Cannon, have demonstrated the fantastic skills I've outlined above. Unless the Blackwell adherents succeed in their efforts to stampede the convention, which seems highly unlikely despite emotional displays on the convention floor that accomplish little except to brighten the drama for the television viewers, the candidate chosen here in Philadelphia is almost certain to be one of the two men observably equipped for the job—if anybody is. Which is not to say that there is nothing to choose between the two, but that whatever choice is made is likely to be a good one, helpful to the party in terms of victory and to the country in terms of the future of us all."

"Nice to have friends," Jake commented. "He doesn't give you a thing over Cannon."

Alec rose from the table and shrugged into his coat. "Well, let's go out and demonstrate that we *have* something more than Cannon." He waited, already impatient during the two seconds it took Jake to push his chair back from the table. "Let's dance a little faster on that tightrope."

"Good morning, Senator," his secretary said rapidly as soon as he appeared in the doorway. Alec answered but didn't slow his progress through the crowded room, whose every surface was heaped with piles of campaign literature. She went on talking to his retreating back. "And one more thing —should I try the Speaker again now?"

"Later." He spied Bob Kneeland, one of his assistants. " 'Morning, Bob. What's Delaware doing?"

"Caucusing."

Alec frowned. "Let me know as soon as you've got word."

"I have the rough copy of your acceptance speech, Senator," his secretary interrupted, offering the sheaf of typed pages.

"Thank you." Girard shoved it into his inside coat pocket. "What's for now?"

"Illinois in the coffee shop," Jake Ruffing said. "Let's go."

Returning to his headquarters from a half-hour with the man who could probably deliver most of the Illinois delegation's votes, Alec said, "Later," to a group of television correspondents stranded amid their equipment outside the door of the suite, and ducked inside. "Get me Mrs. Girard, please," he told his secretary.

Waiting in the bedroom of the suite, with the telephone to his ear, he made his long body comfortable on one of the rumpled beds and reflected without bitterness that his calls to Andy might very well be the only times that he was alone. "Mrs. Girard, please," his secretary told a Langwith servant, her voice clacking metallically in his ear. Alec leaned back and lighted a cigar, holding down the pack of matches with his elbow while he struck one. "Senator Girard is calling."

Alec, looking down, discovered that he had planted his elbow smack in the middle of his own smiling face on the matchbook, and grinned. Then Andy's quick, breathless "Alec?" broadened his smile again.

"Hello, darling. How're my womenfolk?"

"Lovely. I haven't seen Elizabeth all morning. She's out doing something terribly important with Daddy."

"And the other progeny?"

Andy laughed. "He's quiet, but obviously eating. I've been ravenous for a week." She hesitated, then asked uncertainly, "Is there anything— I mean, you don't usually call this early—"

"Just a wandering impulse, I guess. Or convention nerves." He grimaced. "If it's the latter, it'll be cured by tonight, anyway." He blew out cigar smoke, watched it hover, and said in a different voice, "It's all right, isn't it? If I change my telephone schedule, I mean?"

"Idiot." The laughter went out of her voice after a moment, and a dutiful note crept in. "Alec? How is it going?"

"Delaware is caucusing. Illinois is resting easy, I think." Leaning back against the padded headboard of the bed, he discovered that the edge of it was hitting him in the shoulder blades; he shifted uncomfortably, but failed to improve matters much. "Tell me what you're doing."

But Andy had become nervous during the small silence. "I read Gil's column this morning," she rushed on without hearing. "Are you really doing all those difficult things?"

"Probably. Gil's accurate, you know. But he has a little too much imagination. It's not nearly as anguishing as he makes out."

"Alec?"

"Yes?"

She hesitated. "Don't you— I mean, you sound as if— Don't you want to talk about it?"

He examined the question and the ash on his cigar. "No, I don't, really," he said in some surprise. "I'd rather talk about what you're doing."

"Well." Her voice was bright, but Alec smiled, knowing she was going to do some thinking about this later.

"Are Carol and her husband still there?" he asked.

"They left last night." Having Carol around had, oddly, done little or nothing to decrease Andy's loneliness. Examining her feelings as she saw the Donnellys off, she had noted with surprise that she was in no way affected.

"Why so soon?"

Andy giggled. "Well, you may find this hard to believe, but Henry has to go to a convention."

"Good Lord. Not this one, I hope."

"It seems that neurosurgeons have conventions, too." Andy thought it over and added, "Maybe it's all doctors, or all head doctors. I forget just how it's classified. Anyway, he has one coming up in New York soon, and he has to finish something before it opens. But they both reminded me, darling—they wanted to be sure we understood that the offer of their house as a refuge still stands."

Alec closed his eyes and thought with some longing of the Donnellys' large house in a Philadelphia suburb of green lawns and a tradition of quiet. "It's good of them. But they haven't any idea what a shambles comes in my wake."

"Yes, they have," Andy insisted, alarmed by the weariness in his voice. "And they mean it. Alec, you're to take them up on it. You *must* need to get away from that bedlam. When is the last time you had a decent meal?"

Girard laughed. "About five minutes ago. It was the second breakfast. And I have two lunches and two dinners coming up." He listened to what he had said and added, "Maybe literally."

"Ugh. Well, you don't seem to be lacking in quantity of food, anyway."

"The quality isn't up to your standards. But please stop thinking of me as underfed, at least."

"I suppose it's useless to mention rest and other creature comforts," Andy said tentatively. "Oh well, I'll repair the damage when the convention is over."

"Yes, darling," he said with sudden warmth. "I know you will." He looked at his watch and sat upright on the bed, swinging his long legs over the side. "Take care of Junior."

"Of course." Her voice was soft and resigned.

He hesitated, hating to leave her so sad. "You're still sure it *is* Junior?"

Andy laughed, and Alec's face brightened at the sound. He stood up while she spoke, ready to be on his way. "I'm sure," she said. "Thank you for calling, darling."

"It was a distinct pleasure," he told her gravely. "I'll call you right after the roll call tonight. Hug Elizabeth. Regards to your mother and dad. Okay?"

Andy sat very still when she had hung up the phone, looking out at the flower-laden, fulfilled countryside beyond the windows of her father's study. The trouble with love, at least when it worked both ways, was that it led to the benevolent lie: was he helping her to cover up an inadequacy by saying he didn't want to talk to her about the details of the Philadelphia whirl? Or was something wonderfully lucky shaping up—a niche for her, a task she would be happy and satisfied to fill? To be the place where Alec could get away from it all was what she really wanted most, she told herself honestly. Could it actually be that he wanted it, too?

She pondered the question, shifting restlessly now in her father's leather armchair, her pretty face pale and attentive as she struggled for understanding. At last, a decision came—or, at any rate, a knowledge of what would be needed to make a decision. She straightened up and reached for the phone. As she dialed Dr. Williams' number in Washington, her eyes were calm in a quiet, determined face.

Andy broke the news toward the end of lunch, which resulted in nonconsumption of dessert, at least by Elizabeth Langwith. "But to go to the convention hall tonight. All those people—" Her hands shook a little as she laid her crumpled napkin beside her plate. "It can't be advisable."

"The point is," Andy said firmly, "it's not inadvisable." Laughter lurked in her look. "If you understood politics, Mother, you'd know that that's quite enough for tremendous decisions." She pushed back her chair and stood up. "I'd like to finish some of the telephoning before Elizabeth wakes from her nap. Excuse me, please?"

Jake Ruffing's protesting voice finally wound to a stop. "That's quite all right, Jake," Andy said finally into the phone. "There's really no need for me to speak to Alec now at all. If you'll just have someone take care of the arrangements—" She waited patiently, not listening to most of his reply. "That's very kind of you, but there's no need to worry. It's all been worked out at this end." She waited again, thinking about the dress she was planning to wear. "Yes, Luke, hello. It's D-O-N-N-E-L-L-Y. But—that's not for the press, is it? I'd hate to cause the Donnellys any— Oh yes, I see. I'm sure you *will* try." She made her voice warm and truly apologetic. "I do most awfully regret burdening you and Jake, and I know you'll do your best to make the whole thing as un-messy as possible." She listened to Messenger's assurances, which sounded quite genuine now, that it would be a pleasure to have her aboard, and then she hung up. Her lips were curved in a smile as she left the study. She walked lightly, and she had to keep herself from running up the stairs as she went to speak to her daughter.

Her happiness faltered only briefly as, on the plane, she remembered in sudden terror the small backache on the plane from Chicago that had heralded the destruction of last December. But she didn't *have* a backache, she told herself practically, and this baby was farther along. She shook off the small fear: it was right, it felt right—and she wouldn't let that get lost in the fact that it was also new and frightening.

If Carol Donnelly had known all along that under Andrea Girard's softness and beauty lay a steely will, Henry Donnelly had a chance to learn it that evening. Without much hope of being obeyed, considering the tension she must have felt as the roll call on the convention floor began, he ordered Andy to keep her feet up. "I don't know whether she knows it," he had said to his wife as they rushed out to meet their last-minute guest, "but I couldn't do a thing for her if—anything happened. Except stop her from bleeding to death. Maybe," he concluded gloomily.

"Alabama, twenty-nine votes," said the rolling voice from the television set on the Donnellys' screened porch—and Andy, to Henry's surprise, stretched out on the flowered chaise with her feet up. As nearly all the Alabama votes were announced for Tom Cannon, her eyes traveled to Alec's immobile figure, hunched in attentive shadow against the bluish light of the set. Carol tugged at her husband's hand and drew him indoors, so that the Girards could be left alone with the decision. Neither Alec nor Andy saw them go.

"How can he be so calm?" Carol asked her husband as they paused uncertainly in the gloom of their own dining room. From the porch, Alaska could be heard giving its nine votes to Girard.

"Well, he's done everything he can," Henry said reasonably. "Now he's either got it or he hasn't."

"But it can go on over and over again, can't it?"

Henry took her hand and led her toward the stairs. "Listen, let's watch upstairs—I don't want to miss it. No, I think Alec's got it set up so he gets it on the first roll call or the whole thing looks rather dim."

"How do you know?"

"I don't really know anything. Except what I read in the papers. But it's his best strategy. Cannon is too close behind him for Alec to fool around if he has any choice."

As more than half of California's eighty-one votes went to Blackwell, Andy moved her head toward the figure of her husband, but her body remained in obedient repose on the chaise. Alec saw the small motion out of the corner of his eye, though, and said tightly, "It's okay. Three more than we thought." A tangle of swift thoughts flashed through his mind, strangely mingled: pity for her ignorance, which would cause her to suffer over the loss of votes that had been unobtainable from the beginning; annoyance at the necessity to reassure her; and respect for her silence and control. But these reactions came and went very quickly—he had no time at all now. His whole body was tensed toward the television set, his mind was empty and waiting.

"*Idaho, thirteen votes,*" the roll call proceeded. Alec looked down at the paper in his hand and added scribbled numbers swiftly. "Girard and Cannon are neck and neck at this point, a quarter of the way through the roll call," said the smooth voice of the television commentator.

Alec stood up and came over. "We're a handful of votes ahead of what we figured," he said tersely. He went back to his post without waiting for a reply.

The gentleman from Illinois with whom Senator Girard had shared a second breakfast that morning delivered nearly all his delegation's sixty-nine votes. That *must* be good, Andy thought, if Alec was still concerned about the state this morning. But she felt helpless—logic was little good to her. The votes of some big delegations weren't cause for rejoicing, presumably because they'd already been counted on. Yet when Delaware had cast its eleven votes for Cannon, she'd glimpsed disappointment in Alec's guarded look.

Missouri's thirty-nine votes went to a favorite son, as did Minnesota's thirty-one and Mississippi's twenty-three, leaving the score much as it had been after Michigan had delivered the majority of its votes for Alec. "Girard is ahead by a substantial margin," the commentator said excitedly. "He may be within sight of a majority on this ballot." Over his pictured head, numbers shot into place on a board like lemons rolling on a slot machine.

"*North Dakota, eleven votes.*" As the leader of the delegation cast his small group's votes for Alec, the camera picked up a wildly swinging sign that read enthusiastically, if inaccurately, "Vote Gerard."

Ohio dropped its total of sixty-four votes into Alec's column, and Andy Girard became aware, at last, of a certain painful problem in her hand. Uncurling it to look, she saw that her engagement ring had turned slightly and been forced against her little finger, leaving a red mark, when she had unconsciously clenched her fist. She spread her fingers and righted the ring, wrenching her mind away from the memory of the mark on Betty Kimball's hand, that awful day in the winter. Andy took a deep breath of the summer air, weighted with the sweetness of honeysuckle, and was reminded that much was changed.

"Pennsylvania, eighty-one votes." They went for Alec Girard, and during the subsequent roar from the television set, Andy saw him busy again over his little piece of paper. After a moment, he raised his head. "It looks possible," he said clearly. Over his right ear, the Speaker of the House of Representatives, looking irritated, pounded a gavel while tiny Pennsylvania figures danced in the aisle. The camera moved then to other states, still waiting their turn.

"Isn't that Jake?" Andy asked.

Alec looked up attentively. The camera, moving past a still-uncalled delegation, blurred the man standing next to the chairman. Then, as though the television people had noticed the resemblance, too, the camera went back and picked up the man again. It was indeed Jake Ruffing, and he was grinning broadly.

Alec Girard put his pencil down, tucked his little piece of paper in his shirt pocket, and said to his wife, with surprising gaiety, "It could be. It could very well be."

"Girard has seven hundred and fifty votes, with seven sixty-one needed for nomination," the commentator shouted. Looking at her husband, coming toward her now with easy assurance, Andy was still trying to decide whether he meant that he had it on the first ballot when the roar threatened to tear the television set apart, and he had, he had. Alexander Wardwell Girard was his party's candidate for the office of President of the United States, and the Speaker wasn't even attempting to maintain order for the moment.

Andy and Alec were still smiling at each other wordlessly when the Donnellys burst onto the porch, and Alec kept on smiling at Andy over Carol's shoulder while she was kissing his cheek. Then Carol flew to Andy's side and the two women embraced. Alec accepted the glass Henry Donnelly was offering him, and Henry carried the tray over to the ladies. Standing beside the chaise—on which Andy had, at last, dared to sit up—he raised his glass and offered a toast to "the next President of the United States": it was the very first thing, Andy thought, that made these four people gathered here not just the Girards visiting the Donnellys, any time. They drank, and then Carol, glancing briefly at her husband, hurled her glass at the brick half-wall of the porch. Henry followed suit with his, and Andy and Alec, grinning at each other, emulated their host and hostess. As was only customary, on any quiet evening in suburbia.

In the sudden silence after the shattering of the glasses, the wail of a siren was heard outside. "I think—" Alec said tentatively.

It was beginning; the last ordinariness was over. Andy stood up to face it, but fear licked at her thoughts; the shards of glass glinted in the corners like tears as Alec walked forward to meet his escort.

The siren faded, and Andy went upstairs with Carol to get ready for her appearance at the convention hall. She looked calm and lovely, but her hands were very cold in the warm July night.

In the corridors behind the scenes at the convention hall, young Mrs. Girard, chic in a pale blue suit (which would look white on television) with a loose jacket that encompassed her pregnant state without making an elaborate point of it, had to stifle an impulse to cling to the cool cement-block walls. If there were this many people in the back corridors, she thought in horror as two Girard aides ushered her carefully through the crowds and eddies—even down here among overhead pipes and outside the doors of the furnace rooms—what could it be like when she finally met Alec again? She felt desperately alone among the wildly excited people around her, all of whom looked a little afraid of her.

And they looked exhausted, too, she noted, as Jake Ruffing appeared before her and reached for her hand. His own hand felt hot and bony. He turned, pulling her after him through a doorway, and light slanted across his face; Andy decided he looked like a concentration-camp survivor and forgot her fear in her pity. The loudspeaker in the hall boomed suddenly and indistinguishably and she jumped. Someone beside her put a hand on her arm to steady her; she shrank, shamefaced but helpless, from the touch. *I wish the baby would move,* she thought in pure panic. And then she was on the platform, pinned among the merciless lights.

Flowers appeared in her arms, and a pulse of terror beat in her throat. She looked for Alec and found the lined face of the Speaker above her and shook her head to show him that she couldn't hear what he was saying. Then she saw Alec: he looked transfigured, his arms outspread—as if he were being crucified, Andy thought, stumbling forward fearfully. Alec turned and reached for her, clasping her elbow and bringing her to his side at the front of the platform.

Noise, unbelievable noise, broke over her then like a tidal wave, and she held herself very still in it, trying to believe that she would not drown. The Speaker's wife, a matronly woman in a dowdy straw hat, leaned around and said something, but Andy simply shook her head at the kindly face. It was not possible to hear, and it was not possible, she thought— nerving herself, at last, to look straight out over the scene—even to see anything you could really believe in. The blurred pastels of thousands of summer dresses ran through the picture like spilled, melted ice cream. Red streamers seemed to split the air like heat lightning above the surging and roiling in the aisles. Everyone in the world was in motion at once, but no one was really going anywhere. Hopelessly frightened, Andy clung to Alec's hand, though he was as strange, as much an alien, as all the rest. Unbelievably, in the midst of the din, he was conducting a calm and apparently even humorous conversation—several times he ducked his head and grinned as though in acknowledgment of a joke—with the Speaker. Who had wanted Tom Cannon to be nominated, Andy remembered, wondering whether it always felt so lonely when your mind snapped.

"The crowd has gone wild," an excited but conversational and controlled voice said near her feet, and she nearly jumped. She could feel the vibrations through the soles of her dark-blue summer pumps. "Senator Girard has just presented his beautiful young wife to the convention, and it set the cheering off again." She looked over the edge and saw the man, wearing a headset like a little boy's wintertime earmuffs.

"The Speaker is still gaveling for order," the television man told his audience, and Andy realized that the loud thumping to which she had not quite been listening was not, after all, her heart. "Senator Girard's full-dress acceptance speech is scheduled for tomorrow, but he'll probably make a brief announcement now as soon as the Speaker gets the crowd quieted . . ." Andy, watching the television commentator over the edge of the bunting, saw that a fluff of white confetti on a stick lay where it had been tossed, its white tendrils snaking over his shoes. The man was in his shirt sleeves, and his shirt was dark with sweat at the middle of his back.

Alec looked down at her a little apologetically but without saying anything, and let go her hand. She clutched at her flowers, wondering whether they were visibly trembling in her grasp, and watched Alec raise his arms for silence. Amazingly, the crowd began to hush, but it took a long time for all the swirling colors out there to settle into visible, recognizable groups of people, and the groups were still not stable. Andy looked down at her bouquet and saw, finally, that it was red roses. She would have liked to smell them but she was afraid of how it might look to the television viewers, so she stood as still as she could manage, hoping it would somehow look still to the viewers. Could they see that edge of fern flickering with her trembling?

Then Alec said, "Mr. Speaker," and Andy put a bright, attentive look on her face as the crowd, suddenly quiet, listened to the strong boyish voice of the man beside her. Cautiously, she drew in a long, deep breath, and the muscles in her legs lost their aching tension; relief filled her body like seawater running into a hole on the beach.

Deep within her, the baby moved quickly—a swift, blind flicker of confident motion—and Andy Girard smiled so radiantly at the Speaker's wife that that goodhearted woman said to her husband, as the crowd roared into applause over something the candidate had just finished telling them, "She really *is* beautiful, isn't she?"

"If there's one thing clear in this hall at this moment," the commentator confided to his audience, "it's that they love Alec Girard, the American scene's young man with the mostest, who may get even more. Certainly, there's a very good chance that you are looking at the next President of the United States. But, whatever happens next November, the handsome fellow with the beautiful wife on your television screen right now can really be called the man who has everything."

Nine

The men who didn't have everything were still at work trying to get as much of it as they could—though with a certain summer listlessness—while one candidate rested briefly, trying to forget delegate arithmetic, and his probable rival began doing sums at his own party's convention. Ralph Ferris was having it easier than Alec Girard had, though: his party's hard-bitten regulars were aware that Ferris rubbed some voters the wrong way, but he was also the only potential nominee who had had national exposure, and it was a built-in advantage over Girard no one was apt to discard.

The knowledge of that fact robbed the second political convention of any element of suspense, however, and made Ann Taswell's assignment to cover it prove not quite the plum she'd anticipated. Because the managing editor of the *Washington Tribune* was an old acquaintance of the Girards, he was bending over backward to assure coverage of Ralph Ferris; thus, the solid news chores of the convention had been placed in the hands of no less than Martin Halloran, and the talented Miss Taswell had been added to do the "color."

"I can find color, all right," she complained by telephone from Philadelphia. "The only trouble is, it's gray." She listened while her superior argued that the ME felt very strongly the need to be above reproach: Ferris was likely to sulk anyway, and he must be given no grounds for charging favoritism. "I know, I know," Ann said impatiently. "The ME's not the only one, after all." Gil Kimball, who was in the same position—if not more so—because of his friendship with the Girards, had been haunting the convention hall with the earnestness of a fledgling whose job depended on turning up a story. "Listen, you tell the ME something for me: tell him Kimball's lying in bed in his hotel room, writing a column about an interview with a TV commentator who's just interviewed another TV commentator. Go ahead, tell him. I'll wait right here. And I'll be packing."

It was, as she had guessed, the convincer. "The old man just drew the line, Annie," said the voice from the *Tribune*. "Come home."

"I was putting my hat on."

"Look, there's no possibility of Ferris's pulling something interesting by way of a choice for Vice-President?"

"Nobody thinks so," Ann said. "But what the hell can happen that Halloran can't manage without me? Unless Ferris decides to ask Martin Luther King, I mean."

The editor said wistfully that that would be the day, and hung up. A little dreamily, perhaps. Because, though the possibility was considerably smaller than the chances of being struck by lightning—and the chances of Dr. King's acceptance of a place on Ralph Ferris's ticket were not only nil, but some sort of minus quantity—only a move as startling as that seemed likely to lend any drama to the proceedings. There was never an awful lot of drama in the choice of running mates, and every drop had already been wrung from Alec Girard's designation of Senator Tom Cannon, who had been his chief rival for the nomination. Even there, most of the excitement had stemmed from the fact that those most outraged—chiefly, liberals who couldn't abide Cannon's southern accent—had most ready access to the channels of public communication; but they were, as always, noisy rather than knowledgeable and, as always, fell before the facts. There were only two shops to trade at, Girard's and Ferris's, and the liberals would never take their trade to Ferris. Which Girard knew—as he had also known that those who had backed Cannon for the nomination could take their trade to Ferris; they still might, but it was not as likely with Tom Cannon on the Girard ticket. So Girard ignored the votes he could count on and bargained for those he needed, and his liberal adherents seethed for a while—thus creating, as a byproduct, a handy stir of Girard publicity—before they woke to reality.

One of those who seethed, though not in public, was Marian Farland, who announced confidently that she could *not* vote for a ticket that included Tom Cannon—and then agreed meekly that she could not vote for Ralph Ferris. Her husband and Gil Kimball—who, with his wife and Paul Morisot, had dropped in at the Farlands' on Kimball's last between-conventions night in Washington—nodded at each other, checking off the typical liberal voter. They nodded again, with less satisfaction, when Marian went on to say airily that *nobody* would vote for Mr. Ferris, actually, because as soon as you looked at him you said, "There's a man who doesn't mean me any good." Whereupon Kimball and Farland, with Betty as moderator, launched into a debate on the size and significance of Ferris's built-in handicap.

Paul Morisot sat upright on one of the frail chairs that had come with Marian from her Georgetown house and were never used by Will Farland because they did not permit sprawling. Morisot listened politely while the air grew thick with politics, and he even asked a few questions; but as the debate grew more esoteric, he was tacitly excused from attention, and thus was set free to study the large, unframed abstract over the bookshelves. This, like the others of Marian's paintings hung in various places around the house, reflected her psyche or spirit or whatever—they wouldn't have been any good at all if they hadn't—and were open to the world's judgment: a great many people passed varying amounts of time in the Farlands' house. But Morisot's stature made him something else again, and Marian, seeing his survey during the evening, had felt rather painfully vulnerable. For a moment, she wished absurdly that she were very dressed up, presumably so she could be somehow better armored against what he might say than she was in her flimsy summer dress and bare legs. But it was ridiculous: he was the gentlest of men, and in fact, she and Betty had agreed, when they listened to Morisot speak with open affection and admiration of Andrea Girard, that he talked with a warmth other people were afraid of.

Impulse and violence, Morisot was thinking, amazed by the strength and daring he saw in the abstract even more than in the other work: the size of what she had tried was awesome. He looked at the tiny woman who painted so hugely, saw her fear of him, and said something flattering, quickly, about her use of color.

"I couldn't get to green." She seemed startled that she had said it.

Morisot nodded, understanding how so much explosion must set her yearning for its opposite. Particularly since she painted in a way very typical of muscle-flexing young men—accepting no limits, brashly biting off more than they could chew—but was neither young nor strong. Morisot guessed that she had probably never weighed so much as a hundred pounds. "To arrive at green requires many years," he told her kindly, thinking that it was no wonder she longed for rest. "Patience, also."

"But I want to *win*," she said, emboldened by relief. It was good to be known.

Perhaps she would, he reminded himself, remembering suddenly the small, wiry, effeminate man who had been—of all things—a director for the cinema in peacetime, and who had proved one of the bravest and best fighters in their wartime guerrilla band. All its members had been as hungry for victory as any painter—but it always took more than only a great waiting, and more than even an ability to plan and a detailed knowledge of weapons and terrain. The little Mrs. Farland had those, thought the man who had once led brigand-heroes: all her paintings revealed a good concept of design and of what was required to execute it. But there was no way to see in them whether she had also the energy, the dogged strength that was no part of size or muscle but was needed to lurk and strike and, if necessary, come back again and again. . . .

"One does not win beauty by assault," he said gravely, looking at the painting that was a half-victory, like a daring raider who succeeded in breaching the defenses of the enemy depot but couldn't make it all the way back with the stolen supplies. She had taken a wound, but not a grievous one. He smiled at the absurdity of the analogy for a woman who was so plainly not a warrior but a prize of wars. And then he thought of *Andréa,* who was also pretty, likewise *spirituelle*—and possessed of a hidden strength. He shrugged: who knew, really? "It is another kind of fighting," he told Marian, in case, just in case, she had somewhere the needed capacity for the kind of war it was, in which you had to be able to live on short rations, tend your own wounds, depend on your own eyes and ears, and above all, keep moving. "The winning is—a little at a time, you understand?" He gave her the information; she could use it or not, as she was able.

"Yes," said Marian into a sudden shining. Behind her in the room, somebody mentioned the Electoral College.

They had all dispersed after that evening: Morisot to a summer workshop out west at which, for a few weeks, he would talk a little to artists and look a lot at mountains; Kimball to the second convention at Philadelphia, to which the country was reacting with boredom and perhaps resentment at missing its regular television diet. Or maybe it was paying less attention to everything: in the East, at least, people moved slowly in suffocating heat and, if possible, just marked time.

Except Will Farland, who noticed climate no more than he noticed food, and who had a lot to catch up on at the office because he had been dispatched, at the end of the previous month, to make commencement speeches and other appearances in swing through several southern states. It was the sort of thing he did well, but it was as taxing as any other lecture tour. And, for Farland, it was expensive: the citizens who called on the State Department for speakers were duly supplied, but any fees they paid went into the Treasury, and Farland delivered his speeches for his regular pay plus a per diem travel allowance that had been set a generation ago and had to be supplemented from his own pocket if he cared to eat as well as sleep. In addition, he had increased his financial losses this time by sending for Marian, whose solaces were not paid for by the taxpayers, even inadequately. But there was something about lonely southern hotel rooms, Will said on the long-distance telephone, that made him feel like a Bible salesman. Marian, who had never known a Bible salesman, knew desperation when she heard it, however lightly put. So she caught a plane and spent a week lolling around those dreary hotel rooms like a gun moll waiting for her man to come back from a holdup.

Apparently Will didn't sound like a Bible salesman in his speeches, some of which were picked up by the wire services and thus came to widespread attention. One of the causes of Will's current busyness was that the speeches had also come to the attention of Jerry Rosenberg, who called, reminded Will that they had met at the Kimballs', and wondered whether it was possible for Will to drop by for a talk. Farland, as a civil servant, was forbidden by law to engage in partisan political activity; but there were probably few men alive who understood so clearly as Will Farland and Jerry Rosenberg what, precisely, was and was not allowed under the provisions of the Hatch Act. Thus Citizen Rosenberg inquired of Citizen Farland about matters that had been reported in the public prints. If anything Rosenberg learned turned out to be of further use—for example, to his employer, Senator Alexander Girard—that was not a direct consequence of any act of the civil servant Farland.

The civil servant's wife knew only that life was quiet in the house on Mackintosh Place these days, and Will's frequent "staying late at the office" only made it a little quieter. Dick had gone off to camp after a frantic interval during which Rosa and Marian—and then, in Marian's absence, Ann—had sewed RICHARD W. FARLAND tags on an endless pile of garments. Now Dick was represented in the household only by a weekly postcard that he was required to write and that usually sounded like it.

Sharlie's ever-blaring radio was mercifully silenced for the summer, which contributed greatly to the quiet. Charles Grayson, who had never remarried, roved the Far East all year and came back to the States for his annual vacation with his daughter, who never failed to delight him even when she also daunted him. If Grayson was not quite as rigid in the matter of compulsory postcards as the counselors at Dick's camp, he was nevertheless considerate of his former wife and desirous of maintaining the amicable relations that allowed him his weeks with Sharlie. The postcard Marian found waiting at home at the end of one summer workday was typical of what was ordinarily wrung from Sharlie by "Daddy." (Who was Grayson, as distinct from Will Farland, who was "Dad." This nomenclature, devised by Sharlie soon after her mother's remarriage, had held up surprisingly well.) It was addressed to "Everybody, 1028 Mackintosh Place NW, Washington, D.C." and the message half of the card had no salutation. "The Pacific is my favorite ocean," it began unequivocally. "Also they have keen kids in California. I got a new flammingo sweater. Daddy sends love. P.S. I lost Dick's address. P.P.S. Hi, Petey!"

"I done read it," Rosa said, as Marian came into the kitchen and held the card out to her. "You set down, I give you some ice tea."

Marian sat down obediently, her bare legs in their brown-and-white spectator pumps stretched out beneath the table with a freedom possible only in so many absences. She dabbed at her damp neck with a limp Kleenex and turned over the card to look at the picture. Which proved to be not of the Pacific Ocean but of some deep-blue-green cypresses that were impressive but had brooded similarly on last year's postcards from California, too.

Rosa poured iced tea from a glass pitcher painted with tulips and set the tall glass before Marian, who was wondering wearily how many "m's" should properly be in "flamingo."

"Them kids about run both houses out of ice," Rosa said, nodding toward the sunny back yard, where Peter Farland and his friend Tommy tended a lemonade stand.

"What they're selling is mostly melted ice," said Marian, who had been, briefly, a customer. The large dark-red pulpy flowers fallen from the crepe myrtle at the corner of the house made the yard resemble a bloody battlefield; she had downed the dubious drink and fled the scene.

"They got to be makin a pile. They been sellin all afternoon." Rosa sat down with her own glass of iced tea. "I got to talk to you," she said abruptly. "I was hopin you be comin home early enough."

Marian looked at her, actually seeing her for the first time that day. There were greenish shadows on the café-au-lait skin, and the black eyes were dull and tired. "What is it, Rosa? You don't look good. The heat getting you?"

Rosa stirred her iced tea with a long plastic spoon. "Ain't that hot, this part of town. You be surprised how cool this house stay." She watched the grains of sugar swirl and settle. "I ain't sick, but I got this here eatin at me." She put the spoon down and said quickly, as if the words needed to be hurdled, "I got to talk to you about Bettina."

"What about Bettina? What's she been up to?" Rosa's elder daughter was older than Sharlie, and thus was less well-known to Marian than Trixie, who was Sharlie's contemporary.

"I told you she been goin to summer school."

"Yes. She flunked math and had to make it up, didn't she?"

Rosa nodded. "Well, she ain't been goin. The school lady call up last week, but I didn't figure to tell you till I gone to see her." She pushed her glass away, folded her hands on the table, and looked down at them instead of at Marian. "Make a long story short, seem like Bettina—well, the school lady say she ain't been goin to school much all year."

"Then where has she been going?"

"Don't nobody know for sure. Most, she just hang around with that bad bunch she took up with. They don't go to school, none of them, but don't nobody rightly know much what they *do* do. There's two or three been throwed out of school already, and two girls is pregnant that I knows of."

"Oh, Rosa, I don't think it can be that bad. Have you spoken to Bettina about it?"

"Sure." Rosa's eyes were suddenly wet. "She tell me, all right. She say, 'I'm sixteen now, Mama, and I know what I'm doin.'" Rosa unclasped her hands and began to trace the stem of a morning glory printed on the tablecloth. "She *don't* know what she doin. But she got no respect for me, so I can't do her no good nohow."

"Don't cry, Rosa. We'll do something about it."

"I be through cryin, Miz Marian. I been studyin over it all week, and I got it figured what to do." Rosa raised her head. "You don't know nothin about it, but me, I seen when girls start out this kind of way, and I knows where at it ends up. And I wants different for Bettina," she said strongly. "Where I worked, I seen how they do when it happen in them families. When them girls start with stayin out of school and all like that, they people gets special doctors for them. They gets they girls straightened out, so it don't end up with the Juvenile Court. I figure to do for Bettina like that. But I just don't know how to get started, Miz Marian."

"I don't know either," Marian said slowly. "Bettina hasn't really done anything yet. I mean, she's only a truant, not a juvenile delinquent."

"She be a delinquent soon enough. I ain't about to wait till she have to go to court like her friend Louella. That Louella, she ain't no good for Bettina. She got no pride in herself." Rosa tightened her lips. "I know they's somethin better to do than wait for things to get worse. I needs to find out how to do it."

"Well, there's a woman at the *Tribune*," Marian said uncertainly. "Janet Rice. She writes all the stuff about— Well, anyway, she deals with people who work with adolescent problems. I don't know where this fits, but she would know who's the person to see, and that's really what we want, isn't it?"

Rosa nodded, her face clearing at once. "That the idea," she said briskly.

"Do you need money?" Marian asked doubtfully, not sure how it could help here. But money had always been what was needed to cope with the servants' problems in her mother's household. "I have two hundred dollars—"

"I don't know about money— I probably got more left over come the end of the month than you got. But don't matter what it cost, I ain't about to let it happen."

"All right." Marian saw that it was, at that—the black eyes looked lively and confident. She sat in puzzled silence, wondering about this sudden sight of Rosa, who had always been familiar, in the strange guise of a secret researcher, anthropologizing in the homes of the city, learning the rituals and incantations. It made Marian feel creepy, and she had never felt creepy with Rosa before. "Rosa? I hate the idea that you've been—oh—"

"I know what you thinkin. Like I been spyin, kind of. Well, mebbe so. I asks you if I needs to know, but ever'place else, I do got to find out by watchin how they do." She smiled suddenly. "I ain't had no other way. And I figure it the same way you learned, too, ain't it? Only you done it all when you was little. Now, you don't hardly know you know."

It was true, Marian saw. She had absorbed, somehow, a thousand knowledges, some of them now inapplicable—her mother had always had a great deal more than two hundred dollars. But just by being, by living in a home where it was assumed everything that was needed could be obtained, she could now move confidently where Rosa had to feel her way. "I thought it was different, for you. Different from the others," she said slowly.

"I be luckier than most."

"But even for you," Marian persisted, "it's very hard, isn't it? To be a Negro?"

"Some. A lot of it come from just bein poor, though."

"But you just said—"

"I got more money, and I got good sense, too. But people's poor all around, where I live. All the kids Bettina ever knowed is poor." Rosa looked at Marian's bent head and added tentatively, as if equally unsure of what she meant and what would be understood, "Even after you gets enough so you ain't exactly poor, you still— Some hangs on, seem like. Some things just stays missin." She hesitated. "Mr. Farland," she said, very softly, "he know."

But Marian didn't hear, for she had caught sight of the postcard lying on the table. "Sharlie." She looked up at Rosa with her eyes full of dread. "I wouldn't know what to do if Sharlie—"

"By the time Sharlie get to be sixteen, we be experienced." Rosa laughed. "That so, ain't it? So you just stop, Miz Marian. Before you gets yourself all—"

"Rosa!" Peter, who knew nothing between a stentorian bellow and an inaudible whisper, had chosen the former. He slammed the screen door open so hard that it flew back against the wooden railing of the small square utility porch. The dachshund shot in through the opening, discovered Marian, and began ecstatically wiggling his rear while his rough tongue licked her legs. "We gotta have more ice, Rosa."

Rosa got up and started around the island of shelves toward the shiny rank of refrigerator and stove. "Your daddy be bound to need some ice for his drinks when he come home. How about you close up your stand for today? It be dinnertime soon anyways."

Peter looked outraged. "Ten hundred people are getting off the bus. We're making a *lot* of money."

Rosa emptied the contents of an icecube tray into a clean waxed-paper garbage bag. "Well, this here your last tray from this house today."

"It may be the last thing he gets at all," Marian said ominously. "If he doesn't know how to ask any more politely than he just did."

"Oh, Boltaflex." Peter clapped his hand to his forehead. "I forgot my pleases again." He snatched the bag from the counter. "Thank you, Mrs. Rosa Little," he said with show-off formality. Then he flung his arms around her skirts, banging her thigh with the icecubes. "Big Mrs. Rosa Little," he teased, and let her rumple his hair.

"You somethin, you is," Rosa said fondly, coming back to the table. "But you ain't changed my mind none. You still out of business when your daddy drive up, you hear?"

"Okay." Peter hurled his half-naked body against the screen door, which slammed open again. The little dog bolted through it, abandoning the delights of licking Marian for the enticement of immediate escape. His busy black tail whipped Peter's legs as they ran down the steps together. "Here I come, Tom," he shouted unnecessarily. "Hey, pardner, here comes the iceman." Turning to catch the door before it slammed, Marian watched his red shorts flickering among the abundant green of the yard like the plumage of a cardinal and thought of how confidently he had come and demanded, with what assurance that all doors would open to him. It was easy to learn to say "Please" and "Thank you" if you were Peter Farland. She saw suddenly how much easier it was than if you were Bettina Little.

"That chile disgrace us if he don't quit slammin doors," Rosa grumbled. "Look like he must act better when he go play with the little girl over to the President's house, or he wouldn't gone but once."

Marian laughed. "I don't want to shock you, but I'm afraid Elizabeth Girard slams doors too."

"That a fact? Well, now." Rosa was clearly encouraged.

"Besides, her father isn't President. There's a little matter of a national election. All Alec Girard is, so far, is a candidate."

Rosa dismissed this with a contemptuous flick of her hand as she gathered up the glasses. Marian, acknowledging it for the caviling it was, got up also and asked for an assignment.

"You can get them clothes in off the line. This weather, they dries in an hour."

"All right." But Marian turned suddenly, with her hand on the door. "Rosa. 'Them clothes' isn't good grammar. You have to say *'those* clothes.'"

Rosa looked at her with the pleasure of one who receives a gift of love. "'Those clothes,'" she said carefully. "That right?"

Marian nodded, and they both smiled their thanks.

Ten

The group of old, lovely, widely separated houses whose owners get their mail and derive their domestic servants from the little town of Kingsley, Vermont, represents an exclusiveness so exclusive that it doesn't have to exclude anyone. The lake, five miles long, spring-fed, and blue, is largely invisible to the world, unless the world happens to be flying over it; most of the roads around it are private and are built, maintained, and protected by the denizens of the houses. These are, for the most part, people who have money in unimaginable amounts, but for whom money is only a means to buy all the blessings of nature and art. Kingsley Lake doesn't exhibit all the characteristics of a community, for it lacks the formality of an organized viewpoint; it is, simply, a gathering of the very rich of substantial family history, worldly achievement, and reliable taste.

You don't buy property at Kingsley Lake in the ordinary way: usually you are given some by those who are already there, as the Owen Langwiths gave to their granddaughter Andrea and her new husband a pleasant five-bedroom honeymoon "cottage" in a grove of evergreens; but, very occasionally, you are approached subtly by a representative of the charmed world and it is indicated to you indirectly that, if you cared to, it would be acceptable for you to take over the holdings of an old family that has, alas, finally died out.

It was by this latter course that John Alexandre Girard, a gifted financier famous as an adviser to several Presidents, came to build a house by the lake. His father, Alexandre Girard, a French stonecutter who had emigrated to the quarries of Vermont and there made a respectable living and become a citizen of substance, had remained all his life unaware of and indifferent to the graciousnesses of Kingsley Lake. John Alexandre had three qualifications for living there that his father had lacked. The first was that he had promoted his father's respectable earnings into fabulous wealth; it is necessary, at Kingsley Lake, to have enough money so that you need not think about it. The result of the financial genius of Girard *fils* was the achievement of this kind of money, but it was the public accomplishments resulting from this genius that impressed Kingsley Lake, where money alone could make no one acceptable, but distinguished public service could help a lot. Second, this son of a stonecutter had been to a good university, and had gone from there to just the right marriage. Agnes Wardwell Girard's family was New England on both sides for generations, and its money came from whaling. In Boston, the Wardwells, though they were respectable and rich, were not top drawer socially because they lacked history; but Kingsley Lake prided itself on not being Boston. Kingsley Lake was imaginative and loved colorful ancestors, especially when their descendants were quiet, pleasant people with excellent manners, a sense of humor, and no social-climber pushiness about them. And third, the Girards had handsome, lively children who were already showing signs of distinguishing themselves at New England's best schools. Their second son, Alexander, was captain of the debating team at the prep school attended by the other sons of Kingsley Lake when it was suggested to his father, at lunch in a small and little-known club in New York, that a rather pleasant little place might be had at Kingsley Lake if Mr. Girard cared to look into it. Mr. Girard did, and sold his home in a lesser area of Vermont and took his wife, two sons, and three daughters to become "the new family" at Kingsley Lake—a title they would have held for at least a generation if it had not been for World War II.

That cataclysm, in which the Girards' elder son perished, shook up Kingsley Lake as it did other societies: the once-slow process of evolution from stranger to native was speeded up first by the war, which made several old families that had long been obsolescent suddenly and dramatically obsolete. Finally, as the postwar affluent society, cash in hand, began to press toward the sacred enclave from all directions, Kingsley Lake gathered to protect itself, calling on all its denizens equally for their services. The skills and connections of John Girard proved more vital than those of some of his neighbors to the construction of the stockade of preference and manipulation that now kept them all safe from speculators and developers; Kingsley Lake recognized this at the time, and thus John Girard began to become, by not dishonorable means, the community's Grand Old Man.

But Kingsley Lake and much of the rest of the world were still younger and more innocent when Andrea Langwith, on a summer visit to her paternal grandparents, and Alec Girard, spending a summer weekend with his family before going off on a long sailing trip with a couple of friends, actually met there. The occasion, reconstructed later from hazy memories, was a cocktail hour at the home of Max Rombero, publisher of a magazine that set intellectual trends and made no money—which last didn't matter because Rombero, a British Jew, was the possessor of three generations' worth of fortune, one of which included a touch of Rothschild.

The Romberos, like all the Kingsley Lakers, lived the brief and beautiful Vermont summer to the full. Their cocktail hour marked the informal end of a day on the lake and was attended by anyone who felt like a drink and a little talk before dressing for dinner. The guests gathered on the wooden deck that extended out toward the lake from Max Rombero's mahogany-paneled study on the second floor of the house, which was built into the side of the hill. People arrived at the side of the house appropriate to their most recent activity—at the front door if they had come from the tennis courts or from a hike along the private dirt road or woodland paths, or up the straggling path to the sun deck if they had come from the lake— and in costumes appropriate to what they had been doing. Thus, in shorts and sneakers, in bathing suits and bare feet, the well-endowed and (perhaps therefore) gracious and gentle gathered to talk a little while they nibbled and sipped. Birds made a bedtime hubbub, the lake took on its mirrorlike night-time glint, and silently, some pale moonflowers opened on the vine that climbed to the deck. It was the loveliest of worlds, full of kindnesses and almost without envies; probably the only thing ever wrong with it was that it was so small.

Andrea Langwith swam the mile and a half across the lake from her grandparents' home to the Romberos' on the afternoon that should have been historic but wasn't. She was followed by a boat that contained her grand-mother, in flowered voile and a large sun-filtering hat, and was rowed by Jascha Menkoff, the Langwiths' next-door neighbor. The world-renowned pianist wore heavy cotton gardening gloves to protect his hands.

Alec Girard, come early from a tennis game with the childless Romberos' visiting nephew, was standing on the sun deck in his crumpled and dusty white shorts and shirt when he saw the group arrive. He studied Andrea's slender figure in its clinging black bathing suit as she pulled off her cap, shook out her thick damp hair, and bent to help beach the boat. A very good-looking girl indeed, Alec decided judiciously, surveying her as Menkoff helped her into a loose yellow terry-cloth robe; her bare brown legs flashed in the lowering sunlight as she climbed the path. Alec recognized old Mrs. Langwith, guessed that the girl must be a granddaughter, and decided, after he got a closer look at her big dark eyes and wide smile, that you would surely buy Coca-Cola if you saw her on a billboard drinking it. Then he turned away from the lake, toward the blue-shadowed hills in the distance, and answered his friend's remark with a quip.

Though he would have been an unobservant fool if he had not been struck by her beauty, it was not surprising that young Girard made no effort to approach the pretty girl who was now greeting Edith Rombero. For all the girls Alec Girard knew were beautiful: he would no more have bothered with a girl who was not beautiful than he would have tolerated clothes cut poorly or machinery that didn't work. In time, that afternoon, as the dark-blue shadows lengthened over the lake and the loons began to call in the rushes, he was presented to the latest beautiful girl: Alec said something polite, Miss Langwith replied equally politely, and they went their separate ways. Jascha Menkoff, who was fond of the Romberos' Bald-win, wandered indoors and shortly thereafter could be heard playing Chopin's Waltz in A Flat Major more slowly and lovingly than he would in concert. The lilting notes hung in the still and lovely air as Alec made his adieux and went home to dress for his date with a young actress doing summer stock in

Vermont. Andrea, waiting for Menkoff to be ready to leave, flirted a little with the son of a famous architect and forgot Alec Girard instantly.

He was a freshman congressman from Vermont when she met him next, some years later, at the wedding of a college friend; but neither of them remembered that afternoon at the lake. Nor did that second meeting take, either: young Representative Girard was ten years older than the colorful and much sought-after debutante, Andrea Langwith. He was gravid with the problems of New England and the country and he had no time for the frivolous and restless set of which she seemed to be a devout member. He had no occasion to change his attitude, which added up to mild scorn, until he had met her repeatedly in Washington, a few years later still, when Gil and Betty Kimball had begun their determined effort to matchmake between Andrea and the Congress's most eligible bachelor, now representing Vermont in the Senate. By that time, Andy had become less of a playgirl and Alec less single-minded, and among the discoveries about each other that began to emerge from their repeated encounters was the long-lost memory of a cocktail party on a long-ago afternoon, as night crept silently toward Kingsley Lake.

The Kingsley Lake home Andy's grandparents had presented to the newly married Girards was at the opposite end of the lake from their own, on a hillside behind the elder Girards' rambling white house and lakeside acres. A straggly path curved down the hill from Alec's "cottage" to his father's big white house and its wooden dock, filled all summer with the lounging or active bathing-suit-clad figures of Girard children and their progeny. Agnes Girard, mother of many, was quite accustomed to being the grandmother of even more. As little Elizabeth came down the path, the stones rattling under her quick, moccasined feet, each morning of the August after her father had been nominated for the office of President of the United States, her grandmother hugged her and turned her loose among the cousins playing ball or paddling in the lake under the supervision of Girard aunts and uncles and old family employees, to whom another Girard grandchild was a further responsibility but an enjoyable one. When Alec, resting and planning his campaign, took time off to go down to the lake to swim and collect his daughter, he came by the path if he was coming alone; but the footing was too uncertain for Andy, now six months advanced in pregnancy, and the descent too precipitous. So, when Andy came, they walked along the driveway behind their house toward a secondary road that marked the end of the Kingsley Lake enclave. From there, they drove their white convertible along the state road briefly, until they turned off at the winding driveway that led to the elder Girards' front door.

On the other side of the state road lay Wenake Gorge, its wild beauty protected by the United States government, which had, under the lash of Max Rombero's crusading editorials, declared it a national preserve. Where the road curved past the lip of the gorge, a parking area had been hollowed out to accommodate The People, who now owned it. From there a path led to two or three rustic picnic tables for the use of the never very numerous citizens who cared to come and view their communal possession. But it was still, most of the time, only local people who came to stand, usually silent and awestruck, and watch the river tumble violently through the rocky channel it had carved, thousands of years ago, out of the granite hills. On both the steep sides of the gorge, everything that was determined enough managed to grow: the nearly vertical walls were thick with trees, growing out at any angle that would allow them to grab a little life-giving sunlight from the thicket of their neighbors. Deep and cold and far between these cliffs of survivors, the beautiful, deadly river ran swiftly and forever; its roar, which could be heard at Andy and Alec's house as a steady background sound, was like surf, except that it didn't come and go but was relentless and incessant. The butterflies that were everywhere else in the neighborhood avoided the gorge, whose sucking air would have pulled them to death in the river. Even largish birds, if caught in that strong downdraft, could escape only by a frantic beating of wings that, with luck, bore them up enough to reach the safety of one of the great trees that overhung the lip. And yet, and yet— among the murderous dangers, little patches of wildflowers survived, gifts of the wind, irrelevant and innocent as children at play at the scene of a disaster.

After the convention in July, an exhausted Alec, longing for both rest and constructive action, had been condemned to have neither during frustrating weeks in Washington, where a special session of Congress held him bound. As the weeks passed and his opponent for the Presidency made hay while Alec sat at his desk on the Senate floor and accomplished nothing, either as senator or as presidential candidate, he grew increasingly silent and depressed. Andy, reading the morning *Tribune* and noting that none of the legislation her husband had sponsored—at least some of which might have provided campaign arguments for him—had a chance of passage, watched him in silence and with an aching heart. For the first time since he had set in motion the great organized effort that had culminated in winning him the nomination, Alec Girard was bitterly contemplating the possibility of defeat in the election—which was no way, certainly, to start a campaign.

In the house on O Street, Andy struggled to keep her own vexation from becoming still another demand on her tired husband and went to work determinedly at the task of shoring him up. Mutely but steadily she offered food, rest, distraction; he took it all absently, his thoughts grim and elsewhere, but he thrived on it nevertheless. Emboldened by her partial success, she insisted with gentle steeliness, once Congress had at last shut up shop for the summer, on her promised vacation at the lake. Alec, despairing but honorable, could not refuse. On the day that Ralph Ferris was, by the newspaper reports, being wildly cheered in a state whose electoral votes were absolutely essential to Alec Girard's careful campaign strategy, the Senator from Vermont, looking a little grim, gathered up his wife and daughter and flew off to Kingsley Lake.

And it worked. Because he was a graceful man who made his decisions and wasted no time in repining, Alec Girard joined August in Vermont, becoming a wholehearted member of the rapidly waning summer, a citizen of play, a subject of joy. The campaign waited, but he closed his eyes to it; surrounded by family, friends, and flowerings, he lived his week of summer as if it were forever. Piggybacking Elizabeth home from his parents' house in the late afternoon, he held carefully on to her bare feet against his chest as he swung along the path where ferns brushed at his trouser legs. The little girl, tanned and golden-haired, clutched a red ball that sat above her father's thick hair like an absurd crown; she talked incessantly, in the voice of a small bird. At her right and left the poplar leaves trembled, but she rode in the deepest safety known to man.

"Package for Mrs. Girard." Alec knelt beside Andy's chair and tipped his daughter off his shoulders. The red ball rolled from the child's grasp and came to rest at the edge of the sloping lawn, where a reddening maple spoke of autumn.

"Hmm," Andy said. "This package is inadequately wrapped."

"Better go get dressed, kitten," Alec told Elizabeth, patting her little bottom. She pouted, but she went.

Andy reached over to the other lawn chair and handed Alec his shirt. "You, too," she said. "It's starting to get cool."

"I'm warm." He took the shirt away. "I've been creating, and it's good for the circulation." He put his arms into the sleeves, but left it dangling open.

"Whose adventures this time?"

"Dudumber the Cucumber. I've got him in imminent danger of being carried off to the pickle factory, and I can't for the life of me figure out how to rescue him."

"Well, you have till after dinner," Andy consoled. "You'll think of something."

Alec did. Dudumber was saved at the very doors of the pickle factory, it turned out, when the manager, whose papers were blowing about in the wind, realized that a fat cucumber would make a fine paperweight and snatched Dudumber from the loaded dump truck standing in the yard outside. At that point, a triumphant Alec piggybacked a happy Elizabeth off to bed. Leaving Andy smiling alone in the living room of the cottage as she stood at the big window and looked out at the black night: she hoped Alec's invention wouldn't flag—though it seemed a lot to ask, after his virtuoso performance tonight—because, to tell the truth, she was growing fond of Dudumber.

She noticed the flashlights bobbing up the path just as she was thinking how too bad it was that Alec should have now acquired a fan with a long attention span. She went out onto the lawn to greet her mother- and father-in-law as they emerged from the woods.

"We thought we'd just stroll up for a little," Agnes Girard explained. "Are we too late for Elizabeth?"

"I'm afraid so. But do sit down. Would you like to stay out here or come indoors?"

"Oh, I'm warm enough after that hike," the elder Mrs. Girard said. She flopped into one of the lawn chairs, and added accusingly to her husband, "If you hadn't stopped to see whether that was a porcupine you heard, we might have made it in time for Elizabeth."

John Girard looked up at the bright-orange disc of the rising full moon. "Well, it sounded like a porcupine," he argued mildly. "And that's what they call a porcupine moon." The distant light glinted on his steelrimmed glasses and highlighted the white hair standing up around his head like ground mist.

"Don't know what you'd have done if you'd caught up with him, if he was a porcupine," Agnes said. She dismissed the subject then. Like Alec, Andy thought, his mother was not one to repine.

"You about set for the big doings, Andy?" her father-in-law asked.

Andy shook her head. "I don't think I ever will be, somehow. It feels more like something that's all over than something just beginning."

"You've got no call to be bothering Andy with all that. She's busy enough, just having her baby." Agnes Girard impaled her husband on a sharp glance and turned to Andy. "Let the men worry themselves about the headquarters, dear. You and I, we'll just watch the leaves turn."

"They're not beginning so early this year, are they?" Andy said. "Maybe we're going to have a long summer."

"Long or short, it'll be over before we know it." Her father-in-law looked at Andy squarely, defying his wife. "All summers go, sooner or later." His voice was gentle, but firm.

"Leave her be, Johnny," Agnes commanded. "You can't do everything with bulldozers."

Alec came toward them in the warm beam of light from the house. "Mom. Dad. Can I get you a drink?"

"We've had our dinner, and we've had our drinks, and the only thing we were lacking was a little walk, so we sashayed up for a few minutes, just to talk," his father told him. "Figgered we aren't going to have too long now for sitting around, just the family. This time next week, isn't it, your first speech out west?"

"You ought to see your grandmother's russet chrysanthemums," Agnes Girard said hastily to her daughter-in-law.

Andy accepted the offering gracefully. She and Agnes discussed chrysanthemums determinedly while Alec and his father explored the complexities involved in setting up the campaign headquarters. The conversations crisscrossed contrapuntally in the quiet, producing the intricate satisfactions of the fugue, in which all voices respect the directions of the others. When, not long after, the elder Girards gathered themselves for departure, Andy had arrived at a state of content that inspired her to accept with pleasure Alec's invitation to "come along for the ride" while he drove his parents home. He went to get the car, and Andy excused herself to leave word that they were going out, after all. She walked quickly, if a little clumsily, across the lawn to the house that, though it was not really small enough to be truly a cottage, was not large enough to require anything but a minimal domestic staff.

If the young Girards' menage at Kingsley Lake was grander in some respects than most people are accustomed to, it still represented a rather simplified life for Andy. Daily help came from the village, and servants could be borrowed, in a pinch, from her mother-in-law. But normally they were not— when the household retired to Kingsley Lake, only Pierre and Jeanne Champagne came along. Pierre had been valeting Alec since the days of a backrow desk in the House of Representatives and the crowded leisure hours of a bachelor establishment in Georgetown. At the Lake, there were few valeting chores to perform for the vacationing gentleman who spent his days in sneakers, ancient trousers, and an occasional shirt. So Pierre, a Kingsley native, vacationed also during these stays.

Two years ago on one of these visits, Pierre had taken unto himself a bride—which meant that Andy Girard, by the unwritten rule of her society, had at the same time acquired an obligation to find a place on her domestic staff for the bride. As it turned out, Jeanne was a pleasant young woman who was content to work part-time at the O Street house. When the Girards came to the cottage, Jeanne took over, even to doing the cooking, while the family was "roughing it." It was a satisfying arrangement on both sides: Jeanne enjoyed the change in routine and was always happy to be transported to Vermont whenever the Girards chose to go. And Andy was quite content to do without her Washington cook's incomparably greater skill and experience and enjoy the simple life with the help of the loyal, reliable young woman who "belonged" to her household in the same sense that Pierre's father had "belonged" to John Girard and Pierre himself had been "inherited" by Alec. In short, all hands might be said to have reached the unstated conclusion that, though they wouldn't have supported feudalism for a minute, voluntary feudalism was a satisfactory scheme indeed.

"All alone, Jeanne?" Andy asked from the kitchen doorway. The dishwasher hummed companionably in the lighted warmth, and Jeanne looked up from scrubbing the sink with cleanser.

"Ay-uh. Pierre went down to town to play cards."

"We thought we'd drive Mr. and Mrs. Girard home, if you don't mind listening for Elizabeth."

"Sure thing. It's a nice night. Mrs. Girard," she added suddenly as Andy turned to go. She hesitated, despite the encouraging "Yes?" Then she shook her head and plunged: were they going to stay up here from now to election, or would they go back to Washington for a while?

"I'm not quite certain, Jeanne. There're some things I want to get done in the house before the baby . . . When do you need to know?"

"Well, I was thinking," Jeanne said shyly, "to put my checkerboard pie in the contest at the Fair. That'll be the end of this month. If we're here then. And if it's all right with you."

Dismayed by the possibilities of additional publicity, Andy pondered the question and finally asked what Pierre thought of the idea.

"Well, they got a system where you just have numbers, so nobody knows whose pie it is till after. Pierre, he says it's okay, but I got to expect some people to say it's because of the Senator if I win."

Andy laughed and said Pierre, who was a more experienced politician than either of them, was probably right. "I'm sorry about it, Jeanne," she added.

Jeanne folded her dishcloth and hung it up. "It'll be worse when we move to the White House," she said philosophically. "So I guess I better get in the contest now if I can."

"You go ahead and enter," Andy said quickly. Her soft voice held a faint note of indignation not directed at Jeanne. "We'll plan the trip to Washington around it." She turned to go and then paused in the doorway. "If your checkerboard pie doesn't win, we'll demand a recount." If politics had unexpected costs, she was thinking as she went out, it also undeniably widened your vocabulary.

As the convertible drew up in his driveway, John Girard helped his wife out of the car and then kicked at a pile of the bluestone chips from the driveway heaped like a miniature tepee on the edge of the lawn. "Dratted kids," he grumbled. "They'll kill the grass."

Agnes waited calmly on the doorstep. "He's been saying that for forty years," she told them. "Twenty years here, twenty years in the other house. Maybe more. Two generations of kids anyway, and they haven't killed the grass yet."

As Andy leaned out to wave good-night, the defender of lawns was still arguing that only his eternal vigilance maintained the liberties of the older generation. Andy smiled at his son's profile. "Let's not go right home. It's so fine."

"Right." Alec swung the car down the state road and they drove in silence through the black and twittering night. In the sudden glare of the headlights, the roadside was thick with summer and heavy with growth. Like me, Andy thought, watching the green tunnels open before them as they sped through the night.

"I feel good about leaving you with them," Alec said suddenly. "You don't mind? If you'd rather be with your mother . . . ?"

I'd rather be with you, Andy thought rebelliously. "Well, you know Mother," she said slowly. "Your parents are better able to cope with this awful circus we bring wherever we go."

"I know." He slowed, then made a U-turn to put them back in the direction of their house. "We're doing something about it, though, and I think it'll work. Luke had a little talk with the press yesterday."

"Oh?"

"Sort of offering them terms. We'll provide everything they need to make their life easier if they'll agree to cut down on the—er—individual initiative."

"Like those photographs of Elizabeth and me at the lake?"

He nodded. "Telescopic camera, or something. I think we can take care of you as long as you're up here. Washington's a little harder. We really have nothing to bargain with, with the local boys."

"Luke's very good, isn't he?"

"Oh my, yes," Alec said warmly. "They all are—I have a dozen good men for Ferris's one. In addition to my regular staff." He shook his head. "I wouldn't have believed so many people would volunteer so much."

Andy listened to the low roar of the gorge grow louder on their right. "I don't think Ralph Ferris is a man who makes friends," she said.

In the parking space near the gorge, Alec turned off the motor and looked at Andy in the moonlight. "I wasn't, either," he said slowly. "I don't know how to say it, but it has something to do with you."

"Nonsense," Andy scoffed. "Half the people helping in your campaign were friends of yours in college."

Alec looked steadily at his hands on the steering wheel. "Yes, but it was different. I'm good at my trade, and so is Ferris."

"There's an enormous difference."

"Yes, there is," Alec agreed, matter-of-factly. "Now. I think there wasn't always. Everything used to look to me like a news photograph—good and clear, but black and white. And limited. You brought the color." He got out and went around the car to help her out. She held his arm as they walked slowly over the carpet of fallen pine needles toward the lip of the gorge. "And more dimensions," he continued. "And more fun."

Andy stood still, holding his arm, her eyes dreaming over his face hollowed by the moonlight. Above them, the night whispered in the tops of the trees. Below, the endless waters rushed through the gorge.

"What I've always been good at is strategy," Alec went on. He seemed almost to be talking to himself. "But something happened in West Virginia, I think. The strategy was important—two years' worth of work was riding on a decent showing in that primary, and we all knew it. Without it, I wouldn't have had a prayer for the nomination." He hesitated. "Yet, all the time, I was looking around at the people, so poor and so proud. You could hardly believe some of the things I saw there." He looked down at her then. "No, I guess you could. What I mean is, *I* wouldn't have seen them—I wouldn't have seen anything but the strategy—if it hadn't been for you. For something I think I learned from you."

"Oh, Alec."

"Maybe what I'm trying to say is, I really wasn't fit to be President when I first started trying to be."

Andy touched his cheek lightly. "You are now, darling. You most certainly are."

Alec nodded. "Yes, I think I'm closer," he said quietly. "And closer than Ferris is, anyway."

They moved toward the brink, where a rustic rail fence marked the edge of safety. The roar filled the darkness below. Above, the great orange moon journeyed along the sky; against the faint bluish light the trees were only black outlines.

Alec leaned over the rail to look down into the gorge. "That's mean-looking water," he said speculatively. "The Indians must've had quite a struggle with the problem of getting across."

"I think they must have prayed to the god of the waters." Andy backed away a little and sat down on a large rock, holding her coat around her.

"Maybe." Alec sounded unconvinced. "But I'll bet they tried to find a way anyhow. Canoes, logs, attempts at bridging it."

And there you would have been, Andy thought, politicking at the pow-wow. The chief Indian, scheming and trying, persuading reluctant braves, planning all-out assaults. "Couldn't they just stay on this side?" she asked softly.

Alec turned back and looked at her. "No. Not ever, Andy."

Andy clasped her hands tightly in her lap, suddenly sick with sadness. He was right, she knew: but she held her breath against the fear that she would cry out, shamelessly, in protest against it. In defense of staying on this side, looking and listening, living out lives nourished by love and small triumphs. "Of course," she said finally. She put a hand behind her on the rise of the rock to lift her heavy, unbalanced body. With a swift rustle among the dry pine needles, Alec came to help. As he reached down, the baby in her belly moved swiftly, sharply against his outstretched arm.

Alec cried, "There he is!" in the high, excited voice of a little boy, and threw himself down beside her, leaning his ear against the bulge under her coat.

"He's getting very big," Andy said, smiling; his delight was irresistible, contagious. "He kicks a lot."

"Does he?" Alec's face was bright with interest. "More than Elizabeth did?"

"A little, maybe. It's hard to remember." Andy watched him as his questions continued: when Alec delighted, it meant, almost invariably, this kind of swift, comprehensive drive for information. She tossed her own question into the flow at the first pause. "Do you care whether it's a boy?"

"Oh, I guess it'd be nice to have a son," he said carelessly. Then he returned to his researches. "Is that his foot? Do you think he does it because he's swimming?"

"Probably."

"My God, it's ridiculous how little I know about something so important," Alec said disgustedly. He picked up a handful of pine needles and let them fall out through his fingers like sand. "It's a good thing you'll be with my mother."

Stored safely with the women of the tribe . . . Well, why not? It made sense, Andy knew. She had a swift vision of Alec, wearing a headdress of feathers, his torso painted brilliantly, Indian-dancing away down the trail while she and Agnes Girard watched him go. She got up then, with Alec's help, and held his arm, answering his rattle of questions as best she could as they made their way back over the whispery ground.

"Do they think he can hear?" He helped her into the car and turned to look back at the gorge. "I suppose if I *were* an Indian and I couldn't think of a way across, myself, it'd be a comfort to know that my son might."

"All right," Andy promised, laughing up at him. "I'll take care of it, while you're busy around the council fire."

The valedictory note in Andrea Girard's voice in the dark beside the gorge may have been accurate but her vocabulary was not, at least not exactly. For most of Alec's councils of war were behind him by that time: a sprinkling of party braves still sped up the path to Kingsley Lake to confer with the new chief, but the major powwows had been held in the house in Georgetown during the futile special session of Congress. Alec's running mate, Tom Cannon, and Dan Daniels were both senators and therefore also leashed to Capitol Hill. The Cannons had paid a formal call, and then Daniels, accompanied by his wife, had come to complete the burying of preconvention hatchets—pragmatically speaking, at least. Mr. Blackwell, Alec's predecessor as the party's nominee for President, had arrived to offer his services, which were accepted with thanks: millions of Americans had cast their votes for him four years before.

Senator Kenneth Youngblood, whose pre-West Virginia comments had attracted a sizable number of converts to Girard, now led an even larger flock—consisting in part of Senate colleagues who either would have preferred the powerful Cannon or had been afraid to incur his wrath—to Alec's office, where all offers of help were being matched to open speech dates in key states. Members of the House all faced campaigns themselves, of course —but those who thought they could either help or be helped "registered" with Representative Bruyette of Vermont, who was planning minimal campaigning for his own House seat. In addition, a Washington lawyer whose fame was not wide but very deep walked into Volunteers for Girard headquarters in Washington to offer, with maximum publicity, the services that had been valued by the party's candidates for a generation and for almost that long had been regarded by the opposition with respect verging on fear.

When the Girards had left for Vermont, smaller and very exclusive councils of war were held at the home of Jake Ruffing. Jake's always-worried look reflected, this time, a genuine anxiety not unlike that of a commander whose troops are being held too long in barracks. The "troops" he was worrying about really boiled down to Alec Girard: Jake's experienced eye told him that the candidate was tense and tired and had somehow lost or mislaid the rhythm that had swung them up to and through the convention. Such a mood in the candidate had a way of filtering down through the whole organization and taking the fine edge off it. So it was with relief that Ruffing saw Alec off on what he hoped would be a healing, if brief, lull—but he spoke of his fears only to the inner circle as he prepared to dispatch them to their chores around the country.

Luke Messenger and Dan Healy, each with his own corps of assistants, would leave at once; Jerry Rosenberg and his squad of writers and researchers would stay in Washington, picking brains like Will Farland's and availing themselves of the services offered by numerous skilled volunteers in that Oxford of political journalism, until all the major speeches were blocked out and ready for variations to be written around their themes as campaign needs arose. Then Rosenberg would take them to Vermont for review.

When Alec and Andy said their gentle temporary farewell among the pines by the roaring waters, this review—and all the conferring, editing, and rewriting it had entailed—was just over. Rosenberg had arrived in Kingsley with reference materials, a file of Ralph Ferris's public utterances classified by subject matter, and assorted other instant-library impedimenta of the speechwriter. With his usual indifference to appearances, Rosenberg had packed most of this into, of all things, a toy chest: having recently had occasion to buy a cheap, unpainted, and capacious container for his small son's toys, he had realized the box's potential for his own campaign travel needs and simply bought himself another.

Andy, confronting for the first time this raw-wood object that would be so often in her husband's presence until early November, had wasted only a moment in staring at it in grim dismay before she began to work on it. Fortunately, the chest arrived on one of the few days Paul Morisot was spending with the Girards before he left for New York and a temporary job as consultant for a museum there—an assignment he'd taken as a way of staying in the United States until the election was over. Andy and Paul knelt together in the sunshine on newspapers spread over the elder Girards' flagstone terrace and worked away, he at a chaste Grecian border carved with more care than the cheap wood merited, she with paints and brush. When John Girard strolled out to examine the project one day and solemnly reproached Morisot for not having chiseled dollar signs into the decoration, Andy sat back on her heels and laughed so merrily that her father-in-law's careful poker face was quite dislodged.

When the chest was finished, dried, and repacked, the absentminded Rosenberg bore it away without comment; Morisot, who traveled as far as New York with him, reported to Andy later by phone that Rosie still hadn't remarked any change in the converted toy chest by the time he dropped Paul off and set out for the West Coast to await Alec's arrival a few days later.

"Everything's been turned back to the women and children around here," Andrea was writing, a week after Alec left, in a letter to Marian Farland. "At least, temporarily." She put her pen down and picked up Marian's long, newsy letter from which all mention of the campaign was quite remarkably absent. Andy doubted that even the apolitical Marian, whirling in Washington, could be unaware that Alec was not doing very well; Marian was as transparent as she was warmhearted, and Andy was certain that the letter's presence and length resulted from knowledge of the detail its author markedly omitted.

". . . that rusty red, at least the way it printed out in the color pix," an unnumbered page began. Andy remembered that it was about her dress, the one in which she'd been photographed in her Georgetown garden, and didn't bother to hunt for the beginning of the sentence. "If I remember right, the dress itself had more yellow in the red, which is okay for you but terrible for some of the rest of us, so I hope the copyists pick up the color from the papers. Maybe you could hide away the real dress—just till they get the $17.98 models started, huh?"

Let 'em copy Mrs. Ferris, Andy thought of writing in reply. In an interview, that prim lady had managed to hint delicately that Mrs. Girard spent small fortunes on her clothes—thousands, one gathered, that would be better used to feed starving babies. The elegant Mrs. Girard looked down at her green paisley-printed smock and gray maternity skirt and tightened her lips in dislike of politics and even more in dislike of the emotions that had been inspired in her. Then she returned her attention to the prattlings of the likable Marian, who was going on for another page about the problems of outfitting Sharlie for the new term at school.

"After Sharlie, Rosa's daughter was a delight—or is it that anyone else's daughter is always better? Anyway, we've got her all set and she's about ready to go. Rosa went up to Pennsylvania and looked over the school—it's the Catholic one we could afford because it was endowed. Well, Rosa says the nuns are just marvelous—they smile and never raise their voices, and they never give an inch. It's the perfect combination for Bettina—plenty of authority, yet with nobody visibly pushing her around. It was tricky for a while, getting her to agree to go, but I think the new clothes may have swung it. Besides, Bettina's no dope—I think she knew she was heading for trouble, and I don't think people *want* to ruin themselves if they can help it. Anyway, not if somebody comes along and hands them a ticket out of it.

"I had to go up to New York (right after Rosa got back from Pa., which made Will surly—he likes to do all the coming and going) to cover an opening, which was pretty dreary. I don't see how you can like hopping around between Washington and Vermont; I hate not staying in one place. But I ran into Paul Morisot, and he made things a lot better. We played hooky after a long, arty luncheon—the kind with speakers and all the food drowned in floury sauce—and he had this wonderful idea: we took a cab up to the Museum of Natural History and I stared at a huge, hairy mammoth while Paul went to prowl among dinosaur bones. It was all a great relief, and very restful—I just barely made my plane back, but it was worth it. He's a fine fellow, isn't he? He took me out for big gloppy sundaes—I thought nobody but me was so mad about ice cream! He said you were flourishing, which was good to hear. But I miss you—and so does Betty, who sends love. Gil didn't, because we were playing anagrams, and you know he doesn't love *anybody* when he—"

Andrea dropped the letter in mid-sentence because of the vision it called up, of everyone squabbling happily over the wooden letters. She swallowed hard against the tightening in her throat that was so like boarding-school homesickness and turned back to her own description of her women-and-children world. "I'm as stay-put as your fondest dreams, Marian," she wrote. "I won't be doing any 'hopping around' for a long time—if I did, I might miss Alec, who may touch base here from time to time." That sounded self-pitying, she knew, and she didn't care. But she thought that was enough of it, and changed the subject.

"In Paul's version of your day in New York, he reported the luncheon more alarming than dreary. Apparently he could cope with the Phil Colbys, but you were a problem with your great eyes and devastating questions. Paul thinks you have an unerring knack of locating artists' weaknesses or compromises, and I suspect he's right. But I also suspect that, deep down, he's just shocked at the idea of being put on display at lunch. In his native province, they take their eating very, very seriously.

"His version of your visit to the museum was also a little different: isn't it true that you almost missed your plane because you insisted it would be discourteous to leave without dropping in on the Hall of North American Mammals, since you were one? Paul mentioned this with some distress because he hadn't been able to refute your argument. Like many Frenchmen, he's intensely logical—but I admit I didn't think you were."

I'm a North American mammal, too, Andy thought, with the querulousness of someone left out of a party. But she laughed and didn't write it. Nor, after a second's consideration, did she write that although Morisot's interest in dinosaur bones was no surprise to her, his passion for ice cream was news indeed; she decided it would be more fun to confront him with this remarkable change in his tastes when she spoke to him next.

But she sobered when she thought of what she would like to write and couldn't, to Marian or anyone, because it was necessary to support it alone until it went away: there was no other way. If Alec took the beating that seemed, as of now, to be looming, it would be up to his wife to put the pieces back together. It was hard, and lonely; but, she thought—as she wrote that she missed Marian, too, sent her regards to all of them, and signed and sealed the letter—the more you tried, the easier it got. She looked at her watch, and it was time to get on, so she did.

Eleven

In the kitchen of Rosa's apartment in Washington, thirty years separated the oval formica table, at which Trixie Little sat doing her nails, from the rest of the equipment. The refrigerator, tiny by modern standards, was topped by a slatted cylinder containing the motor; the sink and stove were raised on skinny legs of metal from which the enamel was chipping. A striped cotton skirt was strung on a wire to cover the space beneath the sink in which the garbage pail was stored, but nothing had been done to hide the area under the stove with its cracked linoleum darkened by years. At the moment it was occupied by a very black one-year-old in a stained undershirt and grimy training pants; he sat upright and quite still, except for leaning over to bang each of the four supporting pillars of his retreat with a long wooden spoon. He listened carefully to the sound of each, then put the spoon down beside him and sucked his thumb, his round, coal-black eyes contemplative.

Bruce Fisher lounged in the doorway, holding a sweating golden beer can and watching the steam rise from the large kettle on the stove. With his rather narrow face, close-cropped hair, and spade-shaped beard, he looked like an apprentice Mephistopheles—an impression aided by the perpetual sneer he wore. "If you ask me nice, I'll take you to the hootenanny," he told Trixie's back. His voice bluffed, expecting rejection.

Rosa turned from the sink, where she was shucking corn, and surveyed with disapproval his torn T-shirt, tightly fitting jeans, and the sneakers from which a brown toe protruded. "You leave Trixie be. She only a child. Anyway, she already got somewheres to go."

"She may be only a child, but I see she's not too young to be enlisted as a handmaiden of the Establishment."

"It make more sense to help with the election than sit around singin," Rosa said mildly.

The baby crawled out from under the stove, carrying his spoon, and pulled himself upright by holding onto one of the legs. He tottered and sat down hard, arranged his face for a howl, and then sucked his thumb instead. No one noticed him. When he had recovered, he crawled around the table and the tubular-steel legs of the chairs and established himself beside the refrigerator, where he proceeded to knock on its legs with his spoon. The sound he produced was a dull thud that didn't interfere with conversation.

Trixie held up her pink-tipped left hand, tilting her head to evaluate her manicuring skill.

"Very nice," Bruce drawled from the doorway. "You're coming right along, kid. Couple of years, you'll catch yourself one of the nice light-skinned lawyers over at Girard headquarters." His voice was loud with contempt. "Learn to paint yourself real pretty, you too can grow up to be a liberal."

Rosa looked over to see whether the water was boiling and noticed her daughter's confusion out of the corner of her eye. Bruce's jibe had scored, she saw, and smiled as she rinsed the corn under the faucet. Trixie's assiduous attendance to her twice-weekly chores for the Volunteers for Girard Committee was easier to understand now. Rosa dropped the corn into the boiling water and turned the flame down under the pot. There were worse things for a young girl to dream about, she told herself grimly.

Trixie said, "You better be studying for your exams instead of hanging around drinking beer." She held the little brush poised over her finger, but she didn't turn to Bruce. "You flunk out, where are you then?"

"Where I am is, I don't get my M.A. Big deal. I cry all the way to my ditchdigging job."

"You talkin foolish, boy," Rosa admonished him. She sat down at the table opposite Trixie, took up the dress she had left there, and resumed her sewing. Everything was finished but this hem—if she got it done tonight, she could get it to Ann Taswell a little ahead of time. Her fingers dipped toward the fabric as quickly as the head of a tiny feeding bird, and the almost invisible stitches were smaller than its track would be. "When you got that scholarship, you got gold," she told Bruce without looking at him, keeping her eyes on the sewing that, along with Marian's extra articles on New York art shows, would help to make up for Bettina Little's lack of gold. The tuition at the special school in Pennsylvania was small by comparison with what you had to pay at others, but Marian and Rosa would have to round up writing and sewing assignments at least once a month to make the money nevertheless.

"Oh sure. Fool's gold." Bruce drained the beer with his head thrown back, his Adam's apple moving silkily under the brown skin of his throat. He tightened his fingers on the empty can, looking at Rosa insolently. "You know what that M.A. stands for?"

"It stand for a good chance in life."

"Men's-room Assistant, that's what it stands for."

"B.A., that's Bowling Alley." Trixie giggled, showing off her sophistication.

The baby crawled over to Rosa and pulled himself upright by holding to the seat of her chair. She looked down at him absently, still wearing the frown she had directed at her daughter, and saw that he was tugging at his little pants. "Here you, Bruce," she directed, "you come get this baby and put him on the pot right away, hear?"

Bruce put the beer can down on the drainboard and came over quickly. Rosa was telling the baby, "That right, Gregory. You a good boy, tell Aunt Rosa when you got to go." Bruce lifted the baby, swinging him high, then tucked him under one arm and tickled the fat little belly that stuck out between shirt and pants. The baby laughed and so did Bruce.

"Maybe you see if his mama home when you finish," Rosa called after them. "If she ain't home, bring him back."

"Oh, Mama, you know she won't be home." Trixie put the little brush back into the bottle, holding her fingers carefully splayed out as she tightened the lid.

"Well, if she ain't I ain't leavin him by hisself. We put him to sleep on the sofa."

"Then where're you gonna sleep, Mama?"

"I ain't ready to go to sleep yet." Rosa laid her sewing down and looked at her daughter curiously. "Trixie, what this-here 'Establishment' Bruce keep talkin about? You learn about that in school yet?"

"Oh, Mama, that's not something you learn in school."

"What do it mean, then?" Rosa asked patiently.

"Well, it's sort of like an expression." Trixie looked at her mother's waiting eyes and saw that the question couldn't be dismissed. "It means like the people who run things. The government, and all."

"Like the President?"

"More than the President, Mama. All of them."

"The State Department, too?"

"Well, sure. Oh, you mean Mr. Farland? Sure he's part of the Establishment. Miz Farland too, 'cause she works on a newspaper."

"The Establishment," Bruce announced from the doorway, "is what's got its foot on your neck." The baby, sitting on Bruce's arm, chewed delicately on the edge of his torn T-shirt.

"His mama not home?" Rosa sighed. "Trixie, you heat him up some of that soup in the icebox." She stuck her needle into the hem and began to fold the dress. "I ain't listenin to nothin bad about Miz Farland," she told Bruce. "She my friend, and I ain't seen no foot on my neck." She got up and took the baby.

"Well, you work in her kitchen, don't you?"

Rosa put the baby down on the floor in the corner, out of the way of the traffic, and supplied him with an empty pot and three clothespins. Smiling angelically, he dropped the clothespins into the pot one by one, then dumped them out and began again. His small black face was studious and intent.

"I work for Miz Farland, she work for somebody too," said Rosa, straightening. She spoke mildly, but when she caught sight of Bruce's answering sneer, her temper flared. "I be good for doin housework; Miz Farland, she be good for writin in newspapers. What I want to know is, what you good at, boy?"

Standing at the stove, Trixie said angrily, "Oh, Mama. How do you know you couldn't be a better art critic than her if you had her education?"

"I don't guess I *do* know. Fact is, though, I ain't had her education, and it ain't Miz Farland who stopped me from goin to school." She looked from one to the other of the youngsters, searching their faces for some sign of relenting. "Why must I hate ever'body luckier than me?" She smiled, asking them for good humor. "I be too busy to live."

"You talk like a handkerchief-head, Miz Little," flashed Bruce.

"You do, Mama."

Angered, Rosa swatted at them with the dishcloth she was using to wipe off the table. "Don't look like education do you kids no good, you talk so foolish." She waited, struggling to recover her authority. "That soup ready now, Trixie. You go on and feed Gregory, so you have time to eat too before the meetin."

"The holy, precious meeting. Go do your duty, Trixie. Get Alec Girard elected President. That's real important, that is. Makes a big difference which one of them ofays gets in."

"Trixie, get the phone book for him to sit on." Rosa picked up the baby and waited, eyeing with exasperation above the small bobbing head this Bruce who knew what was good grammar and foolishly, deliberately, wasted it. "Mr. and Miz Farland, they for Girard," she began.

"So naturally you gotta be, too."

Rosa put the phone book down on the plump, plastic-covered seat of a chair, set the baby on top of it, and pushed him closer to the table. "No, I figure for myself," she answered evenly, but with obvious effort. "I figure he do more for the colored people." She tied a dish towel loosely around the baby's neck as Trixie sat down beside him and began spooning the soup into his eager mouth.

"Girard ain't about to do nothing for nobody, the way he's going," Bruce said with some satisfaction. "They say he's laying eggs all over the place. Not just the other side's saying it, either. He sounds like he don't know what he wants to sound like, if you ask me. Don't matter anyway." He spoke more quietly, with less anger but bitter conviction. "Neither of them's for us. Nobody in this whole damn country's for us."

Rosa was draining the corn by holding the pot over the sink with the lid tilted. Steam rose from the narrow opening like a genie. "You better go study some more. You ain't learned but half your lesson." She set the pot back on the stove, its lid still tilted.

"Meaning what?"

"Meanin if there ain't enough room in a house, you go to work and build onto it. If you blow it up, ain't *nobody* have no room." The baby was knuckling at his eyes, and she leaned down and took his hand away gently. "Take a couple of these chairs in the front room," she commanded Bruce before he could reply. "Put them by the sofa so he don't roll off. Here, Trixie, you put this here baby down to sleep, and mind you don't forget the rubber sheet. Then you get your supper, hear? I be goin to see how Bettina doin. Bruce, if you hungry, you sit down to some supper with Trixie, hear?"

"Thank you, Miz Little, but I don't think—"

"You livin on Cokes and potato chips, you get sick. Mind what I tell you, Bruce. You eat with Trixie."

"Yes, ma'am."

He was a good boy, Rosa thought, listening to the sounds of the pair putting the baby to bed as she went down the long narrow hall leading to the apartment's only bedroom. One glance at the disorder in there was enough to dampen her pleasure. She sighed and began with the collection of objects littering the double bed. Folding clothes and storing them rapidly in drawers, she asked Bettina cautiously, "How about you leave that wait a little bit and come in for supper?"

Bettina dipped two fingers into a widemouthed jar, collected some of the viscous bluish stuff, and applied it to a small hank of hair held taut between the fingers of the other hand. She caught the slimy drips dextrously; then, satisfied that the hair was anointed enough, she began to smooth it around a pink plastic roller. Rosa paused, watching almost hypnotically until the resulting pink-lined sausage was thoroughly skewered with a pink plastic pick. Bettina picked up her hand mirror, turned her back to the large unframed mirror on the wall over the modernistic bureau, and studied the reflected back of her head. Rosa looked from the matching comb and brush, unscarred by use, to the almost-full, brand-new suitcase—a going-away present from Marian Farland—that stood open in the middle of the bed. "It all right to put the comb and brush in now?"

Bettina said languidly, "I decided to leave that junk for Trixie. Maybe she'll like it."

Rosa, who had given her daughter the set for her birthday, bit her lip and turned away. She lifted the suitcase without closing it and set it on the floor. Then she gathered the movie magazines scattered over the bed into a neat pile. From the cover of the top one Elizabeth Taylor stared, lilac-eyed, at the dirty white plastic whorls of the radio, which was emitting a steady, nervous rock-'n-roll harangue.

The wallpaper in the room, a legacy of a long-ago tenant, was printed in a violent all-over design in which fishing rods and creels, rifles, tennis rackets, and other sports equipment were flung against an unconvincingly knotty-pine background. Time had faded all this to a vague tan with blurs of muddy color, but Rosa noticed, as she watched Bettina bend to peer at a torn-out magazine page stuck on the wall near the mirror, that the lady in the picture had a gun pointing at her head from the adjacent wallpaper. Under the lady there was a drawing of a head, divided into sections and intricately numbered. Bettina studied this schematic carefully, like a builder consulting a blueprint; then, satisfied, she began on the next curl. The noise on the radio gave way to an announcer's rapid patter in which the word "hurry" occurred often.

"I don't want no supper. I ain't coming out of this room till that Bruce is gone," Bettina said sullenly, still looking into the mirror.

Rosa smoothed the clean white candlewick spread over the uneven surface of the bed. "What you got against Bruce?"

"He thinks he's so great, just because he goes to college." Bettina's triangular cat face was distorted with spite. A tall, slender girl with long legs and narrow hips, she was much prettier than her sister. Her skin was as light as Rosa's, though it had a yellower tinge, but she bore no other resemblance to her mother. "Him and his stuck-up girlfriends. Can't hardly tell they *are* girls, with them pants all the time and no makeup."

"Colleges ain't nothin to be stuck-up about," Rosa said slyly. "Anybody can go that finished high school."

"Who needs it?" Bettina shrugged. "Louella says they're all Communists in college."

"Don't tell me what Louella say," Rosa flared. "I ain't got the time of day for that tramp."

"Don't you go calling my best friend a tramp!"

Rosa took the girl by her narrow shoulders and swung her away from the mirror. "You listen to me, Tina," she said firmly. "That Louella, she end up on the street and we both know it. Maybe Bruce act some sassy, but he got brains. Louella, she never be nothin but scum."

"Not like me, huh?" Bettina freed herself and turned back to the mirror, but her hands were shaking at their task. "Get shipped off to the sticks to rot, 'cause you and your fine lady Miz Farland got together and fixed it. Why'n't you get me dyed white while you was at it? That's what you're doing anyway, trying to make me live like I was white. All of a sudden, our way ain't good enough for you any more."

"No." Rosa stared blankly ahead at the window, afraid to look at her daughter. The dingy paper shade, drawn to the sill, had a triangular tear; a similar one on the other window had been mended with white adhesive tape. "It ain't, and that a fact. I ain't about to see you livin like a bug, one day at a time." She turned her head and studied Bettina thoughtfully. "You want to live nice, too, same as I do—what else you readin them magazines for? But it ain't white and black—everybody got a right to live nice."

Bettina tied a rayon scarf printed like leopard fur over her curlers. "You talk like Bruce—all them rights."

"Ain't nothin wrong with what Bruce and them talk, only they don't tell it all. We got rights like white folks, but we got to be willin to live like them other ways, too."

"Yeah. Like with money."

Rosa shook her head. "Money sure be a help, but you put the Farlands right here in this here apartment house and no more money than people here got, and they still be different. They ain't about to throw garbage in the halls."

"Miz Farland is an angel, I already know that," Bettina sneered.

"No, she somethin better, she a lady."

"I be a lady too, if I get me some of those dresses she has."

"Sure." Rosa smiled at her daughter. "You be a lady, too, but not by no dress. You learn to be like Miz Farland—she do her work, pay what she owe, take care of her things and other people's too. And she don't do ever'-thin she feel like doin. You figure how to be like that, you get the dresses."

"How you talk, Mama." The girl turned away with a theatrical laugh, but Rosa was satisfied with the thoughtful look of her. Though not with herself, for she was aware of not having told the whole truth. Even if Bettina learned all she needed to, Marian Farland's world might still be closed to her—including, perhaps, the pretty dresses her mother had unscrupulously dangled before her. Rosa sighed. Who knows, who ever knows? Lots of things might be different. And, anyway, whatever the girl must face when she tried to make a place in the world, she would be better able to cope with it once she had an education and some judgment. It was hard to imagine, looking at Bettina now, but it was even possible she'd forget about the pretty dresses.

Bettina muttered something and went out of the room, her white robe brushing Rosa in the close quarters as she passed. Rosa heard the bathroom door close and, reminding herself that she needed to do better with her other daughter, moved over to Trixie's desk. The girl had finished her homework, as ordered, but she'd left her books jumbled and her notebook spread open. Rosa straightened the pile of books; the top one was covered neatly with sturdy brown paper on which "Beatrix R. Little" was written gracefully and legibly. A school pennant was tacked to the short wall of the corner in which the desk stood; on the other, Trixie had taped white shelf paper over the active tumult of the wallpaper to make a more suitable background for the painting Marian had given her—a light, delicate oil showing a farmyard with chickens and a pair of small, foreign-looking stone buildings under a soft, pale-blue sky. Over the scene lay a kindly yellow light that spoke of peace and warmth. Rosa glanced from this to the one on the opposite wall, a painting on blue velvet of a full moon above a forest and rushing stream, and knew that Trixie was right to think this nicer, though her mother didn't know why. Rosa touched the painted surface lightly with her forefinger, thinking of the man who must have dipped his brush as she had seen Marian do. Maybe it was because one man made it and there was no other picture exactly like it, she thought.

Bettina came back into the room and Rosa turned from the picture to the notebook on the desk, but the scene lingered in her mind. She would like to be, someday, in just such a sunny yard, scattering feed for those chickens. Someday, when the girls were grown, if she could only save enough money . . . She shook herself free of the thought and began to study Trixie's homework. She checked to make sure that the name, date, and class number had been supplied. "I. Properties of a solution," the homework began, and Rosa scanned it, uncomprehending but approving of the neatness and the orderly shape of the outline. She turned the page and frowned—on the next page the writing was crossed out in three places, and the date was missing from its prescribed place in the upper right-hand corner. Tightening her lips, she pushed the looseleaf mechanism and lifted the page out. "Trixie," she called in her high, sweet voice. "Where *you?*"

"Wherever you are, you better hide," Bettina said softly. "Here come Mama with blood in her eye."

Rosa laughed, pausing to survey her elder daughter fondly. When she started toward the doorway again, Bruce was knocking on the half-open door.

"*Come* in," Bettina said languidly, without turning from her mirror. "The door's open, as you can see."

"How true." Bruce's eyes flicked over her before he turned to Rosa. "Trixie's getting the baby a drink of water, Miz Little. She'll be in in a minute. And I wanted to tell you his mother's home now."

"Bet she's been down at the Black Cat all evening," Bettina said.

Bruce nodded, his eyes still on Rosa and holding a question. "Looks like she has, all right, Miz Little. I don't think she knows Gregory's not there, but I left a note in case she thinks of it. I didn't think I better take him back."

"No." Rosa sighed. "Leave him where he at."

"My mother doesn't approve of such goings-on," Bettina announced, whirling to face them. Her eyes sparked with defiance. "Though she's served the liquor at plenty of parties where the ladies got just as drunk."

"I don't think so," Bruce observed. "It'd be pretty hard to match that performance."

Rosa said sadly to her daughter, "They ain't left no babies home alone, cryin in a empty apartment, neither."

Bruce still hung in the doorway, openly watching Bettina now. "All set to go, I see."

"Just about. I have some last-minute chores, of course."

"Of course," he mocked. "Say, do they let you get mail from men at that convent?"

Bettina threw back her head and laughed in careless merriment somewhat flawed by the fact that she was covertly watching herself in the mirror. "They better. I'm not taking *vows*, you know. I'm not even Catholic."

"Let's run a test." Bruce's studied carelessness was a more skilled performance. "Suppose I drop you a line, say, next week."

Bettina shrugged. "If you wish."

"Well, but you'll have to answer or I wouldn't know whether it got through or not."

"I expect I'll be pretty busy. There's a rather heavy academic load up there."

Rosa, watching the two like a spectator at a tennis match, stared at her daughter in hardly hidden amazement. Where had she learned to talk like that?

"It would hardly be a test of their policy if I couldn't ascertain whether you received it," Bruce was saying.

"I suppose you're correct." Bettina considered the merits of his argument, posing with her hand on one slender hip as she thought. "Very well, then. I'll make it my business to reply."

"Good. I'll be expecting to hear from you." Bruce turned his attention to Rosa. "I better see what's holding Trixie up, Miz Little. Would you like me to wait and walk her over to the headquarters?"

"That be a good idea, Bruce."

"Okay. See you around, Eartha," he told Bettina, and vanished.

Rosa said meditatively, "He a good boy. He just talk silly sometime." Then she saw her daughter's dejected face. "What ailin you, honey?"

"Oh Mama."

Rosa came quickly across the small space and clasped the girl to her. Poor baby, she thought, if they don't treat her right I go up there and take her right out, money or no money, "Hush now, baby. Tell Mama."

"He'll know, Mama," Bettina wailed, her voice muffled.

"What he know, honey?" Rosa shifted the girl a little so that a curler would stop digging into her shoulder.

"Now I have to write to him and he'll see how I spell and all. He'll know how ignorant I am."

Lord, Lord, Rosa thought, you never knew what would do it. Patting her daughter, she looked into her memory of the past few months as if she were lifting the lid of a packed trunk. By the time she'd told Marian about the problem, she'd already studied it long enough and hard enough to make her sick. And then, after that there'd been that snooty woman at the *Tribune,* and then the whole jumble of strange white faces that would have been—she knew it, even if Marian didn't seem to—just stiff and bossy if she'd gone alone.

Rosa shook her head a little in reproof for this thought—it wasn't fair, because at least some of the time it hadn't been only that Marian's face was white. Certainly with that fine social worker they'd come to at last, it was Marian herself—the believing way she had when she asked for help—that had started Mrs. Social Worker digging and hunting and telephoning until she'd found these nuns who specialized in problem girls. And certainly that psychiatrist had not had color on his mind—though he'd talked about it, about problems Bettina might run into, and not just paid it no mind like Marian. Rosa smiled, remembering how she had hardly been able to listen to the man for wondering what her own Mama would say if she knew Rosa was sitting there big as life in a *psychiatrist's* office . . .

Rosa held the girl away from her and tilted the woebegone face up with a finger under the chin. "Don't you take on, honey. You ain't ignorant."

Bettina twitched away. "You don't know, Mama. Them girls he knows—"

"Never mind them girls—*those* girls he knows. Listen, if you can't write nice now, what you think you be studyin in that school?"

Bettina brightened. "I did say I'd be busy, so I don't have to answer right away."

"Sure. You got time, and they got teachers." Rosa smiled at her daughter and received a watery answering smile. "You ask them polite, they tell you how to spell what you want. See?"

"I see, Mama." Bettina winked at her. "Maybe I'll find somebody to help me. The nuns got nothing against romance, for other people." She stood up, her narrow face glowing with a vision. "Time I come back, those girls'll be from Dullsville. With my looks and all, once I get brains—" she paused, scanning imaginary rows of grieving girlfriends cast off by Bruce "—he's just not going to *see* them, standing there with their blue jeans and their bare faces."

Rosa stood up, patted her daughter's shoulder again, and went back to the desk to get Trixie's homework paper. When she left the room, the memory of the sunny farmyard in the painting traveled with her down the long dark hall.

III

Jousts and Skirmishes

"And glorying in their vows and him, his knights
Stood round him . . ."

Twelve

"There is simply no excuse," Alec Girard said slowly, for him, from millions of television screens, "for the fact that in this country and this year, a child in Appalachia cannot get the milk he needs." The bright eyes looked directly out at the viewers; the clear, still somewhat boyish voice picked up speed as Girard rattled off the sad statistics of distressed areas in West Virginia and Pennsylvania.

He was getting a little fast again, Jake Ruffing thought, and considered signaling the candidate to slow his pace. On second thought he decided to leave it alone—Alec's ability to summon up the figures on demand commanded respect, and the rapidity of his summary was actually valuable in conveying the speaker's own lack of regard for his feat as a feat; what was coming across was Girard's own view of expertise as a handy tool, but only a tool. He stood quite still and clearly at ease, speaking without gestures and with some urgency, his whole manner that of a busy man with matters of importance to impart—and that total effect was probably more valuable than trying to make sure that the slowest listener kept up. Cocking an eye at the image on the studio monitor, Jake decided against distracting Alec with signals of any kind. Just let him rip.

"I believe that if they are once told clearly, without the fuzziness of false optimism, about this state of affairs, the American people will not elect an administration that will permit it to continue." Alec's voice was quiet, but confident and decisive. "We are going to buy that milk from the farmer who has it to sell and get it to the child who needs it." His right hand descended sharply, in one of his rare gestures; effectively, it closed the subject, dooming anything Ralph Ferris said in reply to the status of a postscript.

Jake glanced over at Rosenberg, who was watching Alec on another screen in the glassed-in booth; Rosie's face was hidden, but the sprawl of his long body bespoke contentment. If I were a drinking man, Jake thought happily . . . and then let it trail away because he wasn't, and just sat there watching Ralph Ferris hint that Alec Girard was being of aid and comfort to the enemies of the United States.

Ferris was dark and intense and there was no stillness in him. "They don't have to run down this great country of ours, as long as Senator Girard will do it for them. This great country, I say; for, under the guiding hand of President Winkler, we have risen to a level of prosperity unknown in the history of the world." It was a campaign speech, and habit gave Ferris's voice a mindless will of its own, like a horse heading for its stable; he waited unconsciously and almost imperceptibly for the burst of applause at

the Winkler name, and there was none, of course, because this was a debate
and its only audience a panel of reporters concentrating on impartiality. The
tiny pause threw the timing and emphasis of the rest of his sentence off
and imparted to the figure on the screen a faint impatience and disappointment, like a man waiting for a train that hadn't come.

Rosenberg pushed a scratch pad along the formica countertop under the
monitor sets. Jake read the scrawled "Superman vs Mr. Coffee Nerves"
and nodded agreement, but Rosie had turned back to the screen without
waiting. Ferris, still giving off that odd impression that he was hopping
around, was tagging his opponent with all the sins of his party; included, it
appeared, was a lack of reverence for free enterprise, which seemed a poor
idea against a candidate who, the whole country knew, was a beneficiary of
his father's skill at free enterprise. Ferris's dark face was lighted with the
joy of the debater, and he was doing well at scoring debating points.

Ferris was, in fact, making the kind of speech Alec had not been making
on the hustings. Jake Ruffing sighed slowly, letting the air out of his lungs
with a sense of luxury awaited and attained at last. Because it had all come
out okay, but it needn't have—it had been a risk to launch his candidate
into hostile territory, and Jake had taken it. The West Coast areas in which
Alec had started campaigning were largely Ferris territory; those that were
not, were no-man's-lands in which mines sowed during the battle for the
nomination remained to be set off by the unwary. Tom Cannon and Dan
Daniels were both out campaigning vigorously for Alec right now, but what
they had said when they were fighting him could not be entirely unsaid:
much of what Ferris had been throwing at Alec tonight, for example, was
little different from the content of Daniels' pre-campaign speeches—except
that the sins Daniels had ascribed to Girard were now being put forth as
typifying both Girard and his party.

The practice of politics is not unlike the game of bridge in that as much
may depend on playing a card at the right time as on having the right card.
The ace of trumps will always take a trick, to be sure—but only one trick,
unless it's used skillfully. Jake Ruffing had employed the bridge analogy on
the recent afternoon at the Vermont headquarters when Bill Bruyette had
taken him for a stroll by the lake and a tentative probe of the Ruffing
strategy.

"Look, Jake, he's laying eggs by the dozen out there. You know it, I know
it, and I know you're not going to bridle when I say it. I'm out of line now
and I know that, too—and I hope you also know that I'm not speaking for
anybody but myself: you're the strategist of Alec's own choice—"

"But you don't think he's chosen well," Jake said, smiling without looking
at Bruyette.

"The point is, Alec thinks he's chosen well. What I think doesn't matter,
except to me. That's why I want to know—if you want to tell me anything
besides to go to hell. Which is your right."

Jake dismissed the protocol with a wave of his hand. "I'm laying off my losers, Bill, that's all. Where he is now, the only way they'll go for him is on a bandwagon anyway, so I just figured that's the place to let him do his losing."

"But is it the time, Jake?" Bruyette hesitated. "I mean, if you start him off by damaging his confidence—"

"I know. It's a calculated risk." Jake looked out across the lake. "I'm trying to hedge it as much as I can, of course, but Alec's bright enough to know he's not going over. If I were handling Ferris—which God forbid—I'd do the exact opposite, because Ferris is the type who needs reassurance. Things have got to be going well for Ferris to get going well. But my boy—" Jake smiled at his own use of the fight-manager's term—"has more—well, heart." This time both men accepted the vocabulary without hesitation. "Knock him down and he not only gets up, but he gets up figuring out what he did wrong instead of crying because he got knocked down."

"What's he doing wrong, Jake?"

Ruffing shrugged. "I'm only a practical psychologist, Bill, not a practicing one. Roughly, I think it has something to do with the fact that he's talking too much like a President and not enough like a fellowman." He silenced Bruyette's beginning interruption with a quick gesture. "I know—that's what worked in Wisconsin. But in Wisconsin they were *seeing* the fellowman while the President was talking. It's not possible to tramp the whole U.S. the way we did Wisconsin. Television is the answer, of course, but we can't spend all that dough until we're sure the people are listening—we could end up with our pockets empty while Ferris saturates the TV channels in the last two weeks."

Bruyette said moodily, "So that means Alec has got to come through in newspaper quotes."

"Sure. And he can be quotable as hell, you know that."

"Yes, but not folksy. Jake, if you think Alec is ever going to start talking about the 'little woman'—"

"Not that way, no." Jake held out his arm so Bruyette could see his watch; they turned back toward the house. "But sooner or later he'll start talking like a man instead of a public institution."

"Talking like Alec is what you mean, isn't it? And you think if he gets mad he'll come out swinging." Bruyette sighed. *"If he gets mad. . ."*

It was more complex than that, but Jake had let it go at that. If Alec Girard got mad the way Ferris did—little, hopping, fuming, frustrated—it wouldn't be the way. But Alec was different: anger brought energy but no visible heat. An angry Alec rolled up his sleeves and got rolling, and it was a spectacle Jake Ruffing was willing to bet the voters would be inspired to go out and vote for. But how to assure it?

Seeking the answer, Jake had maneuvered to do something Will Farland had spoken of, though in disapproval, at the Kimballs' house nearly a year ago: move the problem from where it is to where you wish it were. Farland was correct in condemning it in foreign policy, but it was a good idea in a campaign: if Alec Girard's style was ideal for the television audience, then move him to a television audience. And if you need a confrontation to bring the man out of the institution, then get a confrontation. It was here, Jake knew happily as he sat in the control booth and savored his triumph, that his disadvantages had turned to advantage: it was probably quite likely that Ferris's advisers, who were thoroughly aware that more of the nation knew Ferris's face than Girard's, would never have agreed to the exposure of a national debate unless they were convinced that Alec would lose; if they thought he had an even chance, the encounter would not have been worthwhile for them. Ferris's scouts must have reported, accurately, that Girard wasn't going over on his West Coast trip—thus providing the necessary inducement for the Ferris camp strategists to agree to the debate Jake Ruffing had been proposing but carefully not pushing.

And now the losing card had won the Girard team a trick. Jake Ruffing trusted his own judgment, and his judgment said that Alec Girard had already swamped his opponent.

"The idea," the brisk New England voice said matter-of-factly, "that how the United States looks to the rest of the world depends on slogans or accidental circumstances or even conspiracy and cloak-and-dagger doings—which has been a favorite notion of the administration—is foolish to begin with and may in the end be quite dangerous."

You and I, was the unspoken message of the quiet voice that would not stoop to outright scorn, of the handsome, serious face of a man too intelligent to play games in working time—*we are too busy for nonsense and too grown-up for tricks.* Jake sat up suddenly in his whirly chair, glancing over at his companion; Rosenberg's face was invisible, but Jake could see the movement of the stubbly skin under the ear as Rosie began to smile.

"Propaganda has severe limitations when it's stacked up against truth," Senator Girard said quietly to the most exhorted people in history. "By and large, we look to the rest of the world pretty much the way we are, just as I know what kind of man my neighbor is from what I've seen of him, not from what somebody tells me about him. If we want to be regarded by our international neighbors as generous, the simplest and most foolproof way is to *be* generous, to demonstrate by our laws and our customs that we have significant concern for our poor, our elderly, and our unfortunate citizens. Let the whole world see us as we are: a nation pleased with the advantages of leisure, but not about to confuse a life of ease with the so-called American way of life."

Rosenberg was bent forward now, his arm braced on the counter, scribbling on his pad like a schoolboy. But Jake Ruffing sat at leisure, his work at least temporarily done, free to enjoy the promising future. He was too cautious to take it for a certainty, but he welcomed the bright, growing hunch that all the rest of the winning tricks in this bridge game were in Alec's hand.

"The American way of life is not a simple thing at all—it's much more complex than can be described in thirty seconds. But its major component is a kind of energetic discontent, a marvelous legacy from our forebears. This nation was made and preserved by idealists who were not and never would be content with simply cutting themselves a slice of comfort: those who were that easily satisfied stayed where they were. We are the descendants of the discontent, who had the imagination and the courage to pull up stakes and try for a better life in a new world. All these migrations—into the country, across the country—required imagination and courage and determination enough to cross oceans and venture into untried wildernesses; these qualities have been passed down to us just as surely as the land and the family Bible were handed down. Imagination, courage, and determination have made America a great nation already, but they can make this nation greater still. I remind you, my fellow citizens, that we have not exhausted our capacity for greatness, that it is there as it has always been, ready to be used again and again. We have more important things to do than sit around admiring the pictures in our family album. We will not, we cannot, use the blessings of a good life to achieve only national complacency." Girard paused, his look as demanding, as urgent, as his words had been. Then his face relaxed. "Let's get started," he said, and stepped away from the podium.

Home free, said Jake Ruffing to himself in his glassy cage.

"Hot dog!" the learned and articulate Rosenberg pronounced in quiet awe.

"All Bruyette would say was 'We have met the enemy and they are ours,' " Alec said into the phone. "Just sat there and kept announcing that."

Andy choked on the last gasps of laughter. "Oh, Alec." A few leftover gurgles threatened. "Oh dear. Why didn't you tell me when you called that night?"

"Well, for one thing, it probably hadn't happened yet. I called you as soon as I'd shaken hands with Ferris and swept out. But anyway, it's taken a couple of days to catch up with Rosie—he came out here ahead of me. So I didn't hear the story until late last night. Then we were sitting around that fancy little trunk he carries around—you know—"

"I know," said the fancy little trunk's decorator.

"Well, it reminded him. Have you seen Bruyette since he got back?"

"No. Your mother told me he'd phoned, but he's out campaigning for himself this week, I gathered. I'm surprised now that he was in condition to."

"Oh, he wasn't that drunk, Andy. As a matter of fact, Rosie says he doesn't think Bill had much to drink at all. According to Jake, it was mostly psychological." Alec hesitated, then went on lightly. "My own hunch is that Bruyette actually flew out here for the debate so he could stand by to pick up my remains. I think what got to him was relief more than alcohol. Still," he added ruefully, "I wish I'd seen it."

"How did they get him to bed?"

Alec laughed. "Well, apparently he just sat there on that trunk proclaiming this great victory and of course Jake was—well, you know Jake: he was charging around screaming at everybody about overconfidence and let's get this show on the road. I had been tucked into bed right away in my little nursery," he said without bitterness, "with Healy posted outside the door in case I wanted a drink of water."

Andy made a small consoling sound.

"So it seems that finally Bruyette agreed to go to bed if he could shake my hand. A notion that Jake was hardly about to go for, even weakened as he was—I forgot to tell you, there was an earlier interlude in which Bill had chased him around the room, trying to kiss him on both cheeks." Alec's voice broke. "Which Bruyette considered the only appropriate form of congratulation."

"Oh no."

"Oh yes. That must've been a sight . . . Anyway, they got him to compromise on looking in at me as I lay asleep in my little trundle bed. So Healy and Rosie helped him in and he stood in the doorway with tears in his devoted eyes and watched me breathe in and out for a few minutes—"

"Alec, stop."

"Andy, I swear it. Well, Rosie does. In the end, Bill saw the wisdom of not waking me, and they bundled him off to his room. The next morning, he flew east and I flew west." He sighed. "It was an inspiring tribute. If a little unrealistic. We have a long way to go yet."

"Pooh. Here in Kingsley, we know what we know. Pierre's even made a down payment on a souvenir stand."

"A souvenir stand?"

"For the tourists who'll be coming to visit your birthplace. Oh, don't worry—he's not abandoning Washington and us. He's going to be the silent partner in this business."

"But I wasn't born in Kingsley," Alec protested.

"That is a consideration Pierre has decided to overlook," Andy told him grandly.

"He'll lose his shirt."

"Not according to the best business advice."

"Oh? Whose? The boys he plays cards with at the firehouse?"

Andy laughed. "No, darling. Your father's, as a matter of fact." She listened to Alec's groan and then added wickedly, "So you see, you'd better cream Ferris."

"I'd better *what?*"

"Cream him. Don't you dig?"

"Andy! What in the world have you been doing up there?"

"Eavesdropping on Mary's children, for one thing. Don't you like my new vocabulary? Acquiring it has just about made my week."

"Poor Andy," Alec said soberly. "It isn't very lively for you."

"Oh, it's not too awful," she assured him quickly. "I don't mind, really. Your mother's hairdresser did my hair a new way, and I'm very elegant. All sorts of excitements, really."

"Yes," Alec said dryly. "All sorts. Particularly when Elizabeth gets loose."

"Oh, Alec, it's my fault, I guess. I'm the one who gave her permission to go with the other children to visit Calvin Coolidge's house. I thought of it as just—well, an outing, and educational." She heard the crackle of paper at the other end of the line.

Alec's voice glinted with amusement as he read aloud the results of Elizabeth's outing: " ' "My daddy's going to be President of the Newnited States just like Mr. Coolidge," Elizabeth Girard confided to an interviewer yesterday. Asked how she knew this, Elizabeth turned her bright-blue eyes, so like her father's, on the questioner. "My mommy told me," she said with the finality of a three-year-old.' "

"I didn't, you know I didn't," Elizabeth's mommy protested. "I only said we hoped—"

"And Elizabeth heard only what she wanted to," Alec interrupted. "It's a phenomenon I've seen before."

"Darling, we've got her thoroughly muzzled now, so it won't happen again. But I wasn't there then, and a very quick-thinking woman from one of the magazines just happened to ask her precisely the right question." Andy hesitated. "I know it looks so . . . icky. Has it done an awful lot of damage?"

Alec chuckled. " 'Icky,' it seems, is not all bad in politics. Our staff psychologist, Dr. Jake Ruffing, says it did wonders for my image. With Ferris running around the country telling people I'll cost them their life savings if they vote for me, Elizabeth has gone and tied me to the parsimonious President Coolidge in the public mind. Innocence by association. Also, Luke says it humanizes me. A thought-provoking judgment, that one, don't you think?"

"I hope you made it clear to them that we don't intend to let Elizabeth—"

"I put a stop to all dreams of future statements from her."

"Effectively, I hope."

"Madam, believe me," Alec assured her. "I simply pointed out that Elizabeth is perfectly capable of saying something tomorrow that would tie me in with the Communists. Then I confided to Jake that I'd once said, in her hearing, that Kaslov was a shrewd politician. He turned pale. I think we can be sure he won't count on Elizabeth as a campaigner."

Andy giggled. "Well done. Anyway, you don't need her. I watched the debate, too, you know. You were marvelous, and Ralph Ferris is an awful little man. You're quite right not to let him be President."

"I'll do my best to stop him," Alec told her gravely. "Especially now that Pierre . . . Tell me, how much does he have riding on my nose?"

"Six hundred dollars, I think."

"As much as that? Okay. Tell him I'll try to keep his money safe. After all," he added thoughtfully, "I can't let my father's reputation as a business genius suffer, either. Mother would have to take in washing . . ." His voice trailed off inattentively and then resumed, as if he had suddenly remembered something delightful. "Andy? About that elegant new hairdo—"

"It's going to be on a magazine cover. They were taking Mrs. Ferris too, so I wanted to be dazzling."

"That's a dubious statement," her husband said. "I understood you looked with disfavor on a life motivated by politics."

"Alec, I never—you're right, of course. I must be becoming—"

She sounded so shocked at herself that he thought it had probably been a mistake to tease her. "Look, I'm willing to make an honest woman of you. How would you feel about dazzling me?" He heard her catch her breath. "Now listen. This is only if you can clear it with the doctor, of course. But if he okays it, would you consider joining me when I get to New York?"

"Yes," said Andy immediately.

"There'll be huge crowds," he warned, and then added, "We hope."

"Yes, anyhow."

"Everybody will stare at you."

"I don't care. Yes, yes, yes."

Characteristically embarrassed, Alec said awkwardly, "All right," and then changed the subject at once. Gil Kimball had sent regards, he announced as though it were a matter of great immediacy.

Andy's smile was knowing. But she only asked politely how Gil was.

"Somewhat travel-worn. The press has a rather elaborate system—a kind of revolving pool, so they take turns riding the plane with me. If Gil's turn comes up soon, I'll get a little longer to talk to him. The Ferris camp must be hell on the press: Gil looks awful. But don't let it get back to Betty, will you?"

"And how do you look?" Andy asked. "After weeks of insane meals and no sleep?"

"I look incredibly handsome. I have bright-blue eyes, so like Elizabeth's, and—" He broke off. "But you'll see for yourself."

Andy said happily, "Yes, I will."

"And my sleep, as I told you, is so elaborately provided for that I miss all the fun."

"Dear Jake," Andy said gratefully.

"Maybe I ought to send dear Jake back to be top sergeant at Kingsley. You probably shouldn't be up this late. Get to bed, Andy. I'll try to call earlier tomorrow."

Andy, who had enough sense to quit while she was ahead, agreed meekly that she would go right to bed and said good-night. She hung up the phone, pirouetted clumsily around the cottage's small bedroom, and then curled up in the big bed with a novel and read for several hours about somebody else's far less satisfactory marriage.

Thirteen

If it hadn't been the day the county fair's baked-goods entries were to be submitted, Andrea Girard might not have read Gil Kimball's column until her *Washington Tribune* appeared in the mail the next day. But the young Girards' cottage at Kingsley Lake was all but shaken on its sturdy foundations by the anxiety of Jeanne, who, having baked two checkerboard pies for practice in the past week, was now at last about to bake The Entry.

A bride's home on the morning of the wedding would not have been so replete with nervous manifestations and near-tears; in addition, the necessity for anonymous submission of the pie provoked a series of intrigues, negotiations, and last-minute rendezvous-setting that kept the telephone ringing almost constantly. It took Elizabeth Girard about as long as any three-year-old to sense the household tension—thus, by the time she had breakfasted, she had already begun to add to the tension in no small measure by charging about the house with the noisy rambunctiousness small children use to find out whether grown-up tizzy means that the sky has fallen. The handiest way to stabilize the situation was to remove Elizabeth, so by eleven o'clock Andy was watching her daughter and a cousin rearrange the bluestone chips in their grandfather's driveway. This operation—which consisted of filling buckets, transporting them a few feet via tricycle, and dumping them to the accompaniment of loud calls presumably representing the mating cry of the earth-mover—clearly did not require parental participation, and after a few minutes of sidewalk superintendence Andy wandered into the headquarters she normally visited only rarely. She borrowed a copy of the *New York Leader* that a campaign worker, arrived early that morning, had stuck in his coat pocket as he departed from New York late the night before. Settled with it in her mother-in-law's morning room, she turned to the editorial page in the hopes of finding Gil's column, since the *Leader* was his home paper; when she spotted the familiar brooding photo, it was a little like a letter from home. Then she saw the bold italic headline, "All Right for You, Girard," and she began to read quickly.

"Elizabeth Langwith Girard has, at the age of three, all the virtues of her parents and no drawbacks whatever," Gil began. "Photogenic as her mother, she is not shy and makes no attempt to dodge the press. Articulate as her father, she is not hampered in her public statements by a tiresome dependence on shifting realities and probabilities: where Senator Girard says 'Hopefully,' Elizabeth simply says 'It will be.'

"With all this beauty and punch, you can see, Elizabeth makes the ideal subject for an interview. So, while being scooped at any time hurts any red-blooded, poker-playing gent of the working press, the recent exclusive interview with Elizabeth by a lady from a magazine is a really staggering blow.

"I have nothing against ladies from magazines; some of them are even pretty. But there they sit, watching the bright leaves fall in Kingsley, Vermont. Comfy and well-fed in the local inn, they troop over at their leisure to the sprawling mansion of Senator Girard's parents to survey the hustle and bustle of the Senator's headquarters or to watch the Girard grandchildren at play. Unharried by imminent deadlines, these magazine types may, if they wish, write a few hundred words now and then about how the sun sparkles on the lake or what Andrea Girard wore to a tea party. I have heard that the Senator's mother, under the impression that these people are working and need their strength kept up, treats them to coffee and cake and other yummy snacks. There is an entirely creditable rumor that *Life,* for one, makes its gals take turns covering the Girard enclave at Kingsley Lake because they tend to gain an average of five pounds per stint up there; the *Life* image, it seems, requires slender reporters.

"But not gaunt, apparently—otherwise we hollow-cheeked types who've been following the whirling-dervish candidates around the country would all have been gathered to *Life*'s four-color bosom. I'm not complaining, really— I knew what I was getting into when I stood, shifting uncomfortably from one flat foot to the other and trying to look bright and enterprising, by the desk of a midwestern city editor who was wondering whether it would hurt to take me on. At least, I think I knew, though I suspect what I had in mind was Pulitzer Prizes rather than catching buses and planes, trying to get the coffee down before the paper cup melted, and working out a lucid interpretation of the candidate's farm-price proposals while worrying about whether my luggage would get left in Kansas City. Journalism—particularly during a presidential campaign, and no matter which candidate you're covering— has its hazards, but growing a paunch is not one of them; I've been trailing Ralph Ferris and now I'm trailing Alec Girard, and I speak the nonpartisan truth. God bless the kindly doughnut and box-lunch ladies of both parties, but haggard is still the word for Kimball.

"Mine is a great job, though—and I wouldn't trade it for anything else even if I knew how to do anything else. But I am entitled to a tiny whine, I think. For if ever a story could be described as pure velvet, a reportorial freebie, any interview with Elizabeth Girard surely qualifies. She speaks up loud and clear and not even her worst enemy—can there really be an enemy of Elizabeth?—could say that she equivocates. No hidden meanings to uncover, nothing to research, interpret, or explain—and guaranteed readers all over the U.S. So is it fair, I ask you plaintively, that we travel-worn, dirty, unshaven camp followers should be barred from the orchard when such a journalistic plum is ripe? Is it just, is it kind, is it *human,* for Senator and Mrs. Girard to hand Elizabeth over to a magazine lady luxuriating in Vermont?"

Laughing, Andrea pushed the folded newspaper away and stood up. She hesitated only a moment, then she went over to her mother-in-law's desk and found a scratch pad and a pencil; she collected the newspaper from the table and pushed open the sliding door that led to the patio. Somebody's bulky white sweater was lying on the lounge out there. She put it on, snuggling gratefully into its warmth before she settled her heavy body among the bright cushions of the lounge. Below the huge bulge at her middle, her slim legs and bare feet in dusty navy-blue sneakers looked absurdly schoolgirlish. She held her pencil poised above the pad while she reread the last paragraph of Gil's column. Then she smiled, put the newspaper down, and began to write intently. Wisps of her dark hair escaped from their constraining ribbon and tickled her forehead as the cool autumn wind frisked across the flagstones. She tucked her hair back with her free hand and went on writing.

A carbon copy of Andrea's letter, typed by a secretary who thoroughly enjoyed the task, was delivered to Jake Ruffing in Ohio that evening by Bill Bruyette, who returned from his Vermont congressional district the same day. Jake looked first startled, then dubious, and finally as fatuous as a new grandfather surveying a little blanket-wrapped bundle. Carrying the letter, he charged, with his characteristic half-run, though the partly open doorway into the bedroom of the hotel suite.

The candidate was lying on one of the twin beds in a T-shirt, worn khaki pants, and no shoes or socks. He was plying a much-bitten yellow pencil among the pages of a typed speech and muttering to himself. "Not 'mendacious,' " he said positively. He crossed the word out, and the pencil tore a hole in the paper. He looked at the page disgustedly, said, "Untrustworthy," and wrote something in above the tear. The pencil went through the paper again, and Alec, with a weary exclamation but without any sign of temper, put both pencil and paper down on the bed beside him and looked up at the man he called his "handler."

"I know," he said. "Ferris'll be looking for me to lead with my left."

Jake grinned. "We have a secret punch, it looks like." He waved Andrea's letter at the recumbent Senator. "You saw this, I take it? Andy's *chapeau* in the ring."

Alec dug in his heels and raised himself to a half-sitting position on the bed. "I saw it." He smiled. "But I didn't have any advance warning, if that's what you mean."

"What brought it on? Just Elizabeth's getting involved?"

"Maybe. Or maybe she figured out that we've got to have forty-seven electoral votes out of New York. Or maybe— Jake, I never said I could run Andy, you know. Only the country."

"You know what I think? I bet it's the spirit of Princess Nat asserting itself. Blood will tell." Jake turned to go. "I've got to lay on your new volunteer's press conference. I hope she won't quail when she sees the size of her audience."

"Leave me your copy, will you?" Alec asked. "I don't know what I did with mine. I'll bet she will quail," he added gloomily. "She's probably thinking in terms of Gil Kimball and a couple of his playmates." He took the letter and lay back on the bed, propping the pages on his abdomen. He waved at the departing Jake and began to read his wife's letter to the editor of the *New York Leader*.

"I am so deeply moved," it began, "by the plaint of your columnist Gil Kimball that I'd like to offer an explanation of the recent interview with my daughter Elizabeth.

"First, please tell Mr. Kimball **it** was not a policy decision. The 'magazine lady' about whom he is understandably bitter must have been just as surprised as anyone else when Elizabeth, struck by the fact that the reporter was wearing a scarf like one I own, marched over and initiated a conversation that was not only unplanned but also unnoticed by the grown-ups in charge of the children's outing. Also, if it will make Mr. Kimball feel any less aggrieved, the magazine lady's interview with Elizabeth was not so much of a freebie as he thinks—the reporter got an exclusive story, it's true, but she also underwent an extensive, severe, and probably unethical cross-questioning about her wardrobe, family, and other items of autobiography; my daughter, it seems, was at least as much interviewing as interviewed. I wasn't there at the time, but my sister-in-law, who noticed Elizabeth's absence and went to round her up, described herself as 'going to the rescue.' When Elizabeth's aunt found the pair, the interviewer (rather flushed, it is reported) was nervously trying to explain just why she didn't have a little girl three years old. It seems clear that it wasn't Elizabeth who was rescued.

"I don't imagine it's difficult to understand our reluctance to allow our daughter to talk to the press. Just as Elizabeth is convinced that her daddy will be the next President, Senator Girard and I are convinced that Elizabeth is a very charming child. We'd like to keep her that way, and we're not sure we can if she is exposed to the flattery of having busy men and women hang on her every word. I'm sure parents everywhere can understand our horror of children who are conceited, self-conscious show-offs and our determination not to let the unusual circumstances of her life spoil our lovable, friendly, and—I blush to say—apparently thoroughly inquisitive little girl.

"Yet even a heart of stone would be melted by Mr. Kimball's wail. I know what it's like to try to keep up with Alec Girard, and I'd like to do what I can to try to make it up to Mr. Kimball and his colleagues, who deserve a freebie after their cross-country ordeal. So, since I'm planning to meet my husband in New York next week, I wondered whether, in lieu of Elizabeth, I would do for an easy background story if I promise to try to speak up loud and clear, and to be unequivocal. And, in view of that heartrending history of box lunches and coffee in paper cups, I'd like to invite the hardy troupe of campaign correspondents to a sitting-down lunch, with tablecloths and china and other amenities. As I've had only spotty success in the past in assuring my husband's presence at mealtimes, I can't promise that he'll join us. But I'll do what I can—at the least, perhaps I can wring a promise from him to do nothing that requires reporting while his hard-working camp followers are enjoying a leisurely lunch."

"As a luncheon, it lacked tranquillity," Andy reported resignedly to Paul Morisot, the day after she had entertained the press. "For one thing, Luke tells me everybody who had ever worked in any department of any newspaper managed to get in. I gather that the man who manages Alec's campaign finances won't allow my name to be mentioned in his presence any more. It seems that, thanks to me, we fed half the population of New York." Her smile faded. "Paul, in a way it was frightening—I hadn't expected such masses of people. But they say I didn't do badly, and most of what I read sounded at least kind." Her eyes laughed a little again. "The press, like anybody else, apparently feels kindlier on a full tummy. On numerous full tummies." She sighed. "But even the press luncheon looked cozy by comparison with the parade crowds. Alec *did* warn me about the crowds before I agreed to come to New York, though," she added conscientiously, "so I suppose I have no right to complain about the parade ordeal. Did you see it?"

"I look on the television in the restaurant," Paul Morisot said. "Everyone comes from his table to stand before the machine—it is aloft, you know?" His hand swept up and out, indicating the height of the set in the restaurant; unconsciously, his eyes also assumed the look of devotion the arrangement had caused. His mouth hung loose and faintly wondering, in exact if unintentional reproduction of the appearance of the random collection of New Yorkers who had left their lunches to go and look at the image of the parade. "The little Marian was pained. She wished, instead, to go out and find the street and see you for herself. But I had some fear for her safety in the crowd."

Oh dear, thought Andy. She smoothed the skirt of her garnet-colored maternity dress so that she could present him with her profile and keep her incipient laughter invisible. The little Marian would doubtless have ended up not only undamaged but ushered to a front-row spot and snuggled in some gallant's overcoat against the autumn chill.

"She is so small," Paul was explaining. "And then, of course, we had not yet finished with our lunch." His voice indicated that while one might possibly run some risks in the protection of the *petite,* one would hardly abandon all standards. "But we saw on the television that you rode with Alex in an automobile between tall buildings. The shadows were of amazing purity, do you know?" His hand, sketching in the looming walls of New York's financial district—the tall, close buildings that had cast such interesting shadows —halted in midair as he recalled that Andy might be interested in something else. "You appeared to be happy," he added judiciously.

"I was happy, though I was frightened, too. They were so close, on all sides. Sometimes it seemed—I don't know—as though the sides of the car would buckle. As though they might crush us." Andy shrugged apologetically. "Ridiculous, isn't it? There I sat with my lap full of flowers, among thousands of people who'd been standing there for hours just to get a sight of us. That's hardly anything to be afraid of, is it?" Her slow smile was rueful. "Maybe I'm only half-converted. I see both sides, and it's uncomfortable."

She saw that this side, at least, didn't understand. "So many people," she amplified. "All those eyes, watching so closely. But it's only fair, you see." She spread her hands, her face suddenly earnest and very young. "To be the wife of the President is a very important thing. Why shouldn't they look me over carefully? They have a *right*."

"Perhaps," Paul said gravely. "But the public life deprives the private one."

"Yes, but the public life also insures the private one. I think it'll matter a great deal to the private lives of a lot of people if Alec becomes President of the United States." Andy grinned, mocking her own uncharacteristic "platform" manner. "And it'll certainly matter to our private life if he doesn't. Unfortunately."

"*Andréa*." Paul said it reprovingly. "To live with Alec is to live within the phenomenon, as he does. Surely you know this. Other men's work may be either more or less private, as they wish, but Alec's work must be public. How should he concern himself with the making of balances on this subject? A man of talent does not *wonder* whether he should work. Alec is content to be at once public and private." He smiled at her like a hopeful teacher. "Like other men, he wishes to do his work, though it is different from other men's."

"Well, I know—sometimes. But I still bargain. I guess I mean to pay as little as I can, even though I'm becoming resigned to loving a phenomenon." She nodded as sternly as though Paul had objected. "I'm not entirely sure how to go about it, but—some of my previous 'experience' applies, doesn't it?"

Paul caught the reference and joined her in laughter, but he also noted with approval that there had already been some change: he'd talked to her on the telephone the day the newspapers had carried the interview she was quoting now, and she'd been less than amused, then, at the way her once-restrained husband had let the world in with a quip. Pressed by questions from an airport crowd about the absence of his wife, Girard had said shyly that "her job"—which, of course, everyone understood to mean her pregnancy—was keeping her at home. Then a middle-aged lady with only kindliness in her face asked whether he wasn't worried about leaving Mrs. Girard at this time. Alec looked down into the questioner's eyes and said swiftly that Andy was with his mother—and then added, with a sudden grin and to the crowd in general, that he thought Andy was more worried about him than he about her. "After all," he told them, "I've never run for President before. But she's got experience at her job." And he ducked into the plane, leaving them laughing.

And leaving an image, Paul thought now, that was a great deal closer to the private Alec inside the public phenomenon—which had been almost all that was visible up to then. Paul bent a thoughtful look on the almond sherry Andy was handing him and dismissed Alec, who had extra dimensions and could encompass his problems without help; it was *Andréa* who must re-shape herself, somehow, to encompass a wider world. She had begun to change: already she could smile and wave from the car, accepting the friendliness in the noise and the ranked bodies standing under the shreds of paper falling like snow. So she had, somewhere during these months, learned to widen her warmth without narrowing dignity. But, most important, the gay dancer was still there . . . Paul, who believed earnestly that that must not be lost, sipped at his wine in content.

Until he heard the question she was asking. No, he couldn't really, he told her, come to Kingsley for the big night. He set down his glass and agreed that it would indeed be a unique experience. He thanked her again and stood before her speaking vaguenesses, hoping he didn't look as ill at ease as he felt.

He did, though. Paul's hands, hanging empty by his sides, always looked emptier than anybody else's hands, Andy decided. He was frowning, too, which was not like him. She believed his explanation of why he couldn't get away until the day before Election Day, but it made no sense that he would head for Washington then instead of Vermont. Finally she just asked him why and waited quietly, her hands in her lap and the filtered light glowing where it was gathered to the garnets at her throat. When he told her, reluctantly, that he wished to see a piece of work he had done a long time ago, she knew at once that it had to be *"Fin Fond."*

The sculpture, one of Paul's earliest successes, had been bought by a friend of Andrea's father, another of those quiet rich men who took shelter from the world in the Virginia countryside near the Langwiths' home. The owner, a philanthropist and patron of the arts, had recently lent it to a Washington showing of postwar painting and sculpture. It was a fine piece of work, though not a great favorite among museum viewers: though difficult in its near-abstraction, the title—translated, roughly, "The Utmost Depths"—made the intent clear enough to anyone, but the trouble with it was, as Andy had thought the first time she'd seen it, it gave you a cold grue the moment you laid eyes on it. It began with a massive, vaguely circular block of polished pearly white, suggesting a promising whole like a new world dawning. But between this and the center, the stone grew increasingly darkened and rough; it seemed to move inward in loose but tightening circles toward the huddled shape thrust forward in the middle—a gray and pitted hump of misery, barely discernible as human, cringing, trying to lose itself in the background. While the stone itself narrowed down to almost parallel ridges like rough bars, coldly and relentlessly pushing the figure away from its wide, glowing beginnings. The time was, as the title stated bluntly, the very end: there was nowhere, absolutely nowhere, for that small, scarred mass to go any more. If you looked at it long enough, you would surely begin to weep.

Andrea studied Paul's closed face. "Why now? You haven't been bothered about Denise for years." It was a silly question, she knew as soon as it was out: what mattered was not why. "Paul. She was a destroyer. You had no obligation to join her in her desrtuction. She wasn't even your wife any more when she turned the destruction on herself."

"She was no longer my wife because I had failed her." Morisot's eyes were pained.

" '*Sauve qui peut.*' "

"Which is an inappropriate sentiment for a lover, no? That I did save myself proves I did not love her—or I did not love her enough. I have not forgotten," he added quietly, "that I was joyful when she left."

Andy nodded because it must have been true; it would have made no sense not to be happy, free at last of the woman who had made of herself an immovable barrier between Paul and the work that was opening up to him. He had simply stopped listening to her when there was no way to mollify her rage, and, at last, unable to be content with the dutiful decency of a husband who could not love her any longer, she had divorced him. When Andy met Paul, Denise was already pathetic—a shrill, bitter woman remarried to a drunk who beat her. Or so Alphonse Lenard had told Andy: Denise had, Paul's friend gossiped indignantly, a life full of catastrophes for which she demanded, and got, money from Paul, though he could hardly bear to look at her. And, young as she was, Andy had known the correct word was not "though" but "because." When the catastrophes became too frequent and too large for money, Denise took her life—and even Paul could not truly find it tragic. No one missed Denise because no one needed her, he had told Andy. Then he had clasped his hands, wringing them so the knuckles stood out. "But once she was young, ardent, exciting—and there is no one but me to remember."

"Paul. What is this about, now, after all these years? Denise was sick. You knew it then. Have you forgotten it now?" They had discussed Denise's sickness, and it was Paul himself who had been wise in tracing the course of it: in the *Résistance,* with its small underneath fear, day after day, that death would come today, he and Denise had been children clinging together for comfort in the dark. And then, when they had had a chance to fight, there were the thrills, and Denise was an adolescent thrill-seeking in a way that was admirable because the society around her needed adolescent thrill-seekers. In the end, perhaps because there was nothing to make her change, she kept the daily fear and the need to destroy. If Paul, born with a maker's gift in his hands, could not help seizing the chance to stop destroying and begin making, Denise could not help standing in his way. He had arrived at that conclusion on the way to "The Utmost Depths"; the sculpture might sadden and dismay its audience, but the man who had made it had already surmounted that stony pain.

"I think now that I understood only the end," Paul said slowly. "I see I must understand all that lay between the beginning and the end."

To make another statue? Andy wondered. But not a memorial—he had finished with memorials, Paul had said publicly not long ago, explaining his refusal of a commission by his own government. Perhaps there was something he wanted to make now that he couldn't make with his hands . . . He could not be asked: he would permit more to Andrea than perhaps to anyone, but even she couldn't enter the walled kingdom at will. Already he was turning to her with a bright smile that dismissed her. He finished his sherry and said he had to leave, which she knew was true, and that she had many things to do, which she did. Andy sighed and offered him the punning French farewell that refers to faring well at table. But it was not a joke and they both knew it: he bent to kiss her hand, acknowledging by this unusual formality that he knew she wished him to be nourished happily.

Turning back to smile at her from the doorway, Paul thought the gentle folds of her dress—swung from a yoke just below the shoulders, to leave the outlines of her figure indistinct—made her look like an upside-down flower. Then he went his oddly troubled way and Andy went back into the room to take up politics again in her new, oddly untroubled way.

Fourteen

On the Saturday night before the first Tuesday after the first Monday in November, the junior Senator from Vermont cast a last look at the "Hangman" game being played on the back of an envelope by two of the correspondents in the press bus and guessed—correctly, as Gil Kimball did not at first and was nearly "hanged" before he did—that the word was "mastiff." But Alec kept quiet about it and got up obediently when Dan Healy put his head in the door and said "Let's go, Senator," adding kindly that it was just one more now. Girard observed quietly that by a happy coincidence he had, he hoped, just about enough voice left to deliver The Speech one more time and left in Dan's wake.

Gil guessed "f" desperately and then grinned, because with those two final "f's" looking at him it had to be either "pontiff" or "mastiff," and one more guess would clear that up. Outside, the candidate said, "I've come here tonight to ask you for one of your most valuable possessions: your vote. What I offer you in return is an end to the indecisions and ineptitudes that have kept this fertile valley chained to—" The Consolidated Press man reached across and closed the window—they all knew what this fertile valley was chained to, because Jerry Rosenberg had produced his usual summary of favorite local gripes and frustrations, dug up a quote from a Ferris speech promising a rival town salvation first, and stirred them carefully into Girard's "whistle-stop" speech, which they had all heard hundreds of times; the current variation on the theme had been typed, proofread, and duplicated before the newsmen finished breakfast this morning, and a copy had awaited each scribe with his second cup of coffee.

On Sunday Alec Girard went, photographed, to church and offered his swollen and discolored right hand to be shaken by first the minister and then his flock. Back at the hotel, Dan Healy tended the hand with the hot packs the doctor had ordered while Jake Ruffing paced the floor, not quite watching Ferris going to church on television, urging the candidate to relax and defying anyone else even to dream of it. The only time Jake did not look worried was Sunday night, when the taped five minutes of President Winkler speaking kindly of Ralph Ferris turned up on television channels as regularly as station identification. Rosenberg, who had dubbed this the "bar mitzvah bit," studied the bland, genial features of the President for the umpteenth time and shook his head gloomily over the fatal charm.

"Too late," Jake insisted. "Just about a week too late. The voters have stopped listening." Before that, no one could recall having seen him smile for at least a week.

Monday was very difficult for anyone in the Girard camp to remember accurately, for the senses could not retain any firm impression of so much and so constant motion and noise. Everyplace became blur, Jake Ruffing's bark was everysound. At the end of it, Alec Girard stood tall and quiet with his thick hair coppery in the lights and learned how far the cheers of his followers, packed into the final mammoth rally, could go to lighten weariness.

On the steps of the town hall at Kingsley—a white, spired building like the pictures in everybody's history-book chapter on the American Revolution—Andrea Girard stood a little stiffly under the terrible lights, wearing a loose dark coat that made her look not only not glamorous but close to anonymous. She kept her trembling out of her voice as she began "On behalf of my husband" and she put all the gratitude she could manage into her final thanks to "all those who have given so freely of their hopes and efforts." But she still sounded a little shy and tentative, and Luke Messenger, though he didn't tell her so, thought her "I hope you will cast your vote for Alec Girard" lacked punch. Not sincerity, but punch—there was no doubt that she meant what she said, but urging a course of action on strangers was, for her, so close to discourtesy that an embarrassment nothing could overcome had drained all passion from her words. Oddly enough, Alec, watching it in the last of the endless string of hotel suites, and Paul Morisot, in Washington, came to exactly the same conclusion—that Andy looked beautiful, and startlingly French.

On Tuesday afternoon Marian Farland concluded a rather disturbing telephone conversation during which she tried to persuade Morisot that the reason she couldn't have lunch with him tomorrow had only to do with the related facts of the election and her employment on a daily newspaper; in the end, she thought, Paul had believed her—but she was sure it was less because of anything she'd said than because he'd heard how disappointed she was. The thought troubled her while she sat in silence as Will drove them out to the Maryland suburb in which the Farlands, because they owned a small piece of property, were able to claim a "voting residence." She had never been able to follow the distinctions between this and "legal residence," or the other legalistic squirmings by which Will, and others like him, managed to get around their disfranchisement as residents of the District of Columbia. But it had always, before, struck Marian as exciting and faintly illicit, as if they were living in Prohibition days and driving off to find a bootlegger. Today, however, she was seeing the frustrating and ridiculous side of it again, and it was in an irritated tone that she asked Will, as they got back into the car, whether they really had to show up at all three parties tonight for the "empty exercise" that political celebrations became in Washington on this one day. There might be some point in an election party in any other city, town, or village in the United States; but she could see none whatever in voteless Washington.

Will said peaceably that maybe they could skip one party, and added, "Anyway, we can get home first. You're always complaining about not seeing the kids. Well, tonight we can see them."

Since the polls didn't close until seven o'clock anyway, there would be no returns to watch and analyze for some hours—so this hardly represented a real concession by Will. Marian didn't say it, though, because one glance at him made it perfectly clear that his anticipation and elation were great enough to armor him against any needles she might produce. He was jab-proof, wife-proof.

He was conscientiously "spending time with the children" while Marian finished dressing for the evening; when she came downstairs she found Sharlie literally sitting at Will's feet, sharing the hassock with Dick, while Will held forth in enormous detail and with thoroughly evident enjoyment on the Electoral College: its origins, arithmetic, and effects on past presidential elections. Elaborating some of the remotest possibilities the voting totals might produce, detailing provisions of the Constitution never called on and never likely to be, he looked and sounded like an old astronomer exhorting his students to consider a planet whose existence was only deduced. It would have been touching, Marian thought, except for the fact that, if he'd had no available children, Will would have delivered exactly the same lecture to the Fuller Brush man or anyone else who dropped in. Marian studied Will's rapt disciples with a more attentive and perceptive eye than their mentor's and concluded that Sharlie was thinking that Dad was terribly handsome and Dick that Dad was awfully smart—and that if she asked both of them, this minute, which amendment to the Constitution provided for a popular vote for President, she would embarrass them.

Though she was not exactly good-natured, Marian was not given to tilting at windmills or to holding a grudge against them for turning when the wind blew; thus, once she had resigned herself to the fact that tonight was for going where she was told, looking pretty, and being quiet, she let the basic gaiety attached to the simple business of being dressed up and at a party take over. But by midnight and the third party she had abandoned any effort to follow the proceedings and was pondering quietly in a corner the question of whether Dick's tonsils would have to come out this year. They were proving too troublesome, and you could go on giving a child antibiotics just so long . . . She closed her eyes, sighed, and wished she could talk to Andy, who knew that tonsils were important.

At midnight, Alec Girard had the same desire, although not for the same reason. It had been a long day, beginning with the traditional trip to Kingsley, where he and Andy were photographed arriving to cast their votes; but the day's pressures were not, for the first time in a long time, primarily on Alec. Now the center of the stage was other people's for a while—those whose business was getting voters to the polls, watching the polls, checking returns, and all the other mechanics of party politics. Jake Ruffing was still in motion, of course, and everybody was still working: having done by 7:00 P.M. Pacific Time everything they could think of to persuade voters to the election of Alec Girard, they were now bending every effort to making sure that every one of the votes was cast and counted.

In this effort, Alec himself had little part. Back from town, he shed his sober business suit and took a long nap. After lunch, he took Andy out on the lake and rowed in circles, talking about nothing in particular, until Elizabeth woke from her afternoon nap. In the late afternoon, Alec appeared in the headquarters at his father's house, went on to dine informally with his staff at the Romberos' house, and then bore Rosenberg off to his own cottage for an hour's conference. Rosie escorted Andy down to the elder Girards' when he left, and she had not come back to the cottage by the time Alec strolled down the path through the woods to join his staff in watching the returns that were finally beginning to be interesting if not conclusive. At headquarters he heard that Andy had been seen here or there; but no one seemed to know exactly where she was now.

When the candidate entered the inner sanctum of his headquarters, he found occupants of the disordered room—which had once been the elder Girards' quiet family dining room—lying across every possible surface like toppled statues. Bill Bruyette, though, was still erect; perched on the battered campaign war chest, he was surveying the scene with the irresponsible amusement of a leprechaun. And Jake Ruffing was awake, of course—he was sputtering furiously into one of a row of telephones crammed onto the dining table, which had been pushed back to the wall. Luke Messenger, who should have been the one on the phone, was fast asleep in an incredibly uncomfortable-looking suspension of his tubby body between two small chairs.

Bruyette greeted Alec with a nod. "Looks like a taken town," he said dryly.

"Not quite, it seems. Or is Jake just drilling to keep the troops from getting rusty?" Alec crossed the room to the television set, on which a famous commentator was mouthing mysteries, since the sound was turned all the way down. He tried to right a bronze bowl of red and yellow apples that was tilted on top of the set, discovered that it wouldn't sit straight anywhere on that crowded surface, and carried it over to Bill's perch.

Jake's hoarse voice resounded in the silence, filling the room with a brief sentiment that managed to give equal time to obscenity and blasphemy. Bruyette winced. "The press is incarcerated at the firehouse in town. Some of them appear to be getting restless."

Alec put the bowl down on the wooden chest beside Bill and bit into one of the red apples. "No," he said incredulously. Chewing, he waved the apple at the silent television set. "Who muffled the great opinion-maker?"

"He's just killing time," Bill said. "Waiting for California."

"Aren't we all?" Alec ran his free hand through his already tousled hair. He stuck the apple into his mouth and held it there, his strong white teeth gleaming above the shiny red, while he used both hands to tuck his shirt into his rumpled Army suntan pants.

"You look like a pig at a feast," Bruyette remarked wearily. And then added, with exaggerated respect, "Mr. President."

"Please. 'Senator.' Until we hear from California. Maybe for some years after that."

" 'Thane thou art,' " Bruyette recited, " 'and Cawdor, and shalt be—' "

"Go soak your head," the candidate said mildly. He looked around the room at the utilitarian machinery of communications, uncompromisingly ugly in the bright light. In the corners, where the light was dimmer, the polished wood and lovingly cared-for appointments of a well-furnished home lurked sadly, unceremoniously jumbled together like aristocrats in the tumbrils. "Good Lord, has my mother seen this place?" Bruyette shrugged, but Alec's eyes were on his grandmother Wardwell's brass candlesticks, lying on their sides behind a typewriter.

Ruffing hung up the phone and turned to them. He looked even more untidy than the candidate. "Alec. I'm glad you're here. I've got some suggested changes for your statement—"

"Later, please," Alec interrupted. "I came to look for Andy."

"She went for a walk," Bruyette offered.

Alec held the apple poised, halfway to his mouth. "At this hour?"

Bill laughed. "I think she found the decor in here a little depressing. She'd probably rather look at the lake."

Not the lake, Alec decided, his feet crunching on the gravel of the drive as he walked toward the back of the house. Suddenly sure of where his wife had gone, he reversed his course and headed for the road in front of the house. If she's walked all that way, she'd better ride home, he thought then, and came back to the parked cars. The blue Plymouth with a "U.S. Congress" tag belonged to Bill Bruyette, and the keys were in it; so, also, was an abandoned sweater, which Alec appropriated along with the car.

Where his father's property met the road, he put the left-turn blinker on without thinking, and then, as the little flashing green light on the dashboard caught his attention, he laughed aloud. He watched it going on and off, busy and ridiculous in the totally empty blackness, while he took the last bite of his apple and threw the core through the open window. It described a high, looping arc and disappeared into the pine woods at the roadside. A newspaper photograph flicked in his mind—President Winkler throwing out the first ball to open the baseball season—and he thought, I'll have to practice. Dreams of glory, he jeered at himself as he took out his handkerchief, wiped apple-stickiness from his mouth and hands, and balled it back into his pocket. The handkerchief, of fine lawn and delicately hemstitched, looked like gentility fallen in the world.

Alec pulled into the parking area near Wenake Gorge, the tires slithering softly on fallen pine needles. He turned out the lights and got out, closing the door softly, and then stood by the car, letting his eyes become accustomed to the sudden blackness. There was no moon. Cold blue starlight pricked at the vault of the sky, beautiful but not useful, offering design but little light. Feeling happily alone for the first time in a very long time, Alec stood tall and tired under the stars, listening to the steady roar of the restless waters in the gorge. A scamp of wind, brisk with the chill of Vermont autumn, tugged at his hair, bringing reality. As objects began to take shape in the darkness, he set off up the path, ducking under reaching branches of the black trees. Under the roar of the gorge, he heard the slithery sound of his progress among the fallen leaves and drying needles lying in the path.

He stopped suddenly, aware of a similar sound up ahead, and then dodged irritably as the beam from Andy's flashlight threatened his eyes.

"Alec?" Her voice was low and uncertain.

"There are only two people who would be idiotic enough to wander around here at this hour of the night," he announced positively to the rustling blackness. He saw her coming then, a dark bulk against the faint, starry light, and reached for her. He touched the sleeve of her coat and slid down it to the hand that held the flashlight. He took the metal cylinder and shoved it into his back pocket with his free hand while he pulled her toward him. "Are you out of your mind?" he asked crossly. "Suppose you fell, alone out here."

"Oh, Alec." She put her head down against his borrowed sweater. "Don't fuss."

He stroked her hair. "I *will* fuss. Why on earth did you decide to walk all this way?" His gentle fingers rubbed the back of her neck.

"I didn't decide to," she said reasonably. "I started to walk and after a while I was almost here. So I came the rest of the way."

"Try to remember, will you, that you promised me I'd come out of all this with one victory guaranteed."

She raised her head a little, without dislodging his hand, and peered up at him. Her eyes gleamed in the darkness. " 'One victory'? You haven't—"

"No, we're still ahead, but not enough; we may have to wait for California. Come sit down." He led her over to the rustic picnic table and held her arm while she lowered herself onto one of the benches attached to it. "What *were* you doing here, Andy?" His flush of embarrassment was lost in the sheltering dark. Feeling like a bully, he persisted anyhow. "Please. I want to know."

Andy caught at his hand, brought it to her cheek for a moment, and then let it go. "I was thinking about—a long time ago."

Fallen leaves rustled in the light wind, a small, foreground sound against the steady roar of the gorge. "Not meditating on the implications of being First Lady?"

She looked dismayed. "I don't like that name—it sounds like a kind of pushy attempt at royalty." She picked at a splinter of wood on the slatted tabletop. "But I *was* meditating on the implications of being Mrs. Girard, I guess. I was remembering a night, 'way back, when I was driving home from the Kimballs'. You had called me from Vermont to ask me to a movie. On the way home, I was thinking about marrying you."

"As it happens, I remember that conversation. I spent it falling over my own words." He grinned wickedly. "I also remember that I hadn't yet said a word about marrying me."

"Pooh. I'd been thinking about it for a long time anyway. But that night I decided to stop."

"The prospect didn't bear thinking about."

"No, really," she said. "I decided it was fruitless to go on examining the implications—you know, how would I like being a senator's wife and all that sort of thing." She paused, and then went on a little hesitantly. "I suddenly saw the point. Which was that I wanted to be Mrs. Alec Girard, whatever Mr. Girard happened to be."

Alec nodded. "And all the implications, adjustments, considerations—"

"—would just have to fall in line." Andy grinned then. "It's called 'staying loose.' "

"I made a serious mistake," Alec told her, "when I left you up here among the school kids."

"I didn't get that from them. I got it from one of your camp followers. A television fellow."

"An even more corrupting influence." Alec sat down on the bench opposite and studied the pale blur across the table: the face most known to him of all the world's faces was reduced to an anonymous gleam of eyes, an occasional flash of smile. "So you've decided to stay loose about being— about the White House."

"Yes. The central point is still the same as it was that night."

"Thank you," he said quietly.

She answered with equal seriousness. "You're quite welcome."

Alec sighed, stirring restlessly on the hard bench. "I ought to take you home. You shouldn't be up so late." He looked at her quickly. "How do you feel?"

"Fine, if you mean him." She patted the bulge under her coat. "But me— I feel a little lonely. You know, there's nobody, really, who can understand exactly how it is, this waiting. Except Mrs. Ferris, I guess." She made a small grimace. "And I don't find that endearing."

"Politics makes strange bedfellows' bedfellows," he said apologetically. He sobered then and went on, "You know, it's not all as dark and tortuous as you think, darling. If we make it, I mean. It's not a bad job—no commuting to work, good pay, and you get to see all the parades." His smile flashed in the darkness. "I'd be home to lunch, too."

"I know," Andy said seriously. "I thought about that."

Alec jumped up, laughing aloud. "You confuse my every logic. It's fascinating." He held out his hand to her. "I was joking." His voice was very thoughtful. "But you weren't."

"No, Alec. I wasn't." Andy let him help her up, but then she stood still, digging her heels in like a rebellious child, when he tried to lead her toward the car. "No. Please. I won't go till we've had a look at the gorge."

"A moment ago you were talking like a very bright woman, you know? Not to say, helpmate to a distinguished public servant." He stared down at the dim contrary bulk of the indescribable Andy. "And now, out of the blue, a juvenile delinquent."

She smiled slowly at him, her eyes confident. "Please?"

"Oh Lord." Alec put his arm around her and turned her toward the path that led to the lip of the gorge. "I have no character. It's a good thing Kaslov isn't beautiful."

Holding her hand, he went ahead through the aisle of trees that blotted out the sky. " 'Age cannot wither her, nor custom stale her infinite variety,' " he told the darkness—and meant it exactly as earnestly as Shakespeare's Antony had of Cleopatra. But Alec's Cleopatra was very pregnant. So he said, "Watch that rock," instead of going on with the rhapsody. He waited for her to catch up, then moved ahead slowly. " 'How did you and the Senator pass the time while the votes were being counted, Mrs. Girard?' " Stumbling a little over an erupted root, he stopped and held the flashlight over the spot until Andy was safely past it. " 'Well, actually,' " he went on in a falsetto exaggeration of her accents, " 'we went on a darling little hike up a mountain in the dark. It was terribly slippery, but really smashing fun. My husband delivered the baby himself, of course—he's so talented that even with a broken leg, he managed beautifully.' " He broke off and leaned back for the real Andy, giggling behind him, and pulled her up beside him into the clearing.

Nothing was ever so open as that high and deep night, the sky arching illimitable, the canyoned earth at their feet. They stood in silence, side by side under the far starlight, while the black waters tumbled wildly below. After a long time, Andy said slowly, "It always makes me think of that old prayer. You know—'Dear God, be good to me. The sea is so wide, and my boat is so small.' "

A leaf fell and Alec caught it before it could be sucked into the downdraft. It was true, he thought—here, as at sea, was that immensity before which no man is big—but she had always missed, so far at least, the fact that the man who'd made that prayer was actually at sea in a boat. "You build the best boat you can, and you learn all the seamanship you can," he told the woman who hung back from voyages. "But you go to sea. You always go to sea."

"Aren't you afraid, Alec?" It was not, of course, what she meant—if anyone knew surely that he had been afraid sometimes, it was Andy. "Typhoons come, and the best boat founders."

Alec dug his sneakered toe into the carpet of pine needles and considered how to answer her real question, which had to do, he thought, with whether it was all right with Alec Girard if his wife was human enough to be afraid. "Typhoons are what the fellow was praying about," he said gently. He looked out over the gorge for the last time and then began to lead her away from the dangerous depths and starry immensities too great to endure for long. For Andy, anyway. It was awesome here, but the awesome was present in more places than she knew, and it was not to cower before in any case: you did what you could, as best you could, and then took your chances. He didn't think of it often, but it occurred to him then how much younger she was, and he wondered if that accounted for the difference.

And she was burdened, he was reminded as they negotiated the difficult way down. When he had helped her into the car, he leaned through the window to look in at her faint gleams in the double darkness. "Are *you* afraid, Andy? About the baby, I mean?"

"I don't think so, darling. A few months ago I was, a little. But now . . ." She sighed. "You get so tired of waiting. Now I just want to be delivered, you know. Of the burden." Her broad, sweet smile lighted the darkness. "I want to see my baby."

Alec nodded, relieved that that wasn't it, and went around the car and got in. As he turned the key in the ignition, Andy said, "Besides, this time you'll be there."

"I'll be there, darling. Now let's get you to bed." But when he drew up in front of their house and helped her out, they lingered anyhow. "If you don't need me, I'll go on down and rejoin the nail-biting."

"All right, Alec."

"Get to bed right away."

"Yes, sir." Andy pulled his face down by tugging at his ears and kissed him firmly. "And thank you for taking me to the gorge."

Alec laughed. "A pleasure. But have you noticed? Every time we talk there, we define the same difference."

"What difference? Last time we talked about the Indians, didn't we?"

"Sure. And it was the same point."

"Tell me. I haven't the analytical mind. What difference do we keep defining?"

"The one the French parliamentarian celebrated so memorably," Alec told her gravely. "The one between men and women. Get to bed."

Andy turned obediently and pushed the house door open. She looked at him anxiously in the lamplight from the hall. "You'll wake me?"

"Of course." Back in the car, he leaned out the window and called to her as she stood in the doorway, waiting to see him go. "You're right, you know. You haven't the analytical mind. *Vive la différence.*"

Fifteen

Alec was smiling to himself as he whipped the car into his father's driveway and jumped out, slamming the door noisily. He took the broad front stairs three at a time, with nothing of weariness in his face or body. When he came into the dining room the pall of smoke hit him and he exclaimed and threw open a couple of windows. The television was blaring, but only Rosenberg was watching it, and he looked more skeptical than attentive. Luke Messenger was still asleep. His recumbent form in its precarious berth had apparently become so familiar a part of the scene by now that people seemed to be using it as a handy place to put things—like a discarded sweater, not spread out as if a motherly hand had covered the sleeper but simply abandoned there. The candidate, as adaptable as any man, promptly shed the sweater he had found in Bruyette's car and added it to the inventory on Messenger's abdomen.

Alec asked for Healy, and Rosie said, without turning from the television set, "Inside, keeping the secretaries from hysterics. He left a folder for you over there, and don't forget to sign the picture for the head telephone girl."

"Over there" was a wheeled metal typewriter table. When he dislodged the folder, Alec found the picture of himself and the head telephone girl; a memo slip clipped to the top reminded him of her name, and he wrote it and added "With thanks" and his signature. The rest of the folder was mostly telegrams, clipped together under scrawled labels: "Senate," "House," "Govs." "Labor," "Negro," "Business," "Friends." A thinner pack labeled "Dignitaries" seemed to consist heavily of erstwhile hopefuls for the nomination—including Lloyd Morris, who had early given up his own plans in order to back Alec; the selection also included Dan Daniels, who should have already made it back to "Senate," according to returns from his state. "Friends" began, not surprisingly, with Paul Morisot; but included, a little surprisingly, was Betty Kimball, whose husband was immured in the Kingsley firehouse with the rest of the sweating press and by now probably did not share her earnest good wishes.

Alec turned to comment on wives with minds of their own to Bruyette, who was flipping through what looked like a speech draft. But something new had been added to the room's bedlam, and it distracted him: a huge coffee-maker, looking like a rather battered robot, tipped dangerously among precarious towers of thick white mugs waiting beside it. Alec cocked an eyebrow at the monster. "When did that thing land?"

Bruyette tucked his short, bitten pencil behind his ear. "You wound me. It's our family samovar, brought out of Mother Russia by my grandparents, who were fleeing before the Bolsheviks."

"Looks like they didn't flee fast enough." Alec went over and poked an inquiring finger into a massive dent on the aluminum side of the great percolator. "The Bolsheviks hit it."

Jake Ruffing had darted in, fluttering to something like a pause at Alec's elbow. "Don't you guys ever cut out your fun and games? This is a solemn occasion, for God's sake."

"That's the best kind," Alec assured him.

Jake sighed. "Cannon called. I said you'd call back when you came in. You missed one false report that President Winkler was about to issue a congratulatory message; I phoned, and it was a mistake. Ferris cut down your lead some more, but it's been holding steady for about an hour."

"Why the hell doesn't he concede?" Bruyette asked.

Alec said, "Why should he? He hasn't lost yet."

"There is that." The Congressman yawned. "But this thing is beginning to lack audience interest. Except for statisticians."

"And me. And Ferris," said Alec.

Jake said, "Ferris made an interim statement an hour ago. Maybe you ought to reconsider, Alec." He spied the slumbering press chief and snorted with impatience. "I thought I woke him an hour ago, goddammit."

"Let him sleep, Jake. We don't need him now and we will later. As for Ferris, one of the reasons I didn't vote for him is that he doesn't know the statesman's first rule: when there's nothing to say, shut up."

"Hear, hear." Bruyette rose, stretching. "If I can't sleep, I'm going to eat. Come on. There's a spread in the kitchen."

"Your mother and your sister Agnes," Ruffing explained. "They've been—"

"What?" Alec exploded. "I told them to go to bed hours ago. My mother has no business being up at this hour. Where's my father?"

"In the kitchen, too." Bill Bruyette grinned. "He says he's helping your mother but actually he's making book. Last time I was out there, he was giving seven to five on Salskin County, North Dakota; three-and-a-half to one on a town of six hundred population in the upper-left-hand corner of Tennessee, and—"

"Stop, you're discouraging me. Does my word count for nothing around here?"

Bruyette said from the doorway, "Wait till you're commander in chief. You can haul 'em all up before a firing squad. How about if I bring you back some soup?"

"All right. But speak to my mother curtly, in spite of her gray hairs. Remind her who I am."

"Not me. Your father will foreclose my mortgage."

"And listen," Alec called after him, "if Andy turns up, let me know at once. She seemed docile, but with all this rebellion—"

"I'm glad you got her to go to bed," Ruffing said. "Though, this close to their time, they don't usually sleep very well. The baby kicks too much."

Alec looked down at his short, energetic campaign manager with affection. "Is there anything you don't know, Jake?"

"I'm a multi-father."

"You're a man in a million," Alec said impulsively. They stared at each other in some embarrassment, the fond, earnest words hanging in the air between them.

"You better talk to Cannon now," Ruffing said at last.

"Sure." Waiting, Alec watched the television commentator.

Rosenberg said, without turning his head, "One network's computer gave it to you, then the other one's took it away."

Alec looked disgusted. "Bill was right. It's a night for statisticians. The people who matter are tucked in their beds." He took the phone Jake was holding out to him. "Tom? How're you holding up?"

"It looks good down here," his running mate drawled. "Anybody can manage a landslide. It's this waiting around that separates the men from the boys."

"The suspense can't go on much longer."

"Hell, I'm not in suspense." Cannon's slow voice quickened. "We're in."

"Oh? How do you know?"

"My wife told me," Cannon answered promptly.

Alec laughed. "She's been consulting the entrails of chickens, I suppose."

"Senator, I've been watching that woman wait out election returns for thirty years, and I tell you she's the best damn forecaster in the business. She's never been wrong, and she goes all the way back to when I ran for sheriff."

"And she says we have it?"

Cannon snorted. "She don't *say*. You have to read the signs. You know what she's doing right now?"

"I wouldn't dare to guess."

"She's turning out bureau drawers, that's what. And when Lou turns out bureau drawers it means she's decided I'm elected." He paused significantly. "She just started. I went up and looked in on her an hour ago and she was knitting and watching TV."

"Is that what she does when you're losing?"

"Nope. That's undecided. When she thinks I'm losing, she starts talking about my health. When I lost my first race for the House, she started in telling me about how I need rest and I ought to write a book—before half the precincts were in."

"Awesome," Alec agreed. "Women, I mean."

"You can say that again. How's your good lady doing?"

"I just sent her to bed. I've got too much to do tonight to have to deliver the baby myself."

"Pore little thing." Cannon's voice was gentle. "If she can't get to sleep, you tell her to call Lou, you hear?"

"I'll do that."

"She'll toughen up. They all do." The voice on the telephone brightened. "Anyway, you get something out of this campaign even if the voters turn out to've done us dirt."

"I know. I'm counting on it."

"Hope you get a boy. Girls are too hard to figure out."

Alec sighed. "I'll take what I get."

"Yeah. Like the election. The fellows here've been chawing over some old stories of close races. One of the newspaper guys covered one where there was a fifteen-vote margin out of a hundred thousand. Had to have a recount, but it held . . . Oh listen, we're still keeping mum, are we?"

"Yes, I think so. Sorry, Tom. You deserve a chance to crow—you delivered your states comfortably. The holdup is where I did most of the talking."

"They listened, Alec. You'll see."

"I hope you're right."

"I'll be there when you make your victory statement."

"Right. We'll stick to the arrangements we set up. And, Tom—"

"Yeah?"

"Call me right away if your wife starts knitting." Alec hung up on Cannon's chuckle. "Mrs. Cannon has decided we've won," he told Jake Ruffing, smiling, and then stared in amazement as his campaign manager nodded happily.

"Lou Cannon's never been wrong," Jake said.

Bruyette came in with a tray, and Alec took a bowl of soup and began spooning it up absentmindedly, his eyes thoughtful. Somehow, in spite of his record in House and Senate campaigns, these men sometimes made him feel like a dilettante. No, an undergraduate. Studying for a technical degree.

False humility, he chided himself. He saw crackers on the tray and bit into one. It was advisable not to lose track of the facts—deserving or not, he had plans for the country: a handsome structure built on faith and courage and all the old-fashioned virtues he had been so busy touting up all over the map for such a long time. The question was—as it had always been—could he build it?

Bruyette spoke, but Alec shook his head without answering, dismissing everything in favor of his thoughts. Certainly he could build nothing without the help of these experienced carpenters and plumbers and electricians, who know so well how to make things work. I have a lot to learn, he said to himself, smitten suddenly with a brief, sharp desire. It can be something wonderful, he thought, almost sick with yearning. All at once, overwhelmingly, he knew how much he wanted to be President of the United States.

"I'd like to make a speech," he said suddenly. He looked at Jake. "Please get everyone together for a moment."

"The phones—"

"Let them wait." Alec walked over to the television set and told Rosie, "Turn it off."

"But they're just about to—"

"I don't care," Alec said quietly. "Turn it off. Get Dan. And somebody wake Luke." He waited as the room slowly quieted. While they were assembling, he had time to wonder fleetingly whether he was about to make a fool of himself, trying to say the hardest thing in the world. Then he saw that they were waiting, and he began without introduction.

"I'm sorry to interrupt all of you—especially you, Luke—but there's something I want to say, and it's essential that I say it while we still don't know whether we've won or lost. This isn't the easiest speech for me to make, even with a crowd that I can safely assume is for me. And I don't even have a funny story to start out with.

"A long, long time ago, when all this was just a gleam in Ruffing's eye, I told Andy that to aspire to the Presidency of the United States was a form of megalomania. My excuse for it was that I was angry at Winkler—angry at what he was doing to this nation and at how he was making us look before the world. But I'll spare you the details. I believe everyone here has been exposed, a few times, to my views on the Winkler Administration." That drew a laugh, and Alec's muscles relaxed a little. He took a deep breath, and suddenly his discomfort vanished.

"The prospect of Ferris made me even angrier. I still think—in case anyone was in any doubt—that he's not a good thing to happen to the country. And so I think that the job we've been doing has been not only good but necessary.

"About that job, I want to say this: I don't know of any job, anywhere, that has involved so much inspired work by so many skilled men. If we don't win, I guess that's prima facie evidence that we didn't do *something* right. But I'm damned if I can see what it could be. If we lose, I guess I'll have to figure out what went wrong—and then decide whether I can do it differently. But so far as I can see, everybody in this outfit did everything right all the way." Alec broke off, grinning, and added, "Despite anything I may have said in the heat of a Milwaukee moment, Jake.

"I don't know about the rest of you," he continued soberly when the smiles and the turning of heads had stopped, "but I think I may have forgotten for a while, in the midst of the rush and the speeches and the plans, what it was really all about. A little while ago, standing here with nothing to do but let my whole life pass before my eyes, it suddenly came to me that I was surrounded by people who know their trade and give unstintingly of their gifts. I don't know why it took me so long to dig that simple but awesome fact. And I think I may have been too harsh with some of you speech-concocters when I complained about clichés, for I can't do better, I see, when the chips are down. The shameful truth is, all I could think of when I stood here looking around was 'My heart is full.' "

Alec waited out the applause, not looking at any of them. He stared at the opposite wall, struggling for composure, but he could feel that his ears must be bright red. He raised a hand. "One more thing, and then I'll let you go. Forgive me for taking so long about it. This is what I want to say: I got into this because I had a fond notion, and I suspect that the fact that I still have it has something to do with the people in this room. There's something I want to build, and I am grateful to all of you for working so hard to give me the chance. But even if the people permit me to try, I can't build it alone. Win or lose, I need you."

Only a handful of men, but the applause rattled in the room, the sound bouncing back from the walls to descend on Alec like a shower. Bill Bruyette stood at his elbow, Alec saw as he took out his handkerchief and wiped his heated face. "I feel foolish," he confessed.

Bruyette looked shaken. "I don't think I really knew how good you were."

"Then it was all right?"

The Vermont Congressman smiled, his face resuming slowly its characteristic puckishness. "Well, it wasn't up to 'Once more into the breach, dear friends.' But it'll do."

Relieved, Alec started to answer, but he stopped and stared, a little frightened, as the window behind Bill bloomed with huge, sudden white light. For a split second, his nerves remembered their wartime patterns; then they reacted, just as quickly, to the fact that it was not a flash. The light stayed there, and Bruyette, framed in the window, became a figure of white and tinsel. "It's the TV boys. They're out on the lawn," he was saying, when Jake seemed to fly through the air as though blown by an explosion.

Alec blinked incredulously as his businesslike, whip-wielding right-hand man was transformed, before his eyes, to a snake-dancing college boy.

"Is it—" Alec began, bewildered, freeing his arm from the impossible Jake.

"The flash must have come in while we were turned off," Messenger explained. His round face was split with grins, but his voice was calm. "Ferris is on his way to the television studio to make a statement."

"But—is it to concede? Maybe—"

"They were trying to get us from Washington," Jake yelled. "They're holding it until after Ferris speaks, but they've got the telegram from the President." He pounded a tattoo with his fists on Alec's shoulder. "Now are you convinced, goddammit?"

"Cannon," Alec said, simultaneously catching at his campaign manager and ducking more wild swings.

"I called, I called. He and Lou will be on a plane in minutes." The once-imperturbable Ruffing, now clearly mad, was cornered by Bruyette and Dan Healy and carried out of range.

Alec escaped while he had the chance and made his way carefully across the room to where his parents waited in the open doorway with his sister. John Girard leaned forward eagerly, hand outstretched; but at the last moment, as his son neared him, he stepped back and relinquished first place to his wife. Alec bent to kiss his mother's cool, smooth cheek and then stopped to look at her in surprise as he discovered the tears on it. "I *won,* Mother," he said. "You don't cry for *winning.*" His mother shook her head, smiling at him, and went on crying. He had just time to shake his father's hand before his sister engulfed him, shouting something he couldn't possibly hear in the din. He ducked, trying to hold her off, but she clung to him, covering his face and neck with kisses as he swung her around, pleading "Let go, Aggie. Hey!" They whirled halfway across the room, their grapple becoming a dance, until they fetched up with a thump against Bill Bruyette and Luke Messenger, hands clasped, who were doing a weird kind of polka in the glare of white light near the windows. Alec began to laugh helplessly, captive in a maelstrom of noise and motion, dizzy, unthinking, not truly aware of how much time was going by or even, in any real sense, of what had happened.

"We bring you—" the voice of a television announcer blared into the room. Aggie let go suddenly, and Alec saw that Dan Healy had turned the television set to full volume to compel attention. The stratagem worked, and Healy turned the sound down again as the occupants of the room distributed themselves around the set. But they did not grow silent until the image of Ralph Ferris appeared on the screen. His wife stood beside him, her face drawn.

"I have just dispatched the following telegram," Ferris was saying. " 'Senator Alexander Girard, Kingsley, Vermont. Dear Senator: The American people in their wisdom have chosen you to lead them for the next four years. I congratulate you on your victory and I pledge you my loyalty as an American citizen. If I can be of service to you during your term of office, please do not hesitate to call upon me.' "

Ferris folded the paper he'd read from and spoke slowly, his lips tight in a grim face, thanking the people who had voted for him and the members of his staff. *There but for the grace of God,* thought Alec; but then he stiffened. "It has been a heartbreaking effort," Ferris said. "We have not had an easy time . . .

". . . the sacrifices made by my wife . . ." Alec watched in horror as Mrs. Ferris's lips began to tremble. He tried briefly to imagine Andy subjected to this sort of public display, but all he could do was wince as the voice, perilously close to whining, went on seeking pity. Someone put a glass of champagne into his hand, and he nodded absently. When he returned his attention to the screen, Ralph Ferris was helpfully outlining the nation's future foreign policy for him. Alec gasped, and then he began to laugh. He searched the room for Bill Bruyette, found him, and summoned him with a look.

"I know, I know," Bill said when he had worked his way to Alec's side. "The man is not only a cad, but presumptuous besides."

"I can't listen any more," Alec whispered. "It's too embarrassing."

"When I think what you saved us from."

"Let's get out of here. I want to go wake Andy."

"In a minute, Alec. One little ceremony—"

Bill broke off as Ferris called on God to bless his audience. Mrs. Ferris's face, working with her tremendous effort at control, seemed to linger even after the announcer appeared. "Poor woman," John Girard said, and was answered with a general murmur of compassion. Alec looked at his sister and saw that she was crying on her mother's shoulder.

"Not a dry eye in the house," Bruyette said in an undertone. "But a President yet. Oh God."

Alec nodded. The announcer was reading President Winkler's message. Dan Healy was gone from his post, but someone else turned the sound down as a recovered Jake climbed on a chair in the middle of the room and begged for attention. He introduced "our long-suffering host" and stepped down. The sudden silence waited, almost unbearably solemn after all the madness.

"Ladies and gentlemen." John Girard spoke from the doorway. His voice shook slightly. "I give you the President-elect, Alexander Wardwell Girard."

Smiling at them while they drank, Alec remembered all the voices in all the towns, saying "The next President of the United States" to the applause of the faithful. Now, in this crowded quiet, it was suddenly true.

At least, it must be. Alec kept staring at Jake, whose miraculous sanity must prove it, if anything could. "Thank you," he said. In the little cleared space, he looked curiously dignified: a tall man, erect and alone, with nothing about him of the leisure his worn and rumpled clothing bespoke. "I have made my last speech—for an hour or two, anyway. So I will say now only that the people have trusted us, and we 'have promises to keep.' Let's get to work." He sipped from his glass and put it down, watching his father lead his mother and sister away. Rosenberg came over, and Alec told him, "I want to run up and see Andy. She has a right to know where her lares and penates will be installed."

Rosenberg took his arm out from behind his back and held out a small, tissue-wrapped package; its red satin bow was a little crooked. Alec raised his eyebrows and scanned the waiting group. Luke Messenger slipped quietly into the room from the hall, and Jake Ruffing nodded and signaled Rosenberg.

"I have been chosen," Rosenberg began. "Although, this time, by a somewhat less imposing personage than the One who honored my ancestors." He stopped to think it over. "On second thought, it would be more accurate to say that I have been pressed into service by my fellow myrmidons. A notoriously inarticulate bunch, apparently." His glance swept the grinning assemblage severely. "Please, fellows, this is a ceremonial."

"Give him the present, Rosie," Bruyette called.

Rosenberg shrugged. "I was trying to raise the tone around here," he protested.

"Give him the present, Rosie," Messenger jeered from the doorway. "We're not in the rose garden yet."

"Hoi polloi," Rosenberg said disdainfully against the rising murmur. He held out the package to Alec. "High honor," he said in a brassy monotone. "A man who. Small token of our esteem. There, I hit the high points, anyway," he added as Alec took the package and began unwrapping it with eagerness.

Alec turned the small silver box in his hand. It was a replica of the battered toy chest that had accompanied them during the campaign, with facsimiles of Andy's decorations painstakingly etched into the metal. Alec swung the box lid back on its hinges and peered into the interior. "I was wondering whether there was a teeny-tiny *Statistical Abstract of the United States* in here." They laughed, and so did he; but then he caught sight of the inscription and read it aloud slowly as they fell silent. "To Alec Girard from his 'think boys.'" The engraved date blurred before his eyes. He read "November" and then stopped, blinking rapidly at the signatures on the shining surface. But they were waiting. He cleared his throat and arranged his face in a snarl. "All right," he said. "I want to know, who took time off to go shopping?" While they were still laughing, he found Jake Ruffing and shook his hand.

"Honest, we sent Bonnie," Jake said.

Alec turned to Jerry Rosenberg and shook hands. "May I congratulate you on your presentation speech, and I'm counting on you to do it again for the Arab delegations." He moved on, making a ceremonial circuit of the room, shaking hands, offering a brief comment to each man. When he reached Bill Bruyette at last, Alec muttered, "I've got to go home and change. Want to come?" Bruyette nodded and moved quietly toward the door; he waited while Alec paused in the doorway, waved a hand grandly, and ordered, "Everybody go think." Still holding the little silver box, he joined Bill in the dim hallway and they started toward the door.

The front door was open a little, the white glare from outside making it look artificial, something made of cake frosting. Bill put out a hand, keeping Alec back. "Oh brother," he said, dismayed.

Luke Messenger's round figure on the gleaming steps looked like a cherry atop a mound of whipped cream. "It's no use, fellows," he was saying in a hoarse shout. "You're wasting your time. You'd be better off to take that"—he waved a plump hand at the mobile television van bulking in the driveway —"down to the firehouse and wait."

"Give us a break, Luke," a voice pleaded from the darkness.

"I am. Believe me. The Senator positively will not utter until he speaks at the firehouse in"—he consulted his watch—"one hour or thereabouts. I give you my solemn word."

"We know he's in there," a voice argued.

"The Senator," Messenger said decisively, "is with his wife."

"Listen, Luke, is it true that her obstetrician has been called? Is that why Girard—"

"Mrs. Girard's obstetrician has not been summoned, and I don't know where you characters dig up your ideas. Once and for all—Mrs. Girard *is* going to have a baby, but not here and now. And the Senator's simply gone to inform her that he has a new job and they'll have to move."

In the light laughter from the lawn another voice demanded to know when pictures would be taken. "It's four A.M.," it said piteously.

"Personally, I'm fresh as a daisy," the press chief answered gaily. He was promising them "still pix, anyway" when Bruyette tugged at Alec's arm and led him back down the hall, past the dining-room doorway and into the brightly lighted kitchen. Cups and plates were piled in the sink and on the counters. The remains of an apple pie had been left on the scrubbed wooden table. Alec surveyed the disorder and shook his head. He looked dazed as he followed Bill docilely out through the back door and onto the dark porch. Light from the doorway spilled over them in a diminishing half-circle.

The tall man who came toward them from the shadows was wearing a Navy raincoat. "Congressman Bruyette?" he asked quietly, but it was not really a question. Bill nodded, startled. The man spoke to Alec then. "If you'll move out of the light, please, Senator." Alec obeyed, looking at him wonderingly. "Leroy," the man explained. "I'm chief of the Secret Service detail here, sir."

Alec shook the man's hand. "Guess we'll be seeing a lot of you, Mr. Leroy."

"Yes, sir," the agent said impassively. He hesitated, then a smile quirked at the corners of his thin mouth. "May I congratulate you, sir?"

Alec thanked him, grinning at Bill behind the man's back as they followed him. He led them to the edge of the path that went up through the woods to Alec's house, and there turned them over to another agent who stepped from the shadows. Leroy introduced the new man and turned to go, but Bill stopped him. "Tell me," he asked curiously, "are you from around here?"

"No, sir."

"I thought you might be a constituent. How did you know who I was, then?"

Leroy said expressionlessly, "Part of our preparation, sir. We've memorized the faces of all the Senator's associates. Also the family, the servants, and everyone authorized to be in the vicinity."

"Quite a job," Alec commented.

Leroy allowed himself a small smile. "Not really, sir. We've had a long time to do it."

"He can say that again," Alec remarked, as he and Bill walked through the fallen leaves between the looming trees. A third Secret Service agent, who had been stationed halfway up the path, held a flashlight for them as they followed him. With a brief pang, Alec remembered coming up this path with Elizabeth on his shoulders when the long ordeal still lay ahead of him. President-elect, he thought, trying the words out in his mind. It sounds like something out of *The Mikado.*

They came out of the woods and were turned over to yet another Secret Service agent, who emerged from the shadow of the big maple at the edge of the lawn. Alec noticed Elizabeth's little wagon drawn up under the tree, its long handle, from which all the paint had been worn off by a succession of Girard grandchildren, bent back on itself over a dark heap in the bottom. When he had shaken hands with the new man, Alec leaned down and peered into the wagon. It was loaded with rocks, some of them sizable.

"I imagine my daughter will be something of a change for you," he said to the agent. He pushed at the wagon carelessly, but it didn't move; then, intent on his investigation, he crouched beside it, experimenting until he determined how much strength was required to move it. It took a surprising amount. Alec straightened, wiping his hands on his pants. "It's heavy. How in the world does she move it?"

"You wouldn't believe how strong they are," the Secret Service man said abruptly. He looked apologetic. "I've got a couple of kids of my own, sir," he explained.

So have I, nearly, Alec thought. He looked up at the bedroom window and was pleased to see it dark. The downstairs, though, was all lighted. He sighed a little as he neared the door: it took so long to get to Andy, he thought wearily.

But it went fast, he consoled himself as he stood in the darkness of their bedroom, looking at Andy asleep, savoring the last moment before it would become final. He began to take off his clothes absentmindedly, studying his wife's sleeping face. When she knew, he understood suddenly, it would be true. It would be final. He loitered briefly; then he remembered Bill waiting downstairs with the champagne and he smiled and went on into the shower.

He came out in his bathrobe and stood over her, tying the belt. She was sleeping on her back—she didn't like to, but she had no choice right now, he thought, looking at the swell of her abdomen under the blanket. A white frill at her throat moved gently with her breathing. The only light in the room was the warm yellow spilling in from the open doors to the bathroom and the cold bluish starlight that outlined the pair of square, many-paned windows at the left of the bed. In the combined illumination he could just see Andy's sleeping face as he touched her cheek lightly and called her name very softly.

Her eyes opened immediately. Standing over her, Alec could see that they were still dull with sleep and he wondered fleetingly from what depths he was summoning her as he repeated, "Andy." She came back to him then, her face all alert and big with a question. She tried to move, and he smiled so broadly that she could see the answer without waiting for words, while he helped her sit up in the bed and propped her pillow behind her.

"You won," she said huskily, her look roving over his face. "You won?"

"We won," he corrected her.

"Oh." She reached out her left hand, the wedding ring glinting in the dimness; but she took it back without touching him. "Oh, Alec, I'm so proud."

It was a long embrace. He was almost reluctant to come up out of the warmth and sweet smell and the frail shelter of her arms. The excitement beat in him like a pulse: he wanted to go away and begin doing the things he had waited and planned to do, but he also wanted to stay there, just a little longer, and not think. He stood up at last, looking at her with his delighted smile that had, as always, a little wonder in it, as though he could hardly believe his luck. The small rag rug under his bare feet was little protection from the cold of the polished wood floor. After a while, he realized it and said, "I've got to get dressed."

She had to turn on her side in order to get up, but then she stood beside him like a tall, bulky ghost in her voluminous white nightgown. Her feet were long and narrow and very white on the bright-colored rug; he was watching them, thinking about their delicacy, when she took his head between her warm hands and looked into his eyes.

"Are you different, Alec?"

He turned away, a little discomfited by the directness of her gaze, and stared out of the window at the sleeping lawns below. "Not yet." Below the window, a figure emerged from the shadow of the big maple and crossed to the house. Oh Lord, Alec thought, I'd better break the news about them. "Some things will be, you know," he began tentatively. "I hope you're not going to mind, Andy. Or feel a little—hemmed in. It's the law. The Secret Service—" He broke off, waving at the window, and she crossed swiftly to his side and peered out.

"Already?" she asked. "Is that one of them?"

He nodded, taking her hand. "Since the moment Ferris conceded. The speed was most impressive. Look, they seem to be nice enough. You'll get used to—"

"Won't Elizabeth be wild?" Andy tugged at the window, opening it further so she could watch the agent below. "I don't see any guns."

"Well, I'm sure they must have some somewhere." Alec's eyes were bright with amusement, but he asked her quite gravely, "Then you won't mind too much?"

Andy shivered and closed the window. The agent was out of sight. "Of course not." She stared at him as though he had offered some mad proposal. "And Elizabeth will love it."

Alec sighed. How had he ever managed the election, he wondered, if he couldn't call the shots around home better than that? "You'd better get back to bed before you catch cold. I've got to get dressed and go down to town to speak to the faithful. They're gathered at the firehouse, along with the press, which must be making the boys pretty miserable by now."

"I'm not going back to bed." Andy planted her bare feet apart in a defiant posture. "I want to come, too."

"Do you, really? It'll be a terrible crush, and they're all half-potted by now, probably—"

Andy turned him around, pushing him toward his dressing room. "Well, let's not wait until they pass out."

When Alec emerged, tying his tie, the bed was full of dresses, but she had finally chosen one, a bright red, and was holding it up against her, smiling at herself in the mirror over the old-fashioned bureau. "Try to hurry, Andy, please. I'll wait downstairs with Bill, so I can have a private drink with him. After all, he won an election too."

"Of course." Andy looked startled. "I forgot." She pattered toward the bathroom. "Give my regards to the reelected Congressman and pour a small libation for me. I'll be right down."

Alec was thinking of what he would say at the firehouse as he pulled the bedroom door shut behind him and crossed the lamplit hall to the stairs. Then he stopped suddenly and retraced his steps part of the way until he stood in Elizabeth's doorway. The small white bed glimmered in the dim light. He tiptoed around the foot of it, on which a fat bunny danced on a circle of painted grass, and studied his sleeping daughter. The single window of her room looked out on the very heart of a tall tree: last spring there had been a nest for her to watch, only a few feet on the other side of the glass. Now her father heard the swish of the bare branches as he bent and straightened the blanket the child had kicked off. She was lying on her side in a yellow pajama suit that covered her feet. Her legs were drawn up, and one fist was balled under her flushed cheek. Wisps of her fair hair had strayed over her high, round forehead. He started to smooth them away and then changed his mind for fear of waking her—she looked so close to wakening, as though, tensed for a leap, she might jump up at a touch, fully awake and demanding piggybacking. Alec smiled in the dark, standing very tall at the side of the little bed. All the words he'd been thinking had gone out of his head, leaving his mind resounding with two, strangely new, words. "I promise," he wanted to say, there in the dark, with his daughter breathing gently. His lips moved, and he said it silently and without knowing, really, what he meant. *I promise.*

Sixteen

It is the great glory of our political system, as writers on government are fond of pointing out, that the transfer of power from one President to the next is smooth and orderly; thus, the people rest easily in their beds, confident that no coup will cost them their heads (while those charged with the nation's security sharpen up their wariness, just in case a hostile power doesn't quite believe the books). But, though it lacks the fillip of physical danger, the interregnum is not without its excitements, particularly in Washington, where some dignitaries will go out with the old and others will come in with the new. And most particularly among the Washington press corps, charged with the task of somehow obtaining the names of the new officials—or the best guesses thereon—before they are announced. There could be some doubt that the American public is really waiting breathlessly to find out who will be the new chairman of the Food and Drug Administration, but there is no doubt that the city of Washington hungers for such information: the real estate people, for example, girding for a rush of business as undersecretaries prepare to pack, surely yearn to know who will be in the market for the undersecretaries' houses.

On the Friday after Election Day, however, few real facts are as yet available. The President-elect is nearly always in semi-seclusion; he has much to do and is little inclined to comment about it. The working press, badgered by its editors to come up with something, desperately checks and rechecks whispers and rumors, all numerous, and frantically phones Names all over the country. These gentry, who haven't yet been asked but who have also heard the rumors and are precisely as nervous about the whole thing as their interviewers, are implored to sum up their feelings. They wriggle, hedge, or hint—according to their temperaments and degrees of certainty—and their replies are solemnly reported and, if necessary, then discussed at length by the hard-pressed journalists.

The situation is made to order for the likes of Oscar Bainbridge, who prefer to deal in Top Men and fog. The mist in this morning's Bainbridge column had hovered over Lloyd Morris, who was said by some to have been adviser to Alec Girard on foreign policy. Bainbridge spent a few paragraphs on Lloyd Morris's career and then launched into consideration of the possibility that Morris would be appointed Secretary of State. Rational readers accepted from the start, of course, that Bainbridge couldn't actually know whether Morris would or wouldn't be appointed; even the less rational readers—who were under the vague impression that the President-elect would, as all high officials obviously were required to, make Oscar privy to his decision—understood that Girard might not have arrived at a decision as yet. But the interesting fact about the column was that no reader, rational or irrational, could arrive at a clear judgment of whether the writer thought Girard should or shouldn't appoint Lloyd Morris. It was another triumph of Bainbridgean prose.

Gil Kimball had been fooling around all morning, in his office at the *New York Leader*'s Washington bureau, with a fake interview with a hypothetical Melvin Zilch, mentioned as a hot prospect for chief of the hypothetical Office for Disbursal of Recompense (ODOR); but Gil had found that he just couldn't get Melvin to sound true in his head. "The Hon. Melvin Zilch murmured modestly" stared emptily at him from the sheet of cheap copy paper and would not murmur believable words. At last Kimball decided that the auguries were all wrong for the executive branch and caught a bus for Capitol Hill and a possible sidelight on the legislature, where there was, at least, a lot going on: some of the House members who'd been swept in with Winkler had just been swept out by Girard.

The auguries here were very good indeed. Almost the first person Gil encountered in the strangely quiet corridors of the House Office Building was no less than William Bruyette, newly returned to these halls by the voters of the Fourteenth Congressional District of Vermont, and here today, he admitted blithely to Kimball of the Press, to play the vulture over the corpses of some soon-to-be-ex-colleagues. Gil followed the Congressman, turning over in his mind the possibility of doing a column on what Alec Girard had left behind while everyone else was beating his brains out trying to guess what lay ahead. He looked around at the comfortable, well-furnished office and observed that its tenant didn't seem to be in need of scavenging from the departed.

"I'm scavenging personnel," Bruyette told him. He tilted back in the swivel chair at his desk. "These are job-hunting days for the Hill staff, you know, and I heard of a particularly juicy AA who's up for grabs." He turned coy then, refusing to identify or even describe the sought-after administrative assistant on the grounds that it was dog-eat-dog and he was hungry. He had given Alec Girard everything he owned for the campaign and he would be reduced to answering his own phone unless he did some fast scrounging now.

"How's the Senator's personnel scrounging going?" Gil asked casually. "I hear all sorts of people have been asked to drop in at O Street for a little chat." He looked at Bruyette, but the Vermonter only grinned. "Feller who *could* get himself appointed to Girard's Senate seat but doesn't," Gil went on, addressing a framed picture of Bruyette shaking hands with somebody on the opposite wall, "must have a reason, I figure. When I hear that the Governor of Vermont is going to appoint a character who has 'seatwarmer' writ large all over him, I figure further that the decision has been made to run this feller I'm talking about for the Senate when Girard's old term is up, two years from now. Now I deduce—I'm very good at deduction, you can ask anybody—that this feller is willing to hold off on the Senate because his old pal needs him; he can't be moving up himself while he's lending a hand to a chum, right? This here feller must have a few chores to do for his overworked, personnel-hunting friend, who has a hell of a lot of people to find besides a Secretary of State. For example, the rest of the State appointments, roughly speaking, might well be left to a trusty comrade. Correct?"

"Roughly speaking," Bruyette said. He slid open a drawer and pulled out a manila folder. "It's no secret, Gil, that the man thinks the State Department needs backbone. As a matter of fact, you could give me a little information, if you would."

"In exchange for what?" Gil asked promptly. "I hate to seem grasping, but why should anybody buy my column when Bainbridge can tell them Girard's every thought? And I have twin sons with bottomless bellies, and a daughter who'll be marriageable before I can save up for the wedding."

In the ensuing bargaining session, Gil wrested—for attribution but not quotation—the information that no Secretary had yet been chosen for State but that Blackwell and Lloyd Morris had both been vetoed by the President-elect. "For the top spot," Bruyette (who would appear in print as "a source close to the President-elect") emphasized. What Girard was looking for was a tough, experienced administrator without a personal following, so as not to add to the State Department's perennial internecine warfare. And what Bruyette was looking for, he added, opening his folder, was lower-echelon personnel to match. He leaned across the desk with the confidence of a man who has paid his admission and asked Kimball what he knew about Willard Catullus Farland.

"Catullus, for God's sake. I didn't know *that*."

"Well, I imagine he keeps it pretty well hidden from view. But Jake Ruffing says he and Alec met Farland at your house, so I thought you might be able to help me out." The Congressman ruffled through the contents of the folder, which included some newspaper clippings. "Born Alabama—hmm, he's not much younger than Alec, is he? Summa cum laude, but look where—big fish in little-pond college, our boy Farland. But graduate school is Ivy League. Scholarship? Seems likely . . . yes, here it is. Awarded, et cetera . . . Looks as though he could have stayed in academe trailing somber robes. But no, our hero joined the Foreign Service and set sail almost at once. Complete with bride, too."

"She died," Gil said.

"Yes, I see. These dossiers are rather like capsule novels, aren't they? Transferred to departmental service because of terminal illness of his wife—but it looks as though it turned out to be a wise move anyway, because the bureaucracy seems to have been his meat. Ho, *ho*. Did you know our boy was approached by an Iron Curtain country while his wife was dying?"

"No. They're right on the ball, aren't they? Figured he needed money, I guess."

"Farland was apparently on the ball, too—reported the offer to the department's security people and borrowed the money from the credit union. Hmm. Didn't take him long to remarry, did it?"

Gil said defensively, "He had a little boy."

"Yes, and now he has another, I see. Also a stepdaughter. Maybe the new wife turned out to be a spendthrift? Our boy seems to have transferred around State actively—apparently his own idea, too, because each one is a promotion."

"The trail of an able bureaucrat," Gil pointed out.

"Well, sure. Politicians are the chief export of Alabama."

It would be ironic, Gil thought, if Will Farland, as ex a southerner as ever was, lost a chance for advancement because of his southern birth. Gil considered reminding Bruyette delicately that one didn't discriminate on the basis of origin, but it hardly seemed necessary; Alec Girard might have a politician's awareness of ethnic and regional origins, but he could hardly be accused of being influenced by them.

Bill shuffled the papers into a neat stack and laid them in the folder. "So? Everything looks pretty good for what we want, on the basis of performance, et cetera. But is there anything that doesn't show up, that I ought to know about? You know what I mean."

Gil nodded. It seemed clear enough that they wanted Farland as a kind of watchdog in the new, shook-up administration of the department, and he himself thought it a highly intelligent approach, typical of Girard and Ruffing. For though new brooms could be effectively kept from sweeping clean by stiff wrists at lower levels, an experienced man could spot and outwit any such bureaucratic maneuvers. And if, on the other hand, a new Secretary proved so eager to make a prompt record that he imposed unrealistic goals on the bureaucracy, the error could be corrected within the inner councils and without providing aid and comfort to enemy bureaucrats. What Alec Girard wanted was action, but not unreasonable, riding-off-in-all-directions, change-for-the-sake-of-change action.

"Farland sounds ideal for your setup," he told Bruyette at last. And for the future setup, too, he did not say; but the significance of the clippings in the folder had not escaped him: the only time the Farland name appeared in print was when he made speeches. And some of the academic types who had been pressed into speech-drafting service for the campaign were known to be unsuited for or uninterested in the long White House pull. Still, it was, so far, only a Kimball hunch. "The only thing is, I'm not really an expert on Farland. I mean, it's his wife who was our friend originally. We met him about five years ago, just before they got married. She used to live next door to us."

"Well, what about the wife? Is there anything that could pop up in the papers and make us look foolish? You know what I mean."

Gil smiled, because he did—now. No light of publicity was about to be turned on Farland of the State Department that hadn't been before. Some spot more newsworthy had to be in the works . . . Gil covered his smile by kissing the tips of his fingers and waving them at Bruyette like a movie Italian. "How can I tell you about Marian? Marian," he said dramatically, "is indescribable."

"Try," suggested Bruyette.

"Well, let's see— Did your boyhood reading include *Ivanhoe?*" Gil watched the other's nod. "Then perhaps you recall Ivanhoe's two ladies fair, the pure Lady Rowena and the lush Jewess Rebecca? Well, Marian Farland looks like a mixture of the two."

"And you lived next door. Gee."

"Yeah, gee. I, I might point out, am no bachelor. And, if I'd had any trouble remembering it, Marian would have managed to remind me. I've never been the victim of her chilling look, but I've seen it applied, and the Antarctic winter is cozier." Gil sighed reminiscently. "In addition, there was a duenna—a colored woman named Rosa, who's a doll but formidable as a protector of Marian. And besides *that,* there was an ever-present flow of suitors and assorted hopefuls, plus a handful of eligibles in the city room of the *Tribune.* She works there, you know."

"Now you've gone and spoiled it," Bill Bruyette said regretfully. "Newspaper gals, no matter how pretty they are, have a certain repulsive something."

"I know what you mean, but Marian Farland doesn't have it. I think it's because she came in sort of at the top—what gives them that hard finish, that enamel surface you find so unattractive, is the years of combat. By the time they manage to get themselves up from the women's page, they're just not very womanly any more." Gil went on to explain how Marian, as the wife of Charles Grayson, had been spared combat fatigue. "She writes good," he added hastily. "Real good. I don't mean to knock that. But the thing is, the first time she wrote something, Grayson took it and showed it to somebody—you see what I mean?"

Bruyette, twiddling a pencil, said he saw and asked indifferently in a voice that supposed the answer to be "no" whether there was any scandal about Farland's wife's divorce that might rise up and bite them. Gil, who had known Charles Grayson quite well in the pre-Marian days and who therefore had heard both sides of that story, said simply that both accounts matched: Marian had left Grayson for no dramatic reason, and had lived, with her little daughter and Rosa, in a fashion that had not brought her into conflict with the law or caused serious disturbance to her neighbors.

"Charlie kept flying in from somewhere and taking her out to talk it all over again," Gil said sympathetically, "but it never did any good. Seems she didn't love him, or she didn't love him enough to leave Washington, anyway. My wife seems to understand it, but I don't. Anyway, after a year, Marian said she wanted to go out on dates and she couldn't feel right about it if she was still married, so she got a divorce. With Charlie's consent, of course. What the hell else could he do? Relations have remained friendly: Marian apparently always thought he was a nice guy, and while I don't suppose Farland feels exactly chummy, I don't imagine he has any grudges. But if you're pondering all this from a personnel man's point of view, Bill, I guess you've got to conclude that Farland's domestic prospects are not secure by organization-man standards. After all, what the lady did once, she can do again. Though I've seen no sign of it, if that's any help to you. She seems to love this husband, all right."

"Even from an organization-man point of view, it doesn't add up to much of a drawback," Bruyette observed. "Whatever the lady is, she doesn't appear to be a mankiller: Grayson's alive and functioning nicely at his job, isn't he? What is he now, Far East bureau chief?"

They talked idly for a while about Charlie Grayson, who was indeed Far East bureau chief for Consolidated Press, and then about other mutual acquaintances who were not particularly newsworthy at the moment. Gil was getting up to leave when he thought of saying, with some surprise, that if Bruyette had questions about Marian Farland, he should have asked Andy Girard; the women, he understood from his wife, were quite friendly.

"Don't be silly," Bruyette said sourly. "Andrea Girard doesn't have any women friends."

"I read that, too," Gil said. "Aren't people lousy? I had to stop Betty from going out and bashing somebody's head in over that stinking article. She loves Andy." He sat down again and added heatedly that he supposed it didn't count, but as a matter of fact so did he.

"I remember thinking a long time ago," Bruyette mused, "that the role of mate to destiny's tot was a tough one. Poor Andy. I didn't know she knew Farland's wife, and she wouldn't be likely to volunteer it, I guess. I hope to God they let up on her now that the campaign's over, or she'll be even less communicative." He sighed. "I remember when Andy used to just talk, do you? About anything that came into her head. And to anybody she fancied."

"She was a sweet kid. Them was better days for her, in a way."

Bruyette looked at him sadly and began to reminisce about the first time he'd met Andy, when Alec had taken his best friend to call at the Langwiths'. "I wasn't expecting exactly a dog, you know. After all, over the years, Alec had been emerging unmistakably as a sort of all-around top banana. And I'd seen with my own eyes what he collected without even trying— But this, this beautiful, eager, absolute sweetheart of a girl, obviously nuts about him . . ." The Congressman shook his head. "Those big brown eyes worrying whether Alec's pal would like her—oh my. All I could think was that he'd really done it, he'd really pulled it off this time. I mean, it took him long enough to get married. But it was worth it."

Gil rose. "Andy'll be all right," he said gently. "For all we know, she doesn't even mind these snide things written by women. Women understand other women, you know."

Bruyette muttered that he was glad somebody did, and Gil asked him, shrugging, what you could do about it anyway, considering that you had to have another sex.

The Congressman closed his folder and thanked Gil for the poop on the Farlands. "I guess we'd better have them out for one of the Ruffing fun-and-games Sundays, so Jake can have a little talk with him."

"Well, whatever you do, don't let the games include bridge. Not with the Farlands," Gil warned.

"Why not? Don't tell me they cheat."

"No. But she bids whatever she happens to be in the mood for. And he makes it, whatever she bids. Works better than cheating. You can't possibly win."

Bill Bruyette said loftily that bridge was for idiots, and that he himself hadn't played for a week.

"They're such *nice* people," Marian said into the telephone on Monday afternoon. "Not that you'd know it from what I read in the paper this morning—the *Tribune* got onto the names of some of the people who were there, in spite of what I thought were rather elaborate precautions. The story was in the society section and it sounded—well, idiotic. As though everybody shamefully spent the Sabbath running around acting adolescent."

Morisot observed that he knew few people as un-adolescent as Jake and Bonnie Ruffing.

"I know. I suppose it's because we played softball—hey, did you know I distinguished myself? Rosenberg hit what would have been a sure homer, except that I caught it." Her small face shone with adolescent triumph. "Boy, was he sore!"

Morisot said he would have thought she was too little to be a very good outfielder. His voice held amusement, and some pride in the baseball know-how he was exhibiting.

"Well, nobody had enough faith in me to put me on a base, and Jake apparently always plays shortstop . . . I had to jump like crazy, but anyone would have had to jump, really, so I only needed a few extra inches. I guess the ballet lessons I was dragged to when I was a little girl finally paid off. Paid off tremendously, too, because I dazzled my daughter, which is pretty hard to do." Marian sighed luxuriantly. "That's one of the things that was nice—you could wear slacks and bring your kids. You know, it was the first thing I ever had to go to on account of Will that I actually enjoyed on my own."

Jake Ruffing's place on Sunday was a must, Will had called to tell her Friday afternoon, his voice mysterious and excited. She answered irritably that he could go where he liked, but it had apparently slipped his mind that Dick was in the midst of another bout of tonsillitis and she'd have to stay home with him.

"You have to come, Marian. That's final. The kids, too, except Dick. Let Rosa stay with him."

"Rosa has plans for Sunday."

Will said he didn't give a damn, she could just arrange something, and hung up. She had arranged something, of course—Rosa's sister Gloria agreed to come and sit with Dick. But Marian had been angry and rebellious, even when they were packing the remaining two children into the car on Sunday. Sharlie, who'd been wearing chartreuse slacks and a world-weary expression, tightened the belt of the former and removed the latter when they arrived at the Ruffings'; for other guests had brought their children, and some of their children turned out to be the sort of gangling youths of uncertain voice that invariably brought Sharlie Grayson to instant alertness. The hosts had on hand, among their own collection of boys, one of an age to match Peter's, and Jerry and Nedra Rosenberg had thoughtfully contributed their own small son.

Everything had been lovely—space and trees and crisp fall air, and people of all ages having a good time in whatever fashion their tastes dictated. As the light outdoors began to fail, they had all gathered inside and been fed—hot dogs for the children and goulash for their elders. Afterward, the little children listened to stories and played quiet games upstairs under the supervision of the Ruffing baby's nurse, and, in the big room that looked out over the Potomac, the firelight leaped cozily while somebody played a reasonably good cocktail piano and a man who—Will told Marian later and in confidence—was probably going to be an Undersecretary of the Treasury blew an expert trumpet, high and sweet and swinging. From the basement came the brief thunks of Ping-Pong balls and the voices of the older children. In a small room off to one side, Jake played bridge with a tall, quiet man named Hoffman against Rosenberg and Will, who'd been drafted by Jake with a casual "You don't mind?" to Marian. Surely she didn't mind, but she had thought it a silly way to spend your time with all the more interesting things that were going on.

"Maybe you don't know," Marian said apologetically to Paul. "I mean, maybe you're too important to have to go to command performances. But they're always terrible—hours of hanging around, waiting like a soldier, except that I'm not allowed to gripe like one."

Paul laughed, then advised her solemnly that he was important enough to escape some command performances but not all; the French understood perhaps better than the Americans that art was not produced in drawing rooms, but the understanding was not complete. He went on to suggest that she might find many things different in Washington official life once Alec and Andy were settled in the White House.

"We're not allowed to say 'Andy.' " Marian reached for the memo to "all hands" that had come around this morning and read him the instruction that "staffers" avoid referring to the wife of the President-elect as "Andy." The nickname, the memo conceded, had had wide publicity; but in the *Washington Tribune* the lady would henceforth be either "Mrs. Girard" or "Andrea Girard," it was ordained.

Static electricity made the memo stick to the paper underneath; as she lifted the one she'd been reading, she caught sight of the other and was reminded. "I'm so sorry I couldn't see . . . that we couldn't get together before you left Washington." Genuine sorrow was in her voice. "This stupid staff meeting . . . But I couldn't possibly have escaped it."

"We must make do with regrets then, yes? Only I have not, have I? For I wished to speak with you once again before the plane departs." Paul spoke gently and with a little self-mockery. "But I will surely return for the gala in January, for I have arranged it so. In Paris I will complete the arrangements. And I have already told Alec, when I saw him before he left for Florida." He laughed. "And *Madame* Girard, also."

Marian smiled at this dutiful formality and asked how Andy was. Paul, who had taken his leave of her just before flying to New York, said she was formidably energetic, though she seemed rather tired of being pregnant. They had discussed his return, which involved a commission to write some pieces on the inauguration festivities for a Paris newspaper; Paul had been reluctant to undertake an assignment that seemed to him to be based on nothing more than the exploitation of his friendship with the Girards. But *Andréa,* he told Marian with some amusement, had looked on the affair rather differently: she would rather be interpreted to the newspaper readers of Paris by Paul, she'd declared, than by someone perhaps less competent. Alec, queried earlier on the same point, had announced solemnly that he could think of nothing more hopeful for improving international understanding. "So I am to be in attendance as a French journalist," Paul said, and added that Nedra Rosenberg, who was fluent in French, had offered her help if he needed it at the Inaugural Ball, where there would presumably be a rattle of rapid English that might prove daunting.

"Well, I speak journalist," Marian said, unwittingly echoing Gil Kimball, who'd told Paul exactly that the day before. "I'll be glad to help, too."

Paul marveled aloud and elaborately at her kindness and accepted her offer with intense gratitude and without mentioning Gil's offer. Marian was assuring him that he had nothing to fear, that all it amounted to, really, was just getting the names right, when she heard a woman's voice speak in the background. Paul excused himself and said something indistinct, apparently turning away from the phone. But she heard enough of what he said to gather he was suggesting that somebody go and have a coffee and he would be there in a minute—which didn't matter, except that she thought she heard also the telltale pronoun *"tu,"* and she was startled at the abrupt, dismal feeling that invaded her. Paul came back then to say good-bye, and a moment later he was gone; his warm voice that seemed to be filled equally with pleasure and regret still sounded in her ears.

Marian hung up the phone slowly, trying first to banish that *"tu"* and then, failing that, to explain it. Children and lovers, she had learned in school—where they had doubtless said "very good friends" rather than "lovers"—were addressed as *"tu,"* and nearly everybody else rated a *"vous."* Which would certainly include a museum colleague seeing M. Morisot off, she told herself with tightened lips. A vagrant hope that she could somehow ask Andy whom Paul could have been *"tu"*-ing at Idlewild crept in just before Marian finally persuaded herself that this whole line of speculation was not only foolish but unseemly as well.

In command of herself at last, she read over the damned memo, summoning "culture editors" to a conference at eleven-thirty this morning, that had interfered with her engagement with Paul. Music, Books, Drama, Dance, and Art had all been represented at the discussion of the "expected impact

of the upcoming Girard Administration on Washington's cultural activities";
what upcame of it all was boredom, and, in Marian, who normally tolerated
meaningless endeavors rather well, a sullen anger. She might have erupted
into irritation instead of maintaining her glazed silence if she hadn't caught
sight of Music gazing blandly into the middle distance and known instantly,
with that leap into somebody else's mind that sometimes happened, that he
was singing silently to himself. She spent the rest of the conference guessing
at what he was singing, coming eventually to the decision that it was a Bach
fugue. When her ruminations were interrupted, she made a brief and not
ungracious little speech predicting a revival of interest in the French Impressionists.

Marian crumpled the memo, threw it at the institutional wastebasket, and
missed, partly because her favorite copyboy chose just that moment to appear in a manner that would upset anyone's aim: Grant's long face, topped
with the thick wavy hair that was always in need of cutting, hovered just
above the edge of the glass partition setting off the Sunday Department, and,
more particularly, the cubicles inhabited by Art and Music, from the corridor leading to the back elevators. Grant, who was basketball-player tall,
was the only co-worker able to peer over the partition, and it was a pleasant
enough change from the usual procession of shadows against the frosted
glass. But it was a little disconcerting anyway, this visitation by a disem-
bodied head, however benign.

"You look like a giraffe grazing," she told the head. "I'm sorry I have
no peanuts."

"I don't eat peanuts, I eat foliage," Grant said.

"You don't talk either," Marian pointed out. "If you want to get technical."

"True. I'm an atypical giraffe." His voice was surprisingly deep. It had
been a good many years since copyboys were actually boys; but even when
you knew better, Marian thought, you kept expecting them to be little kids,
not twenty-two-year-old kids who had been to college. "I'm also an atypical
copyboy," Grant went on, "because I'm about to offer to pay for something.
It being the end of the day and all."

"Dinner?" Marian suggested, not without disbelief.

"That'll be the day. Beer was what I had in mind. *A* beer, like. Us copyboys—" she saw the shadow of his hand against the glass as he raised it to
fend off her wrath "—all right, *we* copyboys, are about to repair to Georgetown for a beer, a small celebration, and a round-table discussion." He
grinned at her unspoken question. "The celebration is because we've just
wrapped up the last of the election chores—and received the plaudits of
the ME himself for our industry, loyalty, integrity, ingenuity—"

"Please," Marian said faintly.

"Well, then. The discussion is going to be on the meaning of what we
have just seen. If there is any."

"My husband says there is." Marian's tone chided his mockery. "He says things'll be different now, because Girard understands the uses of power."

"Acch, Powerrr." The head became a "mad scientist" movie ad, complete with crazed rolling eyes and snarling lips drawn back over teeth that were, in this case, a little too young and healthy. "Power iss all," it hissed throatily.

"People who think of power as automatically evil should stop and ask themselves whether they really would prefer powerlessness," Marian recited.

"Your husband says."

"My husband says," she admitted.

Grant sighed. "What else does this character have to say for the new day dawning?"

"Well, for one thing, Girard is the first President since Wilson with a sound theoretical political science background." She lowered her gaze because craning her neck was beginning to make it hurt and added thoughtfully, "At least I think that's what he said."

"Doubtless he did. But did he happen to mention that Congress tied Wilson into tight, teeny knots?" asked Grant, who had an A.B. in political science.

Marian, an erstwhile art major, retreated promptly into *argumentum ad hominem*. "Oh well, if all you're going to do is knock—"

"No such thing. I propose to consider rationally, and as impartially as possible, the effect of the Girard Administration on what is, after all, the key question: by this time next year, will I have made it to reporter or to citizen soldier? Any contribution you care to make to the discussion—"

"Oh, I can't," Marian said softly, her face distressed. "I've got to go home. My husband has a meeting or something, and I've got to spring the housekeeper. Can I have a rain check, though?"

Grant nodded carefully, to avoid scratching his chin on the edge of the glass, and loitered briefly to exchange a few guesses on Girard's Cabinet appointments—a subject as compulsory for Washington now as talk of whether it looks like snow at a ski resort. They agreed that it was worth sticking with good old reliable Kimball, who had said categorically that neither Blackwell nor Lloyd Morris would be Secretary of State, but neither of them had any rumor the other hadn't heard. Finally, Grant went off, his head moving along the partition like something on an assembly line.

Listening to him whistling at the elevator, Marian stared down at the surface of her desk in sudden dismay as it came over her that Alec Girard had taken on the responsibility for ordering or disordering the life of real, precious Grant, a lanky boy who thought he could write and very possibly could, who took grammar not seriously enough and a girl who had shown the great lack of judgment to prefer another perhaps too seriously, whose only half-admitted notion of himself as another Thomas Wolfe might be starkly altered by whether, or when, the ever-threatening draft got him. Grant and his shy confidences and embryo talent and awkward love lived, from here on in, under whatever limitations existed in the capabilities of Alec Girard. Appalled, Marian felt suddenly a great pity for Andrea.

And a little shame that she had been so impatient with Will the other night, she admitted belatedly as she gathered her things to go home. But it had been so difficult to follow what Will was saying; talk of Civil Service rules and something called "Schedule C" numbed her mind until it went beyond noncomprehension into sheer unwillingness to comprehend. The only thing that emerged from his restless talking, for which she had been summoned formally into the study when they got home from the outing at the Ruffings', was that Will seemed to be about to change his job somehow —although he also said, when she asked, that he would still be in the State Department.

He roved the small room, picking things up and putting them back without looking at them, and Marian tucked her bare feet under her to keep them warm and waited in the armchair for something that would tell her what he wanted of her. Whatever kind of new job he was taking, or thinking of taking, his talking to her made no sense; if he'd wanted, he'd have moved them all to Ouagadougu without bothering to mention it until the last minute, and then he'd toss it out with great arrays of figures and slogans and anything else needed to convince her that Ouagadougu was precisely where she'd always longed to live. There was nothing of his usual way about him now, she thought, studying him as he pushed the globe on the bookcase with his finger. He looked troubled, and Will never looked troubled: he *acted* troubled sometimes, but he never looked it.

"What are you scared of?" she asked him suddenly.

"Who's scared? I'm asking you because you have a right to a say in whether I give up all this security we have now and become a political appointee, which means I could get tossed out on my ear any time."

"Do you think you'll be tossed out on your ear?"

"No." He let the globe turn without him and spun around to look directly at her. "Okay, I guess I'm trying to hide behind your skirts—to make it partly your fault if I fall on my face. Okay. So I'm scared."

"What of?" she asked again.

"Of the Depression," Will answered suddenly, and then smiled at her in surprise and relief and she understood that she had brought him the great gift to the anxious, the naming of the name of fear. "You know," he began expansively, and it was the old, confident, discursive Will talking now, "Girard made the point that there's a major chasm in this country between those who were too old for World War Two and those who weren't. I think maybe he's on the right track, but his line of demarcation is wrong: it's the Depression of the Thirties that's the dividing line."

He talked on rapidly and happily, explaining in well-organized detail all the legislation that could keep depressions like the one of the Thirties from recurring. And Marian, looking attentive and benign, drifted off into a few bitter thoughts of Annamay Farland, believer in bombast and seeker after status, who had "never regained her health" after the state of Alabama went bankrupt and her husband, once a lofty high-school principal, became a low-caste traveling salesman. Her own health was not all that suffered from Annamay's inability to respect her husband's ability to sell stoves in Depression-devastated Alabama. Marian suspected that it was then that his mother had begun to instill in Will this notion that to look, at all times, like a very parfit gentil knight was the sine qua non of manhood. Not necessarily to *be* one, Will understood—just to look like it. Which meant you could never look scared.

What all this was about, it seemed, was that Will had a chance to become a Girard myrmidon, though apparently not immediately. But the point was, why shouldn't he be scared, if he was considering leaving his own well-tilled fields to go off and serve as squire at court when he wasn't sure how much worth serving the kingdom was? Marian, who would have started from this point to begin with, recognized that the difference between them might have a great deal to do with the fact that Daddy DiGennaro, showing his daughter an apple-seller on a New York street corner as they left Longchamps after lunch, had explained briefly that something called a Depression was troubling the unfortunate; then he had tightened the little fur collar on her warm coat and hailed a taxi so his pretty little Marianna with the long black curls wouldn't be cold. Daddy DiGennaro had been handsome and thoughtful and gay, a power from whom all blessings flowed, and clearly very, very big. To little Tully (who didn't manage to become "Will" until he got to college and away from his mother), studying his books grimly on an always partly empty stomach, it had been equally clear that Dad Farland was growing smaller and smaller every time his wife looked at him, or avoided looking at him. Dad Farland eventually stopped being an unshaven, unnecessary presence around the house and became a series of small money orders sent home from "on the road"—though the bright, handsome boy who embodied all his mother's hopes for rescue was led to believe that it was Annamay's piano lessons to a few farmer's daughters that kept the leaky roof over their heads.

Poor scarred Will, Marian thought, and listened to him saying that his kids had to go to college whether Girard succeeded or not. "But during the campaign, you seemed to think Girard was the only hope of the future," she interrupted.

"Well, we certainly couldn't have Ferris. But Girard is a beginner, really—if he can't make a working reality of his program, he goes back to private life to write his memoirs. But where do I go back to? I wish him well—but the question is, can he support my career?" Will began pacing the small room nervously. "Oh my, oh my, I wish him well—because he's got just about everything it needs to make the thing work. And when it works—" he wheeled around, his hands raised as if in praise and his eyes alight—"oh baby, you *must* see the beauty of the thing, that lovely, exact balancing of the powers. It works like a fine watch, it actually does. It's a bigger discovery than the wheel."

Elegant, Marian thought, is what mathematicians call a satisfying proof. She wanted time to consider this rapture of Will's, but he was rushing on, proclaiming bitterly the size of Winkler's sin in letting the country fall into government by legislature, with all its built-in abuses, uncertainties, and hazards. His bony hands moved jerkily, one up, one down, making a destroyed balance vivid on the air between them.

"Will," Marian said suddenly, "what more do you want?"

It brought him up short. "I want . . . oh, I guess what I want is the sort of in-the-bones understanding that FDR had; but that was like Shakespeare's way with words, and you can't expect it often. But if Girard had Truman's kind of understanding even, the kind that comes of a good brain exposed to years of experience, so it's almost instinctive—"

"It sounds like Jake Ruffing," Marian interrupted.

Will stopped, discovering her suddenly. "Jake does have it, I think."

"Then why does Alec have to have everything himself? Look at all the people who'll be helping him—like Rosenberg, and Jake, and that man who won the Pulitzer Prize."

"Girard's bright, and he can take advice—he's shown that," Will mused.

"Well, then, it's hardly fair not to give him some, since he's asked."

"The next sound you hear," Will very nearly shouted, "will be my wife hitting the nail on the head. Again." He scooped her out of her nest in the armchair and swung her through the air. Then he kissed her enthusiastically and set her down and told her she was marvelous. Marian twisted from his grasp, wondering what she had told him that he couldn't equally well have told himself, and began to search out her fallen hairpins. "You fuss too much," she said over her shoulder. "Why don't you just remember what you love, instead of talking so much?"

Locking up in her office on Monday night, she recalled that airy advice with something like shame for having made it sound so easy. But she had been startled by the discovery that Will did really, truly love the Constitution of the United States of America, with a genuine and unmistakable devotion and even passion. What she had stumbled on, she decided now, was something she had consistently overlooked: some people—like Will, and probably like Alec Girard—experienced the kind of nearly physical joy, invisible but nevertheless there, that was simply aesthetic delight—the same that her office neighbor found in music and Paul Morisot found in shapes.

The Depression apples rose up in her mind all at once, a ruby geometry in the cold, clean air of long-gone Saturday mornings in New York, with Walter Damrosch's children's concerts and then Daddy the courtier, charming at Longchamps. The glowing, perfect apples, beckoning and beautiful, lived in her memory so wholly that her hands moved, clasping each other as they had inside the satin-lined little fur muff that had nothing whatever to do with depressions. What the apples had to do with the Depression had escaped her and always would: she could not really see them with Will's eyes even when compassion led her to try, and in the end the effort itself hurt and deprived her. The apples were completely and solely apples, pyramided and full of sweet juice, and if they stood for anything at all it was only love.

But by the time she reached the elevator, she was saying guiltily that she should have known before that love was not "only" love: Will's love spoke to him, perhaps, in his view of the apples, and if it was different from the one that sang in hers, who was to say which was the valid view of love? She remembered Grant then, as he had stood lanky and whistling in this same spot, and when the elevator came and carried her down, she found herself yearning for the missed security of the society of the copyboys, who had remote and manageable concerns in which she could be of some palpable aid. A girl who turned you down on the phone might not have had any choice, advised Mama Marian sturdily, and could be wishing with all her heart that you'd try again; syntax was not an old-fashioned notion but a way of helping understanding—and of course you care whether the reader understands you, preached Maxwell Perkins Marian to Thomas Wolfe Grant, or what in hell are you writing for?

And then she was out on the dark street looking at dark bulks of buildings speckled with lights. But behind those lights moved either a populace or people, and which it was depended on what part of what she had been thinking was finally true. Alive between the turgid river and the whole sky was this whole city full of apple-viewers, to be learned and loved, and not classified or even, necessarily, understood.

Seventeen

As Marian settled into bed that night with an unreturned Will still only a recurring, apologetic voice on the phone, Grant's prospects as a reporter—in case he didn't find himself in the Army—took a marked upturn. He and a friend—a copyboy on the *New York Leader* who had taken a bus ride to Washington for some Capitol Hill job-hunting—were walking from the beer-smelling hangout on Wisconsin Avenue to somebody's pad on 28th Street; they kicked absently at drifts of fallen leaves and discoursed, their hands stuffed in the pockets of wash-worn pants and their faces stylishly glum. Most of Georgetown had either gone to bed or to back rooms of the narrow little houses; their lights, if any, fell on the walled gardens where next year's spring flowers slept in new beds.

When, on their zigzag course, the two young men turned into O Street, they blinked against the bright beams of light from what appeared to be a double-parked car. It wasn't until they were nearly abreast of it that they recognized it for an ambulance, though a soundless one with its roof light not only not whirling but even dark. Grant stopped dead and, as his friend eyed him seriously, began to search for the number of the house before which they'd halted. Three houses up ahead he could see, as his eyes adjusted to the twin shafts of light, dark, anonymous figures moving between the house's entrance and the waiting ambulance.

"Doubleyou-oh-Wow!" said Grant, in a tight, soft voice. "You know whose house that is?"

The copyboys looked at each other with at least as wild a surmise as Keats once ascribed to the wrong explorer; then, with one accord, they backed away from the scene, enacting an elaborate tableau of indolent and thoughtless youth. It crossed Grant's mind that it might be better to wait and see who was carried from the house—but the lead time was short: Georgetown University Hospital was only a few minutes away, even without siren, and that few minutes, minus the time it would take him to get to a phone, represented the total of his news beat. Once they turned the corner and were out of sight of the guardians of the O Street house and its occupants, consciousness of that slim margin of time hurled the boys through the dark streets too fast to allow breath for goat-cries. When they reached their destination, Grant's phone priority was unquestioned. *"Washing—"* was as far as the operator got before he barked, "City desk—hurry!" He recognized the voice of the night-shift copyboy who answered, and his, "This is Grant!" was a shout of triumph.

"So? How-do," was the unimpressed reply.

"So there's an ambulance in front of a certain house on O Street Northwest. In Georgetown. The number is—"

"There's an ambulance—*what* number?"

"You heard me," Grant said. His free hand reached, of itself, for the hat it wanted to push back on his head. "I see you know who lives there, huh?" The question was both unnecessary and unheard—in the quiet city room, the night editor was making very good time, for a middle-aged man, at broken-field running between the empty desks toward a wildly wigwagging copyboy.

The excitement beating with the pulse in Andrea's throat was not unlike the kind she'd felt on the night of her debut, as she came down the long staircase of her father's house. Only this time there would be no stairs—Dr. Williams had been adamant about having her carried down, though he'd also been sympathetic to her horror of the crowds an ambulance would bring. Since there was no need for split-second timing, there would be no siren, and there would be every effort to keep her trip to the hospital from public attention. But she would go in an ambulance; on that he was firm.

A panicky doubt about the assumption that there was no need for split-second timing assailed her when the next pain hit, so soon after the last one.

She let her mouth go slack and panted, as she'd been instructed; her hand was still on the telephone, and when she let go after the pain let go of her, her hand left damp traces on the smooth surface. "Early or not, it sounds like we're in business," the doctor had said, and then of course had begun his qualifying remarks, because he could hardly say for sure until he saw her. Andy watched the last of the dark imprints of her hand evaporate from the telephone and ordered herself to turn her attention to her next move. Alec would be notified—"We ought to at least tell him to stand by," the cheerful voice on the phone had decided—and Dr. Williams would meet her at the hospital.

The small arrangements, now, were up to her, and she had very little time. Elizabeth must be provided for. A bag must be packed. Appointments must be canceled. She forced herself to think of small, immediate details. When Irene appeared, she listed the things she would want at the hospital in a strong, clear voice, smiling at the girl's wide-eyed excitement. When she had to, she waited out the pain, sitting very still. When Irene had left the room, she picked up the phone and dialed the Ruffings'. The pain struck again while she listened to the steady whirs, and sweat prickled on her upper lip as she clenched her hand on the telephone.

"I'm sorry if I've awakened you," she began after Jake's fuzzy, "Hello."

"Not really." His logic was as blurry as his voice. "We just got to bed—" He broke off as realization dawned. "Andy! Is it—?"

"We think so," said Andy happily. At the other end, she heard Bonnie say something. "I'm going to the hospital in a minute and I—"

"Honey," Bonnie's voice broke in, "Jake's getting dressed. He'll call Alec right away, and he'll meet you at the hospital. It *is* Georgetown, isn't it?"

"Yes. But there's no need—"

"Is Elizabeth asleep?"

"Yes."

"Then there's no point in waking her now. But I'll be there when she wakes up, unless Alec is. Okay? Would you like me to call your mother?"

Andy, waiting out another pain, closed her eyes against the sudden longing for her mother. Well, not *my* mother, actually, she thought realistically; what I want is just sort of a general mother. "I think not, thank you," she said carefully. "There's bound to be some—er—spotlight, and my mother would only be distressed by it."

"All right, Andy."

"I think I ought—they'll be here any minute," Andy said weakly.

Bonnie had heard the change in Andy's voice. "Sure. You just wait and do exactly what the doctor says, and you'll be fine, honey. I'll be by tomorrow to see you and the boy. You hear?"

"I hear." Andy smiled as she hung up.

She was still smiling faintly as the ambulance attendants maneuvered the stretcher carefully on the stairs. Her cheeks flushed with a sense of the indignity of being carried, prone and helpless, into the street—where, incredibly, a few dark figures had somehow gathered, despite all attempts at secrecy, to peer avidly around the barrier of the Secret Service. Andy turned her face away quickly, hot with embarrassment. But, as the stretcher was being lifted through the gaping door of the ambulance, she opened her eyes wide and stared straight up at the great trees whispery with their dry burden of few, dead leaves; the curve of their high branches, nearly meeting overhead under the starless, smoky sky, held the comfort that lies in whatever has known much coming and going and yet has itself remained. In the ambulance she watched the streetlights flicker past and thought bitterly that Alec should be here and tried not to think it. Then the pain hit again, and she forgot to care.

They let Jake Ruffing in to see her after a while, as she lay in the hospital bed in a wrinkled, scratchy hospital gown, feeling a little like a sacrificial victim readied for esoteric rites. But the sight of Jake made her giggle: his shirt was, quite obviously, a pajama top; a doubled-over sheaf of typewritten papers protruded from the big pocket of the dirty raincoat folded over his arm; and both pockets of his coat, which did not harmonize with his trousers, sagged under the weight of the bulging objects within. "The doctor says I'm doing fine," she told the familiar face leaning above her, its habitual look of impatience deepened by anxiety. "Don't look so worried."

"I've gotten hold of Alec," Jake lied. Silently he cursed both Alec and Bill Bruyette, who had, he'd been told, decided to go for a moonlight sail. "They're arranging to fly him back." The Coast Guard was on the lookout for the two carefree sailors and their Secret Service escort, and a flying boat was warming up against the moment they'd be sighted.

"Thank you, Jake. I'm so sorry to have put you to all this trouble."

"You just take it easy, honey. Nobody's going to bother you—the Secret Service people are right outside your door. If you want anything, you—"

"I don't want anything, thanks." She closed her eyes. Except Alec. Except her baby. She remembered Jake and her duty and opened her eyes to smile at him. "Tell Bonnie thanks, too. I'll ask them to phone as soon as the baby comes."

Ruffing snorted. "I won't be home." He grinned at her then and began lifting things from his pockets, holding them up in front of her one by one. "Cigarettes. Extra cigarettes. Plentiful supply of matches. Chocolate bars. Chewing gum."

"Oh, Jake. You needn't—"

"Newspaper. Papers from the office—I'd rather work than read the ancient copies of *Today's Health* that they keep in the fathers' room."

"Jake, you're not—"

"Oh yes, I am," he said firmly. "Unless you throw me out in favor of someone else. But I warn you you'll never find a better-qualified guy. I'm an expert hospital pacer with five successes to my credit. You want a boy, don't you? Well, I've paced out five boys. Where can you get a man with a better record?"

Tears prickled behind Andy's closed eyelids. She tried to speak, but she could manage only a small sound, something between laughing and weeping. She heard the nurse come in, a soft shuffle of rubber soles against the floor, and say, "I'm afraid that's all, Mr. Ruffing."

Andy opened her eyes and tried weakly, one last time. "I couldn't let you—"

"Hush, Andy. I'll be here till Alec comes." His dark eyes scanned her face, almost pleadingly, but her silence forced him to speak the bald words of love. "You're not having a baby by yourself, hear?"

He went out then, almost scurrying. I hear, Andy thought, and was comforted. I'm not having a baby by myself—a man of my family is in attendance. The tears beginning now were almost entirely self-pity; oh Alec, how could you?

"We're coming along fine," the nurse said. Her hand on the bulge of Andy's belly was warm and firm. "Take a deep breath," she added quickly. Her voice offered warning of the pain before it came and Andy obediently took a deep breath and rode the great wave.

"Here comes the doctor now, honey." It was a new nurse, a little one. Which proved some time must have gone by. It was a form of measurement, like light-years . . . Andy tried to smile through swollen lips. The pain loomed, and she stiffened in fear; the nurse put her hand in Andy's. "Try to relax."

"Try to relax." Alec was laughing at her. "Look at the others." His arm was tight around her and she was holding very tightly to the bar in front of her but she was afraid anyway, shamefully afraid, as the roller coaster rattled to the top of its climb and began to swoop sickeningly toward the lights of Glen Echo below. Down there, the people of Washington, wearing silly straw hats and licking at swollen pink and white blossoms of cotton candy, wandered at leisure from shooting gallery to miniature golf course. Behind her in the other roller-coaster cars girls screamed, high and delighted, their voices lingering among the leaves that were so close overhead, and the men with them laughed and tightened their embraces. Alec, who would never have thought of taking her to Glen Echo, had been delighted with the idea when she suggested it; now, rejoicing in youth, love, and anonymity—for the moment, Senator from nowhere—he hugged his girl and laughed into the face of the wind.

If you want to, if you really want to, you can keep from screaming, Andy told herself grimly; nothing can make you do it if you mean it hard enough. She held her teeth together until her jaws ached, and it worked: she breathed shallowly as the car climbed again; she rested while it rocked along over wooden rails under the leafy trees and the gentle summer sky. Then it was all beginning again, and she said to herself, Now you've seen that you can do it. She tightened her muscles again and made herself small in the circle of Alec's arms . . .

And Alec wasn't there, he was nowhere. No one held her safe and she was rocketing downward, faster and faster, with water in her bones and nothing left but an enormous warning: "Don't Scream ANYHOW." Where was Alec? Alone, alone, she fought with all her strength to remember the rules.

"That's the first sound she's made, poor thing," the little nurse told Dr. Williams as Andy whimpered aloud. The other nurse wiped Andy's wet forehead with a cloth, her hands very gentle.

The doctor straightened, began rolling down his sleeves, and said it would be better if she made some noise; he stood by the bedside, watching the pain-twisted face with its closed eyes, and thought it would help if she could be a little more relaxed. The white cloth that covered her hair was wet with sweat around its edge. Dr. Williams sighed. "We're getting there, but I wish it could be a little easier on her." He bent down so that his mouth was close to Andy's ear. "Mrs. Girard." Her eyes opened slowly, then widened quickly at seeing him so close. "You're doing just fine, Mrs. Girard. Do you understand?" She moistened her lips and nodded, and he went on, "But it'll be a little while yet. So we're going to give you a little something for the pain."

Hurry, Andy said to Alec, if you hurry you can make it—it will be a little while yet, didn't you hear? She was grateful for the sharp pricking in her arm, the something for the pain, and she summoned her resources to say, "Thank you," to the nurse who was withdrawing the needle. The girl smiled at her and said impulsively, "Don't be afraid, Mrs. Girard. We'll all help you."

Oh, I need help, Andy screamed silently. Around the bar of the crib-like bed, the fingernails of her clenched hand met its palm, stinging like the hypodermic. Where was Alec? He had sent Jake to take away the ring, the beautiful square emerald Alec had given her when it was all decided and they were engaged. When was it Jake had been standing beside her bed, holding the ring with its winking green fires? He wrote on a paper that he gave to a hospital person and then he took the ring away, and if she didn't behave properly, she couldn't have it any more. But I'm trying, she moaned, I'm trying hard.

"Sure you are, honey, sure you are," the little nurse crooned. "Just you take it easy, it'll all be over very soon now."

"You haven't been on this wing for a while," the other nurse guessed.

"No." The girl shook her head. Crisp black curls climbed the back and sides of her pointed white cap. "You forget, if you're away for a while."

"Well, she's an exceptionally good one."

"I know." The little nurse put a hand on the swollen abdomen. "It gets to you, doesn't it, how they suffer, poor things."

The other smiled. "Just remember she'll have forgotten it by tomorrow. Once they see the baby, it's all okay."

The baby, Andy thought, startled, waking with a huge start from a long, empty dream. The baby, where was the baby? Suddenly, every inch of her body seemed to wake to life. She saw the pain coming and dived into it as into the curl of a wave, not thinking of hurting, or Alec, or the past, or the future. There was nobody, there was nothing except this great barrier, and it must, *must* get out of the way. She bent all her strength, mindless, pushing against it.

"Get Dr. Williams," the little nurse said sharply. She snatched her hand from the heaving belly. "Quick. She's starting."

"Oh, she can't be."

Andy opened her eyes. "Please get the doctor," she said quietly. "My baby's coming."

"He said he was going to talk to Mr. Ruffing," the little nurse told her colleague. She pushed the button on the call buzzer that was looped over the head of the bed. "Easy, Mrs. Girard. Try to go easy. We're getting the doctor now."

"Hurry." Andy closed her eyes and went to work again. She had moved the barrier a little. She could do it. She could win. She took a long breath and gathered strength confidently. The excited voices of girls in withered-looking tank suits filled the echoing gym; she curled her toes on the rounded edge of tile and grinned down at the clear, unreal, faintly lapping water.

"Doctor, quick," the little nurse gasped as the white-uniformed resident appeared in the doorway. "All of a sudden, she just started—"

Andy opened her eyes once onto the frieze of hurrying figures and saw a reflection of herself, a small white spot on a table surrounded by busy people, in a great mirrorlike lens on the ceiling. Dr. Williams was a pair of dark eyes over a gauze mask. "Okay, Mother," he said cheerfully, "a little more and we've got him." A hand pressed down on her belly. All the lights danced in the mirror over her head and behind all the masks were smiles. A voice said "Let's go-o-o!" and Andy opened her eyes and her mouth and dived headlong into the midst of the pain.

Something was over her nose and mouth; she would have fought it away, but she hurt too much. "Just breathe in," they said and she realized all at once that this meant no more pain; she sucked at it greedily, as if it were a drink on a hot day, and a voice behind her said with gaiety, "Don't *drink* it, honey." Overhead, all the lights and colors melted into a rainbow circle and were blotted out.

Alec Girard grabbed the pilot's hand and shook it, grinning foolishly. His hand was cold and damp. The Navy officer, a little startled because the handsome face had shown no such strain, returned the grin shyly.

"Is there anything about—my wife?" the tense voice was asking.

"Just that Mrs. Girard is resting comfortably. And your son is fine. That's all the radioman reported, sir."

The recently retired Senator from Vermont flopped into one of the plane's worn and utilitarian seats as though someone had suddenly untied all the muscles of his legs. "Resting comfortably." He spoke to himself—but then, as his voice rang out in the silence, he remembered. "Thank you, Commander. Bill, have we got something we can pass around by way of— Commander, would we— I don't want to disrupt the routine, but—" He subsided, lost to them again, as Bruyette came forward, stooped over under the low ceiling, and began to speak to the pilot.

The second officer looked up when the pilot returned to the cockpit. "What'd he say?"

The pilot grinned. "He said the same thing we said—'How's my wife?' "

"Hmm. That's not going to sound very historic."

The pilot settled into his seat. "I'll take over. You go get a piece of the celebration Congressman Bruyette's passing out. What in hell did you *expect* Girard to do, make a political speech? He's sitting there staring into space—he looks like somebody slugged him. But happy, if you know what I mean."

"I know what you mean." The second officer tugged at his tie, straightening it. "But my wife won't." He took up his cap and began to wriggle out. "What the hell, I'll make up something."

"He's not too little, is he?" Alec asked Jake Ruffing as they shook hands beside the plane. "I mean, because it's early."

"Six pounds. Didn't they tell you?"

"Is six pounds—enough? Elizabeth was almost seven."

Jake put his arm around Alec, urging him along. "Six pounds is just fine. He's a great boy—wide-awake when I saw him. I don't know who he looks like, but he's kind of like Andy around the eyes—you know, that big-eyed look."

"Did you talk to her? What did she say?"

Jake laughed. "She was stoned, absolutely loaded to the gills. She said, 'Alexander Wardwell Girard, Junior.' Then she giggled, and I thought she'd gone back to sleep. But just as I was about to go, she opened her eyes and thanked me formally for my help and sent her regards to Bonnie."

"Didn't she ask for me?" Alec's voice was offended.

"Listen, I'm telling you, she's totally loopy. The doctor told me she fought all the stuff they gave her, and then it seemed to hit her all at once after it was over."

Alec climbed into the car after Jake. "You'd think she might remember me," he said mildly. "In the circumstances."

"Williams said he doesn't even think she'll remember talking to me. It figures. Two minutes after she knew who I was—she must have, she mentioned Bonnie—she looked me straight in the eye and said, 'Daddy, Richie took the ball. And it's *my* ball.' Who's Richie—her brother?"

"Yes." Oh, poor Andy. Thirsting for the sight of her, Alec asked irritably, "Can't we go faster? There's no traffic this time of night."

"Take it easy, Senator. She'll be asleep for hours yet."

"Of course." Alec smiled apologetically and sank back in his seat, his long legs stretched as far as they could be in the confined space. "Sorry." Alexander Wardwell Girard, Junior. "Oh my," he said to Jake. He couldn't stop smiling. "Oh my."

"Alexander Wardwell Girard, Junior," the Senator remarked to the Secret

Service agent who'd flown back with him, "won't give his father the time of day." He stared through the glass at the sleeping infant in the plastic crib. The tiny hand was clenched above the blue, tucked-in blanket, and Alec repressed an impulse to point out to everyone in sight the perfection of the fingernails.

Leroy said, smiling, "He's tired, sir."

"Yes. Of course." Alec turned away slowly, unwillingly. He looked back once, shook his head, and said to no one in particular, "A very remarkable thing."

He spoke to the reporters patiently, but with the same dazed, indrawn look. "No, I haven't. She's still asleep, and I don't think she ought to be awakened, do you?"

"How do you feel, Senator?"

"I don't know how to describe it, but I recognize it. I felt this way twice before—when I got married, and when my daughter was born."

"Did you expect a boy?"

"Well, my wife has never broken a promise to me, and she was planning on a boy."

A woman reporter asked, "Is it true, Senator, that naming the baby after you was Mrs. Girard's idea?"

"Yes, it was. I hadn't definitely agreed to it."

"Well, is it settled now?"

The President-elect grinned at them. "When she's brought in a perfect baby, weeks ahead of schedule, do you think I'd argue with her?" He waited out the laugh and then said, "I think that's enough now, if you don't mind."

"Senator, couldn't we have some pictures—"

"Later, if you please," Alec said firmly. "And not here. There are other patients in this hospital, you know, and I'm afraid we may be disturbing them. So, if you'll all go with Luke Messenger, I'll see you later."

He escaped to the door of Andy's room, but, as he was about to go in, Jake Ruffing called to him.

"One minute, please, Alec. I don't like to be carrying this around."

Alec took the emerald ring and looked at Jake over it, puzzled.

"They took it away from her because she was thrashing around so, they were afraid she was going to damage it. I don't think she knows it's gone, though. I signed for it, so if you'll tell them you've got it back—"

"Right." Alec hesitated. "Jake—thanks."

Ruffing blinked foolishly in the bright light of the corridor. "Nothing to it, Dad. I'm an old hand." He yawned elaborately. "Okay if I go home and get some sleep?"

"It's okay," said Alec gravely. "It's quite okay."

The room was already full of flowers. The nurse got up from the armchair, saying, "Mr. President," in a hushed voice.

Alec looked frightened. "Is there anything wrong? Does she need something?"

"Oh no, sir. Mr. Ruffing just said he wanted somebody with her in case she woke up."

"Oh. Thank you, I'll stay with her for a while."

"Would you like me to turn down the other bed for you, sir?"

Alec grinned down at her, wishing she would hurry up and go. Andy was a still, long mound under a green blanket, and he wanted desperately to be alone with her when she woke. "Thank you, no, I'm too excited to sleep. I'll just sit in that armchair, if I may." The courteous words, the patient voice, urged her toward the door. "Yes, thank you. I'll call if I need anything. Thank you so much for your care of Mrs. Girard."

He breathed in thankfully as the door moved slowly shut behind her helpful whiteness. He looked longingly at the extra bed as he went by it, tempted to stretch his cramped legs; but Andy was lying with her face turned away from it, toward the window, and he wanted to see her more than he wanted to lie down. He slouched in the armchair, looking at her dark eyelashes fanned out on her pale cheeks and twiddling the ring between his thumb and forefinger in his pocket.

"It's not difficult to understand, really," Dr. Williams had said, "if you use the old-fashioned terms. That is, Mrs. Girard is a young woman in perfectly good health, but she has what we used to call a frail constitution."

"Is that what made it happen early?"

"Possibly. Does it matter? The baby is not what we would call premature, even technically."

"No, I suppose it doesn't matter." Except that he hadn't been there, hadn't been with her, and he supposed he wanted some excuse. "Just that it caught us off guard, that's all. But there's no reason why Mrs. Girard can't stay in the hospital as long as you want, Doctor."

The doctor smiled. "I foresaw a little trouble if I had to convince her on my own, Senator. But she needs rest badly," he went on soberly. "She was very tired before she began the birth."

"Well, the campaign and all—we tried to have her take it easy."

"Of course. I'm not unmindful of your special problems, Senator. What I'd like to suggest is that we keep her under mild sedation for a while, so that I'm sure she gets a good rest—"

"Without having to fight her all the way."

The doctor laughed. "Something like that, yes."

"Of course. I'll see to it. But— She will be all right, won't she?"

"Certainly. Oh—what you're thinking of is future pregnancies? Well, it might be easier if the next one didn't coincide with the presidential election."

Which was in conflict, Alec had thought—grinning dutifully over the little joke as he shook hands—with the gospel of Luke Messenger. Congratulating himself after the election on his superlative public relations coups during the campaign, Messenger had somehow managed, through a line of foggy reasoning further fogged by alcohol, to include the proper use of Andy among his triumphs. According to his text, she cost potential votes from women because she irked them by being too good-looking. "But pregnant," he had declared expansively, "takes the curse off. They forgive her for being pretty. Right away, they're on her side."

It was Rosenberg, who seemed to be rendered even more logical by alcohol, who had pointed ungenerously to Luke's error in taking credit for this maneuver, even supposing there was anything whatever to the galloping assumptions involved. He had indicated Alec with a wave of his glass. "Our Leader, you'll admit, is the man behind that triumph of imagemaking."

"I try to think of everything," their leader had murmured modestly amid the laughter. And untruthfully, he added now, remembering his own doubt about the advisability of another pregnancy so soon after the miscarriage. The Florida moon unhinged my reason, he defended himself, and then he listened to the orderly voice in his mind citing the numerous visits he had made to Florida, man and boy, without exploding the population. He shook his head: putty in the hands of—"a wisp of a girl," he'd said to Bruyette, a very long time ago on a night in Vermont. He couldn't hope to run Andy, he'd told Jake in a hotel somewhere—just the country. That statement, at least, needed amendment, he decided a little grimly: it might not be easy, but Andy needed a little governing. He looked at her sleeping face—and discovered, abashed, that it wasn't sleeping any more. Her eyes, huge in the white face, were exploring him lazily.

"H'lo, Alec. Is there anybody here?"

"No, darling. Just me."

"That's good." She sighed. "I'm tired of being on show."

"I'll bet you are," he said soberly.

"Did you see him? The baby?" The dull look vanished from her eyes.

"Yes. He's beautiful, Andy."

"You can say that again, old buddy," she said, and her startled husband remembered Jake's description of her as "totally loopy" and realized that it was accurate. "Mos' beautiful baby in the house."

"Right," Alec said, carefully not laughing. "You can say that again."

"Right." She closed her eyes. Suddenly they were open and staring at him demandingly. "So can I have it back, then?"

"Have what back?"

"My ring." She wet her lips and went on pleadingly, "I was very good, truly I was. I hardly cried at all. And nobody saw."

Alec took the ring out of his pocket and swallowed the lump in his throat. "Andy, they only took it away from you so it wouldn't get spoiled." He searched her face for evidence of comprehension. "Do you understand? It's yours, all the time. Forever and ever."

"Okay," she said cheerfully.

He lifted her hand and slid the ring onto her finger, next to her wedding ring. "It's all right to cry, Andy." He kept her hand in his.

"Is it? Is anybody here?"

"No, there's nobody here. It was always all right to cry, though. You don't have to be better than anybody."

"Yes, I do," she insisted, in her thick, drunken voice. "I always do." In contradiction, the tears began to move slowly down her cheeks. "Even when it hurts, a lot."

Alec bent and kissed them away. "Sweet Andy," he said into her hair.

She pushed at him feebly. "No. Go 'way. Bad, bad Alec. You promised you would be here, and you didn't come."

Protest sprang to his lips, but he checked it, studying her petulant, childish face soberly. Finally he said quietly, "You're right. I said I'd be here and I wasn't. I'm very, very sorry."

Andy smiled like an angel, lifting her hand slowly. Still watching her, Alec helped her—he laid her cool fingers against his cheek and held them there. "It's all right, love," she said softly. He held tightly to her hand, afraid for a moment that he would fly apart with his own love, his own weariness.

They stayed that way for a long time, in silence. Then Alec said brightly, "But you kept your word, Andy. A fine boy baby, just as you promised."

She sighed. "Do you think Elizabeth will like him? Can we name him after you—please, Alec?"

"Yes, darling. Elizabeth will love him, he's beautiful. And yes, you can name him anything you like."

She drifted off, away from him—he felt it in the limpness of her hand even before he saw it in her face. He put her hand back on the bed and tucked it in under the blanket. She woke a little and said something, but he couldn't make it out. He was looking at his watch when she opened her eyes again and said distinctly, "Alec, stay here."

He fought the impulse to give her that, and anything else she wanted. "No." His voice was firm. "I'm going home to tell Elizabeth about her new brother."

"All right. But come right back."

"I'll come back, Andy, but I won't be here all the time. I want you to stay here by yourself for a while."

"No!"

"Oh yes. Andy?"

"What." It was a rebellion, not a question.

"I want you to do as I say—"

"I don't want to."

"Even if you don't want to." He met her mutinous look with severity. "*I'm* in charge. You seem to have forgotten that."

She lowered her glance, peeking up at him through her lashes like an old-movie coquette. Alec stifled a grin and continued to regard her sternly.

"All right," she said at last. She sighed, and moved her shoulders under the tucked-in blanket. "I think I'll go to sleep some more."

"Good." Alec bent and kissed her cheek. He watched her for a moment and then started out of the room, his shoulders sagging with fatigue.

"But," said a cool, clear voice from the bed—a voice startlingly without sleepiness—"I want a whole lot of new dresses."

Alec kept his profile toward her. "Some," he conceded. "A few, maybe."

"A whole bunch. And one shaky one right away."

"*What* kind right away?"

"A shaky one. White. With fringes all over." She was propped on one elbow, the other hand busy in explanation: at least some of the shaky fringes, Alec gathered from her gestures, would be at the bosom. "A dress that wiggles when I dance."

"That sounds lovely," he said hastily, hoping she would lie down.

She didn't. "Shimmy, shimmy," she amplified. "Very tight. All sway-ey. You know?"

"I know." Judged by his voice, he was in need of oxygen. "All right, you can have it. If you lie down, right away."

"Two of them," she said cagily. "A gold one, too. With . . . dangle-bangles, that's what." She nodded, satisfied with her choice. "Takes dangle-bangles to unstuff stuffed-shirt New England," she announced owlishly.

Listen, Tondelayo—Alec caught himself in time and said, "A gold shaky dress, too. All right." Dangle-bangles, indeed. "If you're down in that bed," he went on ominously—she let herself down quickly and lay very still under the blankets—"and asleep in five minutes." He came over and tucked the blanket around her with a skill left over from a war. "Tell you what. If you're very good, you can have three dresses."

Her eyes were crinkled shut. "I'm asleep," the small voice announced, and added, "Nice Alec. *Three* new dresses."

"Two shaky dresses," he said casually, trying to keep from his voice the laughter that had arisen with the thought that she might just possibly remember this little scene. He'd give ten to one that she wouldn't admit it if she did. But, just in case, he added, "And another one for the Inaugural Ball. Right?" Her lips tried to say, "Right," and didn't quite make it. He watched her for a while, wondering where she'd ever got the idea it was the dangle-bangles that did it; then he realized she had never worn anything that could remotely be described as dangle-bangles, and it came to him that though there might be less *veritas* in *vino* than everybody thought, she unquestionably had the cutest unconscious he had ever met.

Eighteen

Only two real questions must concern the readers of Washington newspapers, Alexander Girard, who read them closely every day, decided as he surveyed the last of the batch that had been sent to him at his father's

Florida home. From the front page to the editorial page of the *Tribune* the single major preoccupation was who would be who in the new administration—besides the Secretary of State, who was still the chief Who. Opposite the editorial page, Gil Kimball wondered at length what Alec Girard was planning to wear to the Inaugural Ball; thanks to an alert Secret Service, Kimball told his readers breathlessly, a nefarious agent of *Esquire* had been caught redhanded trying to plant a wiretapping device in the workshop of the President-elect's tailor. Behind the Kimball column, the society page demonstrated the validity of his parody by speculating lavishly on what Andrea Girard's ball gown would be like. Old news photos of Andy in a variety of non-maternity dresses were offered to show possible preferences in cut and line. They went all the way back to her return from her honeymoon and demonstrated little beyond eclecticism and a certain openness to experiment, but the pictures had at least the virtue of lightening the dreary columns of print.

Washington's tabloid newspaper, which affected a lowbrow slanginess that it took a highish brow to manage so well, managed to slip in an old photograph of Andy in a bathing suit at Kingsley Lake, waving and smiling and looking quite thoroughly marvelous. A hand not tied by memos about dignified references to the imminent First Lady had slugged the picture, "What Andy Won't Wear to the Ball" in bold italics that looked as gay and lively as the picture's subject.

All three Washington newspapers had, of course, come up with photo spreads of the Smithsonian's exhibit of gowns the First Ladies of the past had worn to inaugural festivities. Alec, glancing at the last of them, noted that none of the dresses looked the least bit "shaky." Wondering briefly whether the Smithsonian would ever forgive him if it knew what he had done to the course of history, he left the press to its speculations and went to keep a swimming date with his daughter.

Elizabeth Girard, after a week of conscientious openmindedness, had come to the regretful conclusion that the much-advertised baby brother was really a good deal less than he had been touted. A certain tender regard for her mother's feelings prevented her from reporting this conclusion to the obviously besotted Andrea. But, as her father surface-dived and came up with Elizabeth on his shoulders, she looked down at the top of his wet head and decided that he could be trusted with her dismay. Thus, when Dan Healy appeared to notify the next President of the United States that the confab he had summoned awaited him on the terrace, Alec demanded an extra few minutes to finish the one in which he was currently engaged. After he had summed up the thrust of his argument (which amounted to a pair of reliable generalities, viz., that you can't tell a book by its cover and that it doesn't pay to ignore wisdom handed down by those gone before), Elizabeth, who had been listening carefully even though she was building a sand wall at the same time, agreed to suspend judgment for a while longer and see whether the creature wouldn't become a little more interesting. She observed calmly that what she had found most convincing was the report that she herself had once been as limited as this baby brother: it was not an easy thing to credit, but her father had proved trustworthy in the past, so she would go along with him now. She watched him shaking his head as he left, and she concluded that he must have water in his ear.

Alec welcomed the gathered "think boys" and their new apprentice, Will Farland, and listened to a number of reports in silence before making half a dozen rapid decisions. He confided to them the discovery he had made in the Washington newspapers and expressed regret that he wasn't ready to make the State appointment final yet and thus leave the field to Andy's dress. "Meanwhile," he nodded at Luke, "why don't you throw them a couple of Defense and Treasury Undersecretaries?" Messenger murmured that the Christmas advertising would soon help out with the newspapers' problem of too much space for the mere marking of time; but, after that, it would be a kindness to the press if a picture of Alexander Wardwell Girard, Jr., could be managed, since even the new Secretary of State wouldn't quite stretch all the way from Christmas to Inauguration. The President-elect agreed to speak to his wife about it, noting with amusement his roly-poly press chief's obvious relief at not having to approach the Gorgon himself, and Messenger took himself off to get off a few releases—from one of which it would become generally known that a new Undersecretary of the Treasury had paid for his college degree in economics by playing trumpet in a highly regarded jazz quintet.

Before he adjourned the meeting, Alec brought up a recent Bainbridge column in which Senator Kenneth Youngblood had been suggested as a possible Secretary of State. He sought, and got, reassurance that his own view— that Youngblood would be more valuable as chairman of the troublesome Senate Foreign Relations Committee—was entirely shared by the Rhode Island Senator. "Oscar was just fishing, and without a license," Dan Healy summed up as he led the visitors out.

Except for Jake Ruffing, Jerry Rosenberg, and Will Farland, who went for a walk with Girard and reported on a bridge game with one Harold Hoffman two weeks ago at Jake's house. Rosenberg and Farland had won, but the consensus was that Hoffman had taken every trick that was coming to him and refrained from trying unneeded finesses; that he had been apparently unperturbed by his partner's somewhat unconventional bidding and, even more important, had adjusted to it speedily; and that he had shown marked ability to adhere to his planned strategy in the face of various seductive "errors" committed by the enemy. Jake, who had been dummy a good part of the time and had spent it observing his partner closely, thought Hoffman had been quick to take the measure of Farland's apparent boyishness and Rosenberg's absentminded air and had reacted with appropriate distrust. Jake noted that Hoffman had at least twice wrenched the bidding around so that he and not his partner would be playing the hand; it was not clear whether these maneuvers resulted from suspicion of Jake or a correct judgment of his ability—

but in any case it showed Hoffman to be unhampered by false modesty. Alec listened carefully in near-silence and then thanked them; on the way to the car, he let the others go on a little ahead and then told Jake that he thought he'd like to get corroboration of the extent and nature of Hoffman's financial holdings from John Girard, who was flying down for Christmas. Jake nodded and said glumly that, from what they had found, Hoffman would have to practically pauperize himself in order to serve the public.

So would he, Alec suggested, if there was any truth to the estimates he'd been reading of the cost of Andy's ball gown. He launched into an analysis of the shortcomings of the press as they hurried to catch up with Rosenberg and Farland.

Catching up with Dick Farland had been the central endeavor of Marian's day, or at least that part of it not pledged to the *Washington Tribune,* and her evening was devoted to providing a parental presence at the Hemingway Garrison School Dramatic Club's performance of a Gilbert and Sullivan operetta. All the performers except Dick—or so it seemed to Marian, who was bitter—were applauded by pairs of parents; two by two, decorously dressed and displaying the correct degree of casual pride, they clapped, murmured at and were murmured back at by faculty representatives, and carried off their flushed, triumphant offspring for treats at the Hot Shoppe. Only Marian's sense of humor saved her from total sourness: standing on the steps, she suddenly saw the orderly procession as passengers debarking from the Ark, with each male-and-female trailed by a noisy, gesticulating adolescent reminder of how long ago it had begun to rain.

That didn't apply, of course, to Richard Willard Farland, owner of a treasured shirt of blinding fluorescent green and a carefully cultivated blond "pompadour"—but not of any parents, unless you count a small, weary, substitute mother. Whom he seemed to accept with the absentminded pleasure appropriate to his age and sex, Marian thought gratefully, and noted too that he accepted the absence of the other half of his original pair of parents more cheerfully than she did. For, though he did say wistfully once that he sort of wished Dad could've seen him, he brightened at once. "That's what happens if your father is an important guy, I guess. You can't let a war get started somewhere because he's got to go to a school play," Dick assured Marian, who would have been perfectly willing to let the war go ahead and happen. Blind to her seething, the boy who had been Kitty Farland's baby and then Marian Farland's little son and who was now rapidly becoming his own man closed the subject with an incisive summary: "I mean, I guess a guy like Dad—well, he has to be where the action is."

With the help of various guardian angels, Marian rose to the occasion by suggesting that Dick could sing a few of the songs for his father when affairs of state permitted that worthy to return; she kept the irony out of her voice successfully, and Dick was cheerfully practicing "A Magnet Hung in a Hardware Shop" when she turned the car into Mackintosh Place. " 'A sil-ver churn, a sil-ver churn,' " he caroled, his voice as shrill as it was unreliable of pitch. " 'If I can whee-dle a knife or a nee-dle, Why not a sil-ver churn?' " He broke off to explain to her that it was because a magnet won't prevail with silver—and then he broke off that explanation to lean from the car window and approve her performance at turning into their driveway. Then he sat back, satisfied with his educational achievements, and studied the sleeping bulk of the public library in silence while Marian cut the motor. She was reaching for the light switch when Dick said dreamily, "You know, someday I'll be telling *my* kids how I rode in a *car*."

Emotions and revelations rushed over Marian like the swift darkness as she crossed the yard slowly, wrapped in a huge wonder and a small fear: it was like turning over a stone and discovering, all at once, a whole busy insect life going on underneath—a going and coming, birthing and dying, an ordered society with all its daily balances. Going on all the time, while you walk by it every day on your way to work.

It was that remark, more than all the veerings and probings with which Dick's conversation had been replete, that fed Marian's fury after Dick had been complimented for the last time and sent to bed. She ran a warm bath and lay in it for a long time, trying to enjoy what had been enjoyable: Dick, it was clear, was smitten with one Lucy; with elaborate casualness, he had pointed her out to Marian at the Hot Shoppe. Not that Marian, an ex-belle, had had any trouble locating the girl Dick had described as "sort of little and bouncy": there she was, complete with toss of head and twitch of short skirt, and even the silver glint of the braces on her teeth highlighting the come-on giggle. "Never mind," Marian had told her son, sighing. "I know which one's Lucy."

For Lucy was a belle, all right, and Dick was faced with problems. Some of which he outlined to Marian on the way home: with his voice indicating nothing but a researcher's interest and usually with his gaze directed at the scenery beyond the car window, he had inquired delicately into the delicate matter of how one asks a popular girl to a movie ("On Saturday afternoons, after her piano lesson, she's allowed to go to the movie with a boy") without running the risk of too much rejection ("You can't tell, is she laughing at you or not, you know what I mean?"). Marian, who knew quite well what he meant, had silently smoldered with the injustice of this kid's need for a father and managed to contrive a sample invitation, based on the movie rather than the company, that rather resembled—though she didn't know it—Alec Girard's solution to a similar problem in courting the glamorous Miss Langwith, who'd been older but still definitely a belle.

But it was all too much for a single warm bath to deal with, and even while the waters were still gurgling away, some of Marian's anger had begun to return. She decided, trying to be fair, that part of it must have something to do with the difference between Dick's brave image of Will standing with a finger in the dike, personally holding back the tides of war, and the actuality—what he was really doing, she would have liked to tell

Dick, was sprawling in a room that happened to be in John Girard's Florida home but could just as well have been anywhere else so far as Will was concerned, and kingmaking with Jake Ruffing, who was equally indifferent to his surroundings. And indifferent to time, which was indeed a river, and on which Dick Farland sailed, more rapidly than his father thought, toward unknown future seas. And needed advice from old rivermen who had been, personally, through the tricky currents. But Dick had to make do with Marian, a librarian handing him a book about seamanship, because Will couldn't see that here, here, was where the action was. . . .

Standing barefoot before her bedroom mirror in her camellia-red nightgown, Marian brushed at her hair as ruthlessly as though it belonged to an enemy and tried not to weep for the earlier, sillier Marian preserved for posterity in the photograph on the mantel. Where it was spring, according to the pink dogwood in full bloom on the church lawn, and the new Mrs. Farland wore a royal-blue silk dress, a matching veily hat, and big frightened eyes; her husband, grinning, held her hand as if it were something he'd mislaid and just found after a long search. The shadow of Jim McGrath, a distinctly amateur photographer, darkened the grass before the couple; behind them, fuzzily out of focus, Ann Taswell stood on the church's shallow step with her arms full of her own and Marian's purses, flowers, and the newly signed marriage certificate. You will observe, Marian observed icily now to the absent Will, that I am the only one taking the whole thing seriously, while you seem to think it's some kind of party . . . She raked the brush through her hair, stubbornly banishing her sudden memory of the other pictures, in all of which she had been either smiling or laughing outright. The choice of this photo from among McGrath's efforts had been a victory of artistic conscience over vanity: it was the best composed, although she herself had looked prettier—and happier—in any one of the others.

To admit this would have been only fair, but Marian was not interested in justice. She slammed the hairbrush down and thrust her feet into her black mules. We are householders and parents, she said to the laughing man in the springtime of a handful of years ago, and it's winter now and the storm windows haven't been put up. And a boy who hasn't got a father out in the audience, applauding at his big moment, probably hasn't really got one at all. You can't just fertilize an egg and then swim away like some kind of goddam fish, without taking any responsibility—

She remembered guiltily at that point that nobody had shown enough responsibility to turn the thermostat down, and the heating bills were backbreaking. As if Will were about to come in and score off her, she scampered out of the bedroom. But she was only halfway down the stairs when she heard the dogs begin to mutter restlessly in the basement. She came down a few more steps so she could see out the front window in the hall. The white light on the roof of the cab flashed on as it pulled away from the curb, and the dogs, recognizing the footsteps on the porch over their heads, began a noisy welcome. Marian straightened and stood waiting with one hand on the banister, poised and graceful and scornfully refusing to make one move to greet a homecoming fish.

It was worth the struggle to get home, Will thought as he opened the door and saw her standing on the great old staircase with her face small and white in the cloud of long black hair and her creamy shoulders above that red nightgown. He had bought it himself, deliberately choosing one of the shorter kind so her legs would show, and rejecting any stuff on the bosom that would get in the way of just Marian, visibly round and firm beneath the gauzy cloth. The way she looked in it, you could eat her with a spoon, he told himself as he paused in the hall to smile up at her and hand her the flowers he had brought. But he kept the judgment to himself, because he had once tried it aloud and it had been declared "vulgar"—and the look that accompanied the word then had been remarkably similar to the menace that was messing up this pretty pose now. It was yonder-peasant-who-is-he time, Will recognized, preparing for war while he accepted the greetings of the dogs, advised them authoritatively to cut it out and go back to sleep, and shut the basement door on their leaps and whines. Coming back through the dining room, he stopped briefly to push the thermostat pointer down a notch, but his mind was on broad tactics. He would begin, he concluded, by brazening it out.

So he said with the warmth of a television charmer, "Baby, the sight of you makes it all worth while."

"Makes *what* worth while?" She held the large yellow chrysanthemums in a loose, indifferent grasp.

"You don't know what it took to get here. The flight I counted on was canceled—poor visibility—and I kept hopping trains and taxis and wheedling and twisting the arms of overworked depot clerks." He looked at his watch and grinned triumphantly. "But I made it. It's not your birthday yet, not by a few minutes."

My God, Marian thought, he expects to be greeted as a hero. The outrage rose in her throat so swiftly and suddenly that it choked off any possibility of speech, but it was too much to be borne in silence. She raised her arms and threw the flowers at him like a god hurling a thunderbolt. They scattered, a few landing on the stairs, the rest littering the hall. Only one hit Will; it rebounded from his shoulder and landed on the bookcase, its round golden head dangling pathetically over the edge of the top shelf.

"Well," Will said coldly, "now that you've made a hell of a dramatic flourish and a satisfying mess—care to tell me what it's all about?"

"I think you know what it's about." Her lips were tight, but the voice that issued from them throbbed like some kind of dangerous machine. "You can't seriously believe that you can dash off to play your silly games, grossly neglecting your child, and then come in here and be welcomed like a returning hero."

"It figures," Will told an invisible watcher at his shoulder. "A guy struggles home to his wife, bringing her flowers. So naturally that proves he's a louse."

"Flowers! Maybe that's what's wrong with you." She nudged one of the fallen blossoms with her toe. "You think you can hand me these juiceless, overblown hothouse things and have me fall all over you and forget."

"Forget what, for God's sake?"

"Forget that if you'd spent any time at your home you'd have seen the real yellow chrysanthemums we had growing in our own back yard. They came and went without your ever so much as glancing at them." Her voice rose, warming itself with its own hatefulness. "Home is where I live, where the children live, and where you don't live. *This* is where *you* live." She kicked at the flower. "With this ridiculous, overpriced substitute for the real thing. And the shame of it, the *horror* of it, is that you don't know any better than to offer it to *me*. If you think it's acceptable to me, you don't understand me at all."

Will tested, not hopefully, the possibilities for the light touch. "Apparently I don't, darling." He rocked back on his heels, looking up at her like Romeo in the balcony scene. "But I'd like to. You're so beautiful." It was true, he noted wryly: fury did things for her, and more than she knew. He looked at her breasts swelled, the nipples defined and pushing at the cloth, and wondered fleetingly whether it made any difference what kind of passion set off the machinery.

"Oh, *oh*." Marian wailed as though she had just been stabbed. "I was right. You don't understand me, you don't understand what you've done—"

"It seems to be pretty serious, whatever it is." He hadn't really believed this could be dodged, but he'd had to try. "Like gross neglect of my child. Which child was it, by the way?"

"Look, Will, turn it off, will you? If you can, that is. Try to remember I'm not a force or an influence or an ethnic group."

It was when she got witty that he couldn't stand her, he decided abruptly. He was in for it now, the whole bit, and his own anger began to take over. "I asked you a simple question, and—"

"—there's some kind of fish does that, I think. Just fertilizes the eggs and swims away. Finished. Gone."

"You better look it up, baby. What really happens is, the female eats him." He was outshouting her, even if his knowledge of marine biology wasn't much better than hers. It occurred to him dimly that he might be thinking of a spider, and then he thought she probably wouldn't know the difference anyway. He listened to her telling him that he had, or was supposed to have, functions beyond the merely biological, and told himself coolly that since he wasn't the one who had fertilized the Sharlie-egg, at least the field was narrowing down. It struck him that he'd been swimming around in Dick's vicinity for a hell of a long time and had paid pediatrician's bills and possessed canceled checks for everything from diapers to blue jeans to prove it—and then he remembered that old fertilized-egg Dick was supposed to be in some goddam thing at school today . . . "All *right*," he yelled suddenly into the midst of her diatribe. "What in hell is this all about? That I missed some goddam shindig at the kid's school, is that it? Well, so what? I had more important things to do. I'm not a shoe salesman, you know."

"Neither were the other fathers, and they all managed to come. This is Washington, remember? You know who's president of the P-TA at Dick's school? The Postmaster General. And he managed to be there tonight."

"The Postmaster General," Will said coldly, "has plenty of time on his hands right now. In a few weeks, he'll be out of a job."

"So? His son is better off than yours, though, Mr. Big Shot. *His* son has a father."

Goddammit, she was doing her best to make him blow up. Violence would earn him nothing but her scorn—but so would letting her get away with this sort of thing. Either way, the odds didn't look good, Will calculated gloomily. "Marian!" Something still might be gained by a quick change of pace. "Please, let's not talk like this. I am Dick's father, and I want to be a good one and you know it. If you think I'm wrong about something, can't you say it quietly? I promise to listen."

Her knuckles were white on the banister as she fought to match his effort at calm. There were things she wanted to tell him, she reminded herself, and they were more important than the mere expression of her own anger. "All I'm trying to say, Will, is that tonight was a big moment, a very big moment, for Dick. You should've been there. He was entitled to it."

"Look—choices have to be made. I had a job to do, and it was a big moment in Florida today, too, as it happens."

Marian shook her head, her eyes pitying him and yet pleading with him. "Don't you see? Dick is only twelve years old once, and very briefly. He needs you. *You*, and no substitute. With Dick, you're the only one who can truly fill the job—you're unique and irreplaceable. Jake Ruffing or somebody else could've done whatever you did in Florida today. But only you could have been there for Dick tonight. You missed it, and it's missed forever."

I'm just tired, Will Farland told himself hastily, interposing the thought before anything else could get in. Obligingly, weariness rolled over him like a wave; but it broke in dismay. Despairing, he fought back as well as he could. "You tell me," he shouted at it, and her, "how it happens like this. Until the minute I got home I was a good guy, struggling against difficulties to do something nice. Yet the minute I walk in that door, I'm a bum again. In Florida people were asking me what I thought, about things that matter." He came around and began to climb the stairs, helping himself with his hand on the banister. Then he stopped, a little below her but still not looking at her, and asked her with biting fury, "Who's right? The rest of the world respects me. But to my wife I'm only and forever a slob."

"*Respect?* Respect you?" Marian screamed at him, her eyes ablaze. "Respect what, for God's sake? A chess game, a strategic maneuver? *I'm* right, that's who. I don't respect you, I never will, and you can't make me, you two-bit demagogue."

That's it, Will said to himself. As though someone had pushed a button, his arm snapped forward and he slapped her smartly across her face.

The sharp sound stayed in the sudden silence, occupying it wholly and devastatingly. And then Marian crumpled on the step at his feet, weeping noisily. Sick at heart, he looked down at her and saw the red slash his fingers had left on her white cheek before she buried her face in her hands and her hair descended around her like a symbol of grief. He stared at his hand, hanging limply by his side, and then moved it slowly toward the bitter sound of her tears, meaning to stop them, somehow, by the gentleness of his touch. But, even as he reached out to stroke her hair, she winced away quickly. The shuddering rejection, so clearly unthinking, called him a monster more loudly than if she had shouted it, and it could not be tolerated or argued about—it had to be denied, at once, entirely and furiously. He rushed past her on the stairs, fleeing from the accusation; before he reached the top step, he had succeeded in believing that he was not, in fact, a monster, but a victim. The horror converted to a more comfortable anger, he fled across the hall and slammed the bedroom door on the sound of her weeping.

His hands were shaking as he untied his shoes. Goddam her, why wouldn't she learn to be a wife? He ripped at his shirt, unable to get it off fast enough, and then forced himself to lay it down slowly and carefully. He stood above the bed, buttoning his pajama top, and thinking, *I love the goddam woman and I always will*—but bitterly, because it was a sentence of doom: there was no way he could please her, and he had to have her. But it would take a syndicate to provide what she wanted: one man—one tired man, he told himself, sitting down on the side of the bed—simply couldn't be all the everythings she demanded.

In the silence he could hear the sound of her weeping, and pity for her flooded away much of his anger. She exaggerates everything I do, he protested. But I am what she says—a compromiser, a conniver, a slapper of Band-Aids on the forever-bleeding body politic. Maybe it's no coincidence that I had to have a woman who simply sweats truth—but it's a hell of a thing for her to have to live with.

Will got up and got a cigarette from his coat pocket. She was like the canary they used to carry into the coal mines so it would faint when the air was unsafe: a good thing for the miners, but a little hard on the canary. Only Marian didn't faint in the presence of the phony—she screamed. He opened the door to the bedroom and listened, and thought about going down to get his toothbrush, which was in the attaché case he'd dropped in the hall. Ah, the hell with it, he decided, and got into bed and lay there stiffly, trying to tell himself that he was going to sleep, that he would brush his teeth in the morning, that he would talk to Dick in the morning. *I sat you down right there in the next room*—he reminded the noisy sobbing on the steps—*and told you what I was going to do.* If she had any objection, she should have said so then. He closed his eyes firmly, shutting out, with the light, the fact that he knew Marian too well to believe she could understand the implications of his joining Girard's camp. She would make no connection between that and his missing Dick's play, and he knew it. She would make no connections at all if she could avoid it—everything to her was an isolated event.

But *I* can make connections, he said to himself suddenly, sitting up, cold with fear. She could walk out, damn her—she really could, in her nightgown, at this hour. He lay down again, telling himself reasonably that she wouldn't. Even Marian wouldn't—

He stood at the door, not knowing how he got there but knowing thoroughly and dreadfully that, though it was insane, the fact was that she *could* leave him, and if she once decided to, that would be that. It was necessary to do something, right away, before she got to thinking about it. How am I going to hold onto her? he asked himself piteously, trying to be sane, while every muscle in his body seemed to be tightening in panic. I'm so tired, he told himself pathetically— Maybe she would notice how tired he looked, he thought as he started down the stairs.

He sat down on the step beside her, but he didn't touch her; she had cried harder at his approach, but when he sat there in silence, she began to quiet a little. When he thought she might be ready to find out what he had come for, he said, "Darling, I'm sorry I slapped you," loudly enough so she could keep on crying moderately and still hear him.

She took her hands away from her face and held them cupped as if to catch the tears. "Will, I know you can wheedle a knife or a needle. But I'm a silver churn."

Will regarded her with speculative interest. He had no idea what she was talking about, but she had communicated something useful to him nevertheless. Somewhere in the meaningless words, he had heard a useful truth— she wanted to be a knife or a needle. He settled quickly on an appropriate negotiating stance. Something tough-sounding, but that would open discussion, and that could be climbed down from. "I shouldn't have hit you, I should've spanked you. As is fitting for a naughty child."

"Really? What should I have done? What's the proper response to egocentricity?"

They glared at each other, side by side on the step, with the two truthful statements hovering between them. All out now, Will counseled himself— move in fast, lay it on thick. "For a bright fellow, I can be pretty stupid," he said humbly. He looked earnestly into her blotched face, thinking that he had never seen her so un-pretty.

She turned away from him, said something he couldn't make out, and began to cry again, but softly now, without self-pity or drama. Will's accurate ear picked up the note of real grief, and his blood chilled. "Baby," he said desperately.

"Please don't, Will. I see through you."

"Marian, please. Darling." He was so frightened that he spoke without planning. "Don't see through me. I beg you. See me instead."

She put her hands down and stopped crying. Afraid of her look, he dodged as she began to turn toward him; he snatched up two chrysanthemums from the steps and held them out to her. "Please. I apologize most humbly, most abjectly."

She took the flowers, her reddened eyes probing at him. "What is it you want me to see, Will? Surely not just elaborate apologies?"

Now. "I want you to try to imagine what it's like to start out as I did— so poor, so nobody. Then maybe you can see why it goes to my head, just to be even a bat boy in the big league." She was listening to him, her lips parted and her face softened; with hope rising every minute, he launched himself like a diver. "I'm a fool. I'm so busy feeling important that I forget what's really important. But, if you try, you can see that there's a reason for it."

"Oh Will."

"No, you're right. You count, Dick counts, home counts. Who's in what post in what department in the next administration—"

"Oh Will, I didn't mean that didn't count."

He shook his head. "It doesn't, not really. It doesn't matter a damn when it's stacked up against the most important thing in my life—that my wife wants me home. But I forgot it today. I was doing what you said, playing my games; I knew I should leave in time to get here for Dick's thing, but I saw a chance to get in just one more lick for my side—if I'd left, they might have decided the other way, and I'd spent a week talking my heart out about this particular thing. I thought I had to clinch it at any price."

"Did you, Will? Clinch it, I mean?" Marian's eyes were glazed with exhaustion.

Will took in her limpness and concluded that it was safe to put his arm around her. When he tried it, she came a little stiffly at first. "Yes, I clinched it. But it wasn't worth the price." He felt her yielding then and he raised his other hand and smoothed her hair back from her face. "If I'd thought about it, I'd have known that. The trouble is, I was too excited to think." The red mark had faded from her cheek and so had the blotches left by her crying. Her face was so pale that it worried him a little.

She smiled. "Don't tell Dick you were only politicking. He thinks you were holding back the dogs of war."

I may have been, Will thought irritably, suddenly sorry for himself because she could not or would not understand that. But he was not such a fool as to risk his victory. He tightened his arm around her shoulder. "Baby."

"Mm?" She yawned.

"Happy birthday," he said into her hair.

Marian opened her eyes and smiled at him, and abruptly he fell in love with her again, drowning in the blue-green depths of her eyes. "I'd like to be able," he said solemnly and a little shakily, "to pick you up and carry you off to bed, like a hero. Since I'm a bum, you'll have to walk." He stood up and reached down to pull her to her feet. "But I love you, so I can at least help you."

"You've carried me upstairs, you know," Marian said sleepily, leaning against his arm. "I'm no heavier than I was last time."

I may not be as strong as I was last time, Will did not say. "Starting from solid ground, I can. But not from a narrow step, partway up. We'd land in a heap at the bottom."

He swung her up, though, as soon as they reached the landing, and he carried her into the bedroom and laid her down on the bed. She was so exhausted— He wondered, sadly, how long she had been raging helplessly, wearing herself out, before he got home. In the lamplight, he saw the shiny track of a tear down her cheek and rubbed at it gently with his thumb. Then he put his arms around her and held her, kissing her face and throat very gently, not trying to stop her slipping away from him—because it was also, he saw with rare, unselfish love, from the remnants of her own un-happiness.

The real hero, Marian kept wanting to say: the one who calculates, so I don't fall downstairs and get hurt. It was too hard to speak, because there were still sobs left in her. After a while, it was too hard to think, too. In the morning, when I pick up the flowers, she promised, I'll remember it.

Will looked at her black lashes unstirring, the small rise and fall of her breast, her outflung hand with the fingers loosely curled. Carefully, he eased his arm out from under her, sighing with relief. He pulled the covers up, studied her with something very like envy, and turned off the light. Then he went into the study and sat down in the armchair and rested and smoked a cigarette in the dark and thought briefly about Alec Girard, who was not always dancing on the edge of a precipice. After a while, he decided he could sleep, so he got up and went into the bedroom and climbed gingerly into his side of the bed. Marian lay with her back to him. He turned on his side and put his arm around her a little above her waist; the warm, round breast burdened and comforted, against his hand. In a minute, he was asleep.

And then, in what seemed only a minute more, he was coming frantically awake, smothering, his heart pounding in terror. He opened his eyes on darkness, grabbing for consciousness, and found himself—at last—in his bed at home, half stifled in warm, soft womanflesh. She was lying heavily across his chest, her tears wetting his shoulder while her fingers dug into his arms. He brushed the strands of her long hair out of his face, holding her with his other hand and making soothing murmurs while he tried, fuzzily, to figure out what she was talking about. Finally, she turned her head and spoke into his neck and he heard her clearly. "Willie, Willie," she was saying. "Oh Willie, hold me tight. I'm going to be old."

Farland the Fool, he charged himself, stroking her, feeling her body quiet under his practiced touch, finally waking enough to grin in lonely amusement into the dark as it became evident that he wasn't as tired, actually, as he'd thought. "Baby, beautiful baby," he said softly. He lifted her off him, put her down on her own side of the bed, and pulled down her nightgown. This woman, he thought wryly, could raise the dead—and wished he could share the joke with her. But that was not what was wanted at the moment. He said, "Lovely baby," and bent his head to her breast while his hand parted her thighs. The feel of the softness on both sides of his hand soon brought the old, usual, welcome drunkenness. He laid his body over her quickly, desperately, as though he was afraid she might go away. Somewhere in the back of his head, though—behind his lips and his hands and the must-have-it growing enormous in his loins—a calm, scorekeeping voice repeated scornfully, "Farland the Fool. So that's what set her off."

$\mathcal{N}$*ineteen*

In the palmy, balmy Florida December, Andrea, barefoot and wearing a sarong-like bathing suit splashed with big, brilliant flowers, would have looked not unlike a travel poster for a South Sea island if she had only stood still. But her walk, as she crossed the patio of the Florida house, was so rapid and determined as to resemble a chase, and there was no languor in her eyes. When she burst into the pleasant room in which her husband was conferring with Dan Healy, Dan took one look and beat a hasty retreat, making for the glass doors at the other end of the room so as not to cross her path.

Alec decided at once that no preliminary conversation would be either necessary or desirable, so he contented himself with simply asking her what he, or someone else, had done.

She must have been out of her mind in the first place, Andy said bitterly, to let him talk her into installing the baby at the opposite end of the house from her bedroom. Alec tried to say he'd been told firmly that she must have rest and he didn't think she'd get much if she could hear the baby every time he peeped. The flood washed him away, however, before he could get more than half of his statement out.

"And now I find—" Andy's voice shook with barely controlled rage "—that I have to beat my way through a human picket fence even to get into his room."

"If anyone has been offensive—"

"Nobody has been offensive, except by *being* there. Am I to understand that my baby is required to live as though he had a contagious disease? This is totally impossible, Alec—I never bargained for it and I won't have it. Do you know, there were *three* men standing directly outside his windows—

outside the windows *alone?* It was a fortress, and it was unbearable. I insist—"

Alec took her by the shoulders and eased her into a chair. "It's only temporary. Let me—"

"And Elizabeth's ridiculous train of escorts—are they temporary, too?" Andy's dark eyes were smoldering. "Miss Page told me Elizabeth called out to the men this morning to 'stop dawdling.' Everybody thought it was very funny, and I suppose it is, but it's also unpleasantly bumptious, isn't it? But Alec, what in the name of heaven is she supposed to think, except that these men must be some kind of idiots? How can she respect grown men who apparently have no work to do, who just stand around all day and can't even seem to keep up with her and Miss Page when they go for a walk? Can't you see how it looks to her?"

"Andy, please. I was going to show you this a little later. I assure you, things won't be as bad after a day or so, certainly not the guard on the baby's room." He held out a paper with a few lines of writing on it and an official-looking stamp up in the corner; as Andy took it wonderingly, she saw that it was a photographic copy, the stiff paper cracking where it had been folded. "Read it," Alec urged. "But calmly, please. With a sense of proportion."

He watched her quietly during the brief time it took, for there wasn't much to read—only a few short ugly lines announcing that the writer was aware of the plot to establish a Girard dynasty in the United States and intended to put a stop to it. Unless Girard at once "resigned" and "turned the government back" to Winkler, Alexander Wardwell Girard, Jr., would be "liquidated" in the interest of the national welfare.

Alec waited until she raised her head and said softly to her stricken eyes in the drained face that the matter was in hand, in fact in the hands of experts, and that the identity of the writer was very nearly established; he was a psychotic who had, in fact, written a letter a few years ago threatening to poison Winkler's grandchildren unless the President increased the amount of certain disability pensions. Which stipulation had practically led the Secret Service to the writer. "So you see, he's too sick to be even effectively crafty, and certainly to be capable of any serious effort. Hardly a real menace." He saw her question coming. "All this rigmarole with the guards is just insurance against the outside chance that it isn't the same man." Or that the guy hadn't somehow managed to avail himself of any or all of the ordnance that was so insanely within the reach of anyone able to print a name on a mail-order blank . . . But she didn't have to know about that particular idiocy. "While they check it out thoroughly, you see," Alec went on smoothly.

"I see." She bent her head to study the paper again.

If she had to be told, Alec thought, it was better that she saw the copy rather than the original. The duplicating process blurred the smeary, penciled letters only a little, but it did much to blur the effect; the distance it lent, and the presence of the official stamp, established the fact of control, of a professionalism at work, and reduced the thing to its realistic size. The infant who had yesterday managed to blunder his fist into his mouth and celebrate by crossing his eyes a little more than usual could not possibly be taken from this house by anything short of an army with tanks. Neither could Elizabeth—and since she was probably more intelligent than the writer of the letter, she could probably outwit any attempt to coax her away from her nurse, without whom she didn't leave the grounds anyway.

"He's only a poor wretch, darling," Alec said aloud. Even when we win glorious victories, he thought bitterly, there's no end to the war damage.

"It's all safely part of the past by now," Alec told Jake Ruffing on the phone a week later. "And of course they took that elaborate guard off the baby as soon as they established that it was the same fellow." He sighed. "It wasn't difficult, you know—for one thing, he'd left his fingerprints all over the letter. And he couldn't have done anything at all—he's a patient in a locked ward at a veterans' hospital."

"I read a little two-sentence thing about some kind of court proceeding."

"Well, we have an open society, Jake—all charges are on the record and so available to the press. But Luke says the papers are very responsible about this sort of thing generally—there's no hard news in it, and they know that a lot of talk has some kind of snowball effect on other nuts, so they just do their minimum duty and let it go at that."

"How's Andy?"

Alec said slowly, "She surprised me, you know? After the first minute or so, she pulled herself together and got right to work on the problem. She had a talk with the head of the Secret Service detail, and I don't know what all—oh, for one thing, she asked for copies of some things that were written about Margaret Truman."

"Truman's daughter was a hell of a lot older than Elizabeth," Jake pointed out.

"I know. Andy collected material on FDR's grandchildren, too. But this Secret Service protection of the President's family is relatively new, so there isn't enough history to find an exact match for a three-year-old and a baby. It's only since 1905—"

Jake laughed. "All right, I believe you. It seems clear that Andy's not been keeping her researches all to herself. I'm glad she took it that way," he went on soberly, "but I guess I'm not really surprised. She's not lacking in brains. *Or* determination."

Alec said, with pleasure lingering in his voice, that Jake should refrain from nominating speeches because Andy had just signed up for a job with at least a four-year term. "And, speaking of jobs, I think it's about time for us to announce the big one. Are the recommendations what I think they are?"

"I think Rosie's is. I talked about it with him and Farland yesterday," Jake said slowly. "Farland ducked, of course. Not that choice, if you know what I mean. Not while he's still working there."

"Of course. And you?"

Jake hesitated. "I have a certain impulse to duck, myself. It's kind of big."

"Right. But are you prepared to go as far as a recommendation?"

"Oh yes. And an observation."

"Which is?"

"Congratulations."

"Thank you. I hope we'll be very happy." Girard's voice held laughter. "How're you doing on the other prospects I sent you?"

"We ought to finish up right after Christmas. With a big party for all hands."

"I wish we could come," Alec said wistfully.

"I know. I wish you could, too. After—next month—things'll get a little easier."

"Mm." Girard did not sound convinced. "Listen, Jake, I think you ought to run down soon if you can make it."

"You're going to stay in Florida then?"

"For a while, I think. The—er—light seems less strong here. But Andy's coming up right after New Year's."

"Oh? Clothes?"

"Well, that. But she has an appointment to—er—look over the new house. The lady who lives there now is going to show her around."

"That should be a happy tête-à-tête."

"Oh, I agree. I'd love to hide behind the arras. I'm not too happy about her running around quite so soon, but I guess she knows what she's doing. And she does have quite a complex chore on her hands, so I'm sure she'll really appreciate the tour. In a way."

"Sure. Listen, do you need me before New Year's Day? Unless it's pressing, I'd rather hang around home for a while."

"No, it can wait. New Year's Day will be fine. I'll be talking to you before then, though. Oh, and listen, Jake."

"Yes, sir?"

"Maybe you ought to bring Farland down with you. Unless you think not."

"Oh, I think so. He's turned out to be a good boy to have around."

"Right. See you then. Love to Bonnie."

Jake hung up the phone and stood up. Out of the corner of his eye, he noticed the puddle left by the edge of his snowy boot heel on the surface of his desk. Whistling softly to himself, he pulled his shirttail out and wiped it away. The soft, warm flannel absorbed the dirty water satisfactorily. He left the shirttail hanging out to dry while he dialed Farland's number. "Will," he said without preamble, "your presence is requested in Florida on New Year's Day. Can you make it?"

Will paused briefly. "I guess so, but not for long. I have a meeting toward the beginning of the next week."

Ruffing said he was sure that would be okay. "How about the home front?"

"I'm currently riding on a wave of new understanding," Will said wryly. "For a few weeks anyhow, I figure I can do just about what I want."

"She'll shape up," Jake assured him. "They always do. Besides, she'll see the evidence writ large—the man has decided. He ought to be announcing it today."

Will sighed. "It was a good choice. I'm glad."

According to Gil Kimball's subsequent column on the announcement that Harold Hoffman would be the Girard Administration's Secretary of State, it was more than a good choice; it was, Gil said, the kind of idea that after somebody had it you wondered why nobody had had it before. Here was a fellow who, as the son of a one-time ambassador, had been brought up in daily confrontation with what foreign policy meant abroad, at the point where it was taking effect; who, as head of a great industry's foreign division, had seen for himself the intimate interrelation between trade and foreign policy; and who, most recently as chairman of the board of the influential Institute of Foreign Relations, had participated in the framing of criteria for organization and personnel of all the government bodies dealing in foreign affairs—including, of course, the State Department. The only thing that could have taken Girard all this time, Kimball speculated, was the problem of overcoming his discomfort at the prospect of asking a top businessman to accept the chickenfeed salary that went with one of the world's biggest headache jobs.

Gil's column provoked a cold fury in Ann Taswell that morning because, as it happened, that was one of the mornings on which she felt that she wrote as well as Gil did, and it was the morning after she'd learned she wasn't likely to be given a chance to show it for a while. In a time when the eyes of everybody in the world are directed to the national government, Ann gets assigned to do a series of features on the District of Columbia! It was dirty pool, at the least. Later that day, she dropped in on Marian, who could be drafted to listen sympathetically to this horrendous example of the apparently forever-unchangeable determination of men on newspapers to keep all women writers' noses firmly tied to the women's page. She found the *Tribune*'s art critic deep in a handwritten letter that was several pages long and that was, Marian said as she tucked it back into its envelope before Ann could see anything of it, from Andy Girard. Ann cocked an eyebrow and asked whether there was anything interesting, and Marian told her Paul Morisot had said the public life deprived the private one.

"Listen," Ann said irritably, "I don't mind a one-shot dabble for the inauguration festivities, but if he's going in for phrasemaking, I won't look on him with the same indulgence."

"Well, it wasn't public phrasemaking," Marian mollified. "Apparently, he said it only to Andy."

"I should think she'd already have known it." She asked what Andy herself had to say.

"She says boy babies are different."

"Well, I should think she'd already have known that, too. Care for a cup of coffee in the—ugh—snack bar?"

Boy babies presented tactical problems you didn't expect, somehow, Marian said. And she'd be down in a couple of minutes. When Ann had gone, she unfolded the letter again and went on reading what Andy had said about some rather more complex discoveries.

"Originally, I was all focused on seeing Elizabeth as a prospective prisoner in the White House and how could I spring her, you know? I reasoned that by going to nursery school every morning she'd have at least one chance a day to get away from specialness. But I see now that I had it backwards: the minute she sets off for nursery school in the morning, she'll be special until she comes home. Actually, the only place she really can have anything like normal freedom will be within the White House grounds, where the supervision is so broad and general that it needn't intrude on her directly. Once she gets off the 'reservation,' the Secret Service has to concentrate on her specifically. So I've figured out by now that the only way Elizabeth is going to get to be in nursery school without an agent at her side is if the nursery school is at the White House. I hope both you and Nedra, to whom I'm also suggesting this, won't feel that you're being asked to assume my adversities—things won't be any different for *your* children from the way they would be anywhere else. But they will be different for Elizabeth.

"I've got to come up for an appointment with Mrs. Winkler, who's going to show me over the White House, on Jan. 2, and after that I'll have a better idea of what's available and what will be needed in the way of physical facilities. I've done a little preliminary research on the question of teachers and what other children might fit well, but I'd like to have us all get together when I have more information. Would it be possible for you to come by O Street at about four on Jan. 2 so we could talk about it?

"Marian, I want you to know that if for any reason you don't want Peter to come to a White House play school, I won't be offended. But I must tell you, I hope to make a very persuasive salestalk. Please let me know if you can't make it on the 2nd, and I'm sorry to have to drag you out, but you know."

Marian looked at the clear, lively signature and smiled as warmly as though it had been Andy herself. As she rode down in the elevator, she realized with surprise that there was a tightness in her throat, the sort that came with looking at certain fragile, antique bibelots. Or anything lovely, and rare, and representing a kind of proof that people had evolved to the point of producing something more elegant than was required just to sustain life. It occurred to her suddenly that this protectiveness now was somewhat fierce, and thus not really like her—it had a feeling of coming to her at second hand . . . Paul Morisot, she remembered wistfully then, had not been afraid of talking about Andy like a Valentine.

She joined Ann, as promised. But it was a good thing Ann was with grievance, because Marian was, at the moment, distinctly short of anything to say.

"I couldn't think of nothing to say," Bettina told her mother. "I was all right till it come into my head what an important man he was. Then it was like the cat got my tongue." She hung her good velvet dress on a hanger and carefully closed its zipper. "I feel like I shamed Bruce," she said gloomily. "I shouldn't a gone, I guess. With all them—those college people."

Rosa beamed. "Honey, you talk so nice since you been goin to that school. And you look nice—like a lady. It do my heart good."

"It's not bad, up there." Bettina tied the sash of her robe, her voice carefully indifferent. "I can't say I'm exactly looking forward to going back, but who does, after vacation?" She shrugged. "Like the judge was saying at the party—"

"To think you been to a party a judge was at," mused Rosa. "Maybe it do Trixie some good to hear that. Set an example, like."

"Well, Bruce says the professor gives this party for his students every year on New Year's Day. It's called a 'At Home.'"

Rosa was still marveling. "A colored judge."

"'Negro,' Mama," Bettina corrected her. "'Colored' is like—well, like baby talk."

Rosa sighed. "Who'd a knowed that Bruce go with important people like that? It show what education can do." She got up from the bed, smoothing the spread with her hands. "I got to go in the kitchen, baby, I got my greens on the fire." She paused and looked at her daughter in sudden doubt. "Tina?"

"What, Mama?"

"You still like greens?"

Bettina turned and hugged her mother swiftly and fiercely. "And biscuits, too? Oh, Mama."

"And side meat," said Rosa, extricating herself after a while. "My, it been good havin you home." She eyed the girl hesitantly. "You want to go back, Tina?"

Bettina turned toward the mirror and began to brush her hair, her face hidden from her mother. "Yes, Mama," she said slowly. "I think I better, if it's all right with you."

"It all right with me, baby. Long as you happy."

"I think—" there was a note of discovery in the girl's voice "—I *know* I'm not done learning what I need." The doorbell sounded at the other end of the apartment, and she whipped around in sudden panic. "That's Bruce. Oh, I ain't near ready."

"You take your time." Rosa was nearly out of the room when she heard her daughter call to her. "What, hon?"

"Remember what I told you, Mama."

"Remember? Oh, about the drink?"

"Yeah. Fix it like I showed you, hear? And watch out which glass."

Rosa smiled at the cracked wall of the apartment's tunnel-like hallway. "I be careful, Tina. I'll fix it real nice." Carole Lombard and William Powell. Irene Dunne and Cary Grant. When she opened the door, she was still trying to think of some more late-movie couples from whom Bettina had probably derived her notions of gracious living.

It wasn't William-Powell-Cary-Grant-Bruce, but Louella, huge and plump and dark. Her elaborate oiled and stiffened coiffure above a black, bulky pea jacket was suggestive of a costume drama about a highborn lady rescued at sea.

Rosa tried, and failed, to insert herself into the wedge of the partly open door. "Bettina, she expectin company."

"Do tell. And how you keepin this evenin, Miz Little?"

"Fine, thank you. Come on in, Louella," answered Rosa as the girl pushed past her and started down the hall. She watched the heavy haunches in the black pants moving away from her and chided herself for not being trusting enough. Two of us got to learn things from that school, she told herself severely. You could get your children a hope of something better than Louella, but you had to step out of the way and let them do the choosing in the end. If Bettina really wanted to exchange the evening she had planned for a round of bars with Louella, there was nothing further her mother could do about it.

But Rosa, summoning up a picture of her daughter in her white silk robe, was almost confident that Bettina wouldn't. Certainly, some troubles lay ahead—the rebellious Bruce, for example, would not be easily or frequently led into exposure to the soirées of Washington's Negro intellectuals; Rosa's lips twisted in suppressed amusement as she remembered how clear it had been that the enchanted Bettina was missing the boy's mockery of the gathering to which he had taken her. But the troubles would be of a very different kind from those that had threatened six months ago. Thanks to the gentle, unswerving sisters at the school. And to luck. And, first of all, to Marian Farland.

Impulsively, Rosa turned to the phone and dialed the number that was relatively unfamiliar to her, since she answered it with much greater frequency than she called it.

"Hello?" The voice was breathless. Marilyn Monroe, Rosa decided.

"Sharlie, this Rosa. Can I talk to your mama?"

"Oh, Rosa. Mom's not home. She had calls to make. For New Year's Day, you know. But where she'll be, mainly, is at Sven Halversen's." Sharlie was reading the name, it was clear. "You want the number? It's a hotel, so after the operator answers you have to ask—"

"Never you mind, baby. I got no need for the number. Your daddy still home?"

"No, she went by herself." A quoting note crept into her voice. "Since meetings are held on business days, obviously the preparations for them have to take place on non-business days."

"What you talkin about, chile?" Rosa asked, startled.

"That's what Dad said. Mom was sore because he went back to Florida today and it's a holiday."

"Then who there with you children?"

"Nobody," said Sharlie proudly. "I mean, me. *I'm* sitting with Peter. I'm getting paid, too."

"That a fact?" Rosa's face clouded. Doubtfully, she told herself that Marian knew what she was doing. "Where Dick?"

"Mom says he doesn't need any sitter any more, and he can do what he pleases as long as he behaves responsibly."

Rosa grinned as the last two words echoed Marian's voice. "Well, he be near as old as you. Peter mindin you okay?"

"Fine," Sharlie assured her. "He's taking his nap now."

"Mama be back soon?"

"I don't think so. Ann's coming over for dinner. She'll be here sometime this afternoon, Mom said."

Rosa smiled. So Marian had hedged her bet after all.

"I've got to peel the potatoes for dinner," Sharlie was continuing. "I don't really think cooking ought to be for the same price as the baby-sitting, do you? But since it's only peeling the potatoes I've decided not to raise the issue. *This* time."

"Well, your mama givin you the chance to get experience so you can sit for other people," Rosa pointed out. "So it only fair you do a little somethin extra."

"That's right, isn't it? Well—did you want Mom to call you, Rosa? Is anything wrong at home?"

"No, hon. Ain't nothin wrong. Everythin fine." The words sounded so good to Rosa that she repeated them. Then she added, remembering her duties to Sharlie, "You suppose to say, 'May I take a message?'"

"I forgot. May I take a message? There's a lot more to baby-sitting than you think."

Rosa nodded, racking her brain for a suitable message. But it was too big to say. "Jus' tell Mama Rosa call up to say 'Thank you.'"

IV

Within the Walls of Camelot

"The fair beginners of a nobler time"

Twenty

The southern undertones of the city of Washington could be heard in many of its daily encounters: in the soft, slurred speech; in a certain acceptance of ignorance and violence; in the way taxi drivers, policemen, and spectators at baseball games still used the word "nigger" when intending only mild hostility. Except for unpublicized pockets of *haute couture*—or aspirants to it—known only to the Andrea Girards, the fashions to be found in even the most expensive shops leaned to the fluffy, and the sign of the white glove was rampant.

But perhaps nothing about the city was so southern as the perennial mass despair of officials and citizens alike at the appearance of snow. Washington was administered by House and Senate committees charged with the care of the District of Columbia and its taxpaying but unrepresented citizens, and the chairmen of both committees were usually southerners. Thus, any D.C. functionary applying for snow-removal funds when the city's budget went to the Hill in the balmy weather was met with a chorus of drawled *"Mañanas"* from gentlemen who expected to be lining up votes in Louisiana or Alabama when the snowflakes zeroed in on the District.

Nearly everybody who worked for the U.S. government in Washington was actually from somewhere else, of course (the natives were largely in the real estate business), with the result that in every snowstorm an aristocracy of expertise would emerge rapidly. The soft southern voices ceased to answer telephones; but statisticians and economists who had originated in large northern cities and were accustomed to municipal hardship would get to work, though late and wet and cursing a bus system that afforded no shelter to the waiting—and waiting, and waiting—passenger. The midwesterners were usually the top of the heap, though: a bureau chief born in Minneapolis and graduated from the University of Wisconsin tended to own boots, ear-muffs, and snow tires, and to be capable of driving comfortably all the way downtown at twenty miles an hour with his foot a respectful distance from the brake. Parking places close to the office being, for once, easily obtainable, he would usually arrive in excellent spirits to find that he must make the morning coffee himself because the pretty little girl from North Carolina who served as his secretary was using up her annual leave being "snowbound" twenty blocks away. Thus, if you called a government office at nine o'clock on a snowy winter work day, you would probably be answered by a mid-western-accented male who didn't know how to work all the buttons on the phone.

To be perfectly fair, though, the snowstorm that began in Washington the day before the scheduled inauguration of Alexander Girard would've been a bit much to handle even without the city's traditional snow-neurosis. For the Inaugural Ball and the preceding fêtes and galas, with entertainment produced and provided by famous Hollywood experts and starring the youngest, handsomest President and prettiest First Lady in contemporary memory, had attracted to the city more visitors than the cherry blossoms of a dozen Aprils. Hotels were jammed to capacity and taxis would have been hard to find even with dry streets and balmy weather. It was a day of bigger and better, and so—alas—was the snowfall, which simply went on and on, beautiful and relentless.

All the city's inadequate snow-removal equipment had to be directed to the task of clearing a path for the official ceremony on the morrow; likewise, all the individual heroism that municipal crises call out—the telephone workers and policemen and bus drivers who Make it Somehow because they are essential—was directed to this same end. The District's small police force was responsible both for steering the retiring President and his successor through the streets and for guarding and guiding most of the nation's dignitaries, come to town to cluster in one small, overcrowded area of one small city. Understandably, the cops had little time for the average citizen, who was left to tackle on his own the problem of getting home through the thickly falling snow. If he made it at all, he could then rise up refreshed on Inauguration Day and consider ways and means of getting to work.

If you work on a daily newspaper, you find some ways and means, for snowfall-heroics are expected of you. Except for the outdoors editor, who was totally cut off from the world in his woodland home an hour's drive away in the wilds of Maryland, nearly everybody on the *Tribune* staff came limping in at some time during the working day. In costumes ranging from the dashing to the drably practical, they improvised transportation or simply slogged through the snow. The gathering of news was no problem, for the way of those who wrote both the simple facts and the historic-occasion appreciations of them was smoothed as it was for the dignitaries they trailed. Desk men and composing-room workers, having got to work, simply stayed there, living off the countryside: the *Tribune* snack bar and whatever an intrepid scout or two could carry back from whatever was open. And, of course, as the day lengthened and supernumeraries of all departments straggled in, life got more luxurious.

By the time the managing editor pushed open the door of the TV editor's office in time to catch the 6 P.M. re-run of the inaugural ceremonies on the set in there, he had some considerable success to contemplate. On the whole, the *Tribune* had done nobly through the hectic day: performance might have been precarious at moments—particularly when, just after the inauguration ceremonies and while copy still had to be run back to the office, a whole new snowfall began—but it added up to satisfactory, and quite up to Inauguration Days in the past. The ME had been a reporter when Franklin Roosevelt was sworn in in 1933, so he had quite a record for comparison. He remembered that cold and slushy March inauguration quite clearly, and he tried to remember now whether anyone had mentioned the weather when the "Lame Duck Amendment," which shifted Inauguration Day to late January, was being debated.

The copyboy who was sprawled in the office's visitor's chair got up quickly and offered it. The ME thought briefly about being democratic and declining, but he was fifty-seven years old and dead tired, and he decided that age has its privileges even if rank may not. So he thanked the boy, lowered his burly form into the comfortable leather armchair and cast a quick, summarizing look around. The TV editor's office, all its upper walls glass, rode like a small crowded lifeboat on the just-quieted waters of the city room; by now, the action was submarine—down among the fast-moving men with dirty finger-nails and caps made of folded newspaper. The big job was almost done; what remained, at least for those who worked on this floor, was a tying-off of loose ends, a few second-thought observations, and a general necessity to hover in case of emergency. And a brief rest period for those who would cover the inaugural festivities in a few hours. The watchers here, then, would be those with a little time to kill, on their way to work, or on their way home. And one at work—the *Tribune's* TV editor, who sat at his desk, making occa-sional notes on a folded piece of copy paper.

The ME waved to a pair of ski-capped editorial writers visible through the glass as they passed the office on their hopeful way home, checked the screen briefly and discovered that what was going on was only some praying, and then swept the office with a sharp, administrative glance designed to dislodge anyone who was supposed to be somewhere else. A sports department lad with a handful of dangling galleys made a small sound in his throat and scurried out as the ME's wise eye fell on him. A kid from the library with a wire basket of clippings hesitated and then stood his ground: after all, he was clearly visible through the glass if his boss wanted him, and the ME al-most certainly didn't know his name. The three day-shift copyboys propped against one wall reminded themselves that they were legit—this was slack time for them, and besides, they were visible if needed—and returned to their horseplay but tried to make their jibes wittier than ever now, in case the old man was listening. The managing editor relaxed, settling comfortably into his chair.

On the screen, Alec Girard, hatless and coatless, was moving the last few inches of his long journey to the Presidency. At the far left of the picture, his young wife, who had kept her head bowed for a moment after the prayer had ended, raised it now; the camera caught the look, composed and proud, that went out quickly toward her husband before she settled back into a photograph of any pretty, well-dressed woman in a pretty hat behaving nicely in the audience at a speech. Beside her, Lou Cannon, the wife of the new Vice-President, snuggled in a mink coat, middle-aged and content and motherly.

The TV editor said, "Marvelous shot of Winkler," and wrote on his paper. The ex-President, hatless in the cold, looked uncomfortable; his bare head,

its fine wisps of hair ruffled by the cold wind, was pulled down into the shelter of his dark overcoat and the white silk scarf that looked hastily tucked
in at the neck. His expression was pleasant, kindly, and babyish. It was indeed a good shot, the managing editor thought, summarizing perfectly the
man you couldn't help liking even while you knew that he might prove the
most dangerous threat the young country had ever known. "Deadly innocence." A *Tribune* editorial writer had used these words to describe the
appalling risk to the public welfare in President Winkler's well-intentioned
ignorances; the consensus at the editorial conference had been that it was
good but went too far, and the writer had accepted the verdict.

The new President began on the part of his speech that the ME described
to himself as "Dearly-beloved-we-are-gathered-here"; he had heard it before,
and he mentally tuned it out for now in favor of watching and thinking. This
was, after all, the first time in his long life that the President being inaugurated was younger than he was, and it had been bringing him—and not only
him, he was pretty sure—some thoughtful moments ever since the election.

The book editor pointed with his chin at the television screen. "There's a
guy whose shoes I wouldn't be in for anything."

The managing editor, who thought at first that his colleague meant the
President, was surprised but inclined to agree. Then his eye caught the indicated figure—a tall, hatless man in a gray overcoat, totally inconspicuous in
the audience. But the television camera selected him without meaning to:
except for the former President, who appeared almost unaware of his surroundings, and this man in the gray overcoat, everyone in the picture was
turned, however slightly and by whatever attitude of face or muffled body,
toward the speaker. But the Secret Service agent's alert look roved slowly,
scanning everything except Alec Girard. The camera passed on, picking up
once again an undisturbed vista of solemn but peaceful attention among the
famous and warmly wrapped, and the ME smiled silently at the departure
of his own momentary feeling of suspense. It's a re-run, he reminded himself
—you know how it comes out; nobody shot at Girard. Nevertheless, he felt
relieved.

"Look, there's Youngblood," said one of the copyboys.

"The hell it is. That's all diplomats over there. Probably the Soviet second
secretary or something."

"I bet we handed the Russians a laugh, yesterday and today," the third
copyboy remarked. "They must have been holding their sides, watching the
U.S. government struggle heroically to get the President a couple of miles
down Pennsylvania Avenue. At home they've probably got this much snow
in the spring."

The managing editor glanced at the speaker, smiling a little. The boy was
exaggerating, of course—but he happened to know that Washington's repeated snow dramas did in fact usually provide the Soviet diplomatic corps
with some innocent merriment. More important, though, was the evidence

of imaginative thinking in the youngster's observation. It was attractive, and boded well; the ME filed away a mental note of which kid it was.

The copyboy said "Here it comes" and sat up attentively. *"We no longer believe,"* said the young, earnest President on the television screen, *"that what is alien is necessarily barbarous."* This was the part of the speech, the managing editor remembered, watching closely now, that had begun with a quotation from Archibald MacLeish: *" 'It is true also that we here are Americans: that we use the machines: that a sight of the god is unusual: that more people have more thoughts: that there are progress and science and tractors and revolutions and Marx and the wars more antiseptic and murderous and music in every home' . . ."* The *Tribune* front-page story on the inauguration would feature Alexander Girard's description to the world of the nation whose leadership he was assuming. The managing editor waited for the key words to come, free to study, as he had not been before, the reactions of those at the scene—and now, of his fellow watchers as well.

"We are a young nation," the crisp New England voice said decisively in the crisp, blowing air, *"yet old in experience of orderly self-government, of transferring power without revolution. We are a free people, yet we resist anarchy as sturdily as we resist tyranny. We are a peaceful people, yet we have performed prodigies in war, and won."*

Applause spattered. In the pale shaft of sunlight that picked out the figures in the front row of the audience, Andrea Girard sat very still, her hands hidden in a small fur muff. The wind lifted her dark thick hair, but did not dislodge the little fur hat. The managing editor studied her steady, pure profile and downcast eyes, and he thought Andy looked a little frightened.

". . . a people who, having learned in infancy the joys and obligations of citizenship and found them comfortable and valuable, tend to extend them. Our nation is not a jealous master: it frees its citizens for all the other memberships of a full life. Thus, we here are members of the community of parents, an international body that will not tolerate the hunger of children." Applause began again, but the strong voice rushed on, overriding it. *"We are farmers, joined with all farmers everywhere in opposition to the laying waste of harvests. We are artisans, citizens of the ancient republic of craftsmanship, dedicated to the fashioning of intricacies and therefore opposed to the bluntnesses of destruction. We are scientists, enlisted for the duration among the forces of seekers of knowledge, who need the long look—and so, are hostile to the short view required by war."* The applause began somewhere out in the massed and huddled audience and rolled in over the speaker, silencing him. The camera closed in on his handsome face, waiting with its characteristic look of controlled impatience.

The book and music critics exchanged pleased, startled glances. The managing editor saw it with some amusement: nothing shakes them like literacy, he thought cynically, but he was pleased by the implied support for his judgment in selecting quotes from the speech to feature in the story. It had what inauguration speeches always had, if you boiled it down—the warning to the world that we want peace, but we will fight. But the language sparked just often enough into the mind-catching word, either fresh or simply unexpected, and it was being uttered by a thoughtful man who listened to what he was saying. "Charisma," the managing editor concluded, studying the tall, waiting figure at the podium, was, like "existential," a word he would rather not hear any more. And maybe it was not necessary, anyway, to descend into magic for the explanation of what was going on: a man of dignity spoke with dignity and it called up a dimension of dignity from the people. The only magic in Girard, maybe, was his loving use of his native tongue.

"Somebody said Jake Ruffing wrote it," a copyboy said. The tentative remark attempted to establish the speaker as one on the "inside," a position beloved of would-be reporters; yet the voice was shaken, clearly doubting its own claim to knowledge.

Another shook his head disbelievingly. "Not in a million years. I could believe Jerry Rosenberg, except there aren't any figures or dates."

"Then who?"

The music critic leaned over them and said softly, "Could you gentlemen entertain the possibility that he wrote it himself?"

The managing editor caught the little man's eye and winked, then turned back to the set. The President was hugging the podium a little now, his gestures smaller and more incisive as he began to outline the projects that would appear on the front page of the *Tribune* in a list of brief paragraphs, each introduced by the round black "bullet": education, housing, civil rights, all the old year-after-year, Congress-after-Congress topics that had been planks in Girard's, and nearly every other President's, campaign platform. The ME smiled, only half listening now, as he caught sight of the long horse face of the new Vice-President on the television screen. Tom Cannon, who had made a career of revealing only when it suited him the good mind camouflaged by his folksy manner, would be more at home with these trees than with the noble view from the mountaintop the President had offered earlier. Respect showed in the wrinkled features of the big Southerner, and it was easy to see why: the man who was speaking was laying down a program with authority and confidence, and Cannon, the redoubtable bred-in-the-bone politician who would, if he had to, certainly have served all those years in the Congress for nothing but the love of it—Cannon's pleasure in the presence of demonstrated political leadership was always immediate, thorough, and bipartisan. Now, listening, he looked like a music lover hearing a concert by a genuine prodigy.

Like me, the managing editor thought wryly, Tom maybe forgives Girard for making him an old man, as he's made all of us, so suddenly. Only Tom at least got to be Vice-President in the process; all I got was older, and fast. Ah well, he told himself, I may not be too old, at that—because he had a definite feeling that running a newspaper in Washington this year was going to be a hell of a lot of fun. And sharpen everybody up, too: a quote from

Secretary of State Harold Hoffman, for example, was goddam well going to have to be accurate, or vengeance would be swift and competent. He looked at the old ex-President, a white, expressionless face above a dark coat, and thought without regret of the soft and easy journalism that had been possible —and had therefore, as Gresham's law prescribed in economics, driven out the good. In that muddled administration the few competent men had been like raisins in a bland cake. Poor old Winkler—let's get him down on his ranch and leave him there with the gifts those who liked things undisturbed were wont to shower on him; with luck—and who could help wishing it to him?—he would never know what a dub he had been. But it was time now (the ME remembered that President Girard would say later in his speech) to stop relaxing from the war and its aftermath and get on with building the advanced society Americans wanted and were entitled to. I want it, too, by God, he thought with sudden surprise: by God, the man has charisma. Grinning, he closed his eyes.

And opened them immediately as he felt the stirring of air by his chair. The drama department secretary crossed the room in a graceful leap and was halfway to her desk before the old man heard her telephone ringing and understood why. He watched her small, firm plaid behind twisting rapidly between the empty desks out in the nearly deserted city room; then he stopped watching and watched the copyboys watching her, instead. The entrance of his own secretary, middle-aged and corseted, did not distract the three young men from their survey, he noted.

"Just wanted to remind you you've got to get dressed soon," she called to him from the doorway. "I'm leaving now, and I was afraid you'd forget the time."

"No, I won't, I promise." He remembered the snow then. "How will you get home? Will you be all right?"

"I can walk—and one of the photographers is going my way, so I'll even have an escort. Don't give it a thought." But she smiled her gratitude because he had. "Good night, chief. Have a ball at the ball."

He thanked her, but his eyes were on the television screen again. President Girard had finished his glowing notes on the new domestic America—most of which depended on a biddable Congress, which he lacked, and he knew it —and he paused now before taking all the final threads of his speech in hand. The wind lifted a feather of whirling snow across the corner of the picture, while, cold and exact, accidentally in its center as the camera moved to a close-up, the gray Secret Service agent searched steadily beyond the tall figure of the President. The managing editor shivered, and wondered how Girard could stand it for so long, coatless in that temperature. Long underwear, of course—and probably he was full of adrenalin, pumping into his blood by the gallon, behind that assured and handsome face.

"*It has been pointed out*," the President said slowly, almost conversationally, "*that this administration is led by, and will be staffed by, young men— young, as youth goes in politics.*" He smiled a little as the ripple of laughter rose in the crowd, but his eyes were still serious. *"Let me point out that the men of our age, and a large percentage of our contemporaries, are first of all survivors: we are the ones who fought the great war and came home, perhaps leaving better leaders under grave markers half around the world."* He shifted almost noticeably into higher gear, riding the end of the applause as though taking advantage of its momentum.

"Should've had a crowd shot there," the TV editor said suddenly. His voice, loud and irritated, jerked the eyes of his visitors toward him with violent unanimity that bespoke their absorption in the speech and embarrassed him. He colored, scribbled on his paper, and muttered something nobody heard.

". . . among the lessons we brought home from that war," the President was saying urgently. *"For example, that there's not much point in the old, slangy 'What's in it for me?' Because we learned, the hard way, that what's in it for me is you, and what's in it for you is me. If we didn't know it before, we knew it very well by the time we collected our discharges and began to look over the scene back home: what happens in the life of every you makes a difference to the life of every me. Wherever, in this country, that has been forgotten, one of the sicknesses that now demand our attention has grown and threatened our national welfare."*

Girard waited for them, his hand dropping from its familiar punching gesture to rest on the podium. When he began again, his voice was not urgent but thoughtful. *"And, for the final lesson we brought back with us from the wars, we are indebted to the fact that they were not our wars alone: we fought as one country among many, in unified commands combining the resources and skills of all the Allies. And we learned this: a babel of tongues is not a problem when what they are talking about is much the same thing— a way of winning, a wish for home, a hope for peace. In the terror and the boredom and the loneliness that was war, the minds of many nations met in one aim, one longing."* He lifted his head and gave himself to them, young and sure and earnest in the sparse sunlight and the strong wind. *"We have begun to learn how small we are, all our many nations together on our one whirling world, under the eye of our one God. With His help, we will never forget."*

"I feel all—funny," the little drama secretary told the music critic. Her bright sweater looked brave but tentative, out of step with the wet eyes and uncertain mouth above it.

The music critic, who had five children, nodded at her kindly. "Your only trouble is, honey, you're too young to remember any speeches but Winkler's."

Tell her to take a cold shower, the managing editor growled in his mind; the poor kid is suffering from a hot flash of patriotism. No wonder she doesn't recognize it, he added, holding fast to his cynicism because of the lump of excitement in his own throat. Suddenly he wanted to get dressed and go to a ball, by God. He got up quickly and turned to the TV editor. "What did you think of the sound quality?" Not really listening to the answer, he watched the kissing and handshaking going on on the screen, noting that Alec Girard—unregenerate New Englander—did not kiss his wife but only held her hands for a moment, looking down at her gravely.

The managing editor moved with as much briskness as he could manage toward the door of the little glassed-in office, steering skillfully between the comments of his staff. Everyone seemed suddenly gay, ready for a holiday, he thought wryly, but it wasn't a holiday. The wisdom of years asserted itself— somewhere, he told his bubbly party feeling, probably in an efficiency apartment near 25th and K streets, a little old lady is writing a politely furious letter to the *Tribune*. When it gets here, we'll learn that, though she's been a subscriber for thirty years, during which she has borne patiently with our errors and inadequacies, she has just about had it now, because this morning in the crossword puzzle, 73 across and 73 down were transposed. A quick check will reveal that she is absolutely right, and the mailroom will be notified at once; its staff, which remembers to a man the day there was a mistake in the bridge column, will groan and call in anybody who's on leave.

In the sanctuary of his office, the ME looked at his dress clothes laid out neatly on the sofa. For tonight he was free to be Joe Citizen (well, Joe Minor-Big-Shot): the remaining Big Question of the evening, Andrea Girard's ball gown, was not his to answer, and the photographs of the ball gown were not his to take, rush back to the *Tribune*, or choose among. Tonight he could be, like everybody else, part of the chorus in the opera where the townspeople gather in the square. Not opera, he said to himself then—more like soap opera. But maybe the best damn soap opera ever. He sat down and began to untie his shoe. Can Alec Girard—no, young and handsome Alec Girard— lead the little old lady on K Street to a new Jerusalem?

Maybe, maybe, his party spirit said, rising indomitable under the weight of dailiness. He eased his foot, swollen after the long day, out of his shoe and sighed with pleasure. It would be worth watching. Amen, and amen again.

Twenty-one

"Be careful of my dress," Andrea Girard warned her daughter. She shook the folds of palest green chiffon and the tiny accordion pleats fell into place. The soft sweep of cloth down from the narrow traces of gold rising under the bosom and girdling her waist was as free and graceful as it had been before Elizabeth's molestations. Relieved, Andy wondered whether she'd spoken too sharply to the child; she eyed the small figure, encased from toes to neck in warm, pale-blue, one-piece pajamas, but she could detect no sign of injury.

Elizabeth sat in the middle of the floor, her legs folded tailor fashion, and examined her mother with a proprietary air. "You look like a picture in a book."

"Really?" Andy adjusted the filmy scarf, neither quite white nor quite green, that shrouded her throat and shoulders and floated away behind. "What book?"

"That big red read-to book. It has that story about the Spartan boy."

Andy nodded, taking up her lipstick. "Well, this dress is made like the ones ladies wore in ancient Greece." She touched her upper lip briefly and then stopped to amplify, "That's where the Spartan boy lived."

"Oh. Is this your best party dress?"

"Yes. Do you like it?"

"It's pretty. But I think you should've got a pink one, like my best party dress."

"I like pink party dresses, too," said Andy, wondering whether her hair didn't look a bit stiff in its unaccustomedly elaborate coiffure. "But the last President's wife wore a pink dress to the ball, and my dress would be right beside hers in the Smithsonian; I thought two pink ones would look a little —ridiculous."

"What's a sonian?" Elizabeth straightened the worn plush ear of the pink and blue stuffed rabbit beside her on the floor.

"*Smith*sonian. It's a kind of museum. I'll take you there sometime soon. They have all the Presidents' wives' inauguration dresses there, as well as—"

"You mean they're going to take your dress away to put in the museum?" Elizabeth's blue eyes blazed.

Andy looked down at her, surprised by her outrage. "Well, after I'm through wearing it, of course."

"I won't let them take mine!" Elizabeth sprang up, snatching up her toy as though it, too, were threatened with confiscation. She stared at her mother with defiance. "It's *my* party dress."

And you're no mollycoddle, unlike your mother, Andy thought, surveying the small rebel. "Nobody's going to take your party dress, Elizabeth," she said firmly.

"Not even for the museum?"

"No. They collect only the dresses the Presidents' wives wore, not their children's."

"Well, all right. But it isn't fair."

Andy said softly, "It is, though, Elizabeth. Do you remember what I told you? All the people have an interest in the President, the new one and all the old Presidents too. They can't all be in all the things that go on when a new President is inaugurated, so things are saved to show everybody a little bit how it was."

"I don't think it's such a great thing to be President," Elizabeth said thoughtfully. "You have to move out of your house, and they take away your best party dress."

"It *is* a great thing," Andy insisted. "But you have to give up something to get great things."

Elizabeth pulled on a strand of her hair and thought it over, pushing her lips in and out—like, Andy remembered, suppressing a giggle, Nero Wolfe, the fat detective of fiction. "Well," she decided, "I'll be a President's child. But I don't think I'll be a President's wife."

Alec came in just too late to hear that one, which was a pity, Andy thought, storing it away to tell him: shades of Margaret Fuller accepting God. She looked at Alec, tall and imposing in his white tie and tails, and decided he must be the handsomest President in history. At the very least.

"It's only in the corridors that there's even the faintest indication we've just moved in," he told Andy. "Marvelous feat. Bill and I've been taking the grand tour. You've wrought miracles, darling."

"Thank you." Silently, Andy begged forgiveness of all the backstairs workers for whose labors she was blandly accepting credit. "You must've been up on the third floor. That's where we dumped the boxes we didn't have time to get at."

Alec nodded. "I went to see what the children were up to. Elizabeth, I was told, was gadding about." He frowned at her with mock severity. "The baby was—"

"He's eating his bottle," Elizabeth interrupted. "I came to help Mommy dress until he's finished."

The President said gravely, "You've done a marvelous job, too. I have never seen your mother looking lovelier."

Andy, fastening her long gold and emerald earring, made a face at him in the mirror. "Thank you, Mr. President."

Alec grinned, then crossed the room and reached for her. "I want to be sure you won't float off somewhere. You look so—"

"Daddy."

Alec sighed and looked down at the child who had marched into his path and now stood, straddle-legged and determined, between her parents. "Yes, Elizabeth."

"I don't think it's fair. Sandy isn't even any years old yet, and he stays up later than I do."

"You're still up," the President temporized. He looked at his wife for help.

Elizabeth dismissed the statement contemptuously. "That's just because you got President. I mean all the time, on regular nights, I have to go to bed and Sandy gets up to eat a bottle, and I'm the big sister. It isn't fair."

"You used to have a bottle late at night when you were a baby," said Andy. Her face showed that she was thinking hard.

"Yes, but I didn't have a big sister," said Elizabeth. "So it wasn't unfair to anybody."

"I see what you mean," Andy murmured. She glanced at Alec and shrugged her tanned shoulders faintly. "I'm sorry, Elizabeth. I'm afraid that's just the way it is with babies—they do have to be fed late at night for a while." Her dark eyes appealed for understanding. "But it's only for a little while. In a few months, he'll be put to bed much earlier than you, and he won't be taken up again until morning."

Elizabeth sighed. There were so many things to accept, Andy thought sympathetically, watching her daughter swallow the defeat. She knelt, careless of the Grecian folds of her dress, and hugged the small protester, smoothing back the fine fair hair.

"Look, kitten," the President said suddenly. "The thing is, the baby doesn't know he's up late. He doesn't know what time it is, you see."

Elizabeth pried herself out of her mother's embrace and peered up at her father, hope growing in her face. "He doesn't even know about bedtime?"

"No," said Alec. "Certainly not."

"Then he doesn't know he's staying up later than his big sister?"

"No. And I'll tell you something else."

"What?"

"He won't remember it, either. He's too little to remember anything that happens to him now."

Elizabeth asked her mother, "Won't he remember the other house?"

"I'm afraid not," Andy said gently. "I wish he could."

Elizabeth smiled reassuringly. "That's all right—I'll tell him about it."

"That will be very nice."

"But," Elizabeth added, looking at her father, "I won't tell him he stayed up later."

The President said decisively, "I wouldn't." He held out his hand. "May I escort you to your room? I know **my** way around quite well now. We'll leave Mommy to do whatever she thinks she has to do—which will certainly amount to gilding the lily—while I take you upstairs." Leading her out, he said over his shoulder to Andy, "Darling, please? Remember—Bruyette is cooling his heels downstairs. And driving will be a slow business in the winter festival out there."

Andy promised to hurry and kissed Elizabeth quickly. She blew a kiss after Alec, too, but he didn't see it; he was busy explaining what "gilding the lily" meant.

She was as good as her word—gloved, glittery, and all collected when he came to get her after a few minutes. In the small elevator, Alec said in mock despair, "Whatever will we do if Elizabeth grows up to look like you? An army of Secret Service agents with drawn guns won't keep the suitors out of our hair."

They crossed the brightly lighted hall, their footsteps echoing. "If she doesn't run away from home before that," Andy said. "I don't think I handled that sticky business of the comparative bedtimes very efficiently. It's a good thing you were around."

He grinned. "It would be too silly, wouldn't it, if the politician's children had to go without negotiations."

"True. But maybe you'd better teach me, Alec—unless you plan to be on call for nursery emergencies."

"Face. That's the whole secret." He had been joking when he began, but suddenly he was more thoughtful than amused. "Even in the nursery, I guess, face outranks fact." He shook his head. "Very remarkable, really."

Congressman Bruyette, waiting for them with a tray of drinks in the oval Blue Room, looked attentive and a little ill at ease. The walls were covered in deep-blue silk with a repeated gold motif, and gilded eagles surmounted the long windows under which uninviting chairs, spaced out by footed urns, were ranged uncompromisingly around the edge of a bare, polished floor. Andy eyed Bill dubiously, trying to decide whether he looked more like the curator of an ice rink or a trainer of eagles. In either case, his relief at their arrival was understandable.

"Mr. President. *Madame.*" Bruyette lifted Andy's hand and kissed it ceremoniously.

Andy twinkled at him and dropped him a slow, graceful curtsey.

"Hey," the President protested. "This here is a democracy here. You two're getting carried away."

"*I* certainly am," said Bruyette. He looked at Andy with awe. "It's a good thing you're already elected. Every woman at the ball will throw herself on the floor and kick her feet and scream."

"How'd you get the drinks?" Alec handed one to Andy and took his own. "I was too timid to try."

The Vermont Congressman came to attention, his glass lifted. "The President."

"The President," said Andrea. On her bare arms, little goosebumps rose suddenly.

The President thanked them with dignity. But when they had touched the glasses to their lips, he smiled suddenly at both of them. "To beauty and friendship," he said. Andy looked at Bill and saw that she wasn't the only one who felt the way she did.

"Let's shove off," Alec said as soon as they had finished.

"Okay." Bruyette sighed. "It'll be a pleasure not to have to fight the impulse to whisper."

"I know," Alec agreed. "All the time we were poking around, looking into the rooms, I kept expecting somebody in a uniform to appear and throw us out."

"You can throw him out," Bill reminded him. "You're commander in chief. That means boss of all the uniforms."

"It's hard to remember."

"Pooh," said Andy. "I don't have any trouble. I'm all ready for any flunky who tries to evict me: I'll just draw myself up to my full height—" she did, and looked down her nose besides "—and say 'That's quite all right, my good man. My husband is the junior Senator from Vermont.' "

Their laughter eased the stiffness. But something was going to have to be done, Andy reminded herself as she slipped her arms into the sleeves of her long ermine coat. Even Bill couldn't stand still in one of these rooms without looking like a sentry. There *must* be a way to remove the museum hush and leave the dignity.

She was mulling over the possibilities when the long black car moved smoothly out of the White House grounds and into the snowy street.

"I wouldn't have liked to be the one responsible for clearing this mess," Bruyette remarked. "Even as much as they have."

"There's supposed to be a limit to the snow," Andy said suddenly. She smiled at Alec and began to sing a snatch of one of the songs in a popular musical. " 'And there's a legal limit to the snow here—in Camelot.' " Her voice was soft but clear and accurate.

"Then somebody goofed," said Bruyette. He nodded at the great heaps of snow that lined the avenue.

"Camelot just got started," Alec apologized. "Give us a chance, will you?" He took a folded packet of paper out of his pocket. "Turn on the light, will you? Let's let the people see Andy." As soon as the light came on, he began reading, stopping once to ask Bill, "Did you put in the comment on Jefferson's inaugural address? Oh yes, here it is. I see it." He fell silent then, his eyes moving rapidly over the pages.

Let's let the people see Andy indeed, Andy thought, peering out of the window as their car moved along slowly in the center of a procession of three. She turned to Alec, but his eyes were gobbling the contents of the papers like a hungry boy attacking a peanut butter sandwich. It wasn't that he had lied —he simply saw a way to get two kinds of mileage out of having the car's interior lights on. She could not resist, suddenly, the desire to touch him: searching, she spotted a tiny wrinkle in the collar of his overcoat and straightened it gratefully, her white-gloved hand lingering for an extra pat. Alec smiled absently and went on reading. Andy took her hand away and winked at Bill Bruyette. Anyway, she told herself philosophically, Alec knew she was there.

Bruyette said, "With you shining all over the place—and us got up in dress uniform, so to speak—it reminds me of your wedding."

The car crept by the red bloom of a fire in a battered container that looked like an oil drum; there were many of them, at intervals along the wall of snow, each surrounded by huddled figures. Whenever the car came abreast of a group, all the figures would turn into silhouettes, standing between the fire and the car with nothing distinct about them except their lifted arms. "It must feel quite different to the spectators," Andy replied.

And, she realized suddenly and with interest, it felt quite different to her, too. She remembered, a little ashamed of it now, the way she had shrunk back from the mass of faces and lifted hands as she and Alec emerged from the church in Kingsley. Summer is quick in Vermont: the August wind that blew her grandmother's veil away from her shoulders and then quickly back again—so that it looked, she saw in the photographs later, rather like a

Grecian drape—had the brisk breath of autumn in it; the year had lolled long enough, and it was getting down to business. They're all well-wishers, Andy had reminded herself, and straightened and walked proudly, for all the people to witness that she accompanied, but did not lean on, her new husband. Who grinned companionably at the crowds, like a baseball player who's hit a home run and is frankly proud of himself.

"Part of Camelot is people," Bill said quietly. "That's why there are always spectators."

Andy nodded. "I know. I feel—different—about them now. I'm glad they're here." She smiled at a white, scarf-shrouded face caught in a sudden leap of firelight and meant by it both a welcome and a plea to be welcomed, to Camelot.

"Jefferson wrote a better speech than I did," Alec said unexpectedly, "but I'll bet I get gentler handling from the press. In his day, they hadn't heard of honeymoons for new administrations."

In the other car, the one after the wedding, the Alec for whom a honeymoon had not, at that moment, been a mere metaphor, said, "Welcome back, Andy," when they were finally alone and on their way.

The recent Miss Langwith eyed him nervously. "Where have I been?"

"Beats me." He took her hand then, his thumb exploring the new wedding ring. "All I know is, while I was still dancing a jig because you'd said you'd marry me, you disappeared among the women and never emerged until just now."

"Oh, Alec."

"Well, that's not quite fair. I remember, you did ask me one day about the address of some second cousins in Canada. But I think it was only because my mother and sister had gone shopping."

"Did you get the name, Andy?" the present Alec was asking. "Harry Simmons."

Confused, she came reluctantly out of the summery past. "What about Harry Simmons?"

"Alec wants him for the information agency," Bill explained. "But Mr. Simmons is a little hesitant about taking a whopping cut in his income, uprooting his family, and becoming a target for hostile newspapers."

"Oddly enough," Alec added.

"I'll bring him and his wife over at the ball," Bill went on. "Maybe it will help if Andy smiles upon them."

"Instead of my customary snarl?"

"Andy." Alec frowned at her.

She bent her carefully coiffured head and watched her gloved fingers playing with the clasp of her small, dull-gold purse. "I'm sorry. I suppose." It came to her then, quickly, out of nowhere—a knowledge of how it must feel to be Mrs. Simmons, wondering, were there good schools for her children in Washington, would she be able to make friends? "I really am sorry," Andy said, raising her head even though the shameful flush still lay on her cheeks. "I'll try. Do they have children?"

Bruyette answered her, but she wasn't listening. Alec's quick, contented smile was enough, for the moment. "You know what Maude Winkler told me," she reminded him. " 'Politics isn't for we women.' "

Alec looked at her soberly. "That's what I meant, you know. We couldn't leave things to people like that, could we?"

"I know. I'm sorry I make trouble. But the absurdities keep intruding."

"So do the needs," Alec said gently. His eyes were open to her, with all the love, understanding, and courage there to be read—a map of a Camelot where all roads led to justice and all citizens were precious.

The car slid to a stop and a thousand flowers of light were blooming over them. Bruyette had disappeared, and she was out of the car and walking between faces and the waves of applause, like a movie of the wedding run in reverse—going in now instead of coming out, going from being private to beginning the public pageant, instead of the other way round. And no longer virginal in white, she said to herself, smiling, smiling at herself and them simultaneously. Neither leaning nor lagging, she walked beside her husband.

They paused among more lights. Alec was shaking hands. Somebody was taking her coat, and she stood patiently awaiting the next move in the pageant, elaborate, absurd, and fun. She looked out at the vista of dressed-up people waiting beyond the empty expanse of spotless carpet, in the great room they would enter. Then the music started; jolted into half-laughter, half-tears, she heard it and recognized "Hail to the Chief." Tom and Lou Cannon fell into step behind them and they paced into the welcoming cheers as though wading into the sea, participants in some obscure but ancient ceremonial presided over by the flashing eyes of cameras. And then Andy was sitting in a great, brocaded chair beside Alec leaning back in another just like it; he was grinning and lighting a big cigar. The music was a pulse rather than a sound; she knew they would begin a token dance soon and wondered how anyone would be able to hear the music. Lou Cannon, her gray hair in sculptured curls like something made of spun sugar to decorate a cake, was screaming words at Andy: concentrating hard, Andy finally made out, "Isn't this fun?" Laughing, abandoning the soft voice of a lifetime's habit and training, she leaned over and screamed back that it was, it truly was.

Twenty-two

"Alexander Girard, who told the American people, 'Let's get started,' may set the same impatient pace at home," Ann Taswell wrote in the *Washington Tribune* of February 1. "These days, the White House rings with the sound of hammers and the hasty calls of workmen. The language of the latter is careful, for nobody can be quite sure that the slim figure in brown slacks and leather jacket won't suddenly appear among them, clipboard in hand, to ask in the soft voice that conceals first-class executive steel whether it wouldn't be quicker if—

"Housewife Andrea Girard seems to have been struck at once by the absurdity of food-preparation and serving arrangements that would have her family living much like the residents of a rooming house, who have to go down to the corner drugstore to get so much as a cup of coffee. Mrs. Girard's predecessors couldn't have been happy to discover that the 'family dining room' was downstairs and barely separated from the Mansion's public rooms; however, perhaps because she is the mother of the youngest children to inhabit the White House in many years, the latest First Lady's dismay took the form of action. The new private dining room on the second floor is still lacking final, or even semifinal, touches, but at least there's a working pantry: food can be prepared or kept hot, and a bowl of alphabet soup can be served to a hungry little girl. That it makes sense is unquestionable, but that it could be done in less than two weeks is very nearly incredible. Without applying any visible pressure, and certainly without raising her voice, the First Lady has the workmen scrambling as though they were building Noah's ark and it was already starting to rain."

Sharlie Grayson, whose monthly chore it was to clean up and keep up to date the bulletin board in the Farland kitchen, didn't get around to her February 1 stint until a few days later. By which time the author of the above tribute to the new "let's get started" spirit was herself material for the bulletin board as a newly elected president. The association of Washington women journalists had formed some years ago, when it became clear that the National Press Club—despite the high percentage of liberal, up-to-date, forward-looking, equal-rights-conscious citizens among its exclusively male members—was not going to depart from its policy of segregating itself against women; Marian Farland thought the women's group had the somehow forlorn air of a Jewish country club and, in fact, when pressed, pronounced it a "ghetto" and refused to join. But Ann had joined, had worked faithfully first on various committees and later on the ladder of the organization's executive offices, and finally, after a year as first vice-president, had not unexpectedly arrived on the top rung. She was inaugurated as soon as the membership had recovered from its chores on behalf of an earlier and more famous inauguration. At the subsequent dinner, Ann made a witty speech pointing to President Girard's clear record of non-discrimination against women. A new era had dawned, she assured her listeners gravely, in which it might no longer be necessary for female members of the Washington press corps to contemplate an appeal to the UN Commission on Human Rights.

The nation's new Chief Executive, who was the guest of honor, made an off-the-record reply avowing devotion to and respect for women in journalism and produced a "proof" that brought down the house: "Alexander volunteered for the staff of the school newspaper last month," a prep school headmaster had written in a long-ago report to Mr. and Mrs. John Girard. "Despite some unreliable spelling, he seems to be enjoying his chores. However, in view of the fact that his enthusiasm exactly coincided with the preparation of our special anniversary issue, in which we were joined by a girls' school, perhaps we should withhold judgment on the depth of his devotion to journalism."

His mother, the President explained solemnly, kept things.

The clipping that Trixie Little was standing on the kitchen steps to thumbtack to the bulletin board was briefer than the event it reported. Under the headline, "Press Women Elect," Ann's pictured face looked cool—and as austere as the account that followed, which quoted from the most general of her remarks and offered a smidgeon of biography, and then closed with a one-sentence paragraph: "President Girard congratulated Miss Taswell in a brief, off-the-record address that brought laughter and applause."

"Right up there—that's good," Sharlie directed. Trixie leaned on the thumbtack successfully and then climbed down.

"Ain't that just like her—she never said a word about it." Rosa shook her head over the mystery of Ann's taciturnity and then made for the other end of the kitchen to begin assembling dinner.

Sharlie was looking at the handful of papers she had taken down: last month's duty list; a December fuel oil bill on which Marian had written in red, "Everybody please note and keep basement door CLOSED. PLEASE"; a "Peanuts" cartoon featuring Pigpen and Charlie Brown in a contretemps relevant to a recurring problem between Peter and Dick Farland; and a full-page newspaper photo in uncertain color of the President and Mrs. Girard arriving for the Inaugural Ball. Sharlie walked slowly over to the trash basket and threw in everything except the picture, which she carried back. She stood, holding it at arm's length, and sighed.

"Oh my," said Trixie, joining her. "She sure looks like a princess. That's ermine. It's what princesses wear."

"Oh, don't be silly," Sharlie scoffed. "What's so great about Andy Girard?" She grinned suddenly. "All she's got is a million dollars and looks like a movie star—"

"And a rich, handsome husband."

"And a rich, handsome husband who's the most powerful man in the world. It said that in the paper," Sharlie argued, though nobody had disputed her.

Rosa said softly, "They both got education, too."

"You name it, they got it." Trixie sighed, studying the President's look of pleasure and his wife's openly joyous smile. "Anything she hasn't got, all she has to do is ask for it anyway."

Rosa pursed her lips but thought better of speech. Andrea Girard, she wanted to say to her daughter's envy, had probably risen earlier this morning than Trixie and would almost certainly work later than any grown-up Trixie; but there seemed no way, without getting herself dismissed as "square," to point out to the girls the effort and sacrifice that went into much of what they were admiring.

Sharlie planted a smacking kiss somewhere in the neighborhood of Alec Girard's white tie. "Oh face it, girl, face it," she advised Trixie breathlessly. "They're just the most."

"They are," said Trixie with an air of having just stumbled on the exact, perfect word, "absolutely positively finally the most."

Rosa looked from one of the ignorant, foolish, and beautiful little girls to the other. "Maybe. But look like it don't hurt you-all to remember: the most cost the most." She listened to the undeniably square sound of the words hanging on the kitchen air and then quickly, because she was afraid of being cast into outer darkness, added an offer of milk and cake. When they accepted, she sent them off to wash their hands, got out the remnants of the cake that had survived Dick's after-school snack, and then stood in front of the bulletin board to use the few minutes' interim for her continuing study of the list of Cabinet officers.

The exercise was part of the education Rosa had set herself to obtain because, as she reckoned it, none of the youngsters would listen to what she did know unless she also knew more about what kids learned in school and people read in the newspapers. It seemed strange that before she could say what she knew—that it was a good thing to cook and serve food to hungry people or that there was a fine feeling that came with doing what you ought to, whether it was paying your bills or cleaning up the kitchen for the night or just holding your tongue when you might needlessly hurt someone's feelings—she'd have to know what was going on in Congress. Yet that was more or less the way it was: if she didn't qualify, they dismissed her without hearing what she said; she became the loved but outgrown, and they got their advice on how to live from somebody more up-to-date.

So Rosa stood now with her hands on her hips, saying over and over the name of the new Secretary of Labor, whose department ran the employment office downtown known as "the state office" to the women in her neighborhood who repaired to it to pick up a day's cleaning work from time to time.

The next day the gently redoubtable First Lady reported to the mothers of its students that the play school could shortly be opened on a three-days-a-week basis. In a few weeks the facilities would be ready for the full-time five-morning routine, but meanwhile children, teachers, and mothers would have a chance to try things out. Marian promptly passed this on to Rosa, who had been the recipient of most of Peter's "Is it time yet?" queries; they were as steady and wearing as water dripping on stone, and Rosa's, "Glory be," represented truly prayerful thanks to a delivering Providence. Marian laughed and said she still hadn't figured out how to manage Peter's transportation, but she would chauffeur him on the first day and after that she'd have another day to work something out.

However, on the red-letter February morning, Will Farland announced abruptly that he would need the car after all. Marian opened her mouth, closed it at once, and after a long moment managed to express, tight-lipped, a hope that he could at least manage to drive Peter and his mother down to the White House. With the faintly injured air of a reasonable man unjustly taken for an unreasonable one, Will acceded.

Marian dressed with extra speed to allow time for negotiations concerning Peter's homeward journey at noon. By the time Farland shut his wife and youngest child into the car, an emergency commitment had been obtained from Rosa's brother-in-law, Claude Jones, to pick up Peter in his taxi. But it had been necessary to telephone the sleeping Claude, who worked nights; it would be necessary to notify the school, so that Claude could be passed through the White House gates; and it would cost a couple of the few dollars that remained of the household funds this close to the end of a pay period.

Peter, an observant child, noted during the trip that no words were addressed by his mother directly to his father and that those she addressed to him were on the gushy side; their tone of rather stagy sweetness might have caused him some worry about what to expect at the school if he hadn't seen instantly that he wasn't the cause of her behavior. Nevertheless, he was unsettled enough to allow Marian to hold his hand when his father let them out of the car and, though he disengaged himself prudently before meeting the teacher or any of his fellow-students, he checked to make sure that his mother was somewhere nearby anyhow.

His chauffeuring done, Will drove up Pennsylvania Avenue into Georgetown, sticking to the heavily traveled thoroughfares so as to benefit by traffic lights set to aid the rush-hour drivers going in the opposite direction. Canal Road was one way heading downtown at this hour, so he took MacArthur Boulevard, a wide street with a dividing strip of withered winter grass. On the other side, autos by the hundred crept and dashed, maneuvering around buses veering like water bugs on the surface of a pond, but Will's side enjoyed almost a Sunday emptiness: he passed only one bus, filled largely with the dark faces of Negro maids headed for the Maryland suburbs. By the time he turned onto Chain Bridge, the subtle sense of privilege that invests the driver proceeding at will—while, across the median, others wait and inch and wait again—had begun to lay a certain peace over his nerves. When he arrived at Jake Ruffing's house just across the river, he still looked unhappy, but not worried.

But, less than half an hour later, Jake was looking very worried. "The only thing is, it's so soon." He shoved his hands into the pocket of his plaid woolen bathrobe and stared moodily out at the tangle of trees that, though they were now only bare purplish smudges against the leaden sky, still kept the road and its Washington-bound bumper-to-bumper traffic an invisible abstraction.

"It took exactly one week for the old hands to set up a handy bypass arrangement," Will said urgently. "You understand, Jake, Morris works hard— he's there early and he stays late. But as I say, he's forest-minded—and meanwhile, they're planting the same old trees exactly where they used to plant them. Those trees grow very fast indeed—by the time Girard feels it's time to take a look at the ground, there'll be full-grown thickets in his way." Will handed a State Department form over Jake's desk. "He's a nice fellow, Jake —friendly. 'Call me Lloyd.' And even imaginative. And he's found some good people—"

"Which was what he was made Undersecretary for, principally."

"Sure. But the department's first Undersecretary has administrative duties —which, I gather, is why I was made his Special Assistant."

Jake sat down at his desk and studied the paper. "Teach him, for God's sake."

"I can't, Jake. I tried, but he was just kindly tolerant of my nitpicking." Will nodded at the paper. "By now, I don't even get much chance. That little move went around us entirely, for example. We're indebted to Jim McGrath, who's an old friend of mine, for any knowledge of it at all. He sent it up to my office—a 'routing mistake,' you understand. Except that my secretary is no fool, and Jim knows it. She knew it didn't get to us by accident."

Jake studied the paper, a routine State Department "housekeeping" order that put a Middle East office staff at the disposal of the expert who had been persuaded by Lloyd Morris to survey and report to the President on a recurring difficulty. Jake's eyebrows went up as his gaze traveled down to the final numbered paragraph. "What's this mean—'Funds will be allocated under'—a whole string of numbers?"

"Nitpicker," Will told him almost happily. "What it means is that the new guy is effectively hamstrung. Because when the funds come from that string of numbers what comes along is a prescribed order and routine—for one thing, it means he'll have to deliver a summary of his report over there, before he sends anything back here, and by a stipulated date. After that, of course, if the boys on the spot don't like it, or him, he'll be spending the rest of his time inside offices, dickering with Americans. Because, under the same order, he's also subject to review, security approval, and God knows what else." Will sighed. "Why go on? Eventually, he can get back to the President and whisper what he actually saw, I suppose—nobody's going to drop him in a river or shoot him. But it'll be damned eventually. And it'll be questionable whether he'll have had a chance to see anything."

"I take it there are freer ways of funding this guy's trip." Jake picked up a pencil.

"Well, McGrath knew it, didn't he?" Will saw the smaller man's poised pencil and questioning look and spelled Jim McGrath's name for him as he wrote. "This sort of thing goes on, you know, Jake. You have to expect it, certainly with a change of administration. I caught a few, the first week or so. But since then, Lloyd's made it clear that he doesn't want to be bothered with paperwork. So the bureaucrats obligingly route it around his office, and nobody has to be afraid that I'll pounce on it. It just never gets to us. You see—"

"I see, I see," Jake interrupted. "I get the goddam picture." He threw his pencil down. "What about Hoffman?"

"He's beating his way through the cobwebs as fast as they weave them around him," Will reported. "I hear. But his hands are full. And maybe tied? After all, he wasn't the one who appointed Lloyd Morris. Even if he knew, it would leave him in a rather sticky position." He waited, but Ruffing was silent. "Anyway, I've—uh—taken steps to see that he hears something, at least."

"I'll bet you have," Jake said matter-of-factly. "But nobody else, I hope to God. You know damn well any talk about this, just yet, would be . . . Remember, there was once a possibility of Morris's running for the nomination himself."

"All the frontrunners would've had to drop dead first."

"All right, but what I mean is, he's not without followers—noisy ones. If any of this gets out, there'll be a whoop and a holler that'll tie the President's hands." Jake's dark face was gloomy. "It's a good thing he takes bad tidings well. If I worked for Winkler, I'd be banished for bringing in news like this."

"I know what you mean," Farland said. "I find a good many of Lloyd's visions attractive myself, you know." He shook a cigarette out of a package. "But you haven't much of a chance of keeping it quiet. I'm not the only one who can see the waters rising."

"All right, all right. But meanwhile, you've got to keep your finger in the dike."

Will blew smoke. "I could get drowned," he said quietly. "I'm already more than a little wet, Jake—I'd hate to have a handwriting expert check Lloyd's signatures on some of the papers he was too busy theorizing to get around to one day and too lofty to notice the absence of the next morning. If you follow me."

"For Christ's sake, don't tell me."

"All right, I won't. But I'm running risks, and I lack protection. Assistant secretaries outrank me, you know."

"Girard pays his debts," Ruffing said.

"If he knows he owes them."

Jake looked at him expressionlessly for a moment, and then amusement and something like respect chased each other across his dark, impatient face. "Don't you trust me, Will?"

"You more than some." Farland crushed out his barely smoked cigarette. "But I've got dependents: wife and three, two dogs, the Credit Union. So I have to stick to what I'm good at, and trusting is not what I'm good at."

Jake pointed with his chin at the typewriter beside his desk. "Okay. Give it to me and I'll take it up to the White House today. You can put your thumbprint on it if you want." He opened the drawer of the desk and fished out some paper. Watching Will wind a sheet into the machine, he said quietly, "Look, I know there are easier things you could've done with your —er—observations."

"Less unlovely, anyhow." Will wiped nicotine-stained fingers across his eyes and down his narrow face. "Lloyd is a nice guy, and I haven't slept much, trying to decide how to dump my ugly burden." His long legs wrapped themselves around the legs of the typewriter table with the smooth familiarity of a cowboy mounting a horse. "I must say, I felt better once I'd decided to be a big boy for Girard and Country."

"We've got a President now who's a big boy himself." Jake got up and offered to go forth and demand coffee of his wife. But he turned back as Farland began to type rapidly with three fingers. "Will."

"Sir?"

"This is just to ease your mind. Morris will kick and scream, of course, and it's going to be difficult to get him to leave without pulling down the temple walls—"

"It'll mar the honeymoon, all right," Will interrupted. "You'll have to find some fancy way to kick him upstairs, I guess. I'm glad it's not my headache."

"Don't be too sure it won't be." Ruffing brushed this aside. "But what I wanted to tell you is, Alec may not be as surprised as you think. At the convention, he was a little unhappy with Lloyd Morris's foreign policy recommendations. For, as it seems to have turned out, exactly the right reasons: he thought they were too much vision and not enough 'how.' "

Will had heard this from Gil Kimball the preceding July and had taken it into account in deciding on this morning's move. He smiled broadly. "Thanks, Jake. It helps, a lot."

Two hours later, stoked with Bonnie Ruffing's fresh coffee and blueberry muffins, he arrived at his office whistling cheerfully. His secretary followed him into his office and rattled off the few facts needed most immediately, like a first officer giving the captain the ship's position: Mr. Morris had liked the speech fine and was now, at this minute, sitting on the platform at the Americas Society, waiting to deliver it. Mr. Kimball had called, and so had Milt Mannering of the *Washington Herald*. She saw Will's alert look at that and added that no, she didn't think it was anything but routine fishing. "And, Mr. Farland? You remember you said yesterday that if I wanted to take a little extra time at lunch?"

Will remembered, as she did too, that what he had actually said was that maybe she ought to take time off for a nice long lunch with her old friend on the seventh floor. Her old friend was Harold Hoffman's secretary and had been his predecessor's, and represented the "steps"—to insure that the Secretary of State heard of the problems his first deputy was creating—

that Will had mentioned to Jake Ruffing. He smiled at his secretary and told her to have a ball, he wouldn't do anything while she was gone that she couldn't undo, and then he propped his feet up and inquired how the old friend liked her new boss. His secretary told him without any expression in her face or voice that her friend was finding Mr. Hoffman very interesting to work for because he seemed so at home in a big organization. "He's quick to pick things up," she said sweetly. "And grateful for helpful suggestions." She reminded Mr. Farland that he had a meeting with Commerce at two o'clock; in case she hadn't returned by then, she'd leave the material he would need.

As she left Will smiled, took his feet down, and dialed the *Washington Tribune.* He gave the art department's extension and received only half a dozen fruitless brrrs in return. He was about to hang up when something clicked and an impersonal voice said that phone didn't answer and who was calling, please?

"This is Marian's husband, Pearl," said Will, recognizing the voice through its uncharacteristic formality.

"Oh, hi, Mr. Farland. She had to do a news story today—some artist suicided. But I was supposed to take her calls in case it was something about the little boy. That's not what you called about, is it? The city desk could probably find her if—"

Will said no, never mind, thanks; then he added that she might tell Marian, if she would, that he would be going home on time tonight, he thought, and would pick her up unless he heard from her. He exchanged another few words with the cheerful Pearl, who was—like Marian—a working mother, and who had been helpful before with the small emergencies resulting from the coexistence of a job and three children. When Will hung up, he lavished a moment of contemplation on the record of Marian's "arrangements." It really was not possible to go into the technical detail with his noisily unpolitical wife; but, thus far, he had clocked examples of her use of ententes, détentes, pacts, alliances, and covenants.

Even as her husband sought her, Marian was concluding a new diplomatic maneuver—her slickest, too, for all that it was impromptu. And hurried, for she was late to work: it had taken Peter a while to verify that Elizabeth Girard was indeed, as advertised, a fellow-student in the new school. Marian had remained in the vicinity, like a sort of social security card, until her son established himself—which he manifested by suddenly giving her a look that not only sent her on her way but very nearly denied any acquaintance with her.

By the time she got to her office the broken body of Gaston Martigny had already been fished from the sea cove into which, it seemed clear, the French painter had hurled himself from a rocky ledge far above. The wire story was only bare facts, and cautious about saying it was suicide, for there had been no note; the *Tribune*'s own library had yielded clippings of reviews of his work but only a very little biographical information, and most of that was about recurring quarrels in the French intellectual community on how to—or whether to—punish Martigny for alleged collaboration with the Germans during the Occupation. This had been held as a shirttail for the wire story, just in case the *Tribune*'s art critic didn't show up.

When she did, she found herself ordered, in her capacity as a writer, to produce a page-one story and a longer evaluation for the obituary page; as an editor, she would have to make hasty plans for a full-page piece in the Sunday "brains section" (designed for readers believed to be willing to read longer and deeper) and for the accompanying illustrative matter—always loosely called "art," but in this case probably consisting of some. As a reporter, it was incumbent on her to get statements from officials and acquaintances of the late great, as well as to dig up and bring back to the nest such information useful for allocating newspaper space as plans for memorial services and commemorative exhibits. This triple demand, coming on the first day of Peter's school, easily rated as adding up to a fair-sized crisis-type day, and a late start wasn't any help. Ingenious, corner-cutting "arrangements" seemed indicated.

Phil Colby of the *Herald* was already talking to the French Embassy's press attaché when Marian Farland of the *Tribune* arrived. Colby crowed a little about that as they emerged, each with scribbled notes and a glossy photograph of the late Martigny. In their shared cab, Colby expounded on how this sort of front-page, stop-the-presses bit separated the dilettantes from the Guild rank and file. Marian took this with such meek good grace that his conscience seemed to smite him: as the taxi drew up before the *Tribune* building, Colby offered to take her to lunch—and maybe he could give her a hand, his apologetic voice said behind the words. Marian bestowed a brilliant and undiscriminating "Last Duchess" smile on Colby and the driver alike and trilled, as she stepped from the cab holding a swirl of skirts with a graceful hand, that it was terribly sweet of him but unfortunately she had someone probably waiting in her office right now. Paul Morisot, as a matter of fact, she added liltingly—and then nodded at Colby's unspoken inquiry: yes, Morisot was going to do a piece for Sunday for her. She paused, yearning for a bracelet that would tinkle, and then added, "Isn't that divine?" Fighting giggles, she fled to the busy shelter of the snack bar, where she ate something that tasted like cardboard and washed it down with some warm blown water while she threw a few notes together.

"The first thing they always scream is, you're riding on your tail," Ann Taswell had once said bitterly of her male competitors; the echo of her friend's complaint troubled Marian as she rode up in the elevator. She wrestled with the charge, which seemed possibly justified in this case—at least in the sense that she suspected that Phil Colby had also attempted to reach Morisot this morning. However, there were a couple of howevers, Marian told herself quickly. For one thing, Colby had a wife to take care of inconveniently timed school debuts. For another, Marian had it from

Andy Girard that Paul thought Marian a more perceptive critic than Colby, and preference based on merit was above reproach. And in any case, she argued as the elevator door parted for her and she started down the narrow back corridor, her relations with the French sculptor were probably not what Ann had meant by her unlovely phrase. She slowed without thinking about it and glanced over her shoulder to make sure all the doors of the quiet rooms in which editorial writers sat and thought were shut; then she bent and smoothed one sheer stocking along her leg and tightened the garter to keep it that way. Her relations with Morisot were—disturbing, she admitted as she straightened her slip and smoothed her skirt. But the disturbance predated and was irrelevant to this simple business arrangement and therefore didn't matter: whatever her relations with Morisot, they weren't sexual, and they certainly weren't going to become so for the sake of the *Tribune.*

Twenty-three

Paul Morisot had a clear idea of his tribal responsibilities in relation to the death of Gaston Martigny—to dress soberly, speak eulogies, and defend the reputation of the departed—and he was prepared to carry them out. The painter had been no father-figure, but represented something closer to an Emeritus Professor, controversial and towering, who had once occupied the chair Morisot held now; thus, the sculptor's own feelings were comfortably approximate to those duty required him to express publicly. But, if he was not in emotional disarray over either the death or its demands on him, Morisot had nevertheless a private problem, which he had not yet had time to solve perfectly, with the most troublesome of emotions—the guilty rapture of survival that follows on a death in one's own ranks. Paul knew this phenomenon well, and what was more, he knew he knew it—because, for reasons that had nothing to do with Martigny, the sculptor had recently been giving much thought to the lessons of his past. Long ago, an imperfectly understood impulse to celebrate upon the body of a woman the cruel joy of being alive when others had fallen in combat had led Morisot—who had not ceased to be a *bourgeois* when he became a guerrilla—to an inadvisable marriage. By now, the lesson was, at last, absorbed. But even if it had not been, or if his logic had been overcome by this morning's surge of survivor-passion, he was far too quixotic to allow it to affect Marian Farland, who was certainly the last woman in the world he would make love to with any implied stigma of generalization or impersonality. That he was there in Marian's office, turning from his survey of her bookshelves as she came in, was proof that he possessed both the intent and the capability of control of wandering impulses; otherwise, he never would have consented to help her out of her editorial dilemma.

Marian was startled when she saw him: he was so impeccably clad, so trimly pressed and snowy-linened, that she trembled on the edge of tagging him "dapper." And then, immediately, she saw that that wasn't the difference, that something had been added besides the distinguished-mourner costume. Up to now, their meetings had always been marked by gaiety, lurking even in the grave, intent look with which Paul watched her being cute over luncheon tables. But now it was suddenly gone, and the reason he was not dapper was that he was a little terrifying. She put out her hand, as the lady should when greeting the gentleman, and said "Paul, this is so good of you" before she went on, briefly, about how she was sorry to be late— which was all the way things were supposed to be. And then she stopped, because he hadn't said it wasn't good of him or that he didn't mind her being late, or anything else he was supposed to say. He hadn't, as a matter of fact, said anything at all—and yet something frightening was happening to her, and the gentle man she had thought she knew was a stranger.

He was not, of course: it was only that he was not the same man this morning as the one who for some time had been politely grounding the electricity between them so as not to alarm the lady. And if he was correct in his estimate that he could not be shaken into impulsive action, he was still, as he took her hand, unexpectedly shaken enough to forget both niceties and his customary disguise. Thus she was seeing, first, what had not been there before, a need for reassurance that didn't normally live in him and was quite momentary—and second, the enormous, encompassing hunger for her that had always been there, but under wraps. Now, abruptly, he had forgotten everything but stuffing his eyes with her as a starving man might stuff bread into his mouth, and then going back to taste more slowly. Meanwhile, he went on holding her hand—not shaking it or kissing it but just holding it, with his thumb moving a little over it in the small stroking by which he learned absentmindedly the shapes of coffee cups.

Well, that tears *that*, Marian said to herself, abandoning all her pre-entry ruminations with hardly a regret. She tried to keep it light, commanding herself sternly not to stick her bosom out like a goddam movie starlet; then she tried to keep it romantic, devoting her attention to the way his dark hair curled crisply away from his temples. And then, with a sudden clear sense of her own hunger, she simply let him assuage his.

Though she could never have let herself know it, her undoing was largely a legacy from her years with the hungry man Will Farland. For, so long as Morisot only wanted, he was not different from a good many other men she met, and she could successfully keep him classified as an unanalyzed "disturbance"; it was only to a needy man, not just a wanting one, that she was accustomed to responding as a lover. So now, as she gave up in one crackling instant all her defensive vows, pretenses, and poses, she had no idea why. But it was shockingly clear to her that if he took a notion to make love to her right here, right now—amid the glassy walls with the wastebasket probably in the way—he would run into no objection of any kind. And he knew it: she saw, besides the hunger in his eyes, a huge delight and a little flicker of fear; it occurred to her (quite accurately) that he might be afraid he *would* take a notion.

It was all over in a moment, actually. Morisot was a strong and stubborn man, and he had decreed; Marian was a woman who yielded, to edicts as well as to impulses. So she didn't rebel when he smiled—a very slow, very sad smile that effectively grounded the troublesome electric charge. She didn't understand all the causes of his resignation (one of which—probably the cause of the smile—was a wry realization that he had had it with any other woman from now on); but she knew all she needed to know for the moment. She said "Paul" on a faint note of reminder, to wake him to the fact that he was still holding her hand. If she was afraid now, though, it was not of what he might do but of what he might be.

"Marian, Max says this is the best he can do with the Gallery prints without color. He wants you to look at it right away and—" Grant had been talking as he came in, which gave the pair in Marian's office a moment to disengage their hands. But Grant still seemed to find their pose a little disconcerting. "I'm sorry. I didn't know—"

Marian, wondering vaguely where she was getting it from, produced enough aplomb to present the copyboy to Monsieur Morisot, who was going to do a memoir on Martigny for Sunday. Then she spread the pictures on her desk and leaned over them, concentrating on making the least unsatisfactory choice among a number of unsatisfactory possibilities. At least until color photographs could be processed, which would take several weeks, poor Martigny's farewell appearance would be less than he deserved. "Oh, I wish we could do better. These are so—muddy-looking." She stirred them with her forefinger as distastefully as though the mud were literal; but she also regarded with equal distaste the nice clean glossy photo of the painter that had been supplied by the Embassy.

"Max wasn't happy," Grant reported. "But you know if he says that's the best—"

"I know. Max can do anything," Marian said to Paul. She laid the protective sheet of copy paper over the photographs and clipped them together. "Except maybe miracles." She held the packet out to Grant. "Tell him thanks, but I'll have to think of something else. We've got to have pictures, but I don't guess we really have to commit a crime to get some."

"I have a photograph of Martigny," Paul said. "Would this be of aid?" He produced an expensive but battered-looking wallet from the inside pocket of his impeccable coat and Marian, waiting while he thumbed through its contents, smiled at this unexpected view of the man who would probably go on carrying the same wallet until somebody gave him another fine new one for some Christmas. He held out a snapshot, brownish at the edges. "Is it possible, perhaps, to divide this—so? And reproduce only this half?"

Looking more than ever like a large, ungainly bird feeding among marsh grasses, Grant bent to study the picture over Marian's shoulder. The snapshot was clear, which was promising, but it was crowded. Paul might have a point, however—for Martigny, a big man with a face that looked hewn of some rough stone, stood over at one side, almost by himself. Marian and Grant reached simultaneously for papers on the desk and laid them on the picture to experiment with possible croppings.

"Hey, we get leg art for the same price," Grant said, and Marian noticed for the first time that the white blur of legs appearing over the painter's shoulder belonged to a girl sitting on a ladder; the dark robe draped over her shoulders in no way interfered with her otherwise total nakedness. Marian took the framing papers away and looked at the picture as a whole for the first time: at its center was a rather amorphous sculpture, a huge stone of the general shape of a woman with a hand on her hip and an empty oval for a head. Through the hole created by the crook of her arm was thrust the head and upper torso of a much younger and somewhat tousled Morisot; he held a tilted wine bottle from which he was pouring a steady and apparently accurate stream into the open mouth of a bearded man in a sweater, who was clinging to the statue near its base. A small dark woman in a dancer's rehearsal leotards was sitting on the floor below the drinker; her arms were clutched about her bent knees, her head was flung back and her mouth open, and she appeared to be lending nothing to the proceedings but laughter.

At the other side of the hulking statue, though, Martigny was clearly not amused. He stood with his feet planted firmly and one hand on his hip, not unlike the statue except that he had another hand, which appeared to be steadying the ladder, and a face, on which was written a light disdain and some impatience. The girl on the ladder was craning forward, apparently to see around the statue; her breasts hung ripely, the toes of one of her bare feet were curled around the ladder, and what was visible of her face under the forward fall of long hair wore something of the look of a mother hoping the boys weren't going to tear their pants climbing around on the stone.

"Yours?" Grant asked, and Marian looked up with interest in the answer, for she thought she had recognized the bearded man as the painter Alphonse Lenard. Which made Paul the most likely perpetrator of the statue, but it was hard to believe he was responsible for it; it said nothing and *was* nothing, really, except a massive cliché of the once-fashionable mannerisms of sculpture.

Paul said, "No, no," in some surprise and then laughed and shook his head to make the point again.

Marian saw now that Grant was pointing at the naked woman, and she smiled for his bright eyes and the faint pinkness in his cheeks and the vision of "artists and models in Paris" that lay behind them.

"That one . . ." the Frenchman hesitated, fishing for a word, and then grinned happily. "She is my buddy's chick."

Marian heard the stifled choking sound Grant made and spoke quickly to cover it, though her own lips twitched with suppressed laughter. "Why don't you take this down and see whether Max can get enough of the naked lady out so it'll be suitable for a family newspaper? Monsieur Morisot will want this back, so they'll have to make their own negative first."

"It need not be returned," Morisot said quickly. "Only—please, nothing will appear except Gaston?"

Marian looked again at the laughing girl in the leotards and didn't need to ask, "Yours?" Whoever she was, she was Paul's, all right—or had been, many years ago, and he didn't want to keep her picture any more. Or didn't need it? Wishing fiercely that she either didn't want to know or dared to ask, Marian sighed and looked up—and read on the copyboy's face the unmistakable sneer of youth, in which disappointment is always so heartbreakingly apparent. Poor Grant. He had almost had a hero, a wine-and-women Bohemian for his fantasies; and then it had run smack into the ideals of political-science-major Grant, who saw his almost-hero first fraternizing with a Nazi sympathizer and then trying to avoid being publicly identified with him. "It's the statue," she said quickly to the boy, without stopping to think. "He doesn't want the statue—" She broke off, belatedly aware of the discourtesy of this public psychoanalysis.

But Paul was smiling at Grant. "I have learned," he said quietly. "I have already paid once for this folly." He glanced down at the picture and began to tell them about Martigny, then an established artist—no friend of the younger Morisot, but dutiful toward talent. He had come and surveyed the statue in silence, while the sculptor waited, surrounded by his friends. "Alphonse and his model came in, bringing wine, a necessity for whatever the verdict would be," Paul was explaining.

And the girl in the foreground, Marian thought? She looked at the slim body in its revealing costume—another necessity for whatever the verdict would be? The verdict was clear in Martigny's face, though it had obviously been rendered before the picture was taken; Marian sternly put away speculation on what had happened after.

"He said, 'Why do you wish to imitate your inferiors?'" Morisot sighed. "It was a good help, and I remember for a very long time. But I do not believe I need it any more. You comprehend?"

Marian looked down at Gaston Martigny's disapproval again and understood it better: there was shock in it at this youthful mocking of art, which, good or bad, was nevertheless holy in the big man's eyes. The young men cavorted, and Martigny, neither funloving nor girl-loving but only and exclusively art-loving, watched them briefly before leaving them to their nonsense and going back to work.

Marian handed the photo over to Grant and watched him twist his way out of the cluttered room. Paul must have gone back to work, too. Soon and faithfully and eventually successfully—at least so far as his work was concerned. Whether he had entirely surmounted the loneliness that might be the

price of what he had made was another question: he was a good man who
imitated no one any more, who loved and was loved by others; but he
must be almost forty, and he had neither wife nor child. He had worshiped
the muse devoutly, if not as devoutly as Martigny, who would not stay to
play. Yet Martigny, at fifty, had ended on the edge of a cliff on a bright,
sparkling morning when the solstice was come and gone and all the rest of
the world was almost certain of spring.

"Paul?" He turned from his examination of her office, which he seemed
to want to know in every detail. "Paul, is it certain that Martigny killed
himself? I mean, there was no note."

Morisot spread his hands. "If to live is insupportable, what should there be
to write?" He looked at something that was not in the room with them,
and when he spoke his voice was gentle. "He was a man with only one
wealth. When that was gone, he was too poor to live. Gaston fought bravely,
Marian. Perhaps he prayed. But it was gone from him, and he could not
make it return. Surely you know that he tried, most earnestly."

Marian nodded, thinking first of the clear, pure line and quintessential
color with which Martigny had begun to change a whole world's way of
painting and then of the swaggering embarrassments he had offered in the
last few years. A new work by Martigny could not be ignored; but it had
been for her as for other critics a painful exercise to point out how far
short of that early exquisite simplicity each new rigid slashing canvas was.
But, yes, Martigny had tried. Right up to the end. Marian saw suddenly how
important this fact was to Morisot, product of a society whose ideal of
prouesse demanded not success but the valor to try, against terrible odds if
need be. The boyhood hero of both Morisot and Martigny had been, probably, the legendary Roland, who would not blow his horn to save himself
because his comrades would be summoned into danger . . . But Marian was
a product of a pragmatic land, and a tenderhearted woman as well. "Maybe
if he hadn't been so alone," she said. "I mean, there we were, all saying
discouraging things—"

"I dislike to be insulting, *Madame*, but critics do not kill artists. They
wound us in the pocket sometimes, but no more than that."

"Never in the heart?"

"It is more difficult than you think. I myself have been scarred by some
attacks." His hand slashed downward obliquely across his chest, beginning
high at the shoulder, in a dramatic demonstration; Marian, an opera lover,
appreciated and smiled. "Even directly over the heart," Morisot said, and
shrugged. "One loses some blood and then one heals, yes?"

Yes, if one has the friends and the girl and whatever else one needs,
Marian thought. And everybody's respect. "If he hadn't collaborated during
the war," she said. "It set everybody against him so."

" 'Everybody,' " Morisot said shortly, "is a fool. Gaston collaborated with
no one, all his life." He looked at her in silence. "Do you not see?" His
voice said she must. "It was of no concern to him who managed countries, in

what uniform. He could not be troubled to resist—it was more important to work."

"But you cared—"

Paul made a sound of mild disgust. "I was only a boy. They take me, they—" he mimed rapid cuffs and straight-arm blows, all as contemptuous as they must have been painful "—and they send me to a prison to stay for I do not know how long. At first, I am ashamed. And then . . ." He shrugged. "Young men, most certainly young men who have not yet been . . . reassured . . . by women, cannot endure to be for long on the bottom of the world. So they must make a fight."

Marian suppressed a smile. Virginity—and most delicately put, too—was an ingenious explanation of heroism, but she didn't quite believe it. For one thing, she knew from Andy Girard that Paul had got married at some point before the final end of the war in Europe—so presumably he had gone on resisting even after being "reassured." For another, she suspected him of being a veritable, certifiable hero on many counts and not all of them in the past; from hints she had heard today, she gathered that Morisot would find his future affairs marching more easily if he were willing to cooperate with the desire of some of his country's bureaucrats to sweep Gaston Martigny under a convenient rug. "I don't think you could've been like Martigny, even when you were a boy," she said.

"That is my hope," Paul said quietly. "But how do I know? Gaston was already at work, but I was only a soldier still. Perhaps I also would have said to them, 'Do anything you please, but leave me to work.' When one cannot know, one should not condemn."

A social scientist might have noted with interest this glimpse of a certified war hero who apparently thought of soldiering as an activity for boys. But Marian was drawing conclusions, this time, about the man rather than his society. *I* can know, she said with certainty, if without science, to the judge who waited in her mind. Paul could not have been like Martigny, ever—because men who care, and take risks, don't get that way suddenly. As if a door had opened on a tableau, she saw how he had been waiting, at the painful cost of the long absence from his home and his work, standing out in the open with nothing to hide his guilt behind, gambling everything, while she had a whole structure of responsibilities and obligations to protect her. Because if he was free to love as she was not, she was also armored against loss as he was not; her loss could be painful, but his could be total. He was a brave man, but it was a bad cause, she said to herself with her lips trembling a little: what could be said for a love that, if it was not denied, would deprive so many, would disrupt and molest duty and all other loves?

She looked up at him suddenly, with all this knowledge in her eyes. His face tightened, closing over all expression, and his body stiffened too, the shoulder hunched, the arm bent and guarding; as he took a step toward her, he looked very like a boxer who has taken enough punches and now means to carry the fight to the other fellow.

"Don't, Paul, please." It was an unthinking response to a perception rather than to any knowledge, and equally unthinkingly, she added, "Not now." And then she stood there, staring in horror at the shameless admission and the pleasure in his eyes that told her he had not missed it.

He had dropped his guard at once: his ringless hands swung loose and empty at his sides. "I am sorry to trouble you so," he said gently. He seemed to think that was an explanation; certainly it was also dismissal. "And now, we must work, yes?" He eyed her typewriter, from which a tongue of paper stuck out, and asked whether she had another machine so he could start. "I must attend a gathering at which it will be decided how sad France may suitably be for Gaston." He indicated his somber garb. "But—I have an hour yet." He looked more cheerful at that thought.

Marian regarded sourly this foreigner to both her language and her trade who proposed to tackle a Sunday piece with such insouciance. He was really too much—she flattened her hands on the desk so she wouldn't slap him. And then she looked down at her hands and acknowledged that what she really wanted to slap him for was, simply, showing up too damned late. And if he was "sorry" to trouble her, that it troubled her was all he was sorry for, it was clear. It was also clear that he had no intention of ceasing to trouble her. She threw him a black look, but Grant saved him then by appearing suddenly to report that the picture had been approved—with heartfelt thanks for the contribution to their naked-lady collection—by Photography. Marian consigned M. Morisot to the copyboy, to be led to a typewriter, and then turned back to her own, for it was out of the soap opera and into the salt mines. Will Our Gal Friday Get This 700 Words Done on Time? was the question for today's episode, not Is She Falling in Love with Paul Morisot?

She typed with every appearance of industry for a while and then let her hands fall and swiveled her chair away from the machine. Nothing was gained by telling herself fairy stories: there was little point in worrying about whether she had fallen in love with Paul, and soap opera would never be a good medium for practical questions like how to stop things right here. She knew the answer to How Can Our Gal Friday Stay Out of Bed with Paul? all right. You did it by erecting whatever defenses you had—in this case, time and inertia and distance—and then you bloody well stayed behind the barricades. The whole thing wasn't her line of work; but she was going to have to do it, and Paul was clearly not going to help her. She saw herself running, twisting through a forest by taking advantage of whatever she found growing there, until she reached—what? The broad plains of virtue?

No, but until he had no more time. She knew from the way he talked of his home in the spring that even if his work didn't make him run out of time here—and how could she cope with *that* guilt, on top of all the others?—the coming of spring would, and it wasn't all that far away. Meanwhile, he'd probably have to fly back to Martigny's funeral: if Martigny was officially snubbed, it would become a matter of honor for Morisot to appear, with all his medals clanking, as chief public mourner. So then maybe he'd be gone for, say, a week. Which would be one week that was safe. And then, the week after, she'd have the curse—now *there* was a handy rescue. And then there was the still open question of whether Dick's troublesome tonsils would have to come out . . . With the help of menstrual periods and tonsils, she could, with luck, remain an honest woman, safe from his predatory wiles until she was sprung by spring.

Hah. That decided, she set to work fiercely, hammering at the typewriter that could be safely punished for times out of joint and other sins of passage. But when she read over the last, unfinished sentence of the review she'd been working on, it became clear that not only her morals were shot, but also her prose style. She stared for several seconds at the muddy gibberish she had produced before she yanked the paper-and-carbon package from the typewriter and tossed it at the trashbasket. If this was what virtue was going to mean, it was hardly worth it.

By the time Paul came in, neat and unruffled and well within his allotted time, she had thrown out two more tries; and if the coolly businesslike gesture with which she waved him to a chair required effort, it was only because she would have preferred something more violently hostile . . . And then she read what he had written, and after that she first wanted to shout and then couldn't stop smiling: Gaston Martigny was beautifully, exactly revealed, in a graceful prose that simply celebrated and mourned the man, and neither because of nor in spite of anything at all. Gratitude for Martigny's gift to the world glowed in the words, and an ache for his pain shone like a benevolent light over the truthful description of the terrible, futile efforts of his last years. A man is only a man, was the message that awaited the reader: this man, who did some wrong, was a cad and a coward and also a pioneer and a sufferer, loved no one enough and so was loved by no one enough, and left what he had to leave; we need not admire him but we must respect him because he did, always, the best he could. As a statement, it was loving and wise. And if it was nearly unbelievable that any piece of writing so simple and complete could have been done so quickly and coolly, no editor in his right mind would have laid a finger on it.

Its author knew he had done well, Marian saw, looking up from the paper with her eyes a little wet to tell him, in answer to his question, that everything was spelled right. If it wasn't she would tend to it later—now, it was not possible to do anything at all but keep looking at this man who stood before her to take his leave. He waited for her dismissal so he could go to his "gathering," because he did what he had to do, this dark and neat and very nearly dapper ex-brigand, perfectly correct except that he was wearing the same smile she couldn't make go away either. He looked too happy to have to see her cry, so Marian made him go away.

And then she put her head down on her desk and, like a tired fighter waiting for the bell, concentrated on hanging on until the next small rescue.

Only, if he didn't have to go to France, she thought wearily, traitorously, she'd just better get the curse early this time.

By the time she had finished cramming into the remaining few hours of the working day the chores she should have had all day to do, the resulting resentment, plus ordinary fatigue, had done a great deal to resolve Marian's distress: what had been temptation at two o'clock became, by five-thirty, to all practical purposes unimaginable. As she left her office to meet Will, he was an image of sanity and safety, a tall bulwark of morality seen in the extra glow of his wife's guilt feelings and his unwitting role as innocent victim.

An objective observer might have guessed that there was no way in which Will Farland could do anything but win that evening. But he managed to dissipate his advantage, beginning with the first moment he picked Marian up in front of the *Tribune* building. His bad temper was apparent at once, and his wife's unusually patient attempts to dispel it had no effect. Except possibly to increase his desire to talk about what was bothering him— which he did, at length and with bitterness, as they crept through the home-going traffic.

What it was all about, Marian gathered dimly, was that Lloyd Morris was still, or again, impossible. Will had bitched all through the Winkler years about "limited minds informed by McGuffey's Reader"; now, for reasons that were not clear, Lloyd Morris, a bright man and one of the nation's best-known liberals, was just as unsatisfactory. Morris and his down-to-earth, re-assuringly unglamorous wife had given a party for his staff as soon as they'd settled in: not only had Marian found him a friendly, likable, and thoroughly interesting man, but Will had also seemed to warm to him. But now dear Lloyd had become Mud—and apparently because he didn't con-sider the State Department's paperwork as holy as Will did. Marian glanced at the mask of fury that was Will's face and decided against saying that he seemed difficult to satisfy.

However, when he drew up at a traffic light and turned to her angrily, charging her with failing to listen, she was stung into reply. "I *am* listening. Only—if Mr. Morris thinks those papers aren't important enough to bother with, he may be right. You've been there a long time, and people get wedded to—"

"He is certainly, and maybe dangerously, dead wrong," Will interrupted. "Foreign policy is carried out by way of unimportant pieces of paper, for God's sake. This is the very point that Girard was one of the few guys smart enough to grasp: the gap between the policy stated in a President's formal address and the actuality that finally emerges. You can't just make a foreign policy. You also have to make it happen."

Marian's tolerance for being harangued was not high even when she was engaged in a deliberate attempt to find nothing but good in Will. Or maybe it was simply that violence begets violence: "You can say what you like, but what comes through smells of plain, old-fashioned disloyalty," she snapped. In her voice was a passion even she couldn't understand.

"Jesus Christ." Will closed his mouth obstinately and drove in the silence that is too angry for speech. But he couldn't quite make it all the way home. "Has it occurred to you," he burst out at last, "that if I say something exists, you might entertain the idea that it really does? Even if it doesn't coincide with your comfy schoolgirl notions?"

I am goddam sick and tired of having that "schoolgirl" thrown at me, Marian announced silently to a passing tree as the car turned the corner onto Mackintosh Place. "I'm afraid it hasn't," she said evenly. The blue spruce in the yard loomed ahead, a comfort in the bareness and a promise that there wasn't much longer to go; for the remaining few minutes, surely, she could behave.

Probably she could have, if Will had not chosen that moment to usurp the role of the adult partner rising above bickering. "You do remember, don't you, that we're having dinner with Oscar Bainbridge tonight? We'll have decent time for dressing, for a change." His voice was so controlled, so conspicuously willing to shelve the quarrel for reasons of superior rationality, that it left Marian no place to stand but petulance.

"I'm not going. You'll have to make my excuses. I have a headache." The moment the words were out, she developed a pounding headache.

Will's thin veneer of maturity splintered promptly. "Haven't you heard? Diplomatic headaches are old hat." He pulled the car into the driveway and set the brake, smiling nastily.

"Nevertheless, I imagine that you can manage to go ahead and spend an evening being 'sources close to the Administration' without any help from me and my schoolgirl mind."

"Undoubtedly. Perhaps I'd better start right now." Will leaned across and opened the door for her with a swift violent motion that bore signs of hasty diversion from an impulse to slap her.

"Perhaps. Thank you for the ride." She swung her legs out.

"It was really no pleasure."

"I must thank you again," she said witheringly, "for your courtesy."

His fair skin flushed. "I've told you before that I'm no gent. So don't count on being able to shove me around."

Marian was out of the car now. "I'm beginning to be more than a little bored," she drawled insolently, "by the 'I'm-just-a-rough-hewn-country-boy' bit." She turned away, her high heels uncertain on the frozen, rutted ground.

Will leaned from the window and said with hate, "The daughters of the rich have bored me for a very long time." He slammed the door that Marian had left open, then started the motor up noisily. She heard its wild roaring as she ran up the broad wooden steps, pounding them as though she had it in mind to stomp them to death. He was backing the car out of the driveway as she opened the door.

"Mom's home!" Sharlie sang out gaily from somewhere upstairs. "Hey, everybody, they're home!"

Dad had to go back to the office, Marian rehearsed hastily, leaning against the closed front door. She worked at arranging her face for the children, frantically as she heard the racket on the stairs above her. Finally she was ready—poised, smiling, sick with longing for the dream with which she had been at play, sick with hatred of Will because she stood here alone and it was all his fault.

Twenty-four

"Will did, too, leave work on time. It was one day last week, I think." Marian watched the soda bubbles dance in the highball Gil Kimball had just handed her. "I remember I circled the date on the calendar."

From upstairs came a wail: "Mom? I dropped a stitch!" Betty Kimball muttered something and disappeared. They heard her footsteps overhead briefly while Gil was explaining that his daughter had recently evinced a sudden desire to learn the womanly arts but was proving rather a clumsy student.

"What's she knitting?" Marian asked.

"A muffler," Gil said. "For Paul Morisot. He stayed with us during Inauguration, you know. And Rosemary fell in love with him." Gil smiled. "When my sister was her age, she fell in love with Nelson Eddy. If you live, things get better, don't they? After all, Paul sculpts good and he writes good —unless you ghosted that Martigny piece for him?"

"About a third of the way through, he made it 'singular' when he meant 'single-minded.' And, oh yes, there was one word that should have ended with 't-i-o-n' and he'd written 's-i-o-n.' "

"I thought so. Oh well, a Renaissance man, I guess—maybe he can design a flying machine too, for all we know. And a free spirit, living the simple life. No palaces—a studio and a little house and a woman to cook for him, back in his native village."

Marian jiggled her glass, sloshing bourbon dangerously, and considered an item she'd read in a syndicated gossip column that morning about this hero of the simple life, currently in New York to talk with an enterprising publisher who wanted him to write a book. "It seems to me I heard tell of a French actress, Aimée Something. Now playing in New York. Not cooking for Morisot, though. I think he's roughing it at the Algonquin."

"Is he going to do a biography of Martigny?" Gil's voice held envy.

Gil probably wouldn't get to write his precious biography of Senator Youngblood until the last young Kimball was through college, Marian thought sympathetically. "No. Notes for a commemorative thing of some sort, though." Martigny, it seemed, had a wife—and had apparently dropped in for two brief visits some years ago. The resulting children, Marian observed dryly, needed money Martigny had not provided, and Morisot seemed to feel some kind of tribal obligation.

"All right, so nobody's entirely a free man. Still, he has a choice—he can take time off to write a book, which is more than I can do."

"Maybe you could if you'd cut down Rosemary's wool money. Let Aimée knit the mufflers."

Gil looked at her curiously. "Why so bitchy?"

"I'm not, I'm just being a critic. Your portrait of a latter-day Thoreau sitting by a pond in southern France doesn't do for Morisot shooting his cuffs urbanely all day and painting New York with painted women all night."

"Oh for God's sake—you know how those gossip gals are: the guy goes in for a sandwich, he's night-clubbing. And this cookie he was with is a singer, with a press agent. Or maybe it's true—I wasn't awarding him the chastity prize." Nor was Morisot intended for it by Mother Nature, if credence could be placed in a somewhat envious remark dropped by Bill Bruyette. Gil wasn't above repeating cloakroom gossip from the Hill, which this technically was—but its origin was the locker room, which was out of bounds generally, and particularly with Marian, who could get awfully prudish awfully fast. Gil grinned at her silence. "Moralizing is an extension of editing, if you ask me," he said boldly to her averted face. "Live it up a little, and you won't correct other people's sexual grammar. Tell you what," he offered, "I'll even show you how. If we can start right away," he added prudently. "Before your husband shows up."

"I couldn't think of putting you to the trouble," Marian said. "Though Will's appearance is questionable for hours yet."

"Lloyd Morris didn't strike me as such a Simon Legree."

"Mr. Morris was probably home and in his slippers a long time ago. Will lurks in the office after Morris goes home. Maybe he's photographing documents to sell to the Russians."

"Cut it out," Gil said sharply. "That's not funny."

"I'm sorry. I'm just fed up, I guess." Secrecy isn't nice to live with even when it's not espionage, she thought rebelliously; there was something unknown, and maybe almost furtive, about Will's activities these days that made her want to run away into any sunshine. She looked at the leaping colors in the fireplace at the other end of the room, and the memory of Paul Morisot's dark eyes peering out from under the hood of a Western High School sweatshirt took all the warmth out of the fire. "This is the most wintry of Februaries, Gil," she said sadly.

"Oh, come on. Not with the offers you have, baby. Like now is the winter of your discontent made glorious summer by the son of Cork."

"Betty once told me your people came from Limerick," she said flatly.

Behind her smile, she wondered why she had never known a man well without his calling her "baby" sooner or later.

Kimball shook his head. "There's an example: haven't I told you my wife doesn't know the real me?"

"Nobody's told me that for hours." Marian stopped abruptly and turned to him with all the fooling gone from her voice. "Gil. You're such a very *nice* man." Her eyes were huge with something he didn't have time to understand because she reached up quickly and pulled his face down to hers and kissed his cheek.

"Holy jumping Jesus," Will said from the doorway.

Gil said primly, "You *might* knock."

"Sorry, old man. It was thoughtless of me. But Bert was going out just as I was reaching for the doorbell, so I forgot my obligations." Will fixed Marian with a stagy glare. "I don't mind your screwing around behind my back, but I've told you again and again, columnists carry *diseases.*"

"Bert was going out?" Gil asked. "Listen, did you see whether he took the car?"

Will addressed an invisible judge hovering somewhere off to his right. "Guy comes up out of the sewer after a hard day's work, finds his friend kissing his wife. Guy reproaches the guilty pair, and what happens? Wanton wife stands there giggling shamelessly. Red-handed lover calmly asks wronged husband for bulletin on whereabouts of his own neglected kid. I ask you." He lowered his severe look and impaled Gil on it. "Actually, Bert stepped into a small saucer-shaped vehicle and soared straight upward. I would've stopped to gawk but I didn't want to be late for the wife-swapping. Which reminds me. Where's my share? Betty!" He roared it so suddenly that Marian jumped. "On the double!"

"Wait a minute," Gil said. "I'll untie her."

Betty Kimball came into the living room carrying a highball glass in one hand and a bowl of nuts in the other. "I have it all ready for you, Will," she told him soothingly. "But you mustn't be so impatient. It's a sign you're getting addicted, when you can't wait." She tried to hand Will the glass, but he was bent over, shaking with laughter; startled, she turned to the others and found them equally dissolved. "What did I say? Gil, you stop that right away and tell me the joke. Marian!"

I *knew* it would get better, Marian told herself happily over her second drink. She lay folded into one of the chairs by the fire, with her legs draped over the arm and her shoes toppled on the floor beneath and listened dreamily to Betty's lively description of the parliamentary goings-on at one of Georgetown's pair of highly articulate and actively civic community organizations.

"So then this man got up and said if the gas station was allowed to put up a sign like that we might as well give up on Georgetown. He's the one who's always saying things like that, though, so nobody—Gil, what *is* that man's name? He lives on 28th Street. You remember him—he always gets the floor and makes those 'either-or' speeches . . ."

"Patrick Henry," Will said smoothly.

"Pat—oh, Will."

"As a matter of fact," Gil told him, "we have a Henry Clay, too. Though Georgetown's vying forces usually prove too much, even for a Great Pacificator who'd rather be right than President."

Marian said mildly that Betty made it sound very interesting, and fun, too, and that the men ought to direct their great satirical wits elsewhere.

"I'm not being satirical," Will objected. "Don't you remember, I told you on the way to the Inaugural Ball that we had proof right before our eyes that man was truly a political animal, even in conditions favoring anarchy?"

"You said a lot of things. It took us about two hours to cover a ten-minute distance. Hours of empty whiteness, like Antarctica." She thought of the strangely beautiful snowfall that had demolished all ends and beginnings; buildings with few, scattered lights grew suddenly and apparently at random out of a landscape without sidewalks, curbs, or streets. She had sat there, warm and protected in her ball finery, while Will wrestled their car past the stalled autos of the less skillful; once an abandoned bus, its lighted windows full of ranked hats and torsos, had appeared without warning as the Farlands' car crept up over the crest of a blind hill. Cursing wildly, Will wrenched the wheel and ran them into the safety of a bank of snow, while the bus faces and the bejeweled lady in the car stared at each other in equal helplessness. "Well, it was certainly anarchy," Marian admitted now. "But I don't know how political people were. Most of them just waited for rescue." She shuddered. "Or blew their horns maddeningly, like one fellow behind us when you and that other man were trying to get a stalled car out of the way."

"Every society has a couple of those," Will shrugged. "After a while, they run their batteries down and it shuts them up. But sitting still and waiting— what's wrong with that? Those people in the stalled buses, for instance— they're not citizens of a precarious South American republic, but of an ordered democracy. So they're not given to rushing into the street and rioting. They've got a whole history of proof that somebody in charge will show up to take care of things."

"Sooner or later," Gil amended.

"Okay. And you can add 'smoothly or with fumbles,' too. But if they don't like it, they'll vote out the guy in charge."

"Not in the District of Columbia," Betty pointed out.

Will sighed and exchanged a sympathetic glance with Kimball. "Okay, so residents of D.C. can't vote." He began to tell Gil of his impromptu traffic direction on that wild night, when he and another man had undertaken to unscramble a specific, one-block-long problem. "The interesting thing was, everybody obeyed us, though we had no authority at all, of course."

"What did you wear to the Home Rule luncheon?" Marian asked Betty.

Gil inspected the women in silence briefly before observing to Will that if *Lord of the Flies* was to be believed, the desire for organization was short-lived.

"Well, the real problem, of course, was a hat. I didn't want to wear a big one and seem pro-hat, but I couldn't find a real little one—"

"Oh, *Lord of the Flies*—I said organization, not a socialist heaven. And they were children, remember. Sure you need a level of competence to support the original urge—"

"Those almost invisible things on the back of your head, like Andy Girard wears—"

"And maybe a common enemy, like nature for the American frontiersman, or hostile Arabs for the Israelis. The snow on Inauguration Night represented—"

"Yes, what is it, Annabelle?" Betty asked. "What's the matter?"

All the crisscross of talk stopped at once. The heads turned toward the maid, framed in the arch leading to the dining room. "Miz Kimball," Annabelle said into the sudden silence. "They said it's the White House calling. They waiting for you to come."

Betty hesitated. "Are you sure they said *Mrs.* Kimball?" The maid nodded, big-eyed, and Betty rose swiftly and followed her to the kitchen.

"It's a gag," Gil said, without conviction, into the room's silence.

But it wasn't, Betty's look told them as she came in. "It was Andy, all right. She wanted to know, would we mind if they dropped in."

Marian looked at Will. "We'd better—"

Betty said quickly, "No, please. She asked whether we were busy, and I said you were here and we were all just sitting around. She said it sounded swell and could they come and sit around, too. She seemed so—well, wistful. I think she'd be hurt if you left."

"Oh. Oh, of course. Poor Andy. They haven't had much ordinary fun lately, I guess."

"Well, let's just not make any fuss, then," Gil suggested. "Okay?"

Okay, but carrying it out was something else again, Marian thought grimly a little later. The living room was too Grand Central, it had been decided, so they'd all moved downstairs to the recreation room. Which had more privacy, but also cheap and sturdy furniture meant to survive the children's parties. And where Marian, sitting like a lady with her shoes on and her legs crossed demurely at the ankle—as she had once been taught and now seldom remembered—peered into the dark of the laundry room in which the bulky washing machine loomed whitely and tried to think of a way to reassure Betty, who was unhappy about the pair of cheap black-and-white plastic chairs with black iron legs. "Let's just relax. Everybody knows this isn't your best furniture."

"Sure." Betty jumped up and began to smooth the cover on the studio couch so that the black and white and green stripes would be straight. She took a pile of *Congressional Records* off the homemade wooden coffee table and stood there with the journals in her hand until Marian got up and took them away from her and put them up on top of the battered upright piano, moving aside an old wine bottle with a few dried stalks of marsh grass sticking out of its neck.

"That advance guard of Secret Service men is a little daunting, isn't it?" Betty said tightly. "I was afraid they'd want the children bound and gagged."

Marian said she doubted it, but that they might have to sedate Annabelle. She looked speculatively at the white rings that glasses had left on the closed piano lid and that she had never noticed before; then she hid them from sight by opening the piano, but there was nothing to be done about the similar marks at the edges of the keyboard or about a long burn where some pianist had forgotten a perched cigarette. "Now come on, you know what Andy wanted—just to come visiting in her friends' house."

"I know." Betty started to sit down on the couch and then remembered and crossed to one of the chairs. Marian, equally determined to preserve the precision of the stripes, sat on the old round piano stool. Both women jumped nervously as the door at the top of the basement stairs opened, but sat back again when they heard Will's voice explaining that the Secret Service didn't have too much to worry about when the President did something on the spur of the moment like this—they just checked the entrances and then sort of loitered.

Gil set the tray of drinks down on the coffee table. "I had to taste the bourbon to show the guy it wasn't poisoned. Every bottle. That's what took so long."

"Oh stop it, Gil. And don't sit down on the couch till they come."

He raised his eyebrows. "Honey, just relax, will you?" But he waved Will to the one remaining chair and sat down on the floor. "For God's sake, let's not just perch here like birds in the wilderness. Anyone for Twenty Questions?"

"Oh please, no." Marian jumped to her feet. "I can't sit still. Let's dance, or something with some moving around in it."

Will said dryly, "We're already practically playing charades. We might as well go all the way."

They agreed on charades almost at once, though on the teams more slowly. Marian held out for men vs women over the objections of Gil, who claimed that the women's mind-reading ability gave them an unfair advantage. But he soon surrendered, and he and Will retired to confer by the piano. Betty and Marian, whispering under the photographs at the other end of the room, had agreed on "Though I speak with the tongues of men and of angels" and were working out the details when they heard the footsteps overhead. They all stopped, looking up at the door at the head of the stairs like Keats's watchers of the skies.

Alec came down first and waited at the bottom step until Andrea caught up with him and stood peering uncertainly over his head with her hands on his shoulders. "All right to come in?" Her eyes were merry. "Skirts and sweaters. Goody." She pushed gently at Alec and he came into the room and shook hands with Gil first and then Will. "I've got flat heels," Andy boasted. "I thought you'd all be flatheeled by now."

"I haven't been home since this morning," Marian explained. "But if we can make you comfy—" She took off her shoes and kicked them under the piano stool.

"Thanks." Andy sank onto the sofa, then tugged at Alec's hand till he sat down beside her. "I hope our circus didn't discombobulate everybody." The anxiety in the nervous joshing was painfully evident; it almost hurt to look into Andy's large, asking eyes.

Marian launched herself to the rescue. "Nonsense. It inspired us to play charades. We were just getting started. You interested?" She was looking at Alec, and her voice carried on when her words stopped suddenly, halted by the need to address him.

Alec observed her fluster. "A simple 'Your Majesty' will do," he told her kindly.

"That seems a little austere," Will said. "How about 'and Honorable Flower of the West'?"

The tension in the room fell noticeably, and a comfortable pre-game negotiation about the rules began. After an argument about choosing teams was settled by drawing lots, the pairs—Alec and Will, Gil and Andy, Marian and Betty—withdrew to corners of the room to confer in a busy conspiratorial hubbub.

The knock on the door froze everyone. "Mr. President?"

Alec frowned. "Yes?"

It was only a tray of drinks, for the Girards—without which, Alec protested, he would be unable to go on. But the joke met with stiff smiles as a trembling Annabelle came down the stairs while they watched in taut suspense, everyone in the room suddenly terrified that she might fall. Betty met her at the bottom like a handler welcoming his fighter back to his corner and took the tray. The maid stood silent, her eyes never moving from the tall figure of the President.

"Why, it's Annabelle," Andy said with not quite convincing gaiety. "How are you, Annabelle? We haven't seen you for quite a while."

"Fine, thank you, ma'am." She swallowed hard and addressed the President in a voice that quavered. "May I offer you my congratulations, sir?" They all looked at the obviously rehearsed words, which seemed to be strung on a clothesline under the low ceiling of the basement. "I would've voted for you if I could," Annabelle added suddenly, and everybody smiled.

"Thank you." Alec looked at her soberly. "I hope you'll find you chose wisely."

They smiled some more, and waited again. It was, Marian thought, hung somewhere between tears and laughter, an act that couldn't get offstage. Then

Andy rescued them. She handed Alec one of the ragged pieces of paper that had been used in the drawing. "It's spelled 'b-e-l-l-e,' isn't that right, Anna-belle?"

Alec found a pen in his inside coat pocket and scribbled rapidly on the paper, bracing it on the edge of the coffee table. When the maid had gone, Andy looked at them, her eyes begging them.

"We didn't want her to," Betty said. "We warned her not to."

Alec said, "She didn't, remember?" He frowned at Andy. "It just happens, that's all." He walked away from them moodily, still carrying the pen, and then suddenly he saw the lighted laundry room and he began to laugh. "Here, let's do it up right." He darted into the small, crowded room, ducking under some towels hanging on a rack suspended from the ceiling, and they crowded after him like children following a leader. Marian, straining on tiptoe, pushed urgently at Will until he moved and let her in, and she saw the President leaning over the bellying curve of the washing machine. "Alexander W. Girard was here," he had written in a large, spiky hand on the smudged wall behind the machine. He added the date, inscribing it carefully, while the laughter rose around him. Then he put the pen away and led them out.

"That's a hell of a thing," Gil grumbled. "If you know a President, you get graffiti over your washing machine. What if the repairman voted for Ferris? You know how hard those guys are to get?"

"Maybe it's washable ink," Andy began in a propitiatory tone that was promptly drowned in hoots from the others.

"You think you're so great," Marian taunted Betty. "Wait till you see whose autograph is on our stove."

"Yes, suh," Will drawled. "What's that general's name, Magnolia Lou?"

"General Electric, Gaylord, honey."

Will slapped his knee. "That's it. He's the one made that gloh-rious stand somewhere up no'th."

"At the New York Stock Exchange," Alec corroborated. "Where he routed General Confusion. Now can I have my drink?" He took a long swallow and asked, "Who's first? It'd better be my team, or I'll have you all up before a firing squad."

But they shouted him down and he submitted with elaborate grumpiness to trial by paper slips again—and then chuckled with delight when he drew the winning slip.

"Power—naked, unscrupulous power," Gil complained at Alec's and Will's backs as they whispered near the piano. "Come on, you've had a whole minute."

"The hell we have," Alec shouted back. "Andy, keep the watch."

"Nope. I'm not on your team now, remember?"

"All right, all right, we're ready anyhow," Will placated.

But the game didn't begin for a while anyway—not until all the glasses had been emptied and Andy and Marian had been threatened, once each, with disqualification for attempted eavesdropping. The two culprits, who were in fact guilty, sat together on the now thoroughly rumpled couch and watched intently as Will took the dried grasses from the wine bottle on the piano and divided the thin clump in half. Then he and Alec lay down side by side on the floor, each with closed eyes and "flowers" on his chest.

"Dead," shouted Andy.

"Wait," Betty cautioned Marian. "They're doing something."

The two prone figures stirred. Each man reached out his right hand, and they shook hands, elaborately, in the small space between them.

"Is that all?" Gil asked.

Will made the chopping motion that indicated "half."

"Is it 'dead'?" Andy demanded.

Alec made the "something like" gesture.

" 'Corpse'?" she asked.

Again, the gesture from the "corpse."

" 'Laid out'?"

"Hey," Marian said. "You can't have so many turns in a row."

Andy looked ashamed. "I'm sorry."

Struck by inspiration, Marian bounced on the couch, screaming, "I have it, listen, listen!" with a markedly greater lack of decorum than she'd reproved Andy for. "I got it. It's 'better beer.' " She looked at the blank faces of the mentally retarded all around her and explained pityingly, " 'Bier.' Like 'funeral.' And they shook hands, didn't they? So they bet a beer."

The frozen faces of the corpses on the floor cracked and Will broke into open laughter.

"Umm. You may not guess it," Gil said, "but you keep on like that and you'll knock them out of the box by making them talk."

"Well, is it just 'bier'?" Marian asked, in the reasonable tone of one who, though in touch with the infinite, is willing to try to get along with the earthbound. The earthbound hooted her down, claiming she had put the same question twice, which was double jeopardy. Alec cowered behind his dusty "flowers," struggling for composure as Andy yelled, "That's unconstitutional!"

The knock on the door was like a bass drum in the middle of the lively fiddles of a hoedown. "Mr. President?" The man's voice rumbled down the stairs as though it bounced from step to step.

Alec sat up hastily. "One moment." He and Will scrambled to their feet and then bent again to pick up the flowers. Alec dumped them on top of the piano and Will brushed frantically at the dust on the back of the President's coat. In their disorganized gestures and waste motion, Marian thought, they looked like a couple of prep school boys about to be caught at mischief by the house mother. Then she was herself being caught up in it as Andy, flushed and desperate, jumped up and began simultaneously trying to smooth her hair and search for her shoes; Marian found the shoes and Betty helped Andy get them on while Alec was saying, "Yes, come," in a strong, calm voice. He crossed the floor, avoiding glasses and ash trays, and met the man at the bottom of the stairs. He stood with his head inclined, listening silently for a moment, then said, "No, I think not. We'll go back and I'll take it in my office." He turned then and looked at them with regret. "Betty, Gil, thank you. I'm sorry, but we must go." His gaze traveled over the group. "Marian and Will. Good night." Reluctantly then, his eyes met Andy's. "Are you ready?"

She walked proudly, though her hair was still tumbled and her cheeks were pink with embarrassment. As she turned to say good-night, Marian saw with pity that Andy was close to tears. "Thank you all," she said faintly. "It's been such fun that I—"

The door at the top of the stairs slammed open, bouncing noisily against the wall. "Hey, Pop, you down there?" Bert Kimball shouted. "Listen, all the neighbors are outside, and a cop wouldn't let me park, right in front of our own house—" He had started to come down without waiting for an answer, but he broke off as he saw the two at the bottom of the stairs. "Oh, hi, Andy. Did you have any troub—" Realization caught up with him in the middle of the word.

Betty, beside Marian, moved convulsively, as though to shield the boy from his own chagrin as he cowered, reddening fiercely, against the staircase wall. Gil crossed quickly and plucked his son down.

"I'm afraid we're the trouble, Bert," Andy said. The room ached with pity for her. Then she grinned widely at the boy. "Or Joe, as the case may be." The familiar joke, an offshoot of long-ago pranks by the Kimball twins, lifted the pall a little, easing Bert's discomfiture at least. But the fun was gone, all of it and hopelessly. Unmistakably, Humpty Dumpty had fallen off the wall.

"Thank you for having us," Alec said, guiding Andy gently toward the stairs again. "We've had a very nice time." His boyish voice lingered on the boyish words.

Marian raised a hand in an abortive wave, but they stood in silence as the Girards walked up the stairs toward the Secret Service agent who held the door open for them at the top. Only Bert was able to gather himself in time; wrenching himself from Gil's grasp, he took a step forward and called out loudly, "Good night, Mr. President."

"In the end," Marian said to Will as they drove home, "Bert was the only one to handle the thing well." She spoke coolly, looking away from him, because relations between them were still strained; but what she had witnessed had been too curious to go without comment. I hope Andy didn't cry, she thought sadly—at least not till she got wherever she finally gets to be alone.

"The resilience of youth, maybe." He glanced down at Marian. "It wasn't all that awful, baby. Don't make too much of it."

He had moved too fast—she was not ready to converse on those terms as yet. "If that's the way you see it," she said coldly.

Will sighed. "Look, Girard didn't get drafted for the job."

Maybe Andy did, Marian thought.

Will tried again. "Hey. Don't you want to know what our quote was?" She tried to stay aloof, but it was too hard. "Was 'bier' right?"

"No, but it wasn't bad." Will laughed. "You know, I could tell you anything I want, and you'd never know whether I was telling the truth. After all, you'd have one hell of a time checking with my partner, wouldn't you?"

"Then what was the word?"

"Andy was close, at one point. 'Body.' "

" 'Body'? What—oh, I see. You shook hands and—"

"Yup. 'When a body meet a body.' We had a lulu for 'comin' through the rye.' "

Marian snuggled down into her coat. "We'd have got it," she boasted.

"You can't prove it now."

"No, I can't." She looked out at the gaunt trees. "I'm glad you're not President."

"You won't believe this, but from time to time I am too. And not only because I'm fond of charades."

"I know you think I'm dramatizing. But it's so awfully sad. Did you see Andy's face?"

"It'll be all right," Will told her. "She's just not used to it yet. She'll get the hang of it." He helped her out of the car and up the steps of their house.

"Get the hang of what?"

Will shrugged. "There are things that Alec Girard could do but Mr. President can't. An evening like that is one of them, that's all."

"Poor Andy."

"She'll think of something," Will assured her. "She won't just sit and pine. You'll see. There are an awful lot of things Mr. Presidents *can* do."

Twenty-five

She and Ann must be in the Chinese restaurant near the office, Marian reasoned, because she could feel the bumpy, braided surface of a piece of jade under her fingers; the proprietor often let her handle the jade he kept for sale in the glass case under his cash register. But something was wrong about the place—there was nothing to eat on the table, and there was such an unaccustomed hubbub that, though Ann was talking urgently, her voice was drowned in a strident, unremitting buzz.

Marian's hand found the alarm clock in its unaccustomed place on top of the upended willow laundry basket that served as an end table in the study. She pushed the button that turned the noise off and then continued to trail her fingers over the bumpy, braided surface of the basket while she shivered in the narrow bed and let herself remember, slowly, where she was. Despite the storm windows outside and the heavy dark-green gabardine drapes drawn across on the inside, the big bay window not only let in an icy February draft but even narrowed and beamed it relentlessly at the bed.

Marian turned on her side between the chill sheets, tucked her cold fingers into her armpits, and told herself with honest rue to remember that it was her own fault she was here. Across the small room, the door that led to the bedroom was open a crack; Will had swung it shut as he left last night, but he hadn't bothered to turn the knob. "I just want to be left alone, that's all," Marian had said, her bare arm flung up to shield her eyes. Under it, she watched him, and saw that he thought he knew what it was all about: the fight over Lloyd Morris and the mutual hard feelings that had never quite got satisfactorily softened. Well, it was and it wasn't, and the same was true of what she had come to think of as "sweating it out until spring"— after which, presumably, some magic would put everything back the way it once had been. Which was a way she wasn't sure she could remember, anyhow. So she had flung her arm up and turned her face away, and Will had said knowingly, "All right, I can wait," and gone to sleep in their bed alone.

After, she was cold in the small, uncomfortable daybed that was more sat on than slept in—that was only a bed, really, when some child was sick enough to need constant, all-night attention. When she sat up and tried to read, her shoulders were cold; when she slid down under the covers, she was too lonely to go to sleep. It would have been worth a lot to be held tightly in the dark and troubling night. But everything was settled, apparently, so far as Will was concerned: he had the answer, he always had all the answers. He had decided that he would wait until she got over what he was arrogantly sure was just pique, and he was insolently sure she *would* get over it. Angry and miserable, she put her arms around herself and hugged herself to sleep in the lonely cold.

Now she shivered her way into her slippers and her long, heavy bathrobe, knowing that the passage of the night had not changed anything, that no triumph had been achieved after all. She shuffled over to the big window and pulled the cord that opened the drapes; outside, the small, silly balcony that you couldn't sit on or sunbathe on was trimmed with only enough ice to lend glitter to its sooty gray but not to hide it. Below, frost hardened the trampled grass of the big yard and its tall, stripped trees. Even the gracefully drooping branches of the big spruce were not so much green as a dulled blue; they looked heavy, artificially fringed and irrelevant in the motionless dead landscape under the motionless lead sky.

She carried her feeling of dread down the hall to the bathroom, where she made the only sounds in the silent world. When she came out, she stood still in the hall, listening to the sleeping stillness and the total silence from downstairs. The door was open on Rosa's empty room, the bed neatly made, the bright-red cover on the armchair unwrinkled, the little matching rug untrodden, the Martian-looking television set silent and unblinking; stiffly posed, gilt-framed studio photographs of Bettina and Trixie regarded absence with set smiles. Marian turned away, shivering a little, aware now that all the silence had a name: Rosa went home for weekends, so it was not surprising that her room was empty on Monday morning, but there ought to be smells of bacon and coffee and there was nothing as Marian padded down the back stairs. There ought to be Rosa, her coat flung down in the pantry because she hurried to start breakfast as soon as she came in, standing at the stove with her apron tied over the non-housedress she wouldn't have time to change out of before the children left for school. There was nothing in the big empty kitchen but dimness and the sound of the dogs whining and scratching at the closed basement door as they heard footsteps. Marian let them out the back door, opened the blinds to the gray world outside, and got out the heavy iron skillet and the bacon, all the time feeling strangely far away from her hands.

Throughout the shifts of the children's breakfast—first Dick, then Sharlie, and finally Peter—she moved with a dreamlike detachment. When at last Will appeared and she launched into her fourth explanation of Rosa's absence, Marian realized suddenly that it was awfully late even for the worst delay in the worst traffic jam. She went out to the phone on the little shelf in the pantry and dialed Rosa's number and stood there dumbly, listening to the foolish, repeated whirring.

At last she decided it was hopeless and returned to the table and her now-cold coffee. Will looked at her over the paper, and she shook her head and said, "I'm getting worried. It seems awfully late for traffic delays."

He buttered his toast. "She probably had to go to the doctor or the dentist or something."

"Well, she would have told me."

"I expect she did, and you forgot," he said contemptuously.

Marian took her seat across from him and tried to read the city news on the first page of the second section, but his casual remark haunted her. Try as she might, she could remember no special plan or arrangement for today; but he was right, she did forget things these days. Feeling not worth very much, she stole a glance at his abstracted scowl and found in it no tolerance for her or anything else. She sighed and offered him more coffee.

"No, thanks. I've got to be going." He noticed her bathrobe for the first time. "You're not going to work?"

"Well, I can't until Rosa shows up; this isn't one of Peter's school days. The five-day-a-week schedule doesn't begin till next week." She stopped because he was paying no attention.

Not to her words, anyway—but he did seem to notice when her voice ceased, because he said that then he'd take the car. Marian made a small sound and he said patiently, "What is it? Do you need the car?"

"I—I don't know. I don't know what's going to—" Will's bony face suddenly looked to her like the carving of a sneer, the absolute abstract essence of scorn. "No, I guess not," she said hastily.

He picked up his briefcase and looked at his watch. To see how much time he'd wasted on her, Marian thought miserably. "Well, are you sure?" he asked, in a voice that congratulated itself on its own forbearance.

"Yes. I suppose. Will, I—" But the anger she had tried to swallow stuck in her throat.

"What is it?" He waited, inspecting her coolly. "You didn't seem to have so much trouble making decisions last night."

"I am trying to please you," Marian said slowly, in a voice that repressed whole operas of emotion, "but it seems to be a fruitless endeavor."

"Forgive me. I had no way of suspecting that was what you were up to." He took his briefcase and slammed out the back door. His footsteps, rapid and somehow furious, passed quickly under the kitchen window and disappeared.

Marian rubbed her eyes with her newsprint-smeared hand and then got up and wearily rinsed and stacked the breakfast dishes, handling them as clumsily, she thought, as she did everything these days. She dried her hands on a paper towel and took Peter upstairs with her while she made his bed, answering his prattle with conscientious cheerfulness that eventually had some tiny convincing effect on her own low spirits. She buttoned him into his jacket to send him off to the public library's morning storytelling hour for preschool children, and then the gray dreads mounted in her again: he seemed small and frail to go forth into a perilous world. She hugged him with restraint, so as not to frighten him, and then she watched him with ridiculous anxiety from the study window as he skipped down the walk and negotiated safely the few hundred yards to the library next door. He had no street to cross, no wild animals lurked on the empty lawns. Insane, Marian thought, dialing Rosa's number and listening hopelessly to the absence over there. Menace, menace everywhere, and not a drop of it was real.

She collected her clothes and carried them into the bedroom to dress, her glance sliding reluctantly over to the rumpled bed. She dressed swiftly in a sweater and skirt, but she left off her garter belt and put on socks; soon she would have to decide whether this was going to be a staying-home day and make some phone calls if it was, but in the meantime, she didn't have to commit herself to stockings. It took an effort to begin making the bed: her hands, smoothing the sheets, trembled with the knowledge that she might never come back there again, where it had all begun with Will and where, she suspected, it had always been sustained. But how did you sleep with a stranger? Whichever of them, he or she, was now the stranger, she added honestly.

She knew as she went into the study that she had left the bed in there for last because she couldn't make up her mind whether to change the sheets. Now she set about making it without changing them, knowing she would be sleeping here again tonight, taking both less than happiness and less than solace. She unfolded the Indian throw that covered the bed in the daytime and smoothed it into place. It was the children's turn now, was what it came down to: their happiness was the only proper quest by this time. She propped the dark green corduroy bolster and pillow against the wall and looked at the little room, restored now at least temporarily to its usual function, through a beginning mist of tears. Sniffling a bit, she decided defiantly that the prospect of a loveless life endured for the sake of the children deserved a few tears; there was nobody here to comment on the follies of self-pity.

Then, suddenly, the phone on her desk rang so impellingly, so sharply, that it seemed to jiggle like a phone in a movie cartoon. She knew, in the instant it took her to dart across the floor, that it was trouble, it was the thing that had been hanging leadenly all morning.

But Rosa was crying so hard that Marian had difficulty making out, at first, what the trouble was, and thoughts of a mutilated Trixie crept icily down her spine. But it was Bruce, she understood at last. And he was not hurt; he was in jail. "What for?" she asked. "Listen, Rosa, *please* stop crying. We'll get him out, but I have to find out what happened. What did they arrest him for?"

"Don't nobody know. They was just waitin for a bus, him and the other boy. The other boy run away. He been hidin all night. Then he come early this mornin to tell me. I gone to the po-lice station and they keep me there waitin and waitin; I try to tell them I got to phone, but they just laugh and say I lose my turn if I come off that bench." Her weak, tired voice hardened suddenly. "They was just havin their fun with me."

"Oh Rosa, honey, you're all wrought up."

"I know I is, indeed I is. When I finally gets to see the man, he tell me they ain't got no Bruce Fisher there, they don't know nothin about him, he must be in some other precinct. But that the precinct them cops come from —the other boy seen the car they got out of. And it rightly the one for that neighborhood."

"Well, maybe they moved him for some reason. Did you ask—"

"That man just laugh and say why don't I go find out. He say they got a dozen or so precincts in the city and I could have me some fun."

Shocked, Marian asked, "Did he say that? Exactly that?"

"Them was his very words, I swear. You know I be a truthful woman, Miz Marian." Rosa broke into sobs again. "They beatin that boy up somewheres, for a fact. And he ain't got no folks here . . . nobody but me, and I ain't done nothin for him . . . I don't—"

"Rosa! Stop that at once. Listen, I want you to get in a cab and come right out here."

"I got to stay and try—"

"*I'll* try. But I can't leave Peter and I don't want to take him down there—"

"No, no." Rosa began to cry hysterically. "Don't you go bringin that baby to this place."

"All right, then you come and take care of him. Come on now, there's nothing you can do there and you're needed here. Doesn't that make sense?"

Rosa said reluctantly, "I suppose."

"Good. Now, give me all the information you have." Rosa gave her the number of the precinct, but she could remember no names of the men she had talked to, and the boy who had escaped had not known the name of the arresting officer. The time and place ought to be enough to establish that, Marian thought, writing down the location of the bus stop on a piece of *Tribune* stationery yanked from her open desk drawer. She ordered Rosa to come straight on out and then hung up at once, to forestall any further delay.

She brought her garter belt and stockings into the study and finished dressing while she waited on the phone. "I'd like to inquire about a boy who was arrested early this morning," she had told the man who'd answered, and then there'd been a click followed by silence. She hunched up her shoulder to hold the phone while she fastened her stockings. It was a long wait, but finally a man pronounced a name she didn't catch and she repeated her request, this time adding Bruce's name. "Nobody here by that name," the voice said.

"But, wait a minute—how do you know?" Marian's own voice was soprano with unbelief. "You didn't even look it up or anything."

"I don't have to look it up, ma'am." She could hear that the man was smiling a little. "I know there warn't no white boys come in here all night."

"Bruce Fisher is a Negro," Marian said coldly and very distinctly, "and I'd appreciate it if you would find out, directly, whether he is being held there and on what charge."

The voice held no more geniality. "Yes, ma'am. May I ask, are you an attorney?"

"No."

"Just a minute." In the background, there was a brief, blurred exchange of men's voices, and then, far too quickly, the man was back. "No such name here," he said abruptly.

"Well, if you've taken him somewhere else, you must have a record of it. Can you tell me, please, to which precinct he's been transferred?"

"Listen, lady, we're busy here and we can't take telephone calls from everybody feels like setting us to look things up. You'll have to follow the regular procedure."

"Well, what *is* the regular procedure?" She spoke sharply, but it never occurred to her that the man would hang up; when she finally interpreted the click successfully, she could feel herself almost literally swelling with rage. "But I'm a taxpayer," she said aloud, her voice shrill with the double futility of the dead phone in the empty house. Biting her lip to keep from crying, she fled into her room and began hastily to put up her hair, but her hands were shaking while she did it. As soon as she'd finished, she called Will; he wasn't in and she left a message, then went downstairs to look in her purse. There was a five-dollar bill and some change. She put the bill into her skirt pocket and was standing by the front door, looking out for the cab, when the phone rang.

She was calm enough when she first heard Will's voice, but as soon as she had finished answering his questions, all the fury and frustration exploded into tears. "You wouldn't *believe* it," she kept saying, about the man at the precinct. "You can't imagine—"

Will said dryly, "Yes, I can. He figured if you were anybody he had to be afraid of, you'd have said so by then. So it was safe to brush you off. All right, listen—"

"Wait. Rosa's here." She gave Rosa the money and told her to ask the cab to wait.

"How is she?" Will asked.

Marian's eyes filled up again. "She looks awful, Will."

"Give her a shot of whisky in a cup of coffee. Then get a cab and meet me at the precinct. You know where it is? Right away now."

"I've got a cab waiting."

"Good." He sounded surprised, though. "Now look, don't take time out for a crying jag, will you? Because I've got a meeting scheduled."

"No," said Marian, weeping. "I won't."

Ten minutes was the time she had set herself, and she made it. She got the coffee and whisky into Rosa, discussed having Peter sent to his friend Tommy's house, and believed, looking at the gray leaving Rosa's skin, that it probably wasn't necessary. Then she said, "I'll call you as soon as I can," and fled to the cab, on time for the first time she could remember. It was a long ride, but that was probably a good idea, because the transition from the orderly, nearly empty streets of the Cleveland Park section to these swarming, trash-strewn sidewalks needed time for adjustment. The cab drew in at the curb a few doors from the police station and Marian rolled the window down and leaned out to look for Will. In a narrow alley between two small, rickety houses, beer cans bloomed in a field of trash, like a crop on a surrealist farm.

Will was lounging nearby, studying a piece of paper. He folded it and put it in his inside pocket when he heard her call and then picked his way across the slowly moving stream of dark pedestrians. Where were they all going? Marian wondered, waiting while he paid the cab. The women with string shopping bags made sense, but the men and boys, calling to one another and strolling as though in summer sunshine, were alien and a little shocking. Across the street an old, very black man tilted back in a wooden kitchen chair against the facade of a shoe repair shop, his battered hat pushed back on his head and his face upturned to the threatening sky. Everything in his pose suggested June and sunshine. It looked, Marian decided, like a stage setting where somebody had mixed up the lighting cues.

When Will took her arm to lead her up the few steps, Marian clung to him, her gloved hand crumpling the piece of paper on which she'd scribbled the few details they had. He glanced down at her critically and said, "Please try to look more arrogant, will you?" He saw the paper, took it out of her hand, and folded it so the letterhead showed. Marian put on a look like her mother's, which was the most arrogant she could think of, and followed Will to the long desk. She noticed that he held the paper negligently, laying it on the counter while he talked, so that the words *"Washington Tribune"* were clearly visible.

The shirt-sleeved policeman behind the long, high desk examined them without curiosity. Will said, "Good morning," and flipped open his wallet. "Farland, Office of the Secretary of State." The impressive-looking card instructed (still in President Winkler's name) all concerned to permit Willard C. Farland—whose picture, in watery color at the upper left, showed him to be unsmiling and somewhat boyish—to pass through all the lines and barriers that would, presumably, be containing the other radioactive citizens in the event of nuclear attack; this preferential treatment, it was indicated vaguely but grandly, was required for the security of the nation. Marian had always cherished a private hope that if the bomb did drop, Will would employ the pass, not to take off for the secret fastness to which he'd been assigned, but instead to beat his way heroically through panicky multitudes to rescue her and the children. Her only revelation of this notion, though, had led to a reply she'd rather not remember but couldn't quite forget. *Why would I?* Will had asked in mild surprise. *You'd probably all be fried by that time anyway.*

"Like to see the commanding officer." Will had held the wallet open just long enough to allow the cop to check the picture against the reality, and to derive a quick impression of high official status. The man's eyes, faded blue under sparse, sandy lashes, now looked alert but troubled. The Washington police had occasional dismaying experiences with foreign diplomats, whose immunity to arrest—a valuable reciprocal proviso designed to protect our own diplomats from harassment in foreign capitals—could be a trying matter in day-to-day civic life at home. The diplomatic community in the nation's capital, if it ran into too intricate a problem with the city's police, appealed to the State Department and things were subsequently ironed out. Usually. And smoothly, which meant without publicity if possible.

The man behind the desk clearly detected the potential flight of a hottish potato that should be caught by someone else, but his slow look revealed the confusion of a limited mentality presented with the unexpected. "Lieutenant Hines ain't here, and he's the one who's supposed to—"

Will broke in with an air of controlled impatience. "Look, I'd like to take care of this right here in the precinct, but if it's going to mean just as much time as going downtown . . ."

The man resolved his doubts in a hurry. "Please have a seat, sir. I'll call the captain." His eyes flicked uncertainly at Marian, but Will had turned away and was leading her over to the highly varnished bench along the opposite wall. The policeman spoke inaudibly into his phone, watching Will, who seated Marian but remained standing himself, looking at his watch with tightened lips.

In a matter of seconds a uniformed patrolman appeared at the end of the long room and held open the swinging gate. "This way, please. Captain Merkel will see you now." He glanced uncertainly at his colleague behind the desk as Will stepped back and waved Marian through ahead of him with apparently absentminded courtesy, but neither of them tried to stop her.

Some kind of quick-change miracle must have been occurring behind her back while she'd been preceding Will down the long hall whose walls—tile halfway up, dingy paint above that—and disinfectant smell reminded her of a public comfort station into which an emergency had once impelled her. For in the captain's office, Will, who had been doing a pretty good imitation of the diplomat von Ribbentrop, had without warning become someone else entirely; he was all but snapping his galluses in front of the county courthouse as he shook hands with the heavy, rumpled-looking man who rose from behind a gray metal desk. The man smiled, cautiously but with pleasure, as Huey Long Will noted genially that he'd read of Captain Merkel's recent appointment with particular interest because they were from the same neck of the woods.

"So you're from Alabama, too, Mr.—er—"

"Dorothy County. A little north of you, I think." Will supplied his name then, pronouncing it carelessly, as though a hint should be enough for his fellow Alabaman, and then introduced Marian with a loose wave that kept her at a distance and told her her response should be a nod rather than the offer of her hand. "Glad you could see us, Captain," Will went on. "This's one of those little clerical problems that could go into months of shovin papers around, but I figured the two of us could go on and get it out of the way in a few minutes."

The captain came out from behind his desk and held Marian's chair, then went back to his own scarred wooden chair, settled down, and expressed his willingness to dispose of problems.

Will had declined a seat; he stood by the room's single grimy window, holding the cord of the Venetian blind but not playing with it as he said softly that first, there was this detail—one of the captain's men had been a little discourteous to Miz Farland on the telephone that morning . . . The lounging pose and drawling speech spoke of ease and familiarity, but his eyes were cold and fixed unwaveringly on the stout man behind the desk.

"Well, we can't have that sort of thing." The captain reached for a scratch pad on his desk. "If you'll let me have the officer's name . . ."

" 'Fraid it's gone and got a little more complicated than that." Will's sigh said that he, for one, certainly wished it hadn't. "You see, my wife works on a newspaper." He paused. "What she was calling about was the arrest last night of a colored boy. When she got the runaround from your man . . .

well, it kind of stirred things up." He turned away to peer at the dim outside world. "Everybody knows, I guess," he said over his shoulder, "how they are about that sort of thing at the *Tribune.*"

Small veins in the captain's fleshy nose were suddenly obvious. He pulled the pad toward him and began drawing a square, a feat that evidently required intense concentration.

Will's tone was conversational, and faintly regretful. "Shame to start a whole rumpus over a little incident like this, but you can understand how people get fussed up. The boy's aunt works for us, you see, so when she came and told my wife she'd been sittin out there most of the night and couldn't find out where the boy was being held or what he was charged with, well of course Miz Farland had to take a hand."

"Relatives," Captain Merkel said carefully. "They always get upset. Especially the women."

"That's what I'd have thought, too. Only thing is, this is a real high-class colored woman—pleasant-spoken and polite. Not educated, like some of them nowadays. And she worked for some right well-known people before she came to us." He paused, examining the cone-shaped plastic dangle at the end of the cord. "I could see right off that she'd be an answer to a prayer if anybody wanted to take off from this little mixup. Make a real good witness, and all."

"Well, we got no call to get into a shootin match." Captain Merkel's southern accent was thickening, Marian noticed with some amusement, as Will's did.

Will smiled. "Trouble is, they're sort of trigger-happy at the *Tribune.* That's why I figured I better come down and see you myself. 'It's some kinda little goof somewhere,' I told my wife, 'and I'm gonna bring you right along with me so you can tell them back at the *Tribune* that there's nothin to it." His smile broadened. "I'm in the Secretary of State's office, you know, and *we're* not understaffed. Still, we have our little snafus from time to time, too." He winked at Marian. "But don't you go puttin that in the paper, honey." Marian stared at him in dumb amazement that apparently passed for acquiescence.

The captain regarded Will thoughtfully when their exchange of genial grins was finished. "I see you understand the problems we got here. Some folks are so quick to jump on us and start yellin."

Will waved an understanding hand. "The way I figured it, soon as I heard the boy hadn't been allowed to make a phone call, was that somebody'd forgotten to book him at all. What with the phone ringin all the time, and maybe the arrestin officer havin to go right out again . . . I said, 'Let's get the details before we start callin up lawyers. It's cheaper that way.' "

The captain laughed dutifully, but Marian sensed the presence of a resistance that hadn't been there before. Under the blue shirt, his shoulders were held a little stiffly as he wrote down the information Will was reading. Had Will gone too far, somehow? She glanced at him and saw that he was measuring the man. "Can't quite make out this street," he said suddenly. He carried her scribbled notes over to the desk and held the paper, with its conspicuous *Washington Tribune* letterhead, under the captain's nose. "No, I see," he said, withdrawing it quickly. "It's 'Jackson'—must be Jackson Circle."

The captain tore the top sheet from his scratch pad and made for the door. "Excuse me a minute. I'll get this tended to."

"What happened?" Marian whispered as the door closed. "All of a sudden, he seemed a little—"

"Ssh. All of a sudden, I raised the price, that's all."

"I don't understand."

Will shrugged. "Just letting the kid go was cheap in return for getting the *Tribune* off his neck."

"And now?"

"I decided," Will said slowly, "there was no reason the boy should have a police record."

"But I never meant—I don't want to do anything illegal," Marian protested.

"Oh hush. All you have to do is sit there and look insulted." He grinned at her happily. "Only thing is, if it actually comes to avenging you in good old southern fashion, for God's sake hang on my arm and remind me I promised my mother I wouldn't be violent." He examined this imaginary scene and added, "*Before* the other guy swings, you understand."

Marian said crossly, "I won't unless you stop calling me 'mah waff.' What's taking him so long?"

"He's got to find out what shape the kid's in." His face twitched with a hunter's attention. "Now honey," he said loudly, "we're dealin with a gentleman here, and there's no call to get upset."

Marian obediently looked upset while Captain Merkel resumed his seat. "Seems there's a little more to it than we thought," he told Will. "There was a little excitement. The other nigger ran away, and while one of the patrolmen was chasing him—"

"We got the right boy?" Will asked softly. He knows that, Marian thought, puzzled; I told him about the other boy.

The captain looked down at the slip of paper in his hand. "Bruce Fisher," he read. "Age, twenty-one. Address, 1314 Ransome Street Northwest. Occupation, student."

Will nodded. "Yep, that's him. He's a law student, you know," he added brightly. "Reckon that's why he knew better than to run away. Or to resist arrest. Any judge'd see that right away."

Marian let out her breath sharply, a small sound in the longish menacing silence. The captain sat very still, looking down at his paper. Then he raised his eyes to Will and said, "I'm having him brought up here," in a flat voice.

"Fine." From Will's acceptance of the statement, it must have been a conciliation. "Well, while we're waitin, we may as well get the rest of the picture. What's the charge?" His eyes, curiously light, bored into the man behind the desk. "You know, Miz Farland couldn't even get that information this morning?"

"Failing to move on." The captain smiled nervously in Marian's general direction. "I hope you know we regret any discourtesy—"

"Well, we may have to discuss that," Will said gravely. "But for now, I'm kinda studyin this 'movin-on' business."

"Now Mr. Farland, you know we don't make the laws—"

"Yes, sir, it's a real interestin point." Will's long fingers twined the Venetian blind cord. "That particular statute can be right useful sometimes, and I'd kind of hate to see it go. But it's kind of vulnerable, wouldn't you say?"

"Seems clear enough here," the captain remarked. "The patrolman told the nig—this Fisher to move on, and he refused to comply."

Will turned to him like a man struck with useful inspiration. "You know, that little statute could use a test. For one thing it's not very uniformly applied, is it? What I could do is—yup, I think I'll go on out and stand in front of this precinct for a while." He chuckled. "I bet I could stand there till I drop and nobody'd tell me to move on. Of course if they did," he added, "I'd refuse, and that would make it another story."

"There were two of them, you know," the captain said. His face suffused with color, he pushed what he thought was his advantage. "Makes a difference with two. They could block the sidewalk."

"That's right." Will welcomed it as a useful suggestion. He dropped the cord and rubbed his hands together. "Why don't we make it a little more interestin?" He nodded at Marian. "Honey, you go phone your office and tell 'em to send down one of their young men to come with me, so there'll be two of us."

Marian picked her purse off her lap.

"Now just a minute," the captain said sharply. He smiled at Will companionably. "That's the trouble with us Reb hotheads. You been real friendly and considerate, Mr. Farland, and I'm not going to let you do something you may be sorry for, for want of a little friendly advice in return." He paused, but Will remained silent. "Now look, you're in the State Department. You get yourself arrested, along with a *Tribune* reporter, and you could be sorry. You didn't get up where you are without knowing that the State Department don't care much for a lot of publicity about their people. Now why don't you take a minute to cool off—and maybe talk it over with your good lady here, because after all anything that affects your job is sure something she'd have an interest in." Merkel glanced over at Marian, confident of support; but she had seen the nasty gleam in her husband's eye. She didn't know how, but she knew that victory was in sight. So she smiled pityingly at Merkel and kept silent.

Will couldn't have been more grateful to the captain, judging by his voice, as he came away from the window. "We raise them sharp, down home," he congratulated the policeman. "But I'm afraid you forgot something." His genial expression vanished abruptly. "It's a new administration, Captain

Merkel, and it came in with a big fat Negro vote. Now I may be in the State Department, but my job depends on a presidential appointment: the way I look at it, this kind of publicity wouldn't do me a bit of harm, would it?" He held the man's glance and said, "Marian!"

She jumped a little at his tone. "You—you want me to phone?"

Will watched his opponent in silence for a minute. Then he asked softly, "You find the whole thing was a clerical error, after all, Captain?"

"Well, sure. You were right, Mr. Farland. That's what I was saying, why have a big fuss over something that's—"

"Right. You'll have Mrs. Farland shown out?" Merkel nodded and picked up his phone. Will waited until he was sure the man could hear him and said gently, "You go on out and sit in the car, honey. No need to call your office yet. I'll be out in—" he looked questioningly at the captain.

"Fifteen minutes." The policeman swiveled his chair away from Will.

"I'll be out in fifteen minutes, honey. With Bruce." The patrolman opened the door and waited. "Fifteen minutes," Will repeated. His gaze, cold and thorough, raked the figure of the young officer. "You take good care of my wife now, won't you?" he asked softly.

"Yes, *sir.*"

The young patrolman who led Marian out to the car and held the door open for her acted as though his life depended on the successful transfer of her fragile body. If I slip on a banana peel, it's all up with him, she thought —Wily Will, the fastest drawl in the District, will hunt him to his death.

Was it really funny? She shifted unhappily in the car seat and tried to pay attention to the faces of the passersby. Will's right, she told herself severely: you won't give him credit for anything he does—you asked for rescue, didn't you? And he rescued Bruce, didn't he? I don't recall that you set any conditions, and certainly Rosa won't give a damn how it was done. Reminded, she put her hand on the door latch, ready to go out and find a phone so Rosa could know. Then she hesitated: suppose somebody was watching and thought she was going to call the *Tribune?* She might be depriving Will of his heaviest artillery, just at the crucial moment.

I can't live as if I were a character in a spy melodrama, she thought miserably, but she sank back in her seat, denying her rebellion even while she was articulating it. They worked, his schemes. And she lived by them—and he was very, very good at it, she admitted to herself reluctantly, recalling his cool fencing, his skillful application of pressure. At no point that she could remember had he actually told a direct lie, but each man he'd encountered had come away with an impression of great forces behind the Farlands. So he was efficient at blackmail, and maybe at some other kinds of unloveli- nesses she just never happened to see: she could not honestly want it other- wise—at least, not today. But she writhed anyhow, aware that it was just as ugly to accept the results while wishing she need have no part of it.

How young Bruce was. She spotted the boy coming across the street with Will following and she scrambled out of the car quickly, smiling welcome at them. Bruce's heavy jacket was badly torn, with one sleeve nearly ripped out and the padding oozing at the opened shoulder seam. There was a long black streak of oil or dirt on one leg of his tan chino trousers. But otherwise, he looked, from across the busy street, like any other college boy in the ridiculous sneakers they somehow managed to wear in midwinter. As he approached, Marian saw that his skin was about the same color as Rosa's— maybe even a little lighter—and his only Negroid feature was the black hair that looked crewcut at first but up close was tight, cropped wool. "How do you do, Bruce," she said warmly, holding out her hand. "I'm Marian Farland. I know Rosa must've spoken of me."

He took his hand—which was not very clean—out of his coat pocket and shook hers with obvious reluctance. "Yes, ma'am," he said in a muffled voice. He ducked his head and Marian saw a large purple bruise on his temple, with a long smear of dirt above it. "I'll go 'long home now."

He looked up at Will. "Thanks for gettin me out, Mr. Farland." There was no gratitude in his voice, which was almost surly. Chilled and puzzled, Marian glanced at Will, but he was opening the back door of the car. Bruce shook his head.

"Oh, get in," Will said impatiently. "You don't want to run around looking like that. We'll drive you home." He left the door swinging open and came around and got into the driver's seat. Bruce climbed in and slammed the back door. "I don't know that you've got anything to thank me for," Will said, without looking around. He glanced in the side mirror and swung the car away from the curb. "I did you out of a possible suit for false arrest, you know. You probably had grounds. But there's no arrest record now."

Marian turned in her seat in time to catch the trace of a smile on the tan poker face. "That strikes me as a largely theoretical suit," Bruce said, with nothing in his speech of the slovenliness of a moment ago. "It looks to me like you got me the best deal that could be had."

"Makes me mad." Will's sudden stop at a red light threw them all forward. "Sorry. I should've gone right on through—I doubt that I can get a ticket for anything in this precinct today." The light changed and he turned right, waiting for a large woman towing two little children to cross. "I'd like to have come out with more than you," he told Bruce morosely. "With the guy's badge. Maybe a few strips of his skin."

Bruce laughed and looked out of the window without answering. He sounded vaguely superior, Marian thought—as though Will were a young freshman and he a wise senior. "You'd better put something on that cut on your head," she advised. "And have you had anything to eat?"

"Yes, ma'am, that's all right." His face was a mask again—dirty, unshaven, and polite. Puzzled by his determined distance, she hesitated; she wanted to ask him to call Rosa, but she was afraid of his reaction. She summoned up her courage finally, for Rosa's sake, as they drew up at the dirt-colored apartment house, its brickwork more ornate than builders had time for these days. Bruce climbed out of the car, looking at her coolly, and answered that he was going to call anyway.

"Why did he dislike me so?" she asked Will at once, as soon as they drove away.

Will slid a look at her and sighed. "Good Lord, did you expect him not to resent you?"

"Why? What did I do?"

"You rescued him."

"But you did it, really."

"That's a little different," Will said shortly. He saw that she was still bewildered. "For God's sake, Marian. Do you think he enjoys being rescued by a woman?"

"But he's only a boy—"

"No, he isn't. He's a man, and he hasn't been treated like one."

Young men . . . cannot endure to be for long on the bottom of the world, Morisot had said. *They take me, they send me to a prison . . .* Marian saw again the swift, stiff motions of his arm: hard, ugly, jabbing gestures that were utterly unknown to Marian had made the feeling of being young and hurt and scorned come to life in her little office, miles and years away from where it had happened. But even then, it hadn't seemed so shocking. . . . Paul was very foreign, and a very *physical* sort of man, like a workman or something. If strange and rough things happened to him . . .

Only the same strange and rough things had happened to Bruce. A student, not a soldier. And *here.* "What happened to him?" she asked quickly. "That bruise—"

"He hit his head when they shoved him into the car. What happened was pretty much what we heard. He and this other fellow were waiting for a bus." Will's lips twisted. "There's one little wrinkle we hadn't heard—seems the kids knew there'd be a long wait for the bus, so they'd stopped at a diner around the corner and got some coffee in paper cups. He had about half of his left when the police car came by. One cop got out and came over to them and asked what they were doing. Bruce said they were waiting for the bus. Then this cop, who'd been smoking a cigarette, spotted the cup, looked in, and just dropped his butt into the coffee; he stood there and grinned, Bruce said. He says it was so quiet there for a minute you could hear the sizzle as the cigarette went out."

"What did Bruce do?"

"Nothing. But apparently the cop's partner, who'd seen it, thought somebody was going to do something. He climbed out of the car and started over, and that's when the other boy took off."

"I'd have thrown the coffee in the man's face," Marian said hotly.

Will smiled wearily. "I know you would. And I'd have had one hell of a time getting you out of jail."

She recognized the truth of this and was quiet, but her throat was filled with borrowed rage. "I wanted to ask you, how *did* you get him out?" she asked, after a minute. "How did you know that captain was from Alabama?"

"Magic," said Will. "I did my homework, that's all. I know some people whose job it is to deal with the police when foreign diplomats get in trouble. They keep up on who's in charge at the various precincts. I got the necessary names and checked them out—and found that the *Tribune* ran a story on the captain a few years ago, in the course of an investigation of some sharp doings. Nothing proved, but he had a rather expensive house for his salary, plus a nice little summer cottage. He must've sweated while the *Tribune* was digging around, so I figured he wouldn't care to tangle with them again, especially since he's just been appointed here."

"Ugh. But how did such a bad man get to be in charge?"

"Look, don't get all upset about—"

Marian put her hand on his arm, stopping him because he was going the wrong way and mustn't get too far off course. "Will, please. I want to understand, not just go around being afraid, don't you see?" She saw at once that he didn't, or he didn't want to, and she said with enormous urgency, "Don't just pet me. *Help* me." But she would have to help him first—it was too hard for him. "Teach me, Will," she begged quietly. "Why do these things happen? How did that bad man get to be there?"

He said unwillingly, "Merkel isn't really a bad man—"

"He wasn't supposed to be the one," she interrupted, suddenly reminded. "How would you have managed if—"

"I have reason to believe Lieutenant Hines would've been even easier to persuade," Will said dryly.

"And you say they're not bad."

"Baby, it's not a *matter* of bad or good. It's a matter of strength of forces, that's all." He sighed. "Look, it's a war, see? And I had heavier artillery."

"And Bruce has none at all."

"That's right." His lips tightened. "Is that what's worrying you? That the cops were being unsportsmanlike? Do you think this is like the basketball games you played in at camp?" His voice was suddenly bitter. "Every girl at that damned camp was there because her daddy was loaded, you know. All the pretty, healthy girls with shiny hair, running around in the sunshine—you-all could *afford* good sportsmanship." He stared down blindly at the beautiful heart-shaped face like something on a porcelain figurine—an *objet d'art* passed carefully from Daddy diGennaro to Charles Grayson and then acquired by Willard Farland. "Merkel, Hines, the two cops last night—honey, they never went to summer camp. They've got no time for playing games, and they never had—they've always been in a war for survival. And where they come from, the Negro is their enemy." He looked at her doubtfully. "He's their competition, don't you understand?"

"No, I don't. I don't see how Bruce was any threat to those policemen last night."

"Baby, in a war, you don't say to yourself, 'Is this particular guy in the other uniform a threat to me?' When you see him, you shoot. With any weapon you have, and to kill if you can. And don't forget that goes for both sides—plenty of cops have got badly hurt in that precinct." Alarm showed suddenly in the eyes of Will Farland, a man who had never owned anything like her before and who liked to play it safe. "Marian? You look—listen, you better go home."

She swallowed nausea and told him she would be all right, and then promised dutifully that she would go home if she wasn't.

"I wish I didn't have this meeting," Will said painfully. "But I can't— you see, with Hoffman out of the country, Lloyd Morris is Acting Secretary of State. And since he doesn't act, that leaves me. The job makes me a little nervous," he went on apologetically, his eyes and his voice begging her to look better, to excuse him for getting her all upset.

She answered this silent plea. "It's not your fault. I wanted to know how you did your magic."

Will sighed in relief. "All right, baby. I'll answer all your questions tonight, I promise. Show you how all the illusions are constructed and even let you examine my tall silk hat." When he had a little time, he could make a better presentation: something vivid, but not too real for her to take. He took a pencil from his breast pocket and then began to fish for a piece of paper because he was a little worried. He shouldn't have let her talk him into—"Look, if you don't feel better, you call me." He found a folded State Department telephone message slip in the pocket of his jacket and scribbled on it hastily, leaning on the dashboard. "Here. If you call this number, you can get me, and you won't have to go through my secretary. But don't bandy the number around now, hear?" His face lightened as he saw her smile. "That's better, right? Now beat it, baby, please, and let me get to work."

By the time she reached her office arguments she should have voiced were crowding into her mind: Captain Merkel had no right to declare a private war, and an unequal one. When his troops were shot at, the culprit was hounded down by society; but when he shot, it was in the name of society. The French called it "staircase wit," Marian recalled as she lifted the phone to call Rosa—this access of clarity and logic when it was too late.

Rosa was too happy to argue about anything. "I makin that man some cornbread right now," she said of Will. "You really got us somethin when you married him."

Marian rolled her eyes at this and listened patiently to Rosa's excited babble about getting Bruce's coat sewed in time for his afternoon class and fixing a feast for the conquering hero Farland. Marian felt the sickness beginning again and with it, this time, a lonely guilt at her refusal to join the celebration. She was behaving like a spoiled child, she told herself after she'd hung up; she had been given what she wanted, and here she was still sulking. But not the way I wanted it, a small, stubborn voice went on insisting in her mind.

She had found an uncertain peace by the time the phone rang and she discovered it was late in the afternoon. From the tone of voice and the occasional appearance of one of Will's characteristic turns of phrase, she guessed that Will's secretary was reading from shorthand notes. Marian listened dully to the news that her husband would not be home for dinner because he was flying up to New York to meet Secretary Hoffman, who was returning from an international conference. She interrupted once, to ask when Will would pick up his bag, and his secretary explained patiently that he wouldn't need one. "He's going to catch the Secretary at Idlewild and ride back to Washington with him. They're taking a sleeper back so they can talk to somebody at the UN late tonight."

"Well, he'll need—"

"All he'll need is a toothbrush, and he can pick that up at the airport," the secretary said. "They'll be working all night on the way back, I'm afraid. They're due at the White House at nine o'clock tomorrow morning." The secretary's voice abandoned her notes and hinted humanly of triumph. "He'll be reporting to the President, Mrs. Farland. With the Secretary of State." She waited for some appropriate response; Marian could almost hear her thinking about poor Mr. Farland, whose wife obviously didn't appreciate him.

"Well, that *is* exciting, isn't it?" she managed. It sounded false even to her. "Thanks very much. And would you ask him to call me in the morning?"

"He has to be at the *White House* at nine, Mrs. Farland. I don't see how he could stop here first, and I don't know where I could leave him a message. If it's an emergency, I could phone the UN delegation—"

"Oh no. No emergency. I forgot about the White House." That tore it, Marian thought, listening to the gasp at the other end of the phone. She thanked the woman again, feeling less than successful in demonstrating that poor Mr. Farland had a wife who appreciated him.

Will's secretary clicked off, but before Marian could hang up, Pearl's voice said in her ear, "Marian? Hold on. I've got your son waiting." A few seconds later, Marian was rubbing her free hand over her forehead and asking carefully, "You need a what?"

"A heart," Dick repeated. "It's my science project. I have a chicken heart that Rosa gave me, and I need one from a bigger animal. To compare."

Which Gilbert and Sullivan was it—*"Take any heart, take mine!"* Marian sang softly into the phone the sweetly descending music that followed, and then began to laugh.

"It's nothing. It's a song from *Pirates of Penzance*. At camp, once, we— Look, don't worry about the heart. I'll talk to you about it later, all right? We'll find something."

When she finally hung up, she went about putting her office to rights with her mind full of long-ago summers of leggy girls in uniform shorts and shirts who put on Gilbert and Sullivan operettas and always said "Sorry" if they inadvertently infringed another's right. Golden girls like Marian—and Andy —who were taught that wealth is a responsibility and learned that nothing is right that is graceless. And who ran about in the sunshine with their heads full of gentle melodies, believing that "Thou the stream and I the willow; thou the sculptor, I the clay . . ." was what love was like.

It was time, she decided, to go home. She put her coat on, felt in her pocket for her glove and found the little folded slip of paper Will had given her. She unfolded it, wondering whether she was supposed to burn it and stir the ashes—the confidential phone number of some secret warren Will had been inhabiting that afternoon must not be allowed to get into the Wrong Hands—and saw there was something written on the other side.

And then a great lump of tears gathered in her throat as she read the three notes Will Farland, in his imprecise schoolboy hand, had written to himself:

"Memo for I.O.

"Draft Cinci speech for Lloyd

"Find out what eating Marian"

Twenty-six

"So that's what one wears to warm a White House," the President said. He closed the door of their bedroom and turned back to Andrea, but with mild dismay replacing delight in his face now. "I was just coming to dress, though. Have I mixed up the time?"

"No, darling, you're all right. I've got to go down and get photographed. I made a bargain—a half hour of taking pictures and answering questions, and then they all go away and let us have our party in peace."

"Is that Luke's idea or yours?"

"Mine." Andy crossed to him and stood on tiptoe to kiss him. "This is not an official party—it's my party. I hope you'll come."

Alec sighed. "I suppose, considering the built-in conflict between Messenger's mission and your determination to keep the children sequestered—"

"Isn't it yours, too?"

"And *our* determination, et cetera—well, it looks as though you and Luke aren't doing too badly toward working out a *modus vivendi.*"

"It takes eternal vigilance, though," Andy said darkly.

"Anyway, yes, I'll come to our party. Most of the time." Alec sat down and began to pull off his shoe, grinning at her. "I'm like a fellow with the GI's, I'm afraid: the party has to be convenient to the latrine and the guests have to be understanding if I absent myself hastily from time to time. But, with those limitations, I can play."

Andy made a face. "I took your special requirements into account, but hardly in those terms. Couldn't you find a less earthy metaphor?"

"I could, I suppose. But my inventiveness has been flagging since I finished another peril in the life of Dudumber the Cucumber. I tried to work for a while after, but I was too drained."

"Oh Alec. You'd better kill him off. You can't go on this way."

"I know." The President wiggled his freed toes gratefully. "At what age do girls abandon their fathers and run off with boys or something?"

"Well, certainly not at four. I'd better go."

Alec caught her hand as she went by him. "Wait. What's this I hear about some ballet dancer coming tonight? You promised me this occasion would be confined to those we've screened for the RH factor."

"Oh, you mean Sergei Borin. I've wanted to meet him for years, and never did. Then it occurred to me that I have power enough to make any hostess's head whirl—I can invite *anybody* to the White House."

"Well, I'm glad you found a compensation for the horrors of living here. But what if this Borin isn't RH-proof?"

"Oh, I think he probably is. You have to take *some* chances."

"You don't say," said the new President.

Andy collapsed onto his lap, grinning. "All right, all right. Wait till the next time *you* sound fatuous."

Alec smoothed his lapful of heavy white silk skirt with a gingerly hand. "Oughtn't you preserve your perfection for the cameras?"

"I considered that it took second place, that sort of thing." Andy peered at him narrowly. "Is the RH factor getting to you?"

"It's different," Alec said. "You've always inspired a Reverent Hush in me."

"Well, it'll be the only one tonight," Andy assured him. She got up, reluctantly, and smoothed her skirt, straightening the narrow panel of soft pink, embroidered with tiny, delicate flowers, that trimmed the low wide neck of the dress and came down the front in a single smooth fall. "Everybody else is tried and found not wanting."

"Yes. Good. Excuse me, but—could I ask, is that—er—ribbon—what is known as a dangle-bangle?"

Andy stared. "I'm not sure I know what a dangle-bangle is."

"Well, then that isn't one?"

"No, of course not." She tried the outrageous word silently. "Alec, really, what have you been reading? This is a . . . sort of a floating panel, I guess. See?" She walked across his line of vision, making the panel float.

"I see. 'Then, then, methinks, how sweetly flows the liquefaction of her clothes.' That thing is some kind of fraud—it looks like a proper subdeb's costume for an afternoon recital of Schubert *Lieder*. And then you move, and it doesn't."

"That's right," Andy said complacently.

"Did I ever tell you you're capable of a terrible lot of guile?"

"Well, certainly more than dangle-bangles." Her voice scorned the word. "You're worse than Paul for picking up silly slang."

"I have opportunities Paul doesn't enjoy." Alec bent his head over the difficult problem of removing his second shoe.

"Apparently," said the cool voice above him.

"All right, you've got me," Alec confessed. He raised his head and grinned. "I did once know a girl who fancied dangle-bangles. Sort of a Tondelayo type, if you know what I mean."

"Not exactly," Andy said dubiously.

"Oh you know—given to dresses that shake and shiver, sort of." He shook his head. "Very attention-getting. But quite appalling, of course."

Andy sighed happily. "It's a good thing you finally proposed."

"Why? This Tondelayo, she was never—"

"I know, darling. It's just that I remember thinking, at one point, that if you didn't show signs of succumbing soon, I was going to have to try something more desperate. Beginning with dresses that shake and shiver." She looked a little grim. "And probably ending with springing out of a pie."

"In the Senate restaurant?" Alec looked her over thoughtfully. "We could use some support on the Hill. Is it too late? If I treat you coldly," he began in a bright, hopeful voice, "do you think you might be inspired to—"

Andy fled. She trimmed her grin down to respectable proportions in the quiet of the little elevator, but she was still a little pink and bright-eyed as her husband's press secretary handed her a copy of the guest list he had prepared for the press. Lucien Messenger, who would be one of the guests, was dressed in evening clothes and a battered fedora; Andy demanded, and got, an explanation as they descended to the press room.

"When I take this hat off, that's all for tonight," Messenger warned the reporters. "I become one of the glittering company."

"It'll take more than that, Luke," someone called out.

"Finish, finish. My wife is waiting for me to escort her to a party."

"Could we have one more with a smile, Mrs. Girard?"

"There'll be no formal entertainment, is that right, Mrs. Girard?"

Andy smiled, outlined the supper menu once more, and confirmed that there would be no formal entertainment. The President was dressing. The guests were all simply friends. "Look," she said earnestly. "We just want to have a party. Like anybody else's party, or as like anybody else's as we can, in the circumstances. I'm sure you all understand and will cooperate. The President needs a little relaxed fun, and this seemed a good way to arrange it." She looked around at them and added, "Please help."

Messenger reached a plump hand toward his hat and thus set off an anguished chorus of protest. The First Lady smiled and spoke, but only those nearby could hear her. "Don't come to the party for another few minutes, please, Luke. I want to check the flowers."

He grinned and took his hand down. "All right," he told the protesters. "Ten minutes more. But it'll have to be just me. Mrs. Girard has things to attend to."

"Will there be ash trays in the downstairs rooms?"

Andy, ready to leave, spun around, attracted by the question. "Ash trays?"

"Mrs. Winkler wouldn't have them. At least not in the public rooms," the reporter explained.

The First Lady and the President's press secretary exchanged a laughter-laden look. "That has been altered," Messenger said gravely. "You may say that Mrs. Girard has no anti-ash tray policy."

He was still hatted, still amiably fielding questions, when Andy finished her survey on the floor above, smiled radiantly at the White House usher who had accompanied her, and dispatched her compliments to the staff. Wisely, she avoided hovering over people who had work to do. But her passage through the polished, waiting rooms did not go unnoticed. "Look at her," whispered the little maid who would attend the visiting ladies. "Did you ever see anybody look so happy?"

The President noticed the same phenomenon as he stepped out of the elevator; his wife, warned of his descent, was waiting for him in the great hall, but there was something about her stillness that implied motion, light and easy and graceful, like a poised butterfly. He tucked her arm in his and covered her hand with his own. "I see you like our new house."

Andy grinned impudently. "If you're engaged in some devious attempt to change my mind about the renovations I've planned, you're wasting your time."

"Wouldn't think of it," he said stoutly. "Who cares if it costs a million votes or so? I've got four years to repair the damage."

"You *are* teasing, aren't you, Alec? It won't cause—"

"It will cause some adverse comment. So, I recall, does the way you arrange your hair." He looked at her thick dark hair, drawn back from her temples into a simple pearl clasp not unlike a child's barrette, then swinging loose and shining below. "Which I find most attractive, by the way."

"Thank you."

"You're welcome. So—it is not incumbent on you to politick when going about your proper business. But I'm astonished to find that you care. I thought the prospect of my being—er—retired involuntarily in a few years wouldn't sadden you."

"I'm a shortsighted fool," Andy said thoughtfully. "I really had no notion whatever of how pleasant it could be when we were finally installed here. All I saw were the drawbacks, but now I find that it may be the best way we ever lived, despite the inconveniences." She laughed. "Do you know, I've seen you more in the few months since you became President than in the year before?"

In Andy's eyes, Alec noted silently, he had become President on a November night in Vermont: everything since, he supposed, had been only details. "It's a good job," he said contentedly, thinking that she might be right, at that. "A little hyperactive but—" He broke off to listen to the servant who approached. "Yes. Thank you." He led his wife toward the door at the north entrance, where they would greet their guests under the great hanging lantern. "Who do you suppose the first arrivals are?"

"The Kimballs. Betty will know that I'm all aflutter."

But it was Bill Bruyette, alone and thus a disappointment to the photographers waiting to record the ladies' gowns for the women's pages. They had their moment after only a brief wait, however: Annette Messenger, on the arm of her hatless husband, whose moon face was imperturbable, wore a ballet-length lavender and black print dress. She looked lovely, but nevertheless her husband abandoned her promptly, once inside, and descended to the diplomatic reception room on the opposite side of the Mansion. Here he waited to welcome two couples, from foreign diplomatic missions in Washington, who were good friends of the Girards and whose presence here tonight was not a matter of protocol.

The flashbulb explosions at the north entrance had hardly faded from sight when the Farlands arrived, Marian a small, quick flame in chiffon that floated so lightly only the camera could still it for the eye. Bonnie Ruffing, poised between the similar wiry black-and-white figures of her husband and Paul Morisot, looked comfortingly placid in bell-skirted rose-colored taffeta, also of the new short length. Jerry Rosenberg was rendered virtually invisible by the elegance of the two tall, slim ladies he had brought: Ann Taswell in white slipper satin striped with dark green and his auburn-haired wife Nedra in a slender frock combining beige and a rich chocolate brown. (But Rosenberg's disappearance was only visual: he hesitated in the most famous doorway in the land to murmur, "I'm not sure we have the right address," convulsing the photographers.) Doctor and Mrs. Henry Donnelly of Philadelphia caused a flurry of whispered questions for a moment until somebody remembered that Carol Donnelly was Andy's college friend. Even more of a flurry, this time with much stage-whispered spelling of the unfamiliar name, attended the arrival of a Georgetown lithographer who'd been the Girards' O Street neighbor; his wife grinned at the photographers she recognized from the days when they'd trodden her flowers and left a litter of dead flashbulbs in her yard. Meanwhile, downstairs, Luke Messenger, with something of a speakeasy-days air, ushered the diplomats and a New York art dealer up to the public rooms.

By the time the Kimballs came, the guest of honor had arrived and the photographers had left. Andy, exclaiming over Betty's dress, led her into the color and movement that had replaced the stately silences of the historic rooms, and said she'd almost given them up. "In fact, Alec may have," she told Gil, peering out over the dancers. "I don't see him."

"I see Rosie, with whom I crave a word." Gil graciously agreed to dispense with being received and steered across the room toward the tall figure of Jerry Rosenberg.

Andy waited till Betty had a drink and then said, "Come let me introduce you to my lion. Did I tell you how shamelessly I snared him? I'd never even met the man, though of course I'd seen him dance. But I wrote him a note."

"And he accepted?" Betty asked in mock surprise.

"Well, every performer likes a fan," Andy returned gravely.

Betty looked around the huge, glittering room. "Where's the music? I hear it, but I don't see—"

"It's in the East Room." Andy grinned. "We've got rooms and rooms. What do you think this is, Georgetown? Although, come to think of it, we had more rooms for living there, even if we couldn't party as grandly. Oh, there's Alec." Her smile faded. "Wouldn't you know? Look at him. And he hasn't even greeted all his guests."

"Well, guests who arrive this late," Betty began, and then she caught sight of the President. Crowded into a corner, he was listening attentively to Bill Bruyette, and it was perfectly clear from their attitudes that neither man was really partygoing. "He's gone," Betty decreed, examining the tableau. "You might as well let him go to his office."

"Not yet, anyway." Andy tugged Betty over to the conferring pair and touched her husband's arm.

Betty said, "Good evening, Mr. President," and "Hi, Bill," in exactly the same tone of voice.

The President laughed. "Glad you could make our housewarming, Betty. Where's Gil?"

"Circulating."

"An activity," Andy said pointedly, "appropriate to parties."

The President sighed. "Put the dice away, Bill. The MP's are here."

"Dancing," Andy went on, "is another highly regarded indulgence at parties."

Bruyette clapped his hand to his forehead. "I have it! They want us to dance!"

The President squared his shoulders. "Never let it be said, and so forth." He took his wife's hand. "Excuse us, please. We're going to—er—cut a rug."

"He's a little out of date," Bruyette admitted, watching them go. "But he's been busy."

Betty sighed, ignoring the comment. "Marvelous. Andy, I mean."

"I know. She trails happiness like some kind of perfume." He eyed Betty dubiously. "You really want to dance?"

"Certainly I do. Doesn't everybody?"

A good many did, anyhow. Andrea Girard, following her husband's rather conventional steps with ease, saw Paul Morisot slide by with Nedra Rosenberg and thought happily that even Paul looked a little less glowery than he had for some time. She glanced up at Alec and found him smiling down at her. "Nice music," he said, apparently forgiving her for shanghaiing him.

Nice Alec, Andy thought, laying her head against his shoulder. Nice friends, nice party, nice world. Under her hand, the muscles at the back of his neck stiffened and she thought determinedly that New England was going to have to unstuff his stuffed shirt tonight, by golly. Certainly among friends, he could relax. She smiled when, after a bit, he did. The music ended and she looked at Alec and said, "It's been a long winter, but spring is coming."

"Oh yes. It does, if you can hang on." He looked out at the others, over her head. "Your ballet dancer is making his way over to claim you, I think."

"Goodness. I hope I'm up to it."

"Please, Mom, can I go play with the fellers now?"

Andy followed Alec's glance to the window embrasure at the far end of the long room and sighed as she counted off Jake Ruffing, Will Farland, and Jerry Rosenberg. "They look like a convention of penguins. All right, darling, if you must. But don't disappear before supper, will you?"

She welcomed Sergei Borin with a bright smile that wobbled a little as he told her he'd asked for a waltz. Then the music began, and the first few measures carried all her qualms away. The dancer came to the waltz with the reverence and knowledge of a poet confronting his native language: Andy, floating in a swift controlled arc as Borin welcomed each measure with a smooth leap, knew she had never waltzed before.

"Look," said Rosenberg with pleasure, interrupting the rapid talk in the huddle. The President was already looking, though—watching his wife laughing as Elizabeth did when he swung her to his shoulder. He awoke to the others after a long moment, turning to them so suddenly that he caught Farland surveying him with curiosity. Taking my measure, the President thought, and who can blame him?

Jake Ruffing turned away from the dancers with leftover fondness in his face and waited for the President to reopen the discussion. But Alec nodded at the enthralled Rosenberg. "Can we get Rosie back from the primrose path?"

"Sorry, sir," Rosenberg said, stealing one last look at the flying dancers. "It's in my blood, you know. My grandmother was born in Vienna—I can feel the ancestral memory stirring—"

"Of course," interrupted Alec, who knew that Rosenberg's grandmother, though indeed born in Vienna, had arrived in this country at the age of two. And, as the daughter of one Harvard professor and the wife of another, had probably done most of her waltzing in Massachusetts. "What runs in *my* blood, I'd like to remind you, is a certain skill at hacking stone. Have you filled Farland in on my proposed quarrying at State?" he asked Jake.

"He has, Mr. President." Will shook his head and looked gloomy.

"Oh. You're not optimistic."

"Well, I think it's an ingenious arrangement. It chips Lloyd out, which is your major objective, and moves a few other boulders at the same time."

"But?"

"Nothing, really, sir. Except that it's a monolithic mass over there. Very stony, indeed." Will grinned. "And, if you can bear the metaphor another minute, Lloyd is one stone who won't just roll away. He'll have to be pushed."

Rosenberg said blithely, "That's where I come in. My shoulder to the boulder, I—"

"Rosie!" The President winced. "Enough, enough." He looked out over the dancers. "Let's go and dance."

"Yes, Mr. President. If you like, sir. But won't people stare?"

Alec feinted a back-of-the-hand at him and set out to look for Andy. The music was starting up again, a gentle foxtrot just suited to his unspectacular talents, when he saw Paul swinging Andy out onto the floor. Alec turned, frowning because he really felt like dancing, and spied Marian Farland's bright, fluttering dress.

He steered her out among the other dancers, surprised for a moment at how much smaller she was than any of the other women—and certainly than Andy—and then they danced for a time with mutual pleasure in the music. Marian craned her dark head back to look up at him and said with naïve delight that this wasn't as frightening as she'd thought. "I never even danced with a *Vice*-President before," she told him solemnly.

Alec laughed. "Nothing to it. Andy does it all the time." He grinned down at her and said he'd half expected to be spurned, as a matter of fact. "I know I've been abusing your patience—making quite incredible demands on Will and sending him home bearded and probably cranky. And meanwhile Andy was moving in and snaring your son. You must be feeling a little beleaguered."

Marian found herself, to her own surprise, denying this rather precise summary of her feelings. But Peter had a complaint, she reported—he had expected to see soldiers at the White House, and all he'd found were policemen.

"Well, if he doesn't mind the homegrown kind, I guess I can find him some," Alec offered. "I don't believe we've had any uninvited foreign troops around for more than a century." The music stopped and he guided her artfully to a halt alongside his wife and Morisot. "I forgot to put my name down on your program," he told Andy. "I suppose I haven't a chance now?"

Andy smiled graciously at the others. "Could you excuse us? It's our song," she added, bland in the face of the orchestra's silence. " 'Hail to the Chief.' It always makes him *so* romantic."

"Madame?" Morisot stood poised like a diver before Marian. The music began—hardly "Hail to the Chief," but instead a medley from the musical *Camelot*—and Marian moved stiffly into his arms. Andy looked thoughtful as she swung away in Alec's embrace.

"I feel good," the President said, demonstrating it with a too-sudden flourish that nearly tripped Andy.

She recovered absentmindedly, peering over his shoulder. He noticed and asked her whether somebody had dropped a tray.

"It's nothing," Andy said, and then added unwillingly that actually it was Paul.

Alec twirled her around so he could see, but all he saw was Marian, whose white, set face bore almost no resemblance to the open, ingenuous one that had recently been upturned to his. "I can't see anything but his back," he said mildly.

"That's what I mean. His shoulders look as though he forgot to take the hanger out of his coat."

Paul did look oddly stiff and uncomfortable, Alec thought; he decided it probably had something to do with all the bureaucratic wrangling over *l'affaire Martigny*. It took a strong man, Alec told himself gaily, to keep limber in the presence of bureaucratic wrangling. He demonstrated his own limberness with a small skipping step of his own on-the-spot invention and said he was sure he knew this song, but he couldn't think of its name.

" 'How to Handle a Woman.' " Andy looked up at him, her eyes teasing. "It's from *Camelot*. Do you want to know the lyrics?"

"Do you think I need to?" Alec listened to the music, which was coming to its end—where the words, as he remembered now, advised, *Simply love her, only love her.* He tightened his arm around Andy, but not enough so that it would be noticeable. "Aren't you satisfied with our Camelot any more?"

"I love it," Andy said happily.

"Good. When do we eat?"

"Oh Alec. After this next dance, all right?" She extricated herself as the music came to a stop. "No, darling. I have to dance with every man here at least once, and I'm not caught up yet. I haven't done Will Farland or Jake."

"I outrank both of them," Alec protested weakly, but he knew it wouldn't wash. He caught at her as she started away. "At least tell me what's for supper."

"Wait and see. No special privileges, Mr. President."

No special privileges whatever, the President thought wryly as he stood at the south window of his oval office staring out at the red aircraft-warning light at the top of the Washington Monument. He looked at the black leafless trees in the foreground and guessed that in summer he wouldn't be able to see the monument at all. But summer was a long time away and this had to be decided now, he told himself ruefully.

He crossed to one of the pair of small curving sofas Andy had added to the long, rather austere room and flung himself down and sat there considering his predicament. The man with the message had been waiting even as his dance with Andy ended; the intelligence service chief, still in his office at this time of night, had been definite when Alec had asked the question on the phone: it had to be at once, there was no time to study the project for himself or to bring his own people in to examine it. He would have to move on the basis of Winkler's planning, or not move at all—and the intelligence chief, he knew, was speaking for the military advisers too when he urged action.

Alec pulled his right leg up and laid it across his left knee, studying his shoe morosely. Most of the Winkler leftovers were not given to calling things by their right names, and the right name of this was an ugly one—a plain assault on the sovereignty of another country in this hemisphere, even if the assault was covert and "unofficial." But a chain of events had already been set in motion: an oppressed people waited for the outside aid that had been promised them, and for this nation, a rare opportunity presented itself to unseat a hostile government too nearby for comfort. Or so said all the evidence at hand, and there was no time to collect new evidence.

The whole thing didn't feel right, but that was a hell of a way to run a country: Alec trusted his feelings, but not his feelings alone. He sighed, a very loud sound in the silence, and told himself that he couldn't expect always to feel comfortable with every decision, that it probably had to be done and he had done it—or would do it at the special meeting he had summoned for the morning. Maybe it would look better in the morning, too, with the light pouring in here through the tall French windows and the sounds of busyness in the corridors and outer offices, available to him the moment he opened his office door. The fact was, it *was* lonely, just the way all the memoirs said.

He got up and pushed open the door that led to his secretary's office, a pool of shadows and shrouded typewriters rendered especially ghostly because no phones rang. The Secret Service agent came toward him through the narrow wedge of light.

"Leroy?"

"No, sir. Cummings."

"Oh, I'm sorry. I couldn't see you properly, Cummings. Look, I wonder if you could have somebody get hold of Congressman Bruyette and ask him to come down here."

"Yes, sir. Mr. President?"

Alec turned back and then he saw what the man was indicating: a tole tray loaded with covered dishes waited on one of the desks. His conscience smote him for his departure without a word to Andy. "Supper?"

"Yes, Mr. President. Shall I take it in for you now, sir? Mrs. Girard instructed that it be left out there until you came out."

Alec found his mouth watering suddenly. "I'll take it myself. And, Cummings—"

"Yes, sir."

"Tell them to extricate Bruyette discreetly, will you? I don't want anybody to cast a pall on the party." Alec carried the heavy tray into his office and set it down carefully on the small table between the sofas. He lifted one domed lid and recognized one of the special dishes, designed to keep food hot, that Andy had used to send his lunch to his Capitol Hill office. It seemed a very long time ago, he thought a little sadly. And then the rich aroma of the lobster newburg reached him, and he unfolded his napkin and began taking lids off the other dishes and setting them down on the floor. Things were looking up, he decided: food for the hungry, company for the lonely. There was absolutely nothing Bruyette could do about his problem, especially in view of the fact that they couldn't discuss it except in hints; it was probably mean to call Bill away from the party just to hold his hand, Alec told himself cheerfully.

Bruyette, ushered in by Cummings a few minutes later, had supped, and exuded a strong odor of good brandy besides. He sat on the other sofa and bowed over his folded hands like an obsequious servant. "You sent for me, sir?" He abandoned his pose for an equally exaggerated snarl. "It better be good. I was just making progress."

The President sighed. "Jest with me, old son. I'm having misgivings."

Bruyette looked over the long, high-ceilinged room with its huge globe on a stand by the window and the gold-fringed American flag behind the waiting desk. "I should think so, in this portentous gloom." He studied his friend. "What is it? 'The hand that signed the paper felled a city'?"

"Dylan Thomas? I thought so. Well, he was no expert on survival. But poets tend to oversimplify power anyway. The name of the game is, sign the right paper and the city won't be felled."

"Well, the power is yours," Bruyette said. "It was transferred to you in correct, constitutional fashion. I saw it myself."

"Unfortunately, the much-acclaimed orderly transfer of power has disadvantages. One of them is that, right now, I have to use transferred research. And a little voice keeps saying, 'Don't.' "

"Then don't."

"Hitler," the President observed, "ran a war on the basis of little inner voices. He lost."

Bruyette said with careful lightness, "I don't mean to pry, but are we talking about war?"

"Well, we're always talking about war a little. But no. Still, people could get hurt."

"People could always get hurt. Remember when you were class president, in prep school?"

Alec grinned. "When I was *finally* class president."

"It only took two tries. And it's the only election we ever lost."

"You're right, of course. On all points, both spoken and unspoken."

Bruyette nodded. "You were a very good class president."

"I made mistakes."

"You made mistakes."

The President looked at his old friend and smiled slowly. "It's been a long time, old wagon-hitcher." *I've decided to hitch my wagon to your star, Girard,* Bill Bruyette had said, sitting with his legs folded tailor fashion in the middle of Alec's rumpled bed. His bony knees pointed aggressively to the far corners of the room in which pennants hung and many solemn words were directed to the long, long future.

"I was a smart kid. Old wagon-hitchers ride smoothly," Bruyette pronounced. "Old stars burn steadily."

Winkler, Alec said to himself, *was* President of the United States, after all. You have to trust to a certain amount of efficiency. Imagination. Just plain good hunches. This time you just can't have your intellectual food tasted for you by the think boys, and God knows you haven't got time to stand there in the lab yourself, testing for exotic poisons. Sign, and pray . . . He stood up, stretching. "I'm finished working. Want to go look up some girls? What's on in town tonight?"

Shared memory laughed in Bill's eyes, but he pursed his lips and appeared to be considering the possibilities. "Let's see. Andrea Girard is giving a party, and it's turning out to be a real do."

Alec shook his head. "I think I'm in bad there." But he let Bruyette propel him toward the door.

"You can win her around, Champ. You always do."

They nodded at the man outside the oval office and Alec said, "Going back to the party now, Cummings."

"Doesn't he follow us?" Bruyette asked.

"Not inside the Mansion. He just tells somebody we're coming. I'd have thought the party would be simmering down by now."

Bill laughed. *"Au contraire.* I think what reshaped the evening, to begin with, was when the Kimballs started demonstrating a new dance—something big right now at their sons' high school. And then everybody started remembering old dances and Andy and Carol Donnelly sort of zeroed in on Morisot. Something from their Paris days, I gathered. He tried a retreat, but he never made it. When I left they were doing that one where you twirl the girl out and then bring her back, you know? I got the feeling Paul didn't mind twirling her out, but—"

"He'll break Andy's arm one of these days," her husband said unfeelingly. "She torments him just the way she does her brother. But Richie Langwith is a phlegmatic type, and Paul isn't." He quickened his pace. "Come on. I'd better leash Andy before he explodes."

"Oh, they've stopped by now," Bruyette said. "Everybody got started on this new one. It's called 'The Octopus'—or it should be."

Alec shuddered. "I suppose it's too much to hope that Andy was watching from the sidelines."

"Well, in a way. She was the first student, of course—"

"Of course. Protocol must be observed."

"—but when I left, she was coaching Sergei and Farland's wife." Bill laughed aloud. "Wait till you hear the music—it's wild. Everybody joined in, then, and I was just getting the hang of it myself when the man came and tapped me on the shoulder."

They emerged into the great hall and Alec winced as the blast of sound hit him. "Good God!"

Bill tested it like a sailor sniffing a breeze. "That's twist music," he pronounced. "Andy must be twisting."

She was, undeniably, Alec saw at once—though there was some question about whether that sound of metal objects falling downstairs could be called music. He moved into the room, staying close to the wall, and watched his wife's cavortings with mingled amusement and dismay. Her pearl barrette had come off, apparently—she held it between her teeth like Carmen's rose and squirmed in a manner that would surely have stopped production among the workers in that Seville cigarette factory. Beside Andy, Marian's orange chiffon scarf flew out like a pennant; somewhere generally across from them, Sergei Borin and Luke Messenger—the latter displaying the surprising fluidity the overweight often bring to dancing—slung their hips in a tempo matching the women's. He ought to make her stop, Alec thought, watching Andy's hand come up hastily to push back her flying hair; this didn't look like an appropriate exercise for a frail constitution. But he hadn't quite enough courage to bludgeon so much merriment with common sense. He was rescued from the need to, though: Andy spotted him, stopped, and began to make her way toward him through the dancers.

It would take her a while, Alec guessed—and vowed that it would also earn her nothing, if what she had in mind was to make him her next pupil. Just in case he would need support, he moved out of the doorway, seeking a wall at his back. He saw Paul a few feet away and sidled over, planning on a plea for aid if it should prove necessary. The sculptor was holding a brandy glass and studying the dancers.

"Must be prime source material for you, Paul," Alec said pleasantly. "I gather from reading art reviews that something called 'mobility' is a good thing to have." He looked out at all the mobility in the sober room and smiled as Farland's wife caught his eye: in her orange dress and constant motion, she looked like an orangeade in a blender. "It's engaging, though, isn't it?"

"Only because it is innocent," Paul observed. "I fear I am not innocent enough to participate. However, it is, as you say, an interesting demonstration of mobility." He grinned up at Alec and then looked away. "If you wish to pursue your studies of the principles of art, you should remember that each element calls into being its opposite."

"Meaning?"

Paul shrugged, keeping his eyes on the dancers. "So much mobility provokes some instant rigidity."

Alec choked, then struggled to recover quickly—Andy had finally made it, though Henry Donnelly was with her and trying to claim his dance.

"A minute," she promised. "I want to find out what Alec's laughing at."

"Nothing, darling," he told her hastily, aware of Paul's interested gaze.

"We were simply exchanging a few mild observations on the human condition."

"Pooh. Come and dance instead."

"No," said Alec in a voice that meant it.

Andy recognized the tone and gave up at once, transferring her invitation to Paul, who demurred on grounds of incapacity. "How do you know?" she argued. "You haven't tried."

"He's not in the mood," Alec intervened.

"*Il faut danser, en tout cas, mon vieux. Courage, mon frère,*" Andy taunted. "*La belle dame se presente—*"

"*Va-t-'en!*" Paul snapped rudely.

Donnelly tugged at Andy's hand. "Come on, come on. You're making everybody stop." The music crashed joyously as he succeeded in propelling Andy toward the wriggling knot of dancers.

Alec decided he deserved a drink and was working his way over to get one when he came on Will Farland and Jake Ruffing, half hidden in a window niche, black-jacketed and sober and talking. He saw them suddenly as Andy had seen him, so many times like this, and began to laugh. They looked up, startled, and Jake said genially, "Mr. President."

"You fellows don't indulge?"

"Too athletic for me," Ruffing said.

Farland stared out abstractedly over the merry inferno. "Hell, is that a dance now? Marian used to do that when she was feeling—good." The hesitation was hardly noticeable, the President thought, watching with amusement; what gave the game away was the flush, easily visible under the fair skin.

"Will, since you're not interested in dancing, a word, if you please."

"Yes, sir."

Alec spoke under the blare of the music. "Are you familiar with the work of our most famous hush-hush agency?"

"In some areas," Will replied. "The rest I deduce from what I read in the papers six months later."

"Have you a high opinion of their skills?"

"Not in general, no, sir."

"I see. Then you wouldn't rely on their estimate of popular feeling in— another country."

"No, sir," Will said promptly. "Not without corroboration."

Alec looked at him, thinking about exploring further. But what was the use, he decided—he had no second team anyhow, no matter how low Farland's opinion of the first. So he said only, "Thank you."

And turned away in time to see Bruyette bearing down on him with a glass. "You read my mind," he said, and drank thirstily. He looked up over the rim of the glass and saw Andy coming. The brassy sound had softened and the musicians vamped while their leader watched Andy for a cue.

"You know," Bruyette said, "that looks like a girl you were telling me about one night. In Vermont, a long time ago." He saw Alec remembering and added, "Old Sobersides."

"Please," begged the pretty girl who had missed a lot of fun by marrying Old Sobersides.

Alec heard the orchestra beginning the one-two-three-*boom* beat and saw the conga line forming up behind Kimball, who specialized in this dance and usually managed to organize it at parties. But probably never before, Alec thought, under a portrait of President Lincoln. "All right, but I'm *not* leading." He looked at Andy with gratitude because she wasn't angry, and then with delight because she was Andy, and added first her and then himself to the line, chanting one-two-three-*boom* as it snaked its way around the stately room. Gil was heading out into the long reception hall, Alec saw, and he grinned, thinking of all that dignity; but he held to his wife's slim hips and kicked out when she did. The line slithered past a startled-looking Messenger, and Alec reached out and pulled him in, turned his head quickly to say, "Deny this, Luke," and turned back so he wouldn't miss the beat.

V

Cracks in the Towered Walls

"Victor from vanquished issues at the last,
And overthrower from being overthrown"

Twenty-seven

The chill February Sunday that followed Andrea Girard's party at the White House was warmed by only intermittent watery sunlight. At lunch with her husband, Andy remarked that she would probably stay indoors this afternoon because the weather looked unattractive, and besides a television network was going to broadcast *La Traviata* and she thought it might be interesting to watch it with Elizabeth. She also said, just before Alec left for his daily nap, that she thought the baby's eyes were going to be brown; didn't Alec think their blue was darkening a little?

Alec fell asleep considering this question and woke decided—no, there was no sign of brown whatever, and his guess was that the baby would be as blue-eyed as Elizabeth. He had no time to impart this decision, though. Dressing with all haste, he managed to get down to his office only a few seconds before Secretary of State Harold Hoffman and his first Undersecretary, Lloyd Morris, were due to be shown in from the west wing entrance for an only recently scheduled call on the President. Alec straightened the knot of his tie unnecessarily, hoped briefly that he would be able to get back to the Mansion in time to watch at least part of the opera, and doubted it; finally he said to himself with a little anxiety and a little more distaste, "Well, here goes," and asked Dan to send the visitors in.

In the living room of his home in upper Northwest Washington, where the chair cushions were pressed permanently into the shapes of his own and his wife's behinds and souvenirs of vacations a dozen years gone were dusted weekly and put back on the mantel, the managing editor of the *Washington Tribune* folded the editorial section of the Sunday *Washington Herald* and asked his wife whether she'd like to see *Traviata* on television. She thought she might, and went to get her knitting while he uncovered the screen from the ingenious contraption of doors and shelves that hid it. He found the right channel and adjusted all the necessary knobs, but the introductory material was still rolling slowly past when his son appeared and announced that there was a phone call. The ME got up, predicting gloomily that he would certainly miss the drinking song, and went into the room his wife called his den.

As soon as he heard Lloyd Morris's voice, he knew very well what it was and that this was going to take a long time. He closed the door of the room with his slippered foot, lighted a cigarette, and listened patiently to Morris, who was an old acquaintance and clearly distressed—and whom he could not help. It was too soon to say this, though, so he only asked, "Where are you, Lloyd?"

"At my office. I came over to prepare a statement, and then I got to thinking about it some more, and I've about decided I'm damned if I'll take it."

"You might *like* the new appointment, you know," the ME suggested.

There was a small silence, and then Morris said, with some bitterness, "I take it that means you don't want to buck the White House."

The ME shrugged: it might as well be got over with sooner as later. "I don't, no, if you want to put it that way, Lloyd."

"How would you like me to put it?"

"Well, I think a fair statement would be that, though I'm not above a certain reluctance to buck all that power at any time and I don't think that makes me a craven coward, on this point I have no quarrel with the President." He closed his eyes on the squawks of outrage and let them go on until he thought they'd spent themselves enough. "Now you know better than that, Lloyd. You're just upset, and it's understandable. But when you cool off, you'll see that Girard has behaved in no way that I—or any other citizen—can properly reproach him for." He listened again, frowning because the outrage was not subsiding. "Now look—in cold, constitutional terms, the President is the head of all the executive departments and that includes the right both to hire and fire, and to reorganize them in almost any way that he damn pleases." Morris began again and he interrupted firmly. "No, you listen. I listened, now you listen. Your beef is that he's kicking you upstairs, and it's certainly true that he is—but what in hell would you like him to do? Of *course* he hopes you'll stay on, of *course* he doesn't want your followers on his neck—but would you honestly want him to keep you on as Undersecretary if he doesn't think you're the man for the job, just because he's afraid of you and yours? I'm trying to explain my position, Lloyd—I'll be through in a minute, and then you can talk. The point is, I can't attack a man who's doing what a President should do: try something, and if it doesn't work, change it."

He bent his head before the barrage and smoked quietly, listening with sympathy for the other man's disappointment. "No, you're right, it wasn't very long, but it's up to Girard to decide what's long enough." He listened some more, sighing, with his hand over the phone, and put his cigarette out, calculating that that made it roughly ten minutes and he'd missed enough of the first act. "For Pete's sake, Lloyd, haven't you ever lost a job before?" He considered saying, *Haven't you thought you might have deserved to lose this one?* but decided against it. "It's an occupational hazard, man—remember, you're not a theoretical liberal now but a practicing politician. And you're not getting shoved aside to make room for somebody with a greater claim to patronage, you know. You—"

"You know I gave up opportunities for myself to put him into office," Morris was saying.

"Sure you did, Lloyd, and everybody knows it, including Alec Girard," the ME replied soothingly. "But a man like you doesn't trade his support for a job like a third-rate wardheeler. Obviously you backed him because you thought he was the right man to run the country. And now this is the way he wants to run it, and he's apparently gone to some trouble to see that you don't get hurt in the process. When you cool off I'm sure you'll see—" Morris interrupted him, so he finished the sentence silently in a way he wouldn't have aloud: *that what you gave up was only opportunity, not the reality, and if you could have made it yourself you never would have handed over to Girard. Now he's paid off and you have no kick coming.*

The ME sat there in silence for some time after he'd hung up, a little dissatisfied with himself because he didn't think he'd been successful in his argument with Morris and a little worried about whether he might get caught in the middle if Lloyd did make a stink. He fought Presidents only reluctantly, but he did it—he'd fought Winkler for at least six years. However, he had no desire to seem to be fighting when he wasn't. He made up his mind quickly, lighted a cigarette, and phoned Jake Ruffing; while he waited, he decided that he would throw in, as a bona fide of his intentions, Lloyd's final remarks about calling Chicago. When Ruffing came on, the ME gave him the information succinctly, stated his own feelings in the matter even more briefly, and hung up with a sense of relief, hoping the commercial was on so he could tell his wife about this without interrupting the opera. As usual, he looked forward to the "thing or two" she always had to say.

Jake depressed the button on his telephone, let it come up again, and dialed Jerry Rosenberg. He talked rapidly for a minute, then Rosenberg broke in. "Where is he, Jake? At his office?" Jake answered and went on talking rapidly. When he stopped Rosenberg said, "Gee, I don't know. If he really feels ill-used, he may—" He sighed. "Okay, I'll get right down there, and I'll call you."

Jake hung up, thought for a moment, whistling silently through his teeth, and then dialed the Farlands' number. It was busy.

". . . and then I remembered seeing that thing on your desk—oh, a thousand times, I guess—and if I figured if you could spare it, I'm saved. Because he really told me about it in plenty of time, and I forgot. And now he'll get a zero tomorrow, and it's my fault—"

Dr. Whittier laughed. "Stop. I'm sold, I'm sold. The only thing is—"

"He'll take very good care of it—but—oh, don't tell me it's something absolutely irreplaceable, just in case. I mean, he has to put it on exhibit or something, and what if somebody bumps into it?"

"Whoa. *Will* you take it easy, Marian? It's not irreplaceable—it's only an ordinary plastic model of a human heart and I imagine you can buy another in any medical supply house if it gets broken. What I'm trying to say is, we're going out this afternoon. We'll be leaving at about four, and there'll be nobody home. So if the boy needs it for school tomorrow, you'll have to get over before—"

She would, she would for certain, in plenty of time, Marian assured the pediatrician. She hung up and the phone rang immediately: Jake Ruffing asking for Will. Marian called Will, went upstairs to tell Dick they were going over to Dr. Whittier's for the heart model and please to put his shoes on right away, then went downstairs to snatch a look at the television set and calculate gloomily that she would certainly miss *"Di Provenza."* Then Will called, and she went up to find him with a suitcase open on the bed. He was irritated when he found that his gray suit was at the cleaner's again and wouldn't come back till tomorrow; Marian had to ask him twice where he was going and what for before he would stop muttering that the gray suit was never there when he wanted it, which led her to point out instances when it had been right on tap. Finally, he interrupted the bickering to shout, in a voice that implied that he'd said it several times—which he hadn't—that he was going to Chicago to mend some fences, for God's sake, and he'd be back tomorrow, so what the hell was the fuss all about? At that point, Marian took the trick by reminding him softly that Peter was taking his nap; leaving Will reduced to silent fury, she climbed to the third floor again to persuade Sharlie to sit with Peter while she was gone.

Marian missed *"Di Provenza,"* which had been a favorite of her grandfather, because the car radio had been broken for months and at the critical moment she was driving back from dropping Will at the airport, speeding along the parkway so she could get to Dr. Whittier's before he went out and then get home in time to release Sharlie, who had a date to do her math homework with a girl who had not forgotten her math book on Friday. *"Ah, quell'amor,"* Marian sang suddenly at the top of her voice, free to choose to celebrate love if she wanted to, whether they were up to it back at the opera house or not. She slowed only a little in deference to a sign that warned, "Speed Radar Controlled." Dick Farland, collector of hearts, looked first startled and then tolerant, as was his wont.

Andrea Girard thought the baritone did a fine job on *"Di Provenza,"* though she had to hush Elizabeth, who developed a pressing question about the baby just as the deep, rich voice was begging, *"Dio mi gui-do."* As soon as the aria was over, she gave Elizabeth her attention and patiently explained that probably Sandy did think indeed Elizabeth was a grown-up: "We're all huge and powerful to him, you see, darling." A lot of water flowed under the bridges of the opera's Paris before the audience concluded its discussion of infant perception and returned to tragedy. By which time a new act had begun and Violetta was nobly pretending to be bored with Alfredo. Elizabeth looked at the heroine dabbing at her eyes with what must have been the scrap of cambric that recurs in all romantic literature and asked why the lady was crying.

Andy smiled down at the baby kicking his feet with incessant, aimless energy in the portable bed on the floor of the sitting room. She told Elizabeth the lady was sad because her lover was leaving—which was succinct, if slightly inaccurate—and then had to hide her face quickly by leaning over the baby when Elizabeth suggested that the lady should get another lover and then she wouldn't have to cry. By the time that act ended, Elizabeth had become absorbed in a puzzle and Andy used the time while the chaste, self-consciously dignified commercial was on to make some notes of ideas she intended to suggest for the new play school; Paul, she thought, would probably not be around much longer, so it might be a good idea to have him come up soon and show the children a few of the tricks with papier-mâché sculpture that had enchanted Elizabeth.

Little Josh Rosenberg, age three, was chasing peas around his plate with a small spoon when his father came home. As he hung up his coat, Rosenberg reported wearily to his wife that it was okay, everything was nailed down and Lloyd had not only seen the light but would calm his agitated admirers. Then he watched the earnest endeavors of the curly-haired child. "Tomorrow begins full-time school for our schoolboy, right?" On the television screen Violetta tossed her head and offered her soprano favors to all comers. Rosenberg watched her briefly, then compared her with Nedra—who was offering only a casserole but who could sing passably too—and decided it was Nedra by a mile.

"Our schoolboy's going out to lunch, too," said Violetta's successful rival. She steered Josh's uncertain hand to success with a final pair of peas. "Did I tell you I worked out a deal with Marian Farland? I'll pick up the kids at the White House and in return she—or her maid, really—will give them lunch."

"Maybe," Rosenberg said. "But you watch out—you're an innocent among old hands, there. Those State Department wives are probably the world's sharpest traders on the domestic front."

In a neat, modern, and curiously static hotel room in Chicago, a thoroughly experienced trader turned his back on his guests to do a little quick thinking while he stripped a hotel glass of its elaborately sealed wrapping and poured himself some ice water from a plastic pitcher; he had little or nothing to trade, Will Farland concluded quickly, because these guys were capable of yelling "Foul" even without any encouragement from Lloyd Morris.

"Let's lay it on the table, gentlemen." Thoughtfully, he directed his words at the youngish political science professor perched on one of the black-covered Hollywood beds. This man, he judged, was the natural leader of the loosely formed group. "You can hurt the President and you can delight the opposition, but you can't keep Lloyd in that job. Girard doesn't want to lose friends, but he's no Winkler—he does what he thinks he has to do whether people love him for it or not. In short—" he smacked the table-top with the palm of his hand "—you elected a President, not an errand boy. Most of us thought you wanted it that way. But if you didn't, there's not a damn thing you can do about it for about four years. And even then, chances are the only choice you're going to have is between Girard and Ferris."

"You're right in saying that we have no place else to go, of course," the professor observed. "But we're entitled to a voice in our own camp."

"Sure you are," Will answered quickly. "And you got one, and you're still getting one. It strikes me, though, that you're demanding not a voice but a veto. You elected Alec Girard to run the government of the United States, which certainly includes the personnel organization of the Department of State. Yet you're acting as though you were a bunch of auto manufacturers and he was the Congressman from Detroit."

One of the other men stirred, frowning. "Lloyd—"

"Needs Girard a hell of a lot more than Girard needs him," Will interrupted brutally. He collected their glances, his voice softening. "Lloyd is one swell guy, I know. I worked for him, and I would again—but not in that job. That job requires a sharpie, which I think you'll agree Lloyd is not; the fellow Girard is moving up to the job *is* a sharpie, and he's *our* sharpie. That's all the choice you get, you know: ours or theirs."

The professor said dryly, "I'm familiar, Mr. Farland, with the text that politics requires compromises. But we happen to think that compromises are what got us into the state Winkler brought us to, and we're determined to stop the whole process, right now, by sticking to what we know is right, right from the beginning."

Lord protect us from our friends, Will thought, surveying the speaker with a respect he didn't feel; from the corners of the room, his sensitive antennae picked up a stirring of disagreement. Your days are numbered, Junior, he advised the young professor silently, and set about giving the opposition a handle. "You're right, you know. About compromises, I mean. Up to a point. But then I begin to hear the baby crying as it gets thrown out with the bathwater. Compromises in politics are something you can't do without, because if each guy simply sticks to what he feels is right—which, by the way, is fanaticism, pure and simple—the whole country sits absolutely still on dead center. Which is no improvement over Winkler." His voice was dextrously closing the discussion. "Maybe compromises did get us into this state, but what'll get us out of it is better compromises, picking them so they work for us. Which is what I did, and you did, when we voted for Alec Girard. He said, you remember, that he'd get things started. He didn't say he'd do it by walking on the waters, and I wouldn't have voted for him if he had. He means to do it by using the tools of politics and government—administration, horsetrading with Congress, executive appointments . . . You know better than I do what those tools are."

He sighed and looked around the room. "I'm for letting the President get on with it. If you think it over and decide that I'm mostly making sense —one hundred percent agreement is not required, as I've been trying to say—then, welcome to the rooters. If you think I'm all wet—" he smiled "—well, it's a free country, and you've already given me all I had coming, by taking the time to listen to what I had to say. In the end, every man runs his own shop, the way he thinks will work out best—and that's as true for all of you as it is for the President."

The men left his hotel room in what seemed to him a friendly mood. Will climbed into his unfamiliar bed with as much satisfaction as weariness, offered up a brief prayer to be spared any more amateurs, and fell asleep.

Rosa Little, already lying abed on the convertible couch in her living room, on which she slept during her weekends at home, was neither quite weary nor quite satisfied. The weekly cleaning of her small apartment had required only a small percentage of her energies and skills; settling down with the inevitable cup of coffee to watch the opera with Trixie and Bruce had given her a mild satisfaction, and she had listened with absent interest to her daughter's summary of the story of Camille-Violetta and her blue-blooded lover.

By now Violetta, having been through a lot of love and music, was lying on a couch, holding a letter in one slim white hand, and apparently reading it—singing, of course, as they seemed to sing even "Please pass the salt" in operas. Violetta had TB, Trixie had explained, and Rosa was wondering who would write such an obviously upsetting letter to such a sick woman . . .

Trixie, silhouetted before her mother in the twilit room, straightened quickly from her lazy crouch on the floor before the television set. Violetta's white garments trailed gracefully as she raised herself on her couch, gasping out her longing for her lost lover while a single violin remembered, heartbroken, *"Ah, quell'amor."* Trixie pressed her thin hands together in front of her as if to catch ecstasy and contain it: love was holy, holy, said the lush music looping into the silence, and Trixie was, as young girls had been for a hundred years, its easiest and first captive. The frail, swelling theme stirred Rosa, too—and even enthralled briefly the love-hungry boy Bruce, who extricated himself only by recalling with determined bitterness that it didn't mean him, the lady hadn't meant him, nobody ever meant him.

"Ah," said Trixie as everybody on stage sang—the remorseful Alfredo and his poor father, Violetta's maid, and a gentleman Rosa wasn't sure of— and Violetta, after a last dying rapture, expired in the arms of her lover. Rosa, who knew when things should end, turned away at once, abandoning both the mourners and her own concern that all those people might catch the TB. Behind her, Alfredo laid back on the pillows the clean and graceful corpse of star-crossed love and cried out his final anguish. Trixie sighed a long sigh and sank back on her heels.

And Bruce, caught with his face naked because Rosa hadn't waited for the very end, lashed out at her in his shame, lecturing her stridently while the curtain closed on the television screen and the applause rose. Violetta returned to life, bowing over an armful of roses, and Rosa asked Bruce whether he was hungry. The question sparked fury. "You and your lily-white Maid Marian," he cried. "That's all she was interested in, too. Stopping my mouth with—Pablum." *With a tit,* was what he had intended originally, but he was not angry enough to use language that would drive Rosa away.

Trixie was turning away from the television screen now, and Rosa smiled at the light in her daughter's eyes and wanted to keep it there. Her impromptu motherhood of Bruce was not exclusive. "It all right," she said, dismissing him cheerfully. "You don't have to be grateful if you don't want."

"Oh, but I am grateful to Lord and Lady Farland, who ride to the aid of the downtrodden. Really I am. I got an education, watching that bloated son-of-a-bitch captain—all right, I'm sorry, Miz Little. Anyway, Farland crumpled him good, and it was a pleasure to watch." Bruce's eyes remembered with bitter pleasure. "And he even gave me a useful lesson, Farland did, when we came out. You know what he told me? 'The thing about a bully,' he said, 'is that he can be bullied. Use your brains and find his handle, that's all.' " Bruce's look hardened. "I'll remember that, all right, and I guess I *am* grateful. It may be the most valuable lesson I've ever learned."

Rosa, who was still learning assorted valuable lessons, turned and turned in her hard bed, trying to get away from the reflected glare of a street light and from the boy's unceasing demands for clarity, order, justice, and other unattainables. You just can't mother the whole world, she lectured herself, and tried to believe it.

In her office the next day, Marian Farland was delivering a similar lecture to herself as, back from lunch, she exchanged her shoes for her office moccasins. Grant had announced at lunch that he was thinking of quitting his job and going to New York to write a novel. Perhaps more tartly than was advisable, Marian had suggested that he pause to arm himself with some knowledge of syntax. To which Grant had replied, jabbing at her with the words, that he would have small use for it when he was drafted. "Hear, hear," one of the other copyboys had murmured, and a flushed Marian had devoted herself to her spaghetti, feeling too frail for the role of sole representative of a world they'd never made.

What was she supposed to say to them, or to her own assortment of children? Seeking relief, her mind turned back to her brief telephone conversation, earlier this morning, with Paul, who had been the only voice in days that made no demands. They simply talked, nothing more: he'd been for a long walk yesterday, he reported, up along the canal, where the path was still rutted and frozen but the slow water moved sluggishly; the river was low, and the rocks looked cruel and enduring. And it could all have been said a hundred Februaries ago, and there was unutterable peace in it. Marian agreed gratefully to have lunch with him and recognized, after she'd hung up the phone, that he'd somehow become a source of peace and rest and that it was pretty funny when you considered how greatly he had disturbed her peace not long ago. Right here in this very office— Carefully, she stopped remembering; that problem had been solved, and she was entitled to enjoy the fruits of self-denial. Which included the peace that came, however oddly, of having just one thing in her whole life in which all struggle was practically finished.

The corner of her eye caught and registered the familiar shape of the shadow on her glass wall, but Will was swinging in the door almost before she realized she had seen him. She jumped up and then stood still, staring at him in confusion and dismay: above the stubble of beard, his eyes glittered as though with fever. His trousers were shapeless and rumpled. His open coat, swung wide by the weight of bulky things in the pockets, revealed a wilted shirt with an inkstain above the pocket like a bullethole that had missed his heart. Disapproving, she stood motionless in the hard circle of his arms, then hung limply as he lifted her off her feet, kissed her soundly, and set her down. His beard had reddened her forehead in passing, and he smelled of too many cigarettes. "Where's your overcoat?" she asked.

"In the car. I'm parked in the twenty-minute spot downstairs." He grinned with a mysterious joy that deepened her displeasure. "Ah, don't look like that, baby. I was at the White House all morning, and I didn't have a chance to spruce up." His hands fumbled at the loosened knot of his tie.

"You went to the White House—like that?" She was more deeply shocked than she could have imagined.

"It's all right, really. I'll fix it. Listen, I've got to go—"

"Where?" she demanded. "Oh Will, if you could see yourself. You look so tired."

"I told you I'll fix it, baby. I'm going home right now and get some sleep. I've got something to tell you, but I won't till later. I'll take you out to dinner tonight, just us, all right? Can I have a date?"

"Tell me now," Marian begged.

He grabbed her instead and held her tightly against him, running his hands down her back. Then he let her go abruptly. "You take a cab home —you got money? Then you get all dressed up, and we'll go out, and I'll tell you then."

Marian nodded dubiously. "I've got money. What did you come for, if you won't tell me?"

Will laughed. "You won't believe me, but I just wanted to see you." He looked around her little glass cage without seeing anything in it. He'd been in her office remarkably few times and never had shown any curiosity; he would hardly begin today, she thought. "Come on, walk me to the elevator."

The tidy music critic came out of his neighboring cubicle just as they passed his door, so any hope of sneaking Will out anonymously was lost.

Torn between laughter and exasperation, Marian indicated the tall, battered scarecrow at her heels and said, "You remember my husband," with no visible shame and only a little defiance.

The day went more hopefully after that: she said almost precisely what she meant to say for her Wednesday piece and at only a little too much length. When she had finished, she strolled over to the *Tribune*'s library to look in an encyclopedia and stopped at the women's page ghetto on her way back; leaning on the swinging gate, she watched with interest and suspense as Irene Tully delicately dislodged her ribboned, intricately wound turban from the sculptured coils of her hair. Both of them held their breath until the hat was safely deposited on Irene's desk and the single strand—ash-blond, this week—that had been disturbed was eased back into its place. Irene opened her purse and took out the notes she'd made at the ladies' luncheon at which, she told Marian, she'd picked up sworn information that Andrea Girard was pregnant, that the President was having an affair with a senator's wife, and that his own wife wanted to leave him. Marian shrugged, said that for all she knew all the items were equally true, and returned virtuously to her desk. Pithy things she might have said about ladies' luncheons interfered with her work for a few minutes, but after that she found her rhythm and worked steadily, blessedly uninterrupted, until the odd silence finally penetrated her absorption and she discovered that quitting time had come and gone.

HE, Rosa reported, making a title of the pronoun, had staggered in the door and up the stairs like a dying man and hadn't made a peep since; she had fixed some okra for his dinner because it was good for the blood, and if Marian could have seen the condition that man came home in, she'd agree that he certainly needed building up. Marian said, over the bickering of her children, that his blood would have to wait till tomorrow because they were supposed to be going out to dinner. "He'll be all right, really," she added. "He loves it."

"Mebbe so. But goin around with nothin in his stomach." Rosa shook her head at consequences too dread for speech. "And his clothes all dirty. And workin day and night. He make money, but he don't live no better than Claude. Be easier to be a cabbie."

Marian thought, escaping upstairs with a drink, that Rosa might just be right, at that. Will was fast asleep. Sprawled on top of the bed in his clothes, with only his shoes and coat removed, he looked like a photograph of a highway accident, or a gangland victim taken for a ride and flung out at the roadside. Marian set her drink on the mantel and took her necklace off; turning to put it away in her bureau drawer, she saw the paper propped up against a perfume bottle and picked it up. It was a White House handout for release the next day, and it began: "The White House announced today the appointment of Willard C. Farland, formerly of the Department of State, as Special Assistant to the President.

"Farland, a career man at State, served most recently as assistant to former Undersecretary of State Lloyd Morris. The new presidential aide is a graduate of . . ."

Marian let her eye rove past the summary of Will's academic accomplishments and past titles and proofread her own name and title. The Farlands, the story went on—expertly touching all the local bases—lived in the Cleveland Park area and had two children in D.C. public schools and a four-year-old. No mention was made of Peter's attendance at the White House school: Andrea Girard's slender hand had weight, Marian thought. She turned to the second page of the release, which contained a short extra paragraph that would undoubtedly be trimmed off by any editor; but she didn't read the paragraph, because under it Will had scrawled, large and triumphant:

Marian—
I love you.
Will

She put the neat pages down carefully, her hand shaking a little, and sped to the study to answer the buzz that indicated a phone call. She told herself she didn't want it to wake Will, but she suspected herself of simply not wanting to think, not just yet.

"Rosa, just a— Oh, Marian," Gil Kimball said. "Hi. Will home?"

"Yes, but he's asleep, Gil. Won't I do?"

Gil said, sounding truly regretful, that she wouldn't this time, he was afraid, because he was columning: in fact, he was after a statement on the White House release. Which he hoped Marian had seen, as he didn't want to spoil any surprises, and he hereby offered the congratulations of all the Kimballs—along with everybody else's, he knew.

"Except Lloyd Morris's," Marian said sharply. "He must find it hard to be polite with Will's foot on his neck."

"I don't think you've got it right, Marian." Gil sounded surprised. "Has Will—"

"No. I just saw the release. I haven't yet been exposed to the silver tongue."

Marian traced with her finger the intricate carving on the wooden screen somebody had brought back for them from India and listened to Gil hesitating to get into a family fight, but actually Girard had had his eye on Will— "Oh certainly," she interrupted. "Why not? Will saw to it that the President was short one foreign policy type." The screen stood in the study's big bay window, hiding the fact that the naked record changer behind it was standing on one of the sturdy wooden boxes the State Department used to transfer its employees' small household goods. All front, Marian noted, sour even in the face of the pleasure of the carved wood.

". . . Girard's whole approach," Gil was saying. "What he's wanted Will for all the time was precisely this skill as a generalist. Alec's always been anti-specialist—he can go on for hours about the evils of the trend." Gil broke off. "Oh what the hell, you're not listening."

"Sure I am." It was only a half-truth. "You're trying to tell me Will's one of the think boys now."

"Well, he's certainly in the biggest political league going. If I go on this way, though, I'll be wasting a column on one reader—"

"Devoted reader."

"Devoted is as devoted does. It's numbers that feeds the family," Gil said ungraciously. "Cheer up, baby. For one thing, life is going to be easier for you now—Will's been practically holding down two jobs at once."

"All right." Surprised, she found that she was, in fact, more cheerful. "I'll have him call you later."

She was smiling as she put the phone down and started back toward the bedroom. When she reached the connecting door she saw that the prophet who was not without honor everywhere except in his own home was propped up on one elbow, rubbing sleep from his eyes. Conscience smote her, and a rush of largely maternal pity finished the job: the next moment, she was sitting on the bed, making little cooing sounds and trying to make him lie down again.

He saw the press release where she had laid it down and said, shamefaced, "I couldn't wait." He began to struggle up again. "But I *am* going to take you out, and in style. Where do you want to go? Name it. I'm a big man now."

Marian said, "You're not going anywhere, Mr. Big. Except into a nice warm bath. And then into bed. Tucked in firmly."

"Where's that blue dress I bought you?" Will bounced up again as soon as she took her hands from his shoulders. "Can you wear it tonight?"

Sharlie knocked at the door. "Dad?"

Before he could answer, Marian, who had heard the phone ring and guessed what it would be about, called out, "Tell them he's not available for comment."

"But it's the *New York Leader*—"

"I don't care who it is. You tell Rosa I said nobody, and I mean nobody, speaks to Dad on the phone tonight."

"Gee, you'd think he was the President or something." Her observation trailed off as she did and Marian and Will looked at each other and laughed.

Will said, "There'll be more. Really, it would be better to go out."

"I know there will. The enterprising Kimball's already called, by the way. But you don't have to answer." Her fingers were busy unbuttoning his shirt. "You can sit up all tidy in your little trundle bed. And," she added, struck with inspiration, "eat okra. How's that?"

"God bless Rosa," Will murmured rapidly. He sank back, pulling Marian with him, and added, into her neck, "And Mummy too."

"Ouch. Will, stop it. You're all scratchy."

"You're supposed to be too overcome to notice."

"And anyway, you need rest."

"Do I? Are you sure?" He took her hand and guided it to the swelling evidence to the contrary. She clung for a moment, oddly comforted. Then the phone rang and she jerked her hand away, and she didn't put it back when the rings stopped abruptly.

Will asked, "Are you afraid it's the vice squad?" He lay back on the bed, watching her. "You'd better take it while you can get it," he advised lazily.

"Why?" Alarm leapt in her eyes. "Oh. You're going away again."

"No. Anyway, not that I know of." He was laughing at her, she saw. "What sublime self-confidence. It never even occurs to you to consider Another Woman."

She wondered why it hadn't—especially since it had been so long for him, too. "We are not the Harringtons," she said shortly, through the ringing of the phone again. "But why the 'Get it while you can'?"

"Well, I'm pushing forty, you know. It can't last forever."

"Oh, for heaven's sake, Will. You're not going to be like those men in the articles, always worrying about their virility."

"No, I'm not going to be like those men in the articles." His hand crept up her leg and tightened on the soft flesh above the top of her stocking. "Better make up your mind, baby. I'll take you out to dinner or I'll stay home—but no trundle bed."

She took his hand away and wrapped her quivering in a firm, camp-counselor voice. "All right, we'll go out to dinner. You go on and take a shower, and I'll change." The phone rang again and she said desperately, through the jangle, "Will, stop it."

"Why? You've got to change your clothes anyway. I'm speeding things up." He pushed her sweater up as far as it would go.

"You could speed things up by getting up this minute and going to take your shower."

"You take one with me. I'm lonely."

Marian surveyed him. "We wouldn't fit," she said practically. "Not if you bring that big thing along. It's a small shower."

He exploded into helpless laughter. She moved to sit up and he felt it and pulled her down. "Jesus, they ought to bottle you—for those men in the articles."

"Will, let me go." The phone started again and she said weakly, "I can't. Not with that going on all the time."

"Not a chance." He ignored both her words and her struggles. "You get me feeling like I could take a town, slay a dozen dragons, and ravish all the local princesses—and then you think you can just murmur that you're not in the mood and get away with it? You should've thought of that before you came hanging over a helpless man, dangling those ripe pomegranates—"

"Those ripe pomegranates," Marian said severely through the ringing of the phone, "were encased in a non-seductive, serviceable brassiere and no threat to your calm whatsoever, until you started . . . Why pomegranates, anyhow?" She looked down at her round breasts, blotched with red streaks his beard had left; they thrust out lewdly between the rolled-up sweater and the yanked-down underclothes. She began to giggle. "I look like a cover on one of those dirty paperbacks."

"You do," Will agreed. "Yum, yum. But that's only the cover. Now, inside the book it goes on to tell—"

"Willie, stop." But she smiled, twirling a wisp of the golden hair on his chest around her little finger, and he slowed his demanding hands and smiled too. "Let's go take a shower." Neither of them heard the phone.

"Ah, that's better, baby." He had scooped her up and was kissing her, his darting tongue inventive and suggesting, and her eyes were closed to the indignity of her rucked-up skirt when Rosa said, "Mr. Farland?" in a rather frightened voice on the heels of her knock.

Marian freed herself with a quick, terrified jerk and called furiously, "Rosa, I said—"

"I know. But—but Mr. Farland, he say he the President."

Will hit the floor like a sailor wakened by a torpedo warning. Tumbled aside unceremoniously, Marian lay in her nest of disordered clothing, listening to the blood pound in her temples. From the adjoining room, Will's alien voice said, "Just a minute, please, sir," and, "That you, Dick? Hang up the phone now, son. I've got it." Marian pulled her skirt down and managed to find enough of her sweater to provide reasonable cover; then she lay there for a long time, waiting for her mind to come back.

Will said, "I see, sir. I'll come right down."

Marian closed her eyes and turned her face away when Will came in, but she felt him sitting down on the bed to put his shoes on. "Oh, great," he said grimly. "Just what I was afraid of. We've pulled a beautiful boner."

She heard him come around the bed and opened her eyes. He was tying his tie. "I'm sorry, darling," he said awkwardly, but his thoughts were somewhere else. He turned and got his wad of papers and his wallet and keys from the top of his chest of drawers.

"Of course." Marian looked at him standing uncertainly by the bed and decided this must be what a call girl felt like if her client had second thoughts. "There's a time for amorous dalliance and a time for affairs of state. Mr. Girard is in favor of the latter, I gather," she said acidly, exacting payment.

She watched Will sizing up the situation; he shrugged, apparently making up his mind that he couldn't win this one anyway. He leaned down and kissed her chastely, patted his pockets, and turned his back on her and her decadent huddle. "Oh, I don't know," he said over his shoulder. "I'm pretty sure he has no *policy* against amorous dalliance . . ." He went out then, briskly, a man with more important things on his mind than a roll in the hay.

Twenty-eight

"I'm sorry about last night, Will," the President said. "I'd hoped you could start out with something of a honeymoon. A little time of gentle dalliance before the world intrudes."

Farland's shoulders twitched sharply for an instant, as though an insect had stung him; but his face, after the briefest disarray, expressed only amusement. "It's quite all right, sir. After all, I was really no virgin." He grinned at Jake Ruffing. "Truth is, Jake was tumbling me in the hedges on moonlight nights before the ceremony."

Ruffing dismissed their nonsense with an abrupt gesture. "All right, we took care of the first aid last night. But the point is, how in the hell could it happen?" His spare figure flapped across the spacious office like wash being reeled in on a clothesline. "I mean, I understand that there are fools. But unanimous fools?"

"Not unanimous, Jake," Girard reminded him. "Farland cried woe on the battlements—or at least caution."

Will was reclining on the end of his spine with his long legs splayed out on the gray-green carpet; he inclined his head in a truncated bow. The President turned away from the others and began reading something on a small table between two of the windows, leaning over it with his weight on his spread hands; black against the light, with bent head, he looked bowed down by grief or trouble.

But his voice, vital and angry, had no such submission in it. "The answer is probably that stupid son-of-a-bitch Winkler. Maybe he didn't even read the goddam thing before he approved it. I understand his staff tried to keep from boring him with business." He turned around. "All right. We agreed last night that the only statement we could make boiled down to 'It won't happen again.'" His voice was calm now. "After you left, I gave some thought to prevention. For one thing, I decided that even though I feel more willing and able than the last tenant, I still can't read every piece of paper that comes by—but I can make sure that what I do read is selected on some sane basis." He nodded at the door leading to his secretary's office. "It's being circulated now. From this day forward, nothing is spared me unless Ruffing, Rosenberg, or Farland says it should be. With initials." His boyish smile lighted the still-angry face. "I may turn this outfit into a bureaucracy yet. But it'll damn well be a first-class one, at least."

"It's a handy bit of preventive procedure, but it wouldn't have helped with this mess," Jake pointed out. "We'd have been stuck with what we inherited, in any case. Except Farland, I guess, and he wasn't working here." He paused in his jerky patrol to inspect the lounging figure of his protégé, his eyes bright with impatience. "Okay, wonder boy, how did you know what all the handpicked intelligence types and the high-class guessers didn't?

That's the *inherited* high-class guessers," he added to the man at the window, who smiled.

Will ran his hand through his brush of fair hair. "I didn't know," he answered slowly. "I just thought they'd left out the guy across the table, though. And if you want to beat him, you've got to figure him out, so you can think like him."

The President looked up alertly. "He's still across the table, unfortunately. So who is he, Will?"

"Feller just like me," Farland drawled. "A two-bit Machiavelli, out of the hills and bound and determined to stay out." He took out a battered cigarette and lighted it without offering the pack. "Feller like that's not about to leave his back door unlocked." He paused, considering. "I don't see how it could happen now, the way things are set up here, sir. You had no choice but to believe what came to you all summarized and tied up with Winkler's okay; but it'd have stuck out like a sore thumb in the original flow of information. Jake or Rosie or I—any one of us would have sent it back and told them to look again."

"What you're talking about," the President said dryly, "is imagination. We seem to have a shortage of it among the experts, and maybe we'd better find out why. It has just been borne in on me, you might say, that a President is pretty much restricted by his information."

"Well, sir, when a certain late and unlamented senator was making headlines hanging the State Department by its thumbs, the word got around that it wasn't wise to say anything in our reports that a congressional committee might find disturbing, even years later. So a lot of people in the field learned, the hard way, to restrict their associations in foreign countries to types who would be acceptable to any congressman, any time. Since foreigners are not really very foreign when it comes down to personalities, what you wound up with was cautious men talking to cautious men and writing guarded reports about it." He shrugged, looking at Girard. "In that sense, you can say that the President, by failing to protect his information gatherers from the bully boys in Congress, sort of restricted his information himself."

"Well, maybe what we'd better do is dig the good guys out of the hinterlands, or wherever they ran for cover during Winkler's day," Jake suggested. "But it might be a good idea to see who's bringing up the new generation, too. We could be harvesting a new crop with precisely the same bugs in it."

"I thought of that possibility." A smile flickered in the President's face. "In another of the notes I made last night, I asked Meyer to take a long look and report. Maybe we can avoid self-perpetuating stupidity. Any more suggestions?"

"Well, along the same line," Will began, and then stopped abruptly as the tall ornate door opened on a flurry of whispers outside. "But I'm *supposed* to," Elizabeth Girard said in her clear high voice to someone behind her. She put her head around the door and the oval gilt knob rode over her thick fair hair like a too-large ornament. "Can I come in, Daddy?"

Her father smiled. "Pray do, Elizabeth."

She advanced quickly toward the desk. Through the door she had left partly open came the muted clack of a typewriter. "You promised me a lollipop, Daddy."

"So I did," the President said gravely. "And I forgot. I'm very sorry." He opened the bottom right-hand drawer of his desk. "Here you are. Which color do you choose?"

Elizabeth stood looking intently into the drawer without answering. The President lifted his eyebrows, then said softly to his visitors, "I'm afraid this will take a minute, gentlemen. But it's important."

Ruffing and Farland nodded. Outside, a telephone rang twice and the chatter of the typewriter stopped. Jake closed the door and sat down beside Will. "Listen, what do you think?"

"Same as you," Farland said, watching the child. "We cut our losses and scram, counting our blessings."

"You mean the Morris thing."

"Sure. It'll barely make page thirty-four now. And if the President is under real attack, everybody'll feel it's no time for party squabbles."

Ruffing started to say something, but Elizabeth's voice rose unhappily. "I can't make up my mind, Daddy. Sometimes I think orange, but then I want purple." Indecision made a small pucker appear between her eyes.

"Purple is grape flavor, if that helps." The President took a lollipop from the drawer and held it up. In the sunlight, the round rich purple glowed behind its cellophane.

"Orange is just orange flavor, isn't it," she said, not asking a question. Suddenly her wide brow cleared. "That's the same as the orange juice we had for breakfast." The President nodded. "Then I'll take purple." She reached for the lollipop. "Sometimes we have grape juice in school."

The President closed the drawer. "I think it's time for school now. Suppose you say good-morning and be on your way." He reached over and pulled up the strap of her pink overalls; sliding down her shoulder, it had produced a curiously coquettish effect.

Elizabeth crossed to the door. "Good morning, Mr. Ruffing," she said obediently. "Good morning, Mr.—" she hesitated, trying to remember Farland's name, and then resolved the problem. "Good morning, Mr. Gentleman."

Jake returned her greeting and gestured toward Will, but Farland warned him off, above her head, as he held the door open for her. She acknowledged the courtesy with a composed nod. Farland smiled, watching her little pink-clad behind disappear into the outer office, and closed the door on the activity out there. "It was an ingenious solution," he told Jake. "I thought we should let it stand. She can be briefed some other time."

"So much for the decision-making process," the President said thoughtfully. "It starts early and it has infinite facets. Sometimes you depend on research, sometimes just ingenuity." He sat down behind his desk and draped one leg over his wastebasket. "At this point, I wish I'd depended on ingenuity rather than research. Well. Where were we?"

"I was about to say, Mr. President," Will spoke up, "one way to avoid this sort of thing again might be an order making ambassadors supreme in their own posts."

Jake asked sharply, "Who says they aren't?"

"I think you'll find that it doesn't work out that way right now. You see, if you start from the premise—which we appear to do—that the only people who are safely anti-Communist are our super-sleuths, why then they would have to know all about the Embassy people. But it wouldn't be safe for the Embassy people to know all about them, would it?" Farland smiled. "So when the President asks the Embassy how things are, the guy answering may have some gaps in his knowledge. Gaps that he doesn't even know exist." He looked at the ceiling. "In the interests of national security, of course."

In the silence that followed, Alexander Girard allowed himself one long, thoughtful whistle. "If I had time I'd go back and apologize for a few things I said during the campaign." He shook his head. "It's a hell of a temptation, though, isn't it? I mean, the man who believes what he's saying is the most convincing witness. I wonder whether we'll ever find ourselves—" He broke off suddenly. "Well. We'd better do a little reshuffling, but we'd better do it quietly—I don't want to look like Winkler, trying to find someone to blame for the mistakes."

"This one certainly is somebody else's fault," Ruffing argued. "You're supposed to be able to rely on those bastards, and they assured you the operation couldn't fail."

"Jake, you're a good workman and it irks you to see a sloppy job," Girard said slowly. "But let's not allow that to confuse the issue. I'm supposed to rely on me. What kind of juice we had for breakfast, and what kind we get in nursery school—that's information." He looked at his chief aide. "I know that when information comes with your stamp on it, it's solid. I had to depend on lesser types this time, and I had qualms. But I'm the one who decided to go ahead and rely on the information."

Ruffing shook his head. "I was afraid you'd take that line."

The President tapped the warm wood of his desk. "Remember an earlier tenant here? Before the demon golfer?"

" 'The buck stops here,' " Will quoted. He slid erect, watching the President closely. "He was quite a decision-maker."

Girard nodded. "I'm beginning to think maybe one of the best we ever had." He smiled. "The view changes when the window you're looking out of is in here."

"You'll do as well," Jake said. He stopped pacing. "Oh well, if you won't listen to reason, I'd better warn Luke." He shrugged. "At least there's plenty of time before the next election."

"Sometimes I think there's hardly any at all," the President said softly.

Ruffing ignored the observation. "I have a few ideas for pulling a brand or two from the fire. Will, can you stand a little heat?"

Farland stood up. "I volunteered for this kitchen, you know."

There was a tap on the side door and Dan Healy stuck his head around it. "Senator Youngblood, Mr. President."

"Yes, Dan. One minute," the man at the desk replied. He looked at his guests. "Well, we've locked the barn, I hope. Fortunately, most of the horses are still left. But if this were a parliamentary government, I'd find myself booted right out of the stable."

"I don't think so," Farland said earnestly. "The people are more imaginative than that. And more patient."

Alec Girard flashed him an ironic glance. "You may be right. About the patience, anyway. How else can you explain Winkler?"

"I can't," said Jake. "So I think I'll go try to explain Girard." He waved and sped through the door to the outer office. Will, following, hesitated and then turned to look back.

"Good morning, Mr. President," he said, with respect.

"What it adds up to," Kenneth Youngblood told some of his colleagues at lunch the next day, "is that Winkler left him this baby. He found it there when he moved in and he had no choice but to pick it up."

"And then it peed all over him," said Senator Fred Carson.

In that afternoon's *Washington Herald*, Representative William Bruyette, who had been urged to comment on his government's unhappy adventure, was quoted as being "extremely surprised to be asked about this, since it clearly is not before the House." He went on to say genially that he'd be very glad to discuss with his questioner the affairs of the Fourteenth District of Vermont.

A southern senator who looked like a matinee idol gone to fat and was, in fact, a walking encyclopedia of contemporary history, told a group of reporters, off the record, that he hoped to Christ the President wasn't a slow learner.

Gil Kimball's best-known fan read his Friday column sitting up in bed and sipping coffee from her breakfast tray. Elizabeth, who had visited her father at his breakfast while her mother slept, had divested herself of only a small portion of her supply of early-morning chatter and was now expending the remainder on her mother. Andy smiled patiently at her daughter, dextrously slid the sleeve of her downy pink bedjacket out of the path of the piece of toast Elizabeth was dropping for the second time, and went on reading with the selective deafness of the experienced parent.

"According to my spy, the second starling from the left in the *Magnolia Grandiflora* on the White House lawn, lights and the presidential temper both burned bright the night early this week when it was learned that a U.S. landing party, come to bring freedom to the citizens of one of our little hemisphere brothers, was abruptly, noisily, and thoroughly shown the door by the forces of the bearded gent who grabbed the government there not long ago. The enterprise ended in chagrin, with the U.S. looking rather like the guy who was assured the husband was away on a business trip, only to find he wasn't. We escaped with our pants full of buckshot, and no glory whatever.

"Now it is perfectly obvious, even to a starling, that President Girard didn't dream up this unhappy little maneuver in the few weeks that he's had to juggle all the problems of the Big Job, so the current rumor that the President inherited the operation would seem to have considerable logic. But no matter which President you care to pin it on, it's equally obvious that the optimistic report on the situation the commandos would find when they got to the beach could only have come from our own so-secret intelligence lads of the Nameless Hushabye Agency."

Andrea's trained ear caught a question in her daughter's monologue. "Was that in the Bugs Bunny cartoon?"

Elizabeth nodded and helped herself to another piece of her mother's toast, this time with jelly. Andrea tried to decide whether Jeanne, who regularly added the toast and jelly to the tray on the grounds that Mrs. Girard needed fattening up, would be encouraged by their regular disappearance and so continue the practice or, on the other hand, begin to worry that Mrs. Girard might gain too much weight and stop it. "Well, then, it was probably a carrot," she told Elizabeth. "Bunnies eat carrots." She abandoned the other question and returned to Kimball.

"Alexander Girard, as those of us who followed him through his campaign dervishing can attest, is a well-organized man, not given to wringing his hands when things go wrong. So I can believe that, as soon as his language had faded from purple to coherent, he ordered an inquiry into how the NHA could have got so wrong. What did they feed their agents, the President instructed his henchmen to find out, that made them so dense?

"Thus it was that two articulate Harvard types in rumpled tweeds turned up the other day to have a look at Trenchcoat Tech, the training school the agency runs in its conspicuous, but addressless, digs over in Virginia. The pair was shown about by the director, No Middle Initial, who ushered them into a classroom in which the students were chanting, in chorus, 'Any-body-Don't-Speak-English-Don't-Know-Nothin.' The teacher, a former scout for the Washington Redskins, was writing the day's lesson on the board: '1 American = 20 Commies.'

"Harvard 1: That equation—

"NMI (hastily): Well, you understand, that's if the American's dropped his gun and the Red has the latest weapon stolen from glorious U.S. arsenals by despicable traitorous atheist spies. Er—would you like to see the gym? (He leads them down the hall. They step aside for squad of brawny young men dressed in lily-white singlets and shorts, who are marching into the gym to their shouted cadence: 'Right. . . . right. . . . right . . .')

"Harvard 1 (looking around): This looks pretty standard—I mean, fellows punching at bags and tackling dummies. Haven't you any more specialized training? After all, your appropriation last year was—how many million dollars?

"NMI: That's top secret. Requires a special clearance. I'll have to check—

"Harvard 2: I suggest you phone the White House.

"NMI (dubiously): I don't know. President Winkler is usually on the golf course around this time.

(*Intermission, while phone call to White House is made. President Girard is not available because he is upstairs watching his baby burp, but NMI reaches chief presidential aide Jake Ruffing, whose brief comment, '$%&'#"*,' clears the Harvards at once.*)"

"What, dear?" Andy said guiltily. "I didn't hear you."

"I said, may I watch the other cartoon?"

Andy looked at her watch. "It ends just as school begins, Elizabeth. Are you all ready for school?"

After a brief bargaining, Elizabeth accepted the award of all but the last ten minutes of the cartoon and disappeared rapidly so as not to waste a precious minute. Andy checked her watch and continued to read.

"NMI (opening a heavily padded door with a key made from the bones of a Foreign Service officer once assigned to China): Here we have our final training exercise, a model of a small-force attack on a certain nameless country, designed to give our chaps a portent of what awaits them when President Wink—well, some future President gives us the word.

"Harvard 1: Well, that's more or less what we wanted to get a look at. Our boss thought there was a certain unrealistic note about some of the information he's received from you people, and he— (He breaks off, staring with his mouth open. At the far end of the gym, a student dressed in a white foam-rubber suit and helmet, with wings on his shiny boots and a knife in his teeth, steps out of a mockup rowboat and pivots up a beach authentic to the last grain of sand. He clutches a carbine, hygienically sealed—including the trigger—in transparent plastic. Ninety percent of the various other pieces of equipment appended from his person were designed for use at a range of a thousand miles or more, and/or in an arctic climate. The other ten percent is stuff he acquired in the field, chiefly through 'midnight requisitioning.')

"Harvard 2: Is that—a student?

"NMI (proudly): Graduating senior. Now watch. (A whistle blows and a man steps onto the stage. He is about five feet tall, bearded and battered-looking; he is barefoot, thin to the point of emaciation, clad in ragged trousers and a drooping straw hat, and he has no weapon whatever—even his fingernails are bitten. He stands still, arms folded on his puny chest, as the student charges up to him and swings a long, looping right, starting from the floor. The peon slowly moves his head an inch to the left and avoids the punch.)

"NMI (chuckling): See? We want them to learn everything doesn't always go just right. (He nudges one of the Harvards, who smiles weakly.) There we go. Now, watch. (The student backs off a few inches, gathers himself, and bares his teeth in a terrifying snarl. The other man falls soundlessly in a small heap.)

"NMI (applauding vigorously): How *about* that? (He produces, from a hidden pocket, a thousand copies of a press release on which can be seen the words 'U.S. Gains' in twenty-four-point type, and four bar graphs with markedly uneven bars.) Briefing, with depth analysis, in thirty minutes, fellows.

"Harvard 1: But—but wouldn't the other guy do something?

"Harvard 2: What's he doing while our guy is landing, for instance?

"NMI: I can get you that information from the computer printout. (He presses a button on his shirt and a stream of paper like a huge adding-machine tape begins to unroll from the ceiling. The men try to make it to high ground, but, within minutes, they are inundated. The Harvards shout '*Veritas!*' as they go under, but NMI keeps mum to the end.)"

Saturday, it had been decided, would be the day on which the trappings required to film a television interview with the President would be least likely to disrupt routine. Alec Girard and the dignified, world-famous commentator who'd been designated to record his views for posterity sat on the two beige sofas in the President's oval office and drank coffee while technicians, who moved with the ease of men doing what they know how to do well, filled the vast room with rubbery cables and called to each other hoarsely in a cryptic language.

"Trenchcoat Tech was cute, all right," the President agreed. "But I thought he rather overdid it. I happen to know the Agency has a fellow on the staff who used to work on the *Harvard Crimson*." He stirred his coffee thoughtfully for a moment. "He's kept in chains, of course."

The commentator laughed, setting his cup down. "You have a natural sense of timing, sir. This is jumping the gun a little on the interview, but I'm curious—have you thought about perhaps going into my line of work when you've finished here? You're the first President who's young enough to have this question come up. I mean, in eight years you'll be hardly ready for retirement. Will it be back to the Senate, do you know? Or can I expect competition?"

"I haven't really thought about it very much, but offhand I'd say Gil Kimball might start worrying about competition. He's pretty good, but he has to work under pressure. My money would give me an unfair advantage, which I wouldn't hesitate to use. I'd give him a run for it."

"You sore at him?" The questioner looked surprised. "I thought he did you a lot of good with that column."

"Hell, no, I'm not sore at him, and I appreciated the column. It was a lovely present, and unexpected—as I'm sure you know." Girard laughed.

"This is not for publication, but my wife is sore at him. I don't think she realized the boost he gave me, so she was inclined to be picky rather than grateful."

"What's she sore about? The crack about burping the baby? I thought he stretched things there."

"Not very much," the President assured him. "My son is a splendid, resounding burper, and it fascinates me—I catch the show every time I can. No, what she objected to was Gil's reference to my purple language." He smiled at the commentator. "I know what you're thinking—of course Gil was telling the truth. It's a classic case of the observer failing to allow for his own presence on the scene. *Her* own presence, I should say." Alec looked at the man opposite him and added, with elaborate sobriety, "Profanity isn't what Andy inspires me to."

"Nor anyone else, either. I was hoping we could get even a single shot of her, just to raise the viewers' morale. You and I are handsome, of course, but for visual interest I'm afraid we don't approach Mrs. Girard." The commentator sighed. "However, since we're supposed to be being typical and she doesn't typically pop in here . . . But I've been thinking of your point about observers. Just in general terms, of course, Mr. President—I wonder what sort of column you'd have written if you'd been competing with Kimball."

Alec blew a cloud of fragrant smoke toward the high ceiling. "Nice footwork. Doubtless you recalled that I said I wouldn't comment on the landing operation, even while you were trying to slide in through the back door. Well, off the record, of course—" he leaned forward conspiratorially "—I wouldn't have made those investigators Harvard men. It perpetuates a myth, you know. Actually, the only Harvard man on my staff is Jerry Rosenberg, and I suspect he went to school there only because his father is on the faculty. Even full professors don't get paid an awful lot, and I don't think Rosenberg *père's Freedom and Society* ever made the bestseller list."

"Well, I asked for it," the commentator said ruefully.

The twinkle in the President's eyes showed that he had heard, but he went on solemnly. "Jake Ruffing is the product of a Midwestern land-grant college—a testimonial to the Morrill Act, I think you'll agree. Will Farland went to some tank-town college in the South; he made the Ivy League on a graduate scholarship, but it wasn't Harvard. Dan Healy never went to college at all; he was dumped out on the world by the Jesuits with a high school education, unfailing imperturbability, and congenital charm. As for Luke Messenger, the story that he has a journalism degree is a canard, put about by—"

"We're ready when you are," the crew chief called out.

The commentator waved at the man and said quickly to the President, "No hurry, sir. Please—take the time to finish your cigar."

Alec smiled slowly. "My hair is smoldering under heaped coals of fire. You've got me this time: I can't be churlish enough, in the circumstances, not to answer your question." He smoked in silence for a moment. "The truth is, I don't know what I'd have written. Though Gil's mythical training school could've been tackled soberly: what we really need is a training school for Presidents, perhaps."

The commentator waited, then prodded him gently. "You don't think the Vice-Presidency provides that?"

Alec shook his head. "I can't see how it would. No matter how the President chooses to define the role, the fact is the Vice-President isn't here— he's down at the Capitol most of the time, usually exposed to things around here only at specified times. No, the more I think about it, the more I become convinced this room is the only possible school. Maybe being an assistant to the President is the best training for the job, because at least you have an idea what to expect. But the trouble is, a good presidential aide is not only a man with a 'passion for anonymity', he's also a fiend for detail— and he develops a habit of acting as devil's advocate, if you know what I mean. Ideas have to be bounced off him. He has to have enough imagination to be outlandish and at the same time he's got to have a sort of professional cynicism—like a good editor."

"It's not the kind of personality that gets votes," the interviewer suggested.

"Well, it can be. Rosenberg, for example, is an extremely effective speaker —assuming, of course, that the audience is not composed of anti-Semites. And Farland has a reputation as a formidable crowd-pleaser; I'm looking forward to his first performance as a member of my own team. But his whole outlook and record are classic examples of the power-behind-the-throne figure. Those fellows are not usually the type to take the risks of campaigning—not for themselves, I mean. Sometimes I think the most truly passionate man I know is Jake Ruffing. But they all tend to be short on the ability to shrug things off." Alec smiled at his listener. "I know you've covered enough campaigns to know how essential that is."

The other man nodded soberly. "I know what you mean, sir. A President has to be both passionate and dispassionate, and it's hard to find one. Fortunately the country gets time to shop around." He hesitated, then grinned wickedly. "Since this is off the record, sir—it's said that Congressman Bruyette gets a good view of life in here. And he has experience at campaigning. Could it be that—well, let me put it this way—that his succession to your old House seat is the beginning of a pattern? I hear he's going to run for the Senate."

Alec said, poker-faced, "On or off the record, I think Bill Bruyette is and always will be an ornament to any office to which the people, in their wisdom, elect him. As for his following in my footsteps—well, I just throw this observation out: Bruyette is a bachelor, and I stopped being one when I was in the Senate. So if he's elected to the Senate, he'd better get a move on shortly thereafter." He paused, then added gravely, "Of course, he'll have

his problems. Andy is not available, and I know of no successful imitations."
He put his cigar out and stood up, stretching. "Should we begin?"

The interviewer sighed. "Somebody'd better tell Kimball to start looking
for another line of work. In about eight years, he'll definitely be in trouble."
He stood and led the way toward the desk.

Twenty-nine

"I hope you'll understand if I'm a little nervous tonight," Will
Farland told the assembled delegates to the women's organization whose
multiple voice, when skillfully gathered into a single determined murmur by
its Washington office, invariably gained the ear of anyone with a campaign
for national political office in his future. "I've got two awfully good reasons."

He did look a little pale, Marian thought, but charming—a tall, lanky,
Skeezix-grown-up, shy but confiding. His yellow hair was already rumpled
and his tie was a trifle crooked. And that handsome-and-motherless air had
begun its appeal, as it always did with women's groups, before he'd even
started to speak; it united his hearers as women, thus hurdling the innate
difficulty of making a single audience out of hearers lacking unity of age,
creed, or place of origin.

"The first is that my wife, who isn't usually willing to suffer my speeches,
has made an exception tonight." Will waited, smiling a little, while the heads
turned and the knowledgeable located Marian among the few women on the
platform. She looked straight ahead, trying to ignore the color mounting into
her cheeks, while hundreds of pairs of eyes under hundreds of flowered hats
accused her briefly and then returned their sympathy to the speaker. *Bastard,*
she thought. But oh, very effective.

"And secondly," Will went on, earnest now, "I realize that this just happens to be the first public speech by a member of the administration since
a certain recent upsetting occurrence. I'm not looking forward to the question period." The laugh began in the seats off to one side in which the working press sat like a jury; it gathered momentum as it traveled through the
room, and it was sympathetic. Marian, the only wry smile in a roomful of
indulgent ones, told herself that "effective" was putting it mildly: he hadn't
said anything yet and he had them in his pocket. His cagey little confidence,
just now, had neatly freed him from having to confront them with a direct
statement on the matter and thus run up against their suspicion that they
might be being sold something. Either he'd escape the hot spot entirely or—
as seemed likely—be able to tackle the job as the honest, forthright lad attacked by a hostile questioner. Marian saw Ann Taswell wink at her almost

imperceptibly and suppressed a smile. She herself was usually Will's partner when they played bridge, but Ann had been the victim, more than once, of his skill at maneuvering the opposition to lead to his strength.

"But I came here tonight to report to you on no single event. I came to tell you, if I can, what it's been like so far, in the few months since you went to the polls and hired Alexander Girard for the biggest job in the world."

The applause at the first mention of the magic name rolled across the audience like tumbleweed. Will looked pleased, pausing to light a cigarette. The press took the opportunity to confer: Marian saw Ann listening with interest to a swarthy man she didn't know.

"I'll say this, first and fast—it hasn't been easy, but it's been exhilarating. And maybe a little noisy. I think we'd all forgotten, after the years when the White House was like a tropical town at siesta time, that people moving around and doing things sometimes bump into each other and knock over the bric-a-brac."

The freeze that had begun in some faces when he'd jabbed at the other party had been cracked immediately by his rapid swipe at his own. They smiled now, trusting him because he mocked both sides.

He gave them no time to notice that his apparent impartiality had actually offered them an image of impotent lassitude on one hand and engaging energy on the other. "We've pulled off some immediate triumphs and made a few mistakes, and on the whole we've got no complaints. I've been reading some of the President's mail and I can say that that seems to be just about the way you all are feeling too."

Marian noted the "you all," which wasn't quite "you-all" but promised to be—and which would go all the way to "y'awl" if he found it convenient; the delegates sat arranged by states in alphabetical order, so that Alabama was right under his eye. She remembered her only visit to Will's tiny northern Alabama birthplace, with its empty, dozing square dominated by a schoolhouse and a church. It wasn't big enough to be a county seat: the courthouse at which Will's father had politicked, briefly and with only minor success, was a few miles to the north. None of Will's family was there any more; his parents, in an uneasy connubiality dictated by the limits of his father's pension, lived and bickered now in a gloomy little city in Kentucky. But Marian had seen, lounging in the rectangular shade of the general store's wooden porch, men who looked like Will; they had spoken in this rhythm, this alternation of the lazy and the forceful, with precisely these diffident gestures.

The women in his audience were not just piemakers and watchers of daytime television, and Will knew it. He leaned forward, pointing the hand that held his cigarette, and spoke soberly to the presidents of P-TA's and devout disciples of Oscar Bainbridge. "Let's face it—we were hard up, in desperate need of Girard's ideas, and his courage and his leadership; and even in this brief shakedown period, the change has been noticeable. Our country had been drifting, at the mercy of every wind and current—and I don't need to tell you, those of us who knew something about the shoals beneath the waters had a little trouble sleeping nights as our ship of state wallowed in circles. Sometimes it seemed to be staying afloat only by chance." He straightened and smiled, radiant with relief. "Speaking for myself, I'd like to say that it feels good, mighty good, to have a captain on the bridge."

Marian joined dutifully in the applause and then, surprised, realized that she meant it.

Her husband shook his head and said ruefully to his cigarette, "But I was going to give a report, not make fancy speeches about the ship of state."

Ann Taswell's sleek head in its small fur toque tilted alertly, measuring the audience's indulgent little laugh. Marian watched her, sure that Ann could add it up as well as she could: Will took no chances, gave nothing unless he got more in return. The "intellectuals," heavily pro-Girard, having been addressed in lofty metaphor—carefully elaborated so that not even the slowest of them could miss the point—were prepared to settle back in comfortable superiority now and let him speak to the groundlings for a while. The lovers of Winkler forgave him because he was boyish and avowedly "nervous" and made shy fun of his own fanciness. Marian's glance, roving the audience, settled on a corseted lady from California, who had paused in her knitting to look the speaker over; her look was motherly, declaring him a nice boy even if he did talk a bit wildly sometimes. That leaves only Marian, Marian acknowledged, lonely and scared in a queasy little solitary cell of dismay.

It got lonelier for her every moment as Will went on, sometimes serious, sometimes merry, always confident—lounging at ease at the lectern in his beloved gray suit. *I'm a high-class huckster for the U.S.A.*, he had said once of his career at the State Department: as one might expect of Will's pronouncements, it was penetrating and accurate. But it had been too "high-class" at State and the whole U.S.A. to sell was too nonpartisan a product for the kind of huckstering he really loved. This was it, for him—it was so clear that Marian could read it from the back of his neck—this outright sell of a particular product. Freed of the diplomat's cautious "It is felt that—" he could be himself, a circus advanceman vowing, in the first person and straight from the heart, that this was the biggest, the best, the most daring and thrilling.

". . . and if you go by 1600 Pennsylvania Avenue on your way to your hotels tonight, I'm pretty sure you're going to see lights burning, no matter how late it is, where the biggest man of all is still at work—on your future and mine."

It was absolutely foolproof, Marian concluded as the applause crashed around the little group on the platform. Those who could take this stuff straight had enough to get happily drunk on; the others—she returned the knowledgeable smile of the organization's president, across the waiting figure of the speaker—enjoyed the spectacle because it made them feel superior. Or, like Ann, because it was an expert performance of an old art: Ann listened to Will, Marian knew, the way her grandfather listened to *Traviata;*

they knew the words and music so well that they became connoisseurs of performance. She remembered her grandfather, a pro-Pinza man, arguing heatedly with a crony who preferred another basso and imagined Ann saying heatedly, somewhere later, "That's as may be, but Farland's legato . . ."

"Alec Girard's got a shopping list," Will was saying. "It was all written up when the Congress you sent us arrived in Washington and began unpacking its bags. What we had on hand to keep us going—that is, what can be done by order of the President—was all mixed and standing in the bowl." The stout lady from California smiled approvingly; the boy had been hanging around his mother's kitchen. "As I stand here tonight, there's a good nourishing stew already simmering on the back of the stove.

"What we need from the congressional store was listed in the President's State of the Union message, which the editorial in your own fine little newspaper summarized very skillfully, so I won't bore you by going over it again. By now some of those groceries have been delivered. The rest, I'm glad to say, are on order." His bony, yellow-stained hand gathered them in. "Alec Girard wasn't kidding when he talked about getting started, and neither was the leadership of the Congress. If there's any dispute between the President and the Congress about *how* to do any one of the things that need doing in this enormous, thriving country, they'll argue it out—as they've begun doing, and as the makers of our Constitution meant them to do."

The Constitution was good for automatic, formal applause. Probably he'd put it in there to give himself time to quench his cigarette: a Farland performance, Marian thought bitterly, left nothing to chance.

Farland had waited for quiet, too, in order to change pace. "I'll tell you what the Congress and the White House are *not* doing," he said acidly. "They're not standing around on the golf course telling each other what great patriots they are—while they compare the latest gifts the lobbyists have sent over."

This time the laughter and applause had the quick, extra enthusiasm of partisanship. I was wrong, Marian decided—it's not the circus coming to town. It must be the Fourth of July, because there go the redcoats. She unclasped her hands carefully and sat back in the uncomfortable, spindly chair, not bothering to listen because what would have to come next was another of the ingathering-of-the-exiles touches that always followed a partisan sock.

She had been wrong before—all wrong about Will: he had never left that dusty, browned-grass Alabama square, the home of slow heat and quick hate, of flowery speeches for our side and a kick in the balls for the others. Where black was black and white was white and all the in-betweens perfectly visible every day were, by unspoken agreement, declared nonexistent. She'd seen him clearly enough, back in their early days when their disparities seemed to mean only new potentials of delight. A mistake in interpretation, but not in vision. I paint better than I live, she thought, remembering the picture she'd done after that visit to the South. They had been to see Grandfather Farland's farm, silent and overgrown; the old man was dead and the settlement of his estate hung in doubt for years while his numerous heirs waited to see whether what they had was salable only as farmland, worth little, or as part of a regional conservation project still in the talking stages but potentially lucrative.

Meanwhile, the land lay unused, slowly reclaiming its wildness, in the long light of that afternoon, along with the big house an earlier Will Farland had built with his own hands to bring his bride to—how many years ago? Standing on the porch, which ran the length of the house, she and Will had peered through dusty windows and seen an iron bedstead, in which Will's father perhaps had been born. Outside the kitchen door a large iron bell hung on a rope—to call the hands in from the fields for meals, Will explained. The fields stretched out of sight, a mass of high, rank growth, but still distinguishably in rows: cotton, Marian supposed, but didn't like to ask, remembering his grimness once when he'd said, "If you've ever hoed cotton, you never want to do it again."

In her painting the shadowed porch sagged more than it actually did, but the tall green ranks stretching away in the relentless heat were as accurate as she could manage. In the foreground at the corner of the house, Will, sharply drawn against the hazy background of weathered wood, looked pasted-on and incongruous. He wore a crisp business suit instead of the tourist slacks and shirt of reality, and he carried a homburg and an attaché case. The black, clearly defined figure from another world stood turned away from the house and the fields, his arm crooked in the attitude of a man looking at his watch.

Oh, I saw, all right, the painter mourned now. But turning away from the fields had never meant turning away from the general store and the courthouse, too, and from all the harangues and blacks-and-whites and rabble-rousing tricks. Will hasn't changed, she reminded herself—but I have: I never used to be disloyal. Guiltily, she began to listen as he began his peroration.

Farland spoke into the hush of the women he had been wooing. "I didn't begin with a story, so maybe I better end with one. Let me tell you about the first formal speech I ever made, when I was the valedictorian of my high school graduating class in Alabama. But I won't tell you what year," he defied them, earning their giggles.

He took the mood down expertly, speaking softly in a seeming reverie. "You remember how it is when you're a kid?" He smiled wryly down at his own hands, folded like a schoolboy's. "We forget how it used to be, I think —how kids used to feel that everything was up to them, including running the world." His bowed head lifted; he returned to them from the mists of the past. "Our Miss Coakley—she was the English teacher, and she was in charge of the speeches—she said we had to have a quotation. Well, I was bound and determined I was going to be valedictorian," he confided. "I hunted through the Bible, the Constitution, and the Declaration of Independence. There was plenty of good stuff, all right, but the trouble was, somebody else would likely find it, too. The competition was rough—espe-

cially from the girls." His smile winked at them. He waited while they tit-
tered, his hands in his pockets.

"Well, I found one that I was pretty sure nobody else had, and I was so
tickled with myself—it never occurred to me at the time that it might be a
little uppity for a kid with his wrists coming out of his good blue jacket and
the taste of a popsicle still sticky on his mouth."

It was just exactly like what he'd done the other night, and Marian knew
it: those who are not taught can learn anyway, as Rosa had demonstrated. So
Marian had been learning to see how he did it—by coaxing away disinclina-
tion, talking away disaffection, until he brought about a slow succumbing.
But Rosa's grammar was still unreliable. And *oh Willie*, Marian was thinking
now, helpless in the face of the little boy and the popsicle. *Oh darling, poor
darling.*

"Maybe it's still uppity," Will told his friends and lovers, "but it sure fits
better in Washington. The quote I finally found was from an Irish poet,
Shaemas O'Sheel, and it went like this, as I recall: 'Yet more remains to do
than all that has been done. And we, we are the doers.' " He held them with
his look while he paused, taking his hands out of his pockets and standing
up straight to be valedictorian. "I think that sums up the Girard Administration's way of looking at things. Both for its little past and its long future."

Applauding with the others, Marian saw them coming to their feet; only
the cries of "Bravo" were missing. Will accepted it all graciously, with an air
of wonder that they were so kind. He left them wanting more and steered his
wife through the crowd that would have coffee before the question period.
The ladies, shoving delicately for front-rank spots, made way for their president, who offered Marian cookies and asked why she didn't go to her husband's speeches; the curiosity, with its faint censure, of all the flowered hats
was represented by their elected spokesman. Will came smoothly to Marian's
rescue, smiling at her proudly as he explained that three kids at home "kinda
keep her jumpin." They twittered; they also promised earnestly to take good
care of her for him while he had a word with Mr. So-and-so. And Marian
was left alone to smile and smile until her face hurt—which was one of
Andy's complaints about these things.

But there were other complaints, and Marian, who could not always think
clearly but saw and heard very well, could feel the anguish of her conflict in
overheard remarks: *Which one is she? Is that his wife? Oh, she is pretty,
isn't she?* There was no legitimate way to be angry because an unknown
woman had said, in a pleased, kindly tone, that you were pretty. And yet,
because the woman's pleasure was for Will, it was not possible not to be
angry: who could bear to be described as, in effect, a piece of Farland's luck?
And yet again, no love is ever to be lightly mocked: the woman was pleased
that Farland's wife was pretty as she would have been pleased to learn that
his house was warm and his larder well-stocked, which is to say she was inspired by warmth and affection, that she wished the fellow-creature Farland

well, and well-served. So he had won from strangers affection and perhaps a kind of altruism, and it was good for everyone to have that happen.

But it demeaned, for a fact—no matter how you argued, what philosophic or sociological or psychological due you paid, and with what justice you acknowledged their right (and that you had, in a way, asked for it), it still made you an object, an artifact. And if you objected, you sounded egotistical or snobbish. Marian listened to Will answering questions from the audience and thought of Andy, who was not at all egotistical, who didn't mind being just Alec Girard's wife, with no career or personal glory—but who writhed away from this something that was so hard to explain, except that it was different from the understandable curiosity of people your husband worked with, say, about what kind of person his wife was. . . .

And that was when Marian caught sight of the clue: the difference was, perhaps, that though these people didn't want to ignore you, they also didn't want to know what you were like. What they did want maybe depended on the state of their mental health—they wanted to see, for the most part, and some to speculate or fantasize or God knew what. And you could go crazy trying to draw lines between the legitimate and illegitimate, decided Marian, who could stay home from her husband's speeches. The fact that Andy couldn't was Andy's headache.

Will was earnestly defending Alec Girard against the implied charge that his own lack of financial headaches might keep him from caring about a lady questioner's retirement pension. Congressman Girard had not failed to care, Farland proved, nor had Senator Girard; examples from the congressional days were neatly topped with a quote from the Inaugural Address. "And besides," Will concluded, smiling at them confidentially, "he's surrounded by fellows like me, who'd remind him. The President's not the only daddy in the west wing offices of the White House, and he *is* the only millionaire."

Andy's obligations were realer, Marian thought—people, after all, had some legitimate claim on the chatelaine of the White House—and Alec was serious and truthful. So was Will, but he didn't have to be trammeled by truth; if he chose, he could be only good theater. Which had its fascinations, but you had to pay for good theater. She listened absently as Will ducked a question from a Louisiana lady about offshore oil—by saying disarmingly that he didn't have the exact quote and then safely misquoting to suit the occasion. He kidded Vermont about its "exports" to Washington and answered a frivolous question with utter solemnity: yes, he had met Elizabeth, indeed he had, and meeting Elizabeth was the major fringe benefit of working at the White House, he would stand on that judgment. . . . And suddenly, his arm poised in the act of pointing out a chosen questioner, he called out with warm friendliness, "Well, it's Miz Jackson, isn't it?" and Marian woke from her half-doze to squint out at the standing figure under the "Texas" placard.

"Watch Texas," Will had muttered as, the coffee hour over, he had gallantly helped Marian up the three steps to the platform. She looked at him, comprehending only his resemblance to an actor about to go on stage; but he smiled, believing that she was enjoying the game. "I'm told they've got one laying for me," he said with the satisfaction of a good tennis player facing a good opponent, and bowed his wife into her chair.

"I recognized you, ma'am," Will was saying genially now. "From your pictures with Mr. Ferris during the campaign. I'm glad to see you now under happier circumstances—and may I add—" he broke off to grin broadly "—that we hope you've seen the light. Now what can we do for you, Miz Jackson?"

"Thank you, Mr. Farland," the woman said rather tartly—which, after all, was just about the only tone he'd left her, Marian decided. "Women Alert for America, of which I happen to be president—" a spatter of applause from her immediate vicinity interrupted her "—want you to tell us whether your Mr. Girard and his fuzzy liberal friends are about to see the light, too. About our sitting there in the UN, year after year, and letting the godless Communists pollute our beloved land with their atheistic attacks on the American way of life." *Wow,* thought Marian, peering closely at the small, stout bundle of energy in a flowered dress on which a clump of orchids bloomed. *A lady Will.* She looked from under her lashes at Will, who had probably been better at it than this even back when he'd been valedictorian but was still, in a manner of speaking, the biter bit. . . . He was listening conscientiously, almost piously, his elbows braced on the lectern and his hands clasped—though Marian had half expected him to be staggering under the barrage. ". . . we have permitted them," Mrs. Jackson was continuing, "to throw everything in the Red arsenal at us while the American taxpayer shells out for Mr. Blackwell to sit there and argue with them. When all the time they're planning to take over the world and filling our reservoirs with poisonous flourides and planting Communist propaganda in our children's textbooks and . . ."

Marian watched her husband with genuine admiration as he let the tirade go on and on while the audience began to squirm and then to murmur. They had not come to hear the tediously earnest Mrs. Jackson, whose thick Texas accents piled up the right-wing clichés relentlessly; they had come to hear the other side's demagogue—the witty, sincere Mr. Farland, who was being so polite and patient in the face of what was emerging, increasingly, as very bad manners. The organization's president got up from her chair and walked over to whisper to Will; he inclined his head with a chivalrous gentleness that contrasted sharply with the passionate venom of the delegate from Texas. Who noted it, Marian saw with some relief, and began to wind down.

"Well, if you wish, Madam President," said Will. He waited, then said regretfully, "Mrs. Jackson, I'm advised that our time is running out, and I do want to answer your question . . ." He paused, looking doubtful, and the unspoken words, *if I can figure out what it is,* swept the room with laughter. Will let it, then leaned in and rescued the Texan before the woman could reap even a breath of martyrdom. "I want to thank you, ma'am, on behalf of Mr. Blackwell, whose talent for speechmaking brought him millions of votes for the Presidency four years ago—when even many who didn't vote for him paid him tribute for that skill." The applause was a mixture of Black-wellite enthusiasm, sheer relief at being able to do anything at all after such a long spell of enforced immobility, and commendation for Farland's correct behavior. "I agree that when we're in a war of words, we couldn't have a better man leading our little squad up there at the United Nations than Mr. Blackwell." He smiled benignly at Mrs. Jackson, who had not said any such thing for him to agree with; voiceless now, she fluttered a hand helplessly.

"But what the lady from Texas wants to know," Will went on soberly, "and maybe some other citizens do, too, is why—since one of the main things we do in the UN is quarrel with the Soviet Union—why we don't just stop bothering. There are several obvious answers: one is that a war confined to words doesn't get our sons' names on casualty lists." He continued quickly, downing the beginning applause. "Another is that the Communists have not taken over the world, whatever they say or whatever the lady from Texas says they say. So we must be doing something right, mustn't we?" He paused, musing at them, but not long enough to allow interruption. "The facts are easy: we're in a fight, sure. But the United States of America has never run away from a fight, any kind of a fight. And what I don't under-stand," he went on a little sadly, his lifted hand holding off their reaction, "what I must say truly shocks me, is to hear the suggestion that we *do* run away from a fight, for the first time in this nation's history, put forth in this brilliant assemblage by a lady who comes to us from the great state of Texas. Where, none of us will ever forget, a little band of brave men fought to the death against hopeless odds—" the prides and sorrows of a thousand Fourth of Julys rang in his voice "—and left Texas and the nation—" his upraised arm seemed to be about to lift them all, and his voice lifted too, not saying now but proclaiming "—the glorious memory of the Alamo."

Texas was on its feet, its face bright with the soaring, magic word, its applause loud and frantic. And then the rest of the audience caught it—and so did the demagogue's wife, standing there clapping her hands for the shameful excitement of the acclaim itself. The mindless roar—triggered by ardors just but irrelevant, by courage long gone and inapplicable, by nothing that really made any sense—went on increasing itself equally senselessly. Carrying along even Marian, whose mind all the time was flinching away.

That flinch, that wince, was what she was trying to tell Will about with her gloomy monosyllabic responses when they'd escaped the mingled odors of perfume and were on their way home at last. It was this twitching people around by their automatic reactions, playing on their deep need for glory—which was probably what had led them all to follow once the conditioned reflex of the Texans to the name of the Alamo had set them off; it was the deft use of others' mindlessness, the contemptuous twisting of honorable im-pulse . . . But to talk like this would gain her nothing, so she simply pointed out flatly that the battle of the Alamo bore no resemblance to any battle we might be conducting in the UN, where we were big and strong and not outnumbered.

"Well, not often and not yet," Will said grimly. "What of it?" He moved through his locking-up chores with weariness. "You don't want us to get out of the UN, do you?"

Marian started up the stairs. "No. Of course not."

"Well, now there'll be some more people on your side. All right, all right," he added impatiently as she started to speak. "The point is, our Mrs. Jackson is going to have a harder time enlisting anti-UN sentiment in Texas than she would have if I hadn't said that. So you've got at least a little piece of what you want, haven't you?"

Not the *way* I want it, Marian thought, struggling against the old sensation of being rushed off her feet to some conclusion that was presented as hers but wasn't, quite. It sounded, she thought helplessly, a little like the tone of brusque reason with which he had ended her small rebellion at sharing his bed. He'd simply pointed out, with that same air of weariness, that she could do as she pleased, of course, but if she insisted on sleeping in separate rooms then he'd have to take the study; whatever his sentiments or hers, he'd said, grinning wryly, it was insupportably ludicrous to have him comfortable in the big bed while she tossed on the little daybed—it would be as though they got on a bus together and he took the only remaining seat and let her stand, strap-hanging above him.

Marian walked toward him now, holding her side of the bedspread, and met him in the middle in the ceremonial that had thus become a nightly ritual again. For it was one thing to make a protest at the expense of her own discomfort and quite another to require Will, who was a restless sleeper, to endure it while she rebelled in luxury. Which ended the use of the bed in the study, for either of them. So he had maneuvered her out of her rebellion's chief symbol—and then, when he'd gained his point, behaved so casually about her presence beside him in their bed that he made her previous withdrawal seem the shrinking of an old maid at nonexistent advances. Not the *way* I meant, she thought again, watching him as he yanked his sock off with the indifferent ruthlessness he displayed toward all inanimate possessions.

"That other stuff—that first question," she said. "You were giving the impression that Girard was above petty politics, but at the same time you were doing the petty politics for him, weren't you?" *It cost something, we learned, and it won't happen again,* he had said succinctly of the abortive coup, Alec Girard's first official mistake. And then Farland had leaned on the podium, his honest face honestly troubled, and said he'd like to say more, he really would, but his boss had said publicly, "I'll take the blame"—and the boss was the boss. And you would have had to be blind and deaf to miss the implication that Girard had inherited the mistake. So the audience clapped for the handsome knight defending his noble king.

Will pulled his other sock off. "So? Everybody realized that."

Everybody most certainly hadn't. But it was true that it had been there to see. He'd had nothing up his sleeve. "But how is that any different from before? It's exactly what Winkler used to do."

Emerging from his undershirt, he was smiling. "Sure. And he served two terms, didn't he?" He saw her face and his smile faded. "Look, are you going to start to wrangle with yourself again? This is no great big truth-versus-expedience torment. All I did was field questions."

Marian slid into her side of the bed. "And all those other things you said —the outright lies and the almost-lies and the slight twisting of the truth— were they all just routine, too?"

The bed sagged on his side. "I don't know what 'lies.' It was all part of ordinary maneuvering, if that's what you mean. Maybe you ought to come more often, so you'd get used to it."

"I can't, remember? I have three kids and," she said with exaggerated folksiness, "y'awl know they kinda keep me jumpin."

Will sighed. "You going to read, or should I put the light out?"

"You can put the light out." All right, I won't lay for you like the Women Alert for America. Or any other way either, she thought, making no attempt to hide her resistance as he put his arm around her.

"I see I'm still poison," he said softly, almost coaxingly. "But you could at least tell me whether I did okay."

It *was* the least, she realized, her guilt like a blow at first, then becoming only another weight to bear her down into the misery of acknowledging that she hadn't even done the least she could do for him. "Of course you did well," she said, her voice unnaturally loud in the dark. "You were terribly effective."

He took his arm away. "Great. Now I can go to sleep, hugging my violets."

Marian said nothing, leaving him his triumphant irony, understanding that it was hard enough for him to lose any encounter. He turned over, muttering a cross good-night, and his genuine weariness brought him sleep.

Tired men sleep better than their bad wives, and idealists make bad wives, Marian summed it all up for the gray rectangle of the window. Schoolgirl idealists, she added, throwing in his remembered jibe against her like poking her tongue into a toothache. The twinge was no more than she deserved—he had been entitled to her approval of his performance; it had been a good one, and she'd been churlish to withhold her applause. It was his job, there was no shame in being good at it. But goddammit, something inside her kept insisting noisily, a little bit of demagoguery is no different from the old joke's little-bit-pregnant. Finally she decided that whatever else there might be in this constant internal dialogue, there was no sleep in it; she got up and, dragging her pillow and bathrobe, went downstairs and fixed herself a long drink.

Though she roved the downstairs rooms of the sleeping house for a long time, by the time she wandered into the dining room, the only thing that was mostly gone was her drink—but not her restlessness, her guilt, her barely suppressed fear that she was living in an air she couldn't breathe. She should have been proud of Will tonight, and in a way she had been—but it wasn't, again, the way she wanted to be. She looked into the bottom of her glass and saw there the words she had shrieked at Will the night he hit her. It was true: she did not respect him. And how could she live with a man she didn't respect?

Night thoughts. It's too late for stuff like that, she told herself severely. She emptied her glass and pushed the thermostat up with a fine disregard for the budget. Then she turned on the television set and found herself in the midst of one of those late-night variety shows. This one's proprietor, a youngish, pleasant man, was chatting with a small, chic woman who had a lively face. "You *are* going to give us one of your songs," he was saying persuasively.

Marian wrapped her bathrobe around her and lay down on the dog-smelling studio couch and then stiffened like a mummy as the guest rattled off a long phrase in French. Marian tried desperately to summon up French classes long past, but only *"moins"* yielded meaning—it had to do with arithmetic, she thought dimly, and finally remembered that it meant "less."

The nice young man came to her rescue, then. Couldn't his guest tell us a little about the song? What did the title mean, for instance?

Marian sat up and stared, with her elbows planted on her knees and her teeth gritted, while the lady told her and all the rest of the folks out there in TV-land, in charmingly accented but quite easily understandable English, that the title meant, in effect, *I'll take less of you because you're so much more than any other man.* "She sings this to her lover, who will not marry with her." The speaker hesitated, then turned shyly to the program's host. "I have tell this so it is understood, yes?"

Oh, quite, quite, said a member of the audience who was not, like those in the studio, laughing kindly and applauding encouragingly—but was, in fact, biting down on her knuckles while the pleasant man assured the lively-looking little lady that she spoke English very well indeed. He asked her how many languages she spoke, and she smiled: she had a round, sweet face, nourishing as an apple, and her smile was positively tasty as she told them a friend had said of her that she spoke three languages: "Paris-after-dark French, show-biz English, and concentration-camp German." She was a natural mimic, was this fascinating little lady in the tight white sequined dress—and when she quoted her friend the phrasemaker, her eyes mysteriously took on some of the gentle laughter that usually inhabited his, and one of her eyebrows even quirked in exact imitation. And Marian knew who she was all right, without the help of the nice young man who was announcing her name while Aimée cuddled the lollipop microphone in her small, competent hands and raised her tragic dark eyes that were doubtless capable of all understanding and began to sing in a warm, low voice that knew very well how to tell so it would be understood, of how much she loved Monsieur More.

Marian switched the channel with a hand gone thoroughly icy and wound up in a scene from something that must be called *Song of Broadway.* She flung herself onto the couch and said to herself that she was prettier than Aimée, much prettier—which was true, but would hardly matter even if she weren't above that sort of thing. This here type chanteuse was, any way you looked at it, a vital, intelligent, and attractive woman—and available to come home to, no? I'd like to know her myself, Marian said to the flickering heroine of a shampoo ecstasy now taking place on the screen: we must have them over sometime, *Paul et Aimée.* I wonder whether they play bridge. . . . The commercial gave way to a heartbreaking misunderstanding between boy and girl and then, after only a moment or two—so brief is love—to a graphic demonstration of how stomach acids eat through assorted objects. Marian, who was certainly being eaten by some kind of acid, clutched at her middle and tried not to think about sexy-looking women in tight dresses who were generous, were obliging enough to take less than marriage, and were undoubtedly quite familiarly *"tu."* She fell into exhausted sleep as Ruby Keeler, given her big chance at stardom, began to tap-dance in net stockings and lots of sequins and a shiny top hat.

Thirty

"I thought, from various things you said, the night of the party and since, that you'd begun to find politics less unpleasant." Alec Girard looked at his wife with worry in his eyes as she sat opposite him in the evening quiet of the upstairs sitting room. She put her "homework" on the arm of her chair and set down on top of it the long yellow lined pad on which she wrote her notes; then she regarded him with such cool, polite attention that he wanted to shake her.

"Perhaps we didn't define 'politics' alike," she suggested. "Would you like some more beer, Alec?"

"No, thanks." He drank in the sound of his name gratefully. Lately he'd become aware that she was the only person he saw daily who used it. He'd noticed it first during a visit to Andy's parents: when his mother-in-law had called him "Alec" it had struck him as slightly strange. Since then, he'd been noticing more—how Jake Ruffing, for example, somehow never called him anything when they were alone, as if "Mr. President" were to be avoided but "Alec" had become impossible. He meant to tell Andy about his discovery— by this time he had quite a list of friends and associates who were, in effect, reduced to saying "Hey, you." But now he knew that there would be no reporting delicious ironies this night. "Look," he said with effort, "I hope you know I really would rather not have this kind of discussion. But if I don't want to talk about a difficulty that crops up, you claim I'm being inimical."

"I appreciate the effort it costs you." Andy smiled—but stopped short, her husband noted, of "Alec." And certainly far, far short of "darling."

"Well, then." His gesture indicated that the floor was hers.

"I should think my reason would be obvious. I simply find it absurd to act as the medium of communication where each side already knows what the other wants to say." She shrugged. "As I understand it, the purpose of the demonstration was to urge you to be against war, which I think it's safe to assume you already are, and to notify you that that pack of women is also against war. I assumed you already knew that, or in any case you could read it in the newspaper. I really don't see what function I could've performed by taking time to see them."

"The function it would've served," Alec said doggedly, "is to make them feel they were being listened to. People have a right to express their feelings, and to know that they're being taken seriously." He looked at her closed face and sighed. "I believe I would like that beer after all."

He stood up as she did, and then he crossed the room, watching her beautiful walk—the firm back, the springing step—until he couldn't bear it and turned away, wanting to look at anything else until he lost the feeling of deep fear that his few quarrels with Andy had always brought. His eye caught her yellow pad on the chair arm and he read her writing absently:

"Luke—

"Nedra Rosenberg tells me she was intercepted by a photographer as she was taking her boy and the Farland child home from school yesterday, and only the intervention of the White House policeman enabled her to avoid being photographed with the children. I find this particularly disturbing because I thought it was understood that under no circumstances were the children or anyone else connected with the school to be molested by—"

And then I molested her, Alec thought, not without sympathy for Luke Messenger, who was the frequent recipient of Andy's handwritten but formally phrased notes. Clipped to the side of the yellow sheet was a briefer note, meant only for her own eyes, that she must have written first: "Get name of WH p'man on duty 12:15 P.M. Thurs, south gate." Tomorrow, some White House policeman would receive a graceful letter his children would cherish. Alec stood above the empty chair, feeling his demands doubly onerous, his position hugely unlovely, in the face of this silent evidence of Andy's careful, detailed work at her job.

She sat down when she'd brought him the beer, but he remained standing, alternately sipping at the cold, bitter drink and prowling the gentle room. He said abruptly into the face of her quiet, "Andy, I know how you work at this and you do a magnificent job. I don't want you to think I'd be so churlish as to complain about an oversight—"

"It wasn't an oversight." Her soft voice closed that avenue of escape. "And I know you're not churlish, Alec."

He wondered, not for the first time, whether she knew how vulnerable he was, how sensitive both to her rejections and her mercies.

"I thought it was clear," she went on, "that my refusal to see the women's peace delegation was entirely intentional. I'm sorry if it caused you embarrassment—I've always tried to avoid that."

"Of course it caused me embarrassment," he burst out, goaded out of his imposed calm. "How could it do anything else, when you snub a group of citizens? I might point out that they were exercising a right granted to them in the Constitution."

"May I point out that I was exercising a right, too? My right to privacy."

"I thought it was understood—" unconsciously, he echoed the language he had just read in her note to Messenger "—that we relinquished some rights to privacy when I took this job." He whirled on her, chopping the air with his speechmaking gesture. "And even before. After all, you married a Senator. I didn't spring this on you."

"I never relinquished my right to decide when it was enough," Andy flared at him. She stood up, tense with anger. "I insist on my right to draw the line when the citizenry starts cluttering up my bedroom."

Alec looked bewildered. "Andy, you're making too much of a routine political phenomenon."

"Perhaps I'm not making nearly enough of it, if it's a routine political phenomenon." Her dark eyes blazed. "I simply will not make gestures based on untruths."

"*What* untruths, for heaven's sake?"

"Well, what do you think is implied in this desire to see me? They come in and plead with me to persuade you to abandon your clashing armor and roaring lust for blood—"

"It's more of a mild yen than a lust," he interrupted diffidently. "Actually, just slapping a mosquito quite dispels it." He studied her face from behind his pose and saw that he had scored, if only slightly. "And I do think it advisable, Andrea, that in your position you avoid the use of words like 'lust.' There's a powerful anti-lust lobby."

Andy went on, ignoring him but with a wicked gleam in her eyes. "Clinging to your arm, I drape myself around your neck and seduce you into the ways of peace by various soft impeachments— But perhaps I'd better avoid that word, too."

"Ouch."

"Well, I'm sorry, Alec, but I simply won't be outwitted. Or chucked under the chin."

"I am not chucking you under the chin. And anyway, if I was I've certainly been painfully chucked back."

"Which is no more than you deserve," Andy said icily. "I think you're behaving contemptuously. I've made what seems to me a quite valid objection to being forced into the position that I can be petitioned into petitioning you on something that you'd be an idiot not to have understood long ago.

I don't see it as citizens exercising rights, or whatever—I see it as a bunch of disorderly women believing you a kind of fool and me a kind of courtesan. I'm sorry if you feel that I'm obliged to lend myself to such tawdriness." Her eyes dismissed him. "I don't, and I won't be jollied and quipped at as if I were merely being whimsical."

She had a damned funny idea of a courtesan, Alec told himself bitterly: at the moment she reminded him far more of Daniel Webster than Ninon de Lenclos. "I didn't intend to imply that you were being whimsical," he said. In diplomacy it was important to remember that a path to peace could open from any point of mutual agreement.

"I'm glad. In that case—since you recognize that I have a serious objection and a right to it—there's no more to be said, is there?"

Just one more teeny-tiny point, madam, thought her startled husband: that I will be master in my own house. Her sarcastic tone and particularly that lofty "no more to be said" rang in his ears as though she had hit him on the head. "Oh, one or two things, I think," he said carefully.

"Really?"

"Such as," Alec Girard said in a voice of deadly quiet his staff would have recognized with instant trepidation, "that I have a serious objection, too. To your being cold, willful, and snobbish." He let the shocked pause extend itself before he went on, with a little more warmth and even a mild attempt at persuasiveness. "I put it to you that you might've met with the ladies and, in perfect dignity, told them approximately what you've just told me." He thought of adding, "a little less graphically, perhaps"; but for all he knew that would come under the heading of treating her contemptuously. So he stood in silence, trying to decide whether his last suggestion had a chance of penetrating her anger. She shrugged and looked away, and when she spoke he saw with despair that it hadn't.

"Well, this discussion is fruitless, isn't it? I think perhaps it's fortunate that I've decided on a little holiday. Then, if any more of your beloved citizens turn up, I'll simply be absent."

Oh no, Alec Girard groaned silently. A picture flashed through his mind of the library of his parents' home in Kingsley. He had come in from the lake—a boy of perhaps twelve, he reckoned. Old enough, anyway, to recognize that a quarrel hung in the air between his parents like a lurking thunderstorm. He waited awkwardly, not knowing how to back out—and then suddenly his mother brushed by him and left the room, walking with rapid strides and her head averted. Alec and his father watched the door as it closed behind her.

John Girard looked at his son ruefully, then turned away with a small shrug. "I suppose you're old enough to begin to collect some data on the phenomenon."

"I don't know what you mean, Dad."

"Women, boy." The elder Girard stuffed his pipe viciously. "Lesson one on the big subject—woman's most powerful argument is the banging of the door."

"Mama? But she didn't—"

"Oh yes she did. You're still too young to hear it, I guess. But you just take your old man's word for it—she banged that door. She banged the hell out of it."

The grown-up Alec Girard thrust a tentative toe against the door his own wife had just banged, ever so gently. "A holiday?" he asked mildly.

She, too, had banged the hell out of it. "Please don't be concerned. I'll be back in time to attend to the next scheduled dinner."

"Andy, please," he said reasonably. "You know I'm not accusing you of dereliction of duty."

"Oh?" The dark eyebrows lifted in the face that had always had some laughter lurking somewhere in it. Until now.

Alec waited. If she said anything, however lofty, however snide, he could move in with praise of the fine job she'd been doing since they'd come to the White House. Of which, he reproached himself bitterly, numerous examples existed. He looked at her with hidden hope, because if she said anything at all, no matter what, he would use it to sue for peace terms—and Elizabeth Langwith's daughter, not Princess Nat's granddaughter, looked back at him and he knew there would be nothing beyond that "Oh?" Knew it, and as he had with campaign disappointments, swallowed the loss and went on from there. "Were you thinking of going down to Florida?" he asked genially. "My parents would be delighted, and my sister Agnes is there now, you know—"

"No. I don't want to go to Florida."

"Then to your mother's? You could get a good rest . . ."

And not be beyond your reach? her dark eyes said with scorn. Alec saw the next defeat written clear and cursed all intelligent women and the fools who thought they could successfully marry them. "I feel awkward about harping this way on the difficulties of being married to me— But, you know, you can't go just anywhere without causing—er—problems," he went on, knowing now that she was leaving the country, that she had concluded (oh, cleverly) that the one thing he could not do was whip over casually to a foreign country for a visit. The injustice of her use of his handicap against him stung him to a slow anger.

"I don't think there'll be any problems, will there, if I go to Switzerland?" She smiled sweetly. "I haven't asked, but I assume it won't start a war or compromise the country in any way."

"Switzerland?"

"Yes, Richie and Cynthia are there now, you know. I do want to see them; I haven't for quite some time."

Her ability to do without contact with her brother, whom she thought of fondly but quite certainly recognized as something of a bore, had always been extensive. "Naturally, you want to preserve your cherished family ties." Alec's voice was thick with frustration.

"Naturally." Her eyelashes fluttered. "Then it *is* all right? I was afraid you wouldn't permit it."

Alec flinched, thinking bitterly of the beginning of this conversation, when he'd been grateful for her use of his name. Being cast as Henry the Eighth was a little hard on a man who'd already found being President a little lonely. "Please don't be foolish, Andy. You're an American citizen in good standing, which means that you have a right to travel abroad." He paused to let his coldness hurt if it could. "And, as you've pointed out so clearly, you have all the usual civil rights."

"Alec."

"Yes?" His heart leaped; but then he saw those big, unhappy eyes.

"About the children—"

"Elizabeth is settled in school, and this is not a school holiday," he said firmly. "I don't think we should treat the business of going to school airily."

"No, of course not." Her eyes were thoughtful. "Then I'll take just the baby."

He could hear, even while she was saying it, that she didn't believe herself. "I don't think so, Andy." His voice was pleasant but there was unquestionable command in it. "He gets excellent care here."

"Yes, of course, but—"

"Then I think it makes no sense to remove him from it. After all, if he's going to be with only one parent, I can't see why I don't qualify as well as you do. I'm a parent in good standing."

A small mutiny was beginning in her eyes. "Alec, you're being quite unreasonable—"

"I was just wondering," he said pleasantly, "whether I wasn't in fact being quite too reasonable. By some standards I may be being positively effete." A vague, wistful thought crossed his mind, of storied husbands who put down mutinies by simply clouting them one; but there were clubs for whose membership he simply couldn't qualify. It occurred to him, though, that Paul, in his shoes, would probably spank her. "However." He squared his shoulders as if preparing to face a press conference. "I'll make my position clear, if I may. I'm saying, Andy, that this is where we live. If you don't want to stay here, I won't force you to: you can go ahead and exercise your rights. But I think you should understand that you cannot also expect indulgences." He smiled emptily, ignoring the disgraceful, imploring *Don't go, oh don't go* that would surely crash through his careful facade in a minute. "May I wish you a pleasant vacation—and I trust you'll let me know its duration. Now, if that's all?"

"Oh, quite, thank you." She moved then, a little uncertainly. She looked, Alec thought, much worse than anybody who'd simply been clouted one. "I'd be . . . obliged . . . if you'd keep me informed . . . about the children . . ."

"Certainly." He crossed the room quickly to open the door for her, and it was very nearly his undoing as he stood inches away from her, staring down at the small faint spray of freckles that were visible only when she was so very pale. "I won't be blackmailed," he said. Miserably, but he said it.

Andrea said with equal misery, "I understand. But I won't be tyrannized."

He opened the door for her and she went out, graceful and stubborn, and Alec stood there in the emptiness she had only begun to leave. Then, brave and stubborn, he went back to the sofa, picked up his folder of papers, and returned to work.

Thirty-one

Paul Morisot ordered the canellone Marian liked, came to a decision about the wine, and then sat back to wait for her in the upstairs dining room of the old, handsome restaurant in the upper reaches of Connecticut Avenue. All luxury and hush and discreet service, with heavy draperies and thick carpets effectively shutting out the hurrying world outside and the footsteps of reality within, the place was rather like a very elegant, well-run brothel, Paul thought. But Washington—and, more important, Marian— seemed to see it as the ultimate in respectability with just a dash of daring, the perfect setting for the long luncheon rendezvous of those inclined to a little tasteful, civilized playing with fire.

Morisot, though, was a simpler man than that, and his intentions were not nearly so limited as those indicated by the decor. The delicious flirtation implied here had never been what he had in mind, and the hunger Marian had discerned in him on the day of Martigny's death was certainly not for a diet of amorous whisperings and flutterings. He had meant, when he'd told her he was sorry for the trouble he was causing her, to express an almost sociological regret for her anguished and so-American writhings over what was only, after all, a relatively unimportant manifestation of a far more important fact; his apology had been, in effect, for his lapse in protecting the lady from what she considered a dragon. But lust was not a very fearful dragon to Morisot, who had slain it in the past in more than one cause and had confidence in his ability to deliver at least a few telling blows whenever it came inconveniently to life again. His confidence was quite justified: a man who has surmounted hunger and peril and survived with the courage to confront, armed with only a couple of tools and a picture in his brain, the million years of silence in a block of stone is not likely to be given much pause by a little localized discomfort.

It was good, though, Paul told himself, that the little one seemed to have managed somehow to come to terms with her terrors; he had no wish to cause her distress in the name of the muted languors this place typified. What he did wish was much simpler, and resulted from the fact that Marian Farland, though someone else's wife, was actually part of Paul Morisot's landscape: she belonged in it just as she was, and she would grow more and more into its color and shape the older she grew. The one in which she lived did not fit her—it forced her into distortions from which she suffered, and it was not impossible that her husband, who was intelligent and probably loved her, knew that even if Marian did not. Paul smiled, considering that in a more civilized society the matter could be arranged by negotiation: an error had been made and must be rectified. In a less civilized society he could either fight Farland or, more likely, offer him whatever number of cows would compensate him for surrendering the use of the woman and, presumably, the potential value of the little Peter—who looked rather like the curly boys riding dolphins in somebody else's sculpture.

Morisot's smile widened as he remembered his brief exchange with Alec this morning. Although speech on the subject was clearly difficult for the Vermonter, he had managed to indicate that "Andy and I have been a little concerned." They had observed Paul's apparently aimless hanging around Washington during a season when he would normally be at home and at work. And now "Andy" was "troubled," Alec said—strangely, undertaking to speak for her in her absence, though Andy habitually conversed fluently with Paul in both his language and her own—because Paul had contracted to write a book, an effort that would take further time away from his real work. And what Alec wanted to say, he mumbled awkwardly, was that if it was a matter of a need of funds. . . . Paul had helped him quickly, then, out of compassion: it was less a matter of money than of a woman—who would be expensive but not, Paul thought, unmanageably so. But who had first to be —um—obtained. Which was a problem in which no friend could be of aid but one that was nevertheless rendered less daunting by the knowledge that friends were concerned. . . . But what if he had said, Paul thought now, that yes, it was most kind of Alec to offer and what Paul would like, please, was to borrow a substantial number of cows. . . .

The waiter appeared suddenly and murmured *"Madame viens"* in reply to Paul's raised eyebrow; the man twitched and poked briefly at the perfections of the table like a mama seeing her daughter off to the ball, and then melted away efficiently because it was no part of his job to spoil lovers' meetings. Paul, with his eyes on the entry and his blood beating a little faster than the act of sitting up straighter in his chair could really require, thought that at this moment, at least, he was wealthier than Alec: for here he had—now, at last—the sight of his love. He rose politely as she approached, feeling other risings, general and specific: the world probably held, he noted, no more effective aphrodisiac than the wordless entrance of Marian. Perhaps because she was always late, she always came hurrying: the dainty high-heeled slippers moved so quickly that the beautiful sleek legs twinkled in his sight; skirts fluttered; slim hands flew to frame apology or dismay; the ripe red-flower mouth opened at once to hasty speech; the dark wings of her hair waited to lift, imminently, the whole exquisite fragile vitality. When Paul took her hand, he felt again, along with the not at all undefined desire to touch her, an undefined need to capture her by this hand, to hold her still at least for long enough to finish looking at her before the fleeting Marian of bright eyes and breathless voice did in fact fly away as she seemed always about to.

Although he knew by this time that there was no gesture by which he could stay her enough—not here, not anywhere except at home with the ancient rocks and the olive trees, in the palette of colors among which her smoky hair and blue-green eyes belonged; there, where the light was true, she could use as it should be used the clear sight she wasted now in observing trends and flaws and mannerisms. She had the wide vision of a child, but the adult energy and resourcefulness that could support it in the making of beauty were now being dissipated in silly struggles with a clock; and her "rest" was only more hurrying—when she should be lying quiet in the soft air in which all her softness would be at home. Paul erased ruthlessly a detailed vision of Marian resting on a certain grassy sward not far from his studio and waited for her to finish her extravagant description of how hungry she was, so he could dive into the torrent of speech for long enough to tell her he had ordered her lunch. Meanwhile, he occupied himself in research into the question of whether the lace edge of slip that had been visible as she hurried toward him was today's only flaw. For her perfection was an illusion of the first dizzying instant: after that, all sorts of quirks and carelessnesses emerged, so that it was never possible, really, to find her exactly the same twice or to reach reliable conclusions about her.

Watching her shudder delicately while she told him with indignation about the chill in the air outside—quite unfair, when it was supposed to be very nearly spring—Paul remembered noticing the first time he'd met her that she always used her body like this, to help her words; the round, high breasts that belonged in the low-necked blouses of his native province must have from the beginning made mock of the sober tailors of her silk shirt, but the shudder now demolished their efforts completely. He took his hand away from his face and let her see the smile he had been hiding. "I have this morning been to visit Alec, and he tells me it will snow," he told her. "In matters of weather, I have found it wise to trust men of the north country."

He didn't listen to what she said then about the man her countrymen had chosen to trust with the whole weather of their lives, because he was smitten with a sudden vivid reminder of exactly, specifically, what he wanted, and with it came an unwanted and ridiculous envy of the man who shared her bedroom. Only a fool or a flagellant would have engaged at any time, and certainly now, in prolonged contemplation of the shared bed. Paul was neither; but it came to him overwhelmingly that to be with her, and not only to be there but to be rightfully at ease there, when she dressed and undressed and brushed out the soft masses of her hair, when she pattered around barefoot, chattering the way she was now and probably tossing bright garments about carelessly—this seemed to him all at once, achingly, very heaven. It also occurred to him that to live in heaven was not necessarily to spend all one's time admiring the decor; Farland, he thought, probably read the newspaper while she dressed—and probably he would, too, after a while, Paul admitted, but right now he would give many, many, many cows. . . . He woke abruptly to the fact that he had left her the whole burden of the conversation while he sat indulging himself in boudoir fantasies, and his face darkened in the beginning of a scowl for his guilt.

". . . and even if Andy had all that madness to go skiing, she didn't have to go as far as Switzerland," Marian was scolding, her voice a little sharpened by her own nervousness. She looked up from the tense business of turning her wineglass in perfect circles and caught his scowl as it was deepening. His dark eyes had lost their gentle look, and his reply, though polite, was cool to further comment even while it revealed his agreement in censure. Marian bent her head before the reproof: Andrea, one gathered, was up to tricks Paul frowned on; but she was his friend and he loved her and by golly, the autocrat of the luncheon table would tolerate no sniping from the sidelines. Marian glanced up to let him see how completely, and how meekly, she had got the message—and found that he had apparently forgotten her in favor of studying the waiter's flat-footed walk and the forward-leaning slant of the lumpy body under its youthfully dashing jacket. *Andréa* might merit a slap on the wrist and Marian might need a little keeping in her place, but Paul had, always, more pressing business than either friendship or love, and he got on with it.

He was such a *noticing* man, she thought with surprise and, from nowhere that she could fathom, a purely physical joy, a softness in her body apparently born of that discovery. For a moment, it was like the awful, ridiculous time that day in her office—such a terrible, simple wanting. That was over now, all that sort of thing, she reminded herself: she had suffered through to a battle won and a decision made. Winter was, to all intents and purposes, the loser on points, and she was no longer clinging to the ropes and hoping for the bell. But for the first time now, she thought, watching her lover at work, she knew the real reason—realer than morality or duty—that it had been necessary to deny love. The people in Paul's province, Andy had said once, thought of being away from home in the spring as suffering a blow to the eyes. It was very simple, Marian knew suddenly: she didn't want his eyes to hurt, no matter what.

Morisot, the noticing man, noticed the tremor in her hand and the hectic color in her cheeks that would gladden the heart of any scheming seducer and wished briefly that he could be a scheming seducer, *tout seul,* and exploit the symptoms. Or else *un chevalier sans peur et sans reproche,* and thus presumably not see them at all. While he asked her whether she would like some brandy, he admitted silently that refraining from maneuvering her into his bed didn't change the fact that he was certainly engaged in a form of seduction. Also, though he was comporting himself with a knightly purity he hadn't attempted since about the age of sixteen, he was neither exactly without fear nor without blame. He faced the truth of all this by deciding against any brandy for himself: a half-citizen in each of two worlds required the full use of his inhibitions.

Marian looked at the dark eyes that reflected more turmoil than their owner realized and decided against the brandy after all—and then, abruptly, against any more of this foolishness of hunting for something seemly to say. "Let's go, Paul, can we? This place is so—Victorian."

He seemed a little startled, but he agreed readily enough. She guessed he knew as well as she did how irrelevant all talk was, and especially in this place, to what was—or had been—between them, the lovely thing that had, sadly, to be denied. And that was that, and no flickers or momentary flareups or twitches of nerve-endings had any real significance.

He had such a deep, velvety voice: a few of her nerve-endings twitched with a kind of envy as she listened to him speaking briefly in his own tongue with the man bowing them out. And then, when Paul was going down the stairs before her, there was a small momentary flareup: she looked at the back of his head and thought, if you could call it thinking, how much she would have liked just to put her hands into that black, springing hair. Then the inner door swung shut behind them, and Paul smiled down at her as they stood, apart from all the world, in the small hushed vestibule. And she saw the stern line of his jaw with the faint shadow of beard and suffered a teeny-tiny flicker as she caught herself wondering unworthily whether Aimée was in the habit of talking to him in one of her three goddam languages while he shaved . . . It was shameful. But it didn't matter: Marian met his somber, wondering gaze and let him see that, though she loved him with all her heart, she had decided to do nothing whatever about it. Then, head up, shoulders back, wearing a composed smile that was a credit to Miss Kingman's School, she waited like a little lady for the chivalrous M. Morisot to open the last door to the everyday world.

But that wasn't what was out there. For outside, it was snowing the very, very beginning of a snow: a fat, wet flake that might have been only the second one to fall looped past, slow and tentative. Then a few more came like a squad following a scout: this place was safe, they could move in. Marian stuck her tongue out and caught one of the new arrivals. It tasted burning, and she said "Oh" in discovery and turned to tell Paul.

And it was then, with the snow army beginning to arrive, company by company, and the soft air full of the rapid thronging fall, that she understood it was utterly, completely, for free, this snow: it was a whole, magic little wedged-in winter; a gift for those who had bravely sweated it out until spring; a tiny holiday from the everyday world for whoever had recognized the need to surrender love. These fat wet flakes wouldn't last past the afternoon, wouldn't change anything, and everything after would go on exactly as it was supposed to. But now here it was, isolate and beautiful and rare: here at hand, to be taken now, a moment for those who could not have a whole season.

Morisot regarded the black of his true love's hair sparkling with snow and thought dizzily that they could not stand here all the afternoon of what was, after all, a Thursday in March and simply celebrate the world and its joys. More snowflakes were glinting in the curly gray fur collar of her short coat, and he brushed at them lightly to occupy his hands in some sober, responsible fashion. He wasn't sure he could afford to believe in what he believed was happening, but first he had to know: he turned her to face him so he could see. What he saw first was melting snowflakes glittering on her eyelashes and then, only then and with fear, her eyes. And all his perfectly usable, heretofore reliable English fled him instantly while he stood there staring down at her with his mind reeling after all the gone words for one, almost any one, to say it with.

Marian with the ache of miracle in her throat saw him knowing, too—and strangely, not doing anything about it. Was he going to make her say it? It occurred to her then that she didn't have the faintest idea how. She looked away from him to frown at her foot, tapping it impatiently like someone waiting to use a phone, and asked herself reasonably whether she really expected him to say, "How about it, baby?" or any variation thereof, in French or English, in lofty or funny. So she raised her head and a snowflake plopped at the side of her nose and she said, "Paul, I want to—go with you. Now."

He was like a passerby caught in a headlight beam by a roadside—a face totally unknown, expressionless except for a small tightening of surprise. "It can be arranged?" He spoke as though his lips hurt.

"Yes." She had no idea what he meant, unless it was something traditionally said at assignations. Maybe there was an etiquette, she thought, wanting to giggle. But something had to be done about the sudden stranger, frozen into immobility. She put her small hand on his coat sleeve. "Let's go for a walk." His arm was like stone, so rigid that she thought she could have chinned herself on it; when she began to laugh, because of this and everything else, he said in the voice of an English butler that she would get wet. She told him she knew, and all the stiffness seemed to go away at once, taking her by surprise: it was as if he had dumped a heavy pack containing, among other burdens, the need to be any longer courtly, restrained, and responsible for both of them. He was so *sudden,* she thought, clinging to the arm that was now quite definitely not made of stone.

Paul told himself that it was impossible, in any language whatever, to have misunderstood her. He began to walk through the curtaining snow, holding her hand and trying to inhabit the rapidly changing universe, whose shape he'd once thought he knew, with this adorable, impossible woman. Only a moment before he had seen what was surely dismissal—and then, with a suddenness that left him feeling that his ears must be flapping, it had become just as surely "now." To control, simultaneously, the stirrings of lust and laughter was difficult, but it was not possible to avoid seeing the delicious irony. For any "now" at all, almost from the first moment he had ever seen her, had been, from his point of view, an appropriate time to make love to her; so it was undeniably funny that what rendered this particular "now" irresistible was precisely the childishness that had made it necessary to protect her. Nothing would have changed for Paul, who did not believe in magic. But the fact that Marian did, and had found a magic permission for herself, magically set him free.

Or it would eventually, he decided: she seemed to be engaged in some kind of internal conflict between a desire to go to bed with him and a desire, apparently, to postpone it. The best way to deal with that was simply to wait: it was a war in which he couldn't lose. But he wanted to win it well, so, while he studied a One Way arrow being steadily rimmed with snow, he summoned to his waiting all information, collected anywhere, that might help his cause. Obligingly then, Andy said snappishly from a corner of his memory that he was "too damned lordly." All he had done, actually, was tell her she couldn't achieve the result she desired with the paintbrush she intended to use; but she had accused him of "issuing edicts." So, said Morisot to himself like a student preparing for a quiz, with an American woman one must avoid lordliness (but surely not also in the matter of the bed? *Incroyable!*). Patience and restraint would be— He frowned suddenly, reminded that patience and restraint could not, by themselves, solve the rather delicate problem occasioned by the suddenness of Marian's decision: it was obvious that she was quite innocent of experience with impromptu afternoon liaisons, and therefore it must be doubted that she carried tucked into her purse any equipment for this occasion. One would think, he thought grimly, that she was quite old enough to know what she was doing. But the intrinsic quality of the stone was a fact with which, always, one began—and the intrinsic quality of Marian indicated the possibility that tiresome details would escape her attention until later. Too much later.

It was not a detail to which he himself had given much attention for a long time: Aimée was, thanks to the scientific zeal of some Nazi doctors, removed from the possibility of pregnancy. And she represented very nearly all his past few years' experience—although Marian seemed to have discovered, quite as suddenly as her magic permission, a blissful belief that impulsive liaisons were a commonplace in his life. Or so he gathered from her trusting air of having enlisted and needing only to await orders. Paul ground his teeth and cursed, silently and impartially, Charles Boyer, Jean Gabin, and Jean Paul Belmondo. And then he smiled down at *la petite* and touched her cold-reddened cheek and suggested as democratically as he could that she must need to telephone and here was a drugstore, no?

He made everything so easy, Marian thought as she dialed the *Tribune* number: he seemed to know always just exactly what to do and he didn't ask you, he told you. And yet, at the same time, he didn't mix up love with rescue and protection and elaborate coddling. For the first time, she was being offered only love, and all the details were left to her. She was watching him through the windowed door of the phone booth and thinking that he treated her like a partner, really, when Pearl came back on the phone to say that most of the messages looked routine all right, and she would hold them. But Ann Taswell had phoned down a little while ago, looking for Marian. Ann's line was free now, Pearl would ring it—

"No," Marian cried, in something close to terror. "Not now. I've got to go —they're starting," she added, inspired. "Tell Ann I'll call her at home tonight."

She crashed the instrument down so abruptly that she could still hear the noise ringing in her head when she finally got Rosa.

"Rosa, everything okay?" But she didn't wait to find out. "Look, I'm taking the rest of the day off. If you need me, you can call my office and leave a message. If it's an emergency, you'll just have to get hold of Will. I don't know when I'll be home."

"Ain't about to be no emergency," Rosa said wonderingly.

"All right, then—"

"Listen, one thing—I has to get off tomorrow night and you got to go out. It say 'Harrington' on your calendar. How you want me to—?"

"I suppose you'd better try to get Gloria," Marian said wearily: a party at the Harringtons' was an exercise she would have preferred to escape. "Or phone the sitter service. Or . . ." Irritation exploded in her, jagged and dangerous. "I don't care, Rosa. Do anything, or nothing. This afternoon, I have no children." Half expecting a bolt of lightning to seek her out in the drugstore, she added meaningfully, "No responsibilities of any kind."

Rosa got the point, after a pause full of surprise. "The truant officer catch you." Her voice held laughter.

"Not if you don't tell."

"I ain't fixin to tell nobody." Marian was starting to hang up when Rosa said softly, "Miz Marian?"

"Yes."

"You have a good time. But you be careful, hear?" She hesitated, and in the silence a door slammed in the house on Mackintosh Place, which was very, very far away. "You got to go back to school tomorrow."

"I know."

Marian hung up very slowly this time and stood still with the lonely truth, that she must leave a way to go back to school tomorrow, before she went to find Paul. Who might have to go back to school tomorrow, too, but who seemed right now to be able to give his whole attention to a row of pseudo-bronze ash trays, each bearing a pseudo-portrait of President Alexander Girard.

When they came out of the steamy shuffle of the store, the snow was still settling like a benediction, bringing quiet and order, trimming all rough edges and making essential shapes of fussy things. A universe of essential shapes was Paul's kind of world, Marian thought, waiting while he paused in the middle of the bridge and braced himself to lean over the cold greening-bronze railing. He turned back then for Marian, who was too small to see much, and lifted her. She slid one arm around his neck and hung in his grasp, looking her fill at the fairyland being constructed on the tangled tree branches along the empty ribbon of roadway below, where lashings of white were heaped along every horizontal arc and silver dripped from the ends of twigs. When she nodded, Paul set her down gently, smiling with the shy pride of a man who has brought his lady love a particularly fine bauble; he seemed happy to be thanked properly for the present, but his hands allowed her time for demur and his kiss held more celebration than demand. When he released her, Marian reached up and smoothed the caretlike quirk in his eyebrow and then put her hand back in his.

Where it belonged, she was discovering as they walked between the old leftover buildings, all their architectural whorls and trims now elaborated and emphasized by snow. The white-topped towers and gables were backdrops for an old story set in a chateau; but Marian was inhabiting a new land, one she had never known, in which it was possible to belong without captivity. She who had always been a pretty to be won, a proof of prowess to be turned in the hands and kept in as much splendor as could be managed —but kept—was now free to stay or go. Marveling at how light freedom was, she exercised it abruptly, stopping Paul in mid-discourse about an unlikely statue of a horse in Lafayette Park: out of the corner of her eye she saw the startled smile of a hurrying passerby before she closed her eyes against pedestrians and the watching windows and the knowledge that they were perilously close to the *Tribune,* from which all sorts of people she knew could issue at any moment. Paul's hands on her shoulders were compelling— but even then, she thought, allowing retreat. She let her kiss tell him she didn't want to retreat.

That certainty had slipped away from her somewhat by the time she was standing before the bedroom mirror in the handsome old hotel where he lived in surprising luxury. She had stared wide-eyed at first at the tapestried chairs with graceful fruitwood legs in a sitting room with high walls and elaborate, delicate molding and trim: this kind of thing was now not only rare but terribly expensive. Her knowledge of that may have been what made the difference, reminding her abruptly that Paul was not a creature of snow-magic but very nearly another kind of legend, a goddam national hero, an item for gossip columns, and probably the recipient of mash notes from little girls. He'd explained, with a haste that only increased her suspicion, that it was necessary to have grandeur when one was lonely and without work to do, and then led her toward the open bedroom door with an ease that convinced her he must spend as much time molding women as carving stone. Then, running absolutely true to form—for it was known that the French were both practical people and also expert at seduction—he had pointed out the bathroom so she could get dry and gone out, leaving the bedroom door open behind him. Left to defend the proprieties from his practical assault,

Marian had retreated to the bathroom to undress and availed herself of the fluffy white terry-cloth robe she'd found among its appointments. The bedroom was dim, elegant, and empty when she ventured out. So she dared to open the robe now and peek at the horrid red line her garter belt had left at her waist. The mark was almost entirely gone; she rubbed at it experimentally and then stopped and let the robe fall closed, just managing to keep herself from clutching it around her, as she heard him coming in.

Paul put his hands into the pockets of the black and white silk bathrobe that had been a birthday present from Andrea and Alec, and that he did not recall ever having actually worn before, and tried to think whether there was anything else he could do, besides avoiding too-sudden nakedness, to dislodge Marian from her obvious fear. He looked at her standing there in the classic pose he had drawn and painted and modeled and carved: woman with arms uplifted, tending her hair. The loose sleeve had fallen back and the sweet white sheltered skin of the inside of her forearm was more pearly than he had ever managed to show it; the angry thought crossed his mind that he had got the figure really right perhaps only once that he could remember, and that time he had help from some especially fine marble. . . . Then he saw her wide eyes asking him what was coming next—and hoping, presumably, that she could endure bravely whatever torments he planned to inflict on her—and he forgot old defeats in contemplating the possibility of a new one. Because, for no reason whatever, the perceptive critic who had marveled in print at Morisot's "enormous tenderness" with an Eve had become utterly convinced that the very same hands, now innocent of mallet and chisel and of any intent but love, represented total menace. He sighed and went to get a towel: while he was wondering what would reassure her—if anything could—or whether he would simply end by ravishing her or killing himself, or both, he could occupy the time by rubbing vigorously at the soaked mass of her hair.

It proved a wise move. At least, he became trustworthy enough so that after a while she peered out from the wild tumble of her hair and said clearly, if not coherently, "Paul, it makes me feel bad."

He dropped towel and aplomb and asked her—his voice indicating that he would kill it, whatever it was—*what* did. He clenched his dangerous hands, impatient to throttle it.

"I don't want to be . . . usual."

Paul summoned what he feared was the last of his control to tell her she was not usual; his voice adding, "Alas," was not reliable. She started to raise her head and he knew it was coming, that look again of the virgin sacrifice, and that he could not hope to be able to bear it. *"C'est moi,"* he said desperately: it might have been *"Vive la France"* spoken before a firing squad, for the way truth-with-its-back-to-the-wall rang through the words. *"C'est MOI."* He pulled her to her feet and held her against him so that perhaps his bones could tell her, and make her believe, that it was indeed he—Paul, who loved her, and not this Don Juan she kept insisting on. In the name of God, he thought: *usual.* His arms tightened in despair because she quivered so, and a thousand pleas, all untranslatable, fled through his mind like a maddened mob. All at once, then, the quivering stopped. Without taking time for giving thanks to any of the deities he had been summoning, he picked up the suddenly pliant body and carried it to the bed.

Whatever he was muttering, Marian knew, was something she wasn't supposed to understand anyway; but the anger in his face as he stared at the red mark near her shoulder required no translation. She understood it: she knew she was beautiful, lying strangely quiet and calm under his dark gaze, and one does not blemish beauty without regret. But neither, she decided, should one murmur that it was nothing and had been necessary besides—or venture to say "Tu-tu-tu-tu" and pat the cheek of such a furious lord. Nothing she had ever done before applied: all she could think to do was close her eyes and wait quietly to find out how things marched in the country of Paul.

In the silence, she heard the small slither as the silk robe slid to the floor; but he didn't join her in the bed. Instead, there was only a gentle touch, a tentative stroking of the damaged flesh as if he might one day forgive himself and maybe allow himself a second chance. She smiled and opened her eyes because she wanted him to allow himself a second chance, and just because it had been a long time without seeing him.

"Do not be frightened," he said quickly. "You must not be frightened."

And that was when it happened, really, the act of intercourse between the naked man standing beside the bed and the naked woman lying on it, and undisturbed, unmoving air separating them. For there is a kind and degree of penetration that is deeper and swifter than any act of sex, and more mutual. And in giving her, nakedly and wholly and authoritatively, the name of his demand, Paul allowed an equal entry. Marian's instant seeing was like a plunge—she saw, suddenly, all of him all the way and all the way back through all his history of enormous gifts that always might also frighten away something he loved; she understood that his triumphs had had costs, and she saw how it was, the plight of those who, awesomely endowed in any way, must tremble before the fear of being only fearsome. The authentic hero who had been frightened all along, though of something she had never imagined, stood over her like a very myth of the conquering male—and stopped to demand what she had been cruelly, stupidly denying him, the right to conquer and not plunder.

They were both so foolishly frightened in their separate ways: in all that crazy walking in the snow, there had not been an ounce of wisdom in anything they had said or done, except the mutual wish to know each other truly. And she had nearly lost that for them at the last minute. The trophy who had always required a hero held out her arms to the hero who was afraid of only taking trophies and said—with her body, as always, helping her words—something exactly imperious enough to assure him of the essen-

tial shape of things: "I'm cold, darling." Only a woman who was so unfear-
ful as to be positively petulant could have put him so neatly in his place as
an ordinary careless fellow.

He couldn't quite believe it, she saw, when he had corrected his lapse from
chivalry; in a way, he knew exactly what had happened to him, that he had
found the land he had thought was somewhere there, over the horizon. His
body hummed with the knowledge—but he was reserving the right to refuse
to go along with it until he had established a rational geography. Lying quiet
in his arms while he explored, Marian thought of old Voltaire insisting on
reason in the face of an earthquake and smiled. But she nobly refrained from
doing anything to speed Paul's obviously imminent earthquake: she let him
map, at his own pace, the latitudes and longitudes of his newfound Indies.

She was free to do her own exploring, though, and the results made her
breath catch in her throat. His body was beautiful—so neatly made, all compact and powerful under smooth, almost polished skin. Except for the white
scar that slashed obliquely across his chest like a shorter, narrower version
of the ribbon worn with formal dress. She trailed her fingers along it, remembering she had thought he was only making a joke, that day in her office. *I
myself have been scarred* . . . She might have known, though: he spoke the
simple truth, even in a secret joke.

Paul leaned on his elbow, tracing with his lips the course of a particularly
interesting topographical feature—and then, with increasing determination
and no tentativeness whatever, the phenomena resulting from his original
foray. And Marian, staring at the scar that was a mocking symbol of all the
secrets that had been withheld from her, found all her ease gone, replaced
by a huge, consuming anger at the outrage recorded here. She touched the
scar, her fingers trembling with her rage at the molesting—somewhere, sometime—of this lean strong body that was meant for her. "Paul? Is this . . .
from the war?"

He didn't answer: the war was of no interest to him at the moment. But
it was wounding Marian most immediately. "Darling? Did it hurt a lot?"

"*Ah oui.* I am a very big hero," said the very big hero indistinctly. He
took her hand out of his way and then, remembering not to be lordly, put it
down on his hip, just above the swell of buttock. "In the same war, I am
also a big coward. Here, I am hurt much more."

She knew him too well now for him to get off with jokes. The flesh had
been gouged: she touched the triangle of indented pebbly skin and found it
was small; but she didn't doubt for a moment that it had hurt him terribly,
and she wouldn't be quiet about it. "Who did that to you?"

"A bad man with a knife."

"Let me see, darling." She craned under his leaning body.

"Later," he said, in a voice that had quite undemocratically decided something.

Which was that she had no more time, no more at all: with the land
sufficiently explored, he was for conquest, not archives. Suddenly he had no

secrets: he was, openly, exactly what he was—fearsome and swift and encompassing. Nerves pricked to attention at a dozen places on her body, and he had a thousand hands and a million mouths; he knew every advantage the instant it was established and returned speedily and in force to double it. Marian struggled against a sense of being totally assailed, meaning to fight this arrogant assumption that she could be taken at will even if it meant fighting herself; she must make it clear to him that she could not be so overwhelmed, so slam-bang conquered. She clenched her hand into a fist to show that she could not be subdued, no matter what. And then, although surely it was only the very next instant, small running alertnesses had broken out all over her; they met together like streams until she was awash and helpless on a flood of waiting. Deep inside her was a swoop and a soar like a bird gliding. Her hands were open and seeking; one tugged at his hair to tell him, hurry, hurry.

"*Madame* permits?" he said absurdly to Madame who lay like the very name of Opening with her lips parted and her arms grasping and her legs arched. She kissed him for thanks, hardly noticing the overwhelming invasion. And then she kissed him for reward because he had asked. And then simply because it was necessary, because nothing must be left out of the darting and flickering and finding everywhere in and on her body. The muscles rippling under the skin of his back felt to her touch as running water looks in sunlight: she thought she was only thinking that and found she was thinking *more, more* instead, and her hands that she had believed were gentling him were, she discovered, writing *closer, closer* on his body while he wrote it in hers. Behind her closed eyelids, she saw the long-ago red apples of a winter day looming in their towering shining, growing bigger, glowing brighter, always beautiful and unreachable.

Only they weren't unreachable any more, because he knew: he knew they were there, and that she was too small by herself, and he wanted the very topmost one, the one she wanted too. He helped her then with his iron arms, she helped him with her grappling legs, and they rose together and reached it. They had it, they balanced it high: everything shouted and they bit into the apple, the good flesh burst through the great red shining and somebody cried out for joy and all the sweet juices ran at once. They ate greedily until there was no more and then licked their lips of the last of it and lay together, waiting to remember.

Marian put her hand to her cheek where there was a dot of cold under the tear left there and thought dimly that she was something different now, and she would find out the name of it when she could. Meanwhile, she lay still and observed the stranger who had folded her body like a scholar closing a rare book and then, leaning above her, kissed her hand in courtly leave-taking. A name for herself came into her head then: "container for the thing contained." She knew it meant something quite absurdly else, but she was too tired to think what. She stirred, meaning to ask him, and he said, "Ssh," and put out his hand to stop her. She smiled, understanding the orders she had meant to follow anyway: she would not move or change, but hoard obediently; she was a true vessel, he should know that.

But he was a dictator, taking no chances, allowing no choices. She breathed shallowly under the weight of his hand on her breast: it was heavy, and he was heavier than he looked, too. Probably because he contained so many secrets . . . But he was no dictator, for he had known what they do not, that a trophy is not a proper noun. With difficulty—because he had made her heavy, too—she turned her head to see what the truth was. And she saw that it was Paul, a workman, who slept close by, his trailing hand like an abandoned tool he would pick up again in the morning. His lips curved in a faint, leftover smile and his eyes had shut up shop for the day. Satisfied then, the true vessel slept also.

One of the secrets of production of a lifetime-sized body of work before the age of forty, and in a life interrupted by many deaths, is the ability to get on with very little sleep: such men live intensely, wringing more than others out of their hours of rest as they do out of their hours of work. Thus Morisot, awakening refreshed after a brief sleep, moved without any sign of weariness and with the controlled energy of a cat. It didn't surprise him that catlike caution was unnecessary, though: he was accustomed to his metabolic difference from most of the rest of humanity, and he turned the lamp on boldly, in full confidence that it wouldn't wake Marian. She hardly stirred as he stood above her, studying first only with pleasure and then with increasing sobriety the small body fallen among the pillows in a pose very like Botticelli's Aphrodite rising out of the sea. The swirling hair was the color of night rather than sunshine, but it had arranged itself as the painter had his model's. The breasts her white hand vaguely protected were rounder, heavier, with dark-brown nipples that had suckled infants; but the flesh gleamed as nearly luminous along the curve of flank, and the inturned leg and slim hand shielded secrets momentarily as secret as any virgin goddess's. And did it with just as much trusting flimsiness, Paul noted wryly while something knocked at his mind, warning him darkly that he would not forget and he might do well to fear: not everything that is innocent is harmless, and the frail can be far from powerless. She was small and vulnerable, but she was a mighty queen of her own land, into which he had rashly ventured.

He left her quickly, before he could consider whether he had become subject or slave, and went into the other room to find out how much time remained. Obligingly, while he frowned out at the new flakes of snow still being whirled before the window, a radio voice confided that it was finishing the five-thirty news and went on to assure him softly that this station was otherwise devoted to music. He prowled silently, a naked man with a joy and a fear, unaware that he was clasping and unclasping his hands the way he did when he began on a new work. In his friend Alphonse Lenard's portrait of Morisot, the wringing hands had seemed to some viewers to indicate prayer; to others, anguish. Both had been correct.

Paul padded into the bedroom and began looking for Marian's clothes because it would be better to get her dressed before he began to talk to her. The music swirled into the room after him, something with a syncopated insistence and a minor harmonic that reminded him of Aimée. With some relief, he stood still and let himself remember the mocking, mobile face he had left spitting warnings at him on a night in New York not very long past.

After all these years, he could hardly expect to deposit Aimée at her hotel with a chaste kiss, night after night, and go unchallenged; realizing it, Paul had gathered his courage, come up for the proffered drink, and said the silly thing he had to say as considerately as he could. And then waited patiently until she had slashed away at him for long enough so he could decently leave.

To go and masturbate, was Aimée's guess, vividly amplified—the better to dream of the American debutante who was, it was Aimée's instant conclusion, the cause of this desire for an unshared bed. Paul had thought even then that she was good, very good: standing there with her hands on her hips, she had magically lengthened her short, competent body to a tall, athletic grace. The husky voice that only hours before had chanted movingly of lost love to a delighted supper-club audience was now nasal and breathy and forming ridiculous syllables: " 'Dah-leeng, I theenk artists are so divine, so ar*tees*tic.' " She flung out her arms, tossing back long shining hair that Paul, flushing with both shame and laughter, was somehow made to see despite the perfectly visible sleek dark head under his eyes. " 'Take me, dah-leeng,' she say. 'Come to me.' And zen—ah *ha,* I am laughing like so—" She showed him how triumphantly she would laugh and went back at once into being the American woman—who now turned away from Paul, peeping at him archly over her shoulder while one hand clutched at the neck of her dress and the other aided her crossed legs in keeping her safe from his ravening assault. " 'Oh, Paul, don't,' " cried Aimée's American debutante in a high, thin voice. From between her narrowed lips came a bloodcurdling giggle. " 'Dah-leeng, you must not *do-o-o* thees, naughtee boy.' "

Paul applauded enthusiastically and turned to go; but there was an encore. He need not expect—said the the throaty contralto, switching now to French —that Aimée would be available to bind up his wounds. He said quietly that he didn't expect that and stayed to look at her because he loved her, in a way that had been satisfactory and pleasant and would have continued to be if only women were interchangeable; she deserved all she wanted of his attention now, even if his admitted folly prevented him from giving it to her any longer in the way that she wanted.

She had recognized long ago, Aimée told him without mockery now, that he wouldn't marry her. Paul nodded, knowing there was nothing to say to this: it was not news, and discussion of it was years behind them. "Good, good, okay," she said in a voice picked up, along with the words, in some agent's office. She bobbed her little head, accepting. But this *tendresse* they had, was it something to throw away for a schoolboy's dreaming? He did not understand, she said tolerantly—and when he came to understand, when he found out what he had let himself in for, it would be too late. He had reason to know, she screamed at him suddenly, abandoning newborn reason before it had barely begun to breathe, that Aimée would have no use for a castrated man. And that was precisely what he was asking for, she informed him at the top of a voice trained to project itself into the last rows of a theater; she sliced at the air graphically in case volume alone wasn't enough to get the point across.

Hoping all her neighbors were either away from home or had no French, Paul told her in a high piping soprano that he quite understood—which had the desired result of making her laugh and also quiet down a little. She came over and put her hard little paw on his shoulder and looked into his eyes. *"Paul? C'est la grande folie, ça?"*

He told her it was the truth and kissed her forehead and fled before the instant return of her wrath, hearing something thump to the floor as he closed the door. He hesitated, worrying a little about her, but he heard after a minute that she was only taking out her rage on a series of small objects, telling herself loudly that he would soon sing a different tune. That he would sing, in fact, *castrato.*

Paul sighed at the memory now and glanced over his shoulder at the sleeping woman who was indeed the *grande folie* that comes to a man once in his lifetime if he is lucky and can bear to invite it. And castration had not proved to be a threat—though it had occurred to him fleetingly that something like rape-in-reverse was threatening him, for he had never been as fully and quickly known to any woman, and it had been a little frightening to contemplate. Still, *tendresse chez Aimée* was doubtless easier in many respects. He sighed and went on into the bathroom, where Marian had probably left her clothes.

The first thing he saw in there were her drugstore purchases, and he made a face at the opened box as he remembered thinking that her fluster over this was close to Aimée's stereotyped prediction. Though Marian was hardly a debutante, this was clearly her debut at anything but connubial lovemaking; still, he hadn't really thought he would hear "Paul, don't." But he had kindly turned his back and studied the drugstore's brummagem, in the name of patience and restraint and to spare Marian's maidenly confusion.

He unwrapped the pristine portable douche bag and screwed the pipes and tubings together experimentally—and then said to himself disgustedly, abandoning women for what mattered, that this thing was a clumsy example of only apparent skill in design. He was lost in the question of devising something that would tuck back into its container neatly while it was still wet, a functional consideration shamefully ignored by the incompetent workman responsible for this, when he turned and caught sight of Marian's clothes. And then he abandoned his engineering researches at once and sat down on the edge of the bathtub to look.

She had hung up her skirt neatly and her blue slip was smoothed over the top of the clothes hamper with exquisite care. And everything else had been folded, even the brassiere, even the stockings, even the narrow little garter belt that didn't lend itself well to folding had been patted into some kind of orderly shape. Each garment was lined up with its neighbor in an exactitude fit for barracks inspection, and in an army more demanding than France's, he thought. There was something so touching about this secret neatness—a punctiliousness that had nothing whatever to do with the woman who was always late and left crumpled paper beside her office waste-basket when her throw had been inaccurate—that Paul put his hand over his eyes for a moment; tears pricked at him as he saw her in there, alone and afraid, delaying while she folded her guilts away devoutly to mollify whoever was about to punish her for wanting to give her warmth and beauty to Paul. *Pauvre petite.* He sat there for a long time, to be sure he wouldn't say "poor baby" or any variation of it to her. When he got up finally, he picked up the clothes roughly, tumbling them from the perfection that would never appease anyway what he supposed was, originally at least, Mama—and then he smiled when the slip slithered in his hand, revealing a triumphantly rebellious safety pin in its strap. If one must be foolish enough to love a childish woman, it was fortunate perhaps that she was not also young.

He remembered to put his bathrobe on before he woke her, though he wondered a little grimly as he tied the belt what his life would be like if he got what he wanted. "Paul, you make the house all dirty with your little stones,' " Aimée's American-beauty voice said in his memory, and he shuddered. But she had gone on warning him just a little too long: " 'Dah-leeng, I must have the new auto, this one is already one-half year old' "; "Paul-*bébé*, it is time to take the doggie to his psychiatrist' "; " 'But dah-leeng, where is *my* swimming pool?' " In the end, he had been less terrified of an American wife than curious about life in Hollywood.

But now he wished, just a little, that Marian would not call him that anonymous "darling" that he had himself heard her use to both Farland and Gil Kimball, which rendered it very nearly meaningless. Aimée's sketch might be several thousand miles too far west and a dozen years too young—and Marian could unquestionably coexist with Morisot's little stones. Nevertheless, he brooded briefly on a lifetime of being properly clothed (and what would she think when she heard his students' joke about *le maître's* summer working costume, "a scar and a loincloth"?) and of trying to think of English words at moments when only one's native tongue springs to mind.

Then he looked down at her and joy rose and bloomed in him: she would learn, he would learn, for already they spoke a little in a shared language. Sighing for the folly of it, he looked around dutifully for something to cover her with before he woke her.

Thirty-two

"Pearl? This is—"

"Oh hi, Mr. Farland," the *Tribune* operator said. "I'm sorry, but I don't know where Marian is. She called in earlier, but I haven't heard since."

"Well, do you know whether she'll be coming back?"

"I don't think so. I mean, she said to tell Ann Taswell she'd call her at home, so it doesn't sound like it, you know? But if you want to leave a message in case—"

Will said it wasn't any crisis, but would Pearl tell Marian, in case she did come in before quitting time, that he was about to go into a meeting and he didn't know whether it would break up in time to pick her up at seven. If she didn't call his office, he'd assume she'd gone home, he said, and hung up with thanks and went about his business with only a fragmentary irritation at his wife's unreliability: if there was something on at the National Gallery or somewhere tonight, she ought to have made a point of telling him.

"He won't be there to talk to—he's out of town making a speech," Marian lied. "Please stop worrying about it, darling. I've got plenty of time before I have to leave." She leaned forward from the chair to which Paul had sternly assigned her.

"Very well." It might be true, and there was no point in open disbelief. "You will dress now, yes? And then—are you hungry? Shall I give you dinner before I take you home?" He looked at her from his careful distance and wondered whether she had been paying any attention to what he had been saying. And doubted it soberly. Vivaldi danced in a shimmer of summer on the quiet air between them, and Paul thought of how she danced when she walked—and how, like her, the music's grace was a strict banishing of everything that did not lend to the shimmer. She loved and was loved, and she was not willing to permit any intellection to darken her summer; she knew exactly what she wanted, and that was all she intended to know.

"No." She pouted. "Paul."

"Yes?" She was so light: when the bad winds blew along the rock cliffs, she would have to be kept in the house for fear she would blow away and be carried to the sea.

"Come here," she ordered.

It was not possible to refuse her, this tiny wanton empress inadequately wrapped in an absurdly large bathrobe slipping off one shoulder. He saw her in profile against the heavy fall of satin behind her and noticed again that neither her face nor her body owned a single straight line. She was all small, sweet curve, from the clear white forehead that was like the ancient mosaic Venus at Toulouse to the last inch of the shapely leg that was too softly molded to be made by any man's hands. He came obediently, holding himself very stiff, glad for once of cover for his nakedness. *"Marianne,* I have told you, we must—"

"But not right now, darling." Her arms reached for him, dislodging her precarious décolletage, revealing curves of snow in which a traveler might lie down—and die, Paul told himself grimly, even if not of cold.

"When, then?" he asked her.

"Darling, *dar*ling, don't be so *grim.*" Her arms met around his neck.

If he leaned over he was lost. He lifted her and stood her up on the chair so that he could at least hold her a little away. The robe swung open and he held her at arm's length, keeping his face just out of reach of all that softness and, like a man dizzy on a height, not daring to look down. "Now is the time to begin," he said.

"Paul, listen. Next week, do you know what? We can have *two* days, I think. Darling? Wouldn't you like that?"

"Very much." There were victories too difficult to win, he thought wearily, and this one might be also too late to fight for. Of great aid in maintaining the gallant restraint he had so suddenly been permitted to abandon this afternoon had been his memory of a useful discovery made as a prisoner: you were all right so long as you planned escape, however wild the scheme; but if you let your mind turn instead to remembering the look and sound of home, you would end by lying on a bunk, helpless to find a way home. So virtue had been supported by self-preservation, and Paul had not been unaware of the risks when he had seized the opportunity to learn the look and sound of home. "And after next week?" he asked, his voice full of his fear that he was already sunk in a prison lassitude. He laid his cheek against one of her breasts and brushed the inner curve of the other with his lips as she moved to let him. And he saw how everything would be put within his reach, just so, by this woman who knew so beautifully how to feed the hungry— with chocolates, with marzipan, with bonbons. Next week's hunger would be met by two days, he thought, sliding his hand down the satiny skin of her back. She would manage somehow, with some lies to someone, and he would make love to her and sleep with her and wake with her in the morning. Once.

"Oh, darling, you'll see. We'll manage other times."

Certainly they would—there would be no "Paul, don't," positively none; she would contrive what she had to. The sweet flesh quivered under his hand, the nipple fed gracefully to him rose to his seeking lips. And it would next week, or next month, and the month after that, and maybe for a year if he was lucky and nothing happened to remind her that she was committing adultery, if nobody said the naughty word that would make it unbearably real for her. And always he would be rewarded for his patient waiting— with everything except what he had asked, a sober and prompt consideration of his plea for a life with her.

"Ah, darling, nice darling, tu-tu-tu-tu—"

A double drunkenness swept him: one made of the rage for this that was within his grasp, a simple need and sweet. The other was a colder fury, and he fought to keep from hurting the soft flesh with the clenching of his hand against whoever had taught her to give herself like this—a beautiful doll to distract intransigent men demanding difficult decisions. He lifted her carefully and carried her over to the bed, trailing her garment of false modesty and carrying with her a much heavier burden.

Paul put her down on the bed not roughly but with enough lack of gentleness to make her eyes widen with surprise. "Let us make it most clear what bargain I am offered." He leaned over and yanked her legs apart, abruptly enough so he thought she wouldn't notice how he avoided looking at what he had done. "It is, quite specifically, for this that I am to wait—no?" He decided against using any of the specific terminology he had been able to add to his collection of English colloquialisms, though several came instantly to mind. "For this," he repeated, and added contemptuously, "Do you think I am so easily content?"

Carefully, he kept his gaze on her startled face instead of the small body displayed as for purchase. She could not believe this, he saw; he thought with panic that it was taking her more time than he could bear to keep his eyes available to her so she could see he loved her and carry that along with the hurt when she turned away. When she did at last, simply huddling away from him with her hands over her face, he was indicted by every vertebra in the miserably bowed back, condemned by the little defenseless white behind and the soft thighs tightened too late. He made himself move away so he wouldn't pick her up and undo it all: if she was to see how monstrous was what she would make of them, it was necessary for him to be a convincing monster.

But he stayed there in the room and spoke to her so she would know he was there and that she had a choice. "I am not to play with, Marian," he said sternly, after he had tested the words in his mind to be sure he would sound harsh but not too harsh. He knew she was crying, and her futile attempt to hide it threatened to break his heart. "When you are ready—" his tongue tripped on the hope of an endearment, but he denied it "—I am waiting."

He waited then, as he had promised—only, when the voice on the radio began to talk, he couldn't stand up and make it go away. He could only bury his head in his hands and try not to hear anything, even the little voice in his mind that was sorry for him. That turned into Marian saying, "Did it hurt a lot?" His aching jaw muscles relaxed in the beginning of a smile as he remembered, because the question about the war was the single thing about making love to her that had threatened to be "usual"—and then he hadn't let it be: for no reason at all, he had told her the truth, that the little wound in the rear had been much more dangerous. It was true enough: a shirt and a coat bundled over his torn chest had hidden it away, but the other was more difficult. His smile faded as he sweated, even now, at only the memory of it, of walking half across a city, under the eyes of police and enemy soldiers, with blood running down his trouser leg—a man with a price on his head who, at all costs, must not be noticed. In the end, he had been saved by his own unfailed nerve, a little luck, and a small rain. And she didn't need to know any of it, except that she was not usual: she was the woman to whom he said, truthfully, what had hurt and what had made him afraid.

The voice from the other room went away and was succeeded by music and Paul looked down at his bare leg and thought about the other bloody time, when he had been no hero at all. The shattered perfume bottle had fallen so slowly, so horribly slowly, from his mother's bureau, and her guilty younger son had left her weeping and run away to hide among the caves before either of them knew he had gashed his leg. His father had come for him: it was easy enough to find Paul, even in the dark, for he smelled alien enough among the earth scents, his bloody pants leg drenched in the exotic perfume. When it was all over, the wound cared for and everything gone except the last of that lingering scent that wouldn't be completely washed off and had driven them all to laughter—what he remembered, forever, was that they had both been punished, Paul and Etienne, for the original crime against property; but extra punishment had been ordered for Paul, for running away. And more punishing still was his father's grave question: "Your mother stood in tears, and you ran away?"

He stared down at his leg and the tiny scar women never asked about and tried to unscramble the day he was a hero and the day he had learned he'd better be, and then both of them from the moment he had become a monster—and suddenly the music was unfurling itself like a flag and Marian's white bare foot was there beside his. He lifted his head a little warily, afraid of what he would find because he mustn't run away but if he had to fight again he would be beaten, for he had no more weapons. . . . And there was no need: she was standing small and straight before him, her face marked by tears but neither accusing nor pathetic. "Paul?" She put her hand up to her tangled hair. "Can you help me, please?" Her calm eyes saw his confusion, and she smiled. "Darling," she finished, making it beautifully clear.

He thought he had never been called anything lovelier or more meaningful. He opened his mouth and then closed it and clenched his jaw against a hundred desires: he wanted to cry on her shoulder, to toss her in the air, to award her the Legion of Honor, to wear her around his neck like a shawl. He did nothing except lead her over to find a hairbrush. He opened the drawer and took out both his brushes because the problem was severe, he thought, blinking down at the difficult mass of her hair. He had begun to close the drawer when he saw her looking at the dark-red leather folder that was lying in there. It was bordered with gold tooling and his initials were curly in gold: he knew that she knew such a thing would not be of his own choosing, and he knew also what she suspected. She looked like an absurd little soldier standing so carefully erect and frowning a little with the effort of asking nothing; he trembled with the strength of his desire to give her something. He reached into the drawer, but before he could touch the folder she was speaking, looking not at him but at it.

"Paul, I must think about it. You know what I want, but it's such a terrible thing."

He nodded. It was indeed a terrible thing to ask—not the divorce, for which he wasted no pity on Farland, but the uprooting of her life to come to him. He believed with all his heart that her home was with him, but to make that a reality now was, he acknowledged, most difficult and painful; if it proved impossible, he would understand. He had told her that, but he had not told her the rest: that she was not made for combat and it was cruel to force her into a struggle when she wanted only to love. To know of his pity would do her no good, though. All she needed to know was that he would not be content with anything less than a lifetime.

"I don't even know how it could be managed," she was saying, with the worry shadowing her clear white brow that should have been allowed simply to be beautiful. "It's so—complicated . . ."

Only in the decision, he told her quickly, must she be alone; after that, the complications could be left to him. His hands, afraid to touch her, clasped each other in that making anguish: the world was full of witful women, but not of women who gave themselves so wholly, without thought or plan or memory. She deserved not to be risked, only to be kept sheltered in a shining "now."

Marian shook her head. "You don't know him. He—"

"I know all I need to know," Paul interrupted, not wanting that "him" in this room. This might be an age of more complex solutions than duels or trading cows for women, but the solutions existed nevertheless. "You must consider essentials, not details." There were only a limited number of things any man, however determined and unscrupulous, could do to keep a wife who didn't want to be kept; Paul told himself that Farland was very likely to do all of them. But if Marian wanted to enough, they would win. "I will arrange—that," he said. "If you decide that you wish me to." He wondered grimly how far Farland would go in the use of the children as weapons.

"Paul, I have children."

"I am no ogre, for children to fear." But it could not be turned off thus lightly. He thought it was better for children when their mother was happy, but there was nothing he could say; he barely knew her children, to whom no generalities might apply. He had never been anybody's father, he admitted, cringing away from the memory of his wife's single incomplete pregnancy: when it became apparent that she would lose the child, two women had come to help her, but it was essential that she be quiet, for they were all in hiding. Paul, useless for anything but brute strength, had been assigned to hold his hand over Denise's mouth to stifle her moans. He had no desire to remember it any more, and certainly no intention that Marian should ever hear about it. Quickly, he interposed the better memory: "I was

a good man's son," he said aloud. If any of Marian's children became his
responsibility, he hoped he could acquit himself with wisdom. Until then,
though, they were her responsibility—and Farland's, and the other man's,
he thought, noting bitterly how many memories there were to wince at—
and Paul at his lordliest would never attempt to decide what would be right
or even supportable for any one or all of them. All he could do was thrust
her into the front line, where all the shooting would be. . . . He suspected
he was having his first experience with castration after all; he didn't like it.

Marian was staring down into the drawer again. "It may take some time
to know what to do," she said tightly. "You're quite right—you have your
own life, and I can hardly expect you to live on the fringes of mine—"

He stopped her, making a furious sound in his throat, and snatched the
folder out and opened it. From the frame on the right-hand side, Elizabeth
Girard in rather droopy shorts smiled enchantingly before a background of
great trees. Opposite, an indecisively shaped but enthusiastically crayoned
red heart had been carefully taped into the frame. "A present for St. Valentine's Day," Paul said unnecessarily. He held it out to her like a job-seeker.

The care with which she hugged him made him feel like a convalescent,
a recent survivor of a dangerous operation. He sat in the chair with Marian
on the floor at his feet while they both brushed the tangles from her hair.
When it was finished, she stood up and kissed him discreetly and he stroked
her hair carefully, so as not to undo the work, and told her to get dressed.

"All right, darling." He closed his eyes against the revelations of the
open robe as she leaned over his chair. He sat there like a grandfather and
wished he felt more like one. "I *am* hungry, I think," she said. "Are you?"

He pulled her into his lap and kissed her, with restraint, and told her he
was hungry and let her discuss with herself where they would go to eat.

"You're tired, darling, aren't you?"

"Yes. I am tired," he lied.

But it was worth it—for she was just as he had thought, and she had
truly forgiven him: she padded about without self-consciousness or fear,
talking and gathering her clothes and her precious hoard of hairpins, humming some of the music from the radio. Paul leaned his head back against
the back of the chair and told himself he had won, he had forced her to be
what she really was, and all he had to do was enjoy his victory. He got up
and got his clothes and took the confining robe off, but he kept his back to
her because he wasn't yet quite able to read the newspaper while she
dressed.

If only Marian hadn't offered a single, idle remark about how much better
he would feel when he had something to eat—by which she meant vaguely,
though he didn't know it, perhaps some red Jell-O—and if Paul hadn't turned
his head with the intention of inquiring, with mild amusement, into what
she believed to be the nature of his malady, everything might have ended
very differently. But he did turn, and before he could speak, he saw. And
what he saw was unbearable, given all the dammed-up anger of having to

be first a monster and then a grandfather and all the time also a gambler staking his new, beautiful, cherished possession with the odds heavily against him. It was too much—the politic course, of intelligent inaction, became physically impossible. Though certainly no thought processes were at work, summing all this up; probably only the cruder sections of his brain were functioning, and just enough to direct his muscles to cover the distance between himself and Marian. Certainly not enough for real speech: what he said as he yanked the brassiere from her hand was neither French nor English, just Sound.

But whatever brain cells are devoted to self-delusion were on the job, for he believed himself to be launched on a limited endeavor—a notion that flouted his every stored bit of memory and learning. A successful survivor of guerrilla warfare knows that it is suicidal to fire a single volley and not move on; a sculptor of skill and passion doesn't take a tool to stone or wood for a single purposeless scratch. And Morisot—of all people—did not put his hands on the body of any woman with such fierce possessiveness and then intend the proceedings to stop. But, incredibly, he believed he had crossed the room only to prevent her, as any civilized man would, from proceeding with a matter-of-fact calm that was barbarous in the circumstances.

An objective observer might have concluded, after analysis, that what had happened to Morisot's poor brain was a kind of short circuit, an abrupt cutting off of thought because thought led to a degree of conflict so insupportable as to threaten the system. For if it takes painful judgment to put up a beloved *objet d'art* as collateral for launching a dream, to turn suddenly and catch sight of the shipper crating it up with careless blows of a hammer is apt to increase the pain and diminish the judgment; besides, the education of a man of lordly temperament to the necessity for standing helpless before an event should be accomplished slowly, with lots of rest periods and preferably without graphic demonstration. So the conflict was bad enough, even without the additional professional accident that had grooved his mind in the pattern typical of men whose work exposes them regularly to the sight of unclad females: the division between a workaday naked woman and a meaningful one is difficult to state in words, but for such men it is decisive. Thus, if what was being done was hard for Paul to look at to begin with, the way it was being done as he turned and saw it was removing the woman from the sphere of love into the course of everyday business: that his *Marianne* should, in his sight, be dressing with all the matter-of-factness of a model finishing an afternoon's work converted Paul's decision, in the blink of an eye, from hard-won wisdom to self-murder—and thus crossed the border from what must somehow be borne to what simply could not be allowed.

The only witness to the sight of Paul, naked and furious and seeming to descend on her like some kind of unholy avenger, was not, however, an objective observer but Marian—a woman never given to analysis and, at the moment, intent on meekness. For, although her ability to refrain permanently from fighting it was questionable, she understood the reason for his insistence on austerity: in principle, she even sympathized, once she saw that what he had been saying was "It's not the *way* I want it"—a text with which she was familiar. She was crossing no border, for she had already crossed the only one that mattered; and to make love to a man and then go about the ordinary routines of living, in his presence, was her accustomed mode of behavior, though it was not Paul's. As she dressed, quickly and efficiently, she was certainly not dismissing him: she was thinking that all this palaver with downcast eyes and folded hands was alien to him; she was remembering the sleeping workman, now replaced by a conscientious mentor with mobile lips tightened against the possibility of saying something too revealing and the speaking eyes carefully silent. And what she was doing, in fact, was behaving like a good wife: she understood her man and knew that this was all terribly hard for him, and she was proceeding as briskly as she could to get him out of it, so he could be comfortable.

Perhaps because, without realizing it, she half-expected him to explode in some fashion, Marian was remarkably calm in the face of a wholly unexpected onslaught by a man with obvious sexual expectations who kept fondling her like a museum curator rescuing an ancient porcelain from a fall while he talked jaggedly in a tone befitting a Hyde Park anarchist orator. If her frightened-virgin look had been inappropriate earlier, it would have been quite logical at this moment. But Marian was not a logical woman: she reacted to everything about him except his angry voice; she remembered *"C'est moi"* without being told, and her body behaved appropriately. Her view, if she had anything so intellectual, was that if he had suddenly been taken with a desire to assail fortresses, it was no trouble to please him: all her doors were open to him any time. The last thing she thought as he carried her to the bed was that it was really quite remarkable that he should have, in addition to everything else, such beautiful ears.

It was not surprising, in the further circumstances, that Paul, having discovered an inviting lubricity, should avail himself of it. There was no decision, since there was no framed intent—except, perhaps, his general, non-unique intent to perpetuate the human race. Though not conscious, it nevertheless prevailed.

That had not yet been, though, Marian's intent. So she opened her eyes as she learned abruptly that his purpose in storming the fortress had been to inhabit it. She blinked at the slashing scar across his chest and said something that sounded perilously like "Oof."

Paul looked at her reproachfully. "You are not hurt." He discovered with awe the miracle of the pulse in her throat—the faint stir in the pale-blue trace under the white, white skin was perfectly visible, perfectly beautiful.

"No, darling. No. I was just a little . . . Paul, you said you were . . . tired."

It was not kind, he told himself, to make it so difficult for her to talk. "I do not always speak the truth," he said, and emphasized it gaily. He grinned, remembering Alphonse's favorite toast—which Paul translated, so as not to be guilty of thinking anything she couldn't understand: *May the good Lord keep you from a talking woman.* He went on making it difficult for her to talk: she should be taught, from the beginning, not to be a talking woman.

"Paul, don't!"

"What?!" His gaiety bubbled into outright laughter. He tested, methodically, the validity of her protest and found it unauthorized, unrepresentative of any of the opinions received from any of the other spokesmen of her body. But just in case the small quiver he detected in the outlying sector of his territory a little to the right was incipient rebellion, he put it down firmly before going on. The music from the other room, cheerful and insistent, accompanied him as he turned with enthusiasm to the subduing of all resistance, among his other occupation duties.

"Paul! You'll *have* to let me go. I didn't do—oh, don't make me say it all. I *believed* you—I thought we *were* going out—"

He kissed her quickly to spare her the need of further explanation and then didn't translate what he said to himself while he was deciding to gamble. He told her gently that it would be all right: nothing would happen. Then he called in all the troops and ordered quiet in the countryside.

But obedience was difficult to command, he found—for now, reassured, she was free to enjoy the new, gentler advance, slower and more delicate and allowing her time to experiment. "I surround you," she boasted. She nibbled at his beautiful ear and moved her hips to prove she surrounded him.

He agreed that he was surrounded: "I shall be quiet in captivity." Silently, he hoped his boast was as valid as hers. He noted with more than a little rue her charming inventiveness, which would have been very helpful indeed to a tired man, and tried to think of something apart from the plight into which telling an easy lie had led him. The sea near home when it was cold looked, briefly, like a promising example. But Marian emerged from it naked and gleaming, and the sun came up: she climbed the rocky path ahead of him, with the beautiful legs twinkling and the pert little behind bouncing just before his eyes and her hair floating around the frail shoulders as she danced in the dancing air, innocently headed right for that hidden grassy sward and begging to be caught and—

He stopped himself just in time, turning the triumphant pounce to just another gentle probe; but all those finely-tuned nerves inside the marvelous warmth had got the real message, and she didn't know she'd better be fooled. He slowed even more, reduced the margin of risk by taking his hands and his lips away from her dangerous skin, and thought about doing a writhing figure in some hard and grainy wood of Saint Anthony at his temptations. Saint Anthony was a frequently attempted subject, but certainly anyone who could survive Marian not even trying but only harmlessly enjoying herself could bring to the problem a special—

"Paul, listen—do you hear the music?"

He breathed a little easier because she had stopped to listen. In the reprieve he had time to marvel at her absolute trust in his assurance that nothing would happen.

"It's the overture to *Merry Wives of Windsor*. We danced to that, that first night, out in the rain. Oh darling, remember?"

He did not remember. But he groaned, realizing that he was almost certainly doomed, because now they were both listening to the lively rhythm. It sounded like some kind of round dance, and Marian obviously liked it: she laughed and sang *"Pum*pumpumpum Pum pum" and began approximately the kind of writhing he had watched her do, from a less trying, vertical advantage, at Andy's party. He had not found it an aid to composure even then.

Faster and faster the music tumbled, with its joyous regular thrusts that neither of them could help echoing, and they both laughed and Marian sang "Pummm-pumpumpumPumpumpum" with her hands fleeing happily along his back. The sea pounded and the sun shone and the fiddlers fiddled faster, and Paul alternately laughed in triumph as he captured his flyaway wanton and ground his teeth as he realized that he would rather be flayed alive than leave this but in another minute he never would . . . And *"Pum*pumpum" said, not Marian, who was beyond singing now, but a dozen authoritative drummers. The dancers, their hands joined, drew closer and closer into the center, narrowing their circle, and trumpets blasted joyously and the sea roared. And the boy who had learned not to leave a lady in tears had learned since if he had learned anything that sometimes you have to let them cry now instead of later— He called on every muscle to help in separating the man from the boy, and *vive l'honneur* . . .

"No!" Marian cried. Her whole body rose against the faint but totally immoral hint of withdrawal at this moment. Her arms tightened fiercely, pulling him down, and she clenched her teeth mercilessly in the flesh between his shoulder and the back of his neck.

He hung in space, flinching from the double pain but holding, holding bravely though in unjust causes—against the design of nature itself, against the woman who surrounded and demanded her just due, against the wailing longbearded prophets warning of punishment for the spilling of seed upon the ground, against the joyous loud pounding music circling toward resolution.

Then it was too much, it was more than could be asked: the damned woman raked her fingernails as far as she could reach down his back, adding the final, insupportable pain. And Paul roared in righteous wrath and taught her a lesson, again and Again and *Again* and AGAIN and *AGAIN*—until she moaned or anyway somebody moaned and he fell exhausted and lay panting on the warm, soft grass while the fiddlers unscrewed their bows and put the violins back in their cases, not forgetting to fold the white silk handkerchiefs they tucked under their chins, and the dancers straightened their skirts and dusted off their shoes and the drummers unstrapped their drums and eased their shoulders after a good day's work and *Marianne* whimpered a little because he was so heavy. He heard this small sound coming faintly through the mist from the sea and he struggled to raise his body because no gentleman ever, said Etienne who knew just how you did it and even with which girls to try—

Paul yanked her to her feet and shook her. Marian blinked at him stupidly, thinking that he was, surely, like no other man in the world. And so mean, too: why wouldn't he let her—? She remembered why then, and touched his cheek reassuringly. "It's all right, darling."

"WHAT?"

He was so terrifyingly *excitable,* and he would be angrier than ever when he realized his hands were hurting her shoulders. "It's all right." She smiled, wooing him away from his ferocity so he wouldn't rage later. "Don't you see, darling?" Her voice lapped at him as softly and seductively as her body had. "It will make it all so easy to decide."

Paul gasped. *"Vite!"* He cursed silently, hunting English words. "Go, at once!" She only stood there in his grasp, looking puzzled; so he turned her around and gave her a smart rap on her rear. "You will go at once and do what is to be done, or I come and do it for you."

She stared at him in horror, believed him immediately, and fled.

Paul shouted after her, in the voice of a vexed teacher, "That is not the way to make decisions!" He collapsed on the bed as the sound of running water began and told himself, with almost as much severity, to stop laughing like a fool and start calculating the odds. The radio music was something gentle and vague now—now that it was too late to save him. Delius, he thought, and Delius was what he felt like: wispy and afloat on a sea of contradictions. One of which was that, somewhere quite out of reach of his orderly mind, he wished it had been possible to let her have her way.

But the chances should be good, he said to himself, matter-of-fact, ignoring small inner voices. It couldn't have been long; there may have been some chemical residue of the other time, when he had not been such a fool as to say he was tired; she was old enough to be perhaps past the greatest likelihood of fertility. . . . He went on gathering a rational man's data until the voice of the knowing Etienne said in a twenty-year-old confidential murmur that thirty seconds was all it took, *formidable*—and Paul reckoned wretchedly that she must have spent a good forty-five seconds arguing. It was more difficult than one would imagine, to command the little *Marianne,* who was not yet *raisonnable.*

The phone rang suddenly, releasing him from his thoughts. He knew at once who it had to be, for he had left orders that he didn't wish to be disturbed and they would be honored in all instances except one.

"Yes?"

Bruyette spoke in his awful French that would have prostrated the Academy to a man—but what he was saying in it was enough to make even

Paul shudder. "Our friend is restless tonight. He yearns for your presence to spark things up a bit."

"Maintenant? C'est impossible." Paul saw Marian come out of the bathroom to stare at him through narrowed eyes while suspicion screamed from every inch of her skin. "I am most occupied," he said hastily, hoping the switch to English would disabuse her of her notion.

It didn't. But she did decide, apparently, on lofty dignity. She turned back into the bathroom, closed the door with ladylike care, and immediately turned on every faucet in the place.

"No, thank you," Paul said wearily. "I do not desire to attend a party."

"Advance notices say beautiful women will abound."

"I do not desire to encounter any beautiful women."

"I should have said," Bruyette amended, *"willing* beautiful women."

Paul sighed. "I do not desire any willing beautiful women," he announced with conviction.

The Congressman knew an unequivocal statement when he heard one. "Okay, it was just a suggestion. Mine. Our friend's is even more bizarre—what he wants is to play games in the gym."

"A moment, please. It appears I have left some water running."

But it wasn't running any more by the time Paul got there, and Marian was marching toward him with fire in her eye and a switch in tactics. "I believe I'll have a word with her after all," she announced sweetly. "We've never met, but we do have something in common." She raked him with a withering look. "Not that it amounts to much, of course."

Paul choked, but he forswore indignation: he clamped one hand over her mouth, tucked her under his other arm, and carried her back to the bed. Where—still silencing her, and stilling her squirming by the simple application of superior weight—he picked up the telephone and said he regretted the delay. He addressed this apology to, carefully, "Bill"; then he let Marian hear the answering voice.

It was okay, Bruyette was saying, but could Paul come? He hesitated. "He's awfully lonely, *copain,* and a little on edge. What with the little woman off globetrotting—well. Seriously, I think running around in the gym might do him some good."

Marian's eyes questioned and were answered; her face soft with pity said that nothing must be denied to poor Alec. She stirred in what had become Paul's embrace, pushing at him with her hands, urging him silently to go, now, at once. He stared at her in honest injury at her lack of thought for poor Paul, who might be hard put to it to run around in a gym right now with the edgy Alec.

But in the end, he agreed, of course. By which time, fortunately, Marian had decided to make restitution for her aspersions of a moment ago. Thus she was busy patting and cooing and producing little repentant kisses, all far away enough from the telephone Paul held cupped at his lips so she didn't hear Bill say cheerfully, "Okay, see you. And you might bring your hair oil, just in case. We could end up at that party yet."

Paul plucked Marian from her remorse and lay with her across the bed, telling himself it was only that she was a patriot. And ignorant: if she seemed to send her beloved forth heartlessly, it was because she herself had never confronted across a court the private Alec Girard—a large, strong, athletic fellow who played games to win. The hero fallen before the battle began tightened his arms around his little expert at reviving the tired and then, resisting all temptation to let her go ahead and do her best, sent her to get dressed.

Answering the telephone in Ann Taswell's neat, attractive apartment was not as much fraught with hazard as *chez Paul,* but perils were evident to Ann as soon as she heard Will Farland's voice.

Although it had occurred fleetingly that afternoon to the snow-blind Marian that she might be seen by someone issuing from the *Tribune* building, the possibility that others who knew her might be making their way toward it had escaped her. Yet it was on Ann's way back to the office, accompanied by a photographer laden with his bulky equipment and damning the snow and the absence of cabs, that she had seen and recognized immediately the back of Marian's short gray coat. The photographer stumbled then and halted their progress and Ann had to help him—which was fortunate, because by the time she was ready to take up her half-formed intention of hailing Marian, half a block away, Ann had had a chance to notice that Marian and her companion were holding hands.

But even as this new intelligence registered, the unholy Marian stopped in the middle of Washington when it was still some people's lunch hour—including, quite possibly, her husband's—and turned to embrace the man who was certainly not the tall, gangling Will. Ann glanced desperately at the photographer, who would certainly recognize one of the participants in this street scene.

"Look, let's cut through there," she said frantically, tugging the man in the wrong direction and pointing wildly at a driveway.

"There? What the hell, Annie. That just goes to that little parking lot behind the Russian Embassy. What's the point—"

The point had, in the end, been attained—after long and nerve-wracking maneuvers. But Ann had worked hard in a cause that she was not sure she believed worthy, and she had not been thanked and didn't even expect her loyal efforts to be known. Which was all right—after all, what are friends *for?*—but as she said, "Oh. Hi, Will," into the telephone now, her voice held a certain resentment against Marian for demanding really too much. Ann patted her hair nervously. "What's up?"

"Marian and I seem to have got our wires crossed this evening," Will told her pleasantly. "I was wondering—she isn't by any chance at your place?"

Yes, but she went out to get a pack of cigarettes? "Why no, Will." Such an attempt was doomed to failure. Besides, why should she even . . . ? And then, a sudden memory lanced across her mind: at the final, hairbreadth moment of risk when the photographer's attention had been successfully diverted, she herself had been fortunate, or unfortunate, enough to see who it was who stood looking down gravely at his beloved. It was only a glimpse, but it was effective as a recruiting poster: Ann had been enlisted then, whether she realized it or not, and even if less in the cause of Marian than simply in the cause of so much love. So it was, at the very least, a Morisot sympathizer who asked now, "Isn't she home yet?" And grimaced, recognizing the idiocy of the question.

Will ignored it. "Well, it *is* getting a little late, and I was beginning to feel a little concerned. I thought I might just call around—"

Oh dear, no: who knew who else might have seen Marian? "Oh, that's not necessary, Will. There's nothing to worry about. If you really are, though, I could probably locate her for you."

"You could?"

"Well, I imagine so," Ann lied smoothly. Morisot sought no publicity, but he was not in hiding, either: the *Tribune*'s city desk was likely to know where he was staying. But Marian might either have flown the Atlantic with him by this time or be still strolling around somewhere, holding hands. If you knew Marian, you knew that anything was possible. "Shall I—" She broke off, thinking that she knew Marian but she didn't really know Morisot.

"No, never mind," Will said crossly. "As long as she's okay—"

"The hell with her, then, right?"

Will laughed. "Your point. But I wish she'd be a little less—indifferent to details. After all, the children—"

"Well, they have you, haven't they?" Ann asked sweetly. Marian was always racing home to be with the kids, coping with them alone like a goddam widow half the time. "You know what? Maybe she gambled that you'd be home tonight."

She had called to say she'd be late, Will admitted, somewhat cowed by Ann's reminder of his own unpredictable comings and goings. But Rosa had forgotten the details of the message, he said; he didn't seem annoyed by this dereliction, though Ann smiled when she heard it. She let Will talk a little more to dispel his annoyance, at least temporarily, before he thanked her and hung up.

Ann sighed and collected her laundry to take it down to the apartment house's laundry room. In the elevator, she warned herself against leaping to conclusions: lots of people kissed people they weren't married to (but not Marian, and certainly not like that). In the vast, shadowy basement, she heaped the washing machine and began adjuring herself to stay out of other people's marital difficulties—even though, as she measured the soap powder carefully, she could hear Marian saying, shamefaced, at lunch one day that she'd had an awful fight with Will (but they've quarreled before, and she never . . .). When the machine was humming, Ann sat on the nearby bench like a lonely traveler in the reaches of a desert and thought that Marian had done some strange things but never anything really *wrong*. . . . I should've guessed it would happen, she decided finally in the echoing emptiness. And if it had to be somebody, she was glad it was Morisot.

Thirty-three

Paul Morisot lay on the mat on the floor of the gym looking, Alec thought, like a man hugging the earth under an artillery bombardment. Or at least dazed by one: for Paul appeared not very interested in anything, even survival. "It is only because I grow old," he was saying. Above the white towel around his neck, his face looked dark and a little puffy, and his eyes were shut.

Sweat gleamed on Alec's shoulders, but his long body still seemed ready for motion. He sat on the mat with his arms around his knees and observed thoughtfully the long scratches on Paul's back; they started from somewhere under the towel and disappeared into the waistband of his shorts. "You know, you should have a son. At the very least."

Morisot turned over onto his back. "I do not comprehend—" he began.

"I was thinking." Alec seemed a little unsure. "Well, I was thinking that maybe you were more disturbed about Martigny's death than you thought."

" 'Timor mortis conturbat me'?"

"Something like that," the bigger man agreed moodily.

Paul blinked at the bright overhead light. "What are the statistics? Approximately another twenty years for us, no?" He considered it. "Less for me, perhaps. The stone dust must have some effect." He tapped his chest.

Alec nodded at the scar. "Whatever it is, your life expectancy is greater now than it was then."

The Frenchman looked first a little surprised and then a little grim. "So also is my ability to find food for a son. Then, I felt great relief that I would not—" He broke off suddenly. "But why do we now discourse on mortality?" His voice attempted a lightness that was absent from his eyes.

"Time," the President said abruptly. "It bothers me more and more. Everything seems to be crowding in, forcing my hand. I want to do so much, and yet it has to move slowly. And now—have you been reading about the sit-ins in the South?"

Morisot looked around unhappily. "Where is Healy? Or Bruyette?"

"Bill's still partying," Alec said, puzzled. "And Dan's gone to church. It's a holy day of obligation, I think." Comprehension dawned, and he grinned. "Oh, I see. You want to call in reserves if I'm about to wander into politics."

He waved aside Paul's interruption. "I know, I know. You're a 'private man.' "

Paul crooked his arm over his eyes. "I will listen, Alec. This is, after all, a holy day of obligation." His voice was gentle, and full of a private wonder.

Alec smiled: those who are smitten late, he thought, are smitten thoroughly. "But you're not such a private man, if the truth be told," he said. "Your 'war decoration,' for example." He looked at the white scar.

"Was not earned on a field of battle but in an alley. And it left a scar only because it was tended by my wife instead of by a doctor," Paul said defensively. "It was entirely a private affair, you see."

"Was it really? What were you doing in that alley?"

Paul said unwillingly, "Stealing."

"Stealing what? Bread? Milk for your baby?"

"Ammunition," Morisot admitted. He sat up, wary and sweating.

"And somebody else was stealing the guns. Wasn't that it, Paul?" Alec leaned in like a prosecuting attorney. "As a matter of fact, it was an underground military operation, wasn't it—the result of planning and organization?"

"It was a simple affair of crime. I steal, I am caught by a policeman, I stab him." Paul said furiously, "I am a criminal. Perhaps a murderer—I did not stay to see whether he lived, I desired only to escape arrest. This is a sinful act, but still the act of a private man . . ." His angry voice ran down under the steady blue gaze of the bigger man. "*Enfin,* it is not enough, I see, to beat me at games."

The President said gently, "I'm trying to prevent its happening again, that's all. I don't want to see Americans slugging it out in alleys instead of in courthouses."

"I know nothing of courthouses. In the *Résistance,* to be arrested was perhaps not to be seen again. Or else—some in our group who were taken said the teeth and the genitals were favored by their questioners for gaining cooperation." His lips twisted in a wry smile. "When I am young, I desire that my future should not be—limited. So it becomes necessary to avoid arrest."

"So you became a criminal."

The Frenchman spread his hands. "And you? You would not have done the same?"

Alec nodded, his face somber in the bright light. "I guess so, once it got down to two guys and a knife. But the point is, you were attacking more than a policeman, Paul. If you had had a vote instead of a knife—" He broke off, looking at the door. "Here's Bruyette now."

The dinner-jacketed Congressman was talking even as he crossed the large, echoing rectangle of the gym. By the time he arrived at the mat occupied by the others, he was dangling his tie. "Up, up and a-way," he caroled. "Who's for a little violent action?"

Morisot groaned and fell over backward on the mat.

"A very effete people," Bruyette observed sadly. "Or are you a pacifist, my good man?"

"*I'm* not." Alec laughed. "As long as it isn't in an alley." He surveyed his old friend. "Shall I change, or will you?"

"Oh I will," Bruyette offered. "This suit's all full of powder and perfume anyway."

As the cheerful noise of Bill's departure faded, Morisot said from under his crooked arm, "Alec, there is perhaps something of which I must speak." He waited until he heard assent. "It is only—it is not of benefit for people, to fight in alleys. Even if their wounds heal." He hesitated. "A man who steals for public reasons—when he is a private man again, he is no longer a man who will not steal." He dismissed his own words with a gesture of disgust for the difficulties of finding the English. "One more thing, Alec. When we talk this morning—"

Girard looked at the half-hidden face, suspecting that the difficulty now was not with language. "I remember, Paul. Is there something you've discovered I can do?"

"No. Only I find now that it is possible I will make you some embarrassment. I regret, but if I must fight, I cannot permit . . ."

"I understand," Alec said swiftly. "If you have to protect me from scandal, that fact could leave you vulnerable, is that it?" He smiled. "Do not disturb yourself, *mon vieux*," he said in a fair imitation of the other man's accents, and then laughed at himself and abandoned Paul's speech for his own. "Whoever the enemy is, you go get him, old son. And don't worry about me. I can take care of myself. *Comprends?*"

Morisot rolled over onto his stomach and said into the mat that he comprehended, and then closed his eyes and added, "Old son." Alec grinned, started to hoist himself to his feet, and saw the livid semicircle on the back of Paul's neck; he winced and sat on his heels, examining the small, even teethmarks covertly while Bruyette's voice loudly summoned one and all to combat.

"I come in a moment," Paul murmured sleepily. "You go—" he raised one hand as if to help himself fish for the word, and the hand encountered the towel he had supposed was hiding his wound. He made a small sound and slid the towel over the back of his neck. "You go hot up," he said triumphantly. "Then I come."

He lay there telling himself for a while to get up, and then for another, briefer, while he commanded himself only not to go to sleep. There was something he had to tell Alec about that alley, because Alec was concerned for the government when he should be concerned more for the people. But it was very difficult to think—and besides, what did it matter, after so long? Denise, who had washed the bloody clothes in the middle of the night, was long dead. And perhaps the policeman was not dead, after all—perhaps, somewhere, a woman cried angrily, "Who did that to you?" and he told her a bad man with a knife and, like Paul, meant himself. Anyone can become a bad man with a knife; Paul, scrabbling on the edge of sleep, couldn't remember whether he had succeeded in telling this to Alec. Or maybe Alec already knew. . . .

Bruyette poked at Morisot's prone body with a toe and then bent and looked curiously at the long pink scratches. "Well, well. Very interesting."

"Laundries leave pins in shirts," announced Alec, who had no idea whether they did. "Vote for me and I'll put a stop to it."

"Not to this you won't, old buddy." Bruyette grinned and knelt beside the sleeping Frenchman. *"Mon amoureux,"* he said softly. *"Je t'adore."* He sat back on his heels, waiting to see what would happen.

Alec observed with relief that nothing did. "I'm afraid it'll take more than that." Privately, he thought that Bill had probably tried the wrong language.

"Well, that's as far as I'm prepared to go," Bruyette said. He stood up. Alec suggested that they leave Morisot to his slumbers while they dressed, and Bill agreed. But he turned back suddenly. "Maybe we ought to leave him a note. You know—'You lost the game, ha ha.' "

Alec shook his head and said he would "question seriously" whether Paul really cared about losing this game.

But a little later, in the quiet of the sitting room on the second floor of the White House, Alec paused in the act of pouring himself a beer and questioned seriously whether it wasn't time he stopped winning games. He set the glass down and went and got, from the drawer in which he'd shut it away with telltale haste, the picture the managing editor of the *Tribune* had sent over to the White House. It was a particularly handsome shot of Andy, Alec thought again as he studied it—better than any of the numerous photographs of her that appeared in the newspapers. This one had proved unusable because the dignitary greeting her, with his hand extended so that he could not be cropped out of the picture, had moved at the critical moment, causing his face to photograph as a sinister blur. "Not for his fan club," the accompanying note had said. "But we thought exceptionally good of Andrea."

It was, indeed—the great dark eyes, lighted with their delicious secret fun, mocked him from the glossy surface of the print. Alec thought he could see why she was a great ad for the U.S.A. He put the picture back in the drawer, wishing he could tell her that it was nice of her to make friends for her country abroad but, as it happened, there were some nearby counties in Maryland that had gone for Ferris in the election; she could usefully stump them, and still get home for dinner.

He thought about that for a moment, sipping his beer, and then marched over to her desk and rummaged for paper and pen. He opened his letter with a report on the children, but his spiky handwriting, with its high ups and low downs, took up so much space that he was reaching for the third sheet of paper before he had finished his account. He scrawled a "3," enveloped it in a circle and continued: "that evidences of an incipient tooth have been pointed out to me, but I've not yet been able to see anything that wasn't there before. However—" He stopped, looking blindly around the hush of the room that she had left so empty, while he considered whether it would be advisable to go on as he'd intended. He'd been about to say *when you put your finger in his mouth, you can feel something trying to bite it;* but the fact was, he'd tried it only when Miss Page wasn't looking and, for all he knew, he might now be about to confess to a misdemeanor. It occurred to him fleetingly that if Andy thought he was doing something bad for the baby, she could very well come winging home to protect her young. But he sighed, put Satan behind him, and finished the sentence weakly with "he's drooling a lot, so maybe the experts are right this time."

He turned then to the gossip of the place: Jake Ruffing had come down with flu and was taking leave for the first time in years—"perhaps I am not a very enlightened employer." Bruyette had dragged Alec to a party "but it was promptly swept by an epidemic of RH, so I left as soon as I could, with only one new observation: when you're with me, everybody stares, but when I'm alone—perhaps because there's less worth looking at—all the eyes are respectfully downcast."

He began another page: Paul had been over often, and had twice met Alec in combat in the gym and twice been defeated by Alec's greater strength and reach, but only once was it a real victory. "Monday he played as though he was trying to kill me, and I finally saw that it wasn't me he was smashing at; I'm not sure whether it was the Germans in Paris, some husband in Washington, or a stubborn muse (which is the muse of sculpture?). Tonight was easier—he didn't have much speed, and that's his major weapon—but he also seemed subdued, and kept having trouble with his English. I recall your saying that was one of the reliable signs that he's about to migrate, so you'd better hurry home if you want to see him."

Alec lifted his pen and looked at what he had written. That "you'd better hurry home" looked awfully bald, even though it was cravenly hung on Paul. But it was smack in the middle of a page: crossing it out would be fatal, and he was damned if he was going to copy his letter over like a schoolboy. He set his jaw and began another paragraph.

"Which reminds me—I don't like to go all heavyhanded, but I'm contemplating sending troops if I don't detect some sign of transatlantic stirring from you very soon. Haven't I been punished enough for my doubtless considerable sins?" He stopped, seeing that his hand was sweating on the pen. That's pretty cheap, he said to himself disgustedly: a threat followed by an I'm-only-kidding concession. Conflict was clear in his handsome face for a moment, and then a flicker of self-pity—why, oh why, did he have to get one whose beautiful eyes were quite so discerning?

He smiled then and seized the pen as though it were about to escape him and wrote swiftly, in a paragraph all to itself, "I miss you"; he looked at it briefly and thought, *Oh hell, in for a penny, in for a pound,* and added, "beloved." Then he folded the sheets rapidly without reading them and stuffed them into an envelope, telling himself that all this haste was necessary to catch the diplomatic mail. The saving skill, the ability to end one thing and begin another whether he had won or lost, that had sustained him through the long rigors of the campaign was beginning to exert itself even as he sealed the envelope: he closed the door on the problem of an intransigent wife, now dealt with for the time being as best he could manage, and entered the room in his mind inhabited by the question whether Fred Carson, junior Senator from Iowa, had been telling the truth or simply hedging when he urged waiting until closer to adjournment.

"How come you can't see that guy was telling the truth?" Bruce indicated the books on the worn table in Rosa's kitchen. "I give you credit. You learned a lot. But you still don't see."

Rosa tied an apron over her good dress and stirred the soup she was heating for the baby. "He only tellin part of the truth."

"What do you mean, part of the truth? Was that or was that not the truth, that the southerners stopped the cloture vote when Congress opened this year?"

She tapped the side of the pot, found it warm enough, and turned the gas off. "They just put it off till the summer."

"Sure they did." Bruce got the bowl down from the cupboard without being told, thumped it onto the table, and thrust an angry face between hers and the slice of toast she was breaking into pieces. "You trying to tell me you don't know when summer comes they'll filibuster the civil rights bill? If you learned anything, you learned that."

"Trixie? Trixie! You bring that baby to eat now, hear? And wash his hands good." Rosa plopped the pieces of toast into the soup and submerged them with a spoon. "Maybe the Senate stop them, come summer."

"With what votes? It takes two-thirds of the Senate to stop a filibuster."

"Bruce, I got a headache. You quit that yellin."

"I'm sorry, Miz Little." The boy surveyed her with real regret. "Here, you sit down with a cup of coffee. I'll get you an aspirin."

Rosa smiled at him. "Later, son. I reckon I just ain't used to meetins. So much hollerin."

Trixie brought little Gregory in and Rosa put him down and began to spoon the soup slowly into his mouth. The familiar action was comforting, in a world grown suddenly very uncomfortable indeed. Beginning with Will Farland last night, white-faced and menacing, hollering at her as he never had—until Rosa, cowering behind a convenient mask of stupidity, convinced him that she'd forgotten where Marian had said she was going. He'd retreated upstairs then, still in a temper, but not of the frantic dimensions inspired by worry; he was angry with his wife because she was not at home and he was, but a simple goof was an acceptable reason—acceptable enough to make him stop roaring at Rosa, anyway. She thought of the black, excited man who had spoken from the floor at the meeting tonight, insisting that there was no hope to be found among the white southerners; no matter how pretty some of them talked, he said, they were all the same underneath. Had

Will Farland in fact found her story acceptable because, deep down underneath, he was at home with the blank, dumb, Uncle Tom face she'd shown him, with the mumbled apology for a job ill done?

She heard Bruce argue, "They've got something to holler about," and she let it lie there while she dodged the splatter as the baby tried to help her feed him. Now she pushed the books out of danger and said stubbornly, "Don't nothin change for hollerin. Only when everybody see somethin real wrong." Her mind slipped to the something real wrong that surely hadn't begun with Marian coming home last night with an air of sweetly vague benignity, speaking to Sharlie and Dick as though she wasn't quite sure who they were but found them charming. Her dreamy air was a dead giveaway, and Rosa, aware that the normally somewhat absentminded head of the household might be less absentminded tonight, had deliberately delayed Marian in the kitchen to get the pink cloud dissipated a little before she floated upstairs. But that pink cloud didn't just blow in from nowhere, Rosa thought: there was the morning when she'd come on Marian fast asleep downstairs before the blank crackle of the television in the early dawn; there was the bed in the study that had been slept in though nobody was sick. Most of all, there was Marian, who maybe wouldn't have delighted the old ladies that did things for the church, but who was no tramp. "The way things goin, somebody bound to get hurt." Rosa said aloud. Then she abandoned dark warning for attention to the problem she could do something about, and added, "I don't hold with all this hate talk."

Trixie said "I don't either," and happiness slanted across Rosa's troubled thoughts like a shaft of sunlight coming suddenly through a window. All at once it seemed possible that everything would come out all right, that the end would be close enough anyhow to what she had been aiming for. She listened, careful not to look proprietary.

". . . and get to know them, we'd see they're people just like us," Trixie was saying. Not hollering, Rosa saw with pride. She also saw that the baby Gregory, whose mother was drunk again, was drooping over the empty soup bowl. Worn out, poor little thing—who knew how long he'd been crying before they'd come up the stairs on their way home from the meeting?

"What people are you talking about?" Bruce was shouting. "The ones who do the voting down there?"

"They aren't all out in the streets picking on the Negro," Trixie said hotly.

"Of course not. Some of them are out campaigning for senators to filibuster against civil rights bills. You and your mother—just who do you think elects these guys? And just who do you think are the only people who can change the way they vote in the Senate? These good southerners you all keep waiting to hear from. Only you can just keep on waiting."

"The Supreme Court decisions," Trixie began.

Rosa gathered up the sleepy baby, for their mutual solace, and rocked him gently, trying to remember about the latest Supreme Court case, but they were always so intricate—injunctions, and court orders to set aside injunctions, and if the Court did nothing, it could be either bad or good for our side, but never the same twice. She saw Bruce's shout gathering and said hastily, "Don't you start hollerin. Mind the baby."

"I'm sorry." Bruce made a visible effort and succeeded. "But a lot of bullying goes on in soft southern voices. It's time to stand up to it, to be a threat instead of being threatened. After all, what've we got to lose? We're not going anyplace anyway."

"Mama, Bruce is right. You remember what that man said in the meeting? The kids who were in first grade when the Supreme Court said schools would have to be integrated ended up graduating from segregated schools. That's how much good the Supreme Court done."

"And remember," Bruce added, "you're the one, Miz Little, who talks about how we need education first, but you don't talk about that county down in Virginia where they closed the public schools so they wouldn't have to integrate. The white kids go to private schools, but there are Negro children there who've probably still never been to school."

They were hammering at her from both sides, with their "Mama" and "Miz Little" and "don't you see" and "all it takes." Her head still hurt and her arm had gone to sleep and everything was shifting around so you'd hardly know it was the same world. She looked at them, at their youth and energy and earnest gesturings and pouring words—and it came to her all at once in her weariness and dismay that one thing was right about it, anyway: they were talking to her, they had not dismissed her and left her behind as Bettina had wanted to do and so many others of their age had done. Maybe it wasn't the same world, but there were things in it that could work out better. And they would need her, even if she couldn't define how, because though they weren't afraid, maybe they should be. They were like Marian, she thought, surprised: lovable and ignorant, walking around with their eyes on the stars—and not enough idea how to look out for dangers on the ground.

"Bruce, you take this baby, hear? He too heavy." Relieved of her burden, she rose and stretched. "I make us some coffee and we talk some more. Like, Bruce, you be tellin me how you change things by goin bus-ridin." She watched him lay the sleeping baby in the laundry basket. "*You* got somethin to lose, son. You lose your scholarship, you lost somethin, all right."

She took two aspirins with her coffee, listening at first as the children explained—interrupting each other, apologizing, then forgetting and doing it again—the aim of the "Freedom Trips" that had been proposed at the meeting. She interrupted them once to say, shaking her head, that it didn't make sense to ask for your rights as a citizen by breaking the law.

"But that's what we show," Bruce argued. "That the law is against us, down there. And maybe when the people in the other states find out, they'll do something about it. But you have to show them, you have to bring it to their attention."

"Mebbe we got no law on our side down there," Rosa pointed out, "but we got laws here. New things that you ain't give no chance yet. This President been tryin to get us jobs, now. Seem to me like that goin about it the right way—a man with a good job, he get listened to."

Bruce said scornfully, "You mean that new employment commission. I heard some southerner on his staff came up with that one." His eyes narrowed. "Hey, I'll bet that was Farland's idea. Was it?"

Rosa didn't know. "I ain't heard nothin about it. But supposin it was? You got no cause to think he be against you, Bruce. Bruce?"

"You'll get mad if I tell you."

"No I won't. Don't you trust Mr. Farland?"

"Sure I do," the boy said slowly. "I trust Mr. Farland to respond to pressure. Quicker than most, because he's smarter."

Rosa looked at him sadly. "You don't trust him because he got white skin. That it?"

"Mama, Bruce didn't mean—"

"Yes he do." Rosa stood up. "Now you tell me, Bruce," she asked in a voice heavy with disdain, "what the difference between you and that Louisiana sheriff that won't believe nothin good about you cause you col— Negro?" In the silence, she crossed the crowded room and put her hand on the boy's shoulder, feeling it stiffen under her touch. "What you lettin them folks do to you, son? You better than that."

They *listened,* she exulted, doing the dishes while they drowsed over their studies in the living room. It was too late for studying tonight, she thought, glancing at the round face of the clock; but they had needed time away from her, to think and perhaps confer. As she had needed this rehearsal. In a few weeks, Bettina would be home from school for Easter vacation, and she could not be forbidden things as Trixie still could. She would need to be argued with, and by someone the others respected.

Rosa dried her hands on the dishtowel and spread out the newspaper on the kitchen floor to dump the food scraps. Andrea Girard, three columns wide, in slim ski clothes and a tight-fitting cap that made her look like an elf, smiled up at the bare overhead light; her bright eyes and wisps of windblown hair spoke of health and fun, enough for everyone.

Rosa finished in the kitchen and went in and roused the youngsters from their listless work. "What say we do like they done tonight—adjourn this here meetin?" she asked cheerfully. "We pass a resolution."

"Resolved, we all go back to work and forget the whole thing, and Girard'll give us our reward in heaven," Bruce said sourly.

"Bruce, you got no call to talk to Mama that way."

"It all right, Trixie. He get mad, just like I get mad too. You think it don't make me mad, what I see?"

"But not mad enough to do anything," Bruce suggested.

"Oh yes," Rosa said calmly. "You be surprised what I be ready to do, mister, when the time come." She collected their surprised glances. "But I ain't sure what time it is, yet. I say wait, give this President a chanct—a couple months," she added quickly, stopping Bruce's interruption. "I got to study some more, study what you say—and I ask you fair, you study what I say tonight."

"That's only fair, Bruce," Trixie urged. "You can't go yelling handkerchief-head at everybody who disagrees with you."

"I got to talk to Tina, too, when she come home, and study what she say." Rosa saw that she had scored with this. "Then we sit down and decide. Right here. Quiet. Not yellin in the aisle how 'I seen the light, O Lawd'." That there got him, she thought—he didn't like the way they carried on either, at the meeting.

"You can't do this by yourself," Bruce warned. But his voice sounded uncertain. "Nor us by ourselves. It takes organization, like an army."

"I know. But we decide for ourself if we join, and how—what our reason, what in our hearts. And when the right time." Rosa thrust out her hand. "If you with me, Bruce, then shake."

But when he shook her hand, she cheated, catching him and kissing his cheek, too.

Thirty-four

As Harrington bent to kiss her hand, Ann Taswell, who was accustomed to exact observation, noted the gray springing like little spurts of water in his black hair. He raised his head and looked at her accusingly. "You're still a Puritan."

"Uh huh. Frigid, too." She looked at the tanned skin of his forehead and wondered whether he had a sort of solstice, when he switched from the sun lamp to the real sun. John Harrington, she had once told Marian, existed primarily to keep bread in the mouths of the wives and children of writers of "inside Washington" stuff, to provide just that titillating lilt of decadence that enlivened the more difficult-to-follow themes of politics. "I really cannot be moved, John," she said calmly, not really expecting belief, as the black-sleeved arm, careless and comradely around her shoulders, began to tighten purposefully. It was a bore to have to dance this *pas de deux* in Harrington's nonstop extramarital ballet—but there was no need to be cruel, she reminded herself, to a poor middle-aged chorus boy. She examined the pummeled-looking flesh that was nevertheless thickening the clean-cut features and the jowls that threatened and would inevitably conquer; lines of weariness bracketed his nose and mouth, and she was suddenly touched by the vulnerability of his face in the lamplight.

"Tired businessmen," she said, stiffening against her own sympathy, "should apply to their wives." She glanced at Eleanor Harrington, talking to

Marian a few feet away, and wished Eleanor would either come and pluck her husband away or release Marian, who would come to the rescue if successfully signaled. Ann moved her arm slightly to block the creeping hand's approach to her breast and told Harrington incisively to go away and play somewhere else.

"Aw, Annie. Don't you want a feller?"

"Occasionally." She had spoken before she thought; she saw it was a mistake. "But not an occasional feller."

Harrington laughed. "That's the latest style, you know. Or, to use a more appropriate language, the *dernier*est *cri*." He halted his maneuvers, apparently finding passion less compelling than gossip. "After all, our Madam President is certainly a trend-setter, and she's dashed off to Europe for a fling with her French boyfriend. So the least you—"

"If you mean Paul Morisot, sorry, John," Ann said, smiling cruelly, "I saw him with my own eyes on Connecticut Avenue yesterday."

"A detail," Harrington shrugged. "So it's not the sculptor. It's the ballet dancer, maybe." Ann started to speak. "All right, all right, so *he's* somewhere else, too. It doesn't matter. You can't get around the fact that she started to walk out on our beloved Alec a couple of years ago. It cost Old Man Girard a million bucks to keep her from messing up the boy wonder's political future." That settled, he reached for her again.

Ann broke into laughter, dislodging Harrington from his certainty. "Okay, so maybe it wasn't a million," he said. "I'm not sure of the exact amount. But the story's true, anyway. Everybody knows it."

"And you, John?" Ann had stopped laughing and was considering him thoughtfully. To say that Andy, because she was Andy, couldn't possibly be bribed to do anything would make no sense to the true believers like Harrington: they had a need to believe in venality, as children must need to believe in Santa Claus. But there was an approach that could get through. "You know something, too, don't you? About the Langwiths, and before them the Carters, and all the time, generation after generation, pots and pots of money?" She saw that she was scoring. "Offering money to Andrea Girard," she said with quiet scorn, "would be about as effective as offering me a free subscription to the *Washington Tribune*."

"Well, every detail doesn't have to check out," Harrington mumbled. He went on slowly, telling her that he hated to descend to "where there's smoke there's fire" and then descending to it, while Ann stared at the back of Marian's neck and tried extrasensory perception.

John Harrington, though crushed, had risen again, even if only slightly: he followed Ann's look and smiled. "Please don't send for Marian, Annie," he begged. "I'll be good. I promise." He shivered. "I don't know how such a sexy little creature can be so freezing, but five seconds with her and my bones don't thaw out for twenty-four hours."

"I don't think she approves of you," Ann admitted.

"I gathered that some time ago." Harrington sighed. "Normally, I'd regard it as a challenge—a woman with a come-hither look plus a 'P.S. Except you, Harrington' could be fatally attractive. But I've known Farland for twenty years—"

"I had no idea you regarded marriage as a deterrent," Ann said in genuine surprise. "It doesn't seem to fit with your—"

"It's Farland as a deterrent."

"Oh." She was disappointed. "If that's all that's worrying you, I don't think he'd shoot."

"And go to jail, or to the booby hatch? Of course not. Why should he?" It was Harrington's turn to triumph. "Honey, this is a political town and Will Farland's a right talented politician. Anybody with a mind to poach on his preserves better have more protection than I have." He saw Ann's disbelief and smiled knowingly. "Listen, years and years ago, when Will was a mere stripling, mind you, compared to the weight he can pull today, a lad at one of our parties got a little forward—well, you know how our parties are."

Ann said, her face carefully frozen, that she knew, and then added that she also knew Marian.

"It was in the day of the first Mrs. Farland," Harrington told her impatiently. "You never knew Kitty—nice gal, more relaxed than Marian. Much more likely to get feeling a little gay, too. And Will wasn't nearly as balmy about her as he is about his little Cuddles now." Ann frowned, and he hurried on to forestall reproof. "Anyway, the forward gent—though, as I said, meaning no harm and maybe even egged on a bit, if you know what I mean—he's still out in Africa somewhere, counting lepers. Every time his name comes up for promotion, so does his file, and what do you want to bet it contains a little something inserted by Farland a long time ago?"

"Oh, come on, John. Will wouldn't."

"All right, but if you want to check it out, you get somebody else to be your guinea pig. Especially now that Farland's working in the White House, which definitely increases the voltage in the electrified fence around his property." Harrington snaked an arm around Ann's waist and pulled her as close as he could before she recovered enough to stop him. "If you were Marian, you know what would happen to me now?" He ignored her announcement that she was Ann, and she knew what was about to happen to him, all right. "Well, for starters, I guess my passport would be lifted." He captured her hands with his free one. "Then—oh, maybe my house would be condemned. I'd be called in to discuss my income tax return. To say nothing of my membership in the Student Fabian Society in my romantic-rebel years." He examined her futile struggles and saw that they were responsible for as much of her embarrassment as the original cause. He doubted that she could bring herself to it, but, just in case, he turned so that a suddenly upthrust knee would be stopped by his hip. "Let's see, now. All sorts of municipal things, too, you know—my driver's license would be found faulty. I'd get a summons for improper garbage facilities, another one for maintaining a fire hazard. My wife picked up for soliciting, my children for loitering, my dog—"

"John," Ann interrupted, "how would you like to see the *Tribune* begin a series on influence peddling in Washington?" She smiled as his grip loosened a little. "I can see Marty Halloran," she suggested, "knocking at your office door Monday morning. To ask what it is, exactly, you do for a living."

Harrington let her go promptly. "I was a victim of passion. I lost my head. Forgive me." He seized her hand and began kissing it fervently. But from a safe distance, so Ann sighed and let him.

Marian, still oblivious to her friend's thought waves, was fighting her own in another corner of the big, crowded room, where she was speculating on her dislike for Mrs. McElroy, whose only distinguishing characteristic was a habit of sleeping with anything in pants so long as it wasn't Rob McElroy. The current choice was supposed to be John Harrington, which was not too unbelievable if you were able to find Harrington believable in the first place. Senator Warren, who had lately enjoyed Mrs. McElroy's favors, seemed happy though deposed, standing with Will and McElroy a foot away in the little whispering cluster that always looked somehow as though they were exchanging dirty pictures. They weren't, though—behind her, Marian heard Will's voice, describing himself as the White House's link to the common man: "They all read *Harper's* and the *Atlantic,* and—I don't know, maybe the *American Scholar.* But several million people read the *Reader's Digest,* and I'm the only one around there who does."

Eleanor Harrington impaled Marian on a bright social smile and asked how she liked having Will at the White House. Assured that it was not really different, Eleanor shook her head, jiggling the long diamond earrings dangling below her black Dutch bob. "Oh Marian, that's not true. I saw your picture on the women's page a couple of weeks ago, greeting some VIP at the airport. Now I know you've been around, but you haven't always made the papers, have you?"

"Well, I wouldn't have been there ordinarily—I was pressed into service. But it was a—new experience." Marian stopped, trying to think how to say what it was like: the endless glitter of glass from the tower, under which an airport man rode on a toy tractor at the far end of a runway bordered by snow heaped like marshmallow sauce. She had kept adjusting her bright official smile that was getting a little worn at the edges as it all went on and on, the scurrying and waiting and mysterious missions of men whose overcoats flapped about their legs. The State Department's protocol man darted about like a sheepdog with a difficult flock, and everybody seemed to be in motion except Alec Girard—who had apparently caused some of the difficulty by suddenly deciding to greet the visitor in person—and Harold Hoffman. Will hunched his shoulders and shifted unobtrusively from one foot to the other, his frozen southern blood doing its best to conform with the

New England President's coatless indifference to the cold. But Hoffman wore an overcoat—either he was still too new in Washington to know that you greeted in whatever costume the President greeted in, no matter what, or else a man with enough courage to tackle the thankless job of Secretary of State would not cower before tradition. Near the official huddle the Marine Band stood very still and brilliantly colored, looking somehow fake.

"It's so—impressive," Marian began to tell them, remembering the way everything had come to a sudden halt as the plane was seen, silver before the chilly sun. It rolled toward them and stopped, and the foreground emptied as the steps were brought forward. From the corner of her eye, she saw Will standing like a sentry in his assigned place; everyone had one, marked on the ground. The bareheaded President, movie-hero tall and handsome, advanced slowly as the door began to open, and the Marines began to play something that was unidentifiable because the wind turned it back into single brassy notes, flying past. The same rush of air flapped the flag, edged in gold; it cut off everything but the figure of the President from Marian's vision. Suddenly she stood straight and tall without thinking about it, not feeling cold but strangely frozen anyway. Some kind of tremor darted through her body and she thought absurdly, "It's the real flag, the AMERICAN flag," with crazy capital letters, as an imaginary voice announced in a rolling baritone, *The President of the United States.*

". . . thought you looked appropriately solemn," Eleanor Harrington was saying.

"I just photograph that way. Actually, it wasn't so much solemn as—well, kind of gay—and courtly." The nursery school, Marian was remembering, had been notified when the party would arrive at the White House, so that Peter Farland could see some soldiers in the honor guard. She looked up at the women helplessly, trying to think of a way to describe the man who would remember and arrange for a detail like that in the midst of his days.

But Mrs. McElroy was looking at Mrs. Harrington. "Marian ought to know. I hear it *is* pretty gay and courtly around the White House these days." Her knowing eye said that Marian's perplexed silence was only, after all, playing dumb. "Things get out."

"What things?"

Mrs. McElroy laughed; when her mouth opened, a long incisor gleamed in the dim light. "Maybe you don't know, at that. He's probably pretty clever about sneaking the lady in."

She looks like a witch, Marian thought. And asked, loudly, stubbornly, "*What* lady?"

"Oh, come off it, Marian. Everybody knows about a certain Frau Senator brightening the President's lonely hours."

"Well, when the cat's away, you know," Eleanor Harrington offered, her earrings swaying.

"Andy has too much self-confidence, if you ask me," said the unasked Mrs.

McElroy. "You don't leave a good-looking man to his own devices while you tootle off to look at Alps. Especially if he has a history of being a hand with the ladies."

Marian felt her face burning. "I have no idea what you think you're talking about."

Eleanor was kind. "Marian's so loyal—"

I am going to hit somebody or I'm going to throw up, Marian was knowing, deep in her churning stomach, when Will appeared magically at her side. He held her arm in a grip that would leave bruises and said accusingly, "I know I'm just part of the scenery in your life by now, but I did hope you'd notice when I asked René to play our song." She was too intent on her struggle for control to say anything at all. Will appealed to the others. "She takes me for granted. Plain old Will, with work-reddened hands. I can remember when she thought I was so romantic."

The piano had actually begun on "It Had To Be You," which was actually their song if anything was, and Marian hung helplessly between lingering fury and beginning laughter. The perfect detail man, she thought, with something like admiration, and said, "Oh Will," with respect.

He was steering her away skillfully. "I don't dance like I did before the housemaid's knee got me, but at least I could hold you in my trembling arms . . . Ladies." He bowed and swept Marian from her captivity and she clung, rescued again. And then he stopped dancing without warning and, in plain sight of the watching harpies, kissed her lingeringly, bending her backward, his hands warm and moving hypnotically on her back. In spite of herself, in spite of her knowledge of the spectators, Marian felt her lips begin to go soft and the initial stiffening begin to melt from her body before she could remind the traitor nerves that this was not the way she felt, not at all, certainly not tonight, maybe not ever. She wrenched away from Will, her eyes stinging with fury as she saw his meaning smile. She wanted to scream defenses, quite sensible, legitimate ones—for five years she had responded to this touch in this way; the brain got grooved, the machinery hummed, and any new discoveries she might have made couldn't change it all at once. A thousand nights and a night, she thought bitterly: with those odds, what else could you expect?

" 'Nobody else gave me that thrill,' " Will sang softly to the music, and Marian opened her mouth to tell him that she hated him and then closed it at once as she saw that this was exactly the wrong thing to do. " 'With all your faults, I lo-ve you still,' " he sang now, and there was a bargain in his eyes. It wasn't hard to read Will, really, if you remembered that he was always operating. He had been, even in his sudden compliance when she had confronted him last night.

Though, at the beginning, he'd been furious. "Where in hell have you been?"

She closed the study door behind her and said, "I went for a walk in the snow."

"A walk in the snow?" He stared at her in total unbelief—for her words, certainly; but even more, she thought, for the fact that she would be such a fool as to attempt nothing more elaborate. "Is that all you're going to say?" He gathered himself like a baseball pitcher winding up. "Because if you think you can just come and go with gay abandon—"

"No, I don't think so," she said in the clear, carrying voice of a public speaker. "I'm sorry for any anxiety I may have caused, or for any disruption of the household routine."

"That's the least—"

"No, it isn't, Will. It's all I'm sorry for. I am not, after all, a machine—if I've diverged from my regular performance once in five years, I don't think I owe anybody any apology. Or any argument either." She moved wearily, crossing to the door of the closet. "I'm tired and I want to be let alone." She took off her blouse and skirt and put on her old flannel bathrobe; that the closet door cut her off from his view could have been only an accidental rudeness. She exchanged her shoes for slippers, tied the belt of her bathrobe, and said, "I'm afraid that's all I'm going to say about it, Will. Now or ever." Uncharacteristically, she closed the closet door. Then she waited, polite but distant, while he laughed and proceeded to save face: she would have made a marvelous suffragette, he told her, and there was no need for her to chain herself to railings, he would give her the vote any time, baby. She smiled and escaped downstairs to Rosa, who would let her alone.

" 'It had to be you,' " Will sang in her ear, and Marian told herself, her cheeks flushed with embarrassment in the midst of one of the Harringtons' parties, that you could see how he might be justified in his maneuvers. She had cut him off from speech and he had chosen this way of putting yesterday, or his guesses about it, in what he hoped was its place: it wasn't important, he was telling her, it was only a meaningless physical phenomenon, a set of reactions that can be started up any time. The fact that it wasn't so was something you couldn't expect him to understand.

She was thinking this pityingly when Will said, "Now they can have some fun at Harrington parties we don't come to." He appeared to think it over and added regretfully, "I guess not, though. We're married. It's not newsworthy when you melt in my arms."

So that was it—the gentle reminder that Farland, the old master, could turn her to jelly. And had the right to, as he had demonstrated neatly: open, official, public rights. Any that she thought she had won had only been what he generously allowed—get it? She got it, and also the bargain his eyes meant: I'll leave it alone, for a price. Marian knew that the price was that her "walk in the snow" must become what Will had decided to call it—a fling, a mistake, like something that happens when people have too much to drink. She looked at Will, her eyes full of fear because he was always right, he always made things happen the way he said. *I am not to play with,* Paul's voice, dark with pain, said in her mind. "Excuse me, darling," she told her husband. "Ann is signaling for rescue."

She routed John Harrington by sending him for a drink—the only gallantry he couldn't deny—and then turned, the rescued rescuer, to the very cool-looking maiden-in-distress, elegant in a slim black dress lit with silver. "Well, your clothes aren't torn, anyway."

"Ugh. I'd like to wash my arm. It's all bedewed with little wet kisses designed to drive me mad."

"They'll dry," Marian said cruelly. "Even the ones that do drive you mad get dry."

Ann had seen Will's dramatic embrace of his wife and thought it looked a little like a perfume ad and was—if Will was up to what Ann thought— a lot of pressure, and not nice. She surveyed Marian with covert sympathy and said John Harrington was a menace.

"All men are," Marian told her absently, and then smiled suddenly and added, "in a way." She looked up at Ann and went on in the voice of a patient mother, "But you can be *too* safe."

Ann sighed. "The lecture again."

"The lecture again. Oh hell, Annie, maybe not—maybe you should forgive and forget the whole lecture. I'm not as qualified to teach as I thought."

"As a guide to a sane sex life, you have it all over John Harrington," Ann decreed. But her eyes on her friend were worried.

"Maybe not. Maybe we're all Harringtons, after all." Marian sounded close to tears.

"Maybe no such thing. Marian, are you listening to me? I hope you're not going to be dumb enough to confuse *what* people do with the way they do it." Ann saw Harrington bearing down on them, tried to think of something she could do for Marian in a hurry, and damned Morisot, who had struck her from the first, she reminded herself, as somehow dangerous: what could be boiling around in the man, she remembered wondering at Andy's party, that made it necessary for him to keep the lid clamped on so tightly? Now she glanced down at Marian and told herself she was being unfair to him—Marian looked subdued, but that might not be entirely a bad idea. She didn't care much for the sadness in her friend's face at the moment, though. She decided abruptly that Marian was in no condition to be exposed to John Harrington, who was looming. Ann said, "Go listen to the music. And don't *think*," and gave Marian a little push in the direction of safety.

Marian succeeded in arriving in the neighborhood of the piano unaccosted, and smiled at René, who was always at the Harringtons' parties, and always at the piano, and played and played and played; he was doing it when you came and still doing it when you left. Leaning against the warm wood in the gentle curve of the piano, she tasted the contents of an abandoned glass and reflected that it was good to have a friend, especially one who offered good, sound advice when you needed it—like when you were just about to be dumb enough to concede any resemblances between the Harrington dewy kisses and the real thing. Ann was quite right, she thought, annexing the drink: it was folly to draw conclusions from the fact that Mrs. Farland and Mrs. McElroy had probably seen the coming of night yesterday from quite similar angles—flat on the back, round heels dug in. But from quite, quite different viewpoints nevertheless. She acknowledged with happiness the sudden warmth somewhere inside her and thought wickedly about asking René whether he could play the *Merry Wives of Windsor* overture. Poor darling, she taunted the absent Paul demurely, I hope you had fun playing ball with the boys after I left; next time we want music not to read by, let's try "The Ride of the Valkyries" . . .

She was listening so intensely to the wild, rapid insistence of that music in her head that what was actually coming from the piano escaped her attention. Until a tall girl in a dress like mermaid's scales began to sing in a throaty voice, and then it struck Marian like a blow to the solar plexus.

" 'Lahk a silvuh dolluh goes from hand to hand,' " the silvery girl chanted, " 'a woman goes from man to man.' "

Marian put down the empty glass and went to look for a place to cry for the terrible truth that there was only one way not to be a Harrington.

Thirty-five

The last of the last snow of the year disappeared under a warming sun that promised more just like itself, the day Andrea Girard came home. As the plane turned above the Potomac River, the trees along the parkway below wore a yellow-green fuzz too faint to be seen, as yet, from the ground. Soon, soon, Andy thought, clasping her hands so tightly that the seams of her gloves twisted against her fingers. Everything was tight, even the skin on her face and the muscles in her legs. As the plane bumped to the ground, she unlocked her seat belt, unwilling to sit still a moment longer. Looking out, straining for a sight of Alec while the plane rolled to a stop, she saw, despairing, that there were too many men out there. Then, suddenly, she found the small figure of Elizabeth, a pink blur with straight legs in leggings, and Andy watched her daughter enviously, wishing she too were allowed to jump up and down. Her lips were stiff with smiling, and her whole body wanted to run. She made for the door, thanking all the people who had been so kind; she heard how breathless her voice was.

The steps were there and she stood at the top as though held in an invisible halter, her hand to the small round hat that matched her beige wool dress; reflected brightness from the sleeve of her short, flared burnt-orange coat slashed across her cheeks and her wide eyes that were searching, searching, while she smiled and smiled. Then it was all over, it was the end of waiting: the way was clear and she broke out, leaving behind the polite voices and the proffered helping hands, and ran down the steps into the sunlight. Elizabeth let go her father's hand and sprinted toward her mother. They were beautiful in flight for a moment among the waiting stillnesses. Then they met on the field and Andy sank to one knee on the damp earth and enveloped the little lively body fiercely, not listening to Elizabeth's mile-a-minute report of something-or-other, not hearing anything at all after the high, excited "Mommy-Mommy-Mommy." She stood up, then stooped again to tuck a flying tendril of Elizabeth's fair, fine hair into the close little cap; when she looked up again, Alec was there with his eyes and his smile and his hair burnished in the sunlight, and all the love in the world was there with him.

She turned swiftly, needing to move, wanting to dance, and saw the nurse with the little bundle of blankets. Elizabeth was clinging to her legs as she looked at her son fast asleep, with a fold of the soft yellow blanket peaked over his head to keep the sun from waking him. His cheeks were round and rosy; his lips, slightly parted, gleamed wetly; his pushed-in nose with its widespread nostrils was faintly pink. Perhaps because Elizabeth squealed suddenly to Andrea to look at some passing airport wonder, the baby stirred as Andy would have taken him; she glanced at the nurse and they waited, held in suspense, as he blew out a tiny wet bubble and slept again. But one boneless-looking little hand had fallen from the cocoon and dangled in the sunlight, soft, dimpled, wristless, disappearing with a roll of fat into the white sweater sleeve. Respectful of his slumber, Andy lifted the hand, kissed it lightly, and tucked it into the blanket. Then she turned to her husband and said, with a sudden steady pounding in her ears, "Oh, let's go home."

He nodded, but he didn't seem to know how to stop looking at her, or she at him; they kept on standing there, smiling and not touching, while Elizabeth danced around them, zigzagging jaggedly like a waterbug on the surface of a still pool. Suddenly she cried piercingly, "Mr. Roy, Mr. Roy," and streaked across to the Secret Service man who had come back with Andy. It was necessary for her parents to remember her then, to watch and make sure that her heedless hurtling body was safely caught. Agent Leroy fielded her expertly, and Alec and Andy woke and began to follow after their daughter, who hung from Leroy's overcoat and went on talking excitedly to nobody in particular.

"It's good to *be* back," Andy answered somebody, her hand warm in the crook of Alec's arm. They paced slowly, he shaking hands, she nodding. "Yes, it was lovely, but it's nice to be home," she said, and the President said, "Glad to meet you," and his wife said, "So kind of you to come out," and the President thanked people and she thanked people. And finally, finally, they were in the car at last and Andy turned to speak to him; but he stopped her by saying huskily, "Please don't go away again." She saw him worry about whether he was being a tyrant and then add, "At least—

not soon," so softly that her heart broke. She turned and held his face between her gloved hands and kissed him on the lips—and then her eyes danced as her stuffed-shirt New Englander twisted away, reddening to his ears, and shouted "Let's go!" at the driver. The car started to move at once and Alec said in a shocked voice, "Andy, for heaven's sake. They'll see."

"Let them," said an unrepentant Andy, who as a matter of fact had seen a flashbulb pop through the window behind him. She sat back in her seat like a proper lady, her hands loose in her lap, and nothing about her demeanor indicated that she was speculating on how he thought his precious citizens thought the children happened, anyway. She swallowed a threatening giggle and sat there carefully not saying anything or looking at him until, as they fled along the road behind the sirens and between the startled, quickly turned faces of people who were only having ordinary days, she felt her hand lifted and her fingers slowly captured. Then she turned her head and smiled quickly, shyly, to show him she understood, before she went back again to being First Lady.

But it was a long, long ride, even at the breakneck speed the Secret Service tried to maintain; the nervous guardians of the President knew his wife's arrival had been announced in advance, and the trip to the airport and back constituted an invitation to trouble that would keep them biting their fingernails until the whole family was safely back in the shelter of the White House. Andy couldn't wait, though—the long thoughts of her faraway nights had led to conclusions that had their own pressure to be told, to be real through being announced. "Alec," she said urgently into his ear under the noise of their travel.

The President said warily, "Not now, darling," and then tightened the clasp of his hand as if to make sure she'd be there later.

Andy dared anyhow. "It took me exactly thirty minutes to pack after I got your letter."

"So that's what did it," said Alec, being President even while he spoke. "I wondered."

"Thank you, thank you, for writing that. I'd have died if I'd had to come home anyway, just because it was time."

He stole a second for a tiny, grinning glance at her. "I'm older, so I figured it was up to me to set an example." He detected her impulse before she could reach to brush his ear with her lips and warned, "Andy, please."

"Yes, darling." She sat back again, smiling because he knew how it had been with her, that she had wanted so badly to come, and because it was lovely not to be a mystery to him. Out of the corner of her eye, she calculated the distance to his freshly shaved, tanned cheek and bet herself that she could make it before he could flinch away. But she had bedeviled him enough, she decided. For now. She looked out of the window at the exquisite pigeons in the park, the frolicsome statue of a man on a horse, the gorgeous shopper with a paper shopping bag from Garfinckel's, the beautiful government workers beginning to prance out of their offices on their way to lunch—everybody, everything, resplendent in the rainbow air of homecoming.

The Chief Usher, turning away from her radiant greeting in the great hall, shook his head in admiration and agreement with the colleague who said breathlessly, "*Some* First Lady we got, huh?" And belowstairs, all afternoon, they were topping each other with examples of her friendly greetings, her meticulous recognitions of this and that perfection that had been supplied for her homecoming. There were miles of corridors and replies, and Andrea Girard seemed to have time for them all. And then, when everything was almost settled down, when coffee had been sent up because everybody had already had lunch and that was all Mrs. Girard wanted (but Jeanne put petits fours on the tray anyway), and the President had ordered in a soft voice and with a very poker face that he not be disturbed until the meeting at three—even then Andrea had time and patience enough to come and help with the gentling of Elizabeth, who had found her tricycle and was pedaling it up and down the hall in an ecstasy of energy.

Now, when the time was finally here, was—if too limited—all theirs at last, she stood just inside the closed door, afraid that there may have been too much absence between them after all. She couldn't speak, so she waited for him, and he waited too, until the sudden silence pounded like surf. Finally the President grinned. "I said 'later,' Andy. Not 'never.' " He held out his arms as for a child who has just learned to walk.

When she could speak, she said, "Alec," very slowly and then forgot what she had been about to say and put quick, shameless little kisses all over his face and neck until he caught her and made her stop. "I was afraid it wouldn't be all right again."

"It stayed all right all the time, Andy." He smoothed her hair.

"I was awfully angry."

"I know you were. You had a right to be, too." He clenched one fist, staring down at it in disgust. "I behaved like some kind of con man—first I told you you could do as you liked about the whole politics thing, and then I kept upping the requirements. And the first time you didn't do as *I* liked, I—"

"Darling, darling, I was so *stupid*." She unfolded his tight fist and made it quiet again. "All that nonsense about I—*my* convictions. I think I even said, God help me, *my* bedroom." She made a fist of her own. "So—unutterably stupid, all those I's, when all the time it was We that mattered. Oh Alec, how can you put up with me?"

"The question that's been bothering me was how I could put up without you." He looked a little grim. "I suppose you figured I would notice when the little cricket on the hearth stopped chirping. Well, I noticed. I noticed like all hell."

"Listen, you were perfectly right about those peace women." She waved off his attempt to speak; she had been planning for too long to say this.

"No, I was all those things you said, cold and snobbish and everything. And if I thought they were foolish—and I'm afraid I still do—I should've met them and told them so. But I didn't understand—I really didn't understand, darling, that they're not outsiders, you see. They come with you. The whole thing comes with you. And I want you, Alec."

"Please, please," he said into her hair. "I can't guarantee I'll never treat you badly again. Only don't run away. I don't want to be a tyrant, I never meant to be. But I—I want you with me."

A long time later, in the stillness of the room that spoke of love and care in all its colors, she said in a voice teetering between laughter and tears, "We sound like 'The Gift of the Magi.' "

Alec inspected this statement with his usual alert interest. "We're a little better off, aren't we? No damage done, in our case. But he sold his watch to buy her some ornaments for her beautiful long hair and she sold her hair to buy him a chain for his watch—wasn't that the way it was? Anyway, they ended up with more understanding, but still just as hungry." He stretched out a lazy arm and helped himself to a couple of petits fours, then made a face, because he didn't like sweets. "We've got understanding *and* provender. Such as it is."

Andy walked to the window and stood with her back to him. "I'm glad to hear there's no damage done, Alec. For just a brief moment before I came home, I was afraid there might be some."

"What are you talking about?" the President asked bluntly. His face had suddenly the intent look with which he listened to questions at his news conferences.

"I rather got the impression that your loneliness—or maybe the injustice of it—led you to . . ." Her careful voice stopped.

"To what? I don't understand what I could have been led to that I didn't write you about." He waited, but she wouldn't speak. "Besides, I must be just about the easiest man in the world to keep tabs on. A visit to your nearest newsstand will enlighten you as to my every waking moment. So what could I possibly have been doing that you wouldn't know about?"

"Not *every* waking moment. Stories get around that the news services don't carry."

"What stories, Andy?"

"Oh, it's too absurd."

"It must be," he said evenly. He looked at her slender back and seemed to make up his mind, for when he spoke it was unquestionably a command. "Let's have it, Andy. What did you hear?"

"I *can't* be going to say this, but—" audibly, she fought tears "—they said you were—entertaining—some woman. Here. In the White House, anyway. I guess not in our bedroom," she added miserably.

He crossed slowly, letting her hear him coming, and took her by her tense shoulders, turning her around to face him but holding her off. "Oh no," he said, discovering her tears with pity and surprise. "Dan said he heard some nonsense, but I never for a moment thought—" She struggled in his grip, but he held her firmly.

"I know. I'm being idiotic. Oh Alec, please don't look at me." He let her come to him then, and she buried her face in his shoulder and went on crying. Alec patted her gently, but his look was not gentle. Over her head his eyes were thoughtful and his lips were compressed in a hard face that softened only as he recalled her suddenly and bent to hear what she was saying into his rapidly wilting collar.

". . . because all the time I knew it wasn't fair, you see. I knew I had no right to get mad and just up and quit on being the President's wife. And when you feel that guilty, you just don't see straight, and—"

"Andy, you're drowning me." He tipped her face up.

"Don't look at me when I'm crying."

"Then stop crying," Alec said sensibly, and watched her try to obey. "Listen, darling, forget the women's delegation. You got a little fed up, that's all. We've been all over that, and we both know we're ready to forget it. But this other stuff—really, Andy, didn't you recognize it for what it was?"

"Recognize it?"

"Well, certainly. It's one of the oldest myths, or folk tales, or what-have-you. Any anthropologist could probably tell you all about it." He grinned at her. "It's the old hero-leader, invincible in battle, ten feet tall, and usually a compulsive stud." He let her go so he could beat his chest *à la* Tarzan. "Every man falls to his spear, every woman to his—well, I think you get the idea."

Andy sniffled, but she was beginning to laugh. "I think you're supposed to be disguised as a swan."

"Can't. The Secret Service has forbidden it—it's too hard to tell me from real swans." Alec looked at her gravely. "I give you my word the only man I've beaten in battle while you were gone was Paul, and I suspect that he was weakened by injudicious womanizing. And the only female I carried home over my shoulder was Elizabeth."

"Pretty poor hero-ing," his wife sneered.

"Alas. But if you don't tell, who'll know that I've spent these weeks hitting the economics books instead of flitting around the countryside planting illegitimate babies. No, that's not the variation here, is it? What was it I was supposed to be doing, rolling in Lincoln's bed with a movie starlet?"

"With a senator's wife."

"Well." He looked down at her thoughtfully and asked, with interest, "Republican, I hope?"

"I don't know. But it would be only seemly," Andy agreed.

"True. Though Lincoln tried hard to be the President of all the people." Watching her hunt in her purse and find her handkerchief, he rested like a man who has worked hard.

"Alec." She looked into his eyes. "I'm sorry. It's just that it hurt. The ugliness—"

"It's not a beautiful job," he said gently. "Just an important one." Then he quoted, " '. . . and the vermin voices here/May buzz so loud—we scorn them, but they sting.' "

Andy said, "But there were some grounds for that gossip in Camelot."

"Ah, well. Every man stands on the shoulders of his predecessors. Haven't you noticed there isn't a single unmarried Lancelot among my knights? I learn from literature. That way, I don't have to worry about whether you're jiving with Jake, romancing with Rosenberg, or—" He broke off. "I'm sorry, but the only thing that occurs to me for Farland is—unsuitable."

"What's unsuitable about 'frolicking'?" Andy asked, wide-eyed.

Alec reached for her, but the knock came too quickly. She tried not to mind as the voice that was itself clearly sorry to interrupt said, "Mr. President, it's—"

"Yes. Thank you. I'll be there directly."

They waited until the footsteps had gone. Then Andy said, "I was a fool. Will you forgive me?"

"I was a fool. Will you forgive me?" the President answered soberly.

"You'd better go, darling." She smiled: they had all the time in the world now.

He turned obediently. "I'll see you at dinner? Oh. One more thing."

Andy had gone to the mirror and was taking off the twisted gold chain necklace she'd been wearing. "Yes, darling."

"I'm really awfully glad you're home. The senator's wife was *such* a bore—and besides, she didn't love me for myself. She was just trying to get her husband a job on the Supreme Court."

Andy made as if to throw the necklace at him and Alec ducked nimbly through the door. But as he rode down in the elevator, looking straight ahead of him, his smile disappeared. In Dan Healy's office, he said expressionlessly, because there were people there, "See you a minute, Dan? Right away." He went on through into his own office. When his appointments secretary came in, he was standing in the middle of the room, studying the eagle woven into the rug. He said, "Close the door," without moving.

"Something wrong, Mr. President?"

"Dan, this is strictly between you and me—"

"Of course." Healy sounded offended.

Alec wheeled around, grinning shamefacedly. "I mean, even more than usual. I want a little hatchet work."

The man who had rung doorbells for Alec Girard's first House campaign let out his breath in relief. "Sure, Champ. You had me scared for a minute. Who is it?"

"I don't know. I want you to find out who's responsible for that goddam story about me and Mrs. Carson—Fred Carson's wife."

"I know the story. But it's kind of hard to track these things down. And you know it's got to be more than just one guy. It's probably quite a crowd, and at least half of them women." The usually merry face, worried now, peered up into Alec's. "You really mean it, though, don't you?"

Alec Girard smiled without humor. "You start a file, Dan, and I don't give a damn how big it gets. I don't care how many heads there are, I want them all on a platter. For future reference." He looked at Healy significantly. "For frequent reference, actually. You get me the names, and we'll give the ladies and gentlemen a taste of that old-time city hall politics."

"I got you," said Healy. "Okay, Mr. President." He went out quietly, happy to be doing something he was good at, thinking about where to cast his line first. Alec would cool off some, in a couple of days. But there would still be a great old Tammany-type fish-fry sooner or later.

Thirty-six

Andrea Langwith, as a good student in a good school, had learned and remembered T. S. Eliot's moving lines: "April is the cruellest month/ Mixing memory and desire." But their application this April was only by way of a passing compassion for others that flitted through her mind and was lost in the gentle wind as she drove her convertible—getting to drive a car *herself* again, at last—back over Chain Bridge after depositing Bonnie Ruffing at her home.

The Secret Service agents in the car behind looked less wary than they had at the start of the jaunt, for the First Lady, to their relief, did not seem to translate her high spirits into automotive recklessness. In addition, her "disguise"—a silk scarf that enveloped completely her thick glossy hair and a pair of enormous sunglasses that compelled the eye triumphantly, making the rest of her face almost disappear—was most effective. So effective that the party had been able to stop at an outlying Hot Shoppe and lunch on hamburgers and milk shakes without attracting attention. In the nearly empty drive-in ranks, the two sober gentlemen in the sedan passed the mustard, commented quietly to each other, and observed with what would surely be thought only reasonable interest the four chattering women in the neighboring convertible; only one of the women looked like anything but a busy housewife snatching an hour while the wash was being dried in the machine, and that one was not the First Lady but her friend Mrs. Farland, who had come from her office and was thus more respectably clad than the others.

Andy stopped for a traffic light on MacArthur Boulevard and looked at Nedra and Marian with her general happiness and a kind of special gratitude besides. For Andy had been learning some lessons in the dark of winter: among them, that the ordinary inanities of speech that are freely allowed all citizens would, if uttered by her to the wrong person, promptly be declared newsworthy and appear in print—where, cold and isolated though correctly quoted, her words would proceed to make her sound even to herself like a stuffed nitwit. So she had come to cherish Nedra and Bonnie and Marian for, in addition to their own characteristics, their determined loyalty: they gave her not only their friendship, but safety for hers.

As Andy said good-bye to the remaining companions of the morning's outing, her gaze lingered—sympathetically, for Andy loved more readily than she moralized—on the oddly subdued Marian. For whom, Andy suspected, April was going to prove only the first of many cruel months . . . But then she turned away, hurrying into the Mansion to do something about removing her "disguise." It was not the way she wanted to be seen by a homecoming husband.

The officials of a western state had automatically requested the President to come out and dedicate their new dam, but they would certainly have settled for the Vice-President or even the Secretary of the Interior. He didn't have to go, Alec had told his wife, it was just that he thought it might be fun. He screwed up his face thoughtfully and said that Ruffing had a spongelike ability to soak up the springs of public feeling, but if you left him lying around the White House too long he got dried out and hard. Complimented on his enlightenment as an employer, he looked down at his shoe and muttered that there were some who might think the new-sprung Girard desire to dedicate a dam a form of vacation from a sparring match with the Congress. But they had small minds.

"We inspected the dam," a presumably sopping Jake said in reply to Andy's polite inquiry that April afternoon, when she greeted the returned voyagers. "It was there, as advertised. Lots of water behind it. The President spoke. Everybody clapped." He swigged the last of the welcoming cup of coffee Andy had provided, offered the abrupt wave that was his characteristic adieu, and darted off to his own concerns, which included a waiting Bonnie and five boys.

Alec said slowly, "It was an amazing thing."

"The dam, darling?"

"Well, I suppose. Miracle of engineering and so on. But I meant the people." He hesitated. "You see it over and over again when you're campaigning, but then, back in Washington, it's different. You forget how remarkable—"

Andy waited, but he didn't seem to be about to go on. "What is, Alec?"

"Oh, I don't know, exactly. They stand there—all along the way—waving, some of them holding up their babies to see." He shook his head. "All so healthy and clean and smiling. It's—awe-inspiring. A very remarkable thing." He broke off, frustrated by the gap between what he had said and what he meant, and then grinned suddenly at his wife. "I had a feeling

that I'd like to take out a picture of our baby and pass it around. But I
thought you wouldn't care for it. For one thing."

Somewhere in the back reaches of Andy a couple of cells informed by
genes inherited from Elizabeth Langwith quivered, then subsided as the
woman who loved Alec Girard smiled and said it would be all right, really,
but just the *picture* of the baby, please, for now anyway. She led him off
for a glimpse of their baby in chubby fact, wondering silently as she walked
beside him whether it was actually Jake who softened and took shape when
he soaked up the public.

Marian Farland sat in her office, divorced from April but unable to stop
smiling at the small wire sculpture that stood among its strewn wrappings
on her desk. Some other time, she told herself, she would put on her critic's
hat and try to decide where among the slim stretches of coppery wire the
knowledge of grace in ungainliness began and how it became unmistakably,
lovingly, utterly Grant and utterly charming. Fluid and gawky, reaching
and shy, the figure craned upward, bearing the eye with it to, somehow, a
guess of success—a conclusion that, however stumbling and however sweetly
clumsy this motion, at the end of it the basketball went through the hoop,
the tennis ball went over the net. Grant himself, looking at this, would
know he probably was going to write the Great American Novel, some
day soon.

Marian gathered the wrappings ineffectually and tossed them in the general direction of the wastebasket, staring hard at the battered surface of the
desk on which, only yesterday, she had painfully—and shamelessly, on the
Tribune's time and stationery—written the stilted note meant primarily to
inform her lover that there was, as she put it after brief thought, "no need
for precipitate decisions now." The aspirins she swallowed had soon put a
stop to the cramp in her belly; but nothing, she had discovered bitterly,
helped the cramp love seemed to cause in her prose style. Nevertheless, she
had gone on determinedly writing him, in a manner quite ponderous enough
for a Bainbridge column, about her decision to explore the possibility of
maintaining her children's situation unchanged even though so much they
didn't know about had changed. She put her pen down and hoped piously
that Paul would derive some idea what that meant, but she doubted it because "some idea" was about all she had, and even without language problems, you had to have more certainty than that before you could communicate. But she could hardly write, "I don't want to be a silver dollar," and
expect to communicate by it that if indeed no more remained of her marriage than a moribund invalid, the patient might still be up to supporting
life for the children of the household. And if it was not, or if it finally died,
a decent burial must be supplied. In the end, she picked up the pen again
and applied it to a series of swift and awkward statements communicating
baldly just about that, and just about as stiffly indicating that Paul could
do what he liked about it. It wasn't graceful, she told herself, but it was the

truth—and then, because she couldn't stand it, she wrote, "I think of you like homesickness," and hoped he would understand that if she could get home she would. But sometimes people had to be exiles.

The reason she had to call him now, though, was that she had to know whether the little Grant statue was an answer, which seemed impossible because he couldn't have had time to make it after he got her note, could he? A hotel voice told her he wasn't in and took the message she was tempted not to leave because she was already ruing having weakened; but she spoke her name bravely enough and then returned to contemplating the wiry Grant with a little more equanimity. And some amusement, too—she doubted that Paul had read the *Washington Herald*'s art column last Sunday, but she had. Phil Colby, discussing a painter who seemed to some critics to play excessively with the physical qualities of the pigment itself, had taken off on a discussion of whether this was such a bad thing, if only it sorted itself out as a passing phenomenon. The early Morisot, Colby told his readers by way of example, had exhibited a similar absorption in his medium, producing abstractions that sometimes seemed as much a celebration of the stone as of the subject. "If, like Morisot's still obviously great but now controlled passion for his stone, the first rapture becomes a way of learning to use the medium tenderly and resourcefully, to live with it fruitfully . . ." Marian smiled, not without a tiny malice, and hoped Paul, having learned to proceed from *folie d'amour* to comfortable domestic relations with his beloved stone, was not going to run off with little snips of wire and leave Colby with his epithalamion hanging out.

When the phone rang, she knew who it was and remembered her perfectly good excuse just in time: after all, if somebody sent you a present you acknowledged it promptly, didn't you? So "When did you make it?" was only the second or third thing she said.

The day after he last saw her, Paul thought; but he'd been contemplating it since he first saw Grant. Only he had to borrow some tools at—he hesitated, apparently remembering switchboards—the home of a friend.

Marian laughed. "The same friend who yearns for exercise?" He acknowledged that it was, and she went on, "I never found out how that game came out, you know. Did you win?"

"Certainly not." Paul sounded surprised, and also somewhat reproving. "I am not—some magic hero, you know. You know?" he asked after a little pause.

"I know, Paul."

"I hope." He did not seem convinced. "I do not always win, even when I am not—ummm—yes, thank you. 'Handicapped.' "

Marian wasn't so sure, though she realized he wanted urgently to convince her. She looked at the wondrous sculpture on her desk and asked, "You got my note? Is that why you sent—?"

"Yes. I desired that you should have—"

"Paul, you know I can't—it's against the rules, of course." It crossed her mind that he might just possibly be ignorant enough of the ways of commerce not to know. "It's—worth a lot of money," she told him maternally. "You probably don't realize—"

"Oh, I realize," answered the practical artist who seemed to want her neither as mother nor baby. "That is why I signed it. You can give it to Grant: if he does indeed leave his employment to write, he will need money. When he has finished showing it to his friends, he can sell it."

"Paul!" She was shocked. "It's beautiful."

"Yes," he said immodestly. "Can a thing that is beautiful not be also useful?" He was very nearly openly laughing at her. "One day, if you permit, I make you a most beautiful omelet pan."

Oh please, yes, some day, she thought, not sure how to keep from weeping with joy because he had understood the plea behind the heavybooted stumbling of her letter. "I hope to permit," she said, her voice very small and subdued.

Then she listened quietly, noticing that it hardly hurt, while he told her he would be going home now—in perhaps two weeks; one of them he would spend in Philadelphia for a visit with the Donnellys. He would make a brief trip to New York—for a day only, he said carefully, adding even more carefully that Carol Donnelly would probably go with him—to complete arrangements for the book he had undertaken to write.

"A book? Oh Paul!" The dead Martigny's pictured face loomed before her. "If you do that, how will you work?"

"In the day," he said calmly. "And the book at night. For a few months, yes?" He listened to the small sound of objection. "Decisions should not be —precipitated—by the lack of money. Either."

"Yes, but if I thought I—"

"That is folly," he said sharply, cutting her off before she could commit an indiscretion. "I am not frail, I assure you." He seemed able to lance into her thoughts at will, Marian thought, as he went on, "I am not Gaston, and I live five kilometers from the sea." His tone said that would do now. "Another thing I must ponder," he went on brightly, "is whether to enlarge my house. Or perhaps build another."

Just like that, Marian thought. *And* tear off another masterpiece. *And* write a book. She remembered Gil's suggestion that Morisot was a Renaissance man, and laughter quivered in her voice. "I didn't know you could build a house, Paul."

"Of course I can," he said quietly. He left the statement for consideration for a moment and then, in a rather different tone, conscientiously explained that naturally his friend Alphonse would help him; he went on to boast of what a marvelous weight of pipes Alphonse could carry uphill, and— Marian knew suddenly that Paul could have built her an ark and carried her away on the flood, and she was overwhelmingly grateful to him that he hadn't, that he had spared her the fate of selfish survival while others drown. "I forgot to say in my note," she interrupted him, "that I'm

glad now you . . . it was arranged . . . so that a difficult decision could be
. . ." *Made the only way it could be bearable,* she thought, but she couldn't
say it.

"I know." His voice altered and she could almost see his slow smile.
"Also, I know you are a little angry."

Startled into abrupt consciousness of it, she said, "I didn't realize, but—
yes, I guess. How did you . . . ?"

"I know because I, too, am a little angry."

Poor darling, she thought, wanting suddenly and very much to put her
arms around him and make it all right. "Oh Paul, couldn't we—" She
broke off for two reasons: the poor darling snapped out a fearfully im-
polite word in French and then followed it with the puzzling but clearly
menacing observation that he would like to be permitted to state a regret
without having his mouth stopped with bonbons, and Ann Taswell swung
in Marian's office door. "All right, I'm sorry. I remember you—made that
point once," Marian said hastily into the telephone, shuddering a little because she did remember. She waved Ann to a chair and managed to keep
her face expressionless while the voice in her ear thanked God *some* hard-
won contests were behind him and went away laughing, for a week anyhow.

Ann recognized Grant in the wire figure immediately and said so, admiring extravagantly and commiserating with poor Marian who would not
be able to keep both this lovely thing and her implied promise to the *Tribune,* which wanted its critics to refrain from accepting gifts. But she wondered silently what Marian was going to do, and not only with the problem
of keeping her reviews free of influence. Ann narrowed her eyes and speculated on how the man who could understand and capture Grant so thoroughly on what must be brief acquaintance would employ his presumably
much deeper knowledge of Marian—assuming he wasn't satisfied with just
making her eyes bright and her hands fluttery, which he apparently could
do by telephone. Ann pursed her lips and waited for Marian to settle down
long enough to listen to something important.

Which was that Ann's series on the brave, sane struggle of the Negro
to bring oppression to an end by nonviolent means had been cited as a
candidate for a national award, and the ME had just asked Miss Taswell to
combine the articles for a special Sunday supplement on the civil rights
struggle in general. Furthermore, the whole thing would be called after her
own term for the movement, "The Tender Revolution." When Ann said
this, the full impact of the fact that these special words—her description of
the remarkable forbearance of people who did not want to hate but would
not be any longer denied—would soon become everybody's came to her
suddenly and, in a second, her eyes were as bright as Marian's, and with a
not very different pride and hope.

For the rest of the month, except for a semi-command reception at which
the director of the National Gallery, some French diplomats, and M. Morisot

had officially told each other and the press how art brought nations together, Marian was successful in avoiding what she could hardly regard as
festivities marking the sculptor's return to France. The reception, at which
she had stood with Phil Colby and clapped her hands politely at the little
speeches, had left her relatively unmoved; the sound of Paul's voice bothered her a little, but his impeccable tailoring covered all scars, and his words
had so little to do with the great stone from which he had hewed meaning
—or with the faraway house to be enlarged or with the eyes that could see
Grant and Martigny with equal love and compassion—that it was not impossible for her to walk and talk and clap her hands as if she were inside a
plastic bubble, or he were.

The private farewellings were more difficult, requiring ingenious manipu-
lations so they could be avoided without causing comment—in the Farland
household or outside. Marian managed, with fair success, to be either absent
or in only brief attendance; each such "triumph" increased her misery. Only
once was she reduced to reliance on that tired stratagem, the "sick headache."

But the one festivity for which no excuse short of confinement to a hospital bed could be acceptable was, of course, the Girards' private, unofficial farewell party. Though Will was not by any means saturated with
State Department starch, he could certainly not have let his wife regard a
White House invitation lightly, unofficial or not. And neither, Marian admitted, could she—even if it were not a matter of Andy. So Marian dressed
with care but chose her less than prettiest dress because Will had bought
her prettiest one for her; she managed, by behaving with the silent circum-
spection of a Japanese wife, to attract no particular comment that she
knew of.

Paul danced with her as stiffly as he had at Andy's first party—a comparison noted silently by a sympathetic Andy, revolving past them in the
arms of Bill Bruyette. But for Marian it became unbearable almost from
the first moment: she wanted to be held closer to Paul as soon as she was
held by him at all; nothing in her could support that small, careful distance
from his body and everything in her screamed at her to get it closed up.
And yet, at precisely the same time and with precisely the same force, she
feared his anger. The result was a collision of impulses ending in a total,
helpless trembling that had nothing whatever of passion in it because it
was all simple physical collapse.

Paul dug cruelly into her back with the strong fingers that could touch
as lightly as a butterfly; his other hand, one promised for the manufacture
of beautiful omelet pans, clenched hers, which was clammy. Muttering that
she should be tranquil—literal translation being all he was up to at the
moment—he danced her through the French doors and out into the sweet-
smelling shadows of the colonnade, propped her carefully, and then turned
and clutched the stone with both hands.

Marian said in a very small, very frightened voice that she was **sorry,** and Paul, a little surprised that he had any voice at all, told her he had not himself much ability to endure such an exercise.

"Paul." She held out her arms.

"Of a certainty," he said. "With pleasure, *Madame*. If you will then permit me to go and find your husband so that you may inform him that you are leaving with me. At once. Tonight." He watched her wilt.

She turned away, looking out over the black stretch of lawn. "You know I can't do that," she said finally, turning back to see whether he did know. He nodded, so she supposed he did. But she also supposed she might very probably slap him if he didn't take his hands away from that stone pillar. Which, she thought nastily—her eyes snapping with the rage that she had found a way to turn on him—he apparently was able to embrace without having to consult a mess of Boy Scout rules. If it wasn't some sexy chanteuse, it was some goddam rock . . . The clear fact that he couldn't be trusted for a minute relieved her of any obligation to obey his orders; in fact, it was simply up to her to find a way. "Darling, listen," she said desperately. "The *Tribune* sent the dance critic to Russia last summer, so certainly if I asked—" She saw his black look beginning, and with a fine instinct for self-preservation, promptly found something to hide behind: "Ann was saying only today that they ought to send me . . ." She stopped, and surrendered. "Paul, please don't look— I—I didn't mean it."

The dance music swirled between them like fog. His voice, when it came, seemed to be full of fog, too. "Why do you wish to make of me always the *jeune fille*, saying, 'I will not lie with you except in a marriage bed'?" His face hardened. "Certainly I will, now that I think again. Come, no one will miss us, we shall go to the gymnasium, where there is a mat on the floor, quite adequate for a quick—encounter—something suitable for under Paris bridges." He took his hands from the stone and Marian suddenly wished he hadn't; involuntarily, her own hands rose protectively to her throat. Paul saw it and nodded with emphasis. "*C'est vrai*—that is entirely possible. If you persist in your folly. If you insist that you must be a whore, I shall first advantage myself and then put a close to your career, I think."

"Paul, don't."

" 'Paul, don't,' " he mocked. "Very well, I shall do no such foolishness myself. Neither foolishness," he added, and laughed. He leaned against the pillar as if for comfort, and then even laid his cheek against it briefly before he said with quiet calm, "I shall not, either, rescue you from the admittedly difficult need to make a decision. Do you understand? However you try, I will—not—rescue—you. *Marianne*, do you listen to me? I will not come when you call me, unless it is to take you home. But then I will fight for you and I will work for you. Always. I will give you gowns, ribbons, furs, jewels, automobiles, swimming pools, whatever you need to prevent you from longing for your native land." He saw her smile and scowled. "You think not? I swear it. Whatever nonsense you desire, I will make it or buy it or steal it."

"What I had in mind," Marian said quietly, trying not to soothe him even though he so obviously needed it, "was a house and a cooking pot and a picture, and maybe a nice dress for Sundays. No, listen—" she stopped his interruption, but without touching him. "I admit that I did have in mind, too—" her voice trembled "—being held when I'm afraid, and also being embraced when I'm not. And I confess I like it when you carry me."

"I will build you a house and keep you safe in it, and I will also make love to you, either purposefully or not. And quite constantly, if I am not in fact required to employ myself at earning automobiles."

"Paul, I love you."

He went on talking as though she had not spoken, but his voice shook with the knowledge that she had. "If it is necessary, I will carry you up mountains every day for the rest of my life and believe myself fortunate. But I will not carry you through the door of your husband's house. Not because I do not love you—"

"I know. 'I could not love thee, dear, so much, loved I not honor more.'"

"Nonsense," Paul said briskly. "That is for Englishmen." He took himself away at last from all the supporting stone and faced her. "Not because I do not love you, but because I will not have less than the most you are. And that is because I also love myself." He clenched his hands and said lightly, "But I love myself less already for whispering in alcoves like a courtier flirting during a ball. And I know that unless I go home soon, I will do it again."

"I'll go inside," Marian said quickly. At the back of her mind a small, amused voice speculated on whether he really could think he had been whispering. "You stay here and rest, darling. You look so very tired." She blushed furiously as Paul began to laugh; he clutched the pillar and told it something terribly funny about bonbons. "All right, you're not as good at resisting geisha girls as you think."

"I am becoming most expert. Soon I will be a veritable hero of the resistance."

"Oh, very funny. Just *look* at you. If I ever saw a man who could use some soothing—"

"Most certainly," he interrupted. "If you will be good enough, then, to inform me when you are ready—"

"On your terms."

"But of course on my terms," he said gently. "Now go, please, my love."

But when she did turn away at last, he looked at that quick flutter of skirt and said, before the twinkling legs could happen to him, "You may have as much time to decide as you require, of course. But try to remember, *Marianne,* it is easier to build a house before the ground freezes."

He was still standing quietly out there by the white stone column, thinking that perhaps he should have remembered to say, "I love you," because she was sometimes so American, when Ann came to find him. She observed silently that the last time she'd seen such an exhausted-looking man was when she covered a rescue attempt at a caved-in coal mine; like those men,

Paul looked as though only a small hope sustained him. She had come to offer him a measure of help—if not to enlist openly, at least to provide some minor Red Cross services, such necessities of morale as a way of obtaining at least news of Marian. Ann made it easy for him because it was so obvious that so little else was, tonight: he was just about capable of a little elementary diplomacy, but that was all it took for the message to be sent and acknowledged.

It was all done very quickly—they had solemnly exchanged addresses, and polite promises to write, and were back in the Red Room before Marian emerged from the powder room wearing a brand-new makeup job that took care of all the damage except her swollen eyelids.

Thirty-seven

"Okay," the President said as his chief aide seated first the Vice-President and then himself. "Let's make it a short wake."

Jake Ruffing bounced up and began his characteristic nervous pacing, like a small animal in captivity. "I'm sorry, Mr. President. If we can't even get a simple majority, we obviously haven't a prayer of ever getting a cloture vote. So if you push on Negro voting rights, the Senate'll filibuster the hell out of you."

Girard turned his head toward the Vice-President. "Tom?"

The big man sighed. "They've got the bit between their teeth, Mr. President, that's for sure. Seems to me Jake's about right. I figure you'll get maybe —oh, fifty percent of what you asked for in the special messages."

The President saw agreement in Ruffing's sharp, unhappy face and wondered whether the congressional committee chairmen would ever realize they weren't members of the opposition party any more. "Meyer sized it up for us," he said quietly. "I've got a 'technical majority.' Which is one of the least viable positions for an executive." He swiveled his black chair around and peered out at the perfect late-May day that he couldn't get to; he was as isolated from it as a traveler in a space capsule. "I don't think the gentlemen on the Hill appreciated my going around them, doing by executive order what they wouldn't give me legislation for. I have a feeling it put their backs up."

The Vice-President stirred. "Look at it this way. Under Winkler, Congress was running the show. He came to them hat in hand for permission to blow his nose." He shook his head. "I'm not sure, if I may say so, Mr. President, that everybody's so sore about the executive orders. You know we've got some southerners—particularly in the Senate—who're bright enough to see that the Negro has to have a fair chance at a job, even if only to keep us from paying out for welfare indefinitely. But you know and I know they can't vote outright like that and expect to be returned to the Congress." Cannon caught Alec's sympathetic grin and returned it. "It feels great, thank you. Sort of like taking off a tight corset. Every time our employment board gets another colored fellow a factory job above the level of sweeper, I feel like drinking to freedom—for Tom Cannon."

Thirty years of getting elected from the South, Alec realized with something of a shock for the length of time, would involve a great deal of corseting for a man like Cannon. Who was, the President thought, almost an archetype, in a way, of what the struggle was aiming for, eventually: Cannon was neither a Negro-lover nor a Negro-hater; he simply applied to Negroes, as to whites, a politician's measurements. Cynicism, if you wanted to call it that— but equal as all hell, totally undiscriminating, asking only results without regard to race, creed, or color. In this respect, Cannon and Girard were substantially alike; the difference was, Alec concluded with a sudden pride in his native state, that in Vermont he could feel that way and let it be known. "But we need more than you can give us through the board, Tom."

The Vice-President nodded. "Afraid so. If you want more jobs and more housing, we'll have to have some legislation."

"But if you tie it into voting rights, the good old coalition of southerners and midwesterners will slap you right down," Jake warned. "You remember the fight over committee rules, don't you? When we tried to break their grip, right at the start?"

"I remember. I had hardly lowered myself into this chair."

Cannon laughed without humor. "We put the screws on every guy in the House—"

"And waved the flag and rhapsodized on noble traditions and won by four votes," Girard interrupted. "We did everything except have Andy go down to the Hill sobbing with the baby in her arms." Which suggestion, he recalled, had been put forth by that advocate of delicacy and restraint, Bill Bruyette.

"And that was with a brand-new President," Cannon noted. "A hundred days is supposed to be the maximum honeymoon, and you're well over the limit."

"Hell, that was no honeymoon." The President grinned. "It wasn't even a fast game of spin the bottle."

Jake paused in his restless wandering to stand by the desk. "Well, at least you don't need your morale raised."

Girard stood up, stretching his arms above his head. "It strikes me as comic as well as tragic—such a classic situation, having to choose between leading responsibly and staying popular so I can get reelected. Like a political science textbook—you know?" Or like the accumulated experience of Cannon, the old pro, Alec amended. "And here I am, a mere beardless boy—" he grinned at Cannon "—beset with all the ancient problems."

The Vice-President, who had wielded Girard's relative youth as a weapon, and often an effective one, while the two men slugged it out for the nomination, laughed heartily and without self-consciousness. "Maybe you been grow-ing up. I don't see you busting into tears at our bad tidings, Mr. President."

"It's too soon to cry. The day's not over—I don't know what else is going to hit the fan. About seven-thirty or so, when everybody's been and gone, I sit down and decide whether to bawl today over foreign or domestic affairs."

Jake shook his head. "You've got less to bawl about than anybody else would have in the foreign policy area. If anyone can move that constipated monster down there in Foggy Bottom, you can."

"In my dreams the State Department leers at me while angel choruses chant *'No pasarán.'* " Alec reached out and set the big tilted globe spinning with a light touch. "So. I can't keep my glorious campaign promises to get the southern Negro his vote—at least not this year. Right? But if I back off and don't try, I may have a chance to assure the Negro anywhere a job and a decent house to live in." He shrugged. "It's not too difficult a decision, is it? Only a hard one to swallow. Unless— What are the chances that I lose even if I prove—accommodating? What've we got to wield?"

"We shot a hell of a lot of our patronage on that opening fight," Jake reminded him glumly. He raised his head and added, "The only poll since your far western trip is due out next week. Meyer has it set for circulation among your former colleagues on the Hill."

The President grinned. "Maybe we ought to look at it first."

Jake said, his eyes on the Vice-President, "I don't have to. I saw the crowds."

Alec put his hand over the lower part of his face, ostensibly to rub his chin thoughtfully, but he was hiding a smile. He himself had first run for Congress about a hundred years ago, he thought wearily; but to the others he was still a gifted amateur for the same reason, or nonreason, that families in Kingsley remained "new" for a generation. Cannon had certainly shared the unspoken conviction of many of his pre-campaign supporters that the Vermonter, as a maverick, a nonconformist rejecting the slow-moving but traditional order of Senate advancement, could not have a just claim to the nomination. Girard had evaded the unwritten rules, he had made an end run around their time-honored huddle—and now, as President, he was proving that he could still be untrustworthy enough to bloody noses by the use of executive power; he bargained, sure, but not until he needed to. And, as Jake was deftly remind-ing Cannon, who had a wider acquaintance in both houses of Congress than anybody in Washington, Girard could go to the people, if he were forced. If a "fireside chat" worked, intransigent legislators beat their way out of offices piled with indignant mail from constituents and appeared, hat in hand, at the White House. *If* it worked, of course. That it was likely to, right now, was the point Jake was delicately driving home.

Listening to his emissary negotiating on his behalf, the President told him-self wryly that it was the distrust native to these men that he had had to cul-tivate. He and Rosenberg, he amended. But the two men bargaining now— and Farland, who was like them—applied pressure as naturally as they breathed. And to their friends as well as their enemies, only altering the amount.

"According to Meyer, our cupboard is pretty bare," Jake was reporting to his boss. "Rosie has some past favors he can collect on. And Farland knows where a few bodies are buried. But these are probably duplications, aren't they?" He turned a poker face on Tom Cannon. "The Vice-President knows everything they know and a thing or two besides, I imagine."

"I've no doubt of that," the President said lightly, thinking that an early Ruffing had probably functioned this way the first time a few cavemen decided to winter together. "What've we got, Tom?"

"Well, now," Cannon drawled, "the senior Senator from Iowa dropped in the other day. Mentioned he had a little something worrying him."

"Good," the President said unfeelingly. He listened to the plight of that unlovely solon, a bind described lovingly by Tom Cannon, who neither relished nor deplored it but simply appreciated its beauty. Eventually, a way was discerned—by stalling just long enough, the administration could get all the juice out of the executive department ruling that had displeased the Iowan. And then yield to him, and collect a future favor therefor. The President ordered Jake to bring about the necessary retreat-with-honor, which wouldn't be either quite retreat or quite with honor, and then asked, sighing, whether Cannon had anything else on the shelves of his store today.

"A few items, but that's the only one that ought to be handled from this end of the avenue." The Vice-President grinned. "Look at it this way, Mr. President. We're still in business."

The President, agreeing, saw the door between his own and Dan Healy's beginning to open. Automatically he glanced at the frame on his desk that held the typed list of his appointments; Dan's interruption meant that he didn't think whatever was next could be held up. The President saw why at once and got up swiftly, smiling and holding out his hand. "I'm sorry. Listen, I'll make it final very soon. On whether we push our quiet little blessings. Meantime, any more information on the chances of success will be a help."

Jake lingered after the Vice-President was ushered out, but Alec said, "Jake, I have to go over to the Mansion."

"Okay. One thing, though. Farland's requested an audience. Shall I ask Dan to set it up?"

Alec halted, surprised. "He doesn't have to—"

"I know you're not that hard to see. But he's either showing the effects of too many years in the State Department or he means the formal request to indicate high significance. My guess is the latter."

"Mine, too. Yes, tell Dan, will you? You wouldn't have a guess about what's on Farland's mind?"

Jake sighed. "No, but I'm sure there's a lot of it, whatever it is. Short of yours, that guy's brain is the busiest in town."

"I hope he's not about to quit."

Typically, Jake answered this half-humorous remark seriously. "Don't think so. He had a walloping offer last week and he turned it down. Considering that he had to borrow money from his bank to pay his income tax, it sounds like he likes it here."

The President began to laugh. "Jake, Jake. Is there anything that escapes you?"

"I hope not, sir," Ruffing said primly.

Alec was still smiling as he made his way through the west wing—a wrong decision, though, he thought: he should have gone the outdoor way so he could see the new garden, and avoid delays. But his smile broadened as he noted the hush that accompanied his passage. Even his personal secretary, whose lack of ability to reject the unimportant was a cross he tried to bear with grace, had learned to allow him to pass in silence. Beats campaigning, he told himself—a candidate couldn't stick his head out of his hotel bedroom, or even out of the bathroom, without being set upon by reporters. He hurried because it was important not to be late to this function, which was one of the kind you couldn't get to when you were campaigning.

"Of course he didn't *know* I wanted to marry him," Andy said in a storyteller's voice. "He *thought* I only wanted to go to the movies with him."

Elizabeth laughed hoarsely and kicked her pink-slippered feet in delight. The story was not only funny, it was also as funny as ever. "Was he ever surprised when you got married to him!"

The block-letter alphabet on the small nursery table was printed in a semicircle above a painted rabbit. "Not exactly surprised," Andy corrected. She nudged her saucer so that it covered nearly all of the rabbit except his pink-lined ears, which were tolerable. "By that time, he was used to the idea. Of course," she added, "Daddy wasn't an easy man to marry. Plenty of ladies had tried to." She traced the embossed "A" with her forefinger. From the corner of her eye, she saw the door open and glimpsed her husband's silhouette. But she kept her head bent over her work. "I had to be ver-y cagey," she went on.

"Indeed?" Alec Girard came quickly into the room and stood, looking huge, beside his daughter's chair.

Elizabeth spun around to hug his trouser legs. "Daddy! Mommy's telling the story about she had to be ver-y cagey to marry you."

The President snorted. "That's what she thinks. That's what I wanted her to think." He leaned down and went on conspiratorially, not looking at his wife's bent head. "The inside story on that little caper has never been fully revealed, you know. Actually, I was even more cagey. I meant to marry her all along."

"You only meant to go to the movies," Elizabeth protested. "That's what Mommy said."

"That's what Mommy thinks. That was the *really* cagey part of my plan."

Andy laughed. "Bainbridge or somebody said the other day that you were subtle and politically daring." She nodded at the empty-eyed doll that sprawled in the chair across the table from her. " '*Politically* daring,' please note," she told the doll. "And 'subtle' is right—I think it must have been the subtlest campaign in history."

"It must have been Somebody, because Bainbridge doesn't write that well," Alec said calmly. "And I don't believe my daring is limited to politics. Besides, whatever Somebody said, a lot of other people are currently calling me too prudent. Try reading the adverse press some time."

"Pooh—what've they got to tell me?" Andy's grin was impudent. "I noticed your prudence, close up, while I was waiting to find out whether I would be an old maid."

"Well, it called for tactics. After all, a beat-up bachelor senator doesn't get the most beautiful postdeb in Washington without a lot of planning."

"I wasn't a 'postdeb.' Really, Alec!"

" 'Postdeb' is what it said under the picture of you and some guy whooping it up in a night club. I remember it clearly: I saw it in the Washington paper just before Bill and I set out to tell the farmers what I would do for them, if elected. The clipping ate through my pocket all during my speech. After that, it ate through *me,* for quite a while."

"You were supposed to see it," Andrea told him without sympathy. "You were also supposed to do something about it. Not after 'quite a while,' but right away."

"I was planning my campaign," he explained. "You didn't expect me just to jump in and start speechmaking, did you?"

Elizabeth banged her spoon on the little table. "You're talking to each *other.* It's not fair—this is my tea party."

"Quite right," the President said quickly. "I know it is, because it said so on the invitation that came to my office." He peered around the prettily decorated room. "I was to take tea with Miss Elizabeth Girard and her friends, but I've not been offered any tea and I see only one friend." He bowed elaborately to Andy. "A mutual friend, of course."

"Please sit down," said the mutual friend politely, indicating the chair opposite Elizabeth. She took a cup from the tray, lifted the small silver teapot gracefully, and poured. Alec folded his big body in enough sections so that it would fit into the little chair and thought that she still had especially pretty arms, smooth and shapely—and usually on display in her characteristic sleeveless dresses, he remembered, smiling to himself because he was a man who admired intelligence. He thanked her for the cup she set before him and began to think about having her portrait painted, sometime soon.

Elizabeth swallowed the spoonful of Jell-O that had made speech temporarily impractical and waved her spoon at the doll on her right. "You forgot her —*she's* a friend."

The President halted, with suppressed amusement, his almost reflex response: by this time, the first thing his muscles seemed to produce when stimulated was a handshake. He offered the doll a truncated bow. "Of course. Samantha, isn't it?"

"A*man*da, Daddy."

"Sorry. My memory simply is not what it was in the days of my courtship."

"Amanda, may I present my father," Elizabeth recited in a monotone.

Andy told her gently, "You've got it backwards."

"You said," her daughter reproached her. "You said, 'Present the gentleman to the lady.' Don't you remember?" Her cross look announced disapproval of capricious mothers.

"I told you, not if the gentleman is President of the United States."

"Oh." Elizabeth showed no intention of apologizing to her mother, but she seemed so wearily resigned that Alec was very nearly moved to apologize to her. Until she said, "I forgot that old PresidentoftheUnitedStates part."

I think she ought to whistle "Hail to the Chief," too, Alec thought of saying then. But he substituted, "How do you do, Amanda? How are you today?"

Elizabeth broke into giggles. "She can't talk, Daddy. She's not real—she doesn't even have real food. Look in her cup, and you'll see it's empty." She ladled another spoonful of glowing Jell-O into her mouth, which was a small, exact copy of her father's, and then smacked her lips, a gesture not copied from her father. "I like Jell-O. 'Specially red Jell-O."

Both her parents gazed at her fondly. The flush of pink along her cheekbones was enchanting, if worrisome, and her always bright eyes now glittered with fever. Andy laid the back of her hand against the high, clear forehead, looked frightened for a moment, and then smiled reassuringly at her husband. "Not much," she said softly. "Not considering it's late afternoon."

Reminded of her invalid status, Elizabeth announced, "I've got the maybe-measles. That's what Doctor Rose said. If I get the real measles—" she favored them with a drama-laden pause "—everybody has to get glamma-glob shots. 'Cause they're supposed."

"*Ex*posed," Andy said.

Elizabeth repeated "*ex*posed" and turned back to her Jell-O, and her father surveyed her mother with respect. Elizabeth sometimes had him at a loss, darting suddenly into reality and leaving him plodding lugubriously behind in let's-pretend, as she had done with the doll, or leaping into the middle of a new subject like the flying grasshoppers of summer in Vermont, but without even the dry whirring sound they warned you with. It would never have occurred to him, he thought, that she meant "exposed." He looked questioningly at Andy. "What's this about measles?"

"Well, there are no signs of it as yet—just sort of general virusy symptoms. But the doctor mentioned it because it's measles season. If it turns out to be, we all may have to have gamma globulin. Do you remember whether you ever had measles? But I could call—"

"Everybody," Elizabeth interrupted, her eyes shining. "The whole school

—all the children, and the teacher, too. And you and Mommy, and Miss Page, and Dan, and—" the thought of the potential stir of which she was the center filled her with such glee that her voice rose nearly to a shriek "—and Mr. Roy, too. *Everybody* has to take *shots*." Visions of the agonized faces of her family and friends were clearly dancing in her head.

A breath from savagery, thought her father, a man who preferred understatement—but there was no way to diminish the size of this fact. Or, he considered, the courage of Andy, painstakingly plying little fig leaves of etiquette in the hope of eventually civilizing.

Elizabeth bit into her single cracker and contemplated the less attractive side of her exalted status. "I hope I don't get the real measles, though. I want to go to school again."

Her mother murmured that she probably would, very soon, and Alec took the opportunity to ask what she liked best about school. When she said "Rest time," he bent his head abruptly and began studying the alphabet on the table with as much care as if he planned to invent one of his own. Elizabeth waved her cracker, narrowly missing sowing her father's hair with crumbs, and began to recount the delights of rest time. Alec said it didn't sound particularly restful, and his wife observed neutrally that sometimes it wasn't, actually.

Elizabeth swallowed the last of her cracker. "One day Peter Farland wanted to sleep with me in rest time. I asked him politely to go away, but he just wouldn't." She licked a final crumb from her lips. "The teacher made him go back to his own mat, all right. At-once-Peter," she finished, in the teacher's voice.

Alexander Girard raised his head from the alphabet and eyed his wife, who said calmly, " 'Nature in the raw is seldom mild.' "

"He shouldn't just come and sleep on top of somebody else," Elizabeth observed.

Andy said she was sure Peter had learned that by now. "That's what children go to school for. To learn." She ignored Alec's eyes asking with interest, *Learn what?*

"Actually," said Elizabeth, in a precise imitation of her mother's use of that word, "I don't care if he wants to sleep with me. If he wants to so much, I guess he can. But he should ask politely, not just come and *plop*."

"Andrea." Alec paused and then said slowly, choosing his words carefully for their distance from his daughter's vocabulary, "I am encountering some difficulty in selecting an appropriate attitude."

His wife suggested that he refrain from selecting any at the moment.

Alec overlooked the interruption. "From one point of view, I cannot but feel that habits of sweet compliance may usefully be implanted in the female in the formative years. However, as *paterfamilias,* it occurs to me that a certain standoffishness is desirable, to avoid—"

"It's difficult," Andy said demurely. "Finding the exact point of balance, I mean."

"Oh, I don't know. It seems to me you managed it with beautiful skill." Alec's eyes held hers. "I remember it distinctly. If a little painfully."

"Alec, please. After all, I was in my twenties. Do try to understand it takes a little time to—er—bring things along."

"Sorry. It's only—I wondered how progressive a school—" He broke off to grab for Elizabeth's spoon, but Andy rescued it first, and steadied the sherbet glass as the child scraped it for the last bits of Jell-O. The head of the family watched their intent cooperation, but he was thinking of Andy in her twenties: a beautiful girl, perhaps a little silly still, but doing no one any harm, really, and having a merry time of it. And then along came the sly Senator, twirling his mustachios, and swept her off her feet: *It won't hurt a bit—just a little campaign once every six years, a fast trip around a small state.* And the silly, sweet slip of a girl believed him—and now, all for love of Alec, she endured the mean sniping of idiots, threats of violence to her children, a house invaded by strangers every morning. . . . If I'd been Andrew Langwith, I think I would have horsewhipped me, Alec said to himself, and then reminded himself that Andy's father couldn't have known. He eyed his own daughter speculatively and thought that *he* knew, though, and any politician coming courting in his parlor. . . . "Andy," he said suddenly. "Are you ever sorry you didn't marry the other fellow?"

"No."

He looked at her quickly, believed her utterly and instantly, and decided to keep an open mind on the subject of Elizabeth's suitors. Just *No,* he thought. No fuss, no fluttering eyelashes, no questions: just *No,* a perfect absolute. A very remarkable woman. He sighed with satisfaction and devoted a moment of thought to the overly ambitious Peter. The boy was young and would learn, either at school or the way an earlier generation had. But Farland ought to have a talk with his son, thought that neglectful father's superior—the boy could be taught, at least, that it's a good idea to try sending flowers first.

Elizabeth had not yet developed her mother's ability to be brief, and she had always had a distaste for conversations that went on without her. She jumped in confidently. "*I'm* sorry I didn't marry Mr. Roy. I like him."

"I think Mr. Leroy likes you, too," her mother replied.

"I know. But he can't marry me. I asked him."

"Did you, dear? What did he say?"

"He said he's very honored, but he's already married. He's even a daddy, did you know that?"

"Yes, dear. Put your spoon down, please. I think Miss Page will be coming for you soon."

Elizabeth obeyed, then frowned at her mother as a thought struck her. "Mommy? Daddy's already married and Mr. Roy is already married—so who can marry me?" She paused, her blue eyes clouded with unhappiness. "I asked Peter, but he's going to marry his mother. He asked his mother if you can marry two people, and she said no. That's right, isn't it?"

Andy seemed inattentive for a moment. Then she said quickly, "Yes, that's right."

Suddenly Elizabeth was close to tears. "Then how can I find somebody to marry me?"

Andy extricated herself deftly from the small chair, lifted her daughter, and carried her over to the rocker. "I don't think you need to worry about it just yet, darling." She sat down with the pajamaed child in her lap. "It isn't time."

Elizabeth clung to her mother, her high spirits gone. "But what about when it *is* time?" She coughed a little, and brushed at her eyes.

"Why then," said Andy calmly, "—when it's time, we'll tell Daddy, and Daddy will take care of it. There's nothing to worry about at all." She rocked the child gently.

Alec got up with difficulty and produced a pencil and a telephone memo slip from the breast pocket of his coat. "Now, just to be sure, Elizabeth," he said importantly. He bent and, leaning the paper on the top of the wide, white-painted toy shelves, wrote quickly. Then he put the pencil away and brought the paper to his daughter.

"Read it, Mommy. What does it say?"

Andy held the paper so Elizabeth could see it while she read the large black capitals: "FIND HUSBAND FOR ELIZABETH."

"You see," Alec explained, "now I can't forget, can I?"

The little girl studied the words critically, then wriggled upright on her mother's lap. "That's 'Elizabeth.'" She pointed, her voice high with excitement. "I see 'Elizabeth.'"

Over her head her parents looked at each other with delight. In the soft light of afternoon in the bright little room, everybody was smiling. Even Amanda.

Alec Girard was still smiling as he reported to the policeman in the hall that he was going back to his office now. A little maid with a tray of silver came out of the family's small dining room, looking like an airbrushed photograph with her figure outlined by the low sun in the west window. She saw him and scurried, and Alec remembered what Andy had told him of her predecessor's household ruling that no servant was ever to be visible to the President. He turned on the maid a smile of enough warmth and brightness to compensate, he hoped, and then forgot her so he could go back to contemplating the picture he had carried away with him.

"It is the universal language," Paul had said once, in the course of a lakeside lecture on elementary art. In Kingsley sometime, Alec thought, and tried to remember when. But it wasn't important—only sometime when Elizabeth was still a baby, and the sun shone and there was more time. Andy lay long and still beside them, probably asleep; her dark head emerged from some kind of fluffy yellow robe. And Alec, who always wanted to know things, was trying to learn something from Paul, who obliged lazily, scratching a slashing oblique in the dirt with a stick. "There is the line—love or war, however you desire to use it." The sculptor's brown hand plunged purposefully as a missile or a lover; then he bunched his fist and drove it suddenly upward, cutting the air between them at the same angle. "You see? The line drives, and—" he picked up the stick again and drew a single gentle arc "—the curve yields. Used with wisdom, they make beauty. But they must always be taken into account, for they are always present." Alec peered at the rough geometry and said he never saw them, and Paul told him to look more at the outlines of things.

Looking at the outlines of what he had just left, Alec thought now that Paul had been right: that universal curve struck directly to the heart of man. In the dainty room, everything about the woman and child had fallen within the curve—the woman's cheek and bosom, the tender downward pose of her bent head, the soft fall of the child's hair over the mother's arm. The man who needed now to put away the curve for the crisscrossing lines that met in his office walked rapidly, glancing out at the May day he was missing, but not really wistfully this time.

VI

A Realm Assailable

"And ever the wind blew, and yellowing leaf,
  And gloom and gleam, and shower and shorn plume
  Went down it . . ."

Thirty-eight

As the Farlands said good-night to the Colbys outside the National Gallery of Art that night and started toward their car, Marian felt a little like Lot's wife fleeing into the desert.

But, for all her longing for the satisfactions she was leaving behind, she couldn't run the risk of turning into a pillar of salt—for there was an enormous agenda that had to be taken up with Will, and the homeward drive represented a rare opportunity to begin. Normally, she wouldn't have been able to combine the responsibilities of career and motherhood so handily. But a few advantages had stemmed from the fact that art had come "in," as Will had once predicted, with the arrival of the Girards in the White House. When the President attended an opening, everyone did who could get an invitation. Including Will Farland—who could now, as a result, be captured for domestic consultation.

The tentative plan to send Peter to boys' camp with Dick this summer ought to have priority, Marian had decided by the time they reached the car. For, in Will's absence, she had yielded to Peter's passionate pleas at least enough to fill out applications and send a deposit to hold a place at camp for him. But then she had begun to quiver protectively, and after that to wonder whether the word was "overprotectively." She thought she'd better find out, and she knew where to begin.

She smiled at her husband's stern profile, remembering his intervention when, as they were driving home with the children late one night from a day at the Ruffings', Peter had suddenly announced that he required a bathroom. Marian stopped him from pulling at his pants and cut off his elaboration of his need to urinate because the graphic detail was unsettling Sharlie. They were passing by the lanes of cherry trees—more Japanese as stark black lines than they would be in blossom in the spring—along the banks of the Potomac; Marian looked out at the landscape of closed buildings and no comfort stations and told Peter he'd have to wait.

"I already waited," he said ominously.

Will said, "Hang on a minute, old man," and pulled the car over to the side of the winding drive. He reached into the back and lifted out his small son. "Jesus," he said to his wife disgustedly. "Three years old and you mean to tell me he's never peed in the woods yet?" He carried Peter off to the bordering darkness among the trees, leaving Marian to contemplate her shortcomings as a mother of men.

The lesson having been learned, Marian attempted now to make up for what she lacked by bringing the current problem of Peter to his father's attention. But when they reached home, it was the rarity of that attention that

445

assumed most dramatic prominence in her mind, for Will made the mistake of displaying innocent amazement at finding Sharlie and Dick still up. Marian had been, for some time, delivering small lectures to herself advising imitation of, for example, Bonnie Ruffing, who seemed to have a lighthearted feeling that when her husband was around it was velvet, a kind of pleasant surprise . . . As soon as Will finished his fatal remark, this educational program abruptly went up in smoke: not more than a second later, Marian was seething with unspoken and un-Bonnie-like comments on fathers so unfamiliar with the household that they didn't even know what time the children went to bed. She had to escape to Rosa to forestall an explosion.

Even asking him about Peter had been a waste of time, anyway, she decided bitterly as she moved about a little later in the kitchen of the house whose master was such a stranger to it. He had failed to offer an opinion on the real issue of Peter's aspirations to be a camper, but had only said absently that he'd find out whether there was enough money as soon as he got a chance to do the accounts. Since his only contribution to the family's accounting in months had been to do the income tax forms, Marian asked herself bitterly what he supposed had been happening all this time; the electricity would have been shut off long ago if she'd waited for Will to write the household checks. The accounts were at least roughly in order, and the income tax had drained surprisingly little money; they could afford to send Peter to camp, and Will could find out if he asked her—but if that was all that occurred to him about the question, the hell with him. Like a widow, she would make all decisions alone.

Rosa, looking small and schoolgirlish in her room with an opened textbook and the blue-lined pages of a notebook before her, had seen the sullenness in Marian's face and probably guessed at least part of the cause. Her eyes speculated worriedly, but she said only that dinner was being kept warm in the oven—and then, when Marian looked blank, reminded, "You said you didn't have time to eat with us, you was going to eat later with him." But Will, it turned out, had eaten something between the office and the Gallery; and Marian, who had earlier come home from work and sat with the children briefly while they ate, then written letters, then tucked Peter in, and then hurried back downtown, had somehow lost both time for dinner and the desire for it. Now she emptied the warmed food into the garbage, wincing a little at the sinful waste, and washed the plates quickly and put the unused silver away, shutting the drawer quietly as a thief, lest Rosa come down and catch her at it.

She sat down at the kitchen table with her recipe box and the torn-out newspaper ad listing the weekend specials at the nearest supermarket and began making out the menus for the upcoming week so she could write up the big weekly shopping list. "Tues.," she wrote, and then, "Beef miroton— noodles—"; she paused to consider a green vegetable. Fresh asparagus was on sale; she had just started to write it when Will appeared in the kitchen doorway, carrying a magazine with his finger tucked between the pages to mark his place.

"Is it really absolutely necessary for me to check the bank statement tonight?" he demanded. "I *would* like to just sit down and read. I don't get much chance."

Marian pointed out patiently that they really had to know for sure how much money there was, and Will sighed and said he supposed so, but it was a goddam bore, and Marian set her teeth in her lower lip so that she would not be able to say that what she was doing wasn't her idea of fun and games, either. Dick's appearance in pajamas to say good-night ended a silence that threatened to go on too long; he dawdled, postponing bedtime, until Marian said it was enough.

"Mommy," he whined, in reasonably good imitation of Peter, "I want a story."

Marian smiled. "You're big enough to tell *me* a story. Tell you what, you go ahead and get into bed—don't forget to brush your teeth—and I'll come up and tuck you in, and you can tell me a story."

"Aw, Mom. I don't know any—"

"Well, think of one. Go on now."

Half pleased, half abashed, Dick tried to duck past his father and then snickered appreciatively as Will's arm shot out to ruffle the precious pompadour even while its owner did his best to protect it. "Your reflexes are still pretty good, Dad," he told Will generously, and scampered up the back stairs, smoothing his hair as he went.

"You hear that?" Will asked. "Raises your morale, a remark like that. Especially the unsaid 'for an old man.'"

"It goes on all the time," Marian said, smiling, meaning to tell him about Sharlie's open patience with the limitations of her aged mother. But then the sound of her spoken words came back to her, and there it was, the implied accusation—and she thought suddenly and furiously that whatever happened she would not turn into one of those, the whiners and naggers and hinters at grievances. So she closed her mouth tightly and picked up her pencil. "Excuse me. I must get on with this. It's getting late."

"I take it," Will said nastily, "that I too am being sent on my way. Only with a polite warning to hurry up and get my nose on that grindstone. Anybody ever tell you you'd make a great top sergeant?"

He waited briefly, but she snubbed him completely, refusing even to look at him, so he shrugged his shoulders and went on upstairs, carrying his look of injured piety like something on a tray, to be sipped at while he labored. His labors would involve more than simple arithmetic, too: Marian might find the accounting tiresome, but managing to keep those dollars in there to be subtracted had its excitements for her husband. If you didn't know that some of that comfortable-looking balance was money that had been borrowed and would have to be paid back, the financial problems involved in sending Peter

to camp must look minimal; Will sighed, recognizing this as one of the drawbacks of keeping his own financial counsel. It was not news to him that the
public, if it is not kept informed, tends to rebel ignorantly. But that was a
price he had long ago decided to pay rather than stir up the kind of flutters
that beset Marian at the prospect of borrowing money—a practice she
seemed to think both perilous and immoral.

Marian waited till Will was safely out of the way and went up to the third
floor, where she paused in Sharlie's room long enough to engage in an inconclusive discussion about whether there was actually any difference at all between a pink blouse and a pink plaid skirt that had arrived in the wardrobe
separately and the matched set of pink blouse and pink plaid skirt being sold
by Woodie's. Then she knocked on Dick's door to keep her appointment.

When she came to sit beside Dick on his bed, he had found a story to tell
her—about the Incas, whose life and times he was studying in school, and
Marian listened with real interest and a deep pleasure in the boy's thin,
lighted face and ready enthusiasm.

"It was a real good deal," he was saying. "See, they could go off to war
without worrying, because everybody else had to tend their land while they
were gone."

"Well, don't we do much the same thing?" Marian asked. "While our men
are in the army, their wives get allowances from the government. Of course,
it isn't enough money, so I guess it still leaves the soldier some worry about
his family. But I don't know, we have so many different other veterans' bene-
fits, maybe it all balances out." She looked at the fair hair against the
propped-up pillow. "You can ask your father about it."

"Sure," said Dick, turning his head away. "He must know all about it," he
added politely.

Marian nodded, understanding. It simply wasn't the kind of thing you
made an appointment to speak to him about, but something you just mentioned when you were with him anyway, driving somewhere or taking down
storm windows or just—around. And just around was something Will Farland had not been, for a very long time. "He's a little busy these days," she
said gently. "But things will loosen up."

Dick studied the navy-blue Washington Senators pennant tacked up on
the wall beside his bed. "Sure, Mom." His voice was expressionless.

"You know, when I went to school, you didn't learn about now the Incas
lived, all you learned was that Whozit had conquered them—"

"Pizarro." The boy turned back to her, surprised. "You mean, you never
studied about the Incas?"

"Not this early," Marian insisted, hoping she was right, but pleased anyway at her success in steering the boy away from disturbing reflections. She
went on trying obediently to remember the old days for Dick, who was discovering the delights of history.

" 'Sugar in the mornin, sugar in the evenin,' " Sharlie's radio sang from
her room across the landing. The voice twanged at exactly the pitch of a

familiar noise behind the dashboard of the car—a vibration, according to the diagnosis, of a loose cable in the speedometer. Marian got up from the bed slowly, trying not to listen to the nerve-jabbing music, trying to turn off the weary calculation that had begun automatically: if I can get Will to give me the car on Wednesday, then I can take it in before inspection is due next week and get the brakes tightened too. Sharlie shuffled out of the bathroom in heelless slippers and a quilted cotton housecoat that matched the pink foam rubber rollers in her hair; she crossed into her room but left her door open—an invitation suitably casual for her age and station. "Down you go, chum," Marian told Dick. "I've got to get back downstairs and finish the menu for the week."

Dick slid down in his bed obediently. "Don't forget chicken. With rice, okay?"

"Shish-kebab," called Sharlie.

"Well, I don't have to do much thinking, with all this help." Marian pulled the covers up around the boy and patted the cheek she was allowed to kiss only on Mother's Day; she crossed to the door and switched off the light. Dick was watching her expectantly, and for no reason that she could think of, she said, "Good night, sugar plum," as she often did to Peter and then began to sing, uncertainly in the face of this more musically knowledge-able audience, " 'Sleep my child, and peace attend thee, all through the night.' " Sharlie's normally unceasing radio went off abruptly and as Marian crossed the little hall, she saw her daughter dive into bed quickly and snap off her light. " 'Guardian angels God will send thee,' " Marian sang with more confidence. She went to Sharlie's bed and pulled up the covers, tucking them in slowly, and kissed the smooth toothpaste-scented cheek in the pause before " 'Soft the drowsy hours are creeping.' " She finished the song stand-ing in the hall between the two dark rectangles of their doorways, her hands held before her, one over the other like a singer at recital. " 'Love alone his watch is keeping,' " she sang to their attentive silence, " 'All through the night.' "

Then, feeling as though she had just donned a fur coat on a cold day, she went carefully down the narrow stairs with her burden of knowledge that these two needed a mother as much as Peter did, if maybe differently; because the load was already heavy, she tried not to weigh their need against the fact that Paul, who did not need a mother, wanted a wife. She put off considera-tion of her own needs and wants—even, she thought, smiling a little wryly at the closed door of Rosa's room as she came out into the second floor corridor, of the fact that, at this moment, she could probably use a mother herself. But Rosa had a heavy schedule of mothering these days and really couldn't accom-modate another orphan at the moment. So Marian refrained from knocking on doors and making demands and continued on down instead to the kitchen, thinking about Rosa's decision and wondering whether, in Rosa's place, she'd sort out demands in the same way.

She'd been shocked, at first, at the idea of Rosa's joining the "Freedom

Trips" into the South that were being planned for the summer. "It's dangerous, you know it is."

"Maybe. It don't have to be. But it more dangerous for them kids than me —I ain't no pretty, light-skin young girl for them rednecks to grab at. And I ain't no hot-head boy with a chip on my shoulder."

"But Rosa—I know it's been slow, but things are getting better all the time. Can't you just wait and—"

"*I* can, Miz Marian. It's Bruce can't, and Bettina. Onliest way in the world I can keep them two out of there this summer is by goin myself. I got them listenin to me—they got to admit I know them people better than they do and I be better able to stir up sympathy without stirrin up trouble." Rosa sighed. "You don't know how hard it been, just keepin them two in school— they was bound and determined they be on the very first bus."

"But what're you going to accomplish?"

"We get the good people to pay attention before it be too late," Rosa said soberly. "I know they got good people down there, and I think we can make them listen, goin peaceful and polite and not fightin. This here preacher got a good idea, but it ain't been easy making them kids listen—" she smiled a little wryly. "This here 'passive' talk don't come natural at their age. But I got 'em willin to let me try, once, my way. If it don't work. . ." She sighed, her round face gloomy. "Well, then I got a agreement to help out with their way. And their way's trouble, big trouble."

"Rosa, you know Alec Girard is on your side. Surely, if you just give him time, he'll come up with something."

"That what I be countin on. I care about the cause, sure, but deep down I just care about keepin Bettina Little out of Alabama, right clear out of reach of those people. I ain't worked all these years so she can be livin down there in a shack, gettin spit on by the trash they got there. And it ain't only Tina and Bruce. That boy sure to get his head broke right here in Washington anyway, one of these days, if he don't learn to hold his tongue. But it ain't long before Trixie follow right in after them, so I better stop the whole shebang now." Rosa smiled. "I be countin on the President to do somethin so those kids never get their turn to go on the Freedom Trip. See?"

Marian stared at her in surprise and dismay. "You're just as much of a schemer as Will, aren't you? When did you get to be such a politician?"

"Maybe him and me, we got somethin out of that air down there— black and white both breathes it." Rosa filled their cups with a steady hand. "And maybe you just learns to be what's needed. Now," she went on, closing the argument decisively, "what we do about Peter this summer? I don't hold with this talk about camp. He only a baby, no matter what he think. Maybe I see what Gloria doin for July, then you take August off and go to the beach with him? You lookin right stringy these days . . ."

It's the same principle, Marian said to herself, putting the recipe box away.

Give when you have to, but no more than you have to: fall back and re-group, which is what Rosa's doing. It was even harder to think of Rosa politicking than Rosa "Negro-ing," as they had come to call it between them, whispering lest Trixie hear them and tell the other stern youngsters of this unseemly levity. Marian, the two women understood, was permitted to be a lightweight, as she had no place in this anyway; all she could do was vote, and that, it had been decided, wasn't enough. But Rosa had a position to defend—a new status, hard-won and easily assailable, with no humor al-lowed, and no communication across No-Man's Land. It never crossed the minds of Rosa's children, who had slowly come to accept some leadership from her, that she was still so unwise as to talk seriously to Marian Farland. Even Trixie, who had always adored and imitated Marian, treated her now as though she were some kind of lovable pet. But Trixie treated her mother with a new respect.

And Rosa was wise to keep it that way, Marian concluded, noticing at the same time that her menus had rice twice in one week. She changed the one in the chicken dinner to potato salad, which they hadn't had yet even though spring was so far advanced, and which Dick liked anyway. And you really had to have rice with shish-kebab. Which they had to have because Sharlie loved it so. Will hated lamb, but, Marian reminded herself as she stowed her menu and shopping list away, the odds were that he wouldn't encounter any of the dinners planned for next week anyhow. She checked to make sure she had arranged for the children to have hamburgers the night of the White House dinner—the only time all week when she and Will would surely be dining in the same place—and scribbled "ch. sirloin (M&W out)" on the shopping list. Then she put everything back again and fixed herself a highball to take upstairs with her.

As soon as she came in, Will, slouched at his own desk, frowning and calculating, asked her whether she had a moment. She answered him politely, remembered satisfactorily what a mysterious $12.84 not identified on the checkbook stub had been for, and then left the room as soon as she could. When she came back to get her robe from the closet, he wheeled about and looked at her sharply; a little fear leaped in her throat, but she went her way coolly, marching down the hall to her waiting bath as if she didn't know his eyes were on her back.

He came into the bedroom after she'd returned and stood in the doorway, watching her brush her hair. "Marian, I'd like to talk to you."

"Certainly." Her voice was muffled by the thicket of her hair. "Did you think about what I asked you—you know, about sending Peter to camp? I wondered whether you—"

"I don't want to talk about kids," he said loudly.

Marian straightened up and looked at him coldly. "It would be better if we could get some of these questions about the children settled now. There's Dick's birthday and—"

"Look, I want you to come in and sit down and talk to me. I've had enough of being fended off with the house and the kids. It's been going on all evening."

"I'm sorry. I'm rather tired."

"Marian, I'm warning you—do you come or do I drag you?" He saw her bare toes curl into the fur rug and the thought flashed through his mind that she might throw the hairbrush she was holding; but he knew instantly and wryly that she wouldn't. Not any more. Which was precisely the trouble. He decided to see how deep this rather frightening control went. "You're lucky I'm feeling enlightened," he added brutally. "Now which will it be, sitting up in there, or flat on your back in here?"

Marian put the hairbrush down with care and glanced over at her bathrobe on the bed. But it would show fear, and that would be a mistake. Give a little, but no more than you have to. "Since courtesy seems to be just about the only relationship we still have," she pointed out disdainfully, "it would seem unwise for you to proceed without it." Barefoot in her long nightgown, she walked by him with as much dignity as she could manage.

No dice, Farland said to himself. He sat astride his desk chair like a movie director and watched her settle in the armchair, crossing her legs discreetly and reaching for her drink. All violence, threats of violence, and hints that I'm bigger are OUT, he told himself while his hands itched to slap her out of her elaborate calm. His eyes noted the panicky rise and fall of the round breasts under the lace bodice; her eyes were huge and brilliant, the way they always were when she was scared, and she gulped at her drink, needing it like a drunk. "I've never known you to try to duck talking over a problem," Will said untruthfully. "You always were the one for talking things over." His voice was gentle, persuasively patient.

"Maybe. I used to be a lot of other things too—a runaway wife, for example."

He stiffened. "Are you threatening me?"

"No, I'm not threatening to leave you, if that's what you mean. I thought I'd made it clear—the children's interests should come first, and they need to live with both of us." She paused. "If we can manage it." She looked down at her hands and laid them carefully in her silken lap. "I think it will be easier to manage if we refrain from this sort of thing. I don't think it serves any purpose."

"And what purpose does your icy silence serve?"

That "icy" is a trap, Marian's combat-ready mind warned; keep moving, don't be sidetracked. "Courtesy and a smooth routine," she said calmly, "have kept many a marriage going—"

"Love works even better, I hear," Will interrupted bitterly. "Or have you run out of that?"

She dodged. "I don't think it's relevant, Will."

"She doesn't think it's *relevant*," he shouted, jumping up. He said it again, declaiming it to the blank windows. "What in the name of God do you say," he demanded of the ceiling, his arm upflung in an orator's gesture, "to a wife who doesn't think love has any relevance to marriage?"

Marian took her hand down from her throat, where it had flown in an involuntary gesture of fear as soon as she'd seen what she'd begun, and tried to watch this like a show. And next time look where you're dodging, she said to herself, trying to make herself laugh.

Will advanced two steps toward her and then stood very still in the middle of the dark-green rug, while his eyes checked to see whether the pyrotechnics display had frightened her. It hadn't, and he kept the discouragement out of his voice for the most part, letting only a little in to enhance the gentleness of the appeal. "I love *you,* you know, and I think that's relevant." There was no visible reaction whatever. She simply sat there, all finishing-school composure, and he knew for a certainty that he could kill her. "Though you don't seem disposed to give it any weight at all." That worked, he saw—or something did; maybe, he admitted briefly, it was the genuine anger that had made him add that last, the remark unneeded by the demagogue, who'd already made his pitch. But needed by Just Plain Will, who had suddenly realized the truth of it. She was like some kind of laboratory instrument, he saw with a sinking heart: the only thing that would make the needle quiver was truth.

"Maybe it has no weight," Marian said cruelly. "Most of the time, it seems to be an abstraction—something you tell yourself down at the office, or on a plane. But the only concrete love around here is around the children, so that's all that's relevant."

"What is this, some kind of Blondie and Dagwood bit?" He turned away, afraid that he really might hit her. "Did I forget our anniversary or something? What do I have to do to make this concrete enough to meet your standards? I don't know who elected you an expert on What Is Love, but if you're going to set standards, then set them openly."

"Please, Will." She stirred in her chair. "This is fruitless, really."

"Oh no you don't, you don't nicey-nicey out of this, lady. I say I love you and you say it won't do—that's all, it just won't do. Like something out of Kafka. I'm convicted of not having enough of something, of not manifesting some mysterious thing concretely enough. Bang. Judged, convicted, hanged. Trial's over."

"This is unjust and ridiculous," Marian said. She stood up gracefully, carrying her drink. "There's nothing mysterious—it's been stated dozens, maybe hundreds of times. We had quite a scene about it once, as I recall. And I don't want another."

"Don't worry, I'm not going to hit you." At least I don't think I am, he thought quickly. God help me. "What is this? Are we going to decline from a lofty discussion to the bit about how I'm neglecting the woman I love?"

Marian said, so quietly that she stopped his gesture in mid-course, "Will, love is attention, and I imagine you know it as well as I do. You give your attention where your true love is, I think. It's not here, and I don't think you can help it. But I honestly don't care any more. And right now I'm getting tired of being addressed as if I were a revival meeting, so if you'll excuse me—"

"So love is attention, is it? I'm glad to have the Word, right from the altar, the pure-white marble altar—" He broke off, reaching out to stop her but pulling his hand back carefully before he actually touched her. "Please. All right, I won't rant, I won't harangue—but let's just take one more minute. Don't go, please."

"We've said everything—"

"Look, you're winning, baby. You can afford to be generous." He smiled at her. "Sit down. There is one new thing this time—we have to get our terms clear. This seems to be a negotiation, so let's conduct it professionally."

She let him wave her back to her chair, but she remained standing. "I'm not negotiating with you, Will."

"Well, you're certainly engaging in a cold war. And what about the fact that I love you and I want to live out my life with you, while you don't give a damn about me?" His voice might have been referring to an item on an agenda. "Wouldn't you say that's an imbalance calling for some kind of compromise?"

It's not true that I don't give a damn about you, Marian thought fiercely, clenching her free hand. Over her lifted glass, her eyes noted his fear, the tension in his body, even while she was warning herself to beware especially the evangelist gone quiet and reasonable. She set the empty glass down, admitting to herself a small, creeping respect for him, for the way his quick mind sought out every advantage; he fought, he would not give up, and you had to respect that. But not surrender to it—any answer would give him what he wanted, an opening to too much. The new Marian, she reminded herself, was a respecter of silence, offering him only the blank wall of her polite presence. He could go on and scrawl on it anything he wanted to; but he could not breach it. She was safe as long as she opened no doors.

"I take it, then, that you agree to my outline of the situation."

Marian ignored him, making herself very busy with lighting her cigarette before he could offer to do it for her. She felt like a traitor to herself—both selves, the real one who wanted to answer and the nicey-nicey one who hated to be rude. Maybe it's time I was a traitor, though, she insisted silently; maybe I've been living under the wrong flag.

"Okay, so what is the compromise being offered? If you won't state it, I will." His voice dismissed her silence as childish, which it was; but it was also utterly defeating for him and he had seen that. He was negotiating from no strength, and he had known it for some time. He threw in one more challenge, as a machine goes on running for a split second after the switch is pulled. "What you offer, it appears, is your presence, and nothing more." He watched her compress her lips and saw that she looked just like her mother—with that snow queen, nothing but a blowtorch would work, he thought grimly, but he went on and had a try at the soft sell anyway. "Well, it's a lot: I get, despite my inadequacies and shortcomings, a mother for my children, a household executive, a social partner. I take it your sudden dislike of me isn't so great that we have to call off our engagements. You'll be able to manage to, as they say, keep up appearances?"

Dislike was not what she felt for Will, but whatever it was, it certainly was not sudden. She had warned, demanded, wept, and screamed, time after time, trying again and again—only to have him shut her up, one way or another, so he could get back to what was important to him, the grass-roots trend in Oshkosh. The bed became a way to silence her—as did the slap, or persuasion, or mockery; the only thing he wouldn't do was listen. Marian wondered dimly why, though she was angry and knew it, she didn't want to scream these accusations at him, as she once would have. And then she found the answer and knew she was safe because she was, herself in herself and without regard to anything else that had happened, finally aware that Will could not listen to her words but only use them. *I am not to use.* She realized only after she had thought it that she was echoing the remembered "I am not to play with"—and she knew, without knowing what, if anything, must come of it, that some kind of small, new growth had followed the last snow of winter.

"I've already said," she told her husband dryly, "that I'm prepared to offer courtesy." It was necessary to post guards, but he was beaten, at least temporarily; eventually, he would regroup and attack from some other direction, but right now she could see him deciding to retreat.

"May I say that it's a cold entente you propose?" He spoke gently. "But I have no choice. I have to accept."

"I'm sorry," she couldn't keep from saying, but she managed to make the words flat. "May I go now? I *am* rather tired."

"Certainly. Except—one more thing. I have to take your terms, as I understand the position, or lose you. Which I'm not prepared to do. But I want to warn you, it'll never work. Don't count on it."

"Thank you," she said coldly. "Good night."

She thought as she climbed into bed that this was what it was like to be a widow, with all sorts of mixed memories pulling you this way and that, but nothing for you to decide because the end had come whether you were ready or not. She turned on the radio and the tentative notes of a Schubert piano sonata ventured softly onto the silence; a small single voice speaking to her single ear, it was more consoling than the generalizations of a whole orchestra. She lay very still, leaving the lamp on but trying to compose herself for sleep, her arms by her sides under the covers like a good little girl, and wondered whether widows were this angry. She heard Will go down the hall to the bathroom and then, briefly, the sound of the shower running before he shut the bathroom door; she began to tremble with rage then, with the unsaid things she would have liked to shriek at the top of her voice —as if it was only safe to feel anything when he was safely out of range, his hearing shrouded by the veiling water. When she heard him coming back, she turned on her side quickly and switched off the light, feeling the muscles of her thighs contract and knowing bitterly that she was still more than a little afraid. Whatever the species of plant whose shoots had broken through the ground, it was not hardy yet.

Will, wearing his bathrobe over his pajamas, came through the study door, looming bleakly with the light behind him. He walked toward the bed slowly and Marian lay still by total force of will, stiff and stubborn as a British soldier in the defensive hollow square—no match, really, for the Fuzzy-Wuzzies howling down from the hills with the night, but not knowing anything else it was possible or honorable to do.

"Maybe I ought to have the clock. I have to get up early tomorrow," said the Black Terror. "Six-thirty, I guess."

"I'll wake you." She felt almost tipsy with relief; there wasn't enough she could do for him, she was so grateful. "I'm up by then anyway."

Will went around to his side of the bed. "Well, if you're sure you'll remember to get me up—"

"I'll remember."

He picked up his paperback book from the table and stood looking down at her with a faint smile. "I take it," he said carefully, "that your program of courtesy does not include extending to me the courtesy of your bed?"

Say "As you like," Marian commanded herself, *and quickly, quickly.* Indifference, stated with speed, was essential. But the redcoated soldier who would hold his position against the fearsome enemy could do only that and no more. No matter how fiercely, desperately, frantically ordered to be truly brave, he could manage only to look it.

Will Farland concentrated on keeping his face so stiff that the wince wouldn't show. Whatever he had thought he'd seen, he must have been out of his mind. Her enormous, frightened eyes smote him and accused him simultaneously; just as it had been the night he had hit her, the view of himself as a monster to be cowered before was unbearable. He turned away with the book in his hand, unable to escape fast enough. "Never mind," he said harshly. "Forgive me for asking." He came back, remembering his cigarettes, and put them into his bathrobe pocket; it was going to be a long night, he thought, his eyes noting the now visible tremor in the small soft body he wanted to hold tight against the monster. The only possible shred of advantage available to him was martyrdom, and he grabbed it." "I'll sleep in the study until—well, until we decide to review the situation." He shut the door behind him with precision and, he hoped, dignity.

Alone in the dark with her triumph, Marian lay there, crying quietly without moving, an exhausted shadow of the woman who had once not hesitated to bawl and brawl. The line of light under the door to the study was a terrible underscoring of loneliness and defeat; she turned toward the little glow from the radio as a wanderer in the cold night of a desert might huddle by his tiny fire.

She was sleeping restlessly, the covers thrown aside, when Will finally became aware of the empty buzz the radio had been emitting ever since the station had gone off the air. He got up from the chair in the study and leaned down to stub out his just-begun cigarette in the overflowing ash tray. Logic was the great friend of long, cold hours, he had concluded, at just about the same time he had concluded his careful analysis of what he was up against. He had wasted little time in mourning the fact that she wasn't Andy Girard or Bonnie Ruffing: he'd known from the beginning that he had a handicap in Marian. The President and Jake were free as he was not; if he wanted to play in their game—and he wanted to, all right—he'd just have to run extra fast to make up for carrying Marian, who would neither send him off cheerfully, like Bonnie, nor learn to come with him, like Andy.

Farland looked at the blue moonlight shafting into the dark room and said to himself unhappily that the truth was, maybe, that Andy had been invited to come along and Marian had only been ordered to. It might have been a hopeless job from the beginning, given the fact of Marian, he told himself, opening the door carefully into the silent bedroom—but the fact was, it had also been a bungled job. He'd known that since before their first big fight, and he'd known he had to do something about it, but he'd thought he had time.

A miscalculation, he thought grimly as he walked over to the bed, and it could be fatal—I was sure I could safely let her simmer until I could get time for her. And I could have, too. Only I forgot that somebody could come in and turn up the heat while I left the kitchen unguarded. He shoved his hands into his bathrobe pockets and forced himself to look at her now, sprawled in sleep in the pale light. That's a lot to lose, he told himself quickly, to excuse the tears that stung behind his eyes.

Okay, okay, it's not lost yet, he reminded himself, bending to switch off the radio, then watching her closely to see whether the sudden cessation of steady sound would waken her. She muttered something and turned on her side. Will ran his eye down the creamy swell of bosom and the smooth silken curve of flank and tasted metal in his mouth. *It must've been cozy on a snowy afternoon, Jack—or, I guess, Jacques.* I bet she looked pretty, all right, he thought grimly—all sprinkled with snow, I suppose, because she said she went for a walk, and you can bet that was the truth: Marian, having decided to break one commandment, would keep all the others assiduously. And then off to bed, no doubt—probably after being fed just enough booze. His mind reeled away from Marian saying to him, once in their early days, "Oh, I am riggish," and covering his face with silly wine-smelling kisses. That's about as *bonne* as *chance* can get, isn't it, fellow—beautiful, available as hell, thanks to a husband who neglects her: one of our natural wonders is Marian, for foreign visitors to enjoy. *But once, Jacques, just once.*

Will studied his wife, reviewing the process by which good ol' logic, the midnight friend, had led him to Morisot—who was a better deal than Bruyette, thank God, because the way Marian was, a man who wasn't around could be beaten. It had had to be somebody unmarried, he'd reasoned; Marian would kick Will Farland where it hurt, once he'd made her mad enough—though, even then, she'd be no lighthearted sinner, he thought with fleeting pity for her—but she'd not hurt an innocent wife. Bruyette was the first possibility if you eliminated an *x* number of men on the *Tribune,* and there was no sense in wandering in that jungle; it might take years to check out all the unknowns there. Will smiled a little, remembering that he'd even thought of Grayson, on the grounds that her tortuous ethics might declare her first husband not adultery. Charlie was too smart to stick his hand in the same fire twice, you would think, but you never knew what that woman could do. However, she couldn't beat geography, and Grayson was more than an afternoon away all the time. But Bruyette had been a problem: Will would have had to begin by finding out whether the Congressman was at the Capitol that afternoon.

Except that the timing made it so clearly Paul Morisot—especially the way she began to droop right after his departure. It was a happy revelation—for the wily Congressman Bruyette could've been quite a problem, considering that quorum calls were infrequent and he had about two years before he needed to run for office again. But Morisot was not likely to be a smooth political operator, and he was very, very far away. And Farland was right here, he reminded Mrs. Farland with silent satisfaction.

He left her for a cigarette then, discovering that the pack was not in his bathrobe pocket. But as he went back into the lighted study, he was thinking a little bitterly that she had been left, on the afternoon in question, for a better reason: Morisot, who had no dependents, could afford to go out to play in the snow, but Farland had to be down in the mines digging for the paycheck. By the time he blew out smoke, though, he had shed that line of thought. He looked down at Marian's "Collected Works"—the scrapbook of her art reviews, in which he had begun doing his belated homework—and advised himself against setting up straw men. The Frenchman was no playboy; he worked, too, and what really hurt, Will admitted unwillingly but necessarily, was that Morisot's work was a kind she understood and respected. He might even be able to ignore her and get away with it.

The enemy forces were strong, Will told himself grimly as he sat down in the battered armchair and read again the *Tribune* clipping from which he —and, a few years ago, half a million readers—had learned that his wife considered Paul Morisot, "here at his best," an irresistible force. "The display of imagination and technique is as dazzling as the result is irresistible: all the awesome powers at the command of his mind and eye and hand are directed skillfully and unerringly to the service of his conviction. A bond of nearly incredible strength is formed between the sculptor and his audience. In the end, I had the feeling that nothing short of Morisot's death or mine could keep him from telling me and me from believing.

"Thus the award committee's description, 'an emotional experience,' becomes a mealy-mouthed understatement. For you can absorb the emotional charge, but that's only the half of it. After, Morisot bangs at your mind anyway, presumably forever."

Jesus, Will thought, squeezing his eyes shut and knuckling at his forehead. Not only was this a fine demonstration that Farland was not the expert detail man he was cracked up to be, but it also made him something of a louse—whatever else was in it for her with this guy now, they had apparently been on the same wavelength even before they'd laid eyes on each other. Nevertheless, he went on turning over pages, working at learning what he needed in order to begin to jam the signal, which he was going to do whether it was a lousy thing or not. Somebody named Tedesco painted "tidily," which appeared to be undesirable; Alphonse Lenard had abandoned his straightforward look at the world in favor of miniaturization of it, which could lead him to "mere hemstitching"; Martigny was like a tenor forcing his voice, which apparently saddened Mrs. Farland; and here was Morisot again, about a year and a half ago, this time with his reach exceeding his grasp and the *Tribune*'s critic softening his failure to attain heaven with the quote from Robert Browning.

Will closed the scrapbook and chewed on his lip for a while, assessing the really alarming communications gap. The truth was, he paid almost no attention to his wife's work and went to almost no trouble for it. She disappeared during the day, when he didn't need her anyway—but, come dusk, she was usually there to listen to the gossip of his world and accompany him to nearly all its fiestas, church services, and condolence calls. Guilt assailed him as he remembered that he had forgotten Phil Colby's wife's name this evening, though Marian had spent long hours not forgetting the names of Assistant Secretaries of State and their wives. And if, coming home from any of her exercises on behalf of Will, she had ever remarked casually that Tedesco was awfully tidy, wasn't he, chances were that she had got nothing for answer but an "Umm" and a pat on the fanny.

Attention comes in kinds, noted the man who guiltily didn't know even what was wrong with mere hemstitching. He switched off the lamp and sat there in the dark, facing up to the disturbing fact that Morisot, who presumably did know, had given her a kind of attention that couldn't be douched away. Marian, well and thoroughly laid, wore an unmistakable glow, and that she had turned up wearing it after a "walk in the snow" was, Will had told himself carefully, a little upsetting—but he would make a mistake if he let himself be sidetracked into jealousy, an oversimplification. Hell, I can't blame you, Will conceded to the man he now definitely wished to kill: what would any guy do when the lady was riggish and had a husband who couldn't get it up? Meaning attention, of course. The kind that had now been decreed to be love.

"All right, forget it," he growled softly, as he began to pace the small room. He could get up the new attention too, if the old stuff wasn't good enough any more. It was too bad about this here type Robert Browning and their star-crossed love, if that's what it was (*besides just screwing my wife, you fucking bastard*), but it was Farland first, with a greater need: the plain truth was, without Marian he had trouble figuring which way was north. So he couldn't afford to let the best man win, in case it turned out to be this character with the dazzling mind and eye and hand and, for all Will knew, maybe a cock to match—after all, her list of Morisot's assets was now out-dated. "Jesus," Will said savagely, shaking his head in the hope of clearing it. *I think maybe you can tell which way is north all on your own, Jacques. But if you can't, that's tough: it's my compass, and I'm keeping it.*

He stopped beating up on himself then and began to consider ways of keeping it, some of which might depend, he thought, flexing his mind like a muscle, on how long he had. The Frenchman would be back, all right—but how soon? A vagrant thought about Morisot's visa crossed his mind and Will laughed silently, remembering what powerful hand could be raised against him if he tried anything like that, and decided it was a mistake to fight new wars with old weapons anyway. This time the defense perimeter would be right at the house's front door, it looked like—but the homely hearthside forces were not without resources. *We are all creatures of habit,* he said to his rival almost blithely, *and her habit is not adultery.* And then there was the big weapon. What could Farland give Mrs. Farland that Morisot could not? Answer: something fast, pleasant, and effective and, though it costs a bit in the long run, keeps the memsahib safely in the compound for at least a couple of years.

He went quietly into the bedroom to have a look at the memsahib, because there was, of course, one catch. But it was a small one, he told himself with growing confidence as he rocked on his heels in the moonlight, grinning down appraisingly at his sleeping wife, who was stubborn but also vulnerable. And who wasn't made for the celibate life. With her, sex was a form of speech, and there was a limit to how long any woman could remain silent. And then there was good ol' habit. If a skilled hand, right now, should urge her just a leetle bit closer to waking, just enough for a murmur, say—he was willing to bet that "Willie?" was what she would murmur. In short, he crowed silently, *what do you bet, mon ami, that I make it into my wife's bed before you jet back? After that, you can feast your eyes on the pretty pregnant lady. You can even go right ahead and bang at her mind.*

Will dropped the image of Robert Browning-Morisot abruptly and devoted himself to a useful fact that had just broken through into his thoughts: Jake Ruffing, the greatest strategist of them all, had five children. Ruffing's new disciple bent over Marian and pulled up the sheet and blanket because the night had grown cool; he had to move her leg to free the covers and he allowed himself a moment's tenderness for the little white naked foot as he held her ankle carefully, so as neither to wake nor hurt her. Then he drew the bedclothes up to her shoulders, resisting a sharp desire to see whether a single, passing, practically accidental touch on the tempting breast would really be enough to wake her. *Cop no feels, Farland,* he told himself with a surge of gaiety. *This is Courtesy Week, remember?*

Or do we think—a snarling voice in his mind said suddenly, spoiling all the fun—we are saving it for the attentive Frenchman? He drew in a deep breath and let it out slowly. There was no point in this kind of thing; it might take eight years to get at Morisot, so thinking about revenge right now was only an unproductive use of energy. What was important was to reclaim Marian, whose intentions seemed to be confused. Will, whose intentions were clear, looked down at her once more, almost coldly, and headed for his (temporary) outcast's bed, hoping he could get at least a couple of hours' sleep. It occurred to him that he had already paid dearly for the opportunity tomorrow's appointment with the President offered. He was planning on it to advance his public life, and he was damned if he was going to let his private life louse it up for him.

Thirty-nine

"You're about a minute early, Will." Dan Healy consulted the round alarm clock surmounted by a sort of mushroom cap; its innocent face and hearty tick had been with him since he was a boy at a Jesuit orphanage, and it was as adaptable as its owner. In a few months Dan's alarm clock had achieved a White House status something like the security arrangements— hardly noticed consciously, yet a fixed condition of the landscape within the west wing offices.

Farland said he didn't mind cooling his heels. "But if you have a second, Dan—I was wondering whether anything was happening about a fellow I recommended to Rosie a while ago. Rosie read some speeches this guy wrote for Dan Daniels during the Wisconsin primary, and he thought—"

"What's this guy's name?"

"McElroy, Robert T."

Healy pushed an imaginary hat back on his grizzled head. "Nothing's going to be happening." The clock ticked busily. "This McElroy a friend of yours?"

"Not now," said Farland.

Healy laughed. "Just as well."

"Look, Dan—"

"Nope."

"No, listen," Will persisted. "All I want to know is, it's not security, for God's sake?"

"Oh." Healy's face cleared. "No. Don't worry. Just an in-house matter."

Will whistled gratefully. "Thanks. You wouldn't," he added, after a pause, "you wouldn't just happen to have a John Harrington on the same list?"

"Gee, I'm sorry, Will, but the list is in the safe."

Farland nodded, recognizing that the answer was yes—the list, it was quite clear, was nowhere except under the imaginary hat of the old pol. And what kind of list it was was also clear. "It's not important, Dan. But the fact is, it's *Mrs.* McElroy."

Healy rooted in his desk and came up with a bag of green jellied mints, which he offered politely before popping one in his mouth. "Man's responsible for his wife."

"Sure," Will said genially. "But this is a little different. They've got a— kind of understanding, you see. She's—um—popular with the boys."

Dan made a face and went on chewing the candy, a jaw-sticking variety that required concentrated chewing.

Will shrugged. "Just thought I'd mention it. McElroy's a good speechwriter."

"Not that good," Healy said indistinctly. He swallowed, looked at his clock, and got up. "I don't give a damn if a guy's wife screws more often and in more places than a traveling plumber. The point is, he's gotta be able to keep her trap shut. Right?" He didn't wait for an answer. "Cabinet Room, and you got fifteen minutes."

"Right," said Farland. "Thanks." Alec Girard wasn't likely to give much of a damn who said what about what; what was likely, Farland was thinking as he left Healy's little cage of an office, was that Girard knew how not to ignore his wife. Poor Rob, he thought, but without any particular pity; Dan Healy was quite right. It was a tough team, but it was a pleasure to play on it.

Two minutes later, he was breathing a little easier about his chances of continuing to play on it—the ball was sailing out nicely over the outfield. It was a promising hit, even if not a home run, and he had at least a couple more at-bats coming before his fifteen minutes were up.

"That's what you get paid for," the President said. "To have a diffuse, generalized hell of a nerve." He was looking out at the rose garden through the tall windows, framed between the straight fall of simple green draperies. His smile had been there when he turned to the window, because he liked the clever balance Farland achieved—a bold, buccaneering bureaucrat was a triumph of a very special kind of civilization. Then something he saw beyond the glass broadened his smile and he turned back, wanting now to enjoy the fun but not to linger unduly at the game. "I take it you don't disagree with my reasoning."

"I don't," Farland said. "That's what bugs me. If I could say I was opposed, it would be simple: I could write a minority report and sit back and wait to be proved right. But your economic approach makes perfect sense, Mr. President: certainly whether a guy gets served in a restaurant matters less than whether he has the price of a meal. I think you're doing more for the Negro's real benefit than anyone has for a hundred years."

"Sit down, Will." Girard sighed. "And no campaign speeches, please. I've already got my vote." He sat down himself, in one of the rank of black leather chairs along the east wall, where staff men and advisers sat during

Cabinet meetings. The larger chair the President occupied at the meetings was directly in front of him now, drawn up halfway down one side of the huge, coffin-shaped table. The inevitable telephone waited at his place, and at intervals on the polished surface of the table, ash trays sat on the edges of their reflections. "What is it you want me to do?" he asked flatly. *And to remember while I'm doing it that it was Farland who urged it,* he added silently. He looked at the tall man perched obediently but uneasily on another chair in the row; above Farland's fair hair the Great Seal of the United States was set into the wall. The President waited quietly for the operator to operate.

"A big, loud, ballyhooed, all-out fireside chat. Straight to the people, demanding everything for the Negro—the whole package."

"You know as well as I do that the answer will be a big loud all-out filibuster," Girard said quietly. "And an early death for the jobs and housing bills I've got Meyer and Rosie sweating on right now. So you must have something figured differently from the way I have. What is it?"

"I don't think the Negro leaders are going to be able to hold their people to the moderation line," Farland answered heavily. "I reckon you think they can, but I think you're wrong. Sir," he added after a pause.

Alec recognized his impulse to reassure his aide for what it was, a response deliberately evoked by that "Sir" and its pointed reminder of their relative positions. *You're the President and I'm taking my career in my hands,* it said bravely, among overtones of high principle and thrilling courage. But the real fun of watching Will do this sort of thing lay in savoring the second layer of skill—the fact that underneath this brave-stand-for-truth pose was, in fact, a brave stand for truth. Which Alec was meant to see, and did. It was all very satisfying, and the President, who had enjoyed being labeled "subtle and politically daring," also enjoyed observing subtlety and political daring in others. He kept his face grave and did his part by adding a small frown. "It's got to be more than a simple difference of opinion, hasn't it? For you to come rushing in to prevent instead of just safely second-guessing."

Farland eyed the flag on its staff beside him. "I smell a revolution, and I'm scared."

"Why? Even our Miss Taswell isn't. She called the revolution 'tender,' didn't she? I thought it was a very good analysis. What did she say about that rally? Oh yes, she found 'an almost tangible cheerfulness and hopefulness—the can-do enthusiasm of a Rotary meeting or a wartime savings bond rally.' Umm—more like that, something about the ignored and despised behaving the way we usually expect only the privileged to behave." He narrowed his eyes, calling on memory. " 'Everything we associate with the middle-class prosperous white American—self-respect, ambition, energy, optimism, good humor.' " He finished the quote triumphantly and smiled slightly as he saw that Farland was genuinely impressed by this demonstration of the impressive Girard memory; then he sighed quietly because Farland was going to be careful not to compliment him on it. The fear of sycophancy, Alec thought, might well be the most trying drawback of his terrifying office: nobody ever said, "That's great," for fear of sounding like a flatterer, and the worst of it was, he had to admire them for it. "Don't you think Ann's right, Will?" Behind his voice, he took back what he had just been thinking, lest the gods punish him for unjustified self-pity. Because there were Andy and Bruyette and Paul, those three who for their different reasons were similarly unafraid; and sometimes Rosie and, less often, Jake forgot who Alec was for long enough to let things be a little normal.

Farland stood up, his long body tense. "Sure she's right, as far as she goes. Which is up to yesterday."

"I thought *I* was taking the long view," Alec said mildly. "That's the point of trying to get your potential revolutionaries jobs and housing and the few other amenities of full citizenship that I can get through the Congress if I squeeze."

"Dammit, it's the short view I'm worrying about." Farland flung away like a rebellious adolescent.

Alec looked at him with attention, for this was no maneuver—a real fear had dislodged the operator. He saw the operator begin to climb back again and waved off his assistant's incipient apologies. "Just what is it you're afraid of?"

"Somebody's going to get killed," Will said miserably. "I feel it in my bones. This thing's about to blow up."

"All right. I've got respect for your bones—I remember they were right when a bushel of earnest reports were wrong. But I can't see that what you want me to do will add anything to what I've already done. We agree that the Negro needs enough political power and economic power so that he can't be pushed around. Any more than any other citizen gets pushed around, that is," the President added dryly. "Now you want me to add a speech that you yourself admit will be largely for advertising purposes, that will stir up expectations I have no way of satisfying—you know as well as I do that I can't make Louisiana, for instance, stop imposing barriers between its Negroes and the ballot. I can't without the Congress, anyway. What you're asking for, then, seems to be only a sort of exercise in demagoguery."

"Why is everyone so set against demagoguery?"

"Because this is a government of reason," the President said sharply.

"The hell it is," Will burst out. "The people are run by their feelings, and we've got these millions of people who feel hopelessly boxed in, who are convinced that every man's hand is against them. Which means the government's. I'll tell you what our Miss Taswell missed," he went on, his voice strained and furious. "These people may be demonstrating the American qualities she talked about, but they're converting the American political way from the party rally to the street rally. They're sliding out from under government, in fact. And while this bunch is, as she says, basically respectable and self-respecting, they won't stay in control of their revolution unless they can produce results."

"What you want me to do is catch up with them and put myself at the head of the procession," Girard said with mild distaste. "Announce myself the leader of what in fact I'd be following. Unattractive picture, isn't it?" He forestalled Farland's interruption. "I know. I'm not necessarily wedded only to the attractive. But the purpose would be only to render respectable a venture you feel has disreputable possibilities. Is it worth it?"

"Lawbreaking is a bad precedent." Will looked equally uncomfortable and stubborn. "It may not be dangerous in the hands of Thoreau. But Thoreaus don't know how to keep it in their hands. You know that, sir."

"Yes, I know that, Will." The President smiled slowly, remembering that he had been told it by a decorated lawbreaker one night in the gym. An interesting combination, Paul and Farland: Girard's active mind explored swiftly, searching out the reason why these two should be more afraid of the consequences of "sliding out from under government" than, say, the tidy-minded Rosenberg, who might be expected to be more upset by disorder of any kind. The difference came to him then—violent men fear violence, and those who wear scars know better than anyone that what is mended is never the same as it was before it was torn. They were curiously emotional about the law, these survivors of oppression or deprivation: Paul always insisted on his "private man" image with the nervousness of a girl defending her reputation for chastity; and Alec was willing to bet that, in any room but this one, Farland would have been shouting and pounding the table by now. The President leaned forward, speaking to the ardent man ardently. "But there are other dangerous precedents. About the Negro problem, I've already laid down in public the proposition that this is a national concern. What you ask—"

"Is a rewording of that statement," Will broke in uncontrollably. "Designed to appeal to the simple emotions of a simple man. An emotional statement, over television, so every guy standing at the bar can feel that you're talking straight to him. And saying, 'Mississippi may have you up the creek, Alabama may be kicking you around, but you have me, and I'm bigger than any sheriff in Tanktown, Louisiana. And I say you're not in a box, because I won't let them nail you in.' "

His voice, high and excited, rang in the bright quiet. The President got up slowly and walked to the end of the room. With his back to Will and his eyes on the portrait of George Washington over the mantel, he asked, "Do you realize what you're asking me to do, what I'd be announcing in addition to the reassurance you have in mind?"

"I think so, Mr. President. I see the distortion you're afraid of."

"I'm afraid of it, all right." Girard turned. "I took an oath to protect and defend the Constitution, not to reshape it. The constitutional relation between the federal government and the states—"

"But the Constitution never envisioned hopeless injustice."

"Nuts," the President said tersely. "You can hardly expect to make a case that the framers of the Constitution were inexperienced with injustice."

"They were looking the other way for it," Farland argued. "Toward tyranny by the federal government, not by the states."

"And you're saying the federal government is the only protection against tyranny by the states, is that it?"

Farland nodded. "Yes, sir. And I see what you call demagoguery as a necessary announcement of that protection. Now, when it's needed."

"But the announcement," the President persisted. "It would have to be backed up with power, wouldn't it? So what you're asking is more than a speech—it's a wielding of federal power, which I grant is probably unavoidable when a state is actively defying the federal government. But here you want me to move first, before there's been any overt, provable defiance. What you're advocating, then, is a kind of preventive war, isn't it?" He waited, but the other didn't answer. "Why do you duck the final question, Will?"

"Because I wouldn't have the guts to be President," Farland said slowly. He looked down at the floor. "It has been borne in on me recently, in connection with other matters, that you're a better man than I am."

Alec shook his head. "It has been borne in on me that I'm a different man, at least."

"Sir?"

The President indicated the pictures on the walls. "Washington. Jefferson. Jackson. The one we need is missing."

"Lincoln?"

"Yes. We'll never know, will we, whether he would've succeeded in finally preserving the union, so that it wouldn't keep threatening to come apart again." Girard looked at his aide thoughtfully. "Will, we come from two different countries, don't you see? In the hills of mine, government is a town meeting—where you raise your hand to speak, and you vote on a resolution."

"And in the hills of mine, government is a revenuer, and you vote against him with a squirrel rifle."

"Yes. Both kinds were necessary to build this union, but it may be impossible for both of them to live at peace in it."

Farland said quietly, "It's the squirrel-rifle set I really came to tell you about, Mr. President. I was afraid you didn't know them."

"Well, I don't, really. But I know they're there. I'm particularly well acquainted with their representatives in the Congress. Who, as you know, can stop most of my legislation to improve the employment status of the Negro. And they will, particularly if I try to impose a heavy hand." The President sighed. "Also, lest we forget and all that—the squirrel-rifle set consists of citizens of the United States of America, and I'm their President, too."

"That's another thing," Farland said slowly. "If Lincoln's unfinished job is ever to be completed—if this union really can be preserved, and sometimes I have severe doubts about that—you're the man to do it, Mr. President. The squirrel-rifle boys didn't vote for you, and they won't again. The Negroes did, but—"

"But they won't next time, unless I go in and tell the state of Mississippi it can't make laws about who sits where in a bus?" Alec looked at his assistant quizzically. "Which you admit I have no constitutional right to do."

"No, sir, but you have indirect rights that would cover it," Will said urgently. "Look, Mr. President, the Negro is taking an incredible shoving around—not only in the deep South. Right here in Washington, for example. It's a piece of luck when they aren't mistreated, just the accident of coming on a good fellow on the police force. But the underlying assumption is of second-class citizenship, and often less, much less. What you're calling demagoguery is simply a way to keep their spirits up, to provide a handle for the moderates among their leaders so the wild-eyed ones don't get to take over. Employment opportunities aren't any use to the types who'd rather throw bricks through windows anyway. If you let them take charge of the Negroes' legitimate grievances, you're going to end up with bully boys on both sides, and I think you know what that will mean."

The President tugged at his hair with one tanned hand. "I have small taste for public emotion," he said slowly.

"I know. But I think you also have small taste for the perpetuation of injustice."

Alec's smile was quick and gay, startlingly boyish before the sober words. "Thank you. But have you thought that perhaps temporary injustices may be necessary to protect the larger justice?"

"If you mean that the preservation of the squirrel rifle's right to keep his foot on the Negro's neck is, in the long run, valuable to the Negro, I suppose I agree, in theory. But my feeling is that we can't afford present casualties to preserve future values." Farland spread his hands. "However, I realize I'm not the guy who has to sign—" He broke off as the President's appointments secretary appeared in the doorway.

"Yes, Dan?" Girard asked.

"The gentlemen from the Hill, Mr. President."

"Hold them for about ten minutes, Dan; then I'll meet them in my office." When the door closed he turned back to Will. "You look unhappy."

"I don't feel conspicuously successful."

"It may be the price of being an honest man," the President said gently. He walked to the window and glanced out. "I imagine what it comes down to is timing. But I'll have to think about it."

"Yes, sir."

"What I'd like you to do, Will," Girard continued, without turning around, "is work me up some instances of the kind of second-class citizenship that confronts these people. Particularly right here, where I can wield some untrammeled power. You did include Washington?"

"Yes, Mr. President. I had some direct experience with it, on behalf of our Negro housekeeper, this winter."

"Right. And of course there's Ann's series. And I think I remember something in the *Tribune* by Marty Halloran—stories on shootings of Negroes by policemen where the line-of-duty defense seemed questionable. Give me a summary by tomorrow, will you, along with anything you think might be useful in the sort of—public display—you've been urging." He grinned teasingly. "And skip the quotations from the Bible, at least until I decide whether I'm going to do anything with the material. Now you look more cheerful," he added.

Farland paused on his way out. "I'm not suffering from a feeling of hopelessness any more," he said pointedly.

The President laughed aloud, his head thrown back and his strong white teeth glinting in the sunlight. "I'll let you know. And thanks." He waited until Farland was in the doorway and then added wickedly, "Oh, don't bother to put in anything about the glorious history of the Green Mountain Boys, Will. I am sufficiently exhorted."

He was smiling when the door closed, but the smile changed as his thoughts went back to Andy's question on a summer night when they had stood listening to the deep waters of Wenake Gorge. Couldn't the Indians just stay on this side, she had asked, and Alec's immediate answer had been "Never." Farland's bones are right, the President said to himself: nobody's going to be willing to stay cut off from the hunting grounds. Even though I'm planning to build them a bridge. All they see is, the powwows go on and on, but they're still not getting across. Sure as hell, some brave will leave the campfire and try a fancy trick on his own. And get hurt.

Farland was brilliant and sensitive, but he could afford the extreme solution; Presidents had better be more cautious. And Paul's experience was with centralized government, which is either all there or not there at all, leaving private men to become murderers in alleys. But a President is different, is a layer in a multilayered structure, with a responsibility toward the states as well as to the citizens. Farland would have the President pretend to more power than he owned. And Paul, if he thought Alec Girard could preserve any man's right to be a private man, was ascribing more power to the President than he owned.

Still, Alec told himself ruefully, when both poet and politician are shouting at you to take action in a hurry, it behooves you to examine the matter carefully, O Rational Man. Rational, but given to the error of the "Gift of the Magi," remember? You can pay so much for the bridge over the gorge that the braves will be unable to see its use any more; by the time you get it built, they'll burn it, out of a kind of conditioned reflex.

Girard shook his head, as though in opposition to a voiced argument. All true, but nevertheless counsels of desperation, maybe. It comes down to doing what you have to do, he decided, but not until you have to do it. Juggle, juggle, toil and trouble. Speed up the bridgebuilding a little, quiet the braves a little, call another powwow, and pray for rain. Wars are prevented by taking small steps instead of large ones, for as long as possible. While building an arsenal, Alec remembered. He found an envelope in his inner coat pocket and scribbled a swift note on it to Jake Ruffing, requesting a summary of the effect of removal of federal funds from Mississippi—which programs could be withdrawn at once, for which could the threat of withdrawal be persuasive? He put the paper away, smiling as he remembered another note he had written recently: "Find husband for Elizabeth" would demand, he suspected, rather less labor than this new memorandum. He opened the French window and stepped outside, letting in a soft wind that minutely stirred the folds of the flags in the Cabinet Room.

We ought to have flowers here all the time, he thought critically as his long strides carried him quickly toward the fragrant corner where he had glimpsed his wife. Then he remembered that there were plans for exactly that, and he sniffed the rose scent happily and speculated, with a pleasant trusting wonder like a child's, on what kind of flowers would come when these were gone. He didn't really care what kind—he simply liked to see flowers growing; but he promised himself that he'd learn the name of each kind because it would probably please Andy.

She was standing with her back to him, unhearing, and he said "Andy" gently, not to startle her. She turned, smiling, and he remembered suddenly a picture of her he'd seen at her mother's—Andy, aged four, with a fat bow in her hair and exactly the same smile in her eyes.

"That's a very pretty frock." It was some sort of pink, and he thought she looked like a flower among flowers. "Will I be reading about it in tomorrow's newspapers?"

"I'm afraid so. I'm about to leave for a ladies' thing." Alec watched her look up at the sky briefly, as if to read the time by the sun, and thought what a small shock of pleasure her soft, almost tentative voice gave him among all the urgent voices of his days. "I think I should've left already," she went on. "But I wanted to come out for a little survey."

"Mm. It's lovely. How was Elizabeth?"

"Oh, quite well, really," Andy said quickly. She read doubt in her husband's eyes. "I know she seemed listless this morning, but I'm sure the isolation has a good deal to do with it. She's a social little creature, and she misses being with the other children." Andy sighed. "In a way, it's a relief to have the school over with for the summer, so she's not constantly reminded. But I imagine it also makes her feel even more isolated. As soon as she's stronger, she can start having a guest for a few hours."

"Well, whatever the doctor okays, of course." Alec traced the edge of a dark-green leaf with his forefinger. "The baby carriage was really rocking out there this morning. I don't like to be a tattletale, but if he was supposed to be sleeping, he wasn't."

"He tried to climb out again, straining madly at the halter. I'm thinking of replacing it with steel or something. He stretches it as far as it will go."

"My son is at the end of his tether," Alec remarked to a nearby rose.

"Like father, like son?" Andy suggested. "Are you out here because you burst your bonds? Or just playing hooky?"

"Oh, a moderate sort of hooky. There are some advantages to working so near home."

"You don't find it—confining?"

Alec studied her briefly. "Apparently you do. Did you ask the doctor about taking Elizabeth to Vermont?"

"Could you go if she could?" Andy looked at him and read the answer. "Never mind, darling. I'm a beast to put the onus on you, anyway. The truth is, I can't take time off for Vermont right now myself. I have a state dinner to finish preparing for."

"Think of it this way. Just about the time we get to retire from public life —unless I get retired involuntarily—Sandy'll be a Cub Scout and you'll be entertaining the den mothers."

"Oh well. By that time we'll be living in a house that's not half museum. A house where all the rooms are just for us." Andy stretched her long body, clasping her hands over her head. "Alec?"

"Yes, darling," he said gravely, but his eyes were full of sudden laughter.

"What's funny?" Andy demanded.

"Nothing, really."

"Tell me."

"Andy, can't I have a private joke? Is there no corner of my mind that you—"

"Oh, I *am* sorry," she said swiftly. "Really."

He looked at remorse lying like leaf shadow over her bright face. "That's better," he said, summoning severity.

"Yes, I must learn not to be so—"

"Demanding," he supplied.

"Demanding and intrusive."

"Possessive," he suggested.

"Demanding and intrusive and possessive," Andy said solemnly. "Tell me why you were laughing."

Alec rolled his eyes heavenward—and found the heavens smiling and sun-lit, too. "I wasn't really laughing at you. It's just that, over the years, I've learned to read you by a few sign and portents."

"And?"

"And one of them is that anything that begins with 'Al-ec,'" he said, imitating her creditably, "with the accent heavy on the first syllable and a kind of pause between them—well, any time you start out like that, it's going to cost me something." He glanced at her quickly. "That's just an observation, of course."

"Of course." Her hair moved against her temple in the light breeze that stirred the roses. "A generalization, so to speak. Not true every time."

"Certainly not," Alec agreed. "For example, sometimes it's followed by 'I've been thinking,' but every so often a 'Wouldn't it be nice if we' turns up. So one never knows."

Andy looked up at him with awe. "How discerning, Mr. President. Because, by an absolutely exquisite coincidence, I *have* been thinking." She put her hand on his sleeve and whispered conspiratorially, although the only figure in sight—a gardener clipping grass at the edge of the lawn—was certainly out of earshot. "And, though it may seem unbelievable, what I was thinking was wouldn't it be nice if we could find a little place of our own, somewhere nearby. So you could be in politician country still, but we could get just a little bit non-public, even for a day at a time?"

Alec covered her hand with his and stood looking down at her sweet face with the fun in it. "Since you're getting such good grades in all your work, and even doing your homework without being reminded," he said lightly, "I think you ought to have a brand-new house, and right away." In the strong sunlight he could see amber flecks in her dark eyes and small imperfections in the skin of her face.

"Oh, Alec. Can I have one *built?* Right from the beginning?"

"Andy, you can build the Taj Mahal if you want it. And you can start right now." The exhilaration he felt when she looked like that—such open, utter pleasure—always made him instantly wary at almost the same moment; he turned away a little, abjuring her as if she were a heady liquor that, taken in anything but prudent quantity, might loosen his tongue. A shout, a leap, or some other behavior unacceptable to Alec Girard, a Vermont man, could be warded off by the judicious use of gallantry. So he said, "Actually, I didn't come charging out here to discuss better homes and gardens." The muted sounds of the traffic on Pennsylvania Avenue entered the small waiting silence. "I saw you out here and it occurred to me—" he smiled at her, waiting straight and tense in the crowd of blossoms "—that there never was a woman who looked quite so—relevant—in a rose garden." He watched the faint pink flush into her cheek. Then she moved and he stiffened in alarm, wondering in quick embarrassment whether she might throw her arms around him in full view of gardeners and the White House police and maybe half his office staff.

But when she said only, "La, sir. How you do go on," and grinned at him, her eyes mocking a little, he was relieved, disappointed, and, finally, convulsed. The woman was a witch; no mere man could hope to win.

He said, "I've got a meeting," and turned away with his mind hurrying his steps back to the office. "See you at dinner," he threw over his shoulder and didn't listen to her answer because he was considering a change in what he'd originally planned to say to the small congressional delegation waiting in his office. In view of Operation Juggle-Juggle, it might be a good idea to try out a little Farlandish exhortation right now.

But, with his hand on the tall window that opened into his oval office, he looked back at Andy. She was still standing there, tall and beautiful; all that unseemly joy she caused would certainly spill over if he wasn't careful. He went in quickly, dismissing her successfully with the wry hope that she wouldn't be too damned late to the ladies' thing.

Forty

"Since June has successfully busted out all over," Gil Kimball notified a nation's breakfasters, "I've decided to bust out along with it this time. Ordinarily, like lobbyists and the proprietors of restaurants near Capitol Hill, I'm tied to the comings and goings of Congress; not until the weather goes from balmy to sultry—a switch that usually occurs overnight—and adjournment talk begins does our hope of freedom begin to stir. Eventually, Washington gets hot enough so that no solon can resist the impulse to mass exodus from this tropical capital, and everything that must be voted on by the turn of the fiscal year gets voted on, however hastily or imprudently. After which, the legislators and the types like me are free to join the proprietors of Georgetown handmade-jewelry shops, and other members of the inherited-wealth set, in some more bearable locale.

"I don't think I'll wait, this year. Because, for one thing, I don't think the place for an observer of the nation's affairs is Washington, this time. With the White House and the Capitol at something very close to a Mexican stand-off, what's important is happening elsewhere, in those faraway places where they celebrate the summer solstice with exotic rituals like burning Negro churches—which anybody can plainly see is lots jazzier than marking the season with an adjournment resolution. I looked it up and I find that I've probably paid for most of Mississippi with my taxes over the years, as well as for a substantial slice of Louisiana and a good-sized hunk of Alabama; they can hardly turn me away when I own part of the place, can they? So, if you'll excuse me for a while, I'm hopping a bus to where the action is. It'll take me a week or so to study the native customs, but I'll write when I get words."

Marian Farland had been a relatively restrained participant in a seasonal ritual that morning when her two sons—or, more precisely as she thought of them, her son and her baby—marched off with the ranks of entraining campers at Union Station. Though everybody, including Dick, forgot it, Will Farland had been seeing Dick off for camp for a couple of years before Marian entered the picture; it may have been for this reason that he was better able to preserve his composure. However, unlike the other fathers in the informal assembly, most of whom settled for leading their weepy wives away dutifully and with an air of embarrassment, Will embraced his with a warmth just this side of ardor and murmured elaborate comforts featuring the word "baby," though not in reference to Peter. Marian extricated herself almost at once and carried her crumpled handkerchief, and a reinforced conviction that there wasn't anything Will wouldn't try to manipulate, back to her office in time for an editorial meeting.

She sat as if she were chained to her chair, believing she was listening, and in a sense she was—if anybody had quizzed her, she probably could have remembered that the *Tribune*'s veteran Senate reporter didn't believe Kenneth Youngblood's upcoming trip to Europe, which the Senator laughingly termed a "jaunt," was really that. She also heard, in a sense, the rueful discussion of the non-news emerging from the last White House state dinner, at which the notoriously rude and hostile senior Senator from Iowa appeared to have dined and otherwise socialized quietly with representatives of a nation he hated noisily every day on the Hill. Marian, who had been at the dinner, was not the only conferee at the meeting who recognized that the victory had been largely Andy Girard's. The young First Lady was both painstaking and intelligent, and she knew how to handle her staff with imagination and firmness; with efficiency and organization behind her, she came down the carpeted stairs on her husband's arm, beautiful and dignified, and her dinner conversation with the visiting Premier seemed to have nothing behind it but a desire to be pleasing.

Marian said nothing while this performance was analyzed, occasionally with a little bitterness, by those who would have found it easier to have a ruckus to write about. But she was remembering too clearly for comfort her own sickening though almost impersonal regret that night, for herself and Will and the cold emptiness into which they had somehow managed to stumble; the knowledge, or maybe the re-knowledge, had struck her while she waited for Will and Jim McGrath to be finished chuckling over a particularly subtle maneuver Jake Ruffing had apparently pulled off in the international version of domestic politics' smoke-filled room. Listening without either understanding or caring—then, and later again, when Will went on crowing to her—Marian had realized how truly hopeless it was. Alec Girard operated very much as Will did, but he could turn off his public life; if Will could ever stop operating, all the rest of it could be borne, maybe. But he couldn't or wouldn't, and Marian told herself it didn't really matter any more which.

She woke to her surroundings when somebody jeered, "Hear, hear."

"The Girard charisma is dangerous to a free press," the managing editor was saying dryly. "Have they now captured my free-thinking White House man? Do I have to rotate everybody to keep my staff pure?"

"I'm not captured," the correspondent replied seriously. "But I am fascinated, I admit. Dammit, fellows, I've never seen a President happening before, right in front of my eyes. I covered Winkler, but he never happened."

"That's the gospel according to Youngblood," said the ME, nodding. "Before the campaign started, I think he looked at Girard like a West Pointer at a ninety-day wonder. But he holds with the theory that the White House makes Presidents."

"I have a hard time understanding Girard." Martin Halloran had covered the White House through the tenure of more Presidents than anyone in the room; he had been a reporter longer ago, even, than the ME. When he spoke, everyone listened. "I can't make up my mind whether he's a political science major studying the book, or a genius rewriting it."

"Well, why don't you go up and do a little sniffing around?" the ME suggested. "At least until Congress adjourns—if it ever does." His glance swept the slouching figures of the others as he rapped an invisible gavel. "And now to culture." He fixed them with a stern glance that held amusement anyhow. "And nobody may be excused."

Marian, unexcused, nevertheless listened with little attention; she did agree, though, to pitch in and help the music critic, who expected to be swamped with outdoor opera performances, by reviewing *La Bohème* for him next month. It occurred to her that working was the only thing she felt good about any more. And then it occurred to her to wonder whether she really knew where she would be next month, and the sound of the meeting sank below consciousness again. When she finally heard her name, she also heard that the ME was saying it for the second time; she apologized quickly.

What about this business, the ME asked patiently while his eyes inspected her with kindly concern, of the peace people who were using a statue by Morisot as a symbol? "Will he make any move to stop them, do you think? He's obviously no pacifist, considering his war record—so do you know how he feels about their use of him? Or whether, in any case, he'd try to stop them because of possible strain on the relationship with the Girards? This peace bunch is somewhat critical of his pal Alec."

"Well, of course, 'The Taken Town' is a powerful symbol for any peace group," Marian said. She folded her hands tightly, a little unnerved by the roomful of solid attention. "But Morisot is—unpolitical. And then there's, you know, when the thing is finished, they don't care about it any more—most artists, anyway. I don't think he'd pay any attention at all. Unless, of course, the Girards asked him to do something about it. And I just don't think they would."

"What had you planned to do about it?"

"Well, I went down and had a look at the photo the peace people have made for their brochure, and it stinks—it's dark and very poor, really. In addition to the fact that 'The Taken Town,' even more than some of his newer work, is meant to be seen three-dimensionally, so you lose half the point anyway in a photograph. So I was just going to say," continued Marian, who had not actually been going to say anything at all, "that I thought Morisot had valid grounds for objecting without regard to any political implications."

"Neat enough," the ME said. "But wouldn't it make sense to get some comment from him? If you can. And maybe from Andy Girard—I have a feeling she may be a little angry about this."

"I'll try."

The ME smiled. "In spite of the latest memo from upstairs squawking about the need for economy, I'll even authorize an overseas call."

"I—I don't believe Morisot can be reached by phone," Marian said, with some difficulty. "I'll have to write." She looked at them blindly. "He—lives in a rather remote village, in the south of France . . ."

"I know, I know," the book editor said dreamily. "I spent my life savings for a teeny visit, a couple of years ago. Rocky hills full of caves. Pools of clear water. Sighing winds. Peace. Imagine living around there, away from the tourists but not from what they came to see."

" *'Connais-tu le pays,'* " the music critic sang softly. He nodded at Marian. "Why don't you send her over to interview the guy, boss?" he suggested generously.

Even after she had been back in her own office for some time, Marian still couldn't get the aria out of her head; it lapped at her softly, its very gentleness more and more unmerciful because her answer to the question was no, she did not know that land. Nor would she come to know its ochres and umbers and its winds and the stone house among the trees, down the hilly path from the square box of his studio, where Paul wrestled with what she could respect. She would not be there when he succeeded in banging, wheedling, stroking, and wrenching animation from the inanimate—or, worse still, when he didn't succeed, when he could use the geisha-girl ministrations he allowed so sparingly. The red-bearded Alphonse, who lived gigantically and worked in miniature, would not be summoned to help with building a bigger house. It was too late, it was all too late. The sudden ringing of the phone was an extra, unnecessary knell.

Charles Grayson wanted to confirm that he would pick his daughter up in New York tomorrow, he said, his voice happy at the prospect; they would stay for a week with a friend at a New Jersey shore resort before heading west. Marian said yes, and then she said that was fine, and she said that sounded nice; all the time, she jotted dutiful notes so Sharlie would be sure to have the right clothes for everywhere her father was going to take her.

When she hung up, she sat there over her list of Sharlie's clothes while the unshed tears gathered and were pushed back, over and over again. Nobody can rescue me from the right, she said to herself, not knowing quite what she meant, but only that she was miserable. And incompetent. She looked at the list again and the prospect of dealing with Sharlie tonight filled her with dread. Not so much the arguments, but the gaiety, the energy. I can't make it, she told herself, I simply can't make it. She began to put her head down on her desk, but the phone rang again. It was later than she'd thought—Rosa had already arrived and was waiting for her downstairs. Marian thanked the guard and fled to the elevator, swiping at her face as she rode down in case any tears had escaped. She peered at herself in the shiny panel that held the floor buttons, and the face that looked out at her was familiar and blank.

"You got to stop what you doin to yourself," Rosa said heatedly, her voice echoing in the dimnesses of the "auditorium" the *Tribune* kept on its street floor for the use of community organizations. "The way you look, you either been cryin or you got a right to been. What's eatin at you like that?"

Marian bit her lip and looked around at the darkened murals, in which rather oily-looking figures disported themselves in civic activities. "I just have a feeling," she insisted. The blue-green eyes offered Rosa their full load of grief and misery. "You won't come back. It won't be the same again. I have a feeling."

"You had a feelin when you was pregnant with Peter. You knew you was goin to die," Rosa reminded her. She waited for a response, got none, and sighed because it was going to take more than this. "Listen, Marian, ain't nothin goin to be exactly the same, ever again. That's true. But I been your friend and I'm goin to stay your friend, and I want to help you. But nobody can right now—that's right, ain't it?"

"You don't say 'Miz Marian' any more," Marian said matter-of-factly.

"You didn't never want me to anyway."

"No, that's right, I didn't. You started it. But why did you stop? It's because of all the Negro-ing, isn't it?"

"I guess. I done brought that from the South, and I givin it back to them."

"You always were equal anyway, Rosa, and you knew it. Now, all of a sudden—"

"All of a sudden I wants to *look* equal." Rosa fanned herself with her newspaper and then laid it down on one of the folding chairs. "And talk equal, too. You know how hard I been tryin to remember the right way to talk."

"You see? You, too. They move in on us—I don't mean only the Negroes, the whole world—and make us live differently. We were happy when they let us alone."

"We were," Rosa agreed. "I remember our little house, when we had little children. But look, Marian, can't nothin stay that way. Negro or no Negro, the world move in. It starts out when the children big enough to go to school." She looked at the pouting face and sighed again. "Sharlie and Trixie, they was equal when they was little. But once they start to school, then Trixie wasn't equal no more. Not my fault, not yours—but they move in on us." She reached out for Marian's cold hand. "Honey," she went on in a pleading voice, "don't nothin stand still. You ain't Miz Marian no more, anyhow. Equal don't matter. But we got older, honey, we grew up. You ain't no more pretty girl comin down the stairs to go out on a date. We grown-up women now. We got daughters almost grown-up women, too." She smiled, her teeth very white in the coffee-colored face. "I got one figures she already grown up. And maybe she's right. Couple of years, I could have me a grand-baby."

"I'm glad Tina found a job in that settlement house, or whatever it is," Marian said, more cheerfully. "We did the right thing with her, Rosa."

"Looks like. We done right to ask for help, anyway. It'll do Tina a lot of good there, this summer. She learn things she need to work in any office—answerin telephones, workin them mimeo—" she stumbled over the word and Marian helped her "—mimeograph machines and all them—*those*—other office things. And besides, she get to see the people Bruce and her always talkin about, and that do a lot of good, too." Rosa tightened her lips. "That boy got a head full of brains, but he don't know nothin. He think you just give the Negro a chance and you got Negro bosses tomorrow."

"Well, why not?"

"Cause they ain't educated, they ain't used to bein in charge. Oh, we got some could do hard jobs; but not most."

"But they are being discriminated against."

"Sure, and we got to put a stop to that. But that don't mean I can go to work on this here newspaper. Even if nobody keep me out because of my color, I still got to know how." Rosa stopped and laughed richly in the gloom. "Equal rights ain't goin to make Ann Taswell out of Rosa Little."

Marian sank into one of the chairs and braced her knees against the one in front of it. From the folded newspaper beside her, Andrea Girard smiled gravely over the round head of her baby. The photograph, made by a world-famous photographer, was beautiful, and so was Andrea's serene pleasure, and so was the plump, cuddly baby. Marian pointed with her chin at the picture and said, "I wish we still had babies," in a voice that acknowledged Rosa's truths.

"Well, we ain't. But we still got Trixie . . . You remember you—"

"Yes, I'll keep an eye on her." Marian smiled. "But tactfully, so as not to offend Bettina."

"And don't you let Bruce—"

"And I won't let Bruce snub me, either."

"Okay. Now leave me give you the keys." Rosa fished in her large white plastic purse and Marian watched her, not listening while Rosa talked about packing for Sharlie and the other household hatches she had battened down before leaving the Cleveland Park house. For good, she's leaving for good, Marian's intuition went on asserting, and it kept her from listening to the words until an insistent question lanced through her trancelike withdrawal. "What?" she asked, startled.

"I say, the kennel called up. How come you puttin the dogs in?"

"Oh. Well, I—I don't want to be tied down. You know. I'd have to come home after work every night. And they'll be lonely all day . . ." Her voice trailed off under Rosa's even inspection. "I don't know yet exactly what I'm going to do," she said unhappily, answering the real question.

Rosa hesitated. "Where I be able to find you?" she asked finally, her voice heavy with meaning.

"I don't know. I just don't know." Marian put her hand to her head as though it ached fiercely.

"Maybe it's a mistake lettin Sharlie go."

"Oh Rosa, don't be ridiculous. Charles just called. He's so eager, and so is she, and they'll have a wonderful time."

"That's not what I mean. Marian?"

"What?"

"Don't you do nothin foolish, you hear?"

Marian's lips twisted. "I always try not to, Rosa. It may come as a surprise to you—and to some other people. But I really try not to do anything foolish."

Rosa said, apparently irrelevantly, "Listen, down South they set fire to a house this Negro couple was livin in. The firemen, they wouldn't come and the house burned down to the ground. Then the sheriff come and arrested the Negroes for arson. On their own house. They still in jail." Her voice was heavy with urgency. "I got to go, Marian. I got to do somethin. Long as them colored got no vote, they goin to have that same sheriff."

"Will you want to be a domestic, after this?" Marian asked baldly.

"That depend. If they doin all right without me by the time the summer's over, then sure. I keep house good, and I earns good money." Rosa smiled. "I don't care about this here status. Not when I got love and money."

"But if things don't change—"

"If they's somethin I got to do, I got to stay and do it," Rosa said simply. She looked at Marian. "Honey, I get you all fixed up, anyhow. You not worryin about that, is you?"

"No. But—you know. I'll miss you."

"Marian?"

"Yes?"

"It's none of my business, except you is—you always my business. So I figure to mix in."

"Rosa, you just said— Look, I have to do what I have to do, too."

"You be sure you have to do it, is all I mean." Rosa's glance was equally weighted with love and impatience. "Marian, you got to learn. When a man doin the best he know how, he got rights."

"Even if his best simply isn't good enough?"

"That's right. Even then. You change what you can and you lives with the rest." Rosa fumbled for words. "A wife ain't a judge. You always tryin to give the children their rights, and that's good. But it ain't all the rights they is, in a family."

"Rosa, I can't stand—"

"Yes, you can. You marry a man, you got to live with him. He got a right to every chance. You don't like what he do, you fight—but he still got a right to a wife."

"Rosa," Marian said desperately, "I'm afraid. He's not a good man."

"No. But he's not a bad man neither. Just a man."

Crawling between heaven and earth, Marian thought. She was a Hamlet, mooning around wondering whether to be or not to be, and all the time Rosa knew where the soliloquy went—the known is less to be feared than the unknown. "I'm going to think about it," she said quietly. "I really am."

Rosa fished in her purse and found a pencil. "Write me down where Ann lives," she instructed, tearing off a strip of margin of the newspaper. "Then I know how I can find you, don't matter where your thinkin end us up."

Marian wrote, not listening to the rest, which was about eating, and sleeping, and going to the doctor to get her blood tested; Rosa's firm belief that everything began and ended with the blood was, like the French preoccupation with the liver, a folk-fetish not entirely unconnected with truth. Handing over the address and taking the keys, Marian promised solemnly to look to her blood and wondered why she had really ordered the dogs sent to the kennel. They would have been happier at the Ruffings', and two more animals would hardly have bothered Bonnie. But then Marian would have to have a legitimate excuse—to be, officially and properly, going somewhere. The trouble with Rosa and me, she concluded, is that we can read each other's minds.

I can't stand this much longer, she thought with swift pain, looking at the round, earnest face of love and comfort that was going away from her, perhaps forever. And wisdom, too—Marian was the one who had been to college, had sat in Philosophy I and heard that life was a moving river; but Rosa was the one who had learned it. Marian broke into the stream of instruction and admonition at random: "Don't worry, Rosa. Please. I'll take care. Only—you do, too."

Rosa was gathering her purse and newspaper, sidling between the neat rows of empty civic chairs, her flowered skirt fluttering frivolously among the dull-brown ranks of virtue. "I be back," she said confidently, and Marian believed her. They paused in the doorway, blinking against the bright sunlight in the lobby. "You havin a hard time right now, honey," she went on. "But you hold on, hear?"

"It is hard," Marian said miserably.

Rosa smiled, her black eyes alight with affection and encouragement. "I know. But you be surprised—when you get it figured out, what's right to do, it get so simple. Real, real simple, Marian. It truly do."

Marian held out her hand, which was trembling a little, and Rosa shook it. And then they both leaned forward impulsively and Rosa kissed Marian's cheek; Marian held her tightly for a moment before letting her go and racing for the elevator, the discarded keys dangling from her cold hand.

Ann was remembering those dangling keys as she sat at the uncluttered desk in her bedroom early the next morning: the symbol had been clearer, in a way, than Marian's words when she'd collapsed in the chair beside her friend's office desk. About all she'd said, really, was, "I can't, I just can't"— and, though it was not certain what she couldn't, the fact that she couldn't could be read all over her, in the gray-looking skin and the droop of her shoulders and the heaviness of her walk as though even her beloved office moccasins now hurt her feet. I should've noticed before, Ann had told herself then—Marian choosing a white blouse with red polka dots to go with a skirt that had a definite, though muted, check pattern represented a crisis of departure from normality, if not actual illness. Untidiness was one thing, but for Marian not to care about line and color meant a lot, and that lot was sad.

Ann sighed and finished the last check of the batch that she had decided to write before leaving for work today; but she sat on in her robe, making no move to get dressed and issue out into the world, because she wasn't sure she was finished with her other intention, which was a half-formed one to write to Paul Morisot. Any noticing she'd been neglecting previously she'd made up for last night when she went home to dinner with Marian to "help with getting Sharlie off." Rosa had left singularly little to do about getting Sharlie off, except simply talk to her; sitting at the big table in the Farland kitchen—where they ate the dinner that Rosa had also left all ready—Ann had almost decided that talking to Sharlie must be what Marian couldn't. And then Will came in, stooping to kiss his wife's unproffered cheek before he announced that he'd already eaten and that he had to go jaunting down to Mississippi tomorrow. In Marian's eyes, invisible to Will but not to Ann across the table, a small light of relief had made it instantly clear that what Marian was afraid of was not Sharlie present, but Sharlie absent—the last member of the household to depart from Marian and leave her alone with Will.

Will accepted Ann's offer to get him a cup of coffee and sat down at the table. But not for long, he said. "I'm supposed to carry the word, and I'll have to figure out what the word is sometime before the plane leaves tomorrow. So I guess I'd better start tonight."

Reprieve, said Marian's eyes while her calm voice dispatched Sharlie upstairs to put out everything for her train case and await inspection.

"I'll take the inspection, Marian," Ann offered as she rejoined the Farlands at the table. "Tell you what, I'll even do the dishes, too. You look so beat— why don't you just kiss Sharlie good-night and call it a day. I'll warn her not to talk to strange men on the plane. I promise."

"You do look a bit droopy, darling," Will observed with mild surprise. "Why don't you grab the offer? I'll work in the study, and I promise not to disturb you."

"I'm not tired, thanks," Marian said weakly. "This time of year is mostly housekeeping for me at the office—odds and ends of notes and interviews, and a few leftover book reviews. I can pretty much skate till the summer art shows at Rehoboth."

Will lighted a cigarette and began by diagnosing Marian's droopiness for them as "empty-nest blues." It was the first year Peter had gone when the other kids did; Will said, smiling, he supposed it wasn't easy to hand over the last baby to little-boy status. "But he is, you know," he told his wife gently.

"I don't know." She was looking down at her coffee cup, turning it in her fingers. "He's still pretty little."

"Darling, don't let's make the mistake of sacrificing old Pete to his mother's nostalgia." Will smiled. "It's the wrong solution to the empty nest. The answer may well be a successor baby, rather than trying to keep Pete in diapers." He patted Marian's hand, which had stopped moving on the cup, and then put out his cigarette and sighed. Things would be nice and restful, he predicted, when he got back from the South; but he'd better get to work on arranging it now.

Ann asked him a few questions about his mission and watched with *aficionado* enjoyment as he answered the questions he wanted her to have asked instead. The kitchen light was bright on his hair, making it almost as yellow as Dick's, and in his easy lounging pose was some of that potential energy, that hint of controlled strength and leashed impulse that, in movie idols, is described as "animal magnetism." That he was a clever man was a tribute Ann paid him at once; he was also a handsome man, unquestionably. She glanced at the small, cowed-looking Marian who would be left to ponder alone for a few days in her characteristic self-accusing fashion the question of whether she was capable of being fair to Peter without Will's guidance, and who, given her age and temperament, could be assumed to entertain a sizable longing for just one more baby. . . . A clever man, a handsome man, and a cruel adversary, thought Ann, who could recognize a war of attrition when she saw one.

Being a war correspondent, the neutral observer watching others get hurt, is difficult at best—and if some of the participants are children, the observer's role can become close to unbearable. Certainly Ann's mission to Sharlie's room to check out the travel preparations turned out to be a severe test of Ann's neutrality. For Sharlie, though forever in motion and apparently talking about nothing all the time, had revealed almost at once a degree of awareness and a width of observation that all but undid her spinster "aunt."

"I know they're wearing clothes less fitted now," Sharlie said, brushing violently at her thick light-brown hair. "But Mother's really overdoing it, don't you think? That dress looks like she got it from the missionaries—and, the way it hangs on her these days, the missionary must've been a size 16." She went on to amplify to a silent Ann the flaws in her mother's couture, her quick voice seeming almost to delight in its own spite. But when she was looking into the mirror instead of at her hearer, the voice changed a little as she remarked that maybe it would be a vacation for Mom just to be left alone for a while. Then she swung away promptly from that much revealed tenderness and went on chattering, applying her sharp tongue to both her parents and both her brothers.

But when she had the last pink roller in place, she said quickly and in almost a mutter that there was a girl at school whose parents were getting divorced: the grimmest part, this girl said, was when they were winding up to it. So maybe Marian was getting off easy by just losing weight.

"Sharlie! Have you been thinking that—" Ann stopped. "You shouldn't let other people's experiences upset you," she finished stiffly, and hypocritically.

"Who's upset? Don't be naïve, Ann. Don't *you* know Mom and Dad are heading for a breakup?"

"Now how would I know a thing like that?"

"Oh, don't snow me," Sharlie said pleasantly enough. "Dick and I talked it over before he left. You know, he thought since I was experienced and all . . . Actually, though, I can't remember how it was when Mom left Daddy—I don't really remember much until we got Rosa, except feeling lonely before that." She took a leaf-green dress from the closet and hung it on the door, the better to appraise it. "But now there's three of us kids, so at least it won't be lonely."

"Sharlie, this is—silly," Ann said, instead of saying it was pathetic. Her throat ached with pity for this knowing young lady who was, at the same time, enough of a child to think it a certainty that she and Dick would be together if the Farlands were divorced. To say nothing of the question of Peter, Ann thought, and wondered sadly whether Marian's dress would look like size 16 if the three children of the household really constituted the firm and portable package Sharlie seemed to visualize. Ann cleared her throat. "Honey, lots of married people go through difficult periods at times. It's a mistake for—youngsters—to try to interpret things like that, because they haven't the experience to evaluate it properly. And you seem to forget that Marian and Will, even if you're right that they're having difficulties, have deep feelings for each other." She made a stab at an ingratiating smile. "That you may still be too young to understand."

"I'm older than you think. Time's been passing since you bounced me on your knee, Ann."

"Well, it's been passing for your mother, too."

"Meaning she's not going to walk out on Will the way she did my father? I don't know." Sharlie hesitated, then dared, "You don't think she'd go back to Daddy, do you? It was Dick's idea," she added hastily. "He asked me how he'd like Daddy. I told him I thought they'd get along swell. Don't you think so?"

Ann suppressed an impulse to shake her head and see whether the buzz would go away. "Charlie's a fine man," she began; but it was impossible—Sharlie seemed to think people just went about airily swapping fathers, and it was too much for Ann. She said so, stringently, and Sharlie got out the shoes that matched the green dress and answered that nothing was unimaginable if they were talking about her mother. Whereupon Ann upbraided her for her "constant" criticism of Marian and was rewarded by another revelation of the curious mental processes of Sharlie Grayson.

For it seemed that Ann talked just like Rosa, who was tiresomely and persistently the "Number One Marian fan"—and what further emerged from underneath this petulance was that Sharlie, though obviously proud of Rosa's southern mission, was far less obviously very much afraid for Rosa's safety. Relieved at encountering a problem she could handle, Ann answered gently and to the point that Rosa would be all right; she was sensible, rather than dramatic—an outlook, Ann added less gently, that Sharlie would do well to consider for herself.

"I'm glad," the girl said, smiling. "I didn't want to say anything to Mom, because I didn't want to put ideas in her head." And then, while Ann was still reeling under the presumption bespoken by this casually maternal concern for one's mother, accompanied by a faint implication that the mother-baby in question was not quite bright, Sharlie added, in a matter-of-fact tone that held incredible tenderness, "She's got too much on her mind now."

Ann got up from her seat on the bed and stood uncertainly, impelled to flight and too conscientious for it. Sharlie promptly appropriated the vacated space for her manicuring materials. "Don't tell Mom I'm doing this on the bedspread, huh?"

Ann opened her mouth to catch the fortunate opportunity, not too frequent in this conversation, to say something practical, sensible, and appropriate to their relative ages; but she'd taken too long to draw breath. "I'm not really worried," Sharlie said pleasantly to the splayed-out fingers of her left hand. "Mom's always done all right by us, if you know what I mean. So I'm with her, I guess." She dipped the brush, trimmed its load against the inner edge of the tiny bottle, and began to paint one fingernail the demure *jeune fille* pink her mother had ruled acceptable. "I hope she makes up her mind this summer, though."

"Sharlie, you really don't know—"

"All right, Auntie Annie." Marian's beautiful child raised her head from her labors. "It's just that I like to know where I'll be going to school, and right now, I'm sort of hung up, you see. But not to fuss—old Mom will muddle through."

Now Auntie Annie looked at her chaste little bedroom clock, discovered with gratitude that it was time to get dressed for work, and decided not to fuss, not to intervene, not to not intervene, and for the moment at least not to write any overseas letters. It was all too bad, but if Marian could manage to keep her marriage in at least some form of operation, it would surely be better all around. (*Would it?* the dark eyes of Paul Morisot asked her then.)

The ME, who had overridden Miss Taswell's protests and dispatched her to report on the Negro society, had been wise enough to know a talent for observing societies when he saw one. Ann the observer of societies proved him right as, lingering at her desk now, she took a second look at the banner that had flown last night over Sharlie's encampment in the embattled plains of Mackintosh Place and read its strange device: *I know more than you think. I know how everything is.* And under it the wide eyes hurting with youth, before which Auntie Annie had quailed, asked the silent corollary, *It isn't really that way, is it?*

Well, sweetie, it is and it isn't, Ann began to explain then, with her pen that was mightier than her tongue. For certainly it was Marian the maternal baby, impulsively distributing abundant tenderness and then, equally without thought, demanding rescue; but it was also true that out of the hubbub of living she created by diving into complexities with nothing going for her but a belief in magic had come, among other things, this Sharlie. Of whom Ann wrote now, slowly and carefully, all she knew for sure so far: "The children of charming children are loyal, loving, and frightened."

But then she put the pen down and rose to array herself to face today, and to consider meanwhile a society in torment: Marian the beautiful, gifted, generous, and trusting—and not tough enough to keep her compassion from being exploited and her innocence from being manipulated. Unless she could learn to compromise and bargain and plan, to cope with the unlovelinesses in order to keep the lovely, she would be lost in spite of all the patriots who would give so much to save her. Gone from among them like those thousands of miles of forests and streams, the spacious skies and fruited plains. . .

But Sharlie—ah, there was another matter. If her airy eclecticism in the matter of fathers had shocked Auntie Annie, maybe that was the price of Auntie's failure to observe what had been happening. For Sharlie's first model had been Marian, who gave love totally; but after that, Sharlie had been learning from her part-time fathers—grace in defeat from Charles Grayson, determination from Will Farland. And then, living off the landscape, she'd gone on to pick up what was around among all the hovering protectors of Marian—which included such oddments as Rosa's sturdiness and Ann's ambition. So if Marian had reproduced herself, all right, in the pretty girl perhaps too quick to pack her bags and set sail, something else had been added. And it might be the necessary toughness, Ann thought. It just could be.

She patted the shining coils of her hair into their ordered loop at the nape of her neck, cast a farewell glance at her neat and silent home, and closed the door behind her. But then she loitered, contemplating absently the little round peephole in the apartment door provided to guard the already-too-safe Miss Taswell against the world, and thinking about that world that might have grown, by now, too big and selfish for those who couldn't play it safe; the tender and defenseless Marian perhaps was best ceded to the foreign ruler who could build a walled castle to keep her in. But—though the impact of shrewd, fluffy Charlotte Grayson on her contemporaries in an ancient village in the south of France was rich in possibilities any observer of societies might find delightful—Ann found herself refusing the image as she emerged into the already hot Washington street. Because it was a hard world a-coming, harder than it had ever been. And this land, she thought passionately, mustn't lose its carping yet adoring, discerning yet credulous Sharlies.

Forty-one

Even the most perceptive observer must first be at the place where something is happening. Ann Taswell's talents were being turned on another aspect of Washington's society on the late-June morning when Andrea Girard came down the steps of the White House's north entrance under the famous hanging lantern. She paused, not minding the tourists peering between the black iron uprights of the fence, not minding that it was clearly going to be hot, and not even minding that she was off to a congregation of ladies, which didn't represent her favorite form of recreation. But what needed a chronicler was that it was not only a beautiful day for Andy but also a unique one, a beginning and an ending—it was, among other things, the day Andrea Girard finally finished becoming a politician's wife and found it fun to be one. It was also a day after which nothing was ever going to be quite the same.

Andy peered through the glass as the car wound slowly down the curved drive and paused at the little white sentry house; she even raised a white-gloved hand in greeting to the people clustered on the sidewalk. Then, on impulse, she leaned forward to ask that she be driven through Georgetown, past her old house on O Street. It was not, strictly speaking, on the way to the old mansion that had been turned into the international students' hostel, where she was to preside at a luncheon. But she had time and she was feeling good, and she wanted, now that she could do it without any undue wistfulness, to look out over the part of the city that was part of her past.

It was easy not to repine, now that the future looked a little brighter. Elizabeth, who had never seemed to get quite well while at the same time not getting any sicker, had at last begun to respond, it appeared, to the latest of a series of medications designed to bring the roses back into her cheeks. Consulting Marian Farland and Bonnie Ruffing, as mothers consult more experienced mothers—only Andy Girard did it in quick corner tête-à-têtes at a state dinner instead of over the back fence on a suburban morning—she'd learned that this sort of thing just happened; kids' responses to medicines were unpredictable, and each time you experimented it took a week or more to find out whether you had it. Elizabeth Girard enjoyed the services of an excellent and well-qualified pediatrician—who had said exactly the same thing, and who had even added, exactly as Marian and Bonnie had, that these flu-ey things left people washed out. But, as pediatricians know and honest mothers admit, only this combination of judgments will quiet the trepidations of a mother who has only four years' experience.

So, though Washington, lazy and emptying for the summer, was certainly not Kingsley Lake, Vermont, it had definite attractions today for a young woman who had been worried and pent-up in her house, even if her house was a very large one. And as the Washington heat increased, the metaphorical but just as uncomfortable heat on Alexander Girard decreased and would come almost to a total stop when Congress adjourned. Whereupon Andy's blessings would include a husband who now had more time than he used to and soon would have more still—in addition to a four-year-old who would soon be frolicking again and a ridiculously cuddly and adventurous brown-eyed baby given to a variety of differentiated gurgles that might or might not be words. Andy had had her doubts yesterday that "kaa" was really intended to communicate the arrival of a limousine headed for the west wing and visible from Sandy's playpen on the lawn; but, in view of Alec's insistence, she had kept them to herself.

The car passed the food market on Wisconsin Avenue where Andrea Girard and Betty Kimball had done their shopping together, two housewives in slacks and sweaters accompanied by Elizabeth alternately riding in and perilously pushing a stroller. Looking out at the bumpy cobblestoned side-walk, Andy thought happily that Alec was "catching on" to fatherhood rather earlier this time, either because he was now experienced or, possibly, because there was something startlingly masculine about the baby, young as he was. Perhaps Senator Girard hadn't known quite what to make of a little girl at the beginning, even when he'd had the time to play with Eliza-beth in the garden of the house on O Street. They were coming to it now, passing the incredibly huge old elm that split the sidewalk and left an indentation that always filled with water and iced over in winter. There, there it was—Andy had nearly had a fall there, the winter she was pregnant with Elizabeth. That same morning she'd been successfully tempted by a small French table, unbelievably curly and fragile, in an antique shop; all the way home she'd been busy inventing elaborate rationalizations to offer Alec, who would nevertheless see that she didn't need the table.

The car slowed in front of the house, with its entrance abrupt on the street, and Andy looked at it like a tourist and thought how happy they had been there—and then, as she scanned the street for a sight of the neighbors, she thought with characteristic honesty that they had also been unhappy there. Particularly Andy, though Alec too had been distressed by their private, incessant tug of war, in which she called perpetually, "Look at me!" while he was looking toward the White House. In that house, too, she had wrestled with the dreads she now knew to have been unrealistic—the White House wasn't so bad to live in, once you got used to that hotelish arrange-ment of the rooms on the second floor, and she had been successful in keep-ing the family quarters safe from invasion. The foolish young wife who had sat and wrung her hands in the house on O Street had been too quick to predict dismays. And arrogant, too, in her assumption that a great unbridge-able chasm existed between her and Alec.

The front windows still had white curtains, Andy noted in her brief in-spection as they drove by. The car wound carefully between the old houses that were like a little French town, and she smiled as she recalled her ponderings about trying to join the politicians—which had kept her too busy to notice that the politicians were joining her all the while. Alec, the best politician in the world, had managed to keep all his promises: he had the Presidency and the baby too, by gosh, just as he'd said he would—even if he'd had to drag a rather difficult wife at least part of the way. And, more than ever, he had Andy, Andy thought.

Refreshed by her brief *recherche du temps perdu,* the First Lady was in high spirits as she stepped from the car before the hostel to be greeted by the Vice-President's wife and then by the Indian girl who was president of the foreign students; Andy paused to speak briefly to the *Tribune*'s Irene Tully and then distributed friendly smiles to familiar faces among the other reporters. She was cooperative with the photographers, posing with a cheerful patience a little like a dog-walker whose progress is interrupted at every tree.

At last, then, she was released and escaped indoors. It was a genuine pleasure to see Lou Cannon, who was a comfortable woman—not beautiful but better-looking than her pictures—with bright, intelligent eyes. But the Indian student looked so sad—as they all seemed to, Andrea thought. She wanted, idiotically, to break into a jig, just to startle and lighten that tragic face. It probably wouldn't work, anyhow, she told herself, and confided to Lou Cannon that yes, she would adore a little wine.

Established with a glass of something pale and dry and light, Andy held court dutifully, listening to the high insistent buzz that always seemed to hang over groups of women. It was better than it had ever been, she knew, looking over the crowd with actual liking for most of them and patience with those she couldn't quite like. The rather pushy little Foreign Service wife, for example—an extraordinarily pretty blonde with a cover girl face and showgirl legs who gave off a disturbing air of tension. The blondness, though once natural, was now augumented; the elegance was too painfully achieved; the air of youth was too intensely dedicated and preserved. Once, Andy knew, the visible strain in the mascaraed eyes would have caused her uneasiness, made her turn away from the woman's too-eager striving for her attention; now she rewarded it with a bright smile, hoping with pity that it would help.

I wasn't a postdeb, she had protested, not really playfully, to Alec at Elizabeth's tea party—but the truth is, she told herself now, I was. Only I'm not, any more. "You don't know how rough it is," Marian Farland had said once when Andy had complained of these tiresome women's things. "No wonder they chatter at you—they've staked a hell of a lot on the encounter." Andrea Girard, who had never in all her life had to live in a situation where her coming or going presented financial problems and who had never had to wonder whether she could get a baby-sitter, had listened with interest and openhearted imagination while an idle conversation became a lesson in life in another world.

"Yes, I'm sure it must be really beautiful at this time of year," Andy said dutifully to the wife of the senior Senator from Iowa; anybody married to that despicable man merited anyone else's immediate compassion, and she gave it freely to his overtalkative, middle-aged wife. But her eyes stayed on the Foreign Service blonde, now being helpful with passing things. It was hard enough to get sitters in the middle of the day, Marian had pointed out, and then you had to get all togged out and drive into town and somehow find a place to park; and when it was over, you had to rush back to the suburbs, stopping on the way to pick up things that had to be picked up today or else, and then climb quickly out of glad rags and scramble up a dinner in a hurry because this kid had to be fed in time for a Scout meeting and that one had to go to the library to work on a school report. "That's if things come out all right," Marian had finished darkly. "If the sitter shows up on time, if the hem doesn't come out of the only dress you can possibly wear, if the washing machine doesn't suddenly break down and flood the basement." Andy smiled with extra radiance at the little blonde because the poor woman was probably having to pay for a sitter out of her household budget, just to be here.

Mrs. Iowa took the smile for encouragement and expanded a thesis that, Andy saw, scanning the group's tight smiles from under her eyelashes, must have been being developed for quite a while. "When the people of this country lived in small towns, they knew how to be neighborly. It's these people from big cities where they ignore the family in the next apartment—"

"Well, now, I don't know," Lou Cannon interrupted. "There's a fellow on my husband's staff comes from New York, and he's always telling wonderful stories about the neighbors he knew when he was a boy." Her eyes on the other woman were amiable and innocent. "Fact, he brought one of his old neighbors in to Tom the other day, to introduce him. Seems our man and this other boy had their bar mitzvahs together." Lou Cannon wrinkled her brow in an elaborate portrait of a struggle with memory, holding them deliberately, in the knowledge that nobody but Andy could interrupt. "Can't think of the feller's name now—Something-berg."

Mrs. Iowa laughed. "Oh, those names. They're impossible."

Andy caught a glimpse of Peggy McGrath's expression and thought that Lou Cannon had just picked up at least one vote for Tom, anyway. She wondered whether the redhaired Peggy, whose helpful presence at the most recent White House state dinner had been noted by the White House's efficient chatelaine, had had a hard time learning not to answer impulsively when wives of Foreign Relations Committee members spoke; the notion came to Andy, swiftly and a little humblingly, that Alec Girard's wife might not have been the only one to have a few struggles with the problems of the public life. "Not really impossible," she said quietly. "My grandmother's foreign name caused a certain amount of difficulty. But it doesn't last long."

"Oh well," said Mrs. Iowa. "That was *French*."

Andy's lips quirked. Almost the last time she and Alec had seen Paul with just the three of them alone together, he had been deploring with tongue in cheek the loss in the French international image. Difficulties arose from being associated in the American mind with Charles Boyer, Paul had said sadly, but Andy could have no idea how much easier that was than to be associated with Charles de Gaulle. "You can bet *I* have an idea," Alec had announced while Andy was saying loyally that Paul was far better-looking than either Charles.

She swallowed laughter now and found that the women were discussing difficult names still, and, out of an obscure desire to oppose Mrs. Iowa, she contributed an anecdote of the problems of being a Miss Langwith. "I was amazed by the variations people managed," she finished.

"There's some people," Lou Cannon said, without bothering even to sound polite, "have trouble with anything that isn't 'Perkins.' "

Peggy McGrath's expression was so like a child watching another child do something naughty that Andy bent her head and buttered her roll devoutly until she was sure she wouldn't laugh. But she almost did anyway. For the lady from Iowa was incredibly thick-skinned, so much so that she managed to find encouragement in that remark to launch on a description of her own genealogy—she was, as bad luck would have it, actually a descendant of some Perkinses—with every appearance of conviction that all the assemblage would be entranced. The Vice-President's wife muttered, "Can't dam a river at flood time, that's all," and Andy's indoor pallor turned quite pink with suppressed laughter. The somewhat faded flower of Iowa, her long beads swinging dangerously above her salad, pointed her sharp nose at them and went on defining for them the good, the true, and the beautiful. The beautiful, one gathered, was largely the province of foreigners and Jews—the former an obviously unreliable crew, the latter of course brilliant but erratic (and tolerated, because some Jews voted in Iowa). Andy went on eating the carefully international food, avoiding the temptation to count the flying stereotypes on her fingers, and contemplating in silence the ushering of art beyond the American Protestant pale.

"Hold on, honey," Irene Tully murmured to the unhearing Andy from the other end of the room. "You mustn't laugh in her face."

"It isn't easy to hold on," said a colleague from a women's magazine. "Besides, Andy came in looking like she'd like to laugh."

"She did look happy," Irene agreed. "Nice. Awfully pretty gal, our Andy."

"Sure. But, with all that dough, who wouldn't be?"

Irene looked at the simple lime-green dress, the minimal hat almost invisible atop the First Lady's thick dark hair, and, though she had a swift doubt about the beautifully fitted pumps she'd noticed, she said stoutly, "She isn't wearing a thing you couldn't buy for fifty bucks."

"Really?"

"Really. Right here in Washington, too."

"Well, you may be right. How about that pin, though?"

"Costume jewelry," Irene said. "Poor Andy—the minute she puts anything on, people start thinking in the thousands. That pin came from Georgetown or Alexandria, and I could afford five of them without even going to the bank."

"Well, you may be right," the correspondent said again. "I'm going to ask her about it later, though."

I hope it's made of the bones of Iowans or something exciting, Irene thought gloomily, because there isn't one damn thing to say about this otherwise. Andy Girard looked beautiful, ate neatly, smiled at people, wore a simple this and a tasteful that. Irene's gaze caught Andy's slim hand with its lovely emerald and she grinned: that was more than fifty bucks, all right. But what the hell, everybody had expensive engagement rings, didn't they? That still didn't make her any different from Mrs. America.

But she was, she most definitely was. Irene thought about it, frowning as she sucked in on a cigarette. Andy was prettier, gayer, better dressed, more imaginative than any other woman in that room—and, though not known to be given to heavy social thinking, probably brighter than most, too. So why not say so? Yet, if you did, you sounded like her press agent—the ME had complained of that, and he was right. Irene crumbled tobacco shards unhappily, trying to beat the problem of how to make this nice woman sound less enameled, while Mrs. Iowa went on and on, almost compulsively, touting up the virtues of the bucolic life with a concentrated, murderous sweetness of voice and manner that inevitably drew attention to the ugly xenophobia lurking in her words.

Such an utter conviction of one's own rectitude is terrifying, Andrea Girard was thinking as she stood, a little later, greeting the foreign students. Like any kind of nuttiness, I suppose—what's frightening about it is that it's an extension of the normal. She spoke slowly to a Pakistani, carefully choosing the kind of formal words foreigners find in English dictionaries. With relief, she addressed a girl from Panama in her useful but not ornamental Spanish and then spoke at a little more length in her fluent French to the next student. The Japanese girl, in a costume Andy suspected she hardly ever wore—the obi looked too tight, as though she'd put on weight during her stay here—said, "It is most honored of me, Madame," and Andrea smiled and said, "I am most grateful that I could come," in unconscious echo of the other's cadences. She posed again, this time in front of the fireplace, which held a large jug of fresh green leaves, with the Indian girl, watching her thoughtfully and wondering how it would be if some of Mrs. Iowa's excessive self-esteem could somehow be grafted onto this overly humble youngster.

It had been a mistake to agree to a final cup of coffee in the drawing room, Andrea saw as Mrs. Iowa plopped onto the sofa beside her with a soft sigh from the down-filled pillows. She arched an eyebrow at Lou Cannon, who shrugged sympathetically, if barely visibly. The senator's wife began on her discourse again, and Andy made the best of it, saying, "I do so admire the women like your grandmother, traveling all that distance in those wagons, all that hardship." She whiled away the next chunk of the peroration by thinking about Alec's grandmother, who had stayed right there in the cold and stony east, helping her husband to wrest a living from that forbidding rock and the New England winter. She's going to say something about "good stock," Andy thought suddenly, a split second before Mrs. Iowa said, "Well, of course, you expect people who know how to behave when you have that good stock." Andy smiled radiantly, in open enchantment with herself, and the woman, believing herself encouraged, went on to point out that there was no substitute for breeding, her voice nudging Andy with a "you and I know, don't we?" intimacy.

The trouble we find ourselves in the world today, Andy guessed, with increasing confidence, a little later, and was filled with gaiety when her increasingly cozy companion said, "The trouble with the world today is that that good stock that was the backbone of our country has been . . ." Andy gave herself five more points and meditated on her next guess while she turned an apparently attentive face to the subsequent deploring of the harm done America by the melting pot.

Untrammeled by seating arrangements now, the Foreign Service wives circulated, though judiciously, never getting too far from the slim, green-clad woman who, one would have thought, was expected somehow to persuade her husband to promote their husbands because the latter had pleasant wives. The ladies of the press—distinguished by their silence and their indifference to the charmed area, which they could enter later—murmured softly but dangerously of their mutual despair. "Why does she encourage it?" Irene Tully asked Peggy McGrath, who could afford to let the others make impressions now while she loitered with the press.

"She isn't, really," Peggy argued. "She's just being nice. Besides, I'm pretty sure she's thinking of something else. And whatever it is, she's enjoying it."

"Maybe her husband. If I owned a man like Alec Girard, damned if I'd think of much else. No wonder she keeps smiling." Irene eyed the colloquy grimly. "Trouble is, our Andy has absolutely fascinated that Gorgon."

"Well, I don't imagine many people listen to the senator's wife so long, or so politely."

"Not unless they're afraid of her husband."

"*Touché*," Peggy said equably. "Maybe Andy's had orders to be peaceable, at that."

"I doubt it. But even if she has, she's overdoing it. All that charm is acting on that old bag like booze on an alcoholic—she'll never stop till she falls over dead."

"Maybe not. Look." Peggy turned away, her bright face interested. "I think Andy started listening. Look at her hands."

The distress that was darkening Andrea Girard's utterly bright day showed in her hands, still lying in her lap, but clenched now. She had been doing well, she told herself, with what she called, to herself, her "privacy sickness" —and she'd been feeling good about it, too. It wasn't so bad, after all, being a politician's wife, and rubbing shoulders with the public wasn't necessarily the impossible ordeal Elizabeth Langwith had always believed it to be. And further, though there were certainly implications of that intrusion into their bedroom—the suggestion that Andy was going to whisper promotion suggestions into Alec's ear, perhaps while cuddled on his lap—it was all, now, somehow funny and maybe even a little endearing. That unhappy interlude during which she had fled Alec had borne fruits in her greater ease now with these crowds of subtly urgent women.

But this, Andy decided, listening with increasing dismay to this horrid woman's disgusting and insistent you-and-I-are-bluebloods chatter—this was too much, was not in the bargain. And even if it was, she decided suddenly, she had had enough. I'll fight it out with Alec if necessary, she told herself firmly, but I'm going to put a stop to this no matter what her husband does to him. She waited, her hands tight, through the next genealogical fatuity, and then said, clearly but casually, "The trouble with genealogy is that it's so unreliable."

How sensitive they were, she observed then; the waiting sudden silence in the room was almost visible. In the glass of a handsome French highboy, Peggy McGrath's reflection flitted toward the central group like a ghost arriving at a séance. Mrs. Iowa was only slightly taken aback—she protested earnestly that not at all, really, Mrs. Girard, there were quite reliable sources, and with some research you could trace your ancestors a very long way back. She herself had found in a little town some records establishing that her great-grandfather, who was a Harrison—

"Oh, great-grandfathers," Andy said airily. "That's what I mean. After all," she added, smiling sweetly at the faintly buzzing queen of the WASPs, "we have only our great-grandmothers' word for the identity of our great-grandfathers, haven't we?"

Among the noticeable gasps was a small, squelched giggle: Peggy McGrath might just as well have shouted, "Go it, old girl." Andy nodded serenely, thinking that Jim McGrath had possibilities that should be drawn to Alec's attention, and turned to watch the slowly purpling complexion of the wife of the senior Senator from Iowa. It was interesting, she decided heartlessly, and smiled around the circle in genuine friendliness as she rose to make her way to the leafy summer outdoors. I'm a wicked, wicked girl, said Elizabeth Langwith's daughter behind her gracious departing speech; and, Alec Girard's wife added with quite restored gaiety, I really don't care. It may even be immoral, but I don't care.

"It may be immoral," Gil said, "and it's certainly unethical. To say nothing of inimical to my whole way of life. Jesus, Jake, I've made a career and maybe a religion of bearing witness to what I see, and I don't mean by that just telling one man over the telephone. I was up thinking about this half the night last night—"

"I appreciate that you're very much in earnest." Ruffing changed the phone to his other hand so he could watch from the window as a pair of bluejays took turns dive-bombing the family cat on the lawn below.

Gil laughed without amusement. "This is my own precious long-distance nickel, so 'in earnest' doesn't even begin to cover it. But I came to the reluctant conclusion that, this close to the boiling point, maybe doing the eye-witness-report bit can be irresponsible. And that maybe I could be effective without being irresponsible if, this once, I told a very small audience how it actually is." He cleared his throat. "Listen, it's awful, just awful. If I could make you see even a little of it, maybe something could get done about it."

"Gil, I know it's distressing. But so is a national police force, if you'll just stop to think about it a minute. Do you really want him to set a terrifying precedent like that if it can possibly be avoided? I know you're upset, but you've got to realize he can't go off half-cocked. The whole structure of law—"

"Jesus Christ, can't you understand? It's the law that's acting illegally. Sure a national police force isn't such a hot idea, but law that's against the citizen is a much worse one."

The victorious bluejays strutted across Jake's field of view as he craned for a sight of the cat slinking away. "I grant you the voters down there seem to have some odd tastes in sheriffs, but you can't let an individual mishap determine sweeping policy. Now you're aware of the problems that could arise if he simply acted on impulse—"

"Listen, Jake, will you just listen? I know it's a Washington summer day up there, with chores to do and people wondering whether Congress'll get around to their appropriations bills before the end of the fiscal year. But down here, it's another world."

"He's aware of that. Why do you think we sent Farland and Rosenberg to look it over? Farland's due back today to report on what he found. We're able to get the picture, too, you know."

"Then here's a picture for your collection. For free, from me. Last night there was a voter registration rally in a small Baptist church here. Forty people, not counting me and a reporter. There were three youngsters from this bunch that's going around explaining how to register—one white boy, one Negro boy, and a white girl. The preacher was giving the invocation when the door banged open and the sheriff and three deputies came in, and the sheriff barged straight down the aisle and right up to the altar. He told the preacher that was enough now, said it was—and I'm quoting, Jake—'time for you niggers to get your tails on home.' At that point, the preacher introduced me and the other press guy, and I think the sheriff was a little upset that we were there. Anyway, he started talking to me, but soft sell, I mean—stuff about how it was only the outside agitators, how their own Nigras were perfectly happy, all that kind of thing. But the soft-sell message hadn't got to his deputies. They were walking up and down the aisles, pointedly writing down the names of all the local people and making remarks that were at best offensive and at worst downright filthy. One of them turned to a local Negro and pointed at the white boy and said, 'He won't be here two weeks from now, but you will, and so will I. You know what I mean?'" Gil shouted into the phone, overriding a small sound from the other end. "No, Jake—I am *quoting*. And I am quoting an officer of the law. I tell you that's what the man said, and he was wearing a gun—and besides, he had this big flashlight and he was swinging it all the time, smacking it against the palm of his other hand. And kind of *smiling*—I was *there*, Jake, I saw it."

"What happened, Gil?" Ruffing asked resignedly. "Did anybody get hurt?"

"Well, I think reporters being there finally got to them. The thing is, after the sheriff and these guys went through the audience making these threats they went outside. We could hear cars coming up and lots of maneuvering going on out there, and I think what happened is the sheriff got them quieted down because of the press but he couldn't get them to go away. Anyway, inside they finished their meeting and sang hymns, and then they filed out—with the deputies standing in the doorway, flashing a light on each face. I heard one officer say to a Negro, 'I'm going to get you, and don't you forget it.' I *heard* this, and I'll swear to it under oath."

"But he didn't get him."

"No. Not right then, anyway. There were whites all around outside, but all they did was curse the people and shout some obscenities at the white girl. The only overt trouble was that the car the girl had come in had a tire slashed. The boy with her was a twenty-one-year-old college student from Pennsylvania. He changed the tire—with these white men jeering at him all the time, for God's sake. The reporter and I stuck close to them and we drove away right on their tail. I'm sure that's why the crowd stopped at jeering."

"It's distressing, Gil, sure. But is it really worth bringing in a regiment for?" Jake heard the beginning of expostulation and added quickly, "Now look, I'm not saying it isn't worth it. But when we get our reports from Will and Rosie, so we have some idea how general this sort of thing is, and, more important, what the authorities have in mind to do about it—"

"Jake, I have not made myself clear, I see. Either that or you're deliberately not taking the point. Points. *One,* if the presence of two reporters diminishes the overt activity, though it's not enough to drive it underground completely, what does that tell you about how clear a look two guys who are known to be White House assistants are going to get—and, on the other side, about how much control the authorities have over these unbelievable people? *Two*—and this one you *really* missed—these *were* the authorities. The men I heard threatening the people gathered in that church *were* the law, Jake." Gil's voice stopped, and then began again with weary determination. "That's why I called, don't you see? Because whatever story some governor hands Farland to bring back to Washington, this is what the law is really doing. Look, I don't want to talk a lot of patriotic jazz, not on my dough—but I hope you see my position. I don't want to stir things up that will get people hurt. But if I write what I saw, and add the question that occurs to me— Where do people go for justice when the law is out to lynch them?—then I'll be adding to the heat." Gil stopped. Then he said with enormous sadness, "And if I don't, I'm very probably managing the news, or something uncomfortably close to it."

Jake Ruffing chewed at his underlip, watching his smallest son entice a squirrel with some peanuts. The squirrel came boldly enough, but the child couldn't wait; he grabbed too soon and the squirrel twitched the peanut away and carried it and his saucy tail up a locust tree. Ruffing sighed and said into the phone that he didn't see that anybody was managing the news or even wanting to, thinking as he spoke that you never really knew what a man loved until you saw what he grabbed for when the house was on fire. Martin Halloran, yes, and even Ann Taswell—but to find Gil this deeply emotional about the trade he plied was a surprise. "Certainly it's the last thing I would do," Jake lied, aware that he would manage the news if he thought it was a good idea and he could get away with it; right now, he didn't, though. "Suppose I do this—if Farland's report doesn't reflect any of what you've been telling me, I'll speak up, pass on what you said. But if you're scared, Farland surely will be, too."

"I don't know. Rosie might, but Will—hell, he was raised down here."

Prejudice, Jake discovered, a little startled, was where you found it, and you found it in the damndest places. Gil couldn't know that Farland had been pressing the President to get into the southern fracas before Johnny-come-lately Kimball had wakened to the implications. Gil would never consciously discriminate against any man on the basis of race or creed, of course, but place of origin, it seemed, wasn't quite as sacredly to be tolerated by the flaming liberal: Alabama-born Farland was, all of a sudden, not quite kosher. Though Rosenberg was. Which might be why he had just written, Jake found to his faint surprise, "Call R. in 4 rept?" on the pad beside the phone.

"Well, be that as it may," he said meaninglessly to fill the waiting, and knew he was going to fly Rosie up at once, just briefly, for a report. And for something like the very reason Gil had implied—because the balance he was aiming at was based on prejudice at least equal to Gil's. If Farland the assimilated southerner could be thought to carry within him a seed of tolerance for white supremacists, the reasoning went, then Rosenberg the assimilated Jew could be nevertheless an extrasensitive detector of the pogrom spirit. Everybody's a racist but thee and me, Jake did not say aloud to Gil, and I've just outdone thee. He struck out the question mark from his note and said to himself that at least he'd never thought he was an idealist.

And then he missed the connection between that mature acceptance of his own fallibility and the sudden increase in his irritation with Gil's obstreperous lobbying. Which was what it was, whether Kimball knew it or not, and Jake was tired of it, he told himself virtuously. "We have to get our information the best way we can, Gil. Maybe nobody's quite pure enough, but I don't see that frantic pressure on the man helps him any." His resentment was more audible than he meant it to be. "It wouldn't be such a bad idea to lay off."

"I never thought," Gil said slowly, "we'd come to this."

"We haven't, goddammit."

"No, of course not. Only my correspondent's credentials up there suddenly get themselves withdrawn—"

Jake interrupted him with a loud, foul oath. "Gil, this is a private call, right? Okay, that was a private statement. I'm not hinting witch hunts, suppression, or any other bogeyman."

"Well, it certainly sounds like it." But the columnist was mollified. "Then what are you hinting?"

"That you remember who we're talking about—what kind of guy." Oh my sweet sister Sue, said Jake Ruffing to himself in utter bewilderment, this guy has lost all memory of Alec Girard. And I'm acting like Girard's mama. "Just stop and think what else he's up against, will you? I don't want you to hate yourself in the morning, that's all." What in hell are we coming to, he wondered, and anger plucked at him again. "What the hell has happened to you? Can't you think in anything but the most lurid terms?"

"Not any more, I guess." But Gil sounded less angry than thoughtful now. "This is lurid country. I don't want to start a crusade, Jake. But I'm scared."

Jake breathed easier, seeing the familiar Gil take shape before him again, a Gil who might allow Alec Girard a presumption of innocence—not to say intelligence. "Look, this is what let's do. I'll see that your fears, and the reason for them, are made known. And as for you, if I can suggest anything without being called names, I'd like to say that you can't lose by waiting. Because if what you saw is typical, it'll happen again. You just got down there—for all you know, it may be a one-shot thing."

"I heard stories from the people at that meeting—"

"Sure you did. But this is all you've actually seen, so far."

Gil sighed audibly. "True. Okay, I'll wait and see what else turns up."

Ruffing heaved a carefully inaudible sigh and thought gratefully that Gil would soon go away quietly and let him have a cup of coffee with Bonnie, who trusted people, before he had to leave. But reprieve was not yet, he discovered, as Gil said, "Jake?" in his ear.

"Yes, my son."

"Democracy is very difficult."

"Hey, now. Why don't you put that in your column? Right away, before you forget it," Jake suggested brightly. "So I can get on over to the office, where they knew it quite a while ago."

Forty-two

Washingtonians would be streaming from the city's exits today like blood from a major wound, John Harrington noted glumly as he attempted to read the morning *Tribune* through his wife's interruptions. Next

Monday was July 4, which made for a nice long holiday weekend that could be made a little longer by taking Friday off on leave, and types like fiscal officers and payroll clerks, who had been working long overtime hours in the usual June rush and had quite a lot coming, would be getting in Harrington's way on the highway.

"This man is the one who does the barbecues for Tom and Lou Cannon," Eleanor was saying. "I realize he comes a little high, but he does everything from digging the pit to cleaning up afterward. And anyway—"

"Yeah." And he was stamped "In Service to the Vice-President," which was enough to up his price for suckers. Harrington inspected his wife, but briefly, because she looked frowsy as hell. "Why ask me now—obviously you've got him reserved. Don't you think I know you couldn't just call this prince of pork at the last minute and expect him to be here on Monday?"

"Well, I thought—"

"Oh for God's sake, don't try *thinking*, not at this stage." Harrington got up and left her there and a few minutes later banged out of the house, telling himself that it had been too late to call off this party anyway. But still, he ought to have made the curt announcement he'd planned—that things weren't looking too good at the office right now and they'd better cut down on the parties for a little while; after all, he didn't have the year-after-year security of a civil servant. He tossed his cigarette carelessly from the car window and decided to hold off on that kind of talk after all—it was important to keep up the front, and maybe he could track down the source of the sudden freeze that was impairing his ability to pay his whopping liquor bills. His name was on somebody's shit list, but whose, and why, had not yet emerged. He sighed, and decided that the last person to talk to about it was Eleanor Harrington. The rest of the way downtown he debated the advisability of trying to tap Farland, who was out of town but, according to his frigid frau, was expected back tomorrow. By the time Harrington arrived at his expensive and shiny suite of offices, he had concluded that it was too soon to let Will know Harrington was hurting.

Farland's frigid frau had risen early in her large and empty house and gone downstairs to make herself an enormous breakfast because she was hungry for the first time in weeks, presumably as a result of the long night's decisions. Will's absence had, as usual, turned out to be longer than the few days advertised—but it wasn't long enough: the looming of Saturday and Will's return filled Marian with so much panic that she had only just strength enough to draw back from the brink. She had more thinking to do, and it could not be done in the state of semi-hysteria inspired by the presence of Will. Turning restlessly in the big empty bed, she had acknowledged that, though she dreaded the meeting, leaving notes on dressing tables or any other variation of comic-strip wives' departures was even more dreadful. Honor demanded that she wait and tell him tomorrow, face to face.

"Oh my," said Ann sleepily. Marian had said she'd been waiting until it was late enough to call, but apparently she had judged Ann's early-morning routine by her own usual one, which was various, complex, and extensive. "I guess you have to do it, but oh my." Still, Ann reasoned foggily, Will would need to report at the White House sometime soon after his return, so maybe he wouldn't have time for a full-length scene with his wife. Also, it was not clear with what intent Marian was asking Ann for sanctuary. Marian was so vague and indecisive these days that it was possible her high-powered husband would need only his smallest skill to render the whole project obsolete in five minutes' debate. "Why, Marian?" Ann asked slowly. "What does 'I just have to think' mean?"

"It means—I guess I don't know what I'm doing." The uncertain voice got stronger. "But I know what I'm not doing. I'm not running away."

Ann rubbed sleep from her eyes and tried to rub away with it the lingering sense of guilty responsibility; it was she who had lectured Marian on the advisability of not running away from things. "But you *are* leaving Will?"

Marian said, after a little silence, "Maybe." And then, after another, "Probably. I'll have to figure a way."

Which means, Ann said to herself, the triangle ends in "a plague o' both your houses"—and here we go again. She wondered whether Rosa knew yet that the bachelor girl establishment in Georgetown loomed once more on the horizon. Where Marian would proclaim that marriage was not for her, and Rosa would cope until some man coaxed Marian out of it. "Look, Marian— I have to make one condition—Will must know where you are."

"Well, I don't mind," Marian said slowly. "But now that I think about it —and I guess I should have, sooner—you may have something better to do than run a first-aid station, and—"

"I have nothing better to do than to help you when you need it," Ann interrupted. "I'm only trying to make sure it *is* help." She listened to the silence. "Look, I think you ought to come here, and I want you to. Because I think you're dreadfully tired and maybe sick, and you need rest and care." And Will wouldn't let up on her for a minute, Ann thought, almost wincing at the vicarious knowledge of that steady, subtle pressure. "Both of which I herewith gladly offer. But I don't want you to think *I* think you ought to leave Will, that's all. Because I don't know what I think about that, and I'd rather not have to find out."

"I know." Marian hesitated. "But maybe I'd better go to a hotel, or somewhere he can't find me. I just realized—Ann, you don't know how he can carry on."

Ann said dryly, "I have an inkling. But he'll find you anyway, sweetie— don't kid yourself about that. And I don't think it's a good idea for you to behave like a fugitive." A little nervously, she decided to take a chance on rubbing Marian's nose in the big question. "Do you have a legitimate complaint or don't you, and if you do, why skulk?"

"That's what I'm deciding."

Ann opened her eyes wide, twisting her face into a grimace of surprise.

Our little girl is growing up, she announced silently to the quiet room—that, oh dear, it occurred to her now, would not be either quiet or neat once it also contained the volatile, untidy Marian.

"I'm not skulking," Marian went on, with a positiveness that amazed her hearer. "And I'm not sick, or even that tired. I don't need to be taken care of, I just need some time and distance."

"Well." Ann recovered quickly. "You're welcome to whatever's in the house, Marian."

"Thank you. But about Will—"

"About Will's carrying on," Ann said firmly, "I imagine he'll do less of it when I'm around than he would otherwise. Now, do you want my car for tomorrow?" She listened, with something approaching respect, to Marian's proposed plan: it had an air of improvisation, but for Marian to plan at all was making history. When they had agreed on a time for tomorrow, Ann hung up and went out to the kitchen to make herself some coffee, shaking her head over the metamorphosis. She returned to her bedroom and sat down at the desk, deciding that if Marian could make it over here, Ann could write a letter. Or maybe what she'd better do is write it first and hold it, because with Marian around it might be impossible to find time and opportunity, or even pen and paper. *"Où est la plume de Tante Anne?"* Ann asked aloud in the silence, and grinned—at least there'd be company, for probably a month or so, to appreciate her wit. Although not that particular example of it— when it came to Paul Morisot, the talkative Marian had managed to be amazingly close-mouthed.

Andrea Girard arrived at a similar observation on uncommunicative loquacity that morning in connection with Dr. Rose, her pediatrician. When he'd mentioned, a week ago, that it might be a good idea to bring in a consultant, Andy had been briefly frightened. Then she'd decided it might well be a manifestation of what she and Alec called "RH," a suspicion Marian had confirmed. "After all, you've been bugging the hell out of the poor guy. Hovering, anxious mamas are an occupational hazard for pediatricians. But when the mama is—well, you know. No wonder he wants a friend to give him moral support."

Andy had breakfasted today in her son's room so she could play with him then and have time for Elizabeth before Dr. Rose was due. When he came, bringing the consultant, she left them to confer after they finished examining Elizabeth. Andy's schedule called for her to open a new recreation center in downtown Washington at midday, to be followed by a luncheon—which meant that the flowers for the tea that afternoon ought to be done before she left the White House. When she came back up to the second floor the doctors were still conferring; while she waited for them she looked in on Elizabeth, who was on the edge of sleep and fell off in the middle of one of her own sentences. It was nearly time to leave then, and she confronted the doctors with carefully controlled impatience that grew less easy to control as the men twaddled along meaninglessly, the consultant saying in several variations that Dr. Rose was doing everything that should be done—which Andy both expected him to say and assumed was true. Finally, she asked whether a brief report could be sent to the President to this effect—hoping wryly that Alec could fathom what "this effect" was—and thanked them hastily and fled, leaving them to be shown out.

As she dived into the elevator, she nodded in greeting to the Secret Service agent, Elizabeth's "Mr. Roy," who was coming down the hall to collect the doctors, she assumed. Dr. Rose came and went without question in the White House by this time, but the Secret Service was careful with any new face, however vouched for. Hurrying to the car, Andy thought briefly that the consultant hadn't looked as though he'd be much fazed by the cloak-and-dagger stuff: he'd scanned his surroundings with curiosity, but not with awe. The car started up and she dug into her purse for her notes on the Washington Negro leader for whom the recreation center was being named.

The President was, at the moment, receiving an informal report—but one whose effect was most clear—from Jake Ruffing on "the agitations of Kimball." Alec listened quietly and then said, "Another one down. I'm feeling more friendless every day."

"You still have me."

"You're just hidebound."

"I do prefer caution in high places," Jake said soberly. "If that's what you mean. Kimball would rather have you be Santa Claus than President."

Alec turned away from the spread-out newspaper on the table between two of the long windows. "Gil can afford it," he said tolerantly. "I suppose I can hardly expect everybody else to keep a cool head. After all, I'm the only one elected to." He sighed a little, fiddling with his framed appointment schedule and then frowning at it as if it had molested him. "But it's hard, having so many people urging me to do what I'd rather do anyway. I'm not temperamentally a holder-outer." His grin lightened the tanned face but didn't cancel all its strain. "As you may have noticed."

"I may have. Tell you what else I noticed, though—you did all right at holding out when we were trying to put salt on the tail of the nomination. You seemed to manage to control your impulsiveness, when that was needed. Even in the face of advice."

"And God knows there was plenty of that."

"Yup. Including Gil's—which was, if you recall, that you ought to settle for Vice-President."

"You should drop in more often." Alec was cheered but still restless; his eyes roved the oval office's space and comfort, but seemed to find not much satisfying. "Okay, I'll stay right here with a light in the window until Farland and Rosenberg come back with reports from enemy country—and Senator Youngblood with a report on what is rapidly becoming our lesser problem." He opened one of the French windows and breathed deeply of the fragrance outside. "I never thought I'd put Europe below Mississippi and Alabama in my list of daily headaches."

Jake laughed. "That reminds me—when I called Rosie, he said to tell you he wants a transfer to Moscow."

"Let him stay in Alabama," Alec growled. "I am kind to my enemies and cruel to my friends."

"He must've figured that, because he said if he can't get transferred, he wants hardship pay. He says if he has to look at hominy once more, he'll join the Air Force."

"If he does I'll assign him to Alabama. He can't get away from my deadly grip." Alec leaned out, surveying the rose garden fretfully. "Jake, do you know of any blue flowers? Some kind that stand up? All I can think of is morning glories, and they twine."

"Blue flowers?" Ruffing stared at him stupidly.

Alec turned, laughing at him. "Caught you, huh? First time you didn't have an answer."

"I have. I'll get you a report on blue flowers—varieties, population, and electoral votes—within thirty minutes, if you really want me to. But why in heaven's name—"

"I just like blue flowers," Alec said rebelliously.

His chief aide regarded him with indulgence. "Hell, that's no problem— we'll call the Park Service and have all the flowers painted blue. If you're powerful enough to keep Rosenberg in Alabama, you ought to be able to get your roses painted whatever color you want." He clicked his heels elaborately. "Now, if there's nothing else, sir—"

"Nothing," Alec assured him solemnly. "As usual, you've met my every need. When I retire, the first thing I'm going to do is write an article for a large-circulation magazine, 'Is Jake Ruffing Really for Real?' "

Jake, at the door, turned back with a smile. "Let me know when you want the research done, Mr. President."

As soon as Jake had gone, Alec's smile faded. He walked over to the table and inspected the spread-out newspaper, although he knew by heart the words that had leaped out at him: "Rep. Bruyette could not be reached for comment."

Representative Bruyette apparently could not be reached by the logic of his old school chum either, his old school chum thought ruefully. Bill could vote any damned way in the House that he pleased and he knew it, but it wasn't like him not to say something, at least. Not that any damage had been done —the proposed amendment to an appropriations bill had been roundly defeated even without Bruyette's help, as Bill had doubtless known it would be. Whatever the issue, there was always a sizable number in the Congress who would object on principle to a legislative rider on an appropriations bill as an unconscionable form of pressure, taking advantage of the fact that the President could not veto part of a bill; unless he was prepared to hold up funds routinely needed to run the government, he would be forced to take the whole package—and thus swallow measures that could not have passed through the Congress on their own against his opposition.

The appropriations bill would now become law without the defeated rider, which had been a feeble attempt to deny the appropriated federal funds to states with segregation laws—which sounded good, but in fact was just a silly exercise, as the President had long since determined. For one thing, even if it worked and funds actually were withheld, the majority of the sufferers would be, directly or indirectly, poor Negroes in the southern states. For another, years of court decisions would be needed to define the loose terminology and defend attacks on the grounds of constitutionality; and even when that was successful, no way was provided to assure enforcement. Thus the rider had been opposed not only by the pro-segregationists and the objectors on principle, but also by a number of congressmen who recognized it as bad legislation, poorly conceived and poorly written, whatever they thought of its intent.

But Bruyette knew all that—and he also knew that Girard's liaison men had been against the rider anyhow because it permitted the weak-willed and the fence-sitters to offer an empty pro-Negro gesture to their Negro constituents instead of backing substantial measures. The additional effects, of draining off energies and fervor from the civil rights advocates and taking up the rapidly vanishing days of the session, made the anti-segregation rider, while apparently liberal in its intent, a net loss to the goal of improvement in the lot of the Negro; only the handful of liberals who failed to comprehend, scorned, or could not afford sensible strategy had voted for it.

That William Bruyette of the Fourteenth District of Vermont voted for it had struck not only the erstwhile holder of that House seat but also the news services as interesting; but their interest had proved equally unavailing, Alec thought a little grimly. Representative Bruyette, who was aware that in the frantic last-minute jumble of Hill activity the press could not afford to pursue any one question for long, had quietly vanished into the warrens of Capitol Hill for the brief duration of the hunt and thus successfully avoided explaining his surprising vote. Which was the Congressman's privilege, his most famous constituent would have been the first to concede; but it wasn't the Congressman's habitual way of conducting himself in relation to Alexander Girard. "Sorry, old son, but I can't go along with you" was not only not an unknown comment from Bruyette but also one he knew to be acceptable, and in a way that silence was not. Because the silence hurt.

Girard sat down in his desk chair and admitted that last, and also why it hurt—Bruyette hadn't done it because of pressure from the Fourteenth District, Alec knew, or because of an overwhelming need to secure the few Negro votes there. What Bruyette's vote meant was that Bill was angry and wanted to make a gesture—not because, like Farland, he thought a gesture would help to head off coming trouble, but simply because Bill Bruyette, who had always been benignly indifferent to Negroes as anything but a voting bloc, now saw them as oppressed citizens taking a shoving around and it

made his blood boil. Alec sighed and wondered whether he was the only one
—besides Bill's mother, maybe—who understood what a simple and thorough-
going Puritan this Bruyette was. Within that thin skin there dwelt, along with
the flippant bachelor Congressman and the shrewd "down-East Ruffing"—as
Andy had once called him—a verray parfit, gentil knight who just couldn't
stand by and see the helpless oppressed, even while he was trying to help
them, without yelling encouragement to them.

Which was all, all known and understandable—except for the silence.
Andy and Bruyette and Paul, Alec had told himself only a short time ago—
the three who were always there and unafraid. Only maybe now Bruyette
was asking out . . . Which was his privilege, Alec added conscientiously; it
was not Bruyette's fault if Gil Kimball had decided to start thinking of Alec
as Genghis Khan in the same week.

Genghis Khan thought wistfully of Paul, who would've been nice to have
around—but Paul had "gone in," which was Andy's term for his disappear-
ances into his work. Alec smiled, remembering his first acquaintance with
this curious vocabulary shortly after their marriage. Picking up an outgoing
letter from the hall table in the new house, he'd noticed it was addressed to
Paul, and on his way out with it, he'd asked Andy some vague question about
her old friend and his relatively new one—how was Paul, or was he coming
over any time soon, or something like that.

"Paul? I don't know. I haven't heard from him in ages."

Alec brandished the letter and said cheerfully that this would probably
rouse him, then.

"Oh, I don't think so," Alec's young wife assured him. "He's gone in, and
I don't think he'll be out for months yet."

She wrote every few weeks, the questioning Alec discovered; but Paul,
once "gone in," didn't answer—probably he didn't even read the letters.
When he was ready to come out, he read up on her news and answered her;
but you couldn't tell when that would be, of course. And Alec had stood
there clutching her fat and utterly selfless letter to the unforthcoming Paul
and wondering about what other amazements were going to come to light
about this new partner in his name and his bed—who, though she awarded
her friendship sparingly, then gave it so unsparingly.

Alec stirred in his chair and debated whether to envy Paul, who could "go
in," which sounded inviting, and be let alone—which was less so. Maybe you
could wrestle alone with a muse, but wrestling with a Congress was a horse
of a different color—was, in fact, a team of horses. He picked up the text
of his Fourth of July speech, which he should have been looking over instead
of contemplating how neglected he was, and concluded unhappily that it reflected the absence from the premises of Rosenberg and Farland. As he
reached for a pencil to make a small improvement, he found his hand stray-
ing toward the telephone that would connect him with the Mansion and Andy
the trustworthy musketeer, the only one left on the scene who would say
"Alec." You big baby, he jeered at himself: can't you leave the woman to get

her hair dressed in peace? He smiled and turned back to the speech and began to write rapidly between the lines, with his forefinger humped like a schoolboy poor at penmanship.

A schoolboy sensation of release was his first response, too, to the familiar sound of Dan Healy at the side door of the oval office. Then a little guilt, as he glanced at his watch—it was time for their daily swim in the White House pool, all right, but he had been goofing off for a while. Nevertheless . . . "Be right with you," he called, forgiving his trespasses. He began to get up from behind his desk. "Okay, let us plunge."

"Mr. President."

Girard sat down as abruptly as though the other man had pushed him. "What's happened, Dan?"

"Dr. Rose would like a word with you. He has a Dr. Snowden with him."

"Doctor . . . Rose?"

"Elizabeth's doctor. I'll hold everything else."

"Yes. Yes, of course," the President said sharply, his throat suddenly dry.

Nothing but courtesy showed in his greeting as he crossed the room to meet his visitors. He led them to the beige sofas before the fireplace and seated them patiently, but the hand on the wood of the chair he sat in was cold and beginning to be damp.

"Elizabeth—" he began tensely, interrogation in his voice. His hand tightened on the chair arm, looking whiter than usual against the dark wood. "She seemed all right this morning." "All right," he thought, his control beginning to desert him, now no longer meant the small pajamaed figure hurtling at him as he sprawled on the bed in his dressing room, trying to read the morning newspapers. "All right" meant, now, that she had smiled at him from her white-painted little bed when he went in to see her in the mornings before he left for the west wing.

"Elizabeth seems to be comfortable. She's napping," Dr. Rose said quickly. "She fell asleep before her mother left." His dark eyes watched his listener kindly while he spoke, his plump body in its neat blue suit leaning forward a little, as if to help in communication. Beside him on the sofa, Dr. Snowden, his face hawklike under black-edged, crisp salty hair that matched his summer suit, sat immobile and attentive.

The President's smile was relieved. "That's good news, Dr. Rose. This thing seems to have lingered so—" He broke off suddenly as his glance fell on the silent Dr. Snowden, and he raised his eyebrows.

"Mr. President, I hope you don't mind our—informality," Dr. Rose said. "I don't know whether Mrs. Girard told you I wanted to call in a consultant. But, after we saw Elizabeth this morning, we thought it best to ask to speak with you at once." His white, very clean hands clasped and unclasped themselves nervously. A heavy gold college ring, much engraved around a dark-blue stone, was sunk deeply into the flesh of his fourth finger; small hairs sprouted around it like wire fencing. "In the circumstances, we also felt it best to—that is, we understood that Mrs. Girard had an appointment, so I'm afraid we—well, we stalled her, I guess, so we could speak to you first. I hope you don't mind these rather—unconventional maneuvers."

"No. I thank you for your consideration." All of Alec Girard was in his waiting eyes.

"Mr. President," Dr. Rose resumed, "in the course of treating Elizabeth, I ordered certain routine tests—to determine the presence of infection, and so forth. Some of the results disturbed me a little, and—"

"But you said she was feeling better," Elizabeth's father interrupted. He stopped then and looked in silence from the pediatrician to his tall colleague. "Dr. Rose, I feel that—Dr. Snowden, you're a specialist?" The voice thinned as if it were being strangled, but it was the President who asked sharply, "In what?"

The tall man stirred, then looked directly at his questioner. "We're talking about leukemia, Mr. President." His voice was flat, matter of fact.

"Dr. Snowden is chairman of the Federal Health Research Institute project on blood and lymph—" Dr. Rose broke off his smooth statement. "Mr. President, please try to listen."

Girard turned his gaze on the little doctor obediently. His eyes were wide with shock.

"I asked for consultation because of a suspicion," Dr. Rose went on, emphasizing the final word. "A suspicion, not a certainty."

Alec nodded. "Yes, I understand, Dr. Rose." His lips were trembling. The doctors waited for him to continue, but there was only silence for a long second. Then he unclasped his fingers, one by one, from the arm of his chair and laid his hand in his lap. The fingers of his other hand, spread on his knee, were digging into the cloth of his trousers. "Gentlemen, please. All the picture at once, if you can. This is something of a—well, doubtless you know. Dr. Snowden?"

The tall man had been surveying the oval office with impassive interest; his eyes surveyed the President now with almost the same quietness. "I think so," he said quickly. "But I'm not sure yet."

"What do you need?" Alec Girard's voice was strong and sure.

"A little time. And, preferably, a hospital." Snowden's lean face did not soften but his eyes, intent on the suffering man across from them, were dark with sympathy. "I need more elaborate facilities."

"We discussed the possibility of moving equipment into the White House," Dr. Rose began.

"It would be a mechanical problem, but I suppose it could be managed," Dr. Snowden said. "But not inconspicuously, which seems to be a consideration. In terms of Mrs. Girard, if nothing else."

"Ah yes," said Alec, in the soft voice of a man with room for no more hurt. "Yes, I suppose there would be no way to keep from telling her if we— What do you recommend, Doctor?"

"My personal opinion is that the uproar of introducing elaborate equipment would alarm both the patient and the mother more than transfer to the hospital. In addition, the presence of other children and other mothers in the same situation seems to make the hospital a more reassuring atmosphere, oddly enough, than confronting this thing in isolation." He fell silent, looking a little surprised at himself. "Of course, that's only a personal opinion," he repeated. "We could consult—"

"No, let's do something without any further consultation if we can," the President said forcefully. "Dr. Rose. Here, or at the hospital?"

"Elizabeth has no fear of hospitals," the pediatrician answered. "All she knows about them, really, is that her mother went to one and came back with her baby brother."

"The baby! My son?"

"No, no, Mr. President, there's nothing to fear," Dr. Rose said hastily. "I checked him yesterday, and he's perfectly well. There's no contagion involved here at all, and even if there were, infants have all sorts of immunity during most of the first year." The meaningless explanation went on, the little doctor laying more words on Alec's wounds like a poultice, watching the effect professionally as he spoke.

The treatment worked; the President nodded gratefully at Dr. Rose. But then his gaze, full of dread, turned compulsively again to the wooden face of the specialist. "What are the chances that she has it?"

"Very great," said Dr. Snowden, immediately and without emphasis.

"Of course." Alec spoke more to himself than to the doctors. "You would hardly have come if they hadn't been." His eyes sought them, questing, in a long probing look that would have been recognized instantly by his staff assistants and others who habitually brought the President information. "If she has leukemia, what will happen to her?"

Dr. Rose said, "There are people walking around who've had it for twenty years."

The President didn't look at him. "Dr. Snowden?"

Dr. Snowden sighed. "Mr. Girard, leukemia is fatal."

Alec drew in his breath sharply and all the color left his face, promptly and dramatically as though it had been bleached by a powerful agent. Only his eyes, drilling through the tall doctor, looked still alive. "When?"

"That can't be predicted."

"I understand that. But—a range?"

"If we get a remission, if we then get another remission, and another—no one can say until we try the drugs we have. Sometimes they work. Sometimes some work and others don't. There's no way to know."

"But there must be a maximum, a minimum." Alec's voice was strangled. "There is experience to draw on." The thin voice grew suddenly peremptory. "What is the range, Doctor?"

"x weeks to x years." Dr. Snowden's eyes narrowed. "Mr. Girard, put your head down," he said sharply.

Surprised into acquiescence, Alec bent his head and then let Dr. Rose press it still farther down, between his knees. The small man's quick, cool hands jerked at the knot of the President's tie, loosening it, and then deftly opened the button at the neck of the white shirt. The dimness before Alec's eyes cleared like blown mist and he saw the weave of the rug, absurdly close up, in individual tufts. Blood banged in his ears, shutting out every other sound. Then his head and shoulders were raised and laid back against the back of his chair and he sat still obediently with Dr. Rose's fingers at his wrist.

"I need to know," he said to Dr. Snowden, still and watchful as an Indian. I'm not making enough sense, Alec told himself, consciously and deliberately rallying his intelligence like a commander of ragged troops. Dr. Rose released his hand and laid it down on the arm of the chair like an object. Alec thanked him and then cleared his throat, which was full of a hard lump that wouldn't move. "I don't want to tell my wife until I must. But she has a right to know if there's any immediate danger of Elizabeth's—" He could not say the word.

Dr. Snowden's quiet, even voice suggested a brief wait for some still-outstanding test results. "As soon as we're certain," he explained, "we can begin the first drug. The achievement of a remission is discernible quickly."

"And—if there is none?"

"They have so many drugs, Mr. President," Dr. Rose said softly. "And new ones being developed all the time."

"If none of them work?" Alec forced the words from between stiff lips.

Dr. Snowden said, "That is statistically unlikely, Mr. Girard."

Girard put his hands together between his knees as if he were about to play pat-a-cake and sat there looking down at them for a long moment. "How soon can you get me a full report?" he asked. He might have been talking to Jake Ruffing. "I'd like a digest of all the available information— data on the efficacy of each drug, whatever you have on how long these remissions hold." His hands sprang apart, one of them chopping the air in his campaign gesture. "If you have it, some advice on how—other parents have—proceeded. Please have the material delivered to Dan Healy, my appointments secretary, with a for-my-eye classification." He stood up abruptly, wavered, clutched at the back of the chair, and recovered his balance. "I thank you gentlemen for your pains in coming here. I know it hasn't been easy."

"Mr. President," Dr. Rose said. "I'm so sorry."

"Thank you." Alec looked at him briefly and then turned to Dr. Snowden. "How close are you to beating it?"

The tall doctor eyed him sadly. "How can that be answered?"

"Of course," the President said. "Please forgive me." He managed a small stretching of his lips that might have been an attempt at a smile. "Dr. Rose," he went on as the two stood up, "I want to thank you again for your consideration of my wife. I should like her kept in ignorance for as long as possible—which will be, presumably, until we move Elizabeth to the hospital on Sunday. Right?"

Dr. Rose nodded and the men turned to go, but Alec stopped Dr. Snowden. "Can you answer this, doctor—it *is* possible that my daughter can be kept alive until a breakthrough on a cure?"

Dr. Snowden looked at him soberly. "That's what we're trying to do, on my project. We have many children up there, Mr. Girard."

Alec dropped his gaze, noticed with surprise that his hand was on Dr. Snowden's coat sleeve, and took it away at once. "Of course."

He waited alone, his hands empty at his sides, watching them go. Not until the door had closed behind them did his hands clench. Then he raised both fists to his forehead and turned away blindly. He was still standing there, tall and silent and helpless, between the gold-trimmed flag and the enormous globe, when he heard the side door open. He dropped his hands and said, "No, Dan."

"Please, Alec."

The pleading voice with its unlikely, unseemly address seemed to ricochet among the paintings of famous victories on the curving walls. Girard turned swiftly. "I'm sorry. The fact is, it's bad."

"How bad, Champ?"

Alec stared at the kind, frightened face and said, as much to himself as to his old companion, "It looks as though we can't win." His hand came up then and punched the air. "But we don't have to lose right away. That's all I know so far."

Dan Healy said into the long pause, "What can I do, Mr. President?"

"Yes." Alec Girard seemed to stand much straighter. "Well, first—Andy is not to know anything until Sunday. That means nobody—" He stopped then, remembering. "Leroy."

"Yes, sir. He's waiting."

"All right. Leroy only. Absolute security—and I mean absolute. And be sure he understands about keeping Andy from—"

"He managed it so she wouldn't know," Dan said. "He kept them at the Mansion until she was gone. Then he called me to get my office cleared out and brought them in that way."

"Good man," the President agreed. His eyes were thoughtful. "Let's make sure that nobody alarms Elizabeth, either—you know, no unscheduled visits."

"Is she going to the hospital?"

"Yes. Probably Sunday." The President paused, a little surprised by the ease with which he could say it. Then he went on, moving on familiar, commanded ground. "Get Cannon to make the July Fourth speech." His hands fumbled, tightening and straightening his tie. "Better have Luke announce that I've got a heavy summer cold—all appointments canceled for the weekend."

Dan hesitated. "And Farland and Rosenberg?"

The President's pale face tightened. "I don't know." He turned away. "Cancel them, too, until I see whether I can—" His businesslike voice wound down like a slowing phonograph record. "I'd like to be left alone, Dan."

"In a minute," the man said apologetically. "What if Andy asks—"

"Tell her it's a diplomatic illness, and I'm too busy for anything. Tell her I'll see her when I can, and I'll explain then. But Dan, for God's sake—" the voice was high and boyish "—that's all now."

The door opened silently, but he knew Dan opened it because he heard the low mutter of a voice on a radio in his appointments secretary's office. Suddenly it seemed to Alec incredible and unbearable that a baseball game, which was what it sounded like, could be going on anywhere at all at this moment. The sound stopped and he raised a clenched fist in fury and then let it fall limply, because there was nothing to hit.

Forty-three

The President's sudden cold caused a small commotion of re-arrangement in the lives of a few people—Lou Cannon, for example, had to pinch-hit for the Vice-President at the Fourth of July rally he had been scheduled to address so that he could go and speak at the one in Washington in place of Alec Girard. But the experienced Mrs. Cannon had been through many political emergencies and, in the end, emerged quite unflurried from this one; and Tom Cannon, to whom orating on July Fourth was very nearly a basic body function, simply added a little more loftiness to his local speech to take into account the presence of the diplomatic corps.

Representative William Bruyette of Vermont called when he heard the news and was reassured by Dan Healy, who regretted that he had to take a message, but orders were orders. Bruyette said he quite understood. "Just tell him his Congressman called, will you? To let him know I'm here to serve him. And I haven't heard from him lately." He hung up quickly, more troubled than ever by Alec's cold.

It didn't trouble Rosa Little, who was serving as a sort of house mother for an impromptu sorority lodged in a ramshackle rooming house in a town on the Virginia–North Carolina border. She attended, along with her charges, a "school" led by a bronze-colored man who, by the age of fifty, had suc-ceeded in making the drawbacks resulting from the darkness of his skin society's losses rather than his. The class learned the exact wording of the Fourteenth Amendment to the Constitution of the United States and a few other matters of federal interest; then they divided into groups to be briefed on the relevant legalities of the communities to which they would be sent— after the holiday, since the knowledgeable leaders were aware that there would be considerable drinking in southern communities and they were not interested in extraneous incidents proving only that sun and beer taken too long in combination can provoke individual belligerence.

Most of the youngsters were good-natured, if noisy; the boys tended to show off when the girls were around and the girls spoke archly to each other in tones of exaggerated gaiety when the boys were around; somebody played somebody else's guitar without permission and had to be made to apologize; and, one night, a white college girl from Illinois dissolved in tears unexpectedly but was perfectly all right again by morning. In the daytimes, various somber leaders reminded them all that they were there to prove to the American people that it was not hoodlums but ordinary respectable people who were being pushed around, so they must be careful to present that picture of themselves wherever they went. And a moon-faced minister with eyes full of pity begged them to remember that hate is as destructive to the Negro as to the white. In the twilight, a mockingbird announced the end of day and a call came across the field like a song; at night, when the group singing had ended and so had the shouts from room to room as the young prepared for bed, Rosa lowered her weary body into the lumpy bed she shared with a middle-aged schoolteacher, who would be taking a group into Mississippi, and thought a little hungrily of home but was very glad she had come. On the last day of the holiday, a white divinity student from Ohio pitched his softball team to victory over a team led by a Negro gas station attendant from the District of Columbia. The losing captain announced that he had just changed his mind about the virtues of integration, convulsing the spectators. Nobody mentioned the changes of plan for the official July Fourth celebration in Washington, D.C.

However, Alec Girard's sudden illness resulted in some problems for Marian Farland as early as Saturday morning. For Dan Healy had reached Farland in Mississippi late Friday to tell him that his Saturday appointment with the President was postponed until, probably, sometime Sunday. Will expressed concern for Girard's health and was told it was nothing serious— only the doctors had figured that, with a holiday coming anyhow, it was a good chance to make the man get a little rest, you know? Will knew. He took the same plane to Washington Saturday anyhow, because it was hard to change plans on a holiday weekend. But he called his wife to tell her of the rearranged appointment, and he knew immediately from her voice that, though she would be there on his return because her intricate ethics demanded it, she would also be determined to listen to nothing he would say. He spent most of Friday evening composing a long letter to her in his head and nearly all the time on the plane writing it down, just in case she would read what she wouldn't listen to.

It was one thing, Marian was finding, to plow on through a session that was bound to be unpleasant when you knew it would have to be brief; but it was quite another to succeed in saying as little as possible to a man who had nothing else he had to go and do at a specified time and also wanted to have as much as possible said. The only thing going for her was that Will was tired—so tired that he had retreated from the last skirmish to lie down on the bed in the study. She didn't really believe he'd fall asleep, but she couldn't quite banish a hope that he would—so, holding to the magic that if she made no noise Will would lie dormant, she shuffled back and forth between her bureau and the open suitcase on the bed with the haste of a fugitive and something like the furtiveness, too, even while she kept reminding herself that she was not skulking.

Stopping to sip at the cup of cooling boiled-over coffee on the table beside the bed, she made a face at the taste and at the whole untidiness of her exit, leaving behind an unkempt house, an unmade bed, and uncertain domestic arrangements—not only for right now, but for after the summer too. The panic began rising again and she stopped and stood where she was, in a shaft of hot sun slanting to the polished floor, and warned herself sternly against getting bogged down in these details. Maybe it wasn't right to flee, but she had waited for all the time she could and done everything she was capable of doing first. And even now, she reminded herself, she wasn't running to a divorce or even to an immediate decision.

The only possible way to do this, she had realized last night, was simply to stop thinking—with the plans all laid on, the immediate details taken care of as best she could manage, what was left to do was to step onto the conveyor belt and be moved to the next stop. Just let all the little wheels turn and bump you along like the grocery packages at the supermarket: clickety-clack, pack the suitcase, put it into Ann's car, and drive the car a few miles across Washington—whatever happens, whatever he says, clickety-clack, out of the store and neatly lined up for pickup . . . If a little demagoguery is acceptable, she thought bitterly as her legs moved obediently on their interrupted journey toward the bed, so is a little fanaticism. She heard Will stirring in the study then. *Don't think*, she said to herself like some kind of prayer. *Don't listen*. Just. Keep. Moving.

Rumpled and unshaven, his feet half thrust into bedroom slippers, Will looked beaten and frantic—a combination that caused his tight-lipped wife some dismay, since the sight of him in the doorway evoked reflex and pity and old habits of reassurance. "Did you read my note?" he asked, being careful to speak quietly.

Marian hadn't read it carefully, only glanced at it long enough to see that it was an impassioned plea for patience and fortitude (as Will defined patience and fortitude), and then she'd stuffed it into her big straw purse to be read later and at a safe distance. But the memory of its cleverness, its smooth exhortation, helped her to recover anger. Several answers to his question occurred to her—a recommendation that he change the letter's salutation and use it for the Alliance for Progress, which was probably a good market for promises to end oppression, or perhaps an openly hostile sneer that there already was too much mail addressed to "Occupant." But these would lead to something other than the waiting conveyor belt, so she took a sweater out of a drawer and told herself she was considering whether she would need a sweater in case an evening got cool, and considering nothing else. She carried the sweater to the suitcase without answering.

"Marian, this is insane. You can't just walk out and leave me to cope with all this." His hand moved outward jerkily, indicating the echoing house where the blinds had not even been drawn against the threat of the already hot sun.

"There's nothing for you to cope with. The children are away and the dogs are at the kennel. You can eat when and where you please. You can take your wash to the laundromat if you don't want to do it downstairs. Or throw the clothes away and buy new ones, if you prefer. You have absolute freedom at last. You don't have to come home at all."

He sighed. "Do you know what you're doing?" He was speaking with deliberate slowness, as to a child or a foreigner new to the language. "Do you have any money? Where are you going?" He waited, but she still didn't answer. "Look, don't be foolish. You know I can find you. I guarantee I can put people on the job who will find you, anywhere in Washington, in less than an hour and anywhere in the country in less than a day." He paused, surveying the clothes in the suitcase; they were folded and packed with exquisite care and intricate use of space, as though no time had been stinted on preparation and planning. "It doesn't look as if you're thinking of leaving the country—but I trust you're intelligent enough to know you can't do *that* without my knowing it."

Mr. Big Shot, she thought bitterly, hesitating with a nightgown in her hand; his tentacles extended all over the place, and he loves it. She wanted to defy him, but there was that promise to Ann. "I'm going to Ann's." She put the nightgown down and looked at him squarely. "If you cause any trouble for her, I'll pay you back if it's the last thing I ever do."

Will watched her pale lips moving in her pale face and knew that what she said was quite true, but it was hardly the surprise to him it apparently was to her. "Oh, don't be a child," he said, making his voice easy and relieved. "Why should I blame Ann? She can't refuse if you ask her, and she may even be capable of talking some sense into you." From that viewpoint, he had already decided, Betty Kimball would have been a better prospect; but he had accepted that Ann was what he would have to work with and his campaign was even now half shaped in his mind.

"Ann is not taking sides in this." Marian looked at him angrily. "Hands off her. I mean it. I will not have her subjected to any of your shenanigans."

"You're melodramatic. And obviously you haven't a clue about what my chief concern is." He started toward her and she jerked to attention, her back at once against an invisible wall. Will cursed himself silently for the foolish move and went on speaking carefully and evenly, holding his hands down with their palms out, his whole posture like someone approaching a skittish animal. "Look, I won't touch you, and I'm certainly not going to hurt you. All I want you to do is turn around and look at yourself in the mirror. Will you do it? Please. Just a look."

"I know I don't look beautiful," she said bitterly. But, mesmerized by his voice, she obeyed, turning partly toward the big mirror over the bureau but warily not turning her back on him entirely. Then she stared, shocked, at what she had not really seen for days, though Ann had warned her. Her hair, limp and greasy-looking, was put up indifferently and clung to her skull instead of puffing out softly as it always had. The colorless face was no more than she expected in the absence of any makeup, for she believed the cosmetic manufacturers who told her she had no color without their help, but, above the soft aqua of her dress, her skin looked frighteningly gray and lifeless. The dress, one of her favorites, was a blouse and softly flowing skirt with a wide matching belt and she had worn it because it could be washed without ironing and because it made her feel good. Now as she discovered the drawn lines in her face she saw further that the deep V of the blouse was pitiless; ridiculously, she wanted to weep about her scrawny neck.

"You see?" Will said quietly. "Yet you won't believe that I'm worrying about you. Baby—" he tried a cautious step forward and then stopped, afraid to lose this slim communication "—I'm *glad* you'll be with Ann. I want to know you'll be taken care of." Her face, turned toward him cautiously, looked suddenly balky; but she was looking at him, and that was more than he had been able to get before, so he tried another tentative move. "Marian, I'm your husband. Surely I'm entitled to want to rescue you when you're clearly in distress?"

She had been looking directly at him, the big eyes frightened and, he thought, a little wistful. But even as he watched with a little hope that he almost had her, almost—her eyes clouded over and she stiffened and half-ran from the room. He saw her go down the long hall to the bathroom and open the medicine chest; she was shaking her head "No" as she began to collect jars and bottles, lining them up on the windowsill. Will thought about following her, then remembered something he had to do. Glancing over his shoulder to make sure she was still busy, he took out his wallet and pulled out all the bills in it. He moved silently across the bare floor to the bed, examining all the compartments of the wallet carefully in the hope of finding some money tucked away before he put a dollar back inside and stuck the wallet in his pants pocket. He rolled the rest of the money tightly and stuffed it down into a corner of her suitcase, patting the red sweater back over it.

When she came back, he was lounging in the study doorway again and he saw immediately that something had stiffened her resolve while she'd been gone. She tucked her toothbrush, a jar of cold cream, and an assort-

ment of other jars and tubes into the appropriate compartment of the suitcase, moving briskly, and then she sat down on the chair and began to
exchange her socks for nylon footlets and her sneakers for high-heeled brown
and white spectator pumps.

Control and competence, Marian told herself, tucking an edge of nylon
under the rim of the shoe, would keep her out of durance vile, and clothes
made a difference—a little girl, shuffling around in sneakers, might be vic-
timized by a con man, but not a trimly dressed woman of the world. She
put her hand on the arm of the chair to get up and put her makeup on; but
she lingered instead, absently stroking the softly curved wood, suddenly reminded that there was more here than Will to be left this day. This home and
its series of decisions made and carried out was a creation not to be abandoned lightly. I am not abandoning it lightly, she told herself firmly, stamp-
ing her other foot into the shoe. She saw how white her leg was and almost
smiled; in the new Washington era, dominated by a vigorous President and
his athletic wife, to be not suntanned by July was to be effete, out of it, left
behind and vaguely dowdy. Good, she defied them, getting up—I want to
be out of it; let them make their goddam new world without me. She went
to the mirror, her skirt swinging against the white legs, and began to paint
her lips with a sure hand.

Will cleared his throat and adapted himself to the new mode he observed. "Look, Marian, if you think you need to get away for a while, well,
maybe that makes some sense. You could use a little rest, away from the
household routine."

Marian studied him in the mirror, her hand poised with the lipstick in it.
It was remarkable how easy it was to deal with, once you stopped cringing
and wailing—here, now, behind this apparently conciliatory statement, was
a sly little attempt to take over her move and make it his. She flashed him a
look of contempt and finished what she was doing without answering.

Will flushed but managed to keep his voice even. "Could you tell me how
long you'll be gone? Or is that too much to ask, in view of all my sins?"
Behind the biting words, his eyes admired her because he couldn't fool her.
The thought that he had to have her, he simply had to, battered him as if an
explosion had occurred too near him, deafening him so that he had trouble
hearing her saying she would be gone as long as it took to figure out what
to do.

"Maybe a week. Maybe for good." She looked around, knitting her forehead in a ridiculous attempt to look practical. "I'll have to make some arrangement about my things. If I decide—"

"If you decide you can't put up with the enormous burden of a man who
loves you and is working his guts out for you."

"Not for me!" Marian shouted suddenly. "*Please* let's call things by their
right names."

Yes, Willard Catullus Farland admitted at last, but I can't without you;
nobody else stops me when I call things whatever names are convenient. He

made an enormous effort, straining as though his life depended on it because he had a feeling it did, to listen to her honestly.

"Power hunger, is that what they call it?" she was asking in a high, tight voice. "I don't know, I don't know. I only know that you may have been right when you said I couldn't succeed in coexisting with it. And I think I also know *you* can't live without it. You can't, can you? It's a kind of sickness."

He nodded soberly, for once and not without timidity answering the question without trying to use it. "I suppose, if you want to call it that, then we're all sick—and Girard is the sickest one of all."

"Maybe. He doesn't even have your excuse—the early poverty, and all that."

Will shook his head. "Money doesn't really have anything at all to do with it, baby."

"That's what I meant—that's what's sick. All it is a love of power."

"Is it so sick? Doesn't everybody want to fight City Hall at some time or other?" He was struck by inspiration. "Remember when you were on that committee trying to get a traffic light near the junior high?"

"What's that got to do with it?"

"It's how it begins, I think," he said soberly. "You want to do something about things, so you exert what power or influence you can. If you're Alec Girard, you run for Congress instead of lazing the days away at Palm Beach. He was just too intelligent to be a playboy. But I suppose the more he tried to do, the more power he needed." Will struggled, against the objective need not to oversimplify, against the subjective observation that they were talking, he had got her talking and there was hope. "You have to get more and more effective. Which means going higher and higher. As high as your capacities will let you go."

"And then what? Suppose you're Alec Girard and you're powerful enough to do anything you want to do. Why do you need to do anything except get your child across the street safely? That traffic light was for our children, and things for us, for our children, for our home are all I want to do something about, and I don't need to get elected to anything for that."

Honesty, Will said to himself with a sick feeling, isn't going to bring us out anywhere that dishonesty didn't; he looked at her, so small and so terrible, and fought down the impulse to grab her, lock her up somewhere, tie her down. "I can't make you see. You can't close the doors and draw the curtains and look only at your own. The rest of the world will throw a brick through your window."

"Why should it?" demanded the daughter of the rich, the coddled princess of many ardent knights. "Anyway, if it does, the police will stop it."

"Not unless somebody tells them to," said the grim witness of a bus station arrest two days before in Mississippi.

"Then let somebody else tell them," pleaded Marian of the white arms ready to cradle.

"I can't." Knowledge of loss, exploding in him, had left a hole through which more could be seen of Will Farland than he intended. He stopped, knowing he had been too much revealed to hope for victory.

She was looking at him pityingly. "I don't understand. I don't want to. I just want to live and be let alone." She began to cry, then, softly and hopelessly. "I don't want power, I want time. There's so little time and so much to see."

He started to put his arm around her and then drew back, afraid. "Marian."

She slammed the suitcase shut and wiped her tears with the back of her hand. "No." She dragged the suitcase off the bed. "Please. I *must* go." Her voice shook, and she was very pale. She struggled past him with the suitcase and he woke from his terror and reached for it; but she saw it as an attempt to stop her and grew instantly frightened and fierce. "Leave me *alone*." Her shrillness hung on the rim of hysteria. "If you try to stop me, I'll—I'll hit you," she cried, threatening him impotently with her purse.

Will saw that she was defending her whole world against its deadly enemy; he also saw that she was almost over the edge and began to worry about her driving. "Please, darling." He smiled down at her, intent on getting her quieted at any cost. "Please, I only want to carry it for you." He reached for the suitcase gingerly; she didn't draw back, but she didn't loose her hold on it either. "Marian?" He folded his hand around the handle. "Let me be this much of a gent, at least?"

She let go and he sighed with relief as he followed her down the stairs; but he was sick with pity as he saw how blindly and stiffly she walked. She stood in the hall, waiting for him to open the door for her, and he saw the joke, saw how ludicrous was this featherweight rebel any reasonably strong man could pick up and put in his pocket, this pampered darling who would overthrow Farland's government but couldn't imagine opening a door for herself—it was to laugh, it was a joke about an anarchist who applied to the government for a permit to throw a bomb because that was the polite way to do it. Will tried very, very hard to remember how funny it was. But all he could remember was his own voice, saying with wonder and laughter, "How *little* you are," the first time he had kissed her, when he'd brought her home to her house in Georgetown and she had promptly kicked her shoes off just inside the door. Little and brave and foolish, his eyes and his intelligence told him, and a lump of tears rose in his throat so that he could not have said, "Don't leave me, baby, I love you with all my heart," even if he hadn't known it couldn't work.

He opened the door for her and followed her down the steps and down the walk between the untrimmed hedges, and he lifted the suitcase into Ann's car and waited while she climbed in and started the motor. Across the street, the mailman plodded by and waved at them, calling a greeting Will couldn't hear. He stood still in the sunlight, nodding back at the gray uniform of order because he was afraid to speak, with his eyes fixed on Marian. She started the car and pulled out from the curb without looking at him and he understood that she didn't dare to and was newly wrung with pity. He watched her drive to the corner, waiting to make sure she would stop at the "Stop" sign; then she turned right and was out of sight behind the solid bulk of the red-brick library. And she had not looked back. Will ran into the house, slamming the door behind him, and sat down on the stairs in the dim front hall and cried.

After a while, he got up and locked the door and windows and went upstairs. He pulled down the blinds in the study and took his clothes off, leaving them in a heap on the floor. Then he lay down on the bed there because, he told himself, he needed to be near the phone; if anything happened to Marian and she didn't show up, Ann would call. Meanwhile, he could get some sleep. He shut his eyes, pointed his sharp chin at the ceiling, and stretched his long, thin body out on the small bed with his arms up and his empty hands behind his head. You said you were going to sleep, he chided himself, and then his heart sank because it was an echo; only it had had a smile in it the other time. And "This is how I *like* to go to sleep," Marian had protested. "Holding on." *Oh, is it*, now? her new husband had not said, grinning into the dark, wondering briefly how long it had taken Charles Grayson to learn to go to sleep in these circumstances and deciding happily, the hell with it, he had her now so who cared.

Will got up, walking carefully around the heap of clothes on the floor and also around the thought of succession, now no longer easily dismissed. He went into the bedroom and found a pair of shorts in his drawer and a bottle of sleeping pills in another drawer and went on out to the bathroom without looking at the bed in which he had learned to go to sleep her way. He swallowed two pills and came back to the study and lay down to wait; then he turned on his stomach and put his arms around the pillow and begged for morning.

Sunday morning came with a clamor of bells, but the earliest was in the home of Dr. Snowden in suburban Montgomery County, Maryland. The doctor, still in bed, listened without comment to the few words of a white-coated lab technician at the hospital and then hung up. He looked over at his sleeping wife almost beseechingly before he took the phone up again and dialed the White House number he had been given.

Churchbells banged in Will Farland's disordered dreams and he woke, sweaty and with a pounding heart, when they became the telephone. He reached for the phone with his left hand because his right was numb from having been slept on.

Jake Ruffing said, "Sorry if it's too early, Will, but I wanted to catch you. I'm setting up a meeting with the man for tonight, but I can't be sure what time right now because I don't know when Rosenberg will get in."

"He coming back?" Will asked foggily.

"Just to report. I think you better get over to the office around eight, though you'll probably have to wait. Okay? And look," Jake continued, typically without waiting for an answer. "I'm afraid I'm going to have to ask you to go back down South again, maybe just overnight. If you could go late tonight, that'd give Rosie at least one night at home even if the man doesn't revise present plans. I know Marian's likely to give you shirted hell, but Nedra's been so patient. If you can possibly manage—"

Farland said thickly, "Don't worry about that. I am completely at your disposal," and hung up.

By the time Jake had completed a series of phone calls and dialed the last number, that of the White House, Dan Healy had returned from church. Jake knew the President's old companion must have been up and about for some time, yet he noticed that Healy sounded much as Farland had.

"No dice, Jake. No phone calls, no messages, for any reason. With one exception, of course—but, unless you're calling from the Pentagon, I don't think you're it."

"Well, can I try later? Dan? What's the matter? You got a cold, too?"

"No, Jake. I don't know. Maybe. Look, I'll call you this afternoon and let you know when he'll be available." Healy rang off abruptly and called Leroy, so that things could be set in motion for the move to the hospital.

The President, who would not be available for some time, watched his wife standing in the middle of the flowered carpet of the Lincoln bedroom, wondered whether he ought to help her to one of the white armchairs, and decided bitterly that there was nothing to do but wait until she found her way through the fog of shock that he remembered quite clearly had also surrounded him two days ago. So he simply stood there, tall and useless beside the frivolous Victorian fantasy of a table that she had so delighted in showing him, only a few short months ago, and watched something like what there must have been to see when Scott's party stumbled stubbornly through an Antarctic gale for no reason except to die a little closer to the goal.

He had no role at the moment, Alec counseled himself, except to be there when she could find him; but first, she had to be alone with the fact. He breathed in and out carefully under the great load of grief in his chest and tried not to remember the role she had immediately and instinctively assigned to him as soon as he'd told her, quickly and brutally because he had himself just learned that there was no better way, about Elizabeth. Her hands had shot out before her as if in defense and a voice not hers had cried out, "Oh, what will we do? Oh, Alec—" and then stopped, suddenly and therefore accusingly. The woman had a right, Alec Girard told himself now, staring at the square, gold-framed portrait of Lincoln on the painted wall: *Oh Alec, make this not happen*, was what her instinct had dictated, and it was a just appeal. I took you from your father's house, he said to her in silence and pain, and brought you through deserts and hardships to a strange land and you came, denying me nothing—not your laughter or your loyalty, your mind or your body. I promised to husband you, to cherish you, and you have a right to accuse: what woman can be said to be cherished whose first-born child is torn from her? Who husbands her who cannot keep her safe from the simplest hunger?

"What will we do?" he had echoed. "We'll fight. That's all we can do, Andy."

Alec swallowed tears again, though he'd thought himself finished with them days ago, and looked at the somber pictured face of the homely President who had known it all, the public and the private tragedy. There was nothing to be learned from the picture, though, except patience—and that bitter lesson waited for him in the white, shocked face of his wife, who stood with her head thrown back as though she'd been struck, her nostrils flaring and her eyes wild. Slowly, slowly, she was fighting her way through the blizzard of terror, and with bitter patience her husband watched her pitiable, fumbling progress. "The baby," she said, and Alec sighed and explained about the baby, as he himself had recently been taught. She nodded and looked down at the floor, still holding herself slim and straight in her white summer churchgoing dress, the cool and elegant dress that belonged to a woman who believed herself truly protected and cherished.

She was coming slowly, haltingly now, along the way he had come—asking questions, trying to find the size and shape of the threat. He answered them patiently from the fund of knowledge he had been acquiring in the past two days and watched some small color creep back into her face, recognizing the symptoms of reviving courage, the hope of hope. He had been there, too, and he welcomed it for her—and prayed silently and devoutly that she would be able to stop at that point and not go on, as he had, past the practicalities and the statistics to the total, frozen, angry knowledge that however it worked out, it could not work out as it had been intended. Coming awake this morning, he'd found himself lying in their bed with his fists clenched and his heart pounding as it had not since the war, in combat with the terrible truth that his child—the lovely, dainty girl-child he had explored as cautiously at first as though she were a wilderness—would never be a woman. It was indecent, the just-awake man in the bed had clapped his hand over his mouth to keep from crying out, that he should outlive his child, that a father should give his daughter not in marriage but to death. He lay with his bones wracked with the pain of it, while innocence in a pretty nightgown slept at his side in an Eden he must darken this day.

Now I know, the President said to himself grimly: it is literally true that I would rather have died than bring this to this woman. He was more than forty years old, and half his life was gone; through all the years and all the knowings, he had remained a skeptical man, suspicious of drama, doubtful of any total assertion. He had never come until this moment to a certainty that there were really things a man would rather die than do.

"Alec." Her voice said that she had said it before. He looked up and saw his prayer had not been answered—the small landmarks he had offered her had not for long beguiled her into hope. She had seen beyond them the size of the endless ice.

She was coming toward him, moving by reflex and memory. Frightened, Alec thought of the sleepwalking Lady Macbeth: *Her eyes are open but their sense is shut.*

"Have you had something to eat, darling?" she asked him patiently, unbelievably.

"Andy?" Alec held his hands a little out from his body, as he had for the plump, intent baby Elizabeth walking proudly but gingerly from Andy to him. But he had known how to help Elizabeth. Now he was uncertain, afraid that anything, even he, could topple this precarious balance.

"Come, let me get you something," she coaxed. "You'll feel better when you've had a little food and some rest. Then we'll talk to Elizabeth." Her eyes widened at the sound of the name and Alec held his breath, almost sure she must awaken now. "We'll go tonight, did you say?"

"Yes, that's right." He hesitated, afraid to speak, afraid to stop in case the sound could help to hold her. "The doctor said you'd both be more comfortable, there with other mothers and children—" His voice wound down to a horrified whisper as she reached him and he saw her, inches away, smiling like a ghastly mechanical doll. His head snapped from side to side in an instinctive search for escape; his seeking glance caught first the white panels of the door at one side of him and then, fatally, Abraham Lincoln on the other. The thought of the other President's wife, who may never have recovered from the death of their child, skewered him like an actual, physical stab, so that there was an enormous sudden heaving deep in the center of his body and it was almost more than he could ask of himself not to turn and run. He put out his hand, as much to fend off this blind madwoman as to touch her, and said "Andy" like a groan. And then he had touched her and she crumpled, the strange mask only Andy's face broken into bits around a red O from which her voice said, over and over, "Alec, stop them, stop them, don't let them, Alec, stop them, stop them . . ."

It was terrible, but it was better; the blizzard raged, but she was with him, she was not lost alone in it any more. He lifted her and carried her over to the great carved bed and sat down with her on the white counterpane, holding her on his lap—the con man who could think of nothing better to tell the frail girl he had betrayed than another lie: "It's all right, beloved. It will be all right." He kept his arms tight around her, hurting her with his strength so that she would know it was there, even if it was no good, not enough to stop them, to not let them.

At dusk, Luke Messenger notified the skeleton press crew keeping a bored watch on the Sunday quiet that a tourist who seemed to be talking wildly had been reported stopped at one of the Pennsylvania Avenue gates. He strolled after the reporters, looking benign, as they streamed toward the comic-opera white cubicle where—it turned out, after a while of confusion and explanation—the White House policeman in charge knew nothing about it and somebody must have made a mistake. With his hands in his pockets stretching his trousers tightly across his ample rear, Messenger led the grumbling trek back to the west wing, remarking brightly as he went on the virtues of exercise.

By which time, several safe minutes had passed since Elizabeth Girard, wrapped in a blanket and clutching her doll Amanda, had been carried from the south entrance of the White House and handed into a green Chevrolet normally used for surveillance by a government security agency. Under the unwashed five-year-old hood, a brand-new engine was tuned like a fine watch, and the whip aerial that looked like a thousand others was the only visible sign of a communications system that was the pride and joy of the United States Army Signal Corps. Cozy between her parents, Elizabeth rode, in the most protection technology could provide, through a landscape lighted by a low red-ball sun. She coaxed Mr. Roy, who sat in front beside the driver, to join the game she and her mother had begun to play, in which you found all the alphabet letters, one by one, on signs and license plates. Her father, who was President of the United States and therefore the one you introduced ladies *to* instead of the other way around, was the only one of the four players who found a "Q." It was on a liquor store in Washington and there was still a long way to go, so they started the alphabet over again in Bethesda and Elizabeth spotted the "E" in the sign for Rockville before she sat back, tired but satisfied. And eager to see the other children she would be able to play with while the people in the hospital were making her all well.

Coming back, her father rode alone in the back of the car, watching the scattered fireworks that were beginning already and praying for a like spark of light, a brief and graceful upward flowering that at best was all there would be of the bright new life Andy and he had made in love, so pitiably few years ago.

Forty-four

"This administration," the Preisdent said rapidly and expressionlessly, "has from the first conceived its chief role in the correction of inequalities to lie in moral suasion, executive order, and enforcement through judicial action. It is as a function of this last that I have requested an opinion from the Attorney General on the entry of the federal government into legal actions arising from last week's arrests in Alabama. Like my fellow citizens, I deeply deplore any interference with the right of individuals to travel peacefully anywhere in our country—no, not 'deplore,' that sounds too impotently wringing the hands."

" 'Denounce,' " Rosenberg suggested, without moving. His elbows were propped on the softly shining surface of the massive conference table in the Cabinet Room; he held his head in his hands as if it were a medicine ball and he was about to toss it to Bill Bruyette.

Girard thought it over briefly. "Okay. Make it 'I denounce without reservation' instead of 'I deeply deplore.' Now then—to travel peacefully anywhere in the country, a right secured to them in the Fourteenth Amendment to the Consti—"

Farland interrupted, "No. Maybe in the questioning, if you want. But not right off the bat." He laid two fingers against the bellying curve of the silver coffeepot to see whether it was still hot enough, and then poured himself some more.

"Why not?" the President asked.

"Because it's too loaded. Down there the very words 'Fourteenth Amendment' are heavy artillery. They mean big, fat, all-out War."

"Well? Isn't war what you were after?" Girard grinned. "Who was it who was parading around this very room, humming 'Marche Militaire' between references to blood and glory? Have you become a Quaker overnight?" If Farland had, it hadn't brought him much peace, the President's shrewd eye observed: Will's long face was bony and tired and only the blond prickle of incipient beard disturbed his marked pallor.

"No peacemaker, I," said Farland, grimacing.

"You ever thought of going to work for *Time?*" Rosenberg jeered. "Asked fortyish, balding Rosenberg."

Jake Ruffing said, "Boys, boys," and then stopped because the President was shaking his head.

You have to let them play a little, he told Jake with his silencing look. They had seen too much too recently, and, flying back and forth between that dusty world full of blows and these elegant rooms full of language, they hadn't had much chance to come to terms with any of it. Eyeing his two aides as they went on inventing newsmagazinish insults for each other, Alec thought Rosie was perhaps adjusting to the frustrations better than Farland— maybe, in the face of the unthinkable, a habit of studiousness offered more support than a habit of striking when irons were hot. Confronted with the impossible fact of being regarded as a kind of enemy soldier within the borders of his own country, Rosenberg found impossible facts of history lying around in his mind to match this one against; whereas Farland, confronted with an impossible fact, immediately began scheming to change it.

Which was why, the President concluded, he had been right to choose Mississippi for Farland and Alabama for Rosenberg, for the missions he was sending them out on again today. Which missions had been defined at Girard's Sunday night meeting with his two travel-weary emissaries and amounted, when you boiled it all down, to offers to the two governors to cut the crap and join the union and in return the President would undertake to save their faces. Because in Mississippi Girard was closer to what he was looking for—an executive not too helpless to negotiate, and a solid constitutional issue to take before the public if negotiations failed. Farland could be counted on for the speed and dexterity needed to play on all the governor's weaknesses and yet leave them unmolested as evidence on which to build a court case. The coax-and-threaten technique, in which you manipulate your adversary's desire for peace while holding him in check with your strength, was like jujitsu on a tightrope; it needed the fancy-dancing razzle-dazzle Farland rather than the chess-strategist Rosenberg.

But Alabama was another matter because the picture was unclear; though Rosenberg would carry the same Girard offer to its governor, Girard was less sure with whom he was trading. So Rosie was doomed to another research stint in Alabama, the President thought unhappily, to watch and measure and eventually determine whether the governor's rook was where it was because he had a devious plan for it or because he was a bad chess player. Once Rosie figured out what the man across the table looked like, Will could probably be sent in to negotiate with him.

Meanwhile, both Will and Rosie were suffering, in their separate ways and to their individual degrees, and Jake—Alec decided—didn't quite understand it. Jake, who had spent a war brilliantly getting supplies to where they had to be, had seen some of the men who finally used them—but not the muddy privates first class collecting illicit puppy mascots in the emptied towns of Europe or erecting in Pacific hellholes signposts pointing the way to "Broadway" and "Main Street."

The President winced as he heard Farland accuse his colleague of "Luce morals" and decided that was about enough. "All right, what about war and peace?" he asked easily.

Bruyette said, "Mr. President, Will's right, it seems to me. If the press conference is supposed to be part of that moral suasion, it doesn't make sense to blow them up before you really begin to talk to them."

"That's true, Mr. President," Farland agreed. "They'll simply tune you out the minute they hear those words." He turned as Bruyette tugged at his sleeve, looked uncomprehending for a moment, and then nodded and passed the coffeepot.

"All right." The President nodded at Dan Healy, tending the tape recorder in the lonely reaches of the far end of the table. "I'll stop it after 'travel peacefully anywhere in our country.' " He shook his head as Healy's inquiring look suggested a readiness to run the tape back. "Never mind. I can work on the opening statement later. Let's get on to the questions." His alert glance swept the group. "Or do you want a moment to refuel first? Dan?"

Healy turned off the tape recorder and came along the table. The President watched him at his impromptu buttling for a moment and then turned away to look out of the window at the lawns and flowerbeds drowsing in the July sun and empty his mind for the coming exercise, which would demand complete attention. It was a familiar routine, like the boxer's ritual knee-bends or the singer's preparatory vocalizing, but this time he couldn't quite manage it. He did succeed in evacuating from his thoughts the one that always haunted him now, but when he turned back to the room, telling himself he was ready, he saw them with their glasses and cups and unwillingly remembered Andy in the first days of the house on O Street.

"I always thought politicians drank all the time," she said, emptying the large but overflowing ash tray on the coffee table into a silver silent butler that might as well have been stamped "wedding present." She looked up at him, her eyes clear and laughing in the wide, smooth planes of her so-young face; her brows were dark and winged and her hair was a brown, close cap. "Now we have oceans of bourbon left over."

"Well, they do drink more at this sort of powwow in Vermont," the Senator told his new wife absently as he packed papers away into a brown envelope. "But beer. And then, not much more."

"It's bourbon in Washington, all the wives said." She got up and brought a tray and began to collect coffee cups. "But here, it was all coffee."

"Darling, it is bourbon in Washington, but not in great quantities tonight. They were *working*." He spoke gravely, out of deference to her earnest innocence and the importance of this, her debut as a politician's wife. "The men who were here tonight have been around for a long time, and those who do much mixing of bourbon and business tend to have shorter careers."

Her laughter was light and free. "Have you ever noticed how everyone has notions about everyone else's profession? Those men probably think all artists drink when they're working, just as I thought *they* did."

"Familiarity does wonders in demolishing stereotypes." Alec took the tray out of her hands and set it down. "Some of the things I heard in prep school about women turned out to be wildly untrue once I began to observe a real woman."

She let him turn her with his hands on her shoulders, but she kept her face hidden from him. "Alec, I hope you don't expect me to believe that you began these—researches—with me."

"But I did," he said firmly. "And I do." He shook her shoulders lightly, making her look at him. "And you do believe me, don't you?"

The tall, beautiful young woman who had been Washington's most sought-after glamour girl, and who was now successfully launched as a hostess to political skull sessions, put her arms around his neck and hugged him with all her not inconsiderable strength. "Absolutely," she said, and that was all she got to say for a while.

The President accepted a glass of iced tea and sipped at it briefly while he watched Jake bolt a cup of coffee as though it had indeed been a shot of bourbon. "Ready? Blah, blah, blah. End of opening statement." He put the glass down on the small table beside the window and stood straight, rocking a little on his heels, before he pointed. "Yes?"

"Martin Halloran, *Washington Tribune*," said Jake. "Mr. President, several Negro leaders in talks during the past week seemed to indicate a certain dissatisfaction with the speed, or the extent, or both, of the administration's activities on behalf of the Negro's struggles in the South. May we have your comment on this?"

"Well, if they've been indicating any dissatisfaction, it hasn't been where I could hear it," the President said amiably. "I think the responsible leadership is well aware that my activities on behalf of the Negro began well before my election and have continued steadily since. Some people may need reminding that one of my first executive orders set up machinery to prohibit job discrimination by any business working on a government contract. But I don't think the Negro leaders are among those people." He nodded at Farland. "Yes?"

"Gil Kimball, *New York Leader*," Farland began, and a small stir was evident in the room. "Sir, since the Negro is no different from any other citizen, I imagine he asks, like the voter in the well-known anecdote, 'What have you done for me *lately?*' Can you tell us what you have in mind to do for him now, particularly by way of putting an end to the current charades in the South—which you yourself, sir, have characterized as unwarranted interference with the Negro's rights as a citizen?"

"I don't know that I'm quite in agreement with one of your implications, Gil," the President replied, his voice even and friendly. "The one that it's I who do things for the Negro. I want to make it clear that it's not a question of my personal favor for his cause—which exists, as I don't need to tell either you or him—but a question of his rights, which are guaranteed to him by the Constitution and the people of the United States and in no way depend upon my personal favor or my party's platform. Even if I thought it was all wrong, I'd still have an obligation to support any citizen's claim to his rights."

Ruffing turned his face toward the tape recorder and said, "Keep that," in a voice loud enough to be picked up.

The President nodded but went on addressing himself to the pseudo-Kimball who sprawled in a chair across the table. "As for what I've done lately, there's a long series of moves, all on the public record, beginning with the assignment of Vice-President Cannon to the President's Committee Against Discrimination in Employment, which I mentioned earlier." He shifted from his role as a President at a press conference to his behind-the-scenes tone and began listing snatches of phrases, ticking off on his fingers the items they represented. "Twenty million jobs—and promotion chances. Complaint and grievance procedures. Ummm. Federal court order to stop those evictions for voting activity in Tennessee. Oh yes—the executive order denying federal impact funds to segregated schools. Which we were able to do by executive order," he added, switching back to his public voice, "and thus were not forced to wait for Congress to act."

"Hear, hear," called the only member of Congress present.

"Wherever it was possible, we persuaded states and counties to abandon discriminatory voting registration procedures," the President orated blandly, even while he fixed Bruyette with a mild glare. "Those who would not be persuaded have found themselves facing the Justice Department in court. This will continue and increase, if necessary.

"A word about this persuasion," Girard went on, his face serious and intent. "I have always maintained that this is a government of reasonable men, and the same is presumably true of the governments of the states. The federal and state governments have an interest in common; whatever the differences in their outlook on the Negro's position in society, no responsible men want to see the streets replace the Congress or violence displace debate. Some of our Negro citizens are angry and embittered and understandably tend to see only what remains to be done: but let us not forget what *has* been done. Informal and fruitful conversations with local authorities have succeeded in bringing about without violence the long-delayed integration of schools in Atlanta, Memphis, Dallas, and other cities, and more will be opened to both races in September—"

"Too peaceful," Bill Bruyette objected. "You're sounding like a Quaker meeting again."

Girard nodded and continued without breaking stride. "Where we have not met with reason, we have acted through the courts once again. For example, early this year, court action protected schoolteachers in one state when their salaries were threatened because they had taught integrated classes. We are, by the means I stated in my opening remarks, moving on all fronts to ensure that the intent of the law is everywhere carried out. I refer, of course, to the federal law, which has been held to be supreme over any state laws that restrict rights granted by—"

Rosenberg said sharply, "You're doing it again, Mr. President—pointing big guns that you're not ready to fire. If we're going to take that line, if we're going to make open war, then why are we still negotiating?"

Alec sighed and let his hands drop, along with his role as performer. "Right. I got carried away, I guess."

"Not bloody loikely," Bruyette said. "I wouldn't say you've been proceeding with anything but the greatest caution."

Alec arched his eyebrows. "You're protesting, old son?"

"You might say that," Bruyette said carefully.

"You have a right to petition, you know," Girard said slowly, after a little silence.

"And you can lobby," the Congressman told him. "If you recall, I even phoned to remind you of my availability to my constituents."

Their stares locked. Girard sighed deeply and then smiled. "Your office or mine?"

"How about on the steps of the Supreme Court building? Just to keep the powers in balance?"

"Right. Do we dress?" Alec began to laugh. "Or just redress?"

Jake Ruffing, who thought that was very possibly the worst pun he had ever heard in all his life, nevertheless looked like a man who'd just had a lucky break. He turned away to leave the two schoolboys to their mending and got himself another cup of coffee.

"Well, *I* don't throw dissenting states out of the union, either," Bruyette was saying to a happier-looking Girard when Jake came back and raised his whip hand threateningly. The Congressman sighed. "Okay, okay. My turn. I hope you'll recognize me in blackface."

Alec straightened, donned his press conference demeanor, and said, "Yes?"

"Carver Jackson, *Press Review*," Bruyette announced. "Mr. President, I know you're aware that Negro Americans proceeding peacefully through several southern states in company with some of their white brothers have been the victims of unjustified, unprovoked, and unmitigated police brutality in several jurisdictions. Many of those who joined the Freedom Trips are now in jail or under indictment in Mississippi and Alabama communities, to choose only two states in which experience indicates that they can hardly expect to meet with justice. I repeat, Mr. President, these patriots are incurring personal danger and expense in a brave test of the desegregation of interstate travel facilities. And I ask you, sir, what are you going to do to protect them from the bigots and fanatics?"

"Mr. Jackson," the President said, his voice deep and slow, "so long as I hold this office, I shall support the right of any citizen to cross state lines without interference. As a human being, I am, like everyone else, sickened and dismayed by the mob violence that has erupted on occasion, particularly the most recent bus burning in Mississippi. And I urge upon those responsible for law and order, in Alabama and in similarly troubled areas, the most prompt and effective action in putting a stop to such outrages and punishing their perpetrators."

"But you won't move in to stop it, is that what you're saying?"

Ruffing said, "Hey, now," but the President waved him aside and went on looking at Jackson-Bruyette. "No, I want to answer—I want to make myself perfectly clear. Mr. Jackson, I deplore, though I understand, provocative behavior that leads to divisiveness and violence—"

"No!" Rosenberg and Farland shouted together.

The President went on, undeterred by the interruption. "—and I urge that it be avoided and forsworn; I want to point out that the movement inspired, as its leader noted, by the doctrines of Christ and Gandhi was totally admirable and totally successful. As a politician, I urge my friends in the protest movement to stick to what works."

"Mr. President," Rosenberg shouted angrily, and jumped to his feet even as Alec nodded at him. "I would like to read to you, sir, a statement from Sheriff Monk Shipworth of Trumpet, Mississippi, who told the press last week, and I quote, 'When outsiders come down here to a peaceful community and stir up trouble by provocative action—' and so on. I ask you, sir, aren't you saying the same thing as this representative of fascist brutality?"

"You haven't identified yourself," the President said mildly. He shaded his eyes with his hand and peered into imaginary lights. "Ah yes, I see—it's Moe Pebble." He smiled, and inquired with friendly interest, "Is it possible that you fellows will someday quit thundering on the left about whose fault it is that we ran out of gas and get out and help push?"

"I know the beautiful liberals irk the hell out of you," Rosenberg said viciously. "But you'll end up with Pebble in your shoe, and it's a long walk to the next election."

"Mr. Pebble," Alec said in a cold, commanding voice, "I am not dismayed to learn that I share a prejudice in favor of nonviolence with anyone at all, even Sheriff Shipworth of Trumpet, who possibly also loves his mother as I do mine. What is important is that I do *not* share some of his other apparent convictions. I put it to you, gentlemen, that criticism of the actions of any people does not yet, in this country, imply throwing them out of the union. That goes for Sheriff Shipworth, and it most certainly goes for any citizens of the United States who wish to travel freely and peacefully within its borders. I am trying to say that I need not approve of their every action in order to insist on their rights, and I make this distinction now because I believe it exists in the minds of many law-abiding white southerners who are not adequately represented by the Sheriff Shipworths." Without any change in his manner, a fellow named Girard, who had gone to college with a fellow named Rosenberg, added, "And you can tell your academic demagogues to put that in their—"

Jake Ruffing's intervening "Mr. President" was somehow marvelously quiet and cultured, summoning those who would fall from debate to invective. Alec pulled up short like a runner in mid-stride and, while the others smirked, managed to make it back to dignity in time.

He nodded graciously. "Of course. The *New York* . . . I'm sorry, I can't seem to recall the name of your good gray archives."

"Sir." Jake's voice wore hornrimmed glasses. "Are we to understand from the statement you have just concluded that you will move to the physical defense of the Freedom Trip people in the event that—"

"Gentlemen," the President said. "I will uphold and defend the Constitution, as I swore I would do. What that means in specific terms depends to a great extent upon what happens. The Constitution applies equally to Trumpet, Mississippi's right to police its own community and to the Negro's right to travel in interstate commerce, and I will not willingly abrogate either right. I do not believe the Constitution gives the national government the right to step in every time there's a breach of the peace, so long as the authorities on the spot are dealing with it promptly and justly. If and when continued and uncontrolled incidents of mob violence occur against a group of people exercising their constitutional rights, and confining themselves to that exercise, then I shall consider that a constitutional obligation to intervene exists and I shall act on it. I urge now that both sides do their best to prevent such an eventuality by the most earnest attention to—no, never mind that last. Leave it at the warning."

"Mr. President," Bruyette called, "are we to take that as a warning?"

"I hope all participants in this matter will take it as a warning, and be guided by it. Civil disorder is painful to the individual and unhealthful to the body politic. And the spectacle of it does our nation, as seen by the rest of the world, no good whatever in terms of incurring respect." The President looked around. "Now, are we going to confine this to one subject? I think perhaps too many people are forgetting that a great deal is going on in other directions, and some of it is just as important and just as directive to our national future as the struggle in the South."

"One more question on this, please, Mr. President?" Farland drawled. "B. U. Collick, *Rural Seedbed*."

"A very thought-provoking sheet indeed, Mr. Collick," the President remarked gravely. "I read it with considerable attention, all during the campaign. As an exercise in humility."

"Sir," Farland said over the laughter, "there have been charges that the Freedom Trip people are being inspired and instructed—and even, it may be, financed—by the Kremlin. As part of their plan to take over our glorious country by fomenting riots and breaking down morality in this grand republic. I hear," he went on, his voice grow suddenly thin and high with outrage, "that on those buses they're *necking*, and under pictures of Lenin."

"My dear sir, I share your dismay, but I am delighted to inform you—and through you, your readers, those upright, solid, right-wing nuts," the President said, in a voice throbbing with sincerity, "that I am familiar with those charges—which are not exactly charges, are they, but an editorial statement in a rather badly printed sheet called *Christian Rectitude*?—and there is nothing to them, really. It's my pleasure to report that the picture thought to be Lenin is actually one of the Smith Brothers, who have contributed free cough drops. The other Smith brother fell down when the bus was hit by the stones thrown by the upright, solid, right-wing nuts of Trumpet, Mississippi. As for the necking, I share your horror." Girard pursed his lips, surveying them all with a gaze gone coldly furious. His voice held onto its light irony, but not for long. "I want to go on record here and now in total support of your group's abhorrence of sex. When I'm sorely troubled with the problems of office, it frequently soothes me like a fresh clean breeze from the subsidized cornfields." The men at the table looked at each other uneasily, as if a toy gun had suddenly been found to be loaded. "I refer, of course, to the probability that if you people keep on with your crusade against sex, you will eventually, like the Albigensian heretics, put yourself out of business through the inexorable results of sheer purity. Bless you, sir, and your people—thanks to their thin lips and tiny minds, we will always have a leaden burden to slow us as we drag our way painfully into the twentieth century. Still brushing off the slime."

"Alec." Bruyette spoke softly, but urgently, like a rider calming an excited mount.

Alec shook his head. "I told you, old son, I get carried away." His voice had recovered, but his color was still poor. "I apologize. It's just that, some days, the problem of coaxing the decent people out of hiding in the South seems downright insurmountable."

"Some of us think it really is." Farland seemed reluctant to say it.

"I know. That's all right. But I think I have to try." The President turned toward them with eagerness; he spoke informally but with the earnestness of an advocate seeking support—and of a passionate man who has been too long restrained. "No state is bigger than the federal government and I can prove it, county by county and case by case—which isn't dramatic enough, maybe, to satisfy people who have understandable cause for outrage. But though it's not dramatic, it's solid. Slow, but inexorable. It beats down the bastards one by one, by making them visibly smaller right on their home grounds for everyone to see. You knock those guys off with an impressive display of power and you run the chance of making martyrs of them, or at least encouraging an underground movement. But if you show them up as powerless to all the people who are now afraid of them, you've got them safely knocked out of the box—for now and for the future, too." The President pounded his right fist into the palm of his left hand, and the soft impact hovered on the unstirring air.

"It's a reasonable plan," Bruyette said finally. "But a political man's plan."

"There are political men on both sides of those street scenes down there. I've just got to hope the political men can gain me the time I need."

Some clues as to what Alec needed time for were emerging, Bruyette discovered when he listened to Act Two of the mock-up press conference. For the President faltered a little when Farland—being, quite effectively, a well-known television commentator—asked him whether the European journey of Senator Youngblood and his Foreign Relations Committee colleagues was connected with rumors that the Russians were planning a new challenge. Had the President "finalized" any plan for such a contingency, the questioner asked politely, or was he awaiting the return of the senators before doing so?

The President squinted at Farland, hesitated, and then said that a report by Senator Youngblood and his committee would be useful and productive as on-the-spot observation by trained and perceptive minds. He added that intelligent cooperation between the legislative and executive branches of the government was vital to the health of the country. But it sounded lame, and Rosenberg was already shaking his head.

"Is that quite responsive, sir?" Farland inquired frostily. "I don't understand whether a policy now exists in regard to a new Russian move—"

"I'm delighted to hear it," the President interrupted smoothly. "And I think that, on the whole, it would be a good idea to leave that doubt. Though I understand and respect the passion you gentlemen entertain for clarity and specificity, I imagine you can understand that some areas are, in the national interest, better left unclear and unspecific at present."

"Oh, I don't think that'll do it," Rosenberg said doubtfully. "Too lofty. Good for a university debate on secret diplomacy versus the people's right to know, maybe."

Jake Ruffing pushed toward the center of the table a leaf torn from his scratch pad. "Don't be an intellectual snob, Rosie. This is how it'll look."

Rosenberg read aloud the headline Ruffing had printed unevenly: *Keep*

Russ in Dark, Girard Warns. "I withdraw my objection," he said admiringly. "I bow to Jake's common touch."

Bruyette watched Alec laugh and went on arguing with himself about what could be the matter: Alec had been through tighter squeezes than this one without crumbling and even without any noticeable chipping away of his good humor; yet now, even when he laughed, there was an edge to it. And that blowup a little while ago, when his characteristic irony had got lost in something close to hysteria, so that he'd begun with a rapier and ended by slashing with a saber . . . A knowledge that was not logical but only something born of many years' experience told Bill something was wrong, very wrong; and the amount of emotion showing in the normally restrained Alec led Bill to a hunch that the something had to do with Andy. Furthermore, why, when the group was only this size, were they meeting in the west wing instead of more cozily on the second floor of the Mansion? Andy was not supposed to be out of town . . . The Congressman wriggled unhappily, feeling a little like a gossip columnist. And then he decided, abandoning the gathering of evidence to stick with the promptings of a deeper knowledge, the hell with it, one thing it wasn't was wife trouble. He sighed, satisfied with this more workable hypothesis—because now it was something he could have a word with Ruffing about afterward. Bruyette might have been out of touch lately, but Jake never was.

". . . whether your family will be going to Vermont for the summer as usual, sir, and whether there's any news of them you'd care to share with us," Rosenberg was simpering in an extravagant falsetto.

The President eyed him warily. "Why yes, Miss Peake," he said slowly. "They're up in Vermont now, and I spoke to my mother on the phone just the other day. As for news, well—this is off the record, of course—" he leaned forward, lowering his voice confidentially "—it seems Mother is a little troubled because my sister Agnes has announced that she wants to marry a Negro. We all feel that, coming at this time—"

The rest was lost in the men's laughter, in which Bruyette joined. But somewhere at the back of his mind, the thought registered that it was odd of Alec to construe his "family" to mean his parents rather than Andy and the children. The little group began to break up then; listening to the departing men who had quarreled and were in many ways at odds and yet still had been held together as a team, the Congressman concluded that, though something sizable was apparently eating Alec, whatever it was had not affected that amazingly quick mind, that impressively dextrous footwork.

The footwork Bruyette admired not only endured but improved at the actual press conference—which, as usual, was far less rough than the "rehearsal"; Alec Girard, never a man whose dignity depended on deferential gestures, encouraged his "think boys" to attack ruthlessly. In turn, because they were armed with a more accurate chart of the President's anatomy than the reporters had, they found and probed brutally at the soft spots. But the official press conferences were less fun than the private ones, too—the witty

President might observe at his powwow that a certain senator's speech was "an example of the humble-jumble school of oratory," but, asked about it by the reporters, his comment would be translated into something rather more urbane. Thus, a House committee chairman who had been dismissed in private as a "senile adventurer" became, in public, a "venerable legislator"— which still reminded everybody that the old man ought to have been retired. But nicely, nicely—that sheathed jab that had made the President's televised press conferences celebrated drew blood, but it never messed up the carpet.

However, at a small meeting in the office of the managing editor of the *Washington Tribune,* the latest press conference was not proving a subject for celebration. Tired and a little battleworn after the full staff meeting, the ME had held back his editorial page editor and the newspaper's political cartoonist to try to seek an understanding within the confines of the tricky command problem of the top offices of journalism—which requires a kind of continuous defining to the laborers in the vineyard of a free press the sometimes conflicting rights to free speech. What the ME was after now was a "wait and see" policy on Alec Girard, for reasons of his own conviction; he was prepared to surrender with a sigh on the matter of the editorial, but the cartoon showing Girard as Hamlet was just too much, he felt.

"It's your paper," the cartoonist said with elaborate indifference—causing mild terror in both editors, for he collected Pulitzer Prizes as a dog collects fleas. "I just draw the pitchers around here," he went on, matching his voice to the deliberate ignorance of his diction.

"Cut it out, Alf," the ME said more calmly than he felt.

"All right." The cartoonist let his propped legs down with a thump. "On the front page the other day you had a photo of a Negro with a bleeding head lying in the street somewhere in Alabama. But on the editorial page, I'm not even allowed to draw a doublet and hose on the guy who lets it happen."

"You're allowed, Alf. And you're allowed, too," the ME said to his editor. "All I'm asking is that you don't do it just because you're allowed. It's easy to attack—hell, half the country is attacking him for not moving, and if the college kids hadn't gone home for the summer they'd be burning him in effigy, I suppose." He sighed. "Look, fellas, I'm not trying to be a little Hitler, I'm asking you to entertain my point of view, that's all. Which is that Hamlet is not a fair allusion because Girard's not indecisive at all. He's made a decision, and he's acting on it."

"I don't call a persistent squirm a policy," the editorial page editor said bluntly. The subscribers to the *Tribune* would hardly rise in protest if he were replaced, and he knew it. He also knew that he was no hero and would not fight to the death; but neither would he lay down his arms until he had to.

"A 'persistent squirm' may be the only policy that makes sense right now," the ME argued, wondering why it was that his subeditor, whose own attitude bore a strong resemblance to Girard's, was unable to sympathize with it or even see it in the President. "Look, you know Alec Girard. Don't *you* think he'd prefer to go charging straight ahead? Wouldn't any politician rather step out like a hero, proclaiming the good and the beautiful?"

"And losing a basketful of southern electoral votes."

"Hell, he could lose those on the basis of his executive orders alone. Where they go at the next election depends on what else there is to go to, and Girard knows that." The ME shook his head. "I'm trying to show you my side, which is that this isn't a political maneuver but a brave try on behalf of a considered policy that he thinks is right. I don't even know whether I think so, too. But it's neither cynical nor indecisive, and I don't think it ought to be treated that way." He sighed. "You and Alf—well, I'm not giving orders; I'm lobbying, that's all."

"If it's for a delay only, I might buy it," his subordinate said thoughtfully. "I admit I have an allergic response to trickiness, so maybe I'm over-reacting."

"I'd say so." Rather than say, the ME added silently, that thinking instead of just breaking out in hives was, in a way, what civilization was all about. Chess was better than war, either within countries or between them.

"Be a pretty poor football game," Alf remarked, "if the only acceptable play was straight through the line."

The ME smiled. "I recommend a little reading in the history of Abraham Lincoln's tricky attempts to avoid the Civil War."

"He lost," said the would-be pragmatist who drew the pictures.

"Right. But it's a different country now. Maybe one that learned something, so it's worth a try to avoid splitting it. Even if the exercise doesn't make Girard look good. Which is something," the ME observed dryly, "he surely knows the value of. So he can be assumed to know what he's giving up." He watched the idea of Alec Girard as underdog enter the attention of the editor, a good man but hagridden by the wistful-intellectual set's fondness for anything believed to be too idealistic for the public. "Now don't let me press you against your judgment," the ME said as he finished doing just that, "but I'd appreciate it if you'd think this over . . ."

When they had gone, he sat alone in his private office, feeling lonely. And sorry for himself, until it occurred to him how lonely it must be over on Pennsylvania Avenue right now.

Forty-five

On the lawn below the wide window of the room in which Andrea Girard was staying at the hospital, a two-armed sprinkler sprayed sparkles in two low arcs, then twitched abruptly and did it again. "Imagine a booster appearing, out of the blue," the President told his wife, his eyes on the sprinkler. "I very nearly fell on his neck in tears of gratitude, only we were in the Treaty Room and the surroundings seemed to forbid, somehow." He grinned down at her. "In your decorating, you seem to have forgotten to provide a secluded nook for sobbing thanks."

"Poor Alec. Is every man's hand really so against you?"

"Nonsense," he said quickly. "I'm coloring it all a bit highly, in an effort to compete for your tender attentions. Actually, Harold Hoffman was with us, too, you know, and he was his usual composed self. But it was after he left that Senator Youngblood made his rather startlingly demonstrative statement." He looked embarrassed. "What do you say when somebody tells you you're being a great statesman, a man for the ages, all that sort of thing—I mean, not from a dais? All I could think of was you saying 'La, sir.' "

"Good heavens, you certainly don't say that!" Andy laughed, but with the muffled, shrouded sound that had so quickly become habitual. As if she expected to hear a small, fretful complaint, she glanced at the connecting door beyond which Elizabeth slept.

Alec sighed, examining his wife with some pain in his eyes. It was like being a new girl at school, she had said when he asked her how it was for her, staying there; the other mothers were polite and wary, and it was understood that she would keep her place. Which was a low one in the hierarchy of tragedy that, despite the cheerful sunshine and the matter-of-fact nurses, still informed the air in this marina in which children—some suffering, some not—bobbed at anchors their elders hoped would hold.

This looked like a schoolgirl's room, Alec thought, surveying the neat single bed and the round table that was littered with fat books like a student's desk when exams are approaching. The student in residence here was doing her industrious if pathetic best to learn all she could as soon as she could of the dimensions of the threat with which she must live. It had already paid off somewhat, Alec acknowledged—without his wife's researches to explain them away, the purplish bruises on his daughter's arms might have caused him more than immediate alarm. There was nothing Andy's instant learning could do, though, to lessen the dismay that rose in him like sickness at the sight of the child's increasing frailty, the lusterless eyes, the white, almost translucent skin. It would be better as soon as the drug took hold, Andy insisted; he tried his best to believe her.

She looked like a student, too, in her simple cotton dress and ballet slippers, with the pink coloring doing something to combat her own pallor. Besides, she was artfully made up, Alec noted, studying her face raised to the searching sunlight in the window; the only clue was the absence of the small golden freckles that would have been visible across the bridge of her nose if her secret skill had not hidden them. She'd been to a lot of trouble to prevent him from worrying about her, he thought, and could hardly bear the touching knowledge of her stratagem; but she was entitled at least to believe she had succeeded. So he kept his gaze calm and unworried as he listened to her talk like someone writing a letter home from foreign places, and he thought his own thoughts.

Which were also a *terra* somewhat *incognita*. At the borders were bits of Youngblood's worrying guess that the Soviet leader was on the spot for sure this time and would have to produce some bone to throw his populace this summer. The devious researches whose results were available to Secretary of State Hoffman confirmed that the upcoming Kaslov address was going to be on the nasty side—maybe even nasty enough to force the U.S. to respond in kind, lest its populace find the government not non-Communist enough. Alec thought ironically that the *Washington Tribune* editorial page cartoonist, who had drawn Girard as a channel swimmer plying nervously toward the beckoning shores of "Adjournment" among a sea of sharks (labeled with names known and honored in the Congress), should have included Premier Kaslov among the sharks; he was the biggest and fiercest, had tasted much blood already, and roved the sea whether Congress did or not.

"This little girl lives quite close by, I gather," Andy was going on with her description of Elizabeth's new hospital "colleague." "Her father works for one of the government offices that've moved out to the suburbs. He's the one who's been over here, mostly—they have two other children, so the mother has to stay home to tend them. The father got a furlough or something from his office."

"Annual leave," Alec said absently. Which runs out eventually, he did not add. But annual leave was intended to be used for vacations and could be accumulated only up to a stated maximum. What would the civil servant who was Alec's hospital "colleague" do when he had to go back to work and all that was left was one tired, frightened mother to be divided between the sick child and the others at home?

"Alec, I want to talk to you, please, about Sandy."

He nodded to indicate his attention, wondering whether she'd been reading his mind; then he saw that she had a sort of prepared presentation, so he waited in silence for her to make her points. But he was thinking that, though he might be swimming between sharks, the thing that hurt was the strangeness of his home waters—not cool, but not buoying as they always had been, whatever else went wrong. We speak to each other now with such care, he thought despairingly: not at all like Alec and Andy, who had addressed each other with this kind of caution in the past only when a serious quarrel was under way. He knitted his brows, agreeing that the baby probably would be better off in the bosom of the noisy, affectionate Ruffing family than in the quiet of the Mansion, where he couldn't count on much besides physical care and the imperfect attentions of his busy father; Alec saw that Andy was trying very hard not to denigrate in any way his supervision of their son, and he arranged his face to show her that he understood, that he knew she didn't distrust him. But behind his arranged face he went on wondering sadly why he and Andy, in alliance against a foe, were drawing apart instead of to-gether. He thought of the awful enemy disease and "Divide and conquer" came into his head, forcing him to disguise a shudder.

Alec watched Andy's eyes and her hands making her case and wondered whether this would be a good place to bring up the problem of telling people, a subject they had both been avoiding. Not that Jake would have needed telling: Jake had a way of knowing everything, and a note from Alec a few days ago—asking for any available data showing whether the incidence of leukemia was in any way correlated with radioactive fallout from nuclear testing—was certainly enough to start Jake wondering why the President was wondering about this at this moment, when no speech or statement on nuclear testing pended. Alec closed his eyes briefly to banish the memory of the long, sleepless night in which the sick thought that he might be even a little respon-sible for his daughter's illness had been only one of many sick and frighten-ing thoughts. The morning had brought only the comfort of reassuring statistics, but it was something.

"I just hate to," Andy said hopelessly but with a faint stubbornness, when Alec mentioned telling people. She wanted to be solaced by others, he could see in her eyes, but not even that at the price of taking the great step, of making the fatal admission. Carefully, he proposed a compromise—the rumor mill was bound to begin to turn, if it hadn't already, and they would let the ground be thus prepared; then, when the promised remission had been achieved, Elizabeth could be at home and walled in while her parents re-leased the intelligence into the somnolence of a Washington from which Con-gress had departed. Andy agreed with an air of postponed dread and a grati-tude so pitiable that it tore at Alec like claws.

Elizabeth awakened then, calling with her new querulousness, and they went in, after carefully smoothing their already careful faces. Alec delivered a chapter of the biography of Dudumber the Cucumber, by request; but he did not, he noticed—and hoped Andy didn't notice—end with the hero in peril, as he always had before. Before Alec took his discreet leave from the hospital grounds, Dudumber, an inch from being snapped at by a hungry turtle, had been rescued by a family of cardinals with a bright-red Daddy and an olive-green Mommy; he had the satisfaction of taking away with him the lively look of wonder the remarkable coincidence of the cardinals—"Just like Mommy showed me yesterday, Daddy," she marveled—had awakened in that pale and beloved face.

The rumor mill had begun to grind even while the President traveled back to his office. For one thing, a Gray Lady, coming with toys to the playroom of this hospital wing, was startled to see a famous face on the slim figure emerg-ing from a door at the far end of the wing, near the back staircase that had recently been closed for unspecified repairs. First Ladies visited hospitals, it was true—but not, the volunteer told herself, her eyes thoughtful, in bare legs

and flatheeled slippers. There had been something curiously at home in
Andrea Girard's costume.

"Something is sure as hell going on," an outraged civil servant grumbled
from a phone booth to the old hand at the *Washington Tribune* who ran the
federal employees' column; even after deciding to complain to the press, the
government worker had been judicious enough to wait until the end of the
day and call from a public telephone.

The *Tribune* man answered courteously; years of putting the column together had taught him to be duly grateful for tips like this. Privately, he suspected that this indignant tale of canceled leave for the day before the July
Fourth weekend—"I wouldn't have made any plans if they hadn't okayed it,
but it was all cleared weeks ago"—and then, outrage upon outrage, equally
sudden orders to report for work on the Saturday morning, would amount
to nothing more than an ordinary snafu somewhere. But you never knew, so
he asked, "What did you say this digest was about?" and wrote "leukemia
studies, updating reports" on his copy paper. He thanked his caller with a
promise to look into it, hung up, and made a note for the morning to call a
fellow in Public Health Service's information office who might be willing and
able to discover what Somebody with enough power to get overtime authorized had had such a pressing need for data on leukemia on the Friday before
July Fourth. Then he read through the proof of tomorrow morning's column,
returned it with a few minor corrections, and cleared his desk. He departed
the premises for the day shortly thereafter, with a cheerful wave for those
around him who were not so lucky as to be features.

Marian Farland, who was a feature, did not avail herself of her similar
advantages but instead hung around in her office waiting for Ann Taswell,
who worked reporters' hours. She used the time to call Bettina Little to check
on the girls and ask news of Rosa. The girls were doing nicely, Bettina was
about to cook supper, Aunt Gloria had taken Trixie to the movies. Rosa had
called once from somewhere near the Alabama border and described what
sounded to Marian, at second hand, rather like an army staging area. Things
were getting organized, Rosa was finding the weather hot but the company
pleasant, and she had warned her daughters—and asked them to remind
Marian—that absence of communication from her in the next few weeks was
not to be construed as alarming: phones were difficult to get to and expensive
to use, and time for writing letters was short. Marian hung up after trading
her own reassurances for Bettina's: Sharlie was fine, Peter had not after all
had second thoughts about being a camper, and Dick had even written a
letter. She also reminded Tina of her changed telephone number, in case she
should be wanted, and the light, gay voice assured her that it was wrote
down.

Marian wondered idly why she'd agreed to go with Ann to the settlement
house "Talent Show" Ann was going to cover for her continuing "Negro in

Washington" story. But when Ann came for her, she trailed along willingly enough, neither happy nor unhappy to be going.

She told this to Ann later, as they drove away from the dark streets among sagging houses, and added that now she was glad she had come. "And I see why you called it 'tender,' too—they're lovely." Once you got used to all the dark faces, among which Ann's silvery head particularly had glittered so strangely, it was just like one of the recitals children's music teachers put on once a year to show the parents what they had been paying for. "That little girl who sang—Crystal, was that her name? It was a beautiful voice."

"Maybe another Marian Anderson. Who knows?"

Marian smiled, thinking of the warm, surprising alto. "It had an odd effect, though, when she did 'Drink to Me Only with Thine Eyes'—I mean, that should be lutes, not velvet. I had a feeling Ben Jonson wouldn't have known quite what to make of it."

"Oh, I don't know," Ann said lightly. "Crystal may have a closer connection with Ben Jonson than a lot of people who sound more appropriate singing his song. Don't forget, somebody found practically untouched traces of Elizabethan English in the whites in some of those southern hills. And it wouldn't surprise me if the blood of a few of them runs through Crystal's veins." She glanced at Marian's startled face in the shifting shadows of the dark car. "Think about it."

"I'd rather not, maybe," Marian admitted. "I prefer to think of oppression as—something more impersonal." She yawned a little and stretched. "Anyway, I've never found the question of what kind of blood is in whose veins absorbing. I'm ignorant after corpuscles, which I understand come in red and white. And you're supposed to have both races."

"Do you want to come back to the office with me? I've got to—"

Marian broke in to say that Ann mustn't worry about entertaining her—it was a pleasure to have nothing particular to do. "If you could drop me off at your place, it would be fun just to fool around." Unbidden, a small wonder about where Will was tonight rose to her mind. "Maybe I'll even do our wash, just to salve my conscience."

Ann laughed. "There isn't a lot of wash in my household, Marian. You forget." She hesitated, and then, her voice saying under the words that this was as good a time as any, she said Will had called again today. "He wanted me to 'talk sense' to you."

"I'm sorry, Annie, I told him not to get you involved. He said he wouldn't, but he's just completely untrustworthy."

"The word is 'ruthless.' I don't mind. I even respect him for pursuing his objective with so much determination."

"I don't want to talk about him," Marian said roughly.

"Well, I do feel bound to transmit his plea—which was that he feels he was a fool, that 'a guy with a wife like Marian ought to have brains enough not to neglect her.' He asks whether a man isn't entitled to try to fix his mistake."

Marian said violently, "I don't care what he said, I don't trust him. I've about decided that, whatever else I am or do, one thing is clear—I'm finished with Will Farland."

"Since I'm in the difficult position of trying to preserve a neutral status, I won't offer any argument." Ann slid the car into the curb in front of the tall apartment house, its glittery white stone front like sugar icing in the street light. "But if my observation is of any use, you are—whatever you may say in anger—far from finished with Will Farland."

" 'We shall o-ver-cuh-uh-um,' " Marian sang, as she had with the crowd at the "Talent Show"; she meant light defiance by it, but she sobered as it occurred to her that she too was oppressed and longing for freedom. She got out of the car and leaned in to say she'd see about the wash and then take a bath and go to bed. She had a lot to overcome besides Will, too, she thought. Like plain homesickness—the nerves in her hands seemed imbued with the remembered feel of rumpled, mudstained jeans whose pockets might contain anything at all, even something alive, but would always contain a single Kleenex that, if missed, would leave its fatal shreds on everything in the wash.

"Why don't I pick up the wash, so you can have a nice leisurely bath without having to hang around and wait? I park in the alley, and I have to come in that way anyhow. Besides," Ann added, clinching the argument, "I can recognize my towels and stuff if they're galloping around in the dryer."

When Marian went in she laid her purse on the coffee table, reminding herself not to leave it there, and turned off the air conditioning and opened the casement windows to the soft night. She puttered briefly and uselessly around the apartment, in which everything belonged in some permanent and well-designed place. She had started her bath, putting in a good dollop of Ann's bath oil, and was in the bedroom, stepping out of her dress—which could go in the wash, if any—when the phone rang.

Will sounded conciliatory. "Baby, I just got back this afternoon and I—"

"I know. Apparently the first thing you did was break your promise not to get Ann into the act," she snapped, ending conciliation abruptly.

"What do you want me to do—fold my hands and sit and weep, like Grayson?"

"You leave Charles out of this. He behaved like a gentleman. You wouldn't understand."

"No, I wouldn't," he retorted. "I come of a long line of non-gents. My grandfather would be ashamed of me because I don't march over there and drag you home by the hair."

"The world now is a little more civilized than the one your grandfather knew about. It was then, too," she added bitingly.

"Maybe. But you might as well understand that I'm not about to allow any more nonsense, Marian."

"You're ridiculous."

"Maybe I am," he shouted. "I certainly feel ridiculous, hanging around like the classic rejected suitor while you're doing the town with some other guy."

"Now you're even more ridiculous." She heard him start to wind up in a tirade, so she just laid the phone down gently and went and turned off the brimming bath. She came back wondering whether he would have noticed, but he hadn't, apparently—and he had also apparently worked himself up considerably while she'd been away.

"Never mind the icy silences, Marian. And don't give me any bullshit, either," he was saying. "I know how they turn up when you need them, so why not now? I turned up when you left Grayson—"

"I wish you hadn't, oh, how I wish you hadn't," she said fiercely. "You can be sure I've learned that lesson," she added bitterly.

"That so? Well, I've learned one, too. I'm going to use my weapons, and they're not insignificant. I've been thinking, and not entirely about peace terms."

"Like what weapons?"

"For one thing, if you think you can collect the children and take them out of my life the way you did with Charlie, you'd better think again." He waited, then he seemed to take her shocked and horrified silence for unbelief. "All right, I'm warning you. If you think I'm bluffing, just try it. I may not win—the courts being the insane mess they are—but I'm sure as hell going to fight."

"You don't care about the effect on the children of a public scandal, do you?"

"Sure I care. But I'm not so sure it would hurt them much to know their father wanted them enough to fight for them."

"You'll lose your precious job if you get into a newspaper stink."

"Maybe. Haven't you been telling me, all along, that you and the children are more important? Well, which way will you have it?" His voice sank to pleading. "Marian, you were right—nothing is any good without Us. For all the use I've been in these miserable weeks, the man would be smart to unload me anyhow. All I want is you—" Is he still at the office, Marian thought. At this hour? A small worry began in the back of her mind about whether he had had any dinner; it would have given him hope if he had known. But he didn't, and he went on, pushing it too far once again "—and I'll do anything to get you back. And the same goes for the children. This is either love or war, Marian—I want it to be the first way, but if I can't get it, by God I'll make an all-out war, you can count on that. And I'm telling you truthfully, and you know it—you're no match for me when it comes to dirty fighting. You'll get hurt, baby, so you better—"

"I don't care to talk to you any more, Will," she interrupted frostily. "This is both fruitless and distasteful."

He snarled, "Of course. I suppose the gentleman is waiting. Or are there more than one, lined up?"

Marian hung up, almost furious enough to slam the phone down. She inspected the contents of the clothes hamper and found there really was enough to wash; but her shaking hands decided her for postponement. The warm, scented bath beckoned and she tore her clothes off in vicious haste, announcing to herself that she'd made up her mind this time for sure, that she never wanted to see Little Hitler again. Let him do his worst—she'd get the children, she'd win anyway. She wasn't afraid, she told herself, trembling with rage and fear.

The gentle waters took some of it away. Peace lapped at her fury as she lay there dreaming of the nice little house she would have, alone with the children in harmony and order, sunshine lying over everything. And Mama Marian coping serenely—a heroine, a Florence Nightingale, a woman dedicated to her children. She was through with all men, she thought, and believed herself even as her body moved luxuriously in the buoyant embrace of the water, aware of more than her mind would admit. In *her* home, she went on assuring herself, nobody would even know whether Congress was in or out of session, and nobody would come to dinner unless she really wanted to see them. It might be lonely, she noted, congratulating herself on her own practicality in noting it—but she was lonely when she lived with Will, anyway. She stepped out of the tub and began patting at her sweet-smelling pearly body with Ann's turquoise towel, wiping Will out of existence.

Will, not quite wiped out of existence but showing some damage, was apologizing to Ann for phoning her twice in the same day, and particularly since he knew she was working.

He hadn't known that at all, Ann thought as she told him it was all right, she was finished anyhow. In case it was in fact what he had called up to find out, she added that she was about to go home.

Will's sigh could have been relief, or, equally, despair. "I called Marian a little while ago. But I didn't do so good."

"Will, you know I won't—"

"I know, I know." He tried laughter, but his voice was unconvinced that there was anything to laugh at. "It's just— I've got to hit the road again, and I hate to leave things like that." He cleared his throat and when he spoke again, Ann could hear that he was smiling. "I prepared a compliment to open my speech with, and then I forgot it. Will you tell her I meant to say I enjoyed her piece on the outdoor art shows? It was witty, but not mean or picky."

He hadn't read it, Ann knew instantly; but she thought his careful lie was touching. "I'll tell her, Will. I'll see her in a few minutes."

He seemed to sense the doubt of his veracity. "I especially liked the photo with it—that painting of a parade by one of the Impressionists."

Ann's eyes narrowed at this attempt to "lend verisimilitude to an otherwise bald and unconvincing narrative." She was sure he hadn't read it, surer than ever now. And besides, the column he was talking about was not Marian's latest, by any means. But he *had* seen it, Ann recognized, and began to wonder whether he had been browsing in the periodical room of some public library. In Mississippi? she asked herself skeptically. "Where are you off to this time, Will?"

"Oh, Rosenberg forgot his lunch or something, so I've got to take it down to Alabama." His voice had switched magically from the lugubrious, struggling suitor's to that of the experienced fender-off of the press. "You know how it is, Annie." Which meant, of course, *That's all I can tell you.*

Rosenberg, Ann thought, and began to laugh because she knew now who had thought Marian's column witty but not mean. And had said so to Will, who stored it away to use in a speech. "Rosenberg," she said. "I see. Tell me, Nedra didn't happen to wrap his corned beef sandwich in an old *Tribune* art page, did she?"

Will gasped and then surrendered. "Well, so much for that try. It's just as well I didn't get it in with Marian, isn't it?"

"You have to get lucky sometime."

"Yeah," he said wryly. "Sometime when *I* go to war, *my* wife will send me news from home, too."

Ann smiled—it was so like Nedra Rosenberg to bolster her husband with intellectual food in the desert. "What does she do, send him the Sunday brains section every week?"

And "Peanuts" for every day, too, Will reported enviously. By the time he hung up, he seemed a little cheered by the prospect of joining Rosenberg, who had all the Peanutses Will had missed.

Ann wondered briefly on the way home what new attempt at peacemaking in the South was afoot, but she put the thought from her because it made her feel unhappy to be piddling around Washington when others were getting big bylines for themselves where the troubles were happening. Whereas all she was getting was a close-up look at the human condition. Which was interesting: for example, love might make the world go round, but it didn't seem to make the gyration smooth—and Farland, who could sweet-talk a Senate committee (so far as that was ever possible), seemed amazingly unaware that he'd never move Marian by haranguing her, or maybe even by buttering her up.

Marian had remained unconfiding and Ann had carefully not pried; but she could put two and two together, and was given to doing so (unlike Marian, who also could but always refused to). The basic problem was, you had to be a politician to get Marian and a poet to keep her—and, thus far, Morisot was proving more adept than Farland at plying the other guy's trade. Morisot's dignified silence, Ann decided as she parked the car and locked it carefully, was an excellent maneuver; making Marian come to him involved a certain risk, but it gave him a much stronger position. Unless, of course, he didn't know Marian's way of getting mad at men who stayed away, and thus was risking more than he meant to. Ann walked lightly down the basement steps, jiggling the car keys in her hand and wearing the look of a racetrack patron approaching the betting window. It was hard to know where to put your two bucks: maybe Paul *did* know the way Marian was and refused to knuckle under to it; maybe Will figured staying in communication was worth losing a few rounds on the telephone . . .

She peered into the vast, cathedral-like silence of the laundry room for the wicker basket she used to transport her wash. There was no sign of it, but it struck her that Marian might have simply stuffed all the wash into a pillow case, so she came into the room and started toward the white machines looming like altars among the great whitewashed pillars.

And then something was pressing powerfully at her throat and there was a great weight at her back, pulling her downward inexorably in spite of her heels scrabbling at the unyielding concrete floor. She threw her hands up and outward in a final attempt at balance even as she knew it was no use— she was down, she even heard the sickening cracking sound as her back smacked against the floor, and all the weight was on top of her. She struggled, trying to roll out from under, and a knee plowed into her middle, just above her waist; all the breath went out of her for a moment and her flailing arms felt as though they were tied to flatirons. She heard loud panting in the silence and thought it was her own, and then she got her breath back and began to scream over the sound of ripping cloth.

"No, oh no." It was something between a wail and a scream, but it wasn't helping—she was so vulnerable, she thought wildly; she should have worn a girdle. Sudden fury charged her with heat and impossible energy. She twisted her body violently and at the same time tore at the creature with her fingernails; her teeth gnashed on themselves, unable to reach the enemy. Then an arm laid along her throat pressed down, heavy and bony, on the windpipe and it was like staying under water too long—her lungs labored, her eyes were about to pop. *No, oh please, no, oh please,* she screamed with no sound. The pressure eased a little, but not enough to draw in breath for more than the little moan as a kind of blind wet fumbling insulted delicate tissue. Her flung arms were being held down, but it meant a little more breath. She used it to cry out when the tiny unseen muscles that were all the defense she had left were overcome. Shame took her, and the lights swam but wouldn't go out, and her own blood was ringing in her ears.

The ringing Marian heard was real—the telephone began as she finished tying the sash of her peach-colored nightgown, just as she was daydreaming of Sharlie's wedding and was reaching to put her arms into the sleeves of the matching negligee. The phone rang like doom, destroying the imagined outlines of Sharlie's wedding dress, and Marian quivered, instantly afraid. But then she remembered—she was in charge of things now and she never needed to talk to Will any more. She could just hang up on him again.

The voice identified itself as the resident manager. If this was Miss Taswell's friend, she had better come at once to Apartment 1A. The woman hung up before Marian could reply. She put the phone down and ran down the small hall, snatching Ann's black silk raincoat out of the hall closet as she flew by, tripping a little in her backless slippers. She put the coat on in the elevator, rolling back one sleeve so she could hold up all her peach-colored skirts while she hunted desperately for Apartment 1A.

She saw Ann the minute the door was opened and pushed past the woman in curlers to the huddled figure on the fat sofa. Ann's clothes were torn and smeared with stone dust; a little blood streaked the white piping on her dark-green dress and some was drying on her stockings. Her hair was frayed out of its neat knot and there was blood on the crown of her head and more of it, in smears, on her arms and the side of her face. Too frightened to know how to begin, Marian focused on the bloody smear slanting down the pale cheek and wiped at it with the skirt of her negligee; but Ann winced a little, so she stopped.

"I didn't look for the wash," Ann said in a flat, dazed voice.

Marian answered stupidly, "I didn't put it in."

The woman had been talking, in small indignant jerks. "This is a very respectable neighborhood . . . The police— Oh my, I don't know what the company will say—how could such a thing happen? It's a very good house, very high-class people . . . " She ran down like a hand-wound phonograph, coming eventually to a stop.

Marian was kneeling on the cheap, prickly carpet, pulling ineffectually at Ann's skirt, which had ripped at the seam. "Oh, Ann, was it—?"

Ann nodded. "Of course." She might have been answering a question about a street direction.

Marian stared at her, too appalled even to cry. She took Ann's hand and laid it against her own cheek. The hand was very cold.

"I don't know why it takes the police so long," the resident manager whined. "You pay your taxes—and they're more every year—and then when you ask even a little something, they take their time."

"Do you have some brandy?" Marian asked her, trying to keep dislike out of her voice. "Or whiskey? Anything."

"Well, I don't drink, of course, but—"

"Get it," Marian said coldly. "And get a blanket, too." Where were the police, she thought, hungry for help, for a man to take charge. Somewhere below conscious thought, she was angry because Will didn't come and do something.

Ann seemed to speak from a long distance away and at great effort. "Don't take on, Marian. Not to fuss." She raised a dirty hand and touched a tear Marian had not known was on her own cheek.

She couldn't bear to see Ann struggle so, trying to say something and failing, and then slowly, like laboring through wet sand, trying again. "Ah," Marian said, "you must've been so frightened."

Ann blinked in evident relief as her daze was penetrated by the words. "I thought he would—kill me." A slow tear rolled down her battered cheek. The woman came with whiskey in a teacup and Marian held it to Ann's lips. She swallowed obediently, gasping a little, and then said again, more clearly, "I thought he would kill me," and began to cry hopelessly.

Marian took the grayish, thin blanket from the woman and put it around Ann's shoulders clumsily and then held the whole wrapped bundle in her arms, patting Ann's back rhythmically as she wept softly. "Hush. Hush, you're all right, Annie." It was something Marian had never thought of—that rape was not death, that Ann was, for the moment at least, more grateful than outraged—and she saw suddenly that it could be a saving point, a means to healing.

"I was so afraid," Ann said, between great sobs. "I didn't want to die."

"You're all right, you're all right, baby," Marian kept repeating, hugging her tightly as she heard the welcome sound of the sirens and listened to the wail coming closer. She wondered whether the police would bring a doctor, whether they would let Ann go home. She thought she ought to go and get dressed, but it was impossible to let Ann go. Even if her friend would let her, Marian had to hold on, keeping Ann warm, keeping away death.

The cops were very big in their blue shirts, both darkened with streaks of sweat. They had things hanging from their belts like Peter at his games; absurdly, Marian remembered that her small son liked to strut around with the tea strainer dangling from the waistband of his pants. The first cop was nasty, she decided, hugging Ann closer as she heard him bullying the resident manager who was giving him Ann's name and apartment number. The woman faltered, and Marian was suddenly sympathetic though she had found her hateful a moment ago.

The second cop was gentle, speaking quietly to Ann so that she raised her buried face. His kind eyes surveyed the damage and he peeled back the blanket a little and looked at her arms; Marian noticed for the first time the lacerations on Ann's elbows. "You hit the floor kind of hard, Miss?" he asked. He stood up without waiting for an answer and glanced at the clotting blood on the crown of the pale head. "You feel all right?"

"Now you told the manager here you never seen the man," the nasty cop interrupted. "You sure about that?"

"I don't know what you mean," Ann answered uncertainly.

"Well now, lemme put it this way—suppose you was out having a beer and you got to talking to this fellow in the bar—"

Marian stood up swiftly, interposing her small angry person between him and Ann. She heard the whimper behind her and she said quietly, "I'm not going anywhere, Annie. I'm right here." To the cop she said with distinct loathing, remembering Will's advice to bully a bully whenever possible, "She was on her way home from work. She works at the *Tribune,* and so do I." Influence, she thought, and added rapidly, "I'm a good friend of Jed Burrows. Do you happen to know him?" She knew it should have been done more smoothly—oh, where was Will, where was some *man?*—

and she was afraid for a moment that the nasty cop would only laugh at her clumsy inexperience, at the inept way she'd plied the name of the *Tribune's* veteran police reporter.

But he didn't. He looked at her uncomfortably, with apology replacing his knowing air, and said, "Yeah, I know Jed. Listen, I didn't mean—"

The gentle cop intervened then. "She's got a head injury," he told his partner. "Better call for an ambulance." He said Marian had better get dressed and then, when Ann wouldn't let her go, he dispatched the resident manager to Ann's apartment to bring Marian some clothes. Marian told the woman that her purse was on the coffee table—smitten with incredible guilt for the fact that she'd left it there despite her good intentions to live up to Ann's housekeeping—and described which were her shoes and a dress that belonged to her.

When she turned back, the nice cop had most of the story from Ann. The assailant had been hiding behind one of the pillars in the big dim laundry room; he let her pass and then jumped her from behind, an arm crooked around her neck. Her screams had been futile—with the basement door shut, it was unlikely that anybody could hear, unless someone just happened to be coming down to wash. (*If I had done the wash,* Marian thought, believing that she was thinking of herself as a rescuer of Ann.) But he was husky, and Ann, though she was tall, was slender and had never been athletic: it was no contest, right from the start. He had said nothing, not a word— She broke off then and began to cry, hiding her face against Marian once more.

"It's all right, Miss," the nice cop said. "You done the best you could." She had now, also—she had remembered more than she thought she could.

Marian flashed him a grateful look and went on saying, "Ssh, ssh, you're going to be all right, nobody will hurt you any more," and wondering fearfully about that head injury. Mothers of school-age boys know something about concussion: Dick Farland's mother tried gently to shift Ann away from her a little so she could see if the pupils of the eyes were uneven.

The nice cop was reading the description to his returned partner: "Colored, eighteen to twenty or so, she thinks. About my height but thinner and wiry, dark pants, striped shirt. She says she tore his shirt, and she may have scratched him—one of her nails is broken and has a little blood under it, but I can't tell whether it just bled when it broke."

"You think it's who I think it is?" The nasty cop didn't wait for an answer. He bent and asked Ann, very gently and with no nastiness at all, "Could you help us a little more, Miss? Try to remember—did you see any marks or scars on him?"

Ann sat up and screwed her eyes shut, but she looked unfrightened for the first time: she had been appealed to as an experienced observer, and she was trying to think. "Yes, he had a—a mole, I think. On his neck."

"Which side?" The policemen exchanged knowing glances.

Ann calculated, seeming to shrink back, and Marian knew why, shrinking also from the picture of the horrid intimacy Ann must evoke in order to answer. Will had a freckle on his neck, just a small brown spot under the skin but feeling no different to the touch; Marian's right hand remembered touching it to see and she realized with surprise that meant it was on the left side—and cringed away from having to see it above her. Ann said in a whisper, "The right side," and buried her face in Marian's shoulder.

"That's him," the mean cop said, and his partner nodded.

"You know the man?" Marian asked, shocked at the idea.

The nice cop said a little wearily that let's say they recognized the description and asked whether Ann would have had a purse. Marian said of course, she had just parked the car in the alley. The other cop went off to look for the purse and Ann stirred and asked fretfully, "Will they come soon? I want a doctor. I feel—" She didn't finish, but Marian knew how she felt; she hugged Ann tighter and asked, over her head, "Can't I take her in and clean her up a little? She'll feel better." The other cop came back then, carrying Ann's purse and the car keys, which she must have been holding in her hand. There was nothing gone from the purse—it had simply flown from her hand and lain there until the cop found it.

By the time the ambulance arrived, the resident manager had come back with Marian's clothes in a little airlines bag. Marian carried it in her hand as she walked beside the stretcher, still in the raincoat over her nightgown and negligee because she hadn't been able to leave Ann long enough to change. But when the ambulance doctor took over, Ann let her go for a minute and Marian said to the nice cop, "Why? If he didn't even want money?" The cop looked embarrassed, but she persisted, her voice low and demanding, because it was somehow terribly important to know. "Look, she's nearly old enough to be his mother." She put her hand on his arm in an unthinking attempt to get past his formality; trying to sound tough, like someone who could be told truths, she hunted for words that would make her "one of the boys." "If he just had—well, hot pants or something, God knows the girls nowadays are obliging enough—"

The cop shook his head. "That's not it. They just want to get back at somebody—that's the way it is, more and more now. Looks like they don't even worry about getting caught." He cleared his throat. "Listen, Miss, I couldn't say anything before—I didn't want to get her all shook up again. But I don't like you thinking we're just mean—I know she'd feel better if she got cleaned up, but it's a matter of evidence." He looked at her besecchingly and then his eyes went to the wedding ring on her hand. "You understand, Missus. We have to be able to make a charge of rape stick."

The significance of that sudden "Missus" flashed on Marian suddenly and horrifyingly and she nodded quickly so he wouldn't explain further. She was a married woman and she was supposed to understand, she saw; and she hated it that she did, that she knew semen dried powdery—it could be collected on a slide, verified under a microscope. Oh God, she prayed, let them give her a sedative, let them knock her out . . . But she knew they wouldn't, not with that smack on the head.

Ann moaned a little as the stretcher was lifted into the ambulance and the nasty cop snarled at the attendant, "For Chris' sake, watch it!" Marian sat in the shifting darkness as they fled through the dim, sultry streets, watching everything in the picture shift before her eyes: the nasty cop was full of inarticulate sympathy and pain, the gentle cop hated hate, the resident manager had chosen the clothes for Marian with intelligence and care and had even thought to tuck a pretty embroidered handkerchief—it was Ann's—into the bag to help raise her morale . . . A poor old woman, frightened for her ill-paying job, sorry she hadn't done better. And Ann was right—she *was* lucky to be alive; the boy, uninterrupted and threatened, must have been stupid not to kill her. Wasn't it the same penalty for rape as for murder? The southern congressmen who were the masters of Washington had done their best to inculcate their mores into its structure of law.

Marian held to the side of the bucking ambulance and looked at her friend —an impersonal casualty of impersonal hate, shrouded in a blanket and lucky to be alive. From nowhere—or perhaps from an English class in Miss Kingman's School for young ladies who would never be bedded without wooing—"The Man with the Hoe" came into her head with its terrible description of the victim-man, the one distorted and made monstrous by the rest of us, the sufferer from "immemorial infamies, perfidious wrongs, immedicable woes." Marian struggled to remember, and Markham's warning question finally came through: "How will the future reckon with this Man?"

The poets dream and the politicians scheme—who had said it, so long ago, on a night of dancing in the rain in the Kimballs' back yard? It could have been the man who was now President of the United States, Marian realized with a sense of shock. The words of the poem jumped suddenly from the bottom of a left-hand page in the anthology with a red binding and "M. DiGennaro" scrawled in ink on the blank first page in a very phony, very fancy, backward-leaning hand.

> How will it be with kingdoms and with kings—
> With those who shaped him to the thing he is—
> When this dumb Terror shall rise to judge the world,
> After the silence of the centuries?

Poets are not too accurate in their predictions, Marian said to herself bitterly, looking down at the white face that had been only that—a white face—to an angry youth with no way to learn the obligations of the strong toward the weaker. It was fine with kingdoms and with kings—old Markham had called it wrong there. It wasn't Andy Girard who had suffered the consequences of the politicians' schemes, but Ann Taswell, the observer and chronicler who had perhaps even won enough sympathy for his plight to change her attacker's future. Marian thought with clear hatred of the grand White House and its carefully protected beauties—sheltered, with its inhabitants, from the consequences that bloodied the unprotected innocent, the helpless man of good will who just happened by when the terror rose.

The ambulance came to a smooth stop in the curving driveway of the hospital and Marian backed against the wall to be out of the way when they lifted the stretcher out and thought, unexpectedly and with unexpected ferocity, of Rosa's journey. Give them hell, she shouted at Rosa in her mind like a fan at a football game, and smiled wanly at the man who held out his hand to help her down. She followed the stretcher quickly, afraid of losing it in the looming bureaucratic immensities, with her head high and her cheeks burning and the long skirt of the negligee Will Farland had bought for his baby doll streaked with blood and fluttering about her naked heels.

Forty-six

This was no sight for Bastille Day, the President thought. He stood in the doorway, between the American and presidential flags on their staffs, and looked around at the beautiful, fragile French furniture of the yellow and gold oval room on the second floor of the White House. Here was the best that was remembered, really, of Louis XVI, who had made the mistake of holding on too long to the Bastille. After all the blood had dried, that gracefully curving white frame with the soft apricot silk upholstery lived past both Louis and the outraged citizens who had stormed the Bastille. The room was all lovely and rare and intricate, from the frieze on the ceiling and the teardrop chandelier to the leatherbound volumes on the shelves in the alcoves; it represented the best, the most satisfyingly artistic, results of a civilization that had doubtless had a great deal wrong with it—sunny beauty purchased at the price of numerous individual squalors. For Americans, it made sense that it was in this room that the President forgathered with visiting heads of state about to be formally fêted, for here was demonstrated the bold American intention to have it both ways: beauty and freedom, the caviar made available to the general—and as a matter of course.

Short weeks ago the President had gone from this room, with his wife on his arm, down the staircase to the great hall to make an entrance behind the flags and their uniformed bearers while the music marched and the waiting assemblage glittered. Awakening this morning, Alec had had a sharp, delicious feeling that it would all happen again, that somehow everything would sparkle again, everything would be all right. He shed the depression of the last few days like a chrysalis, bathed and dressed quickly and breakfasted enthusiastically, and paused in this sunny room more to exchange pleasure than to derive it.

He looked at the golden candelabra on the ornate white mantel and thought pityingly of the deposed Louis whose people had been dissatisfied enough to remove a number of heads on this day some years ago. Even to those who rule by divine right, he told himself gravely, an impulsive populace can be a problem. He shifted under his arm the envelope that contained last night's dole of the cables that daily reported the detailed state of the world, especially the part ruled by Premier Kaslov, who had an impulsive populace to trouble him too. All the evidences seemed to indicate that Kaslov had in mind to stir up a skirmish or two, hopefully minor, in order to take the heat off the failure of his agricultural reforms that would be revealed by the harvest. Distraction by skirmish was a classic procedure for troubled rulers, but a far more dangerous one these days than when any of the Louis were around. It was consoling that Kaslov obviously knew it: he was a dictator, an autocrat, but not a fanatic. The world was undoubtedly safer, Alec concluded, in the hands of a couple of politicians than in those of a totally convinced man, whether he was convinced of divine right or of master race.

A couple of harassed politicians, he amended: he had a restless population snapping at his heels, too, and Kaslov didn't need secret intelligence reports to find it out, thanks to a free press. Ah well, all they could do was refuse to reelect him; at least they wouldn't cart Andy off to the guillotine. Maybe Girard and Kaslov would end up at some international home for rejected politicians one day, cutting up old negotiations. Alec frowned, thinking that it would be a very good idea indeed if he could rescue Kaslov, whose compulsory retirement from power would lead to a new and blunter intelligence at the controls over there. He started to turn away from the room, to take his high spirits on about his serious business, and then it came to him all of a sudden that maybe he could not only rescue Kaslov, but move the world an inch or two toward safety thereby. Because if a flurry of war was out as a means to distract the attention of the discontent, why wouldn't a flurry of peace do the same thing?

The endless, stalemated negotiations to bring an end to the testing that was poisoning the atmosphere—perhaps not as badly as the worriers thought, but fallout was hardly good for you—went on and on in a kind of empty formality that was going nowhere, that in fact constituted only a kind of machinery for keeping opportunity open in case it was wanted. It could be wanted now, perhaps, the President speculated: Kaslov's suspicions, which had always been a prime hindrance to agreement, might well be allayed by the very fact of Girard's home-front troubles; his fellow politician could understand, and might just believe in, the American President's desire to get the heat off. And it was an old saw of diplomacy that where there was mutual need, agreement could be reached.

A dramatic announcement issued soon, simultaneously from Washington and Moscow, could not only distract the discontented in both camps, neither of which was inhabited by a warlike people—whatever the hotbloods on both sides insisted—but it could also actually obtain the suspension that up till now had been unobtainable, an agreement that might not hold indefinitely but would be of obvious physical value for as long as it did hold. And it would have the great, if intangible, value of establishing a precedent: the people sometimes forgot that war was unthinkable—though their leaders had not, at least not yet, thank God—and some of them seemed to believe that peace was. An agreement to suspend testing, however limited its guarantees, could establish a precedent for more actions and, in the meantime, remind everybody that peace was quite thinkable. And not the exclusive property of the demonstrators who demanded it but never bothered with the "How?"

Intent on his thoughts, Alec hurried from the room, right past the two soft, cloudy landscapes by Cézanne that his wife could not possibly have passed without a look, no matter how long she lived with them. As Alec stepped into the elevator, he glanced at his watch to see whether Jake Ruffing would have arrived yet; it was still pretty early, even for a working day. In the corridor where Girard's brisk "Good morning" still hung on the air, the man at the desk by the elevator said into his telephone, "The President is on his way to his office"; a second later, the sprawling building broke out in a rash of small flashing lights, discreet "pings," and high, thin pipings from walkie-talkie receivers.

On a hill just above a hilly village in a southern province of France, Bastille Day was by that time well under way, with lunch over and the dishes already stacked. Madame Berriault, who supervised Paul Morisot rather more closely than the Secret Service did Alec Girard, was wiping the heavy slab of beautifully grained wood from which the master of the house had devised a kitchen table. She plied her scrubbing rag angrily, wondering how she could ever hold her head up in the town again if M'sieu' Paul did not emerge from his workshop today after all. There had been Bastille Days he ignored, but when, about a week ago, he had asked Madame to deviate from her marketing rounds in town long enough to dispatch some money to Alphonse Lenard in Paris, along with an invitation to that impecunious friend to come as soon as he could— Well, Madame Berriault had not felt that she was being rash when, sipping at a farewell glass of wine on the terrace of her friend Thérèse's café, she had allowed to be wheedled from her the information that M'sieu'—probably accompanied by the big red-bearded painter and the latter's, er, lady companion—would attend the Bastille Day festivities.

The town, which was careful not to intrude on the privacy of its most celebrated citizen to an extent great enough to cause him to seek other residence, nevertheless cherished an insatiable appetite for news of his every passing mood. Morisot, paying his taxes and greeting his fellow citizens politely during his infrequent excursions into the metropolis, had little idea how the status of Madame rose and fell in the community in correlation with her success in predicting those excursions. Though he did seem to be aware of her services as an information channel: he had told her exasperatedly once that he was weary of finding nubile females staked in his path, like goats to bait a tiger, every time he went to town; thereafter, he noted, the practice was modified—at least for a while. Nevertheless, it still did not occur to him that Madame, with whom he enjoyed a relationship that quite resembled (although he would have been wrathful had it been pointed out to him) that of an Englishman with his erstwhile Nanny, was also his Grand Vizier.

It had occurred to Aimée, of whom Madame Berriault was thinking with some longing as she wrung out her rag and spread it on the window in the sun. In the pocket of the apron of Madame was yet another of Mam'selle Aimée's discreet, friendly little notes inquiring for news of Madame's health and spirits. The first one, sent from the United States in March, had been accompanied by a little present from New York; Madame had displayed the gift lavishly to Thérèse and the other ladies of the town—a move she now knew to have been an error, allying her with a deposed queen. But there had seemed no harm in it at the time: Aimée had obviously been M'sieu's preference, and the town was pro-Aimée and had been ever since it had become clear that she would not whisk their central celebrity off to Paris. Once it was established that her visits were not pre-connubial, they became, in the eyes of the devoted spectators, one of the conditions necessary to maintain the comfort of M'sieu' Paul, who was understood to be different from other men but not *that* different.

Which conclusion had been reached shortly after he took up residence among them as, at once, a stranger and a son. His own native village had not survived the Nazis—it was a monument, not anyone's home, now—but he was nevertheless a product of the region; his virtues could be claimed and his differences ascribed to his few kilometers' natal handicap, thus freeing the village to look on him with indulgence. When the ancient church had been restored, M'sieu' Paul had come with the other men to help with the work and then contributed an extra couple of weeks' labor at his own specialty: sweating on a ladder day after day, he had diligently carved figures for the doorway that were exact copies of the crumbling ones that the Romans or the Gauls or some other of the long-gone peoples had left as legacy in that shimmering land. Even the most conservative of the local dignitaries, inspecting the work while he eased his parched throat in Thérèse's café, had to concede that Morisot had not even in the tiniest way introduced any touch of dread modernism to the bland triangular faces that were currently held to be those of saints. He might be different, but, artist or not, he was *sérieux*.

Further, the sculptor, though refusing to socialize and known to consort on occasion with politicians in Paris, had nevertheless demonstrated that globetrotting and international friendships could not affect adversely his

French soul, of which love of children is a deep and abiding component. Wandering through the village in pursuit of some supplies he required for one of his building projects, Morisot had come upon the children at play in the school yard and paused to watch them for a while; the resulting meditations produced a gift of ingeniously sculptured playground equipment—including an abstraction that looked something like a heavy-bottomed S, with the upper curve diminished and the lower one exaggerated, that puzzled and dismayed the traditionalists even though they had to admit it was sturdily based and had no sharp edges. One day, though, a very traditionalist six-year-old climbed up the broad, inviting pedestal and curled into that deep, inviting "lap," which the sculptor had ingeniously sheltered from the visitations of birds with the roofing forward curve; the little girl snuggled against the sun-warmed stone for a while, sucking at her thumb and twirling a strand of her hair—and after that, everybody else wanted to. (It was even reputed that a certain sturdy pillar of the community, struggling home from the café one night in an uncertain weather of sobriety, had availed himself of the roomy comforts of Morisot's abstract "alma mater.")

Thus the practical people who lived between the dark mountain and the blue sea, and who recognized the prestige value of having among them a decorated hero of the Republic and flower of French art, were also curiously involved emotionally with the man most of them saw very rarely: he was exploited and envied and occasionally spied on, but he was also forgiven his trespasses against the town's stern beliefs in marriage and in annual appearances at church. What it may well have added up to was love—and therefore the local concern with Morisot's affairs was, though informed with the spice of gossip, nevertheless profoundly kind. So the discussion of the absence of Mam'selle Aimée, which had been being carried on with increasing interest ever since the sculptor's return this year, resulted in steadily more pressing inquiries being made of Madame Berriault as to the state of M'sieu's liver. He had remained too long in the United States this winter, it was suggested delicately, and had possibly damaged his constitution with that country's execrable cuisine; certain vegetables believed to benefit not only the liver but also better-understood systems of the body were pressed on Madame with meaningful solicitude.

Madame had, by that time, received more charming notes from Mam'selle Aimée—the last one accompanied by a little remembrance from Paris—and had for some time been on the lookout for Aimée's successor. None appeared, however—M'sieu' went on working and taking long walks like an Englishman. Madame suspected that the problem would not yield to a change in diet, but she took the proffered vegetables anyway: M'sieu' was, after all, approaching forty, and one should not be incautious in these matters.

The red-bearded Lenard, who was forty but apparently needed no vegetables, emerged from the house's large bathroom, in which his lady companion was supposed to be bathing in preparation for the journey to town, and crossed the neat kitchen to the back door, wearing a grin and some trickling evidence of having been assaulted with a wet sponge. Madame Berriault sighed, momentarily wistful for the visits of Mam'selle Aimée, in which the proprieties were at least formally deferred to: M'sieu' Paul slept in his studio, leaving his house to his guest and her chaperon, and behaved with consistent decorum in the presence of the latter; it was not his fault, Madame had concluded loyally on occasion, that the impulsive Mam'selle kept forgetting to rumple her assigned bed before slipping out of the house into the welcoming night.

Madame eyed the big man who seemed so indifferent to these small but important graces and, swallowing a certain amount of pride, urged him to remind M'sieu' that this was not, after all, a working day. Alphonse said cheerfully that all would be well—Paul was not working, but only writing a letter, and would doubtless be finished at any moment.

What Paul was finishing, Alphonse discovered when he had adjusted his eyes to the cool stone interior of the studio after walking up the sunny path from the house, was a charcoal sketch apparently copied from one of the small clay models baking on the broad windowsill. These little figures of a naked woman leading a small boy by the hand were to be found all about the workroom in a variety of small corrections of pose: here she walked straight forward, perhaps running or dancing; there she trod doubtfully, a hip curved forward but a hesitant backward leaning in the torso. In the drawing Paul was completing, he had given her no face except the pure oval and blind eyes of classic Greek sculpture, but elaborate care had been expended on detailing the way the cloud of black hair grew away from the forehead and temples. What he had done to the body, though, was so shocking that the normally ebullient Lenard was utterly silenced. For, although Paul had clearly made every one of the clay women too small, for some reason, he had also equally clearly made them, with the swift skill in which he had perhaps no contemporary equal, ripely and beautifully Woman. And now, here he was, willfully drawing—with a freeswinging arm and a faint smile on his lips and no look of guilt whatever—what amounted to a pinup girl: glancing frequently at the model, he sketched away murderously, narrowing the hips, giving a pert lift to the breasts he had had the good sense previously to make round and heavy as ripe apples, sleeking down the legs so that they were long and graceful but lacked any of the weight-bearing sturdiness of the walking woman in the clay figure. What Paul was doing, in short, was making an underfed odalisque of the clay Womankind on the windowsill; Alphonse, a man of sensibility and conscience, turned away in disgust.

He soothed himself by turning his attention to the roughed-out statue that dominated the far end of the room; he promptly forgot the vandal at work behind him. The looming stone that would be called "The Leader" was already substantially successful, although there was a way to go before all the metaphorical goals the sketches pinned to the wall were calling for could be achieved. But the major victory was complete: the stone had been hewn so that it appeared to be, from one angle, yielding the tall, strong man's body and, from the other, engulfing it. The head and shoulders were clear and prominent, as was most of the torso; but at the waist the body was pulled backward a little against a barely defined tether that suggested a mountain climber's rope and ended behind and to the right of the figure—where a tumble of amorphous shapes, themselves barely emerged from the stone block, tugged on the rope. The man's leg on that side had been worked free, but not entirely free, so that the line of hip and thigh were as if in relief against the straining mass of undefined figures. But the thigh was muscled and effortful, and successful—for the lower leg and foot came forward, almost as free as the head; the distinct bare foot was about to take a cautious step, with the toes forward and down as if the man tested the ground before proceeding. The other leg was still in the stone: no effort had been made to bring the rest of the body out. But the illusion was rather that the stone had reached to engulf the body; when the statue was finished, this unformed stone would be a polished abstraction, thus enforcing the impression that the human figure had been partly swallowed by monumentality. And human it was, where it was free: the head, cocked a little as if listening but not turning to look back at those who pulled him, was strong and classically heroic—except that it was also under the grip of a plump baby hand, for the man carried a roundly detailed Renaissance child on his shoulders. One of his hands chopped at the air in an oratorical gesture that carried out the forward impulse of the torso; the other held protectively to the little dangling leg.

Alphonse Lenard shook his head, as he had the first time he had seen this, and smiled, as he had every time—for it was a triumph of resolved contradiction, with every forceful element tempered by a gentle one it dominated as the gesturing public hand dominated the tender private one: the leader pulled against what was holding him back, his forward motion slowed but not stopped; the striding thigh tapered down to that carefully probing foot; the chest was strong but not distended or laboring, bespeaking a man working hard but not in vain. Alphonse moved slowly to his right, watching with anticipation as the trick began to work: from a certain point behind the suggested crowd pulling at the rope, the whole picture changed suddenly—the crowd became not a drag on a forward march but a group of rescuers hauling a victim from quicksand or a raging sea. The untouched stone at the other side of the man's body became not monument or eternity or purity, but an ominous, generalized danger from which his followers were saving the hero.

The painter moved directly behind the figure and watched the message change again: now he was looking at a tall, powerful commander. The child's body, so intricately defined from the front, was here only a shape that might have been a helmet; the man's upraised arm, oratorical from the front, was here seen over his own shoulder and was a battle commander's forward-urging gesture to his followers.

From the far side the work was most incomplete, but Lenard's knowing eye, aided by the sketches, translated the chisel-marked stone to the polished, monumental block it would be eventually; he saw it as Paul intended, almost a classic bust of a heroic figure with the head in pure profile, making the face somehow older and only thoughtful. The inturned shoulder hid the straining of the other side, so that the figure would simply grow in dignity out of draped folds of polished stone; the upraised arm, gentled by profile, would be the gesture of a sage who belonged to the ages and was here memorialized for a public square.

The painter muttered an inappropriate *"Merde!"* and scratched his head as he went around to stand in front of the figure again. The gutter word and the vulgar gesture, both apparently disrespectful, were in fact products of overpowering respect for this triumphant capture of triumph without ruthlessness and thrust without violence, of conflicting attitudes of a single body brought into harmony, and finally of the ingenious use of space and the illusion of time that had made a biography of a portrait. It still needed much, Alphonse thought—at least months of labor. But no amount of time and labor would by themselves have wrested the victory of this concept and the masterful trickery that had brought it forth. Alphonse shook his head a last time and turned back to inspect the silly labors the man who had achieved this had insanely descended to now.

If Paul drew a pinup girl, Paul's friend admitted to himself as he peered at the charcoal sketch, it was drawn with talent—he had given to this reposing woman a remarkable quality of impermanence, as though she had been caught in flight and might rise and flutter away. But it wasn't sexy enough; she seemed languorous. And much, much too slender: what was the point of a pinup girl who looked as though she'd need a pillow under her back? The lines of the body were swift and sure and delicate, but all that meant was that Paul did well what he did well; if he was going to attempt this sort of thing, he would have to have advice. Alphonse began disgustedly to give him some. *"Celá—"*

"En anglais," Paul snapped, thinking irritably that Alphonse persisted in proclaiming his desire to improve his sketchy English, yet never voluntarily tried speaking in it. The sketch was a subject on which, the sculptor did not quite consciously admit, he preferred to have his friend comment, if comment he must, in his limited English vocabulary.

"That one—you have made her too—meager," Alphonse transliterated hesitantly.

Paul showed more amusement than his friend thought a conscientious teacher should be inspired to at his pupil's mistakes. "I have no lack of art critics," he said ungraciously. "But I prefer them prettier than you." Then he seemed to remember his pedagogical role. *"Maigre* is not 'meager.' It is —umm—'slim,' 'slender,' 'thin.' Fragile," he added softly while his pupil was stumbling over the difficulties of pronouncing "slim." He debated with himself briefly, then grinned and, observing without any apparent relevance that Bastilles were not breached without daring, lifted his charcoal and dotted in carefully a tiny mole high on the inside of the fragile odalisque's thigh. He sighed because he hated to commit an inaccuracy and the mole was not quite in the right spot. But the real mole was too high up to show in that pose, and it did not suit his purpose to draw the only one in which it would show. So he accepted a slight defeat, laid the drawing down and sprayed it with fixative, and turned to complete his letter to the art editor of the *Washington Tribune* while the sketch dried.

If Paul had followed his impulse, he wouldn't have been at home to receive the letter he was now answering. The careful, apparently aimless note from Ann Taswell had arrived first, and he had torn it open and gulped its chattering introduction, which included bright, cheery news about the Kimballs, the Ruffings, and the Rosenbergs—all of whom he liked and had heard about in Andy's last letter, and none of whom he wanted to read about now. And then the magic name leaped out of the page. Washington was a lonely place in the summer, the normally succinct Miss Taswell had rambled on. But for her it was less lonely than usual, for Marian Farland had come to stay with her— It was some time before Ann's shaken pen pal had subsided enough to read her cautionary amplification of that statement—it seemed that Marian's stay was of undecided duration, etc. etc.

So she had crossed the threshold, but her friend was not sure she would not turn and go back, Paul summarized swiftly. Into his mind leaped an accurate, glittering portrait of the small airplane that plied to and from the resort a few kilometers away: a hastemaking suitor could be aboard in an hour, and, in not very many hours more, could be aboard another plane and winging across the ocean to stir an indecisive lady. . . .

Paul folded Ann's letter and stuck it into the pocket of his American denim pants while he took a short walk outside his studio and conferred with a wind-twisted cypress. The consensus of the meeting was that he would wing over no oceans, if only for the good reason that his chances for acquiring fearsome financial burdens now looked better than ever and he had more need to be a breadwinner at the moment than a courtier. He had no illusions that the silk-clad, satin-skinned Marian would, if she came to him, be abandoning the world for love of Morisot—though he didn't doubt that she thought of it rather like that. But Morisot, with the unpained resignation of a man who has been up against hard fact before, had a rather clearer idea of a future in which trips to Paris would be more numerous than in his lonely past—and also more boring, since part of the time would be spent in hanging around *salons de couture* and much of the rest in dashing across the noisy city to theaters. It was even entirely possible, he knew grimly, that he would find himself living in a Paris suburb and visiting his own province only on the way south for a demure bathe with his bikini-ed Venus and assorted children. He groaned a little, but even this disturbing vision couldn't destroy his surging hope, or the gusto with which he attacked his work because of it.

Marian's letter had taken longer to arrive in France because it had been first sent to some other floor of the *Tribune* building and there translated into French and typed most correctly. Since she clearly had confidence in Paul's ability to read English—the shadowy twists and turns of her letter to him in

Washington, from which he had elicited eventually the information that she was not pregnant, would have been difficult reading for a Henry James scholar —this translation, he understood, was a gesture of formality: a deliberate remoteness, so that he could not detect, because she could not unconsciously reveal, any trace of information about her new status. Or of blandishment or call for rescue. She was most ingenious, Paul had thought, shaking his head —and charmingly courageous: he had said he would not carry her from her husband's house, and she was determined not to ask him to.

Only he had not said he would refrain from standing just outside and coaxing her on, Paul decided. Nor did he have any intention of leaving her entirely at the mercy of Farland's persuasions, which he guessed would be both extensive and powerful. On the other hand, her desire to manage her own affairs most certainly must be encouraged and respected. A nudge, Paul had concluded yesterday, but only a little, apparently coincidental push, was called for.

He set to work to construct a letter that would serve just that purpose. But, though he was a good writer, he was not a professional one; an innocent joy in his own cleverness quite betrayed him, so that he ended with a masterpiece of *double entendre*, in which there was hardly a word that didn't lasso her.

No, M. Morisot wrote the inquiring "M. D. Farland" identified under the signature as "Art Editor," he had no plan to communicate with the people of the peace movement about their use of "The Taken Town." Although he himself was no pacifist, believing as he did that war was, though as painful and devastating as he had tried to show in the work in question, still sometimes necessary—he was aware that he, for example, would fight for something he held dear quite as wholeheartedly as those who were more inclined to general belligerence.

Having thus rapidly dismissed the insignificant, or public, aspect, Paul applied himself to the editor's further inquiry about his work in progress, if he cared to discuss it. He didn't mind discussing it to some extent, he told M. D. Farland ingenuously, but progress on his new work was proving a little disappointing.

At this point, the sculptor took his hands from the keys of his typewriter so that he could put one of them over his eyes to hide from his vision the stone "Leader" that was making a towering liar of him. He succeeded in conquering his own shame at his unscrupulousness, but not the sound of Marian's remembered voice crooning her "poor darling" theme and variations. Paul swallowed, set his face in a sulky pout worthy of any of the French movie idols he had cursed on another occasion, and proceeded to invite some brow-stroking. He was so taken with the concept of a new Venus, he told her: it was to be quite different from Botticelli's young girl coming from the Mediterranean. This one was to be a woman in the prime of life, possibly even with children, borne across wider, rougher seas—well, he didn't want to bore her or take up a great deal of her time. His trouble was, though, that while he had all kinds of ideas for triumphing over all perils and bringing his ideal to fruition, he was, as you Americans said, "hung up," awaiting that vital moment in which one begins a major work.

Still convinced that he was being entirely subtle and devious—which course Marian had left open to him, after all, by giving him the opportunity to reply in French—Paul decided that he had put as much weight on the presumed inattention of the translator as it would bear; he turned now to the problem of defeating what his intuition told him would be an attempt by the foolish Marian, drunk on independence, to go it alone. What was needed, he decided, was some direct appeal to the senses, to cut through the cloud of apparent rationality that she was fond of mistaking for sense. When, after some thought, he came upon the answer, he went back and added to his letter: first, a gracious disclaimer of the intrusion on his time for which M. D. Farland had politely apologized—because, in fact, he would like to intrude even more upon hers. Boldly assuming that she would be good enough to allow the liberty, he was dispatching to her under separate cover a preliminary sketch for the work he had in mind; he imagined she would see for herself that it fell short of the possibilities of the concept, and he would be most grateful for any suggestions the sketch might inspire, if she cared to write. He then paid tribute gracefully to her perceptive criticism and announced himself eager to be guided by it indefinitely. He was, he finished, cordially hers—which, as he signed the letter on the bright afternoon of Bastille Day, he admitted guiltily to himself might well be the only straightforward statement in the entire essay. But he had a goal in mind: it was correct and important that she should, as she had once suggested, be free to give her marriage a decent burial; but it would be incorrect to allow her to believe that her freedom extended beyond that point, and it was most important that she be kept from falling into the error of regarding herself as generally available. She was Morisot's, and no nicety could be allowed to stand in the way of reminding her of it.

Paul folded the letter quickly and sealed it into its envelope, partly because it was in French and therefore vulnerable to the roving Alphonse, who had little sense of privacy; but also, he was anxious to have it on its way to her through all the channels, including the translator. He smiled at the drawing, which would need no translator; it would go directly to Marian, who he knew had no secretary. Not that that mattered—you had to have seen Marian with her hair down to recognize the subject of the portrait.

It occurred to him, blightingly in the midst of his blissful contemplation of his own subtlety and his brightening future, that Will Farland would recognize the subject quite easily. Paul scowled, although not because he thought the drawing would ever reach Farland's attention, and then realized that Alphonse had been asking him about Aimée.

"Aimée will not be coming." Paul deepened his scowl and turned away with his hand over his face, giving the impression of a man too moved for further speech. Actually, he was discovering by the gesture that he still had not shaved. "Never," he said tragically, meanwhile assembling the shaving gear he kept in the studio. "She will never come again."

While the shamefully exploited Alphonse was expressing his regrets in halting English, Morisot carried his equipment over to the stone sink under the window, propped on the sill the kind of wavery square of polished steel used by soldiers, and took off his shirt. He lathered his face swiftly and began to scrape off several days' beard.

Madame appeared in the doorway with the air of one bearing messages, but in view of the delicacy of her employer's operations at the moment, she waited to interrupt him at a safer time. Meanwhile, her gaze roved over the worktable out of habitual need to see what should be picked up; when it encountered the drying sketch, she stared openly—though fortunately unobserved.

Madame had, before taking up residence in this establishment, been relatively unexposed to exhibitions of the female form divine; by this time, she had acquired a certain sophistication in the matter—though she still could not understand why both M'sieu' Paul and Lenard obviously thought Lenard's billowy woman beautiful and used her for a model constantly. Madame's sophistication, however, still consisted largely of not tightening her lips in open disapproval as she glanced away.

But this, this was different—she had no desire to look away from this delicate creature with the long, carefully drawn swirls of black hair who was, though undeniably quite naked, at the same time ineffably ladylike about it. Marian Farland—or Phil Colby, for that matter—could have told her that her impression was the result of extremely skillful manipulation of curves of exactly the right depth, of deft shading that made the shoulder, for example, seem to have only a moment ago yielded the naked breast to the gaze of a special viewer for special reasons. But it hardly mattered: Madame Berriault, though she knew nothing about technique, knew love when it spoke to her, as the unknowledgeable always do—and it spoke here in every stroke and shadow. Poor Mam'selle Aimée, she thought, moving so that M'sieu' would not see that she had been studying the picture. She had considered the possibility of dropping a word or two at court on Aimée's behalf, but this made it hopeless.

Madame saw Paul stop to shake soap into the sink and seized the moment to tell him that since she knew he wanted to hurry to town, she had laid out his clothes in his bedroom; she hesitated and then added that she had taken the liberty of placing the rosette in his buttonhole. He promptly looked balky, and Madame went on rapidly before he could speak, reminding him that it was after all Bastille Day and the emblem of France's honor was really, was it not, a form of decoration the town was entitled to enjoy even if M'sieu' had reservations about it? Paul sighed, agreed not to remove the emblem of France's honor from his buttonhole, and finished shaving; he also agreed, while splashing his face and thereby shutting out the sound of her voice, to whatever else he was supposed to agree to. He assumed it was to dress appropriately, comb his hair, and appear in the village relatively soon.

Which last he did, to Madame's relief as she sat with Thérèse over a glass of wine, watching the more energetic celebrants. She did not know at once that M'sieu' Paul, having had a glass of wine in the studio and another in the bath and another while he dressed in the severe black trousers and loose white shirt and put on the polished slippers, had discovered on the path down to the village that the emergency rations he and Alphonse were carrying would weigh less if they paused from time to time to lighten their load. This scientific inspiration was instantly applauded by the perceptive Alphonse and accepted with a shrug by Alphonse's biddable girl. So that when the three arrived, they contained a great deal more alcohol than they carried. Madame eventually noticed that M'sieu' Paul did seem to be a tiny bit in wine; however, the fact that he had managed by carrying instead of wearing his coat, both to keep his promise to her and to hide his decoration from the world, caused her more displeasure than did a certain observable tipsiness.

But it was hard to cling to censure of this engaging, handsome, and playful hero of the Republic, and Madame inevitably relaxed her stern observation. Paul also relaxed, as the day wore on, though in a rather kinetic fashion that inspired Madame to reflections on whether he had had anything to eat, to absorb all that wine. By dusk, as Paul danced enthusiastically in the square, Madame's fears for his liver were smothered under the pride she felt in the town's affection for its sprightly celebrity: she was assured again and again by strollers past the terrace that the municipality's closest rival, a village a few kilometers farther inland that owned an aged Impressionist, would shrivel with envy.

As the shadows lengthened, M'sieu' Paul concluded the latest of many dances with the schoolteacher, either because she was more successfully staked in his path this time or because he felt more tigerish. As the dancers revived themselves with kisses, their gliding figures and swirling colors clotting suddenly in the cooling air, M'sieu' Paul embraced the schoolteacher and kissed her long and elaborately. And apparently more thoroughly than she had expected, for, rather pink and breathless, she joined Madame and Thérèse on the terrace and sipped silently at a restorative *café blanc.* Over her head, Madame Berriault graciously accepted Thérèse's silent tribute to Madame's skill at reviving her charge's spirits, but she also stored up glory for the future by indicating, with a tiny shake of her head and an almost imperceptible pursing of her mouth, that the schoolteacher would err if she pinned any hopes on this flash of enthusiasm.

As Morisot, protesting that he wasn't sleepy and trying to recite some long, tragic lines of Racine, was being impelled into his bed by the equally intoxicated but still stronger Lenard, Alec Girard was returning to the White House

from his daily journey to the suburbs and doing some thinking involving Paul
—though a Paul quite different from the one declaiming dramatically near
the feet of the statue of a man like Alec.

This was the season of negotiation, the President was thinking as he looked
out at the fullness of a Washington summer with every growing thing complete, laid out, and available to any comer. Behind this open covenant of
bloom openly arrived at, the future gathered, germinating by way of little
underground nourishings whose results would not emerge until the year
swung into at least its next arc. Except for Elizabeth, perhaps.

Alec winced away from this thought and from the memory of the uncomfortable hour with his wife that had become a miserable exercise in avoiding
any specific mention of any specific time in the future while appearing actually to talk to each other. On the surface, Andy was all plans for the future:
she was engaging, her husband had decided, in something like an elaborate
public relations campaign. The round table in her room was awash in bro-
chures and color photographs from the *National Geographic* of the places
she and Elizabeth were going to visit, as soon as the promised remission
began. It was intelligent and resourceful, but it all seemed based, Alec noted,
on the pathetic premise that if Elizabeth could be sold the delights of the
world, she would stick around to see them. "Stay yet awhile; thou art so
fair," was the plea, Alec realized, and wondered whether Andy was remembering the line, too. He thought not; he thought she had begun, as effective
salesmen do, by convincing herself.

But he found out he was wrong when he saw the tape recorder, which had
already been used to archive a story told by Elizabeth to her mother yesterday. That there was no sick failure to recognize unreality behind Andy's
determined planning emerged again during her brief, painful discussion with
Alec about informing what he called "Elizabeth's other people." He and
Andy weren't the only people in Elizabeth's life, Alec had suggested gently:
others had rights in Elizabeth, as she did in them. Whereupon Andy had suggested that Paul be notified, because he had farthest to come.

This observation on geography as a barrier from a woman who had flown
across oceans and found them no substantial deterrent made no sense whatever unless you were Alec and wanted Paul there, too, and for the same
unspoken reason. Paul was needed as a recorder and immortalizer, the one
among those with "rights" to Elizabeth who could most help to keep her with
them when recollection began to fade; what Andy wanted was the biographer
to bolster the frailties of memory, Alec saw even as he heard himself proposing a few days' delay in sending for Paul. Andy agreed for the same reason
Alec had suggested it—to put off acknowledgment of the need, even briefly.

But the colloquy proved she was no more deluded than Alec was: the
journeys she was planning were simply Andy's way of making the unbearable
present bearable. As were the little girl's nightgown with its delicate trim of
narrow pink ribbon run through openwork at the neck, or the gay Quimper
pottery on the dinner tray. Alec had kept his eyes on the softly colored, pan-

talooned figure in the plate on which ignored toast wilted while he listened to Andy and Elizabeth talk their new language, the hospital lingo in which Elizabeth's tongue tripped with startling ease over jawbreaking medical terms or rattled off mysterious sets of initials like a bureaucrat. No, Andy had not left the real world: she had instead joined it and encouraged Elizabeth to learn whatever there was to learn from it; and, characteristically, Andy had set about making it as pretty as she could.

She had, in short, negotiated with the disease—at least to the extent that it is possible to negotiate with something that can have what it wants regardless of what you offer. Alec forced himself to think about his daughter's waxen face, to remember the red spots on her legs that disappeared and then, for no apparent reason, reappeared as though some monster beat her every time her father turned his back. Bright strips of adhesive bandage with pretty designs marked the sites of the constant bloodletting by which the doctors gathered frequent intelligence on the extent of the enemy's damage; his strength was measured by the less frequent bone marrow tests, the latest of which had showed "some slight improvement but nothing significant." Complications resulting from the blood's diminishing clotting capacity were routine, the learned Andy had assured Alec. He understood what her dark, haunted eyes were asking of him and smiled like a television huckster, like a con man, at the little flower face transplanted into a stranger's bed. Elizabeth returned his farewell wave with the hand that was not tied down to accommodate the upended bottle she called, with appalling familiarity, "my Eye-Vee."

The car carried the President of the United States, who understood that the doom of his child could not finally be negotiated, toward his office and tomorrow's negotiations, which might perhaps, with luck, be fruitful. If he couldn't fathom the awful rationale by which the striking down of Elizabeth could be read, he told himself wearily, he could at least try to penetrate the bureaucratic impassivity of the Soviet Ambassador, through whom tomorrow morning he would enlarge his devious approach to the Kremlin. And then he might, especially if he needed an exercise in humility, begin to turn his attention to the perennial attempt to predict the murky determinations of the Congress.

Forty-seven

As the President received the Soviet Ambassador the next morning, the bellwethers of Congress were pasturing in the Mayflower Hotel on Connecticut Avenue. The season of negotiations was in notably full flower here, where the important "when" of the necessary and possibly imminent adjournment of the Congress also meant "what": the natural desire of most of the legislators to end the session coincided with the White House wish to see them depart; but the question was, who would pay what to make it happen. Once an adjournment was agreed on, by that fact the fate of pending measures was also agreed on: some would simply be allowed to die, others would be crammed through. Which would meet which fate was being decided, although not usually baldly, over the spanking white tablecloth and more-elaborate-than-usual Saturday breakfast, by the informal caucus of the majority party composed of "old" Senator Kenneth Youngblood (representing the Establishment of that august body), "young" Senator Fred Carson (representing its Young Turks), and the two senators who spoke for the South (representing a desire to prolong the session) and the Far West (representing a movable bloc of votes available, if its spokesman found the offer tempting, for temporary and specific coalition).

The South, buttering a cinnamon roll in defiance of the recommendations of his doctor, contemplated Youngblood benignly and with no visible sign that he knew the administration was unhappy about the pronouncements issuing with irregularity but reliable frequency from Capitol Hill about the troubles in the South. Old South, a survivor of many skirmishes—some quite deadly—had a very clear idea how these statements interfered with the resolution of conflicts by re-muddying troubled waters every time they seemed about to clear. He was also quite certain that the segregationists would eventually be forced to back down, which caused him regret—but only the unimpassioned regret of the politician, who knows he must lose some of the time. His problem now was to find a way of avoiding strong anti-integration positions, which would return to haunt him when the Negroes of his state began to vote for senator, while simultaneously avoiding offense to the whites who always had determined his survival and still would for a time. Fortunately, this year was not the moment of truth for him; but memories on both sides back home would be apt to be sadly long. Youngblood, he decided while he chewed, would have to have something pretty interesting to offer to outweigh the advantages to this Voice of the South of sitting safely in Washington, regretting in unctuous communications to his constituents that Senate duties kept him from coming home to help out. And simultaneously, of course, holding over the President's head the ax of filibuster—a weapon less formidable when wielded than when simply plied as a threat, keeping measures the President wanted from ever arriving on the Senate floor.

The Far West was faced with less problem than opportunity: his region was not particularly troubled with the color problem, except as it affected Mexicans, most of whom didn't read the newspapers anyway—and even then, only in small pockets in his area had real, ox-gored interest yet been aroused. But it was apparent that the administration, because of its concern with the struggle in the South and possibly for other reasons not unconnected with the trip to Europe from which Youngblood had recently and silently returned, would rather proceed at the moment without Congress looking over its shoulder. The Far West was quite willing to oblige, but of course the administration would understand that the Senator was hardly prepared to be obliging unless some of the major concerns of his constituents received long-delayed attention. Water, now, was a subject that in his territory resulted in Senate seats being won and lost; last-minute congressional action in this area would encourage the representatives of the Far West to go home promptly to pick up their constituents' applause.

Before the smoothly professional waiter had collected the dishes on which bits of scrambled egg were slowly petrifying, the aqueous concerns of the Far West had been dealt with by young Senator Carson, who avowed a sudden interest in a House-passed bill that had been lying neglected on the agenda of the Senate Committee on the Interior all through the session. It was past time, Carson said indignantly, that the bill was reported and acted on. "As amended," the Far West interrupted silkily, and Carson hesitated, then shrugged and repeated, "As amended," in the tone of a housewife who deplores the impossible prices of food but has a family to feed nevertheless.

Over the second cup of coffee, Senator Youngblood outlined with some enthusiasm the White House's plans for a new and marvelous Civil War memorial and, struck with inspiration, turned to the South to ask whether—though admitting he hardly dared hope—the Senator could find it in his heart to help out by heading up the special commission that would choose an appropriate statue. Of course, said the Senator from Rhode Island regretfully, he knew what it would mean to his colleague to be kept in Washington after adjournment, when home and its delights beckoned, but the gentleman was after all the only man who could be counted on to come up with something that was truly representative of America's best by way of memorial—and perhaps his constituents would understand and be willing to sacrifice having their Senator among them during the summer.

The South sighed gustily and said he sure hoped they would, because he guessed he couldn't say no; above the rim of his coffee cup, his red-streaked eyes held admiration for the maneuver, which provided him with the only excuse acceptable at home for remaining in Washington once Congress had been adjourned, and a certain amused curiosity about how Jake Ruffing was going to make the commission disappear when the need for it vanished with the cool of autumn. The old man also, briefly and in passing, expended a small sympathy for those of his southern colleagues who were going to be turned out of Washington with no place to hide. He could rescue two or three, he guessed, by appointing them as his assistants or something; chewing, the South meditated on the most profitable distribution of these favors. Then he inclined his silvered head in acknowledgment of the praises of his colleagues for his sacrifice in the name of history and speculated silently on whether the call for abolition of the memorial project—the call to which the President would promptly yield, of course—would come from the intellectuals or the niggers, which were clearly the only groups Girard ever listened to.

Leaving young Carson to nail down the necessary undertakings that would send Congress home, Senator Youngblood excused himself to make a phone call before the group broke up. From a booth in the hotel lobby, he dialed the home telephone number of an innocuous-looking fellow named Meyer, who was listed on the White House payroll as Special Assistant to the Special Counsel to the President but spent nearly all his working days on Capitol Hill. As the Senator listened for an answering voice, he noticed a waiter leaving the booth just next to his and smiled. There goes the news, he thought, recognizing the waiter as the one who had served his table. Then Meyer answered and Kenneth Youngblood had more important things to impart than his hunch that the rumor mill had just been handed some grist.

The senior Senator from Rhode Island, who had been around Washington for a very long time, just happened to be wrong in this particular guess—but the odds were with him nevertheless. For Youngblood understood what most people, who tend to either underestimate or overestimate the mysterious power of rumor, forget: a rumor, like a radio signal, requires both a transmitter and a receiver to be communication. Some rumors, such as those reporting the end of war or other crises of national concern, are very nearly—if that were possible—generated by the receiver, in the sense that the news they carry is a consummation so devoutly wished by the waiting public that the bulletin is almost pressured into being. Most rumors, though, depend for their viability on what reception awaits them, and the reception, in turn, depends on what advantage lies in it for the hearer—and also what penalty.

By that Saturday morning, the rumor about Elizabeth Girard's illness, for example, existed in a hardly formed embryo state not even shaped by the facts: more people who had heard something about it believed that it was Andrea Girard who was a patient at the hospital than thought it was her daughter. The rumored reasons for Andrea's hospitalization ranged from gonorrhea or an abortion through a "nervous breakdown" to a tragic terminal cancer; but the significant thing about these speculations was that they were all stopped in their tracks by the fact that to be wrong about them would be at least embarrassing and could be excruciatingly painful. Thus, only those with nothing to lose would repeat the rumor—and the crackpots would not have been believed if they had simply whispered the weather report, and therefore diminished the power of the rumor just by repeating it.

As it happened, also, the major source of a legitimate rumor about Elizabeth lay, in this instance, with those least likely to impart the information. For people who work with children suffering from leukemia are, for reasons of their own mental health, assiduous in leaving the working day's concerns behind them. The rumor about Elizabeth Girard, therefore, was both diverted to her mother by the scandalmongers and cut off at the original veritable source. In addition, it arose at a time when most people didn't want to be bothered, which was generally the case in listless, half-empty Washington in July. Since it was also news of a kind that all but the sickest collectors of tragedy would tend to reject, and certainly dealt with people about whom one had better be either right or not subject to proof if one dared to talk at all, knowledge and circulation of it came to depend almost exclusively on an innocent stumbling into the fact by persons going about business that happened to be related to it. For all these reasons—if reason can be assigned to the phenomenon at all—the rumor about the President's daughter spread at a notably laggard pace in the city noted for busy tongues.

But the tip that the majority party was moving toward adjournment was not likely to fall victim to any rumor-strangling circumstances: Kenneth Youngblood, in assuming that the waiter was acting as transmitter for the many receivers tuned to the adjournment-rumor frequency, had on the basis of the record drawn a likely conclusion from his observation. However, he had no way of knowing that a first-time x factor had entered the picture: the waiter the Senator saw telephoning was not an individual entrepreneur with a piece of information to peddle, but something a great deal closer to an intelligence gatherer for an army. After the army was through putting the intelligence to its own use, the news that an adjournment deal had been set up would filter down into the regular rumor channels; for it was a citizen army, and when the councils of war were finished, its members behaved like Washington citizens.

The first result, then, of the waiter's phone call was not, as the Senator suspected, the appearance of a tip in the raucous Washington column that specialized in knowing everything first even if not well; it was instead a hastily summoned meeting in the sleepy heat of a midtown Washington neighborhood where bigwigs were not wont to assemble.

The group had been convened with comparative ease because most of its members had no work to go today: the department store at which one of the men worked as a porter closed on Saturdays in the summer, as did all the downtown department stores, and the closing of the schools had freed another of the leaders of the group, whose July responsibility involved only minor maintenance of the school building (until—and if—the District government got around to finding money for necessary repairs). A housewife in Chevy Chase had received a phone call on behalf of her once-a-week maid, reporting a death in the family; but other women in the group worked for families that had gone away for the summer, abandoning their domestics pending their return as less enlightened people scorn to do with their household pets.

The group sat, sweating and fanning itself, in the church basement and listened as its leaders, having established the necessity to act while Congress was still in session, determined on a move designed to force the President into action and also to cause a certain amount of benevolent stir among the voters at their backyard barbecues. A hopeful faith that just that could be done imbued the closing comments, delivered by a Negro minister.

The gathering stood to speed the departure of its emissaries with a hymn. The two tall black men who would lead the planned march to the chosen Alabama county seat waited on the platform, a little ill at ease—heroes not yet heroes accepting acclaim they had not yet won. But both had been jailed in Mississippi and, like knights blooded in first battle, had proved themselves,

so they had some assurance of their worth to bring to the moment of applause. Their leader shook hands with each of them, and the encouraging
farewells of the group followed them out the door as they headed for the
silent streets and the bus station. The leader drummed his pencil on the worn
wooden table at which he sat and made a mark on the paper before him. He
looked like a general ordering an attack and, in fact, the whole gathering had
rather the air of a much-simplified Pentagon strategic conference—or perhaps
the photographic negative of one, so that whatever would be white at the
Pentagon was black here. The leader jabbed at the paper with the eraser tip
of his pencil, still worrying the single flaw in his plan.

"One hothead can mess it up good, turn the whole thing into a riot instead
of a demonstration. Then we got no case, no sample to show Girard. Seems
silly, don't it?" He grinned suddenly at his small caucus. "All this to educate
one man?"

"He ain't no ordinary man," said a woman in the audience.

"You're right, sister." He sighed. "But I sure hope we picked the right
group to go." He weighed the factors to himself, as a military planner might
go over his distribution of armor, infantry, and artillery. "We got one
minister, a good sprinkling of white college kids, and our own kids all well
trained. And we got Rosa Little with them: she's a sensible woman and the
kids mind her right good." He sighed, put the pencil down, and with Pen-
tagon-like security consciousness began to tear the paper into little scraps
for safe disposal. "Well, we got a certain amount of waiting to do, brothers
and sisters," he said cheerfully, "so let's keep our mouth shut and our heart
high. And if you-all would like to join me in calling upon the Lord—" Over
the bowed heads, he spoke the short, simple prayer that came to him and
then left, shaking hands on the way out, to meet with a priest and rabbi who
might fly down to Alabama to join the group before the maneuvers began.

If the rumor about the adjournment of Congress was free to be broadcast
in ever-widening relays, the rumor about the attack on Ann Taswell, which
was much more readily picked up from transmitters known by each receiver
to be reliable, nevertheless was beamed only within a closed circuit. Although
the Washington newspapers had run their usual brief, quiet, no-names story,
the police watchers on all their staffs who had picked up the item originally
had the name of the victim, of course—and so, very soon, did their colleagues
and the colleagues of their colleagues. But, although the news could go
round and round, it was not likely to go outward: Ann was not only popular
with her peers now, but she had begun her career as a copyholder, which is
the lowest form of composing room life, and was still remembered fondly
by and on good terms with the men who worked in the pressrooms. Indignation burned in the hearts of members of the International Typographical
Union and the Newspaper Guild alike on behalf of their fellow-worker, erstwhile and current; but the writers weren't about to write it and the linotype
operators weren't about to set it. The managing editor of the *Tribune* cursed
for thirty seconds without repeating himself once, when the news was tele-

phoned to him. His wife said she wished Ann had a husband, and the ME, struck by the realization that it was just as well she didn't, was calmed down by the need to think over how in the world you would feel about a thing like that. It occurred to him that, this way, the whole thing could be helped to blow over by an absence of subsequent dramatics.

It was possible that Gil Kimball, whom Marian telephoned for help in getting Ann out of the hospital—"I don't know what to do with her, Gil. She just sort of scrunches under the covers and turns her face to the wall"—was the only member of the Washington press who did not know what had happened. But Gil had flown up from Alabama with a furrowed brow and a sick heart and had snatched up his wife to flee with him briefly to a Delaware beach for a tiny interlude of normality. The telephone message awaiting him on his return—to call Marian Farland at a strange number—was only a mild puzzle until it became a dizzying dismay, like an unexpected blow to the head. Gil's distress translated itself instantly into a professional quest for details.

Marian answered all the questions humbly—including, with some distress of her own, the one about what she was doing living with Ann—and then waited for orders. Gil told her, in a rough voice he meant to be transmitted along with the message, to tell Ann to cut the crap and be ready to leave the hospital when he came to get her because he was only going to come once. Then, because he wasn't sure about Ann's ability to conduct her own affairs if she was behaving as reported and because he didn't trust Marian to know anything of practical value, he delivered a brief rundown on the *Washington Tribune*'s employee health insurance policy and even described the card Ann must have in her wallet. After which he hung up because he had something he needed to check on.

It had occurred to him that Marian was, typically, not enough concerned about the fact that the two women would again be alone in an environment that had just proved alarming, if not outright hostile. After a few phone calls, though, he found that the odd truth was that they would be safer in Ann's apartment than anywhere else: the cops, he was told, always kept a good watch in the neighborhood for a few weeks after this kind of thing. Ann's assailant had been picked up (and found to have raped two other women as well, all in the same neighborhood in the past ten days); but the police, Gil discovered, had found some time ago that even the bare news items the papers printed had a geographical attraction for the sick types who were inspired by the story to go and do likewise. So the cops went there and waited for them to show up—and Gil's newly acquired womenfolk would thus be well protected. By the time he finished that phone call, Gil was reassured; but he was also wondering how in hell it was that Marian invariably converted any man around into a husband.

Meanwhile, Marian—having put the world back in place for herself by locating a man to take care of things (which was what you did with anything ugly or difficult, because that was what men were for)—was operating with the wit she was always capable of once she felt secure as a clinging vine. Although she had scorned demagoguery, she was employing it rapidly and hell-for-leather in Ann's hospital room. She could understand, she said soothingly, that it was difficult for Ann to walk into the Monday morning editorial meeting as if nothing had happened; the ME was not going to expect that. But if Ann would stop cowering and come out, would walk into the *Tribune*, say, in less intimidating circumstances—

"What for?"

"Well—what would you say," asked the demagogue breathlessly, "if I told you it was to pick up your assignment to Alabama?" She smiled happily as she saw this coup take effect and kept her smile pasted on while she set about planning to call the ME and try to make it come true.

"You're bluffing," said the invalid shrewdly.

"You won't know whether I am until you get out of that bed and go to see the man who can send you. The doctor says you can come out any time," Marian went on, keeping herself carefully unmoved by the scabbed face against the pillows. It was a scratch: her children had had thousands of such scratches, and Marian had warned them against picking the scabs off but she had not worried or been torn by pity for them; she was determined to keep her reactions now in proportion with those experiences. "There doesn't seem to be any concussion, which was the only thing that was really worrisome." She paused, thinking that it was very likely that the ME could be persuaded to send Ann if he could see for himself that she was able to work. Work was the best restorative, and what Marian intended was that Ann should get to do her work away from the eyes of her colleagues but also under the eye of Gil. She was pretty sure she could get the ME to see her point of view; she had no intention of arguing it with Gil, who would be presented with a *fait accompli*—he had to be where the news was, and, with luck, it would also be where Ann was.

Marian looked away because she half believed that so much calculation would show in her eyes and asked Ann, in a voice softened by guilt, "How do you feel?"

"Reamed."

Marian winced, but managed to point out calmly that at least there would be no problem of an unwanted pregnancy to worry about. It was so clear from Ann's look that it hadn't occurred to her to worry about it that Marian, who had just recently been quite worried about it (and who, like any married woman of an imprecise turn of mind, always lived with a few nagging questions) was irritated out of gentleness and into what proved to be a more useful toughness.

"Look, you can't cower under the sheets like an outraged virgin forever," she said brutally. "You had it straight in the beginning, and now you've lost it. The—thing itself—isn't important; what's important is that you didn't get killed."

"Rape," said Ann, in a voice that underscored the word Marian had avoided, "is not a mere detail." She essayed a weary smile. "At the very least it's a violation of a pretty basic civil right."

"True. But not an important one. The fact is, you're not a violated virgin. So all you're left with is a pair of skinned elbows—which Peter has three times a week—and assorted other nicely healing contusions and abrasions."

"And a pleasant memory."

"Oh nuts—you don't *have* to remember it, you know. You're making as much of sex as the dried-up types who ban books. It's a simple, mindless act of no particular significance, and too much drama is built on it." Marian paused, wondering why a bolt of lightning—from France, even if heaven didn't care—didn't strike her dead. "The only thing that matters about it at all is the person," she amended quickly, in belated apology to whatever angry gods. She flung her arm out in a good imitation of Farland the public speaker and asked dramatically, "You saw the boy when they brought him in. In all sanity, is he worth remembering?"

Ann wriggled upright, her eyes interested. "Marian, did you think he was feeble-minded?"

"I'm no expert. But he certainly didn't seem to have a dazzling IQ."

" 'I'm sorry I hurt you, lady,' " Ann quoted. "How in hell can you make sense out of that? Is it a split personality or something?"

"Pooh. More likely a foggy brain belatedly remembering that his mother taught him not to hit girls." Marian sighed. "Poor woman. You—and his other victims—are all right, or will be. But that poor mother—"

Ann sat bolt upright, hardly noticing that the sudden movement made her head ache. "I wonder," she said thoughtfully. "What happens to the family when the son does this sort of thing? How do they pay for it? How do they feel?"

"Find out," replied the newest convert to striking while irons were hot. "And tell me. I always believe what I read in the papers."

That other people did, and without troubling to take subordinate clauses into consideration, was the point Martin Halloran was making in the ME's office at the *Tribune* after the Monday morning staff meeting had broken up. Or, more accurately, been precipitately disbanded: Irene Tully of Women's had laid on the ME's desk a sheet of paper with "Elizabeth Girard is up at the Federal Health Hospital. She has leukemia. Andy is staying with her" typed squarely in the middle of the page. Whereupon the ME looked out over the small assemblage, his mind ticking off the nudges and hints that had been gathering—beginning with the tip from the federal-employee columnist about the overtime for gathering data on leukemia—and asked Irene loudly, "Have you confirmation?" Then, without letting her answer, he dismissed all except her and the hard-core inner ring of his staff—the first, second, and third mates of the ship he captained. When he had passed the paper to the editorial page editor on his left, the ME said levelly to Irene, who still stood by his desk like a little girl called to the principal's office, "By confirmation I mean the mother, the father, or the doctor in charge. Nothing less."

"I see what you're after," his second-in-command said quietly. "You know she can't get it, of course. But even if you Philadelphia-lawyer your way out of this by defining confirmation so strictly, you've still got an obligation, just on the basis of an unconfirmed rumor." He looked around as Halloran observed that people would ignore the "unconfirmed" tag and discovered that the consensus was with the old reporter. But they were forgetting the old man, he thought, and went on arguing that the ME would cut his own throat if he ignored this and somebody else turned it in. "What will you gain by—"

"I won't have been the one," the ME interrupted. "That's what." He looked at his subeditor. "Eichmann," he said heavily, "probably reasoned that if he didn't cremate the Jews somebody else would anyway." He saw with tired surprise that Irene was still standing at his desk and waved her away. She sat down in a chair without taking her eyes from his face.

"All right, so I'm nothing but a puny bureaucrat," the editorial page editor said unhappily. "But for God's sake, cover yourself." He challenged the rest of them. "Let's take a vote—don't let him throw away thirty years . . ."

"By the end of thirty years," the ME said dryly, "a man ought to know what he wants to do without advice from whippersnappers." Suddenly he turned a bright, sweet smile on Irene. "Honey, take that look off your face."

"If it were anybody but you—" she began.

"I know." He was still smiling. "I'm the last man *I* ever thought would stoop to 'managing the news,' too." He sobered, and rapped his desk with an imaginary gavel. "Be that as it may—not one word of this, not one hint, is to appear in this paper or issue from it to anybody at all, in confidence or not. When the wire services pick it up, it won't be from here—and it may take them a little longer without our help. I want those parents to have every minute of privacy I can get for them." He stood up, dismissing them. "Right now I'm going out for a walk. I'll turn in my Sigma Delta Phi sweatshirt in the morning."

Grim and silent and burdened with a common secret, they filed out of his office like a band of unhappy conspirators.

An air of happy conspiracy marked the straggling, lively group setting off on the adventure they had been awaiting so long in Alabama. Rosa Little, walking beside her charges like a sergeant of strollers, breathed deeply of the balmy air that would become unbearable in a few more hours and watched the youngsters quizzing each other as many of them had back on their campuses on the morning of an exam.

"Mason County," the girl from Massachusetts sang out. She tossed her head to keep her hair out of her eyes as she listened to a jeans-clad young Negro reel off the voting requirements of Mason County; Rosa was reminded of a colt prancing in the sunlight.

She abandoned them to their practice, which she had already learned to call a "skull session," and let her eye rove over the group, checking on the whereabouts of the five who were to be her personal companions at their destination. The two students, both Negroes, stood out from the others because of their fresh haircuts, their correct suits—the jackets now neatly folded over their arms—and their thorough air of respectability. She caught the eye of the white minister from Connecticut who was to precede her in the Plan C lineup; he was looking at the youngsters with the same fondness she was feeling, and she winked at him happily.

"Yours is the test-case group," the handsome Negro lawyer had told them last night. The police were bound to break up the gathering, they had been warned—on the grounds of impeding traffic, if nothing else. When that happened, they were to obey: they would divide into planned squads of six each, and were to walk in pairs. Two people, walking abreast, could not—the movement's strategists had decided—be declared to be blocking a sidewalk or a road. In Rosa's squad, which had been designed to remove all side problems from the central issue, none of the pairs combined white and Negro: Rosa's own partner, should the two-by-two signal be given, was a middle-aged Negro professor of history, a certified resident of the state who had paid his poll tax, owned property, was free of any police record, and would be difficult to challenge on the grounds of literacy—particularly since he had memorized verbatim, the constitution of the state of Alabama. The white minister's partner was a forty-four-year-old white woman from New York, a teacher of political science in a private school whose official role was to coach aspiring registrants on the structure of the county government. The last couple in the squad was all male and all Negro: a student of the Negro professor—a would-be first voter in the jurisdiction they would test—and a bulky fullback on the football team of a Negro college in the state, but in another county.

"What I told the others about keeping in mind that you are a responsible group of citizens going about the responsible exercise of your constitutional rights goes double—and more—for your squad," their instructor had emphasized. "What we want is an absolutely clear-cut, uncluttered case. The federal government has to underwrite your pursuit of the right to vote, and that's what we want, after all the shouting's done. You people are carrying the ball, and we don't want you hung up on any state or county ordinance: you are not to challenge any law, however ridiculous, or to do anything that could possibly be called inciting to riot." He looked at the white couple from the North. "I want to emphasize to you two especially that you are not to touch any of the others—they may walk behind you, but there is to be no physical contact. You understand me, sir—if Mrs. Little should stumble, for example, you must be on guard against any instinctive courteous gesture."

"It's hard to believe," the minister said dazedly, shaking his head.

"I know it is, sir. But we don't want anybody to claim that you provoked spectators. These boys," he added without emphasis, "know better than to offer aid to your partner in case *she* should stumble."

"It's easier when you learn early," the Negro professor told the minister.

If they were to be so careful to give no offense, Rosa thought, bewildered, what were they here for? To get one, or maybe two, people registered, was it worth abiding by all the demeaning regulations along the way? Maybe they *would* let two such well-behaved Negroes register to vote—they had always encouraged a few Uncle Toms, hadn't they?—but it hardly seemed enough achievement. *Handkerchief-head*, said Bruce's bitter snarl in her mind.

But the lawyer was succeeded by an organizer, a brisk YMCA type with a clipboard and lists and a decisive manner, and the proportions of the plan began to become clear. It was a remarkable achievement in its way: each subgroup served a particular purpose, some legalistic, some psychological. One squad was, curiously, ordered to refuse to give their names to law enforcement officers and instructed to accept arrest with complete passivity. (A Will Farland would have detected the fine hand of the Justice Department in Washington, which had a handy backlog of cases wherein Negroes trying to register had been terrorized; those cases had been left to languish by the previous Administration, but they could be revived as supportive evidence of a new claim that this group's disobedience was based on legitimate expectation of bodily harm.) One squad was assigned to violate the segregation of any public facility they came across on the way: that group was, of course, not expected to make it to the county seat. A well-known Negro actor was the center of another squad doomed to arrest: he carried a large amount of cash in bills the numbers of which were recorded, witnessed, and sealed in a vault in Washington. He was to offer the money as bail, to test the freedom of the bail privilege in the jurisdiction; whether it was accepted as bail or not, federal agents would follow the circulation of the marked money from the moment it left the actor's pocket.

"Penny for your thoughts, Miz Little," said the history professor. Rosa glanced up at his round dark face with rivulets of sweat already tracing its creases and then nodded at the moving mass and said she was thinking it was all like pictures of D-Day in World War II.

The professor laughed and said it was organized by men of far less experience in logistics, and he doubted it would run as smoothly as the novice planners thought. But somebody, he added, smiling, was good at public relations. When Rosa looked puzzled, he pointed up the line at the double squad of bearded and Beatnik-looking college students who marched so far ahead of the rest that they were clearly visible where the road turned. "Whoever costumed them really has a sense of style," he explained. "I don't know that I've ever seen so many bright colors and outlandish-looking clothing of any sort, except maybe in caricatures of the Negro."

"I didn't like that," Rosa admitted reluctantly. "Look to me like they just there to get the people stirred up."

The professor lowered his eyelids quickly to disguise the glint of laughter in his eyes. "Well, now, you'll agree that any citizen's got the right to appear on the public thoroughfares in any kind of costume, so long as he's decently covered. And it's not against the law to be young and—kooky, I believe the word is. As long as you're white."

Rosa shook her head. "I know, but with them goin first—well, it bound to stir things up, that's all."

"You think so?" the professor asked her gravely. A moment later, he excused himself and fell back to confer with his student.

It don't seem right, Rosa said to herself. But the gentle landscape soothed her—on both sides of the road, as far as the eye could see, was green and plenty. The rich black earth gave all and asked nothing, and you would think, Rosa wanted to say to someone, that people could live together in peace where God made it this easy for them. But there was no one to say it to. She scanned the line, found it bunchy, and called out, "Spread out now, come on. Remember we not supposed to bunch up." The youngsters obeyed slowly but with good humor, and she felt like part of the group again—with a place marked out for her and a role to perform, and no right to stand apart and question every little thing. Politics, like religion, ran on faith—you'd arrive at no peace without trust.

She was thinking that that was what she was always trying to tell Bruce, in a way, when the car with the uniformed men in it drove by, herding her and the other "sergeants" off the road and onto the dirt shoulder where the others walked. The car came from up ahead, where the lively, noisy attention-getting double squad was now out of sight; the men were driving on the wrong side of the road and taking no pains to watch out for any pedestrians. Rosa, skipping nimbly out of the way, wondered whether anybody was under orders to get hit by the car. Then, as the police car U-turned sharply and sped back to the head of the column, she decided that this was one event that hadn't been predicted, or she wouldn't have put it past the strategists to set up an accident. Around her, the youngsters cheered the police car raucously as it left them behind, their mockery heavy on the heavy air, and everybody laughed except Rosa's group, already dubbed the "Lilywhite Squad" by its fellows.

But Rosa lost track of her fellow Lilywhites as the day broadened and the formal groups, with no immediate need for their designed coherence, sorted themselves slowly into natural groupings by affiliation of work, personality, or common acquaintance. Thus, in the safety of the unmolested midday, the white minister from Connecticut conversed quietly with the Reverend Hawkins, the Negro preacher who had come from Washington to represent the movement's leader, and the Negro football player held court among admiring college boys of assorted shades and colors. The youngsters to whom Rosa had been "housemother" during those first "school" days on the Virginia–North Carolina border gravitated to her again and she walked easily among them, a comfortable maternal emblem of order.

Priscilla, the Massachusetts college girl who had determinedly toted her squarish leather-covered makeup box through half a dozen states, found her long fair hair an increasing problem in the merciless sun, and Rosa came to her rescue, pausing briefly to make two smooth braids and secure them with rubber bands. Looking at her handiwork as they moved on, it occurred to her that she had made the braids the way her Mama had made hers—starting from the crown of the head—rather than the pigtails she had been accustomed to produce, far more recently, for Sharlie Grayson. I'm back home, she thought, wondering what it meant, and said something aloud about it to the clustered girls, who were educated and might know.

"How long did you live here, Mrs. Little?" Priscilla looked at Rosa with something of the awed curiosity the spectators may have turned on Lazarus.

Rosa corrected the inaccuracy conscientiously. "I lived in Marigold County. That the next one to this." She smiled as they reeled off their earnestly acquired statistics on Marigold County. The numbers told you nothing of how it was: much like this land about them, except lazier and slower, more deeply southern. Here the whites tended to be the lean mountain-men type of Will Farland, different from the plantation-descended whites of her childhood. "There was men in town," she told them, puzzled that it was true even while she said it, "that never worked, not they whole life long." She shook her head at Priscilla's question: she truly didn't know what they lived on. It was only that they bore exalted names and so couldn't work in the hardware store, but only a few of them made it all the way through the university and became the town's leaders and molders. Maybe the others lived on those few, she thought, remembering the plump, soft men who always had time for doing nothing in particular, who—unlike Farland, the hill man who rattled words like a machine-gun—spoke slowly and at length, with long sweeping gestures of hats and mopping handkerchiefs.

Priscilla was talking learnedly to another girl about the effect on children of growing up in an atmosphere of hate and Rosa listened, but it was someone else's biography. She had not felt hated, skipping bare-toed in the dust, except perhaps by her sisters; the men simply had not noticed her. She started to say this and then stopped, recalling that one of them had noticed her eldest sister, all right. Peony, Morning Glory, and Rose—her Mama had picked the fancy names for all the three girls. Peony had become, firmly, Kate as soon as she had left, pregnant at fifteen, to go and stay with an aunt in Virginia. Mama's one reaction to the change had been, "There better be more changes than that with that girl."

"How'd you get out, Mrs. Little?" the white girl was asking, her fair, open face intent on anthropology. Rosa smiled at her absently—for all her pale hair and her greater height, she had reminded Rosa of Marian right from the first; it was probably the voice, she decided now. The bright, interested voice, imbued with the breathy drawl Eastern girls' schools stamped on their products like the purple-ink Department of Agriculture stamp on meat, probed kindly and energetically and never for a moment questioned its welcome.

"My big sister Kate—she sent for my other sister and me." Gloria and Rosa they became in Virginia at the ages of eleven and nine. The old aunt was dead, and they took turns caring for Kate's toddler while Kate worked:

Mama had regarded this as a more than fair exchange, and she had been right. Virginia didn't offer much more in the way of schooling than Alabama had, especially when the two girls had to share it between them—but it was a little better, and it was farther north and so full of hope. Hope was redeemed, too: where in Marigold County could she have met the likes of the handsome Sergeant Little? Mama had come for the wedding, as she had come before for Gloria's marriage to the good-natured, hard-working taxi driver Claude Jones: two long, expensive trips on buses, but worth it, Mama's big tired eyes had said as, each time, whichever daughter hadn't just got married carried her around Washington and showed off the White House with a proprietary air.

God in his Wisdom had taken Mama before he took Sergeant Little, called "Tiger" by his pals, beloved of his young wife Rosa and still unknown to his two tiny daughters, only the elder of whom had ever even heard his voice. Mama, gone from this world secure in the knowledge that she'd done right to send her own little girls away from her, wasn't there when Rosa's tidy world crashed; but Kate was, and took Rosa in with her babies until she was strong again, and Gloria was, and helped Rosa settle in Washington and find a job and an apartment. And then Marian, who was even more motherless than Rosa, had finished filling the emptiness, bringing a brightness and ease to the little girls along with the hand-wringing disorder that needed Rosa. Back at the beginning, when Rosa had first begun regaling her sister with anecdotes about the confused and lovable chatelaine of the house in Georgetown, Gloria had wondered what Mama would ever have made of Marian Grayson, and the conjectured confrontation had driven them both to giggles.

The youngsters around her responded to the whistles faster than Rosa did, although it may have been preoccupation rather than age that hampered her, for the history professor, who was older by far, moved to her side alertly while she was still looking around in confusion. "The sentries," Priscilla whispered, nudging the slow older woman before she herself flitted neatly into her assigned place, farther up the line. In the road, the Reverend Hawkins nodded encouragingly, satisfied as a swimming counselor who has blown his whistle and seen all the buddies' hands raised promptly.

The woman coming toward them across the fields was a real, honest-to-God, literal handkerchief-head—such as Bruce, Rosa thought, smiling, had never actually seen. She was followed by a small, black, barefoot girl whose head was shrouded in the inverted top of a nylon stocking—the cloth stretched as it would be around a plump thigh—with the ragged, cut-off edges knotted into a peak at the top of her head. The marchers relaxed but held their ground, a credit to their training. Their leader came through their ranks and confronted the woman, who was carrying two filled buckets; the child held a large dipper and two boxes of paper cups.

"Dunno we got 'nough for ever'body, Rev'rend," the woman mumbled. Her teeth were mostly gone, so even those whose ears were attuned to the consonantless speech still had difficulty understanding her.

The Reverend Hawkins looked into the two buckets and said, "Lemonade! That'll taste mighty good to us, ma'am. I thank you on behalf of all my friends."

"Set that down," the woman said sharply to the child, who obeyed at once, dropping the dipper onto the road, and then stared, roundeyed and motionless, at Priscilla's flaxen braid swinging down off her shoulder as she bent and picked the dipper up. The woman with the kerchief on her head looked up only as far as the knot on the Negro minister's tie and said hastily, "My white lady done sent it. She say to carry it on down the road. He home today."

The white civics teacher looked over her shoulder at Rosa inquiringly and Rosa translated while the minister was concluding the interview with their benefactor, who wouldn't look at them. She kept glancing nervously over her shoulder; when Hawkins concluded his mercifully brief remarks, she tugged the child's hand and fled. Two of the college boys carried the buckets down the road to where it turned and they would be safely out of sight around the bend. Then the alert groupings broke and the natural ones re-formed, as the marchers distributed themselves on the shaded grassy roadside and waited for the food committee to pass out the lemonade; watered down by an issue from the canteens, it went around successfully. Priscilla held Rosa's cup for her because it wouldn't stand upright on the hillocky bank and Rosa needed both hands to do an emergency mending job on the hem of the white schoolteacher's skirt. "You know," the teacher said, watching Rosa's nimble fingers, "at home, I'd just let it hang—my general rule is to make repairs only in the name of safety and decency. I never thought my contribution to the brotherhood of man would be good grooming."

The Negro student sighed, loosening the collar of his white shirt, and said he himself would have preferred being enlisted in the Beatnik squad, but this affair had certain noticeable resemblances to the army, and maybe the job classification system was one of them. "I'm resigned," he added gaily, "to sweating my square way toward unearthing the so-called good southerners."

"Well, you just seen one," Rosa reminded him. "That white lady, she didn't have to do that."

"Teddibly Christian, wasn't it?" Priscilla asked one of the Negro college girls, and was joined in her mockery by the others.

"It harder than you think," Rosa told them disapprovingly. "It ain't easy to go against ever'body. That lady, she got to go behind her husband's back." She rolled up the leftover thread neatly and put the needle away. "You remember," she said pointedly to Priscilla, "we ain't here to judge them."

The white girl looked as though she might object, but when her Negro companion said, "Yes'm, Miz Little," in a soft, submissive voice, Priscilla ducked her head in silent agreement and held her tongue. Rosa smiled at her and got up; the signal had come to begin moving again. "Let's go, let's go," she called, and then added the more dashing, "His the road." One of the college boys bent and whispered in her ear, and she grinned broadly and shouted,

"Come on, gate, let's agitate," with her voice listening to itself. The result was as self-conscious as a coloratura attempting "Lover" with a night club band, and she broke into laughter with the youngsters.

But a strange core of something like anger (only whatever it was was less than anger) persisted, side by side with the sense of fellowship and the prevailing good humor that walked with the group through the long day. By late afternoon, Rosa had an inkling of what it was, and it startled her. The sentries had alerted them because two cars had passed, each carrying a quartet of white men; faces peered out hostilely at them, but the cars did not stop, or even slow, so presumably these were just people on their way home from work—not particularly pleased to see the marchers, but not disposed to take action. The alarms, close together, had kept them in their assigned groups because they were tiring and even the young were beginning to hoard their energy and restrict their passages up and down the line. So it was to the Negro history professor who was her "buddy" that Rosa unburdened her feelings, softly and hesitatingly, as they walked under the lowering sun.

"All day I been having this feelin, and it don't make sense. Like I said, I done lived here till I was nine. But, you know—it ain't reasonable this place be home to me; it ain't done nothin for me and even my Mama ain't buried here. Everythin important in my life—getting married, my babies, my friends —everything in Washington, and that really my home. And still, when the kids talk mean about this place—" she broke off to wave loosely at the blue swell of mountains that were not much as mountains go and very far away besides. "It don't make sense me thinkin like that. Like I pinin for a place where they never wanted me anyhow." It felt better to have said it, though she was still not sure she had said what she meant.

But he had understood. "Miz Little, home is home, and it doesn't have a thing to do with what happens to you in it." His heavy, aging face brooded out over the landscape. "They never wanted me here either, you know, but it's my home just the same. Emotions are not always open to reason."

"What I got to be proud about, that I get mad when they fun about it, them kids I mean?"

He looked at her thoughtfully. "They're children, making light of what they don't understand, that's all."

Rosa smiled wryly. "I don't understand neither."

"No, but you feel." He walked in silence for a moment, thinking how to say it. "Where you first opened your eyes on the world, that's home, that's all there is to it. Probably the psychologists could tell us it has something to do with the shapes of things you see when you're an infant—that mountain, maybe, means safety and mother's milk to you. So you have feelings of returning home, and they're perfectly natural. It's the others, the white people who pretend this is not your home, who are unnatural. You remember," he assumed courteously, aware that she probably didn't, "that the Jews in Germany went on thinking of themselves as Germans even while Hitler was passing the Nuremberg Laws—the laws that said they weren't Germans. A good many of those Jews could have saved their lives, maybe, if they'd left Germany early—while Hitler was still whipping the German people up, but before he had machinery organized to start killing the Jews. The trouble with a lot of the Jews was, though, that they wouldn't go—they wouldn't leave their homeland, the land of their birth. They either couldn't or wouldn't believe it could also become the cause of their certain death."

Rosa shivered. "That like us here? You think so?"

"No, I don't," the professor said strongly. "If I thought so, I wouldn't be here now. I've got a wife and children, you know—I'd have gathered them up and taken them right out of the country. But I've stayed in the South and brought my children up here at least till I had to send them away for schooling." He shook his head. "No, it's not entirely the same, thank God."

"What the difference?"

"The people. The American people simply are not in the market for the kind of things the Germans—" He stopped suddenly as the whistles blew again and held Rosa back a little so the New York schoolteacher, who had been visiting up the line, could dart into her place beside the white minister. "I was beginning to hope we'd make it to Alameda without trouble," he muttered, hardly moving his lips.

The big man wearing a star that looked like something children send cereal box tops for was also wearing a gun in a holster on his left hip and a club dangling from his belt on the other side. Behind him, another man leaned against the stopped police car holding a carbine loosely in his left arm. Rosa swallowed and tried to hear what the sheriff was saying to their leader, but it was no use; so she looked away, concentrating on the mountains, trying to remember whether she had been aware of them as a small child. Even when the big man began to talk to them through a hand-held loudspeaker, his voice made tinny as it was made loud, she wasn't frightened; everything was happening much as the training had prepared them for. They were being ordered to disperse, for example, on the grounds that they constituted a traffic hazard. She waited beside her partner as the groups began to divide into their rehearsed form up ahead: they knew where they would meet, at a farm on the outskirts of Alameda, three miles from the county seat to which they would march in the morning. The local Negroes who had dared to join them would be waiting for them at the farm.

The ordained amount of space opened in front of the first couple in Rosa's squad and they stepped out confidently in a reasonable stroll, keeping carefully off the road. All at once the sheriff was standing before them, his bull horn held down at his side; he was so close that Rosa could see the beard pricking through on his chin and the red network of capillaries on his fleshy cheeks. He stood with his booted legs apart, halting the Connecticut minister.

"You keepin funny company, Reverend."

The minister kept silent, as he had been instructed.

"The folks back at your church know you're here? Where you from, Reverend?"

Behind the sheriff—"This is Sheriff Floyd of Dorothy County," he had announced importantly in his magnified bellow—a few dark figures inched closer, like interested spectators of any public event; since they stayed in the sheriff's sight, the deputy leaning against the car watched them but didn't interfere. The minister offered his name, his Connecticut address, and the name of his church—all in a flat, even voice.

"So you come down from up north to teach us how we should do, that it?" In the silence, the sheriff pushed his hat back on his head. "You take my advice, Reverend, you be better off stayin where you belong and stickin to your own business."

I am a citizen of the United States engaged in peaceful travel, Rosa said to herself rapidly in her mind, running the words together as a Catholic child might recite the rosary. The minister was not supposed to say it, she knew— not yet; but they were all supposed to think it. Up ahead, over the sheriff's shoulder, she saw the squad that contained the Negro entertainer closing around him as he stood with his back to the scene; he was supposed to get arrested with maximum publicity, which meant not now.

"I asked you what you're doin here with this riffraff, Reverend," the sheriff shouted suddenly.

The minister said quietly, "I am a man of God, sir." He moved a little forward then, putting the schoolteacher slightly behind him, and raised his thin, tired face toward the sheriff. "Whose man are you?" he added clearly.

Rosa felt the history professor's start even as she saw the flush climb into the sheriff's face. She lowered her glance to avoid embarrassing the minister, who should have held his tongue; he was a good man, but he couldn't seem to learn the Negro's kindergarten lesson.

"Sheriff Floyd," said a loud, taunting voice behind the officer. As he wheeled, the same voice chanted, "Sheriff Floyd, gonna be unemployed." Immediately the chant was taken up by many voices, all behind the sheriff, so that his attention was drawn away from the Lilywhite Squad. The deputy approached slowly, his gun lifting; but the little clot of Negro college students in dusty jeans and soiled T-shirts stood their ground in the gathering dusk, chanting gaily, "Sheriff Floyd, gonna be unemployed."

The sheriff waved his deputy back and reached into the group; he dragged out one of the students, holding him by his bunched shirt-front, and said thickly, "You started that."

The boy rolled his eyes like a parody of a movie slave. "Not me, Massa."

"It was you, all right." The big man shook the boy in his grasp.

"I never did. Warn't me." The boy paused, grinned broadly, and added, "You jus' cain't tell one of us from tothuh, can you, Massa?" Shouts of taunting laughter rose from the other students as uniformly as though he were a cheerleader at a football game and they were responding enthusiastically to learned cues. Rosa heard scuffling, but suddenly she couldn't see what was going on; she tried craning, and then she felt the history professor touch her bare arm lightly. The Negro fullback who was in their squad was blocking her view, and she understood then that he was supposed to, that he had planted himself there by plan and she was required to remain silent and invisible behind him.

Their leader's voice, full of indignation, was demanding to know the charge against the boy. "Disorderly conduct," Sheriff Floyd said. "And I'll give you just one minute to get this bunch of jigaboos out of here or I'll take some more with me, too."

Rosa saw the couple in front of her move out and she followed when it was time, keeping step with the history professor. The fullback fell in with his partner behind her. As they passed, unnoticed, the group by the car, she heard the sheriff say in a voice heavy with threat, "I can wait to get you tomorrow, nigger, but I don't have to. You want it now—" There was a sudden flurry and something clanged against metal. "Get him," the sheriff shouted.

"Keep walking," the deep voice behind Rosa said, a foot above her ear. "You keep step, Miz Little."

"What—?"

"Just his partner," said the other student. "You remember, we're supposed to be two in jail at a time? His partner's getting himself arrested, too."

Rosa shuffled obediently along, her eyes on the ground like a convict. She looked up when the professor nudged her: their leader was talking animatedly to a pair of men standing beside a dusty gray car parked on the opposite shoulder of the road. "Who—?"

"Press," said the professor, looking straight ahead. "We don't want those boys who just got arrested to slip out of anybody's mind now, do we?"

His student chuckled behind Rosa. "We'll likely be meeting them in the county jail tomorrow."

"Mebbe. If something don't happen to them tonight," the fullback remarked matter-of-factly.

Rosa shook her head and then stopped shaking it, because that accomplished nothing. But she was still doing it, inside and invisibly, when the day was finally over—when they had been fed and bedded down for the night after a brief service led by the white minister. Their cadre of volunteer Negro teachers was like the working load of scientific instruments carried aloft by a rocket and the rest of them were the jets of flame, the glamorous astronauts, the counting-down voices; in the darkness, the small dedicated group that would melt into the countryside to do the work of coaxing local Negroes to register slipped out of the old farmhouse and went on foot in pairs to the homes of those who had agreed to keep them. Outside, cars passed, pausing and honking from time to time; their headlights swept the ceiling of the square wallpapered room, like the inside of a candy box, in which Rosa presided over the slumbers of Priscilla, the white civics teacher, and three Negro girls. Voices shouted indistinctly, but the sentries gave no warning, so eventually Rosa decided in favor of weariness over nervous alertness and went to sleep.

Forty-eight

The next morning, Elizabeth Girard was given an orange to eat and managed a few segments before she began to cry because it made her mouth sting. She was feeling more cheerful, though, by the time she was taken in her wheelchair for the necessary but frightening business of having a long needle inserted into one of her bones so Dr. Snowden could estimate from analysis of the marrow the size and deployment of the enemy today. Her mother walked beside her, and they sang the little alphabet song, set to Haydn's theme, that has been on the preschoolers' hit parade for a very long time. She was up to "Q-R-S- and T-U-V" as she went by her friend's open door and the other little girl made a duet of "Double-You and X-Y-Z," to the delight of both of them. But Andy's applause had more volume than the combined voices.

The forces and deployment of Rosa Little's enemy were apparent by the time the augmented group of marchers reached the outskirts of the county seat. The sun was already hot, but not too hot, and an air of holiday pervaded the crowd that began right at the town line. A press car followed the marchers, but it was the one ahead of them that contained the photographer who got the good shot of the arrest of the famous Negro entertainer on a charge of disorderly conduct—which offense consisted of singing "We Shall Overcome" with a group of five friends, all arrested with him. He went off without arguing, even waving gaily at the camera. The watchers along the cracked sidewalks were caught up in the general holiday spirit and the specific excitement of the incident and found themselves smiling as the laughing man disappeared into the police wagon. Only for a moment, of course—then they looked at each other, shamefaced, and walked away denying everything.

More members of the press came as the passive resistance squad was being pelted with various foodstuffs by occupants of the Railroad Café on the main street of the town. It was hard to get a good photograph, though—there was the clutter of cars on the street and the blockades of uniformed men and the others whose status as law enforcement officers for the day depended on armbands with strips of elastic that left red marks on bare, hairy arms. Besides, a camera exposed enough to do its work might well get smashed by some joyous missile. The fun of throwing things swept the group like a round of coughing at a bad concert and soon the Railroad Café was denuded of everything that was loose. Its owner, a dedicated law-abiding member of the White Citizens Circle, was close to tears for the first time since his dog had died when he was ten.

A half-full bottle of barbecue sauce smashed the green lens of the traffic light at the circle around the Confederate memorial; for more than a year thereafter, the citizens stopped for a red light but went ahead for a naked white bulb. The *New York Leader* and the *Washington Tribune* were both represented on the scene, but not yet by Gil Kimball and Ann Taswell, who were traveling together but had stopped on their way down to have a look at a Negro church bombed in another town the previous day. A press service photographer, luckier than his fellows, managed to get a shot of a woman in a flower-printed housedress spitting at a Yale divinity student who was being tossed into a truck by three sweating men; she missed his face, though, because he had his head down with his locked hands protecting the vulnerable back of the skull, as he had practiced. The press service ran the picture even though its corner was a little streaked—a child at the curb had waved his Confederate flag too quickly for the camera setting at just the moment the shutter closed.

Everything didn't go off quite as planned for the marchers, of course: for one thing, Priscilla slapped the face of a lout who tugged playfully at one of her long blond braids; he shouted, more in surprise than in anger, and was immediately defended by one of the busy deputies, who arrested Priscilla for assault. This left her admirer a trifle dashed and disappointed, but it was probably better for Priscilla and didn't really do much damage to the plan; she was supposed to get arrested a little later. In the melee—for she didn't go quietly—she couldn't hold onto her precious makeup case, though she tried desperately. As she was hauled away, the white man who had started the whole thing picked the case up from the street and held it dubiously for a moment in the hope that some authority would tell him what to do; all the authorities in town were quite busy at the moment, though, so he settled the matter for himself by handing the case politely to a young Negro girl in the line of march. She took it, too startled for comment, and, since she was one of those arrested quietly, she managed to keep it and gave it to Priscilla when they met in jail.

Things were much quieter by the time the Lilywhite Squad turned onto State Street and began to walk toward the courthouse between lines of buzzing whites. It was like Saturday in town, Rosa thought unwillingly, wanting instead to feel thoroughly alien, as she put her feet down carefully and walked with her head up, like a model. Beside her the history professor, sweat beginning to wilt his stiff white collar, squared his shoulders under the stifling jacket of the blue suit that was too hot for this weather anyway and reminded himself not to clench his hand on the handle of his briefcase. He concentrated on trying to find just that point of ease that fell short of unseemly jauntiness; his attention to the problem brought to his round middle-aged face exactly the right look of calm preoccupation. Ahead of him, the face of the white minister, who had insufficient gift of relaxation for the task he had set himself, was reminiscent of some that might have been seen in Salem, Massachusetts, in the seventeenth century. The civics teacher who paced beside him in sensible low-heeled oxfords surveyed the spectators with a summary classroom gaze that filled many of them with an unfocused but nevertheless quite positive guilt.

Actually the first person Rosa noticed among the spectators was a refugee from the teacher's authoritative eye. He was a small boy, no bigger than Peter Farland, she thought—and actually very like Peter, though less dark—and he was scooping up a precious almost-triangular shard of the green glass from the shattered traffic light when he felt himself impaled by the basilisk eye; he shoved the glass (which was not really glass, but some sort of plastic, he was to discover later) into the pocket of his shorts and scrambled to make himself invisible behind the nearest skirt. It was this scurrying movement that caught Rosa's trained attention, and it took her a moment to remember that whatever he was up to was no business of hers, and then to stop thinking about Peter and the other children that followed the thought of him, and finally to remember what she was there for. *I am a citizen of the United States,* she began to say guiltily in her mind, with the hasty devotion of one whose thoughts have wandered in church.

"I am a resident of this county and this state and a citizen of the United States," the history professor was saying in a clear, carrying voice to the white man who had told him he could not enter the courthouse. A flashbulb accented the sunshine suddenly; it made the professor blink, but its effect on the official was disproportionately devastating. He shouted something indistinct in a high, frightened voice that contrasted beautifully—or miserably, depending on the point of view—with the rich tones of his Negro adversary.

Who was persisting in not being an adversary. "And I have come to seek information on how I may register to vote," he went on, loud, patient, and calm. Rosa stood at his side, looking around at the quiet faces of stragglers on the broad, shallow steps. It was getting across, she thought, her eyes lighting—as she had known they would, the people were responding to dignity.

"There's no registrar here now," the white man in the rumpled suit said quickly.

"That so? I was told that I should inquire here." The professor shifted his briefcase a little, a recognizable portrait of a citizen up against the delays and uncertainties of bureaucracy. "Could you tell me, please, where I may inquire, then?"

"There's no registration now. It's the middle of summer."

"Yes." The voice said that a gentleman was patient with the inadequacies of underlings. "I understand. Could you tell me, please, where I can find out when to register?"

Perhaps because the volume of the professor's voice had fallen a little, a TV correspondent thrust a microphone on a long wire between the two men: he kept it down, not near their faces but simply in the space between them. Nevertheless, the county official jumped as though he had seen a snake and raised his arm as if to brush it away. "I got no time for uppity niggers," he rasped. He looked out at the crowd, his eyes, a little frightened, asking their support.

Rosa heard the general gasp and the specific one that came from one of two women who were not an arm's length away from her on the step. Out of the corner of her eye, she saw the Reverend Hawkins, below, smile brightly and

she understood why: they couldn't have asked for a more stupid handling of
the situation by the enemy. She stood still, staring into the middle distance
like an actress in arena theater who must remain in her role and not allow
herself to be engaged by the nearby surrounding audience. One of the women
said, "Well, I never," almost into Rosa's ear, and it got very hard to hold the
pose.

The professor looked at the smaller man sadly. "I'm sorry to have troubled
you," he said with no particular regret, but definitely a gentleman's gracious-
ness. "I'll inquire inside."

"No, you don't!" the man shouted, suddenly beside himself with the shame
of imminent defeat. "You can't go in there!"

With the press and photographers at their points like a military squad's
reconnaissance men, the crowd surged forward gently, not with menace but
as if everyone wanted to hear better.

The professor said sharply, "I am a citizen of the United States in pursuit
of information about how I may register to vote."

"Troublemaker," someone not on the steps yelled; but the voice sounded
tentative.

"I am also," the professor went on, his voice full of contempt, "a taxpayer
and legal resident of this county. I therefore propose to present myself at the
offices of the county government for the purpose of seeking information—"

"Dirty nigger!" the voice that had yelled before shouted, this time with
more certainty. A rising sound from below began to drown out the professor,
and a Rebel yell from a boy who had climbed onto the Confederate memorial
finished the job.

"Listen," the woman next to Rosa said. "You. I'm talking to you."

Rosa looked at the bouffant hairdo and the pink-and-white, somewhat
wrinkled face below it, and reminded herself that there was this, this respectable woman who wanted to talk to her, not lynch her. "Yes, ma'am," she said
encouragingly.

"Listen." The light eyes bored into hers, anxious and afraid. "Why are
you letting him do this?"

Rosa wondered briefly why, even if the woman thought her the professor's
wife, it followed that his wife would be able to stop him from doing this.
Before she could answer, the woman went on urgently, "What's he want to
start a lot of trouble for?"

"He don't, ma'am. All he wants to do is register to vote."

The woman clucked and turned away from Rosa a little, rubbing her hands
against the gored skirt of her flowered dress, as her friend, who looked a
great deal like her, said something Rosa didn't hear. The second woman
raised her eyes to Rosa and raked her with a contemptuous glance. "Vote!"

"Please," the first woman said nervously. She turned back to Rosa. "If you
people would only stay where you belong—"

Above Rosa and to her left, shouting began, and she saw without actually
registering the fact that the leather-dripping Sheriff Floyd was coming up the

steps, trailed by two men who looked flimsy in Hawaiian-patterned sport shirts. One had almost lost his armband, which had slithered down to his elbow and hung there like the arm bracelets stage Cleopatras wear. But around her and these two women there was a cone of unstirring. "I was born here, ma'am," she said slowly, and added, almost unwillingly, "This is my home."

"You niggers," the second woman began, a braying voice issuing from a sweating face. Her diplomatic friend stopped her with a white, freckled hand on her arm.

"Where you *really* belong," she said to Rosa, appealing, her reasonable look hoping generously to meet reason in return. "You ni—the people of your color," she corrected herself, "should go back to Africa where you came from, and then you could—" She broke off, unable to list the advantages of Africa, but the wave of her hand indicated that votes would surely be among them. Her eyes peered at Rosa, beseeching understanding, flattering her with the offer to assume that she *could* understand.

Two men's voices shouted simultaneously and there was scuffling; but Rosa didn't turn her head. She stood there in the sunlight, tired and polite and respectable, and thought about all the long way she had come while the woman waited, everything about the tilt of her head bespeaking patient hope that Rosa would see the light.

And Rosa was seeing it: *you got what you came for,* she told herself. This was it, the reasonable, fair, well-intentioned white southerner, the one who tried to live like a Christian and deplored violence and would be ashamed when she saw the photograph taken half an hour ago; if she could—if her husband's job or her daughter's invitations or something else close and pressing didn't depend on keeping up relations—she would snub the woman in the picture, the one who had spit at the boy. *Here she is,* said Rosa to Bruce and Bettina and Trixie: *I kept telling you she was there.*

Suddenly it broke upon her, the thought that it had indeed been worth coming all this way for, because she had found out what she needed to know. She took a deep breath, smiled disarmingly at her questioner, and said coldly, "May I remind you, ma'am—I ain't the same color my people was when they come from Africa." She stood there waiting for this to penetrate past the woman's determined saintliness.

But the second woman got the point first. Her red face turned brilliantly purple, all at once and as though someone had spilled grape Kool-Aid over it; she rose on her toes and swung her purse at Rosa, screaming at the top of her voice. Rosa dodged and the move tilted the pink-and-white face of the other woman, the one who wanted her to understand, as though they were dipping on a roller coaster. Suddenly that pink mouth opened, too, and they were both screaming, there was screaming all around but only single words to be heard: "nerve" was one, and "insulted." And of course, "nigger," which had now become "goddam nigger," and then Rosa heard with the beginning of fear that it was a man's voice that had said it. But everything was going too fast for fear—the impact knocked the breath out of her and she lay stupidly on the stone steps, her torso on one and her legs on the one below, panting like a beached fish and looking at a wavering, distorted reflection of herself like the one you see in a polished teaspoon.

Only this, she realized slowly, was a boot, a polished leather boot, and it was moving toward her. She writhed away, feeling the edge of stone like a bar across her back. Somebody was crying, and she prayed that she wasn't the one and tightened her lips against a cry of pain as a hand grabbed her arm and wrenched her to her feet; she leaned into the pull, instinctively trying to lessen the tug that was nearly pulling her arm from its socket. Then she was upright, uncertain and wobbling with her feet too near the edge of the step, and she saw with relief that it was the woman who was crying, weeping and dabbing at her eyes with a crumpled handkerchief while her friend patted her shoulder. With that queerly selective vision that occurs at moments of disaster, Rosa observed that the lace on the handkerchief was cotton and machine-made, and she felt an almost joyous sense of satisfaction.

It was Sheriff-Floyd-Gonna-Be-Unemployed who was dragging at her arm, she saw, and thought about asking him to arrest the woman who had tried to hit her with the purse; and then the joke of it hit her and she lifted her free hand to her mouth so nobody would see her laugh. But she couldn't help laughing—it was just too terribly, terribly funny . . .

"Miz Little, they get your teeth?"

She looked up and found the fullback struggling a few steps below her; he was peering up at her anxiously, his arm pulled back and held behind him by two deputies he seemed to be about to drag upward with him. Rosa took her hand away from her mouth and smiled quickly so he could see she was all right. She called loudly to the boy, "Let 'em arrest you. They can't make it stick." She was rewarded by a vicious tug on her arm.

"We see about that, girl," said a man's voice that might have been the sheriff's. Her arm was doubled behind the small of her back and a knee in her behind started her frog-marching down the steps, her feet only tapping on some of them. Her purse flew from her hand and without thought she turned her head in the direction it had gone and faltered in her rush downward. Another kick came then and a reedy male voice among the watchers said, "Right in the ass. Attaboy," and Rosa began to cry quietly and couldn't go fast enough down the aisle between the jeers.

She was still crying, still oblivious to anything but the shame, when the man behind the desk asked her name. She didn't want to give it, she didn't want to be known here at all, but she began "Rose" before she could stop herself.

" 'Rose' what? Speak up, girl." The voice said its owner was hot and irritated, and maybe even a little ashamed.

She couldn't look at him. Her eyes went beyond him to the small window high in the whitewashed cinder block wall and focused on the green stalks of a variety of house plant she had seen a thousand times; it was growing in a red and white soup can on the windowsill and it seemed suddenly unbearably important to remember the name of the plant. You could grow it in water, but this was in soil—rich brown dirt that crumbed over the edge of the can. The man asked her name again and she thought ridiculously, *I'm trying to think of it*—and then suddenly a name sprang out at her from the can on the window ledge and she said, "Campbell. Rose Campbell," and gave her address as Marigold County.

County officials more public-relations minded than the fool who had barred the courthouse door to the Negro professor issued to the press a neat list of the names of those arrested and the charges on which they were being held. Rose Campbell, Alabama, 36, colored, disorderly conduct, assault, unlawful assembly, and conspiracy against the state, was not thought by the *Washington Tribune* to be of much local interest, so she appeared in agate (without the "colored") at the bottom of the runover of the story on page A16. Thus she came to the attention only of a civil rights organization that was keeping track of possible new members in the South, two proofreaders in the *Tribune* composing room, the old lady on K Street who read every word of every day's newspaper before she did the crossword puzzle, and Alec Girard, whose eye consumed newsprint with the comprehensive swoop of an anteater tonguing in his dinner.

"One wire story had it twenty-four and the other said twenty-five," the President noted as he strolled on the south lawn of the White House with Jake Ruffing and Will Farland. "The *Tribune* made it twenty-two in this morning's story."

"The working conditions for the press down there aren't exactly ideal," Farland observed.

"Yes, I realize that. The point is that about two dozen people were tried within an hour and a half—that seems definite enough to make an impression on the judge." Girard turned to his chief aide. "When do the Justice people think we'll have the decision?"

Ruffing said, "Sometime today. Once we found a federal court judge who wouldn't duck, it was in his interest as well as ours to rule as fast as possible." He smiled. "I guess he'd like to give the people lots of time to forget before the next election. After all, he does have responsibilities as a party leader, even if his own job is safe enough."

The President looked at Farland with admiration. "I suppose we'll have to give you some kind of medal, Will." He blinked at the strong sunlight and took a pair of sunglasses from his shirt pocket.

Farland narrowed his eyes and stared out over the lawn that was like a calm green sea. "If the history professor hadn't been such a clear-cut case, I don't think we'd have got it, even then."

"We were lucky," Ruffing agreed. "There wasn't one damn thing except intimidation of an applicant for voting registration. The guy never even raised his voice, much less a hand. Luke says he talked to the *Herald* man this morning—reporter said the old man is a genuwine, by-gosh hero, and he got a feeling that the crowd was almost with him." His gesture deprecated the breadth of the statement. "Well, you know. For Alabama."

"He's right," Farland said. "No squeeze I could have exerted would've been enough unless the judge saw some backing for the guy, however vague or silent."

The President's lifted face with its shaded eyes watched a mockingbird flutter into a magnolia; the hidden white of the wings flashed like twin hopes and then disappeared as the bird settled on a slim branch that dipped under its weight. "Where do they get these people?" he asked of nobody in particular. "A middle-aged professor of history in a tank-town college. He had an unimpressive record in the war, I read—nothing discreditable, but nothing distinguished either. A man, I'd say, not particularly brilliant or brave—and yet he's got the guts to stand up there in front of that potentially murderous crowd and give us a well-thought-out legal handle." His teeth were very white in his tanned face as he smiled. "He even looked good in the picture, did you notice? Although I doubt that the photographers found perfect working conditions either."

"Care and feeding," Farland answered promptly. "He's a representative of what amounts to a Negro aristocracy: his father had enough money to provide vitamins in infancy, enough local power to keep him safe from overt attack, and enough prestige to get him into a good northern college. Maybe it shows what can be done with the Negro if he can get a few privileges."

"Where did the paternal power come from?" the President asked curiously. "The paper said his father was a minister, but Negro ministers in the South don't have so much automatic status, do they?"

"This one delivered the local labor supply. Unless you wanted to find yourself without farm hands when you needed them, you treated the Reverend with respect."

"Look," Ruffing said suddenly. "Here comes Dan."

The President's lean body jerked to attention. He was beginning a convulsive move across the small space of lawn when his appointments secretary came close enough to call, "Telephone, Mr. President." Girard nodded and said almost brusquely to his assistants, "Please wait." His long strides caught up with Dan Healy and passed him at once.

Farland said, "Seems a little keyed up, doesn't he?"

"So would you be." Jake surveyed Will meditatively. "Now tell Papa. How did you manage to get the judge? Even if it is a clear-cut case, and even if there *is* some modicum of local sympathy—how'd you keep our Negro aristocrat from being buried among the twenty-odd cases tried in a lump?"

"Are you sure you want to know?"

"Come off it, Will. I know you're not dumb enough to pull anything illegal—at least anything illegal enough to bounce back. The President knows it too. Or he'd never have turned you loose down there."

Farland said succinctly, "Blackmail." He saw the alarm in Jake's eyes and added, "No, no. No sex—if it was girls, it wouldn't matter. And I figured if it was boys, the judge's opposition would've dug it up long ago. I reckoned that was out, and so was any ordinary nigger-loving stuff." His eyes, cynical and knowing, registered the other man's wince. "So I concentrated on the question of what else would severely damage his image among the local populace."

"Well, if a homosexual is out and a womanizer is acceptable—graft?"

Farland sighed. "The notion that charges of graft and corruption are viable handles in politics is a feeble one, at best. I put it to you that the man in the street is less shocked than intrigued: he may shake his head, but he's more inclined to admire the rascal's ingenuity than to throw him out."

"Go teach your grandmother to suck eggs. Quit throwing dust in my eyes, Will. An alcoholic?"

"No good. Every third family's got one. I remind you of the very senior nameless representative from a nameless deep-South state who's been a notorious lush for years."

"And he's not unique. I give up, then."

"An informer," Farland said, smiling.

"Of course." Ruffing's voice was full of admiration. "Especially if it's a matter of federal—"

"Bingo." Will stretched his long arms in the sunlight. "Visualize our confrontation, will you? The good judge deplores what our county is coming to and mentions that he knew my daddy—which I doubt that he did, because my daddy wasn't anywhere near in his league. He sorrows that I have departed the hallowed land of my fathers for the service of the 'crowd in Washington'—I quote—but he guesses we need our representatives up there, too, don't we? I put my spoon down gently on my saucer, the way my mother and my wife taught me, and say that service to the federal government has its satisfactions, too. Even"—the lazy, storytelling voice sharpened suddenly—"the little services that go unnoticed and unrewarded. 'As you know, Judge.' "

"Taxes."

"Right. To make a long story short, I offered to see to it that Internal Revenue sends the judge a certificate for him to frame among the other certificates of virtue on the wall of his office. So that the tip he gave them a few years ago would no longer be an unknown and unsung contribution to the national interest."

"Will! Surely he knows Internal Revenue has to keep—"

"The judge is a southern politician, Jake. He knows perfectly well that influence can do anything. We might have to fire the Internal Revenue clerk who made the error of publicizing the judge's tip, but that would hardly do the judge any good, would it?"

"I hope to God you didn't get it from Internal Revenue," Ruffing said. "But I guess I better know, if you've left us open."

"The judge didn't know my daddy, but my daddy liked to pretend he knew the judge, who was—I think—the County Attorney then. As a court-house hanger-on, all my daddy could ever latch onto was the job as principal of the high school. Which isn't one of the bigger favors. So his ambitions were bigger than his capacity," Will summarized cruelly. "But he liked to sound like a big man by pointing to the clay feet of the local idols. I found out later that there was less to Daddy than met the boyish eye." His voice held bitterness. "On the law of averages, though, there had to be some truth in something he'd said. Of course, I had to go get names and dates, but I don't think the judge is going to start even a rumor about federal harassment. Besides, I offered him a little friendly advice—as the son of his old friend, of course. You might say that I persuaded him that the wave of the future was rolling in from Washington. It wasn't too hard—after all, a feller doesn't get drafted into a federal judgeship. And the senator who got the job for him is pushing seventy." Will shielded his eyes with his hand and peered out over the lawn like a baseball spectator. "That Dan again?"

Ruffing snatched the paper torn from the teletype as Dan Healy held it out to him and read aloud the brief report in square capital letters. " 'A federal judge in Alabama today granted the U.S. Justice Department's request for a preliminary injunction to stay prosecution of—' "

"The President wants you fellows back in the office," Healy interrupted. "The Attorney General's on his way over."

Ruffing handed the wire copy to Farland. "We didn't get a thing but the professor. The judge turned down all the others, including the exorbitant-bail question they hung on that damn actor. All the other cases'll have to go to the appellate court."

Will read the report quickly as he followed the others across the lawn toward the oval office in the west wing. The German officers in the plot to kill Hitler must have felt a little like this, he thought—so much effort, and only partial success. He told himself carefully that it was not an exact analogy; it covered only the fact that he had shot his bolt. He had never counted on getting more than a little, and he had violated less than the Prussian military men had: he was a traitor only to a feeling, an obscure feeling of semi-loyalty to a society that had never found him really acceptable anyway. And a poor kind of society, at that—if the judge had had nothing but conviction that white supremacy was right and divinely ordained, he would have been just as wrong but nevertheless admirable, and impervious to Farland, gnawing like a termite at the underpinnings of his white-columned house. Nobody gets sucked in by a con man, Will insisted silently, unless he's got larceny in his heart.

Ruffing, walking with Healy, looked back over his shoulder at his lagging aide and then slowed to wait for him, letting Healy go on ahead. "Dan says our dark reverend has already been on the phone."

Will nodded. "He's worried a jailful, and I don't blame him." He stopped Ruffing with a hand on his sleeve. "Jake, somebody's got to convince the

President that being in jail down there is not like being in jail in Vermont. Anything can happen to those people. Being in the Dorothy jail is like dropping off the edge of the world."

"Take it easy. I know he still doesn't grasp the difference, at least not emotionally—he has a sort of mental picture of Thoreau sitting on the edge of a bunk bed, I think. But, apart from that, something's happening. It hasn't been easy for him, holding out virtually alone—I think when Bruyette couldn't go along with him, it really shook him—and I respect him for it."

"Well, so do I, but there are other considerations—"

"Certainly. I'm trying to tell you I think he's decided that the ones that count are now involved."

"He's still negotiating."

"Just barely," Jake said thoughtfully. "We're not dealing with anybody but the governor now, and I think the President's beginning to make it plain to him that Washington has been pushed just about far enough."

"You don't understand—none of you understand. These guys have been saying that Washington doesn't count for so long, and winning elections on the strength of it, that they've come to believe it themselves."

Ruffing eyed him shrewdly. "Sure they haven't half-convinced you?"

"That's not fair, Jake."

"No, I suppose not. I'm sorry."

"Forget it." Will grinned. "It's the fate of Cassandras."

Jake paused with his hand on the French window that led into the office. "All I really meant to say is, if the governor has to be disabused of any such notion, I know you'll agree that Alec Girard is the one for the job." He stepped back, ushering the taller man into the office before him.

Will stood still just inside, letting his eyes adjust to the welcome softness of the light. The President sat at his desk with one knee crooked over his other leg and his chin in his hand as he listened to the quick, bespectacled Attorney General. He jerked his head toward the door leading to Dan Healy's office. "Get on Dan's extension, will you, Jake? I've got that bastard in Alabama sweating. I've been waiting to talk to him till you came."

Girard's curt voice should be making it clear even to the most self-deluded, Will thought as he listened, that the President was not interested in exchanging chit-chat. "I quite understand the geographical problem, Governor. Nevertheless, you either are or are not in a position to tell me—" He listened briefly, drumming his fingers on his desk top. "Now look, I'm not at the army installation nearest Dorothy County, but I can assure anybody that the soldiers are not going to do anything I haven't given them an order to do. If you can't guarantee a like responsibility for anywhere but the plot of ground you're standing on, then I suggest you get over to Dorothy County at once."

The Attorney General winced elaborately and then grinned at Will, who nodded in sympathy. Nobody who heard that could say that the President was being reluctant to exert pressure: it was a naked fist, aimed right at that outthrust chin. But Will went on listening with an anxious look, wondering whether the Vermonter would have any idea how useful it could be to the Alabama Governor to appear to be pushed around by heavy-handed Washington.

"I quite agree, Governor." The boyish voice had become silky. "If the prospect of such a clash didn't distress me, I wouldn't have been as patient as I have been. I assure you I won't enjoy announcing that you have called on me for aid—" He broke off as the phone sputtered and held the instrument away from his ear until most of the squawks had died down. "No, you understood me quite correctly. If you can't give me your personal assurance of the safety of those in custody, I shall be forced to interpret that fact as an admission of breakdown of law and order and a call for federal assistance. To which I shall respond, as I know the country would want me to."

Will let out a long breath and conceded that there were no flies on Alec Girard. He lighted a cigarette with a new feeling of freedom.

"Yes, the Senator did call, but I didn't feel that he had anything really new to say. I appreciate the difficulties of a constituency with strong views, but—" the voice became loud and threatening "—the minority view of your people—and let me remind you, Governor, that they do represent a distinct minority of public opinion in the nation—has had more than enough consideration up to this time. I don't propose to be patient any longer: your people are citizens of the United States and I'm their President. If you are unable to make that clear to them, then I stand ready to do it for you."

Squawk, squawk, said the voice at the other end of the phone—you could hear the sweat in it all the way across the room. Farland thought without shame for his meanness of spirit that he would give a lot to be Ruffing, listening to the other side of this conversation. He stubbed out his cigarette, twisting it in the ash tray as though he wished it were the governor's arm. Then his hand halted in mid-twist.

"I'm certainly happy that you see it that way, Governor, and I appreciate your offer of help. It's most kind of you, and if you don't mind, I'll take you up on that: I'm sending my assistant, Jerry Rosenberg, down to the county seat—in fact, he should be on his way now. I'll see that he's instructed to serve as liaison, so that it will be possible for you to communicate with me promptly. Just have Rosenberg call—I am available to him at any time." The President listened briefly. "Rosen*berg.* Yes, he's my personal representative. So I know that you'll see that he meets with every courtesy —at every official level. Meanwhile, I'm very glad we had this little chat, and I'll rely on your assurances . . . What's that, Governor? I'm not sure I heard—" The President leaned back in his chair and looked at the other men in the room for the first time. He flung up one hand with its palm out and fingers spread apart and rolled his eyes heavenward in broad caricature of utter amazement. When he spoke, his voice held hidden laughter and nearly open contempt. "Well, I'll tell you, Governor, I'm not really prepared to go into that right now. I'm too much concerned with this affair of interference with individual rights guaranteed by the Fourteenth Amendment. But offhand I'd say this isn't a very good time for your state to be seeking cooperation from representatives of other regions; I'm afraid you're not very popular with the rest of the country right now."

"The governor doesn't believe that for a minute," Will said to the Attorney General. "It's part of the dogma down there that everyone in the country sympathizes with them."

"Maybe he'll believe it now," the Cabinet officer observed.

The President was obviously interrupting a speech from the other end of the line. "I'm sorry, Governor. I'm afraid I can't give it any time at present. Let's wait till I hear from Rosenberg that everything's going quietly in Dorothy County, shall we? Then I might be able to take up smaller affairs such as your suggestion—which is, after all, a matter in which I have no obligation, do I?"

Farland chuckled aloud as the President waited courteously for a brief moment and then began a firm good-bye. It really took gall for that little bastard to think he could lobby now, but maybe it was a good thing— let Girard see for himself just how nutty these guys were. Ruffing came in from Healy's office and shut the door behind him.

The President looked up, caught Jake's eye, and they exploded into laughter. "On *your* nickel," Jake gasped when he had breath enough. "Oh, the exquisite *nerve* of it."

The President took out a cigar. "I guess he figured he had nothing to lose by trying." He was still grinning broadly. "Fascinating, though—like one of those crude paintings, you know. American Primitive, political category." He began to light the cigar.

"I thought our side was pretty primitive, too," Ruffing said. "I think it was necessary, because subtlety doesn't seem to be the governor's forte. But Bam! Pow! Zowie! doesn't strike me as the most complex kind of negotiation."

Girard blew out a wreath of smoke and put his head back to watch it climb on the air currents. "How speaks the left wing?" he asked. "Will? Was my fist mailed enough to satisfy you?"

Farland stood up slowly, his mind sinking in self-pity: why couldn't he once, just once, be part of the celebration? "I think making him have to go hat in hand to Rosenberg was comfortingly insulting," he said slowly. "But Rosie, all by himself, is a pretty slim federal presence. And not a very conspicuous one."

The President laid his cigar on the edge of the ash tray and said quietly to Ruffing, "I was wrong. He's not the left wing, he's a total anarchist." He folded his hands on his desk and leaned over them slightly as though he were about to make a television address. "Will," he said slowly, "what in hell do you want? I got the assurance we wanted. I made the fellow say uncle. There's no reason for any 'federal presence.' " He saw what was in Farland's face then. "You think he means to double-cross us."

"Yes, sir."

Alec Girard tugged at his thick, curly hair. "I suppose it's your bones again."

"Yes, sir." Farland grinned tightly.

The President took up his cigar again. "The man is the governor of a state. If he gives me his word, I've got to take it. I can keep Rosenberg there unofficially, as a personal emissary. But I can't go any farther than that, even if your bones are right."

"You can have your alternatives set up, just in case I *am* right, Mr. President."

"I know. But at a price."

Jake said to Will, "Nobody on God's earth could guarantee that any kind of standby order wouldn't get out. You'd be giving that bastard a perfect excuse to scream bad faith and cut loose with everything."

Dan Healy opened the side door and waited there.

The President looked at him. "Blackwell?"

"They just called from the gate. He'll be in the diplomatic reception room, Mr. President."

"All right, thank you." Girard waited until the door closed. "I'll take five minutes to give his arrival time to sink in. The press boys are probably feeling drowsy by this time of day. Jake, you and Farland—over at the Mansion, for tea? Ten minutes, and don't be late—our Blackwell needs the most careful diplomatic handling, as I think you know. Oh, and Will—before you put your other hat on: I'll think about your gloomy urgings. All right?" He turned to the Attorney General as the others left. "Now, about laying up a supply of marshals against the storm—"

VII

Wars

"The knights and ladies wept, and rich and poor
Wept, and the King himself could hardly speak
For grief . . ."

Forty-nine

"Down here, swelled-head columnists, dimpled TV commentators, and other spoiled darlings of what we laughingly call the communications industry are reeling from severe blows to the ego," reported Gil Kimball in a special story datelined Dorothy, Alabama. "In New York, the home of my home paper, everyone except possibly the Mafia is right civil to the press. In Washington, where I mostly hang out, the merest cub reporter is treated with courtesy by the famous and powerful: if you have a thing against journalists in Politics, U.S.A., you outwit them or mislead them or, if you can, hide from them. But if they find you, brother, you smile. Some of the Maryland and Virginia suburban split-levels are furnished with columnist dolls wearing pins in their vitals; however the blinds are carefully lowered and the windows closed before the evening voodoo chant begins.

"But here in the sullen center of white supremacy, just about the only time a white skin doesn't count is when it's wrapped around the press, and that goes for both genders, too. Not everybody I run into is smitten on sight by my physical appeal, I admit, and some of my colleagues also have faces that don't arouse instant affection in anyone but a few unchoosy mothers; but in all the years that I've known, worked with, and envied the skills of the *Washington Tribune*'s elegant Ann Taswell, I have never before seen her get the cold shoulder, even from an illiterate. I haven't space enough to begin on a description of the divinely fair Miss Taswell, so let me capsule it: I have with my own eyes seen an eight-year-old boy voluntarily comb his hair because she was coming to dinner.

"But even gentle Ann can't make a dent in the hostility that surrounds the fourth estate in this Yahoo Capital, in which I've just arrived after jaunting elsewhere in the Cretin State. I find we are tolerated in the hotel, for reasons that seem to have rather more to do with our expense accounts—which the hostelry taps at a rate that would make Conrad Hilton blush—than with the brotherhood of man. The single café that consents to feed us is run by a fellow whose wife had an expensive operation last year, so he's forgiven by the populace because it's understood he has to make a buck (I use the term loosely). Writers who would have crawled ten miles on hands and knees just for a chance at cutting each others' throats now huddle together in forlorn groups, and nobody but nobody ever goes out on the street alone.

"I've tried to understand it, but it defies logic. Although I can't for the life of me see why anyone in his right mind could believe that we would be residing, however temporarily, in this metropolis unless duty bade us to, the natives nevertheless persist in a tribal conviction that the presence of the press is what's causing their troubles and not the other way 'round. Among their cherished dogmas, I've discovered, is that if we weren't here to tell you about it, the Negroes of this county would cease to (a) want to vote, (b) object to insult, persecution, and economic pressures, and (c) insist on due process, freedom of assembly, and the other constitutional gimmicks the forefathers of some of us—and of some of them—nailed down for all U.S. citizens.

"I hope nobody goes away with the notion that I'm a sensitive soul whose feelings are easily hurt or who grew just a little too accustomed to getting the glad hand from charming, lovable Luke Messenger, the White House pressroom's *maître d'*. Perish the thought: I am as emotionally secure as the next ulcer sufferer, and anybody who wants to glare at me can go ahead and glare. But being well-adjusted can't get me in to see the county records, which are supposed to be open to the public; then, after persistence, ingenuity, and a transfusion from my expense account do the trick for me, guess what? The particular ledger that shows poll tax payments for the year I'm interested in —the very one I had to hand in an application slip for—simply cannot be found.

"I don't think I'm just being neurotic, either, when I object to cooling my heels in the anteroom of the sheriff's office, waiting for him to be 'in,' while first his midmorning coffee, then his lunch, then the first pair of his afternoon Cokes, are borne past me for consumption within. I finally made it, though, after the exercise of devious pressures I won't go into here—and that's where I got the poop about the press causing all the trouble. Right from the mouth of the horse who arrested a beaten civil rights worker for bleeding onto the nice clean streets but couldn't find a single one of the miscreants who fired into a farmhouse in nearby Alameda, cracked the skull of a news service photographer in Hardin, or dynamited a Negro church out on U.S. 38. Maybe the sheriff should try getting out of his office a little more.

"I may be just imagining one thing, though—the sheriff didn't say so, but I got the feeling that I, or any of my colleagues, could easily get a year at the prison farm if we were caught jaywalking. But I'm sure that's nonsense: it's a free country, isn't it?"

Outside the White House pressroom, the waves of questions roiled up by the plaintive Kimball piece were beating against the rotund Luke Messenger, who bounced on the balls of his feet as he stood, so that he looked not unlike a buoy in a swelling sea.

"Aren't you going over the same ground with that one?" he complained. "I've already read you the President's statement, which seems to cover it." He stirred the pool of papers on the massive circular table that had been a gift to the United States from an Asian ally and came up with the morning's handout. "Here it is: 'Freedom depends, et cetera, on information reaching the people'—so forth, so forth. Now—'Denial to the press of access to public records violates'—well, what the hell, you can read. The President disapproves, he roundly condemns, he denounces in no uncertain terms. What else do you want him to do, send the cavalry to rescue Kimball?"

"What *about* sending the cavalry, Luke?" asked Martin Halloran. "The Negroes have presented him with a clear enough case of interference with federal process."

"The President believes it would be a mistake for Washington to rush in any time there's a slipup in handling things on a local basis." Messenger held up a hand against the murmurs. "However—if the local authorities should show themselves consistently over their heads in dealing with the problem and so unable to provide the necessary guarantees of safety to travelers in interstate commerce, or to those in pursuit of matters relative to voting in a national election, then the national government has an obligation to step in."

"Not so fast," a woman's voice complained.

Messenger said, "It's all in the handout anyway."

"Except," Halloran remarked, "whether the President has decided that the sheriff in Dorothy has been consistent enough in shoving people around."

Messenger wiped his wide brow and folded his arms. The knowledgeable, recognizing the implications of the stance, fell silent immediately and waited with pencils poised. Also waiting, though far from knowledgeable, was young Grant, who had been brought to the White House this morning by the veteran Halloran on much the same principle as a mother duck leads her ducklings ceremoniously to the water's edge. The ex-copyboy (as of yesterday) had abandoned the Great American Novel, temporarily, to taste life as a fledgling reporter; he began, today, by noting the press secretary's gesture and its significance. Like the ducklings, nothing much in the way of swimming was expected of Grant at the moment; but he wouldn't set foot in these waters again until he had spent many years wading in such eddies and pools as suburban citizens' councils, government departments, and airport arrivals of prominent travelers. Still, he took note, he stored impressions away—if only because it would be nice, on the way back to the *Tribune,* to show Halloran that Grant had an affinity for water.

"In his telephone conversation with the governor, the President received that gentleman's personal undertaking that the disturbances were being controlled by the county law enforcement authorities and that any further problems would be handled by them also, with the aid of state police if necessary. If that situation should change, the President will be notified and will take appropriate action." The official tone vanished from Messenger's voice. "The man is governor of a state—what do you expect the President to do, call him a liar?"

"But it's true, isn't it, that marshals have been sworn in by the Justice Department anyway?" a wire service man called out.

"The Justice Department would be the place to ask that."

"And I suppose we'll be sent to the Pentagon to ask whether there isn't a standby order out for the troops," the *Washington Herald* said sourly. "Isn't it true that leaves have been canceled at Fort Cassidy? I ask because this is, after all, the headquarters of the commander in chief," he added pointedly.

Messenger grinned. "If you want to know how long the counter girls get for lunch in the five-and-dime on Fourteenth Street, do you ask Mr. Kresge? Fort Cassidy has an information officer."

The *Washington Herald* offered a lurid speculation on Messenger's ancestry before retiring in defeat. The startled Grant watched the press secretary's grave, patient face during the small squall of laughter. "I'm afraid," the roly-poly man observed when he could be heard, "that's history and not in my department. I suggest you check at Archives—" They drowned him out then and Grant shook his head in admiration, then glanced up at his mentor to see whether it was all right. Halloran was laughing with the others and ignored the youngster. He brought the new reporters here when they were hatched, in a tradition that had stemmed from a long-ago single kindly impulse; now it was a kind of anthropological rite, like the Indians sending young lads out into the forest or the neophyte knight's night of prayer at the altar.

The correspondent for Enterprise Newspapers, a chain that included the Dayton, Ohio, *Ledger,* was asking whether Luke had any comment about the congressional quotes the press had rounded up on the Kimball article. Gil Kimball had begun his journalistic career on the *Ledger,* the correspondent reminded them, and the congressman from that district was planning a one-minute speech in the House today to notify the sheriff of Dorothy, Alabama, that Dayton would take it hard if its favorite son were persecuted. The representative of the Illinois district that contained Chicago, Gil's birthplace, was inserting a similar comment in the Appendix to the *Congressional Record,* someone else added before Messenger could reply. "Oh Lord," another voice groaned. "When you think that the mail hasn't even really started yet."

"I spoke to Meyer this morning," Messenger observed without excitement. "He says both New York senators got phone calls from the New York Leader Syndicate before they'd swallowed their coffee. The *Leader* has already had a few hundred telegrams—and, of course, that's just the people who know enough to address themselves to the syndicate. Meyer says the Hill is expecting a very heavy mail in the next few days. All over, of course—Kimball must be in over four hundred papers, including a lot of large-circulation big-city dailies." He grinned at them. "I know Gil thinks he's just Joe Citizen who happens to write for a living, but he could end up by keeping Congress in session all by himself. That's just my own observation, of course," he added hastily.

"What's the President's observation?" Martin Halloran asked quietly.

"Well, he remarked at breakfast that he hoped it wouldn't depress Gil to discover that thousands of people who only clucked a little at the arrests of two dozen civil rights workers in Dorothy, Alabama, were moved to sit down and write their congressmen because the sheriff had been rude to Kimball." He shook his head at the instant, hopeful question. "No, you can't. But you can say, for attribution, that the President was happy to see the national concern for justice. Happy but not surprised. He always knew the average American took the protection of the rights of fellow citizens seriously."

"What about Kimball?"

"Umm—and that Mr. Kimball once again—uh, as he so often has during a long and honorable career of journalistic triumphs—has spoken for all of us in demanding swift and—umm—equitable application of the protections of the law."

Enterprise Newspapers grinned. "It doesn't sound full of overwhelming personal devotion to his old pal. Is he sore at Gil?"

"Off the record, the President finds Kimball a little—shall we say, naïve? His private comment was that Gil could hardly expect them to give him the keys to the city when he calls them the Yahoo Capital of the U.S.A." He laughed, spreading his small, soft hands. "No feud, fellows, really. Just what you might call a difference in point of view: the President is a practical politician, after all."

Halloran nodded. "Yes. Senator Youngblood had much the same reaction —also off the record, by the way—and Gil is like a son to him. A wide-eyed idealist son, though."

"He may be a shrewder politician than the politicians," the wire service man said. "Anybody object if we get on to something else? Luke, how about the Soviet Ambassador's trip home?"

"Well, how about it? People take vacations, even in the land of True Democracy and People's Paradise. Beside, summer may be the only time he can stand the Moscow weather."

"What did he and the President talk about when he came to say good-bye?" The questioner added, irony in his voice, "Which, of course, is something every diplomat does, no? Drop in at the White House so the President can personally wish him *bon voyage?*"

Messenger folded his arms. Proud that he now knew the sign, Grant glanced at Halloran—and then was dashed to find that lanky veteran lounging unmoved, not even troubling to raise his pencil.

"The President sent personal greetings to Premier Kaslov and Madame Kaslov and thanked them, on behalf of Mrs. Girard too, for the beautiful fur carriage cover they sent for the baby." Messenger paused to scratch his graying hair. "Oh yes, and the President also hoped the Premier had quite recovered from his cold and was enjoying his brief vacation at the Black Sea."

"And could he borrow the lawnmower," suggested an ironic voice from the clot of correspondents. "Come on, Luke. Cut the Pablum."

"I don't know what you mean."

Halloran stirred. "Look what we have, Luke: Youngblood and his subcommittee make a sudden jaunt to Europe, including Berlin. The Secretary of State makes an oddly saber-rattling speech. The Soviet Ambassador drops in at the White House. In Moscow, Kaslov makes a fiery little speech designed to settle the stomachs of the Kremlin crowd that gets flutters if they think the Soviets are going soft on capitalism. You with me so far? At this point, both sides have thrown a sop to their bloodthirsty elements. Now—our Ambassador to the UN, who isn't what you might call a Girard crony, dropping in for a game of gin rummy whenever he's in town—"

"The President does not play gin rummy," Messenger corrected, and added, with an air of earnest helpfulness, "Poker, either."

The group stared him down and Halloran continued. "Blackwell appears at the White House for tea. Let's see, what else? Oh yes, of the two presidential assistants who've been working in the South, the one that's brought back—Will Farland—just happens to be the one who used to be in the State Department."

"Farland did a stint there as UN liaison man, too," the *Washington Herald* observed.

"Yes, you're right. So—how about it, Luke? Shall we go on adding things up, or are you going to say something?"

Messenger said, his face blank, "You haven't asked me anything."

"All right, I'm asking: is a peace move being worked up?"

"The President has said repeatedly that the United States is always interested in seeking any road to peace—"

"Oh go to hell," said a voice among the groundlings.

Grant had been watching the thin, alert face of his teacher. He saw with a little thrill, a sense of being present at a historic moment, that Halloran had just come to a conclusion. The long body that seemed sometimes to be held together with baling wire was pulled upright slowly, and the *Tribune* reporter raised his hand with untypical formality and waited to be recognized. Halloran's delighted, observant disciple noticed the wary look in the press secretary's eyes.

"I'm afraid there's only time for one more," Messenger said, and then held his arm extended, pointing to his wristwatch as the mumble of protest began. "Listen, how long do you expect to get for your fishing? It's late enough. I'd cut you off now if it weren't that the venerable Halloran commands my respect. Okay—Marty, and that's all."

It was like a game of Twenty Questions, Grant saw, with only one question left. He watched Halloran figuring out how to get the most mileage.

"Mr. Messenger," the old man said gently. "Can you tell us whether the President has any indication that the Secretary-General of the United Nations has been meeting privately with the UN representatives of this government and of the Soviet Union to discuss a possible agreement on, say, nucl—"

"No comment," the press secretary interrupted loudly. He tilted his head toward them in an effort to sort out the shouted protests. Then his face cleared. "Oh, I'm sorry, Marty," he said. "I didn't mean to interrupt you. I really thought you were through." The note of sincere apology was not intended, clearly, as an offer to reopen the meeting; he went on without giving Halloran a chance to continue. "But I imagine you'd finished anyway."

Halloran showed his tobacco-yellowed teeth in a wide grin and nodded without comment.

"In that case," said Messenger, his voice betraying relief, "I suggest we adjourn—except, wait a minute, here's one bit you guys may have overlooked." He took up a handful of pages from a stack and began distributing them to the nearest raised hands. "Immediate release—the governor of Alabama is ordering the state police into Dorothy tomorrow." He ducked as those still without copies of the release grabbed at the pile on their way out to the pressroom phones; when one correspondent said, "You devil, Luke," as he hurried past, Messenger grinned broadly and bowed a little, like a sixth grader accepting his diploma from the principal on graduation day.

He was still smiling as he instructed one of his pair of pretty secretaries to see that the honored representatives of the press got whatever they needed —"but not what they deserve," he added, winking at the youngster who was waiting for Halloran to finish on the phone—and went on his way along the narrow curving halls to Farland's office. Will was just hanging up his phone in the small, bare, and rather gloomy room, undecorated except for a signed picture of Alec Girard on the wall and an unsigned one of Marian on the desk.

"You get rid of your playmates?" Will asked. He nodded at his utilitarian visitor's chair.

"Can't stay." The press secretary declined the invitation. "Yes, I fed them and wiped their chins. It wasn't too tough today, thanks to Gil Kimball. He kept them pretty well occupied."

"Oh? I haven't read the paper yet. I thought I'd read it on the plane."

"Well, he's all wound up about Alabama. But that's not what I wanted to talk to you about, Will. Marty Halloran has apparently put two and two together about the agreement."

Farland raised his eyebrows. "It's a little earlier than we thought, but it won't hurt anything. And Halloran can be counted on not to go off half-cocked. The *Tribune*'s likely to sit on it until they have something more definite."

"That's what I figured. Still, you'd better keep an eye on their UN man— he's no Halloran, of course, but—" Messenger hesitated. "I don't suppose Halloran got his any way but just by being bright, do you?"

"If you mean Marian," Farland said positively, "not a chance. In the first place, she doesn't know. Besides, she wouldn't care if she did know."

"Well, I thought as much. She's not awfully politically minded."

Her husband tilted back in his chair. "If you gave Marian an association test and said 'Soviet Union,' she'd say 'snow'—and mean it literally, too." Will examined his statement while Messenger laughed. "In fact, I'm not sure what she'd do with 'government,' even."

" 'Paycheck,' " Messenger suggested.

Farland nodded. "Probably."

The President's press secretary sighed gratefully. "Marian's about as politically advanced as Andy used to be. Well, I've got errands, and you've got a plane to catch."

"Yeah." Farland's restless fingers worried a scrap of paper. "Listen, Luke, I just heard from one of my sources—"

"Which are various, dependable, and mysterious. What've they picked up now?"

Will looked at him. "Why is the President sending for Paul Morisot?"

Messenger whistled softly. "And speedy, too—have you got somebody standing guard, night and day?" He examined the nearly bare surface of Farland's desk, avoiding its owner's eye. "Why shouldn't he send for Paul if he wants to? Maybe he needs a fourth at bridge."

"Come off it, Luke. A vice-consul's gone out to Morisot's Shangri-La with a sealed message, to be hand-delivered. Instant transport has been laid on. And it's all hush-hush as hell. What's up?"

Luke shrugged. "I am not privy to the great man's every thought. You'll have to ask him. And he's not here—he's taking some annual leave." He smiled slightly. "Of course, he might be just a teeny bit curious about your private intelligence service, particularly when he seems to want this kept top secret."

Will got to his feet and reached for his briefcase. "He won't find out from me," he said pointedly.

"Well, I've demonstrated that *I* can keep a secret."

"I know. My private pipeline could just come in handy for you, too, some day."

Messenger assured Will that this thought had, oddly enough, occurred to him and promptly withdrew. Farland sat down at his desk again and began taking papers from a drawer to put into the briefcase. No hits, no runs; but he had also got away without errors. Which wasn't bad, considering that he'd been completely out of touch. He smiled a little ruefully, remembering Luke's tribute to the Farland private intelligence service: the fact was, except for items picked up from State Department crannies—including a standing order that anything connected with Paul Morisot was to be brought to Farland's attention immediately—his intelligence service functioned only poorly when left to itself. And Farland, with an hour or so at a time in Washington between flights out of it, hadn't been able to keep the works very well oiled. Whatever was going on was big, all right; but, it was clear from the grim close-mouthedness of Dan Healy alone, it was also *verboten*. Since whatever it was couldn't be any danger to Farland, who was being every day a whiter-haired boy around the White House, it behooved Farland to keep out of unclear waters.

He reached for the phone and then hesitated, wondering whether calling Marian might score as an error. It was almost certain that she didn't know Morisot had been summoned, so Will had a certain amount of time to establish communications before the competition showed up: it wouldn't do to have Paul Morisot appear on the scene while Will Farland was still being washed out of her hair. On the other hand, he'd probably get a brushoff, calling her now while she was at work. He decided against it for the moment and went on filling his briefcase. Tonight, he thought, when she'd had time to read the postcard from Sharlie he'd forwarded from home, she might just be mellow enough to make the try worthwhile. He could just as easily call from New York. He closed the briefcase firmly and reached for his coat.

The President watched a commercial plane sailing over the river from its takeoff and wondered whether Farland was on that one; his assistant's little talk with the Secretary-General's representative was the only thing scheduled for today that really boded success. He turned away from the car window then and read again the note from Jake: "Rev. sez group going to Dorothy this weekend—thinks he better go. With state police there, may be okay, so he's decided not to try to keep the lid all the way on. Sez you'll understand."

Alec crumpled the note and stuck it into his side pocket, understanding quite well: he was the one, wasn't he, who had once said something to Far-land about the leader's necessity to run up to the head of the column when it became apparent that the troops were going to march, with or without him? He dismissed the matter because there was nothing he could do about it—a technique of compartmentalization that Presidents either learned or they perished. As the car turned at the hospital grounds, he was studying the other memo: Paul Morisot, it seemed, had chosen this most unfortunate time to take off on a walking trip to parts unknown. All the information the young State Department man had been able to get from Madame Berriault was that M'sieu' and his friend had announced they were "going swimming" and would be back when they were tired of it. The friend, a painter, had left his "female companion"—Alec grinned as he read the careful words—at Mori-sot's home in the housekeeper's charge; it had thus been concluded by the American emissary's superior that the pair of irresponsible artists would not be gone long, and the young vice-consul had been instructed to wait a few days in the village, while also instigating a discreet search of neighboring areas. Alec looked up from the memo, recognizing the pang of envy he felt for the carefree Paul, and found that he was at the hospital entrance.

"How we disturb people's lives," Andy remarked when Alec told her. He looked at her in surprise, for she hadn't seemed to have qualms about disturbing Paul's—even when she hadn't known she wasn't going to be able to right away, as it now seemed. "The vice-consul," she explained. "He probably told his wife he'd be away only overnight. Now she's stuck and she doesn't know for how long."

Alec shook his head without answering, but with a sudden new realization of what it might mean in terms of family life when he said, more or less airily, to one of his staff, "I'd like to have everything available on that by tomorrow." He looked at his wife with interest, wondering how she picked up these things. She seemed to have become, effortlessly and mysteriously, a minor expert on life as it is lived in the lower echelons of government. He looked around her room at the hospital, a student's room still, and saw that that was the answer: Andy was an indefatigable student; dropped into any situation, she listened and watched and learned. He was suddenly charged with respect for her, and a knowledge that she was important to him in more ways than the ones he had known when he'd told Bill Bruyette, "I have to get married."

Elizabeth was watching television when Alec succeeded in dispatching his wife on an outing to the Ruffings' for a visit with the baby and some relaxation. Including, he suggested, a swim—Paul's idea was an inspired one, and should be imitated. It was possible to have some touch of summer, even if one couldn't have Vermont.

The mention of Paul had been a mistake, though, he saw by her troubled look. "They'll find him in no time," he said quickly. "The people around there probably know all his haunts very well. Besides, there's the female companion left behind as hostage." This brought a lightening to her look; she even smiled as she speculated briefly on that odd pair, Alphonse's girl and the faintly moustached Madame Berriault.

But at the final moment, Andy hesitated about leaving. "Elizabeth—" she began.

"Elizabeth has two parents," Alec said quietly. "I'll be with her till you get back." That did it—she went, reluctant but with a holiday look beginning to warm her unhappy eyes.

Alec lounged in the hospital armchair beside the bed and watched his daughter watching the overly smiling man who was, according to Elizabeth's rapid briefing during a commercial, the Commander of the Cosmic Patrol. The Commander was interviewing a Cosmic Patroller of about Elizabeth's age who had just given his name and address with great aplomb, though he'd made "SilverSpringMaryland" one word. Asked what his father did, the boy said clearly, "He works in the Interior Department and he knows all about Indians. He came to my sister's school and told the class all about them."

Alec wondered whether this program might be one source of Andy's researches into the lives of the citizenry and thought about asking Elizabeth whether Mommy usually watched this with her; but a look at her intense concentration convinced him that it wouldn't be a good idea to speak until the commercial. When the moment came, though, he was too slow; his dulled perception failed to pick up the slight shift between the real Cosmic Patroller from Silver Spring and the model boy who was enthusiastically biting into a slab of bread until the outsized peanut-butter jar loomed up and engulfed the eater. By that time, Elizabeth, who knew her way around in these matters better than her father, had seized the brief and vital moment. "They're really in a telebision studio," she remarked. "Mommy showed me the studio once when we were riding in the car. The Patrollers have to go to the telebision studio and then their pictures come on the TV."

One of the most articulate Presidents in the nation's history could think of no reply to this intelligence report but a meek, "I see."

Elizabeth said, "Daddy," and then paused to size up his mood and bearing.

Apparently they were found promising, because she went on quickly, "Can a President's child be a Cosmic Patroller?"

"Well, I don't know," he said doubtfully, trying to think of some reason besides the obvious one, the one that must be avoided. "I mean, is it fair to the other children? The people in charge can't select everybody who writes, but they certainly would—"

"Oh yes, I forgot about the publicity," she interrupted her astounded father, and then convulsed him by continuing in her mother's voice, "We don't want to gladden the heart of Luke Messenger, do we?" She looked at Alec's dropped jaw and said that well, that was what Mommy had said once.

Poor Luke, Alec was thinking, had been very good about being sternly muzzled without being told why; it occurred to him that Luke probably knew why, and, sadly, that Elizabeth's hospital stay was one thing Luke and Andy at last saw eye to eye on in the matter of publicity. Alec was suddenly grateful for the pretense by the men around him that they were being successfully kept in the dark. Most of the men, anyway—he was almost certain Rosenberg, completely out of touch, didn't know; and probably Farland, who had been kept pretty busy and besides had a tremendous capacity for concentration on immediate crises, had not yet picked it up.

The President summoned his own concentration to his daughter's problem then. The looming space helmet she'd been wearing in the past day or so was issued by the hospital to those children on the ward whose hair had begun to fall out, which was one of the side effects of a drug that, hopefully, controlled the disease. With the ridiculous inversion of all normal values that went with this whole shocking new experience, Alec and Andy had found themselves delighted to see Elizabeth making the elite company of the ward's helmeted children. If the drug did indeed take hold, she would soon be out at play among the other children on the ward—and then, and then. But he turned off quickly any contemplation of the blissful goal of remission: the point was, while she was here, she ought to be as equal as anyone else, Alec put it to himself grimly. He looked at the television screen, found it safe to talk, and asked her what you had to do get to be a Cosmic Patroller.

"Well, all you really have to do is eat Star Twinkles or Munchy Peanut Butter. Either one. Then you're a Patroller. But if you want to be on the TV, you have to get your Mommy or Daddy to write a letter for you. The Commander tells, after the cartoon."

Alec nodded respectfully but in silence because the cartoon had already begun, and decided to temporize with the problem. When the rabbit was shot out of a rocket, however, Elizabeth announced that she had already seen this one; her father turned the sound down at her request so she could tell him about the entrance requirements for the Cosmic Patrol. The letter, it seemed, had to tell who you were and where you lived and about your father and mother—the father who knew about Indians, then, had been no accidental choice, Alec realized—and your sisters and brothers if you had any, and your pets. And why you like Star Twinkles or Munchy Peanut Butter. Elizabeth wrinkled her high, round brow with the new blotches, and said she didn't like the peanut butter but if he could just say about the Star Twinkles for her . . . Alec woke suddenly to the realization that he was being asked to act as amanuensis.

He cleared his throat. "You have just as much right to apply as anyone else, but you must meet all the requirements." She was looking at him uncomprehendingly and he wished vaguely that Andy were here to translate. "I mean, you have to tell the truth. Do you really like—er—Star Twinkles?"

"Yes, Daddy."

He preserved judicial skepticism, with difficulty in the face of her big-eyed solemnity. "Why do you like it?" *It or them?* he wondered silently, sighing under the awesome responsibilities of parenthood—not only ethics but grammar, underfoot on the most surprising paths.

"Well, because."

" 'Because' is not a satisfactory answer, Elizabeth." *Isn't it?* A straggling root of esthetics appeared among the hazards of the path.

She had accepted the rebuke with good grace, and she thought deeply before she answered. Then the truth came to her, and her pale face lighted with the happiness of it. "Because you can get to be a Cosmic Patroller if you like it."

Alec, searching the sunny room for pencil and paper, meditated joyfully on the perfections of the circle and forgot everything except his delight in her until he came on the small blue tape recorder and remembered its mission. He had already been derelict, he knew at once—that dialogue should have been preserved. He carried the machine over to the bedside table and explained that this was better than writing because he couldn't write fast enough; she could just talk in here, he said, handing her the microphone with a heavy heart, and one of the ladies at his office would write the letter for her on a typewriter. He pushed the switch and watched her moments begin to wind.

"That's better, anyway, Daddy," she agreed cheerfully. "Then the Commander won't have to figure out your hen scratches."

Startled, he repeated the description inquiringly. "Where'd you pick that up?"

"From a lady in your office. She said it to the other lady, but she meant you, because she said '*his*' hen scratches."

Alec closed the subject firmly, adjuring her to get on with the letter to the Commander, who was now waving a silent and toothy good-bye from the television screen. Alec, sighing inwardly for the future of the human race, saw Elizabeth dutifully waving back as he turned off the set and urged her to begin. " 'Dear Commander,' " he suggested.

"Dear *Cosmic* Commander," Elizabeth corrected, directing her severity at the microphone in her hand. "I am sick in the hospital now, but I would like to be on the TV when I get better—" She broke off to ask Alec whether that was all right to say and he assured her in a voice that did not tremble that it was. But she ought to begin with her name. "Oh yes," she went on. "My name is Elizabeth Langwith Girard, but I can only write Elizabeth." She stopped again. "I can't write it right most of the time," she reported to her father. "So is it all right to say that?"

"Well, maybe not," her adviser on ethics replied. "We'll have to discuss that. Why don't you just leave it, and we can change it later if you want." Her future, he said to himself gaily, clearly does not lie with Madison Avenue —and then all his gaiety disappeared and so did his voice. It was a good thing Elizabeth had returned to her work, because he was numbed and flattened by the great, dumb weight of that "her future."

". . . in the White House in WashingtonDeecee. My father is President oftheUnitedStates and my mother is—just a lady. I have a brother Sandy that's not a year old yet so he didn't have any birthdays, but he has some teeth and he can stand up holding on. I have a whole lot of pets . . ."

The stricken man in the chair stopped listening and practiced breathing, aware of only a small faint glimmering of thanks that the woman who was "just a lady" had not heard this talk of birthdays. Although, it came to him then, she must hear a good many other things that left this socked-in-the-solar-plexus feeling: a vision of the torture for Andy that lurked in this sunny, pretty room, day after day, tightened the bands that were already clamped around his chest. He stared at the clean, institutional gray wall; it was decorated with get-well cards featuring laughing animals and all purchased by Andy so Elizabeth, who mustn't be known to require get-well cards, could nevertheless keep up with her colleagues. Like the cards, the official hospital nameplate was stuck under the metal strip that ran across the wall at shoulder level. "Girard, Elizabeth L." was legible in the faint purple ink and so was, just barely, "Washington, D.C.," but the rest was rows of letters and numbers diminishing in size like an eye doctor's testing chart. On the other side of it was a color photograph that was indistinct from where Alec was sitting; he narrowed his eyes at it and then recognized the spaceman and Pilgrims Paul had made for a table decoration when they'd all been at the Langwiths' for Thanksgiving dinner. *For dinner,* Alec insisted sternly, banishing the dangerous word "Thanksgiving"—but he didn't remember the accompanying incident soon enough to banish it and it came back, the conversation with Paul in Andrew Langwith's library about loneliness and the unfamilied. Andy had come in then and assured Paul firmly that he was not unfamilied. Alec Girard closed his eyes against the memory of it and the new, certain knowledge that he was unfamilied—he had, at this moment, no one at all, not even Andy. Between them lay this awful knowledge, this terrible need to walk warily around any mention of the future, of Thanksgiving dinners and July Fourths and everything else that came only once a year and therefore fatally measured time. You could not possibly talk to anyone whom you must spare so much.

"I don't feel like finishing now, Daddy," said Elizabeth.

Alec looked quickly, guiltily at the very pale little face, and wondered what she'd been saying. He went to the bed and took the machine away from her. Her hand seemed to him very hot, and she was noticeably tired.

"I wish Mommy would come back," she said fretfully, turning her helmeted head on the pillow. "I wish getting made all well didn't make you *feel* so bad all the time."

Alec stared down at her, holding himself very still, like a man carrying a vessel too full of liquid. "I wish so, too, Elizabeth." It struck him then how furious she must be, somewhere below where she could recognize it, with the parents who were supposed to take care of her and instead let strangers hurt her. "Nobody would blame you for being very angry about it," he said quietly.

Her eyes opened wide. "Not even Dr. Snowden?"

"Not even Dr. Snowden," Alec told her, almost angry himself at this insight into her fear of offending the doctors and nurses who mattered most because they could make her well. "He doesn't like hurting little girls any more than I do."

"But he can't help it?" Elizabeth said, not really asking. "You can't help anything." Her voice held a faint, despairing scorn. She sighed, then. "Well anyway, Dr. Snowden can make me all well."

And you can't hung on the air in the quiet room. Alec Girard, who had never in all his life been hurt so badly, stood still and took the bitter blow of his own powerlessness—and managed the grace to keep from troubling her with his useless regrets.

Fifty

Andrea Girard lay on the hard concrete near the pool instead of on the lush grass only a little farther away, and she knew why she was doing it. First, it was because she couldn't get warm enough, and the baked stone, deliberately roughened to guard the Ruffing boys against accidental slips, held all the violent heat of the summer day. And then, it was hard and rough and more fitting for a warrior than the cool green of the grass. Her very bones ached with the exhaustion of combat; but it was not yet time for rest.

She turned on her side, feeling the hot ridges dig into her naked thigh and the flesh not much protected by the thin fabric of the scanty bathing suit, and watched her son examine some brightly painted wooden discs that stacked on a blunt pole. The discs, graduated in size, had holes through their middles so that, properly stacked on a central pole, they formed a cone. In his only attempt to replace the discs after he had once tumbled them off the stick, Sandy had managed to coordinate hole and pole only one time out of innumerable tries, and besides, since then he had been trying to put a bigger one on top of a smaller. It was safe to conclude, Andy thought, that order wasn't in him yet. But neither was dismay, at the moment—he sat solidly and happily, naked except for a diaper and waterproof pants, in the middle of his playpen in the dappled shade and talked to himself lovingly and at length about the round yellow wood he was intermittently tasting.

He was what made it hard, his mother admitted dully. The feeling of ending had been with her, no matter how she had tried to deny it, ever since Elizabeth had gone to the hospital—maybe even before, when she'd never seemed to get well. It was still unbelievable in its entirety, but Andy had tested herself, alone in the long nights, and found she could believe it enough for working premises: first, that Elizabeth was not going to grow up. And now, since last night anyway, that there might be very little time. Alec had been there today when one of the pretty nurses brought Elizabeth the two pills in a little paper cup, but he'd been distracted by the child's pleasure in the swallow of "Coke" that came along with the unidentified medicine; Andy knew, though, that the medicine was an antibiotic. The disease that was itself a killer left its victims terribly vulnerable to infection: while the small body was being slowly beaten by the merciless giant, something else had invaded— Dr. Snowden's snapping black eyes had seen the danger, and reserve troops had been called in for the new skirmish. But they all knew, and soon the slowly knowing eyes of Andrea had learned, that the fight for a remission of leukemia had now become secondary to an immediate fight for Elizabeth's life. New measures were taken, and the threatening elevation of her temperature had leveled off: but even if this infection was conquered, others could attack before Snowden's legions had succeeded in arming Elizabeth to defend herself. A helpless correspondent at the battle scene, Andrea had almost ceased to cry.

But it was more bearable there where it was going on than here: it was the beginning in the midst of ending that undid her, she knew. She tried with all her soul to accept the sturdy infant son who was now describing to an unseen assistant all the qualities of the blue disc; the reportorial tone of his voice was unmistakable, as were its businesslike cadences—words might be a long time away, but speech was within the grasp of his fat, busy fists. And walking was, too. He had come, almost ignored, largely unnoticed, over all the centuries from crawling to standing; now, when the spirit moved him, he could shuffle around his little jail, holding on and inching sidewise, with his dimpled toes dug into the bright plastic pad. Not for long, and not with any reliability—after a little of it, he plopped down and resumed his investigations and discourses, resting up for another try. But he was beginning—he was *all* beginning. And sometimes it almost couldn't be borne.

Andy turned onto her stomach and propped her chin on her hands to stare out at the untroubled blue waters of the imitation lake, chlorined and confined, and blinked against the tears that she knew were self-pity rather than grief, at this moment. She looked at her thin hands through her lashes, which had rainbows on them, and added loneliness to her diagnosis. She was more lonely than she had ever been in her life, she thought at first, and then revised it—no, only since before she'd met Alec. Once, when she had first come to Miss Kingman's School, she had been bitterly lonely; she closed her eyes and remembered how she and Marian had talked about it, in the little house on O Street. They had both known the feeling—both had been outsiders, at least for a while, walking among the chittering girls who all seemed to have known each other for a thousand years and to have a million marvelous secrets. "You only find out later," Marian had said, "that while you're wandering around worrying about whether your heart will break—"

"And if it will show when it does."

"Well, that probably bothered you more than me—I never gave a damn who was looking. But, you know, all the time, they think you're being haughty? I only found out years later: there was this girl I would have died for a kind word from, if you know what I mean. And all the time she thought I was coming it over her because she was of the threadbare nobility and I was Little Miss Moneybags."

Andy had known exactly what she meant. They had smiled at each other, and drunk tea—survivors of loneliness, secure now, promising each other gaily that their daughters would never be sent to a school for young ladies. Where there were boys around, Marian had summarized, there was a common problem—everybody was in the same worried frenzy about whether any boy would really find them attractive, so nobody could be quite so lonely. As mothers of daughters, they would keep that in mind—

Flinching away from the rest of the memory, Andy nevertheless thought wistfully that Marian could keep her from being alone with this. But she knew she had been right to reject the idea. For Marian would make the sign of the evil eye and run away, probably—just as Nedra Rosenberg would want to do, just as Bonnie Ruffing's eyes, almost wincing away from the sight of Andy, had in mind to do even while they also spoke of pity and kindness. And Carol, her college roommate, was disqualified because she was childless. Andrea put her head down on her warm hands, forgiving them all: no mother could bear to share this, and no one who was not a mother would know how.

She even forgave Alec, who was disqualified on all sorts of grounds—not only, for once, just his job. Andy had seen the other women whose children were with Elizabeth: they were stiff with their husbands, denying, as though some mutual anger stood between them. If she was angry with Alec, she couldn't find or recognize the feeling; but she could recognize that he doubled the pain, and so she cringed from meeting him, tried to tell herself that he didn't realize quite what was happening. Because if Alec knew what she knew, and said so, there would be nothing but pain, moon landscapes of it, stretching as far as the inner eye could see, vistas of desolation from which nothing could possibly be saved and in which nothing could ever grow again. She raised her head and clasped her hands tightly as if she could hold back with them the dread made more terrible by being shared with her husband.

For the first time, it was necessary to be as separate from him as she could manage: it was her only hope of protecting him. And it was her only loneliness since the day she had first understood that she wanted to be married to Alec Girard, even when she still believed it might not be a good idea.

That baby lost before it had ever been more than a medical fantasy, a dot of cells, had parted her from Alec briefly, perhaps, but only until Alec had come and seen and reached for her to bring her back to them. This was not enough death to part them, his eyes and hands had announced to her as he stood in her hospital room with the frightened face he didn't know she could read, and he would not abide the separation. He wasn't alone in his haste to be together again then, Andy observed, turning her head to look at the preoccupied baby—it was the impulsive Mrs. Girard more than her more thoughtful husband who had wanted to begin this new baby right away.

This new baby, thoughtless of his origins, crawled solemnly over to the opposite corner of the playpen and fetched the red disc, taking care to drool on it thoroughly before transporting it. Andy looked at his round, padded rear, confidently aloft as he maneuvered the disc, and forgot pain for a tiny fraction of a second. She turned her head to see the sunlight prancing on the blue water and her heart filled with love and longing for the beautiful lake at home, where her husband lay back on the waters, long and confident, and took his leisure under the far sight of the sky. Borne up, laughing, he floated through her memory for a moment—and then she put her head down and began to weep.

For Elizabeth had appeared in the scene—just such a round, sun-browned baby then as this one was, but not familiar to her father, not as understood. Andrea stood in the waist-deep water, dipping the baby and cooing at her, and Alec floated idly, wearing the look of respectful distance he seemed to don whenever he saw her with the baby—as though she were some kind of statue of Madonna and Child, to cherish but not to touch. She wasn't being quite fair—he'd handled the baby, bringing her from her playpen into the cottage, perhaps, and sometimes he even played with her, preferably through the bars, offering her toys gravely or tickling her plump, ankleless leg gently with a blade of grass. But Elizabeth was still a curiosity to him, Andy was thinking that day as the baby slapped at the water and then laughed at the spray she had made—she was something he experimented with, rather gingerly.

Andy decided in a brilliant, inspired instant, that she had had quite enough of that. With no warning but a broad, exceptionally sweet smile, she lifted the little body, laid it squarely on the Senator's flat belly, and moved out of reach.

She could still almost laugh at will, simply by remembering the totally appalled, really pitiable look of near terror he had sent her before he had to turn all his attention to Elizabeth, who crawled uncertainly up his front, helping her progress by seizing fistfuls of the hair on his chest. He grabbed for the baby, lest she roll off into the water—and then, once she was safe, he noticed that she was laughing, and he laughed too, but with some bewilderment, looking closely into the small, open face so near his.

He could have stood up in that water easily; he could have got to his feet and handed the baby back to Andy, maybe acknowledging a joke but putting a graceful enough end to it, right there. But he didn't—he went on floating in the gentle waters, big and safe between his child and their hidden dangers, while she drooled on his chest and climbed earnestly up to his neck. He floated all the way in that way, holding her with one hand while he propelled them slowly through the water with lazy flaps of the other, and then he lay for a long time on the beach with her, smiling and unafraid—and his wife sat apart and watched them at their discoveries until Elizabeth had eaten really too much sand. She thought she would like to have a picture of Alec Girard becoming a father, but she was pretty sure she wouldn't need one.

Andrea wiped her eyes on the backs of her sunwarmed hands and sat up, bearing her great load upright with her. It was time to put pictures away now, she knew. She felt her hair to make sure it was mostly dry, because it would be a little hard on Elizabeth to know that her mother had been swimming when she couldn't go. Andy scrambled to her feet, lifted the baby out of the playpen, and carried him toward the Ruffings' house, so she could have another few minutes with him while she dressed. He hung on her shoulder, too busy investigating the thickets of her hair to mind the bumpiness of the ride as she almost ran over the uneven ground.

The woman who would have made the sign of the evil eye and run away sat on the edge of the sofa in Ann Taswell's once-neat apartment, in a living room now littered with Marian Farland's shoes in the middle of the rug just inside the door, her newspaper and purse dumped on a chair, her bag of groceries sagging dangerously on the coffee table. The perpetrator of all this subversion of order sat there and sniffled, holding in one grimy hand a picture postcard showing in exaggerated colors a huge redwood tree with a tunnel through it from which a very old-model automobile was emerging. On the back, a dashing though slightly unreliable handwriting that attempted to lean backward but occasionally forgot and that dotted i's with little circles, announced to "Dear Mom and Dad" that its owner was having a "marvy" time. "Daddy's friend is working in a picture and I've been on the set," it went on, with the last three words underlined twice, "every single day—met stars and all—weather is groovy—so are boys." This jagged construction was sealed with three exclamation points like those in display type, with the upper ellipses hollow and the periods empty circles. "Wrote Dick but no answer—sent Smokey the Bear doll to Peter but maybe he won't like!?! Too young for him Mom??? Love forever—Sharlie." Straggling up the side of the small message space in unbelievably tiny letters was the obviously adult-inspired addition, "Daddy sends regards."

Marian laid this confectionery report down on the coffee table and carried the grocery bag out to the neat kitchen, where she put the frozen food into the freezer compartment and the cream into the refrigerator and then left everything else still in the bag so she could come back and fish in her purse for a Kleenex to wipe her eyes with. It wasn't clear to her whether she was weeping with gratitude that somehow Sharlie still believed her world safe and unchanged or with dismay that time was running out and it had not yet changed enough. She blew her nose and was telling herself that she wished she could make some sense, just once in a while, when the phone rang.

The Will who spoke was, at first, only the other half of the "Dear Mom and Dad" of the postcard that was so miraculously like last year's and the year before's. The Marian who said she'd just got it, thanks, and wasn't it—amazing, spoke with warmth and laughed willingly at her husband's comment that he thought it was pretty marvy, too. Perhaps he was encouraged, or perhaps he was too concerned to calculate—or maybe he simply didn't have any more time, because he was calling from Ambassador Blackwell's apartment in New York and people were waiting—for whatever reason, he cleared his throat too soon and said without enough preliminary in a too abruptly businesslike voice, "Listen, Marian, I read in Gil's column this morning that Ann was in Alabama and it was quite a shock."

"Oh, she's all right," said Marian, assuming that Will, who had a wide acquaintance among the press, had picked up the rumor about Ann. It didn't occur to her that Will had been having good reason to dodge the press of late.

"Dammit, I know she's all right," said the man who had spent most of the day holding his tongue while slower people arrived at conclusions he had encompassed long before. "I'm talking about you."

Marian brushed at her dank hair with a hand sticky from summer and traffic. She looked around the dim bedroom littered with clothes she hadn't had time to put away if she was going to make the bed before work—and then she hadn't had time to make the bed either—and it felt so good to be worried about that she almost sank down in it like a feather bed on a cold morning. "I'm all right, really," she said gratefully.

The trouble (as a more methodical Will decided later, when he was analyzing the damages) was that he had been marshaling arguments instead of listening to her voice, so he missed the gentleness of it and consequently the vulnerability to return gentleness. Instead he came on, he told himself bitterly later, like a young lawyer lousing up his virgin appearance before the Supreme Court. Brash, overbriefed, frozen by nervousness into a preset line of argument that should have been altered to respond to the unexpected, he told his wife brusquely that he had agreed to her "somewhat flamboyant" announcement that she could think only under someone else's roof, and to such subsequent shenanigans as hanging up on him when he called to talk sense to her, only on the understanding that she would be in Ann's care. He felt, he said stiffly, that it had been at least discourteous of Ann not to tell him she was going away; but now that he'd discovered the fact, he had no intention of permitting Marian to remain there, alone and unsupervised, and he demanded that she return to their home at once.

Marian said "Un*supervised!*" in a voice that drowned out an Apache raid going on on the television set in the next apartment. Then she went on to instruct Will, loudly and without pause, that one way he could tell the difference between her and the dogs—which he didn't seem able to manage—was that they were the ones who were parked in kennels. What he thought of as Ann's discourtesy was simply Ann's ability to make the distinction that escaped him and that therefore enabled her to regard Marian as something other than an article of stored furniture or an automobile left for repairs.

Will kept trying to say something in what might have been a conciliatory tone had enough of it been allowed to be heard, but Marian was too addicted to her rant to allow it to stop or even to slow down. Behind it, she was aware of two feelings: a combined surprise at Will's uncharacteristic ineptitude and worry about whether it might be a manifestation of illness or exhaustion, and a longing to be collected, precisely like an article of stored furniture. It was the presence of this latter that recharged her harangue on her independent status wherever it threatened to run down—plus, she thought after she had decided she'd covered the matter thoroughly and hung up without giving him a chance to speak, the simple fact that he'd called perhaps ten minutes too soon (before she'd had a chance to turn on the air conditioning) or maybe half an hour too soon (before she'd had a chance to have a nice bath). Full of injury and adrenalin, she turned on the air conditioning and the bath and danced around the living room, naked and energetic and free, while the tub was filling. By the time the bath was ready, she was in such high spirits that she picked up the clothes she'd abandoned, some in each room of the small apartment, and disposed of them with elaborate neatness. In the tub, she essayed the "Queen of the Night" aria without success but without caring much about her failure, and disdained to scramble out to answer the ringing telephone. If it was Ann, she'd call again—and if it was Will, the sooner he got tired of bothering her, the better. Let him conclude that she was out doing the town with some man who was madly in love with her, she decided, making a merry face at the merry face in the medicine-chest mirror as she blotted up just enough water from her body to keep from soaking the floor; another man was the only fate Will ever seemed able to imagine for her, and it was tiresome of him. Doubtless he caused himself suffering with his idiotic jealousy, but perhaps suffering was the unavoidable price of a limited imagination, she said to herself sagely, strutting out of the now-littered bathroom with a jaunty fling of a round hip that was a great deal closer to invitation than the telling-off she had intended it to be.

She was barefoot still, but decently dressed in shorts and shirt, her hair brushed and braided, and she was—on an obscure, belated impulse—making the bed when the phone rang again. She looked at it and then, as it insisted, she went on looking at it without—for the first time in as long as she could remember—doing anything whatever about it. She simply stood there, her hands at her sides and her eyes full of awe at her own daring, and waited for whatever the terrible consequences must be. After a very long while, the ringing stopped. In the utter, deadly silence, Marian backed away from the phone until she was beyond what must be its striking range. And then she turned and ran, flushed with triumph, to the kitchen to celebrate with a victory drink. She had certainly showed Will, and she proceeded to drink to it unstintingly.

As a matter of fact, it wasn't Will she showed—not until sometime later, when, full of alcoholic courage, she heard the phone again from the kitchen and only stuck her tongue out at the distant sound. It was Ann who had called the first time: Ann, who doubtless knew already what Marian was so busily finding out—that independence was heady stuff.

Marian toasted it again now, downing a big swallow in the name of Independence Day and another, for impartiality, to Bastille Day. Then she defined her terms better and did it over, making it a double each for "Willy and Nilly." "Cope by yourself, baby, and if I don't happen to have my hands full of stone when you're ready"—well, that wasn't exactly what he'd said, old Nilly, but that was the gist, all right. Except, not "baby"—that was some other fellow entirely. This one demanded that you come not only in utter nakedness but trailing clouds of maturity . . . She tossed her braid back defiantly but poured bourbon to replace the missing ounces in her glass, because all the rest of the requirements for his course were so stiff, surely no half-empty glasses would be permitted. And it was too dangerous to try to get any soda, especially with that dark, angry face looking at her from the faintly gleaming wall of the refrigerator. "Well, you're the one who wanted me to be so grown up," she said, and boldly toasted Monsieur On-My-Terms: "To adultery." She smiled, giving him the full treatment, and threw in a little wit besides, adding, "His, and hers." But Paul only said again that he would not have less than the best she was. And after that he wouldn't say *anything* no matter how she looked at him . . . You make the adult-ery course too stiff, Marian told him with the fury of a woman scorned, and Madame will not permit. How do you like *that*, Monsieur Great Stone Face? Ho ho *ho*.

She evened off her glass with whiskey again but this time it was because *she* liked things tidy, and if he wouldn't come for her, she could do what she liked. She said so noisily. But Paul only went on looking not amused. So where the hell *are* you, she asked the silence—and then it came to her that he had shut his mouth and thrown away the key, as in nursery school, and she knew why. Giggling, she tidied her glass again and carried it out of the sight of Old Loving-Honor-More, that he said was for Englishmen but *I do not always speak the truth* . . .

" 'But—in spite of all temp-ta-tions, To belong to o-ther nations—' " she sang it in the hall, where Paul couldn't see her. Then she stopped and, tilted slightly against the bookcase, remarked sadly that Frenchman-Turk-or-Prooshian Paul belonged to a nation of men she'd heard about but never met personally: "They lay you and leave you," she announced, her lips trembling. But she recovered: valor was important, no matter what. " 'You remain an En-glishman,' " she sang then, loudly, triumphantly. And even compassionately—because the truth was, they were all Englishmen.

She forgot her glass on the bookcase and padded back to the bedroom, discussing the matter learnedly: what happened was, as soon as you let them be lovers, they started wanting to be husbands. Even dear-sweet-Charles, who had said any time she needed anything, was in California being a father. Husbands and fathers, the whole damned international shebang: it just wasn't possible to find a fellow foreign enough, so the hell with them. She picked up the telephone and inverted it; tilting it into the light from the lamp, she found the little bar that controlled the volume of the ring and pushed it all the way to "Soft." She thumped the phone back into its place and it sat there, rendered harmless—solid evidence that Marian didn't need anybody, see?

Once, she had wondered whether it was because Ann didn't need anyone that nobody ever married her. Now, on the verge of testing the thesis, Marian remembered the remark—and then began to laugh, because if you looked at the matter abstractly and unemotionally, Ann had been having a more active sex life lately than Marian, recently accused of whoring. She took her clothes off and turned down the freshly made bed. But instead of putting her nightgown on she just stood there and asked politely, "Anybody for laying Marian?"

Paul took his hands away from the stone and said quietly that he would put an end to her career—and, suddenly meek, she climbed quickly into the bed and pulled up the sheet demurely, and then lay there smiling because it was a hell of a way to find out whom you were married to. But it was also valid as hell: what counted, probably for some unworthy reason, was who got angry at the whole idea—as opposed to just maneuvering to cut the other customers out. *I didn't mean it,* she had said quickly, to mollify the eyebrow quirked caret-like in the dark wrathful face of the man who made the rules and could make them stick.

She snapped off the light, marking the end of Independence Day, and lay there looking at Paul who knew—how?—that lust alone would not support life, and who therefore held out for clear title to Marian. As amended.

"C'est moi," she said clearly into the dark.

And then the drunkenness caught her again; the world swooped and she rode it dangerously but determinedly, as if it were one of Paul's too-stiff requirements for the course. I won't insist on getting laid if it's against your religion, darling, her own voice said with incredible casualness in her fog-whirled head; but would the Empire really totter if you made a teeny little pass at me, old cock? *Scaredy cat,* she taunted the remembered face of the not-quite-Saint Anthony, tortured on the rack of her body—I made you forget your Boy Scout honor once, and I can do it again. She curled up into a small defensive ball (because you never knew for sure how much teasing

Paul would allow) and the swooping stopped; in the new undizziness, she knew she wouldn't do it again. And besides, she was reminding herself conscientiously as she fell asleep, she had needed the help of the Boston Pops to bring it off, even that once.

Fifty-one

The week that was, for Washington and points north and west, full of peregrinations, encounters, and discoveries, was for Rosa Little, inmate of the Dorothy County, Alabama, jail, too confined for peregrination, limited in its encounters, and troubled by discoveries that came with nausea and departed leaving scars.

In the dank contiguity of the large cell that was apparently intended as a drunk tank, the white New York schoolteacher ceased to be that generic label and became Edith Crane. In turn, the teacher adapted herself to the mores of her Negro cellmates, who had had a bellyful of being called by their Christian names—a mark of good-fellowship where she came from— and learned that, among them, the greater the friendship the more respectful the mode of address. By Friday, she was used to being "Miz Crane" and could say "Miz Little" with no embarrassment of the tongue.

Edith Crane had been a childless widow for more than a dozen years and had been, even before that, intelligent, knowledgeable, and self-supporting in a milieu that was too rushed for chivalry. She had begun work as a gym teacher, gone to graduate school in the summers (and finally, one semester full-time, by living narrowly on her savings and her widow's pension), and qualified as a teacher of political science. But the New York City public school system offered only a job—and a very empty apartment at the end of the day; so, after giving the matter cool consideration, she went to work in a good private school, where she was able to enjoy the comings and goings, the buzzings and quarrelings, that substituted for the constant human contact the luckier found in families.

As co-administrators of the small sad world of their confinement, Miz Crane and Miz Little offered, between them, all that could really be wanted; to Edith Crane's experience with the world and lack of fear of officialdom was added Rosa Little's more engaging personality, a swift intuition that detected the troubled and found without thought the needed word or gesture, and an array of practical skills enhanced by experience at improvisation in imperfect physical circumstances. The women were equal and complementary, in skill and will; the eight young girls jailed with them couldn't have been in better hands, and many of them probably never had been.

Interestingly, though they began from dramatically different frames of reference, Miz Crane and Miz Little arrived simultaneously at the knowledge that their greatest asset for dealing with the situation in which they found themselves was the jailer's wife who brought them food. This burdened, blowsy woman had a grievance: after so many years of being paid for doing very little that she had begun to think idleness was her right, she was unforgivably saddled with a crushing load of chores for all these sudden prisoners. The county law enforcement authorities, themselves prisoners of their own limited background and imagination, had "punished" Edith Crane and the other white marchers by putting them in with the Negroes; when the white prisoners seemed unaware that they were being punished in this way, it became incumbent on their jailers to make the point for them by declaring them, directly and indirectly, *déclassée*. It struck Edith Crane and Rosa Little simultaneously that, in order to snub Edith effectively, their jailer's wife would be forced to converse with Rosa—there was no other way to provide the contrast necessary to demonstrate to the white prisoner her fellow-Caucasian's scorn for her. In addition, a woman with a grievance had to have a place to lay her grumbles, a place Rosa naturally tended to occupy anyway. Thus Rosa became both the personal and social answer for the representative of white power with whom she came into daily contact.

In turn, the woman, with her whining voice and her too-white, heavy legs mottled with prominent veins, became first of all a prime source of news for the Crane-Little administration. So, when Jerry Rosenberg telephoned to the White House toward the end of the week that the promised state police were beginning to arrive, but in amazingly small numbers and with a suspiciously skimpy supply setup for a troop that planned to stay for any length of time, Miz Crane and Miz Little had the report before the President did. For Girard was in his daughter's hospital room when Rosenberg talked to Jake Ruffing, who decided to hold the information until his chief's return; but the news had been handed to the prisoners, along with their gluey stew, via Rosa within half an hour after Rosenberg left the sheriff's office. Earlier, the announcement that federal court judge Hadley Thurston had granted the injunction barring prosecution of the Negro history professor made almost as good time in reaching the confined women.

Their news source was neither omniscient nor remarkably articulate, though, so Edith Crane, at least, was aware of some gaps in their information. Still, they knew that most of the men jailed with them had been taken to the county's work farm. This was dangerous—but the men's names, like their own, had been picked up and duly reported by the newsgatherers, so there was insurance against their simply "disappearing." That their own lawyer had somehow been unable to see the women was explained by the jailer, with a sneer, as a result of the arrests of several other groups "all over the state." Since this had been the plan, the women were undismayed, and the absence of legal advice failed to alarm them because it was a detail they'd been warned about.

But orientation was a small matter, dispensed with early in their incarceration—although not so early that Miz Crane had not already set up certain daily routines, like those that might be established by shipwreck survivors on a desert island, and Miz Little begun to repair damages, physical and mental, among the battered crew. Particularly one, Violet, who may have been not too bright to begin with, probably had always been emotionally immature, and was severely frightened by the circumstances of her arrest. When she finally comprehended that she was really in jail and couldn't get out, she went to pieces. Rosa rocked the girl to sleep for the first two nights, holding her in her arms and singing lullabies as soft and precious as old lace, and continued to issue a judicious amount of coddling and babying thereafter.

A Negro girl with the gift of natural cheerfulness and a talent for mimicry was promptly appointed head of the entertainment committee; Mary Jane had little talent for administration and so was forced to provide most of the entertainment herself, which worked out well for all concerned. The white student Priscilla, who had too much energy and not enough experience with resignation, was a potentially explosive element, the two sage heads concluded: she was therefore loaded with chores that kept her in sight and occupied. Among these was a highly successful seminar in makeup and hair styling—the colors of makeup base and powder supplied by the precious makeup case that was her security blanket were inappropriate for those with the darkest complexions, but the theory of their use could nevertheless be taught and laboratory work could still be done with lipstick and eye makeup. Spirits were lifted by the wonders achieved, and even Rosa, serving as passive makeup-ee for the first session, was dazzled at the glamour of herself with indigo eyeshadow.

Priscilla's other chief assignment was as reporter, stationed at the single barred window high up in the wall to chronicle the activities of the natives in the public square and beyond; she gave the repeaters appropriate nicknames and summarized their, and others', activities with a dry wit and a narrative skill that was a credit, Miz Crane announced with professional generosity, to the Massachusetts schools. Priscilla's description of the "foreign" press in Coventry was so particularly vivid and telling that a special dispensation was granted so each of the girls could have a turn to climb up and watch the lepers walking from the café to the hotel with the streets clearing before them as though they had indeed rung pathetic bells.

Rosa, standing on a bunk so she could see out, was on duty at the window while Miz Crane conducted the morning calisthenics; it was then that she saw Ann Taswell arrive, tall, cool, and uncharacteristically wearing a small beanie-shaped black hat. (This, and its successor, a starched white lace Dutch cap, represented an unsolved puzzle to Rosa, whose intelligence service did not extend outward and backward from Alabama and the present; therefore, it left her ignorant of the small shaven patch around a nearly healed wound on the back of Ann's head.) Rosa had turned away from the window to report her discovery by the time Gil followed Ann into the hotel, so she remained unaware of his arrival and never associated him with the "Mickey Finn" of Priscilla's accounts. Nor did the jailer's wife (who had no known name but did have a notably discontented face and was therefore dubbed "Sunshine") mention the name of the "foreigner" who had printed all the lies about Dorothy and was worse than all the rest of them put together. On his head, Sunshine confided darkly to Rosa, would lie the blood of others; but she either did not know his name or scorned to let it pass her lips.

The attitudes of Sunshine and the other natives who were occasionally in contact with the organized Amazon society of the drunk tank were absolutely unpredictable and apparently patternless, providing thereby a spark of interest but also a sense of dread—until the politically minded Miz Crane succeeded in drawing some correlations between the arrivals of such outsiders as the press and the state police and the attentions of the local constabulary. "The whole thing's shifting our way, Miz Little," she told Rosa earnestly at their evening conference, after the girls had been bedded down. "They're beginning to try to protect themselves. To realize they may eventually be held legally accountable for their behavior. They're not used to that."

Rosa nodded. Without understanding all the intricacies, she had grasped the idea that the more mistreatment she encountered, the better it was for a future legal test; she had been prepared to be unjustly treated. But Edith Crane regarded her with concern, for the latest threat to the order the two women had salvaged was having a noticeable effect on Rosa.

Not that the white woman had been unmoved, either, when the ugly business began. Fortunately for the group's morale, the first victim was a Negro girl of even temperament—a quiet girl, but sturdy. Ordered by the jailer to come along, she went with neither alarm nor defiance. When she came back, she climbed onto one of the slab beds slung high against the wall and lay there with her eyes closed, but she didn't cry or make any fuss. The two leaders exchanged glances and, a little later, while Rosa was using the needle and thread from the teacher's little purse-sized sewing kit to demonstrate how a sleeve should be set into a dress, Edith Crane climbed up and talked to the girl at length in a low voice. When she came down, she indicated quietly to Rosa that it would be a good idea to keep the girls too busy for exchanging confidences. The activities from late afternoon until lights out accordingly were continuous and absorbing, and it wasn't until the supervisory conference, held in whispers in a corner of the musty stone-walled cell, that Rosa found out what had upset the girl.

"I don't know which is the best way to handle it," Edith Crane confessed. "If we warn the girls, we're going to send them off scared—they'll be a bundle of nerves before they ever set foot in the place, and so everything will be even harder for them. And maybe it won't even happen again. But if we don't warn them, I'm afraid they'll feel we let them down."

"We got no choice but to say somethin," Rosa said. "The way they feel ashamed—that the worst of it, ain't it? Well, if we act like they got somethin to be ashamed about, then we makin it that much worse." She sighed, looking down at her hands. "It ain't so much what happen to you, Miz Crane, that do the damage—it more important how you feelin while it happenin."

Touched by the painful learning she saw behind this statement, Edith Crane reached out and patted the hands that looked older than their owner. "All right, I'll talk to them in the morning—I know you'd rather I begin, anyway." She watched Rosa nod and then added slowly, "I'm sorry, but I think it would be better if you were the one to make the protest, though. You may have noticed that you're in better standing with officialdom than I am." Her thin lips stretched in an unamused smile.

"You mean, we go'n talk to the *sheriff* about it?"

"We're certainly going to try. In the meantime, we'll talk to anyone we can. Beginning with Sunshine, or her husband—whichever one turns up with breakfast." Her wise eyes understood, and deplored, the other woman's difficulty. "Miz Little, it's a useful thing to know how to take adversity without letting it swamp you, but we don't let people push us around without a protest, in any case."

Rosa said, like someone trying out a new language, that she guessed they didn't, and went to bed wondering whether Miz Crane was learned or ignorant, or both. In the morning, she listened closely as the teacher addressed the girls, admiring the woman's fluency and understanding that the dry, flat tone and the use of the big words were exactly right to discourage useless panic.

"It seems that the people in charge here have thought up another way to try to make us unhappy, or at least they did yesterday, and I mention it because it's possible that it may go on. I refer to the medical examinations, which apparently include the taking of vaginal smears—a procedure some of you may not be familiar with."

Priscilla was familiar with it, Rosa saw: the girl turned her fair head to one side and studied the floor near her feet, struggling against embarrassment the cool voice was declaring ignoble. Violet looked, as she usually did, uncomprehending; only one of the Negro girls besides yesterday's victim appeared to have made the acquaintance of either the word "vaginal" or the medical technique the teacher was explaining.

"In the best circumstances," Miz Crane went on, "this can be a little embarrassing to the sensitive, since it requires the woman to lie on her back with knees up and legs apart, exposing the genital area. However, it is a normal and necessary part of routine preventive medicine, useful in detecting cancer, for instance, and is ordinarily brief and painless."

Violet, still uncomprehending but now vaguely threatened, came to sit by Rosa, who patted her as one would a small animal, and gently indicated that attention to the speaker was required.

"Now it seems that some of the people in charge here, who may or may not include a real doctor, have been using this procedure for improper purposes." Miz Crane looked around at the sound of the gasp and raised her voice a little. "I want everyone to understand that rape doesn't seem to be involved." She paused to let them absorb this. "In fact, from what we've heard, the only damage is that there has been, at times, an . . . audience . . . looking on, which is understandably distressing for the girl being examined. And it also seems that the person conducting the examination is perhaps a little rougher than he needs to be."

"Miz Little." Priscilla turned a terribly pale face to Rosa. "I don't think I could bear—"

It was Edith Crane who told her, immediately and dryly, that she probably wouldn't have to bear anything; the medical thoroughness was likely to be restricted to the Negro girls. Rosa watched the angry color flood Priscilla's cheeks and discovered for the first time that exclusion from pain could be as painful as enduring it, and that maybe being an innocent nonvictim was tougher than being an innocent victim.

Miz Crane had let them exchange horrified cries for a while, depending on Rosa to keep Violet from setting off a real panic. "Now I want you to listen closely while I tell you what to do. Miz Little and I are, of course, going to protest to the authorities about this, but we can't stop it right away. *If* you are called, and *if* you are the victim of the illegal procedure I've described—and remember, it is not wrong if it is done by a doctor with a nurse in attendance and nobody interested in any aspect of the affair but the scientific—but if you find yourself being spied on during this business by people who obviously have no standing, I want you to make one, single, quiet protest to the person who seems to be in charge. Speak clearly and politely, but firmly, just to make it known that you know they are taking advantage of you. And then do not speak at all—and whatever you do, don't cry or scream or show alarm; in fact, try not to show anything at all but disgust. The best idea is to get the whole thing over as quickly as possible, and to remove whatever pleasure these benighted people get from the performance." She swept the taut faces with a commanding eye. "I repeat, don't make it interesting for them by showing fear. They are not normal men and, for reasons I don't think I'll bother to go into right now, any sign that you are suffering or ashamed excites them and gives them pleasure. We want to take the kicks out of it for them, and the best way to do that is with a quiet disdain—" She broke off as the chairman of the entertainment committee jumped to her feet.

"Like this," Mary Jane said quickly. She sucked in her cheeks and lifted her eyebrows and looked down her nose at her friend. "Like 'I a princess and you just heathen scum.'"

Miz Crane joined the laughter, but her eyes measured it and found it too high-pitched, too extensive for the size of the joke; she looked over and saw that Miz Little had simultaneously recognized the content of hysteria. "Yes, something like that is the idea—only just think it, don't say it. Don't say anything at all except what I told you, and say that right at the beginning. Now, are there any questions? Yes?"

"Miz Crane, what about if you have the curse?"

"Then tell the doctor as soon as you enter the room, and they'll probably send you back. But don't say it if it isn't true, because they may check up. Any more questions? Well then, I have one: is there any girl here who has any reason to think she may be pregnant? Before you answer me, I want you to think carefully. This is not a moral question, but a serious scientific one: don't let shame for your behavior lead you to endanger a baby." She looked around at them, but saw no signs of guilt or doubt. "Good. If there is anyone, though, who doesn't want to speak up now, she should tell Miz Little or me later. Now, one more thing—it's possible that any girl who is a virgin—you all know what a virgin is?—may experience, during the examination, a sharp stab of pain followed by a little bleeding. Do not be alarmed if this happens—it is nothing to worry about and you are not hurt. It is only a natural occurrence—" the formal lecturing voice dropped suddenly "—that should take place in happier circumstances, of course. Well, then," she said, picking up leadership again like an accustomed burden. "Miz Little, do you have something to add?"

"I like to say," Rosa said softly, "that you-all should remember—real men, they ain't like them in there." Her eyes shared generously a happy secret for which some of the girls thanked her; others looked away.

A remarkable woman, Edith Crane said to herself then, and later, when she was pretending to take a nap but actually coming to terms with herself for refusal to believe in the unbelievable, she added honestly that Rosa had proved more perceptive than she had in grasping the situation, too. For Edith had hoped there might be some germ of correct routine, violated perhaps only once or twice, but Rosa had grasped the peepshow purpose immediately and been quite correct. Even the times of day fitted; the girls were sent for, Rosa pointed out matter-of-factly, when the wives were likely to be at home preparing lunch, and again when the women would be busy getting dinner. Well, they were lucky in one way, Edith Crane reminded herself—one of the first victims after the Crane briefing had been the group's chief extrovert, the lively little Mary Jane.

"So I'm layin there like a big ol turkey 'bout to be stuffed, and I looks around and see them faces hangin in the window." She made wherever she stood a stage, and her rubber features reflected everything her sharp eyes had seen. "Climbin over each other up on the screen—" she stretched her neck, her face a mask of eager lewdness "—like flies stickin on flypaper, they was. And me—" her arms with the elbows sharply down, the hands slipped out sidewise with the palms up, were a metaphor for her spread legs on the examining table. "So I says—to myself, Miz Crane, don't you worry, I didn't say nothin to them—I says, 'You come git you'self a look, Jack. It my treat. 'Cause you too poor to buy it and you too sad to win it.' "

The gusts of laughter contained some hysteria still, but even more healing. Behind her closed eyelids that night, Edith Crane marveled on Mary Jane's gift, and then on the way something always seemed to appear that surprised you. The history professor's solid courage, the mimic's saving mockery—and Rosa Little's physical bravery, that very day. She had made the planned protest to the jailer, Sunshine's husband—an unwashed, unkempt man whose dropped suspenders looped over his shrunken haunches like the rigging of some faulty parachute—and Edith Crane had known it wouldn't work from the moment those small eyes turned at the sound of Rosa's soft-voiced opening words; helpless, she'd stood by, regretting her part in urging Rosa to what she thought would be only dismay. Ignorant again, the teacher charged herself: she had expected denial, and, if she'd thought about it, she might even have expected the filthy vocabulary in which it was couched; but she couldn't possibly have expected the blow the jailer aimed at the small woman. Rosa ducked it easily and came in under his still-flailing arm with a fast, strong punch to the sagging stomach. The impact brought an audible "Oof" from the man's vacuous face, and then, as girls scrambled, shrieking with delight, from all the shadows toward the fracas, Rosa said to him softly, "You lay one finger on me and you git a gripe in you belly the rest of you days." The man turned pale, rolled his eyes from her quiet menace to the joyfully belligerent girls, and retreated with haste and without dignity, slamming the barred door even while Edith Crane hurried forward to restrain the girls. All Rosa said about it was "You-all quiet down, we ain't got time for riots" to the girls and to Miz Crane, "Reckon we got to try somebody else. Don' look like he be much help."

Mary Jane's successors had not done as well as she at managing to think scornfully while remaining silent: the women in the cellblock heard a girl screaming, "Oh, please!" during the morning "physical" the next day. Miz Crane and Miz Little looked at each other sickly for a moment before Rosa said, "If we hear her, she hear us," and began to sing "We Shall Overcome" in a strong, carrying voice that brought them all to their feet and into the song. They stood against the bars, singing at the tops of their voices so the sufferer would be sure to hear; Edith Crane, singing too, glanced nervously up the corridor toward the sheriff's office, but nobody came to stop them or hush them. The girl was crying when she came back, and there was little point in questioning her, but Rosa did establish, for the benefit of the others, that she had not been sexually molested. "They brung their *sons*," she sobbed, her head on Rosa's shoulder. "I opens my eyes and a *boy* was lookin at me with my privates—" The rest was wordless tears, and there was nothing to do then but let her cry it out.

When Sunshine came, Rosa went to tackle her. "Please, ma'am," Edith Crane heard her begin and then the teacher left them, drawing the girls to the far end of the cell because the woman would be more likely to be reasonable without an audience. But the schoolteacher thought bitterly then that all she was here for could be summed up in the injustice of Rosa

Little saying, "Please, ma'am," to this slovenly creature whose help they needed.

That Sunshine was powerless as well as unlovely was the conclusion Miz Crane drew from Miz Little's report on the brief conference. "First she try to say the girl only fussin like girls do," Rosa told her colleague. "Then I say she right, of course, only one or two sound like they somethin really bad there—like bringin the boy to see, just say. That make her right unhappy—but she don't say nothin, just 'I know, I heard.' Then the poor thing, you know what she say?" Rosa paused to share the sympathy that was making her own eyes luminous. "She say maybe they get tired of it and stop soon, but then—" Rosa's voice demanded pity from Edith Crane for the woman she was about to quote "—she say, all mumblin, 'That just like the men, dirty. What can anybody do?' She shake her head like she about to start cryin and then she gone so fast I couldn't ask her for the Kotex for Priscilla like we said."

Edith Crane looked at Rosa's soft, pitying comprehension of Sunshine's misery and wondered silently whether there was any limit to Miz Little's strength and then, a little later when she was briefly alone, how in the name of God they did it. Unless it was, perhaps, in the name of God.

But there was a limit to Rosa's strength. It was reached, though temporarily, when the unfortunate Violet was led away for the afternoon session. Rosa smiled affectionately and Violet kept her large, muddy eyes on Rosa until she turned the corner of the corridor and was out of sight. Rosa waved and smiled some more; but when the girl had disappeared, Rosa remained hovering near the door, looking worried and preoccupied, and had to be reminded of her turn in the game of hopscotch Priscilla had scratched out on the stone floor. In fact, Miz Little was so clearly waiting, so noticeably anxious, that it was almost a relief when it happened: the scream came like a clap of thunder into the electric air of a summer afternoon. Wordless at first, it racketed down the corridor between the slimy stone walls like something thrown. They all jerked to attention, frozen in a clump with Rosa at their point, like a flock of wild geese in flight. *"Mama,"* Violet cried piercingly, and then, in a voice that broke of its own fear, "Mama, Mama, oh Mama."

Rosa Little launched herself at the bars and tugged at them, straining to pull them apart with her hands while her feet kicked a tattoo against the metal farther down. Corded veins threatened to break the surface of the coffee-colored skin of her forehead and sweat rolled down her face as she strained violently at her useless endeavor. By the time the others reached her, her white, even, upper teeth had lacerated the lower lip; blood poured down her chin and dripped onto her chest. Her knees were scraped and bloody with their bruising battle with the iron that had surrendered only flakes of rust to spatter her bare legs. When Miz Crane had wrestled her to a bunk and Priscilla had bathed the torn lip with the group's only handkerchief, wrung out in some of their scant supply of cool water, Rosa sighed once; then her eyes closed and she lay so still they thought she had fainted, until they saw the big, slow, silent tears slither down toward her ears. Priscilla handed the wet handkerchief to the girl beside her and fell on her knees by the bunk and wept, too.

Violet's poor comprehension and even poorer memory proved, in the circumstances, something of a blessing. If she was not able to report on her adventure, she was able to be easily consoled—an effect that proved healing for Miz Little, too. Rosa had recovered so thoroughly that she was able to produce a quiet "Thank you, ma'am" when Sunshine, bringing their dinner, added a warm, linen-covered tray and "I made some beaten biscuits," mumbled to no one in particular.

"That right kindly, ma'am. We thanks you."

Sunshine stared briefly at Rosa, then ducked her head and fled, flushed and silent.

Miz Crane scowled at the contretemps and called the biscuits "conscience food. I suppose this is how she soothes herself for not doing anything."

"They delicious," Rosa said placidly. Her brown forefinger prodded the flaky innards of the biscuit knowingly and found them satisfactorily airy. "Besides, I ain't sure she ain't done nothin."

Miz Crane swallowed the satisfactory biscuit and the unsatisfactory situation and planned her evening discourse to Rosa; she was too respectful of Rosa's knowledge of these people to dismiss her opinion, but an enormous cram course awaited the Negro woman. Munching, the teacher meditated on the best way to teach Rosa Little, in a hurry, not to settle for tokens.

Rosa's guess had been quite correct: as soon as she'd finished serving the prisoners their early dinner, the woman they called Sunshine took off her apron and went hesitantly forth to request an audience with the preacher. She interrupted his dinner with her tale, but he understood that she had to get back before her husband missed her. After she left, he felt disinclined to continue his meal. He took his hat and drove out to the home of Judge Hadley Thurston, who was just sitting down to his own dinner, timed according to the town's unwritten social edict: the higher the status, the later the evening repast. The judge listened to the minister's opening remarks and sent for his mulatto housekeeper to take the food away and bring drinks out to the veranda; there, where the judge had not long ago been lessened by his elliptical conversation with the ex-hillbilly Will Farland, he retrieved self-esteem by way of the opportunity presented by his fellow leader of men. The law saw the clergy on its way after a little chat, hospitably walking out to the somber, aging car that was considered suitably unflashy and virtuous for the ministry.

"I'm glad you came right to me, Reverend. Don't you bother about it any more, hear? I'll put a stop to that nonsense right away."

"I thought you would, Judge." The departing guest leaned from his car window. "I knew there was one decent man left around here anyway." He looked up briefly at the darkening sky. "But God help us if there aren't more."

"I know, Reverend, I know. Sometimes I wonder, what become of us, anyway? Before there was all this talk of rights, the town was full of decent people who just *did* right by their niggers and everybody else."

The judge went back into his house and telephoned the sheriff with an order as peremptory as those his father had been in the habit of issuing to Floyd's father. "I'm not about to discuss it on the phone. You just get yourself out here." He ate his dinner hurriedly then, sweating lightly with the haste and with the thought that, but for the grace of God, some of the Communist press currently disgracing the local scene could have picked this thing up and ridden away with it.

Sheriff Floyd, who had been offered only coffee and that rather cool, said placatingly that the law provided for the examinations and he didn't think—but of course the judge would know—it specified in just what room the prisoners should be examined? So nothing really illegal had been going on, and besides, the only complaints could come from the little nigger gals. The white women and that mouthy tan bitch had been left strictly alone. There wasn't no cause for fussin, was there, Judge—when there was no laws broke and the boys just havin theirselves a little fun?

Hadley Thurston hooded his eyes so Floyd couldn't see the judgment that lay in them: the boy was a sure thing to be washed away in the wave of the future, if only because he was too dumb to swim. "You just tell the boys the fun's over," he said softly. He stood up, giving himself the pleasure of dismissing the sheriff. "We can let it go at that, I reckon. As long as I don't hear," he added, very slowly, "that anybody failed to get the message." He let the warning sink in and didn't add, until he was sending the sheriff off with a handshake, that he knew the boys needed their recreation, but they shouldn't be trying to get it for nothing: let them dig down in their jeans for a couple of bucks and go on over to the nigger quarter like their daddies had done. The sheriff guffawed under the stars and raced the powerful motor of the police car so that it leaped from the driveway, scattering gravel.

Fifty-two

At about the time Sheriff Floyd was passing on the bad news to "the boys," Edith Crane was engaged in a more delicate and difficult communication to Rosa; it consisted also of passing on bad news, but carefully phrased so as not to be discouraging. For a fearful suspicion entertained by the political scientist Edith Crane (and, earlier, by the Negro history professor) was apparently proving valid: in political maneuvering, as in any other skill, experience is better than inexperience and professionals operate more efficiently than amateurs. The march had been planned in intricate detail by earnest people, most of whom scorned politics, and—not unlike an amateur theatrical company that begins with a performance of *Hamlet*—their intent had rather exceeded their capabilities. Thus, not all the ambitious projects were succeeding, though, happily, the chief one, the building of a court case around the history professor, seemed to be. But at lower levels, where the opponents tended to be a wily county official fighting on his home ground and a civil rights lawyer from "foreign parts," some local monkey wrenches had been applied to the march planners' machinery.

Mrs. Crane was guessing as she told Rosa, "Apparently, our hosts have managed to slow things down, probably by way of new obstacles put up to hide us from the outside world." But she was roughly accurate, as she was also when she went on, "Our people will work their way through the red tape, though. They must've started as soon as the news of our arrest got out. So I probably won't be with you much longer." She watched Rosa remembering—according to the original plan, Edith Crane should have been released from the jail by now: it had been decided, wisely, to expend the movement's limited funds on bail for those who, like Mrs. Crane, could go from the jail to tour New York and New England and thus raise bail money for the others. "Even if they don't get to me right away, though," the teacher continued, "as soon as the state police settle in here they'll move Priscilla and me to some separate cell or something—they have to, because of their own segregation law, you see." She smiled, but not with the wryness she felt at this explanation of how the other side, too, could be hoist on its own petard. The trouble with political efforts built on faith, she decided, was that the faithful tended to wait for revelation; the local political types had not been slow to observe this and to use it by simply cutting communications between the leaders and the led.

"That sheriff put you with us because he thought it make you mad? Like it was a joke on you? How come they could do like that, if it against their law?" Rosa tried not to look at the enormous cockroach crossing the stone floor behind Miz Crane; she herself would have killed it without hesitation, but Miz Crane got so upset that it was better to let the bug escape than draw it to her attention.

"That's what I've been trying to show you—the county people are little tin gods, as long as you remain under their control." The teacher spoke swiftly, seeing a chance to inspire faith to works. "They can do whatever they please and nobody will stop them. What you've got to do is get yourself and the girls noticed by somebody who's got more power than the sheriff, don't you see? Somebody outside. The point is, the press is paying more attention now than when we were brought before the judge in that farcical proceeding. And you even know this Ann Whatever-her-name-is—

so you've got it made if you can just reach her, don't you see? With the people you work for—"

"They ain't got nothin to do with it," Rosa said stubbornly.

Edith Crane sighed. "You're being quixotic." She saw the incomprehension in Rosa's face but decided not to get sidetracked into giving vocabulary lessons, too; practical political science was enough for one evening's whispering. "Let me put it to you this way, Miz Little: you're wasting something the girls need. Protection you could get for them, just by a piece of good luck, and without disobeying the orders we were given. And not by asking special favors either, if that's what you object to. This newspaper-woman you know would only be doing what she's paid to do if she wrote up what's going on here. In fact you'd be doing her a favor, you'd be giving her a story nobody else has."

"A scoop," said Rosa, who watched television. Pleasure began to show in her face.

The experienced eye of the schoolteacher detected the opening of communication with a student. "That's right. Now you see what you could do? Use your head, and you can help this Ann and our Violet, both at the same time."

"All right. How I do it?"

"Well, what it comes down to is, you have to get some outside force working for you. The Action Now lawyer is technically that, but he's getting pushed around by the sheriff, and maybe will be until a whole series of legal battles are won. Meanwhile, you and the girls have all the material you need, right now, to support a complaint—so why let these people keep you here any longer than you have to? Really, Miz Little, the best way is for you to get yourself in touch with this Ann. Do you think Sunshine—?"

Rosa thought Sunshine certainly couldn't march right up to the hotel, bearing a message for Ann Taswell—not and expect her husband to keep his job. But Sunshine, properly plumbed, could be a vital source of information. Miss Taswell could be reached by a chambermaid at the hotel, or by a busboy at the café where she ate. Rosa mused on this aloud, watching the cockroach now climbing the wall behind the other woman, while Edith Crane listened with amazement as the portrait of an invisible subculture, a black network capable of considerable unobserved communication, was innocently painted for her by Rosa. Who took it, the teacher observed—trying not to feel despairing about the fact—so calmly, so pathetically, for granted.

When decisions were made, Rosa had once pointed out to Marian Farland, things got simple. Things in this case were simplified by outside events that had little to do with the decisive Crane-Little conference among the sleeping innocents, but they got quite simple. For one thing, the salient points of a speech by the senior Senator from Iowa appeared in the local press, and Sheriff Floyd read the headline and the first paragraph and absorbed part of each; then, the jailer saw a way to get revenge on Rosa anonymously and thus without exposing himself to her witch-warning, in the power of which he believed more than he disbelieved. So it happened that the slow-moving routine that had taken so long to bring to Sheriff Floyd's attention the purse Rosa had lost at the time of her arrest was abruptly speeded by the jailer. Watching the sheriff go through the worn wallet now empty of cash, he volunteered the information that them nigger gals in the tank called the woman "Miz Little." He had heard them.

The sheriff held the small white card in his thick fingers and read "Rosa Little" and the address in Washington, D.C. "District of Columbia Public Library," he said slowly. "Will you look at that? In the capital of the country, you got to sit next to a nigger in the liberry." He spoke with the passion of a man who had once borrowed a book from a public library, and his jailer clucked with the alarm of a man who thought he just might want to try it himself someday. Ponderously, the pair checked the list of the jail's inmates and came to the mutual conclusion that one Rose Campbell must indeed be this Rosa Little, library patron, charge customer of Woodward & Lothrop, contributor to the United Givers' Fund, and probably a domestic servant. "This her?" the sheriff asked, pointing to the aproned figure holding a small white child in a color photograph that also contained a well-dressed white mama, papa, big sister, and big brother, most of them smiling. The jailer said that was her, all right, and identified her again in a wallet-size version of a studio portrait with two little girls, one of whom looked quite a bit like her. "Here's her man," the jailer said, flipping aside the smiling face of "Tiger" Little, muscled and enormously alive in white swimming trunks (though unidentifiable—alas for his widow, at the moment—as an Army noncom).

But the sheriff wasn't listening. "Senator Charges Reds Led Alabama Riots" danced in his head like a very special kind of sugar plum. He, too, watched television, and even before that, he had been a devoted fan of *The FBI in Peace and War* on the radio; Communists, he knew, had "party names." He began to question the jailer closely about the woman, hearing nothing but corroboration of his hopes in the report that she was the ringleader of the batch of nigger gals—along with the white woman from New York. It was probably the last item that did it: there was only one thinkable sponsor for a team composed of a white woman from New York and a nigger from anywhere. Sheriff Floyd slapped the top of his desk and rose with the speed and grace of a man of action to seek out the County Attorney, who would be just as pleased as he to present the state fellows with a coup like this when they moved in. But it would have to be fast, if they were to have the Commie safely tagged by that time. He ordered the jailer not to say nothing to nobody as he collected the purse and its contents, reached for his broad-brimmed hat (like those worn by the Texas Rangers, whose adventures he had also followed on radio and TV), and took off in a hurry.

Rosa admitted readily when they questioned her that the purse was hers and volunteered the information that the wallet had contained forty dollars with enough sharpness to insure that they wouldn't find her harmless and decide to drop her; there hadn't been time to consult Miz Crane before Rosa'd been brought into the sheriff's office, but she decided for herself that God moved in wondrous ways to bring buried prisoners to public attention and it was up to her to help Him all she could. The County Attorney looked at the sheriff when she mentioned the money. He said, "Floyd, you're a two-bit man all the way," with disgust in his voice while he took out a dollar of his own and put it into Rosa's wallet; then he told her calmly that she must've been mistaken about the amount she had. After that he proceeded at once to a series of questions about her associations and acquaintances, including the white people in the photograph.

Rosa stared at Marian Farland's pictured face, a smiling blur under her good spring hat, and at Charlotte Grayson with a fluff of light-brown hair and high heels, standing taller than her mother and than Dick Farland, who looked faintly unhappy behind a dazzling shirt and neatly knotted tie. Will Farland, tall and proprietary, looked quite at ease though dressed up, and behind him the prickly leaves of the holly tree in the front yard on Mackintosh Place were definite and shiny. "I done forgot their name," Rosa told the County Attorney, and insisted, in the face of his disbelief, that these were some white people she baby-sat for sometimes—he could tell by the picture, couldn't he, they were going out and she was keeping the baby?—but she couldn't ever recollect their name, she just went when the lady called her. The very intelligence of her argument seemed to make this story not quite plausible, the County Attorney thought; but the sheriff found it a believable portrait of darky ways.

When they pressed on to the organizations she belonged to, Rosa displayed a similar low IQ, which met with similar reactions from the two men. The sheriff was gradually losing faith in his hot case because she was sounding too ordinary-nigger, just a domestic with poor memory. But he revived happily when the attorney's question about why she had come down here produced a spiel about freedom that she could only have learned in one of them schools the Reds kept. When she mentioned the Fourteenth Amendment to the Constitution, her hearers' differences dissolved in the certainty that they had a live one, all right; wheels were turning to bring her to court tomorrow, which was Friday and would guarantee a whole weekend of glory, even while she was refusing to say who had sent her on the trip to Alabama and trying to get away with the bald lie that she had paid her fare herself. The charge would be giving false information to the police, for a starter.

The Crane-Little meeting that night was more of a strategy conference than a general discussion. The teacher surveyed Rosa, dress-rehearsing in all the makeup and furbelows the girls had offered, and wished the swelling on her lip weren't going down so rapidly. Still, if they took her to court tomorrow, it might still be visible. "Now, first thing, you see if you can find Miss Taswell—"

"You said she be there," Rosa reminded her, alarmed.

"The judge has a right to keep the press out," Edith Crane said carefully, "and he might just do that. But he can't keep them from gathering outside the courtroom door. She'll be there, and I'll bet you'll see others you know, too."

"But what if I can't talk—you said I was to be sure to talk to Miss Ann."

"Don't upset yourself, Miz Little. One way or another, you'll come to her attention. Failing everything else, don't forget that our lawyer will be there—with the press there, they've got to let him talk to you, even though they're trying to make it late enough so he can't possibly prepare a decent case. But he can always take a message to your friend without anybody's being able to trace it back to you and take it out on the girls—if that's what's worrying you. They'd expect him to be talking to the press."

Edith Crane, trying to prepare Rosa for the possibility of not seeing Ann Taswell at once, was thinking of routine county justice, which preferred quiet; but she had no idea of the county officials' dreams of exposing a Communist, quick and loud, before the state boys could snatch the glory. Closing the courtroom was just about the last thing the judge wanted to do in this case, and a new friendliness to the press was so apparent that Gil Kimball, taking his place beside Ann in the courtroom, began to speculate on possible reasons for it. That some of the city fathers were a little wounded by what they'd read about themselves in Kimball's column and elsewhere was the reason offered by the editor of the local newspaper, who had tipped off the press enclave at the hotel that tomorrow they could see true Alabama justice in action during the course of a promisingly newsworthy hearing in the county court. The word "newsworthy" had been the pivotal one for most of the reporters, including Ann; but the *New York Leader* had its own staff reporter on the scene to take care of news—what had brought Gil here this morning was the implication that he'd been hasty in scorning Dorothy and its denizens. If they could indeed be just as just as anybody else, it was incumbent on Kimball to come and watch.

Standing for the entrance of the judge, he saw that the balcony was almost empty except for a scattering of Negroes; a woman with a small child was struggling in through an iron door that looked as if it might lead to a fire escape. Downstairs, he noted, sitting down beside Ann and letting the droning buzz around him without attention, the whites entered through an imposing doorway with an elaborate plaster molding surmounted by a bird that was probably supposed to be an eagle. Gil tried to remember in which of the public rooms of the White House a gilt eagle perched above each of the windows; he had shaken Andy out of her First-Lady poise, at the Girards' "housewarming," by murmuring commiserations on the problems birdlime on the curtains must cause her. He watched for a while, but Dorothy County's eagle remained either continent or simply unmoved. If it *was* an eagle. Kimball-the-artist eternally beset by copy editors sighed heavily and told himself to stick to his last.

Ann, who had been sticking to hers, suddenly smothered a gasp. Gil heard the sound and felt the stiffening at his side and was thus led to direct his attention to the prisoner being brought up to stand before the judge— and had to suppress his own gasp when he recognized Rosa. He shook his head negatively by way of caution to Ann because he found the county's new fondness for the press too suspect to believe it would do Rosa any good to have their acquaintance known. Ann wrote "lip" on her copy paper and Gil read it and nodded, returning his gaze quickly to Rosa; he had noticed the swollen lip, but it was only the most dramatic of a number of differences between the woman the County Attorney was currently talking about and the pleasant, trim housekeeper and all-around savior of Marian Grayson's Georgetown ménage. The competent hands Rosa folded before her now in a not entirely successful attempt at composure had spread peanut butter in quantities that must have mounted to at least a ton for Sharlie and her next-door pal Rosemary Kimball, an inveterate moocher from the age of three. He had always known that an Alabama jail was not exactly a health resort, Gil told himself dumbly, and reached for Ann's notes to see what the hell Rosa was doing in there and how come nobody had known and gotten her out.

Since the county's lawyer was at the moment outlining the false infor- mation the prisoner had given to the police, it didn't take Gil long to figure out why Marian hadn't flown down to chew the Alabama scenery. Ann's scribbled summary of the original charges against "Rose Campbell"— "Disord cond, aslt, unlfl assmbl, conspir a/st state"—added up to nothing that would've kept Will Farland from springing Rosa within twenty-four hours. But "Rose Campbell," Gil said to himself bitterly, had had to sit there rotting in that goddam jail. His dark eyes concentrated on Rosa, will- ing her to know he was there.

The first sight of Gil had granted Rosa all the freedom she needed. The note carried out of the jail in her brassiere would reach Ann safely, she knew; the Negro lawyer who had explained that there would be nothing he could do at this hearing, which was only a formality, would get it to Ann, and Ann would do something if those men kept torturing the girls. But Gil was another matter, was more, even, than Rosa had expected. "Looks like everybody reads Gil Kimball," Dick had said at dinner one long-ago Wednes- day night, when half of Washington had been choking with laughter at the Kimball version, that morning, of a USIA translator trying to render Presi- dent Winkler's press conference faithfully into Swahili. Marian had said she supposed several million people did anyway, looking at Will for con- firmation of the guess, and Will had laughed, helping himself to one of the rolls Rosa was passing. "The point is, he's got two readers: Alec Girard and Ralph Ferris. That may be all that matters."

Outside notice was what they needed, Miz Crane had insisted—and one thing Gil Kimball could certainly provide, especially if Alec Girard was still among his readers, was outside notice; it was a pity Rosa Little hadn't done something more important, something more worthy of attention, than just walk down a street beside a brave man and then be impudent to a white woman. She was very ordinary, and she knew it; she answered humbly, then, when the judge asked her why she had given a false name to the police, that she guessed it was because she was ashamed to be getting arrested.

The judge smiled kindly at her, keenly aware of Hadley Thurston's warning that they would have Washington permanently on their doorstep unless they stopped giving the impression they were hounding the niggers. Thurston hadn't known then, of course, about this promising little Communist item—which was just as well: the old man was getting on to an age where he ought to begin to be moved over. But his advice was good—the way to do it and make it stick was not to white-sheet around the place. "Come now, Rose," the county judge said genially. "You know you been arrested before, haven't you?" He waited, but the damned woman didn't answer. He studied the light-skinned face that didn't look frightened enough, saw the swollen lip, and cursed that blundering fool Floyd; maybe it would get by as just Negroid, but why take a chance? Only a jerk would have sent her into court visibly marked up.

Of course, they did provoke the hell out of you, he said to himself, arranging his own countenance to reflect paternal benignity before trying again. "You hear me, girl? I bet if I sent for the records from some other towns 'round here where they've had trouble I'd find you've been there—under one of your aliases, anyhow. Were you in Mississippi in the spring, too? Or does the Communist Party keep you people workin on one state?"

Gil saw that Ann was getting it all, which was advisable—there tended to be considerable difficulty in obtaining records of court proceedings around here—and put his hands in his pockets so he wouldn't rub them in satisfaction. The old boy was going to hang himself for fair if he went on this way: Gil and Ann would probably be two of the least well-known figures who could testify to Rosa's presence in Washington when they got around to nailing down some of those dates. Just for openers, the Secretary of State had dropped in on the Farlands' farewell party for Sven Halversen of the International Financial Organization; there'd been the usual hired crew to do the food and drinks, but Rosa, startlingly proper in maid's uniform for once, had admitted the guests and taken the gentlemen's coats. Wouldn't it be juicy if that night coincided with an uproar somewhere in Mississippi at which Rosa was supposed to be working for the Communists? Also, it was too much to hope for, but he scribbled on his folded paper nevertheless a note to find out whether Rosa had ever picked up Peter Farland at the White House play school. Gil sat back happily then, smiling with anticipation, and with gratitude that the bad old days were over: under the timid Winkler, any charge of a Communist connection, however vague and unproved, might have meant trouble for Farland. But, though Alec Girard was too conservative for Gil's taste in interpreting the Fourteenth Amendment, there was no question at all about his respect for the Bill of Rights. Anyone trying to throw Red mud at Farland via Rosa would run smack into the President of the United States, who had demonstrated devastatingly, the first time anyone had tried, that the era of that kind of nonsense had come to an end.

"You admitted that these were your possessions, didn't you?" The judge's voice was less indulgent now, and it surprised him at first that it worked better that way. All she said was, "Yes," but at least she had answered. He turned over the pictures in the wallet. "This *is* your wallet, with these cards in the name of Rosa Little?"

"Yes. That my name." She had a clear, carrying voice when she wanted to use it. "That my wallet, Judge, and there was forty dollars in it when I dropped my pocketbook. The man done grabbed me—"

"Well now, that's another matter, Rose," the judge said kindly but quickly, careful not to look too openly at the press. "If your money's been mishandled we'll find the miscreants if you can back up your story. We don't let our Nigras get robbed in this city, no matter what the left-wing press says." His white eyebrows drew together and he bent his head toward her: he knew how to be kind if she knew how to be respectful. "I hear you from around here, that right?"

"Yes, Judge."

"And you got these two fine-looking daughters, I see. Guess you'll be wanting their picture back, won't you?" He passed her the photograph and waved away her thank-you. "Now what we got here, Rose? This's a nice-looking little family, too. These your white folks?"

Rosa was ready to answer that, the way she'd explained it in the white lawyer's office; this judge would, like the sheriff, find it believable that she could work for people and not know their name. And then she'd get the picture back, so it couldn't get in the papers and maybe embarrass the Farlands. She began to smile, to fall into the role of the local nigger the judge and his friends might be persuaded by—a good woman, fond of her white folks, and no Communist at all.

It was hard to say exactly what did it: Ann Taswell's almost comically startled look had something to do with it, as Rosa saw her trying to merge the fact of the photograph, which must obviously be of the Farlands, with the notion that they were anybody's "white folks." Edith Crane's lecture to the girls certainly had something to do with it: speak up once, clearly and politely, just to let them know you know. She should have done it at once, but it still wasn't too late. And maybe also the dark, urgent message in the eyes of Gil Kimball, who had changed startlingly from Rosemary's daddy and the Farlands' dinner guest to the sum of millions of openings onto the world for one who had just been discovering how locked up you could be, how muffled and helpless to help the innocent who depended on you . . .

Still, no one of these things, or even the sum of all of them, might have been enough to move Mama's daughter—Rose, the sister of Peony and Morning Glory, born to the ways of Marigold County, Alabama—if the judge had not begun to grow impatient then. Relying on what he had interpreted before as the woman's response to a voice of authority, he said briskly, "Speak up, girl. You're wasting this court's time."

"Judge, I never been arrested before and I ain't no Communist," she said loudly, turning partly away from him to face the filled courtroom. "But I ain't no girl neither." Her eyes went up to the dark faces in the balcony before she continued, raising her voice over murmurs. " 'Miz Little' is the proper way to call my name for them that don't know me. Like you, Judge. And I ain't about to answer no questions till I'm spoke to proper."

The only thing on God's earth that might save her, Gil thought, getting to his feet swiftly while he held Ann down, is that they were being slow to get the point—it was simply too stupefying for them. "Does she mean—" a woman in a broad-brimmed straw hat began to say to her friend, who was too stunned to ply her round paper fan advertising "Status Funerals"; but it was impossible for the woman to say what she understood Rosa to mean, so she fell silent. "Y'all *hear* that nigger?" a man's voice cried uncertainly, near the eagle-topped door. In the well of the court, the Action Now lawyer stood up, his face gray, his eyes checking the doors. Not a chance, Gil told the man in his mind—no way through that crowd.

The judge was rapping for order. "Woman, do I understand you to say—"

"I ain't a child nor a dog," Rosa interrupted him, yelling. Her eyes flashed. "I don't answer no questions unless I called right and proper."

In the balcony, they got it: "Hallelujah!" someone shouted, and the cheers flew up the short distance to the ceiling and showered down again like confetti. On the white audience below, now even further confused by this new evidence of the end of the world.

". . . hold you for contempt for refusing to answer questions in a properly constituted court of the County of Dorothy—" The judge, on his feet now, was drowning out his own words with the hammering of his gavel.

Gil made it down to the well of the court while the startled audience was only just beginning to move. He tapped the sheriff. "I'm Gil Kimball," he began.

"I know you, mister." Floyd's face was scarlet. "I got no time for you, now or ever."

"That's all right, Jack," Gil said, measuring the man, who was big but soft. "I just want to watch you get that woman out of here in one piece. I want to see her safe before I start writing. You understand me?"

"Out of my way, nigger-lover." The sheriff dodged Gil without pushing him and made for Rosa, already in the clutch of two deputies. If they moved fast, they could make it, because the crowd was pushing forward but there was no organization behind these still-startled people. In the balcony the Negroes were singing "We Shall Overcome" with a volume that shook the building.

"Okay, Rosa" was all Gil had time to shout at her as she went through the side door in the midst of the pushing men. But he saw that she had heard him. There was no point in listening to the judge fume right now, so he stood still and watched the Negroes beating it out their narrow balcony door before the sheriff found time to see who they were. Gil checked briefly to see that Ann was okay—she was, wedged in among the reporters shouting questions at the judge—and headed for the telephone back at the hotel.

Later, as they ate a hasty, unappetizing dinner, Gil told Ann, "The White House says Will's in New York. It must be some big deal, because I can't find out where in New York from the girl, and both Messenger and Ruffing are out. I left a message at the UN delegation, just in case. What did you get?"

"They've got her in a cell by herself, apparently."

Gil nodded. "Sure. They're giving her the troublemaker treatment. But I think she'll be safe enough."

"Gil, do you think we ought to call Marian?"

"Jesus, I hate to until we've got hold of Will, so we can tell her he's got the thing in hand. We'll need something to hold her down, and Will is our best hope."

"I know," Ann said unhappily, "but we can't just let her read it in the paper."

"She may not get to," Gil said thoughtfully.

"Meaning?"

"Meaning that if it's occurred to me that this one's a high-court baby, it may occur to the county people, too. In which case, they won't care to box themselves in publicly, any more than they have already."

"I don't—"

"Oh for Pete's sake," Gil said wearily. "Can't you see it can go to the Supreme Court? What's equal treatment? Does it include being addressed respectfully in court?"

"Oh."

"Yeah, oh." Gil sighed. "I think I'll run out and see Judge Thurston. Who must be praying hard for a newsbreak somewhere else today."

If Gil's guess was correct, the judge's prayers appeared to be answered: for, late that afternoon, an enterprising Alabama lad with a camera and ambition to move on to a big city succeeded in working his way through the bureaucracy of the Coordinated Press. Which promptly puchased, and promptly put on its wire, the lad's photograph of the famous Negro entertainer, dressed in a prisoner's uniform at the county farm and wearing, noticeably even in the poorish photo, the marks of recent assault. The shift of attention was immediate: though the story of Rosa Little's day in court still ran in the newspapers, it commanded less attention than the photo of the battered entertainer.

On the 6 P.M. television news, where the process of selection is sterner and perhaps owes less to abstract standards of journalism, everything from Alabama disappeared behind pictures of the county work farm and old photos of the entertainer who was, in a way, television's own. The face, laughing and unbattered, was familiar to viewers; it was not surprising, then, that the television reporters featured the story much as any reporter features the local boy in a dispatch from a war front.

But Gil Kimball's column could revive what the immediate news had passed by, and Hadley Thurston knew it. So Kimball came away from his interview with the judge satisfied that no harm would come to Rosa so long as Sheriff Floyd remained under the judge's thumb—which presumably would be at least until the state police took over. With something of a cease-fire in effect then, Kimball withdrew. Back at the hotel, Ann reported that she had got first a busy signal and then no answer at her apartment; at the Tribune, all the copyboy on duty knew was that Marian's Sunday page had been finished and a proof run off and checked, after which the art editor had taken off for, it was said by somebody passing by at the moment, some out-of-town art show. Kimball nodded and tried Will Farland at home, though just for form's sake. There had been no result of his call to New York (because Farland, told that Gil Kimball was trying to find him, cursed his luck and dove deeper into hiding from newshounds on the trail of the U.S.-Soviet talks), and it wasn't likely there would be any: possibly a few of the 11 P.M. newscasts might mention Rosa's name, but none of them had a picture of her anyway. The news might not reach Farland at all.

But the Action Now office in Washington knew how to reach Bettina Little, so Rosa's daughters, escorted by Bruce Fisher, were on their way to Dorothy by that time. Neither the girls nor Bruce had had any idea that Rosa was in the contingent jailed at Dorothy, and Rose Campbell of Alabama meant nothing in particular to the Washington office of Action Now either. Rosa's family and friends had read the list of names carefully and when hers didn't appear, they congratulated each other on their good luck. This afternoon, the bubble had burst.

Bettina went home from her interview with the kindly man who had broken the news to her and started packing—but for herself, not Trixie. True to her promise to her mother, she'd tried to consult Marian before taking any action at all; Trixie, ordered to "keep calling Miz Farland," had rung the phone at the Mackintosh Place house at fifteen-minute intervals all through the flurry, reporting no success each time. It simply didn't occur to Bettina that she was the only one who had Marian's changed telephone number, so she assumed Marian was out for the evening—which meant Bettina had the right to make her own decisions, because she had to leave right away. Harassed and frightened, she sought help from Gloria and Claude Jones in leaving Trixie behind; but Gloria was almost prostrate with fear for her sister's life, and Claude was too busy rounding up money for fare to rule on procedure. So, in the end, it was all three youngsters who set off for the bus station in Claude's cab. Trixie, worn out with battle for a place in the battle lines, fell asleep soon after the bus began to roll southward. But Bettina cried for a long while on Bruce's shoulder.

Gil, who wanted to catch Rosenberg first thing in the morning, let the evil thereof be sufficient unto the day and went to bed. Ann decided to try Marian in the morning and went to bed shortly thereafter. Sometime in the night, a hotel employee slipped Rosa's note under the door, but Ann didn't wake from her troubled sleep.

Of them all, only Rosa slept peacefully. She had worried briefly about the girls, particularly Violet; but Miz Crane was still with them and they would be all right. And, in a way, it was good to be alone again. The last thing she thought about before she went to sleep was how funny it was that it had taken her so long to see what really mattered—more than jobs, more than votes, more than laws and constitutions and amendments and all the other things that made her head swim. The whole point had been, all the time, to be treated proper: whatever happened to her now, until Gil or somebody could bring help, was less important, than that she had done what she'd been supposed to do all along. It was good not to be all mixed up any more.

Fifty-three

A Washington deep-summer weekend, arriving in the midst of one of the fullblown, merciless heat waves, is something that may be either actively contended with or fled in panic, but it can almost never be ignored. So long as it was necessary to go to work, the population arose, puffy-faced and irritable after sleepless nights, and quarreled its way onto and off the buses, some of which were air-conditioned but seldom in rush hours. Trade fell off in air-conditioned stores because the shoppers simply couldn't face the explosive blast of hot air they knew would await them when they pushed open the glass doors to the outside world. Those who had air conditioning at home cowered indoors, very like polar explorers huddling in their huts during a blizzard—small, guarded units of life isolated and battened down in the midst of a hostile environment.

But when the weekend arrived, it was no longer necessary to endure in order to survive: free for two days of the requirements of breadwinning, suburban families gathered in their community pools and concentrated on remaining half-naked and at least partly wet during every waking moment. The bars of the budget were lifted: daddies foraged forth for hamburgers that could be made more cheaply at home, and mamas who were ardent devotees of the Balanced Meal declared a tired slice of hothouse tomato a green vegetable and let it go at that. The children of upright, conscientious civil servants

and their well-read wives, pillars of the League of Women Voters, ran barefoot through the darkness until all hours while their parents traded con-
science-soothing reminders that the kids had no school tomorrow and it
couldn't hurt, this once.

The citizens who chose to fight back were up at dawn on Saturday morning, summoning prodigies of patience and energy to manage all the logistic
triumphs needed in order to be on the road, equipped and provisioned, at an
hour earlier than they would normally be going to work. In the case of the
Lucien Messengers, this weekend, most of the prodigies were Annette's: with
the exertions of a Sisyphus, she pushed the boulder that was her husband uphill so successfully that, by noon, he had almost stopped issuing ominous
statistics on the incidence of heart attacks in middle-aged men shoved into
the wilderness by crazy nature-girl wives. Exhausted by the half-mile of downward trek from the car and guilty about getting out of town at all, Luke sat
on the stone step before a wooden trail hut on the Skyline Drive in Virginia
and sipped a chilled martini carried from home in a vacuum bottle.

Marian Farland, heading for an art show at Rehoboth Beach in a car driven
by Phil Colby, surveyed the flattish, peaceful landscape of Delaware through
her sunglasses and let her spirits rise unmolested by guilt: she was working,
and the fact that the earning of her daily bread carried her to the sea, for the
sight of which she had been hungering, was a gift of the gods. She patted the
bag that contained her bathing suit and told Phil that no, she didn't want to
stop for a cup of coffee; if she could go swimming before the show, it would
be easier to keep her mind on the pictures. Colby nodded, understanding the
problem, and speeded up, keeping one eye out for the Delaware cops who
prey on refugee Washingtonians heading for the beaches.

In New York, where the heat was noticeable but less fierce and personal,
Will Farland, having checked out of his hotel and stowed his bag, was wandering free and frightened. Climbing the broad, shallow steps of the old
museum, the political man who strove always in the midst of contending
forces was oddly, thoroughly alone in contending with something nameless
and unclassifiable but clearly both fierce and personal. Anonymous and almost at the end of thought, he stood among the Rodins, aware, at first, of
nothing in himself but the need of change, a desperate need, to be met at any
price; psychoanalysts would have recognized his mood as the one in which
people—the hopeful cases, whose chances are good—come to seek treatment.
Will moved at random among the stone and bronze strivings on exhibit in the
museum, seeking a beginning of some healing that he could do himself. He
got his chance, suddenly and without preparation, when he sauntered through
an archway into yet another echoing, open vault and confronted the central
sculpture. *Look at it, don't read about it,* Marian had tried to teach him, but
Farland the Fact Man had never quite been able to make the leap—thus, he
had seen only a slanted column of gray stone before he read the neat white
card attached to the pedestal: "SOLDIER. Paul Morisot." The long-gone
date typed beside the name had been a year of many and recent ex-soldiers.

It was too bad, Will thought, that he hadn't indeed looked at it first, because now there was so damn much shit in his way. He thrust his hands deeper into his pockets, planted his feet right where they were, and stuck out his sharp chin: the way to begin was just to begin. The first result of his determined study of the statue was surprise, because it was not a soldier, actually, but a taut twist of stone—an abstraction, which Will had always believed vaguely was something very new; yet here was Morisot being abstract years ago. And yet his peace statue, that had gotten into politics, was whatever the opposite of abstract was; Will recalled clearly a quite specific, recognizable baby crying in the rubble in Morisot's "The Taken Town."

But the hectoring voice in Will's head insisted "*Look* at it," and he shrugged and left the art-politics of Morisot alone. Making himself just look, he saw the statement in the shape—the forward-plunging stance that leaned into a knifelike point of stone—but he thought that Marian was all wet: without the title, he would never have seen what it was. He glanced over his shoulder to make sure he was alone and then tested out his theory with his own body, holding the pose and comparing it to the statue. That's what it was, sure enough—a bayonet charge. He stood upright again, lighted an illicit cigarette, and paid Morisot a grudging tribute: the Frenchman may have turned his back on abstraction sometime afterward, but he was the first one who had made any sense of it to Will Farland. Even the hole in the stone that seemed to be a requirement of the form, like a union card in another trade, at last had some rational excuse for being: here it was not quite a hole, but almost, and it was where the belly of the soldier would be. Will nodded, grinning a little, as his body remembered for him the sinking, gone-in-the-guts sensation of fear. If that was what Morisot had meant to transmit, he had made his point clearly enough. If, on the other hand, Farland was being too naïvely literal—well, at least Marian couldn't complain that he didn't react viscerally.

Will stepped on the stub of his cigarette and then bent and put the crushed butt into his pocket and dispersed the small trace of ash with the toe of his shoe, so that the pristine purity of the gallery wouldn't be marred by traces of visiting yokels. He rocked back on his heels and studied the sunlight slanting in from the high windows; it looked like the chutes down which they used to dump coal into basement windows, he thought. And then he shook his head in pleased wonder with himself: he was *looking*.

He started out of the place in rather high spirits, but he turned back and surveyed the sculpture again from a distance, trying to find the name of whatever it was he thought he had begun to learn from it. To make the "soldier" gray instead of the white marble of the Rodins was a choice he approved and thought he could understand; but what still eluded him was how that shape, that fluidity of stone that was not the figure of a man but the suggestion of it, had been invested with such desperation and fear. Something, he fumbled, something had gone into it, something so powerful that it spoke nevertheless to anyone who could listen—and, most important, it stood there, waiting to be listened to, a cause and not an effect: it was made, hacked or chipped or carved or whatever they did, of its own maker's attention rather than any discovered need to which a response was required.

"Love is attention," Marian had said, leaving him only that when she began to take herself away from Will's climate—the air of effect and response in which he breathed but she wept that she could not. Will nodded briskly at the statue, as though it were a messenger delivering a telegram, and turned away for good.

Lost among the ancient Greeks on his way out of the museum, he paused to stare at without seeing a broken statue of a god of mischief, wondering for the first time whether it was funny that it had taken Marian's lover to translate her too-specific, too-personal shrieks and tears into an evolved statement that her husband could begin to understand. Tidily, his mind edited the thought, pointing out that though it was the abstract sculptor who had spoken to Farland, the man who had successfully coveted his neighbor's wife had first traveled from the difficult column of stone to the immediately understandable baby of the peace statue. Perhaps what had been needed to mediate between Will and Marian, spokesmen of opposing worlds, was a Morisot, who had journeyed in both. At that point, Will decided it was pretty funny, after all, and that he was hungry. He found the cafeteria, ate absently, and returned, to his own surprise, to continue his cram course among the Egyptians—who would have been as amazed to find themselves in that air-conditioned quiet as Farland was.

Andrea Girard had had time to become unamazed at finding herself in silent halls. Walking, now, the silent halls of the only place in the environs of Washington where it was probably true that everybody was indifferent to the heat, the tall figure in its chocolate brown skirt and tan shirt, tan linen spectator pumps on bare legs, needed only some sunglasses and a bright scarf to be perfectly appropriate as a spectator at a regatta, perhaps: a slim, elegant, athletic woman whose picture inspires dreams and effort in plump, lonely government girls turning magazine pages in their shared apartments. But today, like them, Andy had no place to go. In solemn, tiled rooms like altars to some god of hygiene, Elizabeth, lying on a wheeled table, was being fought for by those who knew how.

Andrea had hovered, an unwanted watcher trying humbly not to be in the way, a hindrance and a reproach, with big eyes that asked questions nobody could answer. Once, timidly, she had accosted Dr. Snowden as he came out with another man, both of them frowning and not speaking. The doctor turned his angry eyes on Andy's long hand with its orange-tinted fingernails, raised by way of tentative apology but looking only frivolous instead, and said, "*Please,* Mrs. Girard"; he stopped suddenly, glancing past her as if seeking help, but there was only the waiting Secret Service agent at the end of the corridor. Andy let her hand fall and muttered that she was sorry and turned away, listening to the words the doctor had forborne to say: *Get out of here and let me work.*

She had fled then, back to the ward and the children she couldn't bear to
see when she first came because they were so pathetic in wheelchairs and now
couldn't bear to see because they were so lucky to be in wheelchairs. The
other mothers plied her with coffee and huddled around her protectively, as
if all they could do for her who was one of their own was spare her as much
as possible the troubling sight and sound of children who were better off
than hers. Andrea was aware of their kindness, but she didn't entirely understand its origin until the father of the child who had come in with Elizabeth
—the child who had responded well to the very first drug tried—asked her if
she wouldn't like to go for a little walk outside.

They paced the ordered paths under the unsparing blanketing heat that
Andy simply didn't notice, though she replied to the man's few comments
about it. Then he offered her a cigarette, and, as she raised her head after
accepting a light for it, she caught the meaning of him and of all the others:
accidentally looking into his eyes, she looked, as sometimes happens between
people, right through them into the whole of the man himself and saw, as a
sweeping searchlight picks up and illuminates hugely and wholly one object
among many, the great gratitude that filled him. She turned away, her hands
shaking with the knowledge that she was, for him and all of them, the hostage
to fortune, that informing all their sympathy was this gratitude to her for
being the one to whom it was happening. The cruel giant who threatened
them all was going to win: the white-clad hero Snowden couldn't kill the
giant, only confuse and bedevil him and so deprive him for a while of some
of his prey. But, though the sick children were one as a combined prey of
horror, their salvation was individual: each parent felt obscurely that every
time another child was gobbled by the giant the odds improved for his own.
The parents lived on the frail hope that each sweep could be the last—that
one of the Snowdens would burst from one of the tiled rooms of long tables
and Bunsen burners and shout that it was over, it was done, every child who
still breathed could be counted a permanent survivor. The men and women
so deeply threatened by magic were reduced to reliance on compensatory
magic, abandoning whatever levels of rationality they had managed before.
Thus they needed Andrea Girard, for she was their surrogate in sorrow. Like
the ancients who chose a king for a year, they showered her with the gifts
of their love and sympathy before sending her forth to be sacrificed for all.

She wasn't being fair, Andy told herself as she thanked the man, saying she
thought she would go in for a while; after all, these parents had not chosen
her as their sacrifice. Responding to a choice they would not have wished to
make, they wished only to be saved from a like one now that it was made.

Andy turned quickly and almost ran back down the corridor with the panicky denial that the choice had indeed been made shrieking in her mind; as
if her loitering presence outside the door guaranteed that it wasn't so, she
flew back to her post. Her flight slowed as her desperation was haltered by
the years of training in looking composed—"Really, Andrea, I can't think
how you could consider making yourself so *conspicuous*," Elizabeth Lang-

with had said about the amateur theatricals, about the essay contest for school polemicists— Her mother's daughter again, Andrea paced the corridor to the wide window at its blind end.

"They've located Morisot, did you hear?" Dan Healy said as Jake came into his office. "He's on his way right now." The cheerful voice stopped abruptly as Healy's pleasure in imparting good news came up against the slower realization that the good news didn't matter.

Jake heard, and understood—but he thought it would make a difference, at least to Andy. Poor Andy, who always got left alone. Jake, who had "paced in" the baby for her, was needed right here, this time. He nodded at the restless figure of the President, visible through the open door leading to the oval office. "Any more on Elizabeth?" he asked quietly. Paul would have to take care of Andy; the tall man hovering near the tall windows needed all the help he could get.

"He called Andy." Dan lowered his voice. "They're still trying to knock out the infection. Jake, what's a hematologist for?"

"Blood diseases, I guess. Besides leukemia." *A very serious bacterial infection in the blood against which she has poor or no defenses* had been the exact words—Jake happened to know—of the doctors' report to Alec Girard.

"The odds aren't good, are they?"

"No." Jake peered in at the unquiet figure. "But they told him that last night."

"He's waiting for Andy to call him back. That's why he can't settle down."

"Yeah. Maybe." Jake said. "Or it could be because of Alabama, or Moscow, or Capitol Hill or—hell, you name it." He sighed, and tried a reassuring smile for the man Girard had once teasingly called "Nursey." "I'll see what I can do, Dan. Take it easy."

Jake was mopping his face with a crumpled handkerchief as he closed the door of the oval office behind him. "Awful damn hot out there," he explained. "Mr. President."

"It's hot in here, and getting even hotter. Mr. Counsel."

"Nice," Jake said bitterly. "Well, could you please come and sit down anyhow? I can't stand the sight of all that energy. What's your good news?"

Girard complied, settling himself in an upholstered chair with one long leg draped over the arm like a teen-ager. "Rosenberg called. Among other jolly portents and local legal excitements, it seems they burned a cross on the judge's lawn last night. Thurston—the federal judge who granted the injunction."

"Ouch. He's more than a federal judge, you know—he's a local symbol of aristocratic rectitude."

"So Rosie gave me to understand," the President said. "He also indicated that the whole escapade was not what you might call outside the general picture."

"What about the state police?"

"Rather curious—they're there but not quite there. He seemed to be having a little trouble describing their role. I finally pinned him down a bit, and I gather that he's not convinced they're going to stay, for one thing." He hesitated. "I also got the feeling that Rosie thought we were not alone. His conversation seemed stilted."

"Oh?" Jake's eyebrows shot up. "If that's so, they're getting bolder than we've been led to believe. Maybe we ought to get the Army in at least for communications purposes." He looked at the President's negative response. "I guess you're right—no sense jiggling the boat unless we're prepared to ditch the governor and swim for it. I'm beginning to think I should've left Farland down there—he could probably tell better than Rosie how much stir is just a hot Saturday."

"Don't. We needed Farland in New York." The President pointed with his foot at the *Congressional Record* lying on the little table between the beige sofas. "If Kaslov's read that—and I imagine he has—he ought to be eager to sign on the dotted line." Jake looked puzzled, so Girard went on. "We reason, don't we, that it's better to deal with Kaslov than what might replace him? Well, if I were Kaslov, I'd figure the same way about Girard right now, and I'd grab the agreement while I could."

Jake picked up the stapled paper book with its solid blocks of old-fashioned type and opened it to the first of two places marked by scraps of paper stuck into the pages. He read quickly, and then looked up in surprise. "Hell, this is only the old Senator from Iowa's dark warning the other day."

" 'If President Girard is willing to stand by and let the Reds fulfill their threat by undermining our beloved land with street riots and—' "

"Please," said Jake. "Spare me. Wouldn't you rather recite 'The Boy Stood on the Burning Deck,' to show off your fabulous memory? What's the point, anyway? We all know the Senator believes the Communist Party is paying the way of every Negro heading for Alabama. Did Rosie say anything about the latest batch due in Dorothy?"

"Uh-huh. The largest force is expected to arrive tonight. The Negro leaders plan to keep everybody pretty busy in church tomorrow, which ought to make things fairly quiet at least until noon."

"Good. By that time, they may be sleepy. Noon on a summer day in Alabama is a little hot for rioting." Jake looked at the President. "Why are we trembling before the jerk from Iowa?"

"We aren't. It's just that he's one end of the spectrum. Look at the other end—I've marked it." He got up and went back to the window.

Jake opened the *Record* where the other slip of paper stuck out, near the back, and began to read aloud: " 'Extension of remarks of Hon. William Bruyette of Vermont in the House of Representatives.' " He stopped, smiling, as he heard Girard intoning the formula with him; then his smile faded when he recognized the note of nostalgia.

" 'Mr. Speaker,' " the President quoted from memory, " 'under leave to extend my remarks in the Appendix'—"

Jake shook his head in severe reminder that those were not, in truth, the good old days; in point of fact, Representative Girard had been a very frustrated fellow, and his former administrative assistant wished that he would remember it right now.

"—'to include an editorial,' " the ex-Congressman was continuing, " 'from the *Newport Telegraph*'—"

Jake interrupted, repeating the name of the newspaper on a note of inquiry. "Is that the guy—"

"Ayuh. He went to school with me. Also through most of the war."

Jake read silently now: "You can probably count on the fingers of one hand the number of times this newspaper has found fault with Alexander Girard in the past. But it is time now, and past time, that our voice should be raised, to ask: 'Mr. President, what are you waiting for?'

"The *Newport Telegraph* appeals to the President, to our Senators, and to our own Congressman Bill Bruyette to listen to the people of Vermont, speaking in behalf of those who are being kept from speaking. In the filthy jails of Mississippi and Alabama, of Louisiana and Georgia, representatives of those who have for too long been denied the rights of full citizenship are now further silenced and abused, left at the mercy of a people who, at their best and kindest, think of the Negro as only a domestic animal.

"Mr. President, Senators, Congressman, Honorables all—we who have been fortunate enough to breathe the bracing air of justice in Vermont, we descendants of the brave and the free, demand that you come to the aid of the sufferers in Dorothy, Alabama. We here rebel against the legalistic shilly-shallying that permits the southern states to be a part of the union when it comes to dams and air bases and Army camps and protective tariffs and all the other prerogatives wrung for them from our taxes and defended for them by the rest of us, yet suddenly untouchably sovereign political entities when it comes to the right of a Negro to vote, farm, work, or just walk down a street without stepping off the sidewalk. Alabama is either a part of this nation or it isn't: if it is, then what is done there is done partly in our name. Gentlemen, we will not have it, not a moment longer. As citizens of the United States of America, we will not permit liberty to be violated, in Alabama or anywhere else in this great republic."

"Did you get to 'this great republic'?" Girard asked. "Oddly enough, the Iowa evangelist uses the same phrase, 'this great republic threatened by the Red conspiracy'—'the hand of the Kremlin'—oh well, you know."

"The guy in Vermont writes better," Jake said coolly. "But so what? Is it Bruyette's putting this in the *Record* that's got you steamed up?"

"Of course not. He has to represent his constituency, doesn't he?" The President sat down in the chair behind his desk. "There's nothing the matter with Bruyette except that he has an exaggerated idea of the powers of the President—and the funny thing about it is, they're just about the same ideas I had until this year. Maybe you'd better start grooming Bill."

"Maybe there's only one way for men of good will to learn." Jake smiled, less with humor than with relief that the President had relaxed. "But I respectfully suggest, Mr. President, that you be in less·of a hurry to establish your succession. Maybe you're too eager to get started as a newspaper columnist."

"It certainly looks easier. All you have to do is write the truth. Like Kimball, for example—was it last week he raked me over the coals for 'teaching the Negro to seek justice in the streets'? Now there's a fine, indignant phrase."

"Oh, Gil," said Ruffing, suddenly reminded that he had several phone messages to call the columnist. But he asked instead, "What did you tell Rosenberg?"

"To call at ten o'clock tomorrow morning. I'd like to know more about those state police and still have time for the Army order in case Rosie's doubts are confirmed."

"You're not going to start with marshals then?"

The President sighed. "No. One of the lessons I've learned in my short unhappy tenure is that if we go in, we'd better go in big. I don't want any more adventures like the tentative little landing operation with which we began—remember? And Jake—I think Farland's advice, that we go in noisy, makes sense, too. So I think we'd better have a fireside-chat TV affair set up to coincide with it."

"You want me to find Farland?"

"Tomorrow will do," the President said slowly. "I'd like to write it myself, but I can use suggestions from him tomorrow. This time, Farland is to this operation as the military advisers were to the landing."

Jake said, "You're going too fast for me, Mr. President."

"Sorry. I'm lumping what represents a lot of thinking." Alec Girard tilted back in his chair and studied the ceiling. "This is sort of a note for my book on the Presidency, I guess. Ready, Boswell?"

"Shoot."

"It has to do with the hazards of advice, Jake. There are some men who should be used for information only—or, in the case of Farland, as a kind of technician."

"Is that what you meant—the comparison between the generals in the invasion and Farland in this?"

"Ayuh." This time the Vermontese was not a joke. "The power of the Presidency is like one of those fabulous weapons they fool around with on the testing grounds—enormous power that we hope will never be actually tried. You see? But it takes a strong personality to resist the temptation to try it out—all the way, with the throttle open. I think something like that was behind the military advice I got on the landing business—deliberately or not, an attempt to seduce me into full use of the powers of the Presidency." He hesitated. "You know, when it dawned on me that the top men of the military services included minds capable of believing of me that I would really prefer all-out war to losing face by having to back down—well, I got scared, Jake. I mean, these are the best we've produced, by a complex competitive system, yet they can think like that."

"That's what you meant when you said they were expert but not trustworthy." Ruffing got up, frowning, and began his characteristic pacing without realizing what he was doing. "But where does Farland come in? He was right when they were wrong."

"Yes, he was, but it could've been just because his neuroses lay on the right side of that one. We may have to end up doing exactly what he wanted us to in Alabama, but it strikes me now that his wanting us to do it right away and without trying anything else first is less an example of prescience than of the presence of a monkey on his own back. I think—if it doesn't sound too way out—that Farland's so ashamed of Alabama that he'd have liked to bring in the biggest weapons and smash it flat." The President blinked, a little shocked at what he had said, and added, "I don't mean consciously, of course."

Daddy turned out to be rather less than met the boyish eye, the light voice had said in the garden: Will Farland, just returned from proving that there was rather less than met the eye in an Alabama symbol of aristocratic rectitude. Jake looked at the man behind the desk with something close to awe and said thoughtfully, "You know, there's nothing on God's earth as thoroughly valuable as a good mind. No, I don't mean only that—Farland's got a good mind, too, but I think you're right, I think he is fighting Daddy, whether in the form of Fatherland Alabama or authority in epaulets. What I mean is, a good mind free to think."

"Come off it, Jake. Who ever is actually free to think?"

"Not many, Mr. President. Not many at all. That's why, if you don't mind, we won't relinquish your second term just yet."

Girard's laughter was genuinely gay. "With the Midwest and New England both firing at me already, how can I lose?" He shook his head. "Sorry, Jake, but I'm afraid that if I have to sign that order tomorrow, you'd better count on moving out of the west wing in less than four years."

Like a housewife who calculates, in the back of her mind, what can be rounded up from the refrigerator for dinner tonight, Ruffing added blocs of votes; he had to admit the rough figures bore out the President's prediction. Certainly the action would give Girard the Negro vote, but he already had that anyway. All he could do was lose votes that had been for him and gain no new ones. And yet, and yet . . . "Make a note for your book about the Presidency," Jake advised. "The best ones we've ever had or will have are the ones who are willing to risk the office for the sake of the job."

When Jake had left, to begin the elaborate arrangements that had to be set up just in case Rosenberg's telephone call in the morning was bad news, the President patrolled his luxurious prison restlessly, wondering what he had defined besides the isolation of his office. What had he said, really, except that power was a lonely business, a slow, sometimes painful, learning to distrust? He grinned suddenly, remembering Andy's saying on Election Night that nobody really knew how she felt except Mrs. Ferris, a thought that gave her no great pleasure. "Dear Pen Pal Kaslov," he began an imaginary letter while he settled down at his desk with his feet on the pulled-out bottom drawer and his writing pad on his lap. "Only you and I can know—" But when he lifted his pencil, what he actually began writing was, "Fellow Citizens, I come to you tonight to report on a legal and moral crisis that threatens all our people indirectly because it has threatened some of them directly."

Andy's phone call interrupted nothing but thought—Alec had stopped writing, but he was so deeply in the subject that he spoke to her almost absently, once she had said Elizabeth was asleep. "Oh, that's good to hear. Everything is so damned tense around here that the very word 'sleep' is welcome."

"Haven't you time for a nap, darling?"

"Not likely, I'm afraid. I feel strongly that I'd like to write this civil rights speech myself, and the time is a little tricky."

"Nevertheless, Alec, you simply must make time for some rest and recreation."

"Isn't that your old campaign speech? I seem to remember hearing it on the telephone in hotel rooms in Detroit, Chicago— Look, what time do you think she'll wake up?"

"Alec, why don't you skip coming out today? No, listen, darling, before you start overruling me. She'll probably sleep for hours, and she won't feel like playing— I mean, she's all dopey from the medication—"

"Andy. She's not—worse?"

"No, really. But she honestly won't know the difference, Alec. So why not be sensible? Take the little time you can spare and go swimming with Dan and then have a nap before you tackle your speech."

"If she's all that busy sleeping, you can come down here and come swimming with me—or I'll come get you. You're prettier than Dan."

"Well, I work harder at it."

You could keep on falling in love with her low laugh indefinitely, Alec decided. "Come on out and play, Andy."

"I'd love to, darling. But could I some other time, instead? I'm so awfully tired—I thought it would be nice if I could sleep while Elizabeth does."

She was a healthy young woman, but frail, wasn't that what that doctor had told him? And she was on duty twenty-four hours a day, every day. His conscience smote him a telling blow. "All right, I'll let you off this time."

"But you *will* hold the job open for me, sir?"

"Ayuh. You can have sick leave for this afternoon. Naturally, you'll have to file a doctor's certificate, though . . . Andy?"

"Yes, darling."

"Call me when you wake up?"

She promised, and he hung up and summoned Dan. "Listen," he began, "I'd like you to get hold of Dr. Rose—you know, the pediatrician." He stopped suddenly, wondering whether his new respect for the value of distrust wasn't getting the upper hand when it began to extend itself to Andy. If she said Elizabeth wasn't worse—"Never mind, the hell with it. How would you feel about a swim, Dan?"

"Sounds swell," Healy said.

"Let's go. And turn everything off except Andy and Jake, will you?"

On the way down to the White House pool, Alec asked, "You remember that guy who bought the *Newport Telegraph* after the war?"

"Sure. Great guy. He really went to bat for us in the House campaigns."

"Well, he just ran an editorial telling me to get the lead out or else."

"Is that so," Healy said indignantly. "Well, I always said he was a jerk."

In the Saturday night gaiety of Dorothy, Alabama, which appeared to depend heavily on bloodcurdling Rebel yells, the small group of press people who'd been in town long enough to have got rooms at its hotel—as opposed to Johnny-come-latelies who had had to find lodging in far-flung motels—sat sober as deacons over their warmish drinks. Somebody wondered aloud whether Dorothy-at-leisure really resembled a frontier town, or was it only that the inhabitants had seen too many TV versions of Saturday night in a frontier town? Gil said his learned friend had the wrong movie: it was actually a tea plantation with the natives working up to something and pretty soon the elephants would begin to stampede. The courtly Coordinated Press correspondent volunteered to rescue Ann if Tyrone Power failed to show. He drew a small, sour laugh.

In the street in front of the hotel, a car that seemed to be full of men drew up with a screech of tires across from the neon-decorated "Grill" from which a jukebox hillbilly had been crying about the sun going down ever since the sun had gone down. The driver got out, leaving the car door swinging open behind him, and crossed the street; and a prolonged mingled shout that sounded like incoherent welcome followed his entrance into Dorothy's bistro. Ann stirred her drink with a slivery wooden paddle and said idly, "The natives are certainly restless tonight."

As if on cue, a sudden enormous silence descended: the jukebox shut off in mid-wail, and in the shattering quiet the small click Ann produced as she laid the little stick down on the pseudo-marble tabletop actually caused her companions' heads to turn in her direction. "What the hell," somebody muttered, but his voice, too, was startling and it trailed away as though the speaker had scared himself. Like inhabitants of some minor Pompeii, they were frozen in the midst of motion: four sweating men and a woman who looked cool but wasn't. Just outside, just beyond the plate glass whose frailty was dawning on those within, the men in the car were equally still before their backdrop, an orange-pink neon celebration of the single word "Grill."

If somebody doesn't move soon, I'm going to scream, Ann thought with certainty and also with resignation. But then somebody did, and it was worse: the man sitting beside the empty driver's seat in the car turned his head slowly and looked at the group in the hotel. Even more slowly, and bewilderingly, with no rhyme or reason but with infinite menace, he brought a rifle up from the darkness of the car and pointed it out the window at the lighted front of the hotel, not aiming it but simply resting it on the edge of the car door. It was ludicrous. It was phony. It was appalling.

"I think," said the Coordinated Press very quietly, "we are supposed to get scared."

Ann, who would almost rather have died than be the first to say anything, let out a long, soft sigh.

"I *am* scared," said Gil. His heavy face, in total blacks and whites, looked like an overexposed photograph. "I haven't been so scared since the war." He thought it over. "Come to think of it, nobody's aimed a gun at me since the war."

The *St. Louis Messenger,* at least a dozen years Gil's junior, offered the useful observation that the rifle was not, after all, exactly aimed right now. "Listen to that engine—that's a valve tap," he added cheerfully. "These people treat their cars the way they treat their women—just run 'em till they conk out."

As a demonstration of insouciance, it was laudable, and as a sociological finding it was interesting and probably accurate, Ann told herself; but it had one most unfortunate aspect. Rat-*tat,* rat-*tat,* went the idling motor she would never have noticed—and from that moment on, it filled the night for her, tightening her nerves as though it had indeed been native drums beating menace in the hills.

Gil looked at the boy with grudging respect. "If there's anything I can't stand, it's an uppity Nieman Fellow."

Rat-*tat,* rat-*tat.* A door banged and the hotel proprietor, a bulky man in a long, flapping apron, lumbered onto the sidewalk and leaned into the car window beside the rifle as the men in the back seat bent forward to hear him. Rat-*tat,* rat-*tat* said the night. The hotel man gestured with his outward hand at the reporters on display, but he went on talking inside the car. Suddenly, across the street, the silence of the Grill exploded in a huge guffaw, from which a shouted question tagged like a wisp of smoke; then, just as suddenly, there was ominous silence again.

The hotel man stepped backward as the car door was pushed open at imminent peril to his ample belly. The tall young man who slid out, gun first, was wearing a handsome cowboy hat with its wide brim nursed into a faint curl on each side. It took time and trouble to make the brim do that, Ann thought irrelevantly as the man approached the plate glass window with a slow, loping walk that she knew she recognized from somewhere, if she could only think something, anything, besides rat-*tat,* rat-*tat.* The innkeeper, backing up before the one-man invasion, was still talking and waving his arms; but laughter from the others, now leaning out of the car to watch the show, drowned out his voice.

The tall young man swept the aproned figure aside with a careless sidearm gesture that seemed to have no force behind it, yet the innkeeper staggered and danced clumsily for a few steps before it was certain that he would keep his feet. From the open car window came a spattering of applause. The man with the gun stopped directly in front of the plate glass behind which the press sat like something for sale. He peered in, scanning them lazily until his look found Ann's.

Ann stared at the long, bony face and knew then that it was Will Farland she had recognized in the walk, and recognized Will again in the confident grin. The man stepped back a single pace, swept his romantic hat off with an extravagance that added all-but-visible plumes to it, and offered her a deep, elaborate bow—a mocking, stagy gesture so full of insolence, assertive of opportunity, of ownership of all the time in the world and nothing to stop the ominous cavalier, that the smoky air above the round table seemed to fill with menace like a cloud with rain.

Oh *shit*, Gil Kimball said loudly in his mind with all the force of his desire not to move. He was a man with a wife and three, he announced grimly in the deep reaches of his mind, and he was goddam well not going to get himself plugged in the prime of his life in this hellhole, miles away from Betty, who would make a lousy widow. And my God, what if she lost the house; had he ever got around to putting it in both their names? Let the wild colonial boy who'd come out of Harvard all Nieman-fattened rise up and redeem the insult to the honor of the press, or of Ann Taswell, or of both; not me, no thanks, said the determinedly erstwhile Studs Lonigan Kimball who had left Chicago a long time ago to become paterfamilias and taxpayer, anagram king of metropolitan Washington. Listen, I'm listed in *Who's Who in America* as a professional coward, he was saying behind a roaring noise in his ears when the state police car slid around the corner. The whipping light on its roof picked out Kimball of the Establishment, marching up to a wall of non-bullet-proof glass on the other side of which a rifle pointed at his suddenly churning intestines.

When the mighty Kimball came back from the can, where he had spent rather a long interval, the swirly plastic drape over the front window of the hostelry had been lowered and the only noise to be heard outside was the jukebox singer, who had rediscovered his sundown complaint. The hero sank into his chair and soothed his gut with bourbon, an unorthodox medication that threatened not to work at first but eventually anesthetized all the agitated coils of Kimball. Meanwhile his companions briefed him: the car's driver, it seemed, had emerged from the Grill to dicker in friendly fashion with the state trooper. "We-uns jest go'n out fo a little huntin," he had shouted, his genial voice audible to the stunned fourth estate. "Now, that's all right, ain't it, Cap'n?"

"Spare me the dialect," Gil told the Coordinated Press. "I get the picture. So they picked up a jug and—"

"And another two carfuls of hunters. They came tumbling out of the Grill, all armed and provisioned, and rode off with a farewell wave to the law. A-hunting they would go."

"But not us, this time—apparently we're not in season," the Nieman Fellow observed. "It maketh me to wonder, though—who is?"

Gil said, "I have a feeling the game laws on newspaper types are recognized only by the state cops, and they're few and far between."

"I don't think the sheriff is going to be much interested in protecting me," Ann told them thoughtfully. "I was over there asking embarrassing questions —about that note I got," she said to Gil. "Maybe that—er, infantryman— was one of the voyeurs whose fun I spoiled." She shook her head at the others' questions. "It's an exclusive. You can read it in the *WashTrib*." She paused. "Listen, Gil, will it make you squirm if I say you were something marvelous?"

"Yup. I nearly died of embarrassment when they pinned the *Croix de Guerre* on me, too."

"Really." Her cameo face flushed with the embarrassment she attributed to him. "I do most awfully thank you."

"It was nothing Hemingway wouldn't have done, my dear." Gil reached out a hairy arm and patted her. "Don't thank me. If you want to be real nice, just witness my will."

"Well, at least I can buy you a drink." She got up gratefully, collected his glass, and went to refill it.

"As for the rest of you slackers—" Gil began.

" 'Slackers'?" the youngster interrupted. "What war did you say you were in, Pa Kimball?"

"My last one," Gil said pointedly. "Everybody got that? You can decide for yourself who's next, but I intend to collect this drink and go write a novel. Something stark, maybe with a bullfight, even."

But after he and Ann had tried phoning Will and Marian, respectively, twice more before they gave up for the night and parted at their sagging doors in the long upstairs hall, Gil decided he wasn't old enough to be Papa quite yet. Whistling "My Wild Colonial Boy" but keeping it soft in deference to the lady next door, he stood before the rather listless fan long enough to dry the sweat and then put his pajama pants on in deference to possible night riders. He locked the door and climbed into the dubious bed, where he concentrated on persuading himself it was not Ann he heard crying on the other side of the thin wall.

When he had that trick mastered, he got to work on persuading himself that it wasn't shameful for a man to be afraid, either. He fell asleep in the process of constructing a small, hopeful drama in which Bert and Joe listened, respectfully, to his carefully modest account of how their Pop had walked right up to this guy—make him a known killer?—pointing a rifle— make it a machine gun? . . .

In Washington Saturday night was gayer, or appeared to be. Will Farland, drinking with businesslike devotion at the Harringtons', examined the party, which was noisy and full of bare arms and almost bare bosoms and yet offered no place where a man could be solaced. By the exercise of a little ingenious research, Will had rendered himself able to explain, with truth, that Marian was covering summer art shows at Rehoboth Beach; since he'd just got back from New York he'd been unable to go with her. But explanation wasn't necessary after the first few moments at the Harringtons'—it never was; one just came and drank and either went away or stayed and sooner or later made a fool of himself. Will went on drinking dumbly, indifferent to which way it ended. It was better than going home to that empty house.

The party at Rehoboth had the advantage that it was genuinely gay—sand crunched under sandaled feet, music lost out happily in its hopeless competition with chatter and certainly with the pound and hiss of the surf; and even if, inevitably, some fool came and joined you, you could stand on the wooden balcony that looked out over the sea and watch the waves obey the moon.

"Well, it has left a certain painterly tendency that shows in the sculpture," Marian said to the slacks and polo shirt that had found her again; she threw out the remark like a keeper throwing a fish to a seal, and the sleek man responded similarly, with happy barks. After the second drink, she began to look at him, and at all the other pretty people, and after the third drink, she danced the twist with a golden brown, boneless youth who spent his days attempting to wrest immortal art from intricate convolutions of metal. The sea wind frolicked across her bare shoulders and through her salt-smelling hair, and she was light and pretty and careless. She ran barefoot across the sand while others followed, warning of sand fleas and other menaces, and got to wiggle her toes in the last of a wave just arrived from Portugal, before they made her come back because it wasn't allowed. It was not as lovely as dancing in the rain with the graceful Andrea and her dark-eyed sculptor friend—but that was long ago, and too much that wasn't good had happened in between. Marian fell asleep in the car on the way back to Washington—to the annoyance of Phil Colby, who wanted to ask her whether she'd heard that Morisot had started fooling with wire sculpture.

Dr. Snowden, who had not had a very gay Saturday night and didn't expect it to improve, lay stiffly on the narrow, professionally smooth bed and composed himself for a brief sleep that would be interrupted for a report on the attempt to bolster artificially the Girard child's dangerously falling blood pressure. If she went into shock, it would be as good as all over—and before he had barely begun the real fight. Because it was impossible not to rage and yet he would be no good without rest, he focused his anger on this specific frustration—the probability of losing this child without making progress on behalf of the other children. He was accustomed to defeat, but this was the hardest kind.

On the second floor of the White House, Alec Girard, who had not the benefit of Dr. Snowden's experience with defeat, sipped his bouillon without tasting it and stared unseeing at the sideboard that had once belonged to Daniel Webster. Who had never become President— "Sometimes I wonder where Ralph Ferris is now," he said suddenly. "Wherever it is, I envy him."

Jake Ruffing made a small sound of disapproval in his throat but didn't stop reading the yellow pages spread out on the polished surface of the pedestal table. There was nothing stingy about Girard, he thought happily— when he decided to speak up, he did it with bells on.

"Because justice is slow, it has its victims," the pointy penciled scrawl said. "Those, both Negro and white, who have suffered at the hands of the brutal and ignorant were part of a necessary process: in a country of law, it is not enough that the presence of injustice be charged, it must be demonstrated. A middle-aged Negro college professor walked through a hostile crowd to present himself formally at the county courthouse in Dorothy, Alabama, in circumstances that made it clear beyond all reasonable doubt that the color of his skin was the only reason he was being denied entrance; a white lawyer in Allentown, Mississippi, in the face of threats and even after attempts on the lives of his wife and children, persisted in appealing to his fellow citizens on behalf of law and conscience; a Negro minister with a true belief in the power of love led his unarmed, unresisting flock into a hysterical mob of screaming whites in a Georgia town to show us all clearly and unforgettably on which side the violence lay and exactly how much less than supreme were the whites who claimed supremacy; in Louisiana, a white editor printed, verbatim, the local judge's unjudicial comments during the trial of a Negro—an exercise of conscientious, rudimentary journalism that cost him his life at the hands of an unknown gunman in the night. These are only a few of the more prominent and publicized of the thousands of acts of individual heroism that had to be recorded before this administration, representing all the citizens of the United States, gained the right to question the activities of state authorities.

"In three of the states I have mentioned, representatives of the United States Department of Justice approached state and local officials with the gathered evidence of infraction of the guarantees provided by the Fourteenth and Fifteenth Amendments to the Constitution. Proceeding on the assumption that elected officials were responsible and honorable men, the representatives of the federal government demanded correction of inequities and reform of biased and unjust institutions, preferring to gain agreement without going into the courts if possible. As happens in neighborhood conflicts among ordinary citizens, quite often the problems were solved and the injustices corrected without resort to law. Where this did not occur, however, the Department of Justice took steps to secure through the courts the rights that state and local officials could not or would not agree to guarantee for Negroes in their jurisdiction.

"Unfortunately, in Alabama the Department of Justice and, subsequently, members of the White House staff, sent as my representatives in a final attempt to uncover reasonable grounds for agreement, were all unsuccessful on the whole, though they did obtain hopeful solutions of problems in some localities. But in Dorothy County particularly, the situation has continued to worsen. As reports continued of uncontrolled mob activity and of unequal application of the law by law enforcement authorities themselves, I placed a telephone call to the governor of the state, in the course of which I demanded that Negro citizens of the United States be permitted to proceed on their peaceful business in and through the state without harassment. The governor assured me that, though there were individual difficulties, he had the situation well in hand; he also said that he was sending enough detachments of the state police to Dorothy County to insure maintenance of law and order there. We agreed that if this effort should be unavailing, the governor's only recourse would be to ask for assistance from Washington in protecting citizens of Dorothy and its current visitors from the lawless activities of the violent and deluded.

"It is as a result of this conversation that I have decided to order troops of the 3rd Army to Dorothy, Alabama, where state and local resources have proved insufficient to secure protection for some citizens. The officers in command of the airborne units that will be dispatched to Dorothy will have orders to seek cooperation in restoring calm but if they do not obtain it promptly they are to employ whatever degree of force is necessary; I expect these orders to be carried out without delay and with military thoroughness. When negotiation fails, force must be used—this is a hard truth, but nevertheless a fact of life.

"To those citizens of the state of Alabama whose wishes and ideals may not have been adequately represented by their elected officials, I offer my sympathy. To the soldiers who will soon be on their way to Dorothy, I say this: as your commander in chief, it is always my aim, and it always has been, to refrain from sending you into action at all, anywhere, so long as possible. But if you must bear arms, it can be in no cause more just and righteous than this one. Nor, so long as you serve in the military forces of this country, will you ever be more definitely engaged in defending the United States than when you are protecting the victims of persecution in Alabama."

Ruffing stood the sheets of paper on end on the table and shuffled them into a neat pile between his hands. Then he laid the stack down with exquisite care, squaring its edge with the edge of the table, and asked genially, "What other little chores did you take care of this afternoon, Mr. Lincoln?"

"You think it's all right?" the President asked. He dug in his trouser pocket and produced another sheet of the yellow paper, folded many times. "Here's another bit I thought of after I finished. Maybe Farland can work it in tomorrow."

Jake unfolded the paper. "It is not difficult," the insert began, "for the rest of the country to recognize the South's special problems in regard to the Negro: we know that the weight of tradition, even of immoral tradition, is very great and that whatever we learn in childhood has a powerful hold, even when maturity reveals to us that it was wrong. Precisely because we have understood that a process of education was needed in those areas where local custom and local law denied the Negro the rights of full citizenship, we have asked the American Negro to be patient a little more, for yet a little longer. By and large, the Negro has deferred to this difficult request; he has restrained his hotheads and generally conducted himself as a responsible citizen. The same, unfortunately, cannot be said for some southern white leaders. Although the patience of the Negro, and of the rest of us who understand that his cause is ours, has been rewarded with progress in much of the South, in part of Alabama, and certainly in Dorothy County, our patience was only providing opportunity for more and more fanatic opposition. Now it is time, therefore, to bring patience to an end, and to remind those who will not revise their regional traditions that the United States has national traditions older and stronger than the segregation laws and the vicious customs that can be honored by nothing but time, if that. I say to all good citizens of all the states of the union that our abiding tradition as a nation was set forth as long ago as 1776: 'We hold these truths to be self-evident; that all men are created equal; that they are endowed by their Creator with certain unalienable Rights; that among these are Life, Liberty and the pursuit of Happiness.' We can allow no more time for the slow to learn these truths."

Jake smoothed out the creases in the paper carefully and laid it on top of the other manuscript pages. "Let me get it all typed up so you can see what it looks like. Then you can move chunks of it around if you like. Although I'd be against tampering with that original ending—the bit about the soldiers defending the U.S. by going to Alabama."

"You haven't said what you think," the President noted.

"Good Lord, is it really necessary?" Jake stared at him in surprise, and then his gaze softened as he saw the weariness in the other man's face. "It's obvious that it's going to make enemies, and also history—and if it doesn't make you President again, it'll be because the country doesn't deserve you. But you surely must know all that. What I was thinking, though—I mean, as me, Jake Ruffing, boy campaign manager—was how in hell the notion ever got around that you were a cold personality."

Girard grinned. "You know, only two things in the campaign really got Andy's goat. One was Mrs. Ferris's crack about the cost of her clothes, which irked her. But the other one, about her reserved and frosty husband, really made her livid."

"Hmm. Next time, we're going to have to get you across as a man of throbbing passion, somehow. After this, it shouldn't be hard."

"You think it'll really do?"

Ruffing smiled—there was no end, apparently, to the anxieties of authorship. "I think it'll do, Mr. President. Maybe we ought to have Farland go to work on it with his common-man touch—as usual, some of it is a little lofty. But it's a damn lofty occasion, so that's mostly all right. I assume, that is, that you mean to come out and tag segregation as immoral, in just those words."

"I mean 'immoral.' "

"Okay, then." Jake stowed the papers carefully in a large brown envelope. "I don't want to get the original manuscript of the second Emancipation Proclamation messed up," he said, wrestling the envelope closed. "I get all thumbs when I feel history breathing down my neck."

The President said dryly, "It doesn't make me feel exactly comfy either."

"No. I know." Jake surveyed the exhausted slump of the tall figure. "How about hitting the hay, Mr. President? If you do have to show up on television tomorrow, we don't want you to look as though you're nursing a hangover."

Girard obeyed, getting up slowly. "I don't know that I'd trust a President who preserved his boyish good looks too well while in office, though." He stood uncertainly near the dining-room door while Jake put the dishes through the serving hatch. "A look of Lincolnesque weariness—" He dropped the light tone abruptly then. "I have more than weariness in common with Lincoln, Jake."

"Yes, I know." He's afraid, Jake thought: he's not afraid to take on the wicked and the violent in the name of justice and law, he's not afraid to risk his hold on the highest office in the land—the office he wasn't afraid to get in there and fight for when all the experts told him he didn't have a chance. And he's not even any more afraid than anybody with a mind ought to be of the officer with the special locked case who's always somewhere around, just in case the word comes that could require Alec Girard to be responsible for the deaths of millions. But he's afraid to walk down the hall and go to bed in his silent house. "Want me to keep you company while you get ready for bed?"

"You know about Elizabeth's—condition." It was not a question, but a deduction.

"Yes, I know." Jake hesitated. "Bruyette knows, too. We discussed what to do about it."

"And?"

"We decided that you and Andy know where we live, if you want us for anything besides our prayers."

"Thank you," the President said simply. He strolled down the long hall to his solitary bedroom, still reluctantly, but Jake's company did somehow help to make it more bearable. They talked desultorily while he readied himself for bed as Jake sat in an armchair, still clutching the envelope that held the speech.

"Jake, I just remembered." Alec rinsed his toothbrush and put it away. "Andy ran into something at the hospital I'd like you to look into." He padded back into the bedroom, barefoot and pajamaed, with his thick hair rumpled. "Can't we get some kind of compassionate leave arrangement for the government employees?" He sat on the edge of the bed to tell Ruffing about the father of Elizabeth's "colleague." "There ought to be some way that the father doesn't have to keep going to work every day when a thing like this strikes the family. I wonder how much good he is at his office anyway, sitting there worrying about his family."

Oh, I don't know, Jake thought, maybe he's managing to write an ode to the rights of man, work out a viable agreement with the Russians, analyze the responsible uses and limits of power, and just manage on the side to consider the plight of an anonymous civil servant who's running out of annual leave. "Let me talk to the government employees' union people. They may have a proposal hanging around already." Of course, Jake told himself, he'd probably have to be Alec Girard to cope with all that—and he'd probably look as though a steamroller had run over him by the end of the day, too. "I'll check into it," he said aloud, hoping to lull that active mind to rest with the promise. Briefly and without pleasure, Jake wondered what Andy was looking like today. "Come on, Senator, let's adjourn for today," he said softly.

The mechanism worked—the instant relaxation that had made possible a mankilling campaign pace was triggered off by the old, almost-forgotten words in the familiar voice. Alec Girard lay back in the bed and closed his eyes. "Jake."

Ruffing paused on his way to the door. "Yes."

"Please thank Bonnie for taking care of our baby for us."

Safe from sight, Jake let the tears come to his eyes. "I will, but Andy already has."

The strained face on the pillow was softened by a smile. "Of course. She would have."

"It isn't necessary, anyway. He's a pleasure and a delight." And someday, please God, he'll be something to you, too, besides a reminder of the unbearable, Jake thought; but it was impossible to offer this man the thought of one child as a palliative for the death of another. It was impossible to offer him anything, Jake decided, even overt sympathy. So he just said goodnight, and left.

"The President has retired," he told the man on duty outside.

"Yes sir. Good night, Mr. Ruffing." The man hesitated. "Excuse me, sir. Is there any more news about—"

"No," Jake interrupted him, and then added the words that could not have been said to Alec Girard. "I'm sorry." Outside its center, grief could be shared. Jake went away pondering this, carrying his archives.

Fifty-four

In Washington's hot, unstirring Sunday morning, coffee was brewing in the cavernous kitchen of the White House and in the west wing's oval office, a pair of Secret Service agents prowled with a Geiger counter, checking for the silent, subtle weapon that could murder the President slowly. Upstairs in the Mansion, another agent carried a piece of special film into the oval sitting room, so that if any of the new dangers that Louis XVI had never had to fear lurked behind the golden graces, their presence could be detected when the plate was "developed." Since only the briefest exposure was required, the man flitted in and out of rooms on his scheduled course, disturbing nothing, least of all Alec Girard's heavy, exhausted slumber.

In the hospital home of the children of death, on the ward where it was never early, Dr. Rose pulled the delicate fabric of Elizabeth's nightgown down over the blotched little thighs and read from Dr. Snowden's face instead of from the blood pressure apparatus how short was the column of mercury. The third doctor, who had been brought in like a relief pitcher in the eighth inning of a lost game, nodded at the nurse who'd called them to read the evidence. She let the air come back into the rubber bulb and laid it down, but she left the bracelet of cloth on the frail upper arm. She waited until Dr. Snowden had straightened, expressionless, and then she moved in and began to smooth the meticulous fold of the white sheet that showed up so terribly the bluish tinge of the child's skin.

The pediatrician who, watched by the happy parents, had once taken into his hands the body of a perfect female infant, aged one day, was less capable of stoicism: Dr. Rose's eyes were anguished as he glanced at the connecting door. "Would you like me to—speak to her?"

Dr. Snowden moved his shoulders in the shadow of a shrug that said he would just as soon be spared if he honorably could be. He left while the third doctor was giving orders to continue the intravenous—because it was against the religion of all of them to give up—and Dr. Rose was deciding to let Andrea Girard, who had finally gone to sleep only a few hours ago, go on sleeping for a little longer. Dr. Snowden went down the hall without speaking to anyone, found a phone in an empty office, and woke up his wife. "I won't be home," he said with cruel abruptness. "She's going." His wife's sleepy voice asked a brief question and he answered, "I don't know exactly what. We've got all the time in the world for the pathologists to figure it out, haven't we?" His wife, who understood that he needed to be silent, let him hang up without farewell.

Will Farland's waking was far less self-controlled. After a moment of gut-quivering unbelief when he opened his eyes to the sight, a few inches away, of a woman's breast, he discovered that the reason it was the wrong size, shape, and hue was that it belonged to the red-haired Jill, lying beside him in a room strewn with her underclothes. Though his heart still knocked with the first instant's panic that he had lost his sanity, had somehow gone from wishing to hallucinating, he figured out readily now the dimensions of his small, manageable problem and decided this was the unfunniest joke he had ever encountered. He slid carefully out of the bed, making a face at the taste in his mouth, and put on yesterday's clothes with haste and indifference, paying no attention to the sleeping girl but noticing, with a ridiculous sense of outrage, that she apparently owned a green girdle. For no reason that he could fathom, he was furious at the idea that anybody would try to pass him off as allied, however fleetingly and however drunkenly, with a woman who wore a green girdle. If he hadn't been in sore need of the coffee he was drinking downstairs a moment later, he would have thrown the cup in John Harrington's sleepy face.

"Well, she passed out and we had to put her somewhere," Harrington protested, "and you'd helped yourself to a double bed. I sure didn't think you'd mind, anyway."

Will ordered him to commit an unnatural and in fact physiologically impossible act. Then he said he supposed he should have known what to expect if he spent the night in Gomorrah. "But you didn't have to undress her."

Harrington giggled. "I know. We couldn't resist. Eleanor wanted to sit up in the chair, just so she could see your face when you woke up. But I thought you might—er—avail yourself of opportunity when you rose—"

"For Christ's sake. I thought I was making a joke about Gomorrah." Will helped himself to a cinnamon roll. "Tell me something, John. Has it ever occurred to you that—how shall I put it?—a woman is more than a cunt?"

"Frankly, no. At least not since I was fourteen."

In spite of his anger, Will decided his host deserved a straight man. "What happened then?"

"Oh, my favorite ethereal princess resulted in a wet dream, just like all the others."

Will laughed, his annoyance leaking away: there was simply nothing to be done about Harrington, as he had tried to tell Marian. At the thought of her, his face froze in a look of horror that drew an inquiry from his host. "Nothing. I just thought . . . what if Marian had decided to drop in, late last night?" He ground his teeth. "I think it might very well have been borne in on you that this joke was as unfunny as I said."

"Take it easy, Will. You know that's not likely—we're hardly your beautiful Puritan's favorite people. Besides, I'd have sworn on a stack of Bibles that you weren't here. Jesus, I've been your friend for twenty years. You think I'd let you down?"

Will choked on his third bun and washed it down hastily with more coffee, vowing never to talk to John again without an interpreter.

Now that Harrington had thought it over, he was wounded. "Anyway, what are you so sore about? What's so awful about having a willing redhead handed to you, all peeled? Natural redhead, too, I'm sure you noticed.

You know, I suspect you of protesting too much." He leered. "Are you certain you remember everything you did, pal? You were awful, awful drunk, old buddy."

"I know. And that's how I know. Old buddy. Sober, I'm only rationally monogamous. But drunk, I'm a fanatic." A glimmering of last night's desperation lighted a far corner of his mind; he remembered the sinking certainty that there was only one place he could lay his hurts, and it would never be anywhere in this house. "Look, I've got to go to work today, so I'd better shove off." Suddenly he wanted very much to be clean, and it occurred to him fleetingly that this might be what Marian felt like at the Harringtons' all the time. "Thanks for a lovely party, and so forth. By 'so forth,' " he added quickly, "I mean breakfast."

Will heard the phone ringing as he pulled into his driveway. It went on ringing while he wrestled with the lock and shoved the door open, kicking aside the mail that had accumulated like snow under the slot in the front door. He got halfway through the dining room on a run before the phone stopped. He cursed with shocking loudness in the empty house and went back and closed the door. Then he climbed the stairs quickly, shedding his clothes on the floor of the bedroom because of his passionate yearning for the comfort of the shower. *Jill,* for God's sake, he said to himself indignantly, glancing over his naked shoulder at the smooth, unslept-in double bed. He found clean underwear and carried it off to the bathroom, suddenly furious again.

It was nearly ten o'clock as Will's air of outraged maidenly virtue was being sluiced from his hide. Marian, for no sensible reason, had wakened at about nine-thirty and stumbled out to Ann's kitchen, pausing on her way to take the Sunday newspaper in from the doormat. She flapped the heavy paper onto the couch and made a pot of coffee, conscientiously letting it perk for ten minutes, during which time she mostly stood around yawning except for a brief, vague hunt for something to eat for breakfast; the hunt was unsuccessful because she wasn't really hungry, so she turned off the coffee and left it to settle. She plodded barefoot back into the living room and picked up the *Tribune* to see whether Ann had a byline—but it was "Rosa Little" that, though it was not prominently displayed, nevertheless jumped out of the page and smacked her between the eyes. Marian fell on the couch as though she had been blown there by an explosion and read the words through twice before she succeeded in taking them in. And even then, she didn't notice that it was a follow-up story.

The first thought she had was for the children, who would surely be frightened to death, since she was. She ran into the bedroom and dialed the number of Rosa's apartment while the pulse beat in her temple with the thudding importance of the pumps fighting for a sinking ship. The whirring sound went on and on, and she began counting compulsively—eight, nine, ten, eleven; Rosa's was a small apartment, and from any point in it you could get to the phone before it rang eleven, no twelve, times. She hung up and dialed again, just in case her clumsiness was at fault; but when she heard herself counting hypnotically again, she hung up on "ten." *Think,* she commanded the new, competent Marian, the one who was no clinging vine. She got a cup of the fresh coffee to help in the process and then left it to grow cold while she found and dragged out the phone book—why, oh why, did Ann have everything so put *away?*—and hunted down Rosa's brother-in-law Claude among the Joneses. She managed to consume half the coffee while she waited, listening to some more of those steady birrs like a dentist's drill; then she slammed the phone down in despair and went back for more coffee. Pacing the living room with it, she saw the newspaper again and it dawned on her how long ago what she had just read must have been written. She turned on the television set and then ran out to the bedroom again and switched the radio on, too; she shuttled between them, twisting dials, but there was no news on either. She collected clothes and began to dress hastily, but stopped midway to look up the airport number—and then, in the middle of that, to find her purse and see whether she had enough money to fly to Alabama. She didn't think she had, and she didn't know whether they let you write checks for airplane tickets . . . Suddenly, she dropped her purse and collapsed in tears, sobbing like a child because they would kill Rosa unless she could do something and there was so little she knew how to do.

It occurred to her then that Will could do a great deal and she went at once and dialed the number of her own house, indifferent to anything but her purpose. When it got to twelve rings and there was no answer, she held out for fifteen, and then for eighteen; at twenty, she concluded bitterly that Will could be just about anywhere. In the living room, the television announcer was reciting the news; but Marian was still in the bedroom, trying Gloria again. This time, just as she was about to give up, the phone was answered by a fuzzy, child's voice that was difficult to hear. Marian summoned all her control and patience and managed to elicit from the little girl, who seemed anxious to get away, that she lived next door and that Miz Jones had gone to church. There was no point in attempting any message, so Marian hung up as gently as she had spoken and went back to the living room just before the news began on the bedroom radio.

They're all at church, that's all, she told herself, getting out crackers and cheese because too much coffee on an empty stomach wasn't good for you. She began to cry again, standing in the middle of the kitchen and swiping at tears with crumbs in them, because the reason she knew it wasn't good for you was that Rosa had said so: Rosa, who held lining the stomach to be second in importance only to retaining the correct thickness of the blood, and who might never offer any more vital information. Marian brushed a cracker crumb from her slip and remembered then that she was going to get dressed to go to Alabama.

"Every now and then, you get it," Kenneth Youngblood said to her from the television screen, stopping her in her tracks. "This sense of a main historic outline among all the things shaping up around you every day."

The television commentator, whose name Marian couldn't remember (but she remembered that Will considered him no fool), said he hadn't thought the Senator was among those who saw the trouble in Alabama as more than just—well, troublesome.

"I don't, of course," Youngblood agreed. "Not in itself. But it's part of a problem I think we'd better look into—one that goes beyond the Negroes, you see, to the question of our national mechanism for response." It was impossible not to listen earnestly and with belief to that thoughtful voice or not to trust the white-haired man whose every wrinkle said it had been earned with honor. Marian sat down in a chair with her coffee cup held steadily now and her bare legs crossed at the ankles like a lady, her eyes on the quiet face of order and reasonable behavior, her hysterical flitting stopped by the sound of an authoritative male voice that might be going to say, any moment, that Rosa was all right.

But the voice was discoursing on something quite unrelated: the discussion had been taped much earlier, before "unrest" became actual bloodshed, before newspaper words meant Rosa. "No, I'm not really ready to think in terms of a constitutional amendment yet." Youngblood understood as well as his interviewer did that a pronouncement on the subject from one of the Senate's chief figures would have a wide reach. "What I'd like to see is a study of means to open this channel of communication, either through an amendment or by some smaller changes. At this point, though, all I can say is that this is what's happening—that a path is being trodden, so to speak, and that it would make sense to build a road where the people are thus indicating that they need one."

"Why won't it do—I gather you don't think it will—to let nature take its course, just let it go on as it is?"

"Because, at the moment, all that stands between us and an undesirable and possibly permanent distortion of our structure of government is Alexander Girard. We're lucky enough now to have a man in the White House who's intelligent enough to perceive what's happening and honorable enough not to take advantage of it, but . . ." The Senator shook his head. "A government that depends for its health on the virtues of one man is in precarious condition. Probably the first requirement of sturdy government should be that it can't be misused by the weak or ill-intentioned."

"We haven't much time left, Senator. If you can sum up for us just what it is about this trend that is disturbing you, that you want people to think about—" The commentator's small, self-conscious laugh recognized the impertinence of his request. "Let's see if I can begin it for you: you feel that because the Constitution now fails to provide a means of redress for grievances when the citizen is up against state and local governments, as the Negro is in the South—"

"There are provisions in the Constitution," Youngblood objected gently. "The trouble is, they're not viable in practical terms. The state officials have all the time in the world to drag their feet in the courts, but the original litigant doesn't—he has to earn a living, and sometimes he has to get out of the state just in order to protect himself and his family."

"So this leaves him no place to go with his protest except to the streets, is that your point, sir?"

"Yes, except that what has been obscured is that when he goes to the streets he actually goes to the President. The White House is the central point of appeal for all those without political power in their communities, and for the disfranchised and disadvantaged. Which leaves the President in the uncomfortable position of having rather more asked of him than he can deliver without taking at least mild liberties with the spirit, if not also the letter, of the Constitution."

"It may be uncomfortable if he's Alec Girard," the commentator said, grinning. "I can think of some politicians who'd like nothing better than to be the people's directly indispensable man, with nothing in between."

The Senator's reply was sober. "Yes, so can I—and let's not forget how many well-intentioned people who don't realize the implications of that role are begging the President to assume it. If that's what the country wants, though—a totally centralized government leading directly to the executive—well, then, I suppose they'll have it. But not, if I can help it, without knowing what they're doing, and the dangers in it. Which includes, possibly, the election of almost anyone who talks soothingly and doesn't bother the people with specific problems. A demagogue, in short. Maybe even a nice, intelligent demagogue—but a demagogue anyway."

Paradoxically, Marian Farland, a natural-born patsy for a nice, intelligent demagogue, had been making one of Kenneth Youngblood while he warned against the possibility. For, though the world of political men may not have been the one in which she truly belonged, it was the one in which she had lived and the world of self-sufficient women was one in which she had only visited briefly. Strangely, then, the voice of Senator Youngblood talking about "the structure of federalism" soothed and comforted her, and therefore bolstered her shaken confidence.

It was to be hoped that the Sunday morning television viewers were being shaken rather than soothed—but while they were still listening to the warning against drifting into totalitarianism, the Senator who had issued it was being shown into the Treaty Room on the second floor of the White House along with Secretary of State Harold Hoffman, to discuss the promising developments in the gingerly attempt to work out an agreement with the Soviet Union. The strain was beginning to tell on the President, Youngblood observed, as he sat at the carved table at which Girard seemed unable to settle down permanently.

The President caught the Rhode Island Senator's covert inspection of him. "I'm a little jumpy, gentlemen. I hope you'll forgive me. I set this meeting for this time because I assumed I'd be through by then with the report on Alabama I've been waiting for. Rosenberg was supposed to call at ten, and I'm afraid I'm a little upset by the delay."

"I don't blame you, Mr. President," Youngblood said quickly. "Have they tried calling from here?"

"We're trying now. I wanted to give Rosenberg enough time, but it seems—"

"Yes, it does."

The President glanced at Youngblood sharply, acutely measuring the older man's concern. "Well, we'll know soon," he said. "It may be just one of those little snafus that try men's souls." With a small effort, he composed himself for attention to Hoffman. "Now. I've got Farland coming up a little later to report on his New York talks in detail, but we already know they went well. What would you think about letting the Secretary-General know—Oh, Dan. Rosie got through?"

"Mr. President," said the hoarse voice in the doorway. "It's . . . it's Mrs. Girard."

"She wants. . . ?"

"Come right away, yes."

The President said to his visitors, sounding like a tape recording of his own voice played too fast, "Excuse me, please. Dan will take care of you." Then he was gone, and Healy after him. Senator Youngblood and Secretary Hoffman went on sitting, shaken with surprise, in the ornate chairs with heart-shaped backs; Dan Healy did not return until after the sirens had begun outside, and then he was openly crying.

By that time, Andy was asking the operator for a number in Kingsley, Vermont, in a thick voice that sounded drugged, although her swollen face looked more like a sufferer with a heavy cold. Outside, in the stifling heat, Luke Messenger sweated in a flannel shirt that had been comfortable in the early-morning chill of the mountains from which the park police had abstracted him—in a helicopter, to the everlasting delight of his sons, both of whom promptly vowed to become Forest Rangers. "You grab one picture," he said heavily to an early-bird TV reporter who had been at home half a mile from the hospital when his office called, "one picture, and so help me God, I guarantee you that you get not so much as a mimeographed handout from the White House until the next administration takes over. I mean it, and if you make the mistake of thinking I don't, I'll hound you till the day you die."

In his "den," the managing editor of the *Washington Tribune* breathed a long sigh of relief when Halloran came on the phone. "Marty, he just left for the hospital. Behind sirens." He hung up and dialed another number, where he gave a terse order and then added quietly, "You better lock up the obit, too, of course." Not that it could take very long, he thought bitterly: he had written Elizabeth Girard's obituary himself; it consisted of few words, and half of them were about her parents and grandparents. He went in search of his wife and found her sitting outside with the newspaper's Sunday book review section in her lap; she was wondering, not very energetically, whether she should get up and make some fresh coffee. The moment he appeared, she knew what had happened; but she let him, because he needed the time, put his arm around her plump shoulders and begin, "Honey, there's some pretty lousy news . . ."

Marian left the commentator thanking Senator Kenneth Youngblood of Rhode Island, Chairman of the Senate Foreign Relations Committee and majority something-or-other, and went to finish getting dressed because that was the first thing to do before going on to do something useful and competent, first about Rosa's children and then about Rosa. She did her hair with assurance, still in her slip because her dress could be stepped into, and tried to get the Little girls once more, giving up after the eighth ring because she was over that foolishness. She was putting away her nightgown, not noticing that she was folding it, as if for packing, instead of hanging it in the closet, when the announcer on the television suddenly stopped describing Senator Fred Carson, who would be next week's guest on *Faces and Events*; at exactly the same minute, the woolly strains of something by Fauré on the bedroom radio stopped abruptly. Marian had started to go to the living room, alerted by the word "bulletin"; now she stood in the hall, her hands folded into the filmy nightgown, and heard it from both sources at once, a stereophonic triumph of inescapable words bowling down the hall at her from both ends until she backed against the bookcase, cowering.

". . . Elizabeth Girard," the demon voices boomed. "The four-year-old daughter of the President is reported critically ill at the Federal Research Hospital. The President and the First Lady are at the hospital now. No more information is available at the moment." Marian broke loose from one of the voices then, fleeing to the bedroom with the nightgown held before her like a shield. ". . . consideration for the other patients, it is requested that listeners refrain from calling the hospital. White House press secretary Luke Messenger emphasized that no news media have any more detailed information, nor will any further bulletins be issued until later in the day. As soon as anything more is known, we will interrupt our programming. Until then, WADC joins in urging, ladies and gentlemen, that you *not* call the hospital, *please*."

Please, Paul Morisot said to God, looking out over the cloud-floored vastness as if he could see it from God's point of view. He clenched his brown, strong fingers in his lap and leaned forward, hurrying the plane that didn't seem to have moved since the radioed bulletin that meant it had become so bad with Elizabeth that secrets didn't matter any more. His dark eyes roved the fluff outside, looking for something with a shape, something that he could understand or make understanding grow from, about a God who behaved like a random madman, an idiot trampling flowers, an inefficient clerk making incredible errors. Somebody tired, or old, or bad had been meant instead: God would discover His mistake and rectify it at the last moment. Underneath the thought lay a fury he believed was prayer—until he caught himself thinking, *If you're hurting her, I'll kill you,* and made himself stop because this was no way to bargain.

His fingers unclenched and his left hand sought and found a small, smooth stone in the pocket of his coat; he held it loosely in his cupped hand, not stroking it but offering it up—*and the woman, too,* he wheedled. The woman and the stone for one small life, surely not important to any reasonable God . . . Sweat pricked out on his forehead and he swallowed hard, knowing that he was not offering all he could but wanting terribly to stay alive.

It was not enough and he knew it; he leaned back against the seat, bitter and almost beaten, and began to attack instead of coax this imbecile God who apparently felt so threatened by one flitting, new, butterfly child or who needed to punish *Andréa—but for what? what did you mean a woman to be, if not Andréa?*—or Alec—*but it was only men he wanted to lead, you fool, he offered no trespass on heaven.* Paul closed his hand around the stone, making of it nothing tender now but only added force for his fist, aimed at the disappointing God who was no better than the childish gods of the Greeks, spiteful and silly and dabbling in everything, finding hubris in every kitchen corner . . . *If anybody committed hubris it was I,* he thought with sudden hope of transferring punishment. He closed his eyes against the images of all the welcomes of the future of home, woman, and work and then he said, in the pink light behind his blind eyes, that if the child were spared he would give up all these for the future and make restitution for the past—and added scornfully that it was his last offer and a good one, as God must know unless He was a complete fool.

Morisot opened his eyes and looked out on the unending, noncommittal fluff of cloud, watching it with the empty look of a gambler who has laid all his chips on a single number and now, with all decisions made, has nothing to do but wait for the answer.

Waiting for the answer, Marian thought of exactly nothing, felt nothing except a pervading, undefined sorrow. "Will?" she asked quietly, seeing him, a stick figure, picking up the telephone in the study, under a portrait of her old nurse. "It's me. Marian." The pseudo-mother of her childhood was safe in the framed canvas, in the limited light the young girl painter had learned from the Dutch masters, and there she would stay forever: derivative, immature, inconsequential, and safe from any more demands of love or bold ventures into unknown truths, in a private world on which no public world could ever intrude.

"I know," Will said with pity. He sat down on the part-time, one-person bed and looked at the litter of newspaper on the floor. "Look, baby, *your* children are all right. Really."

"I hope so. It's more than I deserve." Behind her voice, piano music was skipping expertly. "What's Elizabeth—?"

"She has leukemia."

Marian gasped. "Why didn't you tell me?"

"I just found out," he said, surprised. He had forgotten, he saw, how god-like she expected him to be.

"Will, I just found out about Rosa."

He thought it was better not to tell her he had, too. "Darling, I know you're worried—"

"Willie, take me there. I want to go, right away."

"No." His blood ran cold at the very thought.

"Please, *please.*"

"Marian, the last place to do anything useful about Dorothy, Alabama, is in Dorothy. Don't be childish." Oops, he thought as soon as he'd said it: oh God, that'll tear it.

"Why is it childish? Ann is there. If Ann can be there, why can't I? Why are you trying to keep me—"

"Look, anything you could do, Ann can do. Which, by the way, is nothing. Anything that's going to get done will get done at Sixteen Hundred Pennsylvania Avenue." He wondered briefly what in hell that would be. "Marian, please be sensible."

"I *am* being sensible. Anyway, I want to be, I've got to be. She has to be got out of there." She began to cry then, reminded of the empty ringing of all the phones. "I tried and tried to find you. Oh, where were you, Will? Why did you let it happen?"

I was embracing Paul Morisot, he thought, and refusing to embrace a red-head; I was very occupied.

"The world came in," she was saying wildly. "The world came in and got Rosa, and I couldn't keep it out. I just didn't know how, but I wanted to so much. It came in and got Ann, and then it got Rosa. And now even children aren't safe, nothing is safe—"

"Baby, baby," he said, wrung with pity for her terror. "The children are all right. You're mixing things up." He thought about asking what had got Ann, but she was talking again, the words tumbling all over each other; suddenly he realized that it wasn't English at all. "What's that mean?"

"Don't you remember? Those Foreign Service people who came home from Japan told it to us—they're your friends, not mine," she said accusingly. "*Kamari masu*—that's what happening."

He remembered it then: *It means "Everything is going to pieces, everything is shot to hell. It's what the Japanese said about Hiroshima,"* the man had said, standing in a house somewhere near Chevy Chase Circle. The man who wasn't a Foreign Service officer at all, but a newspaper correspondent, and not a friend of Will Farland but of Charles Grayson. It was November and he was coming through Washington, and Grayson had sent the kids' Christmas presents by him. Will sighed, wondering where to reach for the handle in all this, and then he jerked to attention.

"Willie," she was saying, "you were right and I was wrong. I give up. Please—"

"No," he interrupted, quickly enough to cut her off from saying what he had been dreaming, all this terrible summer, that she would eventually say. He thought he ought to have his head examined, he thought he ought to be made to turn in his Machiavelli button—but he told himself to try it on for size, to gamble for something bigger and better. "Look, you weren't all wrong, and as soon as you feel better, you'll know it and be sorry. You'll be trapped again. So don't say it." He listened to her quiet crying. "Marian, darling, I know you're scared. But you've got to know that I'm scared, too." No fraud, no matter what it costs, he said to himself; she's got to *know*. "Baby, we can kill each other if we go on the way we've been, with me using your weaknesses and you scorning mine." Oh Jesus, sweet Jesus, he prayed. What if it doesn't work out?

"I don't scorn you, Will."

The tears were still behind her voice, but he thought he had never heard such genuine surprise. "Not now, you don't, baby. Right now you need a hero." He flung all cautious operation to the winds. If you believe she knows the sound of truth, he told himself fiercely, then trust her to hear it.

"If you start to bargain, I'll only get mad," she said wearily. "I'll have to give you whatever you want, of course, but that's not the way you want it, is it?"

"If I think that you might get mad, I start operating," he told her humbly. "I'm trying not to operate because that's not the way I want it."

"All right. I'll try, too, Will. What do you want of me? You know what I want of you—I want you to make everything all right."

Lord, Lord, what a beautiful setup, he thought wistfully. "I want you to say 'Come and get me,' the way you were going to, I think. But not so you'll un-say it later." He hesitated, then plunged like a diver entering unknown waters, depending on some skill but mostly luck, thinking, *Here goes nothing.* "Darling, I can't make everything all right. I'm not ten feet tall—sometimes I'm not even six feet tall. There are things I can't do. I'm just an ordinary guy."

"No, you're not. If you were, I wouldn't get mixed up. You mix me up because sometimes you *are* a hero. You take good care of me, Will, and the children, too. You do better than an ordinary guy." Her calm broke. "It's all my fault. I make you—"

"Whoa," he said softly. "There goes Daddy's little extremist, soaring way out of sight. Marian."

"What?"

"I can't protect you against some things. Just as a horrible example, look at what happened to the Girards. I mean, what could he do?"

"And you're no Alec Girard," she said with a crushing practicality that made him wince again.

"No. But I try hard," he insisted; it was true, he realized with sudden honest pride.

"Can you fix Rosa, Will?"

He swallowed. "I don't know, baby. I'll try. I'm going down to the office now. You know I'll try, don't you, Marian?"

"Yes. I know. Willie."

"Ma'am?" He held his breath against the ache in his chest.

"I can't say 'Come and get me,' " she told him sadly.

Kamari masu wrote itself across his mind. "Well, so much for the golden truth." But he had been bred not in the tradition of hara kiri but of the back-to-the-wall fight, his boyhood hero not the kamikaze immolating himself but the brave lad slipping off to bring help to the stockade. "No doubt I'll feel good about having been honest, anyway. Maybe in a decade or two."

"Oh listen," she said in alarm. "It's not that. Truly. Darling, please don't think it's you." Her voice offered cough syrup, chicken broth, red Jell-O: more important than anything else was the need to stop his hurting. "It's me that doesn't qualify. Now that it's not to be just a bargain, it's to be—this good way, I'd taint it with my—well, I thought I didn't have to tell you—"

"You don't!" he yelled, suddenly seeing what she was talking about. If he let her say it, he was done for: an inch from victory, Alabama would take over and do him in, once and for all. "Please don't," he begged her fervently, trying to blink away an image of himself in overalls, tracking down Morisot with a squirrel rifle.

"But I have to. I can't—I mean, I'm not a silver dollar," she said obscurely.

She had to make *some* sacrifices, he wanted to point out. But now what mattered was to keep her from dynamiting everything in the name of truth. "Listen, baby, what went on when the snow was on the ground is all melted away by now."

"No, it isn't. It isn't that easy."

Silently, he cursed her for a Calvinist. "Look—at the time, you were being bullied. Don't argue—you said so, and you were right. Okay. Everybody has a moral right to fight against oppression—which means any kind of fight at all. Underground tactics are the only ones possible against a tyrant."

"Will, I'm not sure it was only—"

"Well, *I'm* sure," he said quickly, telling himself that she sounded at least biddable. He drew in a long breath and let it out slowly. "I know everything I need to know about the old order and I ask you to help me bury it, here and now. I ask you to elect me again and I promise I'll govern better, because I know how now. A new regime. No more tyrant, and," he finished carefully, "no more underground."

In the long pause, he listened to the music in the room with her: the orchestra chased, caught up with, and overwhelmed the piano. "All right, Will."

If she had practiced with a punching bag for a year, she couldn't have hit him harder than she did with that slow, earnest promise ringing with her painful recognition that if he wanted to try, she had no right to deny him the chance. She was an honest woman and he had nothing to worry about, he thought—except how to forget the pathetic resignation in her voice, and how to keep from punishing her for it. A couple of teeny-tiny lifetime headaches.

"Don't feel bad, baby," he said lightly. "You'll just adore government by consent of the governed. All the best people do."

"I know I shall," she said gracefully, with nothing in her voice now but giving to him. Quality folks, he acknowledged, and sighed: home was in sight and was beautiful and was worth everything; in time, the destruction he was guilty of now could become beneficence—in taken towns, once enough time had passed, the survivors sometimes built better. "Come and get me, Willie," she said. And added humbly, "When you can."

"Yes, ma'am. Oh, that will pleasure me greatly, ma'am. Wait for me."

"I'll be here." She was crying a little again. "Willie, please send Rosa home soon."

"I will, baby," he promised, before he could bite his tongue.

For a long time after, he sat on the little bed with his hands dangling in front of him, wondering at exactly what point Marian had known for sure that Willie-hero was going to make everything all right. The second after she earned it by deciding to put duty before love, he thought swiftly—and then erased that pain from the blackboard of his mind; it took up space he needed for writing the record, so he could determine at what point Farland had once more deserted truth for response. "Words is words," he said aloud, and decided to let it stand as a requiem for a good try and a prayer for luck. He got up and began trying to get the place ready for her return, trying to decide all the time whether she'd heard them both swing right back again, after all the fine talk, at the very last minute. Then he told himself not to be a fool—if she hadn't, she would. But by that time, maybe he'd have figured out whether to laugh or cry.

By the time Jake Ruffing called, Will had brought in some flowers from the back yard, where they'd been slowly choking to death among the weeds, and stood them in a vase, where they leaned awkwardly and he didn't know what to do about it. He abandoned that problem and looked in the bottom drawer of her desk. When the phone rang, he was in the bedroom, laying her calling card with its demure "Mrs. Willard Catullus Farland" on her pillow.

"Will, where the hell are you?"

"I was just coming. I figured the meeting on the UN business was postponed."

"Well, sure," Ruffing said irritably. "But this is a hell of a time for you to get technical. We have a television appearance all set up, and an Alabama speech that's too damn long."

Will advised, "Cut it down to 'Get in line or get shot.' "

"He's not going to make that decision if he doesn't have to. We're still waiting to hear from Rosenberg. The speech is just to be a warning that—"

"What time was Rosenberg supposed to call?"

Ruffing told him, and Will sat down slowly in his wife's desk chair, his face very pale. "Jake, listen. If they've cut Rosie's communications off, they've gone over the line: it means the word is out that anything goes. You understand me?"

Jake said wearily, "I understand that you're crying doom again."

"I'm crying murder. If the man makes a speech before he's got troops there, he's going to set off the goddamndest blood bath you ever saw. They won't listen to him unless he's got a gun at their heads."

"Oh for Pete's sake. They know what he can do."

It was like walking through water, Will Farland told himself desperately. It was like trying to handle nitroglycerine with long, clumsy tongs. "They have a way of not adding things up if they don't like the sum," he said quietly. It was important not to sound excited.

"What does that mean?"

"It means that those lickered-up bastards are sure as hell going to decide to teach Washington not to interfere." *Can you fix Rosa?* He had said he would try, but with what tool? He stood helpless, an interpreter ordered to translate literally, when Rosa's life depended on interpretation, on making the ways of irrational men understandable to rational men. "Jake, please believe me. He'll speak a warning, and they'll hear a dare."

"Oh come on, Farland. Nobody's going to buck a force they know can flatten them."

Will fumbled through his mind for an effective threat. A strike would be silly: they could get along without him. He was a technician; he could be replaced. The only tool he had, he decided swiftly, was the good old silver tongue—whistle up the convincer now, or die. "Why not?" he asked lightly. "People did in Budapest, you know. Or are you under the impression, Jake, that men are only fearless in a just cause?"

"No," Ruffing said abruptly. "All right. I've got just one chance to talk to him. What are you trying to get me to tell him?"

One thing about Jake—Will thought, getting to his feet because it was time to go to work—if he was stupid once in a while it wasn't for long. "That if he doesn't have the troops on the spot when he begins to talk, he'll be inviting lynchings. And mob violence. And that, in any case, he hasn't much time."

"All right. But I'm not the guy who gives the orders. You come on down here and work out alternative approaches in the meantime. I've been trying to get the governor, but he's not back from church yet. And Rosie may have some proposal."

You won't get the governor on the phone this day, Will told him silently. And you won't be able to reach Judge Hadley Thurston either: they're both wherever they go to hide when the white hoods are being taken down from the top shelves of closets. Will sighed. This was the best he could do; Rosenberg, if he got through, would do the rest: there's something about the voice of a man who's right there where the mob is that's remarkably persuasive. "One thing, Jake," he said slowly. "If Rosenberg does call, tell him to get out of there. As soon as possible, but certainly before dark."

But when Rosenberg did finally call, his report—brief, matter-of-fact, and inconclusive—didn't inspire such finalities. "It was getting so late I thought I'd better check in anyway, Jake." He sounded faint and very far away. "But all I have is shreds."

"You know what we want to know."

"Yes, and it's clear enough that something sub rosa and unsanitary is going on." Rosenberg outlined his conversation with the sheriff. "So I went over to the hotel and put in a call to the governor. Which has involved a long runaround, adding up to quite a while and three secretaries, so far. In theory, I'm still waiting for him to call me back. But I decided to do a little checking on my own first."

"The governor's trying to avoid us, too."

"Well, he can't do it forever. As soon as I finish out here, I'll try him again. By then I'll have some collateral information, I hope." The slow voice sounded unhappy. "You know how it is, Jake—you want something official before you make a recommendation in a thing like this. I don't want to be just passing on rumors."

"But they seem well-founded?"

"Yes, I guess so. Still . . . it's all so hit-or-miss, you know? It feels like a hell of a way to run a country."

"I know," Jake said, and did. Rosenberg's thoroughness, his researcher's passion for nailing down details, had stood the Girard forces in good stead defensively always, and now and then he had even turned up something that, plied by the offensive team, unhorsed an opponent before he could even ride in their candidate's direction. "Okay, I'll tell the man what you said, and we'll wait for you to call again—what, a couple of hours? I've got to go see him now, so take it easy, Rosie."

"I *am* taking it easy. The trouble is, it looks very much as though the state police are, too."

"Disturbed but not frantic" was what the message amounted to, Jake decided, thinking it over quickly as he left for the hospital. And, given Jerry Rosenberg, he could be disturbed simply by the vagueness of the situation. But, also given Jerry the prompt as well as precise, the fact that he had uncharacteristically delayed phoning indicated that he definitely smelled a rat—one big enough to make Rosenberg more inquisitive than punctilious, even if not enough to make him emotional.

Ruffing walked down the hospital corridor with the gait of a man tired of plying between deaths, and even more tired of weighing people. Passing the improvised press room where Luke Messenger sat with the three men of the press "pool," Jake shook his head at them and noted at the same time that one of the chosen was Martin Halloran, who was a big gun for a "death watch," normally one of the simplest of journalistic chores. He filed this observation away for future speculation and returned to Farland, the measuring instrument with—as the President had pointed out—built-in error. But if the bathroom scale was not accurate, was as much as five pounds off, Jake argued, and it said I weighed two hundred pounds, I'd still be fat. And Gil Kimball, whose built-in errors, whatever they were, weren't the same as Farland's, had said, *This is lurid country.* Suddenly the deputy Gil had described in his phone call rose before Jake's eyes: the blunt weapon in its lovingly adorned holster, the flashlight rhythmically smacking against the hard palm. *He was smiling,* Gil had stipulated, in unmistakable horror . . . And then there was Bruyette, a man not inclined to dispute Alec's judgment— All these Columbuses, insisting the world was round. If Jacob Ruffing, practical politician, knew anything at all, he knew that the world was negotiation-shaped: a vast flatland of pull and counterpull, bounded on one side by tit-for-tat and on the other by quid-pro-quo. Yet it was necessary, sometimes, to believe in what you couldn't see. Which might also, it occurred to him, be bothering Rosenberg.

Through the door as Alec Girard came out, Jake saw the stopped-film stillness of the room where the clinical white was somehow brighter than all the pathetic attempts to color life. He discovered with the dismay with which decent men confront their faulty humanness that he had, unbelievably, almost forgotten; in the back of his mind, where he looked at himself, he acknowledged with shame that it was not, in fact, because he had been just busy but because he had been busy running away. Some confrontations were too much to ask: Alec and Andy, however loved and honored, stood by themselves in the wide circle no other parent could help drawing around them. He looked up guiltily at the President's haggard face under the thick, vitally springing hair and decided to make his pitch quick and strong.

He repeated Will's words, his neutral voice making no attempt to shade them. "I've got Farland doing it both ways, pending your decision. I'm sorry we never seem quite able to come up with something unequivocal for you," he finished, and waited.

Girard wiped his hand across his forehead. "We've been deluding ourselves, Jake. Any cop used to dealing with gangsters probably could've told us—that sheriff has a jail full of people who can testify against him. If he thinks they're going to have a chance to—and if, as it seems, the state police aren't going to police him—why should he protect them? *That* seems unequivocal enough. Farland's right: we're talking about murder."

"Then the troops go in before the speech?"

The President sighed. "Yes."

"When?"

" 'Before dark,' " the tall man quoted thoughtfully. He looked at the closed door at his side, his eyes visibly yearning toward it. "All right. We'll wait till the last possible minute to give Rosenberg time to check it out thoroughly. Find out how late the Army can wait, then schedule the speech for whenever they can guarantee the men will be there. Before dark. In the meantime . . ."

"I'm still trying to get the governor."

"Well, if you get him, I don't want to talk to him," Girard said violently. "The only thing we're waiting for is Rosenberg, to let us know for sure whether the state police are there—I mean, really there. If they are, we'll call our operations off, but he's the only one I'll believe. If the governor calls, tell him that." His angry voice softened then. "And when Rosie calls, order him home—we've abused him enough. Is that all, Jake? You know I—"

"Yes, Mr. President," Ruffing interrupted quickly, to spare him the pain of asking. "I'll see that you're left alone." The President turned away and Jake began, "Please tell Andy—" and stopped, because he couldn't think what.

"Yes." The handsome face was already turned back to its private hell. "If anyone can think of something to tell Andy, let me know."

Fifty-five

"On the whole, we were lucky to get off so cheaply," Jerry Rosenberg's father had written on the V-mail blank that tormented articulate correspondents during World War II; the prescribed square of paper seemed made, though, for the Professor's small, distinct script. "The only abiding effect is that she will be forced to lead a physically inactive life, in which a trip to Symphony, for example, will constitute a major outing. She herself is relatively cheerful about this; she says books may be canned food, but they're food nevertheless. Myself, I think her family had better plan on supplementing her diet with fresh-squeezed experience."

Perhaps because the requirements of the role coincided with his natural turn of mind, Rosenberg, in the years since his mother's chronic illness began, had learned to see new characters and environments as if he were a correspondent, meeting them at once as himself and as an interpreter, looking and summarizing simultaneously; if this habit insulated him somewhat, diminishing his emotional response, it was not to an extent dangerous to his personality and it provided him with a skill the value of which Senator Alexander Girard had had the wit to recognize. The capacious Rosenberg mind was a notable asset in a political campaign; perhaps because Rosenberg's mother was a gifted woman and not by any means uncritical, he had learned to meet rather high standards in the delivery of "fresh-squeezed experience."

As he drove from Dorothy out on the road to Alameda on this abusively hot Sunday in Alabama, Rosenberg was engaged in revising an earlier imaginary report to his mother from, as he had labeled himself, her "correspondent in Gehenna." "I take back what I said about it's being unrecognizable here, because I've just discovered it was only that I was looking at it with an expectation of familiarity—a delusion based on the fact that this place is in the U.S. But once divorced from that expectation, the countryside and the people are perfectly recognizable, all right—I've seen them all before, during the war, in North Africa. The heat and the flies are the chief similarity; but, while there are no deserts as such, there's also an impression of dusty yellowish emptiness in the foreground with lush, tangled greenness beyond, all somewhat echoing Africa. As does the fact that the people move as if they're sick with some sort—or several sorts—of debilitating disease. But it's hard to feel pity for them because they make me nervous in a way I can't describe but can recall feeling about the Arabs working around the Army base in those days: they always seemed to be exchanging some kind of incomprehensible but dangerous communication that wasn't frightening, because we had found them quite unintelligent and incompetent on the whole. But it did keep us edgy."

Rosenberg drove slowly, watching for the turnoff to Judge Thurston's place because he knew it must be here—somewhere about halfway to Alameda—even though he hadn't been able to get any reliable directions. The empty road baked alone under the shimmering waves of heat, as though it had been turned over to the killing, victorious sun. Even the dense green at the sides, which must have been inhabited by millions of small creatures, was silent, dusty, and unstirring—whatever did live there lay panting, presumably under leaves.

"Maybe some of the foreignness that made it all so unidentifiable at first came from the fact that these people are not only American but white; it was especially hard to link them with the Arabs because the brown and black —and many hues between—people who are jammed into the sagging houses of the Negro area here are much more like we were in North Africa. The whole thing is reversed, you see. Very curious . . .

"I know you don't like words like 'ominous' or 'menace' that say but don't explain, so I've been trying to think of what makes these people, the whites, so menacing. All I come up with is the single fact that, though there's a lot of ceremonious smiling, nobody does much real laughing. Whereas, when I drove through the Negro part yesterday, I was like an officer going through the barracks area: laughter and buzzing and a whole spectrum of activities stopped when I appeared and began again in my wake. (Their communications aren't too good, possibly because the place is terribly overcrowded with new arrivals—and another busload arrived this morning, I heard—so I caught, before they could shove them out of my sight, a crap game, a songfest, and a guy sitting on a step writing a letter; you couldn't ask for a combination more likely to stir barracks memories.) "

Rosenberg heard, with amusement, that he had strayed from the unwelcome task of trying to transmit the image of Sheriff Floyd to the easier job of describing the Negroes. He found what must be the road, just behind one of the "Jesus Saves" signs that appeared more frequently here than Burma Shave, and turned down it, excusing himself for his dereliction of duty: after all, he was no Faulkner. And physical description couldn't do it alone. There must be thousands of big men going soft in the middle, with small eyes in a jowly face and an air of unwillingly suppressed surliness rendered particularly irritating because of its thin obeisance to elaborate courtesy. He himself had encountered salesclerks like Sheriff Floyd—dapper, contemptuous, and unlovely in their overdone servility, touchy about status as only those who lack it can be.

Rosenberg, who did not lack status and never had, had recognized with mild impersonal interest that the sheriff was lording it over him in their encounter that morning. "I quite understand, Sheriff. I have orders myself. Mine are to call the President at ten o'clock. I thought yours were to make your office facilities available."

"Well, of course, when we said that, Mr.—uh—Rosen, we just naturally didn't in no way have Sunday in mind. Mebbe they don't take their Sunday serious in Washington—fact is, I heard some stories make me believe they don't take it serious atall. But the sheriff's office in Dorothy been closed on Sundays long as there was a sheriff's office atall. Reckon they just didn't understand—uh—local conditions when they told you that." The yellow teeth bared in a humorless smile had sharp points, as though they had chewed only on mushy food and so never had got ground down. "I reckon that's it, don't you?"

Rosenberg returned the smile, although his had genuine humor; he was entranced with a vision of this man's vision of Sunday in heathen Washington, suspecting it of containing dancing girls and peeled grapes. "Perhaps they didn't," he said pleasantly. "You take all of Sunday off, do you?"

"The woman brings a meal to the prisoners around noon," the sheriff told him defensively. The words reached Rosenberg propelled on a wave of bourbon fumes. "We ain't neglectin them none, sir."

"Of course not." The eyes behind the glasses considered the vulnerability of the small stone building in the midst of the empty square. "How about trouble, though? Don't you have anybody on duty to handle whatever might come up? Or do the state police keep their eye on the jail, in case of any attempts there?" He watched the man blandly, knowing his fishing was awfully unsubtle but guessing it would get by; the sheriff was too eager to demonstrate superiority to give any attention at all to suspicion of the spineless, ignorant "foreigner" who could be so safely snubbed.

"Why, sir," the big man said, "we don't have no trouble on Sundays no way. This here's a peaceful, godfearin community we got here. Any trouble starts here has just got to be outside agitators." He stopped, the narrow limits of his mind too threatened by the size of his secret joke to permit him to continue. He took off his broad-brimmed hat and scratched at his sweat-prickling, graying hair while he jingled his keys in an effort to contain his amusement.

"Well, anyway, with the state police—"

"We ain't callin for no state police to do nothin for us," the sheriff said, scowling into the sun. Resentment at being deprived of his joke topped the older anger that flourished always in the poor soil of his pauperate self-esteem.

"That's another fool notion you-all in Washington got. Them state fellers ain't much, mister."

Rosenberg thought of goading him a little further by challenging this, but then he decided that silence would be more effective as a demand for substantiation.

He was right. "Listen, mister," the sheriff went on angrily. "Mebbe—and mind, I only said mebbe—them fellers can direct traffic in the Baptist Church parking lot today, but I have my doubts."

"Oh? Why's that?"

Finding himself respectfully questioned restored the sheriff's good humor. "Well now, I ain't one to toot my own horn, but—say, you by any chance a drinkin man?"

"Let's say I like a drop," said Rosenberg, hinting successfully at secret debauches. He disguised his shudder at the thought that he might be offered the wine of the country, raw bourbon, warm and tasting of a metal flask.

"Hey now, you'll know what I mean, then. Their cap'n was down to the Grill last night, and—" the sheriff bent double and came up slapping his whipcord thigh in the ritual that substituted for laughter—"would you believe it if I was to tell you he was flat on his ass under the table by ten o'clock?"

Rosenberg clucked. "A man who can't hold his liquor—"

"You said it. Mind you, that's their cap'n, too." The memory of pleasure lighted the seamed face. "Took all four of his boys to carry him out of there —and they wasn't in too good shape theirself, on accounta they'd been seein the rest of them fellers off. Sweet Jesus, it was something. The Grill was livelier'n Niggertown last night."

Under his satisfaction at getting the information he was after about the state police—though it would need checking out; Floyd was not an unprejudiced witness, and besides, he wasn't entirely sober—Rosenberg was aware of an anthropological insight. He concluded his interview with the sheriff as rapidly as possible, because he calculated that the inevitable shift from the palsy-walsy to the truculent was about due, and also because he knew that this florid fool was as obedient as he was dull, and had orders. The man could not be dealt with, so Rosenberg dismissed him, nodding agreeably as the sheriff observed that he guessed he would get on his way to church; it was patently a lie, but the President's assistant had more effective liars to contend with.

Fishing in his pocket for coins as he approached the single telephone booth in the stale, silent lobby of the hotel, a few minutes later, he noted his finding for his mother's benefit: "A curious impression, but I think an accurate one, has been building up in my mind. I couldn't substantiate it with any real evidence, but more and more I get the feeling that the way the whites feel about their 'Niggertown' is that it's forbidden and fascinating. Like a big, noisy party to which they'll never be invited. I guess what I'm trying to say is that the wall of the Negro ghetto here seems to wall *out* as well as in, and it opens up some interesting questions. Could it have been the same in, say, the Warsaw ghetto? Are the anti's wistful as well as wicked—could a feeling of exclusion have something to do with their anger? I really think it does here, but as a Jew without any direct experience of anti-Semitism, I don't know whether it applies there, too."

The governor—his assistant, who lisped, told Mr. Rosenberg of the White House staff with soft respect—was probably either on his way to church or already there. Mr. Rosenberg spoke sternly and then suffered qualms of guilt as the almost fainting voice vowed earnestly that certainly he understood that Mr. Rosenberg would not be calling if it were not pressing and the governor would be most disturbed if Mr. Rosenberg went ahead and reported to the President without consulting him first, yes, he quite agreed to that. He implored Mr. Rosenberg to wait, please, and he would try to locate the governor at once. But in any case, he would call Mr. Rosenberg back at that number as soon as possible, and it distressed him that he had to ask Mr. Rosenberg to wait at all . . . Mr. Rosenberg, fed up with being addressed in trembling, said he would wait, and hung up after making the point again that the sheriff's office was unaccountably closed and he was calling from the hotel lobby.

He began again on the letter to his mother while he sat in a weary armchair from whose broken springs only an equally weary cushion protected his behind: "While I'm muddling around in these socio-something fields in which I have no particular competence, I might as well branch off into psychoanalysis too, and note what I think is called the phenomenon of projection. The whole image of the southern Negro as the whites caricature him amounts to that, I think: when I look closely, I see that it is the sheriff, for example, who is shiftless, sloppy, stupid, easily awed, irresponsible, and in need of direction like a child. In fact, one of the most childlike aspects is their attitude toward alcohol, which partakes of some kind of belief in magic, I think. Whoever called rum a demon did these people a big favor, because it bolstered their comfortable feeling of being taken over by a force greater than themselves and of therefore having no responsibility. A man who is drunk, it has been borne in on me through many, many offhand remarks (not aimed at making an impression on me because the speaker so takes the fact for granted), is excused, is free of all liability for anything he does, and is usually even lightly forgiven—though what is described as 'a mean drunk,' with a disapproving shake of the head, apparently is looked down on to some degree. But you have to be something pretty appalling to be 'a mean drunk' around here: I'm not certain just what; wifebeating, for example, doesn't qualify. Anyway, this arrangement, as I'm sure you can see, opens up all kinds of possibilities for doing things you might be ashamed to do except that you've had a few public drinks first."

Rosenberg's ruminations were interrupted by the telephone in the booth, a loud jangling that apparently failed to alert any hotel functionary. He accepted with some boredom the apologies of another gubernatorial aide—this time a woman with magnolias melting under her tongue—and agreed to wait a little longer for somebody to locate her elusive boss. When he hung up, he decided he really couldn't keep the President waiting any more while some Stanley sought the governor in the trackless wilds of the state capital, so he got out the last of his change and set about calling the White House number. But even this met with no success: the operator was just as sorry as she could be, sir, but all outgoing lines were in use right now. Rosenberg thanked her, refraining from calling her "Betty Sue Jo," which he'd just decided on, discarding "Willie Lou May." He left the booth, forgetting the neat stack of coins he had built on the ledge near the phone, and stood at the big front window of the hotel, contemplating the closed Grill across the street with its one-word sign, never much of a trial to literacy, now reduced to bare tubing like the bent glass straws used by hospital patients who can't sit up. It seemed hard to believe that behind the locked doors and silent houses of this town enough people were busy making long distance calls to jam all the lines, he thought suspiciously; then he remembered the press and decided maybe four reporters calling their desks at once could swamp Dorothy. Only what news could they possibly be calling in, he wondered as the phone rang again.

This assistant, also almost cloyingly polite, was also insistent that Mr. Rosenberg would be called again in a very short time. Agreeing to wait, Mr. Rosenberg decided it wasn't paranoia if there really were little men watching you from the walls, and that it was time to find out why it was so important that he be kept immobilized. He wiped his sweaty face with his handkerchief and picked up his coat, a haberdashery formality he considered necessary for when he arrived but not until then. Then he strode out and got into his rented car and headed for Judge Hadley Thurston's ancestral manse.

As soon as he was well out of the city, he spotted a telephone booth in a closed gas station—so closed that it looked as though it might never open again. His pants pockets were empty, but there was still a dime in his coat pocket. He used it to get the operator—not "Betty Sue Jo," but perhaps a specialist in collect calls?—and heard Dan Healy's voice accepting the charges at the other end; but then there was a series of clicks that irked Taxpayer Rosenberg (why the hell couldn't they have delayed accepting it until they found Ruffing?) before Jake said "Hello."

When Rosenberg hung up, he was a little displeased with his report because it didn't seem to transmit the hovering menace he felt in the hot silence that lay over everything; but he was a man accustomed to accepting and forgiving himself, so he turned his attention to the imaginary report to his mother, which didn't have to be quite as well documented, and was still at work on it when he came in sight of the rutted dirt road leading up a small slope from the judge's mailbox. He stopped the car to put his coat on before he drove slowly on into the welcoming coolness of the yard, shaded by huge old trees, from one of which a mockingbird eyed him boldly.

The judge's hand was papery, making him seem older than he must be; that unexpected antiquity and the easy flow of his courtesies lulled Rosenberg a little. Not much, though. When the judge, shaking hands, said, "I know of your father, of course, Mr. Rosenberg," Jerry smiled and made polite murmurs. But he thought, "My father knows of you, too," and went on remembering his father's ironic description of what he had called the "sucking aristocrat." Professor Rosenberg's son put down the drink he now regretted having accepted, because it was becoming clear this wasn't the kind of man he wanted to drink with, and said bluntly, "A citizen has a duty to his country, Judge, and I don't think you're doing yours unless you stop twisting and give me a responsive answer. Am I or am I not correct in my suspicions?"

Hadley Thurston looked at Rosenberg from lizard eyes in a clay face and gave up. "Floyd is a stupid man. He should have let you make your call."

"Agreed. But hardly surprising. Would any but stupid men be suitable for your troops?"

"Mr. Rosenberg, they are not my troops." He saw the younger man's unbelief. "Allow me, if you will, to indicate for you in what direction the wind blows. We had in custody in the town a northern white lady—a Mrs. Crane—who had got herself involved with the darkies: a very unseemly business for a member of the learned profession."

"You say you 'had.' Who got her out? I take it that's your point."

"Exactly, sir." The eyes came a little alive with the happiness of didacticism. "Now who would you imagine obtained the misguided lady's release from durance vile—if you'll forgive me?"

I won't, thought Rosenberg; you ought to learn to speak with respect of better men, which includes white ladies involved with the darkies. "I would assume—since you mentioned her profession—that it was her school? Or—what is it she teaches—a professional organization, perhaps?"

"Ah, you make my point for me." The old voice was full of satisfaction. "Which is?"

"Which is, my dear sir, that times have changed, and that power hereabouts is no longer in the hands of tradition or learning." He nodded emphatically. "Our Mrs. Crane was released through her academic connections, certainly—but more precisely, through the coincidence that a member of the board of trustees of the school in which she teaches is a director of a large manufacturing enterprise with a factory in this county. Do I make myself clear, Mr. Rosenberg? Please understand that the lady's more—respectable—connections did not fail to make representations on her behalf, and the rather amateurish organization that sent her had also made some ineffectual plans. But the one that prevailed was—well, I see you take the point."

Rosenberg's look suggested an Army chaplain examining filthy pictures confiscated from the barracks. "If your point is that you have no power to intercede against the illegalities—not to say immoralities—apparently slated for some kind of folk festival today, I take it, all right." He stood up. "Now, if I may use your telephone . . ."

"Please, Mr. Rosenberg."

Jerry stared, thinking that he would have thought it impossible to feel pity for a misery that contained so much self-pity; but he felt it anyway. "Perhaps I've made a mistake, Judge. I understood you to be saying that you were powerless, not approving."

"I implore you, sir, not to compel me to what I assure you would be the first inhospitality of a long life."

Well, I'll be goddamned, said Rosenberg to himself: what's bothering him is that he doesn't want to have to tell me I can't use his phone. Something that may have been laughter and may have been anger and may even have been both was in his throat like phlegm, making him want to spit. "I'll reverse the charges, of course," he said with deliberate brutality.

"Mr. Rosenberg, I am an old man and I have noticed before that the young condemn so easily."

"You're approximately of an age with my father, sir. He has noted the same phenomenon, but he's solved the problem by giving the young as little as possible to condemn. And I might add, Judge, that I am not really young."

The judge said in a slow, hopeless voice, "Your father has better fortune than I. He lives in a free society."

"Are you telling me—"

"I am indeed telling you, young man. If a telephone call to Washington went out from my house now, it would be monitored, and reported, and I should—suffer severely." His lips curled. "I put it to you, sir, that you are younger than you think. Control of the press, of communications with the outside world, of education—did you think these phenomena, and all the rest that follow from them, were confined to the other side of the ocean?"

Molested by sympathy again, Rosenberg sat down in the weathered wooden rocker. "Perhaps I did, Judge Thurston."

"Ha. As usual, those who are responsible for destruction fail to recognize their part in it."

"How—?"

"You forced it, my boy," the old man said strongly. His eyes were alight, and even his sparse yellowish white hair seemed to acquire new vitality. "All you people. With your pressures, and your questions, and your test cases—inexorably you forced into the open what was once kept under discreet suppression by—my kind of people. The moment you did that," he cried, wagging a long, very white forefinger, "the very moment you did that, you handed over power to those who do not know how to use it honorably. To the commercial outsiders, who have no thought for what is noble in our traditions, our sanctified way of life—and they, ignorant and afar from the scene, careless of what the fools do so long as they are available for work at the factory on Monday morning, they in turn empower the Floyds and others like them. People of a poor quality, sir, never meant for authority."

"Well, I can certainly agree with that estimate. But I fail to see how we are responsible—"

"You are, sir, you are indeed." The judge's voice shook with passion. "And I charge you with it. It is you who created the problems of which you complain, and for which you attempt to condemn us."

Oh brother, said Jerry Rosenberg—meaning, actually, his father—if this isn't the old bit about how it's the Jews who cause anti-Semitism, I am an illegitimate child. The requirements of honest anthropology struggled against the disgust his father's son could not help but feel. "Judge," he said slowly, "however comfortable the gentlemen's agreements of the past may have been, they nevertheless did not succeed, did they, in killing off the monster?" He waited patiently for some sign that he was understood, but the old man still looked only triumphant. "Judge Thurston. This afternoon—"

"Not until dark," the judge corrected him. At home among his wrinkles was a look of superiority, a joy in knowing more.

"Very well, sir," the patient son of Professor Rosenberg persisted. "This evening, then, there will presumably be illegal activity that will doubtless result in considerable mayhem and possibly murder. Now, regardless of who struck John—I mean, sir, without relation to the question of previous or present blame for the causative factors, I think you'll agree that some action must be taken to stop this from happening?"

The old voice was very tired, very soft, and very self-pitying. "I'm sorry, but I must be away until tomorrow. Today is my daughter's birthday and I am off to visit her and her family. She lives nearly eighty miles from here." He glanced up quickly at Rosenberg. "I assure you, my boy, I speak the truth. This is indeed my daughter's birthday."

Thank God I am not your boy, the dark eyes behind the glasses said; and what's more, I'll see to it that my boy is not your boy either. "I don't doubt that it's your daughter's birthday," Rosenberg said evenly. He stood up. "I don't doubt, either, that if it weren't, some other suitable anniversary would require celebration."

"I am an old man." Somewhere in the somnolence behind the house a hound spoke, as if in corroboration.

"That can't be helped. What can be helped is your indifference to others' rights to live to be old men." He waited, but there was no answer. Rosenberg sighed and let him have it. "May I use your telephone, Judge Thurston?"

Well, at least I rubbed his face in it, he told himself, stopping at the end of the lane to put the top down on the convertible. Even the hot wind it left him open to was better than the terrible contained heat of the car unmolested by any moving air. Driving fast and with what would have been recklessness except that there was no traffic, he spun into the trampled dirt driveway of the closed gas station and jumped out of the car before he remembered that he had no coins left. With an anger uncharacteristic of him, Rosenberg got back into the car and headed at speed for the city limits.

But he wasn't speedy enough, perhaps, he thought after he tried once more, at a diner just inside the town. It was a curious experience: Jerry Rosenberg, first anonymous among students and then anonymous among soldiers, lumped professionally as one of Girard's "think boys" first and then as "White House sources," was a marked man in Dorothy, Alabama, and environs —including a diner that was oddly out of change for a dollar. "Just recently," he began to recount to his mother as he started the car again, "Nedra told me that she'd heard us spoken of as 'that quiet couple in 3B,' and I remember I said to her then that she may be the only person in Washington for whom I'm sharply individualized. I thought I was joking, and I guess I was—Jake Ruffing knows who I am, and so do others of a select few—but now I regard it with a certain nostalgia. I also recall with a new sympathy something I once heard Andy Girard say about feeling eyes on her back all the time."

He drove slowly past the shattered traffic light in the city's center, observing that the landscape now had figures in it, though they were few and lounging. He parked outside the café and went inside to find Ann and Gil. As he'd expected, they were there, finishing a lunch whose lateness resulted from the fact that they hadn't breakfasted till noon, and discussing Rosa; Ann's attempt to see her yesterday had been thwarted by a bland statement from the sheriff that the prisoner had tried to escape and therefore was in solitary confinement. "Well, she's safe enough, even incommunicado," Gil was saying morosely as Rosenberg came in. "For a while, anyway."

The proprietor bustled forward, protesting that he was sorry, he wasn't serving any more, he was about to close, he would have closed already if— Rosenberg, feeling absurdly like a booted Storm Trooper, brushed the man aside with the sudden, and totally unexpected, reply that he only ate kosher food anyway. He could tell that Ann had heard, because her mouth was hanging open when he arrived at their table, which was in fact the only one occupied; but he wasn't sure whether Gil's narrowed eyes indicated specific or general alertness. Without bothering with preliminaries, Rosenberg collected all the change both of them owned, fended off their questions and offers of coffee, and strode out, restraining the impulse to yell "Heil Hitler" at the already unnerved proprietor.

Who rushed over to Gil and Ann and began openly and almost hysterically now to urge the prompt departure he had been hinting at for some time. "What's up?" Gil asked him with frank curiosity, and would not be put off by demurrers. Eventually, his open good humor won out, and the sorely tried man gave up attempts to lie.

"You know I'm not one of them that always wants trouble," he began.

Nodding, Gil accepted this bona fide. "Then what's the stew?"

"I had my windows broke before, I had my place wrecked—cost me more money than I take in in a month last time—"

"Who's going to make trouble?" Gil laughed. "Listen, from what I saw last night, I can guarantee that hangovers will keep the boys quiet today."

"Not in this town," the man boasted. "The way our boys drink, it don't die on Saturday night." He nodded at the almost unpeopled street. "You wait and see—not everybody's done with dinner yet. But after, they'll get started drinking again." He grinned at Gil, giving him credit for some small expertise. "To chase the hangovers."

"What kind of trouble do you expect?" Ann asked.

"Now, how would I know, Miss? Course, I hear tell there's another busload of niggers come in this morning—they just waiting in Niggertown to start trouble." He saw the nervousness in her face and was instantly gallant. "Don't you get scared. Ain't nothing going to happen now. This is Sunday, ain't it? And this here's a godfearing town."

Gil said that, in that case, he would have another cup of coffee and, when the man hesitated, shooed him on his way with a jocular reminder that it would be Sunday for several hours yet. The proprietor muttered that he was going to be busier'n a pimp at a whorehouse tea—"Pardon, ma'am"—just getting ready to close, and then he always had trouble with the shutter for the front . . . But he went for the coffee anyway.

Ann looked at Gil with wide, troubled eyes. "Is it at sundown that the Sabbath's officially over?"

"That's the Jews." He straightened a ketchup bottle. "I reckon maybe it's over when the boys have got enough hair of enough dogs in them. Though, since this is a godfearing town, ma'am, that there sun's got to be a mite lower in the sky."

"I'm glad they talk differently." She shivered, though it was certainly not cold, even in the direct path of the fan that threatened periodically to sail her little hat away. "I was watching them yesterday, going in and out of the supermarket and the five-and-ten—you know, just like anybody's Saturday. And it gave me the willies. But I feel better when I realize that even though they buy the same brand of soap and eat the same packaged cereal for breakfast, they're a different race of people from the rest of us. Maybe that's why they're so terrifying. Isn't the alien always terrifying?"

"Maybe," Gil said soberly to the ketchup bottle. "But I think they are like us. Which is even more terrifying."

Rosenberg, shut firmly into the phone booth in the hotel lobby, was testing a dubious gift for mimicry. He had once auditioned for his college revue with an act that involved imitations of faculty figures; he reminded himself now, a little fearfully, that he'd been turned down. But then that was a more discriminating audience, he said to himself, and listened briefly to the remembered sound of the old man's voice in his head before he said authoritatively to the operator who had just discovered that there were no outside lines available, "Miss, this is Judge Thurston, and I have a mind to call Washington, D.C. Right now, if you please, young lady. See to it, hear?"

He waited, holding his breath, doubting that "Miss" now—"Ma'am?" "Honey?" Would she call the judge? And if so, would he already have left on that visit to his daughter that Rosenberg didn't doubt for a minute? On an impulse, he jiggled the bracket that held the old-fashioned earpiece and shouted in the irritable voice of an old man, "Get a move on there, y'all hear?" and then began sweating again, charging himself with not having the good sense to leave well enough alone.

And then, blessedly, he had them in Washington, and he unburdened himself of his terrifying news succinctly, got the thoroughly unterrifying news that he was to come home, and hung up, smiling. It wasn't until he had opened the door of the booth to let in a bit of the air that was now refreshingly cool by contrast that he remembered "Address Unknown," a short story famous just before World War II; it was in the form of a series of letters from a German refugee in the U.S. to someone back in Germany, and you gathered slowly that the recipient had become a Nazi. But you also gathered slowly that the sender was realizing it, and then his letters began to become gradually more dangerous for the recipient in Germany. Rosenberg couldn't remember whether the German had appealed to the refugee to stop the letters, but he rather thought something like that had been implied. Anyway, the refugee kept on—and the last letter was finally returned to him, stamped "Address Unknown." Jerry Rosenberg consulted his conscience, and it twinged: Hadley Thurston was his father's age. Still, there was no point in assuming guilt until it was certain. He hadn't, after all, talked in Thurston's accent during the conversation. The researcher who lived in his mind pointed out that any eavesdropper would have been too excited by the content to notice the accent, or lack of it, and that logical proof was not required in this un-free society before a man was declared guilty.

What was done, was done. He put in a call to the governor and got the number without difficulty—which meant what? What could have happened to reduce, abruptly, the governor's fear of Girard vengeance? Jake hadn't mentioned any change—Rosenberg put the speculation aside when the governor came on, because he had a job to do: there was some time to gain, if he could.

"I've been trying to reach you, Mr. Rosenberg," the governor said warmly. "What can I do for you? I'm so sorry I was out when you called. I was at church, you know."

Rosenberg began to ask the questions to which he now knew the answer.

The governor's tone sketched the disdain of a big executive being troubled with trifling minor problems. He was sure he couldn't say, he said, what the personnel situation for the county law enforcement people might be. But certainly there was some kind of skeleton staff around, he added, implying that Rosenberg had simply looked carelessly, failing to move the bookcase and peer behind it, perhaps. Of course, he said pointedly, it *was* Sunday, and naturally that made a difference.

"Don't your state police work on Sunday, either?"

The governor said stiffly that they, too, had their appropriate schedules.

"Governor," Rosenberg said in a cold, brutal voice, "we are face to face with a strong probability that there will be riots, with or without a concurrent assault on the county jail. Now—are you able or willing to get enough police to Dorothy to deal with it?"

"Mr. Rosenberg, I have no such reports, and I can't help feeling you're exaggerating. Now, even if I had any grounds for action, there's not much I could do on Sunday—"

"Are you or aren't you going to get some police here?"

"Sir, I resent your tone. I am the highest official of this sovereign state—"

"But not high enough to call the cops on Sunday." It occurred to Rosenberg that the man might hang up. "I'm sorry about my tone."

"Well, I understand that you are overworked—"

"I was going to suggest that you complain about it to my boss. At once." That noise on the line was nothing, Rosenberg told himself—after all, Girard's assistants often listened in on telephone conversations of their chief. Still, "Address Unknown" burned in letters of fire on the pebbly stuff of the phone booth's wall. "Very well, sir," he said loudly. "I'll pass on to President Girard at once your request for his intervention to maintain law and order in Dorothy." He hung up on what he hoped was a gasp, and as he turned to leave the booth he saw what he had missed in his hurry on coming in. "Keep Jesus," somebody who had not had much practice in writing had printed in pencil, "and Jesus Will Keep You." Rosenberg was aware of an instant involuntary pang of sympathy for that gentle teacher in whose name so many horrors were perpetrated. He walked out of the lobby quickly, ignoring a friendly hail from the Coordinated Press just coming downstairs.

As he crossed the square, less friendly observers marked him. Two local adherents of Jesus, representing the real cross Jesus had to bear, had been discussing the weather and the deepening afternoon with a lassitude relieved only when one of them pointed out that Sunday was most over by now and things should be sparking up real soon. Heartened, the other agreed, but mourned the fact that it was necessary to keep the Sunday quiet at all—thus shocking his friend, who admonished him in a disjointed sentence featuring the word "godfearing." His heart may have been in the task of raising up the fallen and leading him to righteous ways, but his attention was diverted by the appearance of Rosenberg, striding across to his car with that out-lander's energy that stamped him "Made in Massachusetts," a son of freedom, born among the elms, bred by lovers of inquiry.

"There's Girard's Jew-boy. That's him, ain't it?"

This guess was corroborated, as was a further guess about Rosenberg's height and weight, two statistics the man most intimately concerned with them had not brought up to date since the last time it had been officially demanded of him. The discussion moved on like lava, slowly encompassing rough estimates of the cost of the tropical-weight suit, the shoes, the handsome Father's Day tie that had been packaged under the forged name of three-year-old Joshua Rosenberg.

As he pointed the car out of town in the direction of the motel from which he was about to check out with extensive if unexpressed thanks, Rosenberg was composing another letter in his head, this time to his wife. He noticed the change in addressee immediately and speculated on whether the desire to be a hero in one's own home had anything to do with the fact that he wrote to Nedra instead of his mother when he felt particularly proud of himself. There was, he admitted honestly, a distinct sense of accomplishment in having brought it off: the U.S. Cavalry would come in time, and the savior of the good guys—if "savior" was a permissible term for a Jew—was Jeremiah Rosenberg of the quiet couple in 3B, father of one and one-third hostages to fortune, and ardent follower of the vicissitudes of Charlie Brown. Rosenberg the historian meditated briefly, but with delight, on the frequency with which the record showed—if read judiciously—that good guys everywhere had always found just such unlikely saviors.

The question of what was permissible for a Jew had by that time been raised by the brighter of the two youths in dialogue in the square. It occurred to him, and he advanced the proposition to his friend, that the ban on Sunday fun could not really be said to extend to Jews, who didn't recognize Sunday the way godfearing folks did.

By the time the philosopher had secured agreement from his disciple, and they had got to their car, Rosenberg had begun to address Nedra on the subject of the convertible; he would soon be turning it in, and then back to Washington and his sober sedan. "I know you would find it interesting to see your scholarly swain tootling around town in a pale-blue convertible," he began, and then broke off, remembering his conservative wife's face, stunned and politely suppressing it, when he had suddenly bought himself a beret last year. He slowed the car to a stop at the traffic light slung across the road like a leftover Christmas decoration and sat there waiting, smiling a little shamefacedly because he suspected himself of possibly harboring a brand-new secret desire for a dashing, out-of-character, beret-type convertible.

The two young citizens of Dorothy, familiar with the back roads and in more hurry than Rosenberg, had arrived at the intersection before him and were poised with their motor running in the parking lot of the Dixie Inn Barbecue, Dine and Dance, closed because it was Sunday. Rosenberg's large head, full of wisdom and follies and triumphs and doubts, was outlined clearly against the sun when the boy raised the rifle his daddy had given him for his twelfth birthday—as *his* daddy had done for *his* twelfth birthday; he took aim as carefully as though the target had not been motionless, near, and defenseless, and squeezed the trigger evenly, as he had been taught. Rosenberg was dead, his head abruptly empty of letters, before the light changed.

The boys got out and pushed the convertible and its occupant, bleeding not too much and fallen sideways on the seat, into the foliage at the side of the road. They gave the car a last concerted shove that sent it down a small incline to a dried-up brook, where its front wheels were stopped. When the lads had climbed back up to the road, from which little disturbance was visible even now and certainly nothing would be at night, they turned their car around and drove toward town without loitering, so they wouldn't miss any of the fun in case it started early.

·

Fifty-six

The knowledge had been plucking at Rosa's consciousness all morning, even though there was no basis for it except, perhaps, the curious quiet of the authorities. And that was not unexpected, she told herself, it being Sunday and all. Still, when by midmorning nobody had berated the girls she began to feel anxious: not very long after she'd been installed in this cell by herself, the girls had discovered that she could hear them if they stood at their barred door and called, though no more than a few shouts could be exchanged before the door to the office slammed and heavy footsteps began in the corridor. The prisoners had to stop then, but they tried again, and so did Rosa. It was too important to forgo—not only the contact with other people but also, she found, the driblets of information about the outside world from Priscilla, perched at the high window of the drunk tank. There was no window in Rosa's solitary cell.

Priscilla was gone now, freed along with Miz Crane—they had called their good-byes and their promises as they were led down the hall to the office, a journey that didn't take them past Rosa's cell. Sunshine, bringing food, had been almost loquacious with relief at their departure: the jail was restored now to its proper function, a container of niggers, and all was at least righter with her world. Who would ever have known, she asked Rosa (but rhetorically) that that fool girl's father was a judge? Kids, she added, and shook her head to show the hopelessness of describing how kids were: you could raise them up nice, as she charitably assumed even judges in Massachusetts tried to do, and then they shamed you like that. You could just feel for that poor mother, Sunshine said, departing with her face almost full of pity, except for the little bit of room that was left for her pleasure with her own good heart and Christian sympathy.

Sunshine had brought breakfast but not lunch yet this morning, which the girls reported was bright and hot; even Rosa's cell, so dank that it was almost cool, was beginning to warm up when a girl's voice called, "Miz Little, there that blond lady." Rosa shouted back quickly to ask where Ann was going before silence could be imposed on them.

"She goin in the café with two men," was the report. "Reckon they git up purty late, just comin out for breakfast now."

Another girl added enviously that they had it easy, all right, and somebody else said she bet they made good money, too—and that's when Rosa noticed the absence of official intervention. The silence from the office was complete—not even a roar for quiet from the deputy who was too lazy to move unless he had to. They had learned that his shouts could be ignored for as long as half a dozen further exchanges before he would drag himself out to stop them.

"She got on a kind of loose middlin-blue dress and that lil ol white hat," the news report went on.

"Lem*me* see." The new commentator spoke up knowledgeably after a moment that, presumably, was devoted to scuffling for position. "That there a A-line dress. Royal blue. Look like cotton, but it likely one of them new goods." The two argued briefly about the material, then switched to an argument about whether the two-piece white dress Ann had worn on her thoroughly reported arrival at the jail yesterday was or was not like one Andy Girard had once been photographed in. Rosa let them go on until they began to grow acrimonious, then she ordered them to settle down to their chores and assigned one of them to lead the calisthenics; when they obeyed, she herself settled down to considering the nature of the silence.

"It been right quiet here all morning," she said tentatively when Sunshine came in with lunch. The food looked better than usual, and so did its bearer, still wearing her dark, decent church dress. A few rising wisps from the neat flattened hair attested that a hat had only recently been removed.

Rosa noticed that the woman was avoiding her gaze. "Sound like there ain't nobody around," she persisted, with a cold certainty beginning to grow like a cancer in her stomach.

"This here's Sunday," the woman said. She looked for a moment as though she might say something more, but she turned and left the cell abruptly.

Rosa ran to the barred door. "They just gone to church," she suggested desperately.

Sunshine stood still in the gloomy corridor with her back turned. "Everybody's off today," she said slowly. "Exceptin for me to bring the meals." Rosa saw the indentations of the brassiere on the broad, fleshy back.

She ate without appetite, stoking her mouth as if it were a coal furnace, and lectured herself busily about her own need for calisthenics. The girls, she told herself angrily, weren't the only ones Miz Crane had meant when she discussed the importance of keeping mind and body in good shape despite the conditions . . .

Rosa laid the spoon down then and stopped trying to think anything but the truth: as soon as she let it in—the admission that the absence of guards was an invitation to a lynching and that those in charge knew as well as she did that the invitation would be accepted—a kind of surprise came with it. Why should she have to die, she wondered, when she was really just starting to learn a few things, to sort of get the hang of life? She was sitting there, puzzling less about the content of her question than that she should dare to ask it at all, when Sunshine came back to collect the bowl and spoon.

"My husband's here till I go," she said from outside the cell before she unlocked the door. She came in cautiously, waiting for a response, and when none came, she added, "I ain't alone. You understand me?"

Rosa nodded, though she was not sure, from the woman's tone of voice, whether the purpose was to warn her against an attempt at escape or to apologize for something.

Sunshine put a black book down on the bunk and picked up the dishes. Rosa stared at the gilt lettering on the cover of the book and traced her finger across the stiff gilt edges of the pages while she waited for what the other woman seemed about to say after her hesitant "I brung you this."

Then Sunshine was on the other side of the barred door. "I give them one." She nodded in the direction of the girls' cell. "Them's Bibles," she said, her voice urging Rosa toward the book. "From the ho-tel."

Rosa looked down at the gift and read that it was from the Gideon Society. She raised her eyes to the real giver, saw that she was being asked for a gift in return, and gave it, though with effort. "Thank you."

Sunshine whispered, "He's here," and turned the key in the lock. Her footsteps, going away, were very loud and so was the sound of the office door and her "Ready." The man's voice was neither loud nor clear, only mumbling something vaguely grouchy, and the closing of the final door was almost gentle.

Rosa picked up the Bible and let it fall open in her hands, but she couldn't make herself read the thin type crowded on the flimsy page. *It don't matter,* she said stubbornly: *It don't matter what it say, I still too young to die.* Behind her eyes, tears began to prickle and she welcomed them, doing nothing to stop them and then encouraging them with blinks and the pity that God should be showing and wasn't.

Wanting to be left to herself and her angry grief for herself, she hated the girls when they first began to call. She let their cries of "Miz Little" go unanswered a few times, telling herself that she had a right. Then she heard them getting shriller and finally the wailing that she knew as Violet began, and she was up in a flash and at the door with one bound, shaking the cool bar furiously.

"You-all stop that this minute," she shouted. "You hear me?" Someone was trying to shush Violet, she heard, but without success: the sobs were giving way to high tentative screams. "Violet, you don't shut your mouth, I make you one sorry gal." It was beginning to work, she heard: Violet was arguing tearfully now, but she wasn't screaming any more. "You a dis*grace,*" Rosa said severely.

"Miz Little, they go'n come for us. Ain't they, Miz Little?"

It was like trying to cure a sick child without being able to touch him, Rosa thought desperately. Then she turned cold with fear because Mary Jane was talking to the others: "They get together and give that lil ol door one great big whomp—'All together now, men'—bang!" The girl's voice thinned and tightened. "And then they bust in and haul us out. We's a-screamin and a-prayin—"

"Shut *up!*" Rosa bellowed. The mimic could really set off the whole batch of them, she knew, visualizing that expressive face, the bright quick eyes, the hands that shaped so vividly whatever they would. Mary Jane's gift could be fatal. Or, Rosa thought quickly, it could be used. "Y'all listen to me. I want ever' last one of you lined up," she called. "Make youself a good straight line right there by that door, so ever'body can hear me." She waited a moment. "I said a *straight* line," she added sternly.

Her guess was a good one: she heard them ordering each other around, accusing each other of spoiling the line, and she sighed in relief because the edge had been taken off the panic already.

"We ready, Miz Little."

"Okay now, you listen. You know who comin? The gov'ment, that who. Ain't nobody be breakin down no door, 'less they want the soldiers to shoot them."

"Ta*dum*-ta*dum*-taDUM-ta*dum*," the little mimic sang. "Here come the soldiers, ridin on their high-steppin horses."

Somebody began to imitate galloping horses with rhythmic clicks of her tongue and somebody else took it up. Rosa smiled and unclenched her hand from the bar for the first time; its cold imprint stayed in her palm and her fingers were still curled. She began to lecture them then—on their folly, their lack of faith. "You think them white trash so big and powerful?" she taunted. "They nothin but specks of dirt, put them aside the President. He got a whole army, and planes and all."

"The President come," Mary Jane elaborated, "and he take that fat-fanny sheriff and he step on him like a bug. Squoosh! That there sheriff-juice runnin out on the floor." Their laughter was high-pitched, but it had their salvation in it. Rosa dismissed the lineup and called for a report from the window, keeping her voice even and confident; but she recognized relief in herself when the girl said there was nobody much out there, just some boys standing around and one couple holding hands. The big man from Washington, she added—the one with the glasses—had come out of the hotel and got in his car, and then the boys left too. Rosa said triumphantly that it didn't look like no meeting, now, did it, and they agreed, laughing. Mary Jane said the lovers sure had no rope on them and hazarded a guess as to what equipment they might have, though, and the others began to guess, too, intent on outdoing each other in daring.

Rosa put a stop to it after it had gone on for a moment or so, because joking couldn't be relied on permanently and it was, she knew grimly, going to be a long wait. She pointed out sharply that this was Sunday and they were not heathen and ordered them to sit on their bunks—they were few enough now so that each girl had one—and listen to Mary Jane read a passage from the Bible. "I start you off with a hymn," she told them, "and then I wants quiet in here. I got my own prayin to do, and then I take a nap. It be a good idea if you do like me, but anyways you get quiet and you just stay that way."

"Yes, ma'am," the mimic called. "What I supposed to read?"

"Anythin. It all good." Absolutely nothing came into Rosa's mind. "You tell Violet close her eyes and open the book. Then you read where she pick."

"Yes, ma'am. We ready to begin, Miz Little."

Rosa closed her eyes in half a second of thanks and then began to sing strongly, " 'A-bide with me, Fast falls the e-ven-tide.' " They joined her when she got to "Lord with me abide" and she led them through the whole thing an extra time before she abandoned them to their church services.

Church services in the small town that provided an unofficial center for the large Virginia estates surrounding it had been over for some time by the time the one in the Dorothy jail began. Elizabeth Langwith, rendered as always a little uneasy by the presence of people who were not either members of her family or servants in her household, caused herself to be removed from among the worshippers as soon as she decently could. As she was driven away from the disquieting strangers toward the reassurance of reunion with her non-churchgoing husband, she glanced back at the little gray building and thought that, without its spire, it would look rather like a cup in the saucer of gentle hills around it. When the car stopped, she stripped off her gloves, thanking the chauffeur with a charming and genuine smile, and made for the house to remove her hat. Her arms were lifted, ready to take the pins out of the back, lift off the hat, and smooth down her hair, as she had been doing every Sunday for endless years, when she was told that her husband would like to see her in the library.

Andrew Langwith, his face very pale above a sober dark suit and his eyes like those of a condemned murderer, led her to a chair with a gentle hand under her elbow before he began to lead deviously into the news she could not possibly confront.

In Kingsley, Vermont, John and Agnes Girard took a walk after church, leaving their daughter Agnes to go home for brunch with a school friend whose father picked the girls up in a station wagon. The Girards had decided early that it was too pretty to take the car, so they'd come to the small white clapboard church in practical walking clothes, including Mrs. Girard's sturdy brown oxfords, which no other woman in town could possibly have worn to church and which no woman in town would ever criticize. The Girards, bickering idly at intervals about the habits of a certain bird and the amount of rainfall three summers ago, wound home eventually when they were tired and hungry enough. Agnes Girard was carrying a specimen of Indian paintbrush, its roots wrapped loosely in a Kleenex, that her husband said would not transplant but that she insisted would—they had agreed to leave the decision to event rather than discussion when they came far enough into their own driveway to see the old car the trees had hidden from them. Bill Bruyette's mother stood on their doorstep, facing out, waiting for them. John Girard quickened his step, smiling a welcome; but his wife suddenly had no welcome for her oldest friend. Unaccountably, Agnes Girard lagged, her heavy shoes crunching slowly on the gravel, managing only with deliberate effort not to tighten her hand on the frail plant.

Ann Taswell was sleeping heavily when Gil Kimball, who had knocked loudly and received no answer, pushed open the door of her room. He saw her lying on the bed in her slip and the front of his mind said bitterly that that was a hell of a goof-off thing while the back of it registered how white and gold and tall and spare she was, like a Viking goddess picked down to bleached bones. He shouted "Ann" in a loud, cranky voice and turned to the washed-out cretonne curtain that hid the row of hooks on the wall the hotel considered a closet. He yanked the curtain aside, then looked over his shoulder and saw her sitting bolt upright. "Get up, for Christ's sake," he shouted.

"Gil? What's—what's the matter?"

"The Nieman kid just found out—the sheriff and his boys are heading for Niggertown. Dragging fire hoses."

"Why?" she asked stupidly. She swung her legs over the side of the bed and begin feeling blindly for her shoes.

Gil snatched a white dress off a hanger, wondering why indeed: there hadn't been a sound or a move from the Negro quarter. Or had there—had they missed something? He discovered that there was another piece to the dress and threw both parts at Ann. "I don't know," he said nastily. "And I'm never gonna know if I have to carry you around." Even if they had missed something, it couldn't have been much: the town was small enough so there'd hardly be a riot at one end of it without the press—admittedly hiding from the smothering heat by playing poker in the hotel—hearing a sound. "Get dressed, will you?" he roared at her, turning around and discovering that she was, that she was buttoning her jacket and reaching for her hat. Now we have a little something to go with the tender revolution, he thought; now we get a quiet riot. He let the curtain fall back into place and discovered that Ann was waiting for him at the door.

The sun, a ridiculous, phony-looking ball on the horizon, stabbed redly at Gil's eyes as he and Ann ran side by side through the streets, past the boarded-up front of the café, and into the confusing streams of traffic. These were the damndest people for togetherness, Gil thought, as a man jogged toward him with a small child on his shoulders; they brought their kids to every riot. He stopped and watched the man pass, apparently headless, with his bright, sweat-stained shirt topped only by the little behind in dirty shorts riding like a hump between his shoulders. Ann called something and darted away and Gil let her go, remembering all at once that she was News but he was Analysis, and Analysis had less need to hurry. He had left his watch somewhere, he discovered when he tried to consult it; the thought crossed his mind then that whatever time it was, it was long past time for Great White Father Girard to get the lead out of his Constitution. "A leaderless people burst into the streets of this Alabama town today like water from a broken main," he began writing defiantly in his head. "As the shadows of dusk began, so did the shadows of violence and fear, lying across the sagging storefronts on Grove Street—" He stopped writing in order to look at how the shadows actually were lying across the sagging storefronts on Grove Street. And then he said aloud, "The hell with this," and began running after Ann as if he were News, too.

She was right on the job, he had to concede as soon as he turned the last corner and found himself behind the ragged line of sweating deputies wrestling with thick gray folds of fire hose. He could see her just ahead, dancing around Sheriff Floyd like a basketball guard around the opposing forward. The big man was pretty well ringed around by reporters, but it was Ann who had him pinned down most thoroughly, bobbing up under his flailing arm, appearing in every direction he tried to turn. Gil grinned, and then choked as the light wind rose suddenly and carried the Niggertown stench straight at him. The smell was decaying pork, old coffee grounds, fish skeletons and used sanitary napkins, watermelon rinds and ammonia, corn cobs and rags that had wiped up vomit—it was humanity in the hundreds after a week of no garbage collection in Alabama in summer, and it was indescribable and should have been unbearable.

Gil stopped, staggered by it, and then forgot it instantly as the noise began: among the black faces ranked on the other side of Ann and the sheriff in their clumsy dance, a voice called something that lobbed like a tennis ball into the empty space. Gil began to run again, with the speed of panic, and then reeled to a stop because what had followed the voice was unbelievably but unmistakably laughter: a huge, mocking, good-natured laugh that rolled backward from the front line of the Negroes to where little brownskinned boys perched in the scraggly trees were leaning down to hear the joke. Gil began to walk forward more slowly, trying to puzzle it out, trying to make some logic of these insane people, both black and white.

He came up beside Ann, thinking that it was curious that nobody had tried to stop him, nobody had asked for his press pass—not important, but another example of the Alice in Wonderland air of the whole crazy town, where yesterday he hadn't been able to take a step without challenge—just as a voice from the crowd called insolently, "It ain't polite to be comin widout no invite. Whar your manners, Sher'f Floyd?" Gil looked at the man who had spoken—thirtyish, with a round black face, wearing a tattered shirt with a printed design that seemed to be made up of sailfish leaping among palm trees; he stood with his elbows slightly crooked, his hands hooked into a leather belt that was the lowest visible point on his body.

Around him were ranged several women, one carrying a baby, and two school-age children. "A plague o' both your houses" Gil quoted silently, remembering the other man in a gay shirt with a child on his—

Suddenly the picture jumped in Kimball's mind like an awkward home movie, and he saw what he had seen but not seen: it was the *back* of the white man with the child on his shoulders, going the other way. He grabbed at Ann's elbow, his fingers slipping sweatily on the new pink skin where her abrasions had healed, and jerked her away from her hard-won spot under the sheriff's nose. She tried to shake him off, protesting, but he tightened his grip on her arm. "Come on!" he yelled in her ear, and began to drag her down the street, away from the deputies and their fire hoses.

"Yah, go on home, Sher'f," a voice jibed from the crowd. "We ain't askin you in." More laughter came, with catcalls behind it.

Ann struggled in Gil's grasp, shouting something at him; she set her heels down so he had to wrestle her along. Behind her, the Coordinated Press man was loping toward them with a wary look on his face, like a law-abiding citizen who wants to do right but doesn't want to get into the middle of a family quarrel.

"Ann, Ann, don't be a damn fool," Gil said to her in a stage whisper.

"But what's the point of—"

"The point," said Gil, "is the jail." He saw in her face that she saw and he shushed her quickly. "Shut up. We don't want to touch it off any sooner than—"

The CP man came up saying, "What the hell?" and Gil wheeled and took his arm.

"Just walk," he said, propelling both of them in what he hoped looked like a casual stroll. "You amateur," he said to his colleague. "Didn't it strike you that there were no white civilians attending the so-called riot?" He didn't mention that it had been a long time striking him, even with the advantages of Analysis's luxury over News's necessity. Then he just held his breath as they neared the square before the courthouse, hoping there was time. If he was right, it wasn't going to come off for a while yet, unless it was pushed.

They came in sight of the square and Gil breathed again. It was like the very earliest arrivals for a concert at Washington's Constitution Hall—a milling around, with greetings and finding seats. But if the Negroes rushed, so would this still leisurely crowd. Gil let go of the other man and Ann and they paced slowly side by side, like people taking a walk on the deck of a ship.

"There's a state cop over there," Ann said quietly. "At least, he was before. I saw him from my window."

Gil said grimly, "He may be all by himself. If he's still there."

"I'll find out." She began to slide away from them imperceptibly.

The CP man said he would cover the crowd and Gil volunteered to try the phone. The informal pool arrangement concluded, the CP man sauntered away, taking out a cigarette, and Gil made for the hotel, trying to look like somebody who just had to go in for a minute to go to the bathroom.

From the window of the drunk tank, Ann's progress across the square was being reported to Rosa, who was still rubbing sleep out of her eyes. "Look like she comin in here, Miz Little," Mary Jane called, and then added in a voice that lacked all her usual gaiety, "Miz Little, they's a awful lot of people shufflin round out there."

It was no use to scold her, Rosa thought wearily; she was making all the effort you could expect of her. "It all right, honey," she said. "They just coolin off, maybe. Maybe it cooler down there." She waited, trying to think. "What they doin, honey?"

"Oh, just shufflin round, kind of. Talkin to each other." The voice, so accurate an instrument for mimicry, reflected as accurately its owner's pathetic wish to be out there—or anyway, out somewhere—just shuffling around and talking.

"Well, that ain't nothin to be scared about. You girls scarin yourself like little kids with ghost stories." Inspired, she added with authority, "Now y'all get on away from that window, and I tell you when it time to report again." She had her doubts about whether her act was going over. "How about mebbe you tell a story, one of them like about the Hollywood stars. Can you tell it loud, you think? So I can hear, too?"

"I try, Miz Little." Mary Jane cleared her throat and began, loudly, and with a sweetness that turned Rosa's legs to water, "Once upon a time, there was a beautiful Hollywood star, name of Pearl. This Pearl, she had golden hair and blue eyes like a bird's egg, and all the handsomest men in Hollywood they done dream about her every time they puttin they head on they pillow . . ."

Rosa touched the stiff cover of the Bible beside her on the bunk and wondered whether she was doing right. They were young and she was responsible for them: her own children—her mind winced away from any more thinking about them—her Tina and her Trixie had Marian to look out for them, and Gloria for whatever Marian was no good at; but these girls had only Rosa to mother them and maybe all she could do for them was lead them to God. And here she sat, listening while the beautiful mythical Pearl ordered champagne—before dinner, Rosa heard, and then found to her surprise that she was able to smile.

She opened the Bible and turned pages, looking vaguely for the Book of Job. But the more she remembered it, the more unsuitable it became for all of them—certainly for the foolish innocents, and for Rosa Little, who was no candidate for trials by God. If He wanted to prove something, she couldn't see that it made any sense for Him to begin with her.

"Miz Little!"

She hadn't realized the girl's story had broken off. She jumped up and ran to the cell door, spilling the Bible onto the floor on her way.

"Miz Little, can we look out? They some noise out there . . ."

Even as she gave permission, she heard it—a buzz of voices, like a convention of bees, all exchanging information. But there was a strain of music in it—a harmonica, she thought—and she clung to that. Nobody brought music to a lynching, did they? The word brought pictures that made the sweat come out on her even while she was waiting for the "report"—she felt the knee in her backside as she was hustled down the street toward the jail on her last day out in the world, and she burned with shame. What if there was more than death waiting? Shrinking and sweating, she thought she could bear to die if she had to, but not in shame, not in a way for her girls to turn away from, guilty and embarrassed, wishing they could forget and then ashamed of the wish.

There were more people now, the girl was reporting. Rosa fought the beginning hysteria she heard, asking them about the harmonica, seizing on the report that kids were there, eating ice cream. Locked in her vulnerable body and nauseated with fear, she chivvied the girls and coaxed them and jollied them.

But she was losing them. "You said they comin to he'p us. You done told us that, Miz Little."

"I did for sure," she called back ringingly. "And they comin. You see."

"When they comin, Miz Little?" cried the voices that wanted to believe, and Rosa shouted back that she had said before dark and it wasn't dark yet. Was it, she added, trying to keep the anxious question out of her voice.

"No, ma'am, not yet. Miz Little! You hear them? They singin about it."

Straining, she heard them then. "When the sun goes down," the voices outside were taunting her, and she sat down abruptly because the burden was heavy even though she didn't think she'd have to tote it long. She rubbed her hand across her eyes, trying to think whether it was time yet to stop telling the girls lies. I guess they goin to get us all right, she said quietly in the gloom of her mind in the gloom of her cell; how long I right to keep tellin them kids it all okay? She thought about Violet, who needed a long time to understand any change, and decided on only a little while longer.

Then she knew what she was going to tell them when it was time. She got up and picked up the small table against the wall, turning it over to peer at how its legs were put on. The nearest one seemed loose when she shook it tentatively; when she tried in earnest to pry it loose, though, it bent and bent like a green branch but would not break.

"Miz Little!"

She dragged the table over to the cell door so she could work and talk. "All right now, we quiet us down with a little prayer."

"They still singin, Miz Little."

When the sun goes down, their voices threatened, and she didn't know how long there was until it would. "Nemmind them. Now y'all say after me, and you see Violet do too, you wait for her, hear. 'Our Father which art in Heaven.'"

"Our Father which art in Heaven," they said, mostly together.

"Hallowed be Thy name."

"Hallowed be Thy name-ame."

"Thy Kingdom come," Rosa said, and then, "Thy will be done." She put her foot on the table and leaned on its bent leg with all her strength, pulling the nails in it till they stretched like elastic bands; but it didn't come off. "On earth as it is in Heaven."

While they repeated it raggedly, with Violet finishing alone, Rosa went and picked up the Bible, hefting it to see whether it would do. "Give us this day our daily bread," she went on, then caught her breath with the pain of the young voices asking, "Give us this day," when she couldn't. "And forgive us our trespasses," she called, and wedged the Bible against the table leg until it was taut. They had caught up by that time and she said, "As we forgive those who trespass against us," and began to cry fiercely and silently, because if it was true there was no forgiveness for her: she would not, could not, forgive them, not if it cost her a thousand heavens. "And lead us not into temptation," she said, scorning the words the people outside had probably prayed only today; but He had led them into temptation nevertheless, or somebody had. She heard the girls crying and she shouted, like a command, "But deliver us from evil," and threw herself on the leg of the table and heard it snap between the pressure of her body and the Bible.

"For Thine is the kingdom," she called, joyously, wrenching the last nails loose and lifting her improvised club in her hands that were striped with the marks of her struggle. *Till the sun goes down,* they sang outside, and she hurried, not able to wait for Violet any more: "And the power and the glory—"

"And the power and the glory," the girls said unevenly but clinging together as closely as they could. "Glory," lagged Violet in a wail like something falling down a high hill.

"Forever and ever, Amen."

Rosa got up and, holding her club, stood erect beside the fallen Bible and bent her head to say her real prayer: I sorry, Lord, but we just ain't about to die like cattle.

"Amen," the voices of the girls trailed. Rosa listened for the end of the sound, ready now for her final speech, whenever the sun went down: "Y'all listen now—if we has to go, we don't go quiet." She ran through her memory of their cell, looking for possibilities for weapons, so she could instruct them rapidly and competently as soon as they were finally through with their praying.

Outside in the charged and still-hot streets, Bruce Fisher pressed close against the shuttered front of the Railroad Café and waited for a couple on the other side of the street to pass, so that he could slip back to his own lines with the report of what he had seen in the square. Fire hoses couldn't stop the people of Niggertown if they found out what was going on; and even if they were eventually stopped, it would take the breaking up of the sundown party to do it. Nobody wanted a lot of people hurt, least of all Bruce, he thought—but black men could not stand there and let their own people be taken from that jail.

Across the street, the couple strolling cheerfully, with their handy picnic cooler for iced drinks swinging between them, disappeared around the corner. Bruce launched himself away from the gritty leftover heat of the stone and sped toward Niggertown, fleet and soft-footed as the Indian boy in a book he'd taken from the library when he was eight.

Fifty-seven

In a plane boring steadily south through bland summer sky, the powerful man John Girard clenched his hands and cursed silently and methodically the pilot, the copilot, and each and every engine part that he could remember. Beside him, his wife prayed equally silently, with her hands folded in the lap that had sustained small, wiggly members of two generations, for a moment to see and touch the child—if, she added humbly, it could be had without causing Elizabeth one additional moment of pain.

Andrew Langwith drove—skillful, desperate, and alone—through the lush landscape of summer fulfillments. His wrists firm as though the car were a spirited horse, he steered among the Sunday families out for a ride in the Virginia countryside, maneuvering for a second here, half a minute there, that hopefully could be summed into a last sight of the wisps of fair hair sweeping back from the high, clear brow or of small hands he had directed in the important task of holding a ball. With bitterness, he fled the knowledge that the child—he never thought of her as Elizabeth, because that was his wife—was at least better off than his own daughter, who had no mother. It was Andrea he prayed for between the ranks of roadside poplars as the afternoon sped before him. In guilt and shame, he thanked God that his daughter, so long alone and deprived, was not alone in this final deprivation, and he prayed strength to the sustaining arm of Alec Girard.

At the nurses' station in the hospital pavilion, Dr. Snowden confirmed nothing and told Luke Messenger furiously, "We never call a patient hopeless. I have nothing more to say." He watched the round man who should have been a figure of merriment walk away slowly and knew this was not an appropriate target for his anger. But he had to shoot it off, get it out of his way, if he was to be able to get on. Elizabeth, he had told her mother—who should be under sedation—could possibly be aware of her parents'

presence; certainly there was a level of communication below speech . . .
Behind his blank, grave face it had occurred to him that if there weren't, his
wife would probably have left him long ago.

But he had no time for speculation: the patient was in shock and comatose,
with a pulse that had been growing steadily weaker and was now so shallow
as to be almost imperceptible. Even with death only an hour or two away,
he would not state the finality; but whatever effort was left to be made could
be made just as well by smaller talents than Snowden's. Other children, their
deaths far less immediate—and perhaps one, today? tomorrow? that would
be the first one not certain—waited to be championed. The tumult and the
shouting would begin in another sector, the one mapped between the silvery
covers of the new chart he studied now: Age, 5 years 3 months; marrow
count, 30 percent. The angry man read the history typed on the page, looking for indications of a viable strategy and trying to waste no other moment
of another young life in mourning Elizabeth Girard, the already slain, left
on a previous battlefield.

In the room of which she was still the center, Elizabeth lay free now of
all the once-hopeful trappings—the mask to help her breathing, the looming
"Eye-Vee" and upended bottles of blood in their racks; only the cloth cuff
that was inflated to measure her failing blood pressure was still on her arm,
half covering one of the ugly flat red splotches of the original disease. But
all that was really left was what belonged to her: the polished dark-green
leaves of the perfect pale roses she would not see any more; the doll Amanda,
glassy-eyed and rejected; the pictured promises of California redwoods that
for hundreds of years had not known death, and of dolphins leaping in the
bluest of faraway seas. And the begging parents, each holding to the bluish-
gray fingers of one of the needle-scarred, cold little hands as if it were possible to complete a circuit that would charge her with life.

She looked like a small, drowned Ophelia, her father thought, angry at the
ravages to her thick, soft hair. The inroad by the drug on the beauty of his
daughter, a few days ago worth everything because no vanity was greater
than the hope of life, now was an ugly, hurting irony. The dusky lips flickered
in a faint smile that spoke of a dream, and Alec looked at the sum of loss—
the unique combination that could never happen again, individual as a
thumbprint—and longed to be with her wherever she was: accepting decoration as a Cosmic Patroller first class? Racing for the sandbox that had
marked her tenancy on the White House landscape? Squatting among her
fellows as Grandpa Girard, looking like Socrates in the midst of his students,
read out the deliciously foreign Sunday funnies from the Boston newspaper?

"She's dreaming," Andy said in a wondering whisper, as though all the
hope of the world lay in this phenomenon.

But not of me, Elizabeth's father raged without words. The child who had
made him a parent had no time for him now. She had done enough for him—
she moved on to her own concerns, leaving him clinging to her hand, beseeching a quiver.

There was one—through their closed circuit ran an urgency like an electric current. Alec felt it, and knew wearily that it came not from Elizabeth but from her mother. Furtively, in case Andy should be watching him, he glanced up at her, wondering with an old despair what in God's name he could do for her. The woman would not let go, she would not accept the evidence before her eyes and in her hand; though the angel of death came with a dozen flashing swords and a hundred omnipotent cohorts, Andrea Girard intended to stand in his path. All Alec could offer Elizabeth was whatever problematic sense of his presence the touch of his hand supplied her as she drifted into death; he gave it, with pain but no doubt. But Andy needed something more of him: she could not be left to drift, because the waters she was entering were not safe.

"She is slipping away from us," he said deliberately, because it had to be said. "Dreaming" was not enough: people came back from dreams. "Andy." He waited, making her lift her head, forcing her to let him see her strange face with the sick skin, the delicate features coarsened by the swollen price of sleeplessness and tears. "Don't try to stop her."

Andy looked at his eyes; her own burned with the dark ardor of the fanatic. "We mustn't let go."

"Darling, we must. You know we must."

"We're her parents." Her voice was husky with shock, outraged as though he had tried to deny paternity.

Who is a parent to a dying child, Alec wondered; but he had to answer her quickly, before she could be lost to him. "Yes. We're helping her." His voice shook. "Andy, it's a—good death."

Her eyes denied him, and he knew she was right: there is no good death. But it was a seemly one, he meant, a gentle and painless one, a soft slipping out of life. "It's all we can give her," he said brokenly, and knew that it was the truth and that he had to be grateful for it. All wrong for a man—who had his summing-up to do at the last, who needed time for the apologies anybody owes—this nursery death was appropriate for a child. "Leave her to be easy in it," he begged Andy, his eyes begging her further to understand. They were Elizabeth's parents; when they held her hands it must be to guide her along the way she had to go, not tug at her with hopeless demands to stay. "We—we have to do the hard things for her," he said. He bowed his head, helpless to explain.

"Alec."

He had been almost sure he felt the difference before she spoke—in a lessening of the conflict coursing through their circuit. The child, it almost seemed, now slept more safely.

"Yes." Like a diver coming up from long depths, he breathed the air that was now without the tormenting tension. Andy was sitting up straight and making an attempt to compose her poor, pretty face with its stung lips; her pathetic dignity made him want to run through the streets, weeping aloud and tearing at his clothes.

"Are you sure?" she asked quietly.

"Yes, Andy, I'm sure." He let his eyes stay on hers until he saw that it would be all right. They would walk now, as bravely as they could, leading their daughter between them.

Andrea reached out and put her free hand in his. "Then—let's do it. The hard thing."

He raised her hand to his lips and then held it against his cheek for a moment. She was right in calling for ritual—and it would help her, he saw. She waited, the good woman, to take her part as soon as he had taken his. *I had to make a speech,* Alec the awkward suitor had said across the miles to his beautiful, tantalizing girl in the springtime of a lifetime ago. He sighed; keeping her hand in his, he shouldered his enormous burden now. He had to make a speech.

"Father," he began, and watched her bow her head. But he went on looking straight ahead, at his wife's dark disordered hair, at the sunlight that came into the window but not quite into the room. "Father, with thanks for the riches we knew in her and for the sunny days of her short life, we . . . commend to you . . . our child Elizabeth—" he heard Andy crying and he shook his head against his own tears "—most innocent and loving and . . . and gay. We beg for her whatever joys . . ." He bowed his head at last, and could not finish a simple speech.

Andy leaned across to stroke his hair with her free hand. On the white sheet of the lightly inhabited bed, his hand lay empty with the fingers curled, but not quite into a fist any more.

They sat there weeping together as the afternoon lengthened and Elizabeth dreamed her way toward an easeful death with her parents helping her as far as they were allowed.

Outside the awful privacy of that quiet room, Jake Ruffing prowled the corridor under the merciful gaze of the Secret Service agent Leroy and his sober colleague. Twenty minutes were gone since Jake had phoned Bill Bruyette to say this was it, as late as the President could wait to order the troops in and still have them arrive before sunset. "I thought maybe you'd want to be here," he'd said miserably.

"Yes. I guess so."

Behind the Congressman's voice, Jake heard the uneven tapping of an unprofessional typist, a flurry-and-silence, pounce-and-pause rhythm that he recognized as Farland at work. "You think you better come and stay with Andy?" he asked reluctantly, because he needed all the help with the speech he could get.

"I thought Morisot would be there by this time."

Jake sighed. "His plane ran into trouble—they had to crash land."

"Oh God. He okay?"

"Not very." The Frenchman had been nearly incoherent on the phone, but it was hard to tell whether with grief or pain or anger, or all three. "His left hand was hurt, it seems—I don't know how badly. But he's on his way again."

Bruyette said, "You didn't tell Andy."

"No. Of course not."

"You've been having it rough, Jake."

"It's not all the rest of it," Ruffing said. "It's—how in hell can I go in there and tell him he has to leave his child, now? It's inhuman."

"You can't, Jake. I'll do it. I guess I'm the one. I'll be there right away."

Ruffing patrolled the corridor with the short, jerky strides a wry President had once pointed to as a burden on the taxpayer, causing undue wear and tear on the oval office's carpet. Jake wasted no time berating himself for his lack of courage, if that was indeed what it was—perhaps, he thought, it made more sense for the unmarried, childless Bruyette to tell the President it was time to leave his wife and child; sometimes it was easier for a man who had never built a house to bomb a house. What worried Jake was the time, and the fear that he might have cut it too close. There was no magic in the technical moment of sundown, and every passing minute might cost a life. Swiveling on his ordered course, he saw Bruyette hurrying toward him now and felt sweat prickly under his hair because, all of a sudden, there really was no more time. He nodded, and sped off to do what was necessary before Bill even reached the closed door.

Bruyette tapped once and then turned the knob without waiting for permission; he paused in the doorway, stopped by the shock of Andy's ravaged face, contrasting pitiably with the raspberry-sherbet color of her lighthearted summer dress. The President sat with his back to the door and didn't turn around, but Bruyette could tell by the stiffening of the shoulders under the trim dark coat that his presence was known, and probably its purpose also. He closed the door gently and said, "Alec."

Alec shook his head stiffly, looking at his wife.

Bruyette took two steps into the room. "Mr. President. It has to be now."

"I have no right to wait," Alec said to Andy in a flat voice that held so much knowledge there was no room for regret. "I told you about it."

"I remember," Andy lied, but only partly. What she remembered fully was her decision in the garden of the Georgetown house: neither of them could have known then that it would come to this, but this was in it all the time and in an obscure way she had known some of it, at least that there was only one life to be divided between the public and the private moments. And only one of them could take precedence: a public man's family must die, as well as live, in a special way.

Alec said wretchedly, "Elizabeth," like a summing up.

I'll be a President's child, Elizabeth had said on Inauguration Night, but I don't think I'll be a President's wife. Andy detached the limp little hand from Alec's. "Elizabeth is a President's child," she said quietly.

"Andy, those down there—in the South—those are the deaths I can do something about."

She nodded, taking Elizabeth's hand to replace him. "I know, darling." She formed the words with wooden lips, a stone tongue. "You have to."

Huge and dark as he bent over the bed, Alec kissed the little face it hurt to look at and then straightened and stood there, needing to leave and needing something else more. His eyes begged it of Andy.

Both her hands were occupied now with the dying child. "I understand, darling," she said clearly. She raised her eyes to his and saw that he knew it was true. But still he hesitated to turn away. He was her rock, but she knew she was his harbor: her eyes, dark and quiet and velvet, promised him return. "Go ahead, Alec. I'll come . . . when I can."

The President stopped at the door to the waiting world and Bruyette handed him a folded handkerchief. Over his shoulder, the Congressman inquired of Andy and was assigned to Alec; the short, decisive movement of her head said that was where he was needed most. He swallowed hard and asked, "Ready, Mr. President?" with his hand on the doorknob. Alec pocketed the handkerchief, nodded quickly, once, and stepped back to let the door open.

"The President has signed the order," a waiting man in the hospital solarium said into a radio transmitter as Girard finished his spiky signature, even more illegible than usual, on the paper the military aide was holding steady for him. He acknowledged the aide's salute with a nod, then said, "Wait a minute," to Jake Ruffing, watching until the precious paper was on its way. After that, he went willingly if woodenly, taking his place in the small procession so like a thousand others in hotel corridors and convention halls, except that the candidate had had to smile and shake hands and parry questions. The Chief Executive need only walk tall and straight between Jake hurrying ahead and Bruyette like a warmth at his back.

Even so, even with decision clear and habit to rely on, Alec's step faltered as they turned the corner and he saw Luke Messenger ahead, whispering urgently to the pool reporters; low sun coming through the great glass doors outlined the men's heads, blackening them inside pinkish coronas, and revealed the long black car waiting to take him irretrievably away from his last moment of Elizabeth. Alec's lips moved, but only Bruyette, a quick, supporting arm beside him, heard him say piteously, like a weakling, "Stay with me."

"All the way," said the voice that had been there all the years, before life was either public or private or anything but a grand and hopeful guess. "All the way, old son."

Martin Halloran of the *Tribune* had seen Presidents come and go and pay many costs, but he thought none like this. He drew his thin old body up to a posture of stiff military attention, his eyes commanding his colleagues—if we are anything, if we are men at all, his look warned them—and they obeyed. Alec Girard walked past them unmolested and apparently unaware, and then, at the last moment, turned back and extended his hand to Halloran and, to them all, the tribute of surrender: he stood there briefly before them, vulnerable, leaning openly on Bruyette, not minding that they saw the tears on his face. Halloran said, "Good luck, Mr. President," exchanging with the President the knowledge of the bitter uselessness of the wish.

Luke Messenger said to the three men, when the glass door had swung silently behind the small procession, "I don't have to say it, fellows," and led them to the press car, where he passed a flask and didn't say it.

"Farland's got the speech all ready," Bruyette reported as the President's car moved down the drive. "You'll have a little time to make changes, but I don't think you'll want to." He went on talking carefully, offering normality like medicine. "It isn't one of the easiest speeches you ever had to make, but it's a damn good one. And the important thing is, the minute you start talking, murders start stopping."

"It isn't the hardest I ever had to make." The President looked back at the white, piled mass of the hospital buildings as the car turned onto Wisconsin Avenue. Then he looked ahead and added, "It'd better be good. It's cost quite a bit."

The waiting motorcycle policemen picked them up, loitered briefly till the press car came in sight, and sped ahead, their sirens stopping all speech.

In Dan Healy's office in the west wing, Will Farland sat hunched before his typewriter, wheeled in on its table, with his feet on the table ledge and the precious copy in his hand. Through the open door to the President's office came the disjointed cries of the television technicians, setting up; the commentator famous for his keen understanding and dispassionate voice crouched on the sofa out of their way and held his head in his hands, trying to empty his mind of thought so he would be able to speak a brief, simple sentence.

Will came to ". . . that the next generation may not charge us with dereliction" and caught up short, wondering whether Girard could manage it. His pencil hovered for a moment, then he decided if Girard could speak at all, he could speak the truth, and the truth was that there was a next generation, present and waiting. Though minus one member.

Sharlie Grayson was one of those waiting—sipping at her ginger-ale-and-grenadine "cocktail" by the edge of a Hollywood swimming pool and wondering warily whether the sweet-faced but rather dowdy middle-aged screen writer to whom her father had introduced her so casually was slated to become her stepmother.

At a boys' camp in Vermont, where the air was cool and already demanding the wearing of fleece-lined sweatshirts with the camp name scrawled on a hundred hopeful chests, Dick Farland sent a scowl across to his brother Peter, who was not standing quite still among the ranks of "midgets" lined up to march to the mess hall.

In the Washington suburbs, mothers were reacting to the news about Elizabeth Girard with typical indulgences for whatever children were around, alive and well, within their sight. Thus Bonnie Ruffing, spooning applesauce from a babyfood jar, only smiled when Alexander Wardwell Girard, Jr.—just bathed and clad in clean pajamas—dabbled his fingers in the contents of the spoon, found the texture suitable, and rubbed the stuff in his hair. Some of the previous owners of the highchair returned his grin, and went on hanging around because their mother seemed to have forgotten she had forbidden it.

In Silver Spring, Maryland, Nedra Rosenberg cut up her son Josh's roast beef into fancy shapes to coax the child to eat—a practice the head of the household had sternly forbidden. Nedra looked pale, and though she thought she had finished crying for Elizabeth, more tears kept threatening; but she knew she was probably overtired. She had been easily fatigued at this point in her first pregnancy, too, Jerry of the comfortingly long memory had pointed out when she'd complained on the phone a few days ago. Thinking of Jerry made her smile; feeling only a little guilty, she bribed Josh to eat his peas by offering ice cream for dessert.

And in the South in the dimming summer light, the troop transports flew their ordered course, bearing the armored young, nervous but instructed, on the way to the precarious peace that is bought by force. And not too soon: in the slowly cooling streets of Dorothy, Alabama, the arcs of spray from the jerking fire hose caught rainbows from the sun as they broke against the dark bodies, moving inexorably and violently toward the violence coming to turn them back. Trixie Little, knocked down but not hurt—not this time—struggled to her feet with her sister's help in a small circle of temporary safety with a radius the length of a board in Bruce Fisher's hands. Trixie was only wet, but Bruce was drowned: in his eyes as he stood guard over his women, ready to swing at anything white, was an engulfing darkness no vote or job or school would dam.

In the flyblown office at the courthouse building, four state policemen—reprieved while the crowd in the square fled to battle at the edge of the ghetto—conferred, agreed that they were no match for whichever force would win out, and prepared to withdraw while they had the chance. Beyond them, Rosa waited, armed and trying to trust.

In Washington, violins sang from Ann Taswell's little radio in the sweet transience of the *Wieniawski Concerto*. Beside a half-packed suitcase, Marian Farland slept like an exhausted kitten on the bed on which she happened to find herself.

In the center of the world, Andrea Girard felt the gathering in the small body, a stirring of energy that must be like the embryo's, launching itself for the plunge to life. She held Elizabeth's hands, offering dependable strength for as long as it was needed, until the child was ready to go alone. In the lowering light, her white arms holding, her white neck bowed, she waited in her curves of tenderness and surrender like the most ancient and enduring of the statues men carve from the formless stone nature leaves in their landscape.

Death will not yield, but the fear of it yields to love. The shining around the sheltering mother and the striving child lighted the coming dark, making it safe for solitary voyages.

When it was time, Andy let go.

ABOUT THE AUTHOR

MAGGIE RENNERT has been a reporter, an editor, a speechwriter for government officials, a book reviewer for the *New York Herald Tribune* and other papers, the co-author of a handbook on English style, and the author of poetry published in the *Saturday Review* and several literary quarterlies. Though now a widow, she was for many years a Washington housewife, mother, and full-time member of that circle she recreates so vividly in A MOMENT IN CAMELOT. She says of these years: "Looking back, I can see that I collected information on the interaction of public and private lives on the Washington scene as methodically as if it were an anthropological study. But that wasn't what I was doing: I was just living. I was there, a functioning part of that society in which Daddy can't make it to his daughter's birthday party because all hell has just broken loose in Suez."

The intensity of first-hand experience, seen with the poet's eye and told with the reporter's skill—these are the elements that make this the most startlingly authentic and deeply moving political novel of recent years.